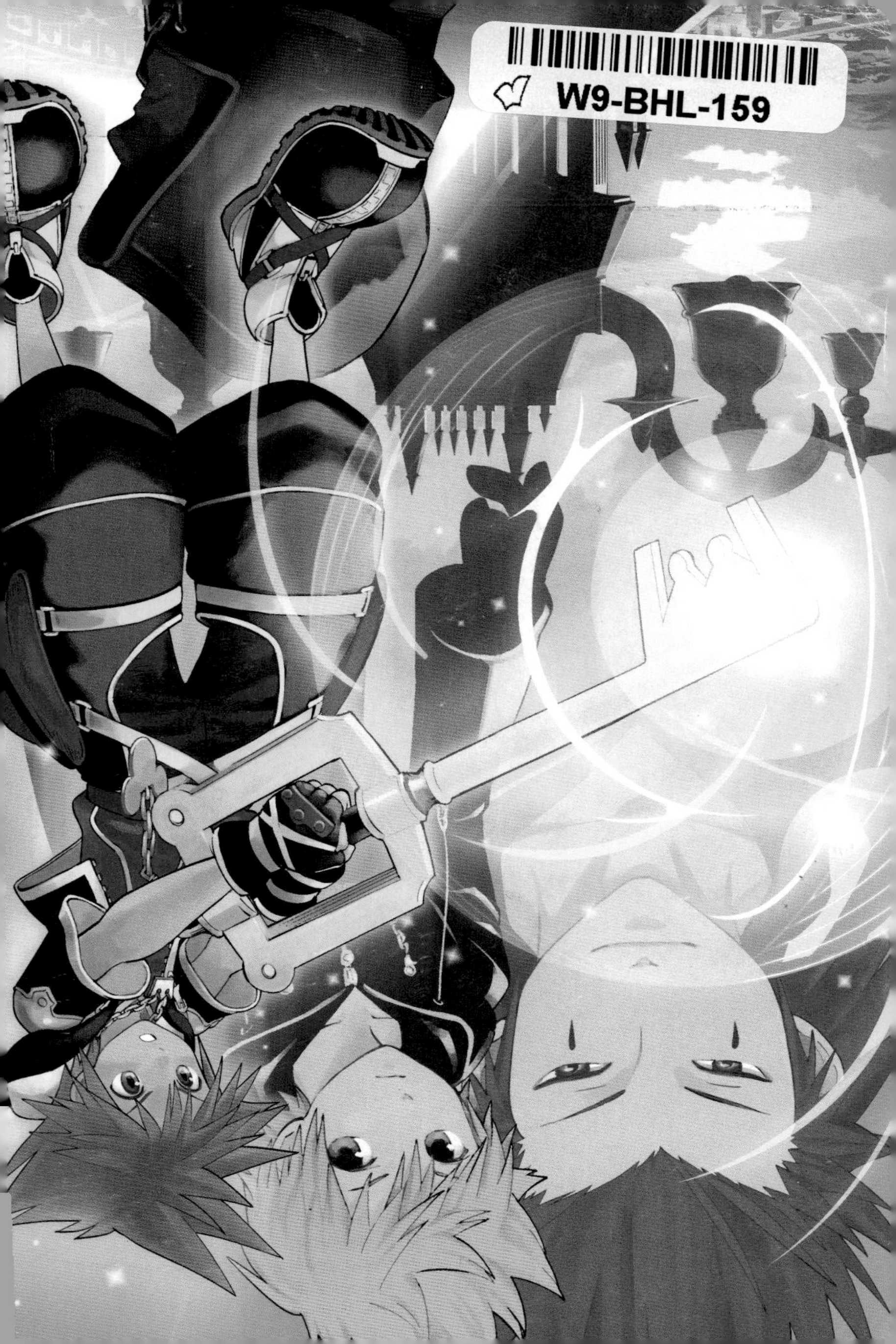

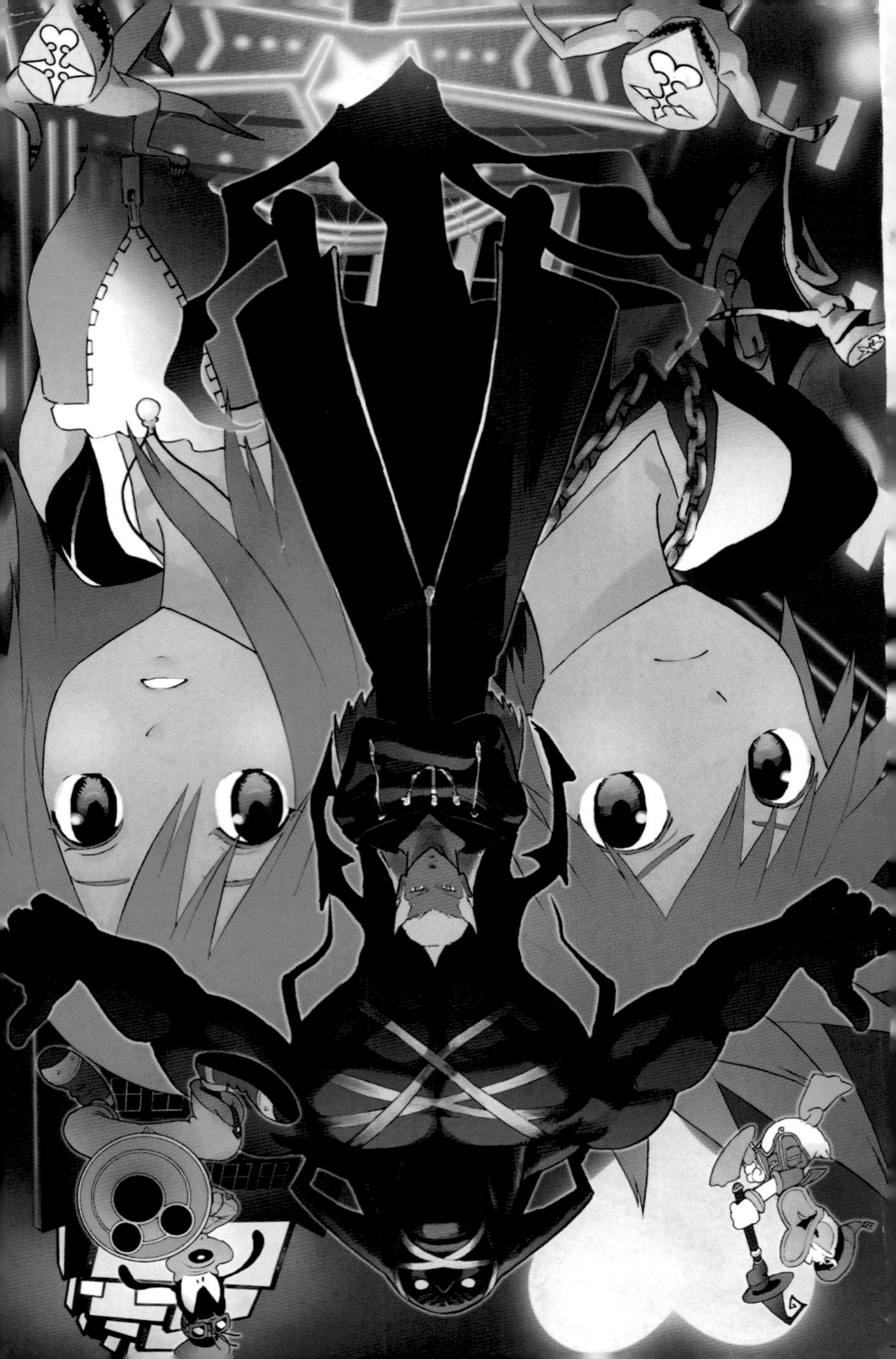

KINGDOM HEARTS II

A scattered dream that's like a far-off memory. A far-off memory that's like a scattered dream.
I want to line the pieces up, yours and mine.

SHIRO AMANO
ORIGINAL CONCEPT:
TETSUYA NOMURA

4

DISNEY SQUARE ENIX

KINGDOM HEARTS

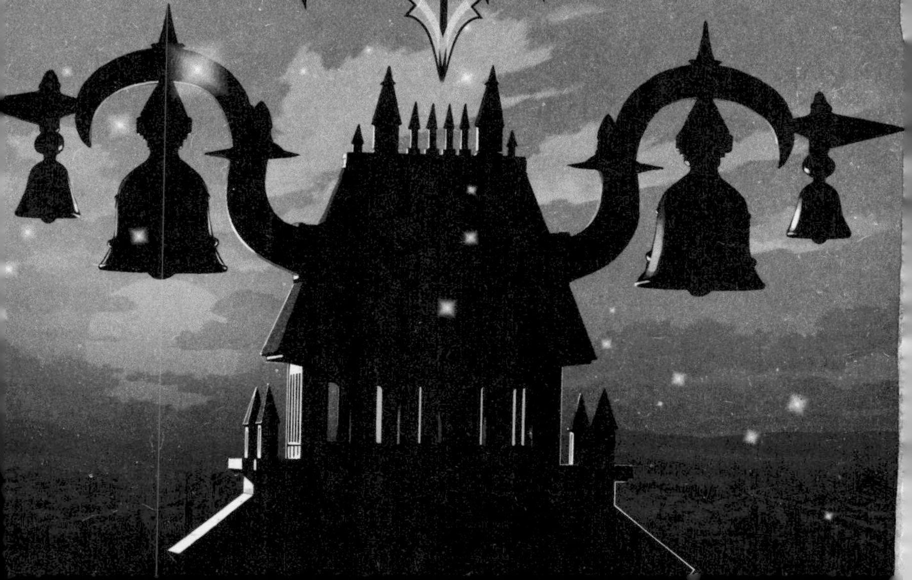

CONTENTS

KINGDOM HEARTS II

Chapter 51: Proof of Friendship

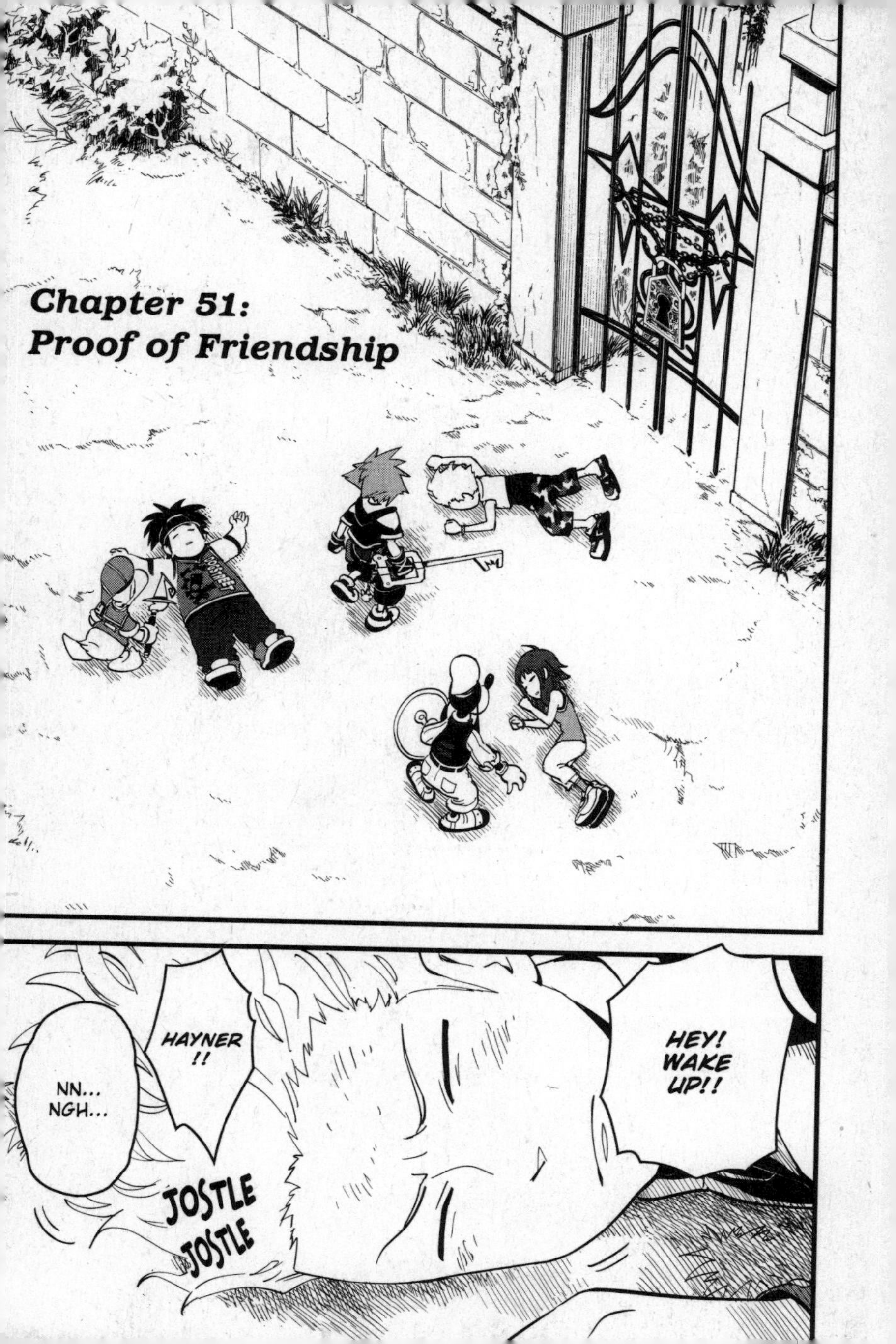
HEY! WAKE UP!!
HAYNER !!
NN... NGH...
JOSTLE JOSTLE

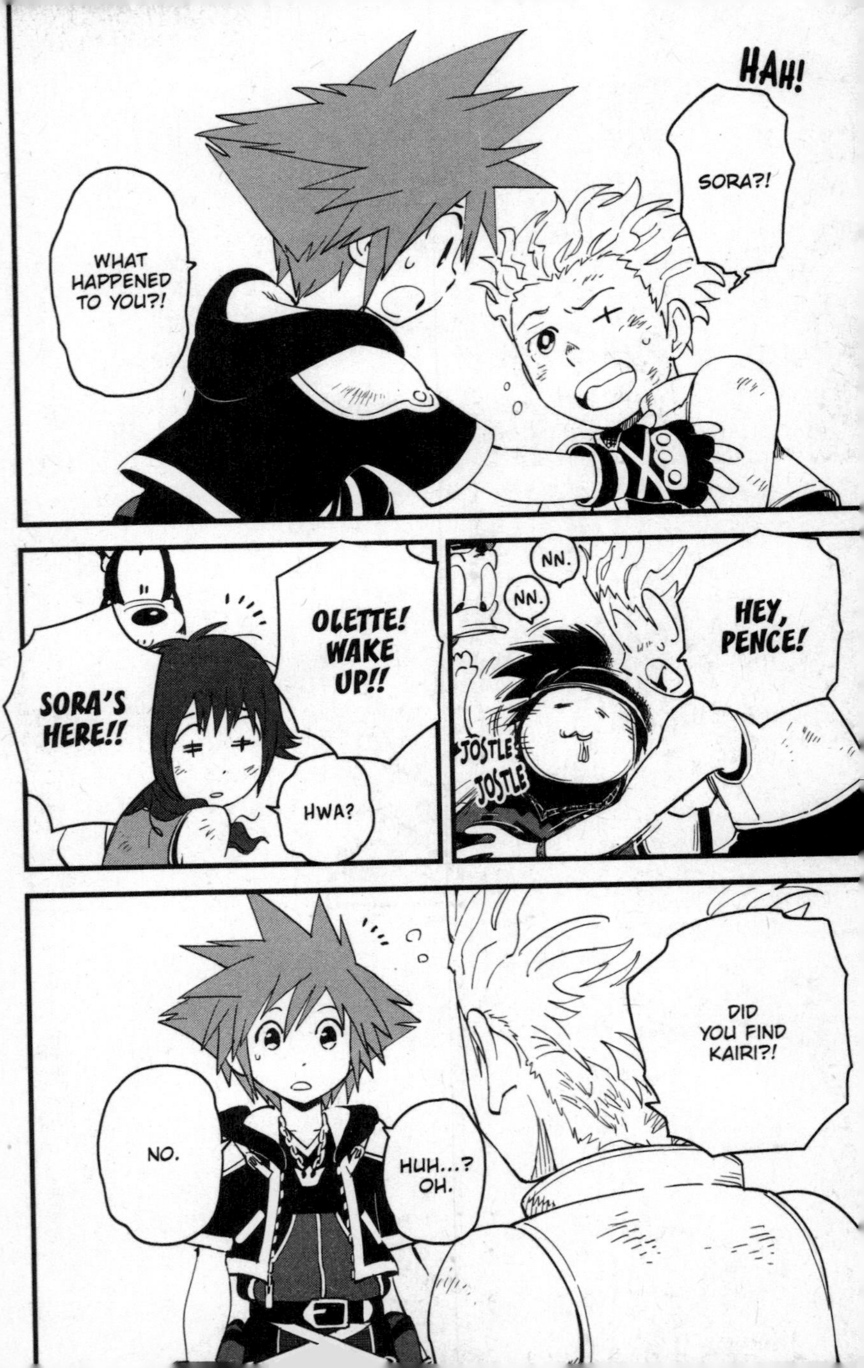
HAH!
SORA?!
WHAT HAPPENED TO YOU?!
HEY, PENCE!
NN.
NN.
JOSTLE JOSTLE
OLETTE! WAKE UP!!
SORA'S HERE!!
HWA?
DID YOU FIND KAIRI?!
HUH...? OH.
NO.

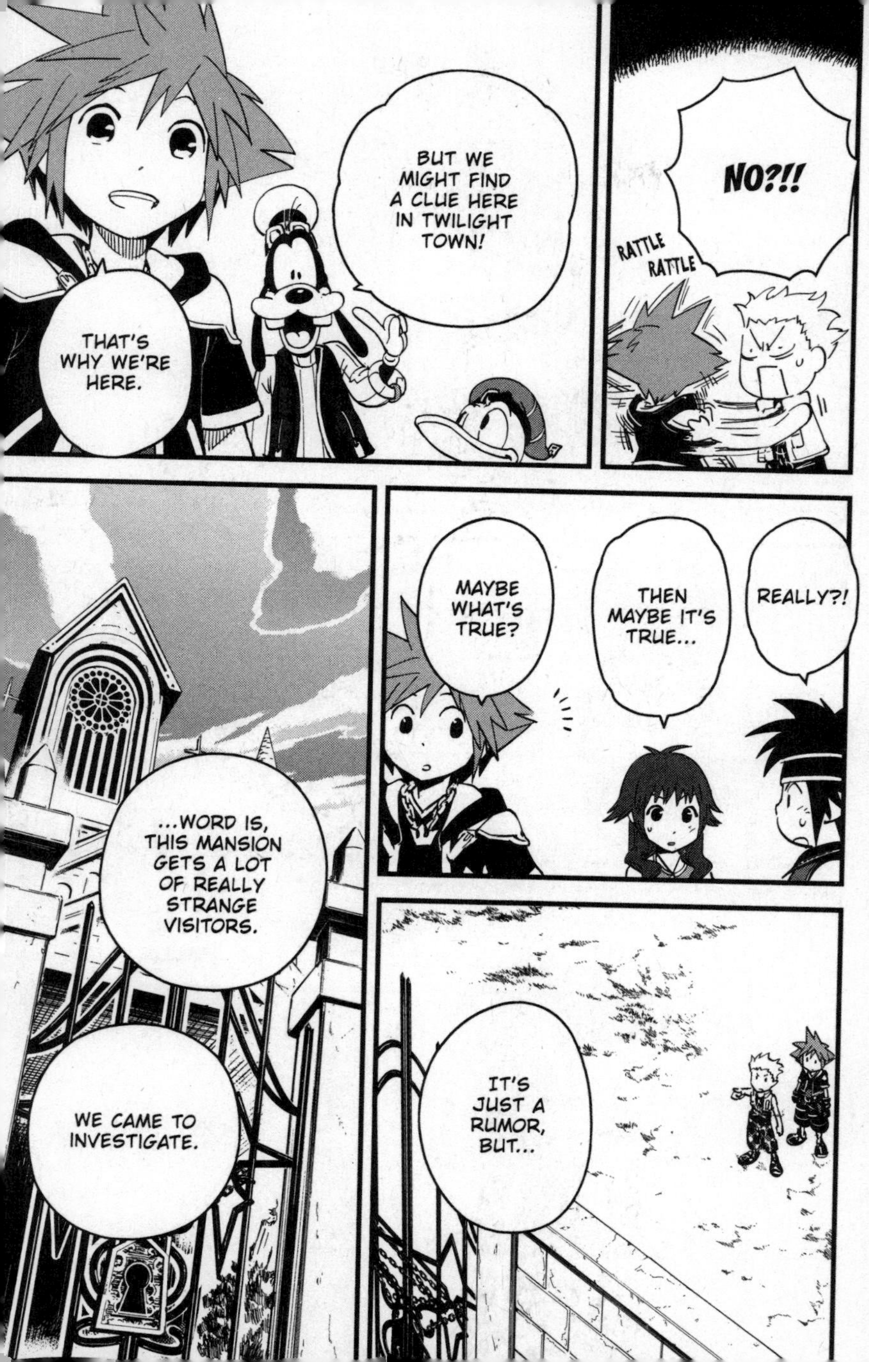
NO?!!
RATTLE RATTLE
BUT WE MIGHT FIND A CLUE HERE IN TWILIGHT TOWN!
THAT'S WHY WE'RE HERE.
REALLY?!
THEN MAYBE IT'S TRUE...
MAYBE WHAT'S TRUE?
IT'S JUST A RUMOR, BUT...
...WORD IS, THIS MANSION GETS A LOT OF REALLY STRANGE VISITORS.
WE CAME TO INVESTIGATE.

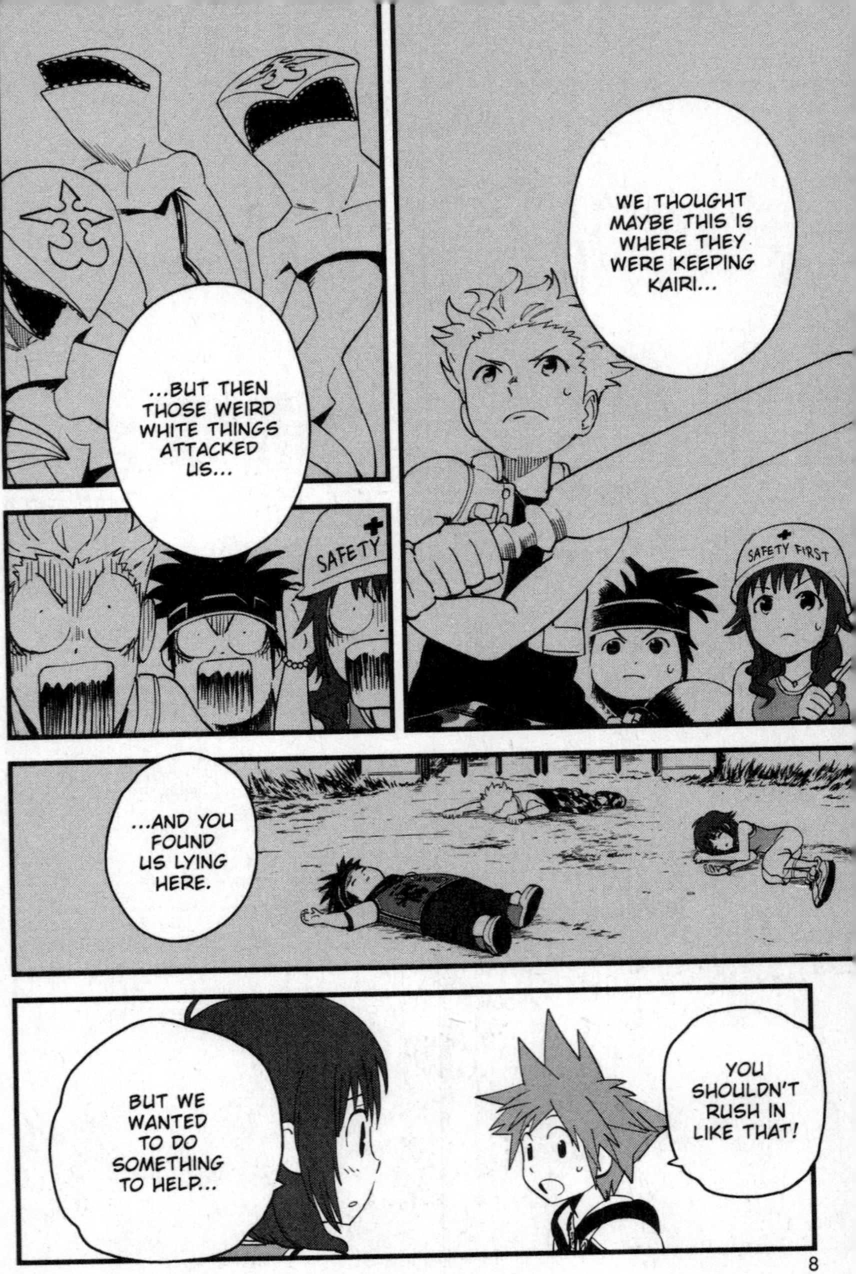
WE THOUGHT MAYBE THIS IS WHERE THEY WERE KEEPING KAIRI...
SAFETY FIRST
...BUT THEN THOSE WEIRD WHITE THINGS ATTACKED US...
SAFETY
...AND YOU FOUND US LYING HERE.
YOU SHOULDN'T RUSH IN LIKE THAT!
BUT WE WANTED TO DO SOMETHING TO HELP...

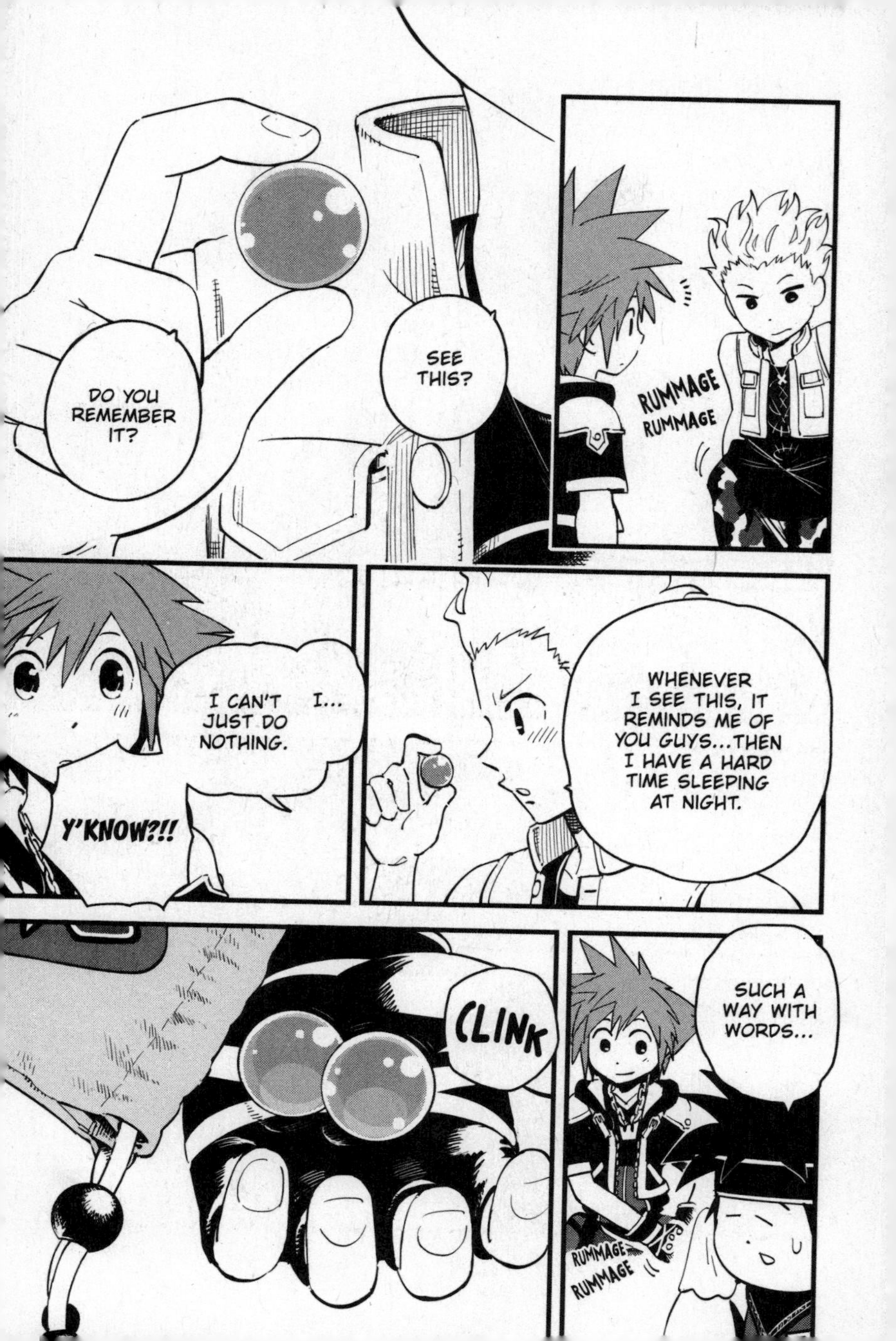
RUMMAGE RUMMAGE
SEE THIS?
DO YOU REMEMBER IT?
WHENEVER I SEE THIS, IT REMINDS ME OF YOU GUYS...THEN I HAVE A HARD TIME SLEEPING AT NIGHT.
I...
I CAN'T JUST DO NOTHING.
Y'KNOW?!!
SUCH A WAY WITH WORDS...
RUMMAGE RUMMAGE
CLINK

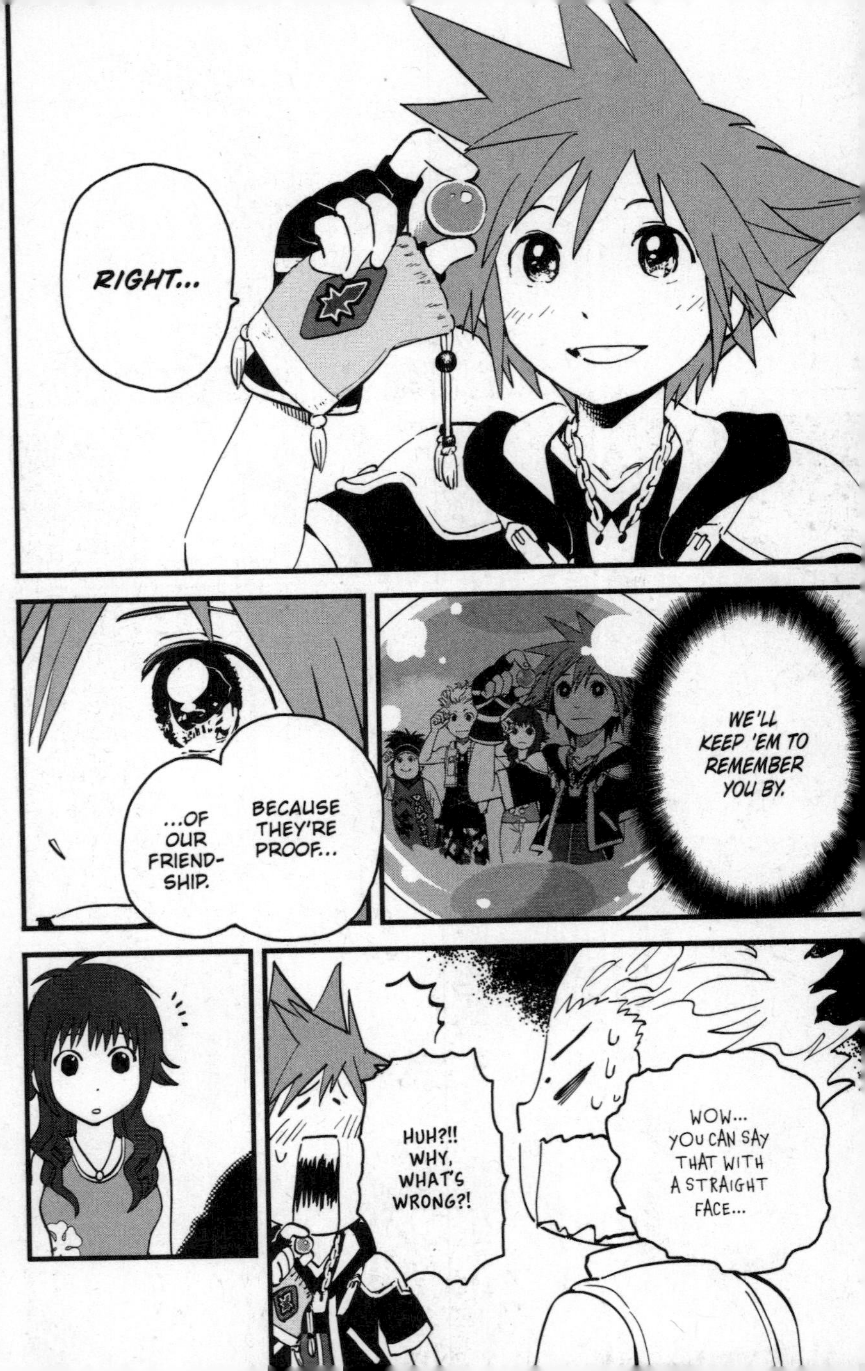
RIGHT...
WE'LL KEEP 'EM TO REMEMBER YOU BY.
BECAUSE THEY'RE PROOF...
...OF OUR FRIEND-SHIP.
WOW... YOU CAN SAY THAT WITH A STRAIGHT FACE...
HUH?!! WHY, WHAT'S WRONG?!

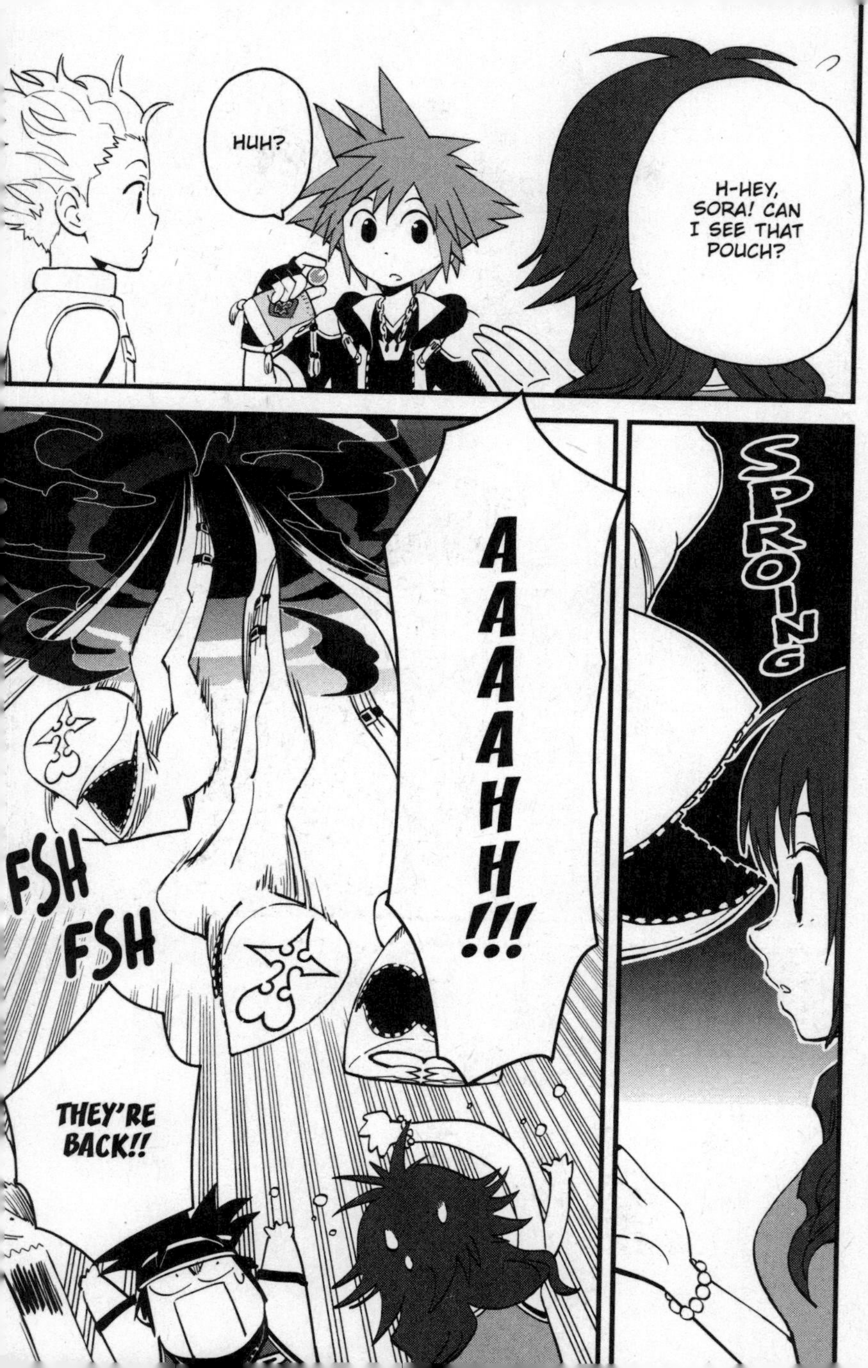
H-HEY, SORA! CAN I SEE THAT POUCH?
HUH?
SPROING
AAAAAHH!!!
FSH FSH
THEY'RE BACK!!

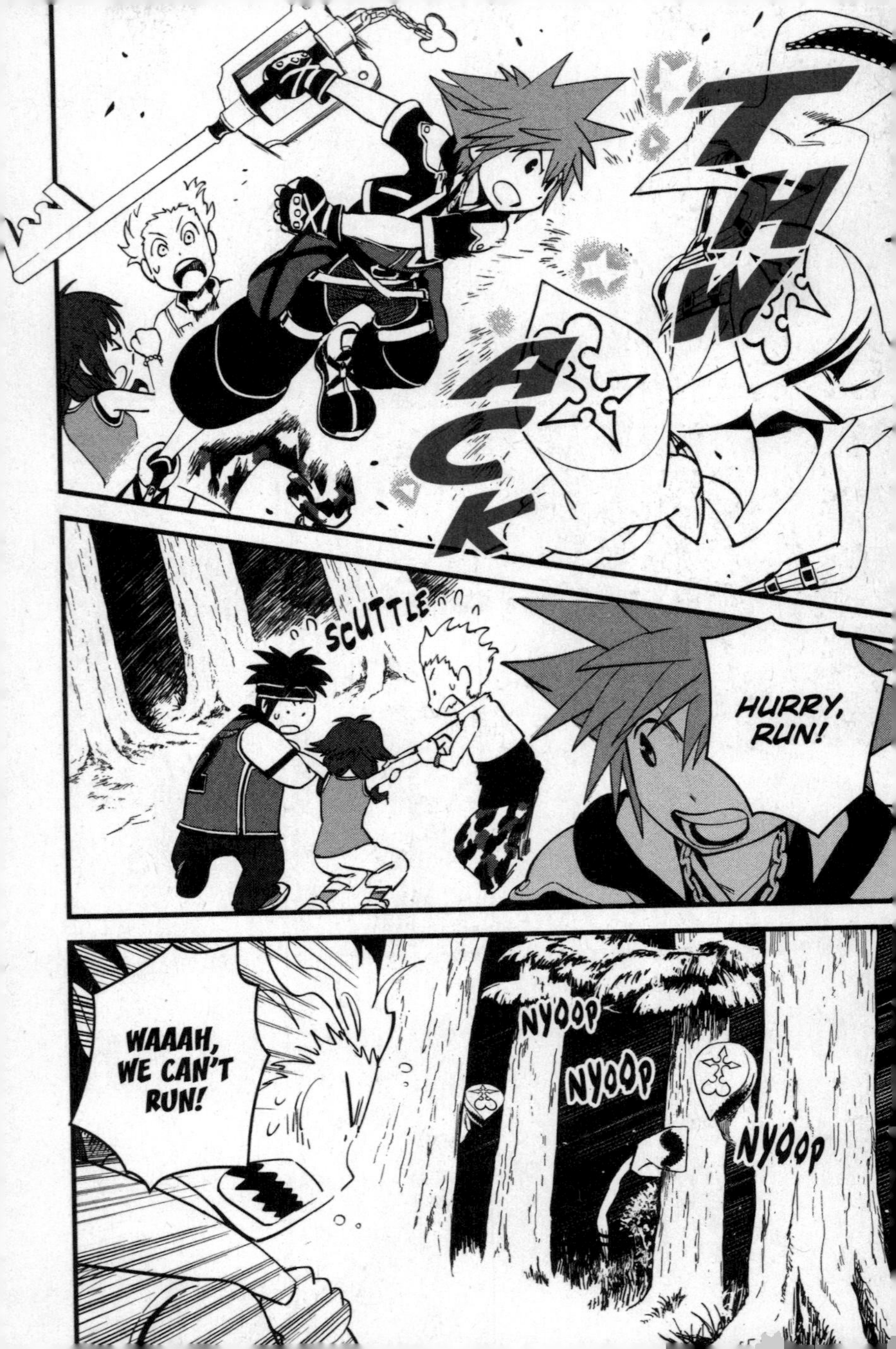

THWACK
HURRY, RUN!
SCUTTLE
NYOOP
NYOOP
NYOOP
WAAAH, WE CAN'T RUN!

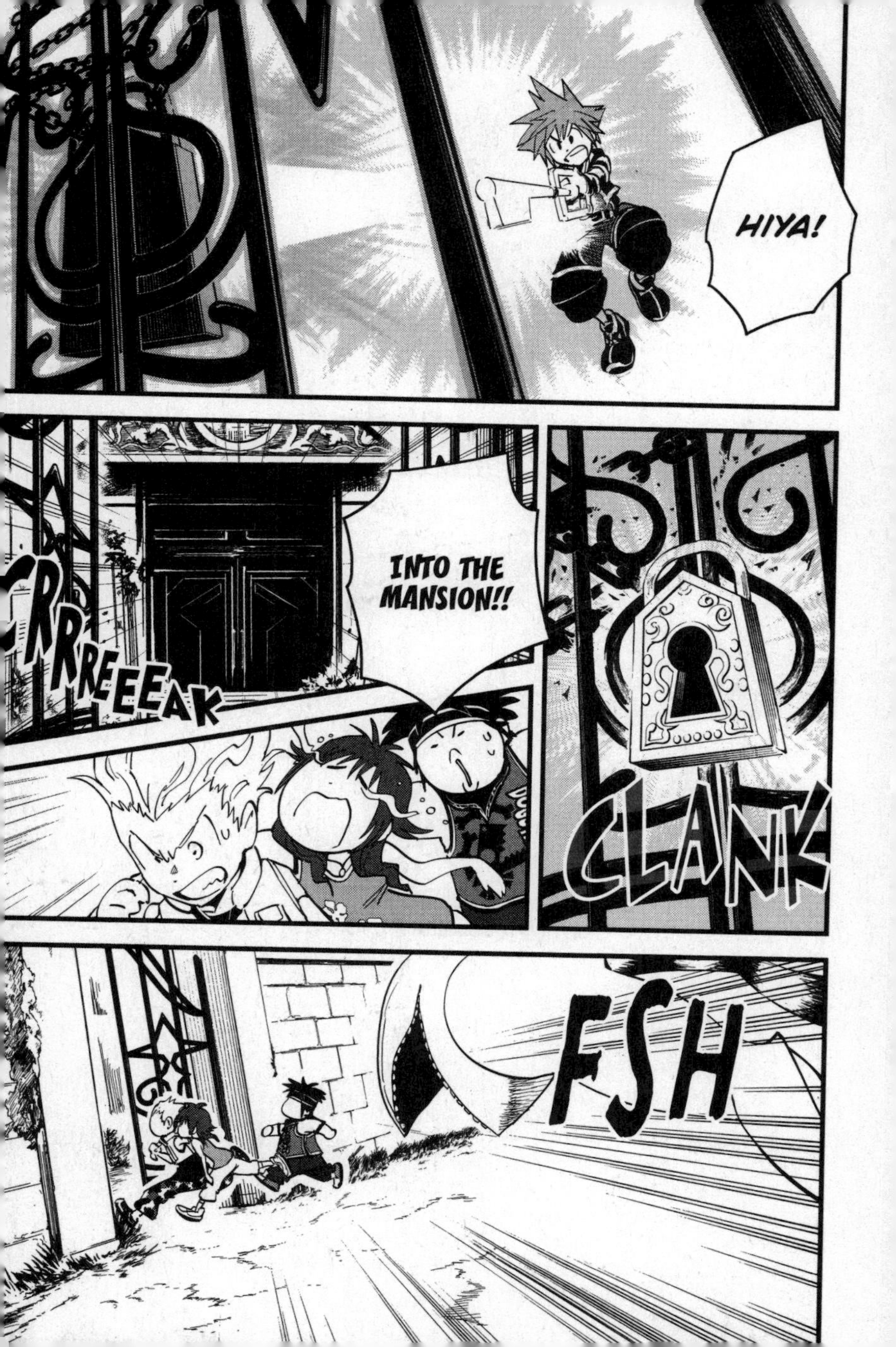
HIYA!
CLANK
INTO THE MANSION!!
CRRREEEAK
FSH

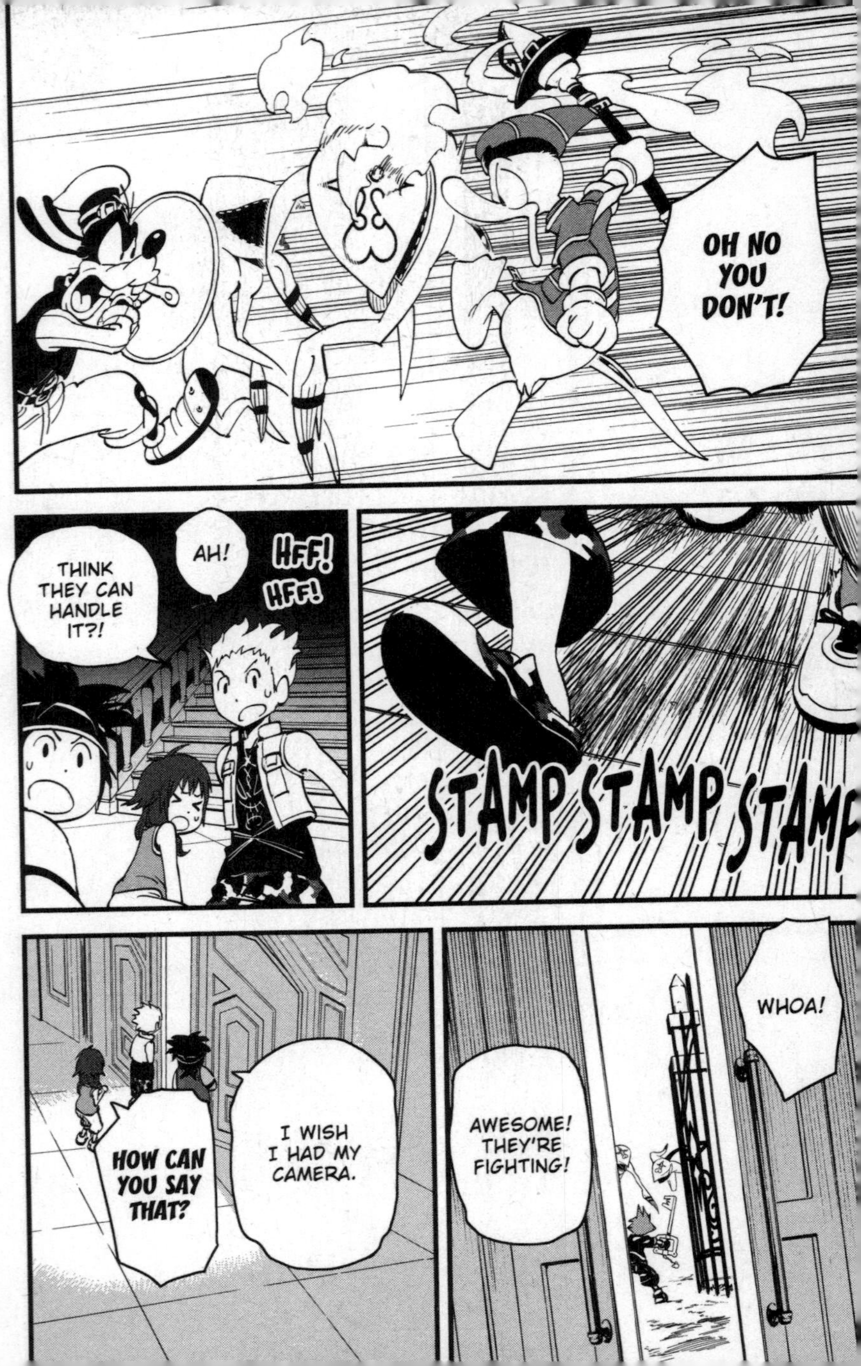
OH NO YOU DON'T!
STAMP STAMP STAM
HFF! HFF!
AH!
THINK THEY CAN HANDLE IT?!
WHOA!
AWESOME! THEY'RE FIGHTING!
I WISH I HAD MY CAMERA.
HOW CAN YOU SAY THAT?

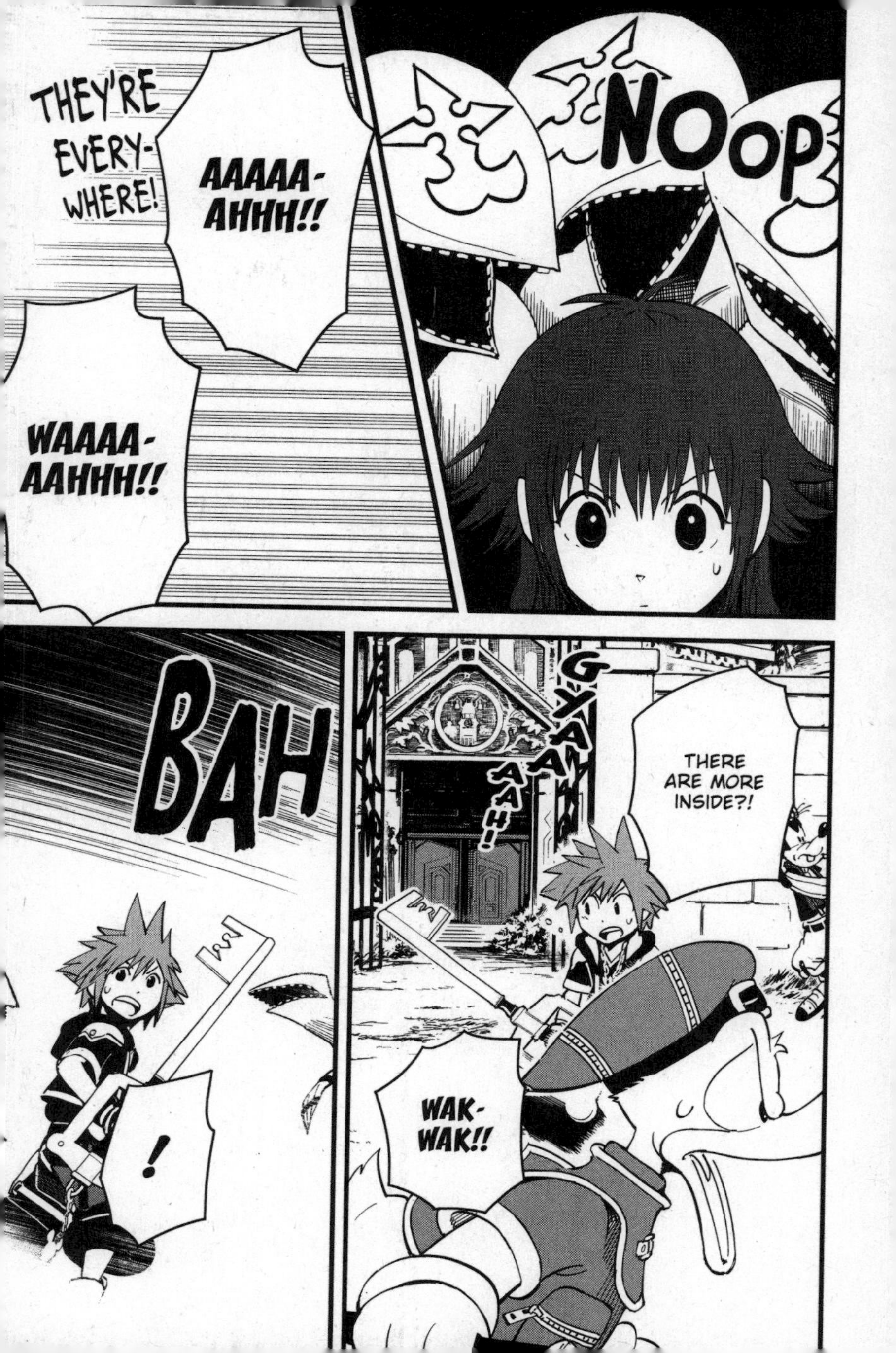
NOOP
AAAAA-AHHH!!
THEY'RE EVERY-WHERE!
WAAAA-AAHHH!!
GYAAAAH!
THERE ARE MORE INSIDE?!
WAK-WAK!!
BAH
!

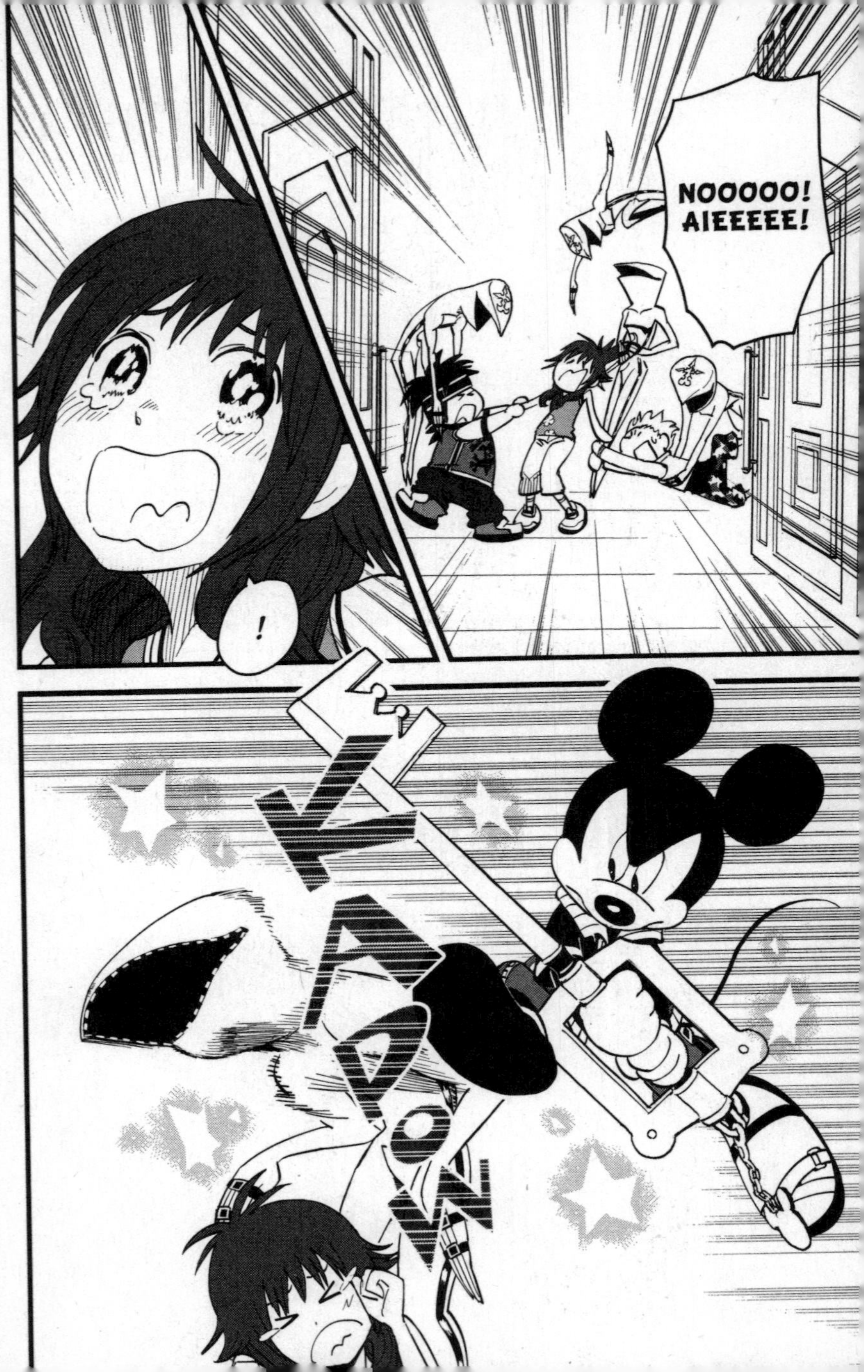
NOOOOO! AIEEEEE!
!
KAPOW

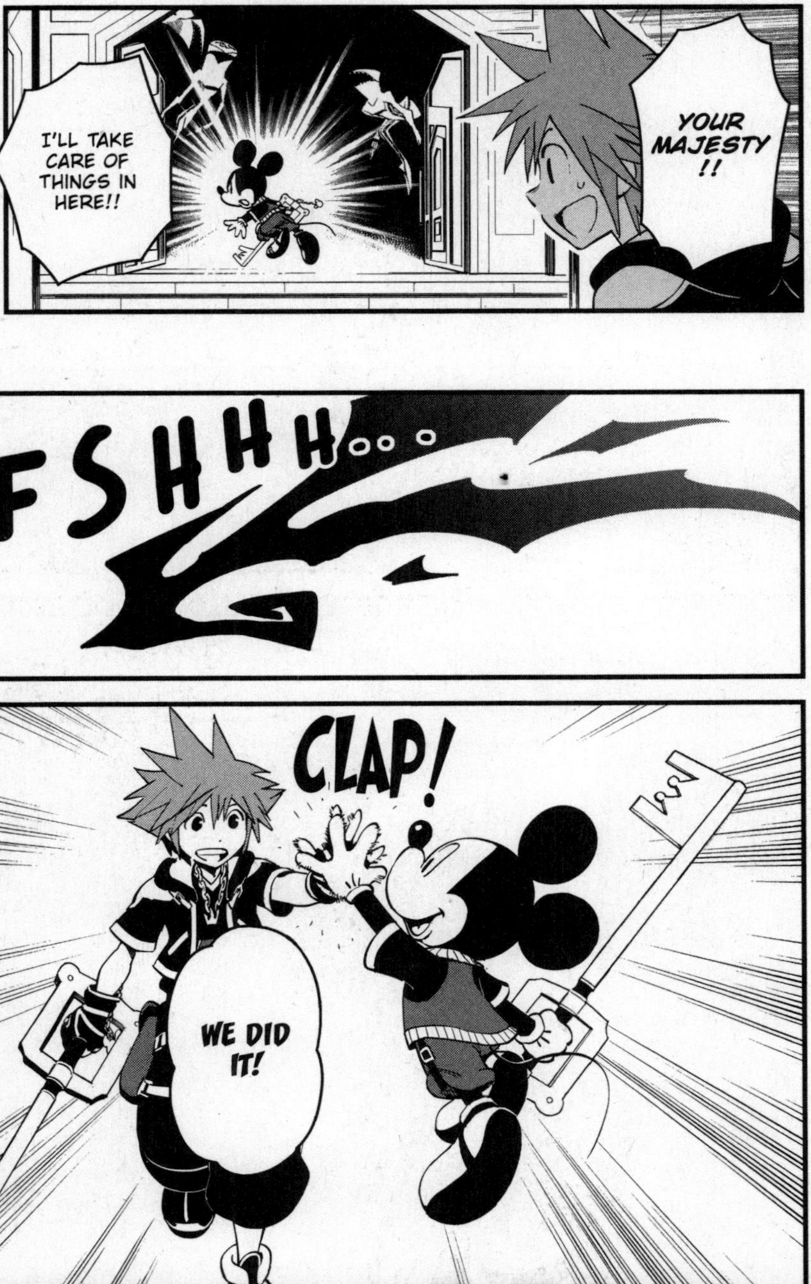
YOUR MAJESTY!!
I'LL TAKE CARE OF THINGS IN HERE!!
FSHHH...
CLAP!
WE DID IT!

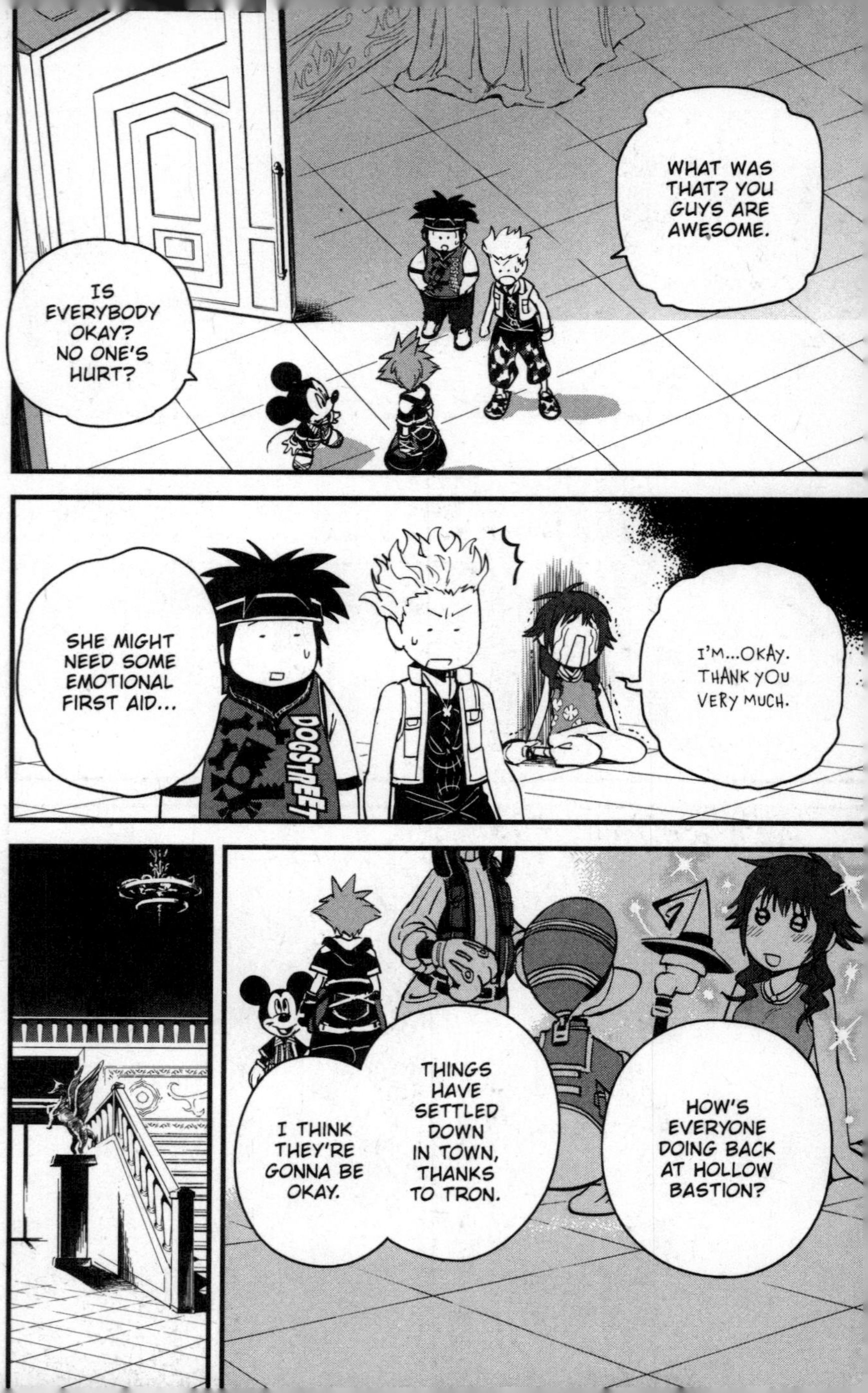
WHAT WAS THAT? YOU GUYS ARE AWESOME.
IS EVERYBODY OKAY? NO ONE'S HURT?
I'M...OKAY. THANK YOU VERY MUCH.
SHE MIGHT NEED SOME EMOTIONAL FIRST AID...
HOW'S EVERYONE DOING BACK AT HOLLOW BASTION?
THINGS HAVE SETTLED DOWN IN TOWN, THANKS TO TRON.
I THINK THEY'RE GONNA BE OKAY.

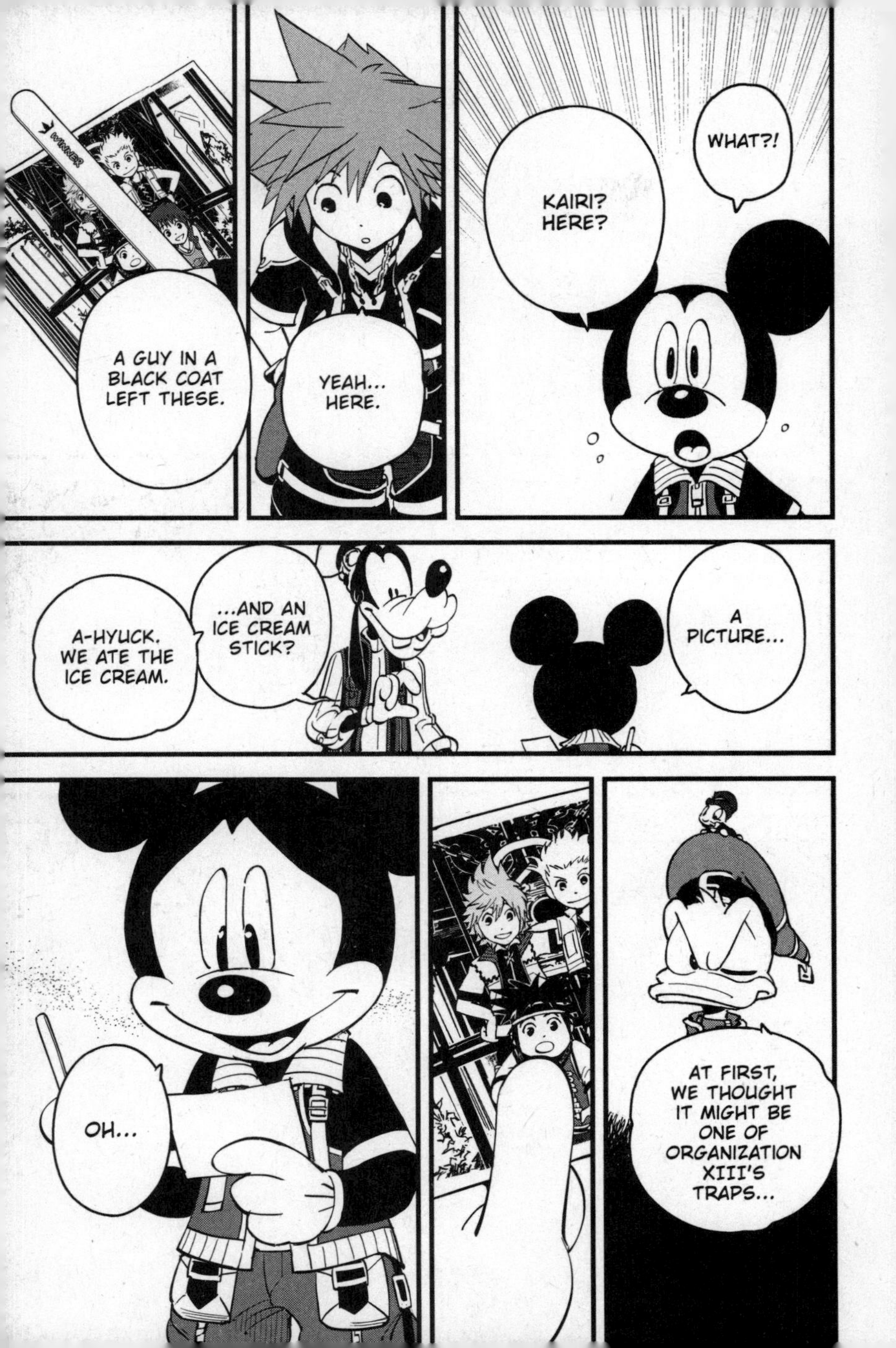
WHAT?!
KAIRI? HERE?
YEAH... HERE.
WINNER
A GUY IN A BLACK COAT LEFT THESE.
A PICTURE...
...AND AN ICE CREAM STICK?
A-HYUCK. WE ATE THE ICE CREAM.
AT FIRST, WE THOUGHT IT MIGHT BE ONE OF ORGANIZATION XIII'S TRAPS...
OH...

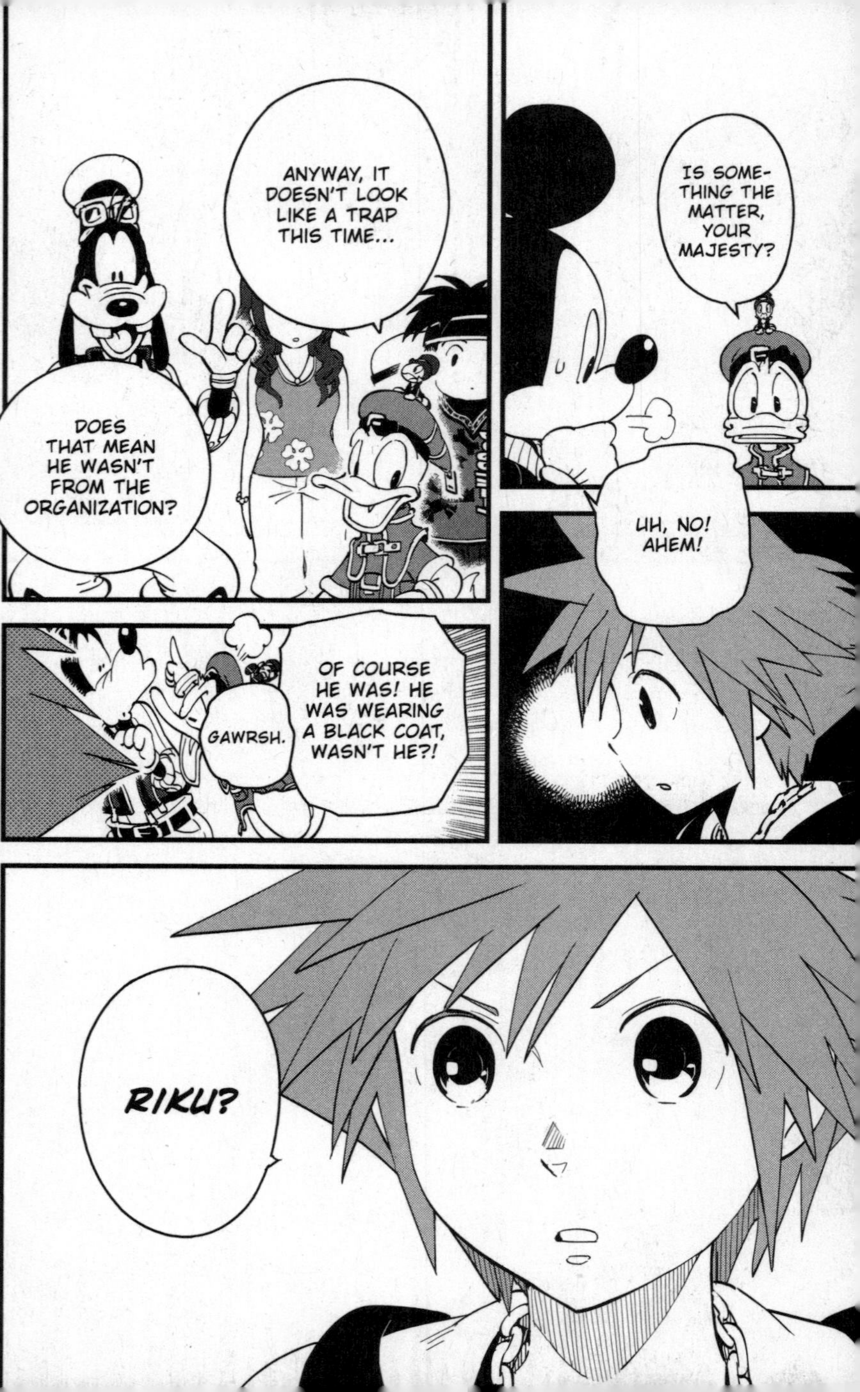
IS SOME-THING THE MATTER, YOUR MAJESTY?
ANYWAY, IT DOESN'T LOOK LIKE A TRAP THIS TIME...
DOES THAT MEAN HE WASN'T FROM THE ORGANIZATION?
UH, NO! AHEM!
OF COURSE HE WAS! HE WAS WEARING A BLACK COAT, WASN'T HE?!
GAWRSH.
RIKU?

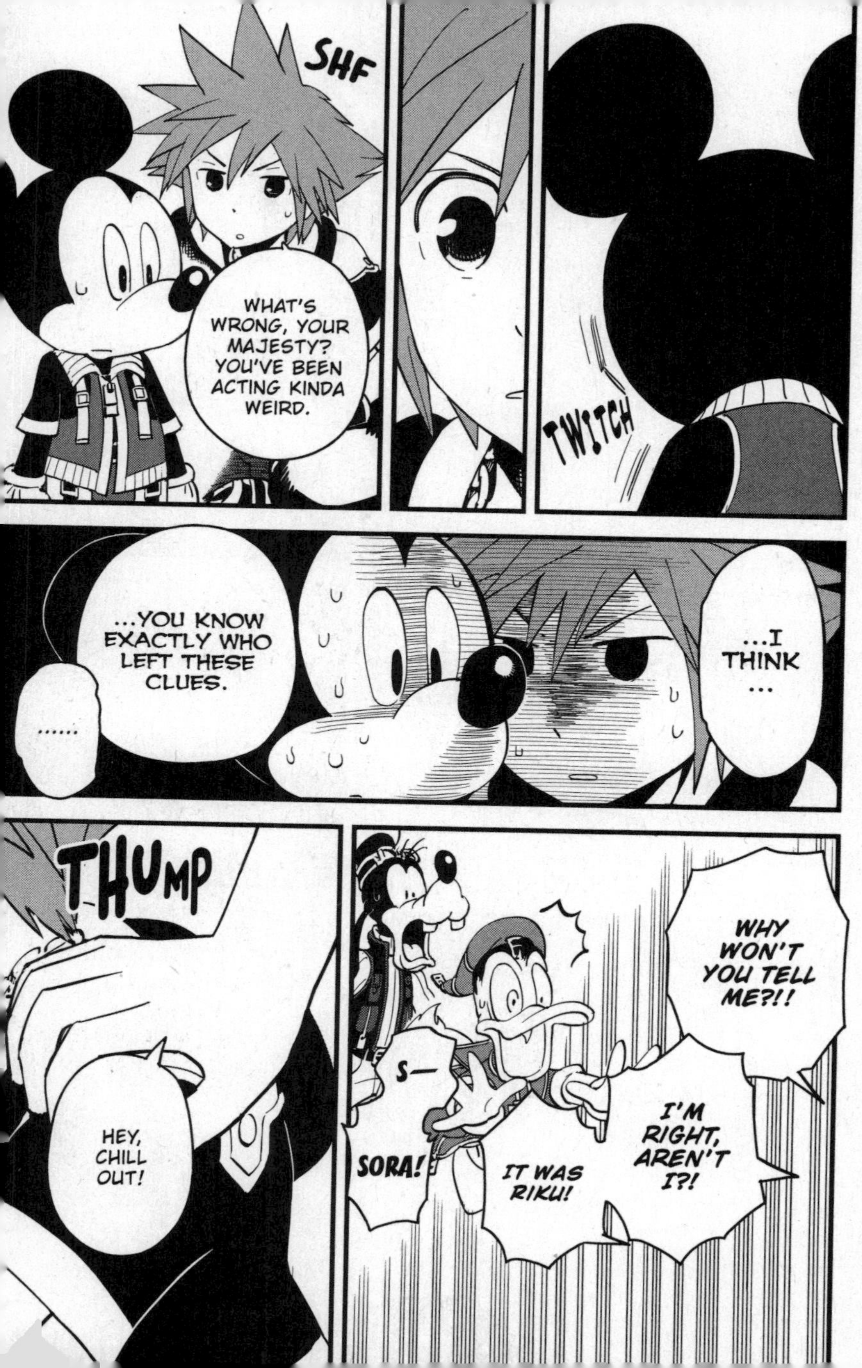
TWITCH
SHF
WHAT'S WRONG, YOUR MAJESTY? YOU'VE BEEN ACTING KINDA WEIRD.
...I THINK ...
...YOU KNOW EXACTLY WHO LEFT THESE CLUES.
......
WHY WON'T YOU TELL ME?!!
I'M RIGHT, AREN'T I?!
IT WAS RIKU!
S—
SORA!
THUMP
HEY, CHILL OUT!

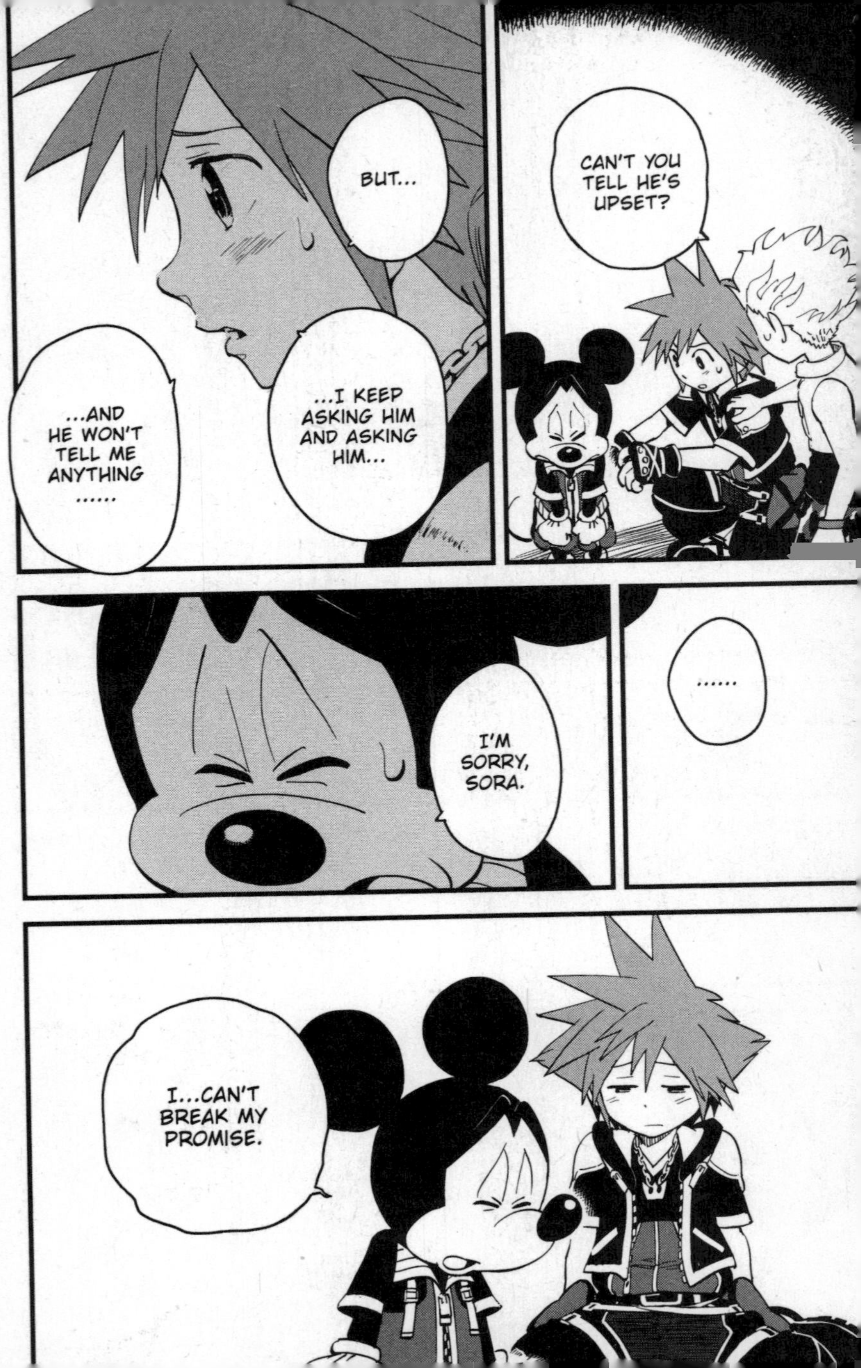
CAN'T YOU TELL HE'S UPSET?
BUT...
...I KEEP ASKING HIM AND ASKING HIM...
...AND HE WON'T TELL ME ANYTHING ......
......
I'M SORRY, SORA.
I...CAN'T BREAK MY PROMISE.

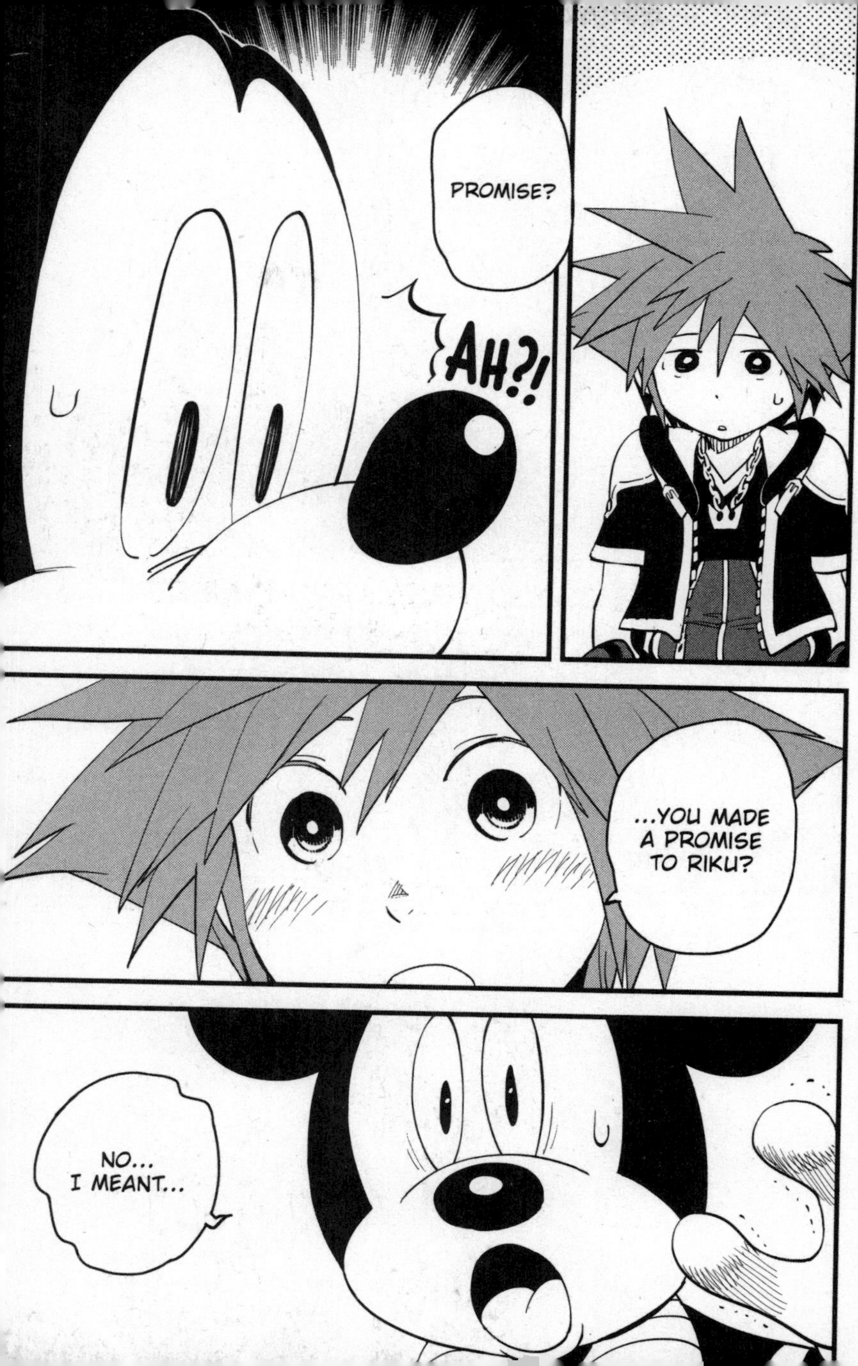
PROMISE?
AH?!
...YOU MADE A PROMISE TO RIKU?
NO... I MEANT...

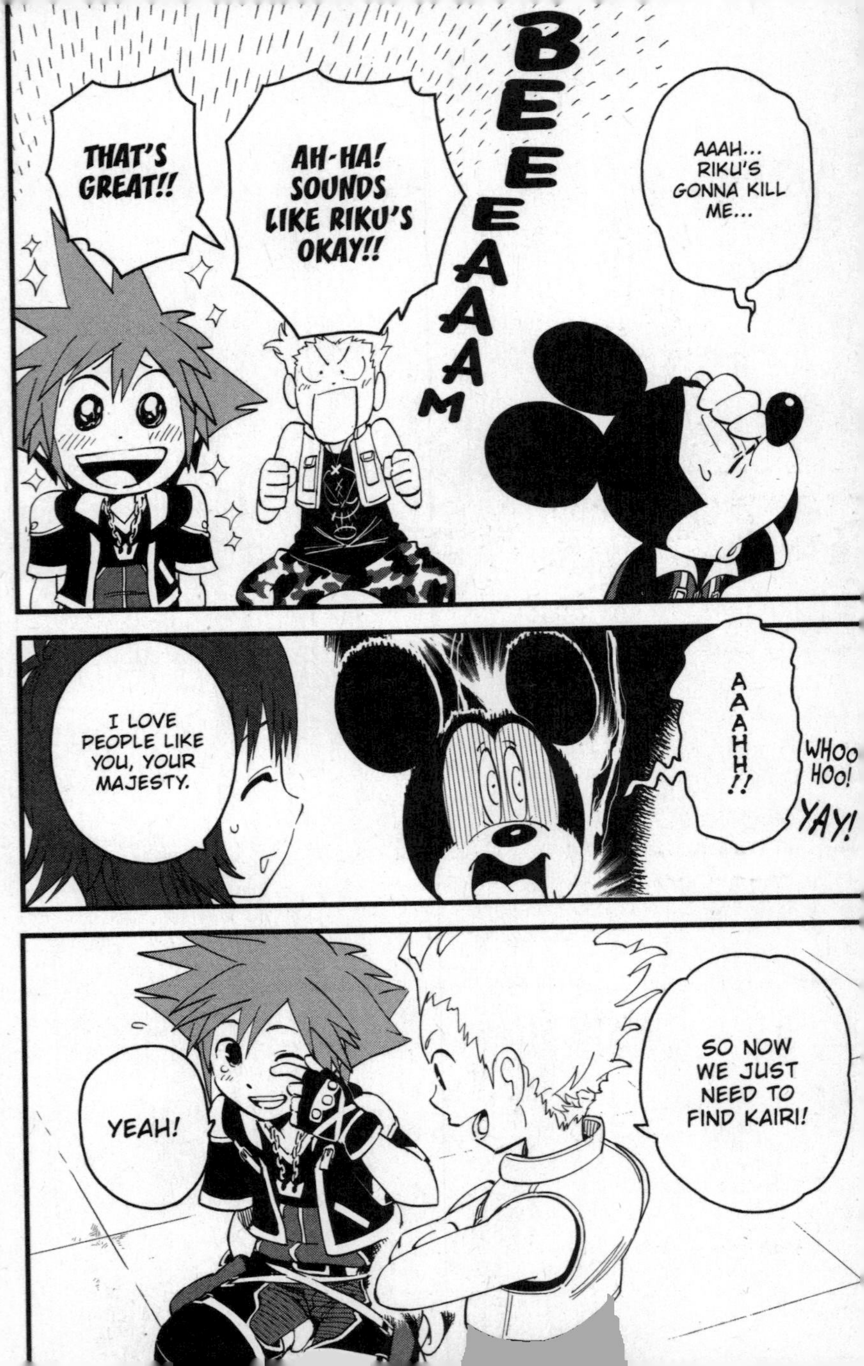
AAAH... RIKU'S GONNA KILL ME...
BEEEAAAM
AH-HA! SOUNDS LIKE RIKU'S OKAY!!
THAT'S GREAT!!
WHOO HOO! YAY!
AAAHH!!
I LOVE PEOPLE LIKE YOU, YOUR MAJESTY.
SO NOW WE JUST NEED TO FIND KAIRI!
YEAH!

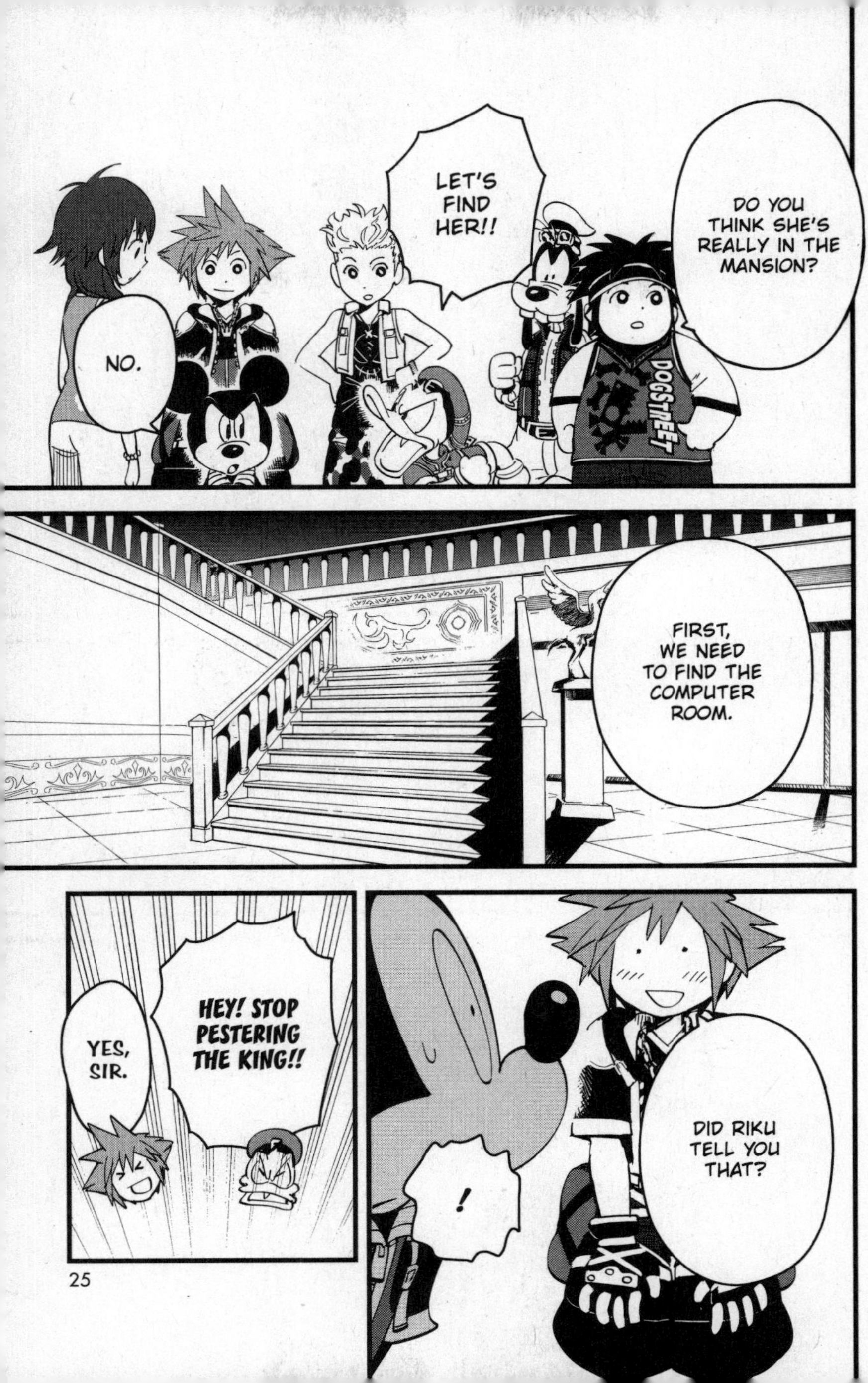
DO YOU THINK SHE'S REALLY IN THE MANSION?
LET'S FIND HER!!
NO.
FIRST, WE NEED TO FIND THE COMPUTER ROOM.
DID RIKU TELL YOU THAT?
!
HEY! STOP PESTERING THE KING!!
YES, SIR.

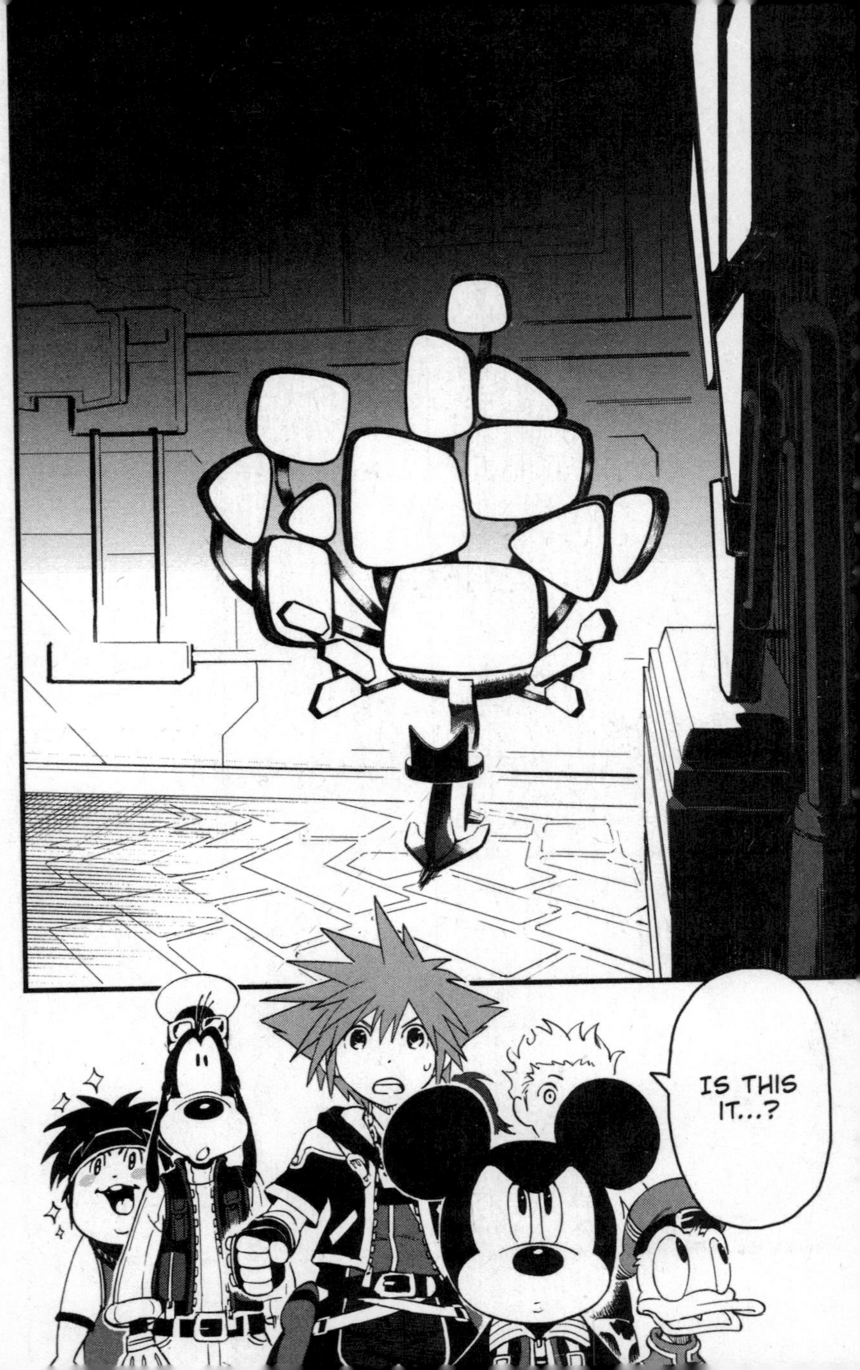
IS THIS IT...?

Chapter 52: The Other Twilight Town

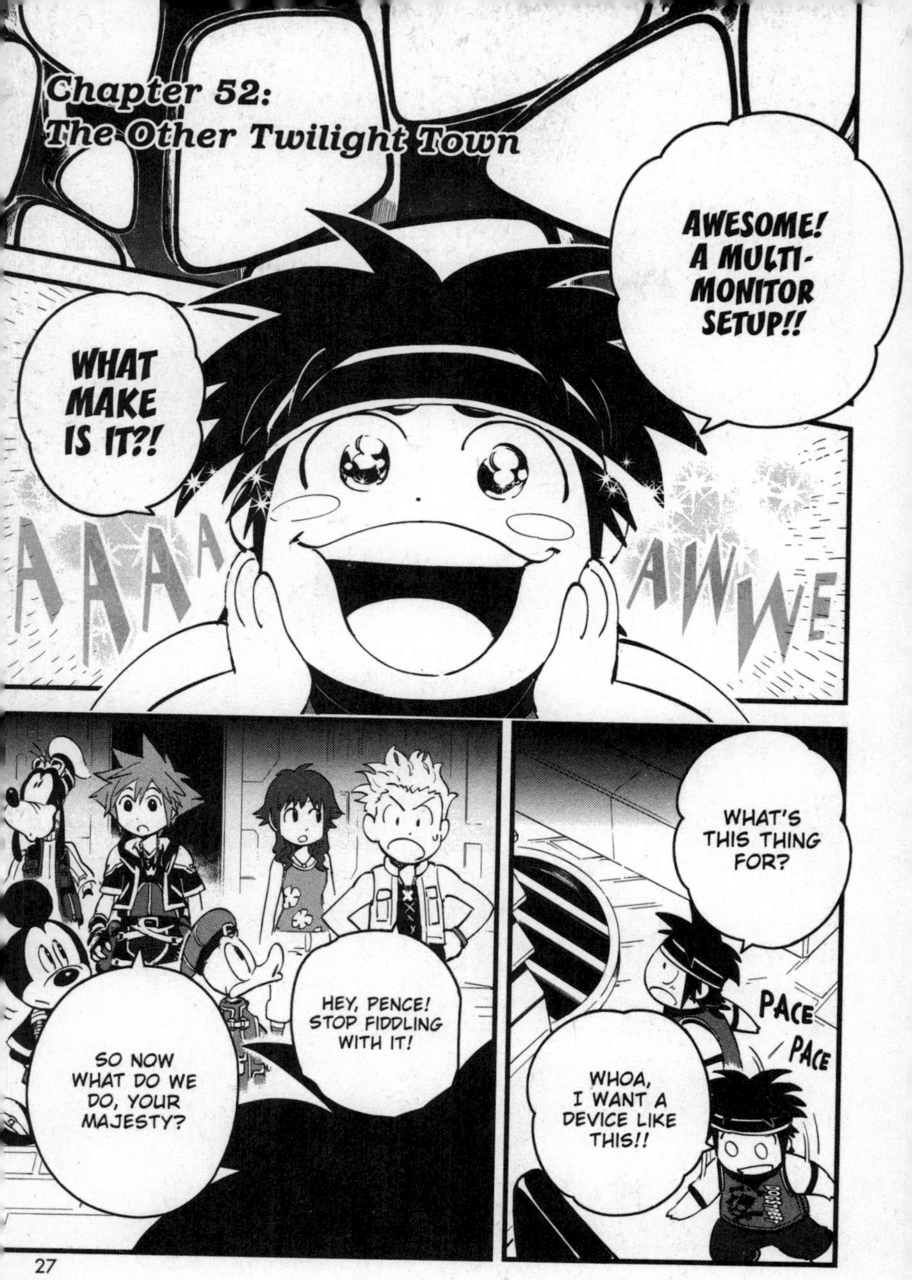

AWESOME! A MULTI-MONITOR SETUP!!
AWWE
WHAT MAKE IS IT?!
AAAA
WHAT'S THIS THING FOR?
PACE
PACE
WHOA, I WANT A DEVICE LIKE THIS!!
HEY, PENCE! STOP FIDDLING WITH IT!
SO NOW WHAT DO WE DO, YOUR MAJESTY?

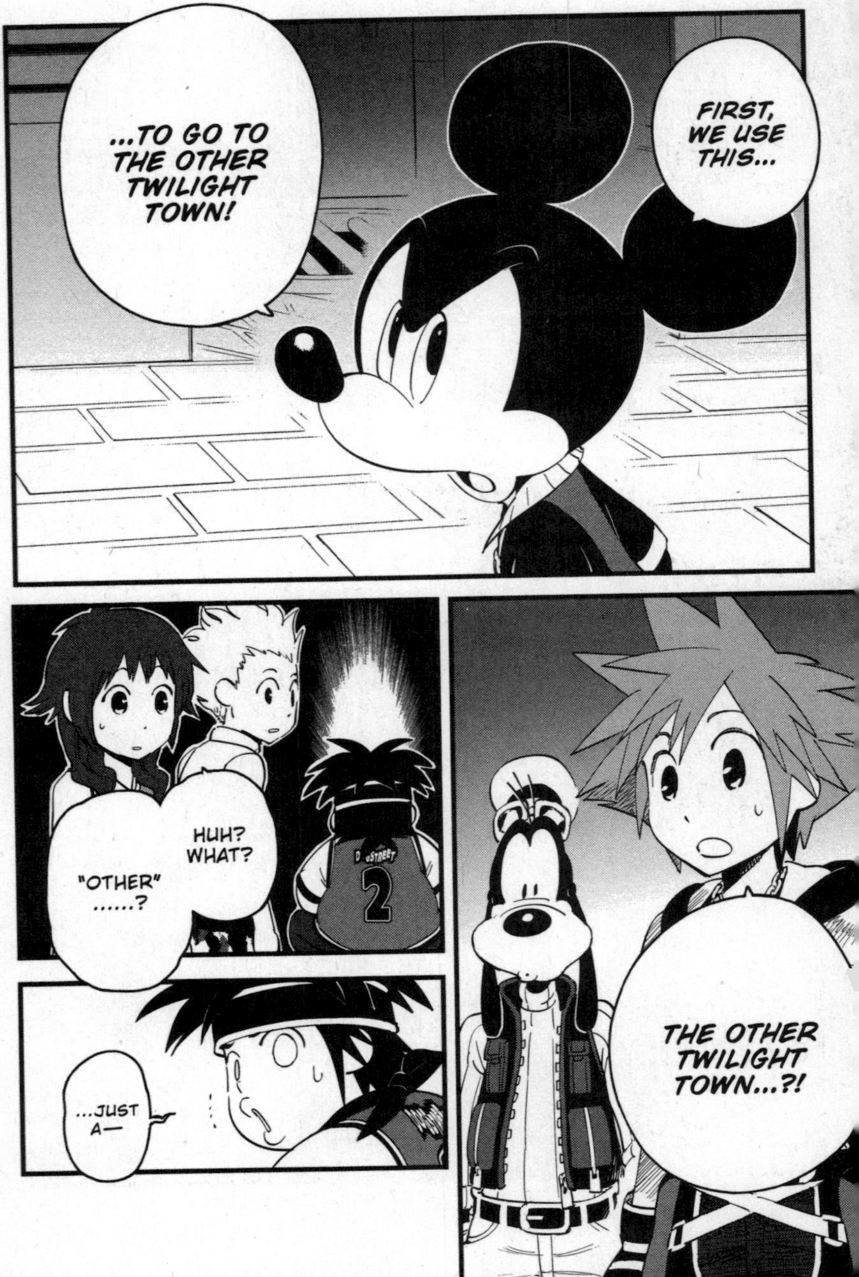
FIRST, WE USE THIS...
...TO GO TO THE OTHER TWILIGHT TOWN!
THE OTHER TWILIGHT TOWN...?!
HUH? WHAT?
"OTHER" ......?
...JUST A—

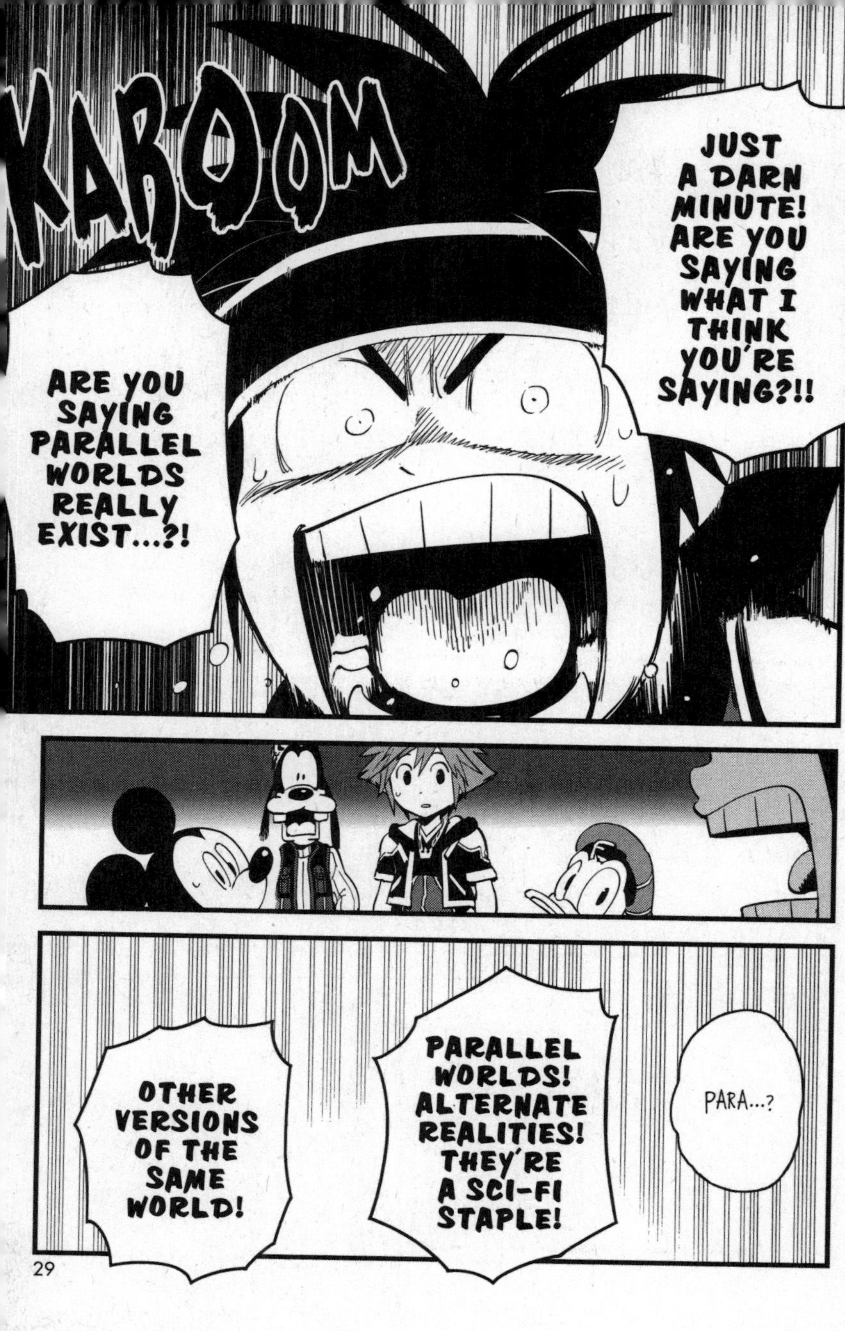
JUST A DARN MINUTE! ARE YOU SAYING WHAT I THINK YOU'RE SAYING?!!
KABOOM
ARE YOU SAYING PARALLEL WORLDS REALLY EXIST...?!
PARA...?
PARALLEL WORLDS! ALTERNATE REALITIES! THEY'RE A SCI-FI STAPLE!
OTHER VERSIONS OF THE SAME WORLD!

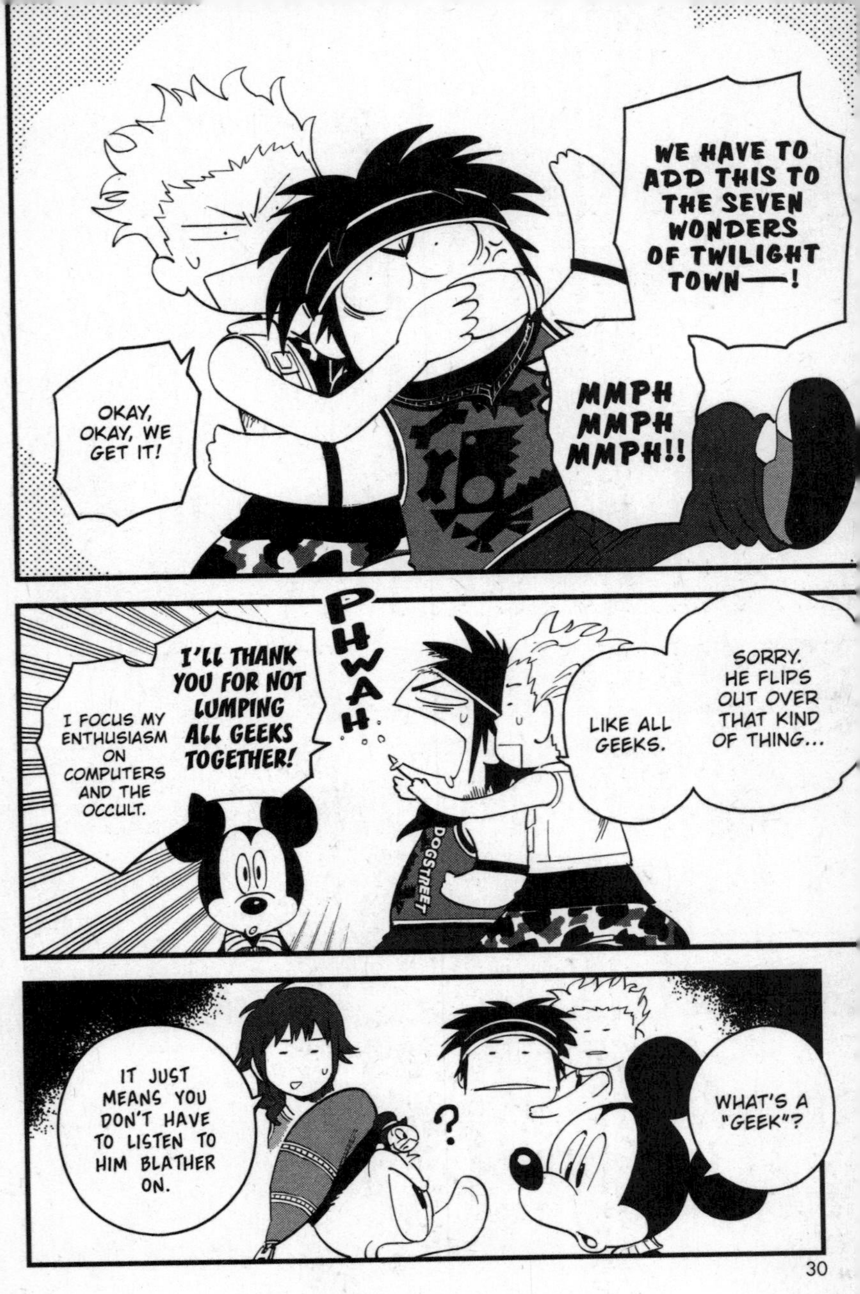
WE HAVE TO ADD THIS TO THE SEVEN WONDERS OF TWILIGHT TOWN—!
MMPH MMPH MMPH!!
OKAY, OKAY, WE GET IT!
SORRY. HE FLIPS OUT OVER THAT KIND OF THING...
LIKE ALL GEEKS.
PHWAH
DOGSTREET
I'LL THANK YOU FOR NOT LUMPING ALL GEEKS TOGETHER!
I FOCUS MY ENTHUSIASM ON COMPUTERS AND THE OCCULT.
WHAT'S A "GEEK"?
?
IT JUST MEANS YOU DON'T HAVE TO LISTEN TO HIM BLATHER ON.

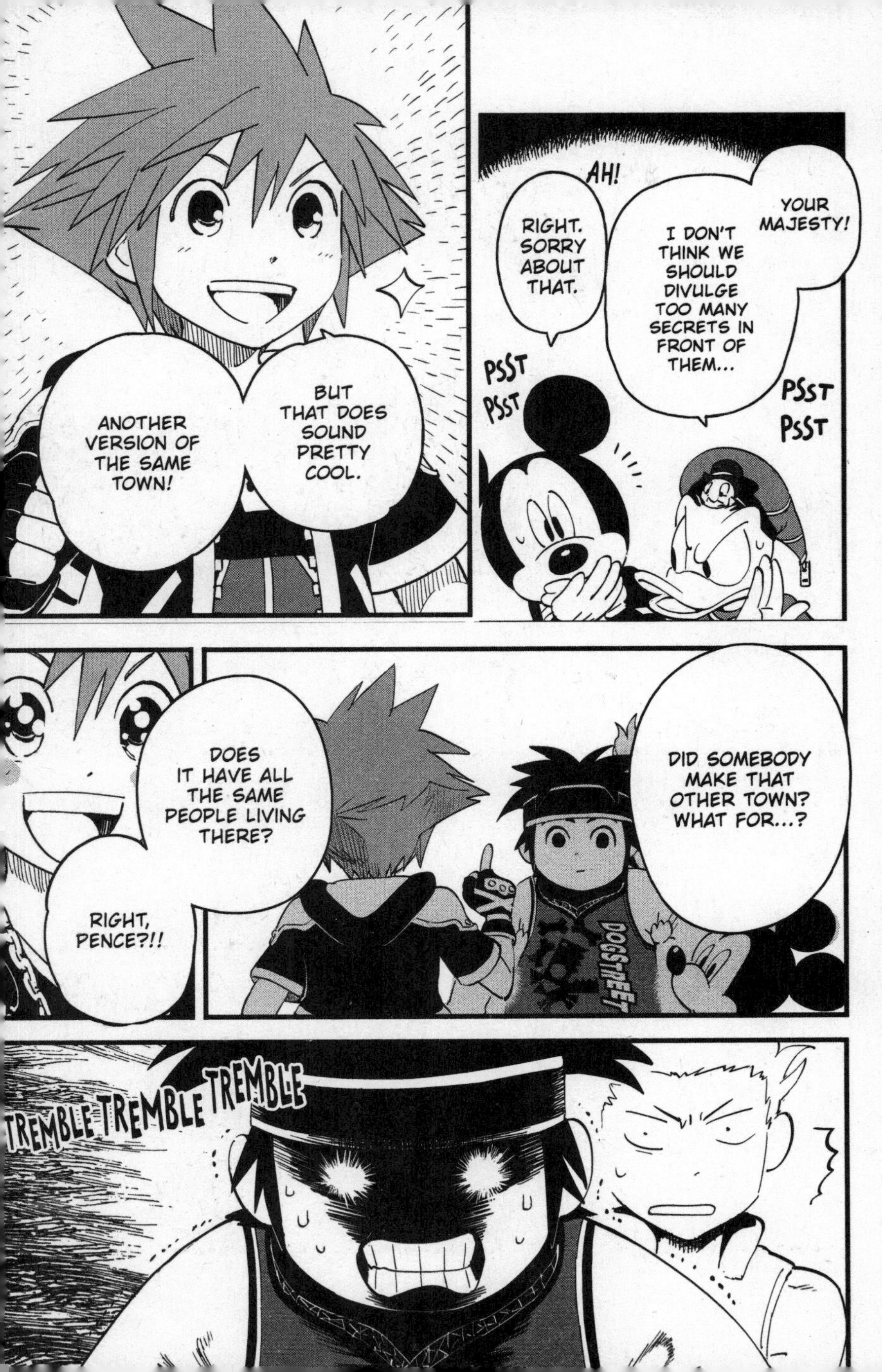
YOUR MAJESTY!
I DON'T THINK WE SHOULD DIVULGE TOO MANY SECRETS IN FRONT OF THEM...
AH!
RIGHT. SORRY ABOUT THAT.
PSST PSST
PSST PSST
BUT THAT DOES SOUND PRETTY COOL.
ANOTHER VERSION OF THE SAME TOWN!
DID SOMEBODY MAKE THAT OTHER TOWN? WHAT FOR...?
DOGSTREET
DOES IT HAVE ALL THE SAME PEOPLE LIVING THERE?
RIGHT, PENCE?!!
TREMBLE TREMBLE TREMBLE

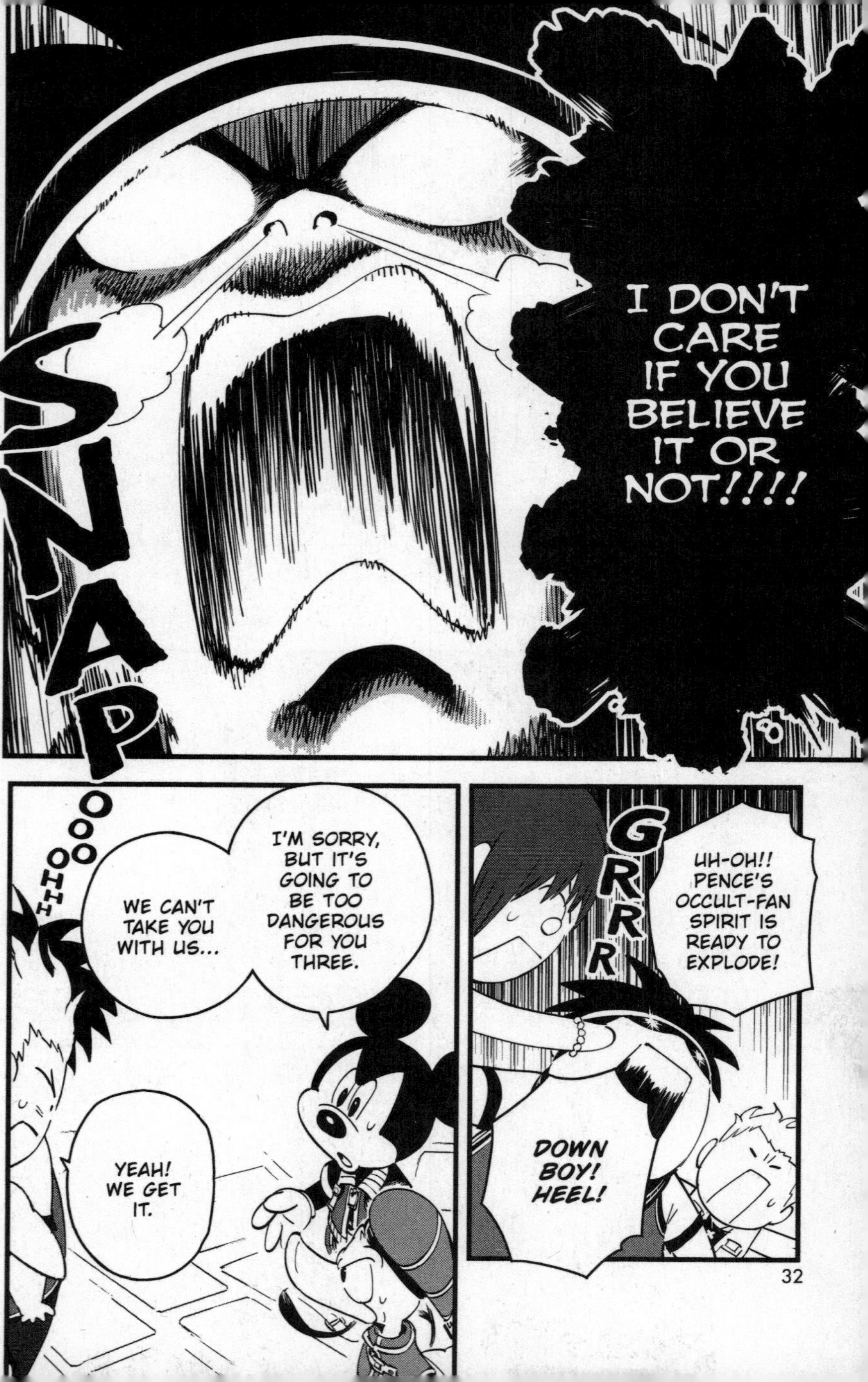
SNAP
I DON'T CARE IF YOU BELIEVE IT OR NOT!!!!
GRRR
UH-OH!! PENCE'S OCCULT-FAN SPIRIT IS READY TO EXPLODE!
DOWN BOY! HEEL!
OOOOHHH
I'M SORRY, BUT IT'S GOING TO BE TOO DANGEROUS FOR YOU THREE.
WE CAN'T TAKE YOU WITH US...
YEAH! WE GET IT.

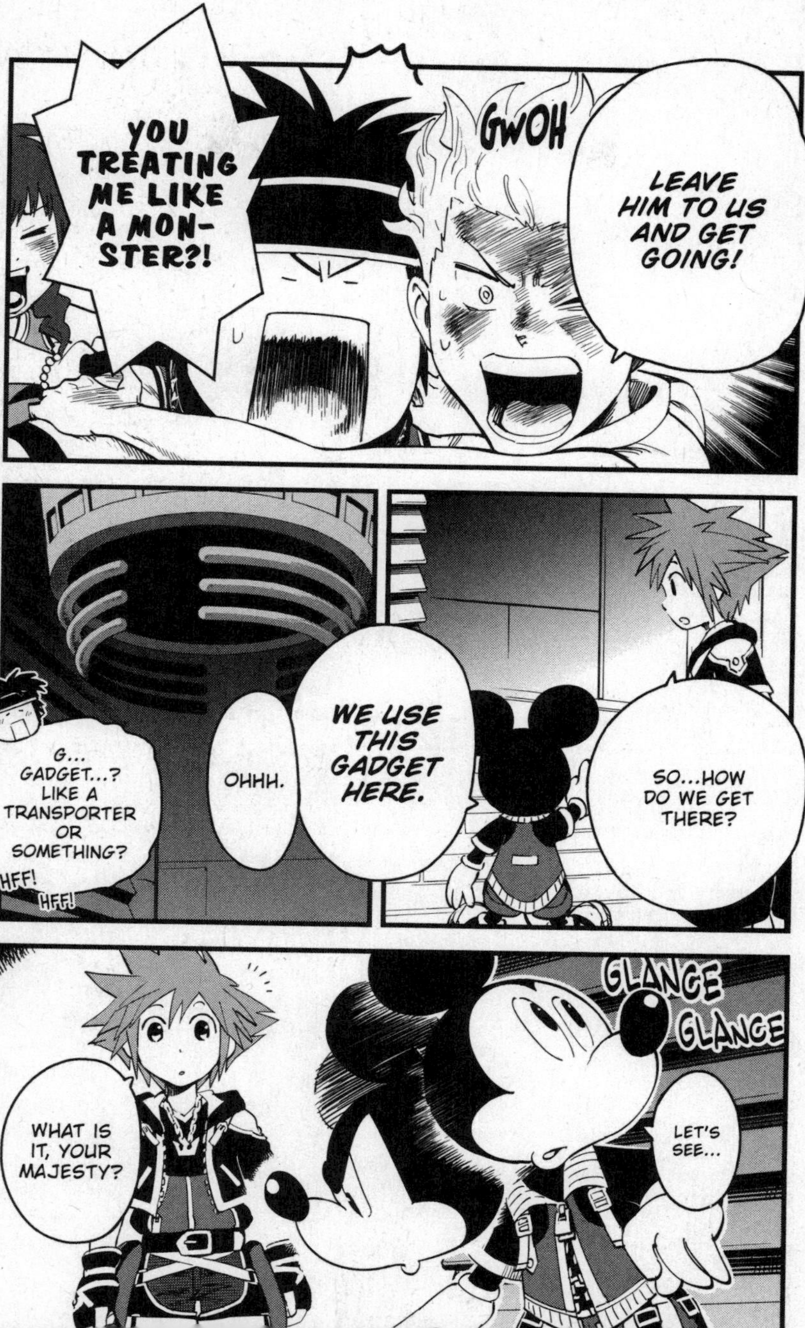

LEAVE HIM TO US AND GET GOING!
GWOH
YOU TREATING ME LIKE A MON-STER?!
SO...HOW DO WE GET THERE?
WE USE THIS GADGET HERE.
OHHH.
G... GADGET...? LIKE A TRANSPORTER OR SOMETHING?
HFF! HFF!
GLANCE GLANCE
LET'S SEE...
WHAT IS IT, YOUR MAJESTY?

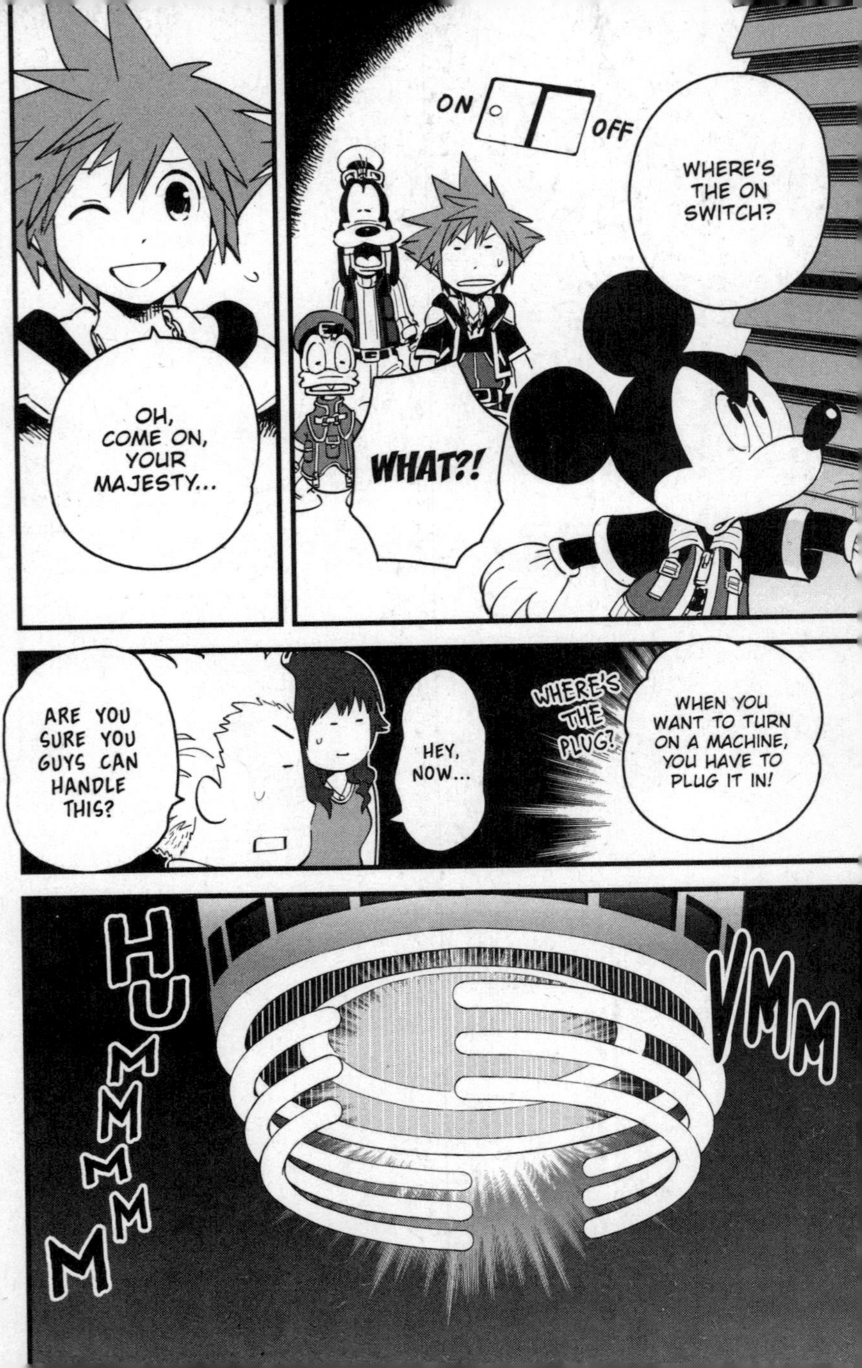
ON
OFF
WHERE'S THE ON SWITCH?
WHAT?!
OH, COME ON, YOUR MAJESTY...
WHEN YOU WANT TO TURN ON A MACHINE, YOU HAVE TO PLUG IT IN!
WHERE'S THE PLUG?
HEY, NOW...
ARE YOU SURE YOU GUYS CAN HANDLE THIS?
VMM
HUMMMMM

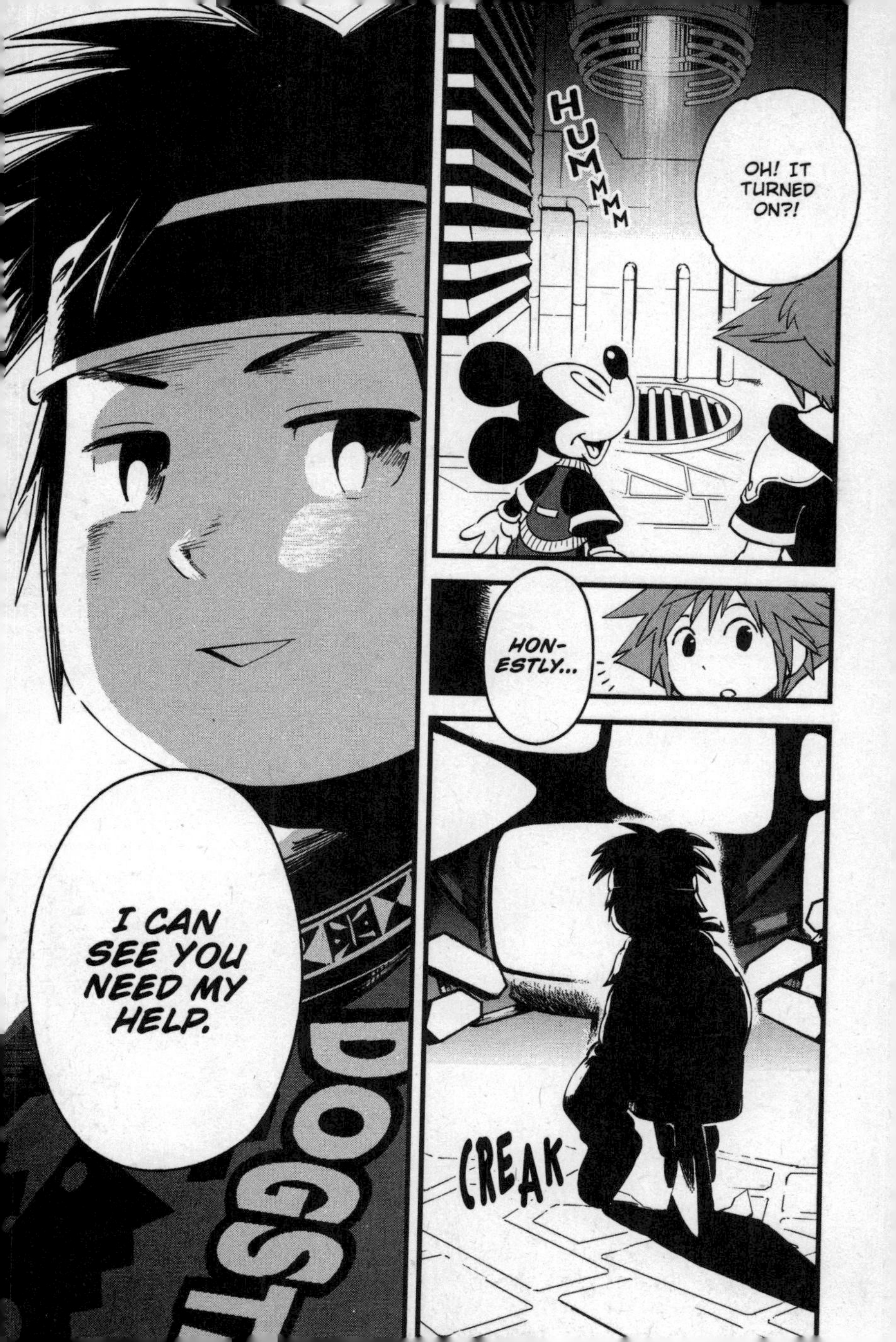
OH! IT TURNED ON?!
HUMMM
HON-ESTLY...
CREAK
I CAN SEE YOU NEED MY HELP.

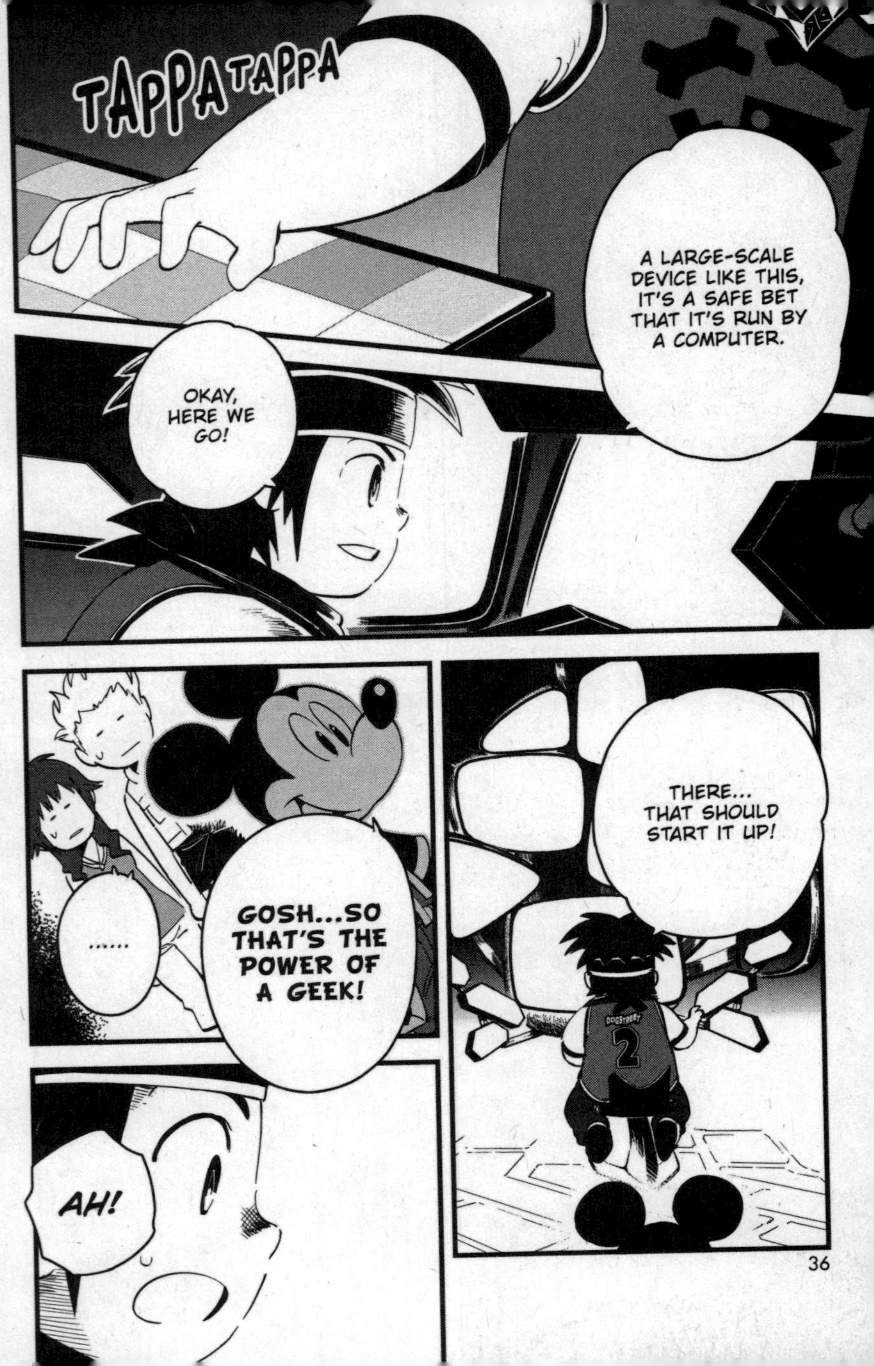
A LARGE-SCALE DEVICE LIKE THIS, IT'S A SAFE BET THAT IT'S RUN BY A COMPUTER.
TAPPA TAPPA
OKAY, HERE WE GO!
THERE... THAT SHOULD START IT UP!
GOSH...SO THAT'S THE POWER OF A GEEK!
......
AH!

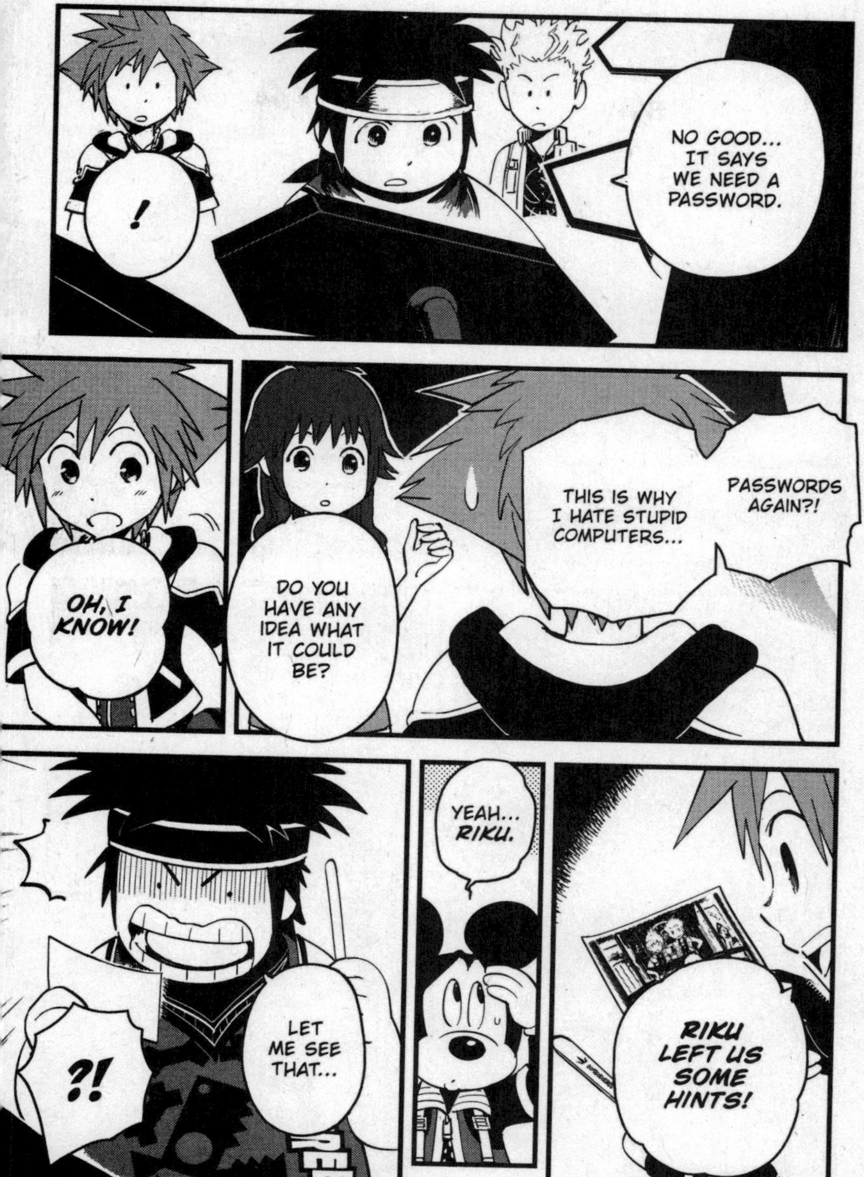
NO GOOD... IT SAYS WE NEED A PASSWORD.
!
PASSWORDS AGAIN?!
THIS IS WHY I HATE STUPID COMPUTERS...
DO YOU HAVE ANY IDEA WHAT IT COULD BE?
OH, I KNOW!
RIKU LEFT US SOME HINTS!
YEAH... RIKU.
LET ME SEE THAT...
?!

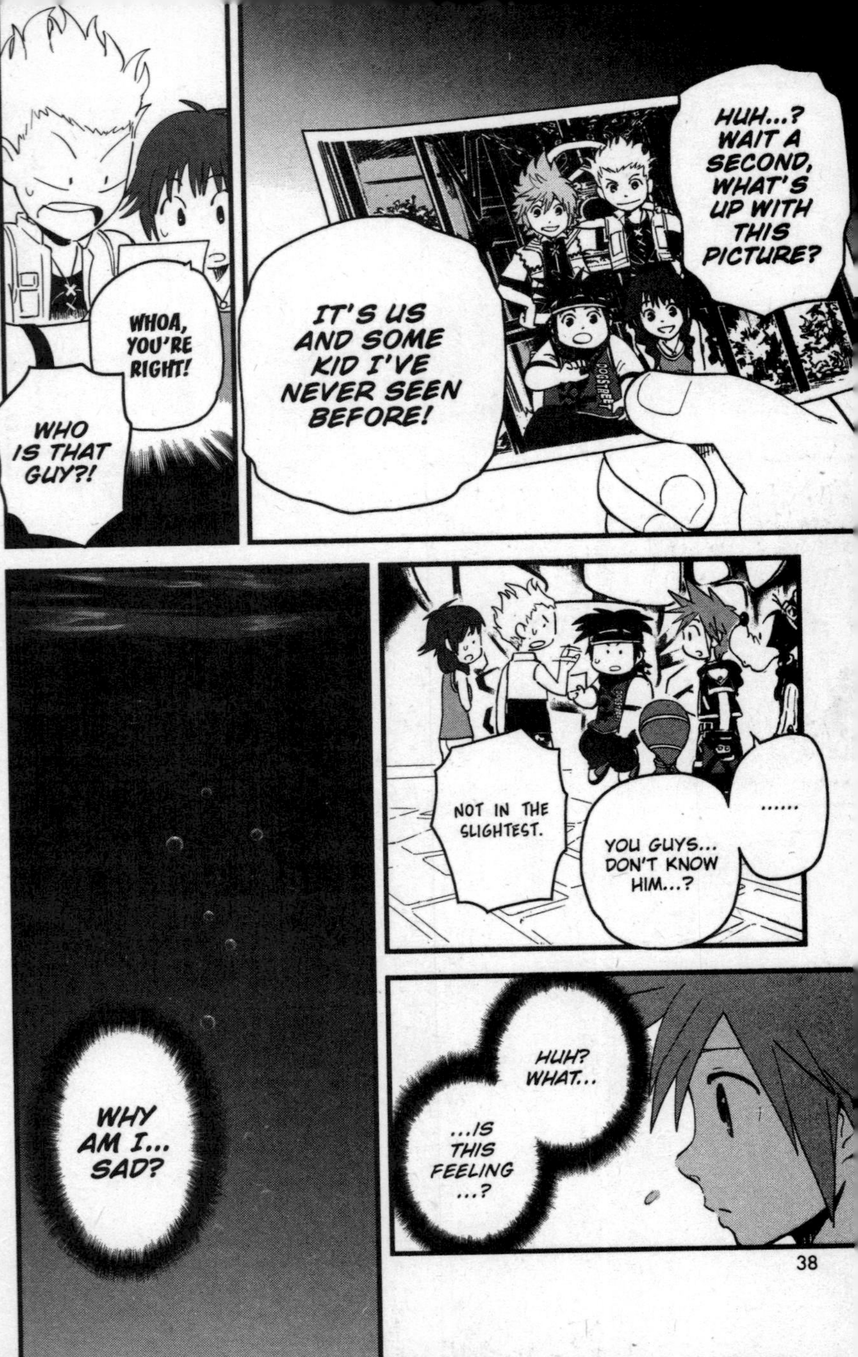
HUH...? WAIT A SECOND, WHAT'S UP WITH THIS PICTURE?
IT'S US AND SOME KID I'VE NEVER SEEN BEFORE!
WHOA, YOU'RE RIGHT!
WHO IS THAT GUY?!
......
YOU GUYS... DON'T KNOW HIM...?
NOT IN THE SLIGHTEST.
HUH? WHAT...
...IS THIS FEELING ...?
WHY AM I... SAD?

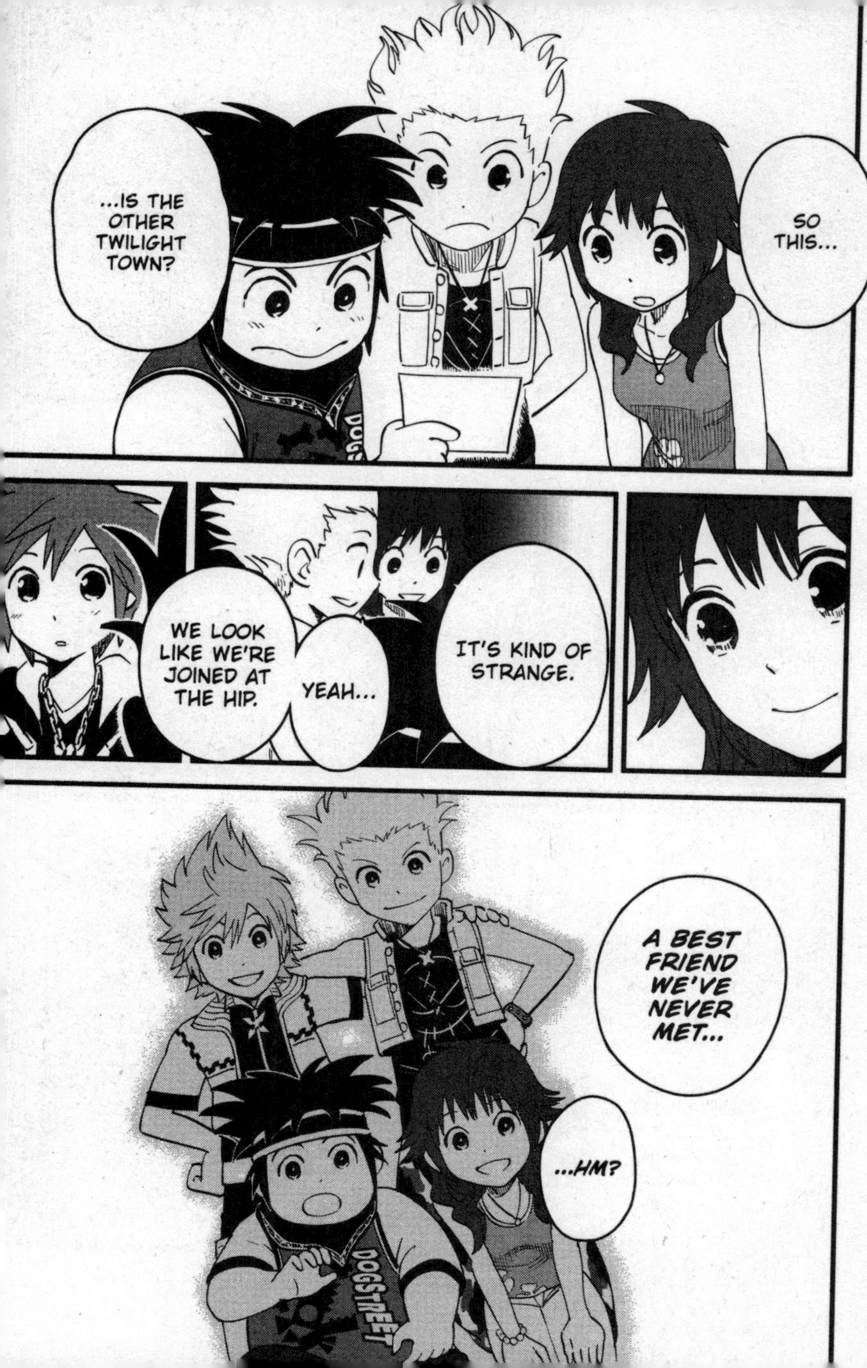
SO THIS...
...IS THE OTHER TWILIGHT TOWN?
IT'S KIND OF STRANGE.
YEAH...
WE LOOK LIKE WE'RE JOINED AT THE HIP.
A BEST FRIEND WE'VE NEVER MET...
...HM?
DOGSTREET

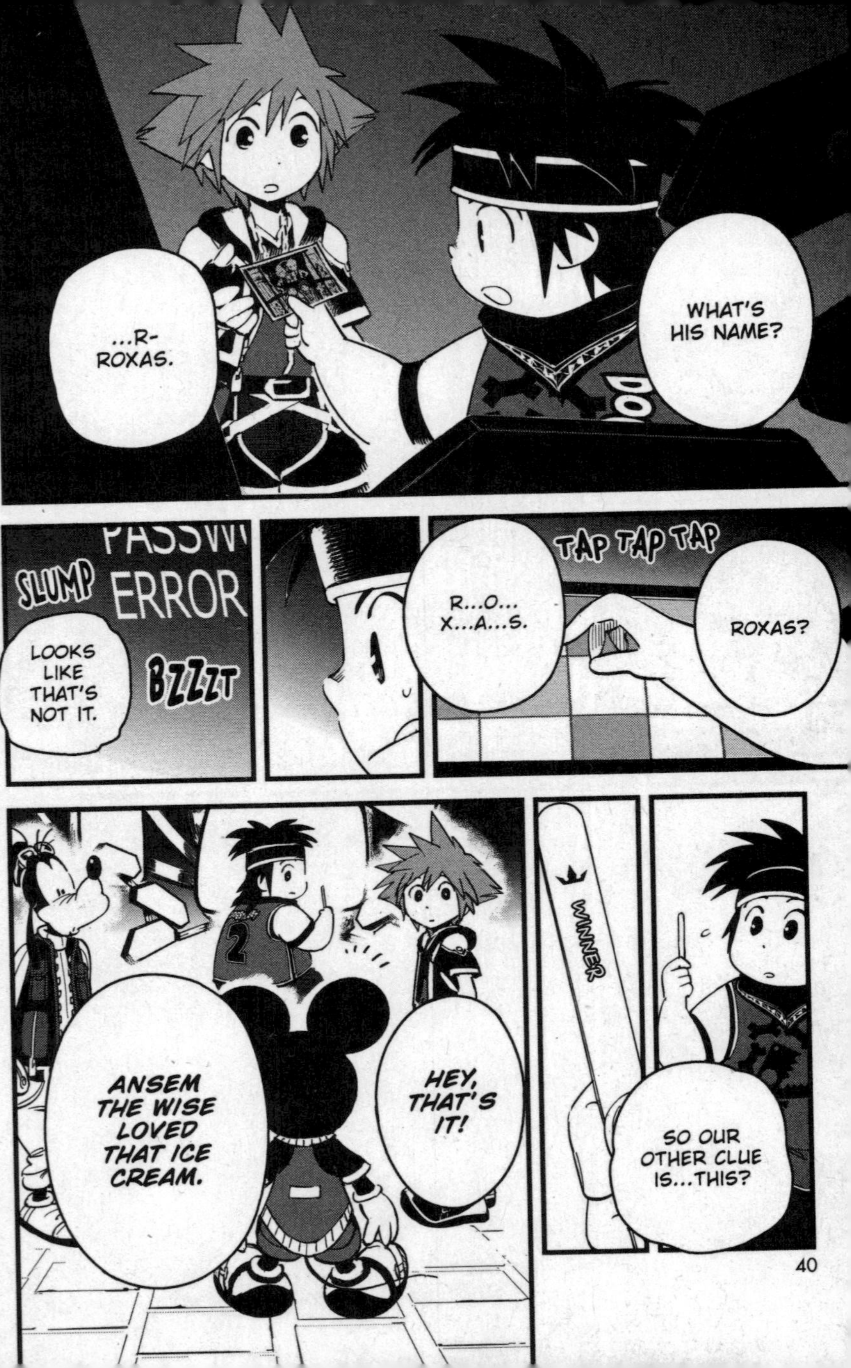
WHAT'S HIS NAME?
...R- ROXAS.
TAP TAP TAP
ROXAS?
R...O... X...A...S.
PASSW
ERROR
SLUMP
BZZZT
LOOKS LIKE THAT'S NOT IT.
WINNER
SO OUR OTHER CLUE IS...THIS?
HEY, THAT'S IT!
ANSEM THE WISE LOVED THAT ICE CREAM.

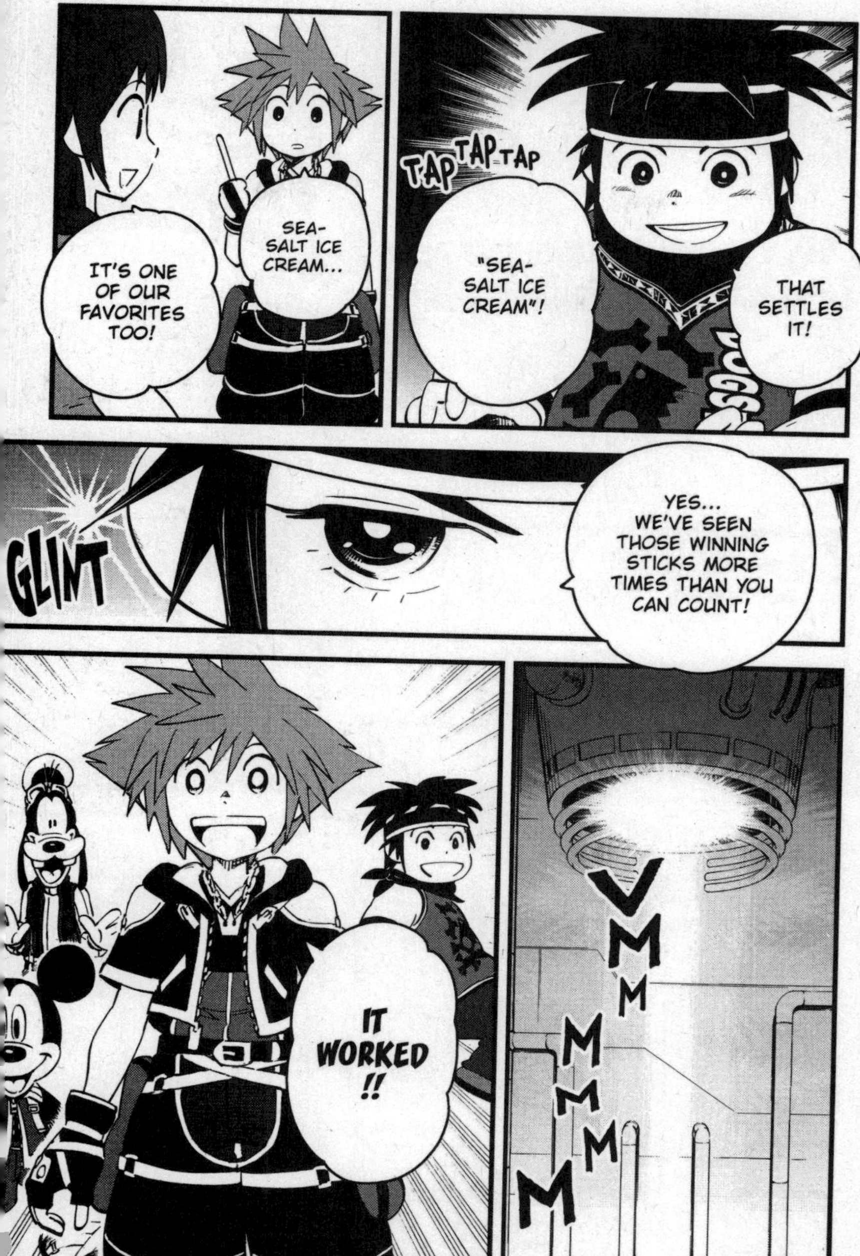
TAP TAP TAP
"SEA-SALT ICE CREAM"!
THAT SETTLES IT!
SEA-SALT ICE CREAM...
IT'S ONE OF OUR FAVORITES TOO!
YES... WE'VE SEEN THOSE WINNING STICKS MORE TIMES THAN YOU CAN COUNT!
GLINT
VMMMMMMM
IT WORKED!!

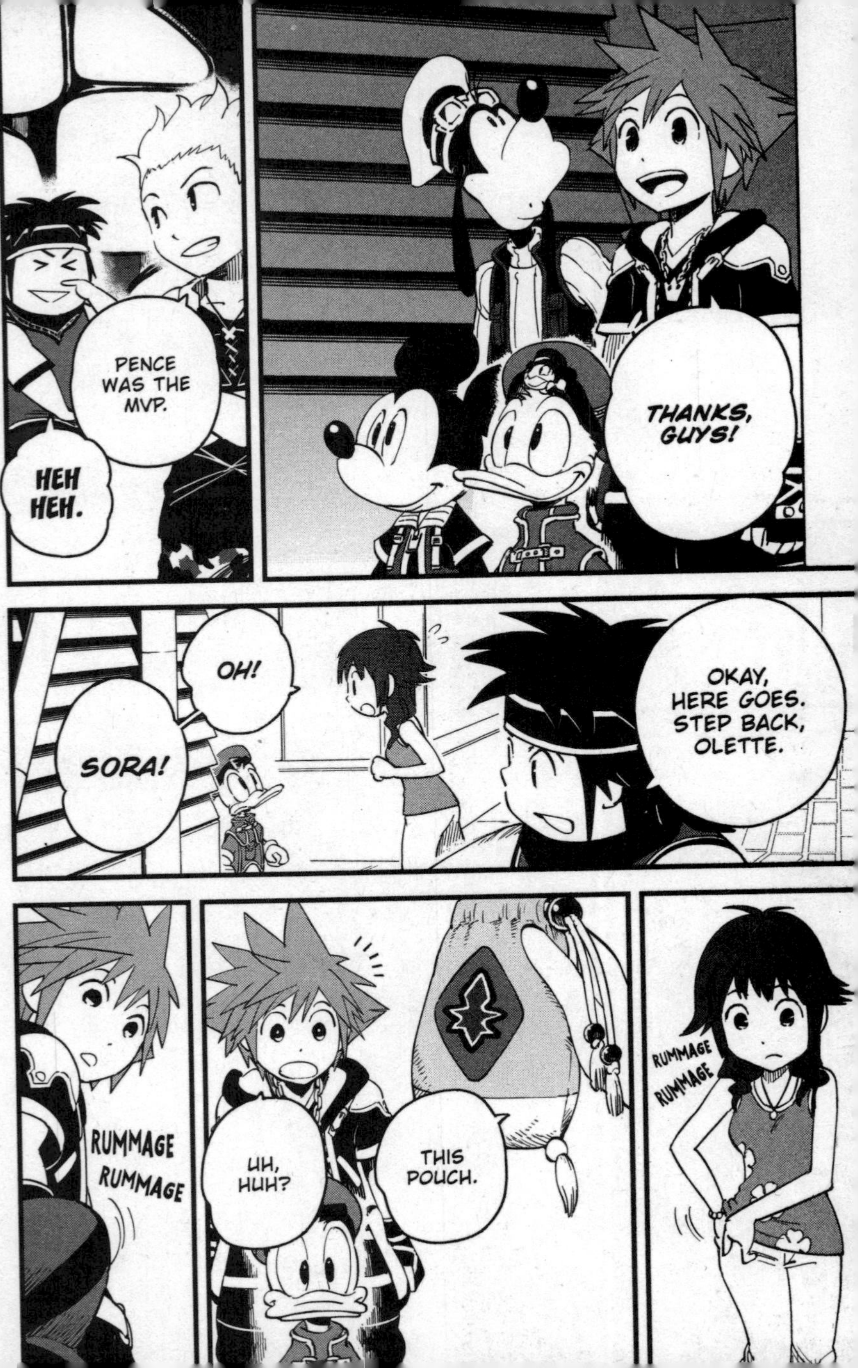
THANKS, GUYS!
PENCE WAS THE MVP.
HEH HEH.
OKAY, HERE GOES. STEP BACK, OLETTE.
OH!
SORA!
RUMMAGE RUMMAGE
THIS POUCH.
UH, HUH?
RUMMAGE RUMMAGE

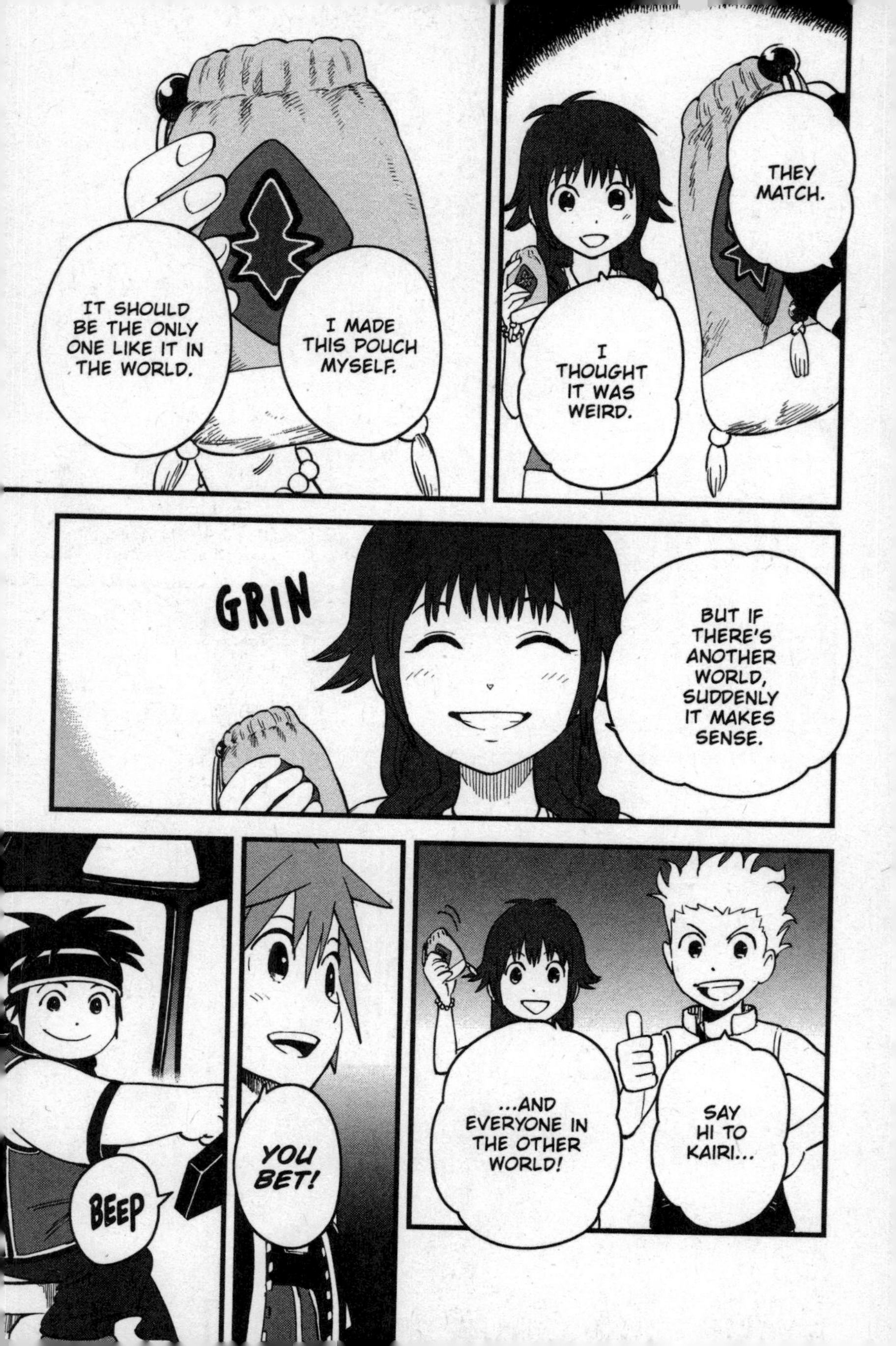
THEY MATCH.
I THOUGHT IT WAS WEIRD.
I MADE THIS POUCH MYSELF.
IT SHOULD BE THE ONLY ONE LIKE IT IN THE WORLD.
BUT IF THERE'S ANOTHER WORLD, SUDDENLY IT MAKES SENSE.
GRIN
SAY HI TO KAIRI...
...AND EVERYONE IN THE OTHER WORLD!
YOU BET!
BEEP

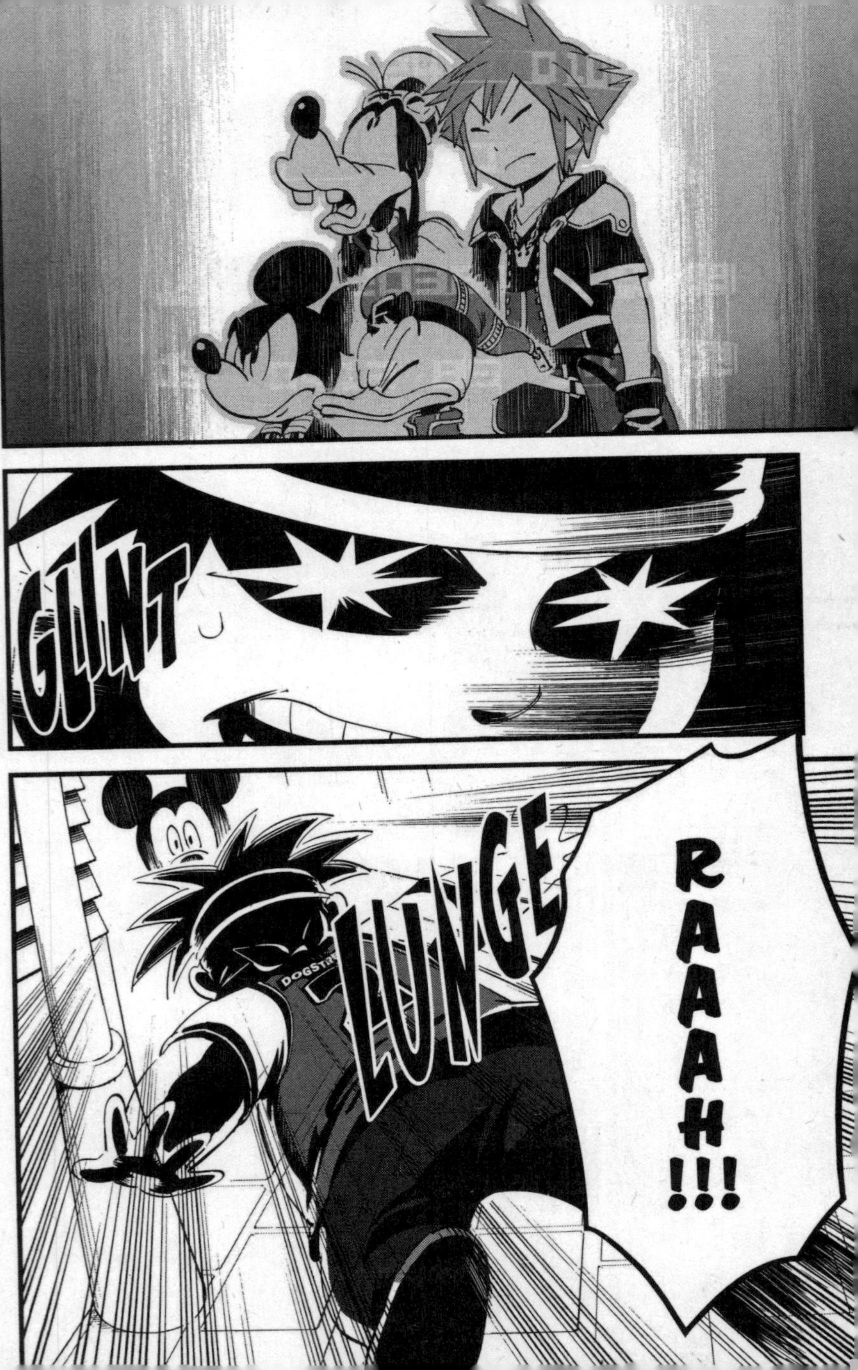
GLINT
RAAAH!!!
LUNGE

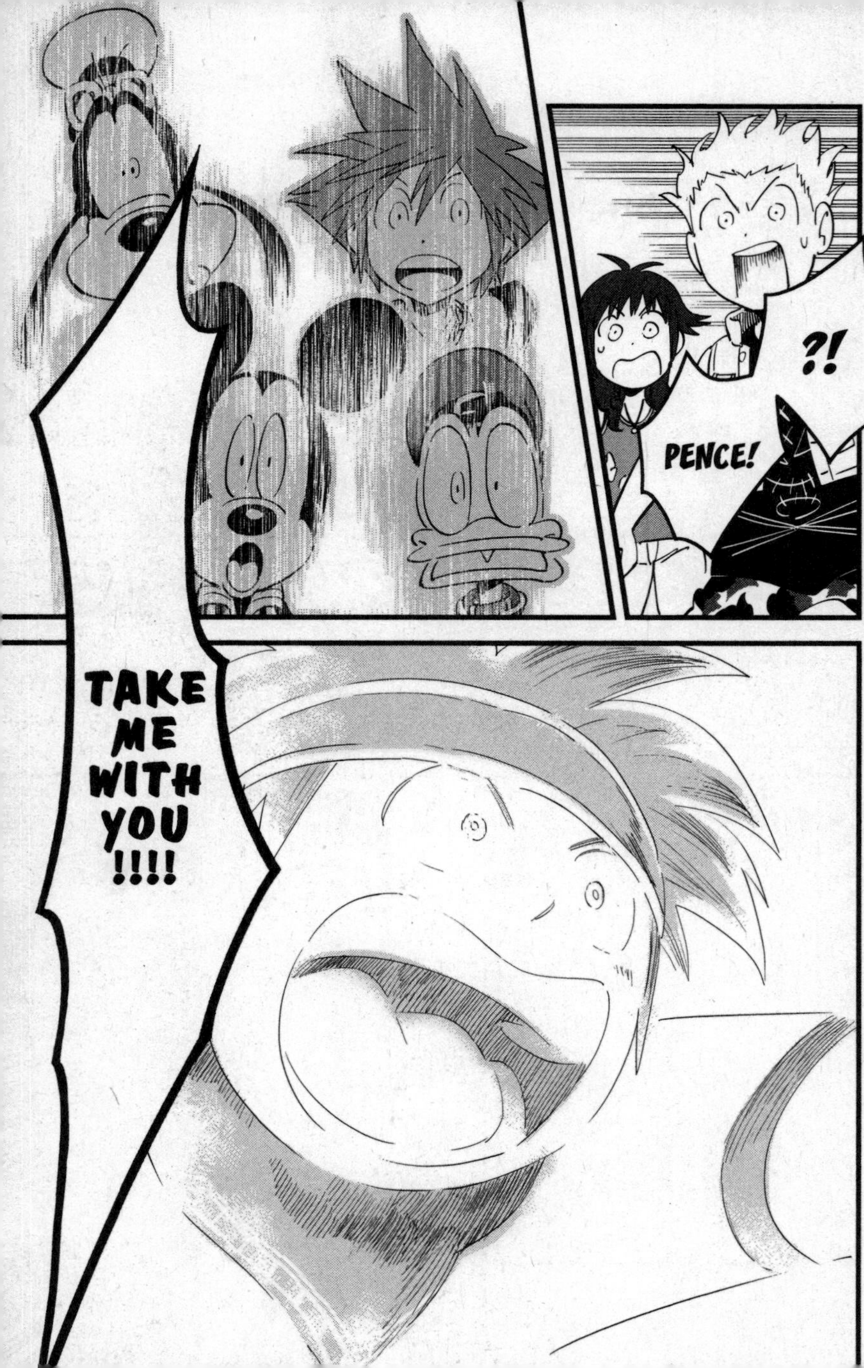
?!
PENCE!
TAKE ME WITH YOU!!!!

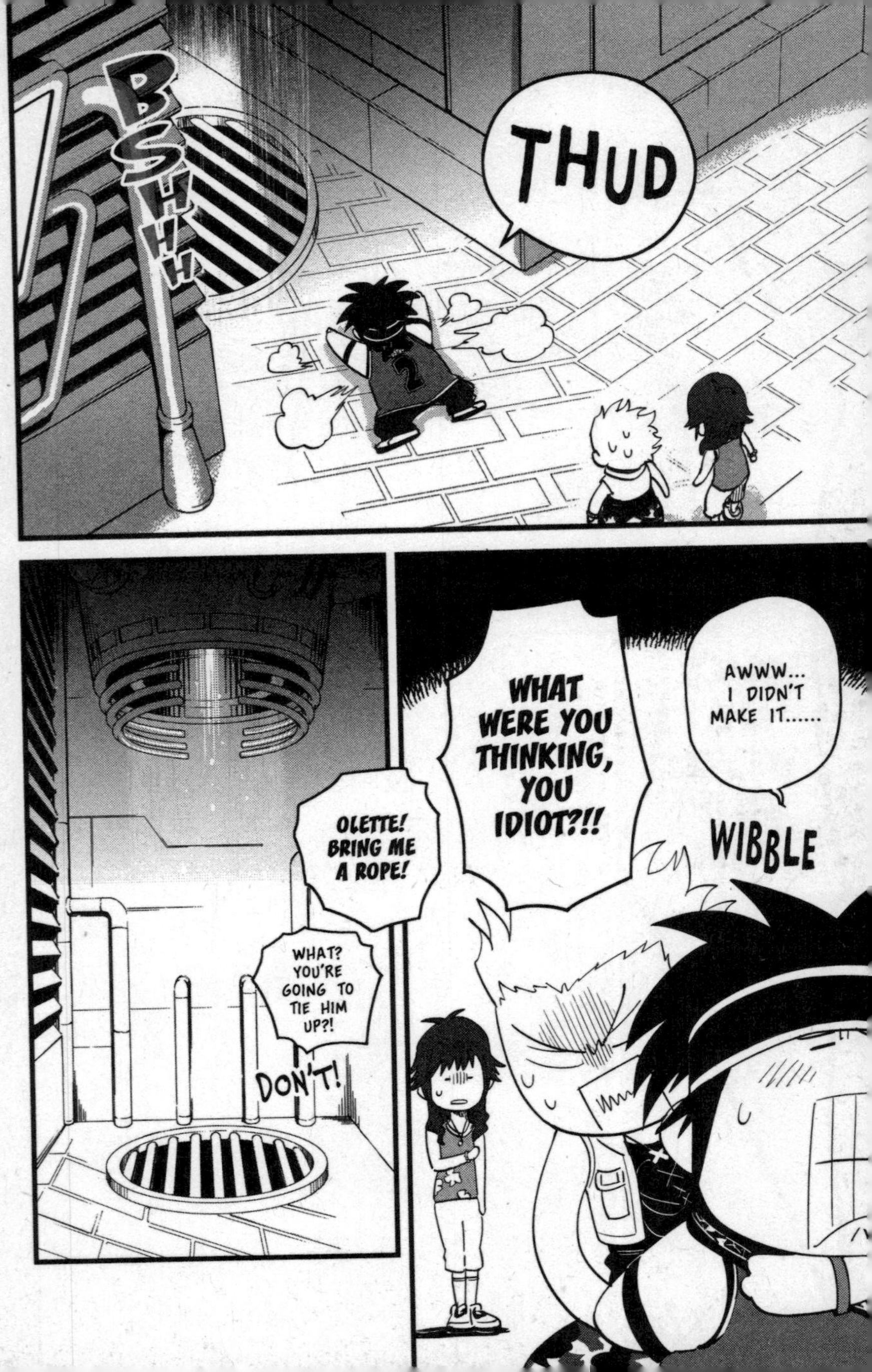
THUD
BSHHHH
WHAT WERE YOU THINKING, YOU IDIOT?!!
AWWW... I DIDN'T MAKE IT......
WIBBLE
OLETTE! BRING ME A ROPE!
WHAT? YOU'RE GOING TO TIE HIM UP?!
DON'T!

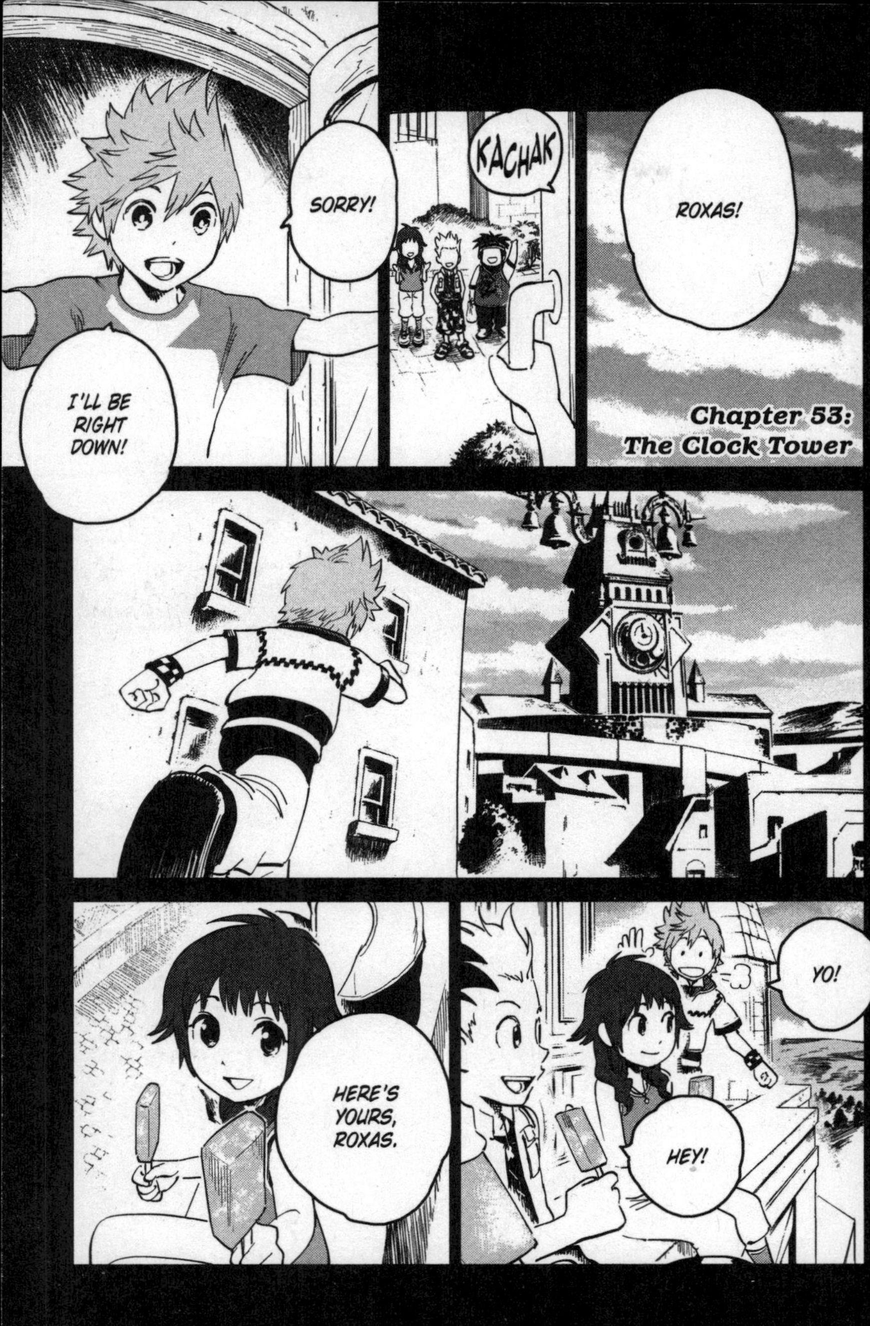
ROXAS!
Chapter 53: The Clock Tower
KACHAK
SORRY!
I'LL BE RIGHT DOWN!
YO!
HEY!
HERE'S YOURS, ROXAS.

Chapter 53: The Clock Tower

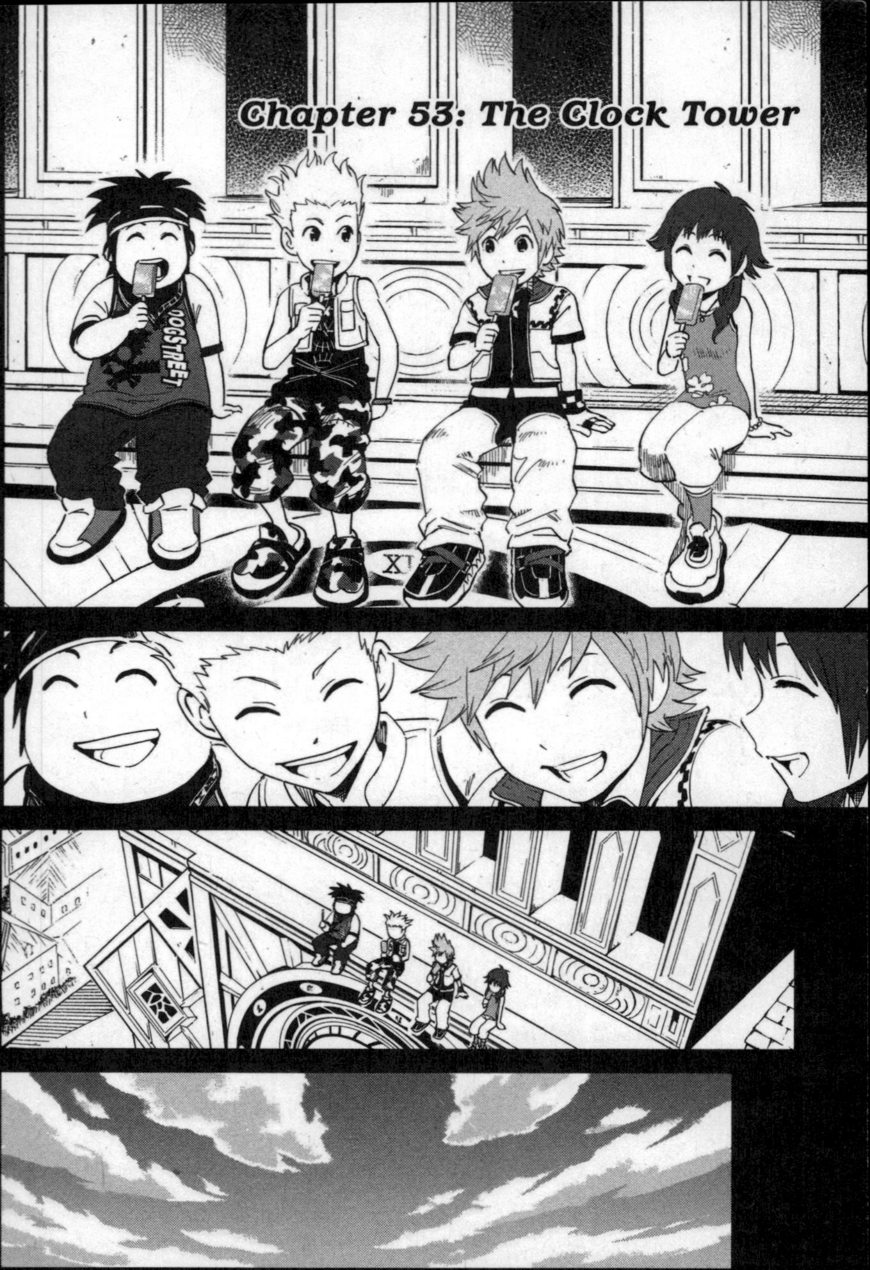

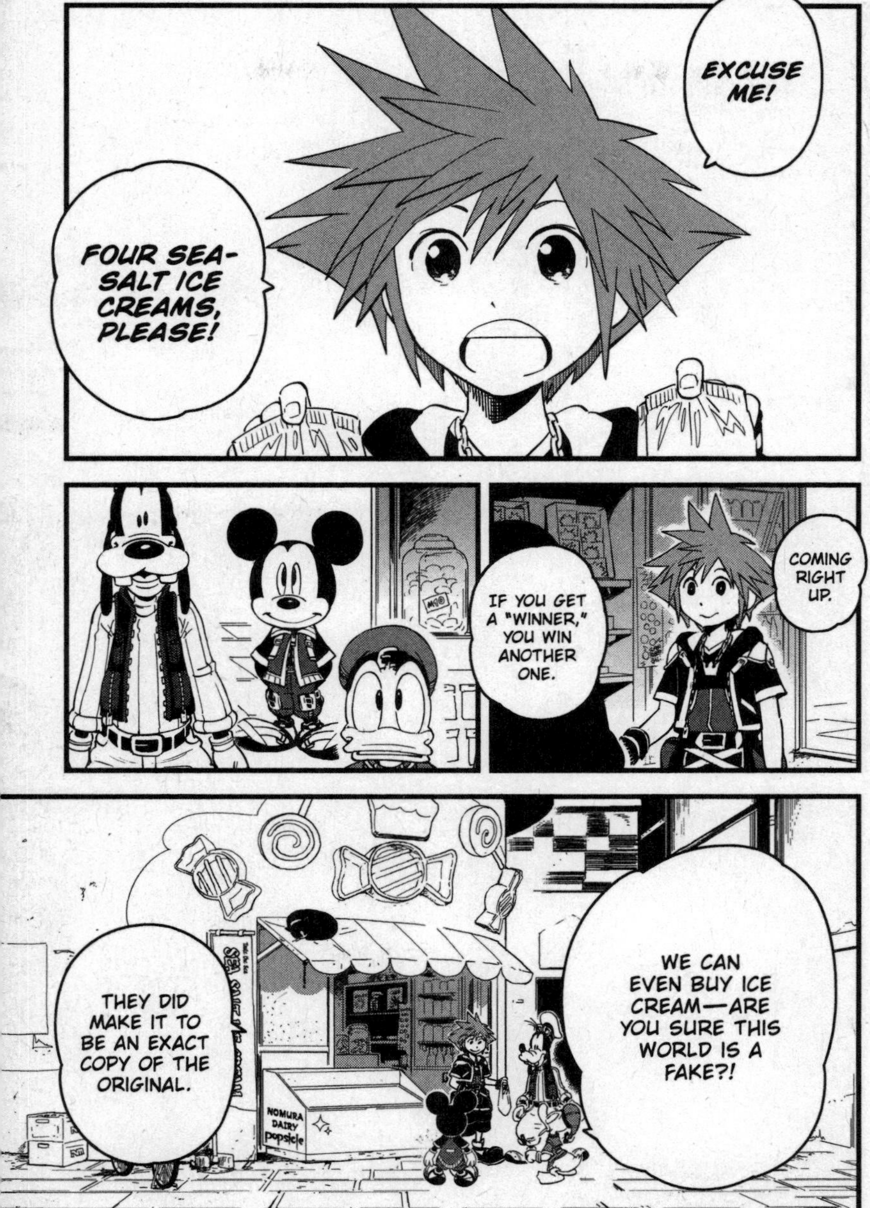
EXCUSE ME!
FOUR SEA-SALT ICE CREAMS, PLEASE!
COMING RIGHT UP.
IF YOU GET A "WINNER," YOU WIN ANOTHER ONE.
WE CAN EVEN BUY ICE CREAM—ARE YOU SURE THIS WORLD IS A FAKE?!
NOMURA DAIRY popsicle
THEY DID MAKE IT TO BE AN EXACT COPY OF THE ORIGINAL.

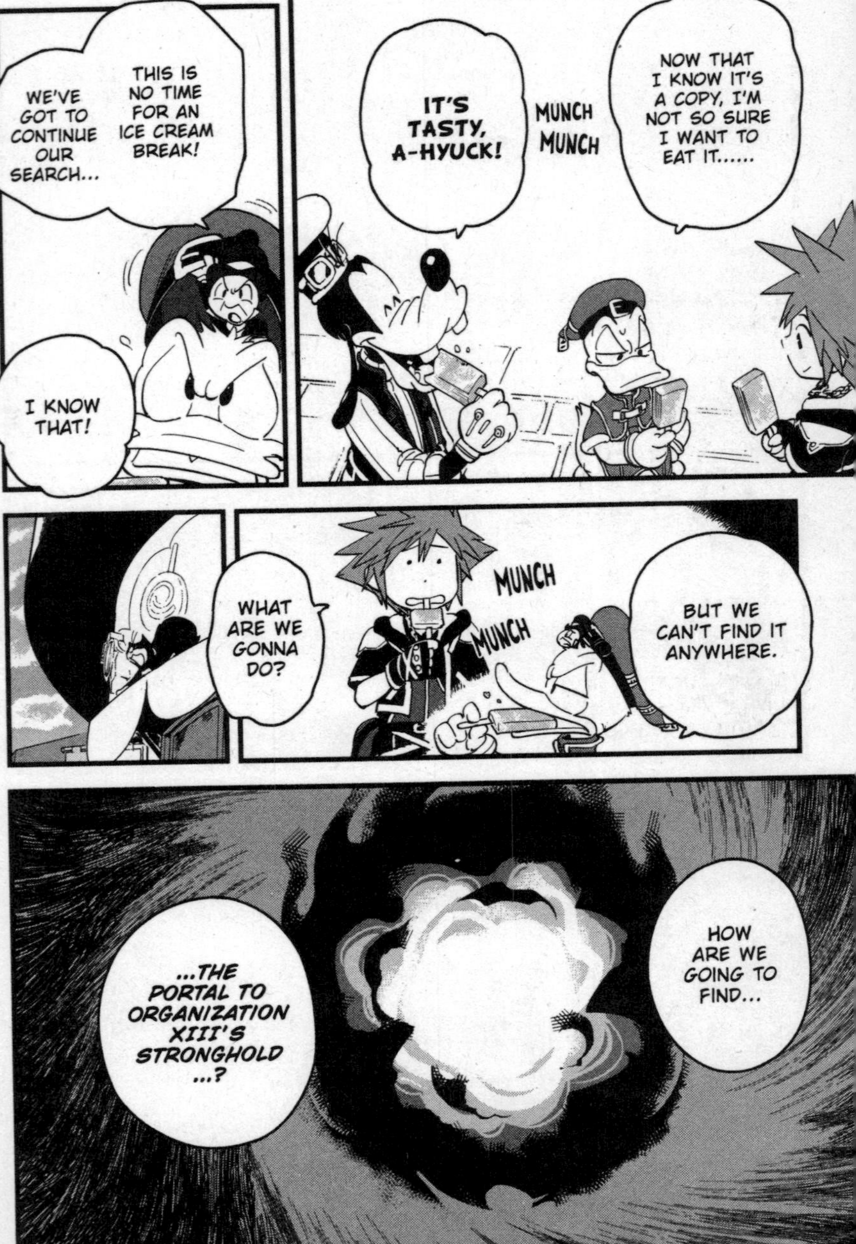
NOW THAT I KNOW IT'S A COPY, I'M NOT SO SURE I WANT TO EAT IT......
MUNCH MUNCH
IT'S TASTY, A-HYUCK!
THIS IS NO TIME FOR AN ICE CREAM BREAK!
WE'VE GOT TO CONTINUE OUR SEARCH...
I KNOW THAT!
BUT WE CAN'T FIND IT ANYWHERE.
MUNCH MUNCH
WHAT ARE WE GONNA DO?
HOW ARE WE GOING TO FIND...
...THE PORTAL TO ORGANIZATION XIII'S STRONGHOLD ...?

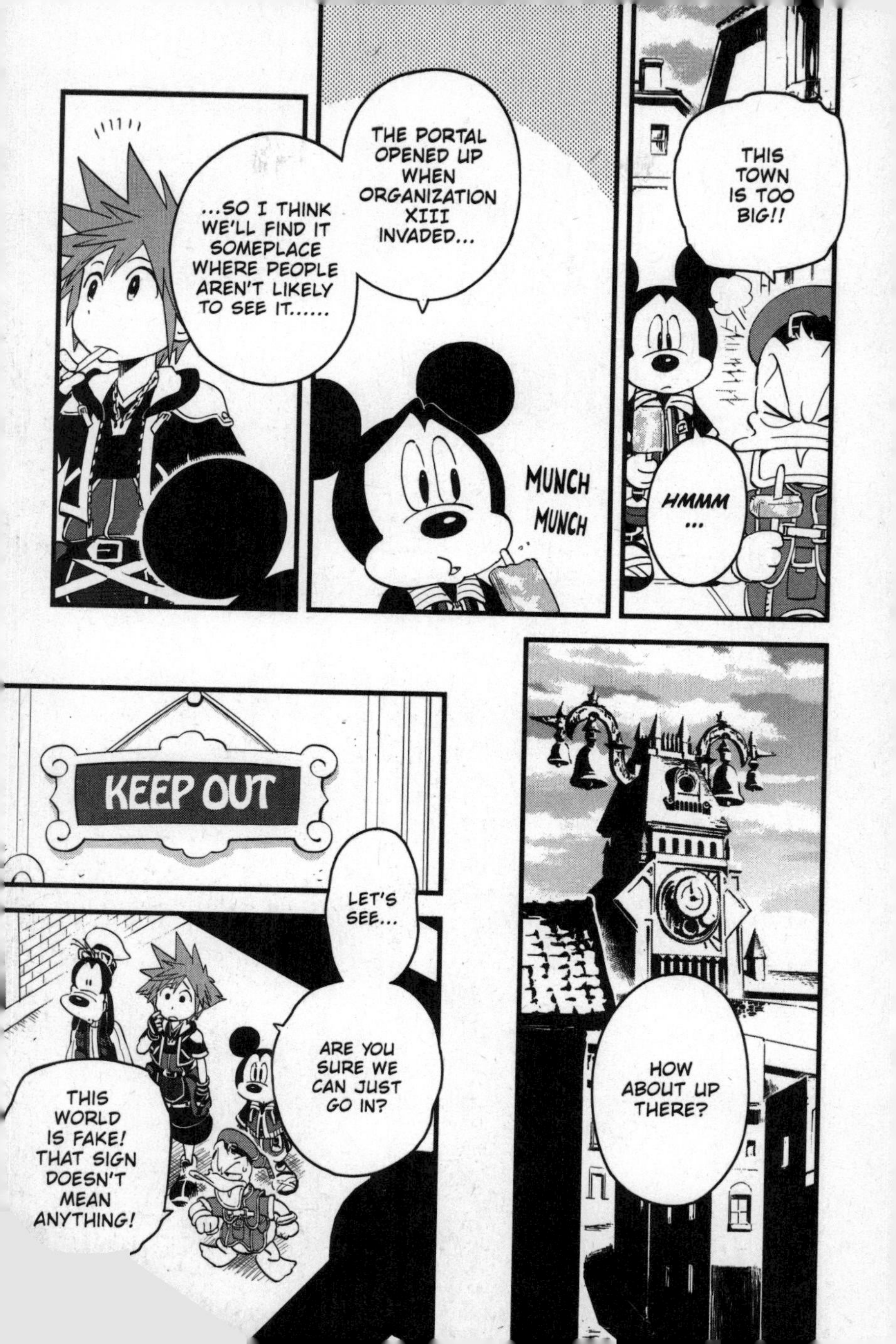
THIS TOWN IS TOO BIG!!
HMMM...
THE PORTAL OPENED UP WHEN ORGANIZATION XIII INVADED...
MUNCH MUNCH
...SO I THINK WE'LL FIND IT SOMEPLACE WHERE PEOPLE AREN'T LIKELY TO SEE IT......
HOW ABOUT UP THERE?
KEEP OUT
LET'S SEE...
ARE YOU SURE WE CAN JUST GO IN?
THIS WORLD IS FAKE! THAT SIGN DOESN'T MEAN ANYTHING!

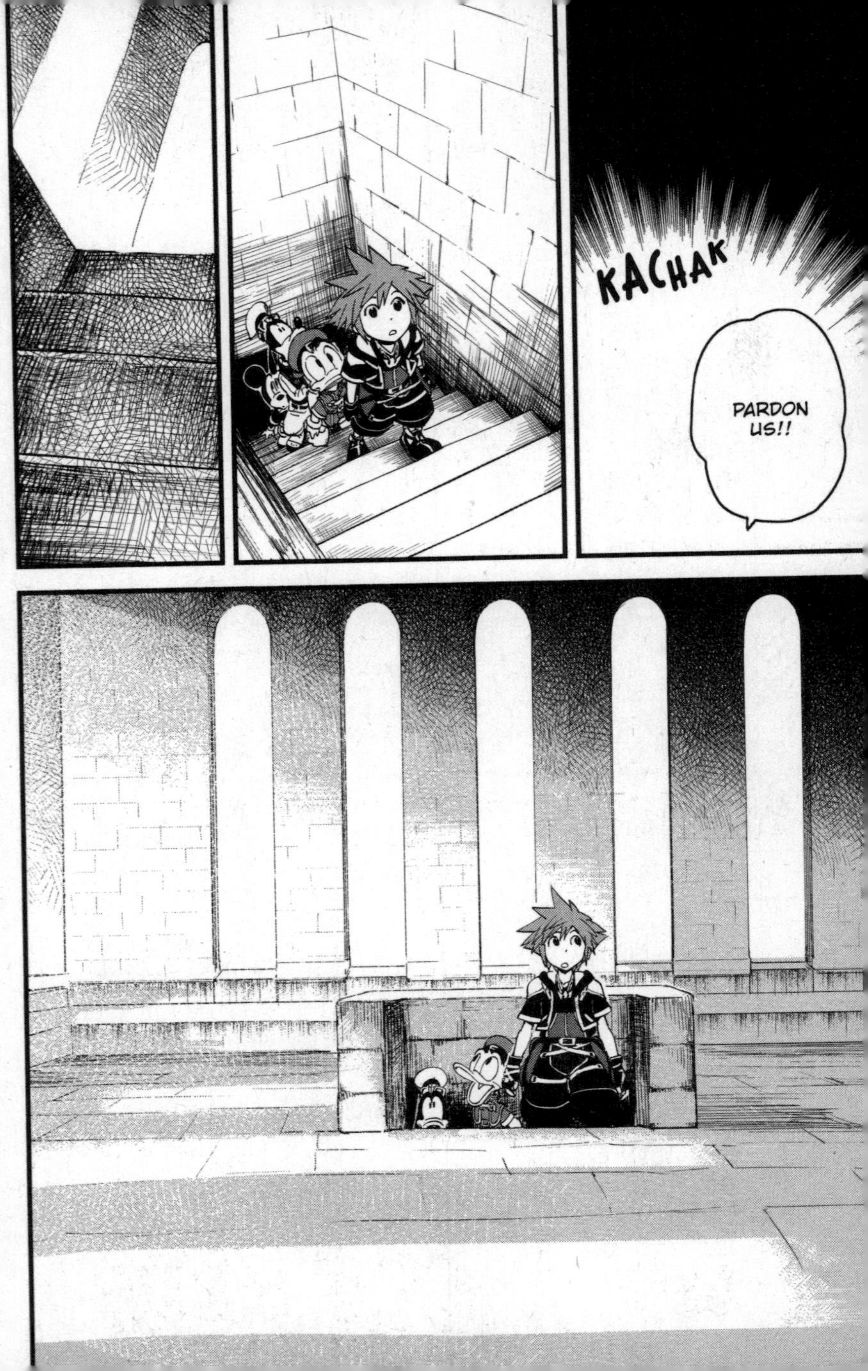
KACHAK
PARDON US!!

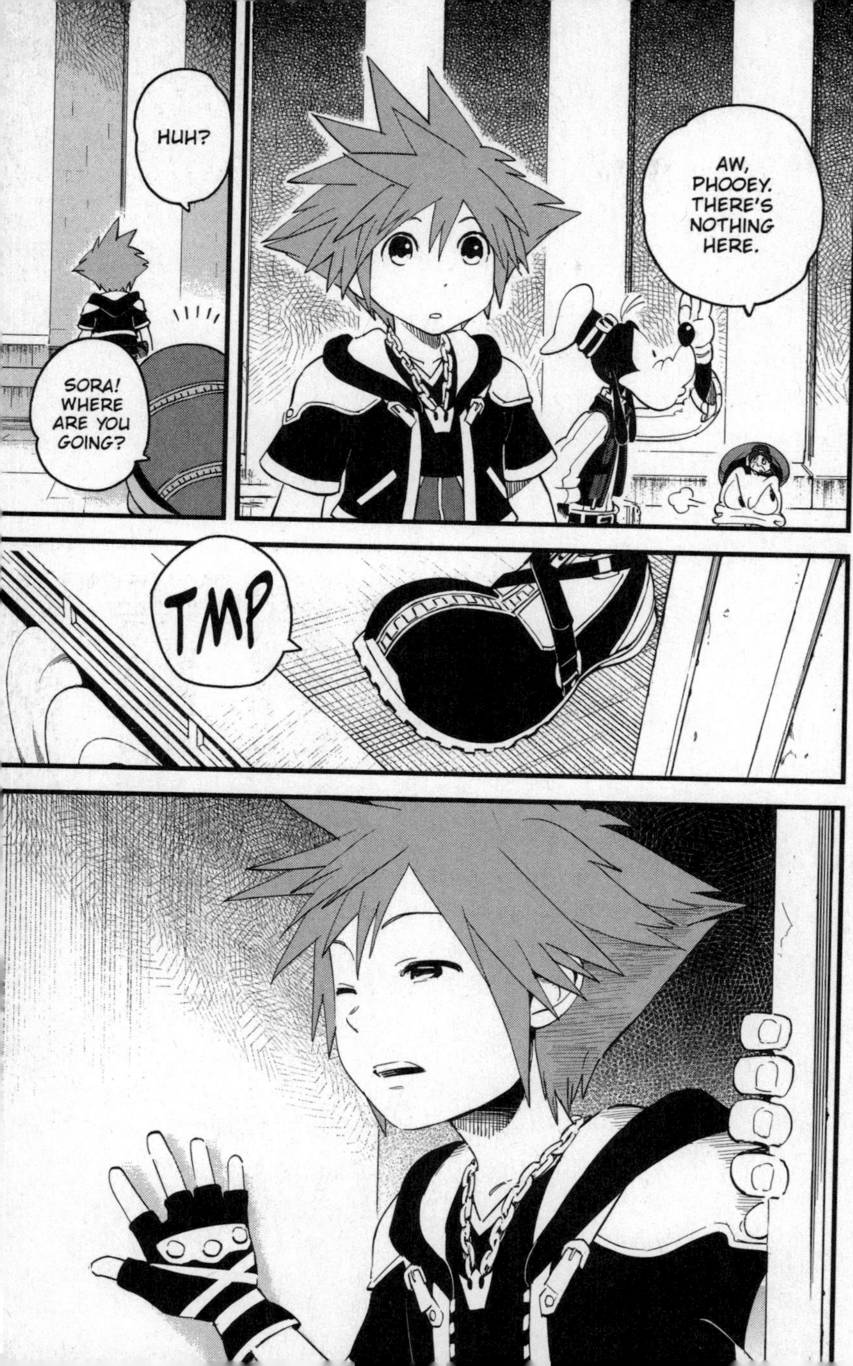
AW, PHOOEY. THERE'S NOTHING HERE.
HUH?
SORA! WHERE ARE YOU GOING?
TMP

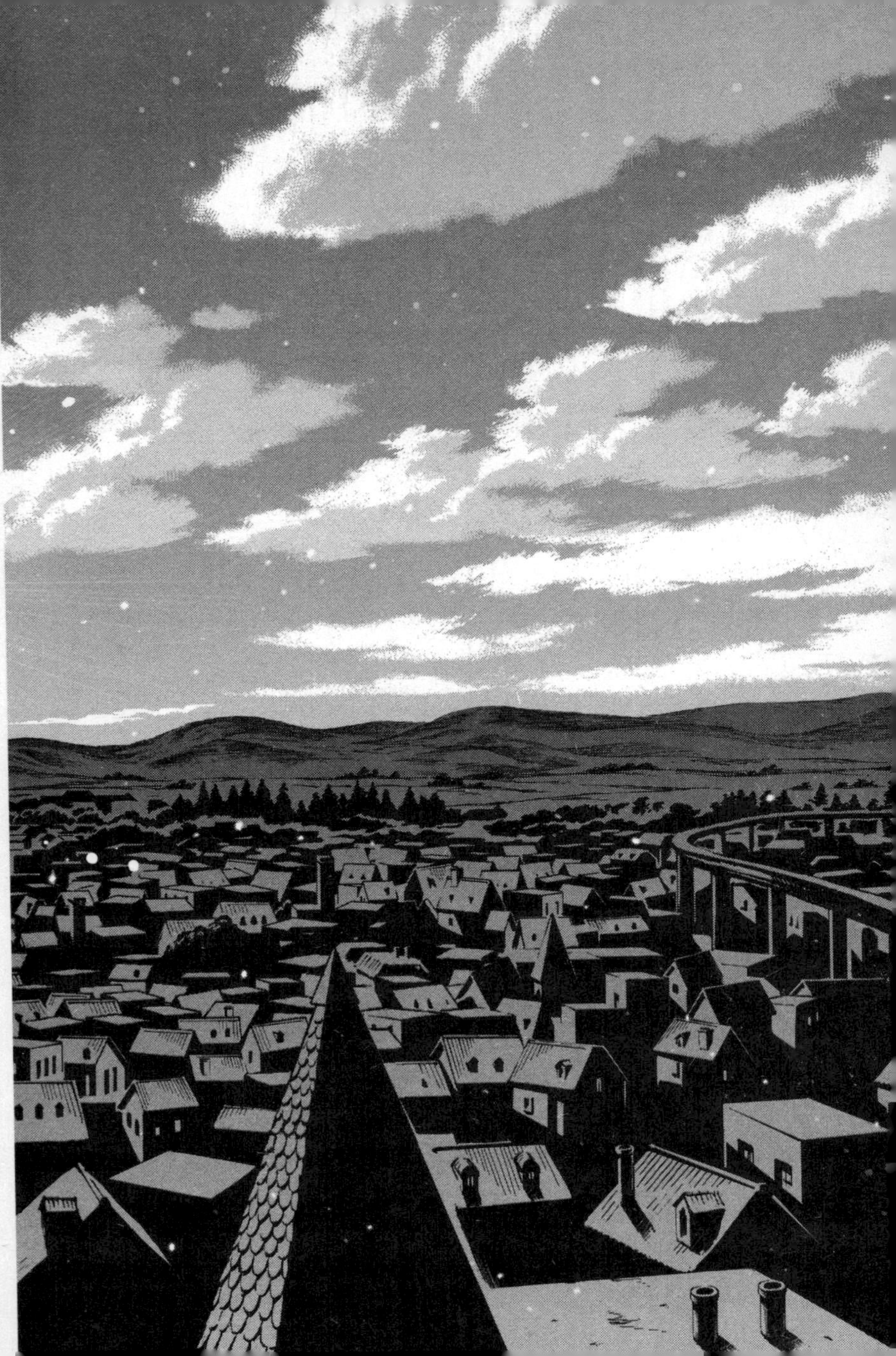

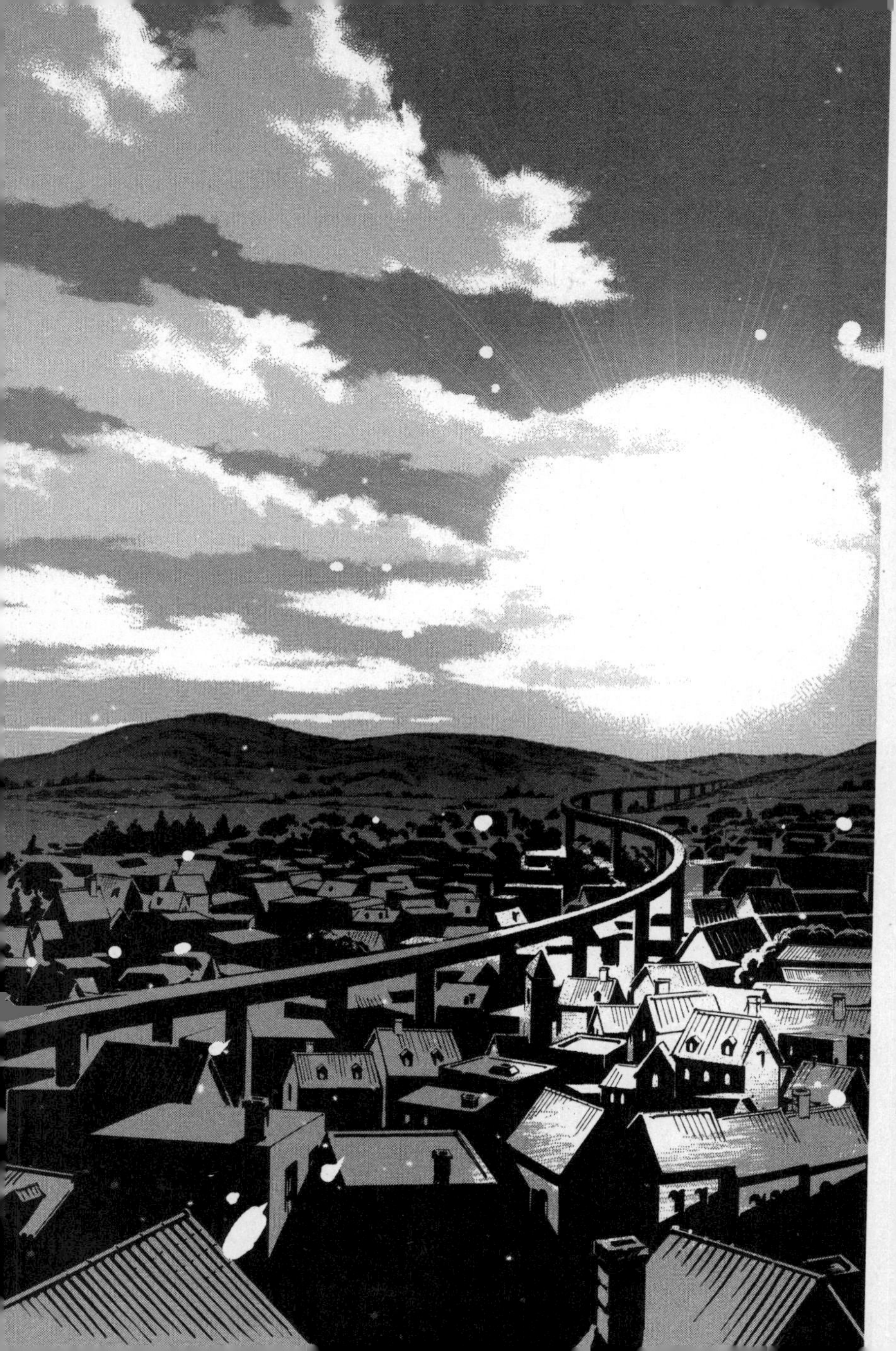

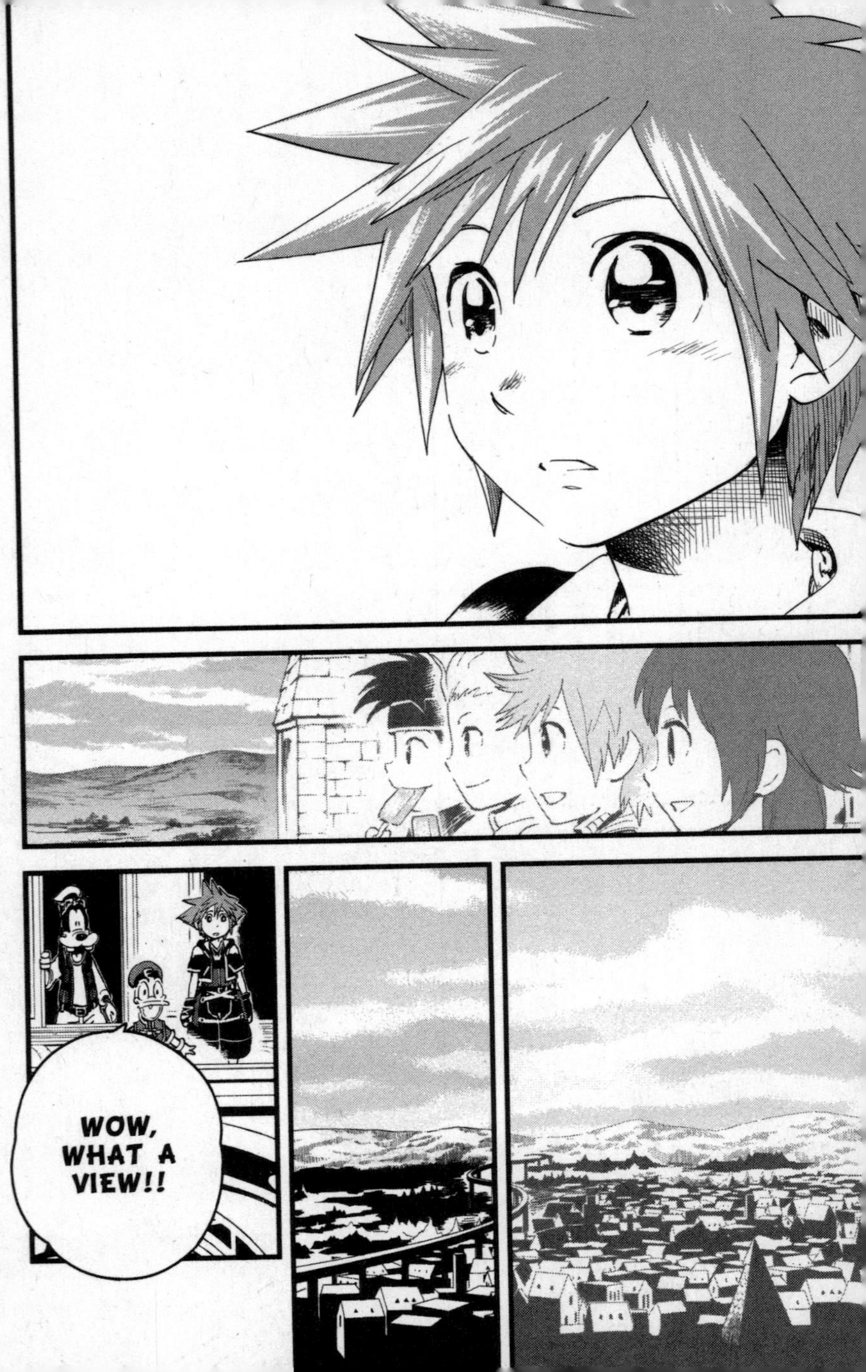
WOW, WHAT A VIEW!!

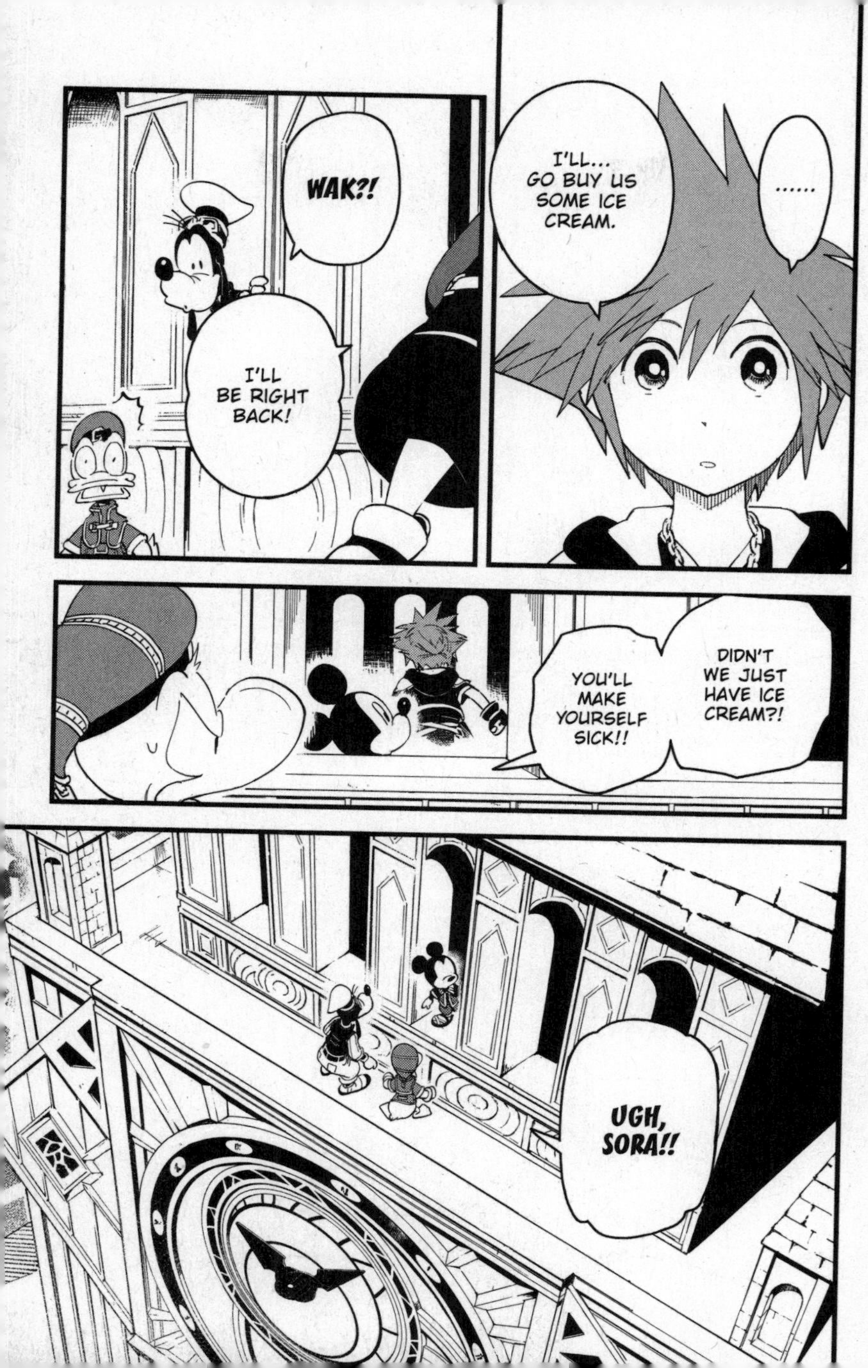
......
I'LL... GO BUY US SOME ICE CREAM.
WAK?!
I'LL BE RIGHT BACK!
DIDN'T WE JUST HAVE ICE CREAM?!
YOU'LL MAKE YOURSELF SICK!!
UGH, SORA!!

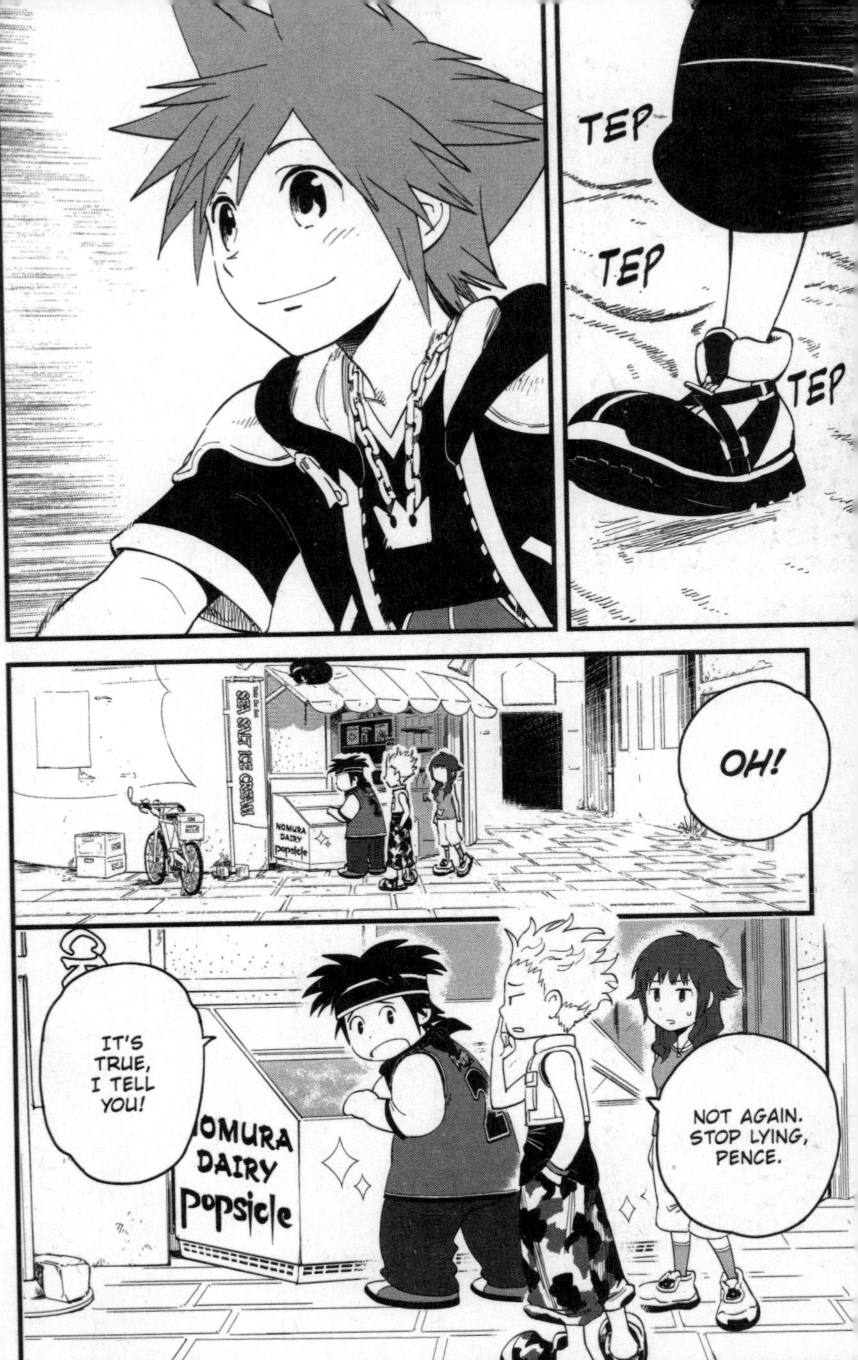
TEP
TEP
TEP
OH!
SEA SALT ICE CREAM
NOMURA DAIRY popsicle
NOT AGAIN. STOP LYING, PENCE.
IT'S TRUE, I TELL YOU!
DAIRY Popsicle

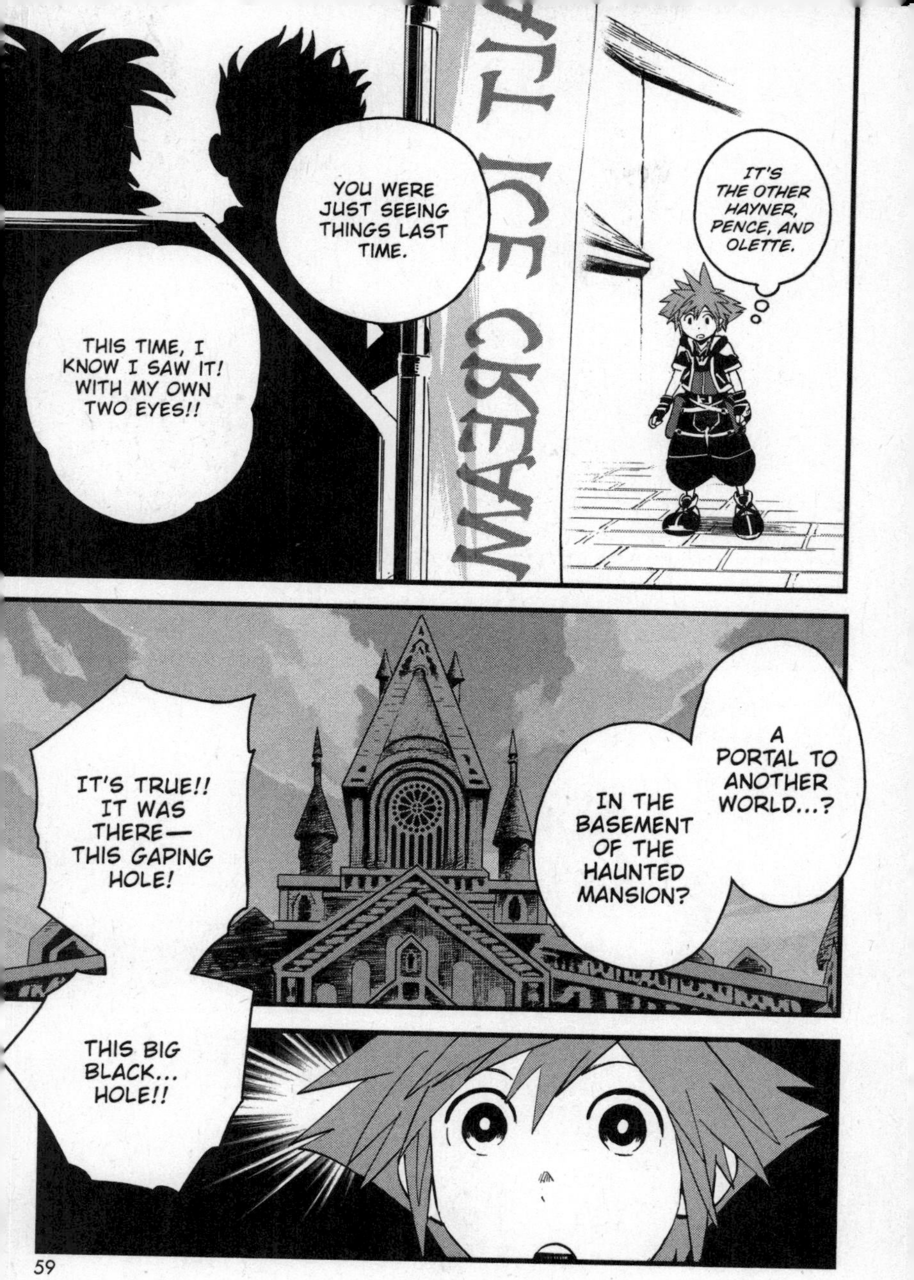
IT'S THE OTHER HAYNER, PENCE, AND OLETTE.
YOU WERE JUST SEEING THINGS LAST TIME.
THIS TIME, I KNOW I SAW IT! WITH MY OWN TWO EYES!!
A PORTAL TO ANOTHER WORLD...?
IN THE BASEMENT OF THE HAUNTED MANSION?
IT'S TRUE!! IT WAS THERE— THIS GAPING HOLE!
THIS BIG BLACK... HOLE!!

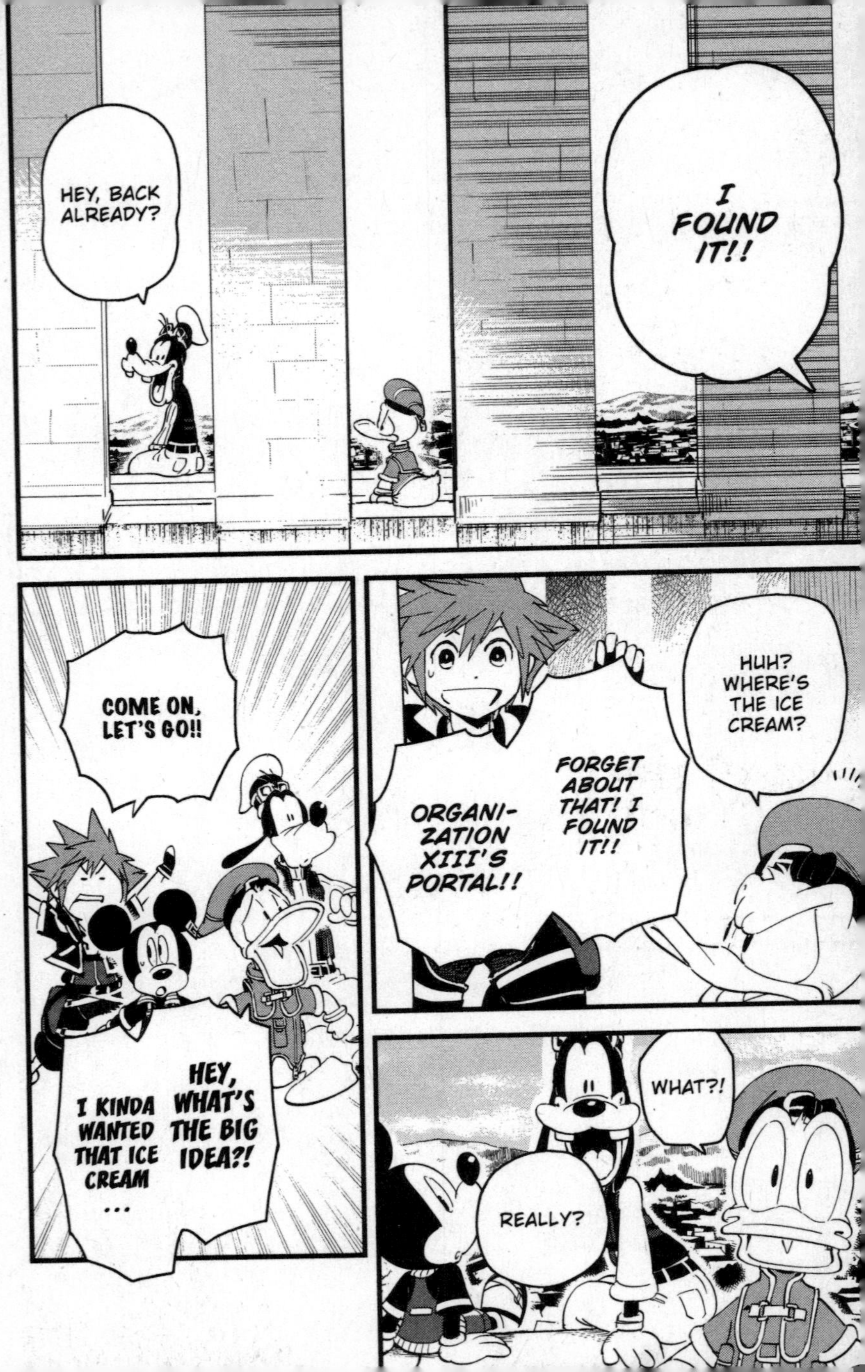
I FOUND IT!!
HEY, BACK ALREADY?
HUH? WHERE'S THE ICE CREAM?
FORGET ABOUT THAT! I FOUND IT!!
ORGANIZATION XIII'S PORTAL!!
WHAT?!
REALLY?
COME ON, LET'S GO!!
HEY, WHAT'S THE BIG IDEA?!
I KINDA WANTED THAT ICE CREAM ...

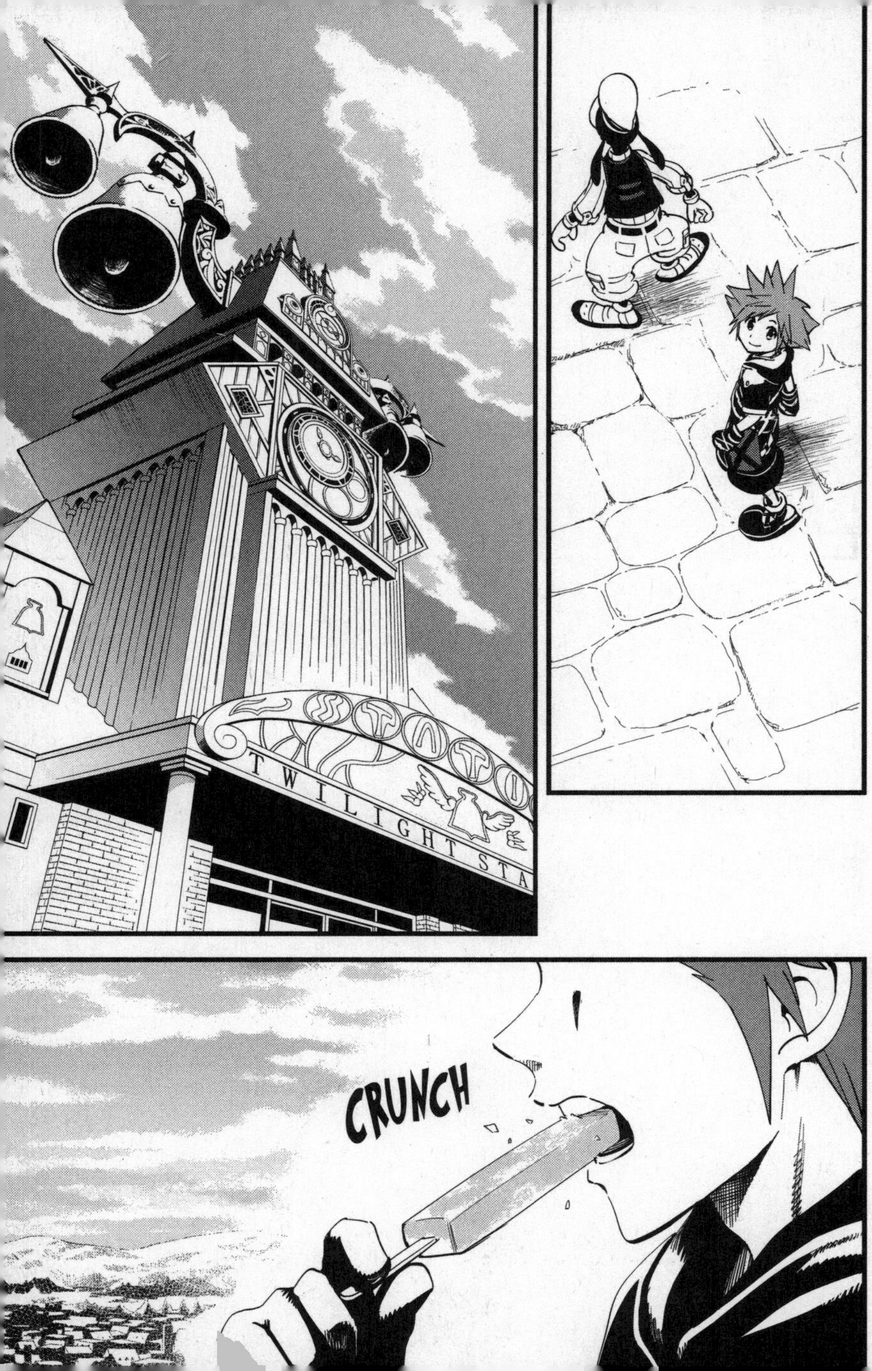
TWILIGHT STA
CRUNCH

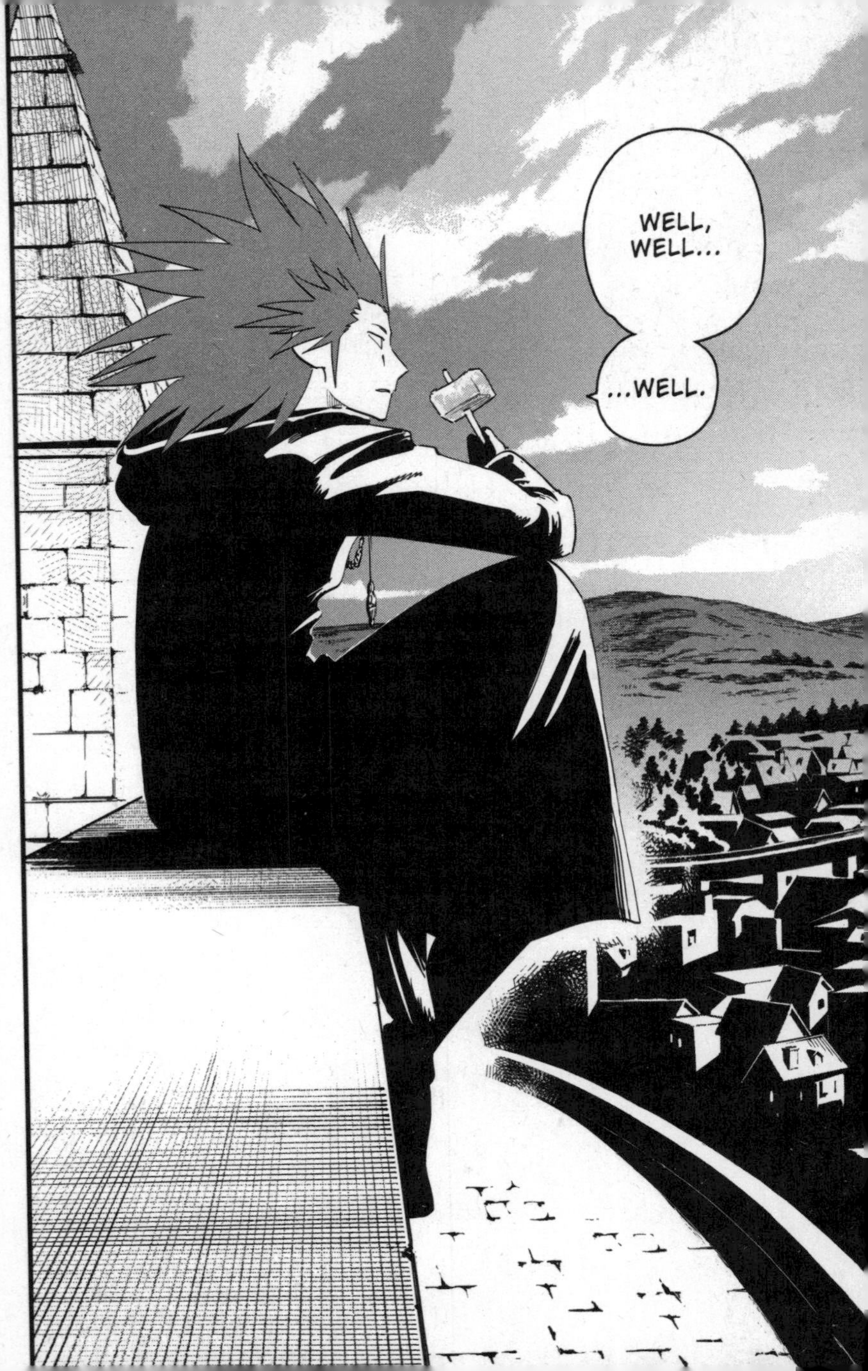
WELL, WELL...
...WELL.

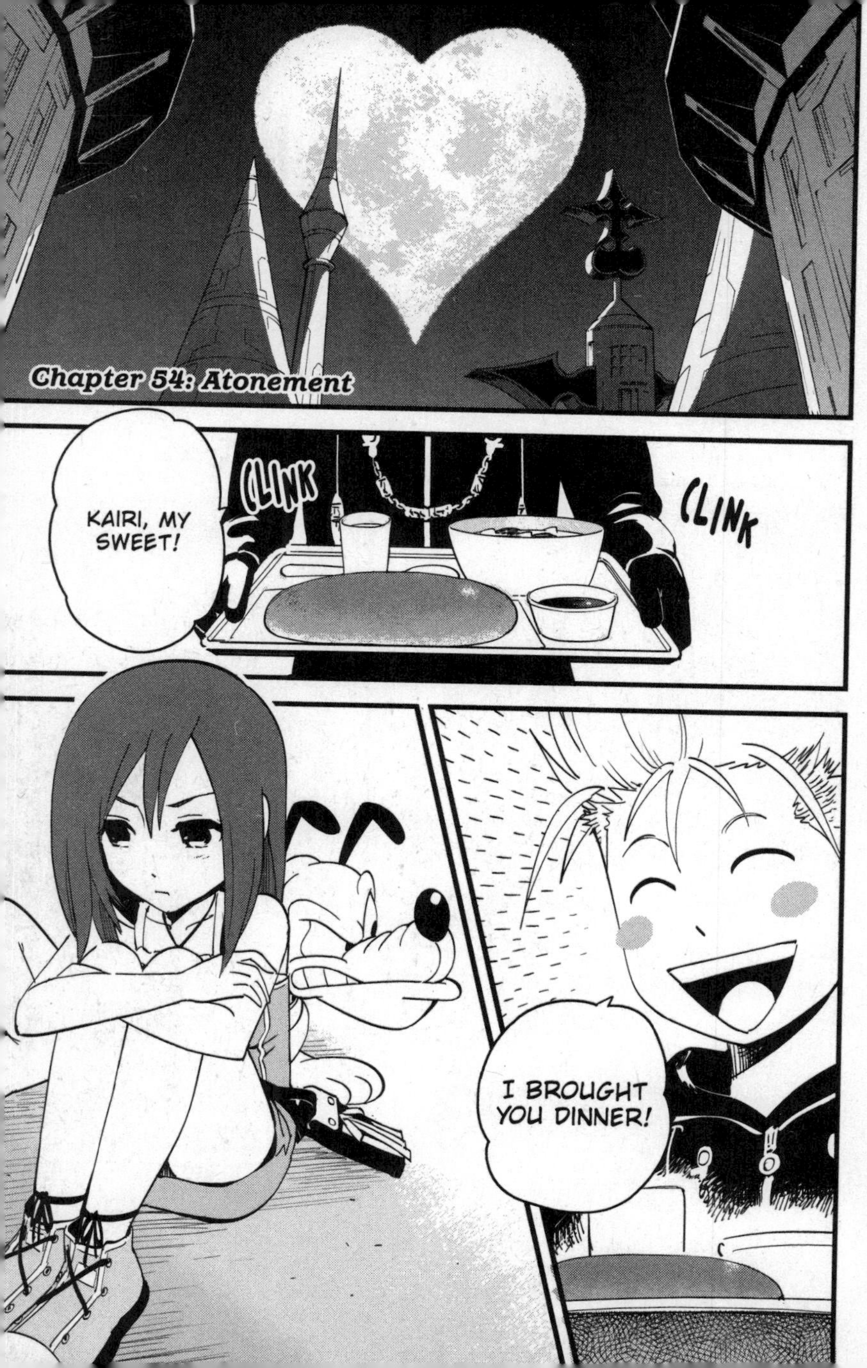
Chapter 54: Atonement
CLINK
CLINK
KAIRI, MY SWEET!
I BROUGHT YOU DINNER!

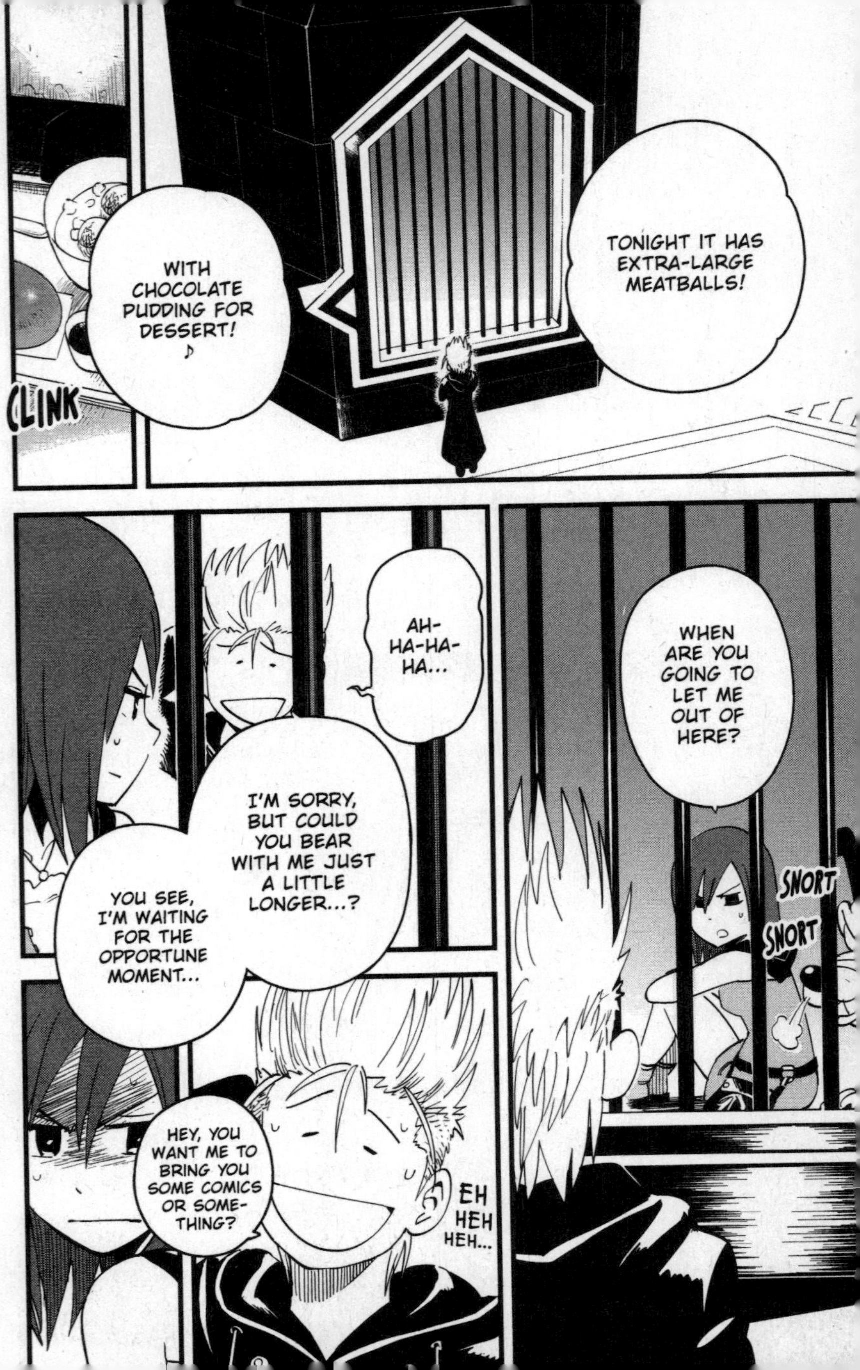
TONIGHT IT HAS EXTRA-LARGE MEATBALLS!
WITH CHOCOLATE PUDDING FOR DESSERT! ♪
CLINK
WHEN ARE YOU GOING TO LET ME OUT OF HERE?
SNORT
SNORT
AH-HA-HA-HA...
I'M SORRY, BUT COULD YOU BEAR WITH ME JUST A LITTLE LONGER...?
YOU SEE, I'M WAITING FOR THE OPPORTUNE MOMENT...
EH HEH HEH...
HEY, YOU WANT ME TO BRING YOU SOME COMICS OR SOME-THING?

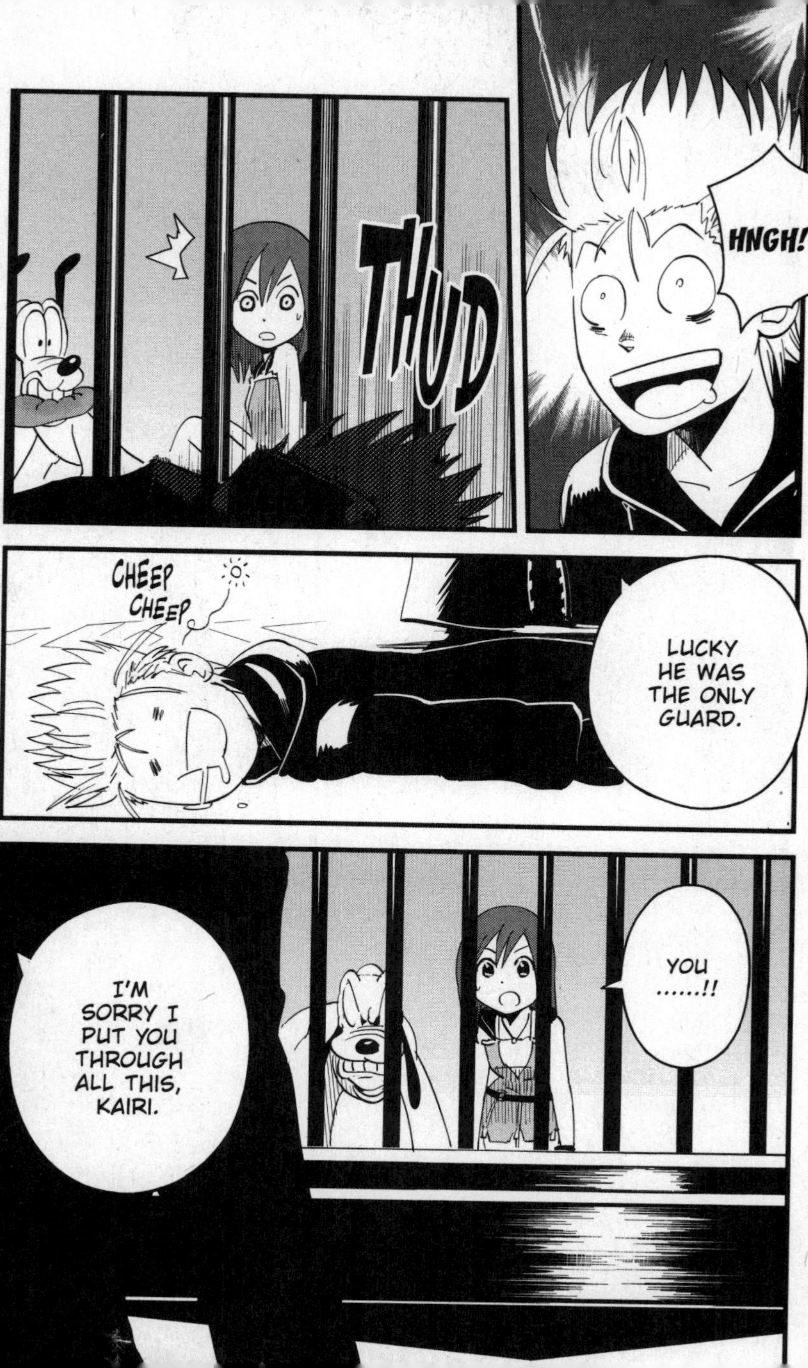
HNGH!
THUD
LUCKY HE WAS THE ONLY GUARD.
CHEEP CHEEP
YOU ......!!
I'M SORRY I PUT YOU THROUGH ALL THIS, KAIRI.

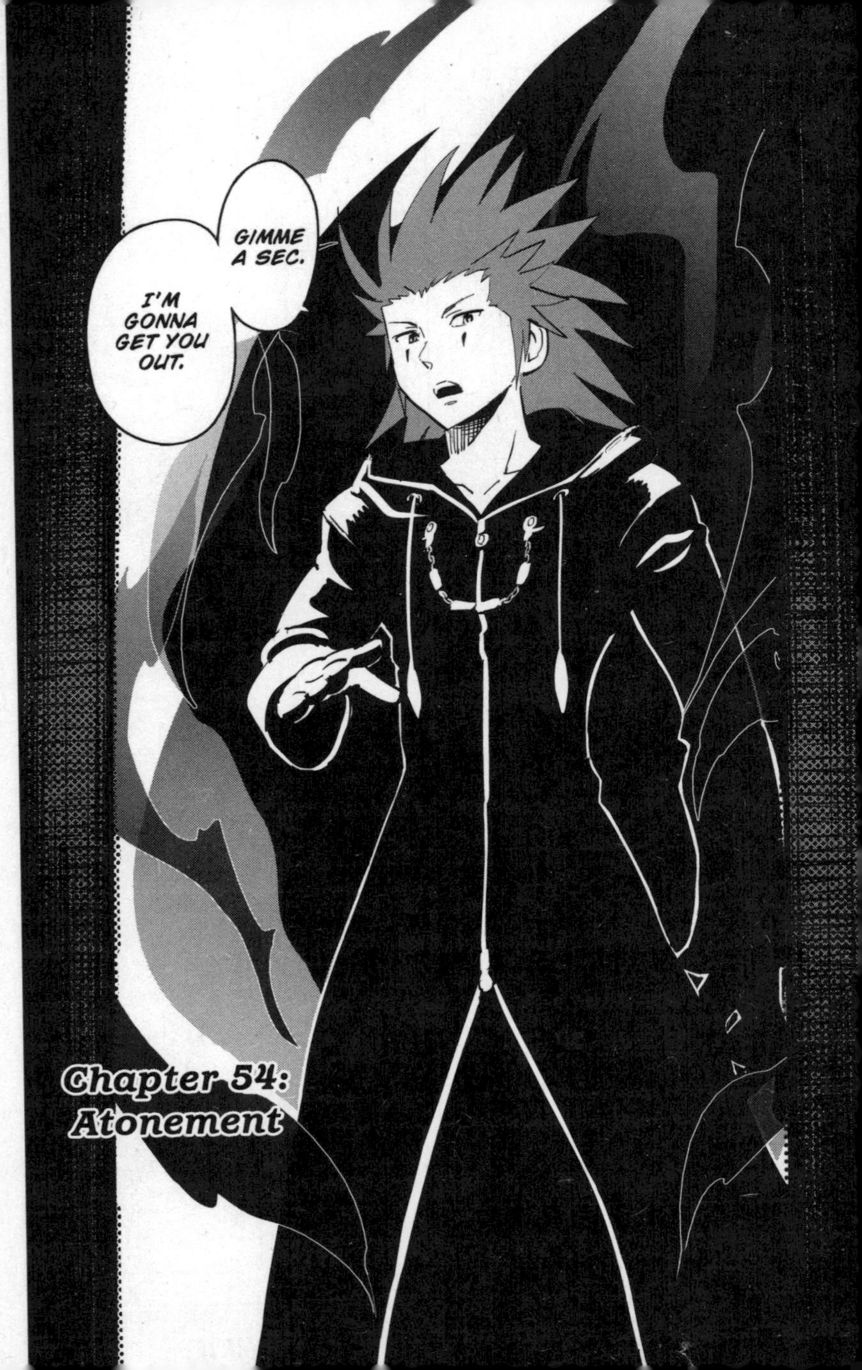
GIMME A SEC.
I'M GONNA GET YOU OUT.
Chapter 54: Atonement

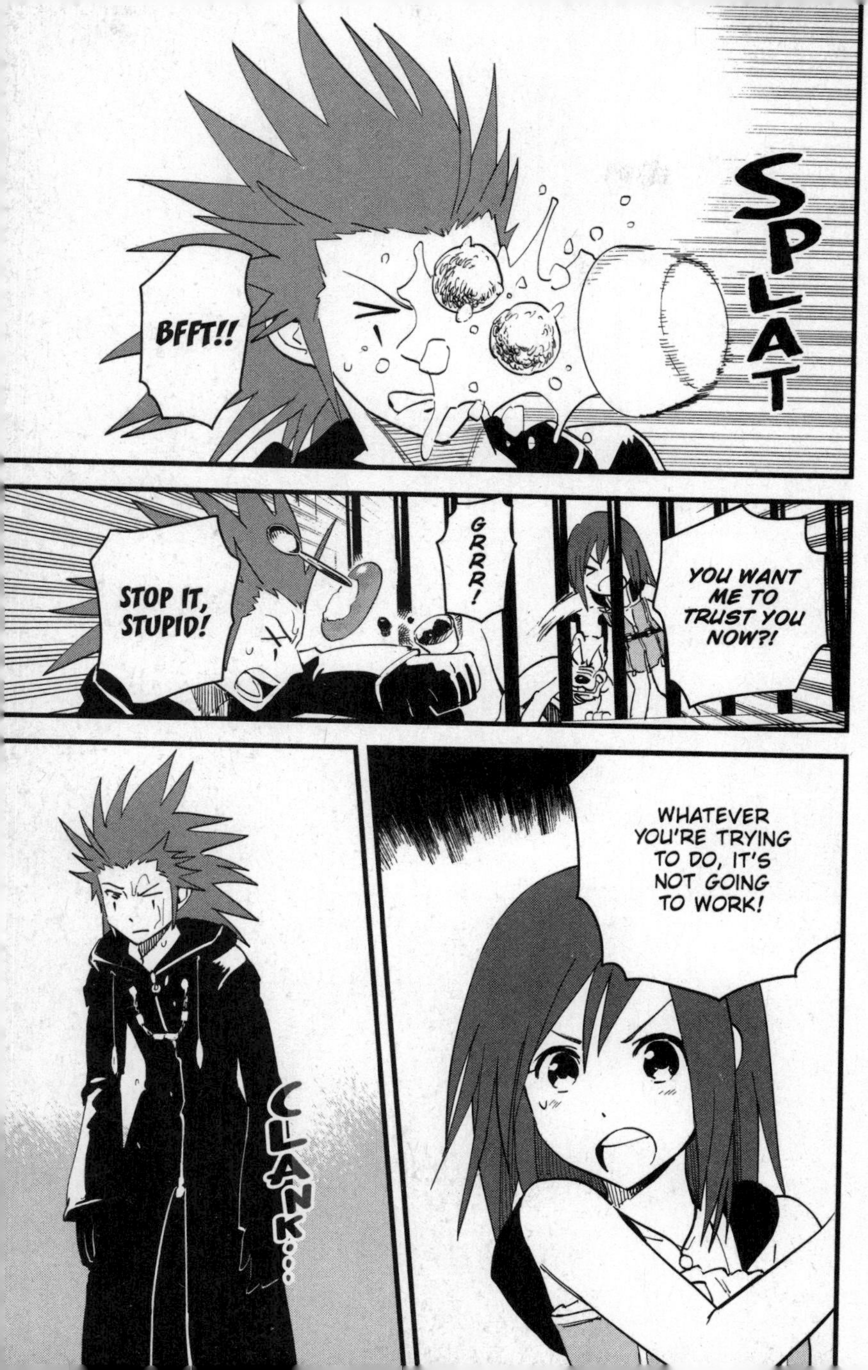
SPLAT
BFFT!!
YOU WANT ME TO TRUST YOU NOW?!
GRRR!
STOP IT, STUPID!
WHATEVER YOU'RE TRYING TO DO, IT'S NOT GOING TO WORK!
CLANK...

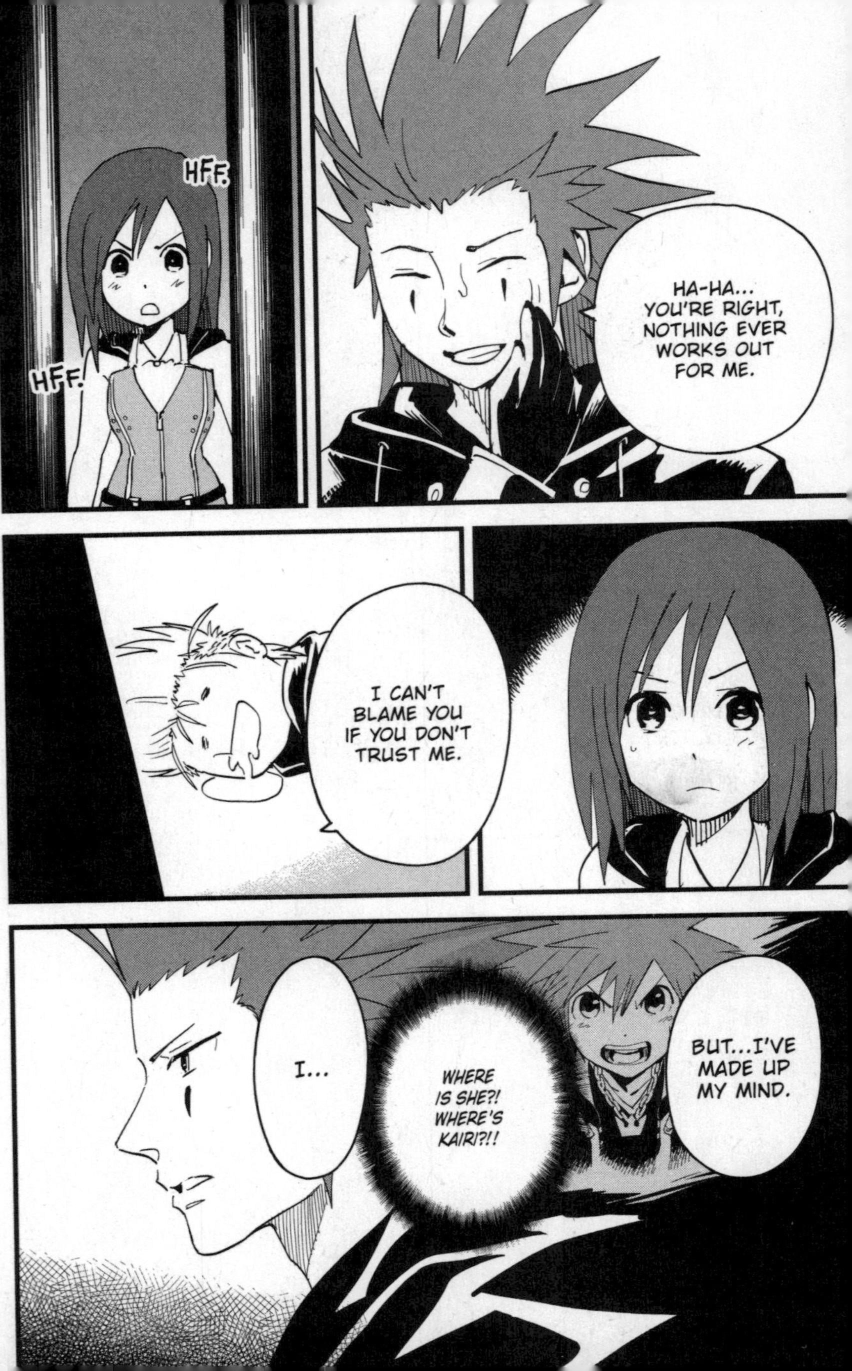
HA-HA... YOU'RE RIGHT, NOTHING EVER WORKS OUT FOR ME.
HFF.
HFF.
I CAN'T BLAME YOU IF YOU DON'T TRUST ME.
BUT...I'VE MADE UP MY MIND.
WHERE IS SHE?! WHERE'S KAIRI?!!
I...

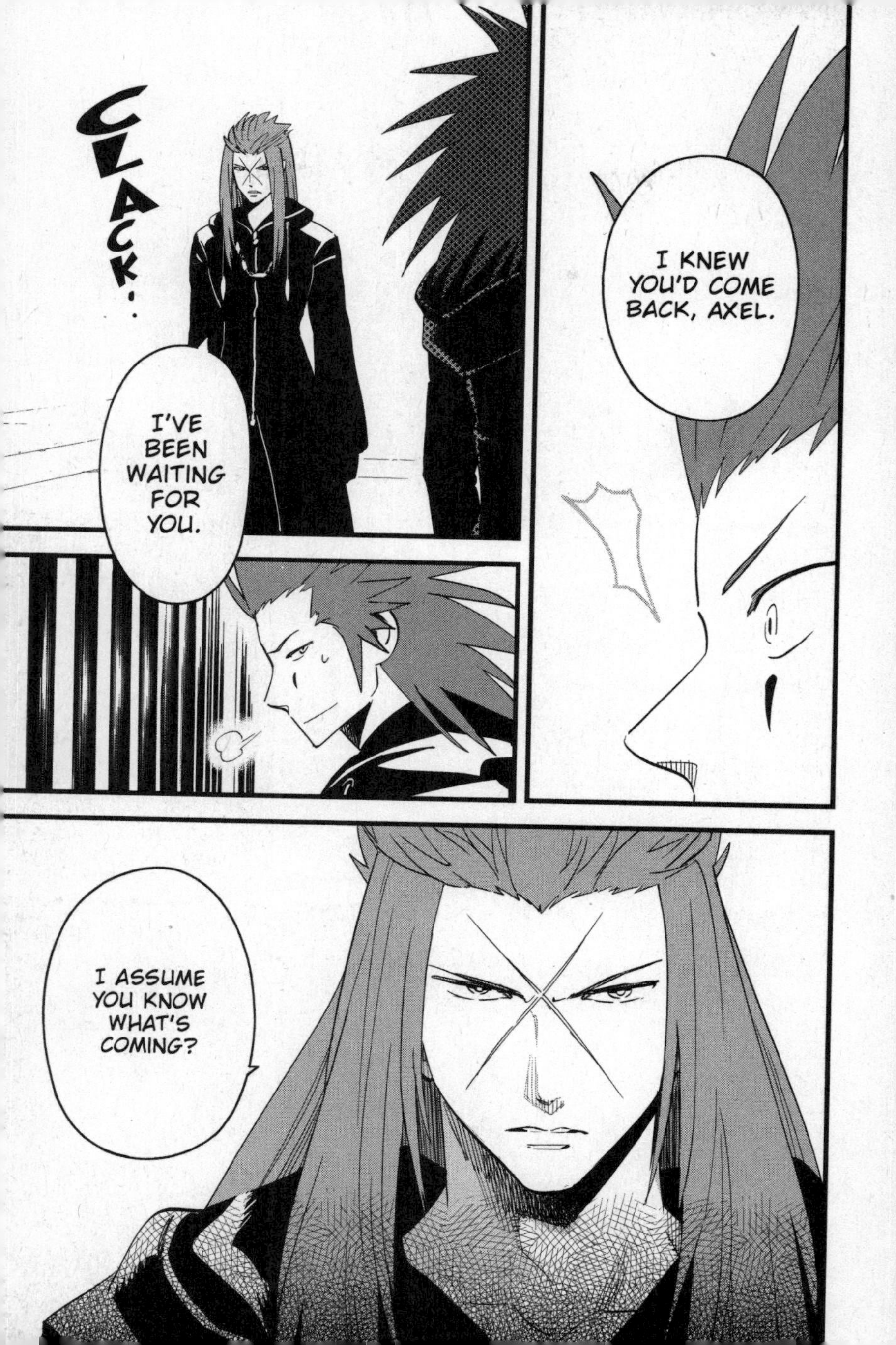
I KNEW YOU'D COME BACK, AXEL.
CLACK..
I'VE BEEN WAITING FOR YOU.
I ASSUME YOU KNOW WHAT'S COMING?

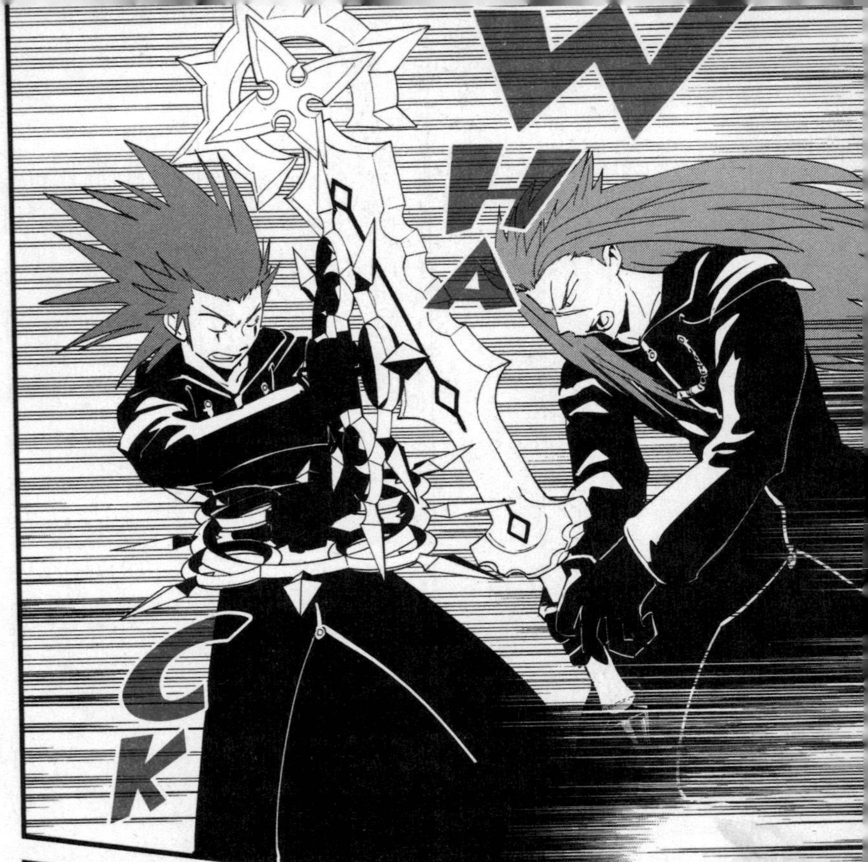
WHA
CK
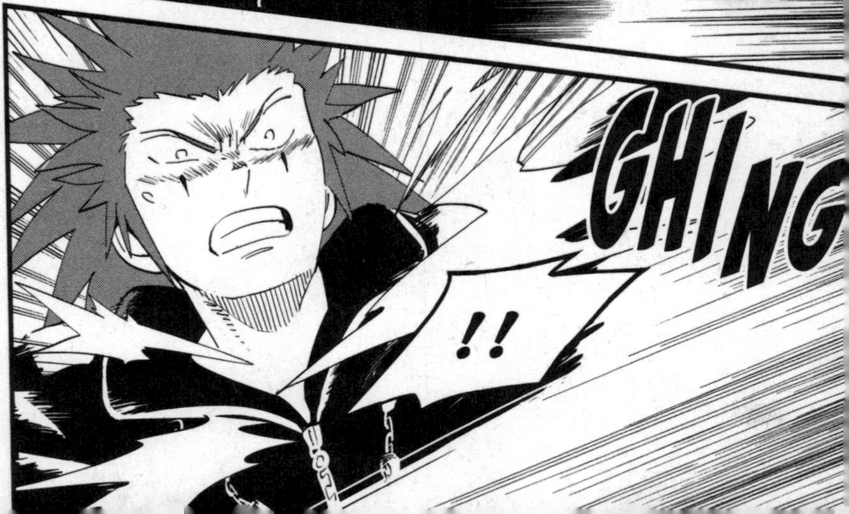
GHING
!!

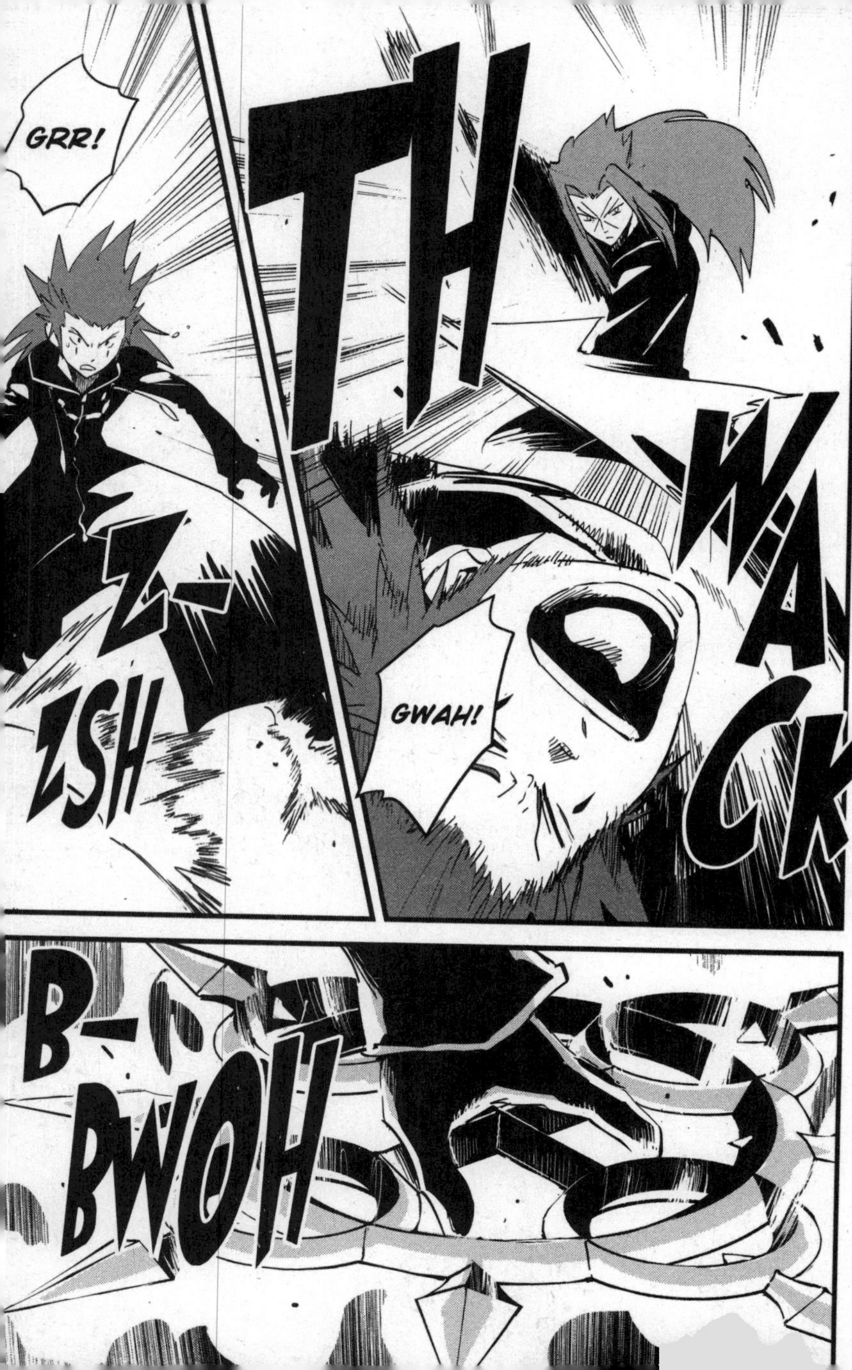
THWACK
GWAH!
GRR!
Z-ZSH
B-BWOH

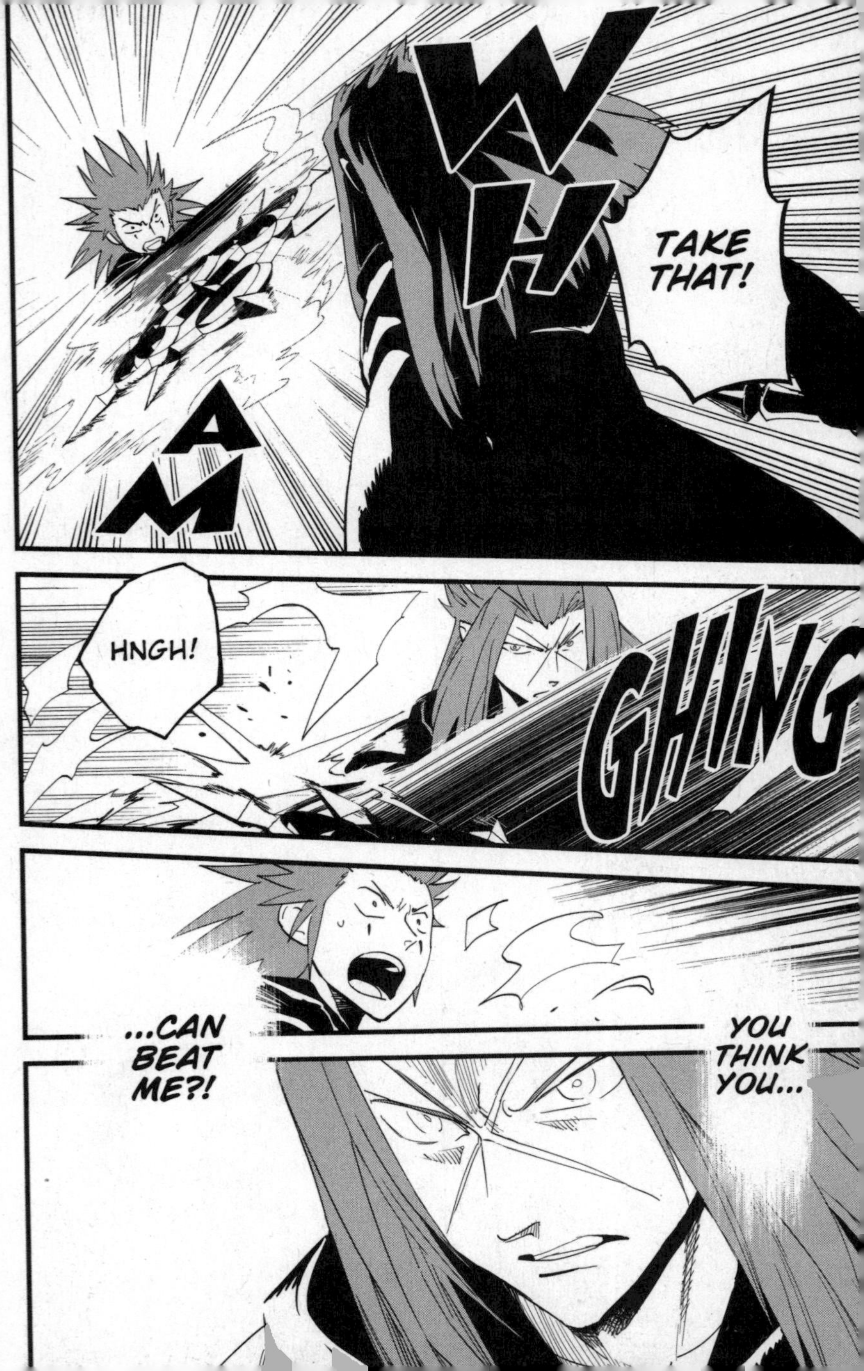
TAKE THAT!
WHAM
GHING
HNGH!
YOU THINK YOU...
...CAN BEAT ME?!

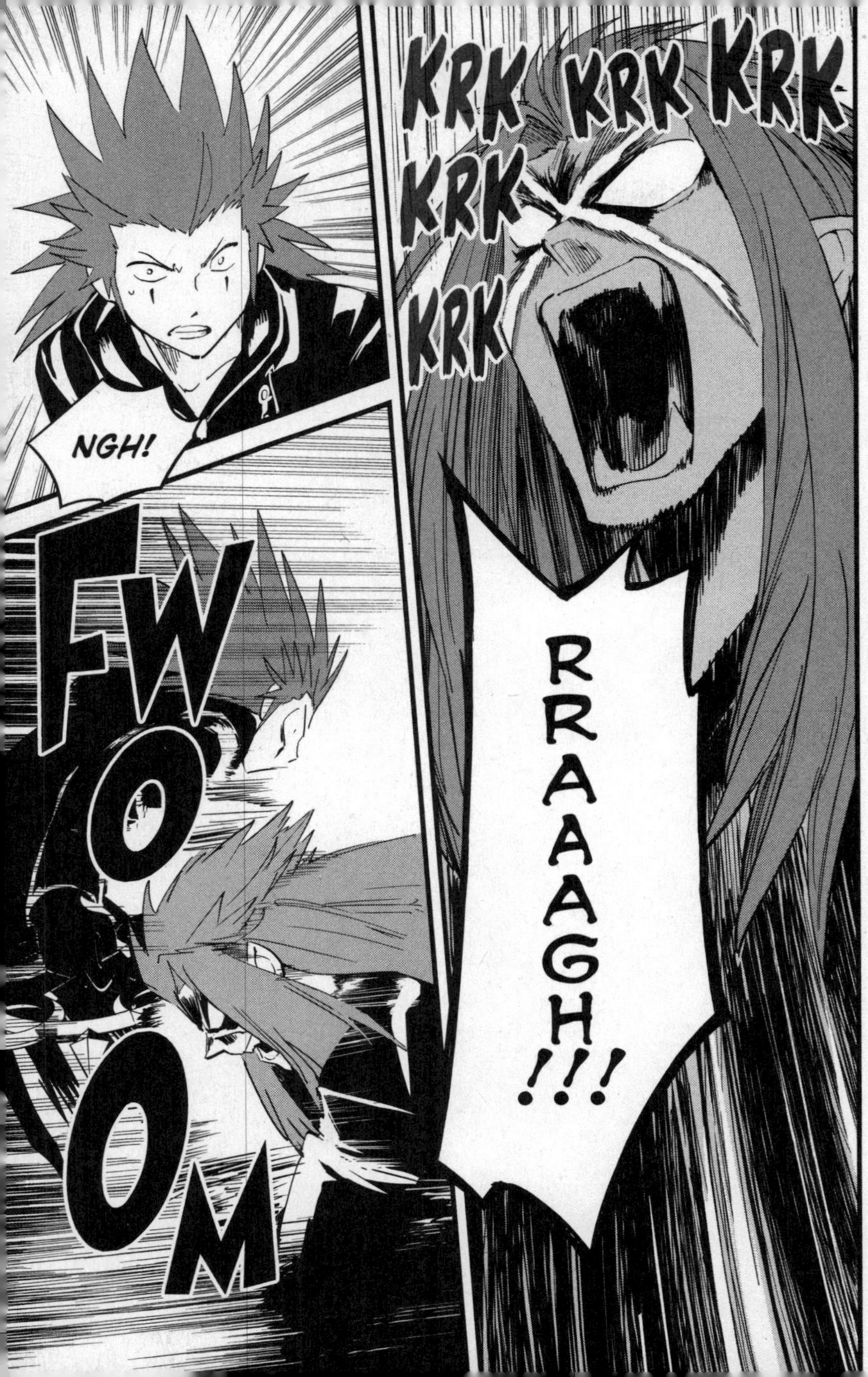
KRK KRK KRK KRK KRK
RRAAGH!!!
NGH!
FWOOM

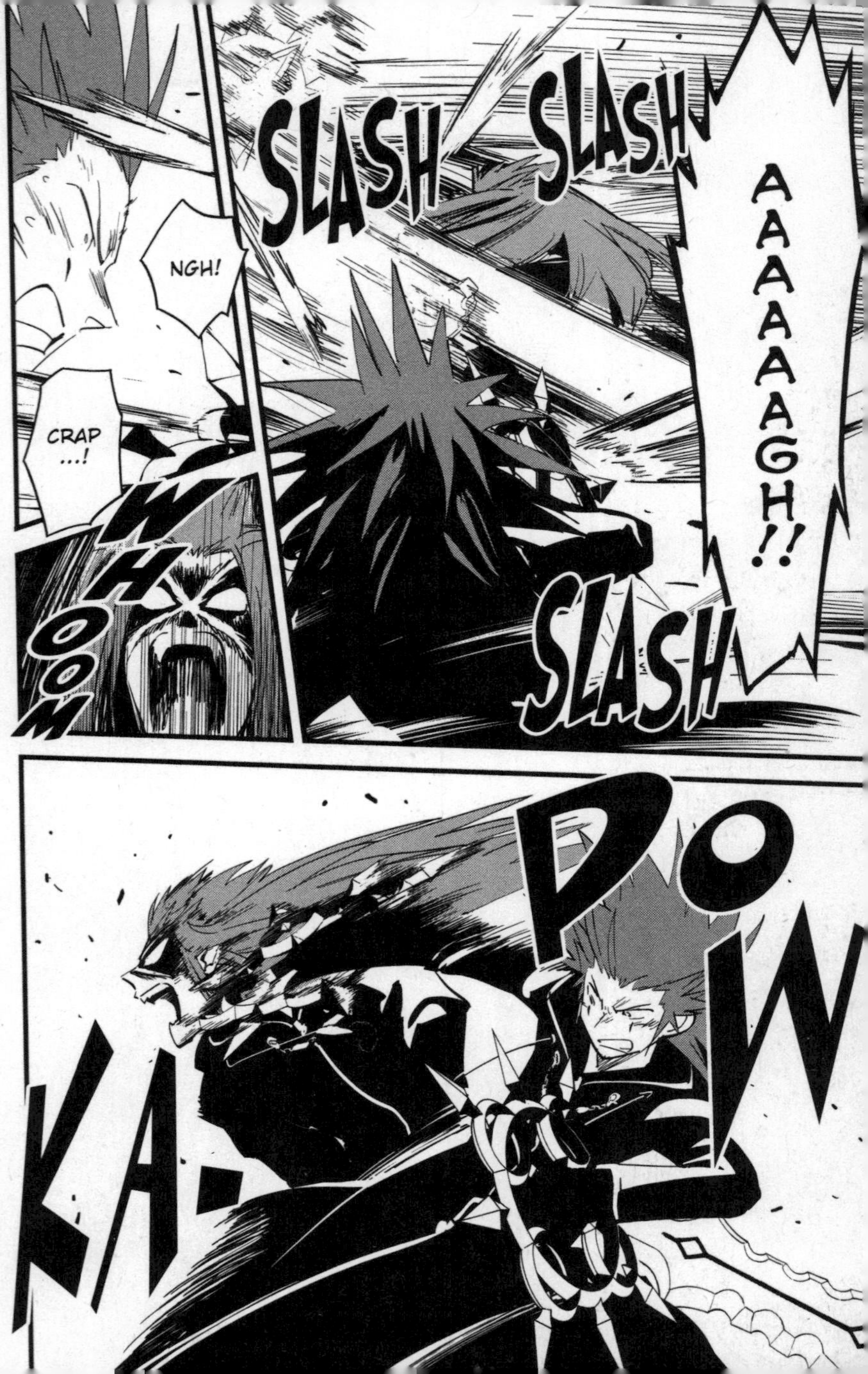

AAAAAAGH!!
SLASH
SLASH
SLASH
NGH!
CRAP ...!
WHOOM
KA-
POW

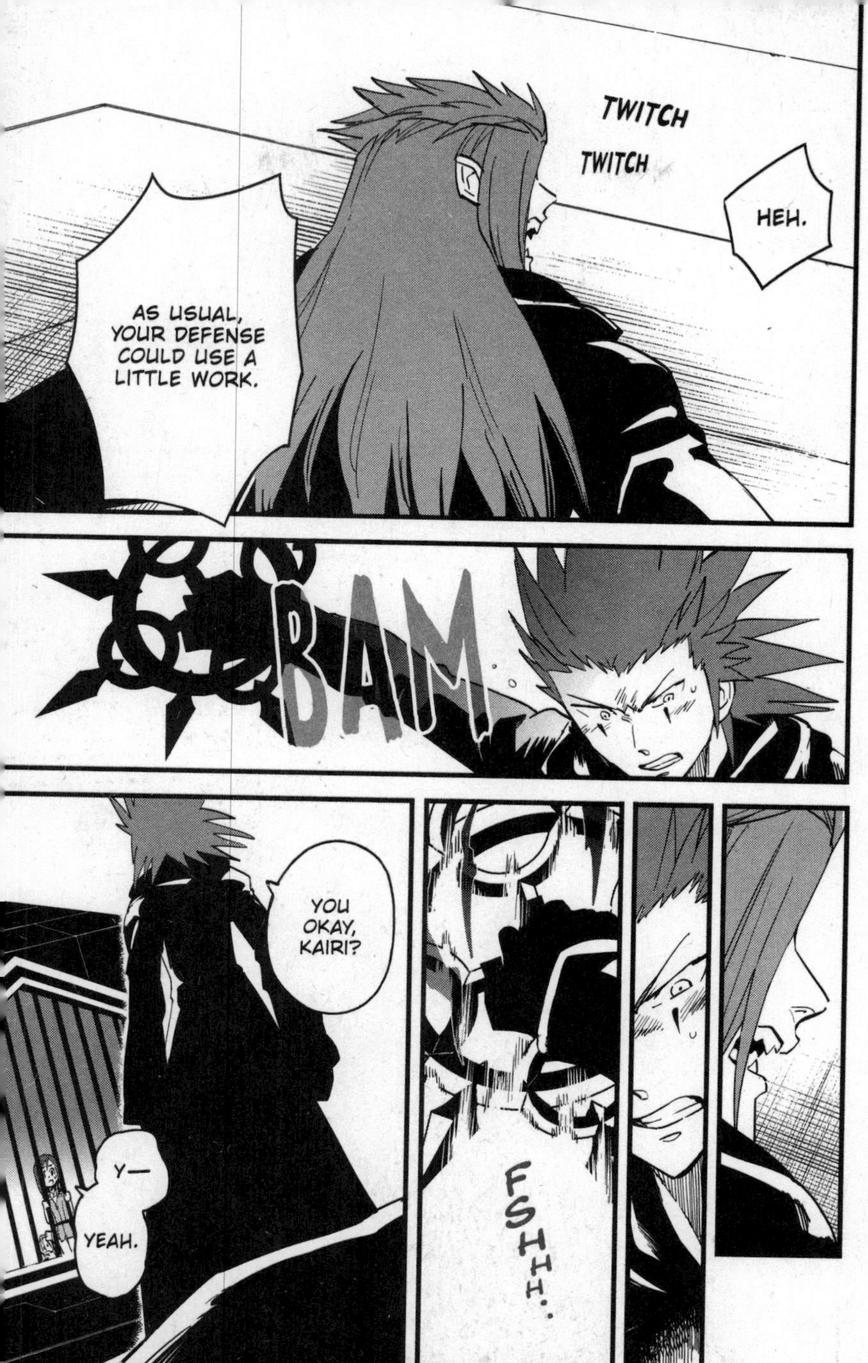
TWITCH
TWITCH
HEH.
AS USUAL, YOUR DEFENSE COULD USE A LITTLE WORK.
BAM
FSHHH..
YOU OKAY, KAIRI?
Y—
YEAH.

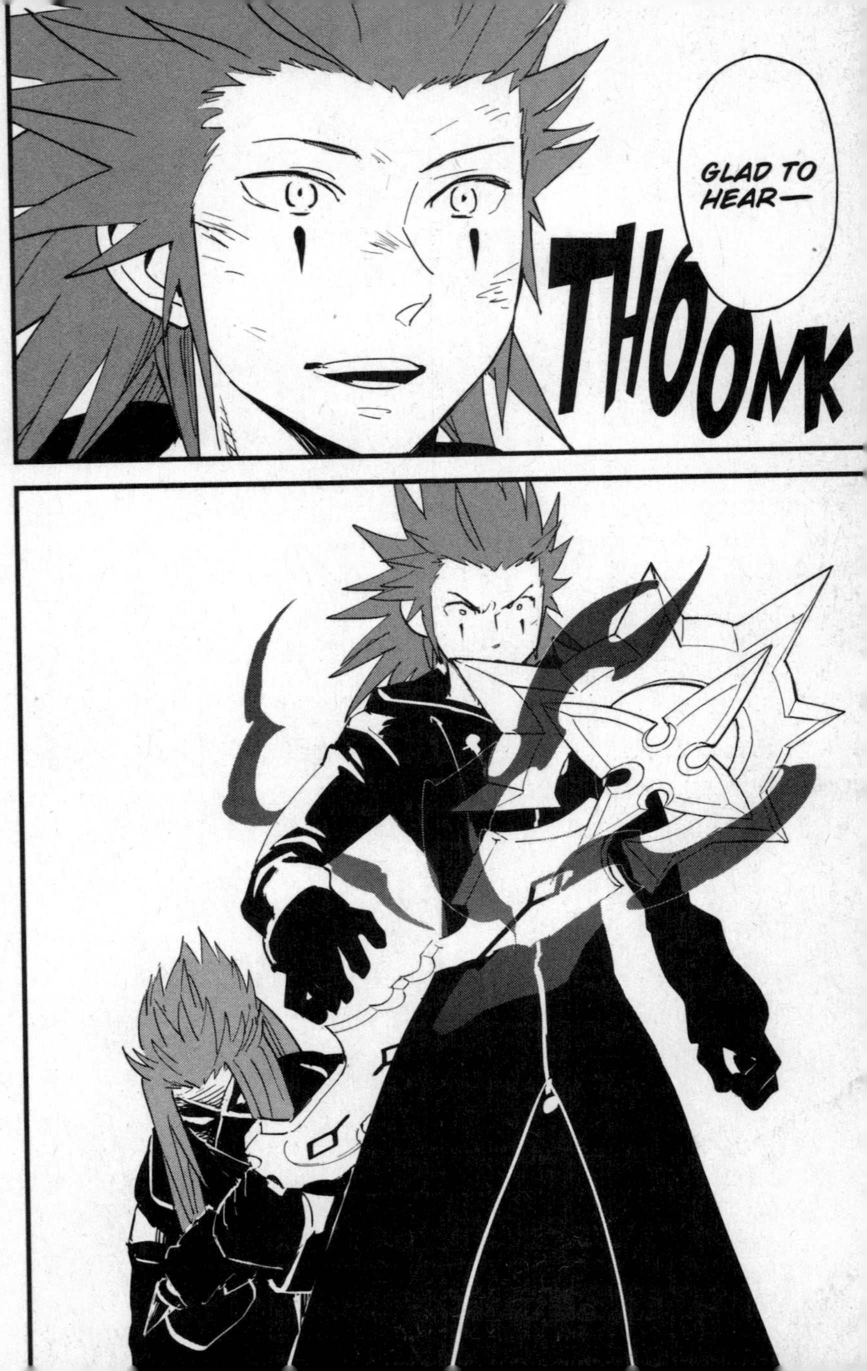
GLAD TO HEAR—
THOOMK

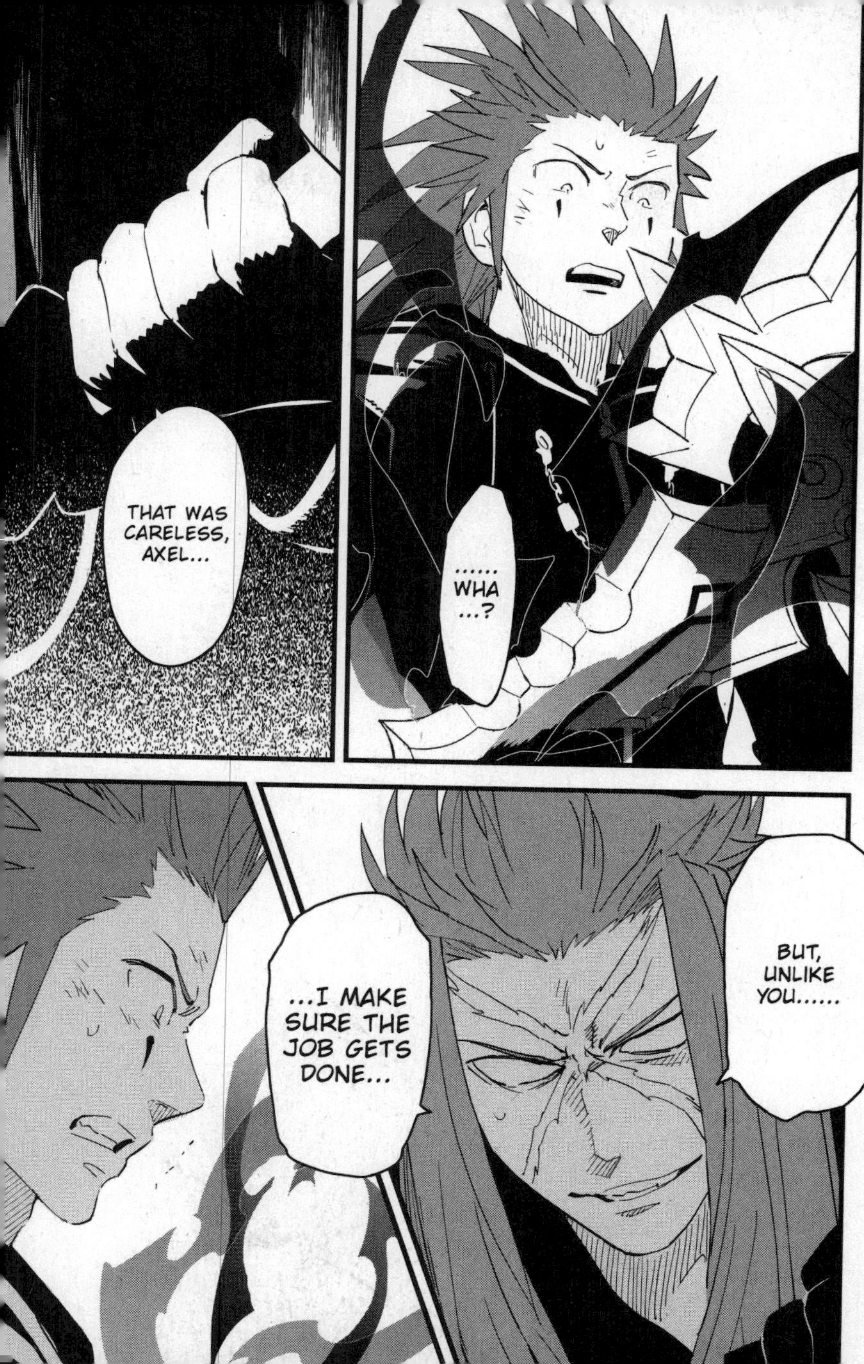
......WHA...?
THAT WAS CARELESS, AXEL...
BUT, UNLIKE YOU......
...I MAKE SURE THE JOB GETS DONE...

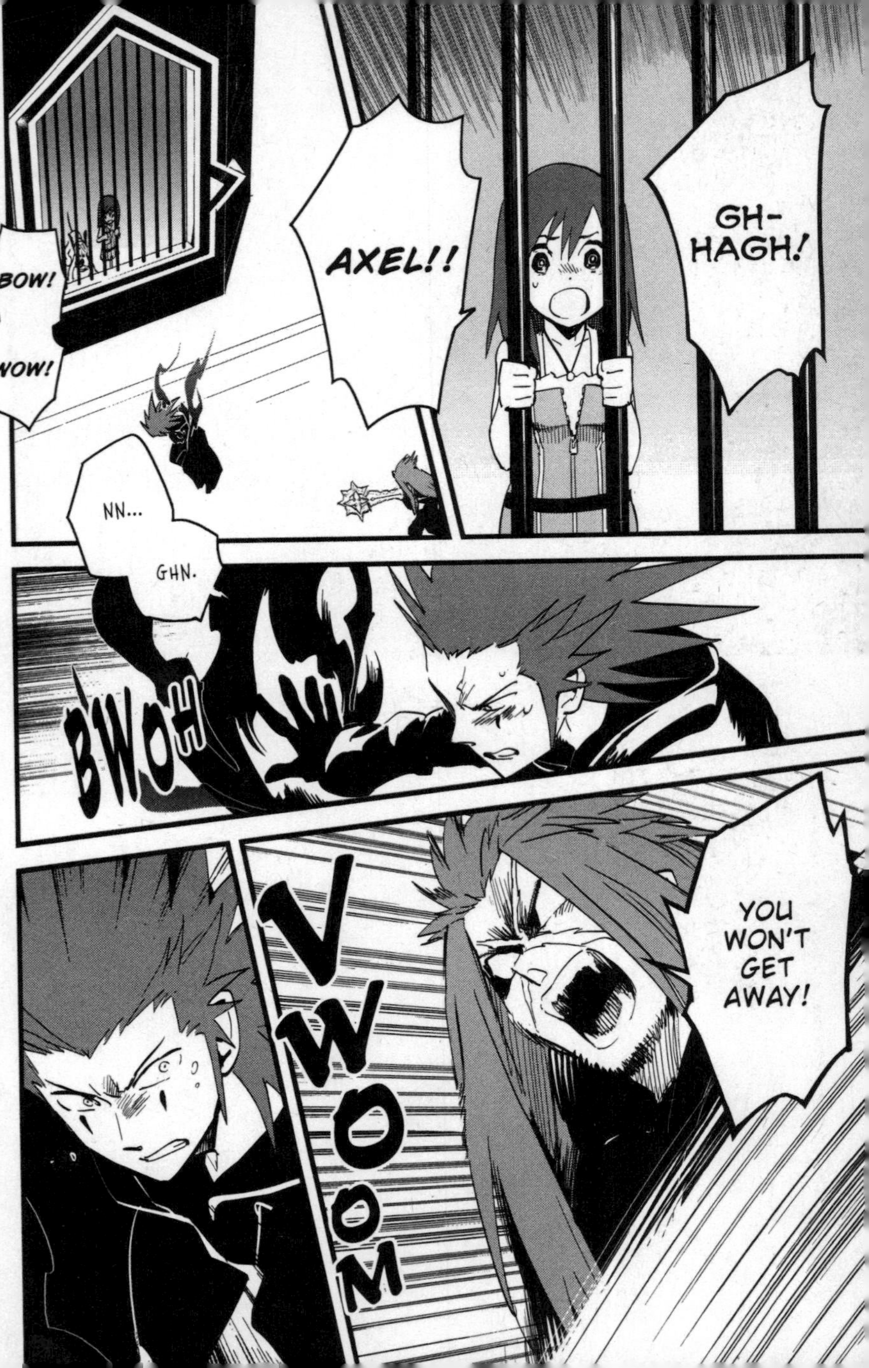
GH-HAGH!
AXEL!!
BOW!
WOW!
NN...
GHN.
BWOH
YOU WON'T GET AWAY!
VWOOM

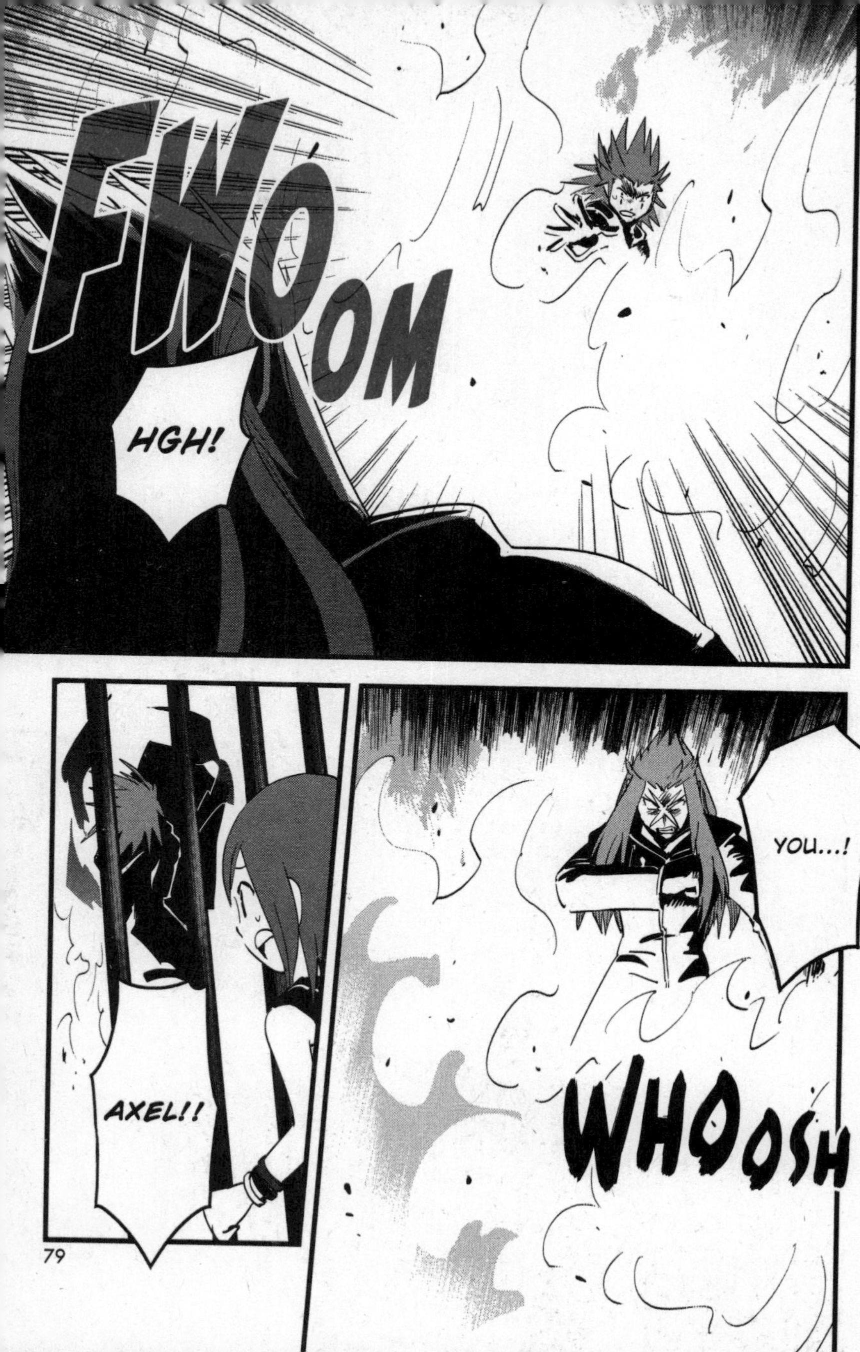
FWOOM
HGH!
YOU...!
WHOOSH
AXEL!!

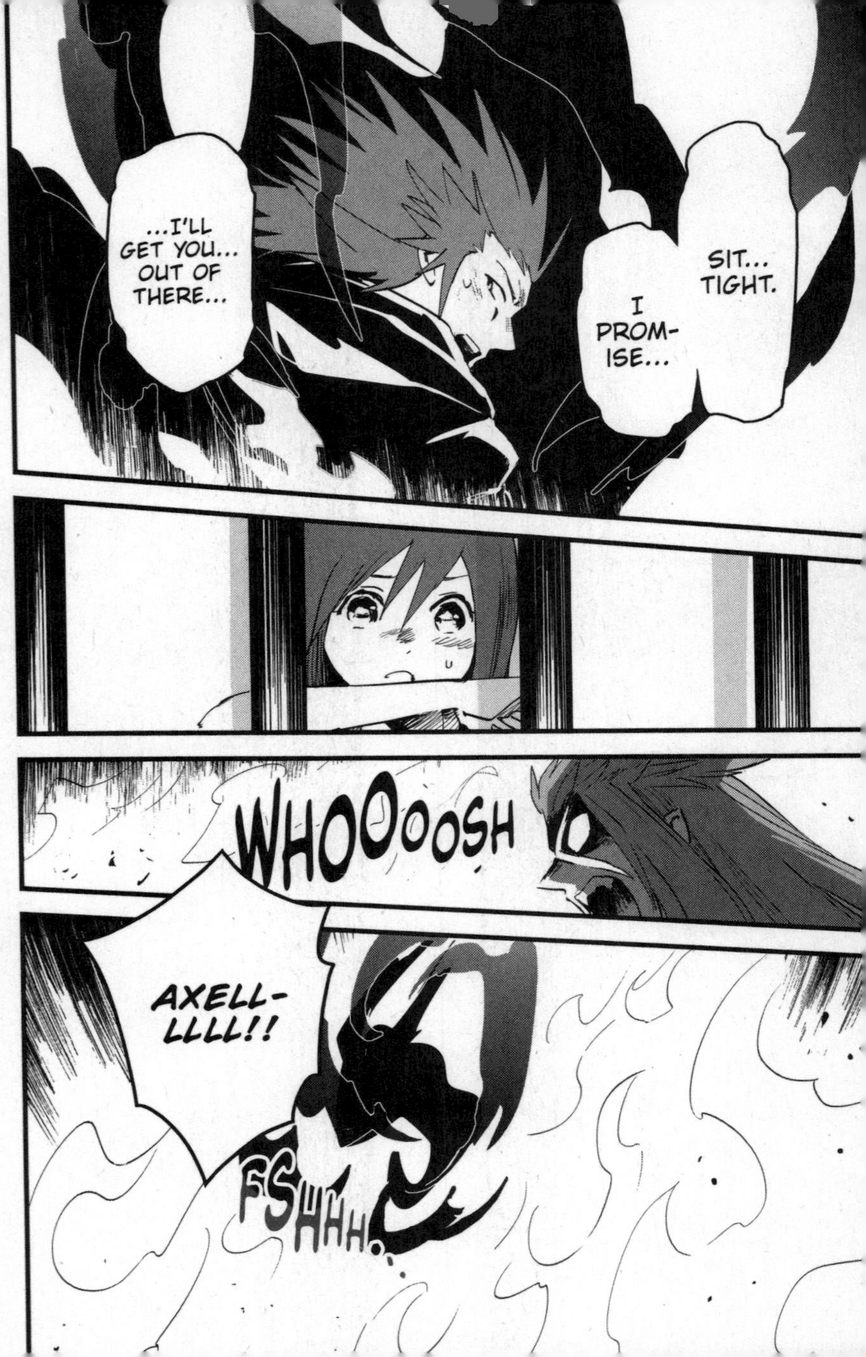
SIT... TIGHT.
I PROMISE...
...I'LL GET YOU... OUT OF THERE...
WHOOOoosh
AXELL-LLLL!!
FSHHH..

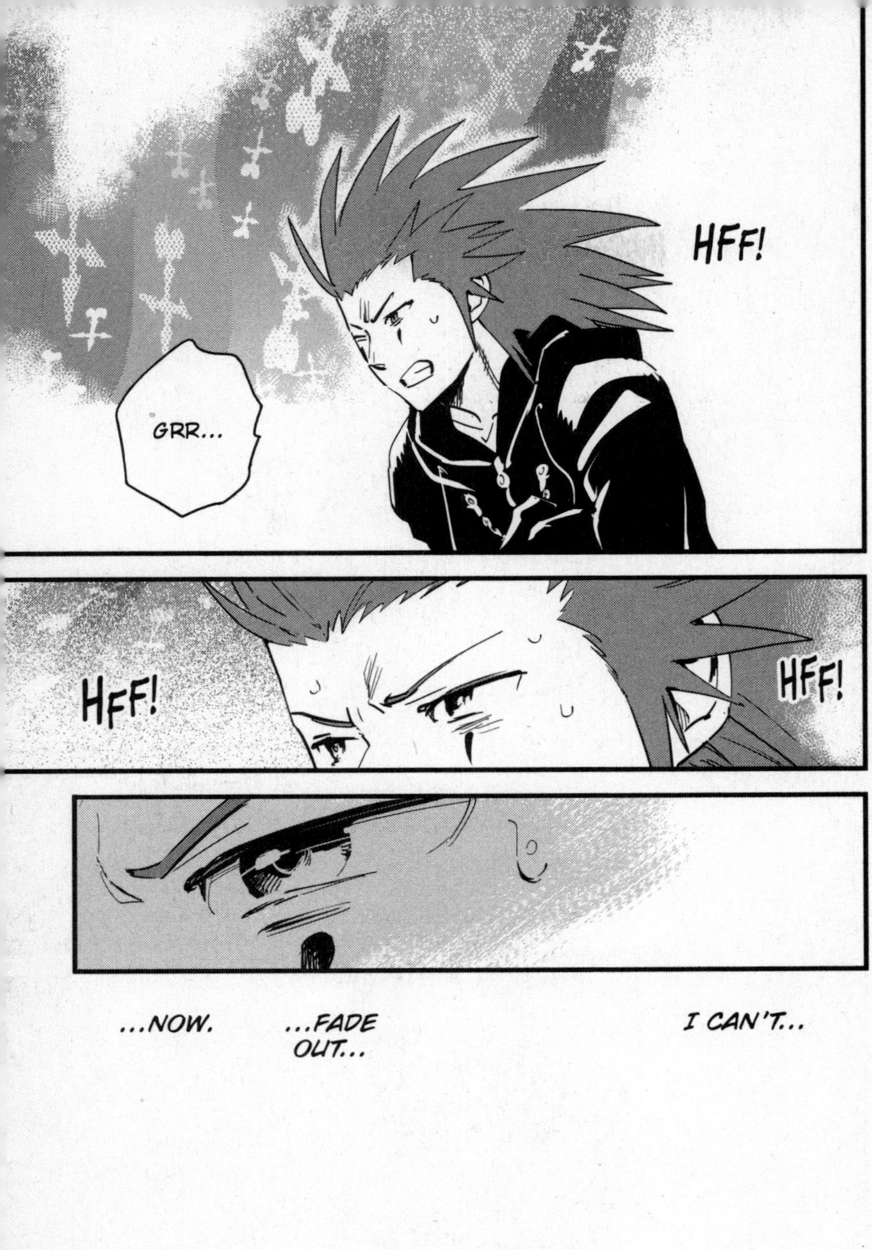
HFF!
GRR...
HFF!
HFF!
I CAN'T...
...FADE OUT...
...NOW.

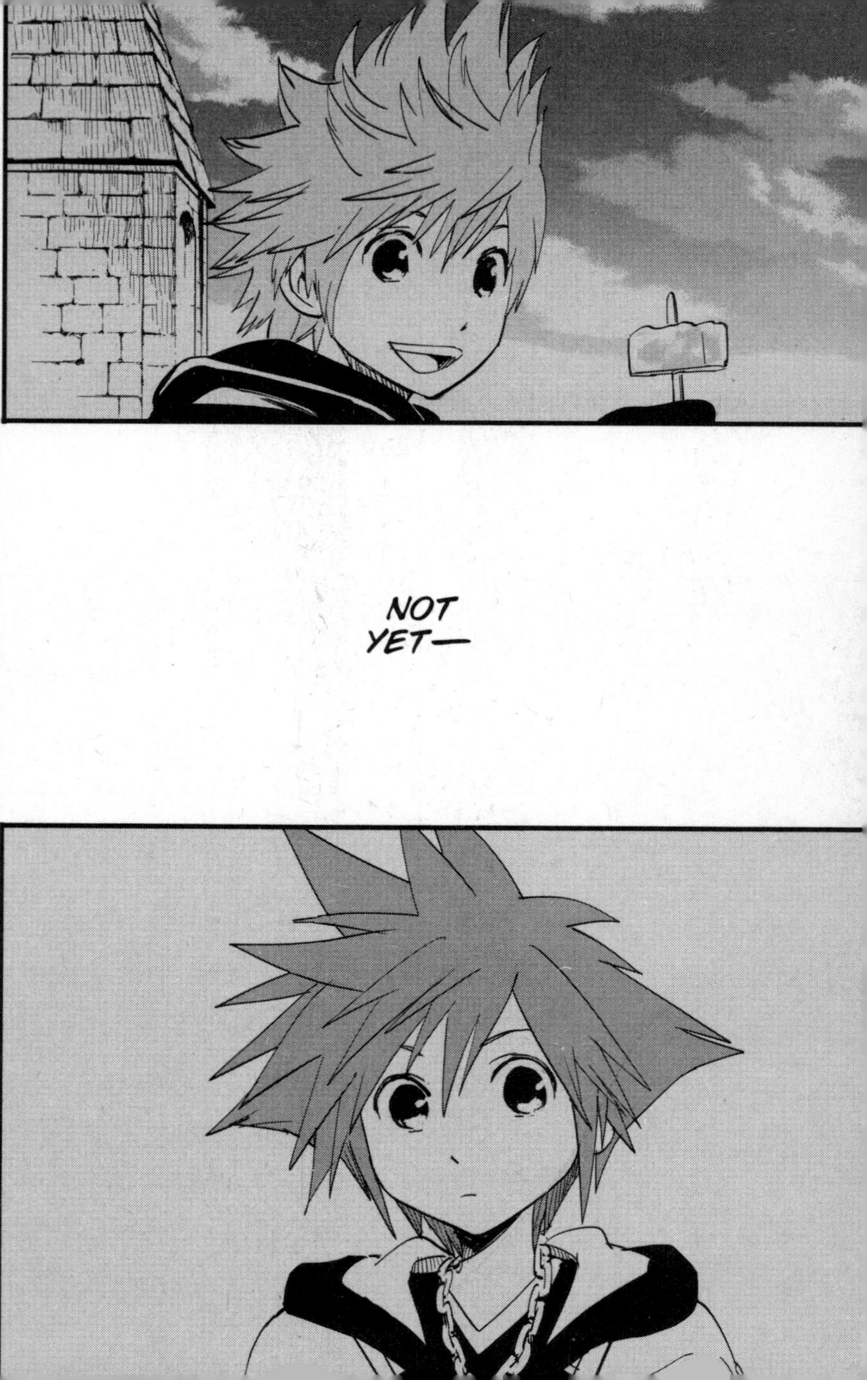
NOT YET—

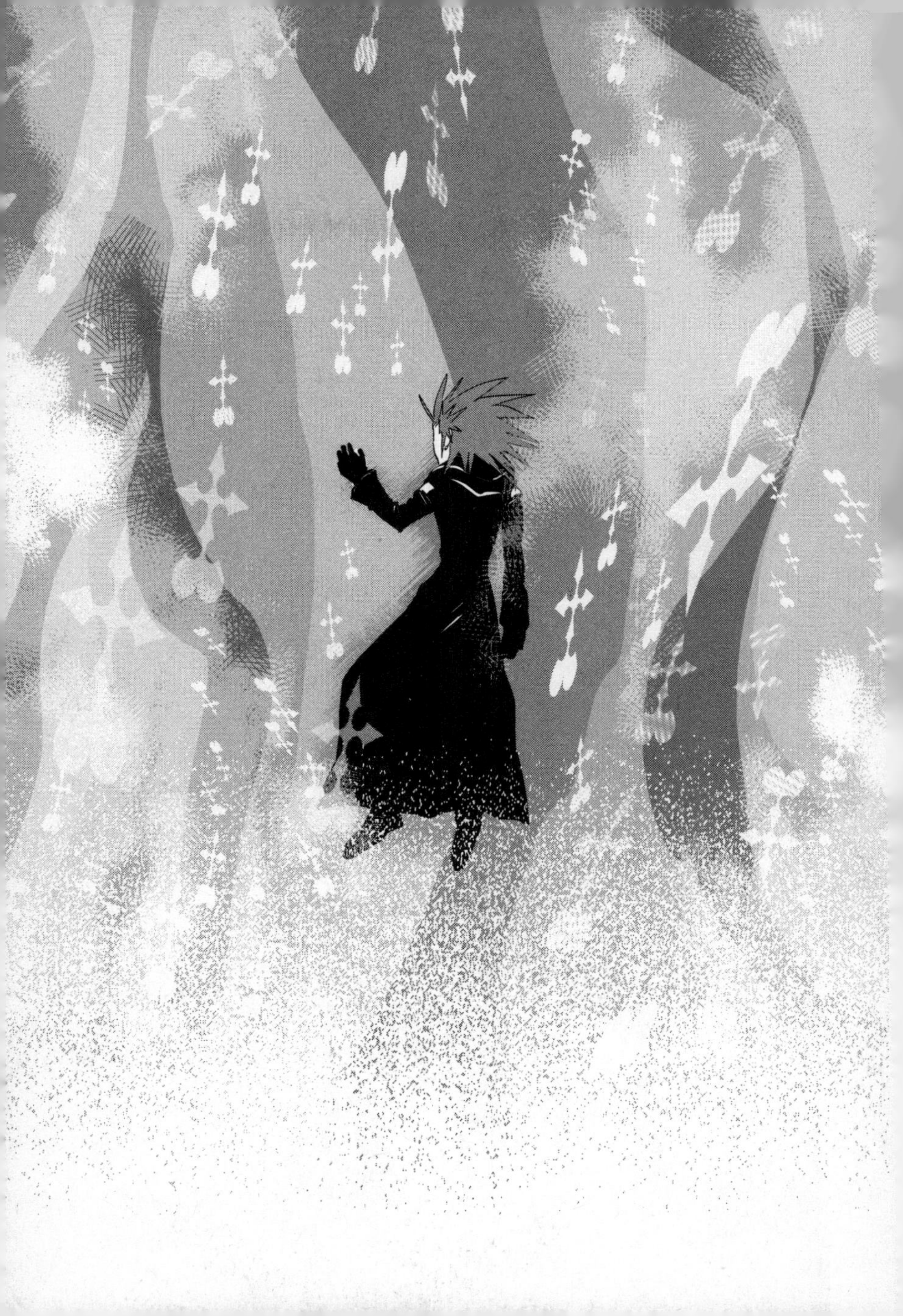

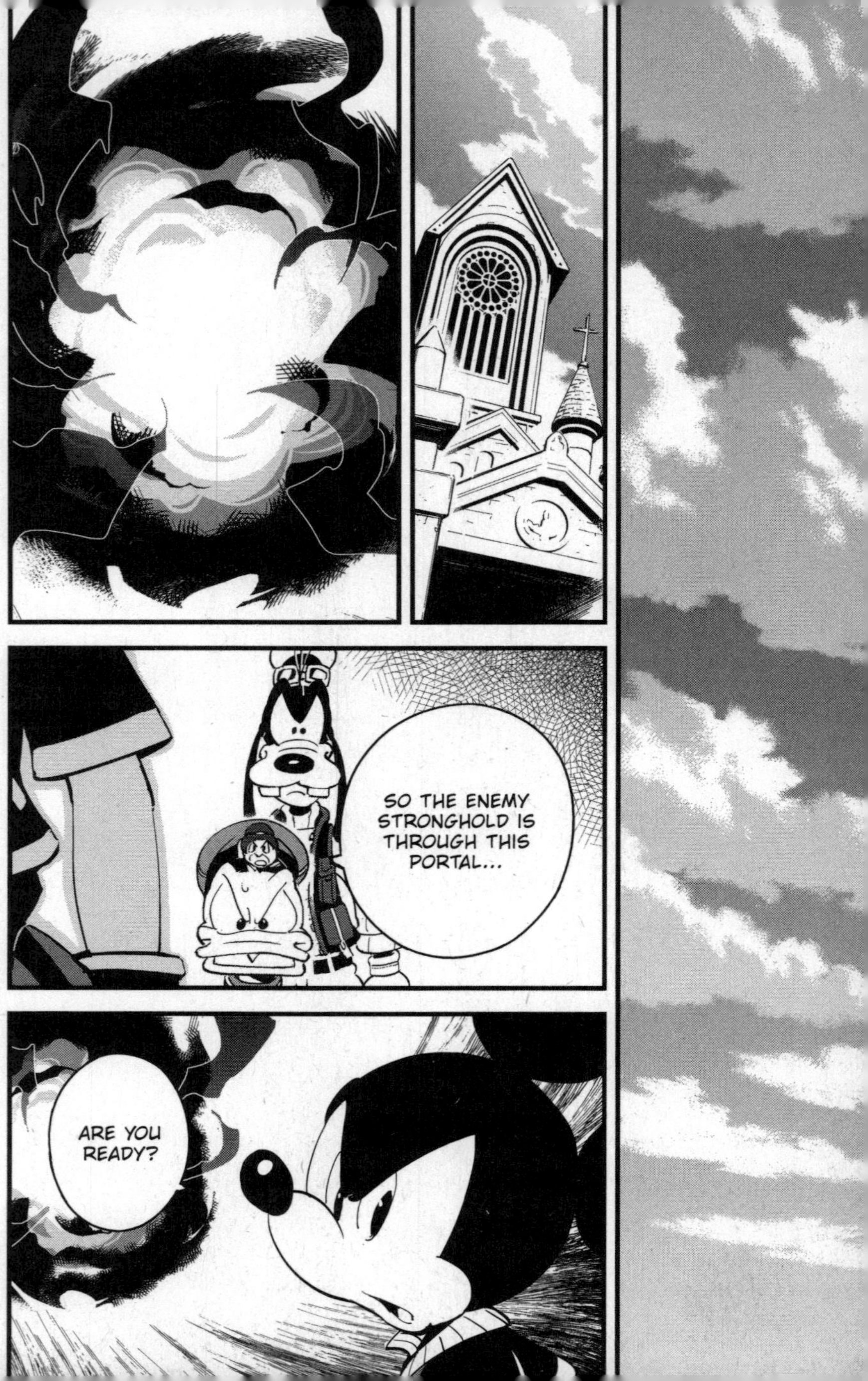
SO THE ENEMY STRONGHOLD IS THROUGH THIS PORTAL...
ARE YOU READY?

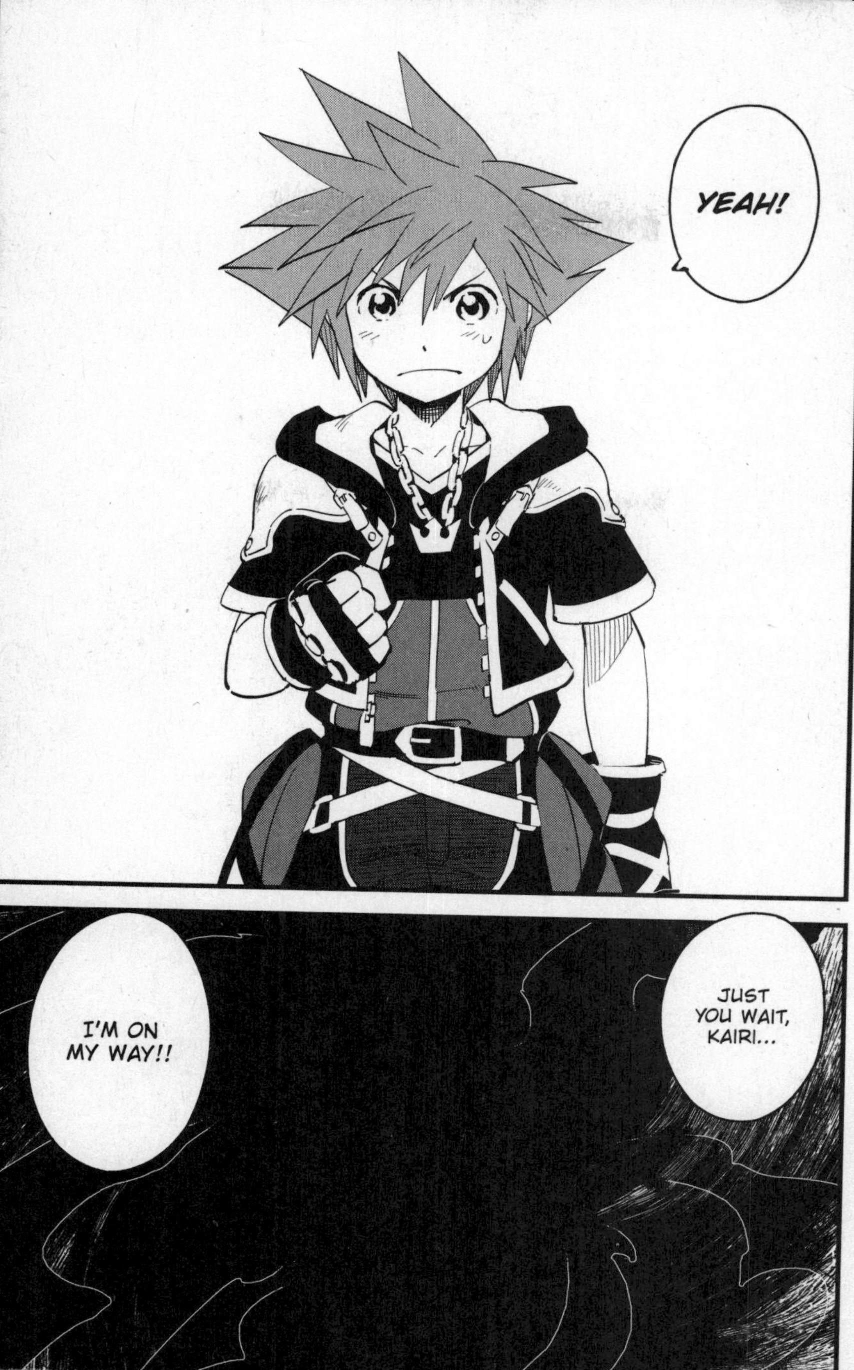
YEAH!
JUST YOU WAIT, KAIRI...
I'M ON MY WAY!!

Disney SQUARE ENIX

KINGDOM HEARTS

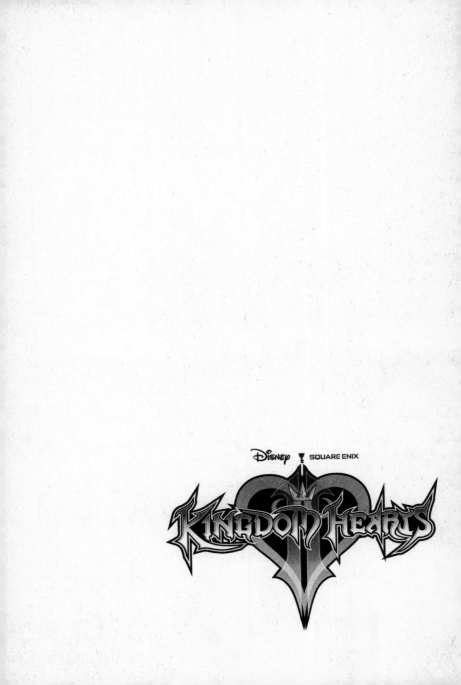

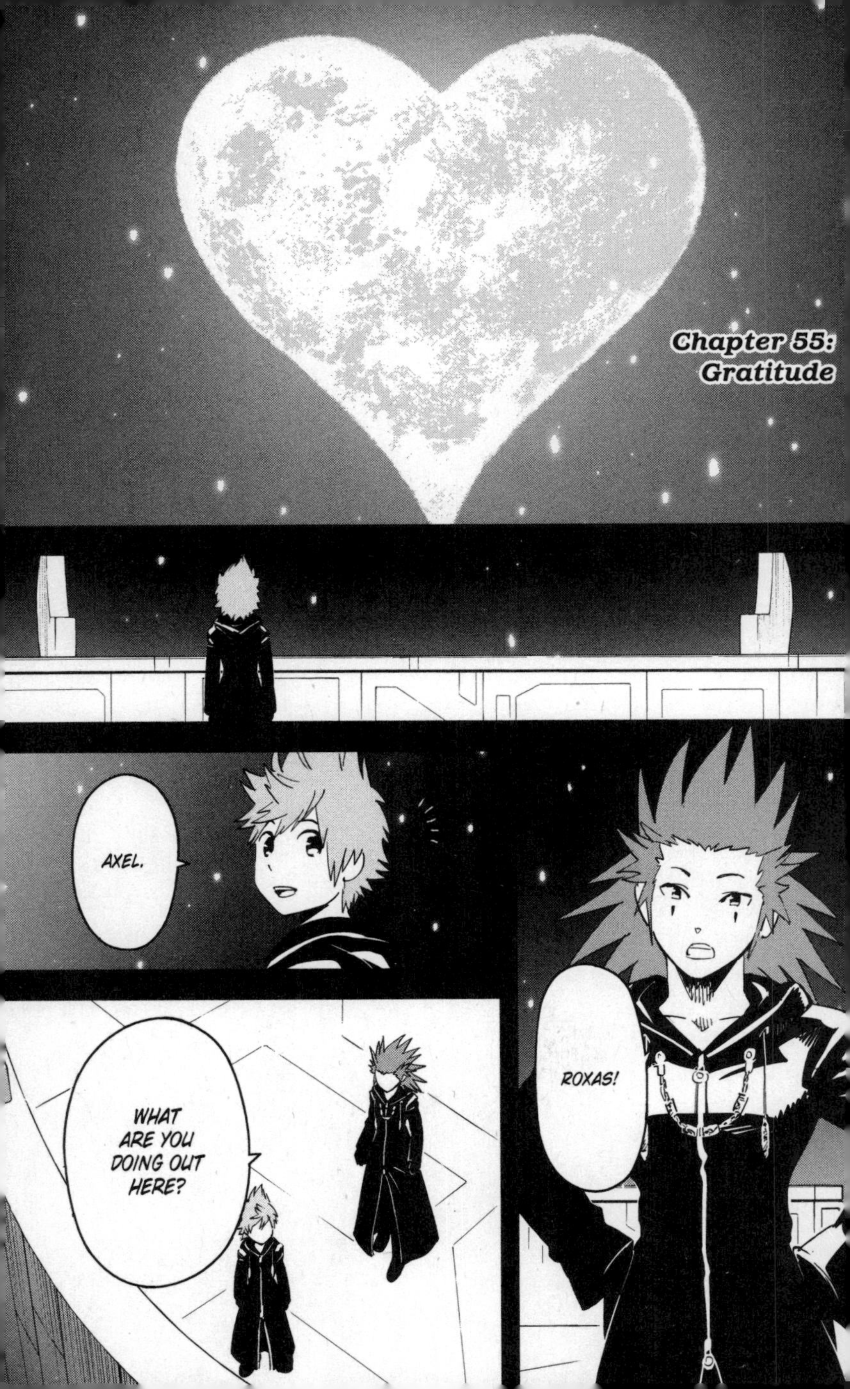
Chapter 55:
Gratitude
ROXAS!
AXEL.
WHAT ARE YOU DOING OUT HERE?

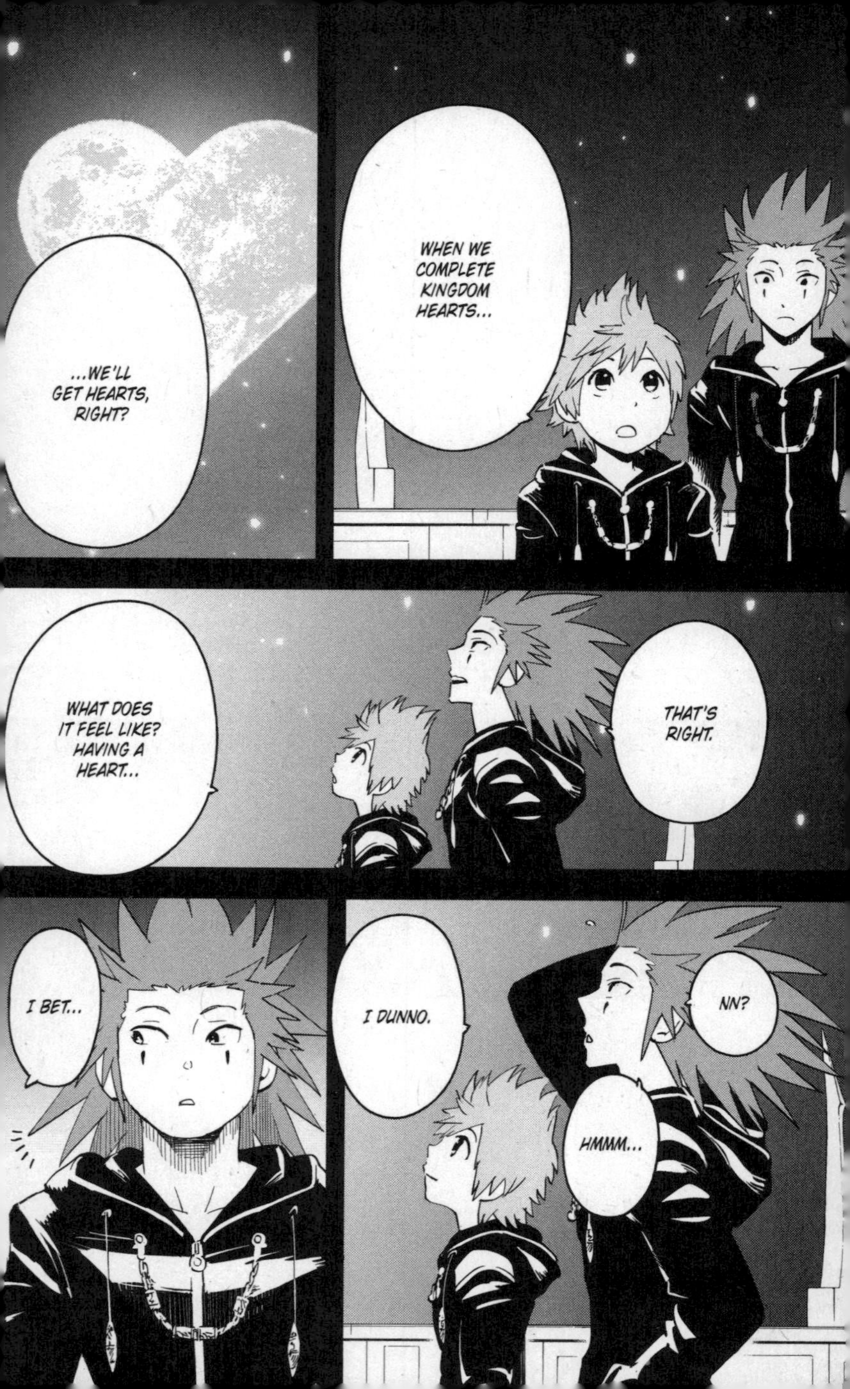
WHEN WE COMPLETE KINGDOM HEARTS...
...WE'LL GET HEARTS, RIGHT?
THAT'S RIGHT.
WHAT DOES IT FEEL LIKE? HAVING A HEART...
NN?
I DUNNO.
HMMM...
I BET...

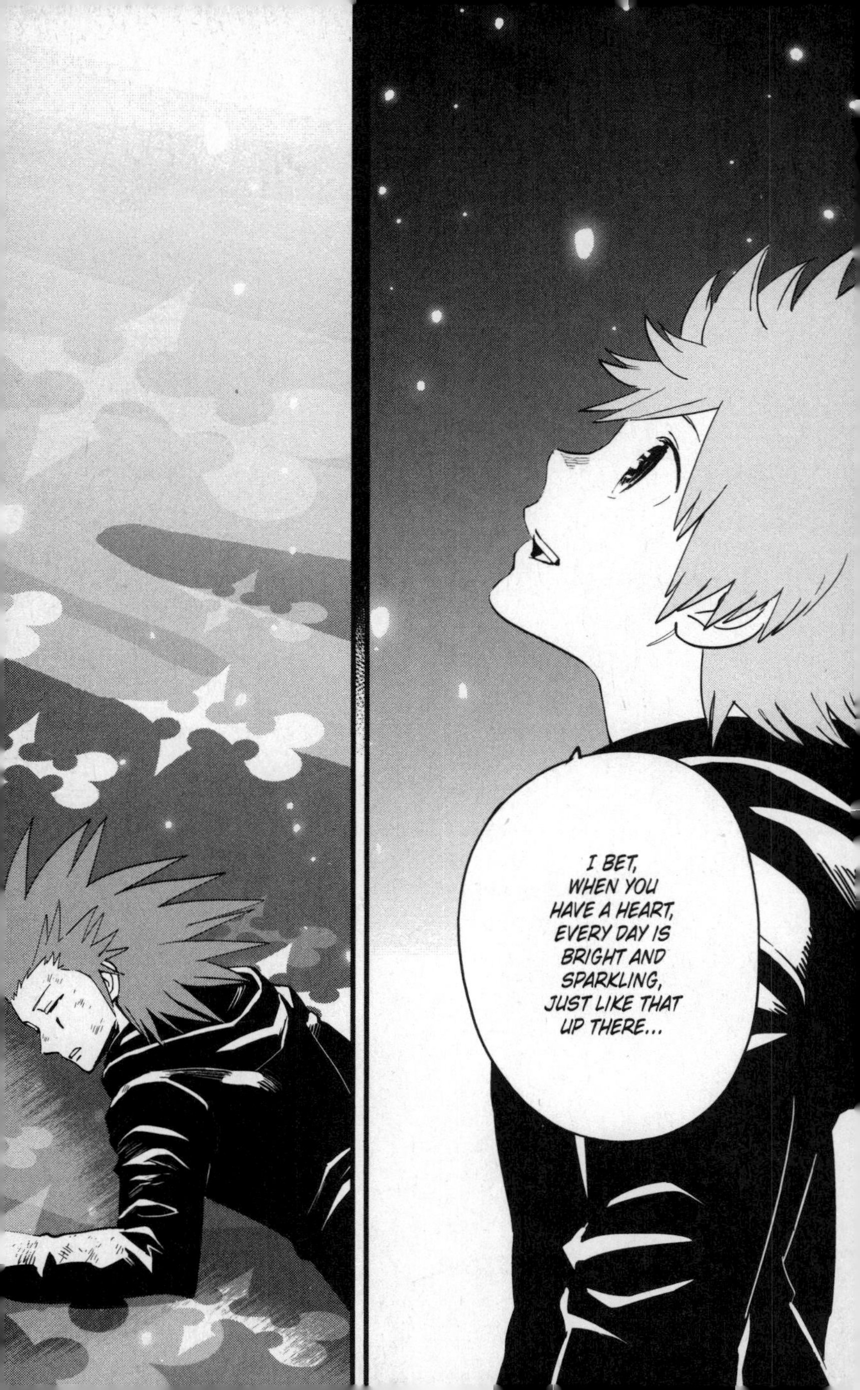
I BET, WHEN YOU HAVE A HEART, EVERY DAY IS BRIGHT AND SPARKLING, JUST LIKE THAT UP THERE...

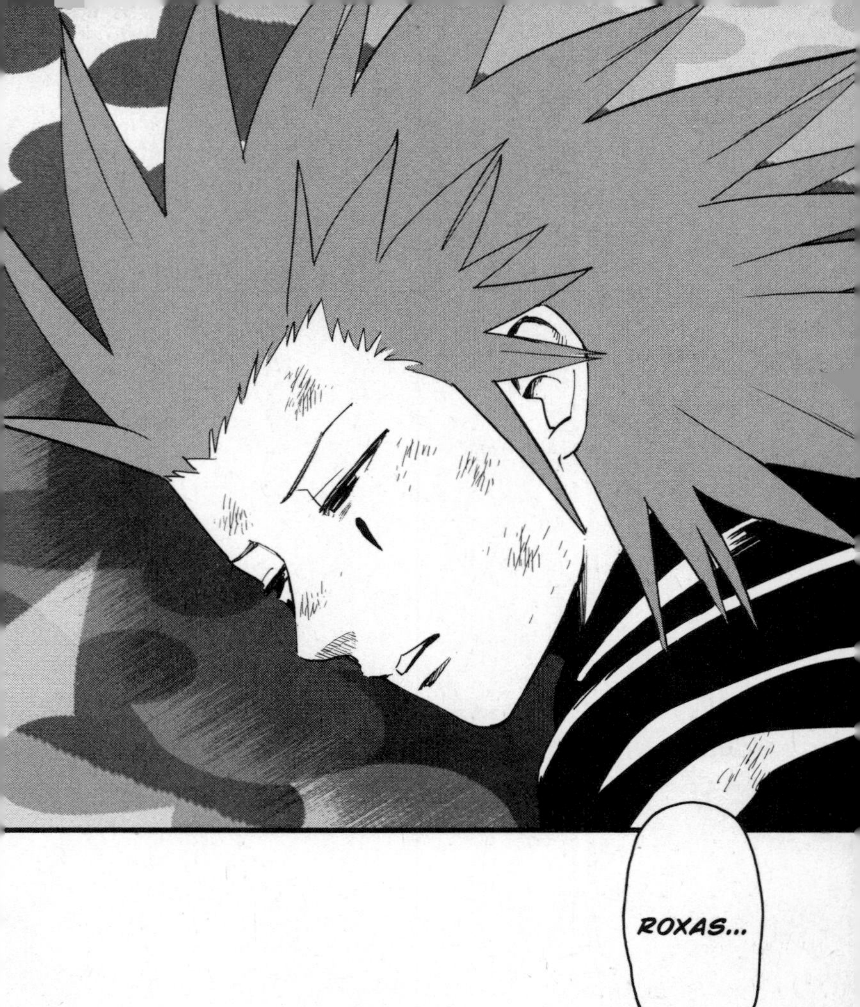
ROXAS...

Chapter 55: Gratitude

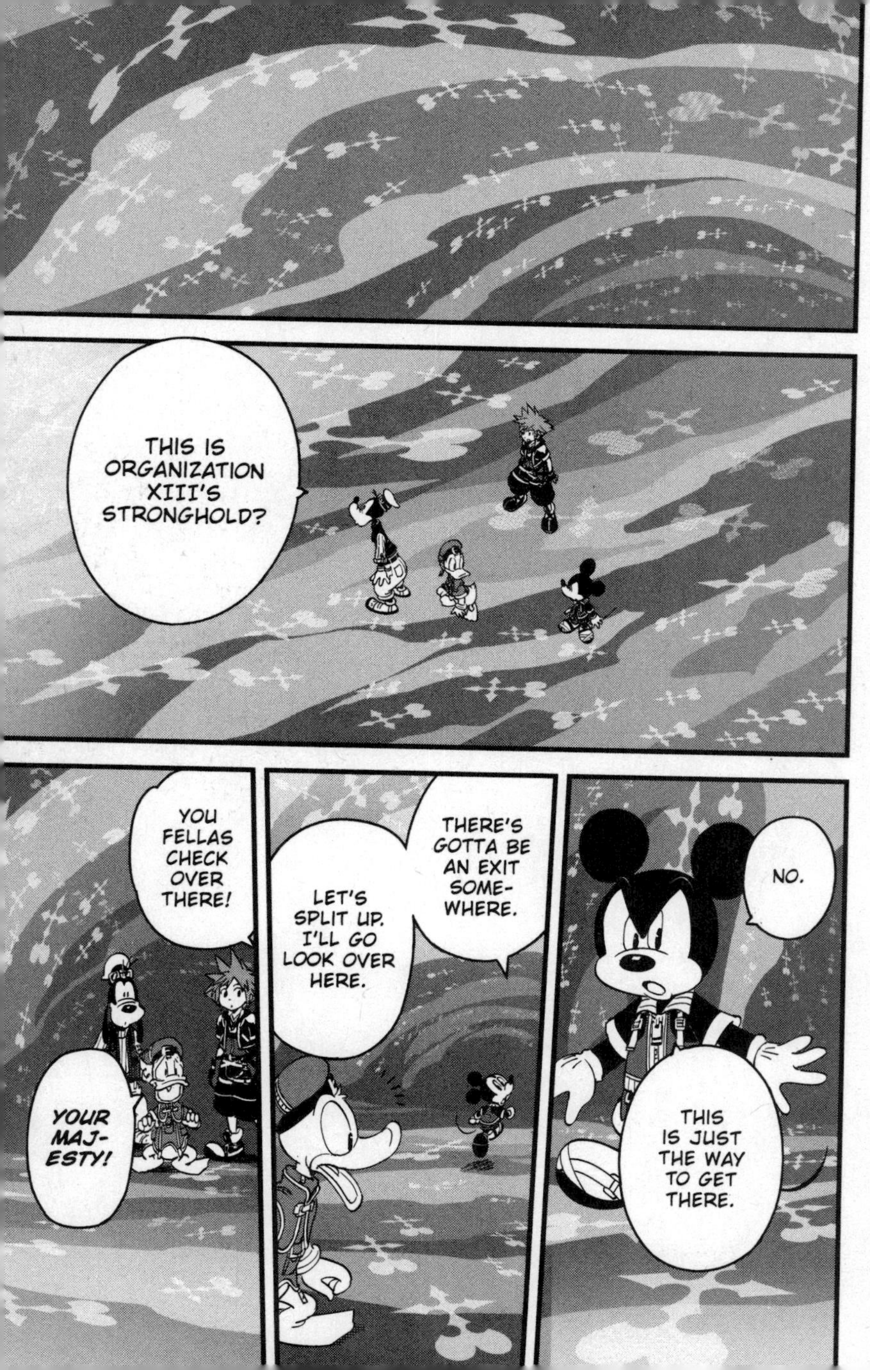
THIS IS ORGANIZATION XIII'S STRONGHOLD?
NO.
THIS IS JUST THE WAY TO GET THERE.
THERE'S GOTTA BE AN EXIT SOME-WHERE.
LET'S SPLIT UP. I'LL GO LOOK OVER HERE.
YOU FELLAS CHECK OVER THERE!
YOUR MAJ-ESTY!

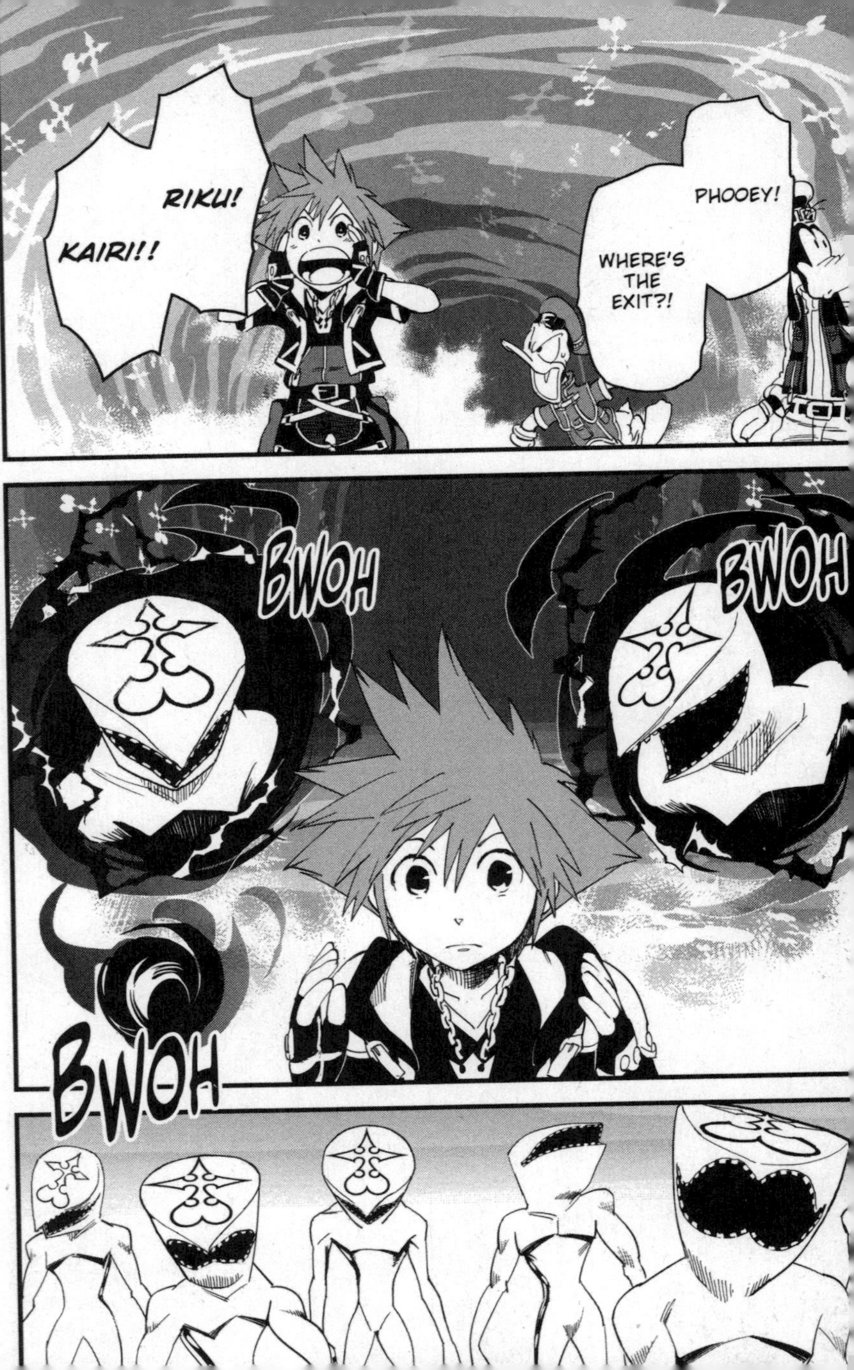
PHOOEY!
WHERE'S THE EXIT?!
RIKU!
KAIRI!!
BWOH
BWOH
BWOH

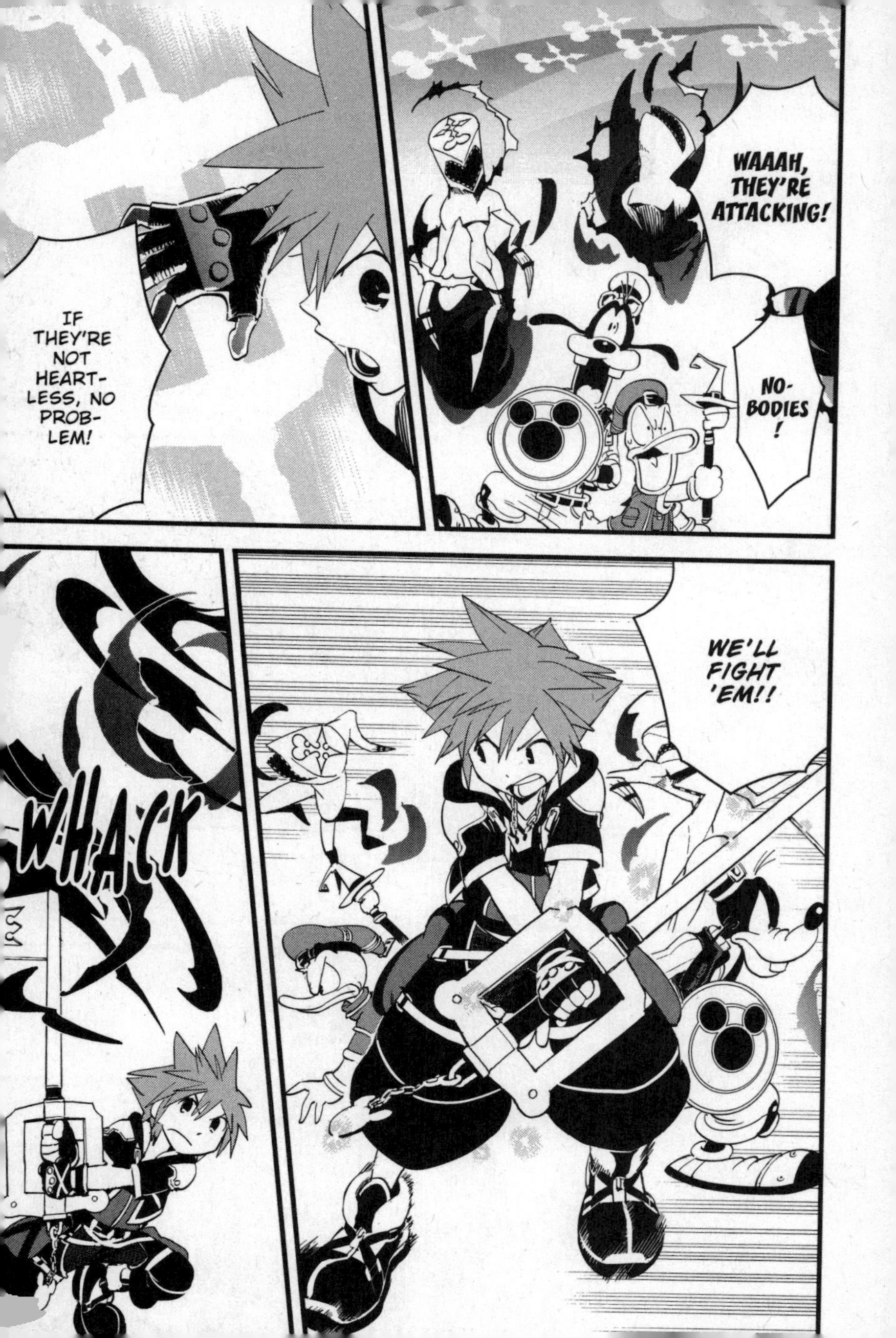
WAAAH, THEY'RE ATTACKING!
NO-BODIES!
IF THEY'RE NOT HEART-LESS, NO PROB-LEM!
WE'LL FIGHT 'EM!!
WHACK

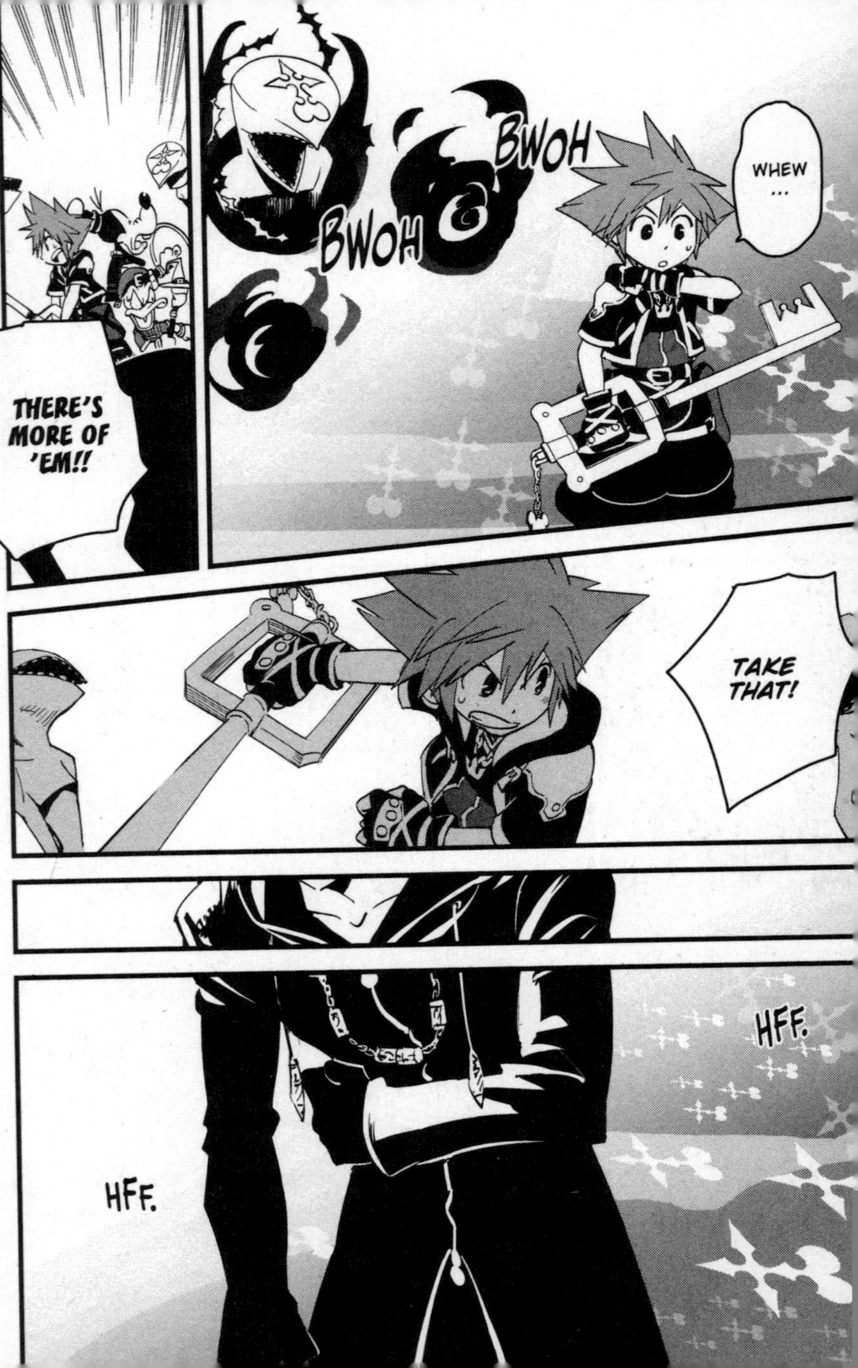
WHEW ...
BWOH
BWOH
THERE'S MORE OF 'EM!!
TAKE THAT!
HFF.
HFF.

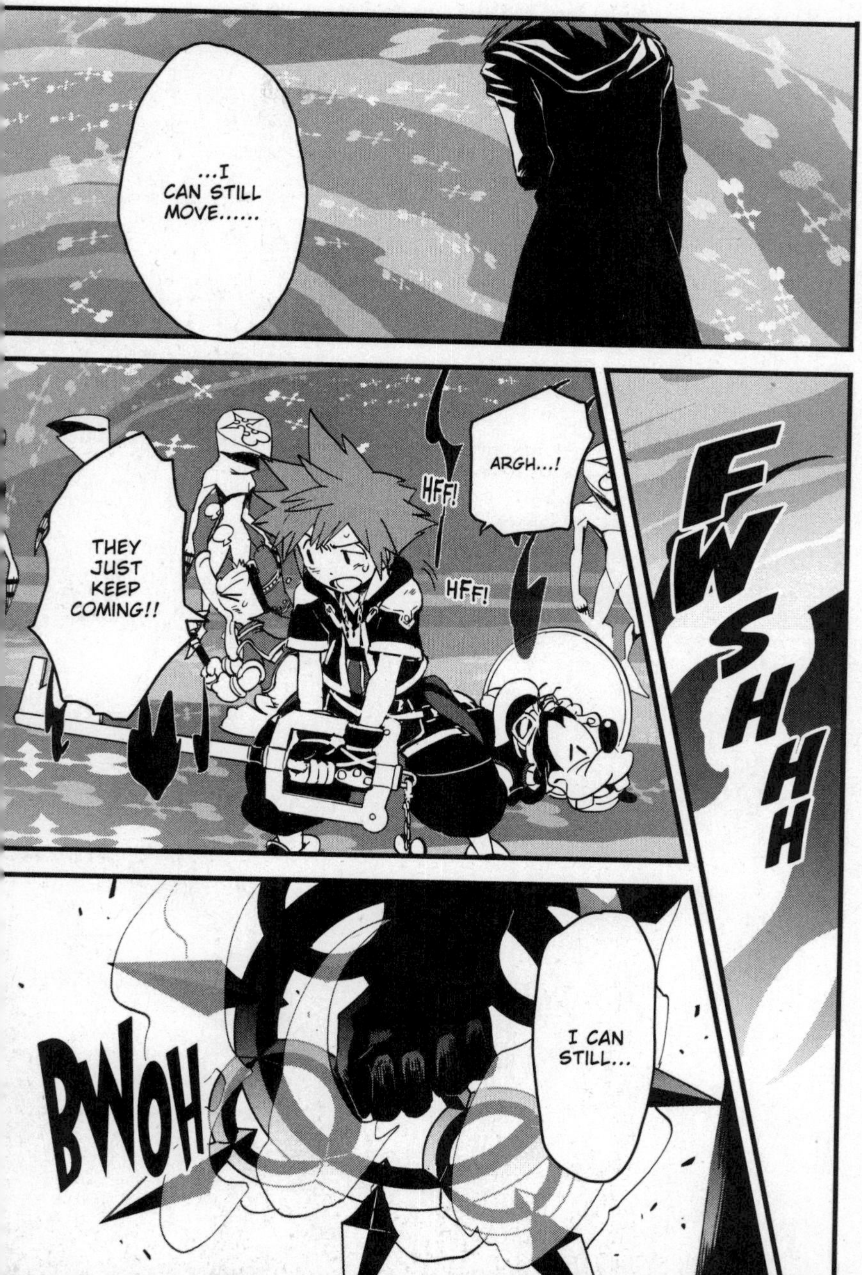
...I CAN STILL MOVE......
FWSHHHH
ARGH...!
HFF!
HFF!
THEY JUST KEEP COMING!!
I CAN STILL...
BWOH

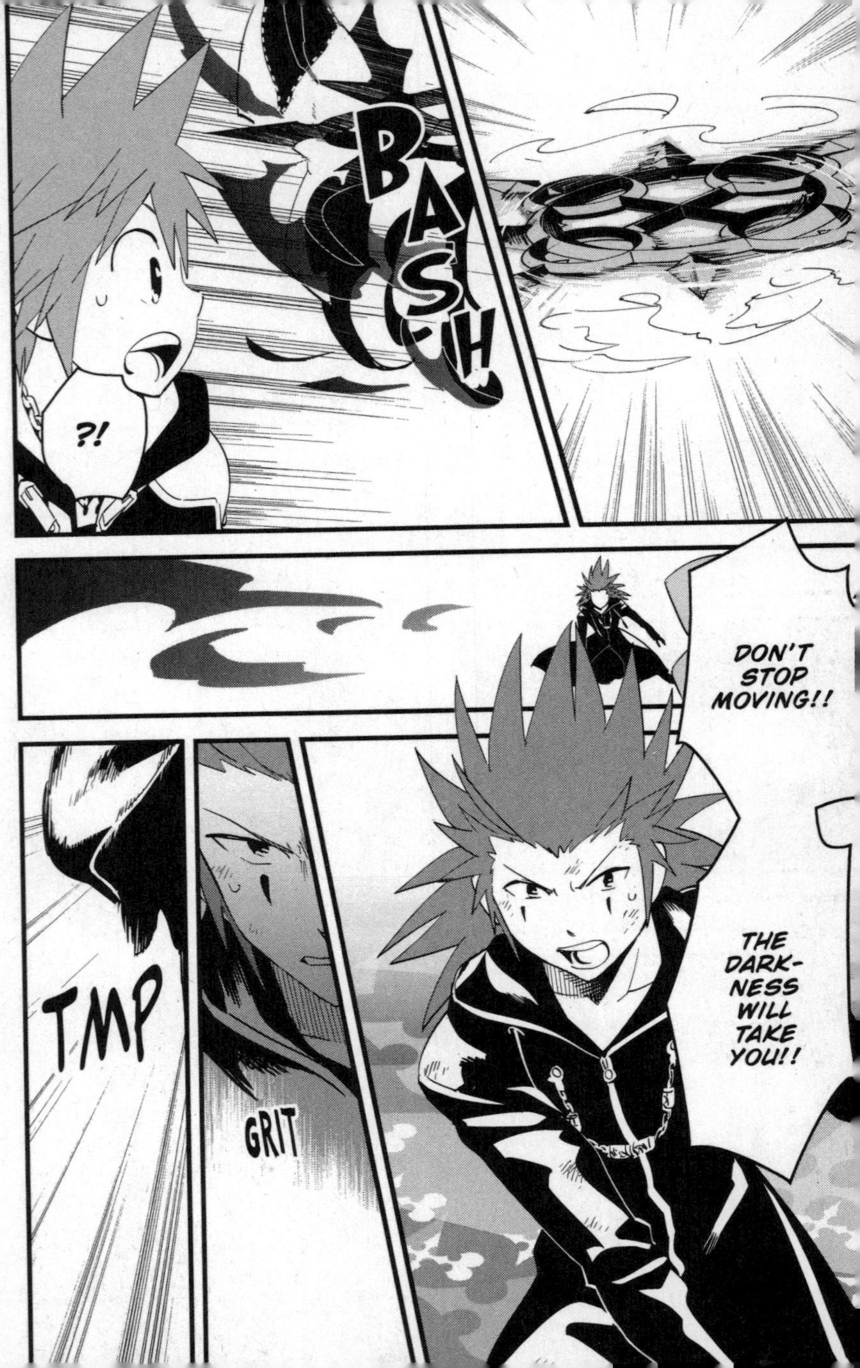
BASH
?!
DON'T STOP MOVING!!
THE DARK-NESS WILL TAKE YOU!!
GRIT
TMP

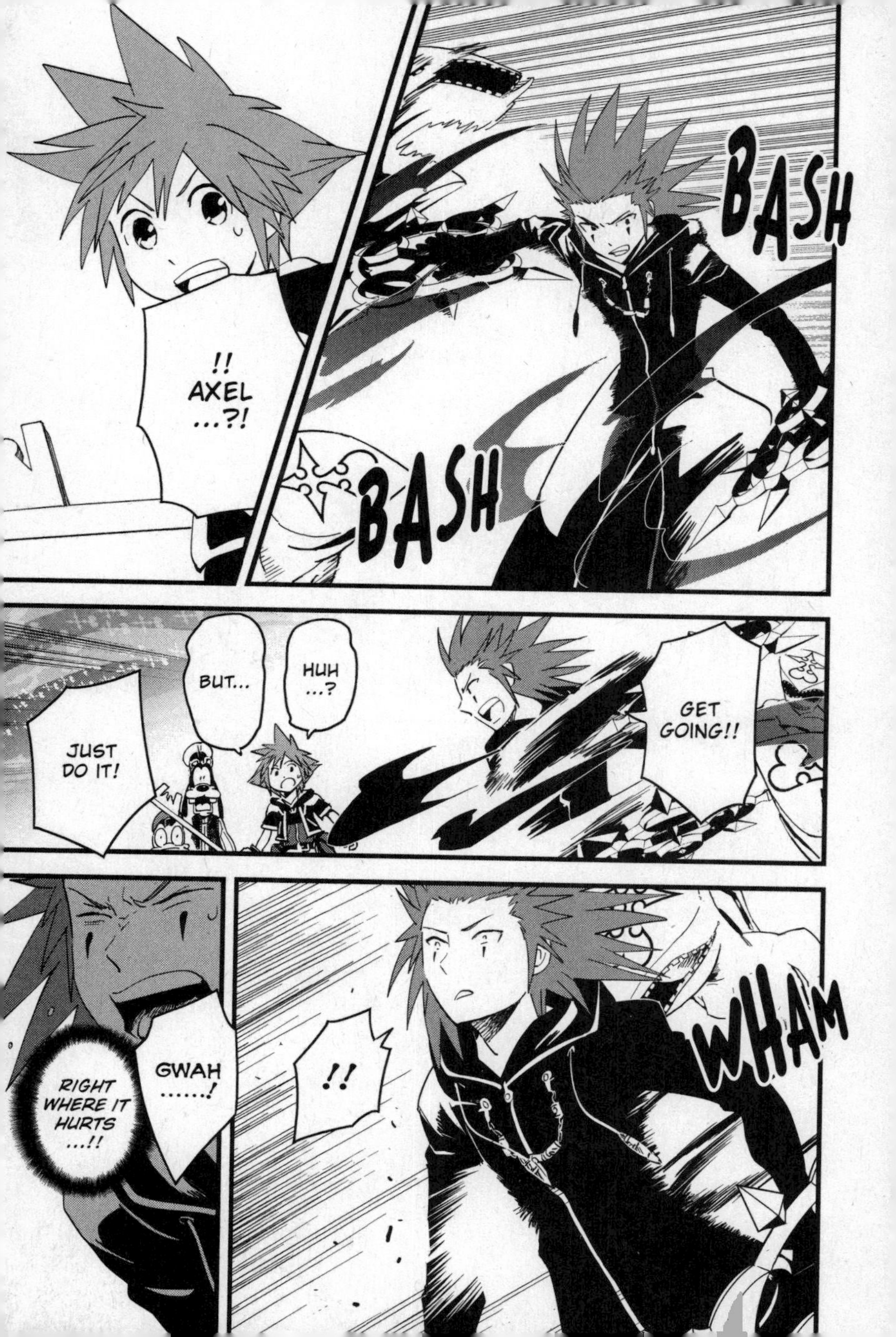
BASH
BASH
!! AXEL ...?!
GET GOING!!
HUH ...?
BUT...
JUST DO IT!
WHAM
!!
GWAH ....!
RIGHT WHERE IT HURTS ...!!

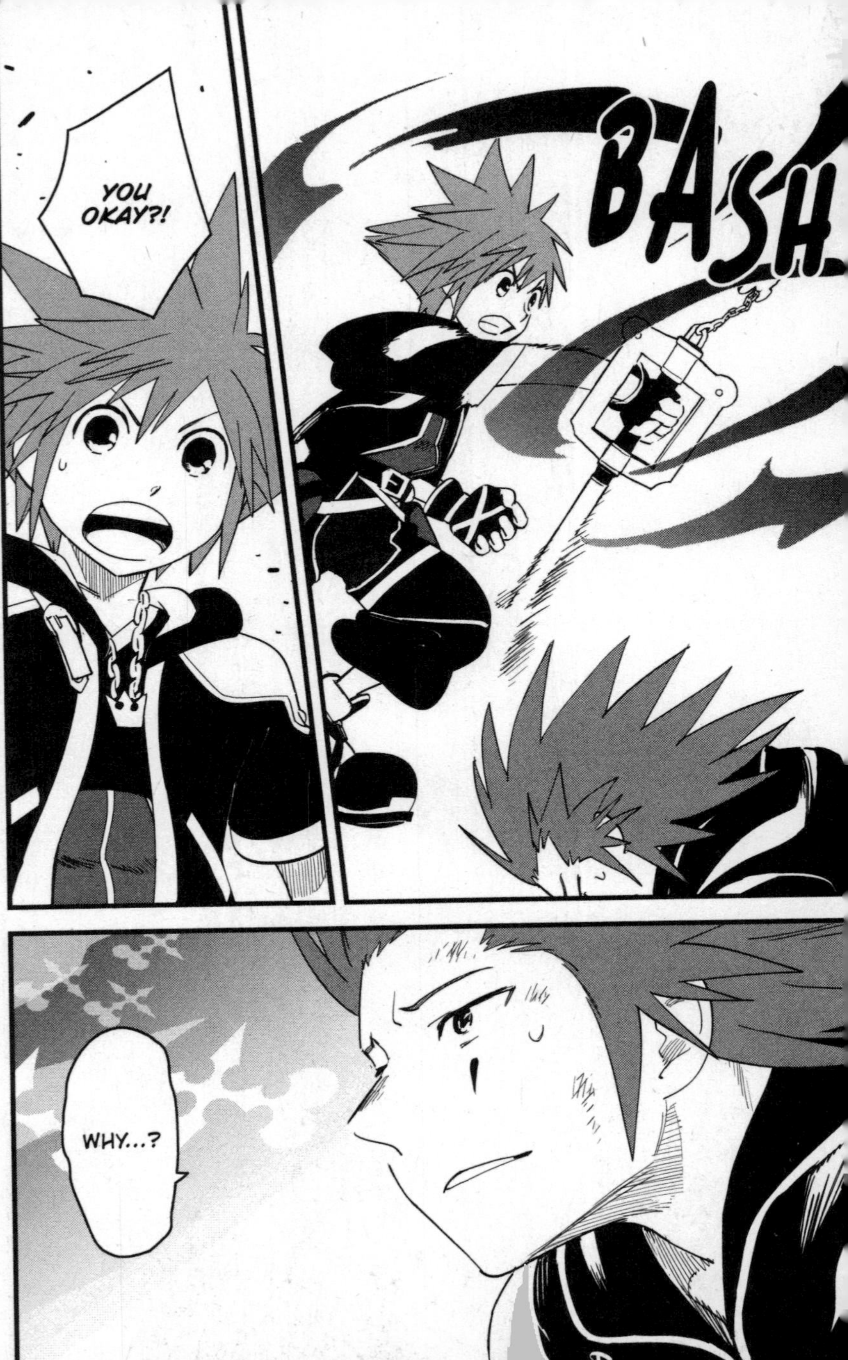
BASH
YOU OKAY?!
WHY...?

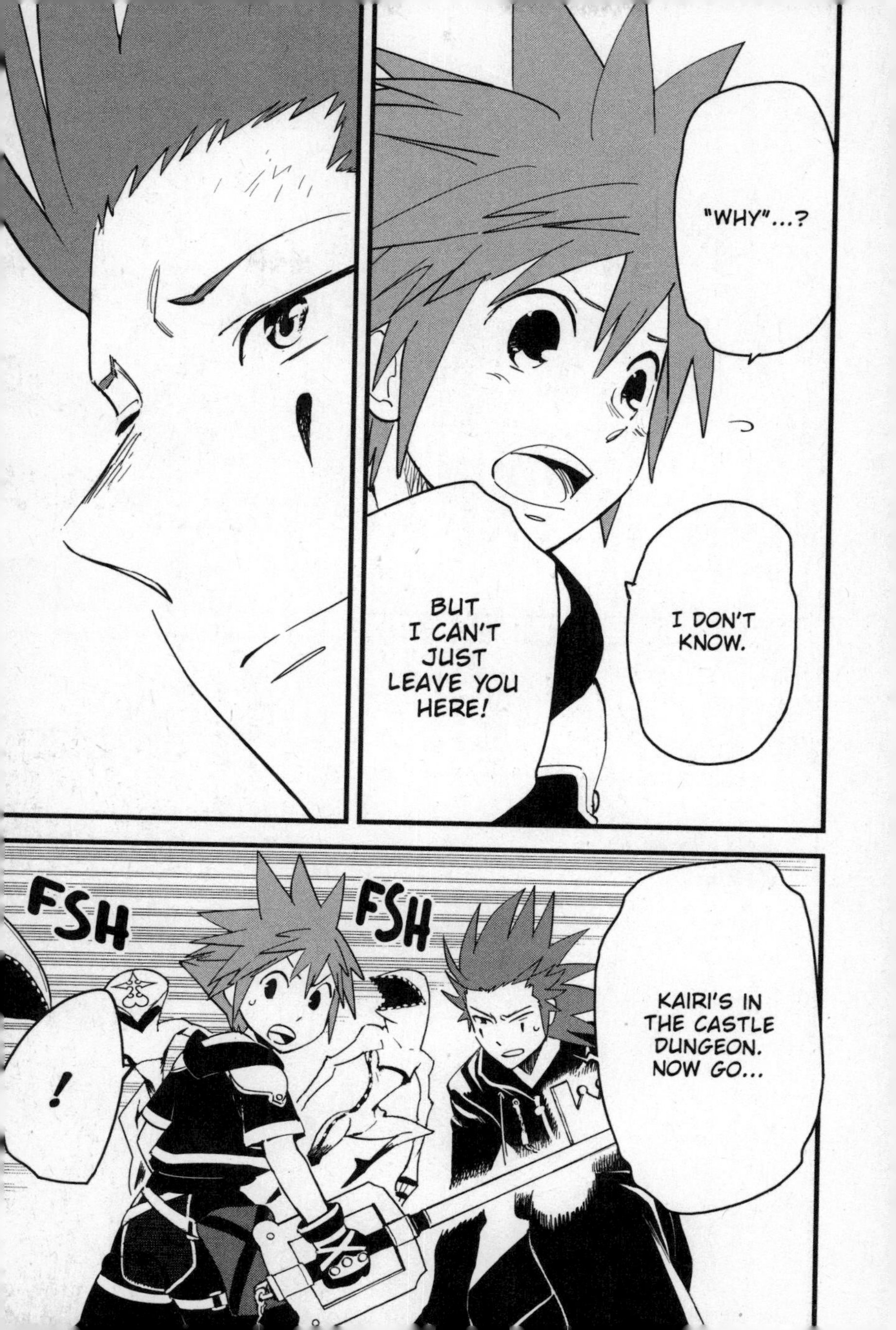
"WHY"...?
I DON'T KNOW.
BUT I CAN'T JUST LEAVE YOU HERE!
KAIRI'S IN THE CASTLE DUNGEON. NOW GO...
FSH
FSH
!

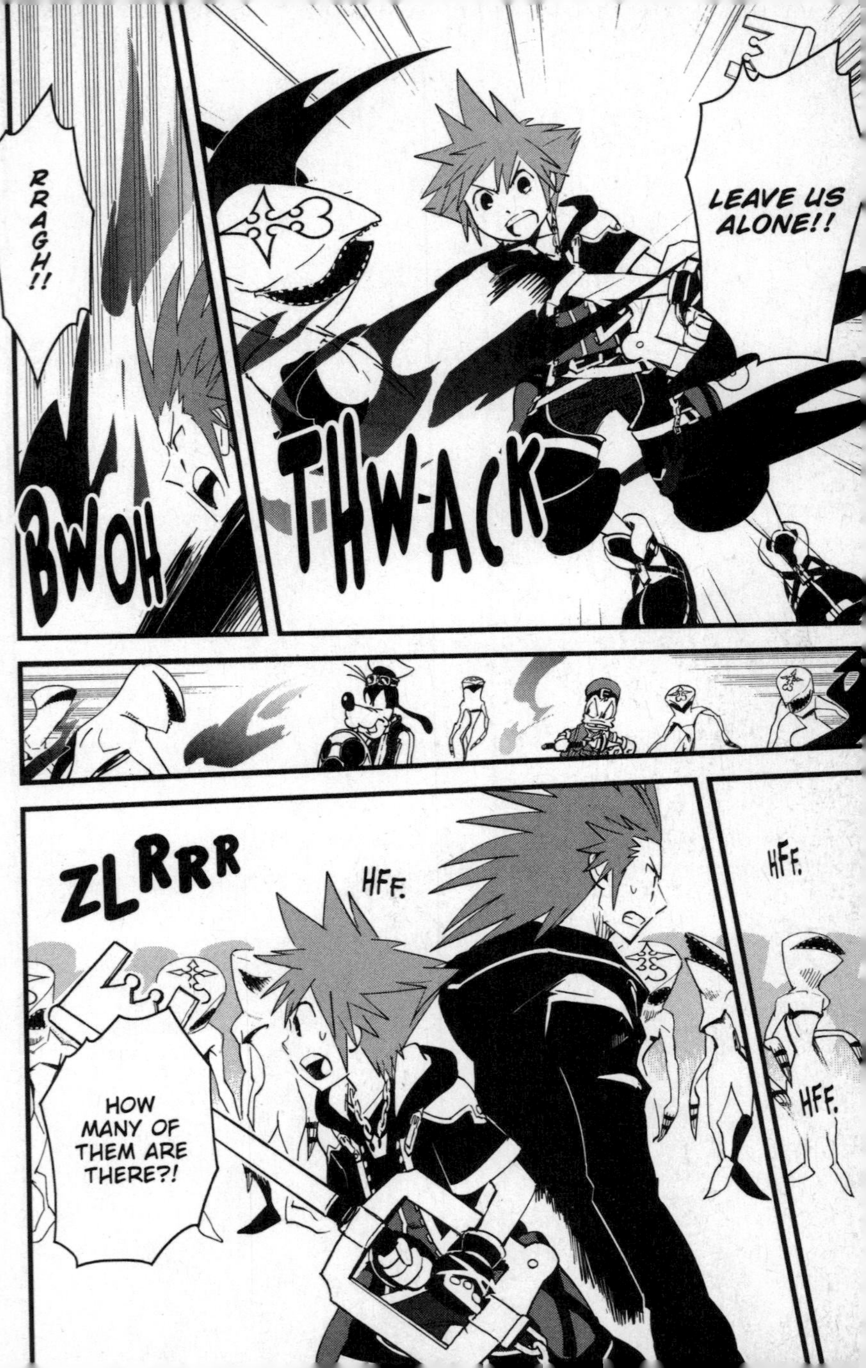
LEAVE US ALONE!!
THWACK
RRAGH!!
BWOH
HFF.
HFF.
HFF.
ZLRRR
HOW MANY OF THEM ARE THERE?!

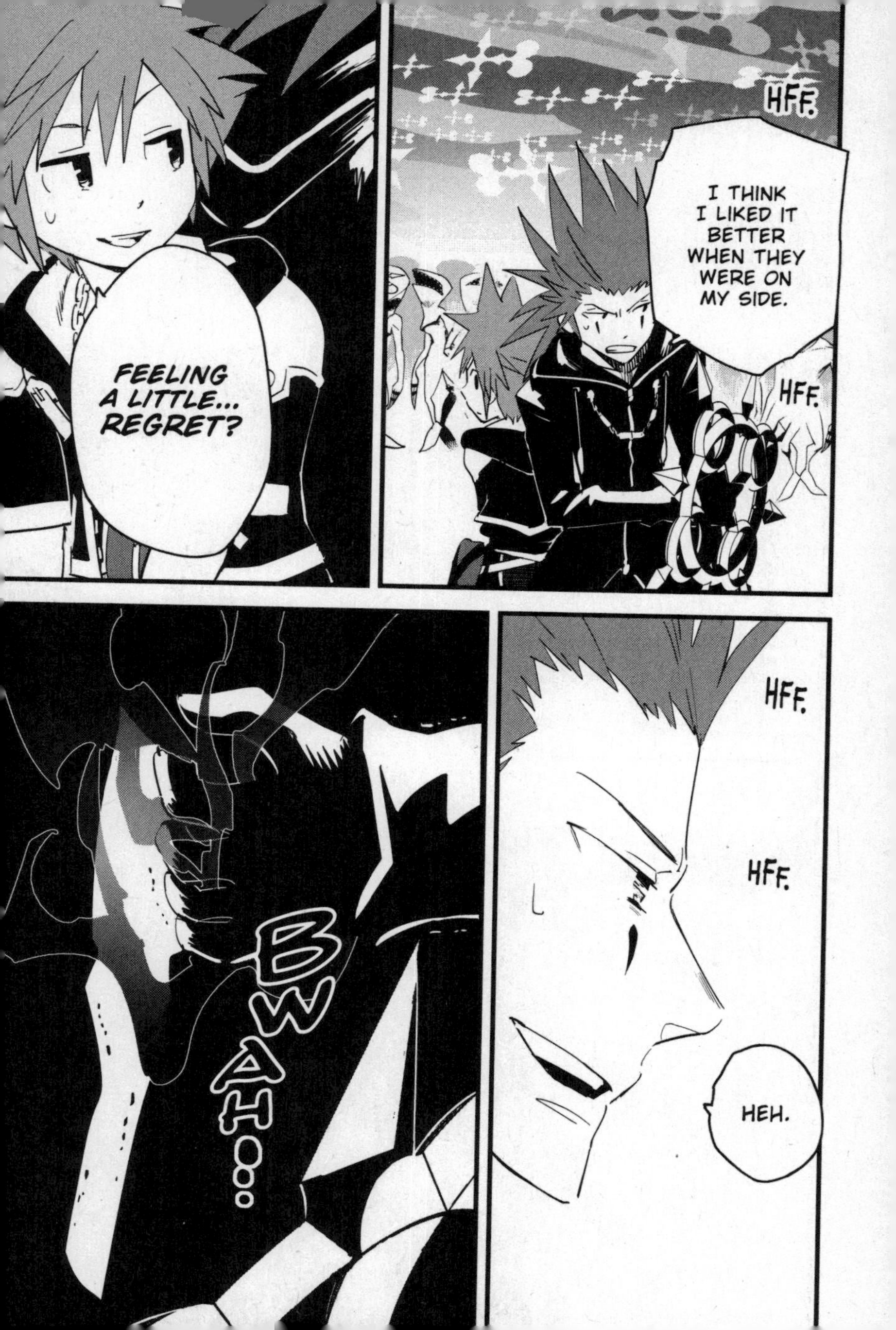
HFF.
I THINK I LIKED IT BETTER WHEN THEY WERE ON MY SIDE.
HFF.
FEELING A LITTLE... REGRET?
HFF.
HFF.
HEH.
BWAHO...

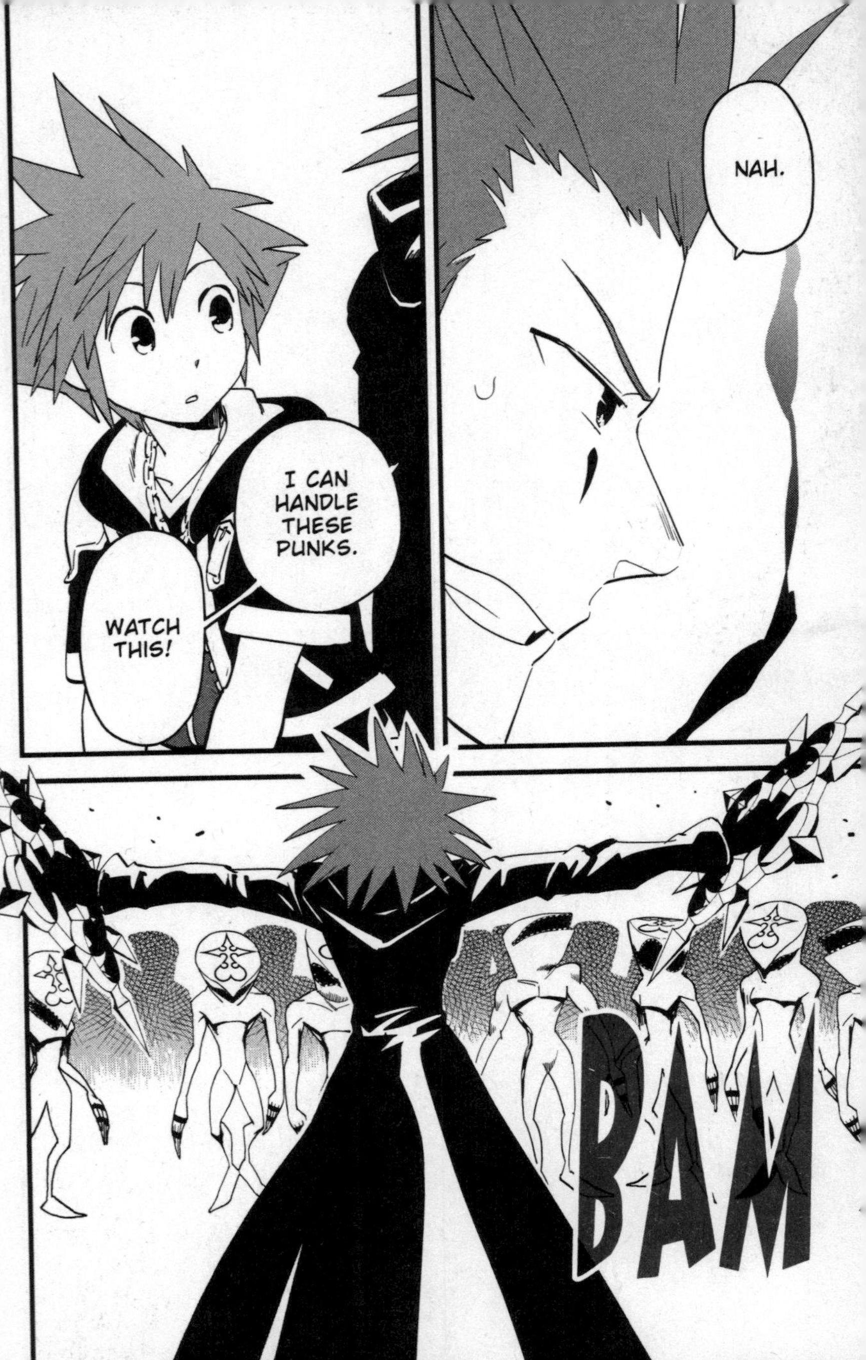
NAH.
I CAN HANDLE THESE PUNKS.
WATCH THIS!
BAM

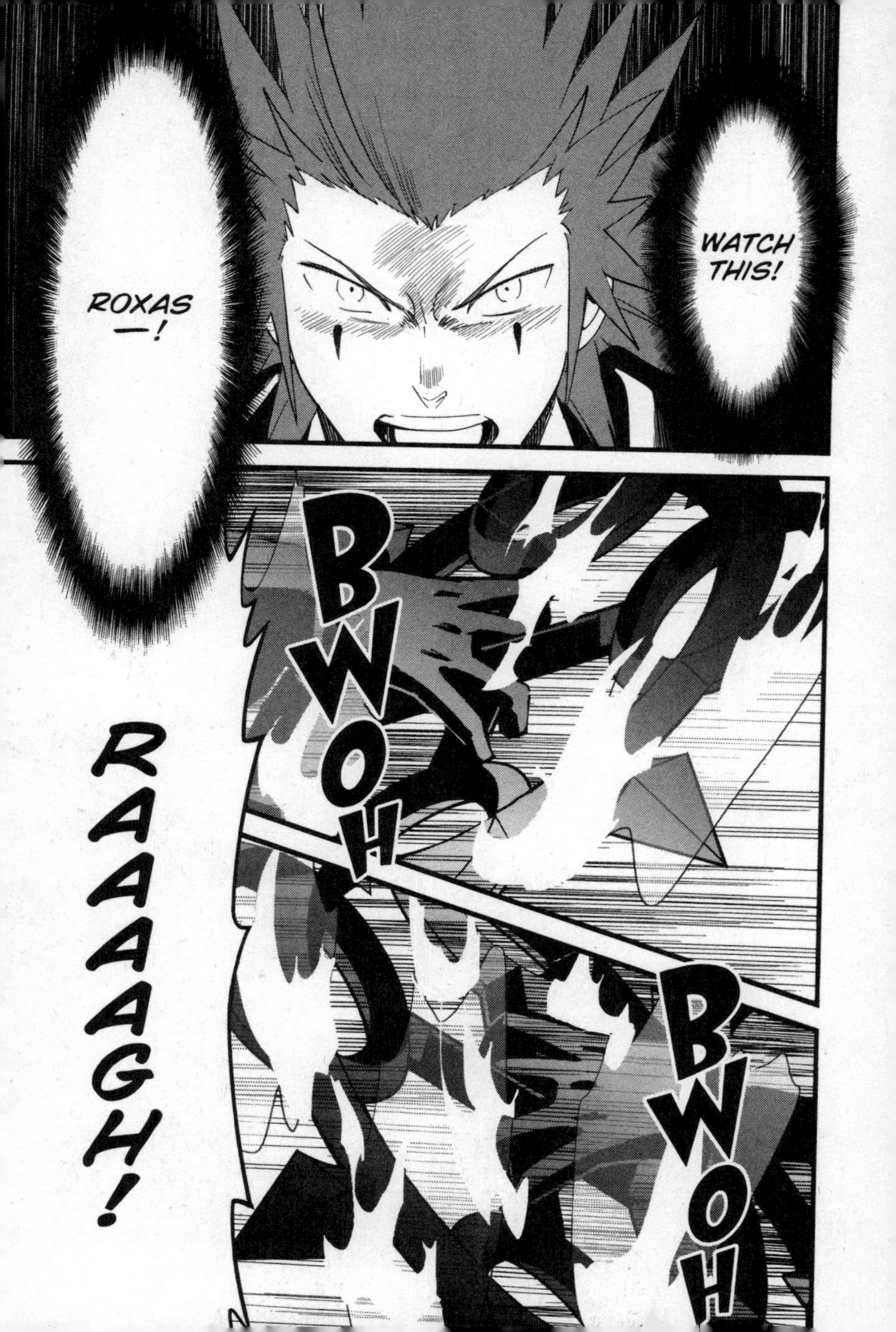
WATCH THIS!
ROXAS—!
BWOH
BWOH
RAAAAGH!

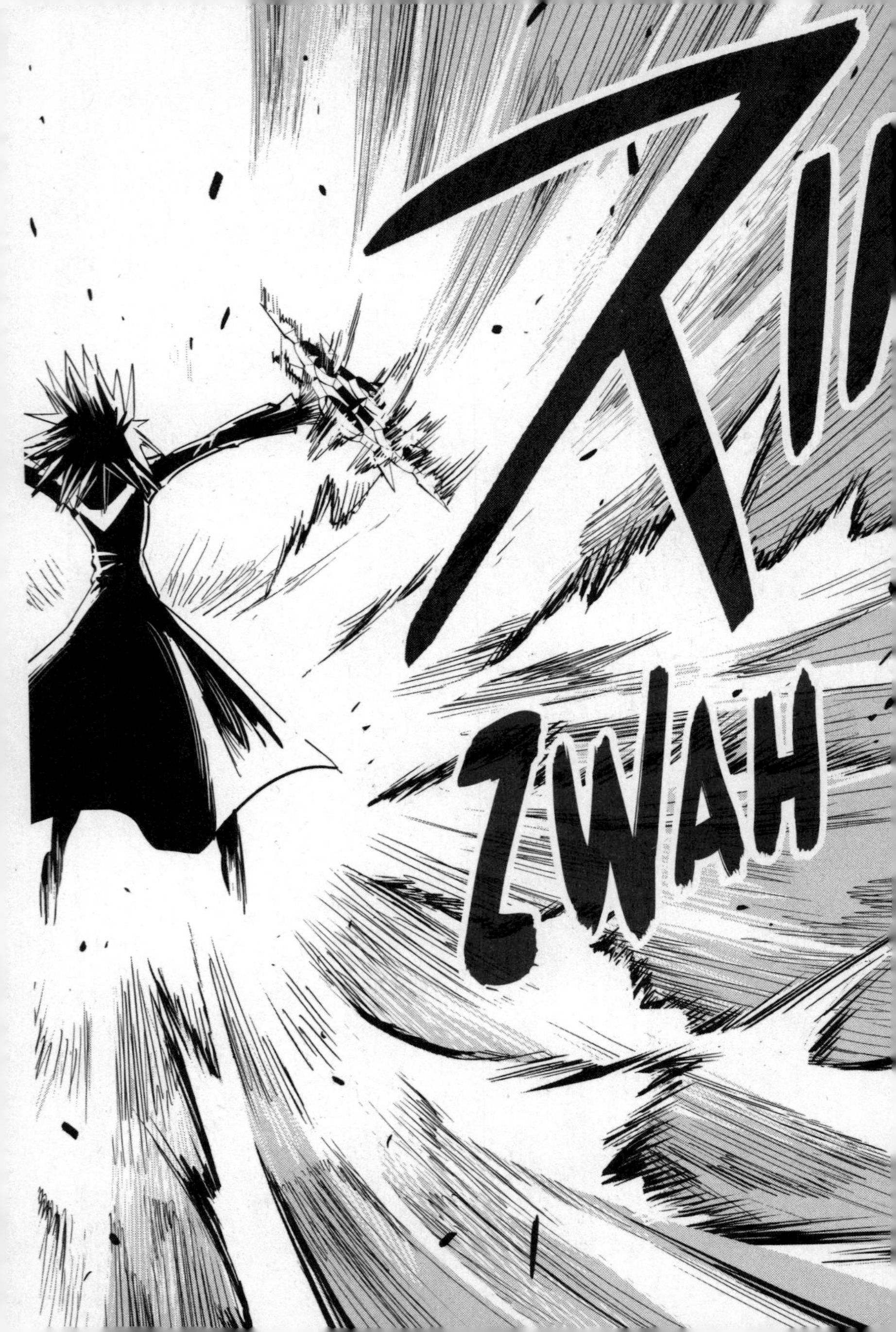
ZWAH

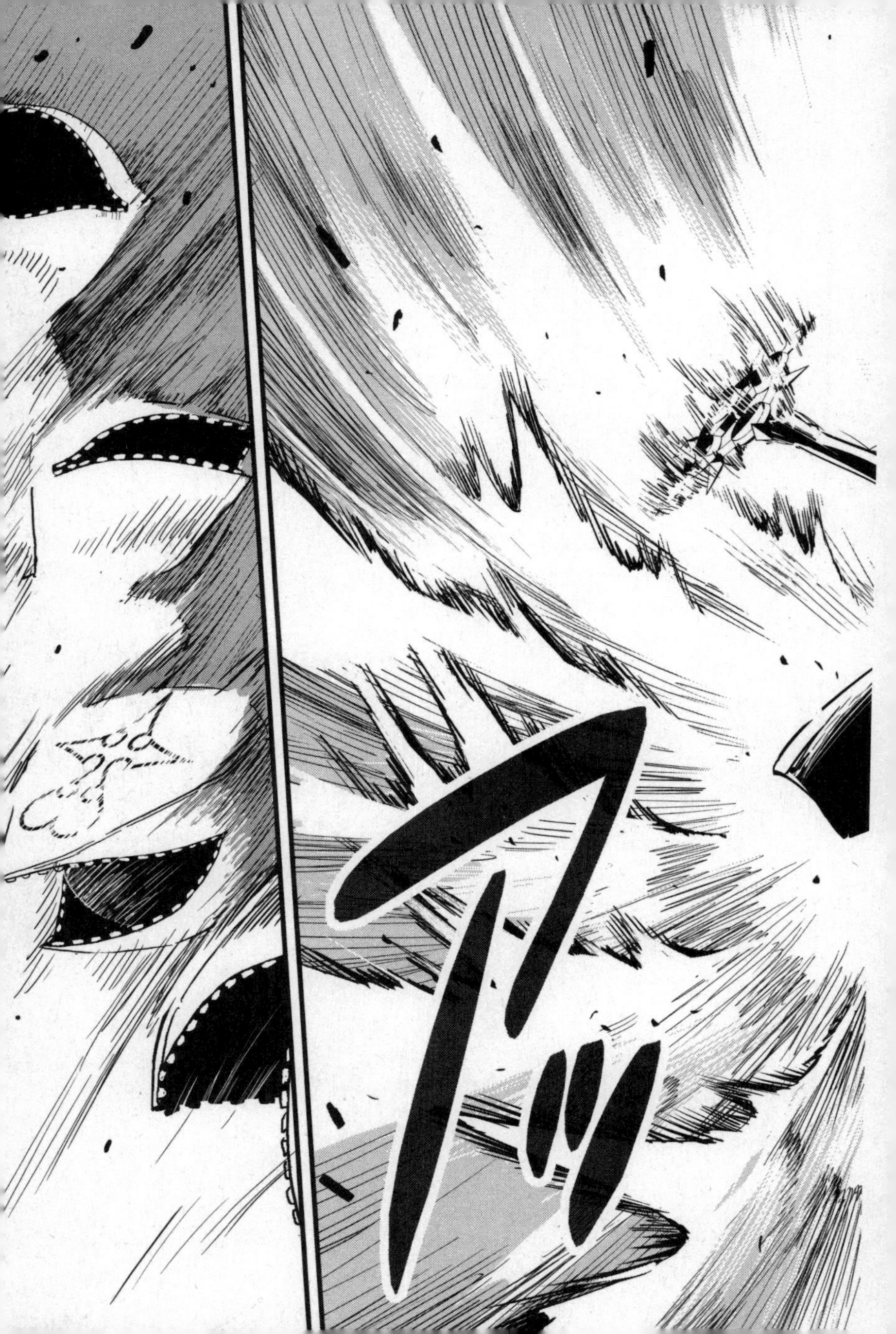

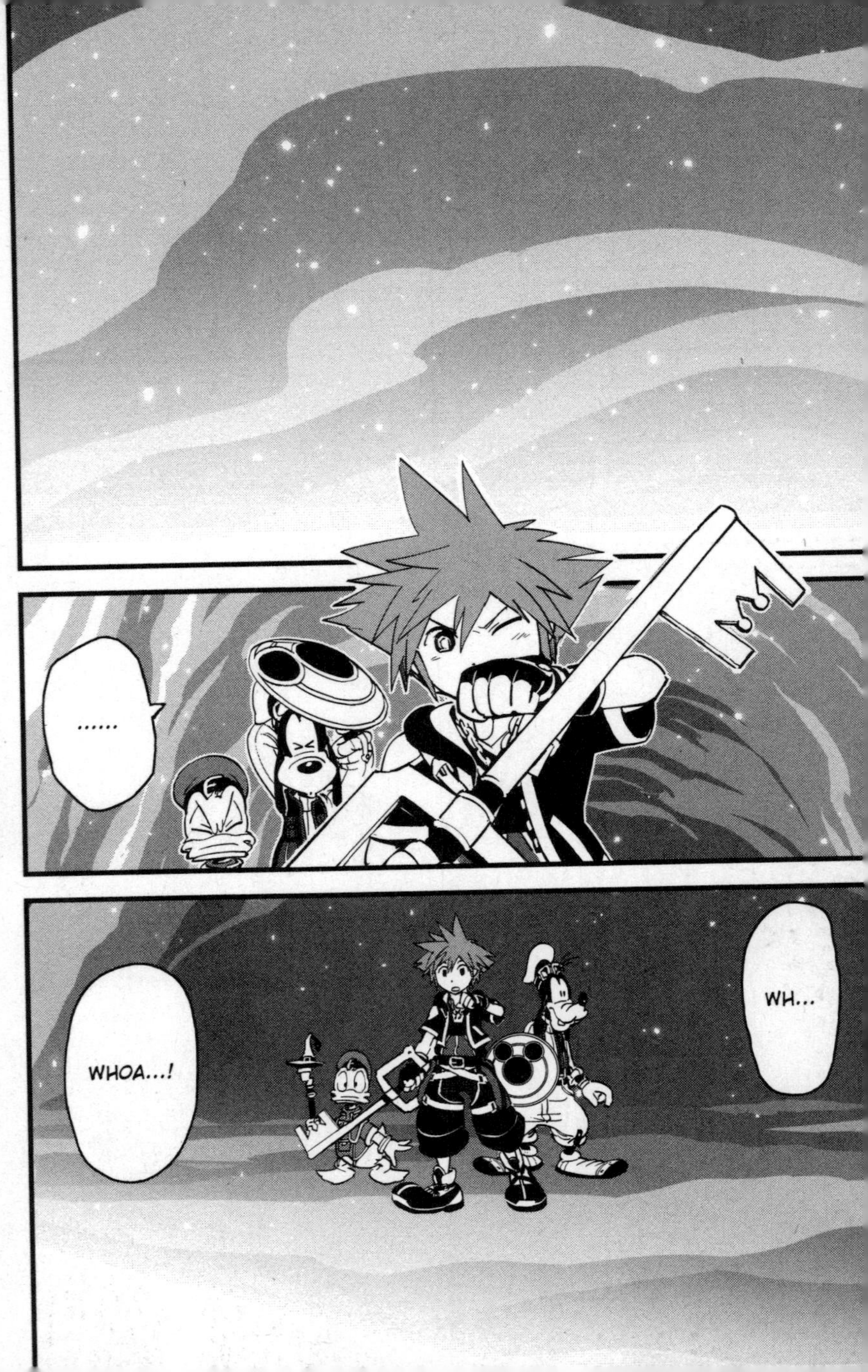
......
WH...
WHOA...!

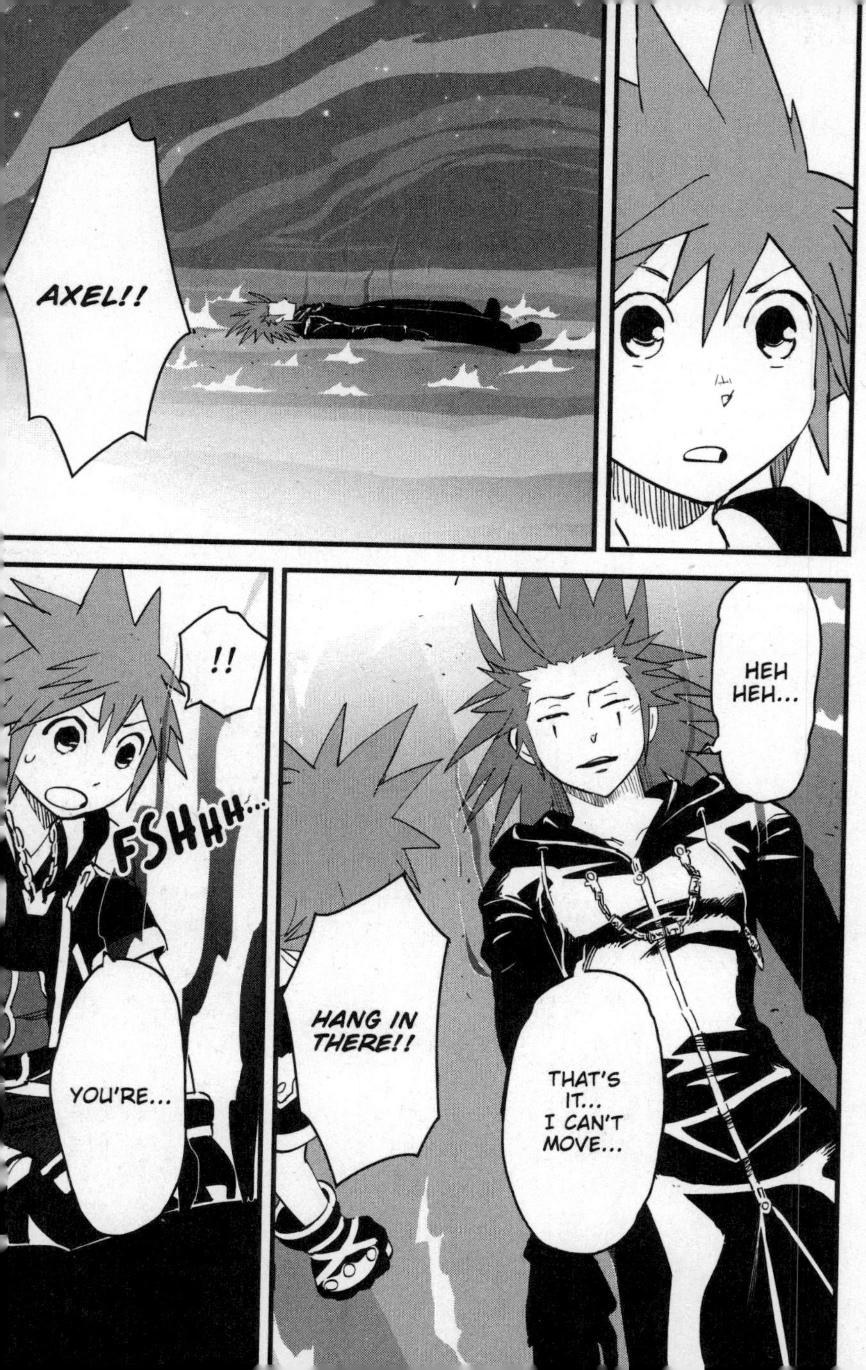
AXEL!!
HEH HEH...
THAT'S IT... I CAN'T MOVE...
HANG IN THERE!!
!!
FSHHH...
YOU'RE...

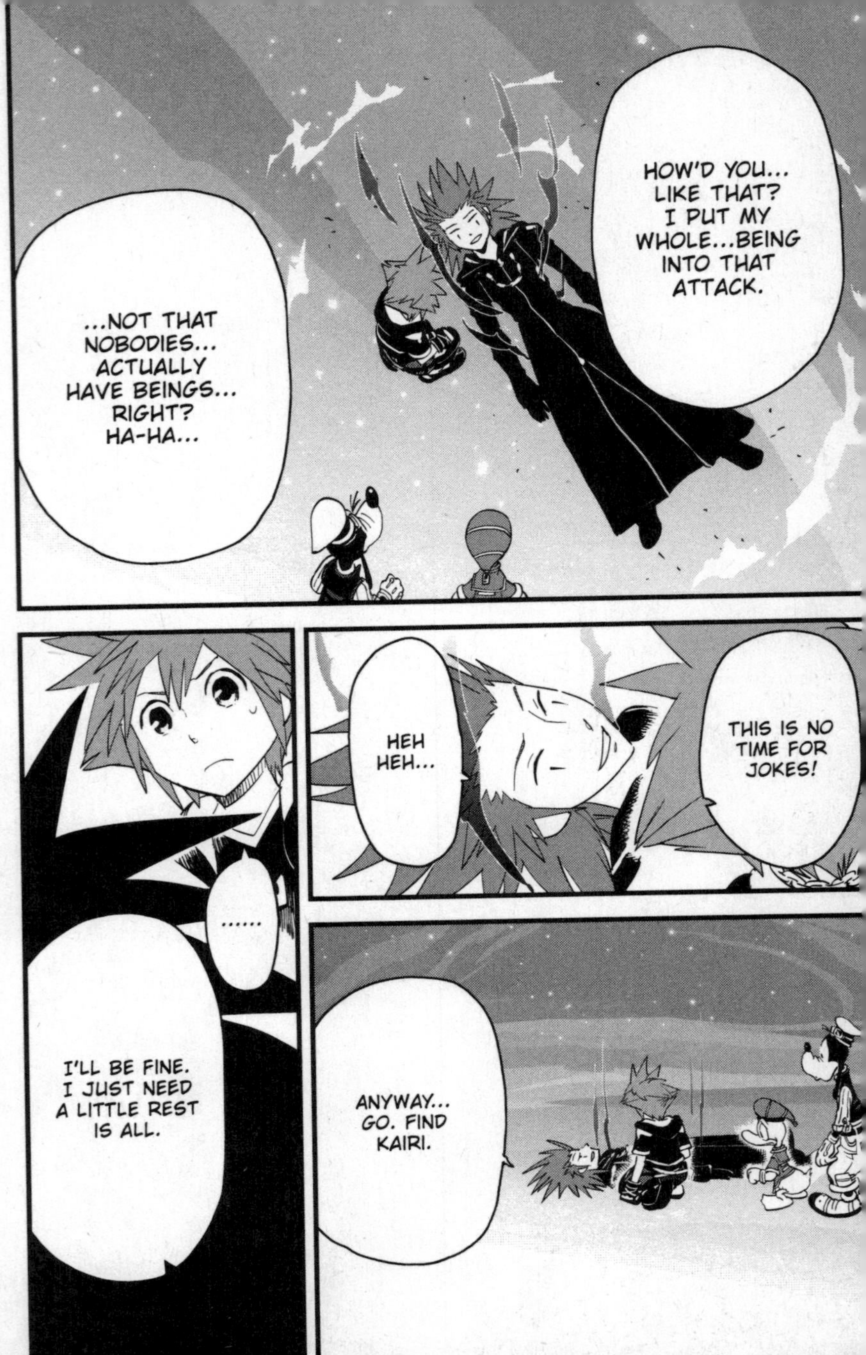
HOW'D YOU... LIKE THAT? I PUT MY WHOLE...BEING INTO THAT ATTACK.
...NOT THAT NOBODIES... ACTUALLY HAVE BEINGS... RIGHT? HA-HA...
THIS IS NO TIME FOR JOKES!
HEH HEH...
ANYWAY... GO. FIND KAIRI.
......
I'LL BE FINE. I JUST NEED A LITTLE REST IS ALL.

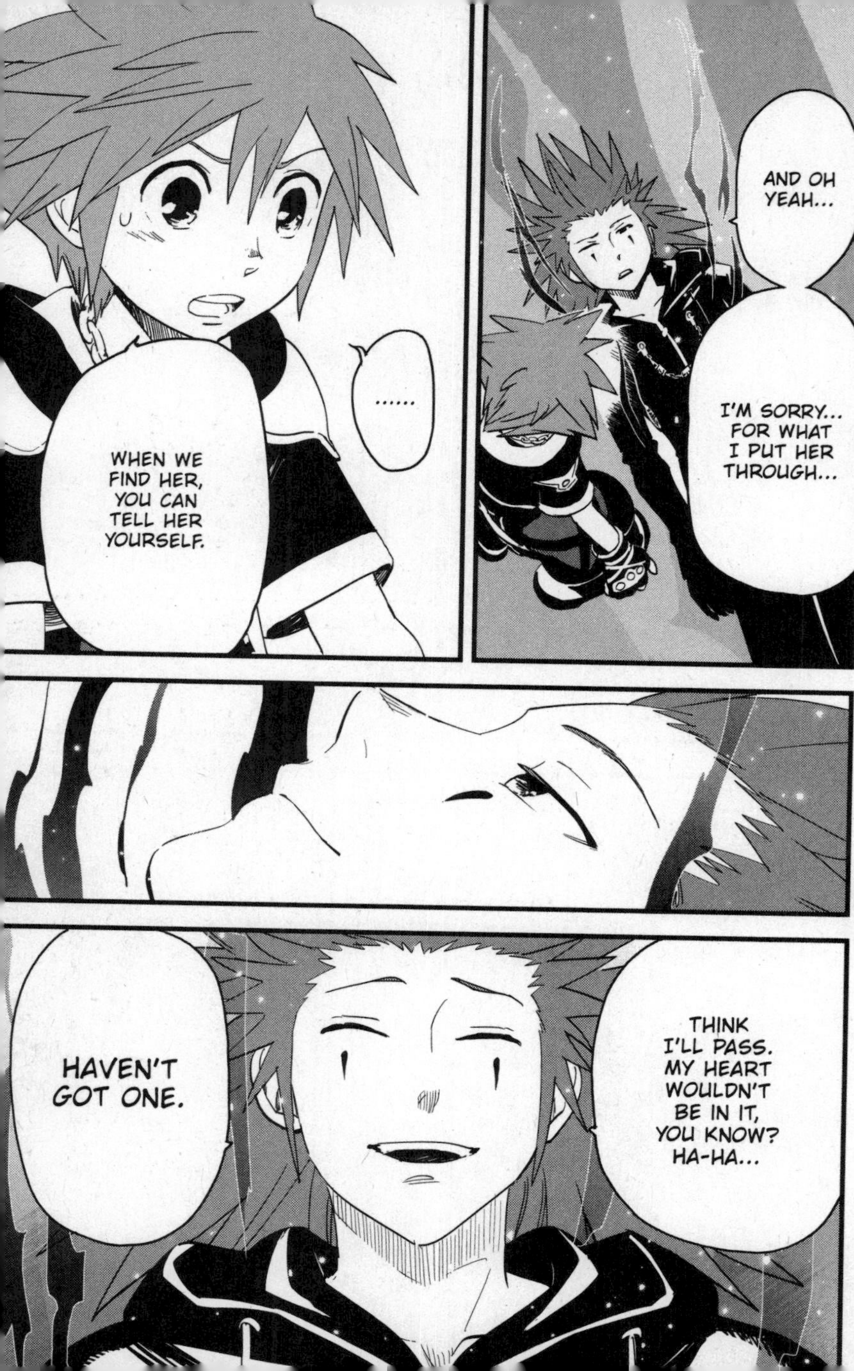
AND OH YEAH...
I'M SORRY... FOR WHAT I PUT HER THROUGH...
......
WHEN WE FIND HER, YOU CAN TELL HER YOURSELF.
THINK I'LL PASS. MY HEART WOULDN'T BE IN IT, YOU KNOW? HA-HA...
HAVEN'T GOT ONE.

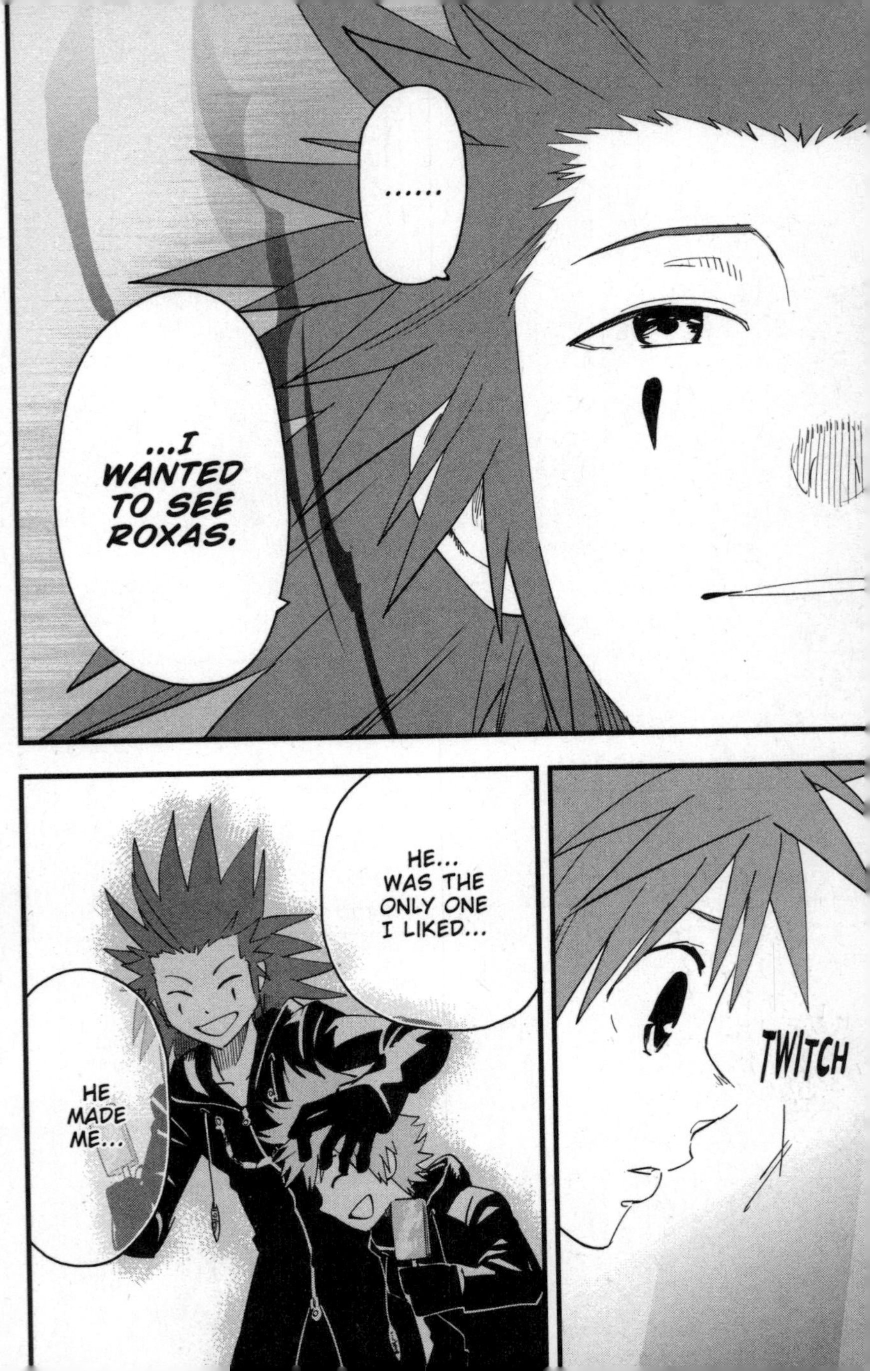
......
...I WANTED TO SEE ROXAS.
TWITCH
HE... WAS THE ONLY ONE I LIKED...
HE MADE ME...

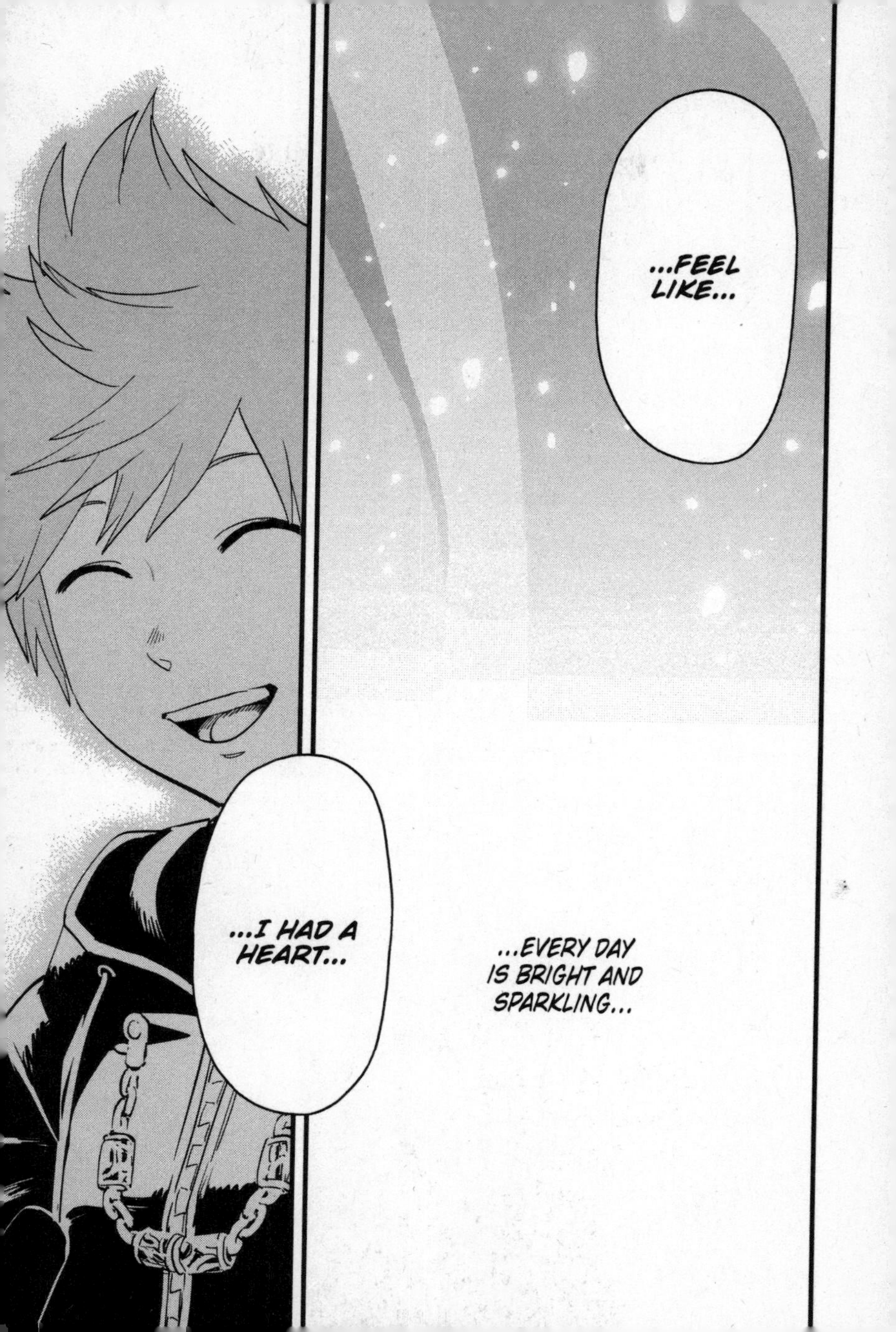
...FEEL LIKE...
...EVERY DAY IS BRIGHT AND SPARKLING...
...I HAD A HEART...

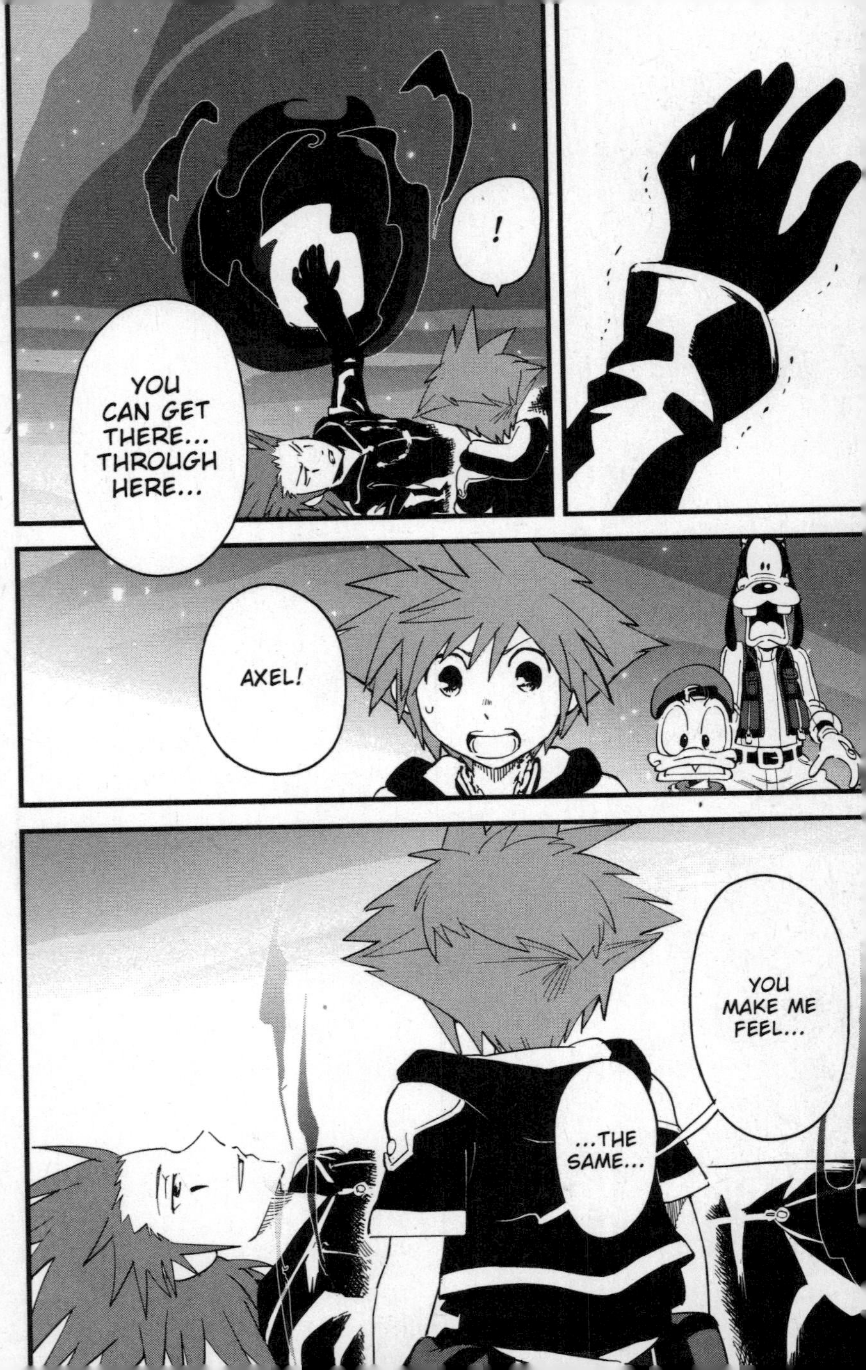
!
YOU CAN GET THERE... THROUGH HERE...
AXEL!
YOU MAKE ME FEEL...
...THE SAME...

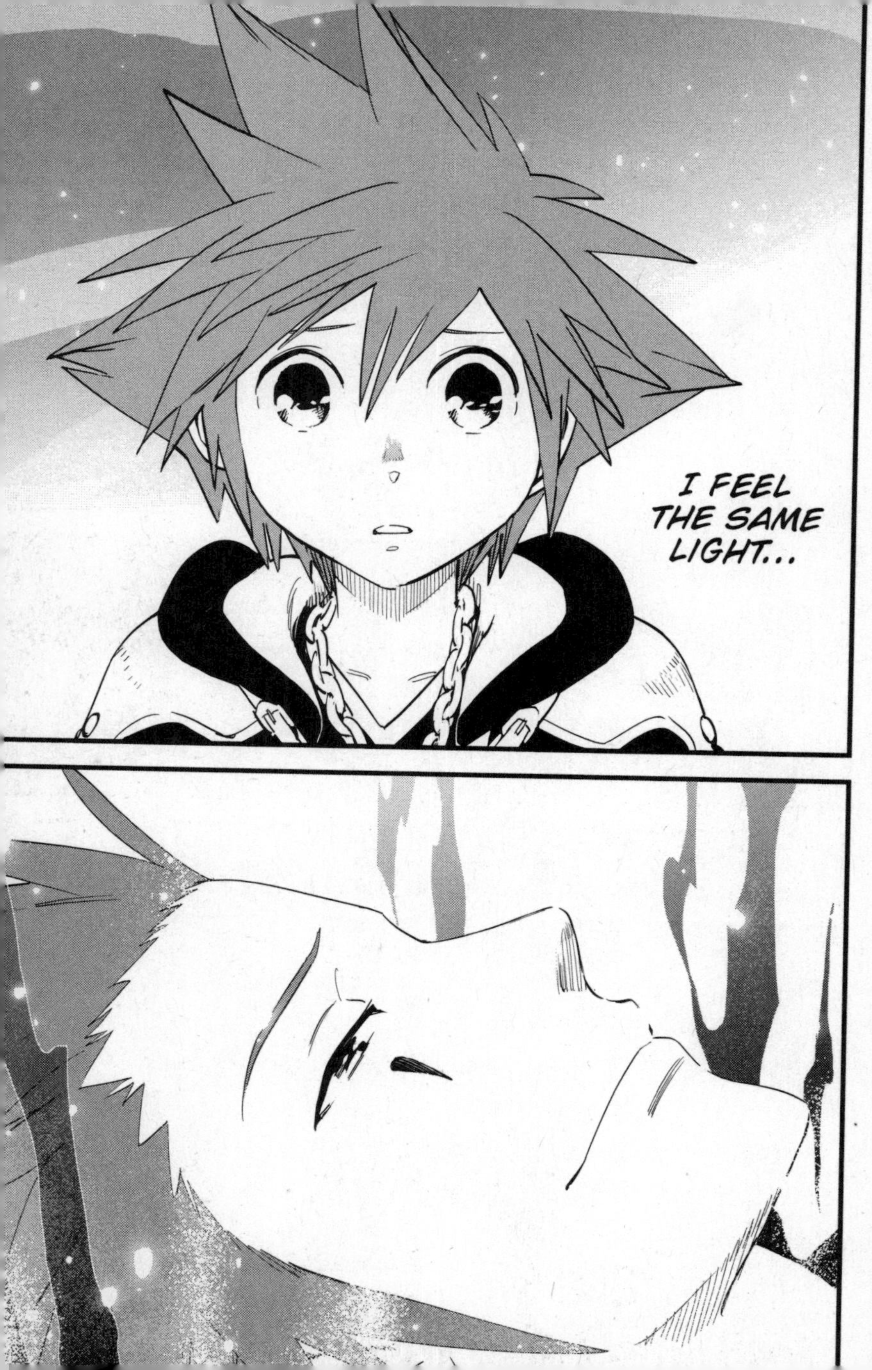
I FEEL THE SAME LIGHT...

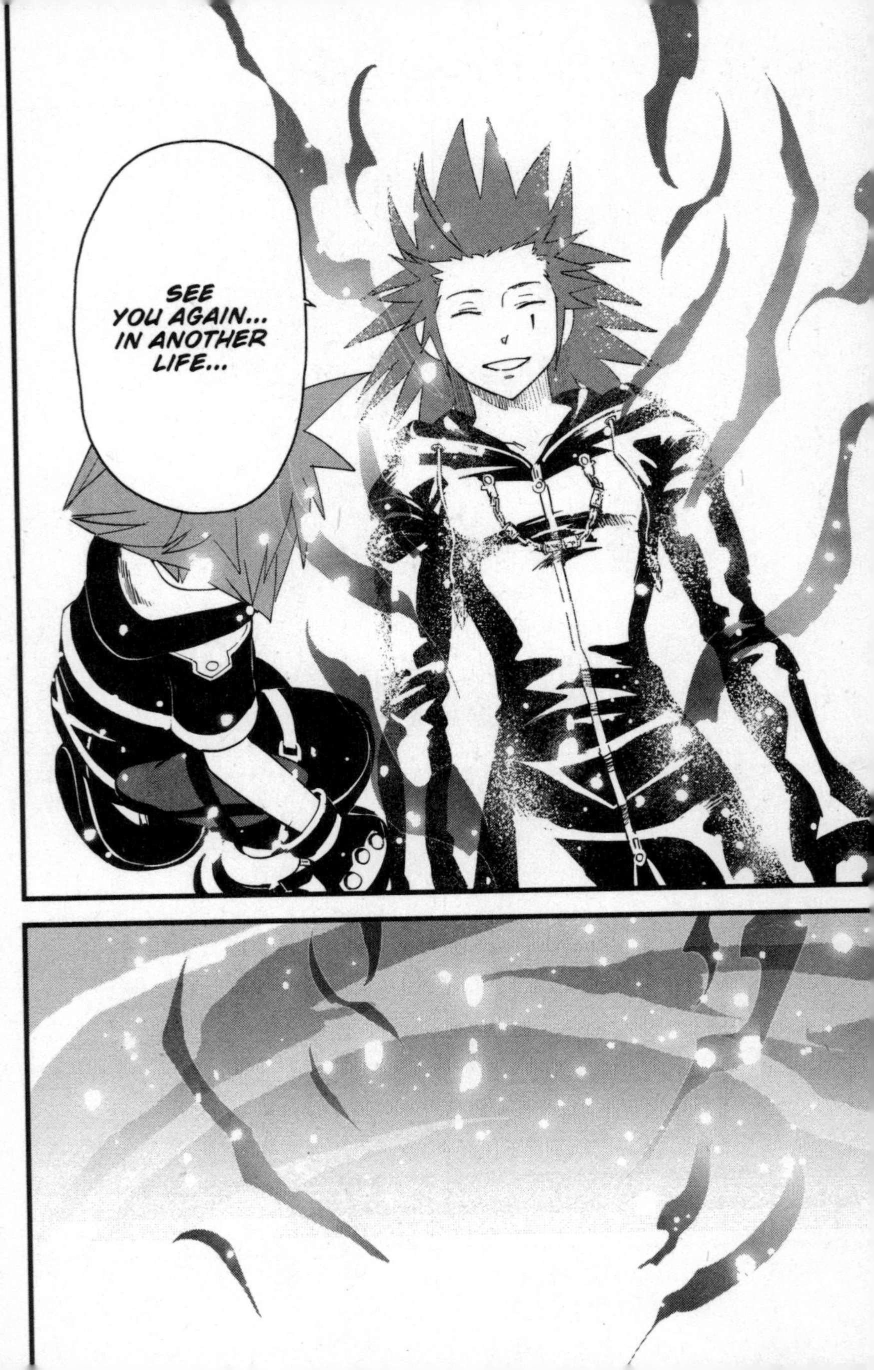
SEE YOU AGAIN... IN ANOTHER LIFE...

Chapter 56: Blending Hearts

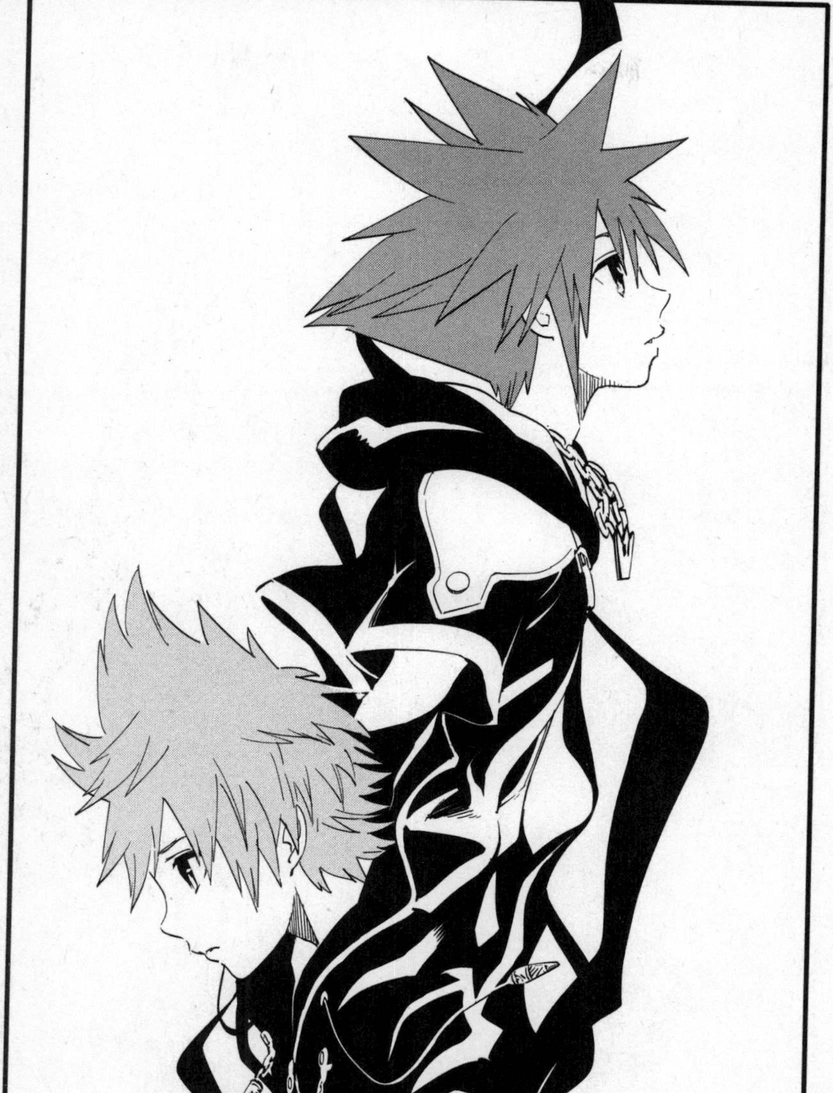

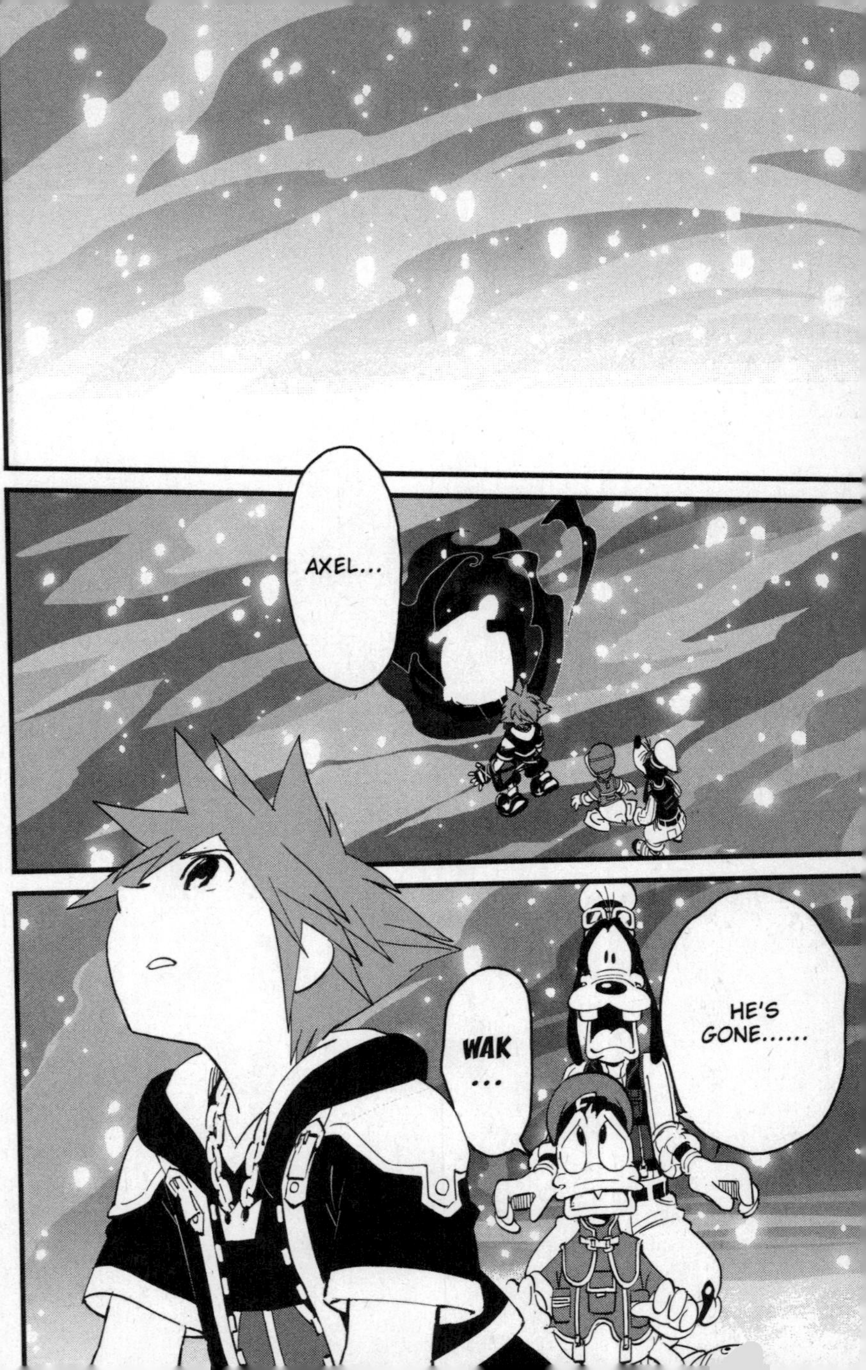
AXEL...
HE'S GONE......
WAK
...

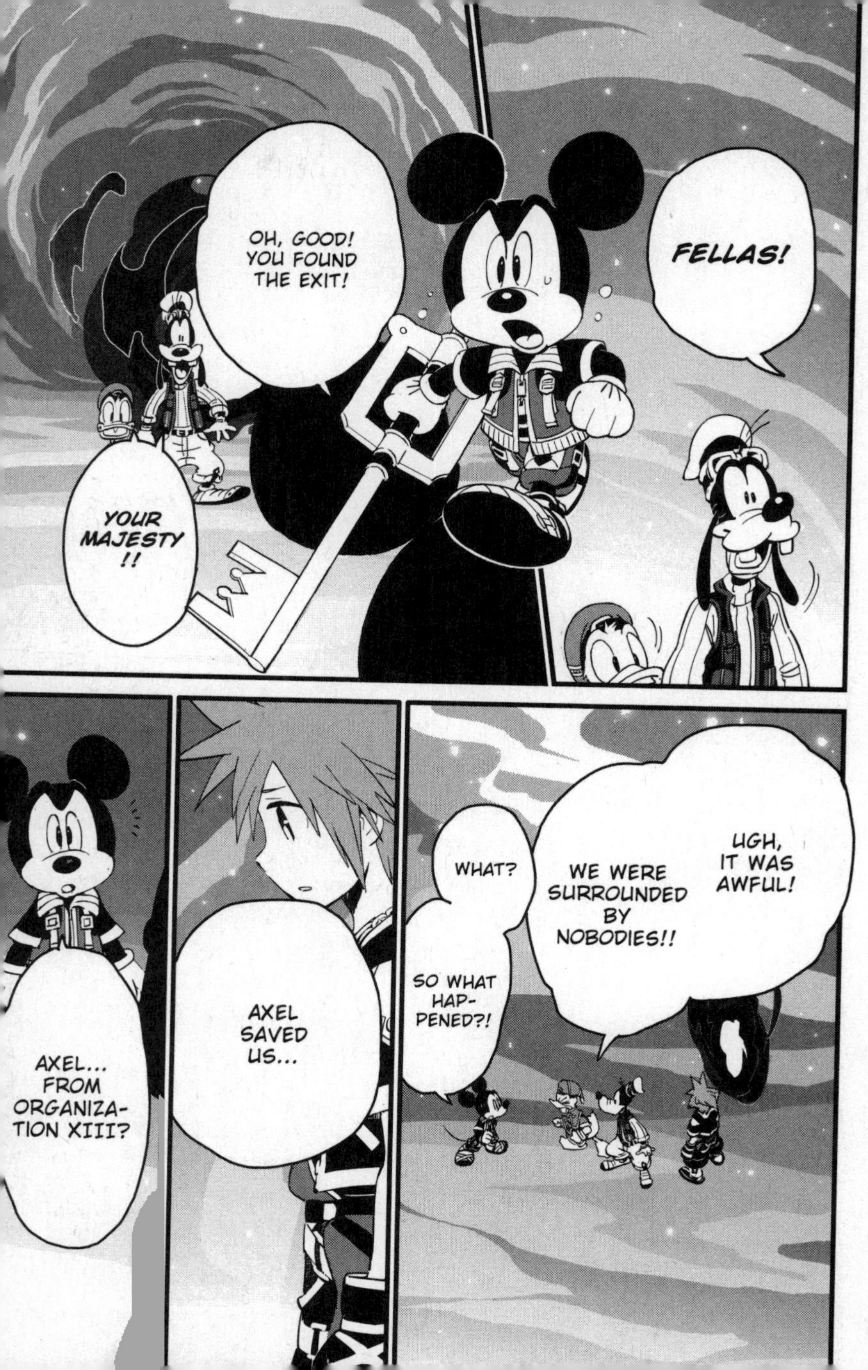
FELLAS!
OH, GOOD! YOU FOUND THE EXIT!
YOUR MAJESTY !!
UGH, IT WAS AWFUL!
WE WERE SURROUNDED BY NOBODIES!!
WHAT?
SO WHAT HAP-PENED?!
AXEL SAVED US...
AXEL... FROM ORGANIZA-TION XIII?

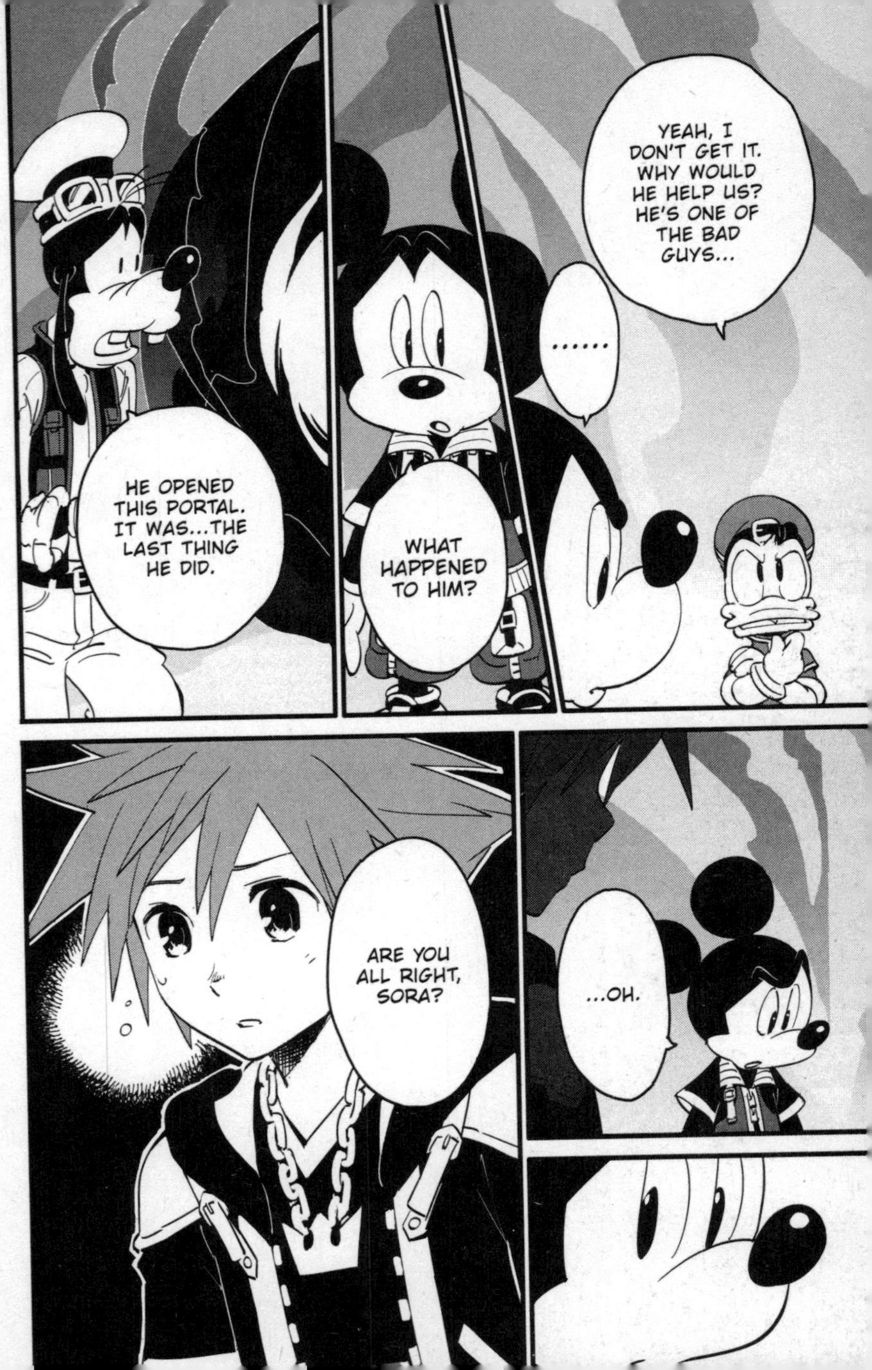
YEAH, I DON'T GET IT. WHY WOULD HE HELP US? HE'S ONE OF THE BAD GUYS...
......
WHAT HAPPENED TO HIM?
HE OPENED THIS PORTAL. IT WAS...THE LAST THING HE DID.
...OH.
ARE YOU ALL RIGHT, SORA?

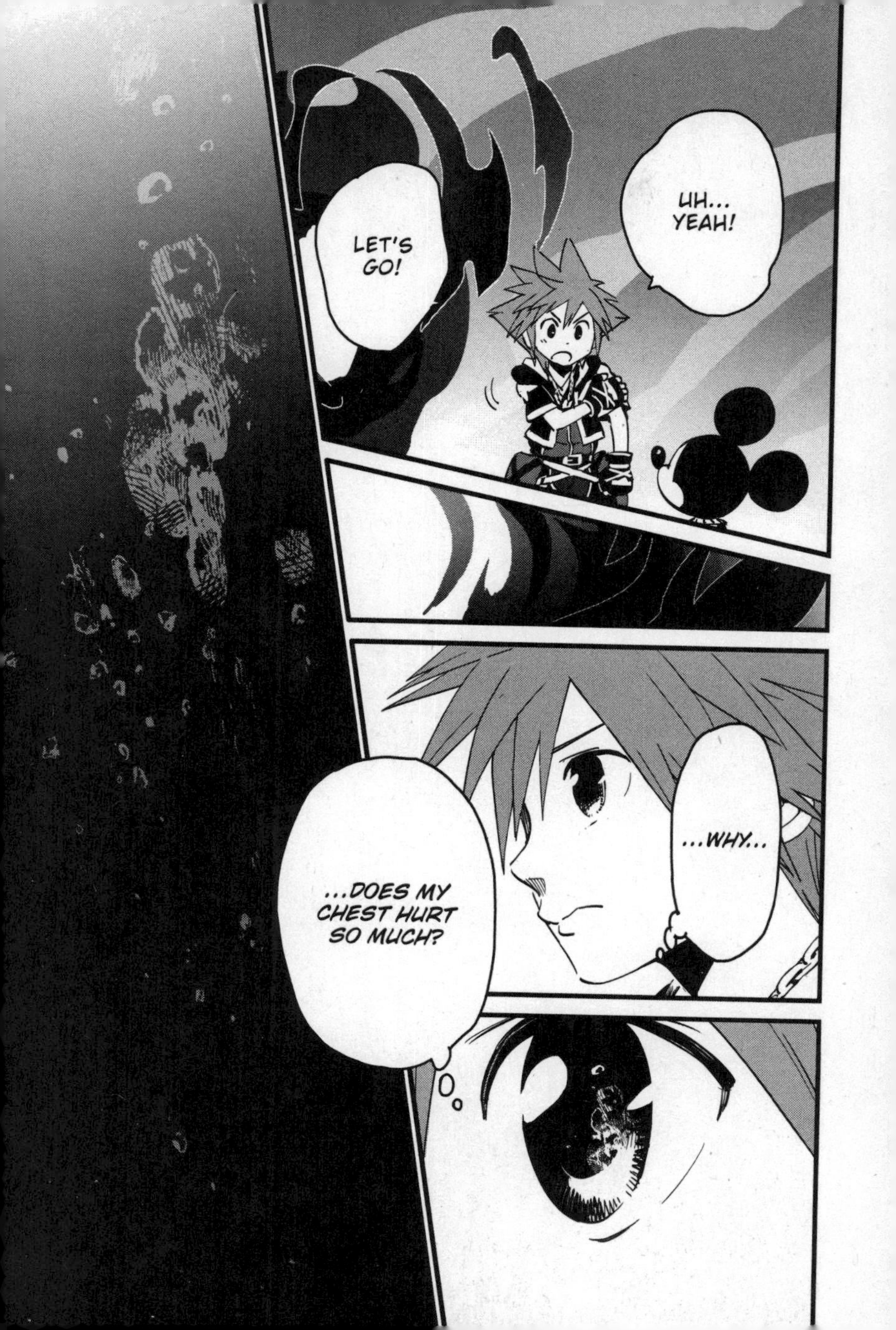
UH... YEAH!
LET'S GO!
...WHY...
...DOES MY CHEST HURT SO MUCH?

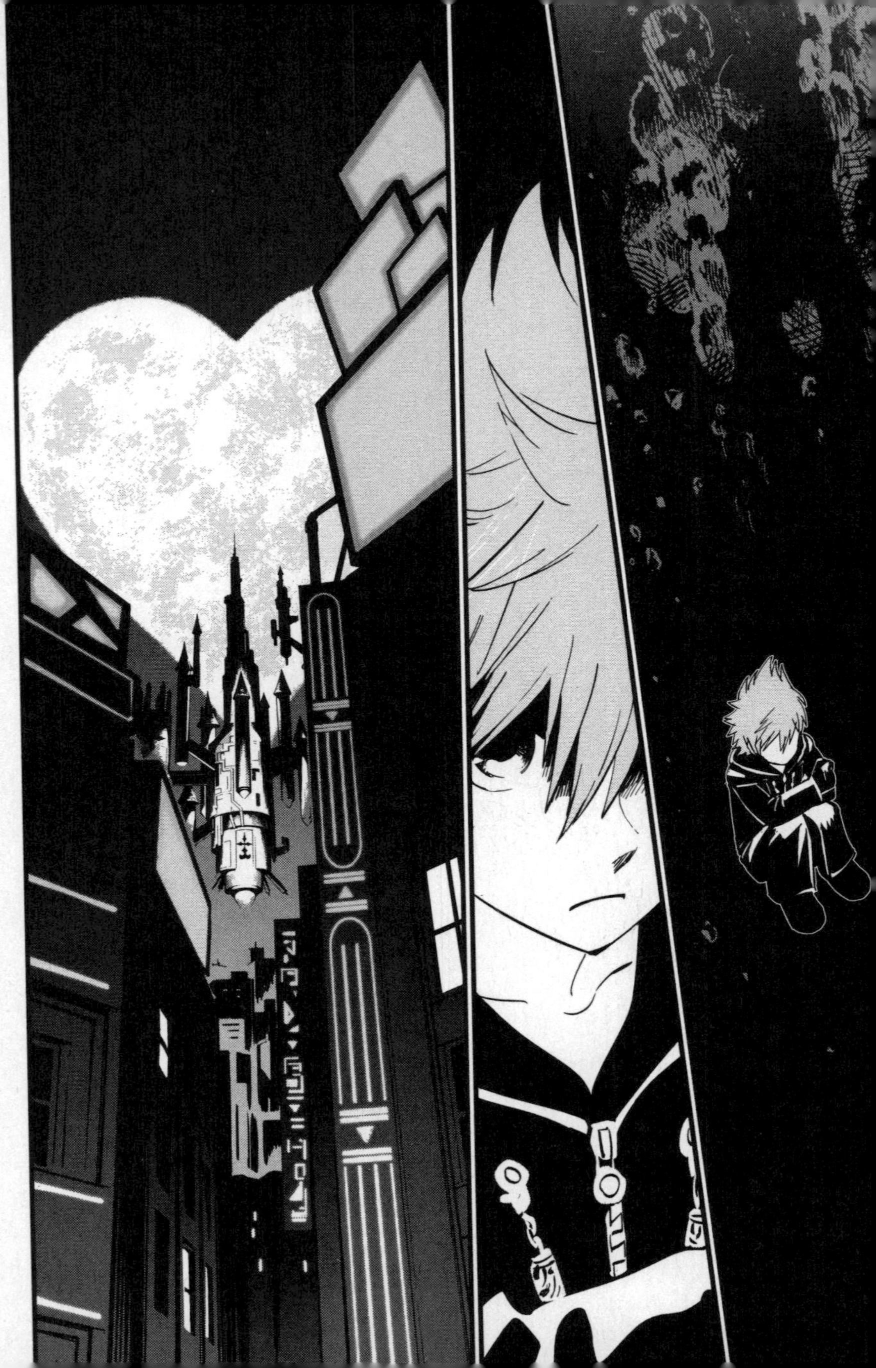

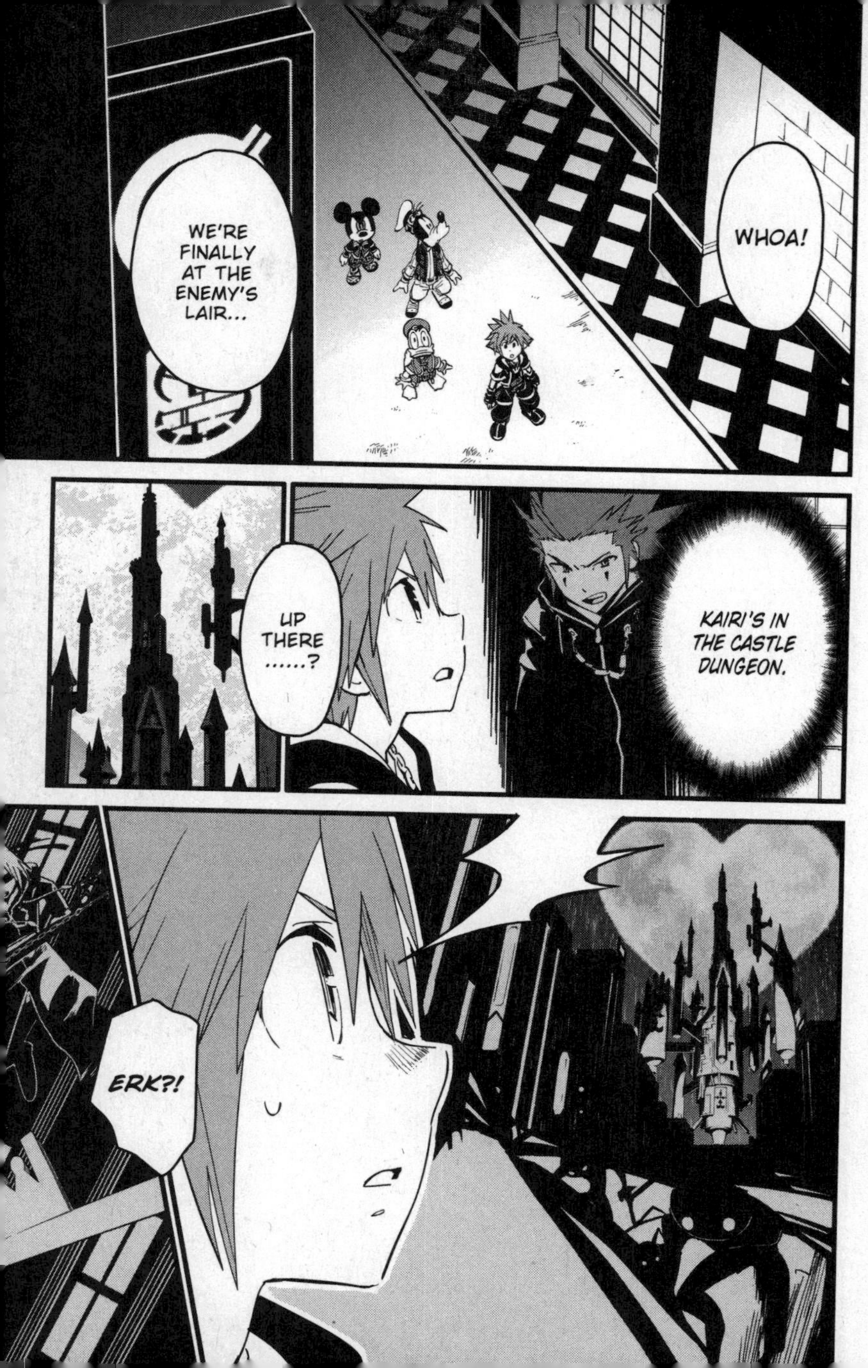
WHOA!
WE'RE FINALLY AT THE ENEMY'S LAIR...
KAIRI'S IN THE CASTLE DUNGEON.
UP THERE ......?
ERK?!

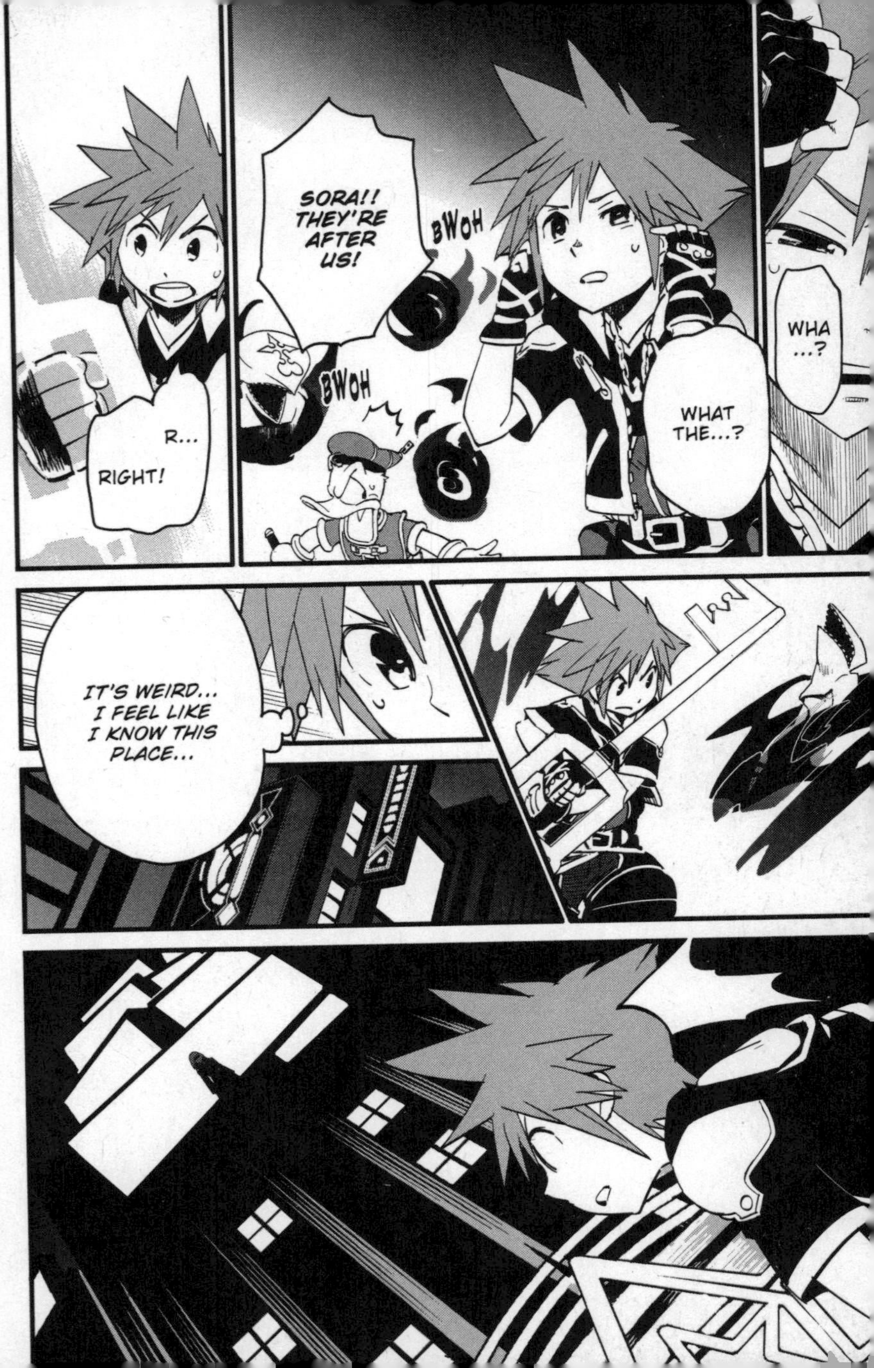
WHA ...?
SORA!! THEY'RE AFTER US!
BWOH
BWOH
WHAT THE...?
R... RIGHT!
IT'S WEIRD... I FEEL LIKE I KNOW THIS PLACE...

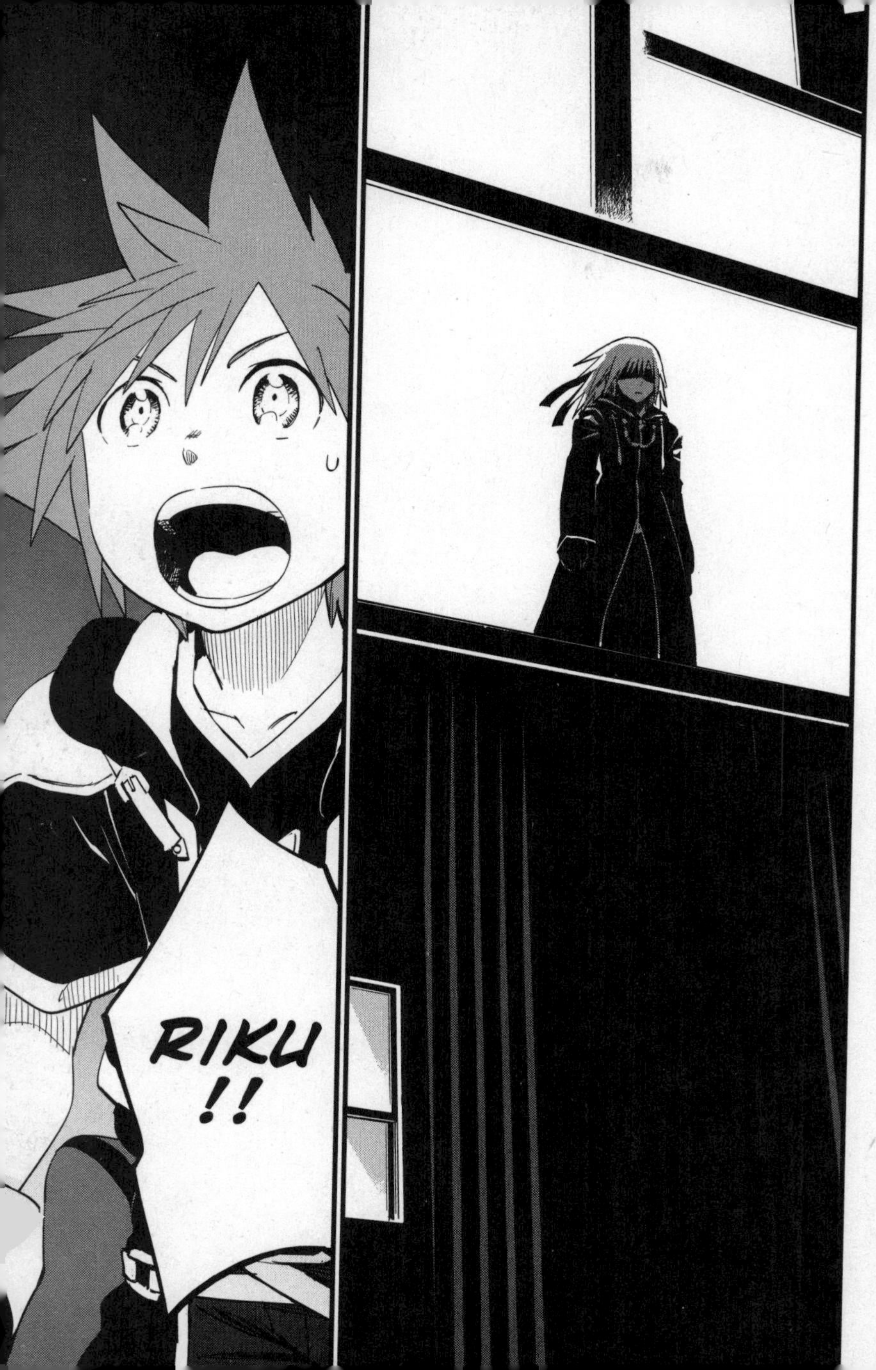
RIKU !!

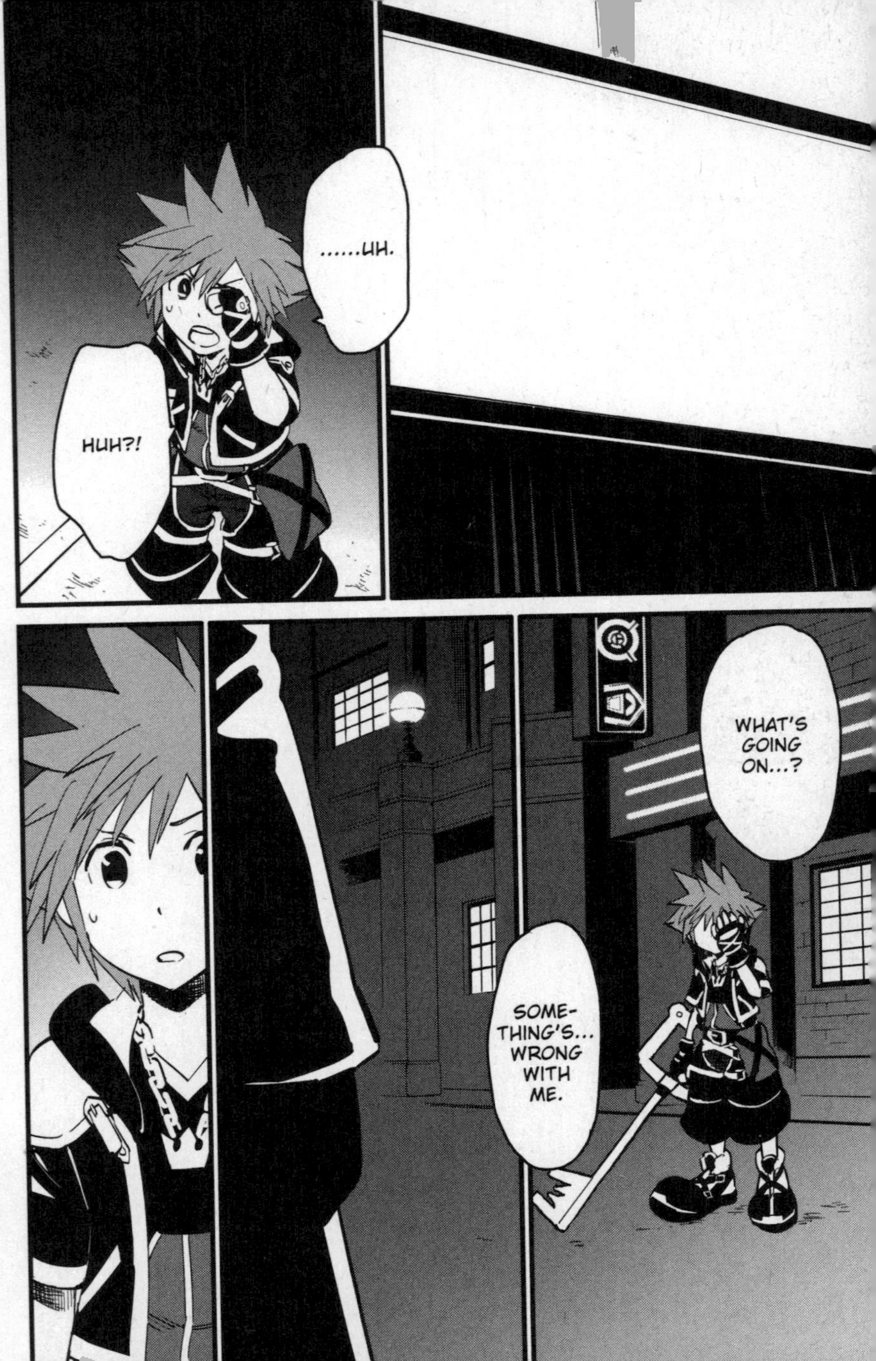
......UH.
HUH?!
WHAT'S GOING ON...?
SOME-THING'S... WRONG WITH ME.

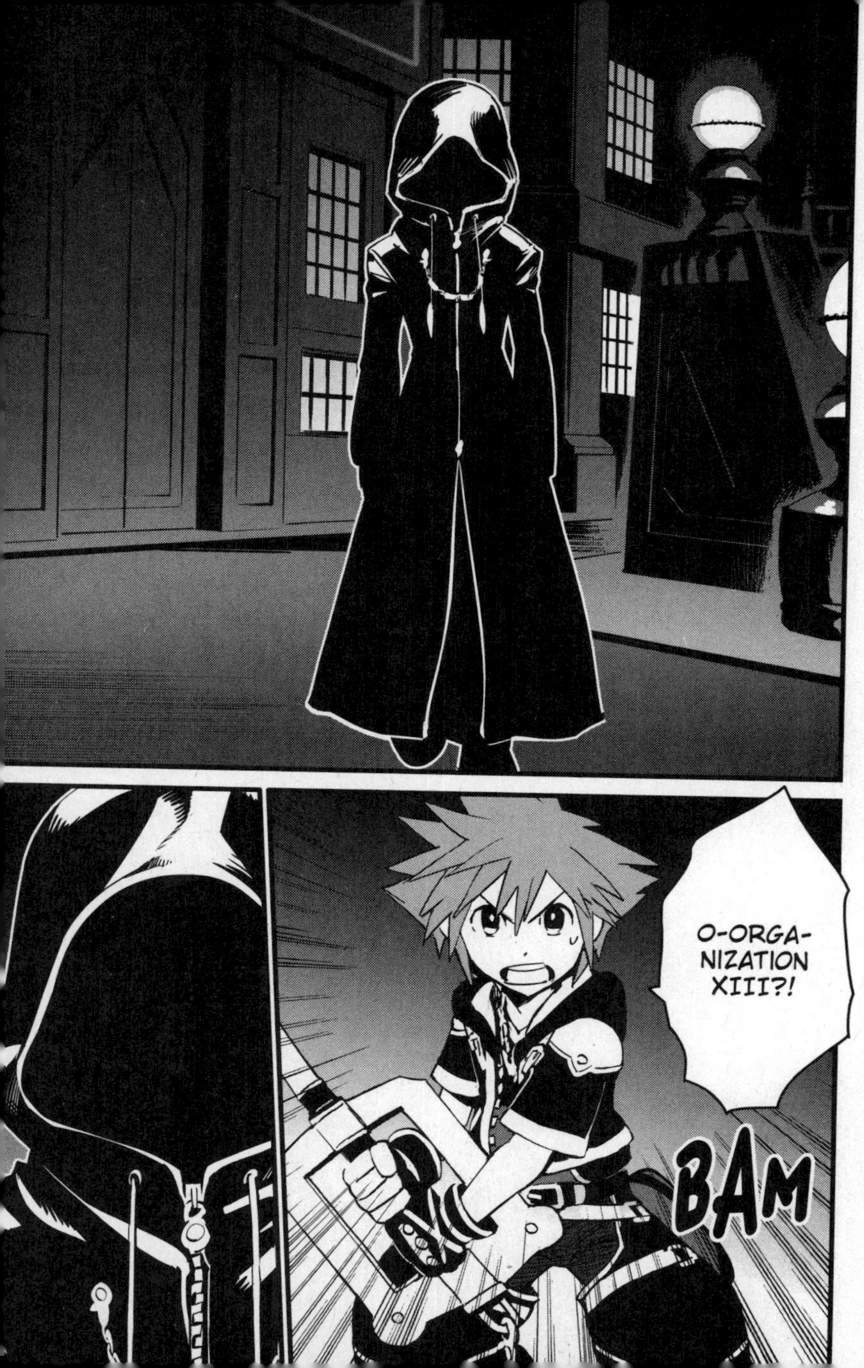
O-ORGA-
NIZATION
XIII?!
BAM

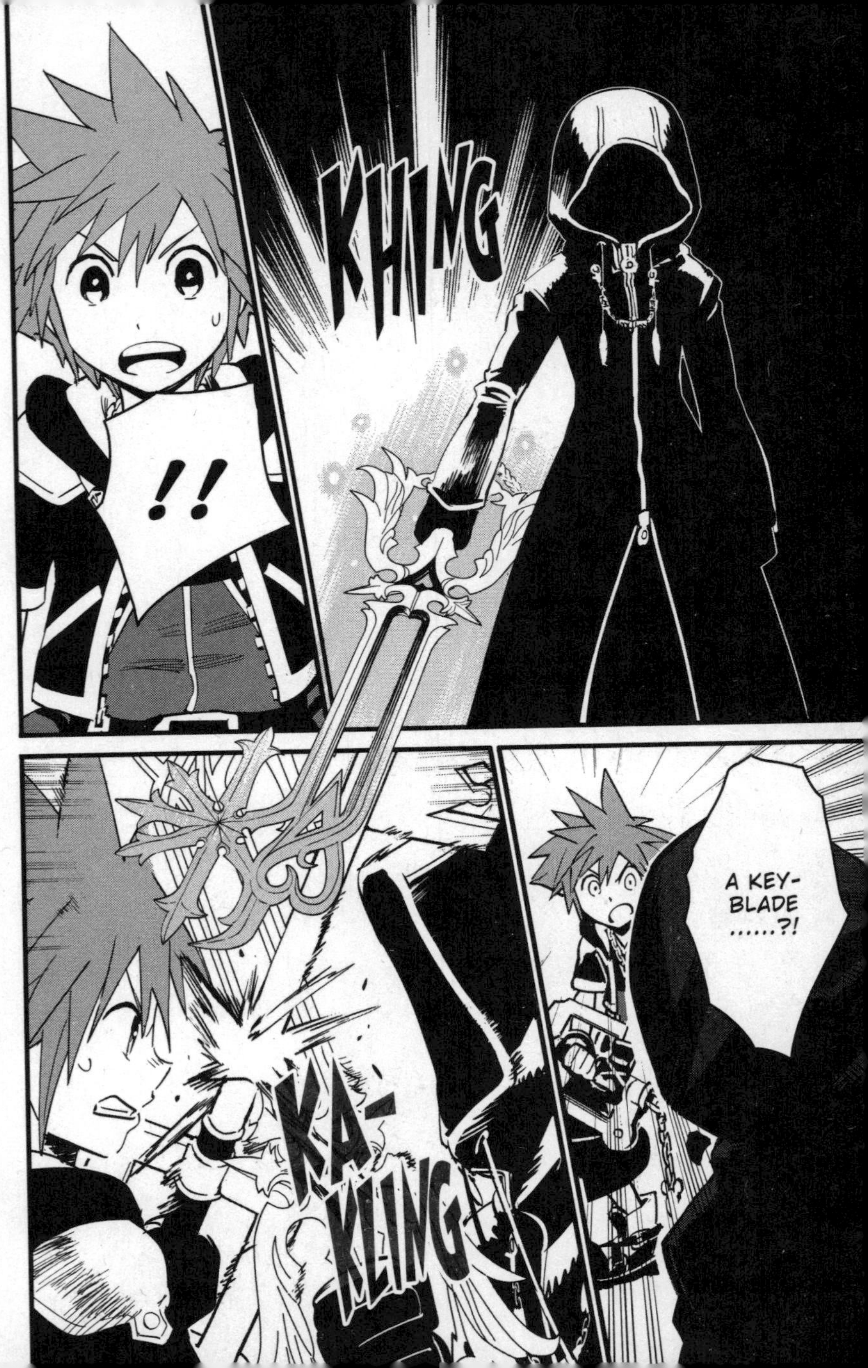
KHING
!!
A KEY-BLADE ......?!
KA-KLING

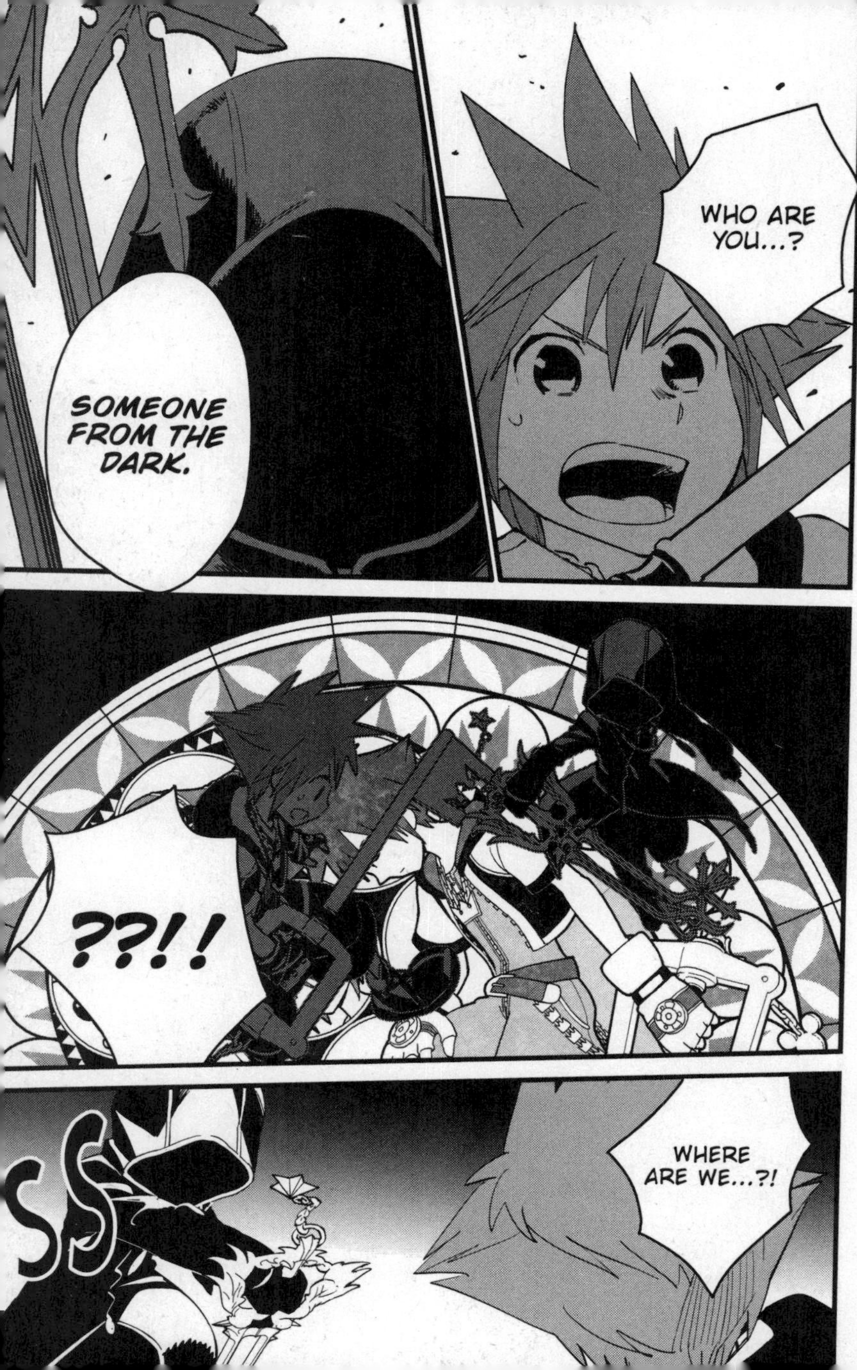
WHO ARE YOU...?
SOMEONE FROM THE DARK.
??!!
WHERE ARE WE...?!
SS

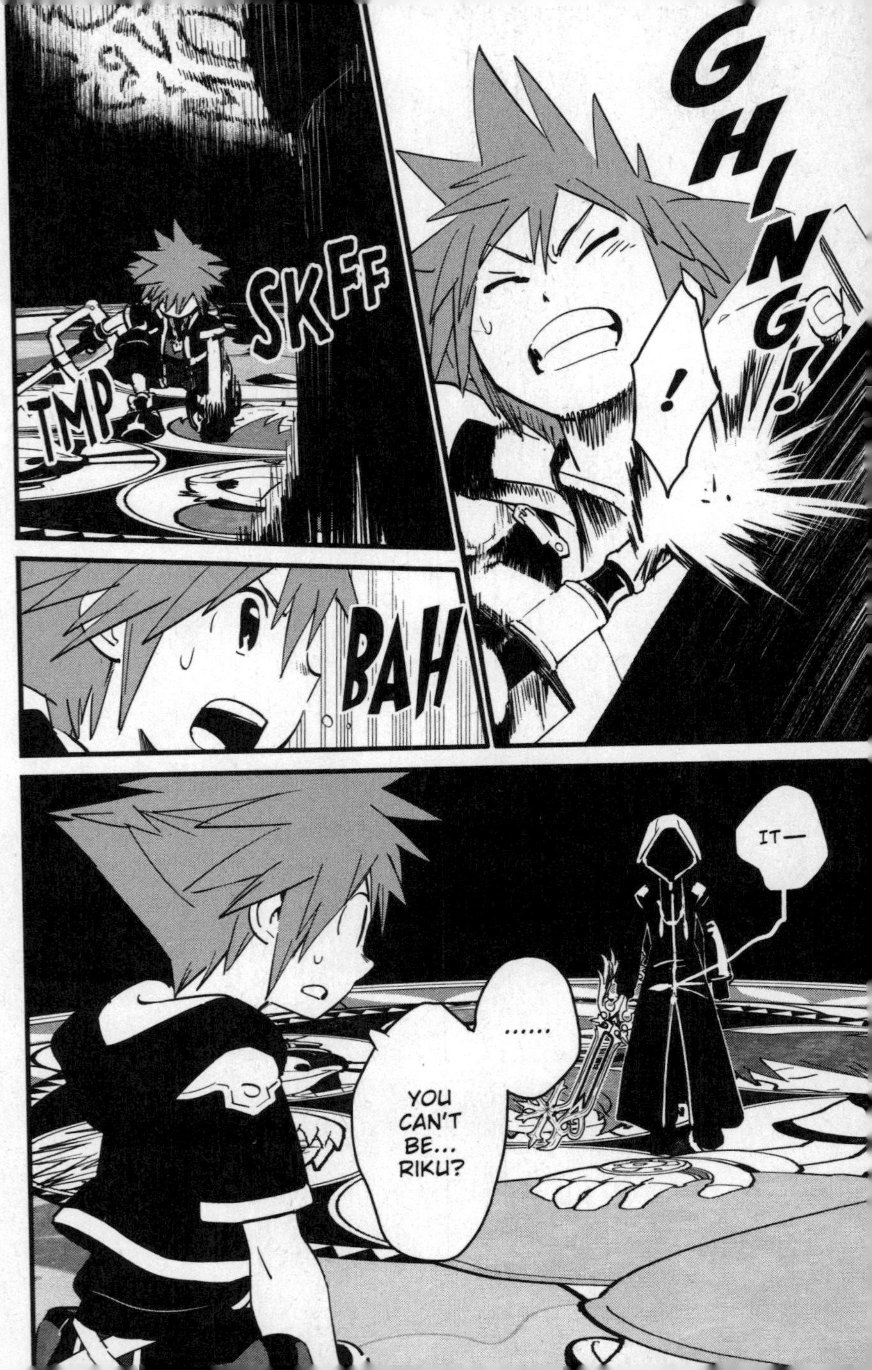
GHING!!
!
SKFF
TMP
BAH
IT—
......
YOU CAN'T BE... RIKU?

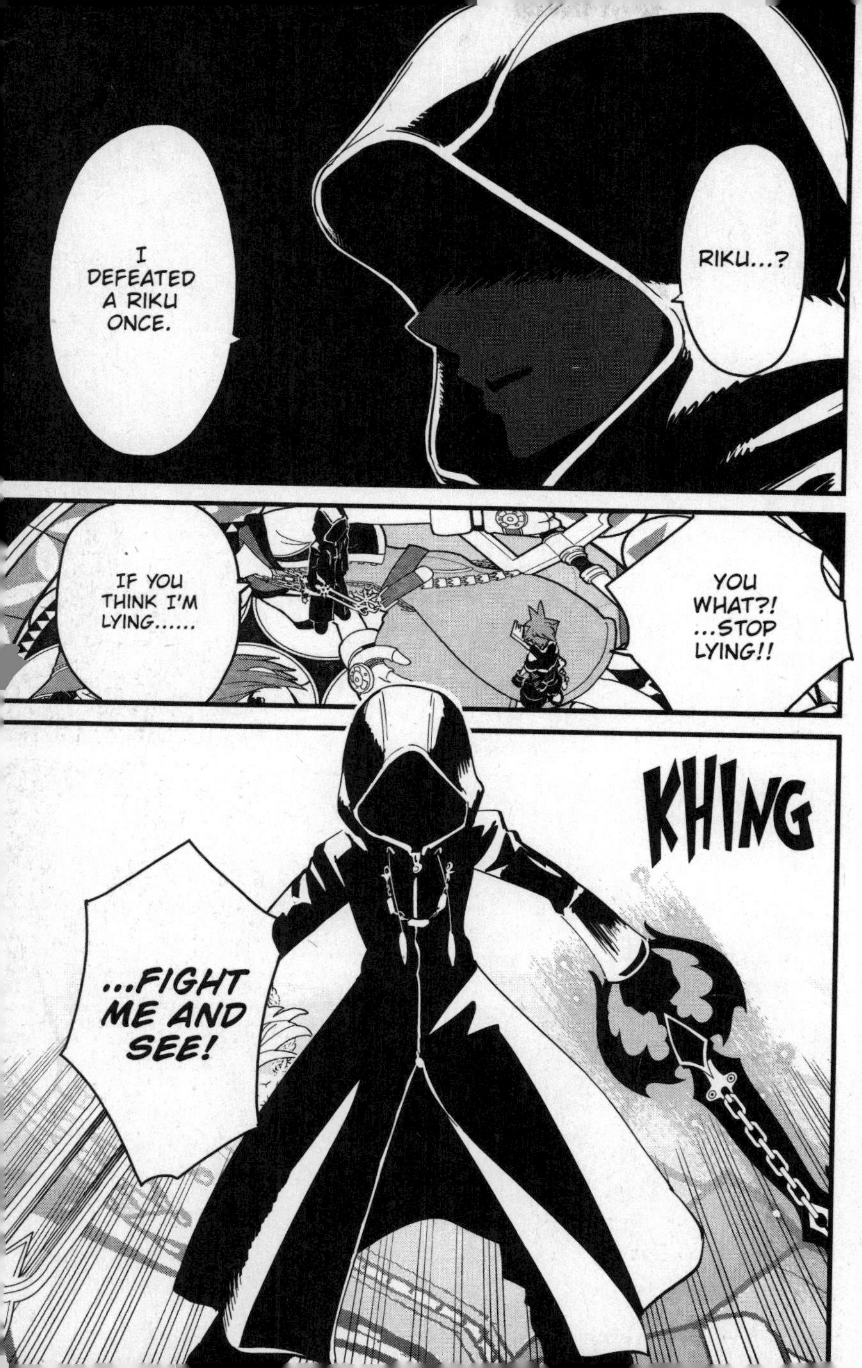
RIKU...?
I DEFEATED A RIKU ONCE.
YOU WHAT?! ...STOP LYING!!
IF YOU THINK I'M LYING......
KHING
...FIGHT ME AND SEE!

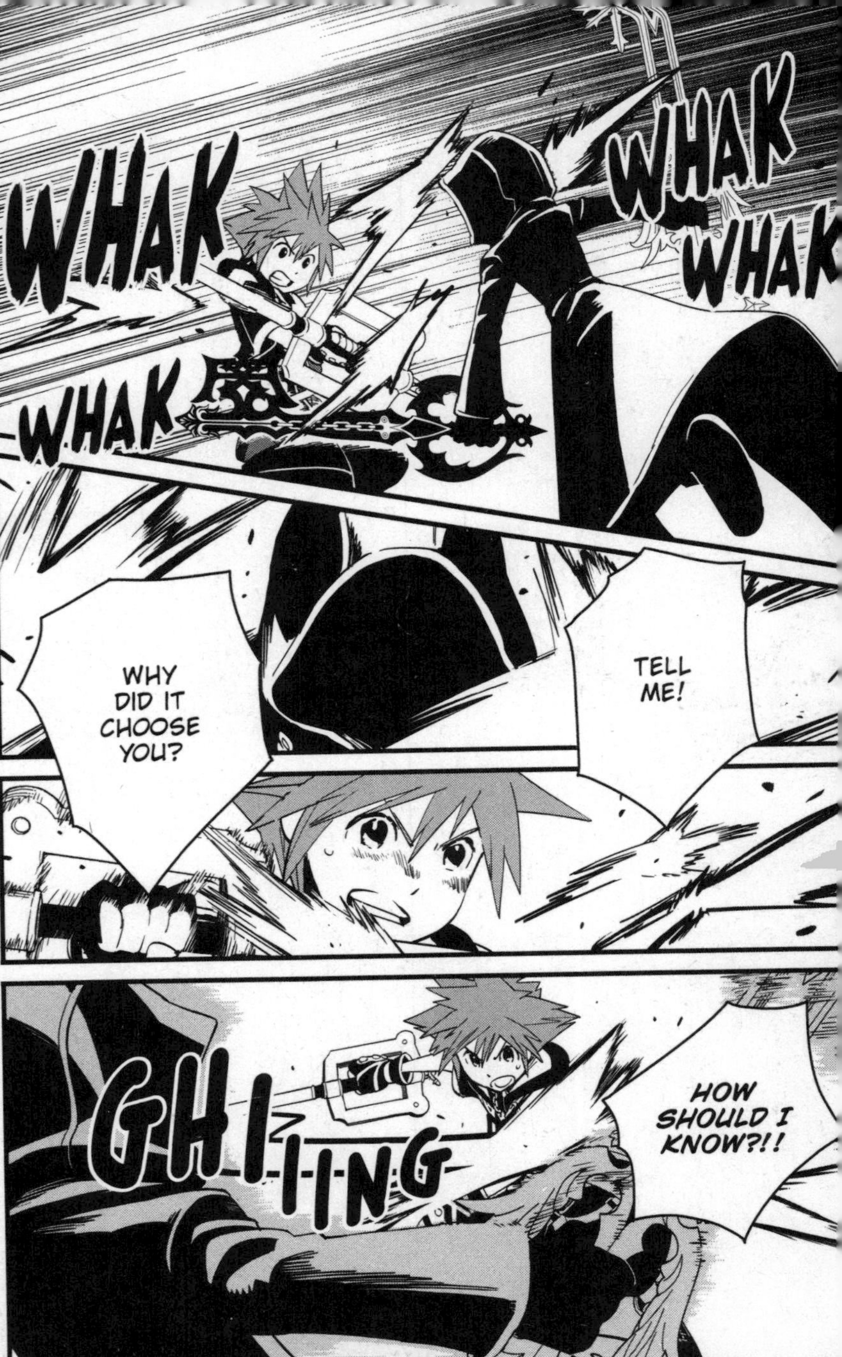
WHAK
WHAK
WHAK
WHAK
WHAK
TELL ME!
WHY DID IT CHOOSE YOU?
HOW SHOULD I KNOW?!!
GHI-I-ING

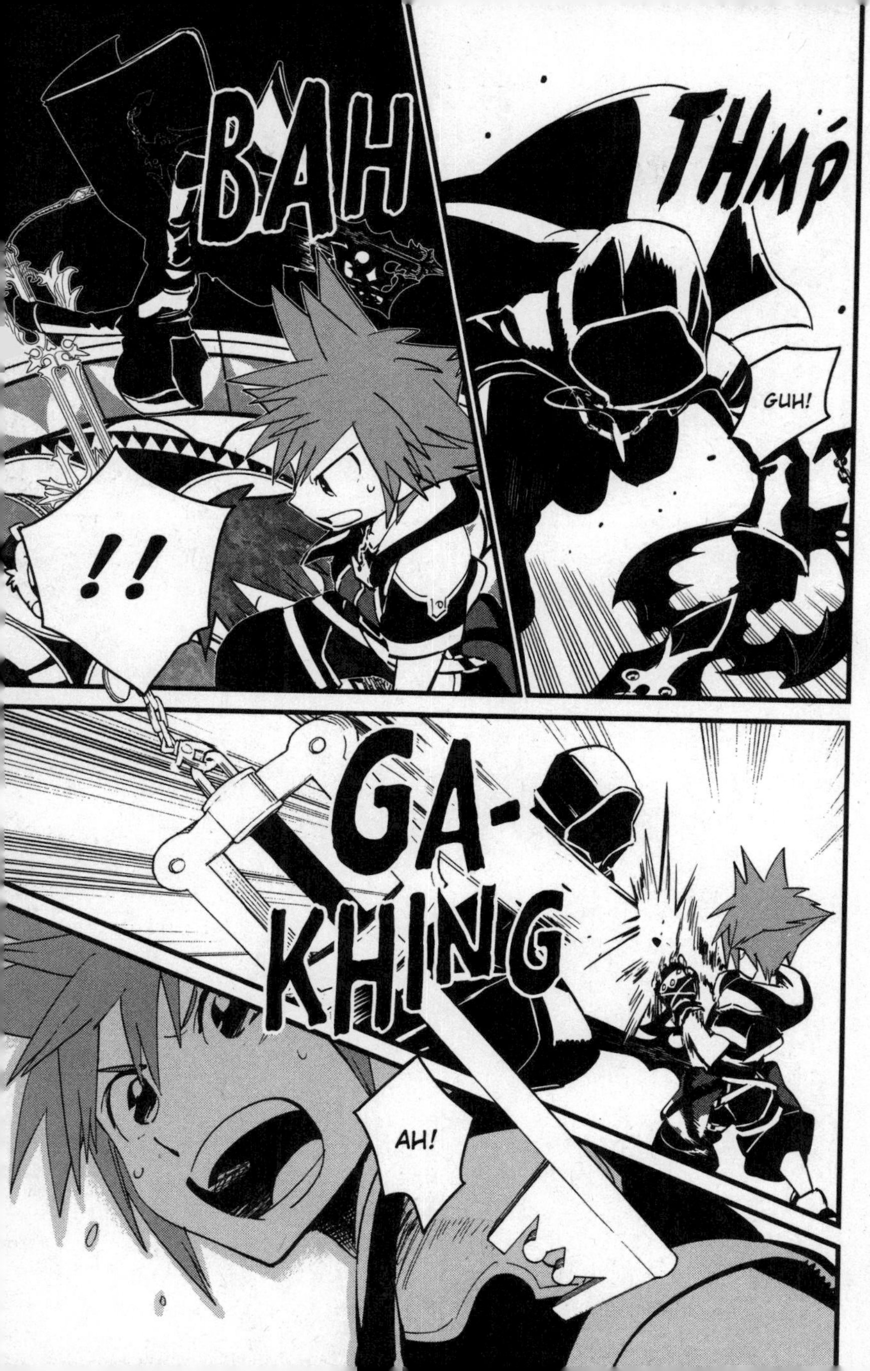
THMP
GUH!
BAH
!!
GA-KHING
AH!

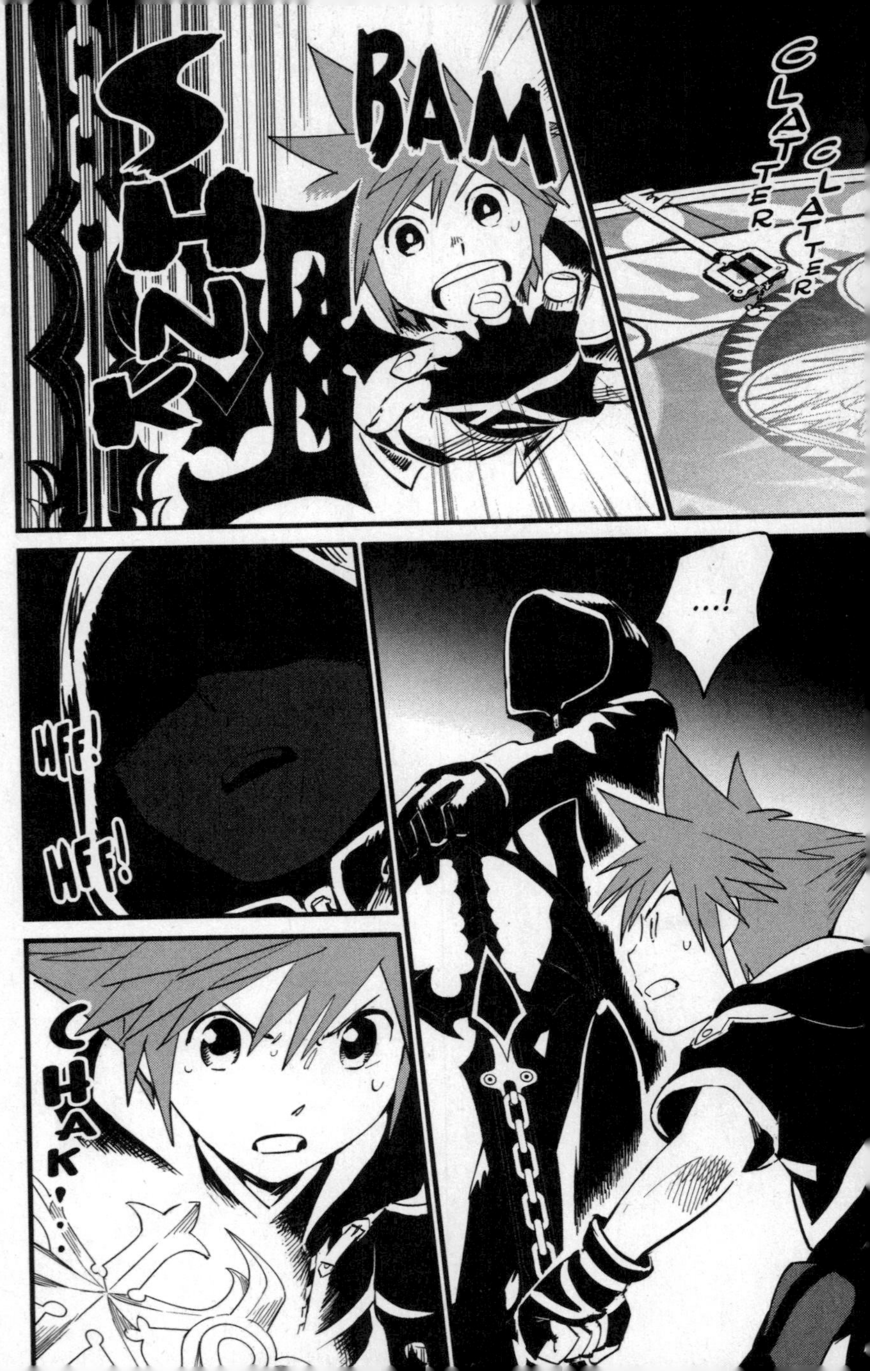
CLATTER CLATTER
BAM
SHNK
...!
HFF! HFF!
CHAK...

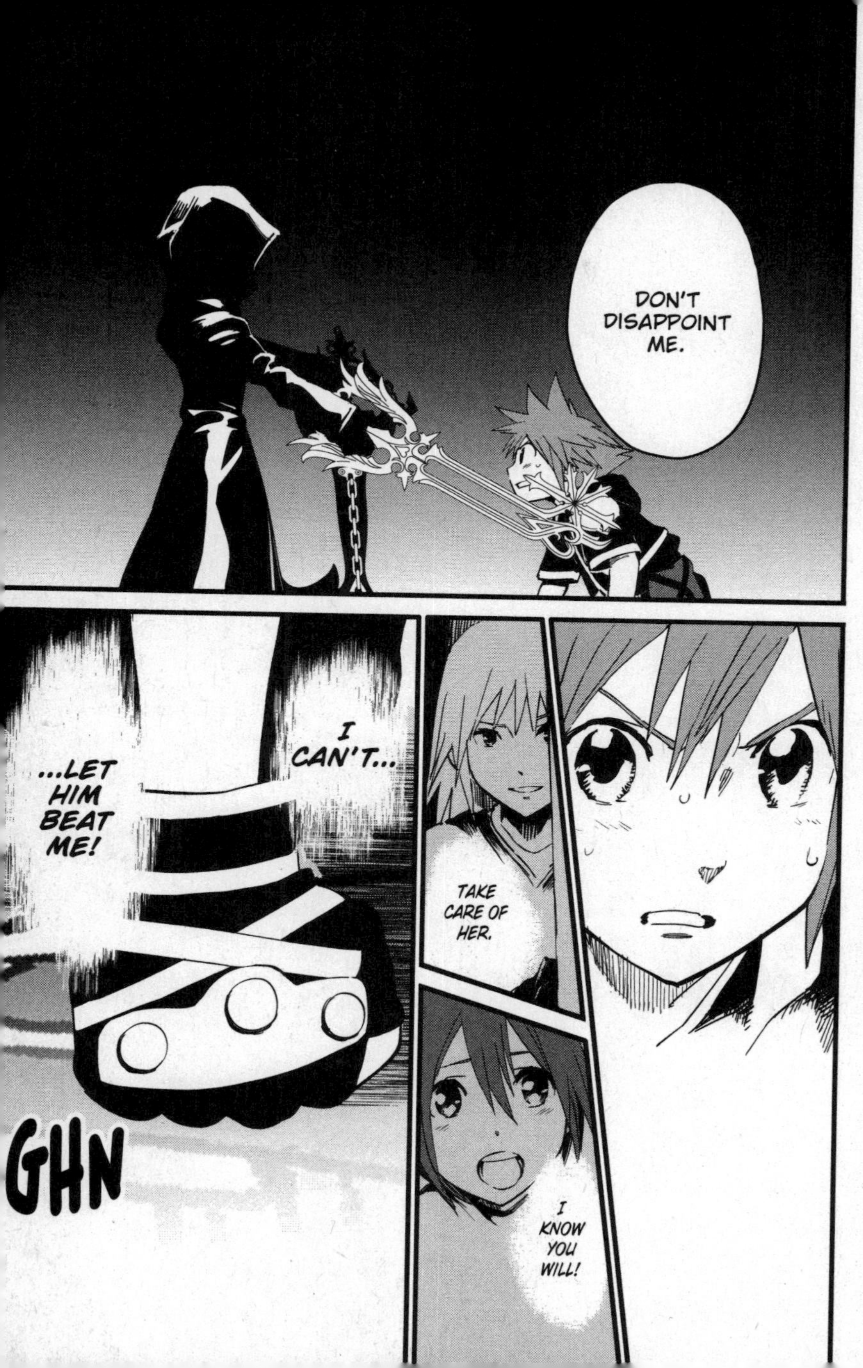
DON'T DISAPPOINT ME.
TAKE CARE OF HER.
I KNOW YOU WILL!
I CAN'T...
...LET HIM BEAT ME!
GHN

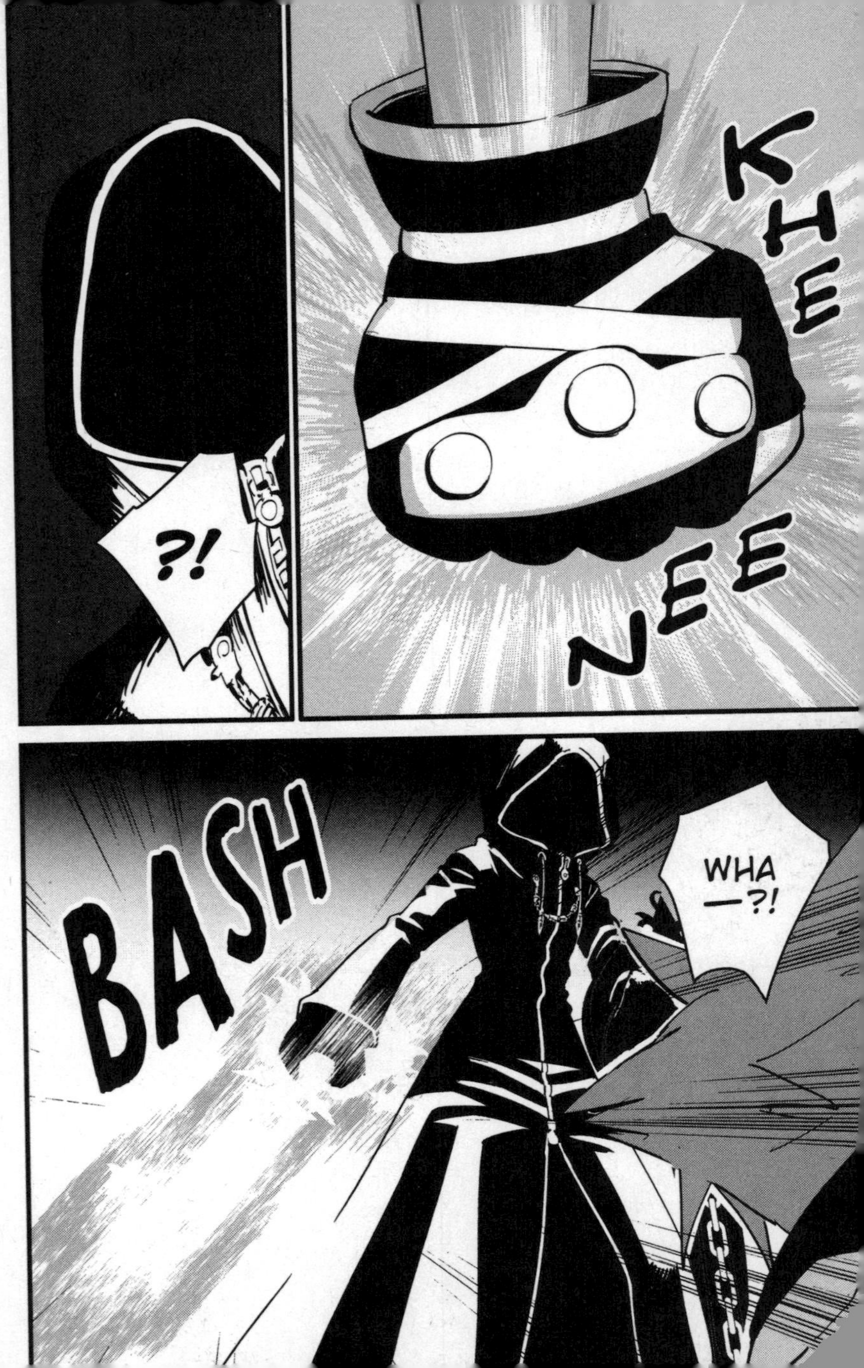
KHE
NEE
?!
WHA—?!
BASH

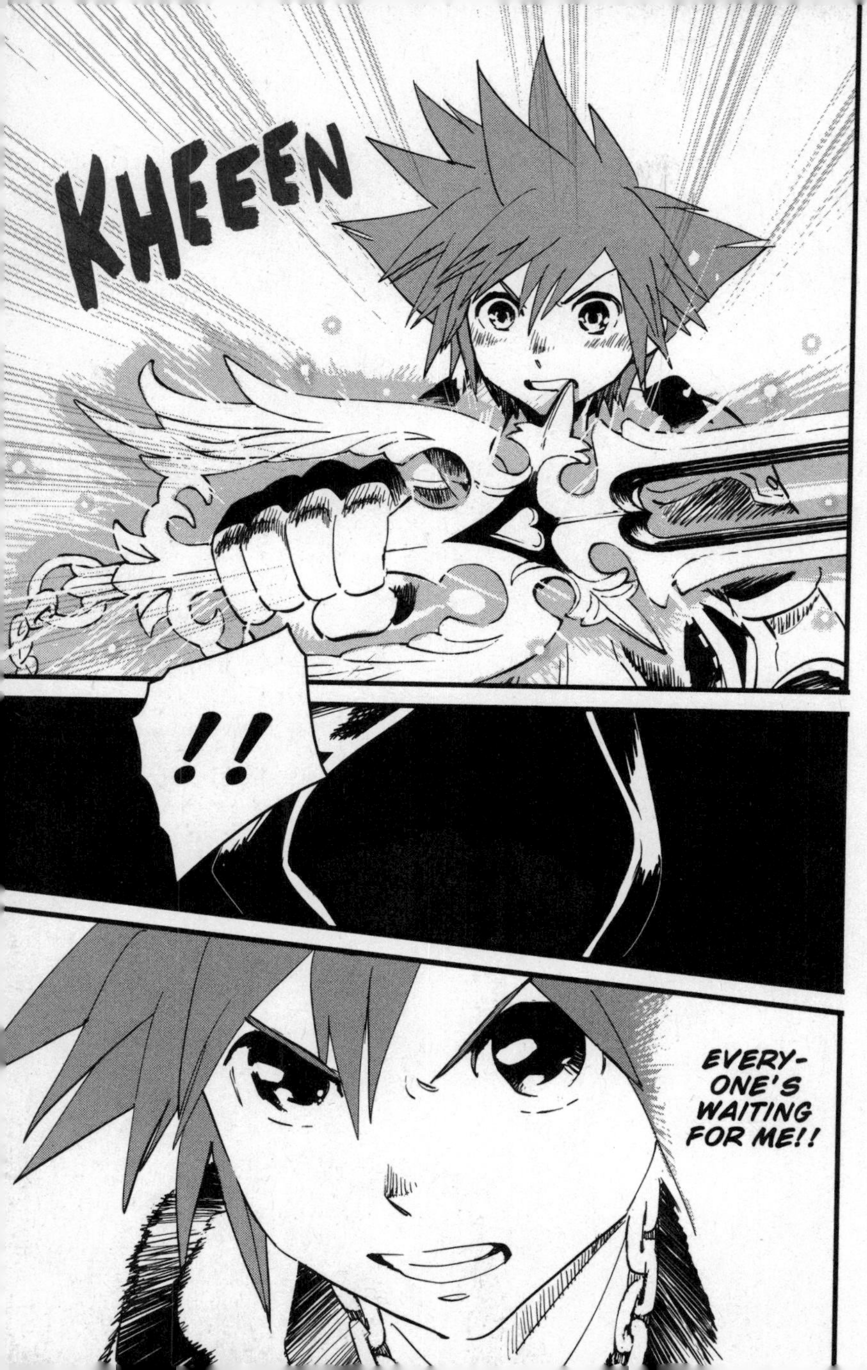
KHEEEN
!!
EVERY-ONE'S WAITING FOR ME!!

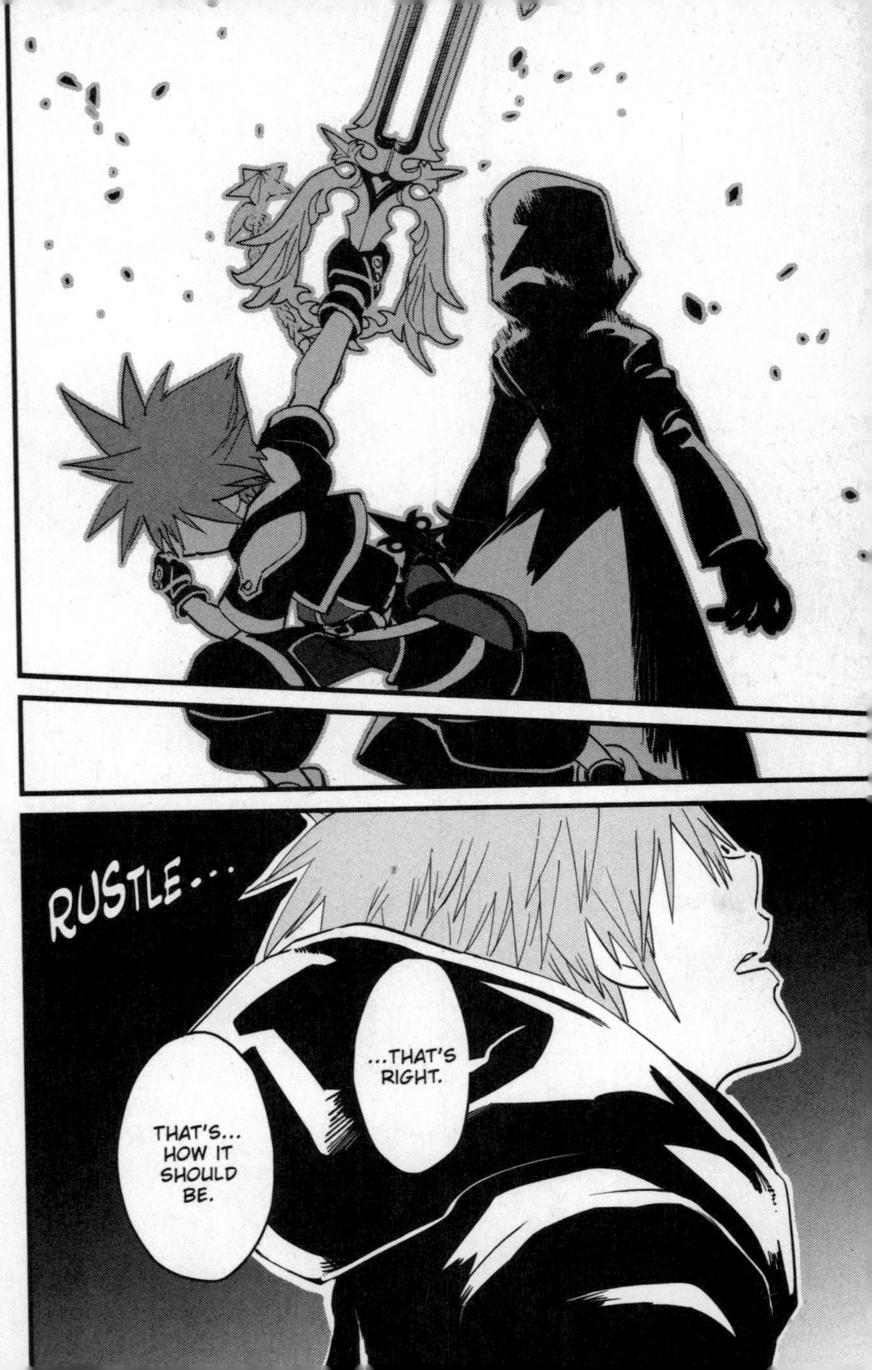
RUSTLE...
...THAT'S RIGHT.
THAT'S... HOW IT SHOULD BE.

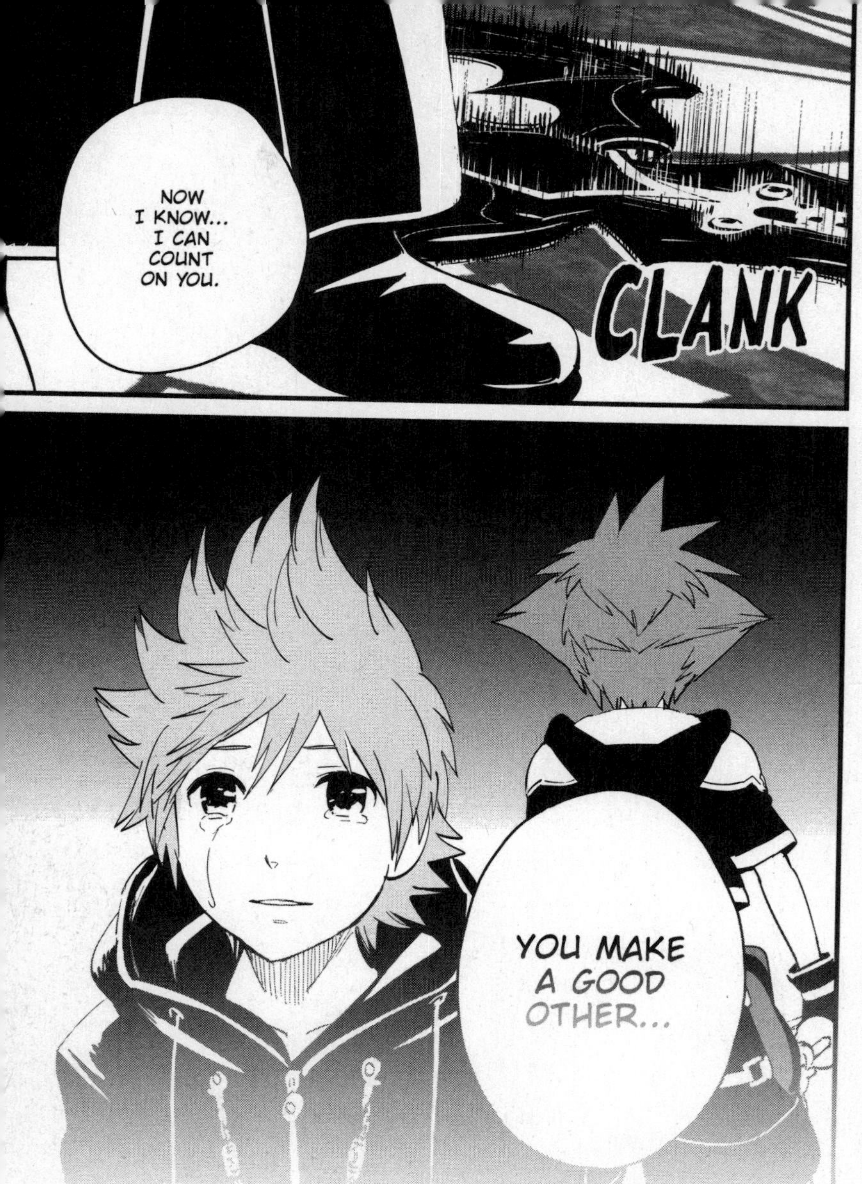
NOW I KNOW... I CAN COUNT ON YOU.
CLANK
YOU MAKE A GOOD OTHER...

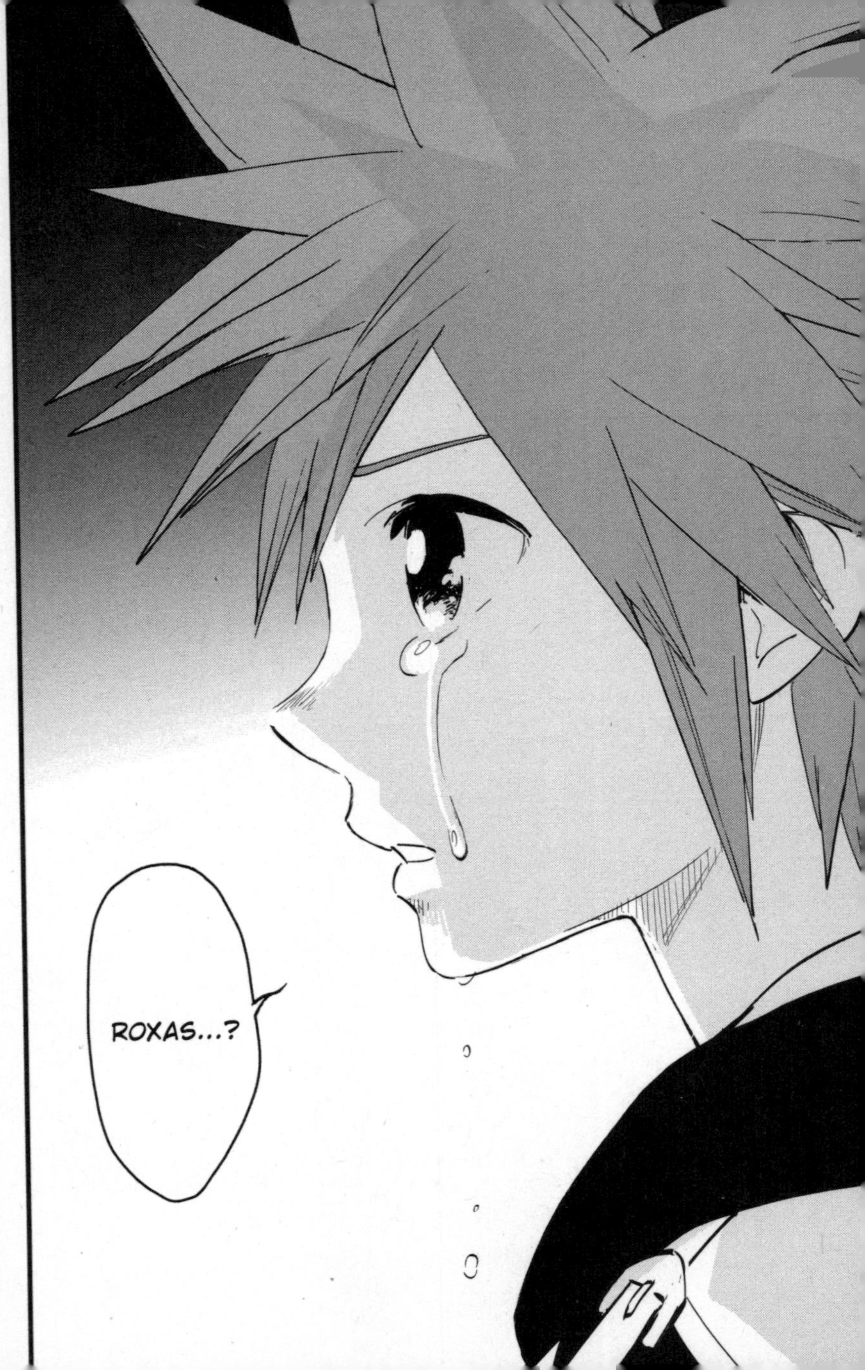
ROXAS...?

Chapter 57: Parting and Reunion

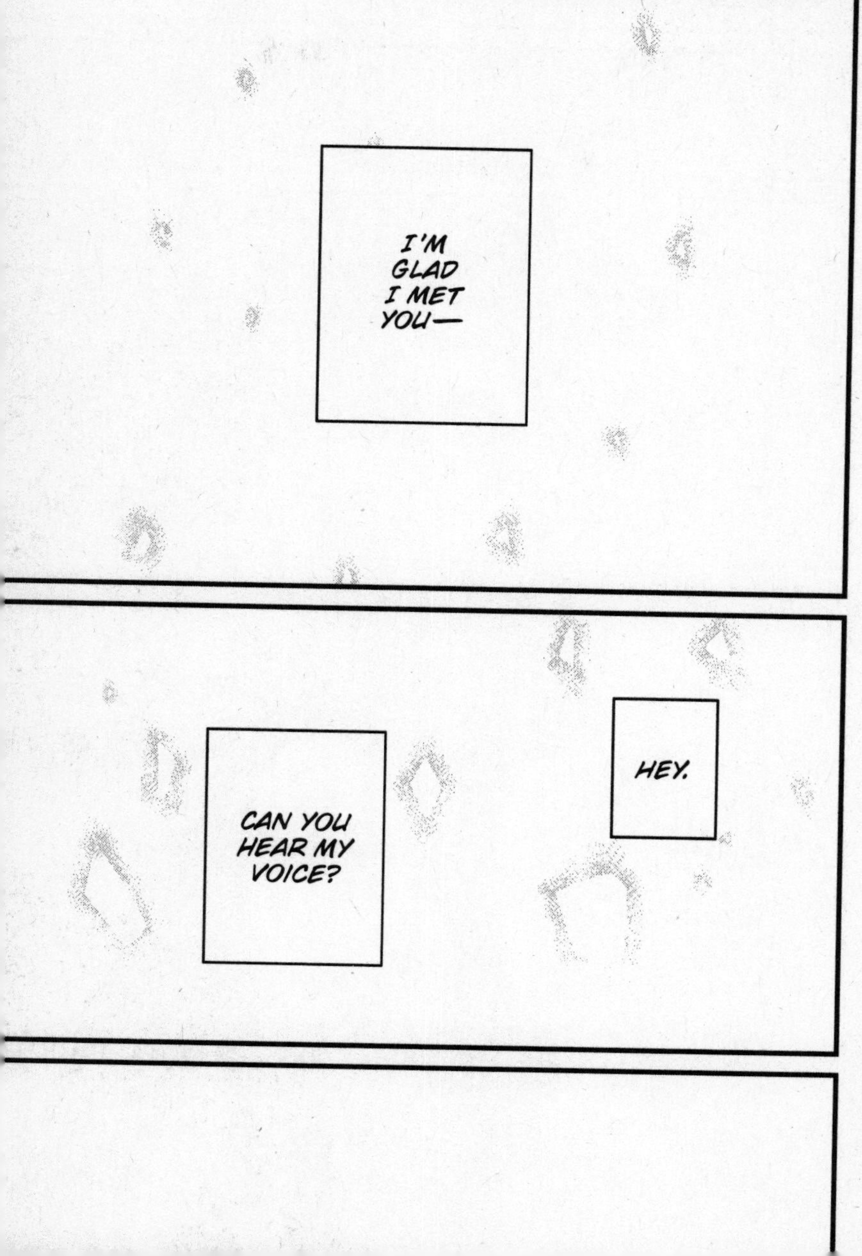
I'M GLAD I MET YOU—
HEY.
CAN YOU HEAR MY VOICE?

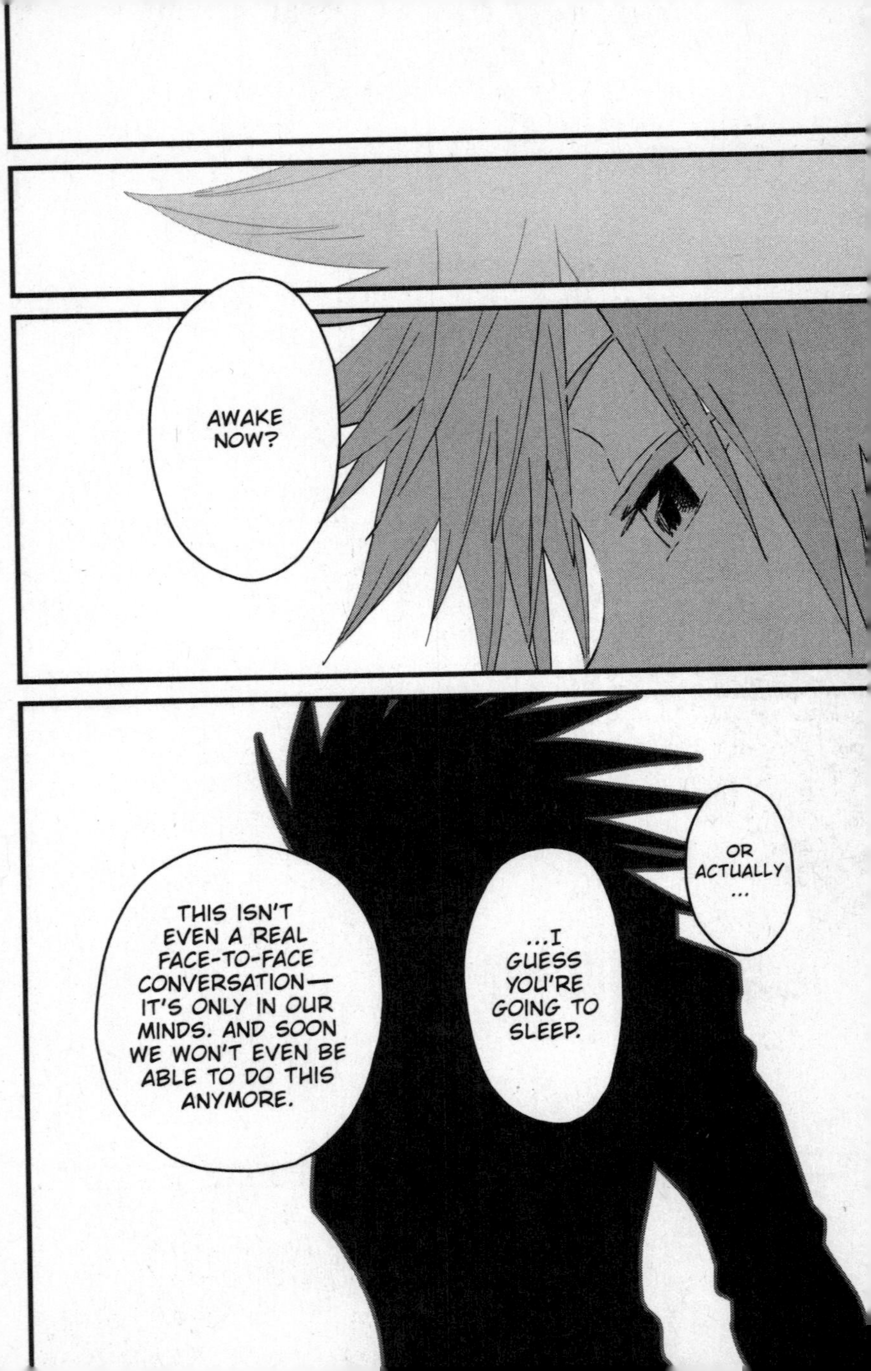
AWAKE NOW?
OR ACTUALLY ...
...I GUESS YOU'RE GOING TO SLEEP.
THIS ISN'T EVEN A REAL FACE-TO-FACE CONVERSATION—IT'S ONLY IN OUR MINDS. AND SOON WE WON'T EVEN BE ABLE TO DO THIS ANYMORE.

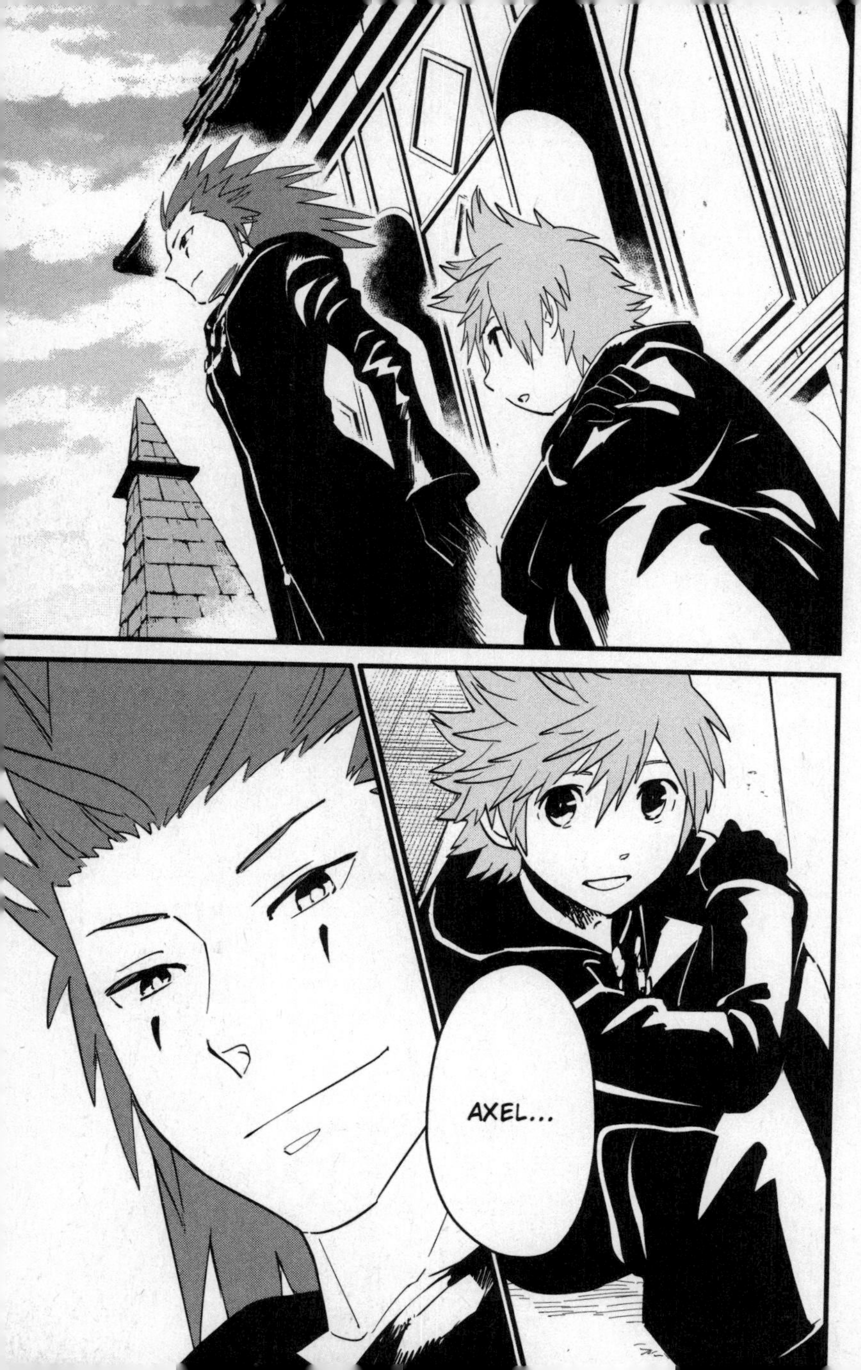
AXEL...

Chapter 57: Parting and Reunion

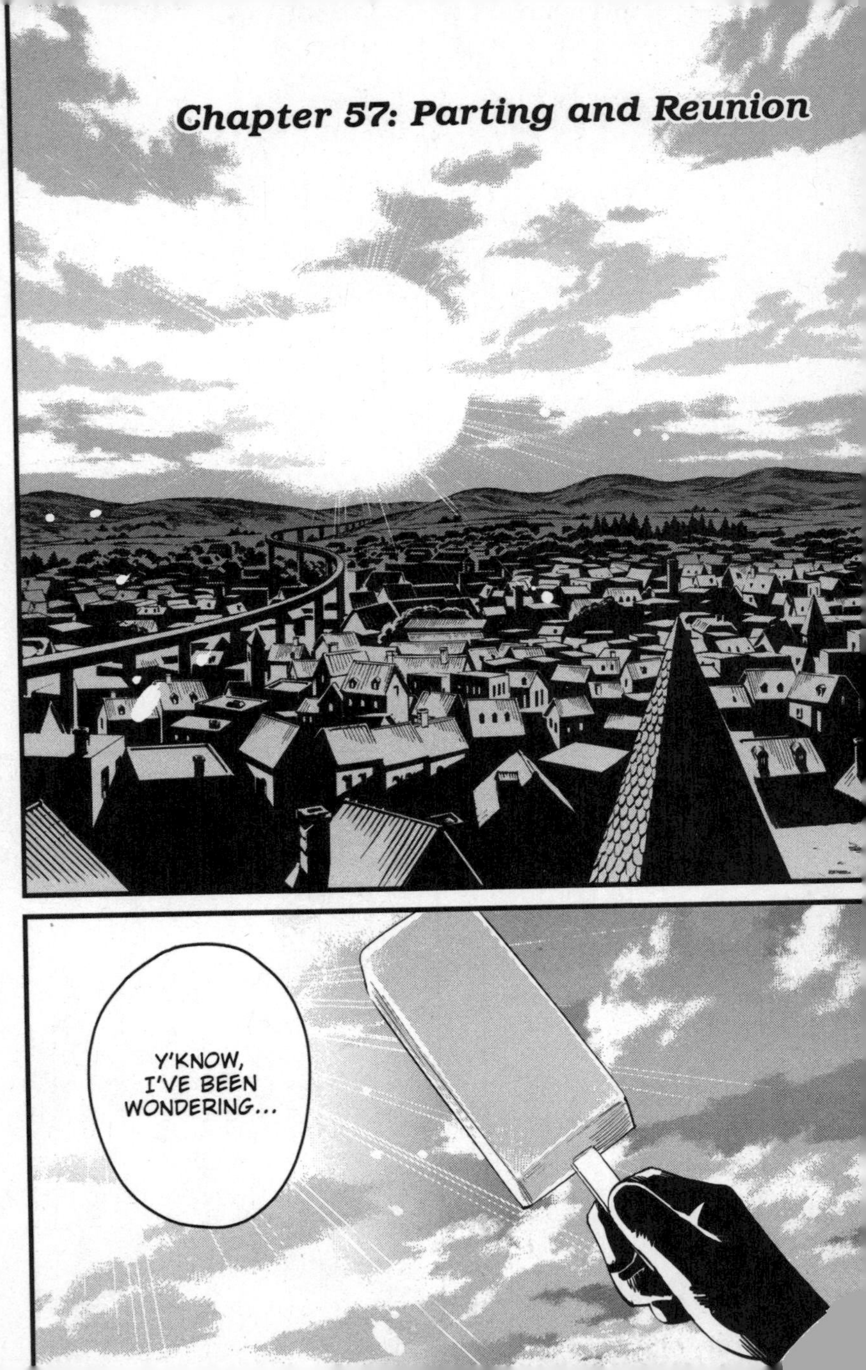
Y'KNOW, I'VE BEEN WONDERING...

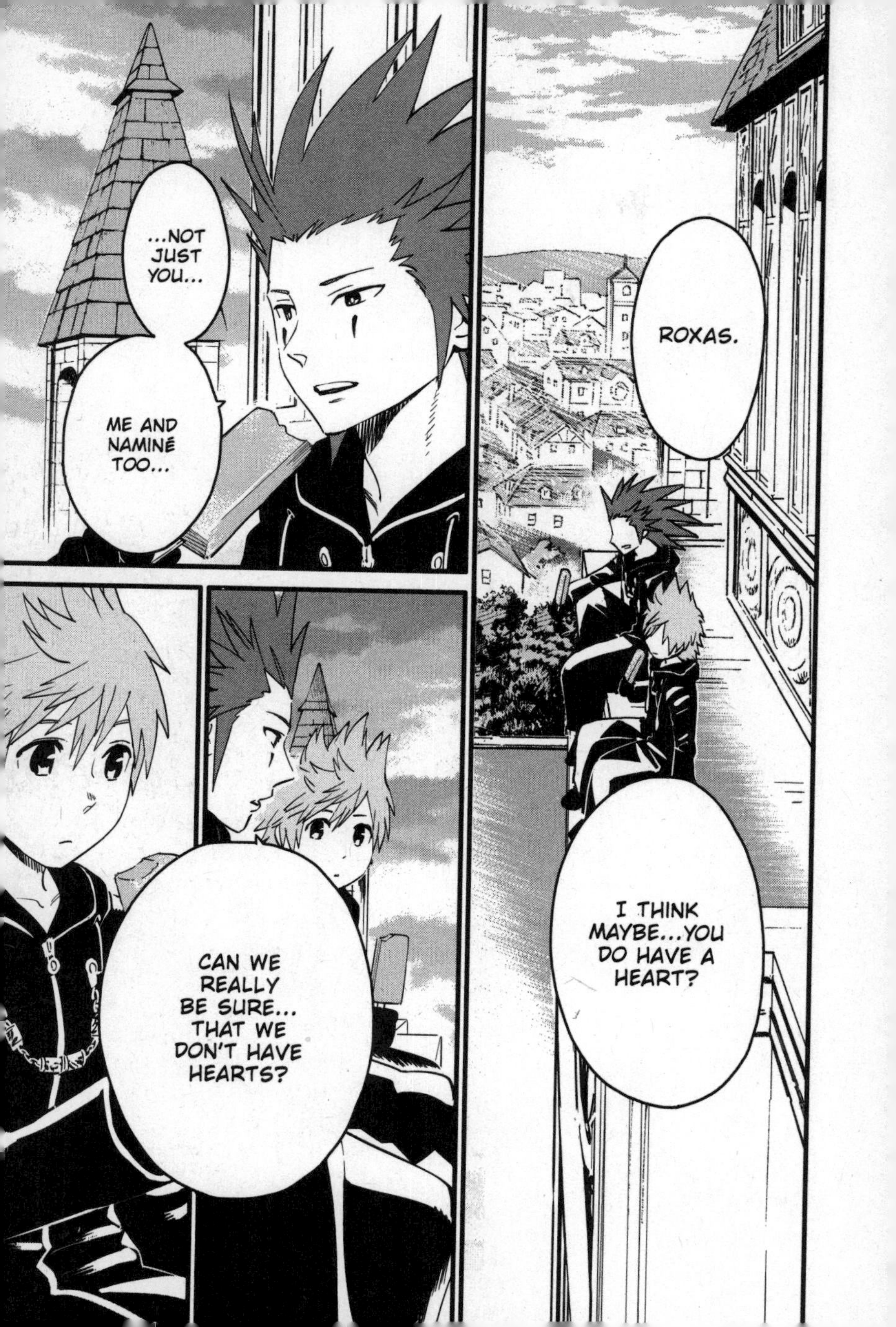
ROXAS.
I THINK MAYBE...YOU DO HAVE A HEART?
...NOT JUST YOU...
ME AND NAMINÉ TOO...
CAN WE REALLY BE SURE... THAT WE DON'T HAVE HEARTS?

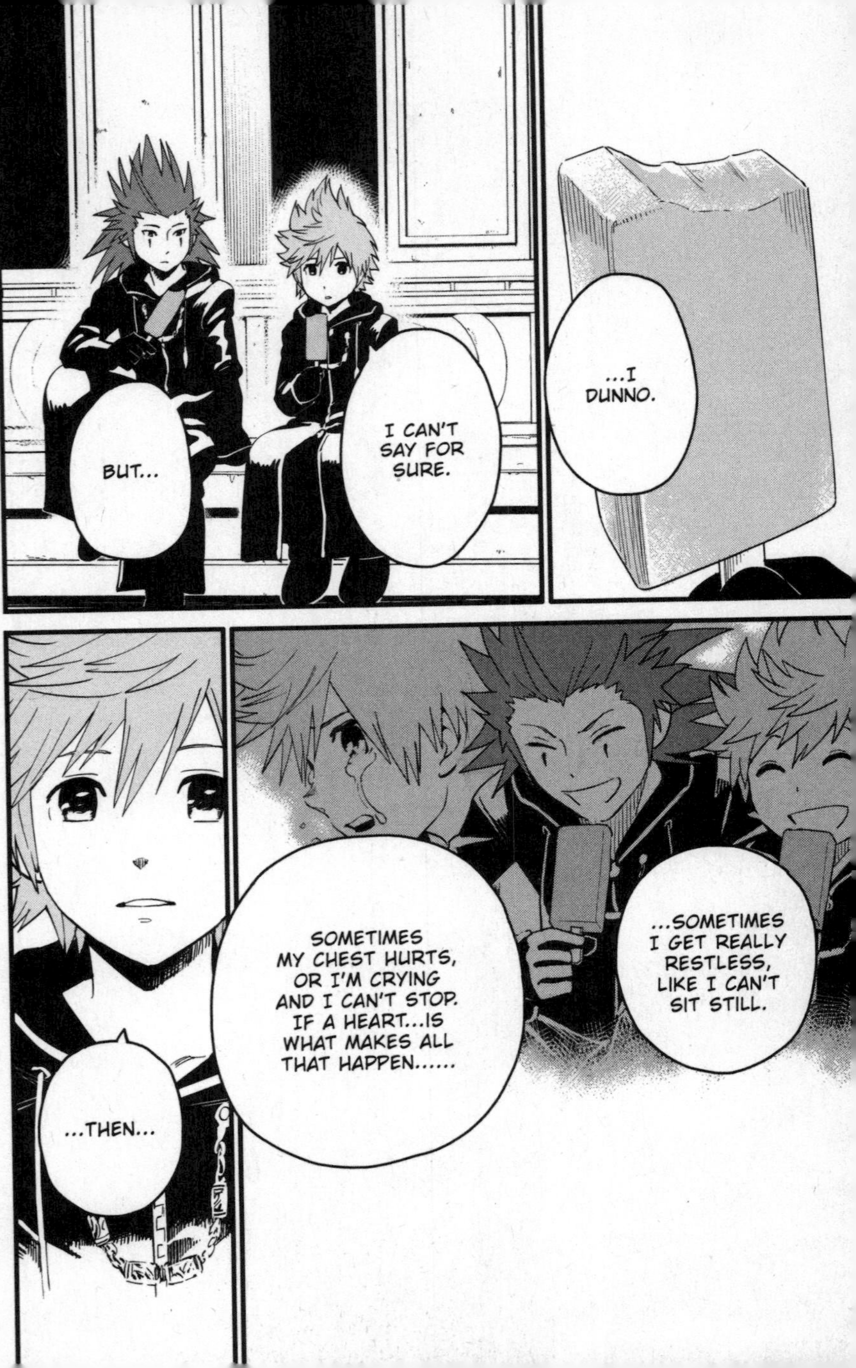
...I DUNNO.
I CAN'T SAY FOR SURE.
BUT...
...SOMETIMES I GET REALLY RESTLESS, LIKE I CAN'T SIT STILL.
SOMETIMES MY CHEST HURTS, OR I'M CRYING AND I CAN'T STOP. IF A HEART...IS WHAT MAKES ALL THAT HAPPEN......
...THEN...

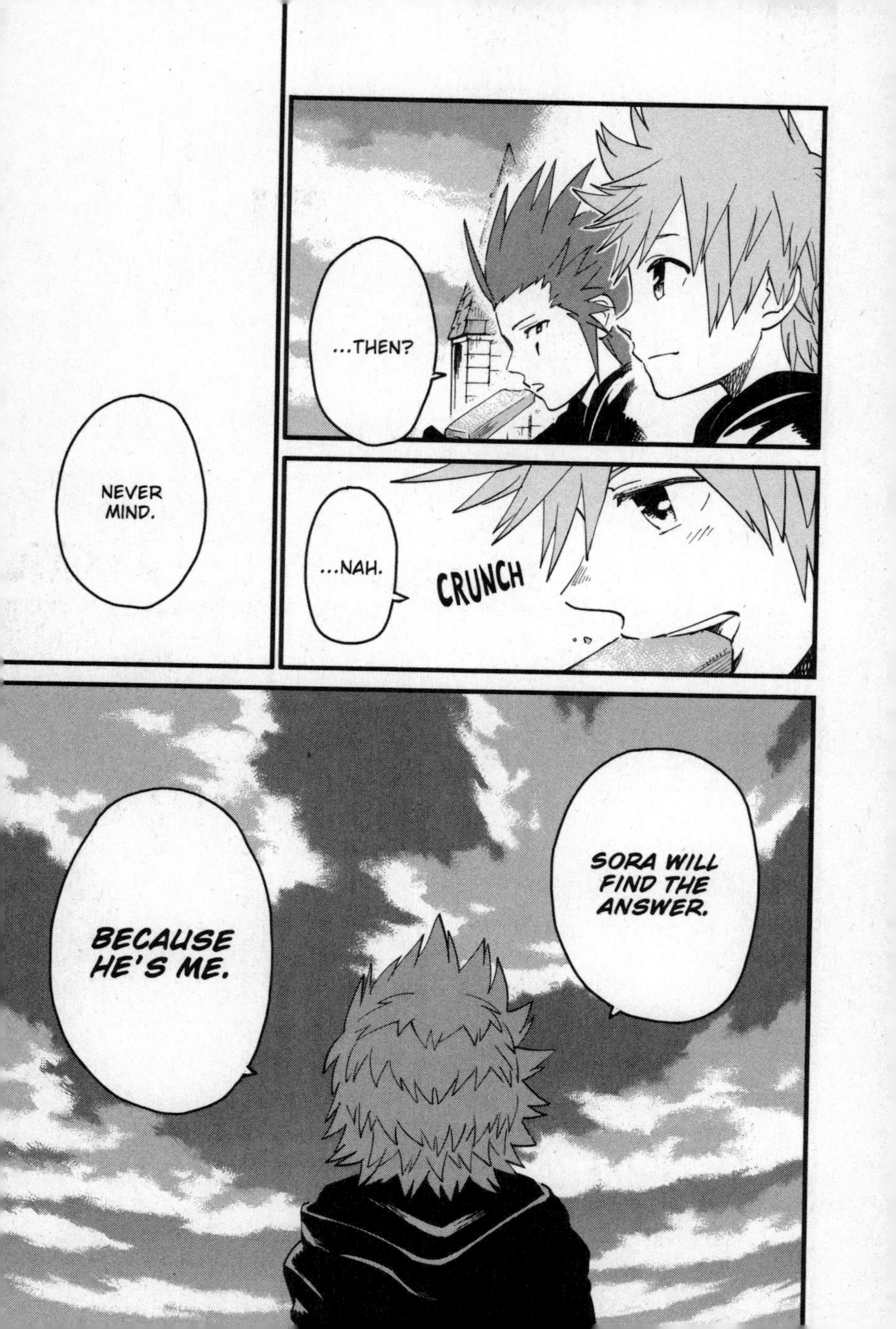
...THEN?
...NAH.
CRUNCH
NEVER MIND.
SORA WILL FIND THE ANSWER.
BECAUSE HE'S ME.

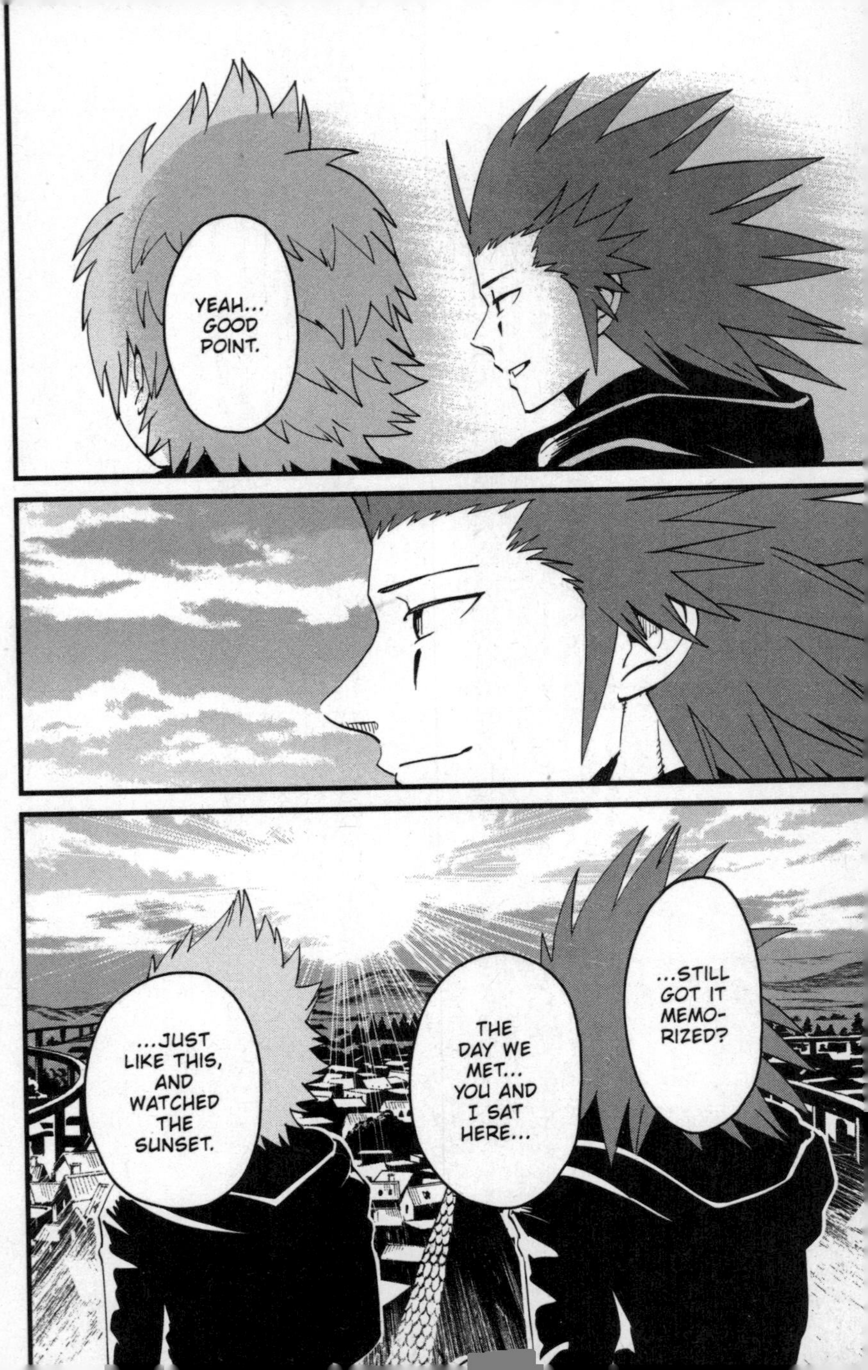
YEAH... GOOD POINT.
...STILL GOT IT MEMORIZED?
THE DAY WE MET... YOU AND I SAT HERE...
...JUST LIKE THIS, AND WATCHED THE SUNSET.

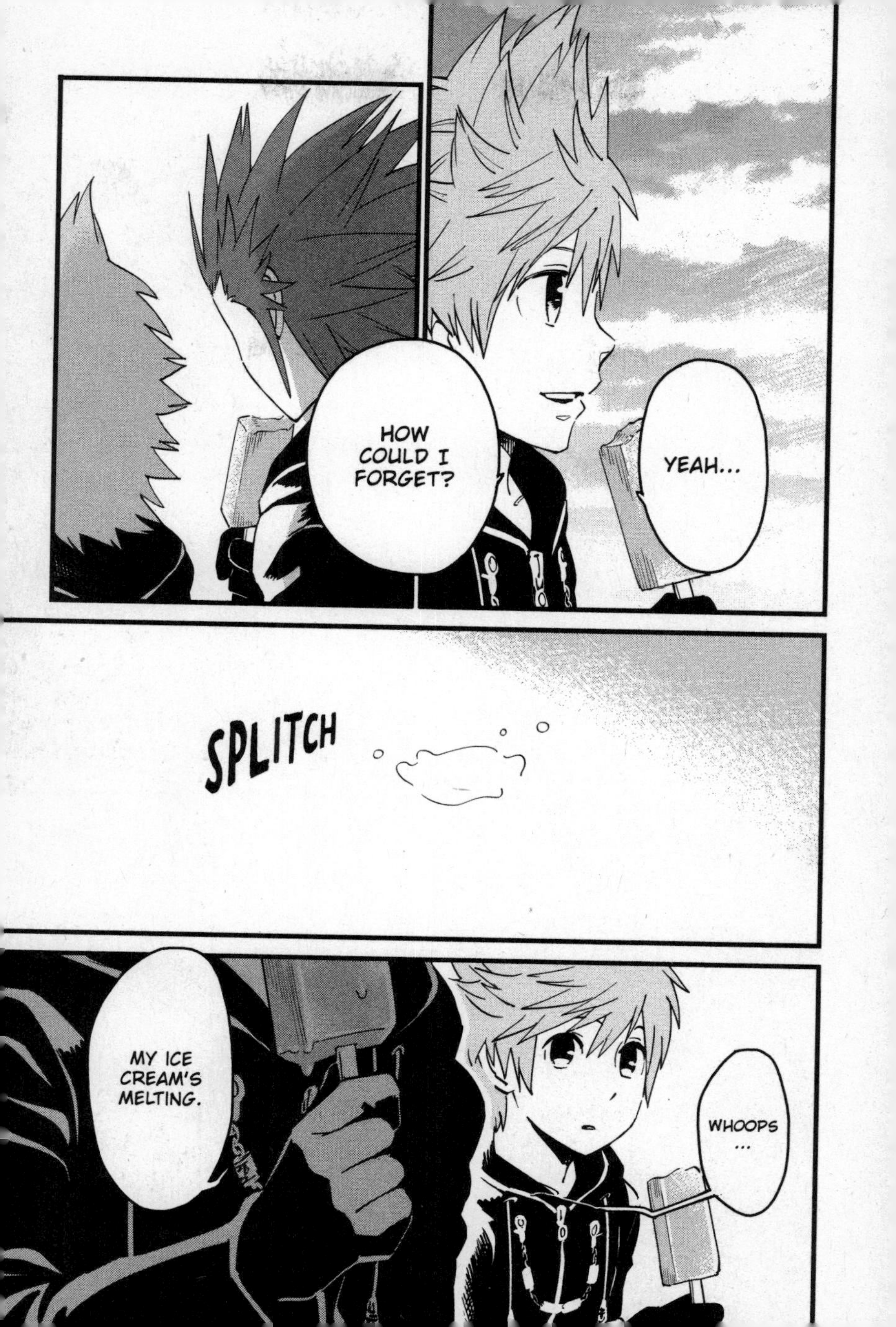
YEAH...
HOW COULD I FORGET?
SPLITCH
WHOOPS...
MY ICE CREAM'S MELTING.

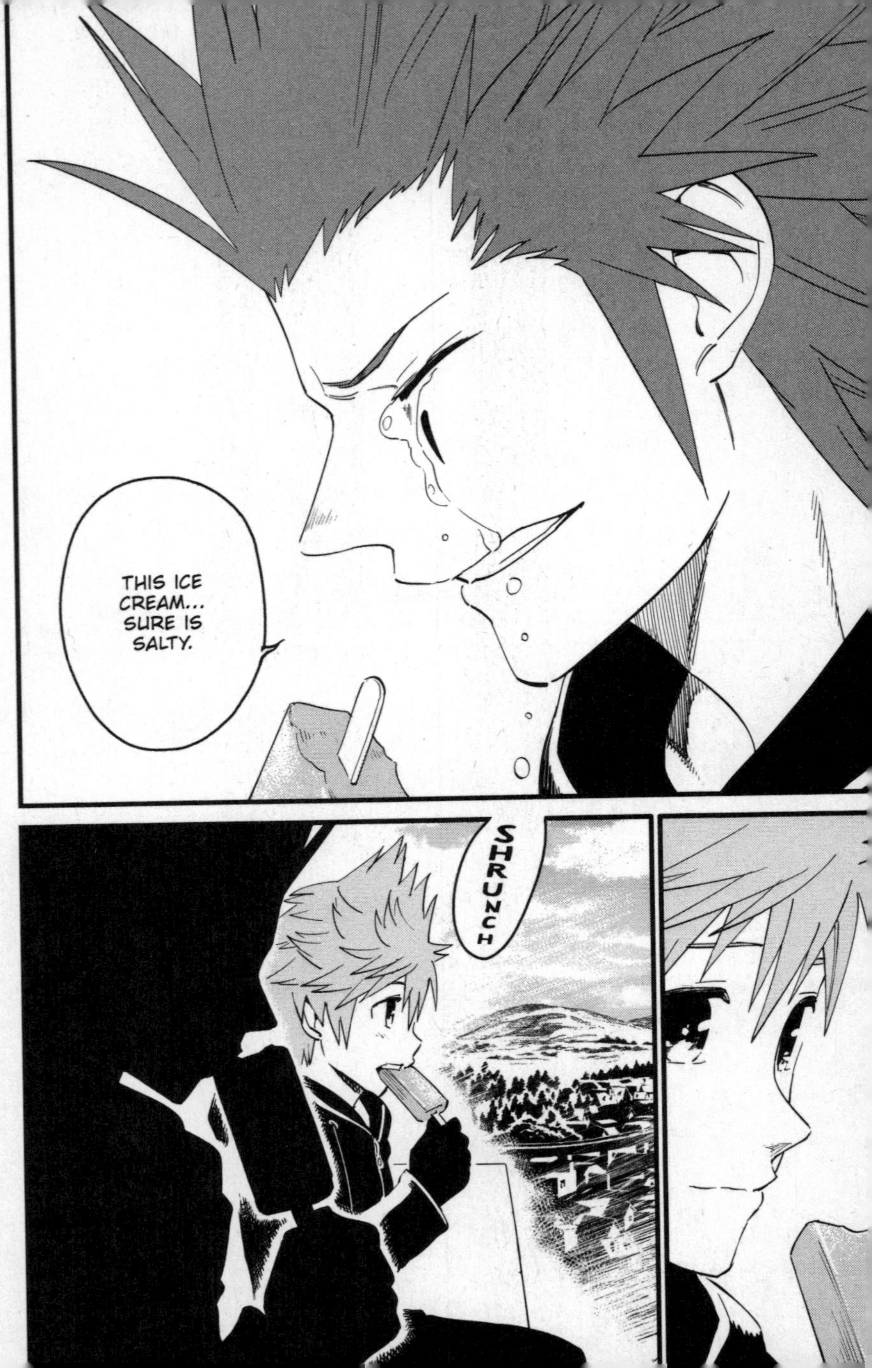
THIS ICE CREAM... SURE IS SALTY.
SHRUNCH

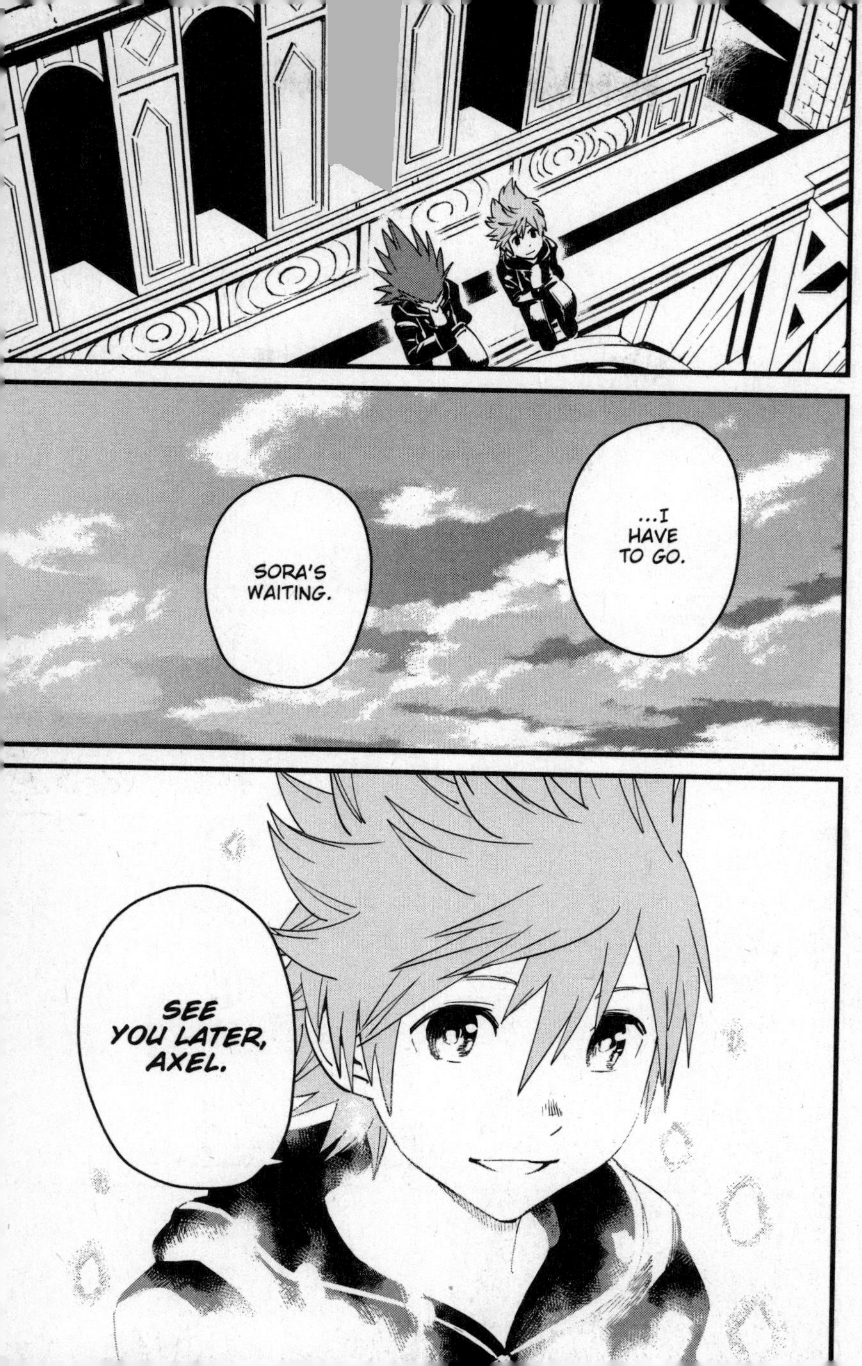
...I HAVE TO GO.
SORA'S WAITING.
SEE YOU LATER, AXEL.

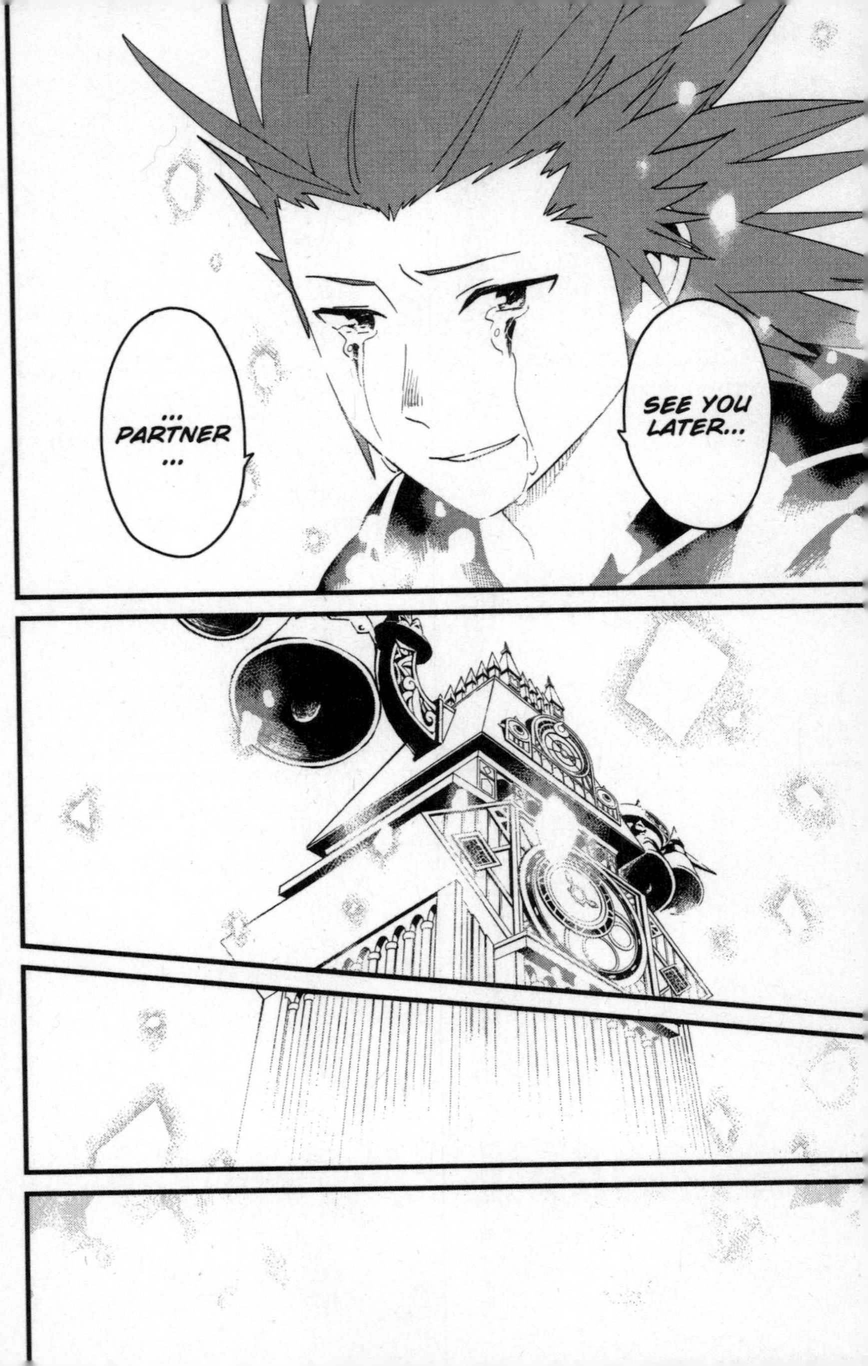
SEE YOU LATER...
...PARTNER...

I'M
GLAD
I MET
YOU—

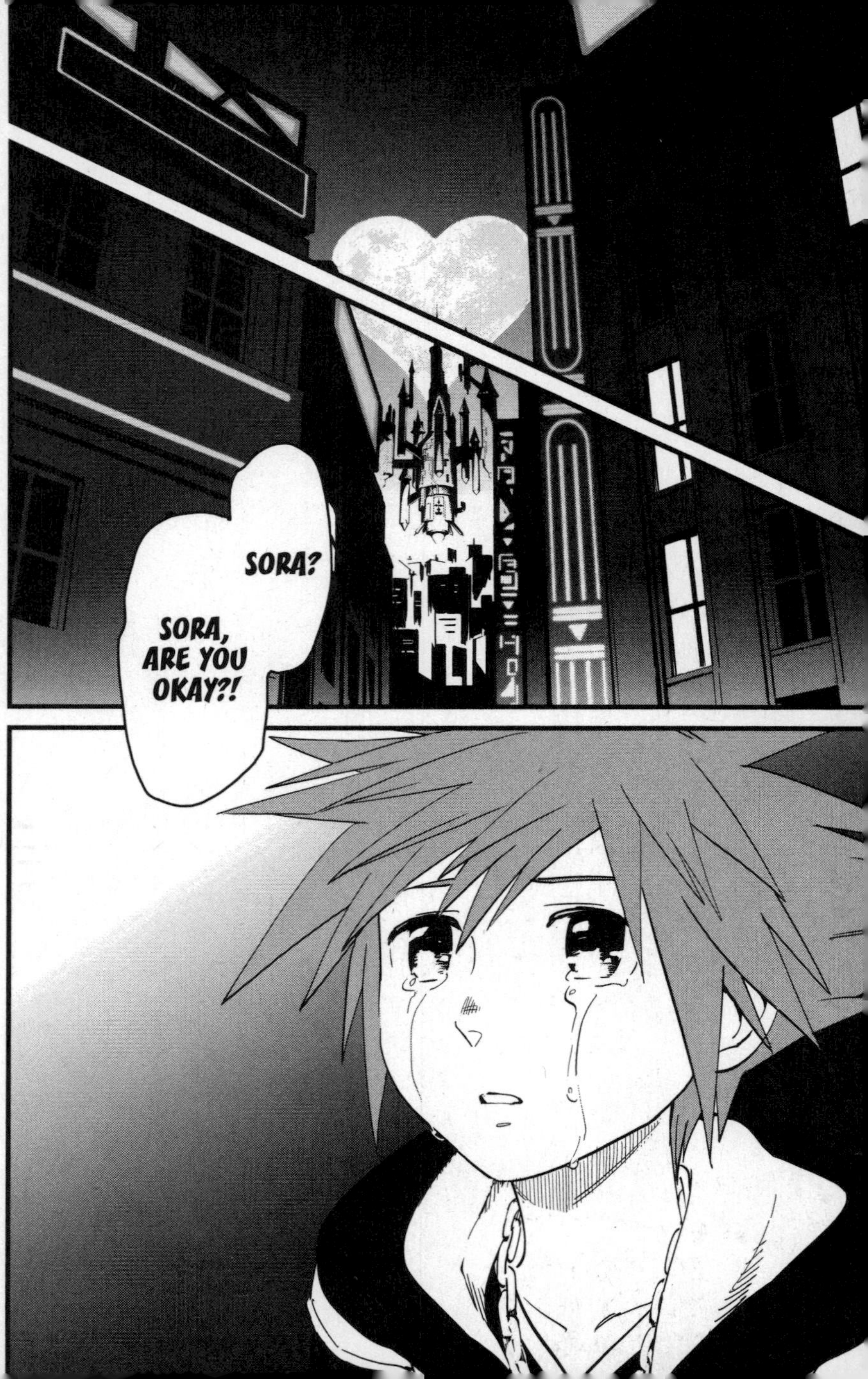
SORA?
SORA, ARE YOU OKAY?!

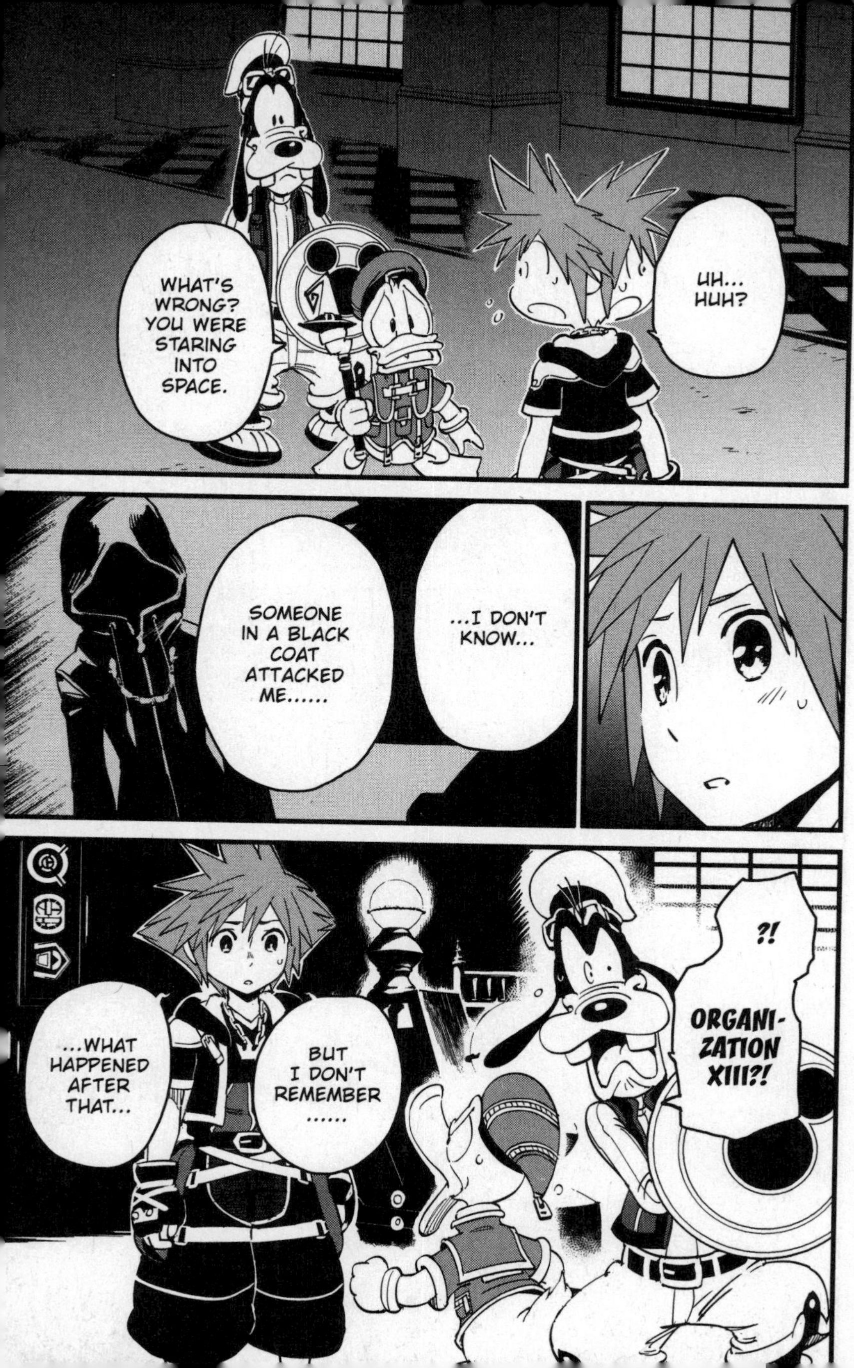
UH... HUH?
WHAT'S WRONG? YOU WERE STARING INTO SPACE.
...I DON'T KNOW...
SOMEONE IN A BLACK COAT ATTACKED ME......
?!
ORGANIZATION XIII?!
BUT I DON'T REMEMBER ......
...WHAT HAPPENED AFTER THAT...

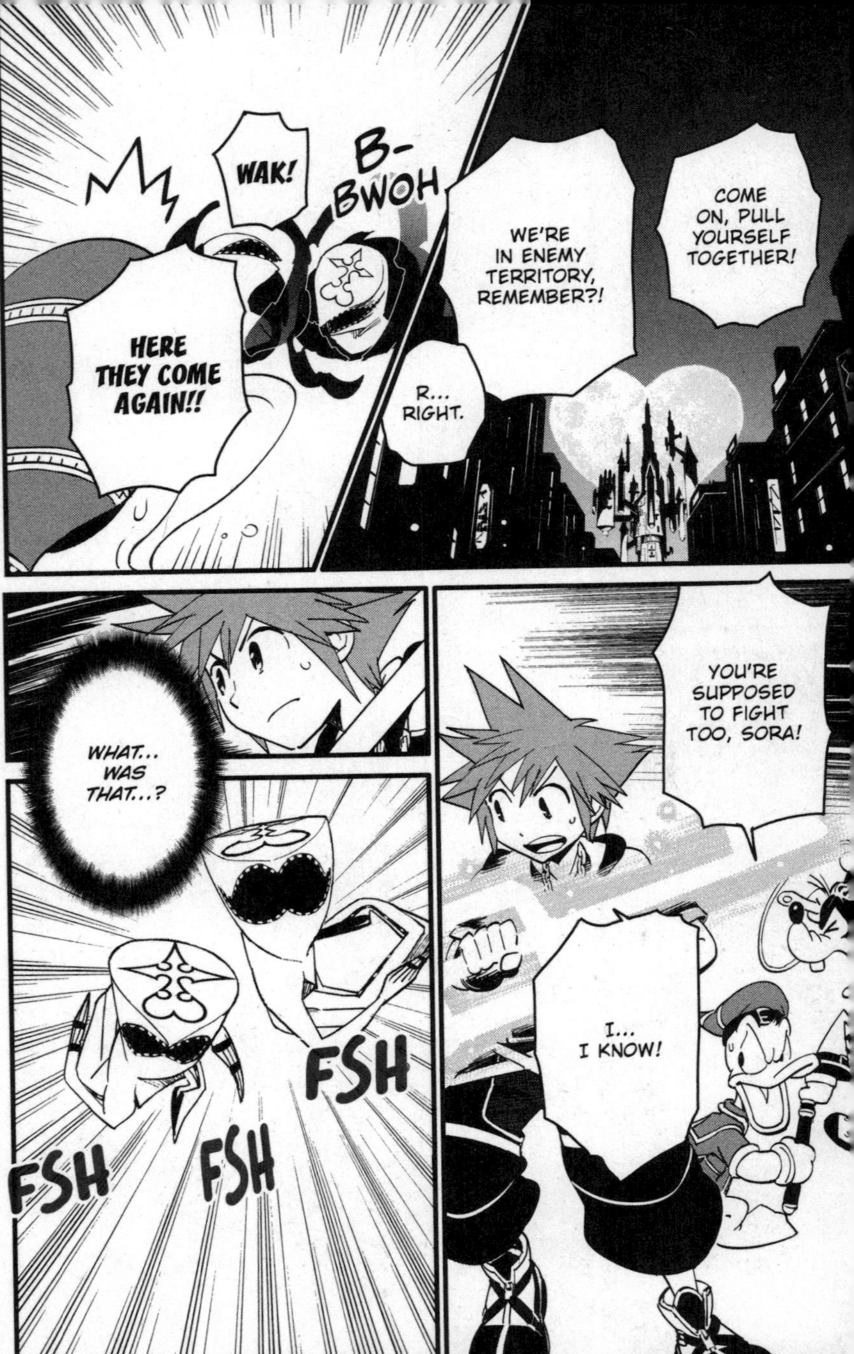
COME ON, PULL YOURSELF TOGETHER!
WE'RE IN ENEMY TERRITORY, REMEMBER?!
R... RIGHT.
WAK!
B-BWOH
HERE THEY COME AGAIN!!
YOU'RE SUPPOSED TO FIGHT TOO, SORA!
I... I KNOW!
WHAT... WAS THAT...?
FSH
FSH
FSH

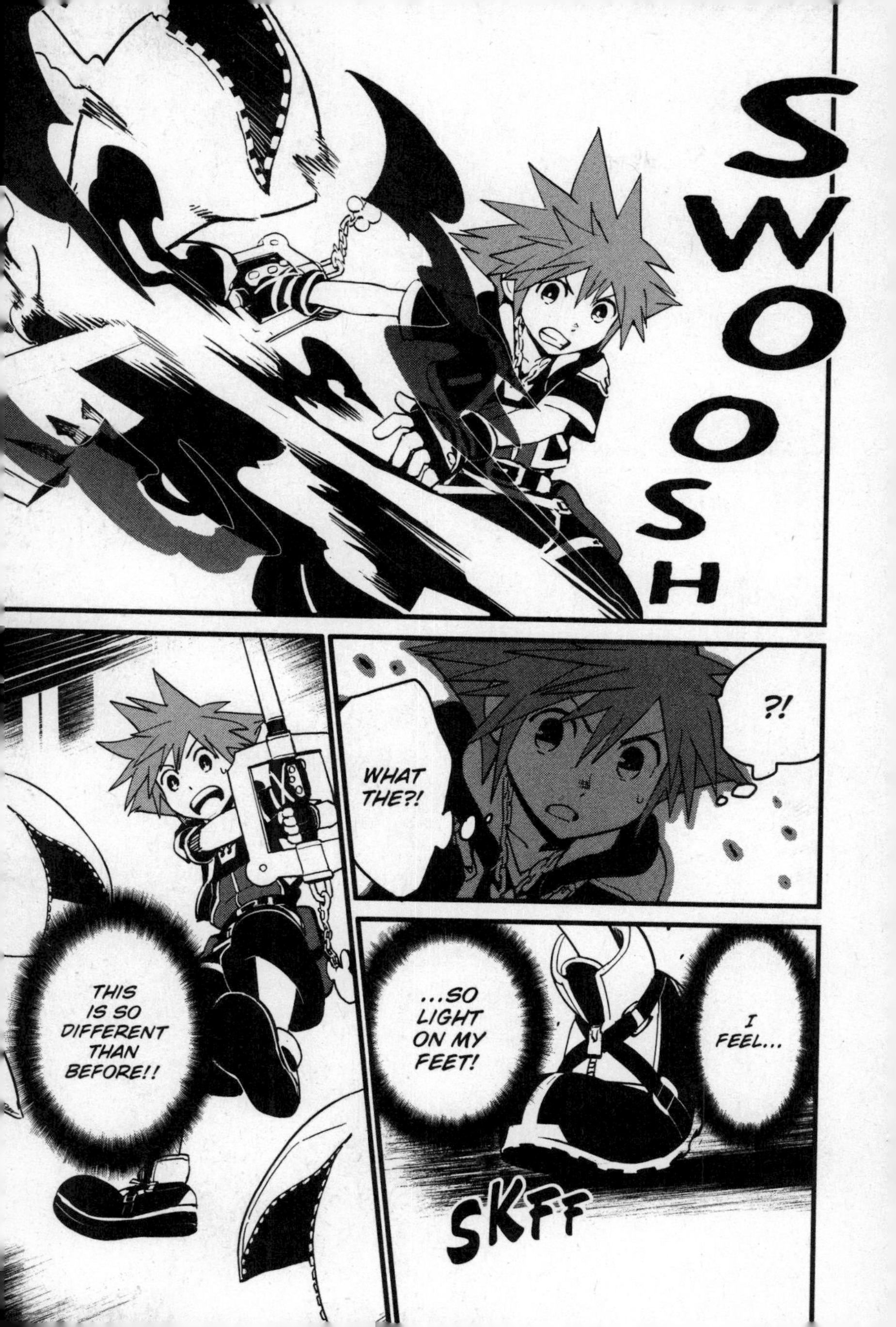
SWOOSH
?!
WHAT THE?!
I FEEL...
...SO LIGHT ON MY FEET!
SKFF
THIS IS SO DIFFERENT THAN BEFORE!!

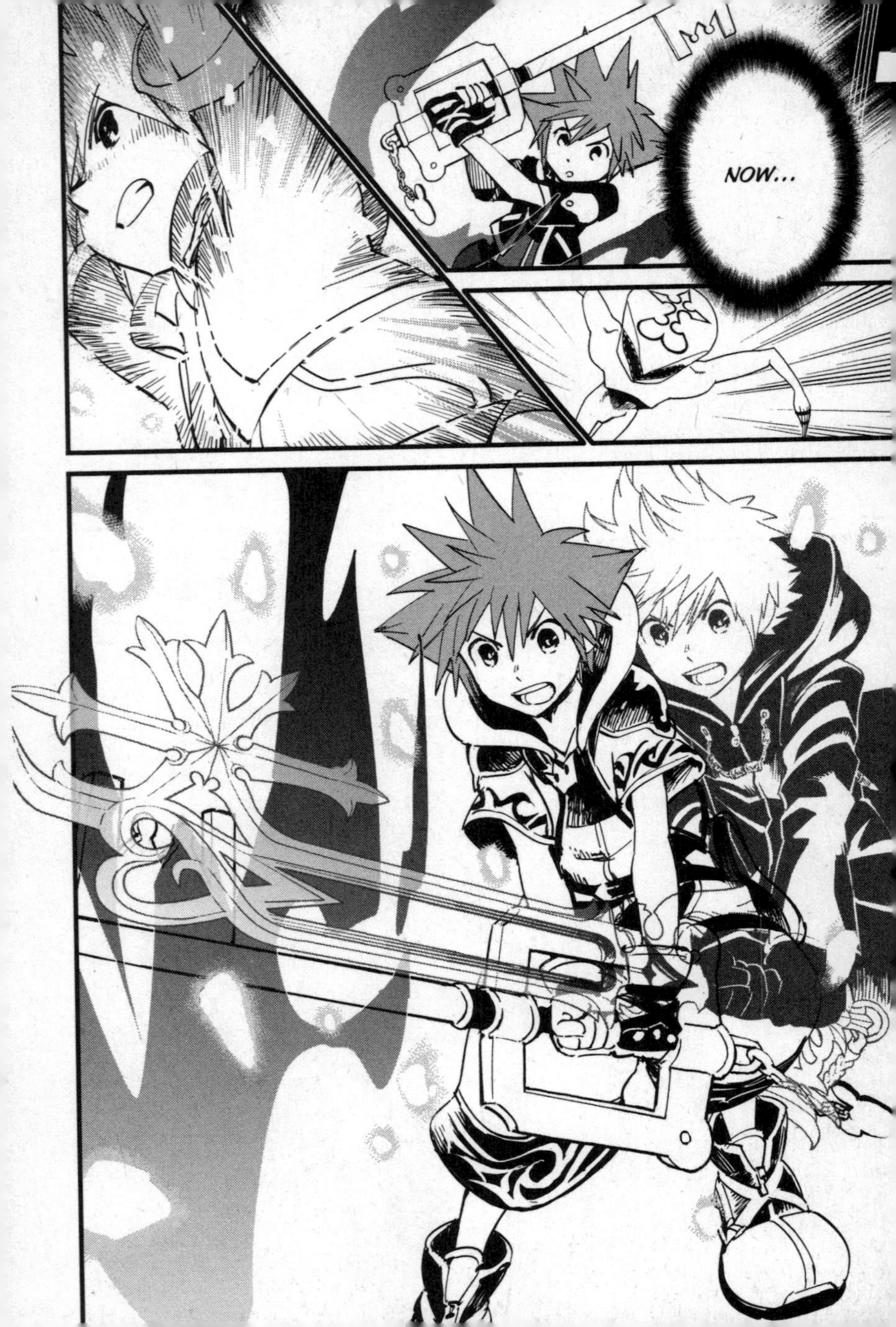
NOW...

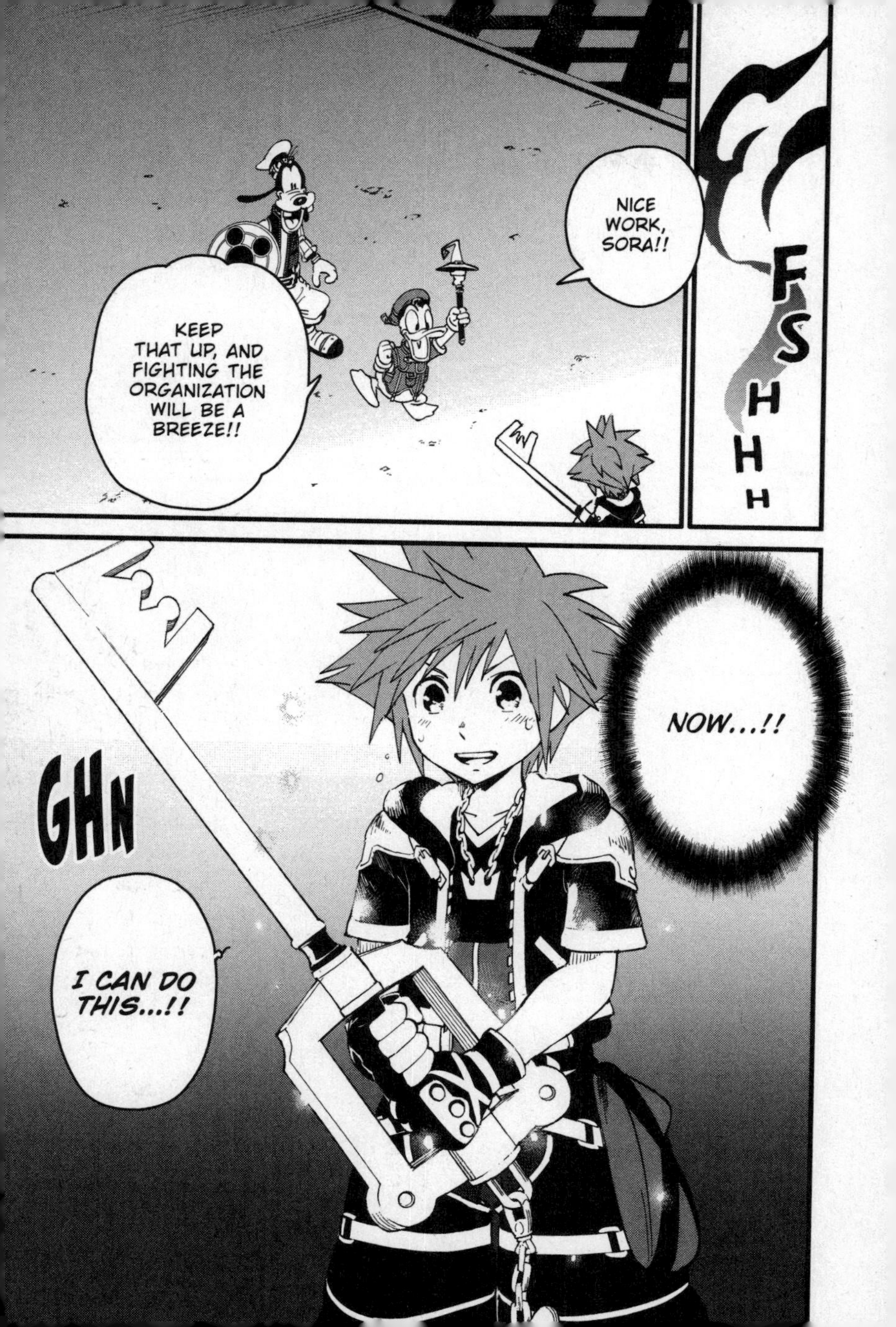
FSHHH
NICE WORK, SORA!!
KEEP THAT UP, AND FIGHTING THE ORGANIZATION WILL BE A BREEZE!!
NOW...!!
GHN
I CAN DO THIS...!!

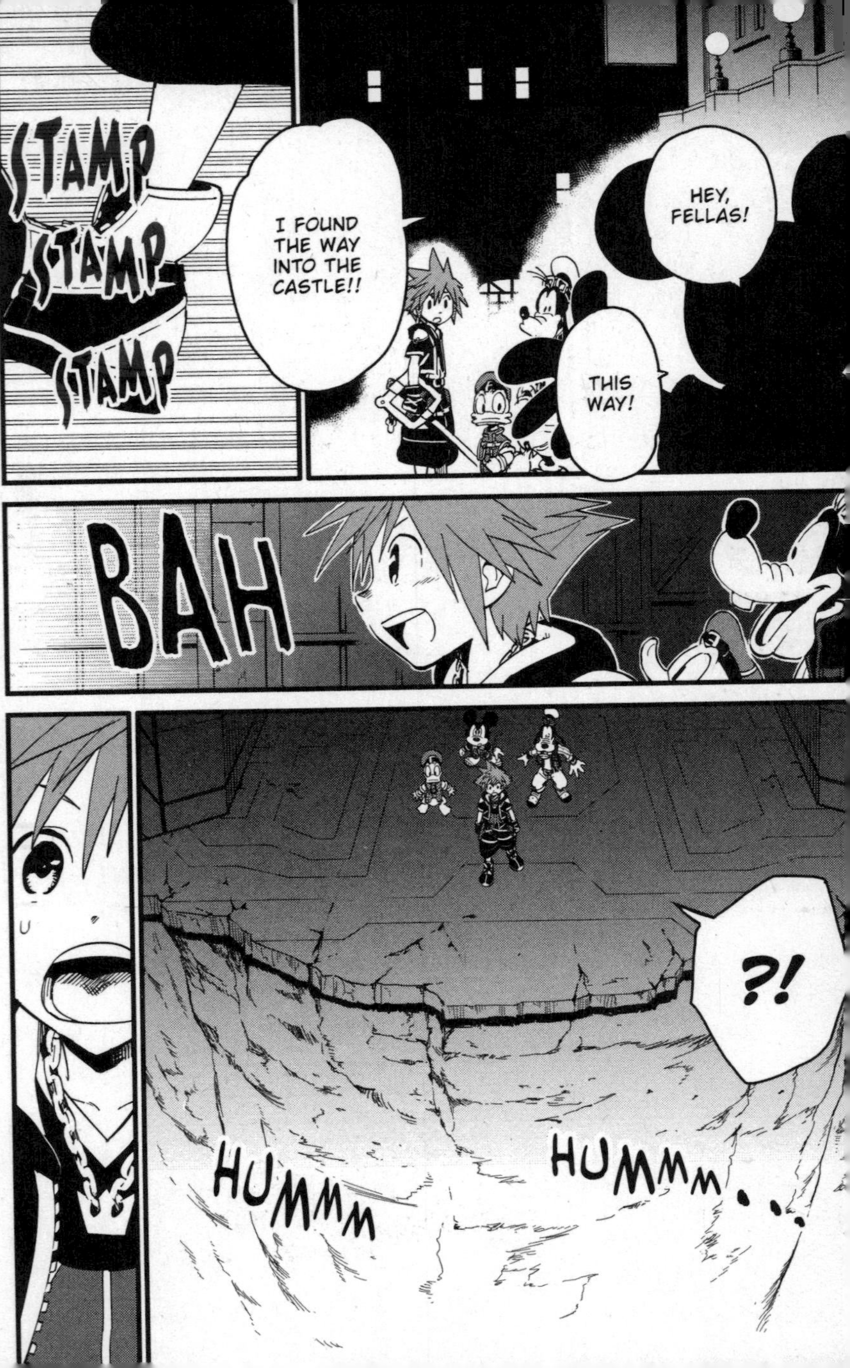
HEY, FELLAS!
I FOUND THE WAY INTO THE CASTLE!!
THIS WAY!
STAMP
STAMP
STAMP
BAH
?!
HUMMM
HUMMM...

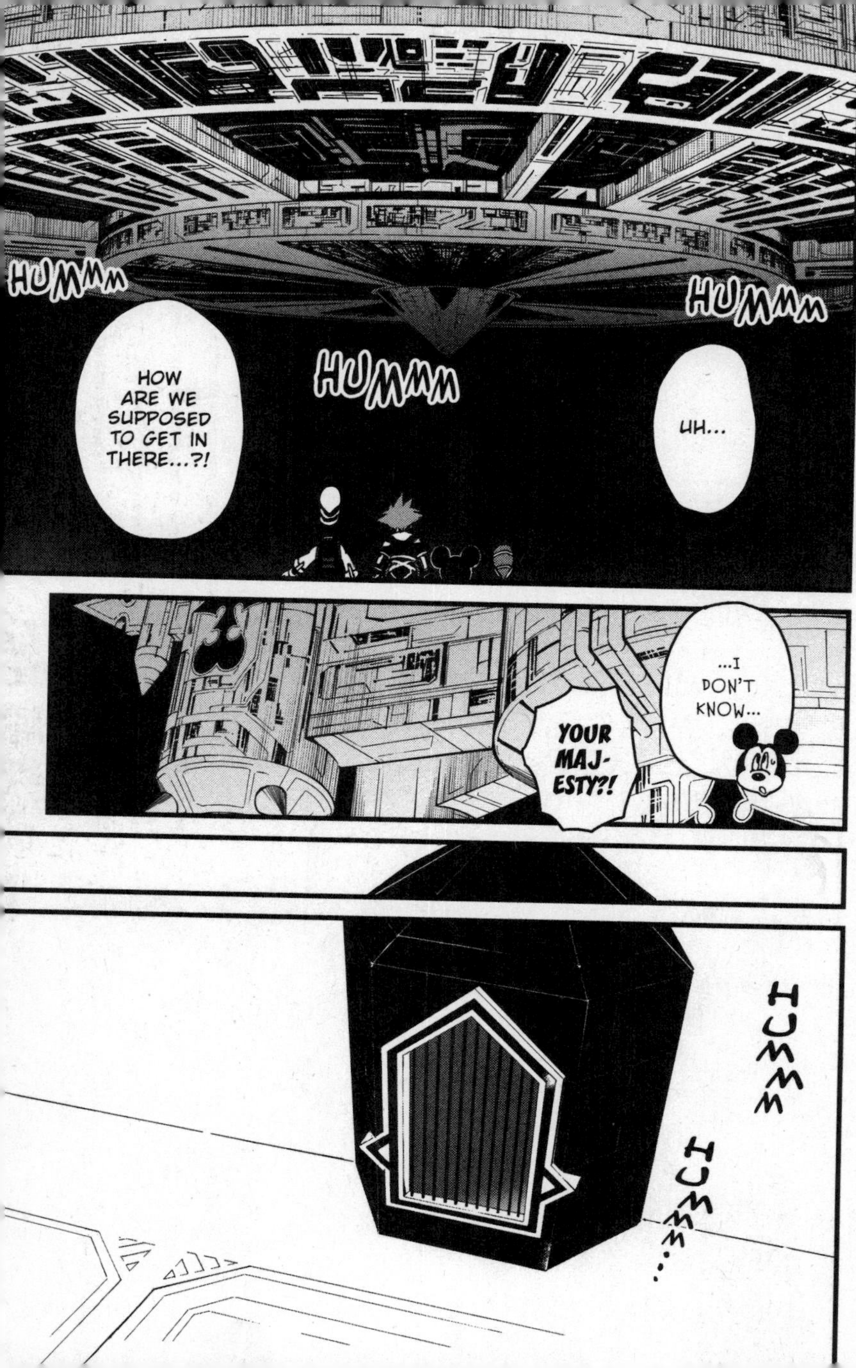
HUMMM
UH...
HUMMM
HUMMM
HOW ARE WE SUPPOSED TO GET IN THERE...?!
...I DON'T KNOW...
YOUR MAJ-ESTY?!
HUMMM
HUMMM...

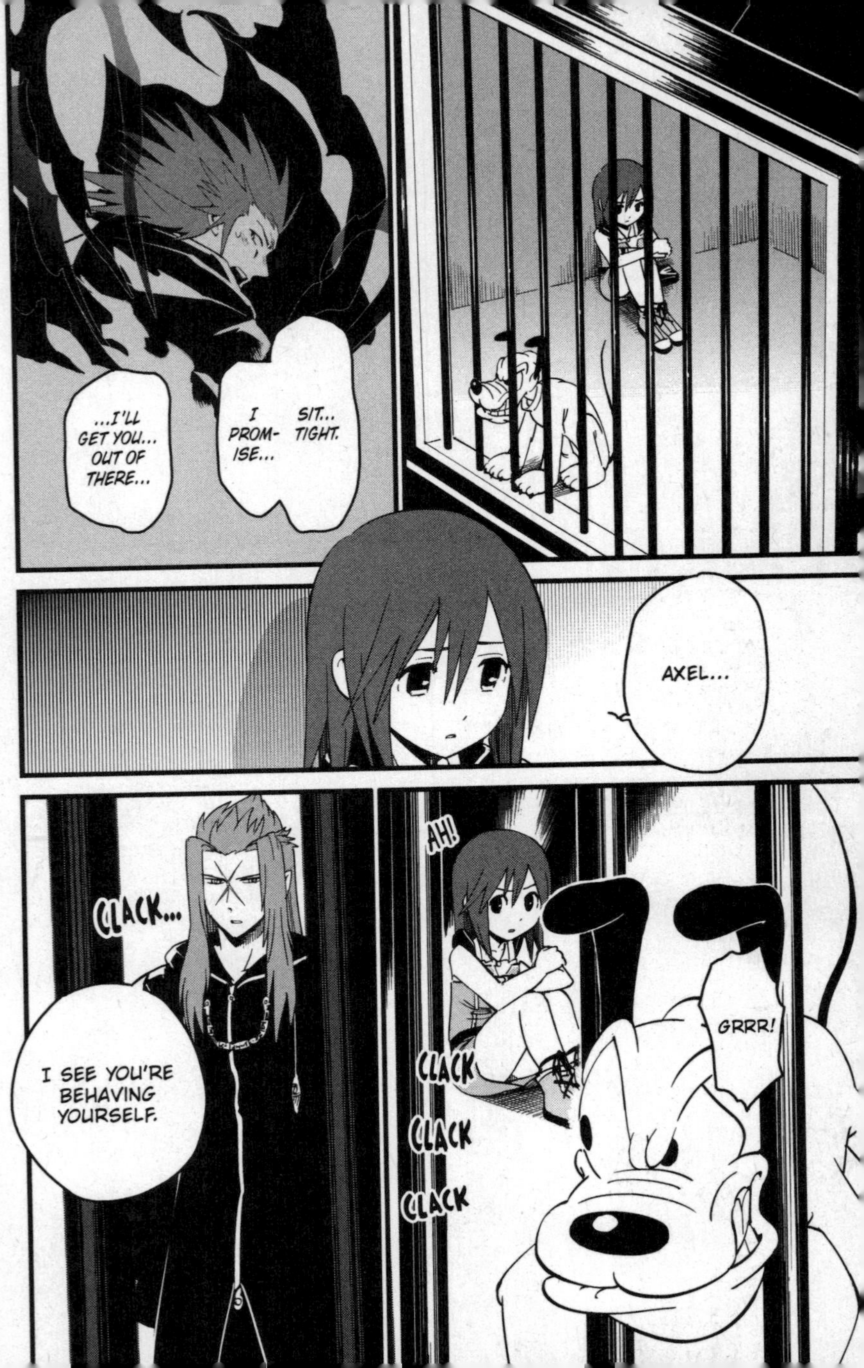
SIT... TIGHT.
I PROMISE...
...I'LL GET YOU... OUT OF THERE...
AXEL...
AH!
GRRR!
CLACK
CLACK
CLACK
CLACK...
I SEE YOU'RE BEHAVING YOURSELF.

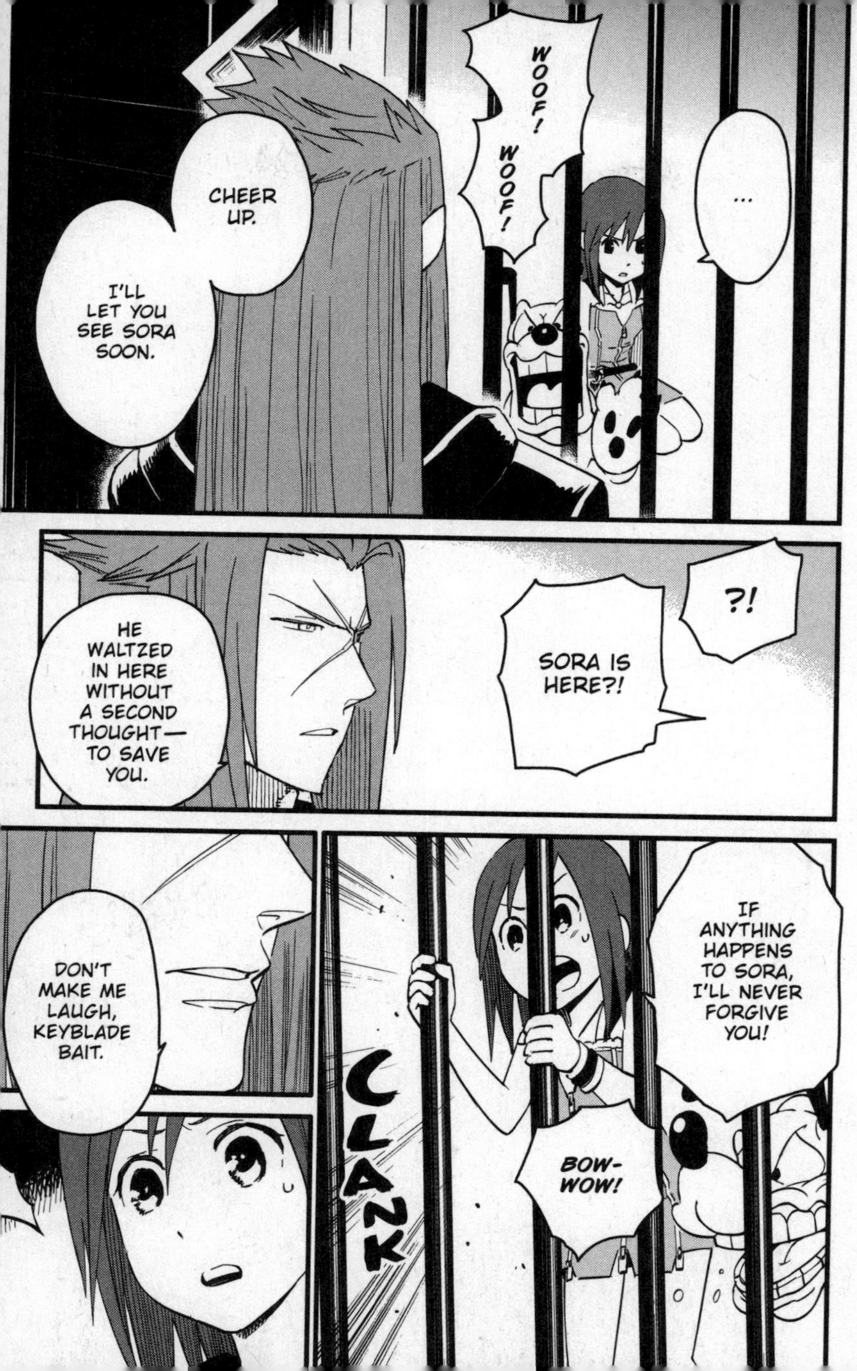
...
WOOF! WOOF!
CHEER UP.
I'LL LET YOU SEE SORA SOON.
?!
SORA IS HERE?!
HE WALTZED IN HERE WITHOUT A SECOND THOUGHT—TO SAVE YOU.
IF ANYTHING HAPPENS TO SORA, I'LL NEVER FORGIVE YOU!
BOW-WOW!
CLANK
DON'T MAKE ME LAUGH, KEYBLADE BAIT.

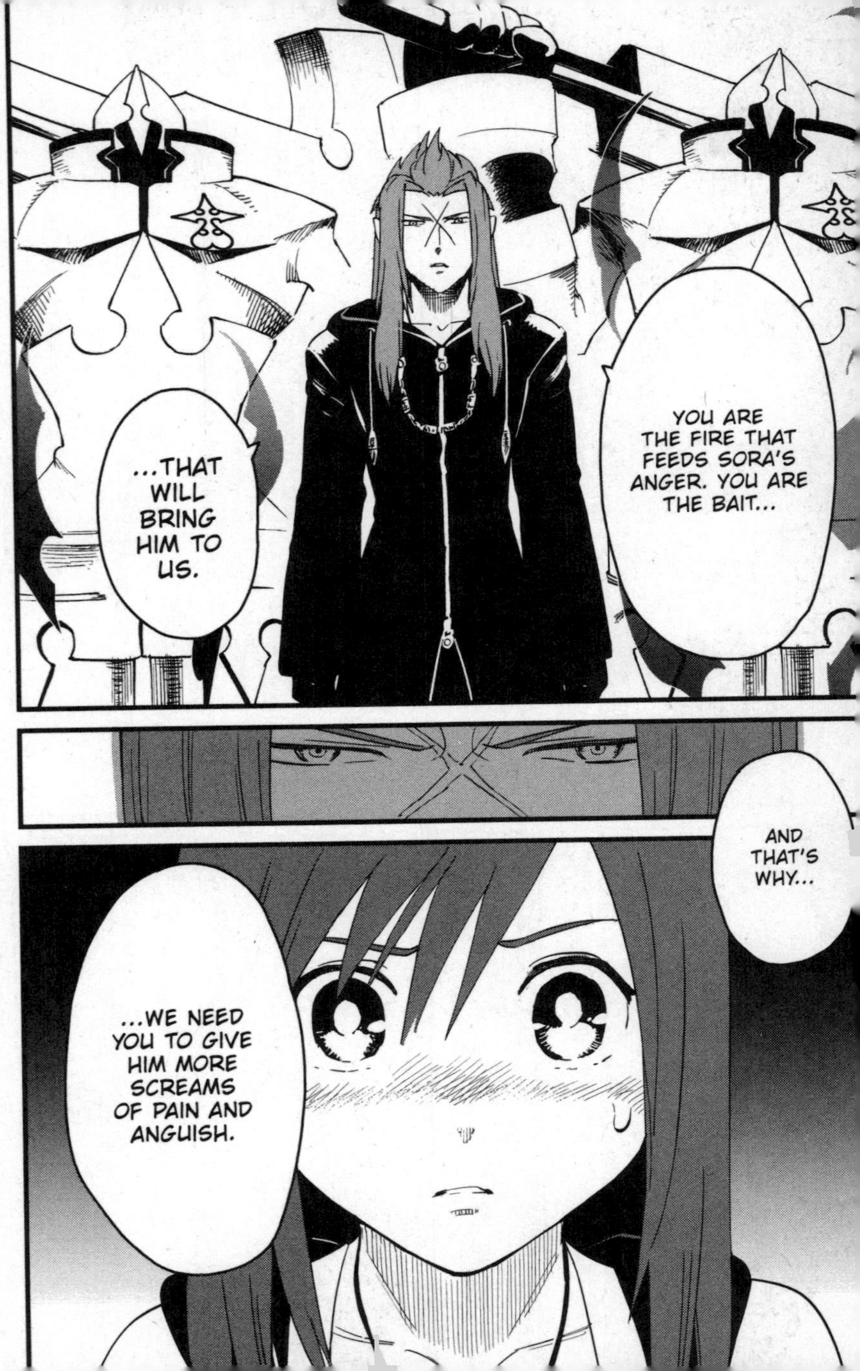
YOU ARE THE FIRE THAT FEEDS SORA'S ANGER. YOU ARE THE BAIT...
...THAT WILL BRING HIM TO US.
AND THAT'S WHY...
...WE NEED YOU TO GIVE HIM MORE SCREAMS OF PAIN AND ANGUISH.

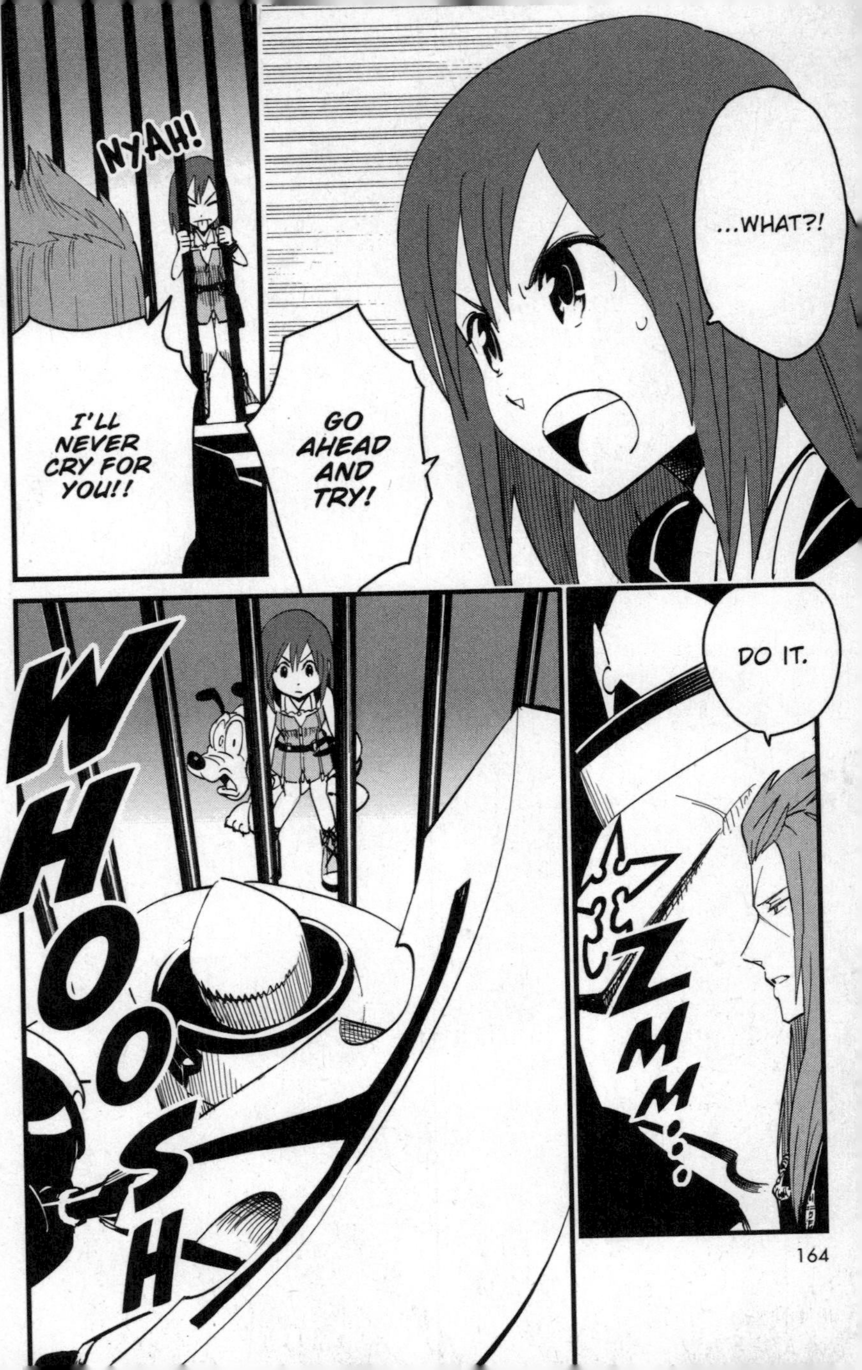
...WHAT?!
GO AHEAD AND TRY!
NYAH!
I'LL NEVER CRY FOR YOU!!
DO IT.
ZMMM...
WHOOSH

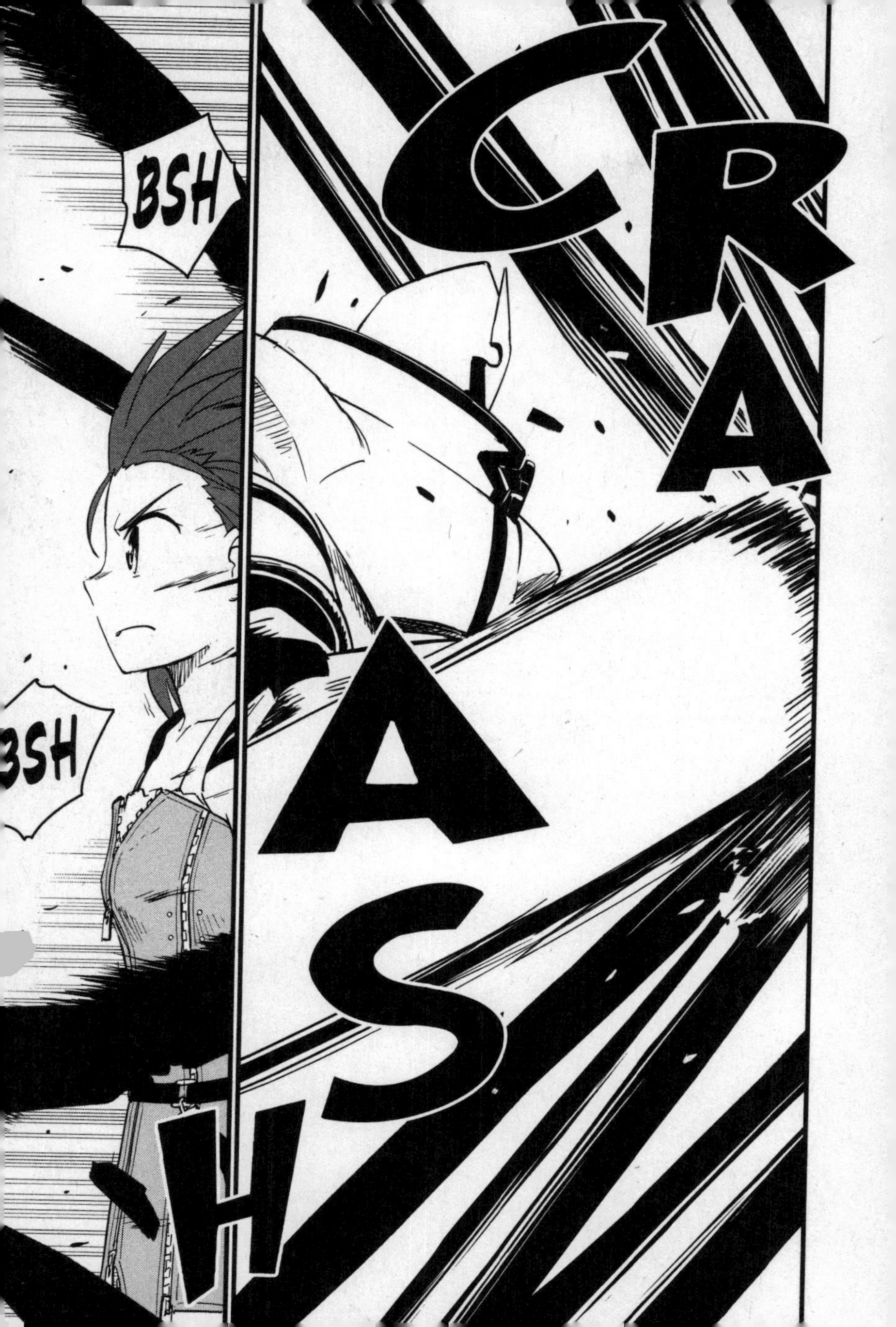
CRAASH
BSH

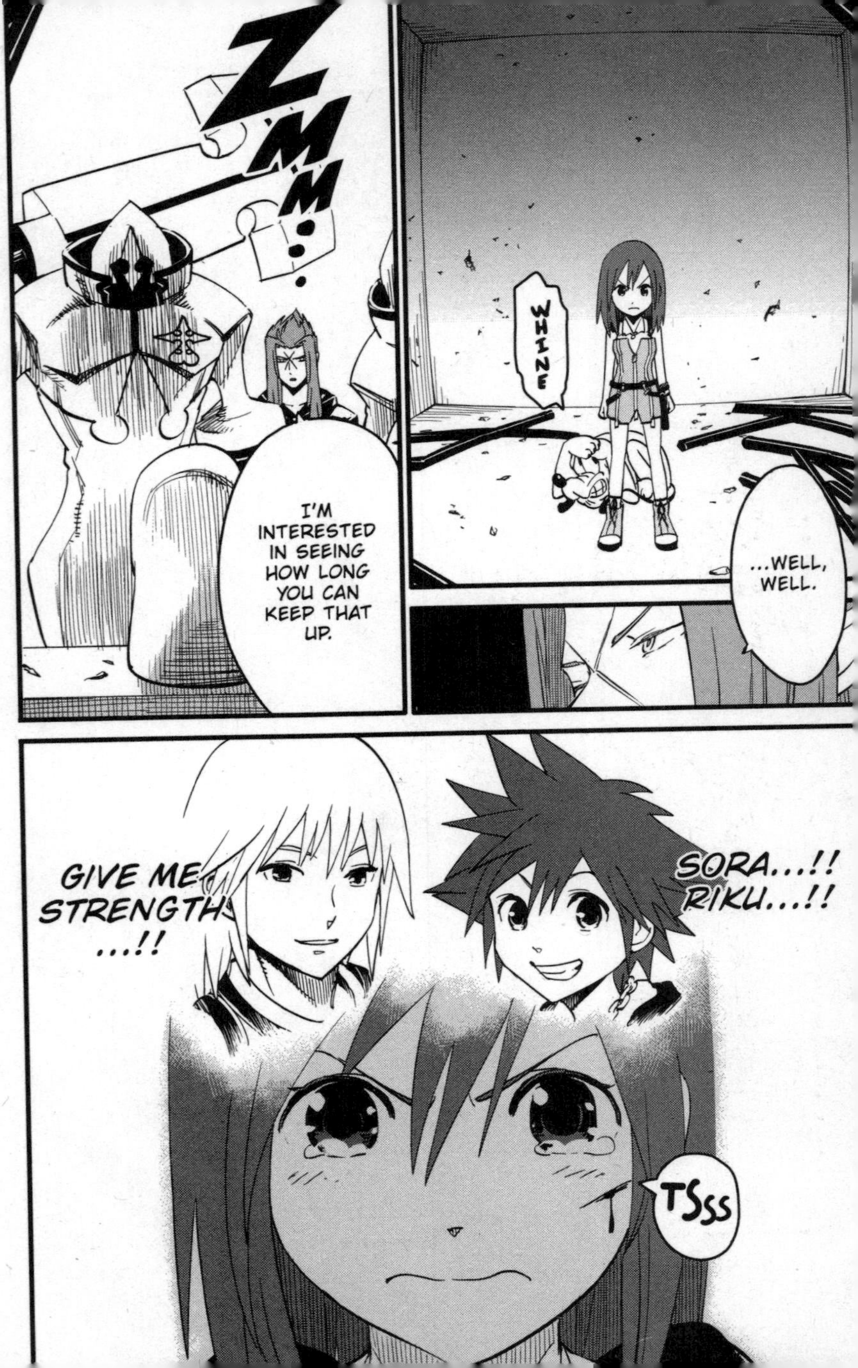
WHINE
...WELL, WELL.
ZMMM!
I'M INTERESTED IN SEEING HOW LONG YOU CAN KEEP THAT UP.
SORA...!! RIKU...!!
GIVE ME STRENGTH...!!
TSSS

Chapter 58: Riku's Secret

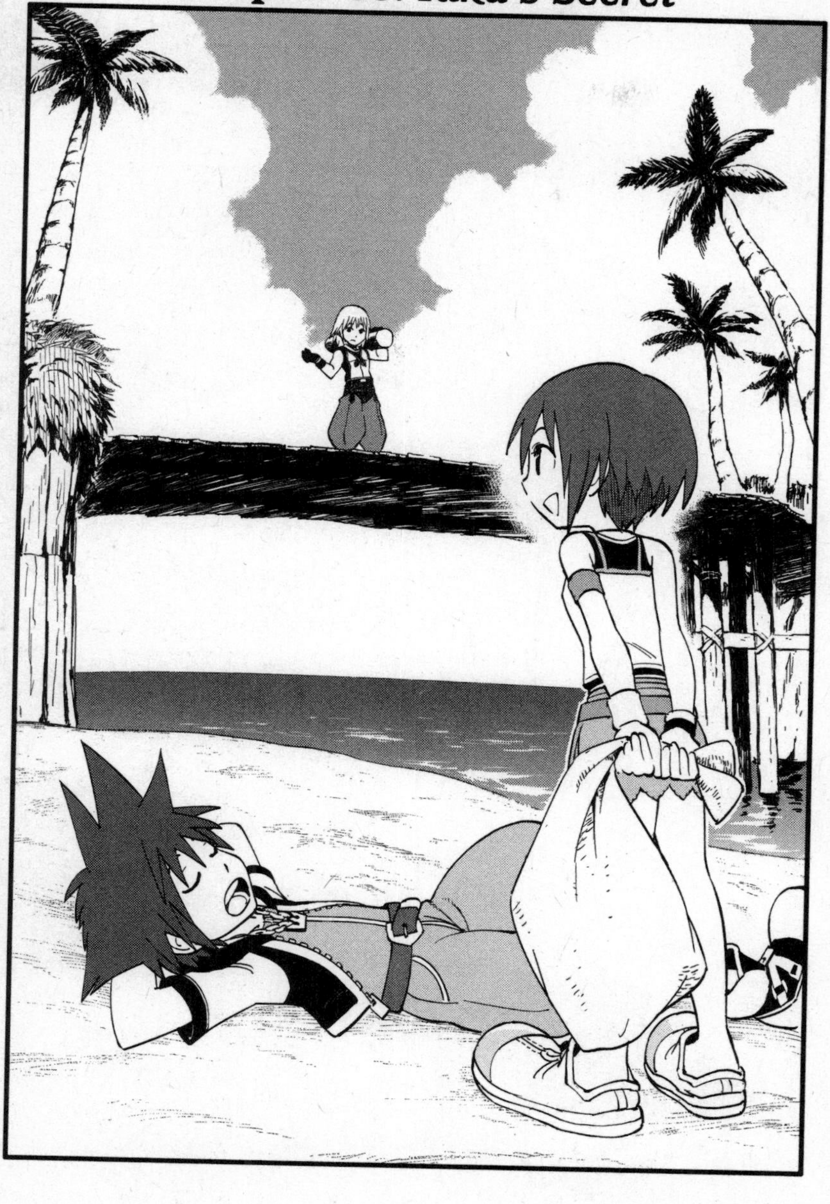

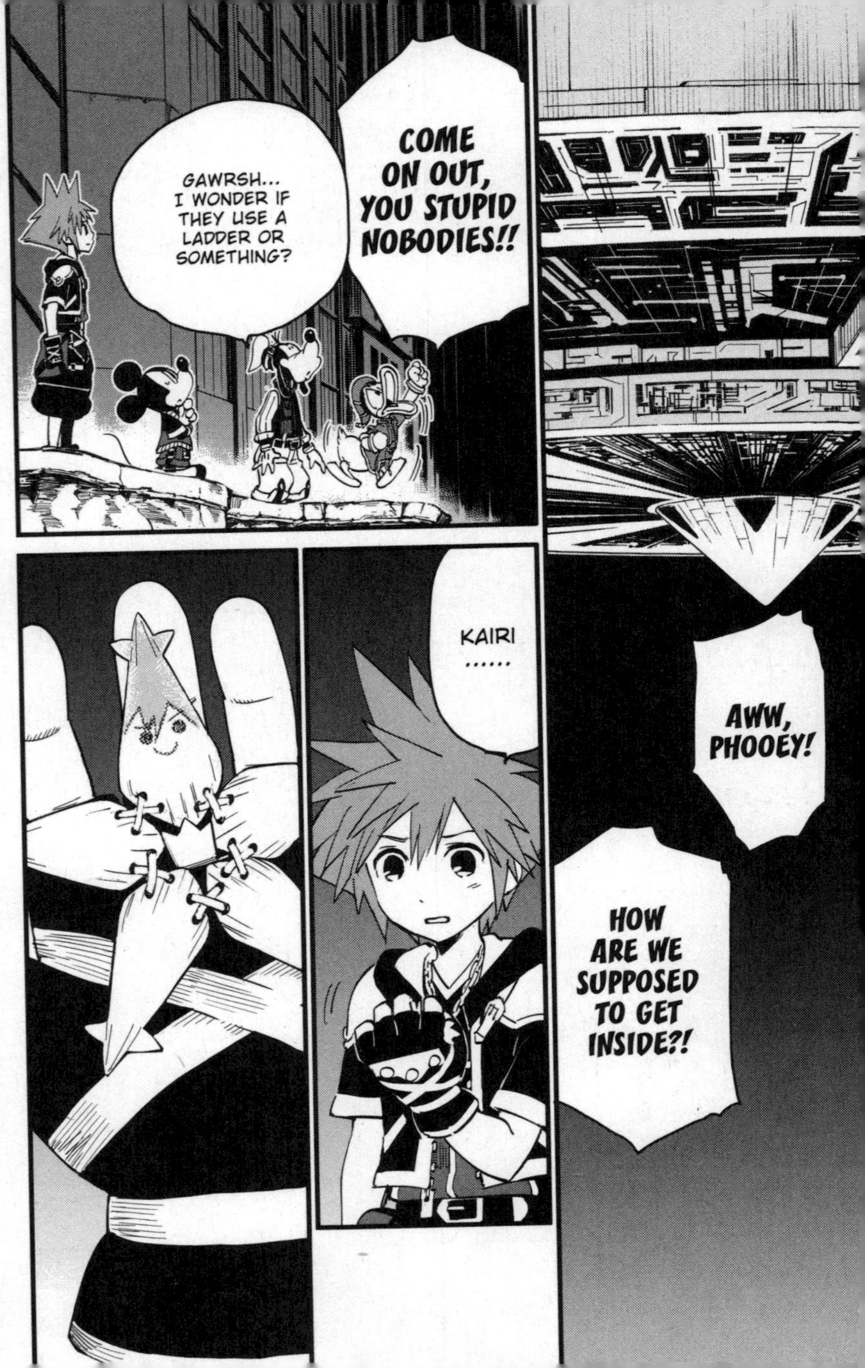
COME ON OUT, YOU STUPID NOBODIES!!
GAWRSH... I WONDER IF THEY USE A LADDER OR SOMETHING?
AWW, PHOOEY!
HOW ARE WE SUPPOSED TO GET INSIDE?!
KAIRI ......

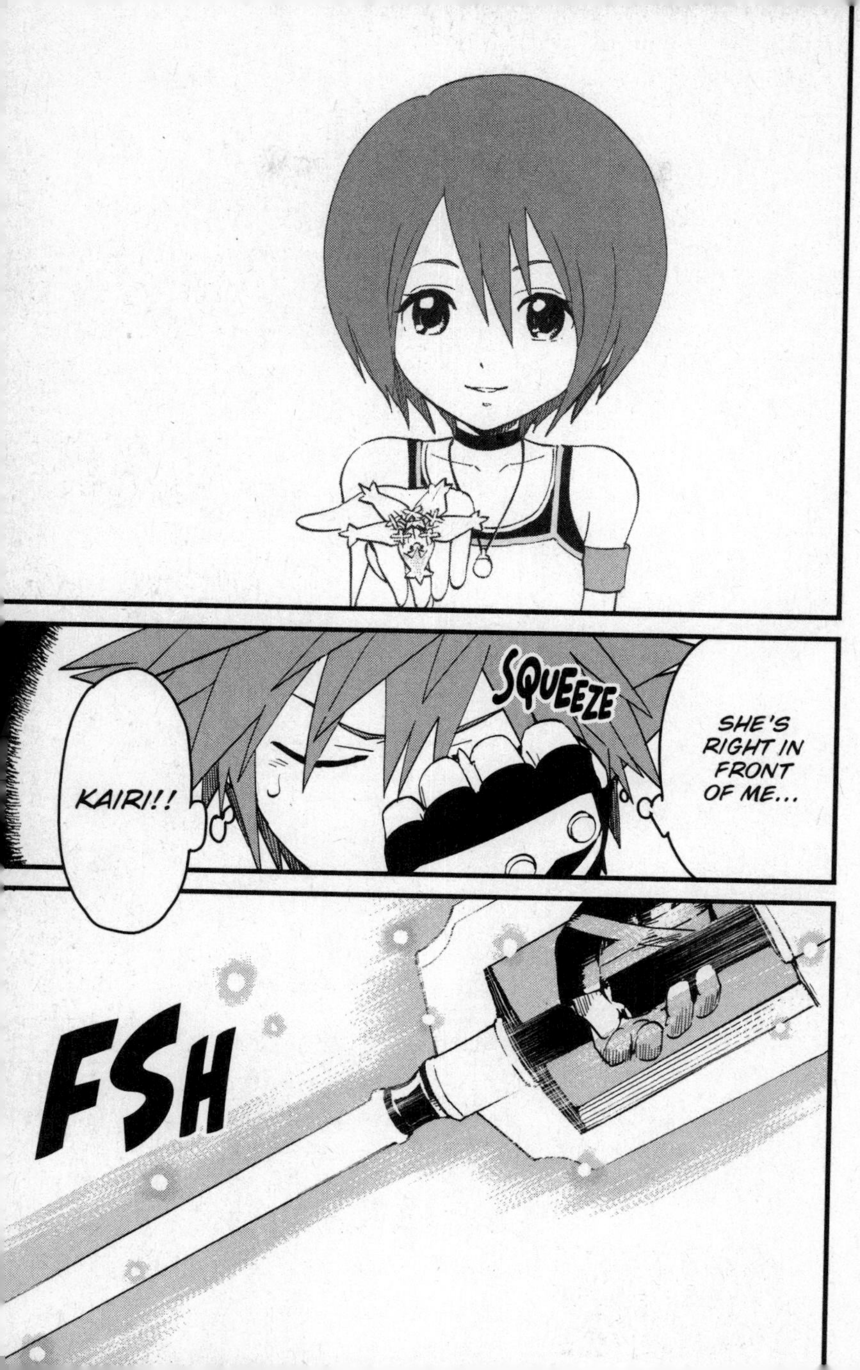
SHE'S RIGHT IN FRONT OF ME...
SQUEEZE
KAIRI!!
FSH

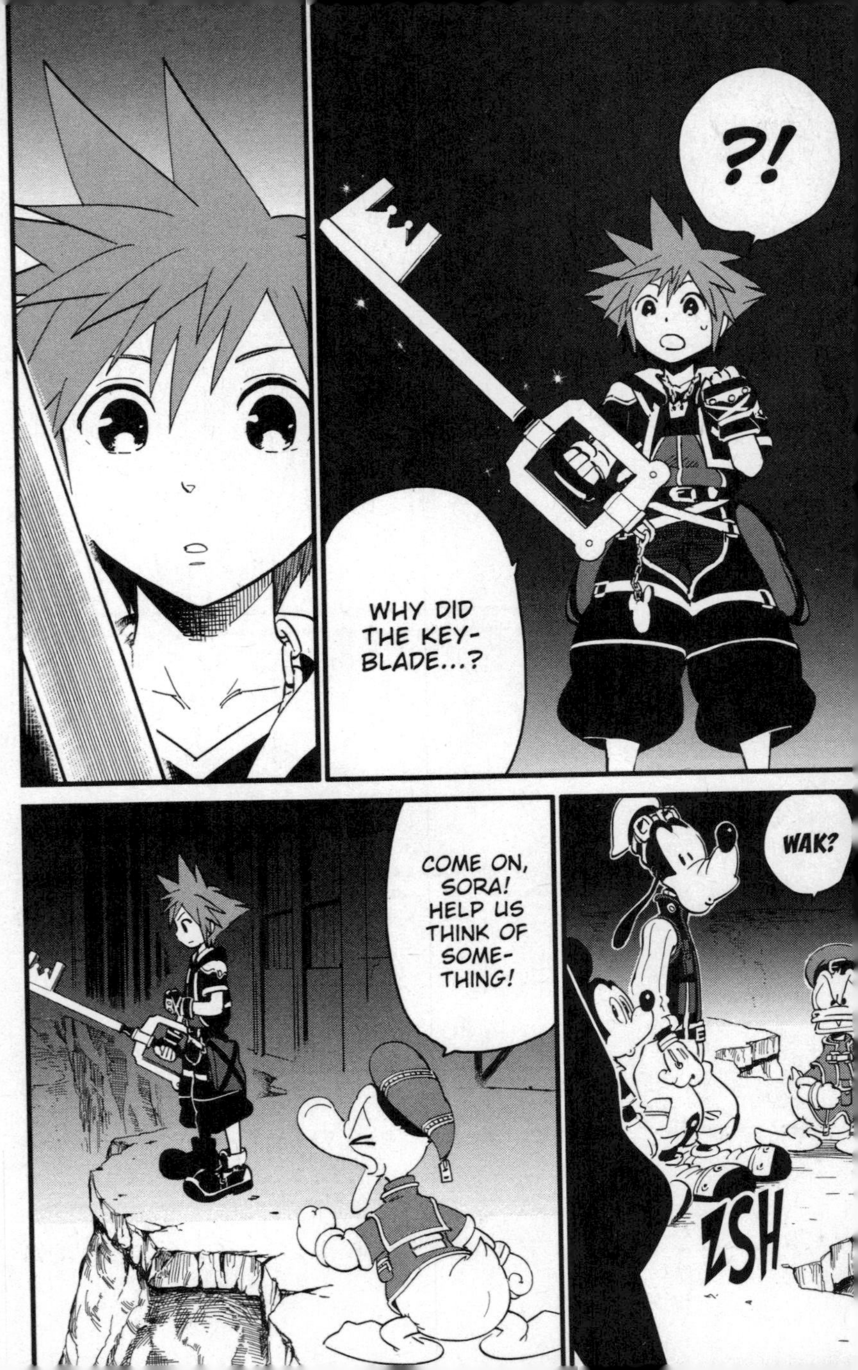
?!
WHY DID THE KEY-BLADE...?
WAK?
ZSH
COME ON, SORA! HELP US THINK OF SOME-THING!

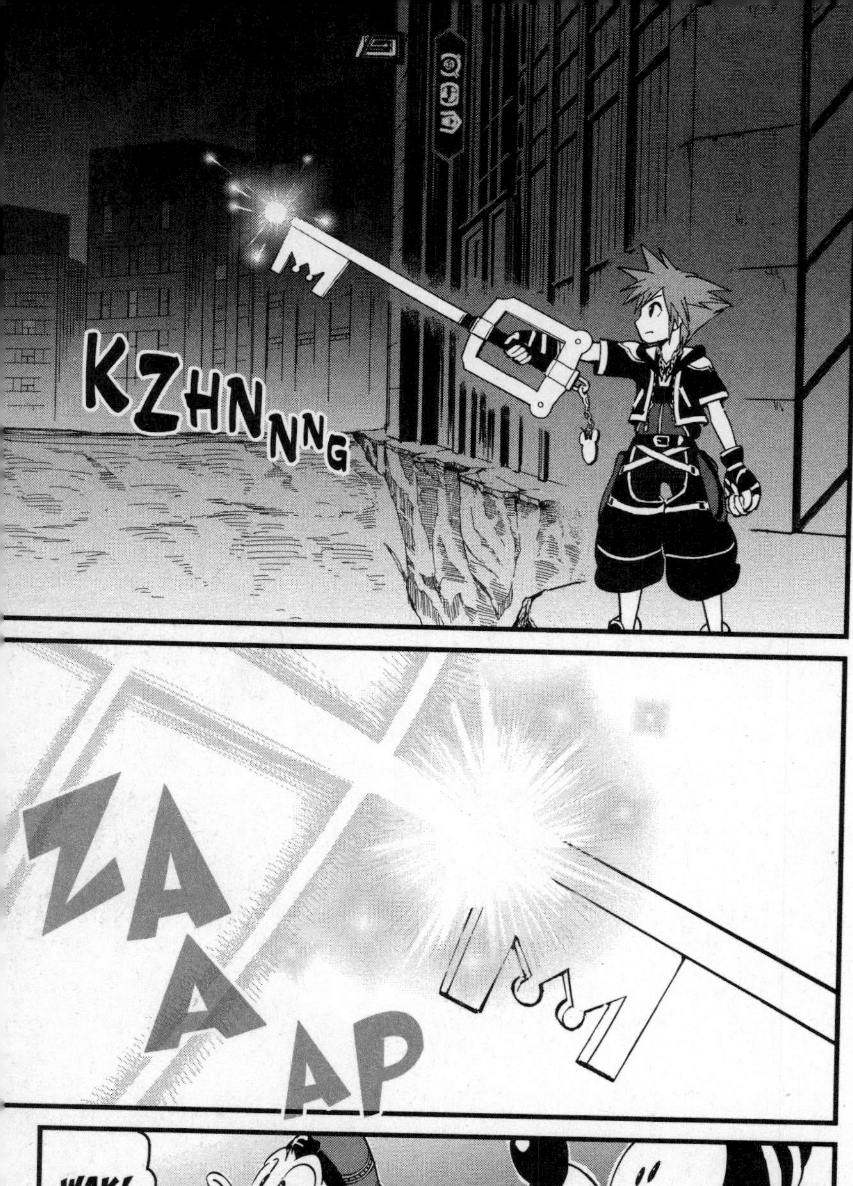
KZHNNNG
ZAAAP
WAK!

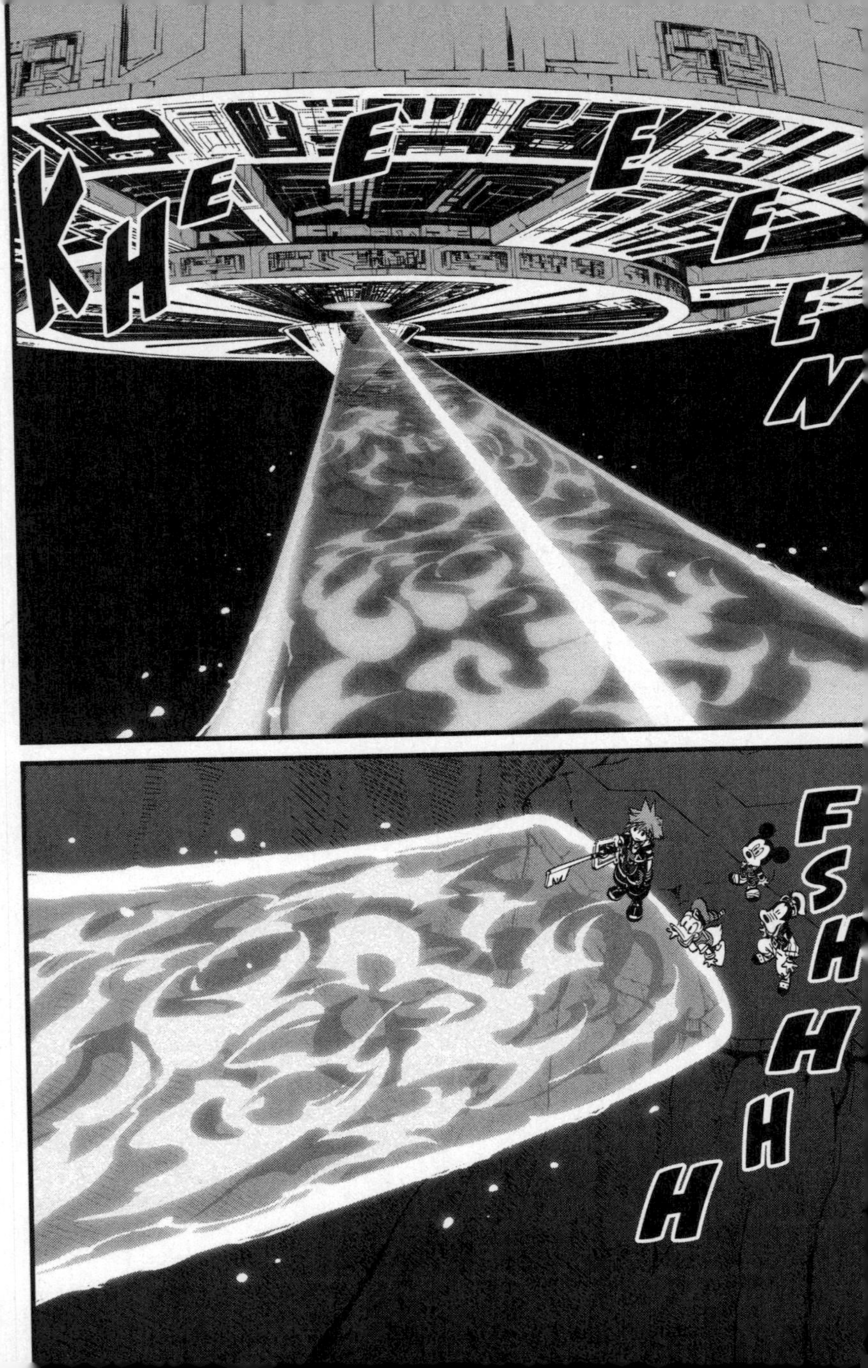
KHEEEEEN
FSHHHH

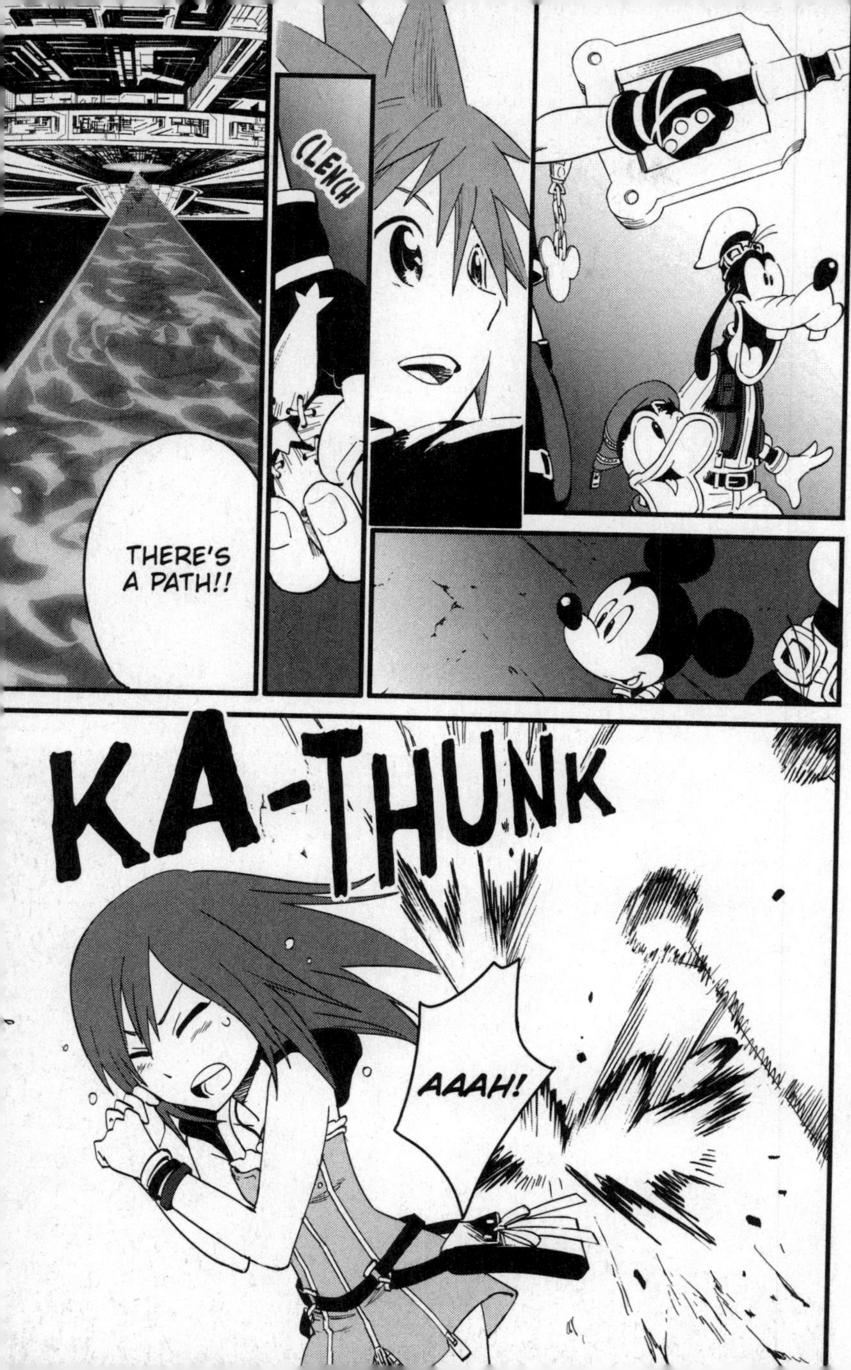
CLENCH
THERE'S A PATH!!
KA-THUNK
AAAH!

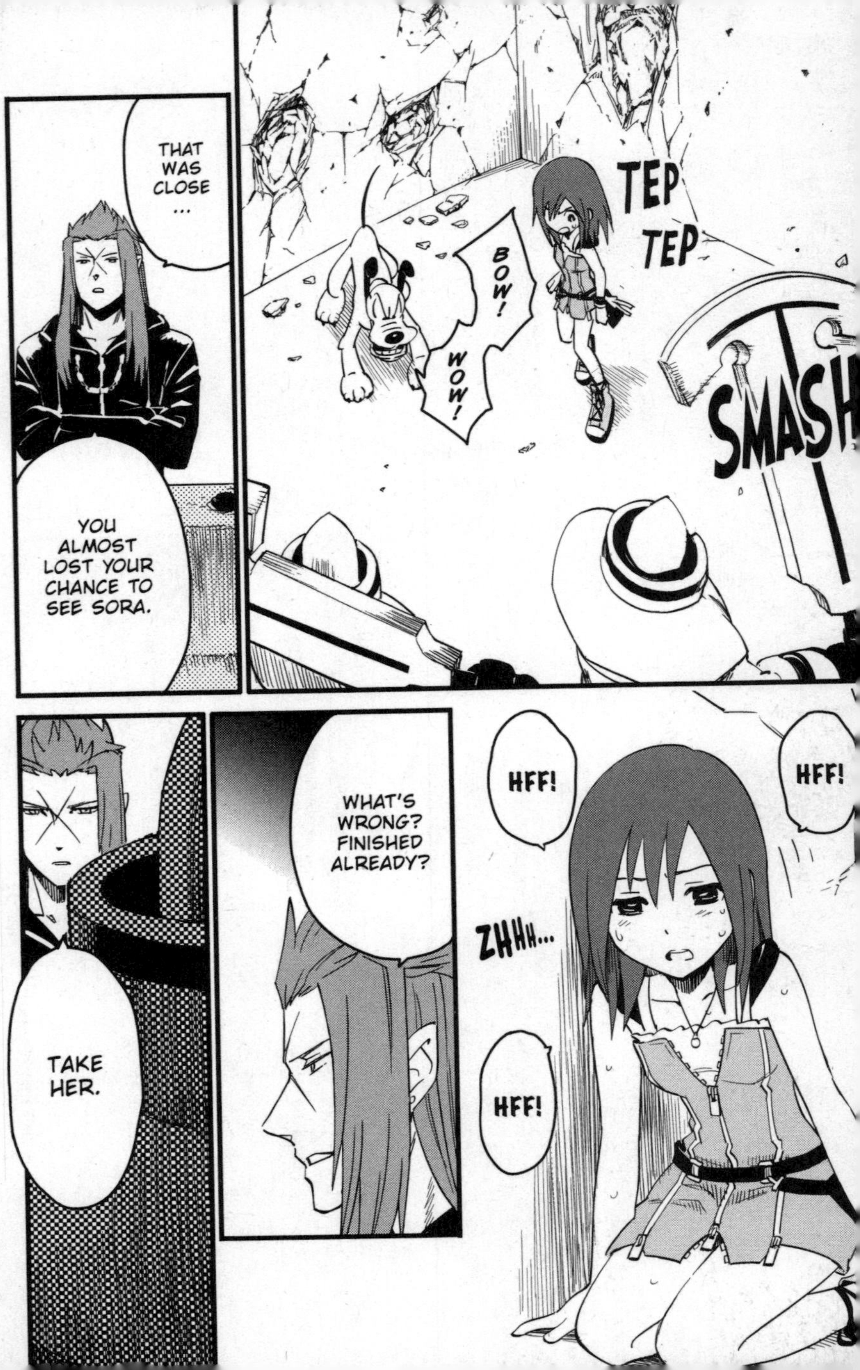
TEP TEP
SMASH
BOW! WOW!
THAT WAS CLOSE ...
YOU ALMOST LOST YOUR CHANCE TO SEE SORA.
HFF!
HFF!
ZHHH...
HFF!
WHAT'S WRONG? FINISHED ALREADY?
TAKE HER.

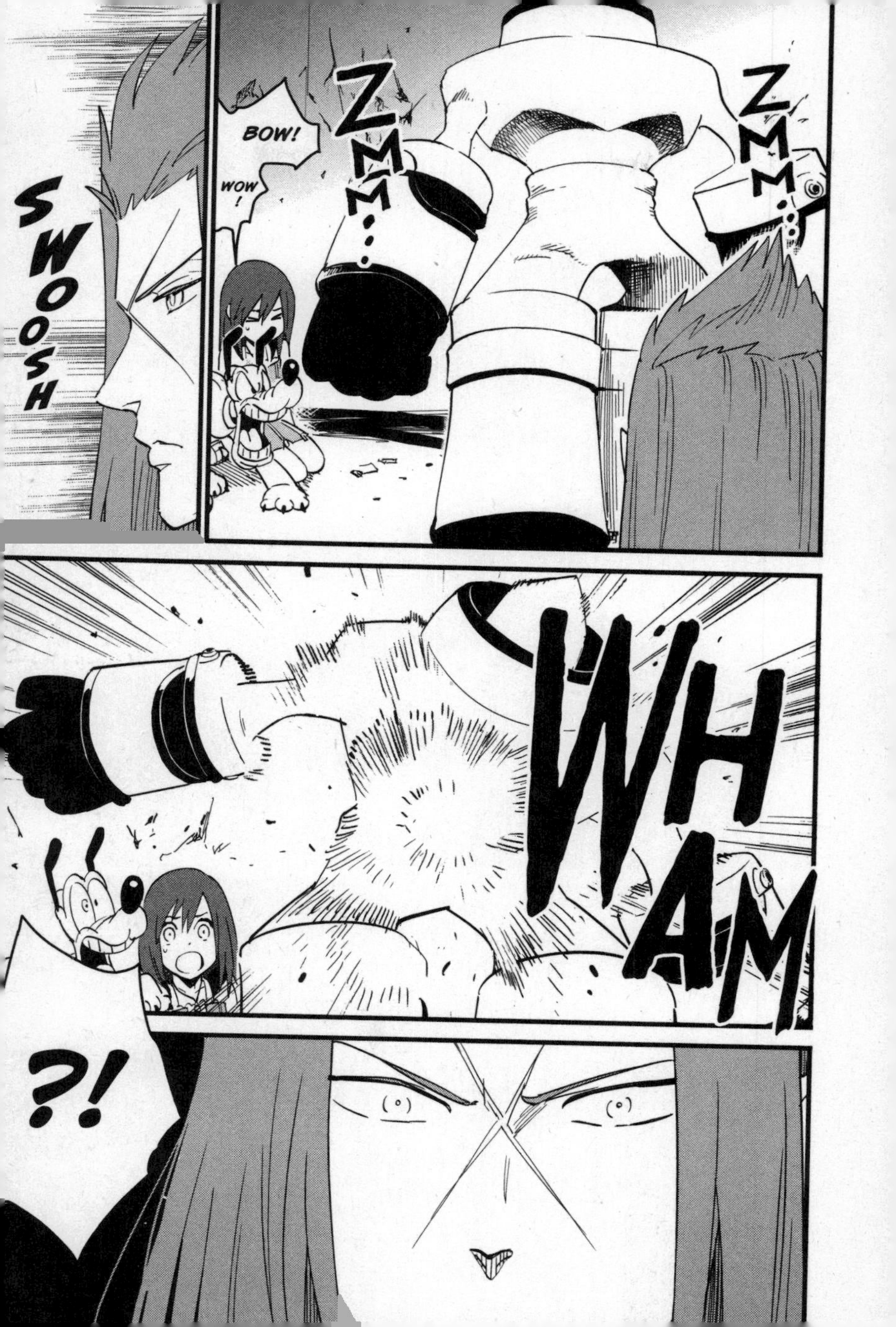
ZMM...
ZMM...
BOW!
WOW!
SWOOSH
WHAM
?!

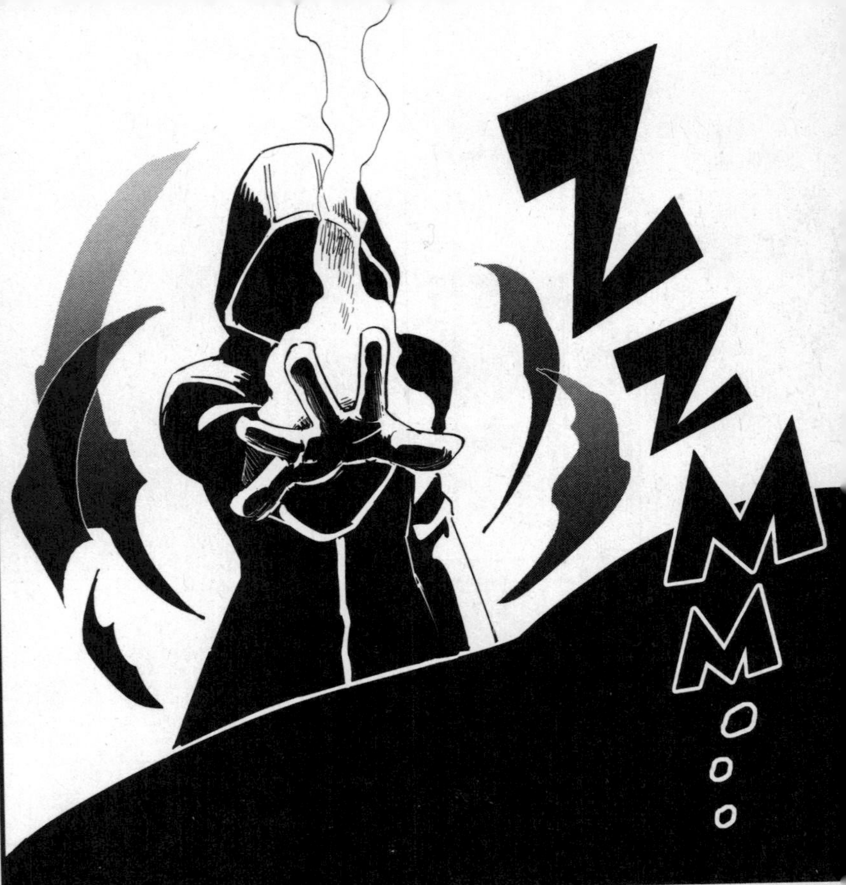
ZZMMMooo

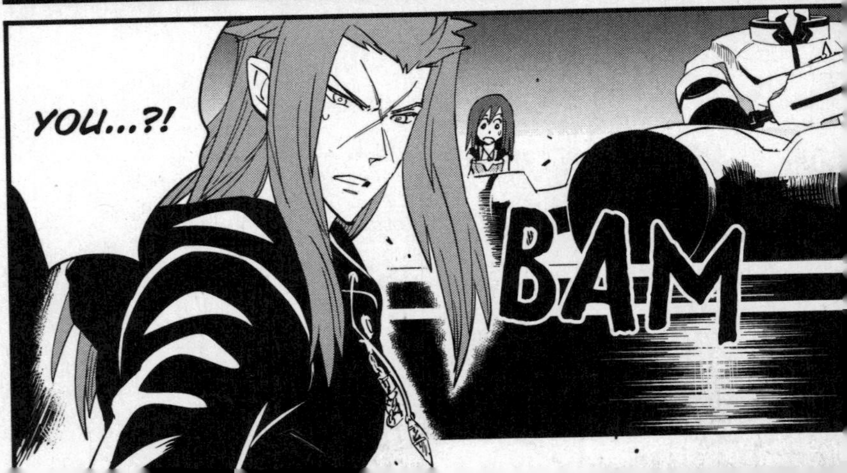
YOU...?!
BAM

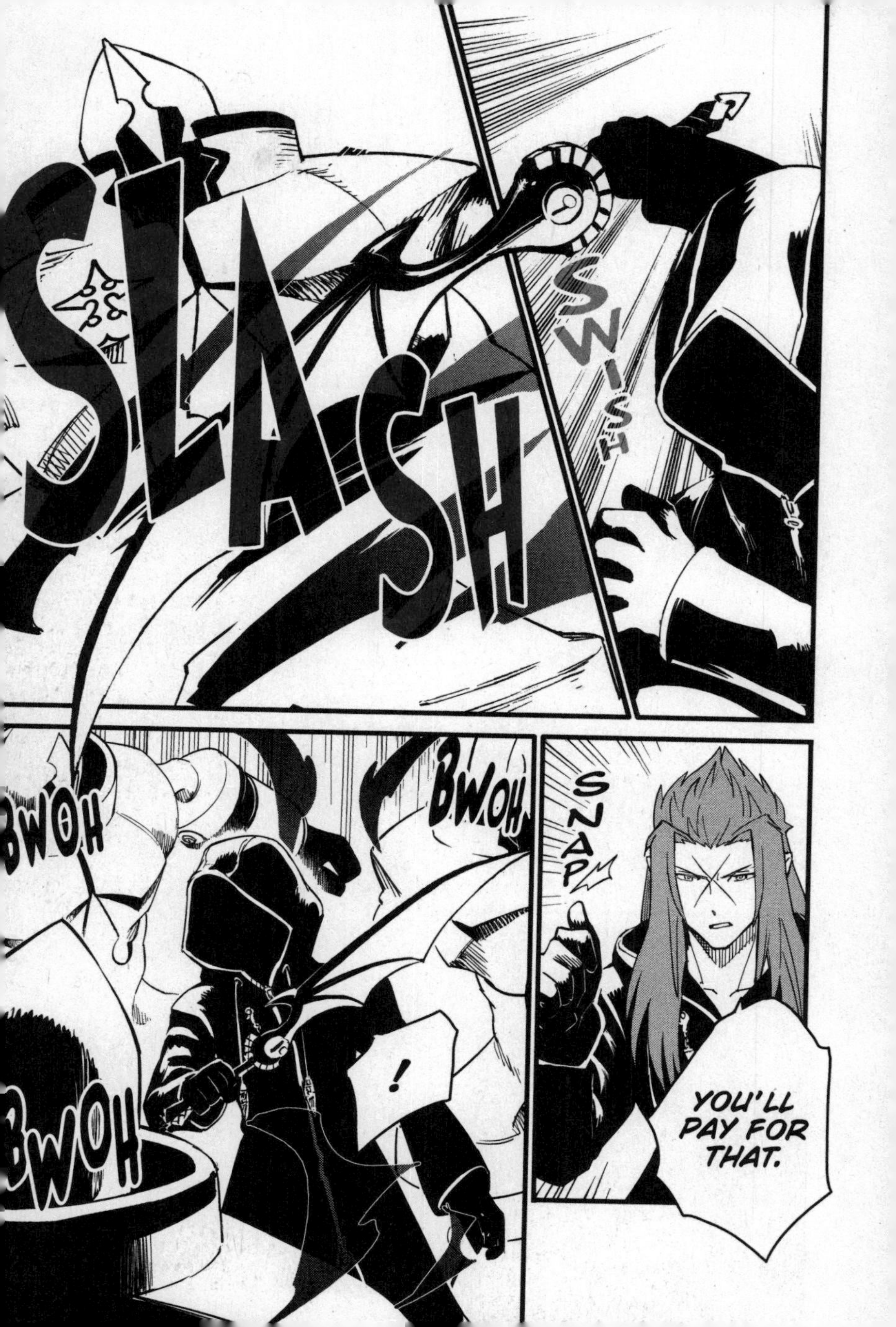
SWISH
SLASH
SNAP
YOU'LL PAY FOR THAT.
BWOH
BWOH
!
BWOH

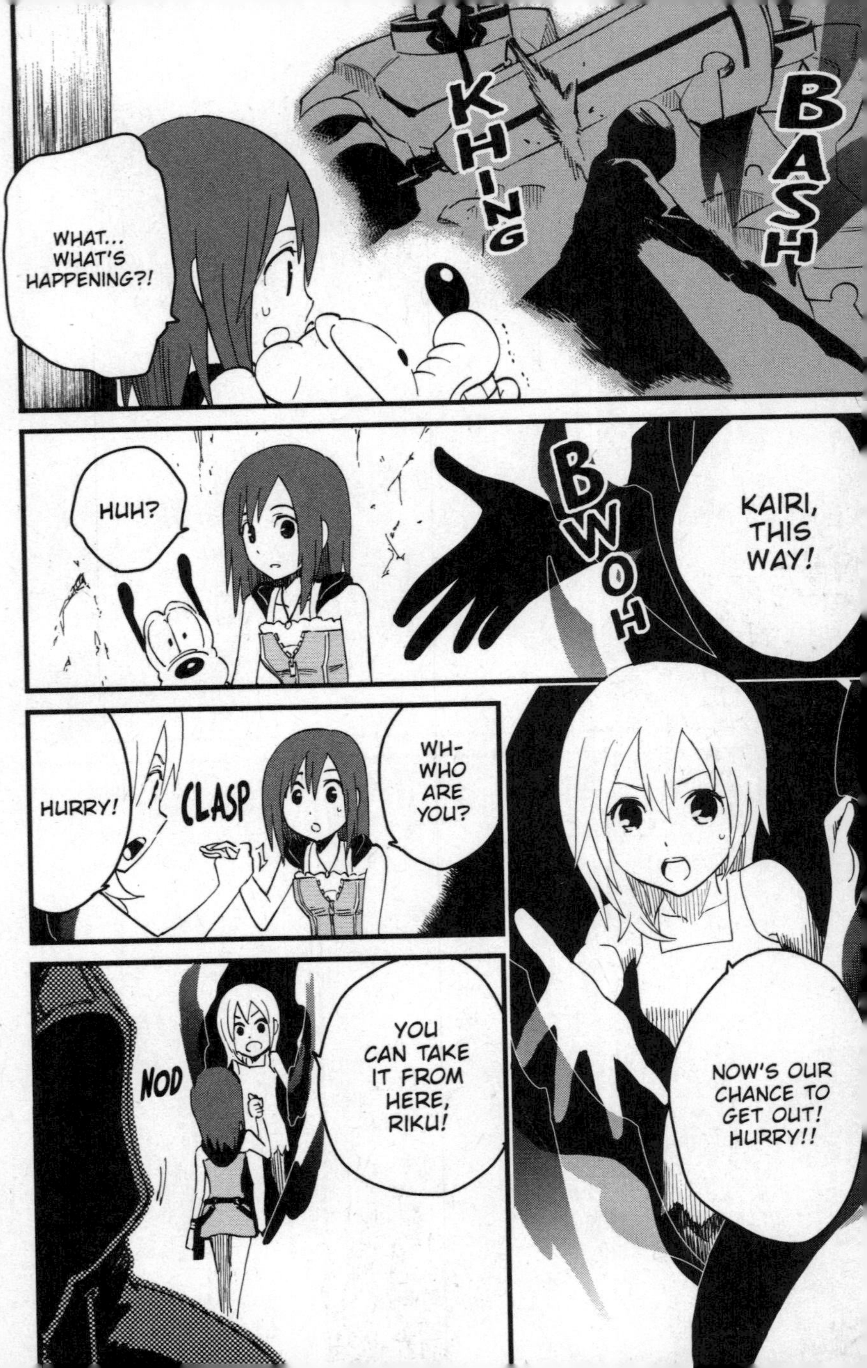
BASH
KHING
WHAT... WHAT'S HAPPENING?!
KAIRI, THIS WAY!
BWOH
HUH?
NOW'S OUR CHANCE TO GET OUT! HURRY!!
WH-WHO ARE YOU?
CLASP
HURRY!
YOU CAN TAKE IT FROM HERE, RIKU!
NOD

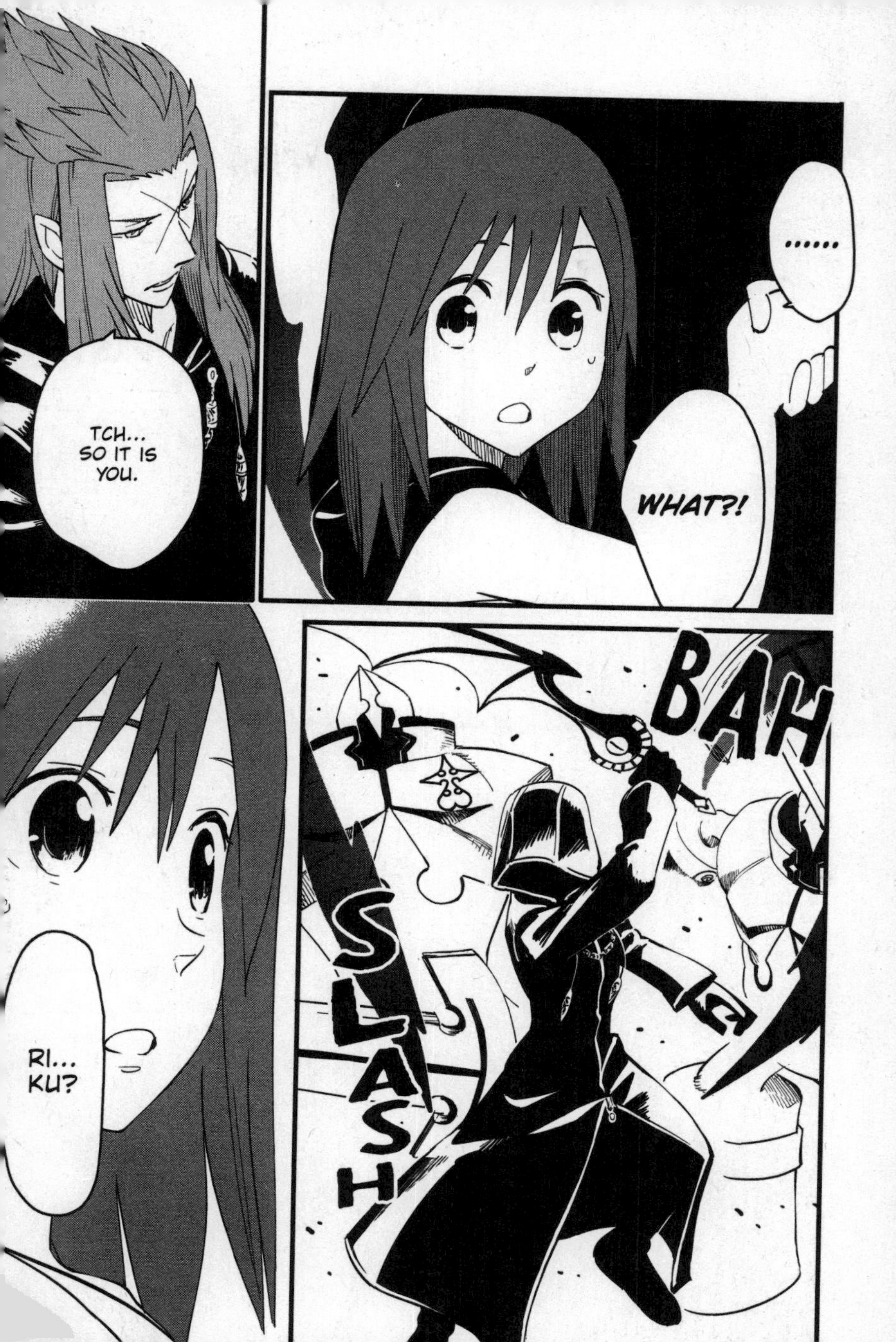
......
WHAT?!
TCH... SO IT IS YOU.
BAH
SLASH
RI... KU?

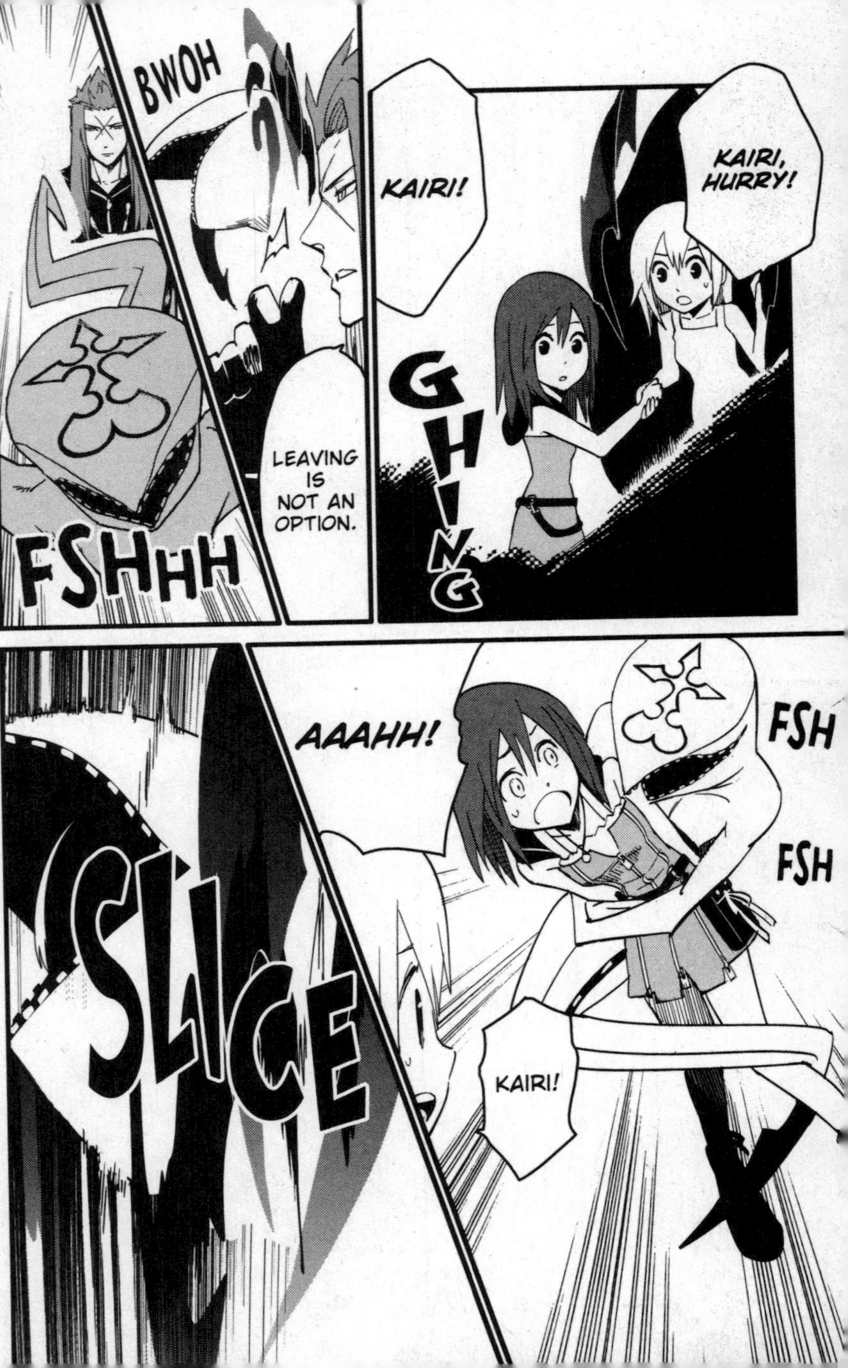
KAIRI, HURRY!
KAIRI!
GHING
BWOH
LEAVING IS NOT AN OPTION.
FSHHH
FSH
FSH
AAAHH!
KAIRI!
SLICE

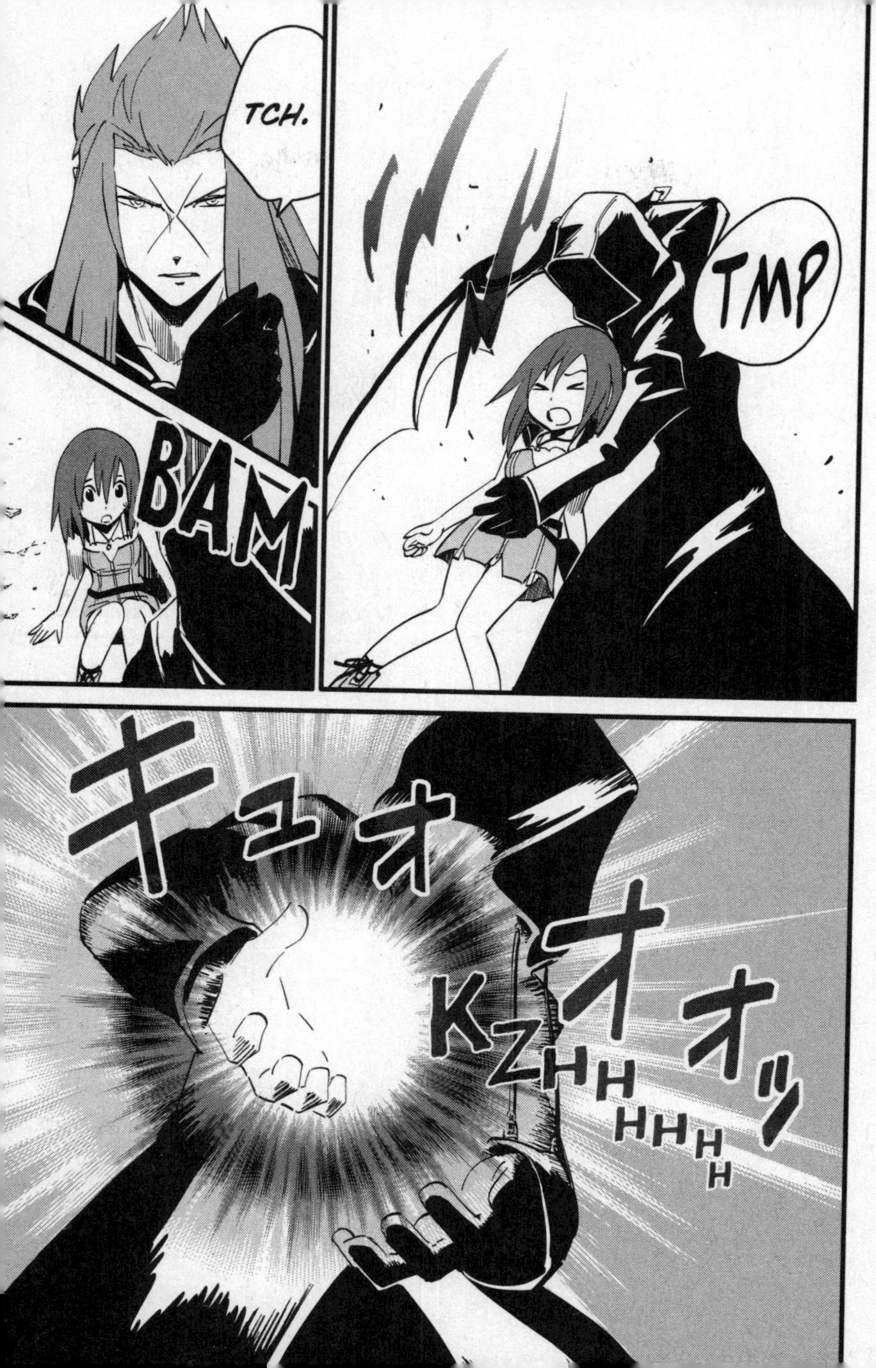
TMP
TCH.
BAM
キュオオオッ
KZHHHHHHH

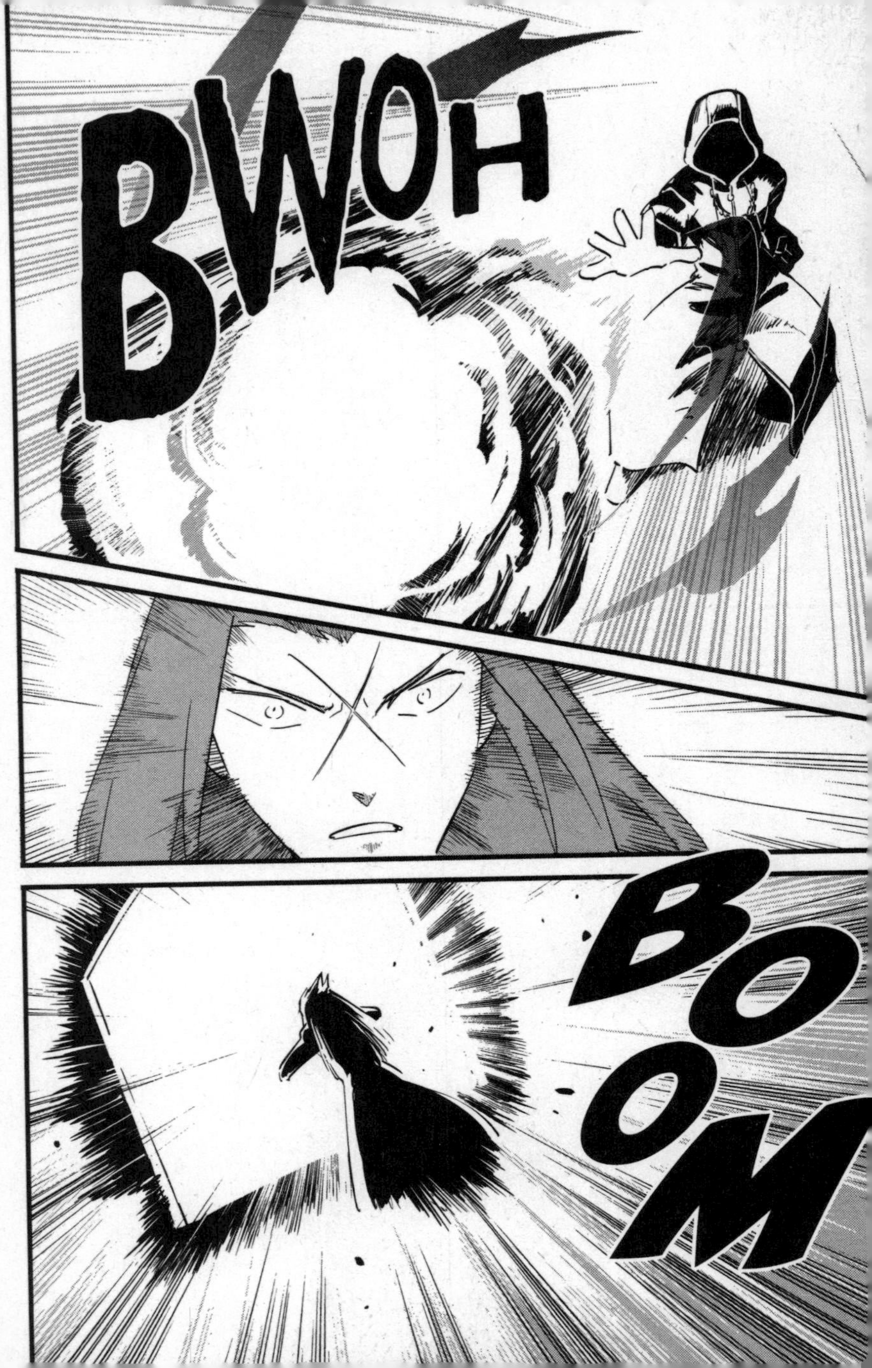
BWOH
BOOM

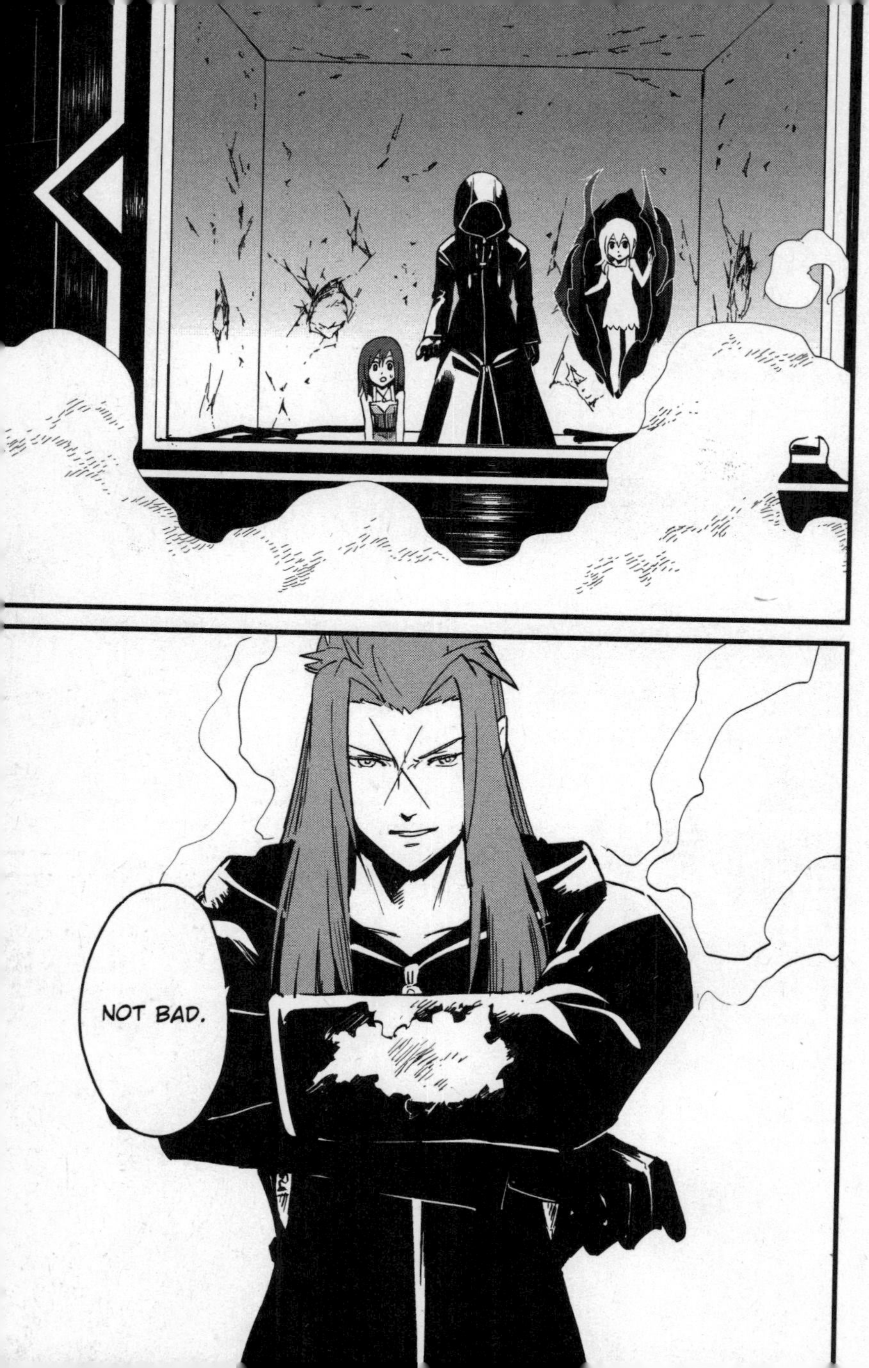
NOT BAD.

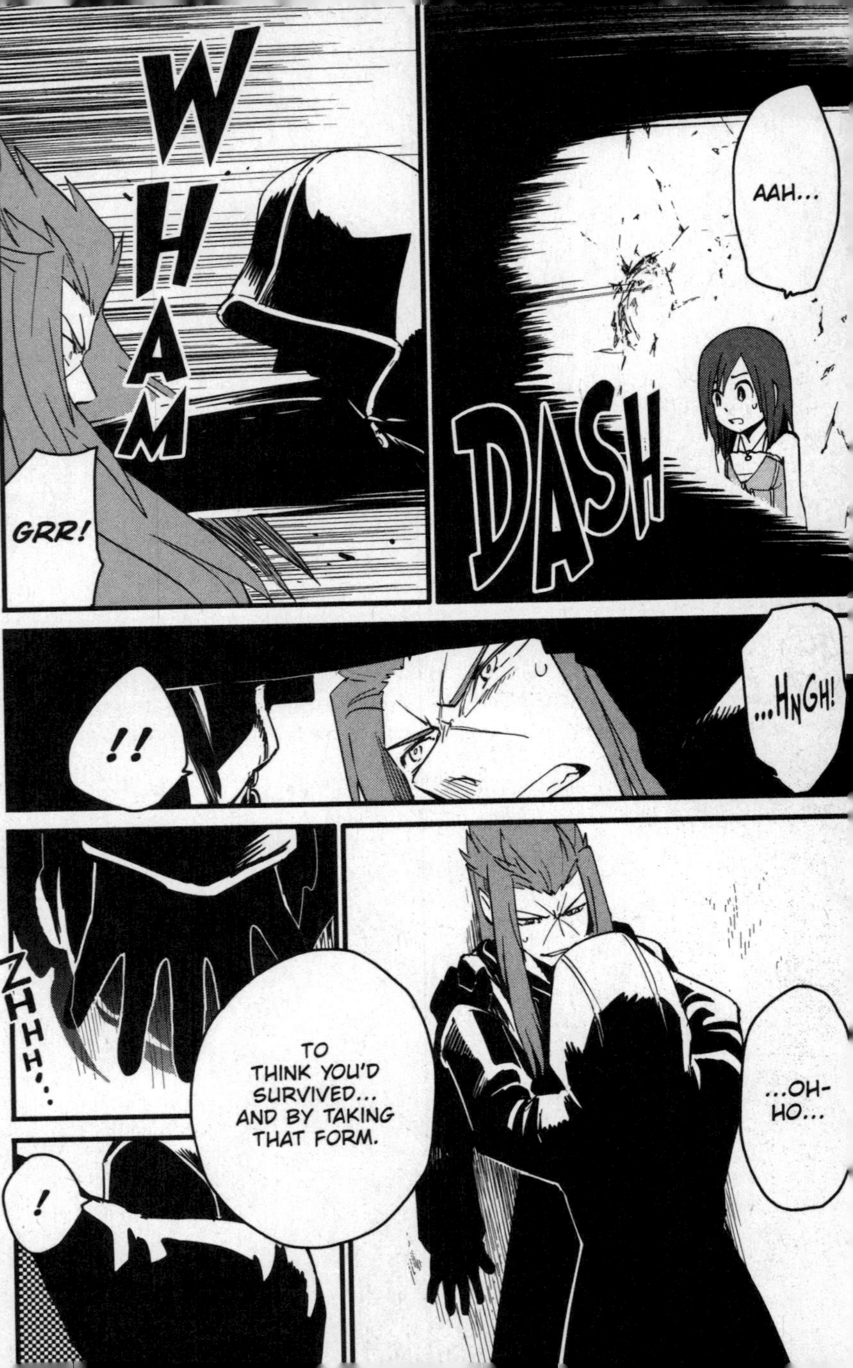
AAH...
DASH
WHAM
GRR!
...HNGH!
!!
...OH-HO...
TO THINK YOU'D SURVIVED... AND BY TAKING THAT FORM.
ZHHH...
!

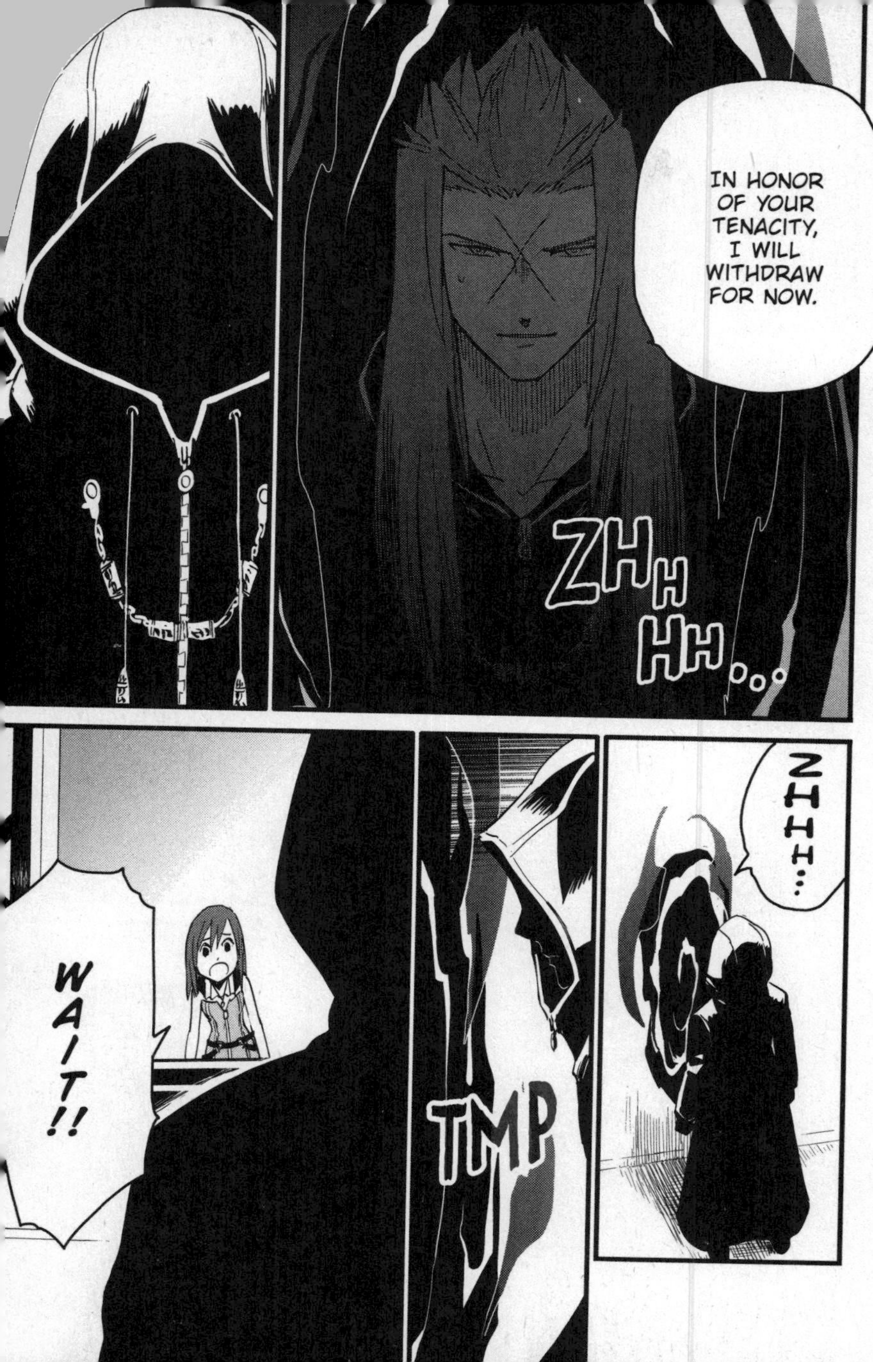
IN HONOR OF YOUR TENACITY, I WILL WITHDRAW FOR NOW.
ZHHHH...
ZHHH...
TMP
WAIT!!

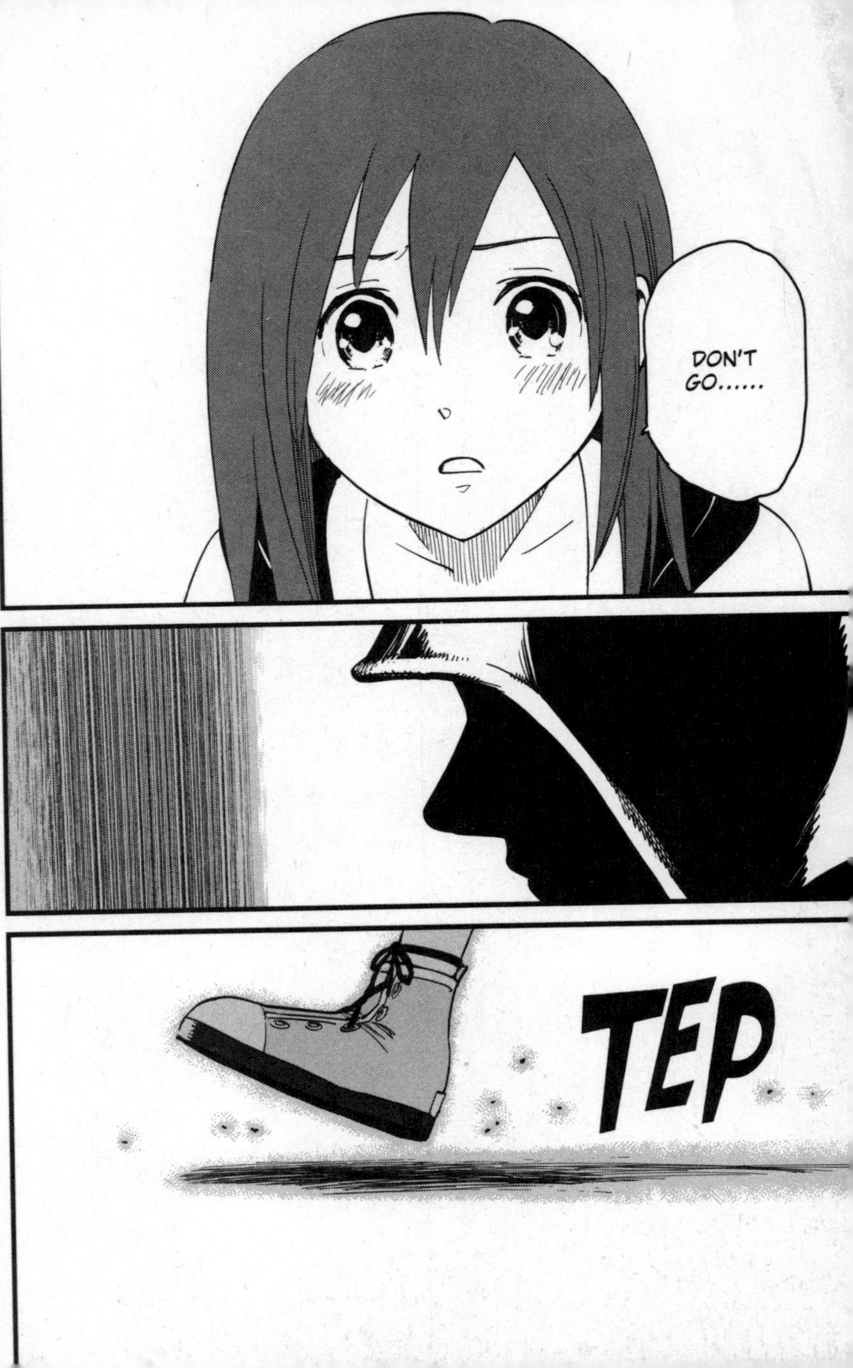
DON'T GO......
TEP

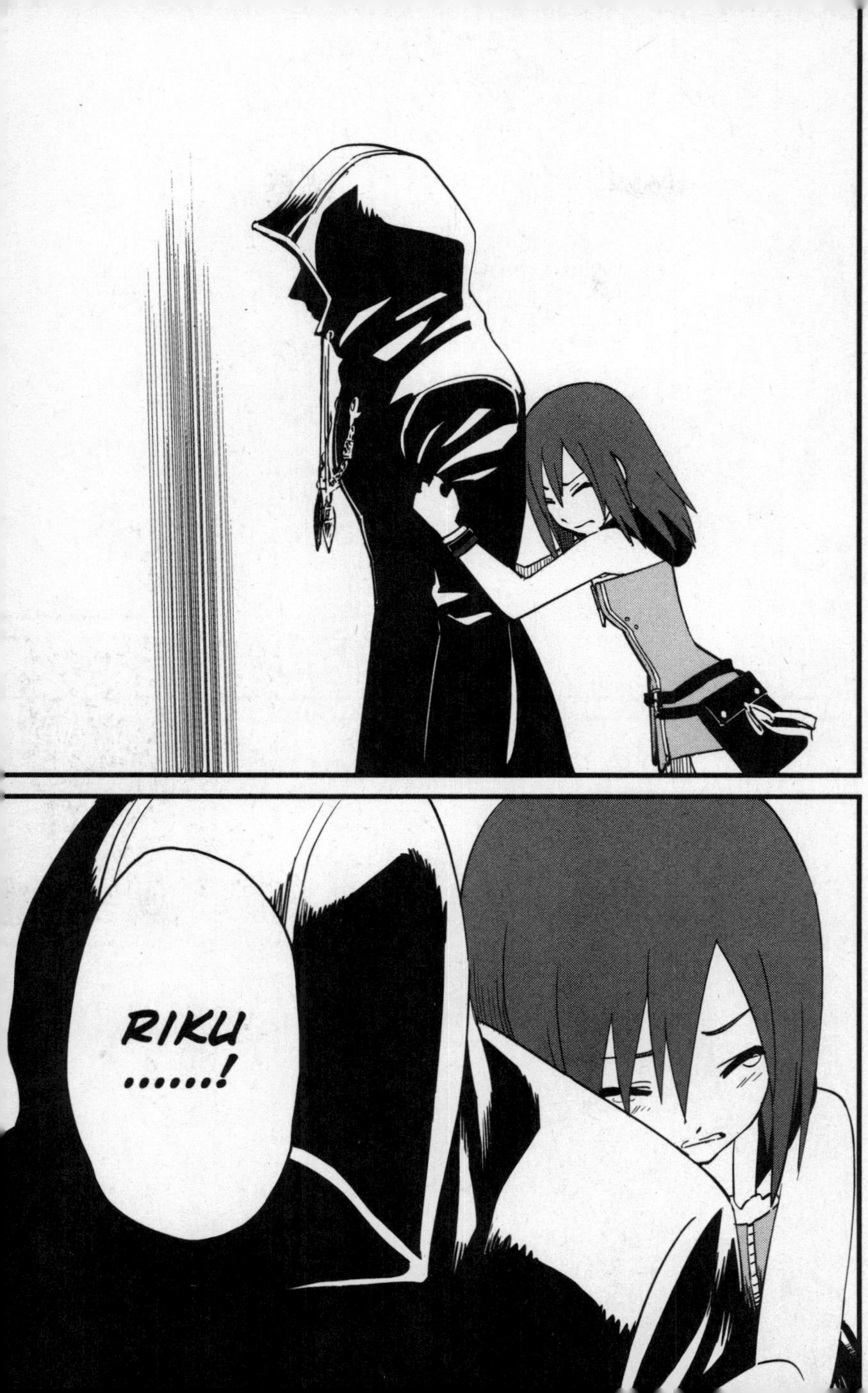
RIKU ......!

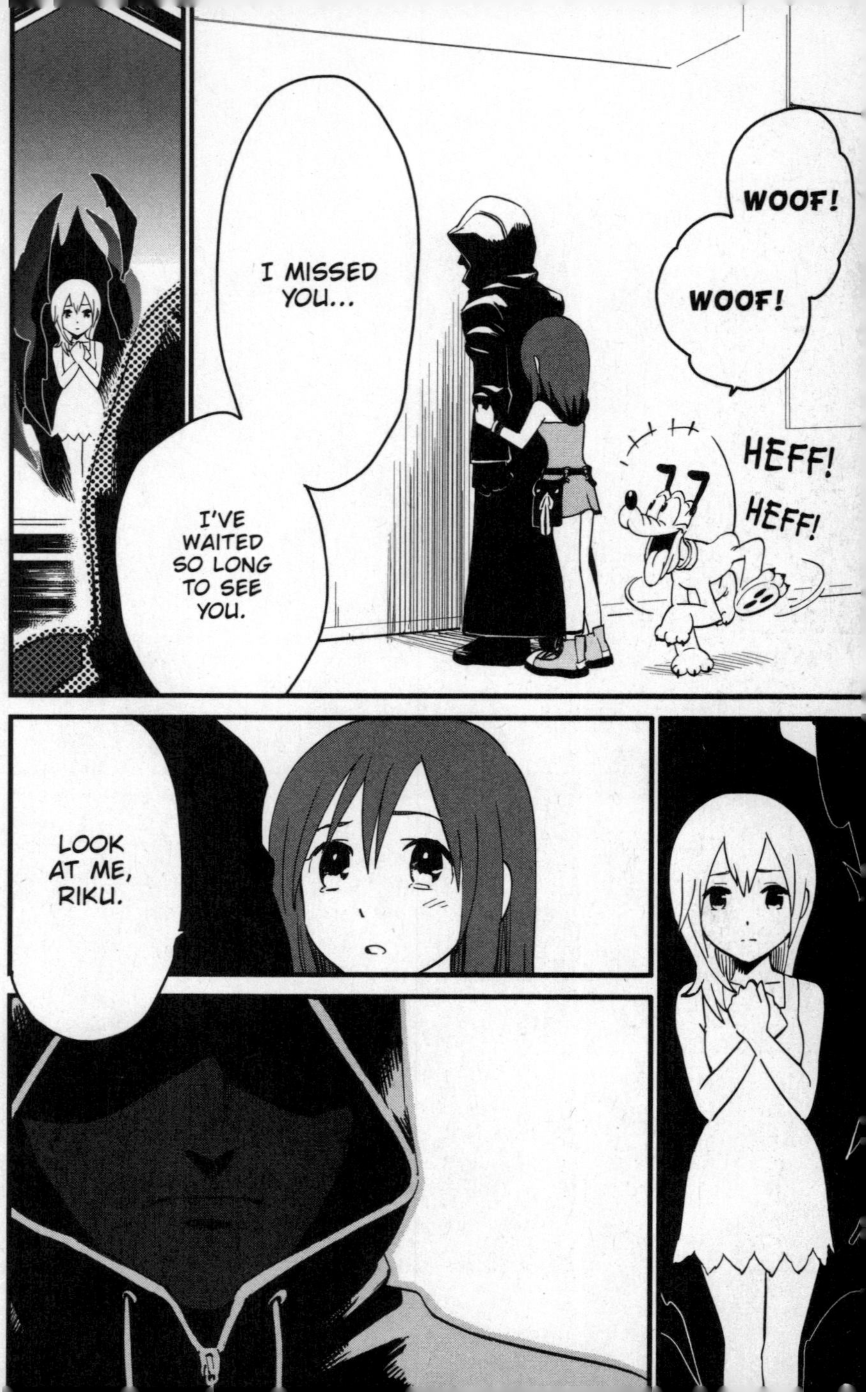
WOOF!
WOOF!
HEFF! HEFF!
I MISSED YOU...
I'VE WAITED SO LONG TO SEE YOU.
LOOK AT ME, RIKU.

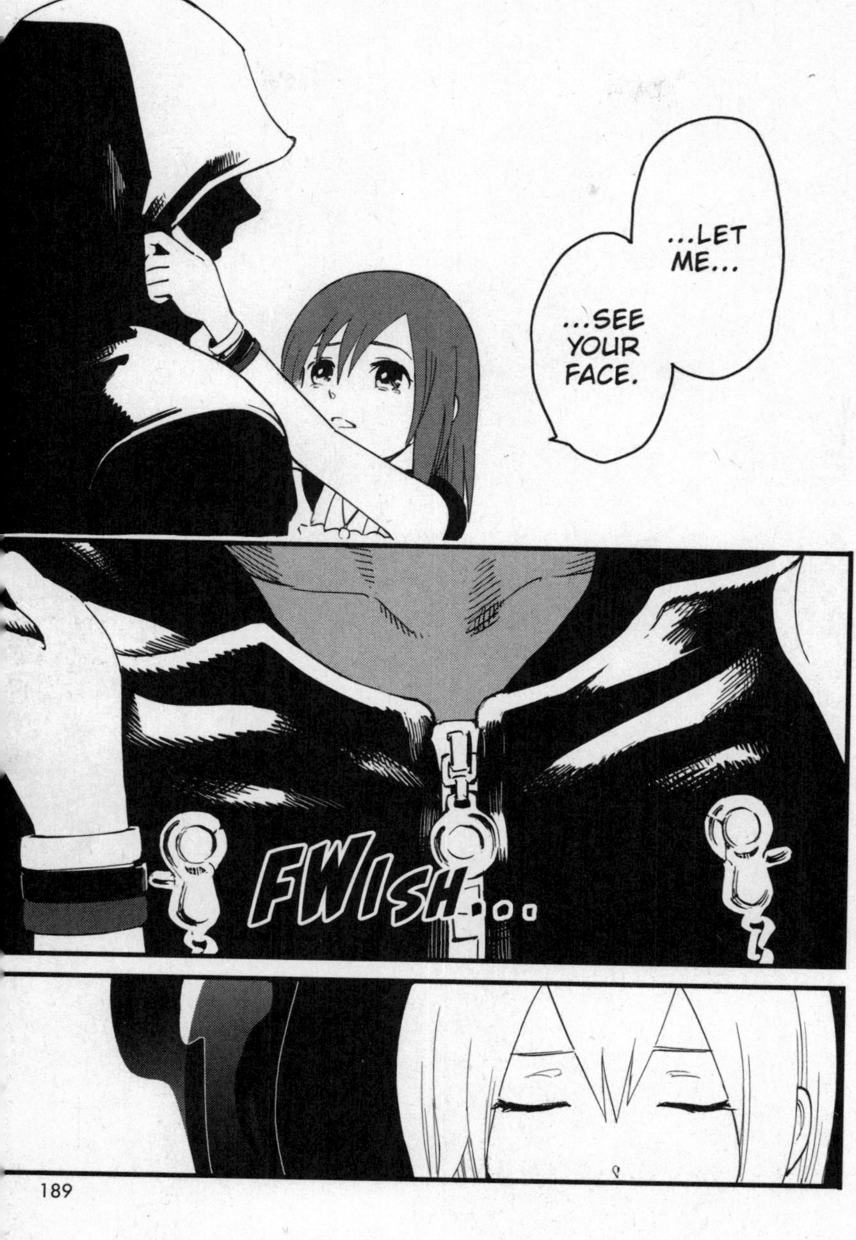
...LET ME...
...SEE YOUR FACE.
FWISH...

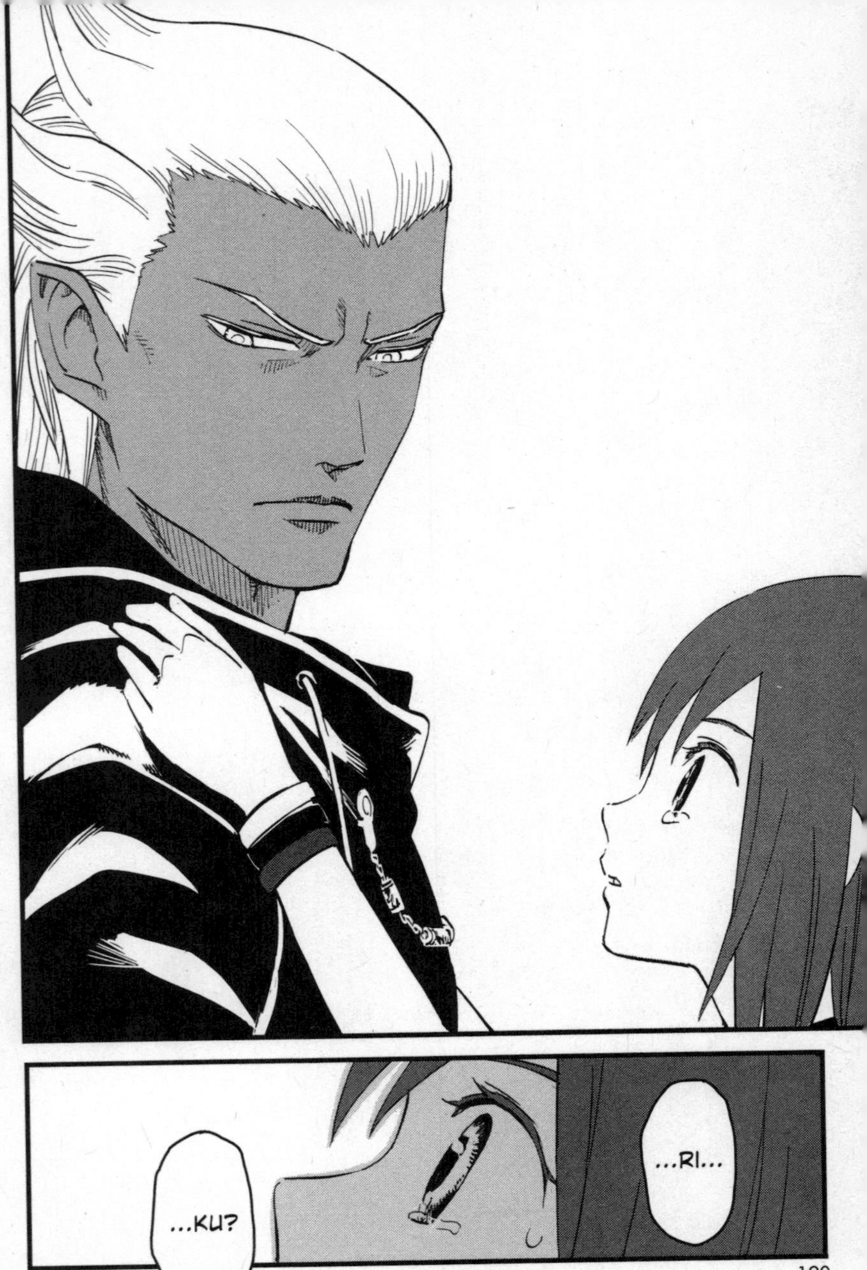
...RI...
...KU?

Disney SQUARE ENIX

KINGDOM HEARTS

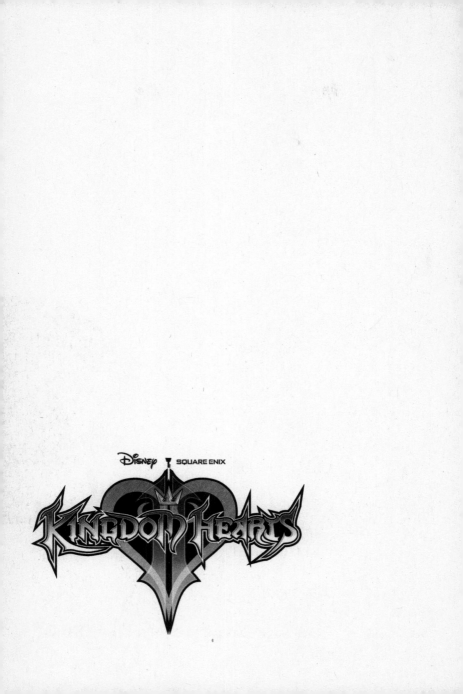

Disney SQUARE ENIX

KINGDOM HEARTS II

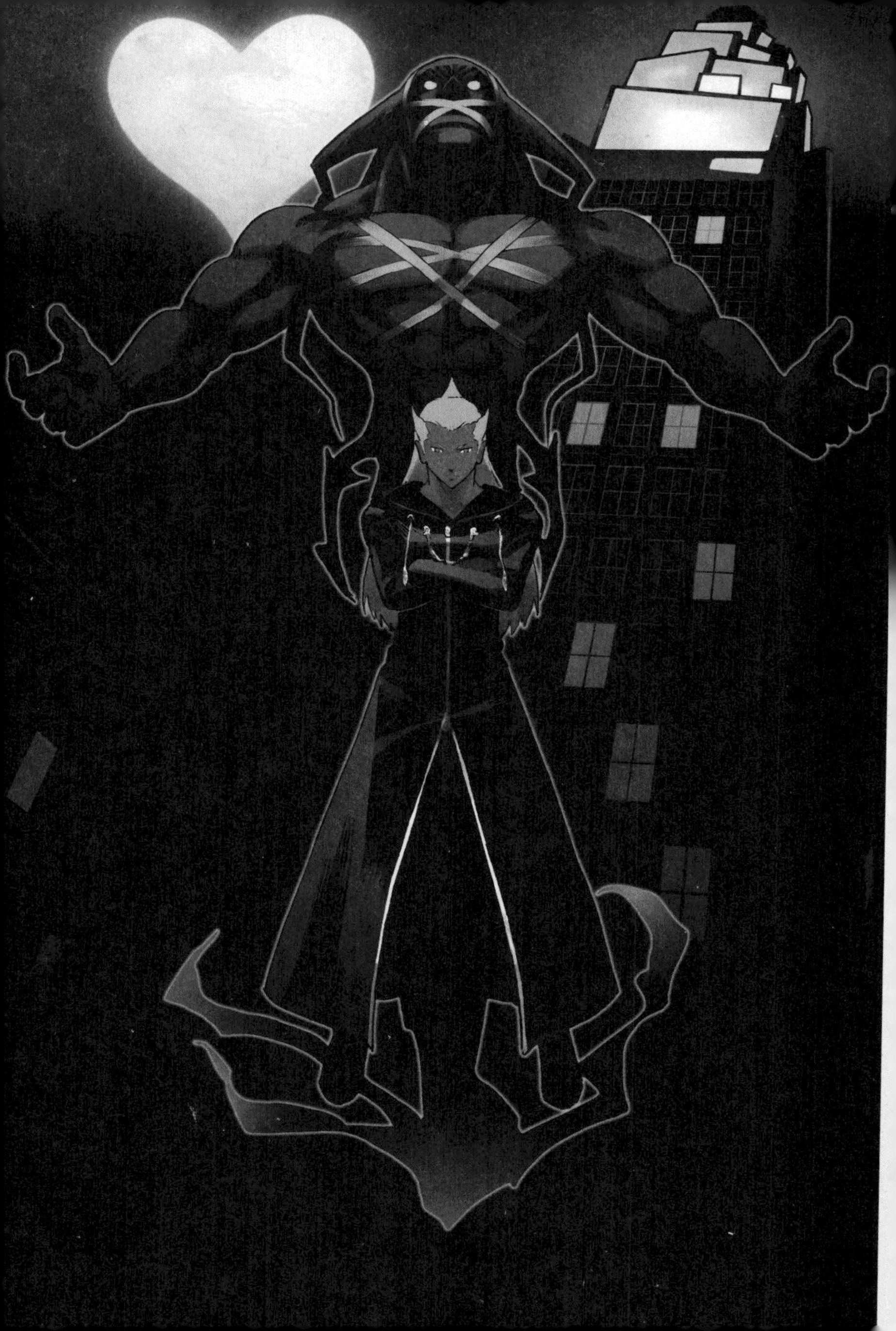

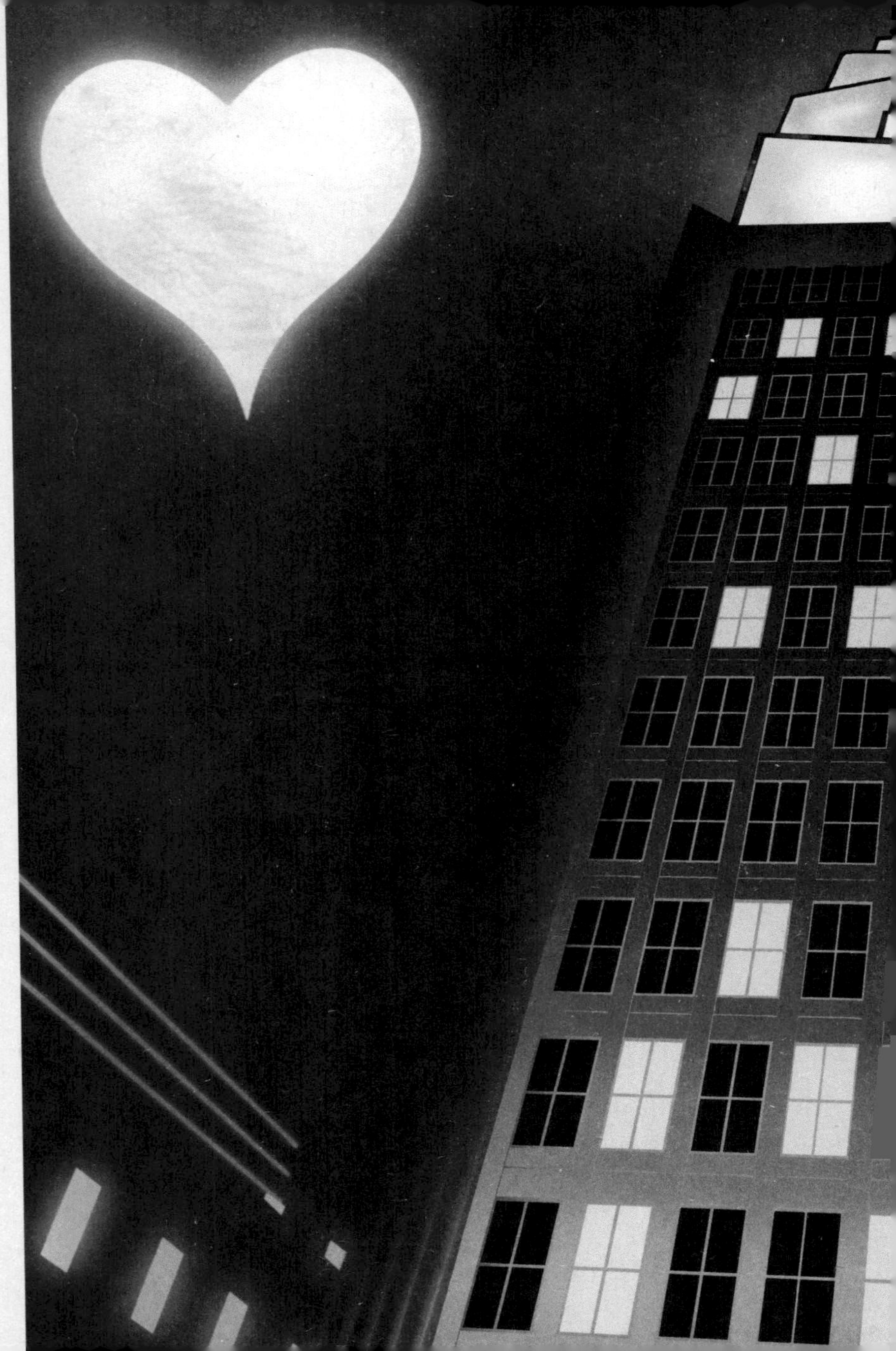

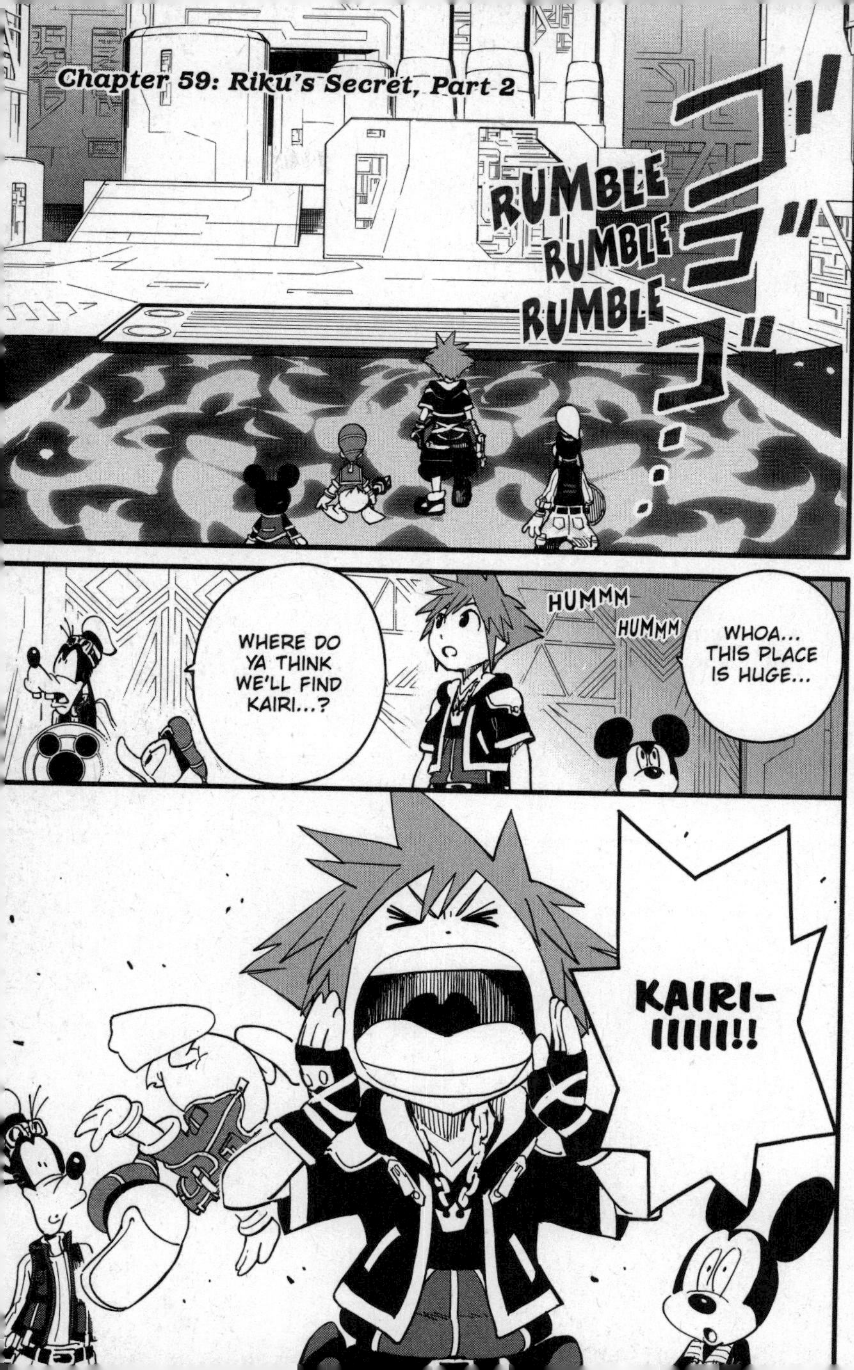
Chapter 59: Riku's Secret, Part 2
ゴゴゴゴ
RUMBLE RUMBLE RUMBLE
WHOA... THIS PLACE IS HUGE...
HUMMM HUMMM
WHERE DO YA THINK WE'LL FIND KAIRI...?
KAIRI-IIIIII!!

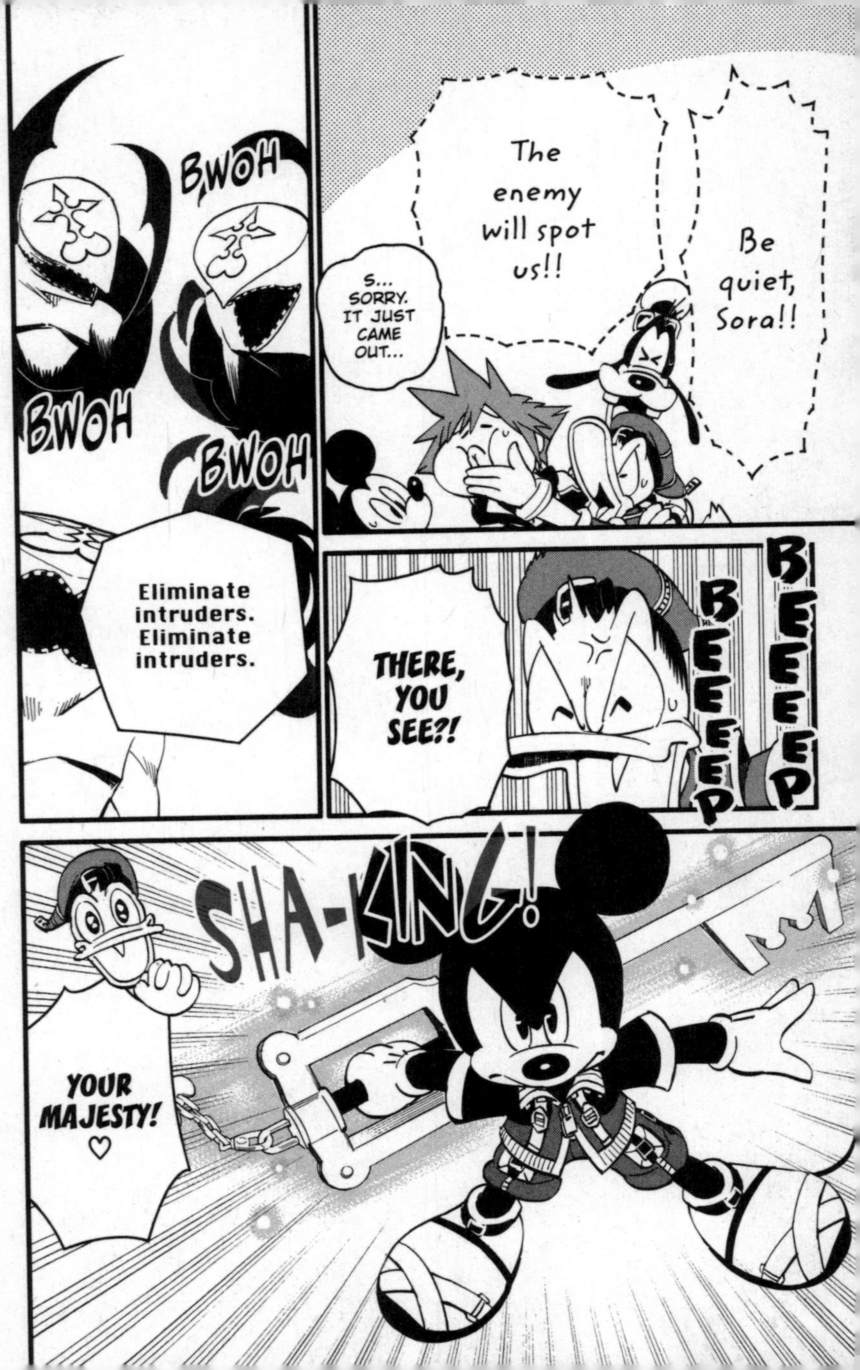
Be quiet, Sora!!
The enemy will spot us!!
S... SORRY. IT JUST CAME OUT...
BEEEEP
BEEEEP
THERE, YOU SEE?!
BWOH
BWOH
BWOH
Eliminate intruders. Eliminate intruders.
SHA-KING!
YOUR MAJESTY! ♡

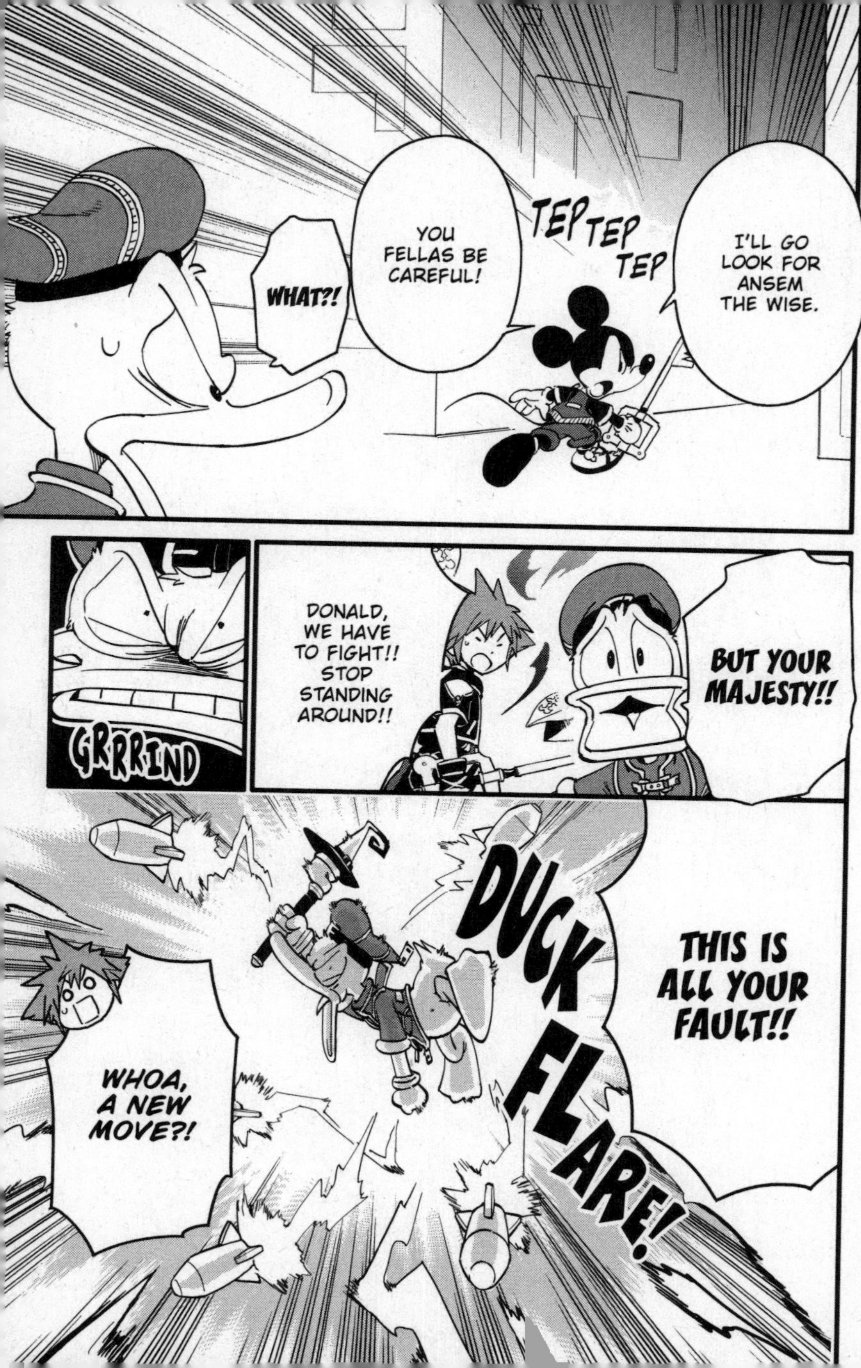
I'LL GO LOOK FOR ANSEM THE WISE.
TEP TEP TEP
YOU FELLAS BE CAREFUL!
WHAT?!
BUT YOUR MAJESTY!!
DONALD, WE HAVE TO FIGHT!! STOP STANDING AROUND!!
GRRRIND
THIS IS ALL YOUR FAULT!!
DUCK FLARE!
WHOA, A NEW MOVE?!

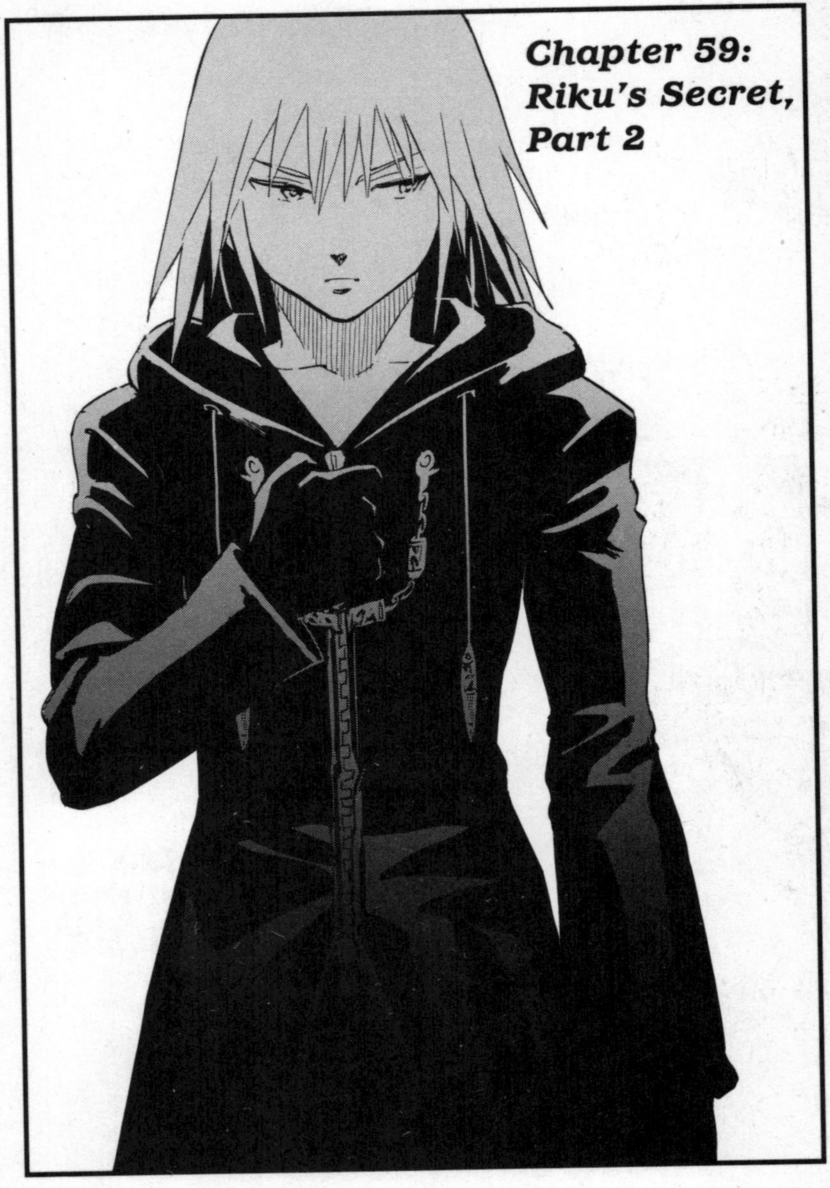
Chapter 59:
Riku's Secret,
Part 2

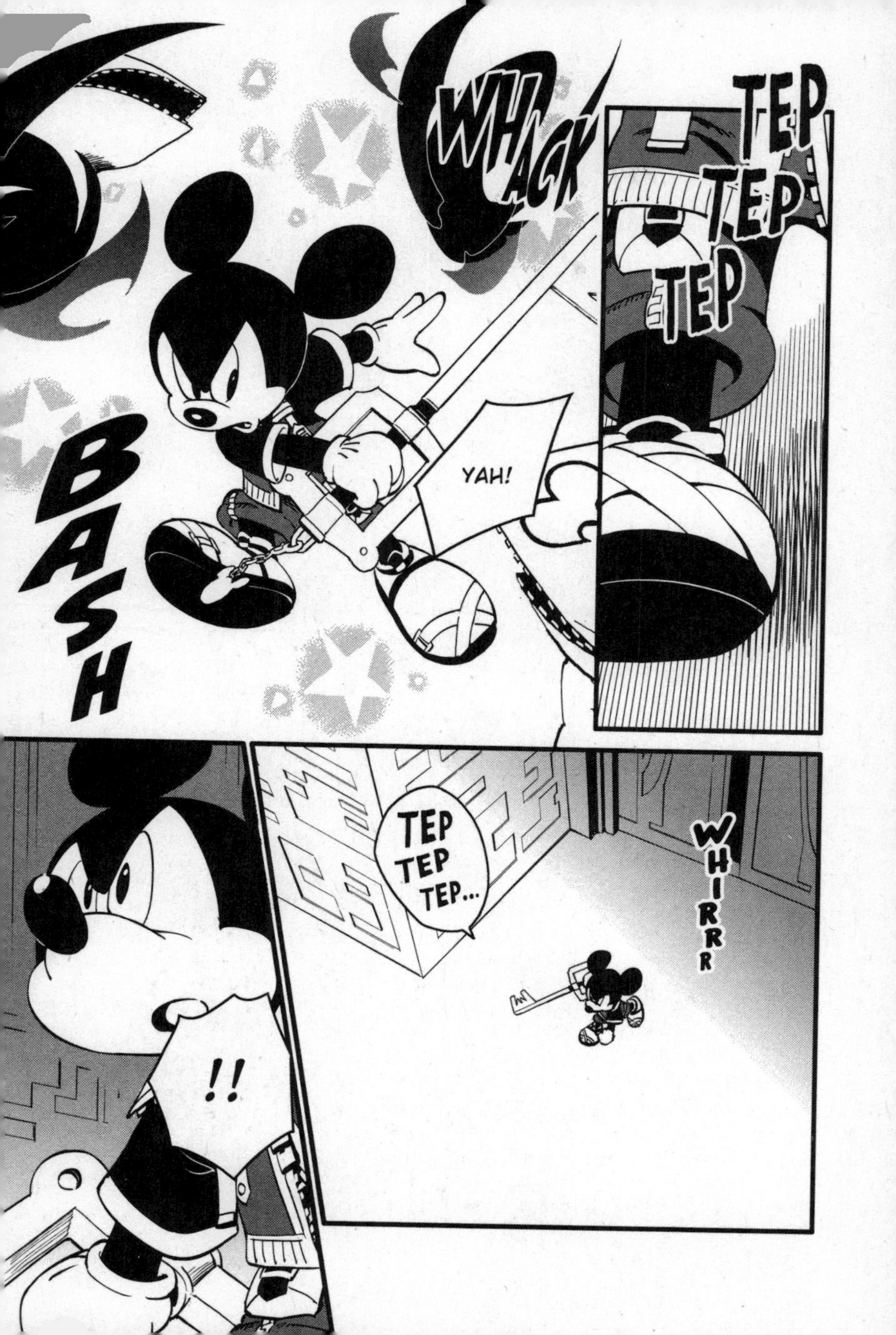
TEP TEP TEP
WHACK
YAH!
BASH
TEP TEP TEP...
WHIRRR
!!

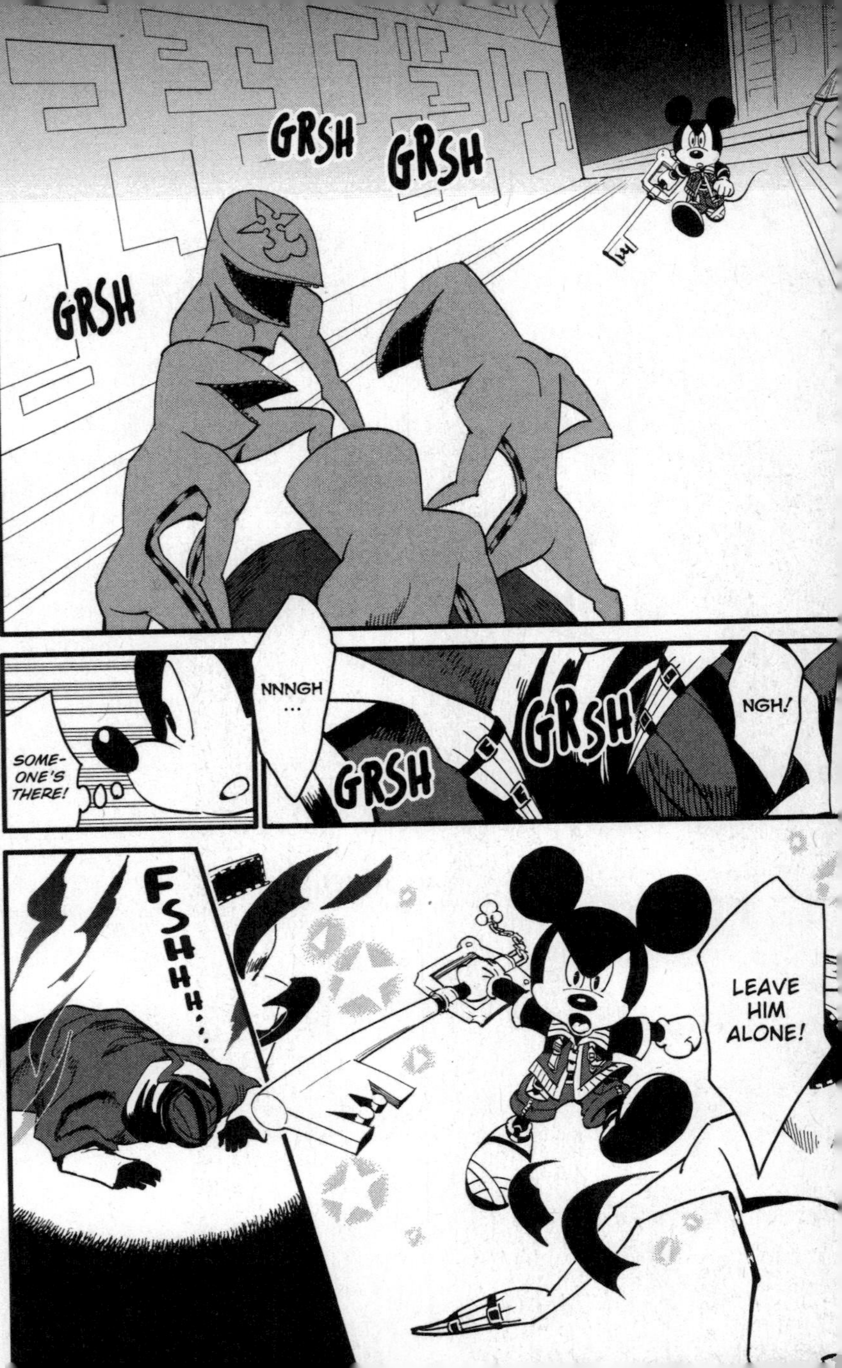
GRSH
GRSH
GRSH
NGH!
NNNGH ...
GRSH
GRSH
SOME-ONE'S THERE!
LEAVE HIM ALONE!
FSHHH...

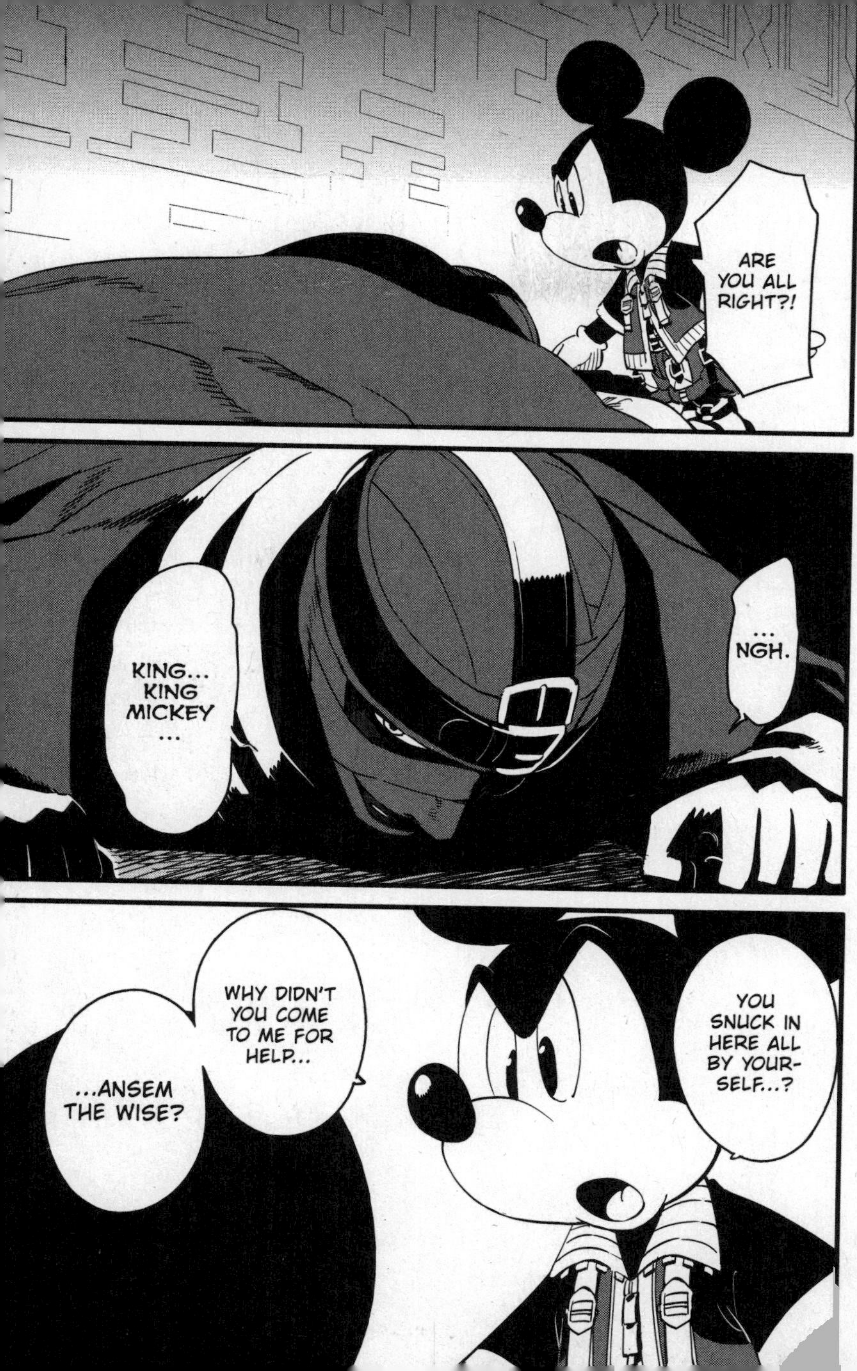
ARE YOU ALL RIGHT?!
...NGH.
KING... KING MICKEY ...
YOU SNUCK IN HERE ALL BY YOURSELF...?
WHY DIDN'T YOU COME TO ME FOR HELP...
...ANSEM THE WISE?

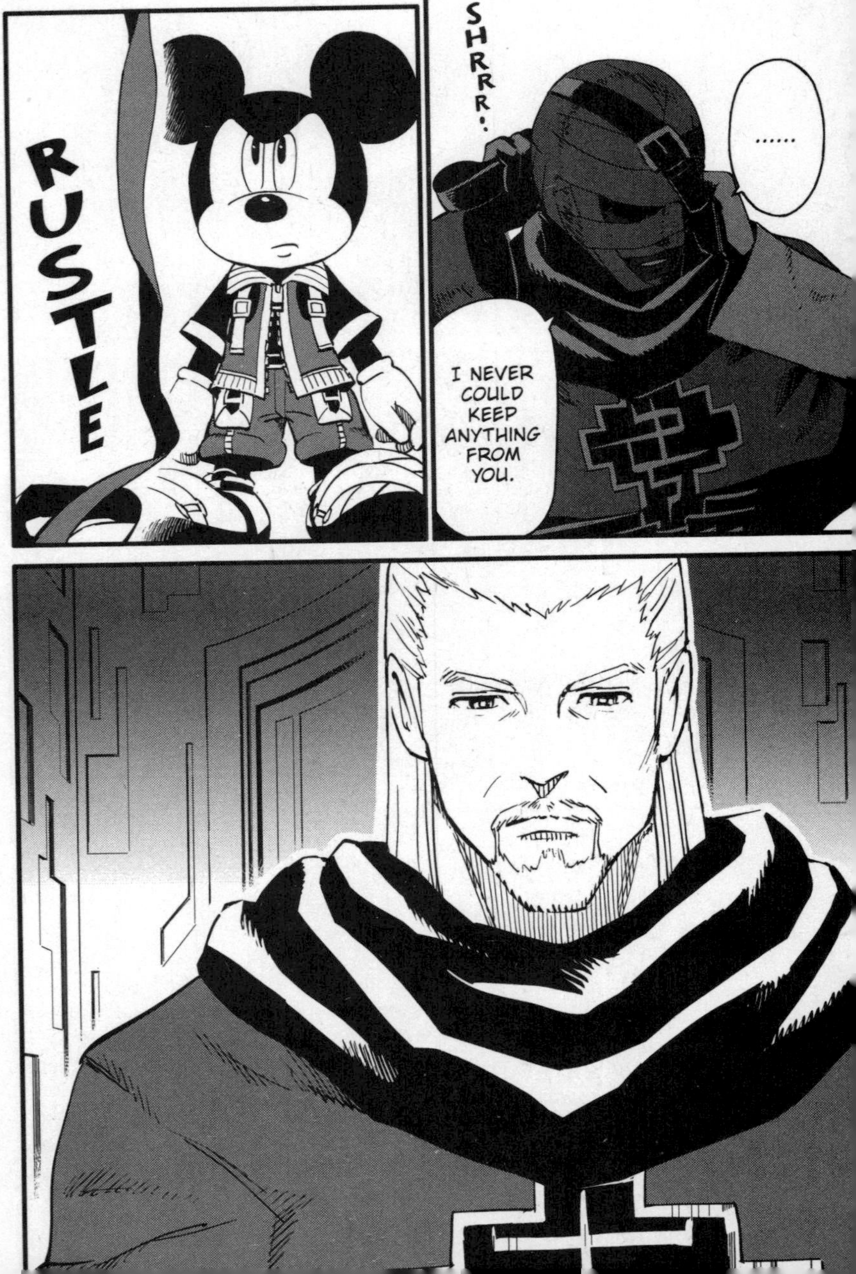
......
SHRRR..
I NEVER COULD KEEP ANYTHING FROM YOU.
RUSTLE

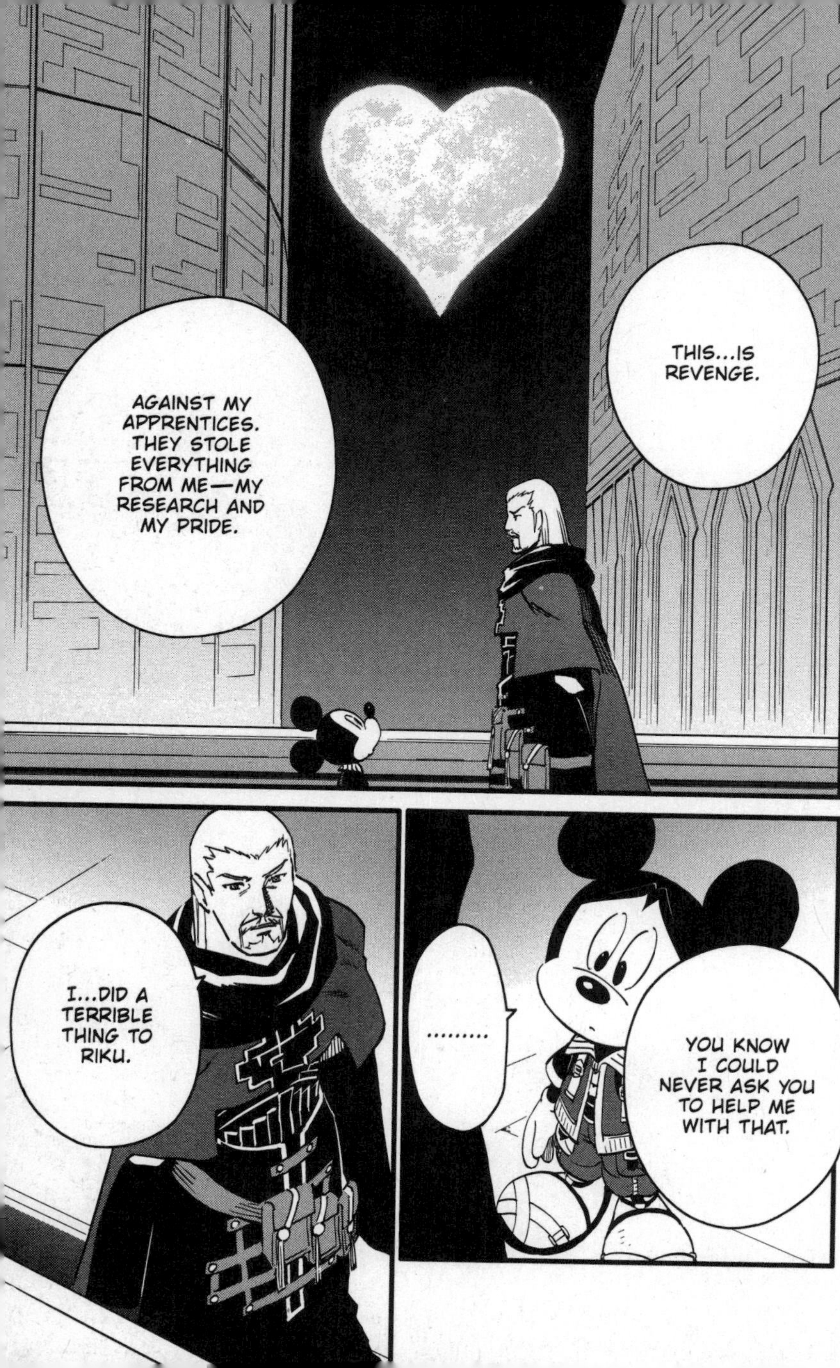
THIS...IS REVENGE.
AGAINST MY APPRENTICES. THEY STOLE EVERYTHING FROM ME—MY RESEARCH AND MY PRIDE.
YOU KNOW I COULD NEVER ASK YOU TO HELP ME WITH THAT.
....
I...DID A TERRIBLE THING TO RIKU.

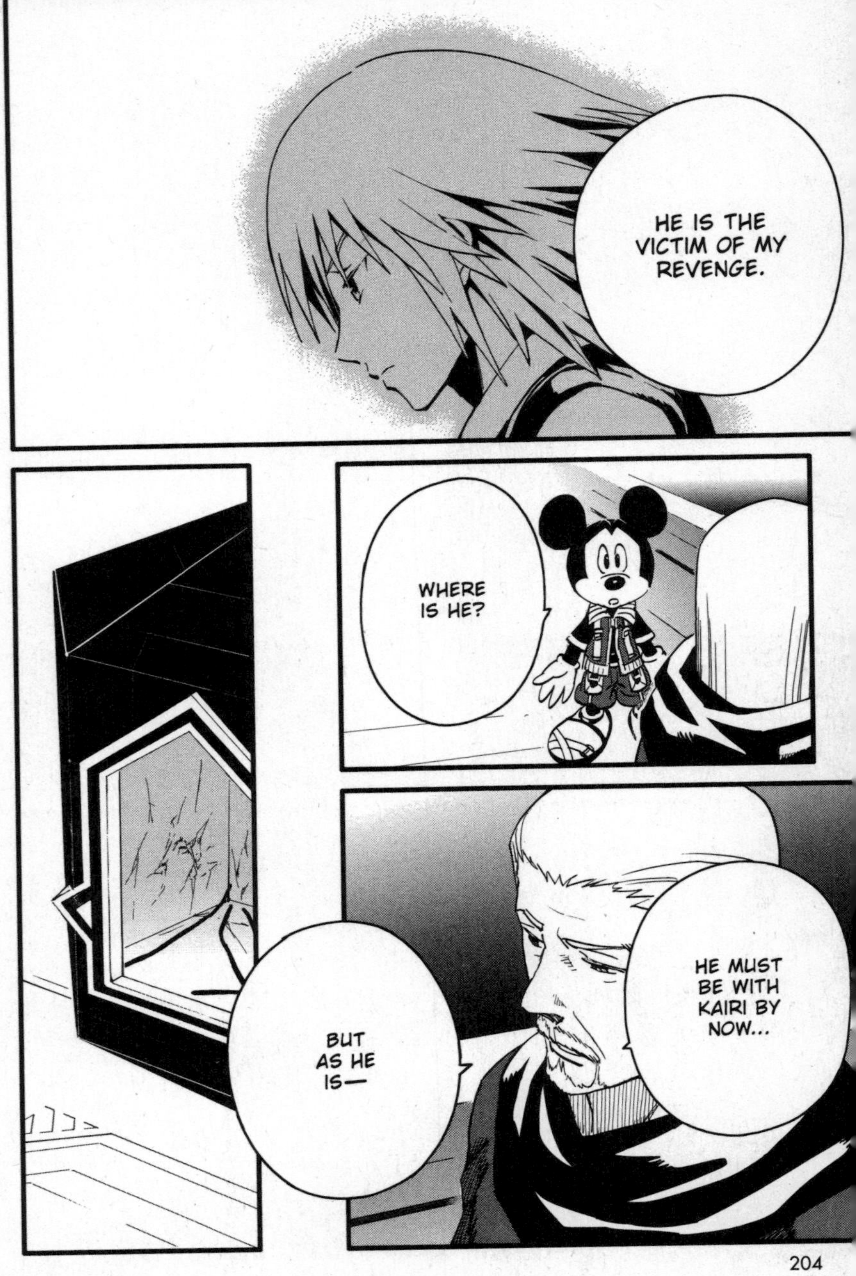
HE IS THE VICTIM OF MY REVENGE.
WHERE IS HE?
HE MUST BE WITH KAIRI BY NOW...
BUT AS HE IS—

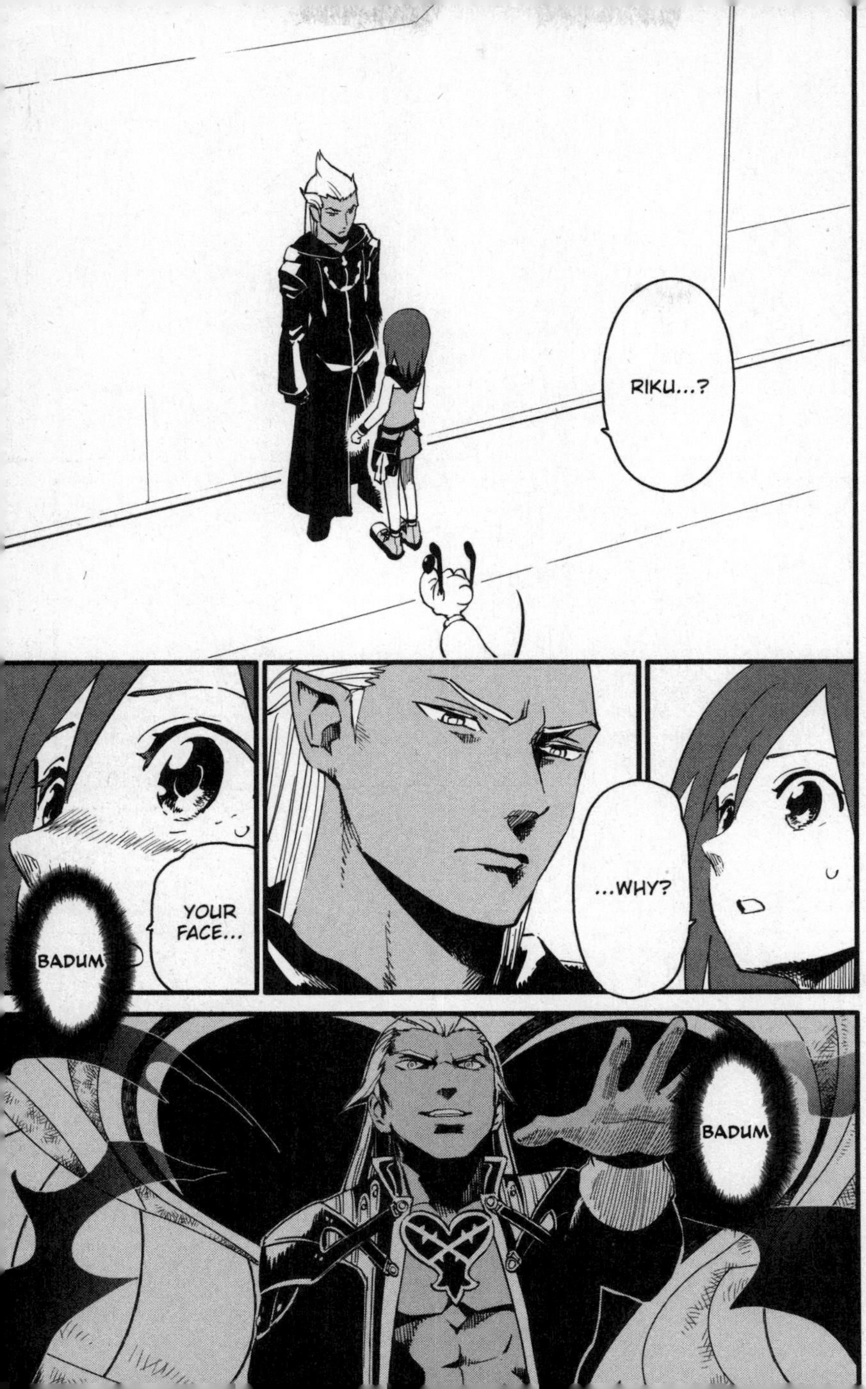
RIKU...?
...WHY?
YOUR FACE...
BADUM
BADUM

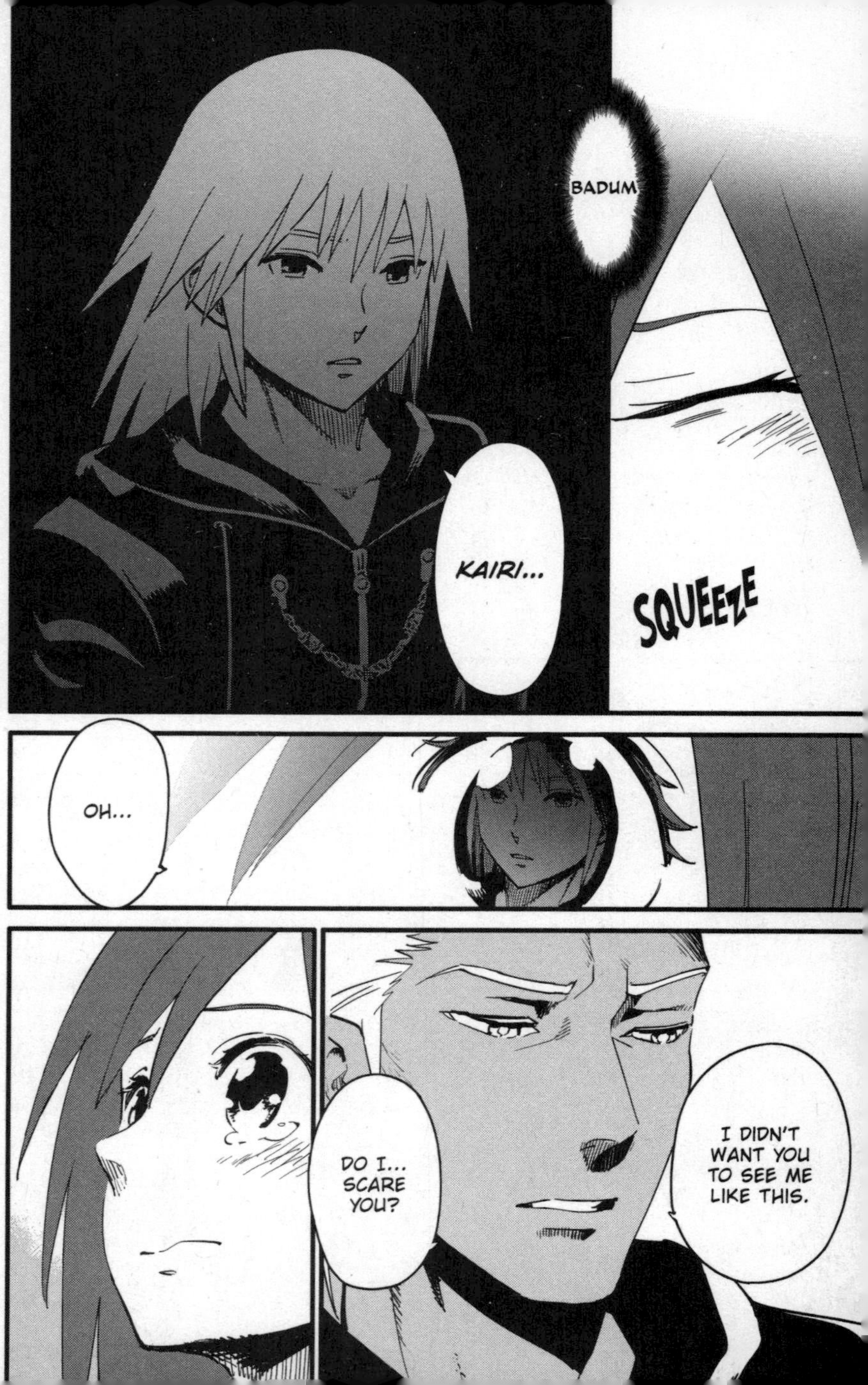
BADUM
SQUEEZE
KAIRI...
OH...
I DIDN'T WANT YOU TO SEE ME LIKE THIS.
DO I... SCARE YOU?

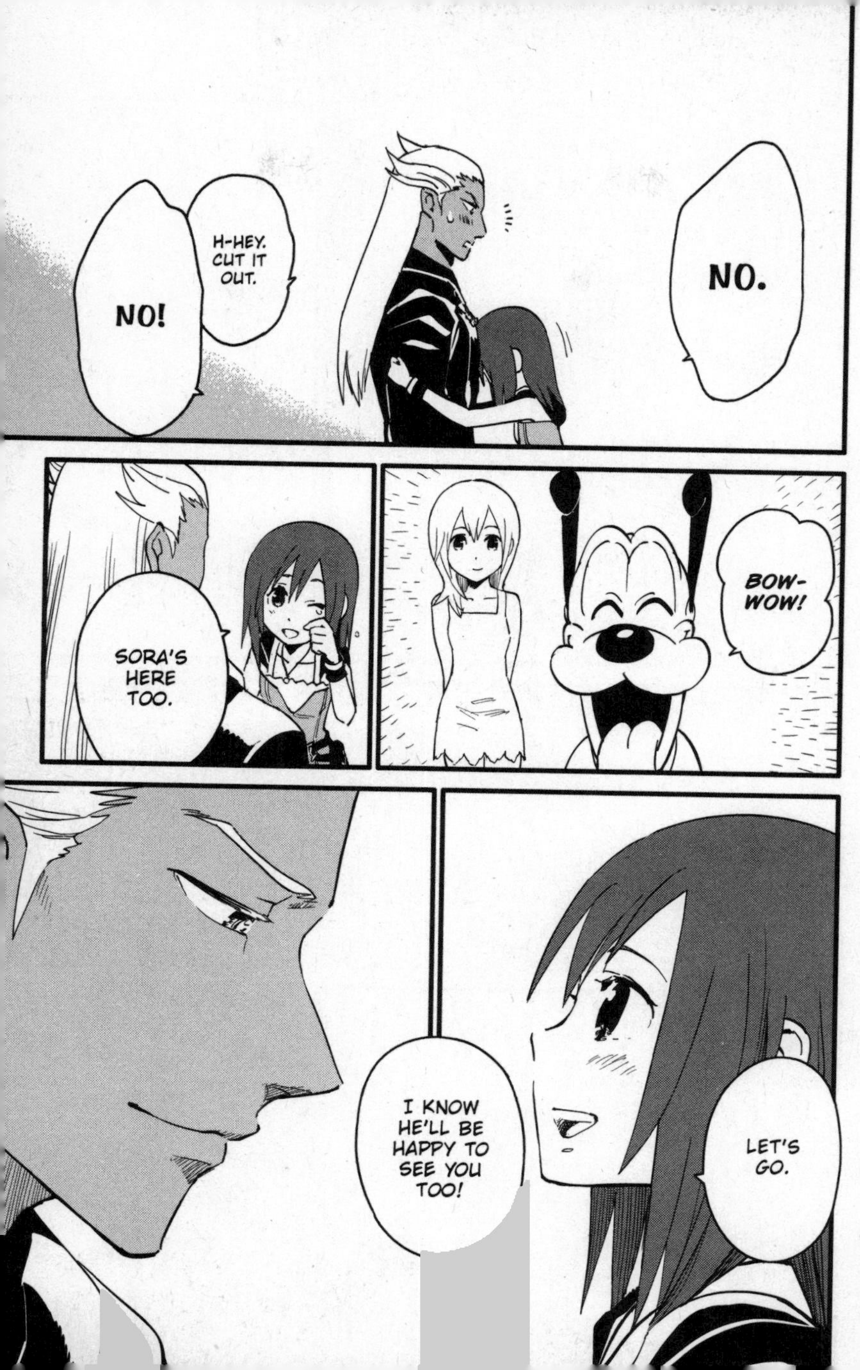
NO.
H-HEY. CUT IT OUT.
NO!
BOW-WOW!
SORA'S HERE TOO.
LET'S GO.
I KNOW HE'LL BE HAPPY TO SEE YOU TOO!

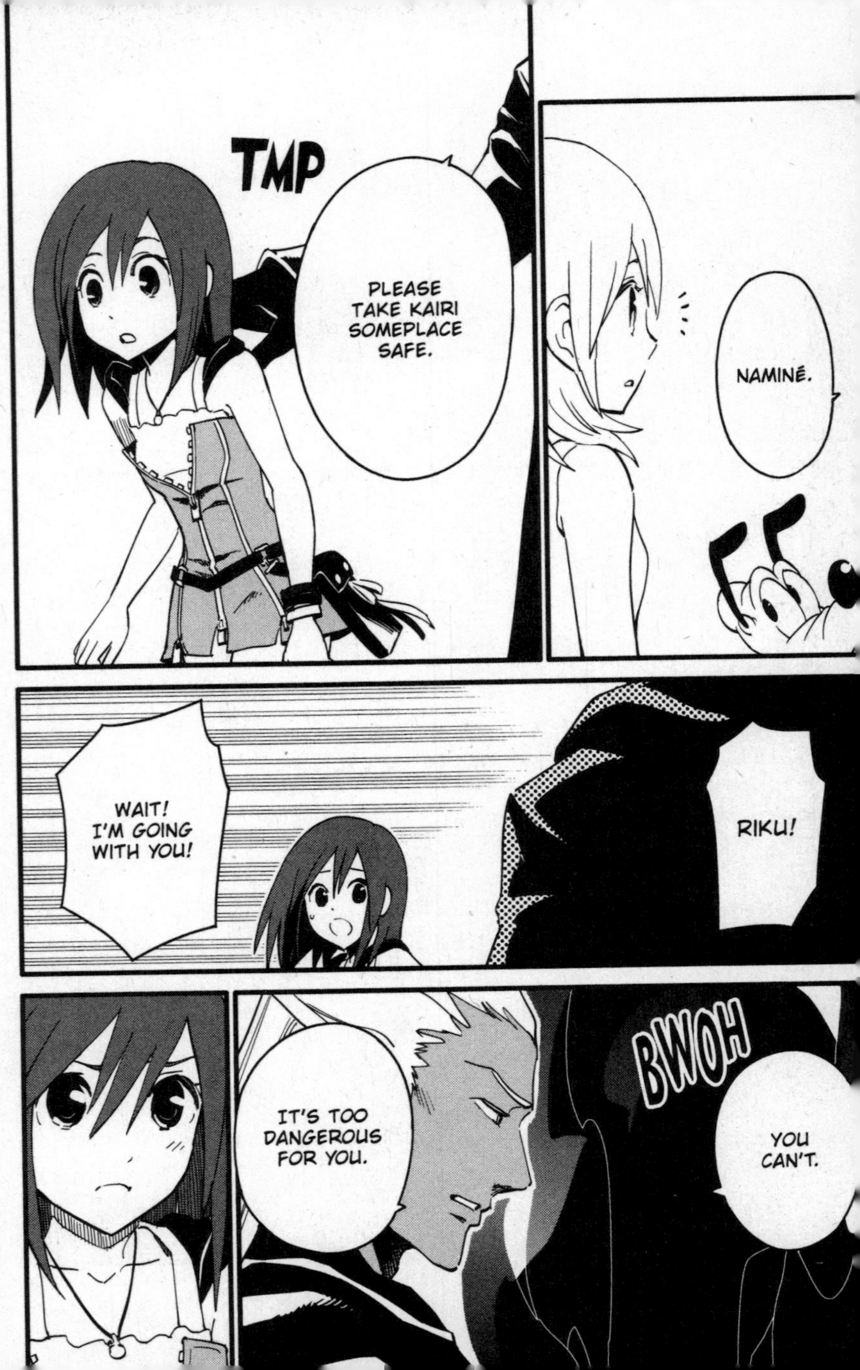
NAMINÉ.
TMP
PLEASE TAKE KAIRI SOMEPLACE SAFE.
RIKU!
WAIT! I'M GOING WITH YOU!
BWOH
YOU CAN'T.
IT'S TOO DANGEROUS FOR YOU.

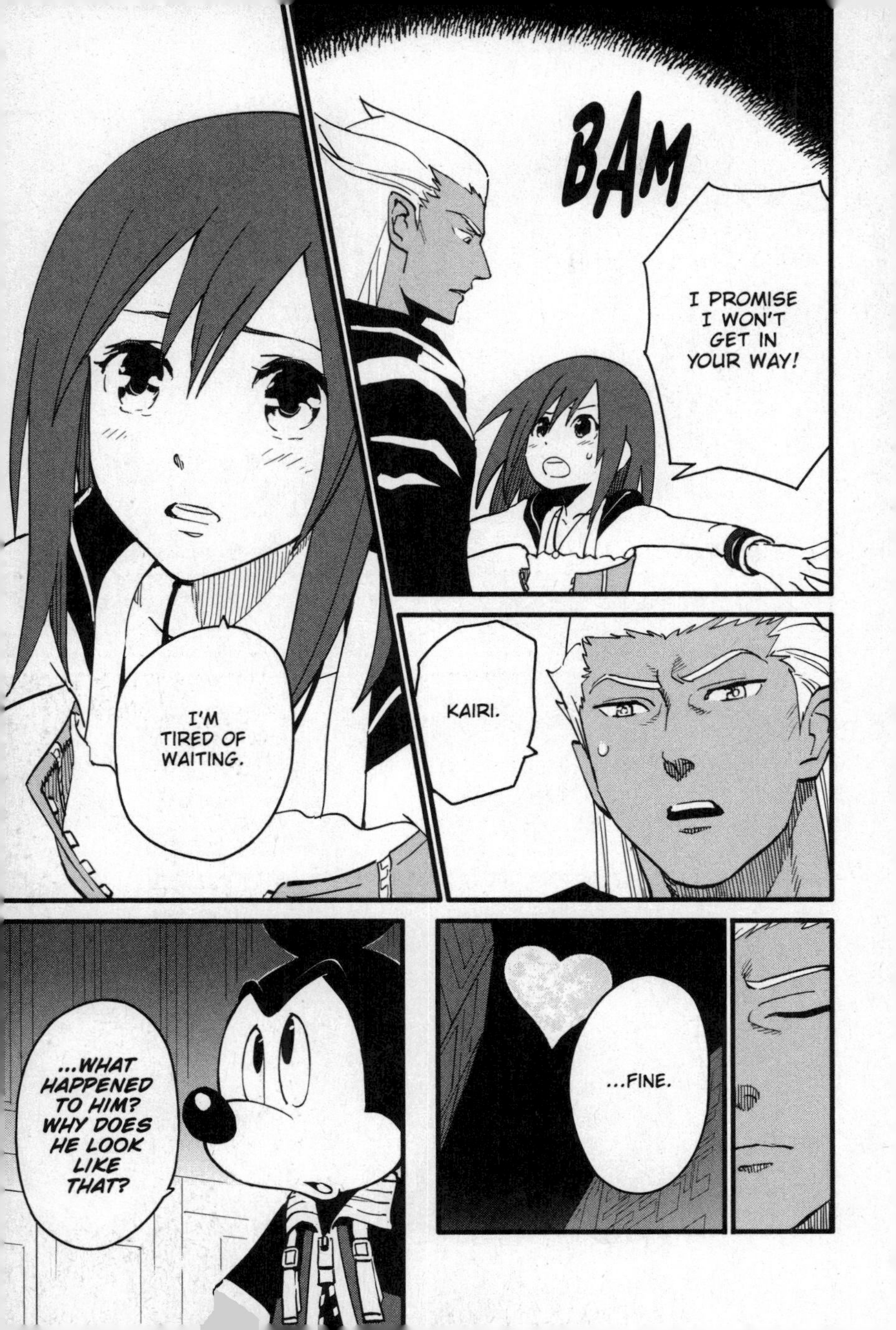
BAM
I PROMISE I WON'T GET IN YOUR WAY!
KAIRI.
I'M TIRED OF WAITING.
...FINE.
...WHAT HAPPENED TO HIM? WHY DOES HE LOOK LIKE THAT?

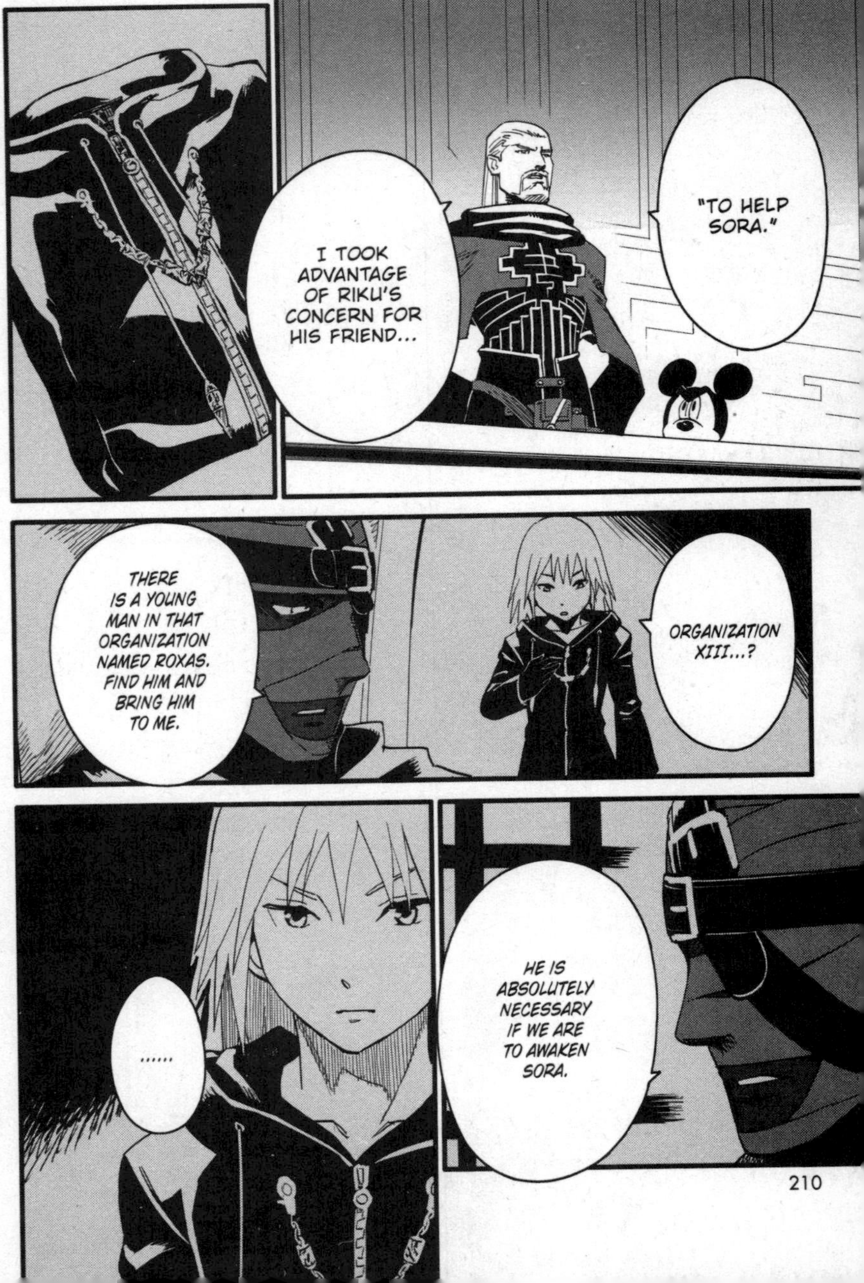
"TO HELP SORA."
I TOOK ADVANTAGE OF RIKU'S CONCERN FOR HIS FRIEND...
ORGANIZATION XIII...?
THERE IS A YOUNG MAN IN THAT ORGANIZATION NAMED ROXAS. FIND HIM AND BRING HIM TO ME.
HE IS ABSOLUTELY NECESSARY IF WE ARE TO AWAKEN SORA.
......

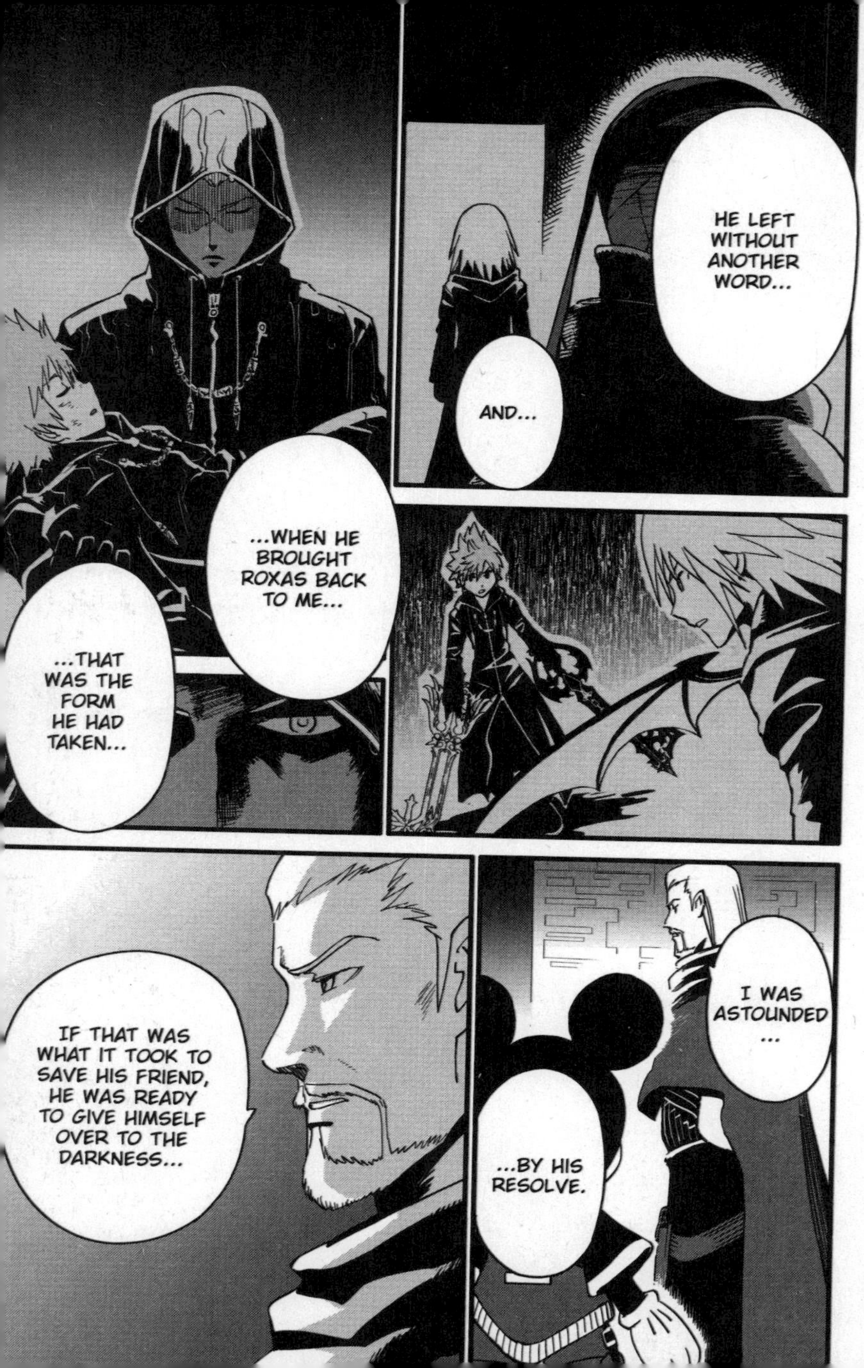
HE LEFT WITHOUT ANOTHER WORD...
AND...
...WHEN HE BROUGHT ROXAS BACK TO ME...
...THAT WAS THE FORM HE HAD TAKEN...
I WAS ASTOUNDED...
...BY HIS RESOLVE.
IF THAT WAS WHAT IT TOOK TO SAVE HIS FRIEND, HE WAS READY TO GIVE HIMSELF OVER TO THE DARKNESS...

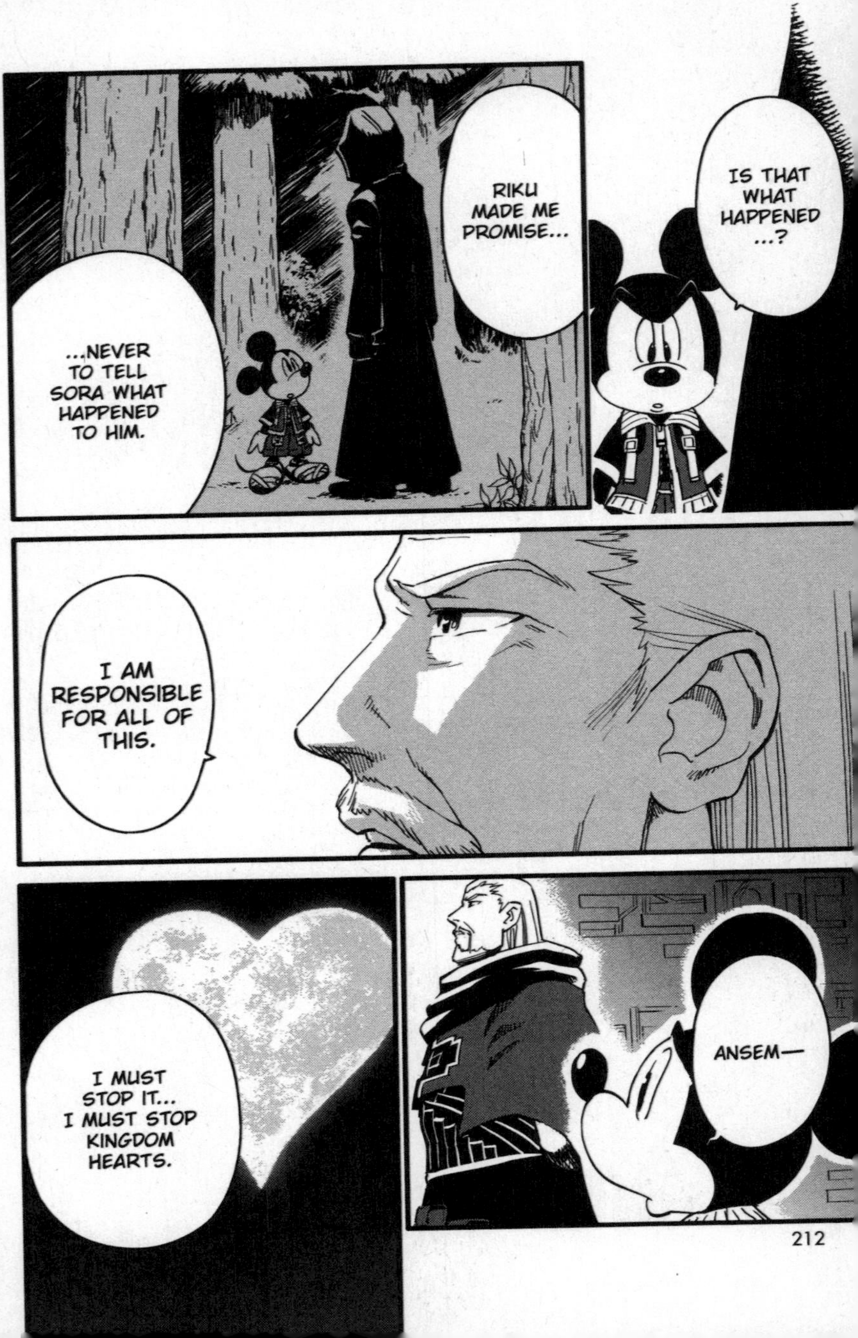
IS THAT WHAT HAPPENED ...?
RIKU MADE ME PROMISE...
...NEVER TO TELL SORA WHAT HAPPENED TO HIM.
I AM RESPONSIBLE FOR ALL OF THIS.
ANSEM—
I MUST STOP IT... I MUST STOP KINGDOM HEARTS.

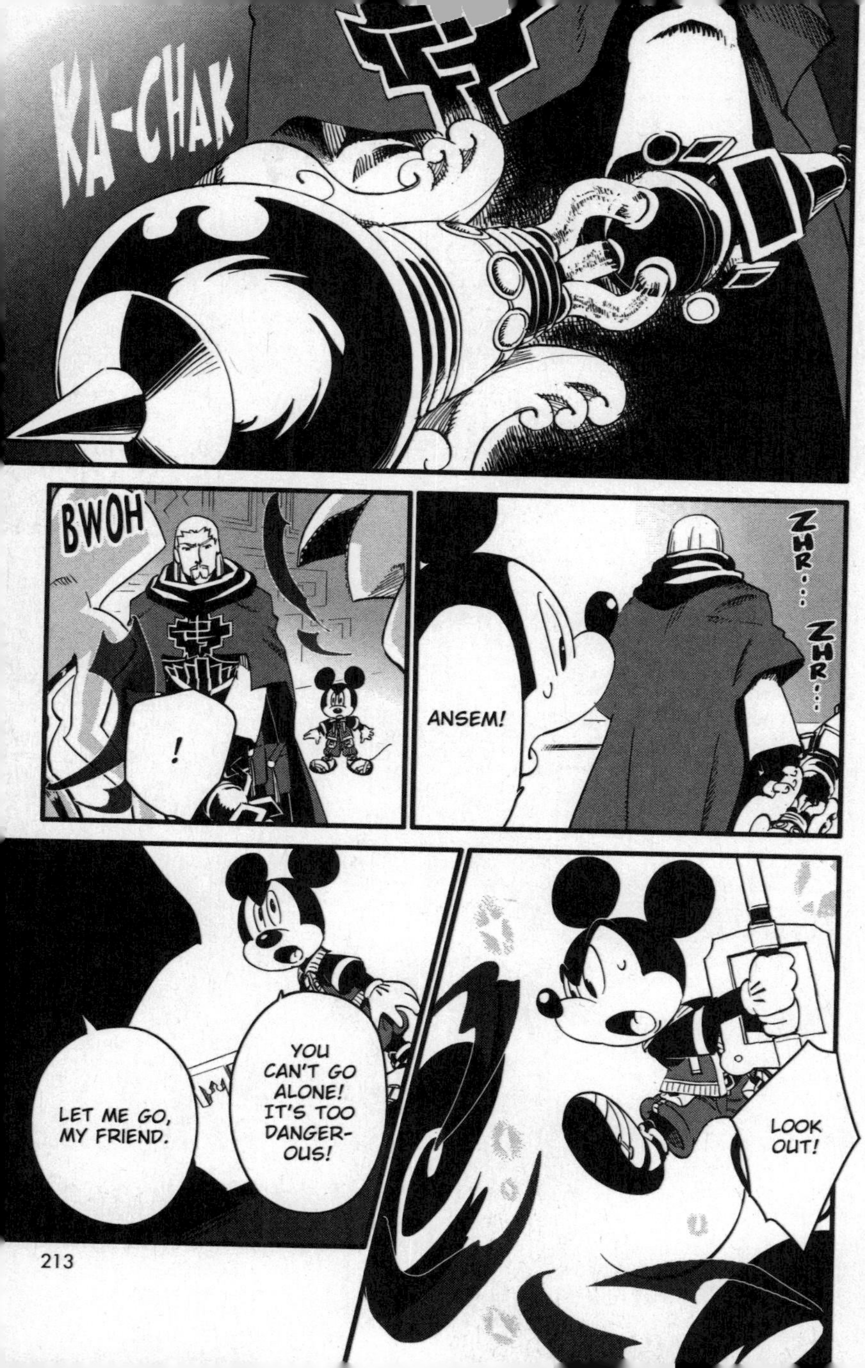
KA-CHAK
ZHR... ZHR...
ANSEM!
BWOH
!
LOOK OUT!
YOU CAN'T GO ALONE! IT'S TOO DANGER-OUS!
LET ME GO, MY FRIEND.

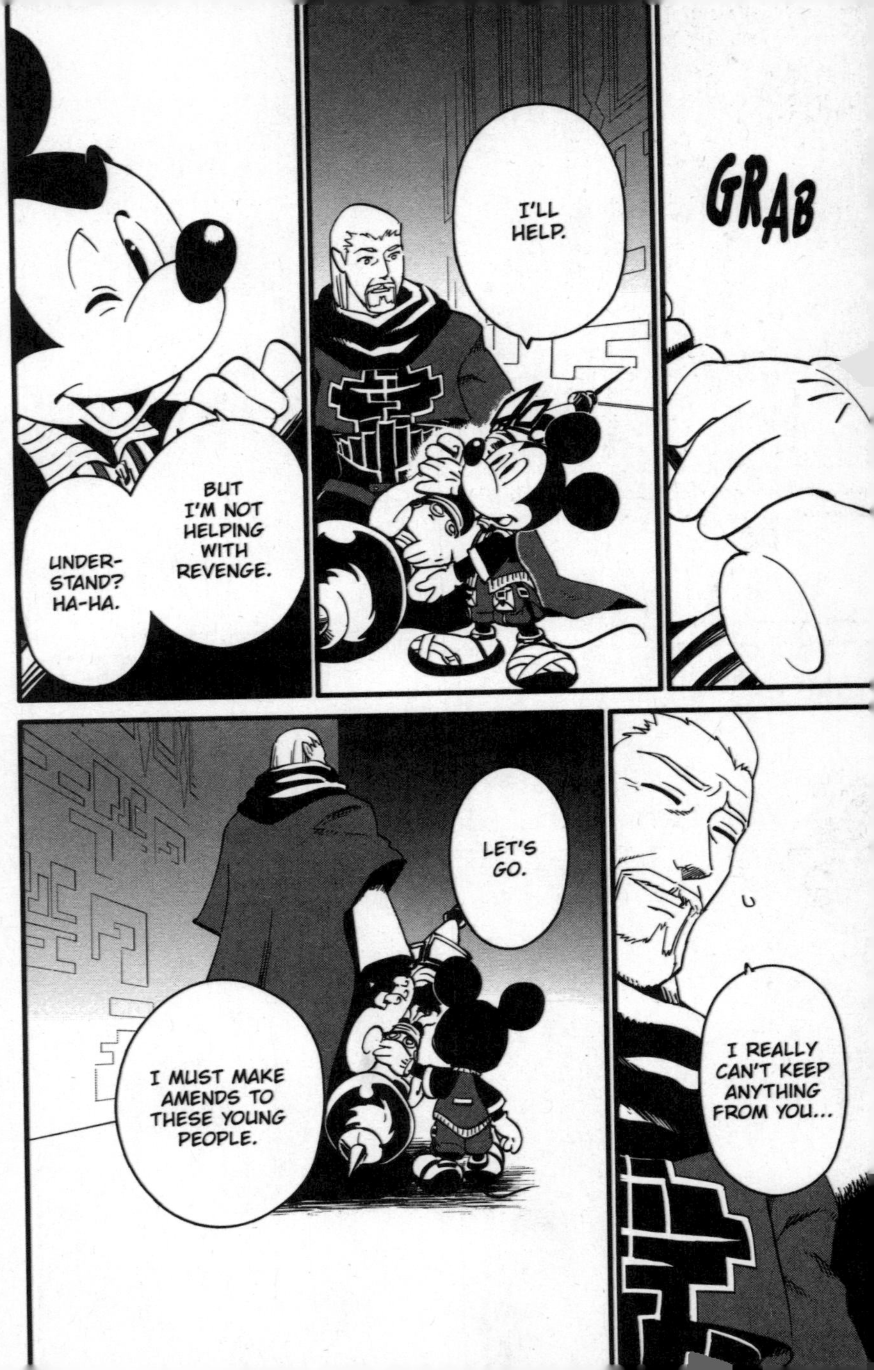
GRAB
I'LL HELP.
BUT I'M NOT HELPING WITH REVENGE.
UNDER-STAND? HA-HA.
I REALLY CAN'T KEEP ANYTHING FROM YOU...
LET'S GO.
I MUST MAKE AMENDS TO THESE YOUNG PEOPLE.

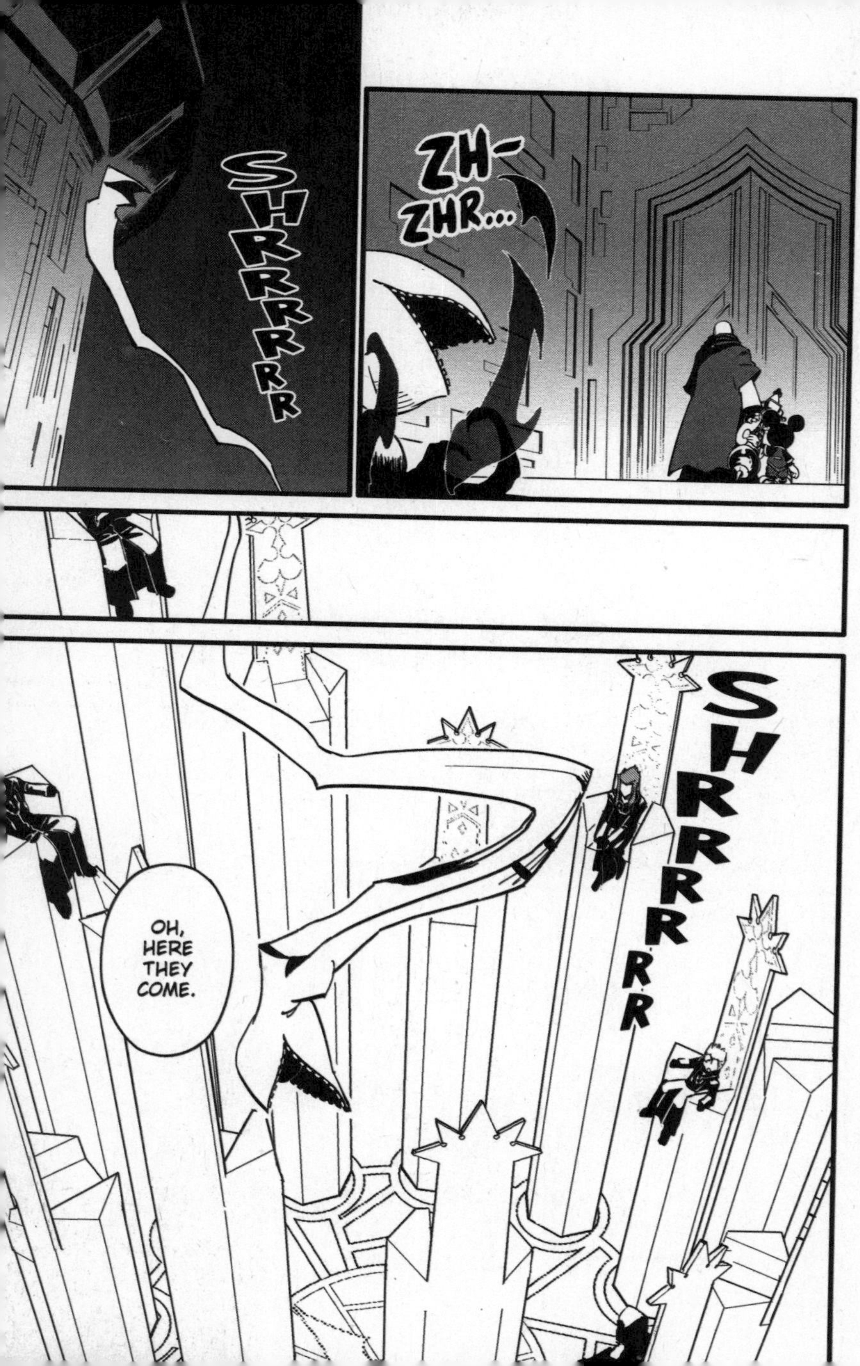
ZH-ZHR...
SHRRRRRR
SHRRRRRRR
OH, HERE THEY COME.

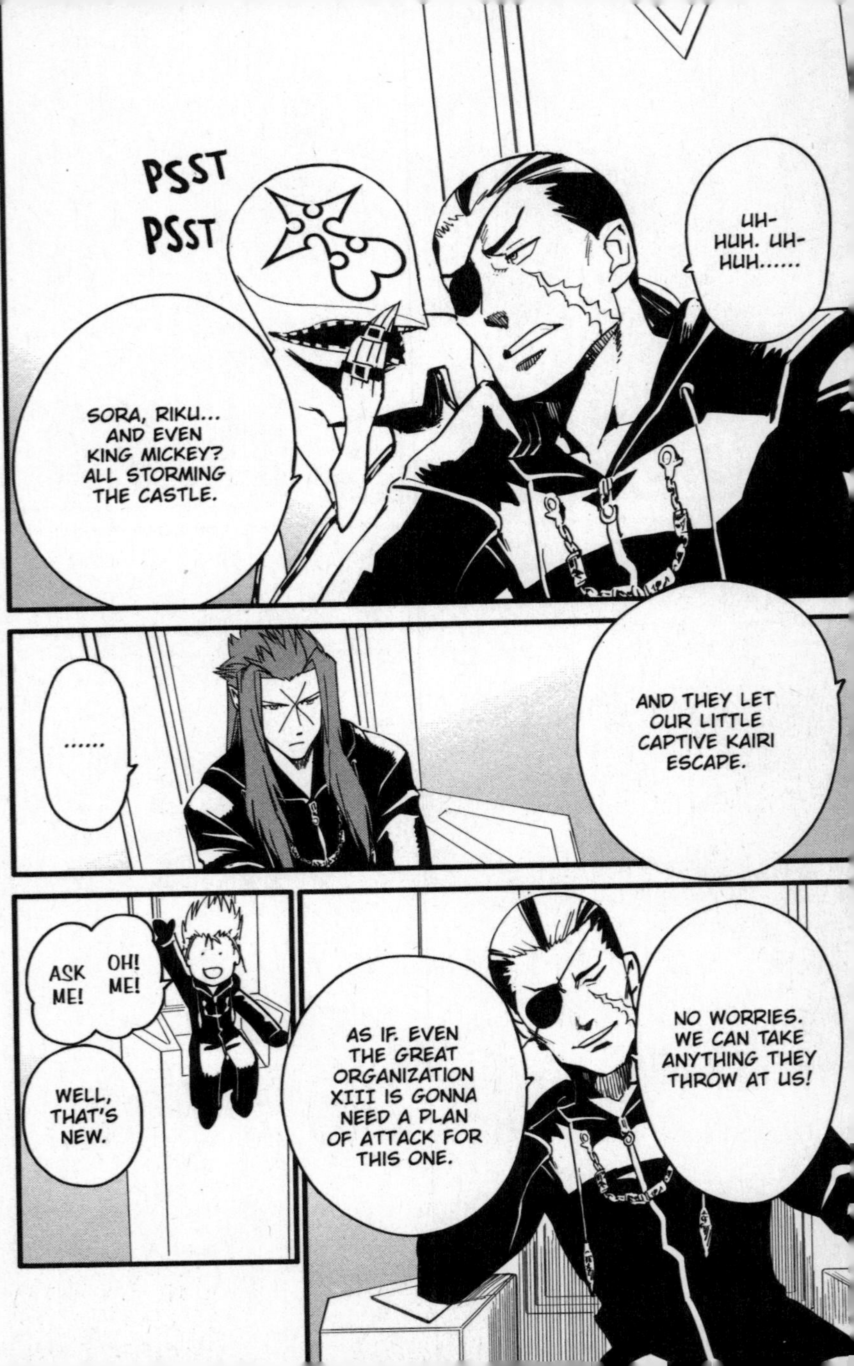
UH-HUH. UH-HUH......
PSST
PSST
SORA, RIKU... AND EVEN KING MICKEY? ALL STORMING THE CASTLE.
AND THEY LET OUR LITTLE CAPTIVE KAIRI ESCAPE.
......
NO WORRIES. WE CAN TAKE ANYTHING THEY THROW AT US!
AS IF. EVEN THE GREAT ORGANIZATION XIII IS GONNA NEED A PLAN OF ATTACK FOR THIS ONE.
OH! ME!
ASK ME!
WELL, THAT'S NEW.

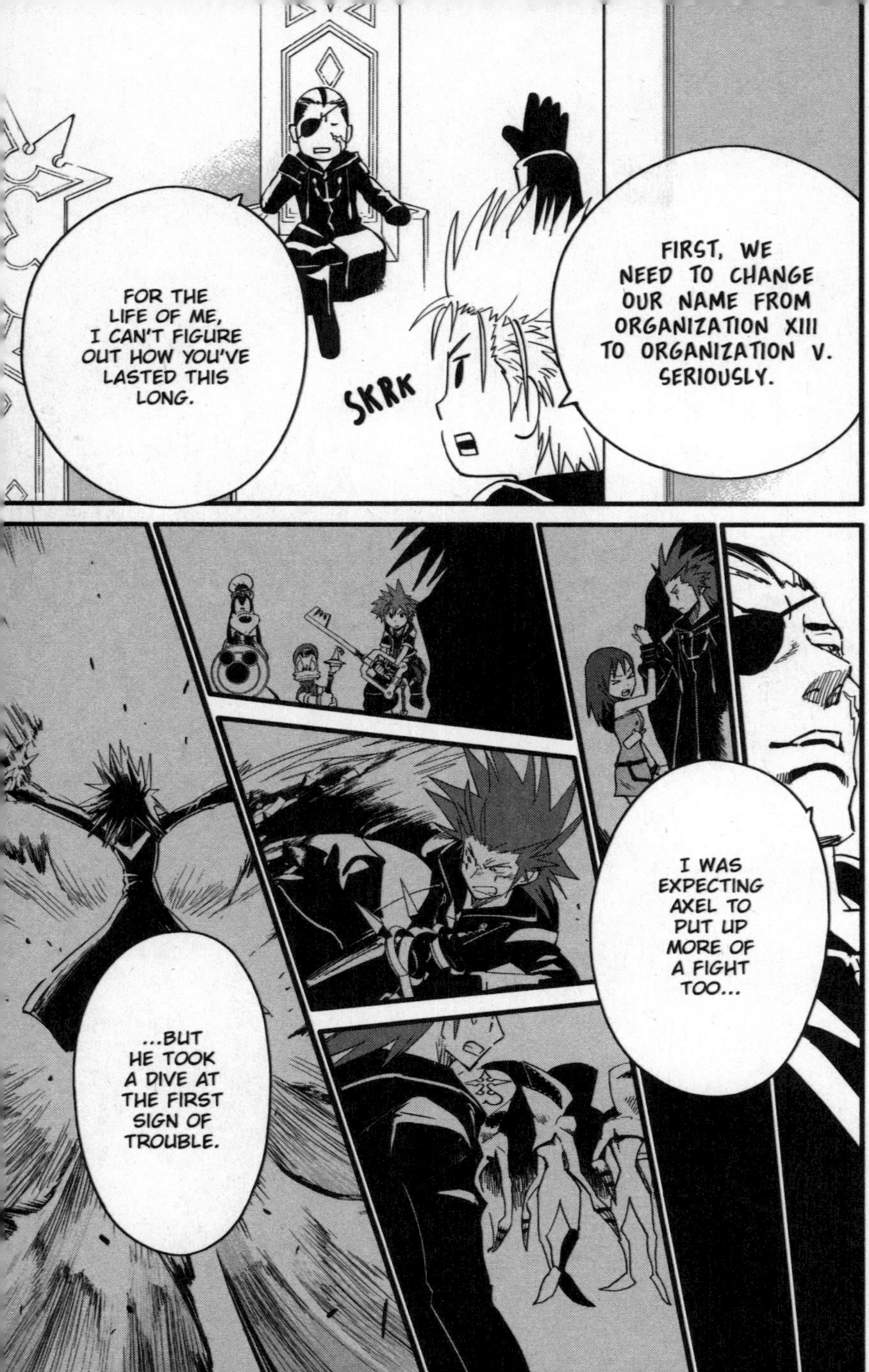
FIRST, WE NEED TO CHANGE OUR NAME FROM ORGANIZATION XIII TO ORGANIZATION V. SERIOUSLY.
SKRK
FOR THE LIFE OF ME, I CAN'T FIGURE OUT HOW YOU'VE LASTED THIS LONG.
I WAS EXPECTING AXEL TO PUT UP MORE OF A FIGHT TOO...
...BUT HE TOOK A DIVE AT THE FIRST SIGN OF TROUBLE.

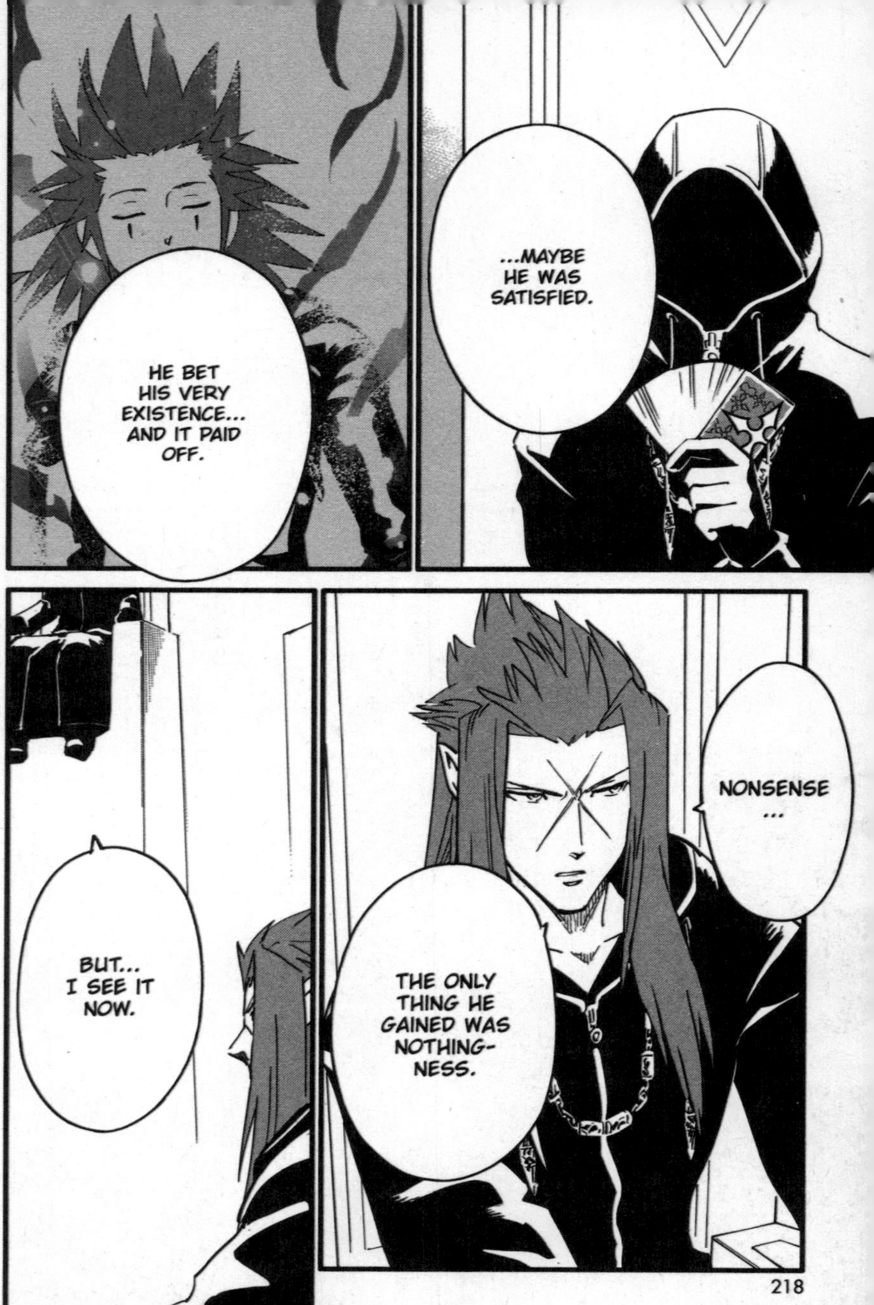
...MAYBE HE WAS SATISFIED.
HE BET HIS VERY EXISTENCE... AND IT PAID OFF.
NONSENSE...
THE ONLY THING HE GAINED WAS NOTHING-NESS.
BUT... I SEE IT NOW.

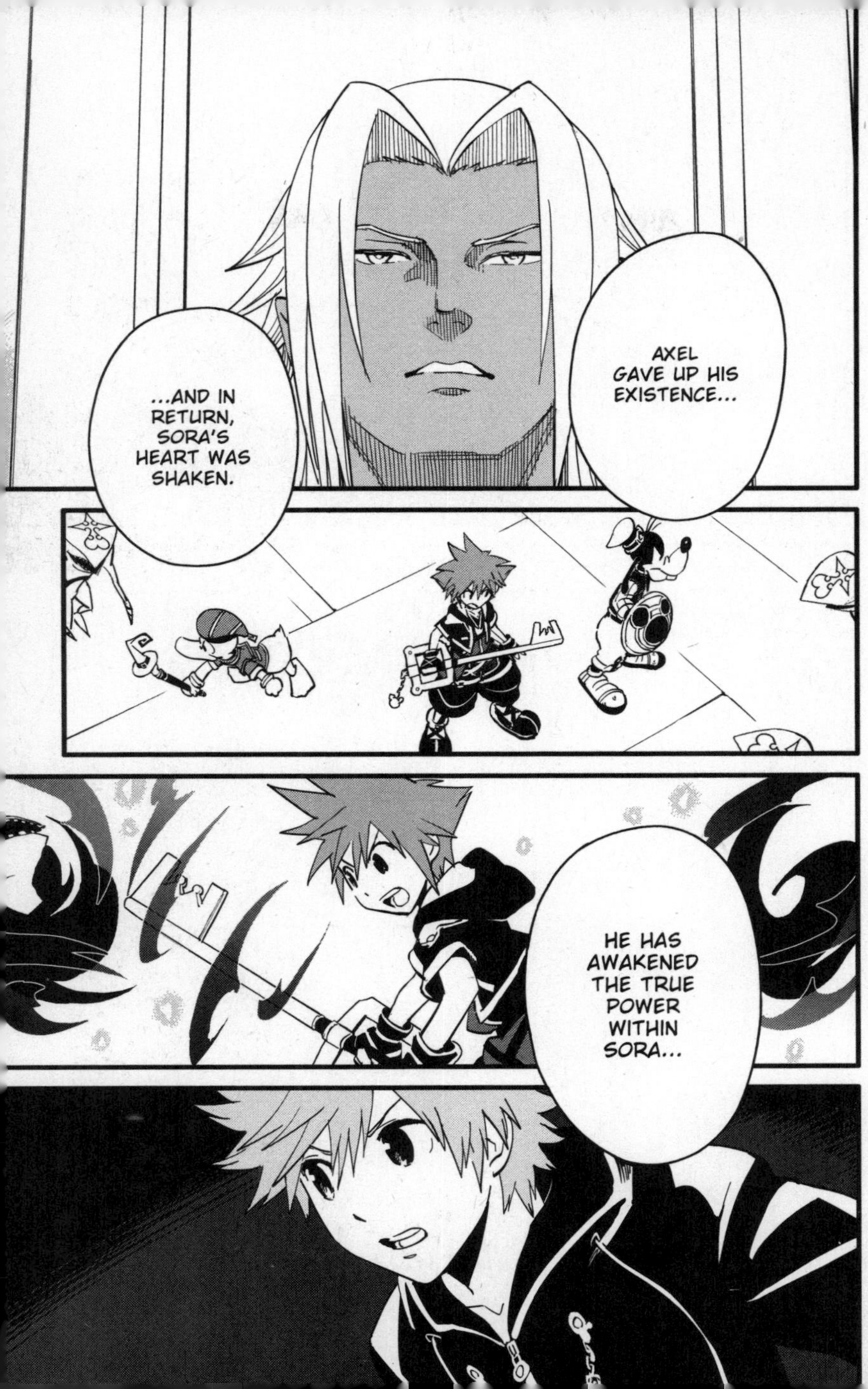
AXEL GAVE UP HIS EXISTENCE...
...AND IN RETURN, SORA'S HEART WAS SHAKEN.
HE HAS AWAKENED THE TRUE POWER WITHIN SORA...

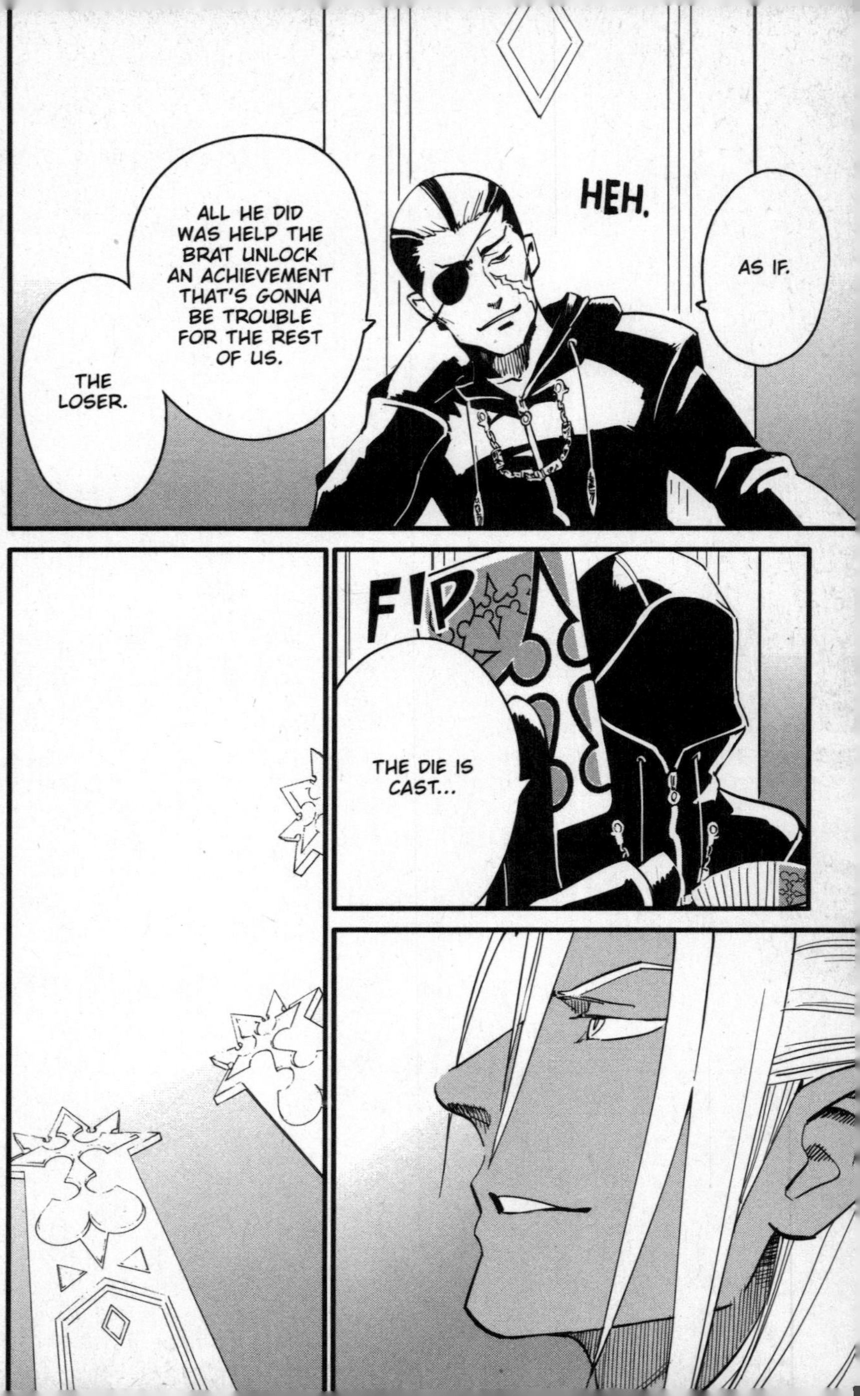
AS IF.
HEH.
ALL HE DID WAS HELP THE BRAT UNLOCK AN ACHIEVEMENT THAT'S GONNA BE TROUBLE FOR THE REST OF US.
THE LOSER.
FIP
THE DIE IS CAST...

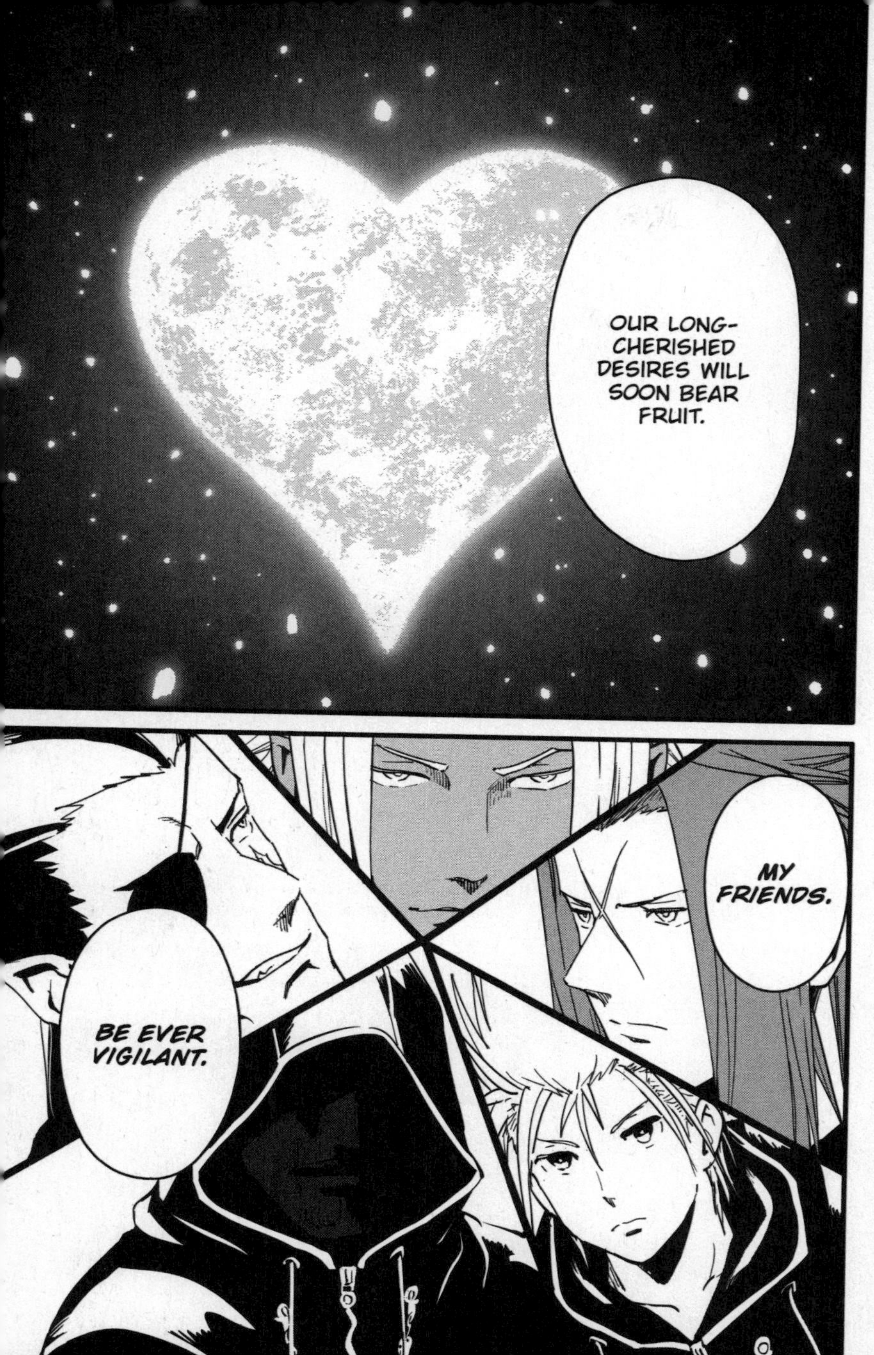
OUR LONG-CHERISHED DESIRES WILL SOON BEAR FRUIT.
MY FRIENDS.
BE EVER VIGILANT.

Disney SQUARE ENIX

KINGDOM HEARTS

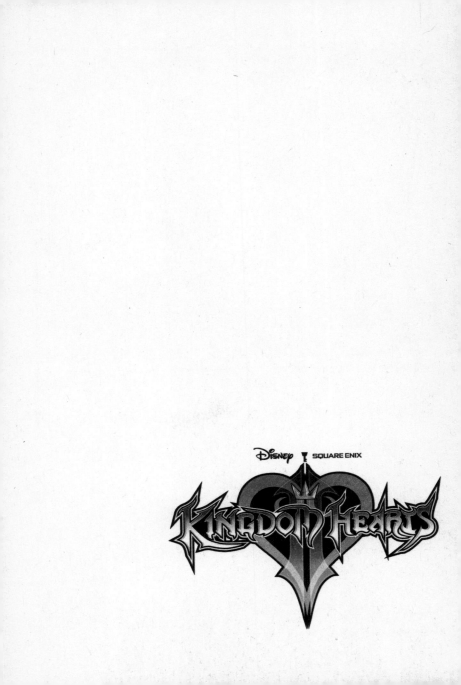

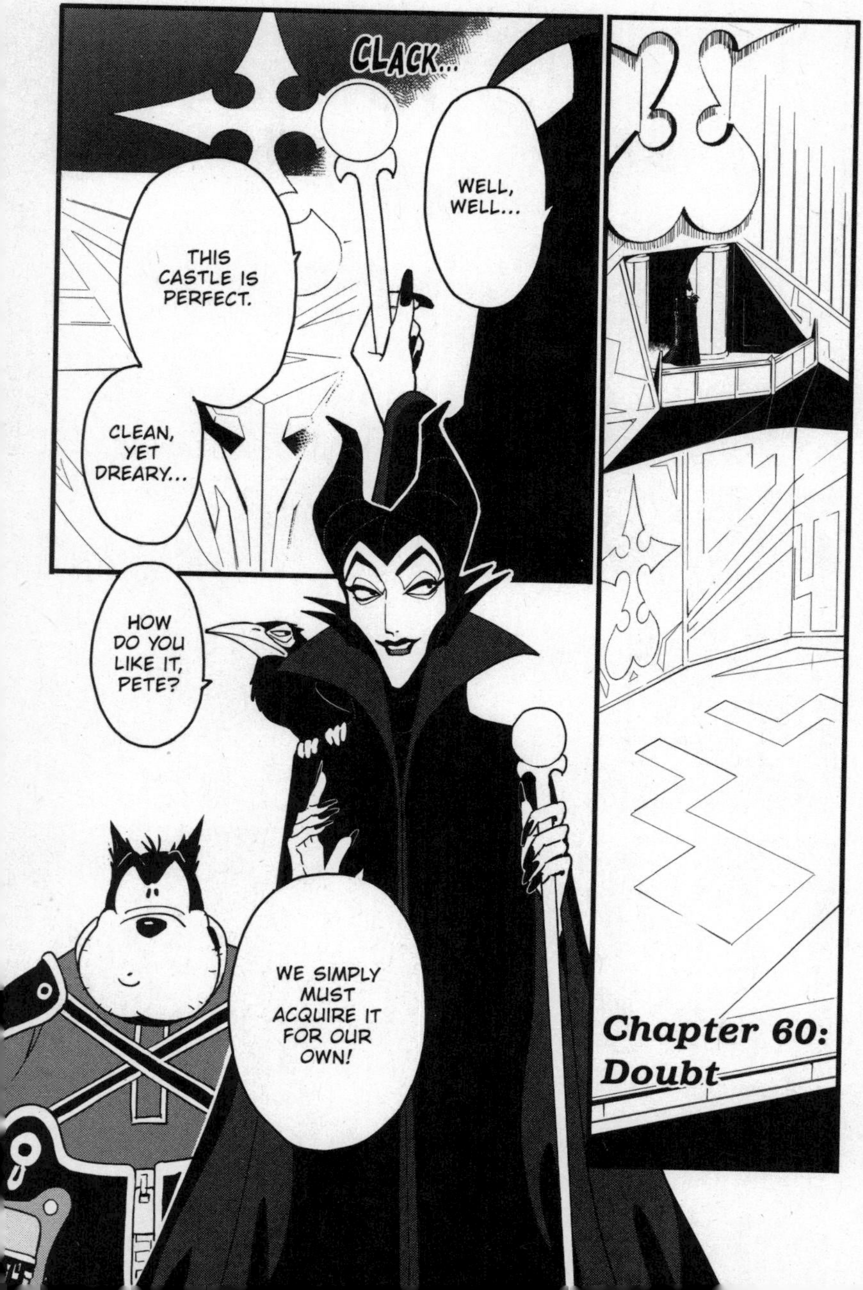
Chapter 60: Doubt
CLACK...
WELL, WELL...
THIS CASTLE IS PERFECT.
CLEAN, YET DREARY...
HOW DO YOU LIKE IT, PETE?
WE SIMPLY MUST ACQUIRE IT FOR OUR OWN!

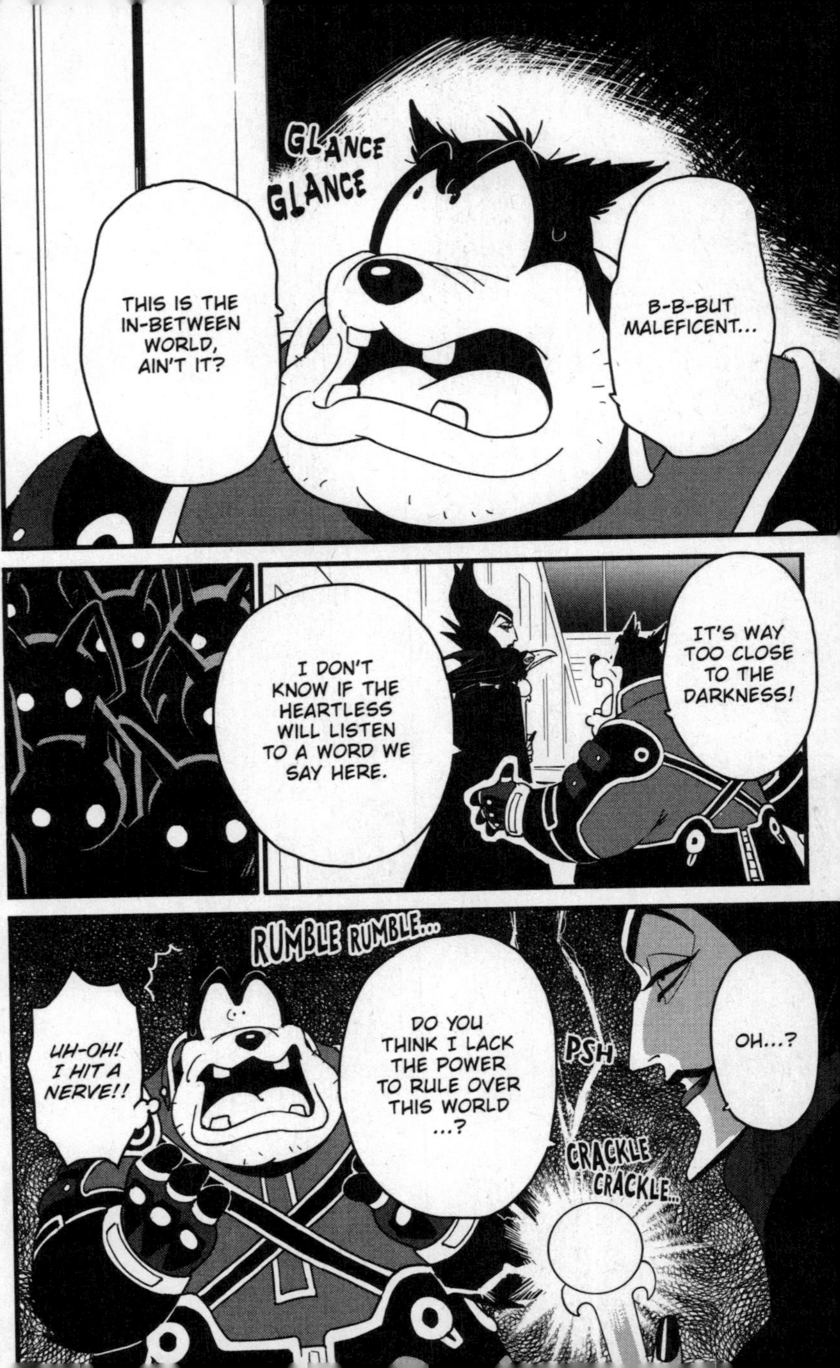
B-B-BUT MALEFICENT...
GLANCE GLANCE
THIS IS THE IN-BETWEEN WORLD, AIN'T IT?
IT'S WAY TOO CLOSE TO THE DARKNESS!
I DON'T KNOW IF THE HEARTLESS WILL LISTEN TO A WORD WE SAY HERE.
OH...?
PSH
RUMBLE RUMBLE...
DO YOU THINK I LACK THE POWER TO RULE OVER THIS WORLD ...?
CRACKLE CRACKLE...
UH-OH! I HIT A NERVE!!

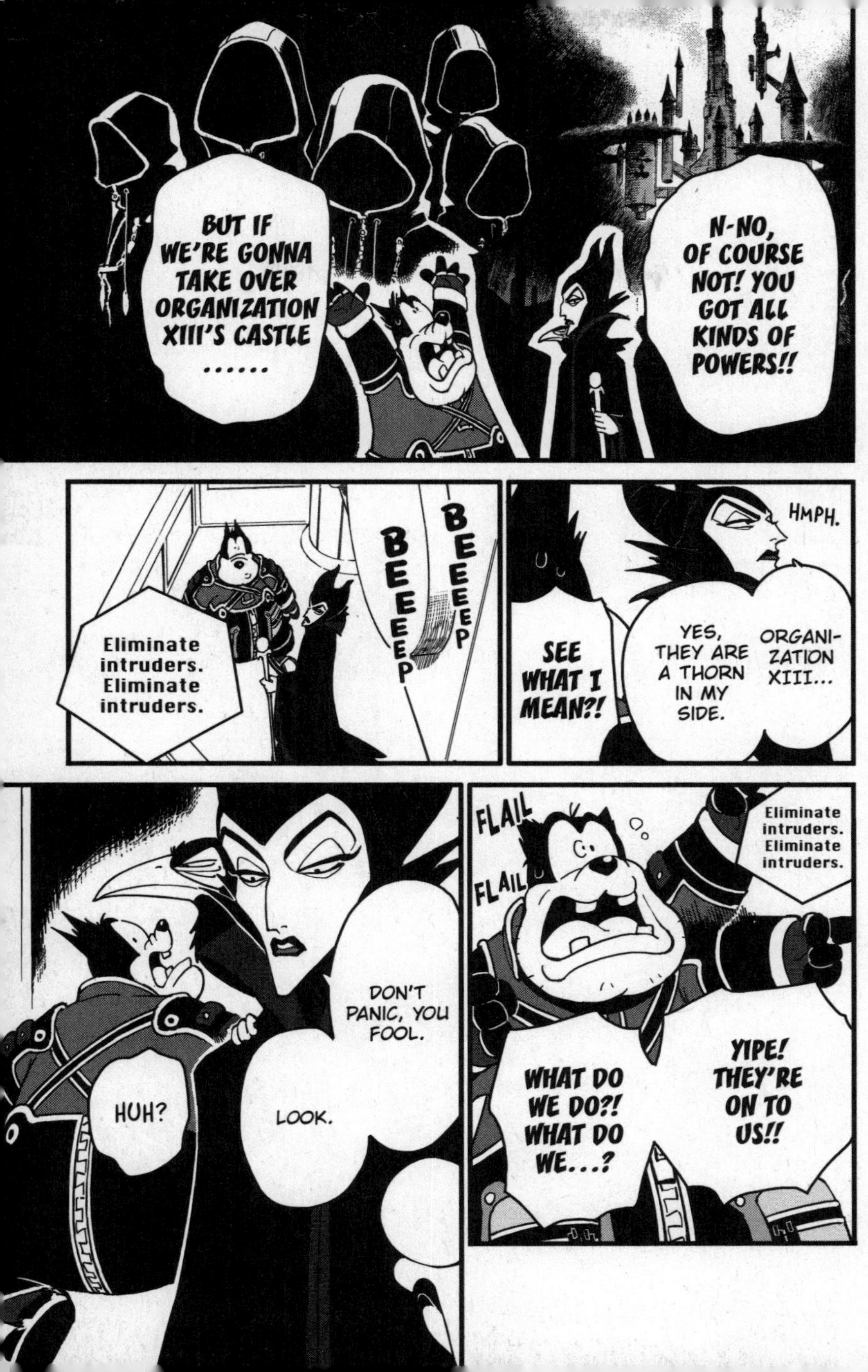
N-NO, OF COURSE NOT! YOU GOT ALL KINDS OF POWERS!!
BUT IF WE'RE GONNA TAKE OVER ORGANIZATION XIII'S CASTLE ......
HMPH.
ORGANIZATION XIII...
YES, THEY ARE A THORN IN MY SIDE.
SEE WHAT I MEAN?!
BEEEEP
BEEEEP
Eliminate intruders. Eliminate intruders.
FLAIL
FLAIL
Eliminate intruders. Eliminate intruders.
YIPE! THEY'RE ON TO US!!
WHAT DO WE DO?! WHAT DO WE...?
DON'T PANIC, YOU FOOL.
LOOK.
HUH?

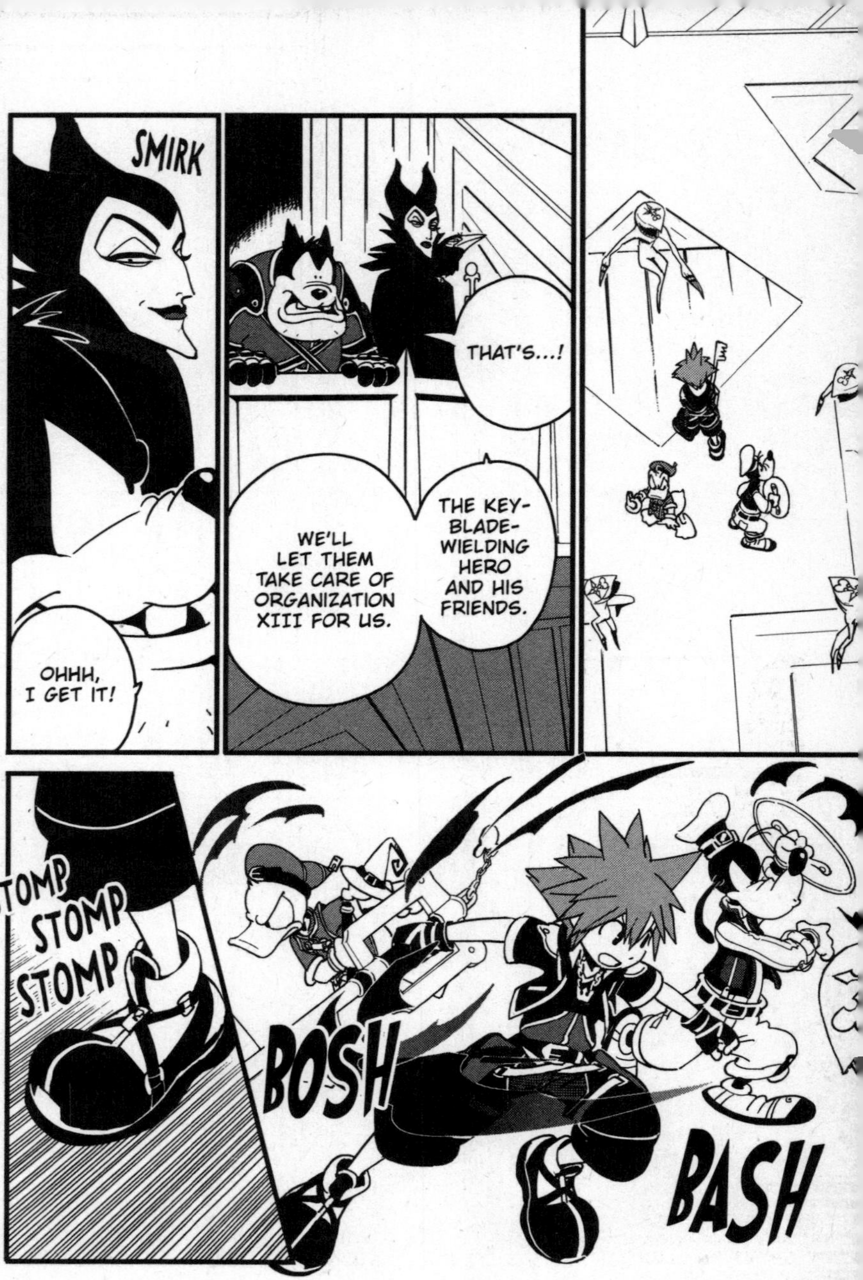
THAT'S...!
THE KEY-BLADE-WIELDING HERO AND HIS FRIENDS.
WE'LL LET THEM TAKE CARE OF ORGANIZATION XIII FOR US.
SMIRK
OHHH, I GET IT!
BASH
BOSH
STOMP STOMP STOMP

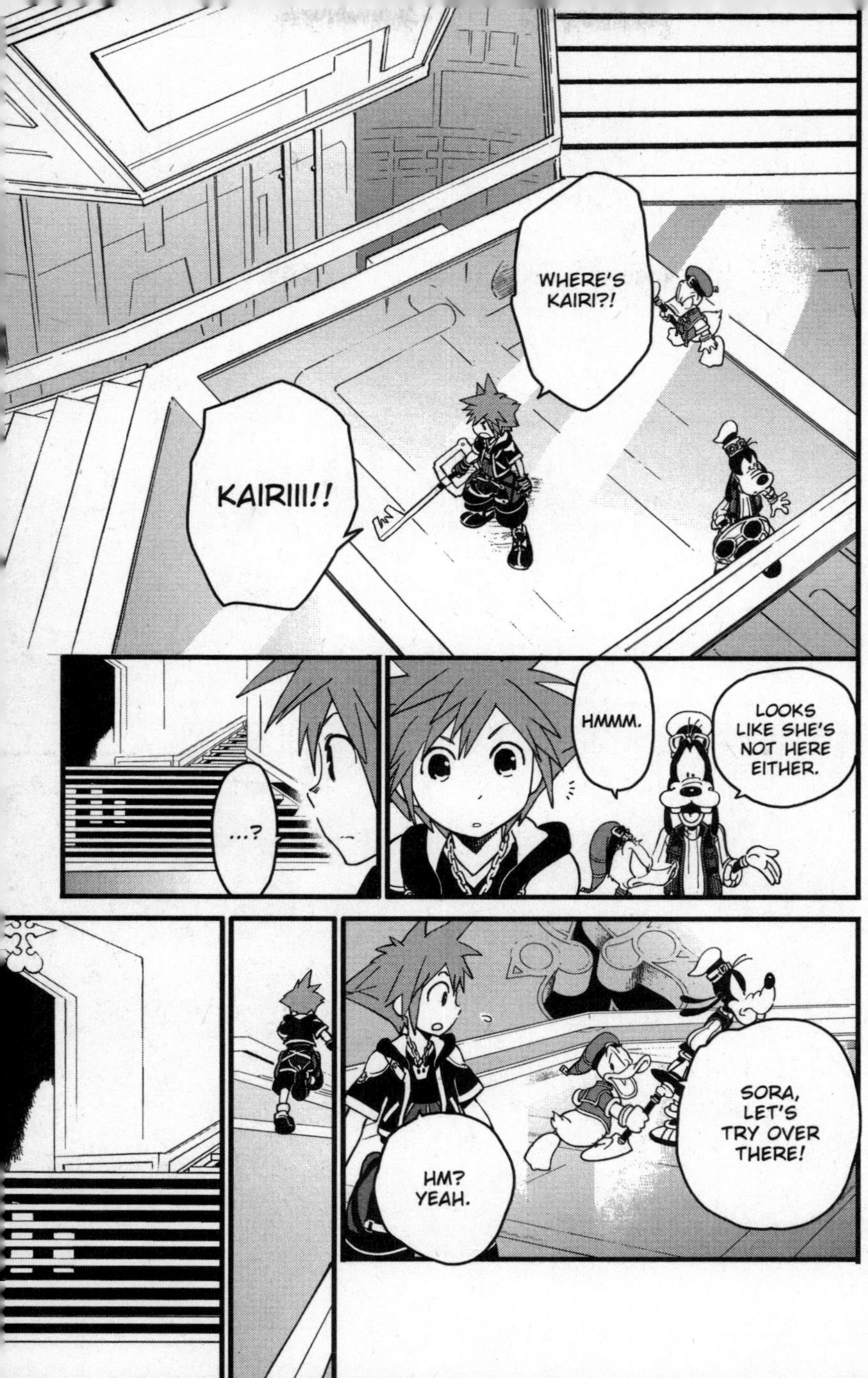
WHERE'S KAIRI?!
KAIRIIII!!
LOOKS LIKE SHE'S NOT HERE EITHER.
HMMM.
...?
SORA, LET'S TRY OVER THERE!
HM? YEAH.

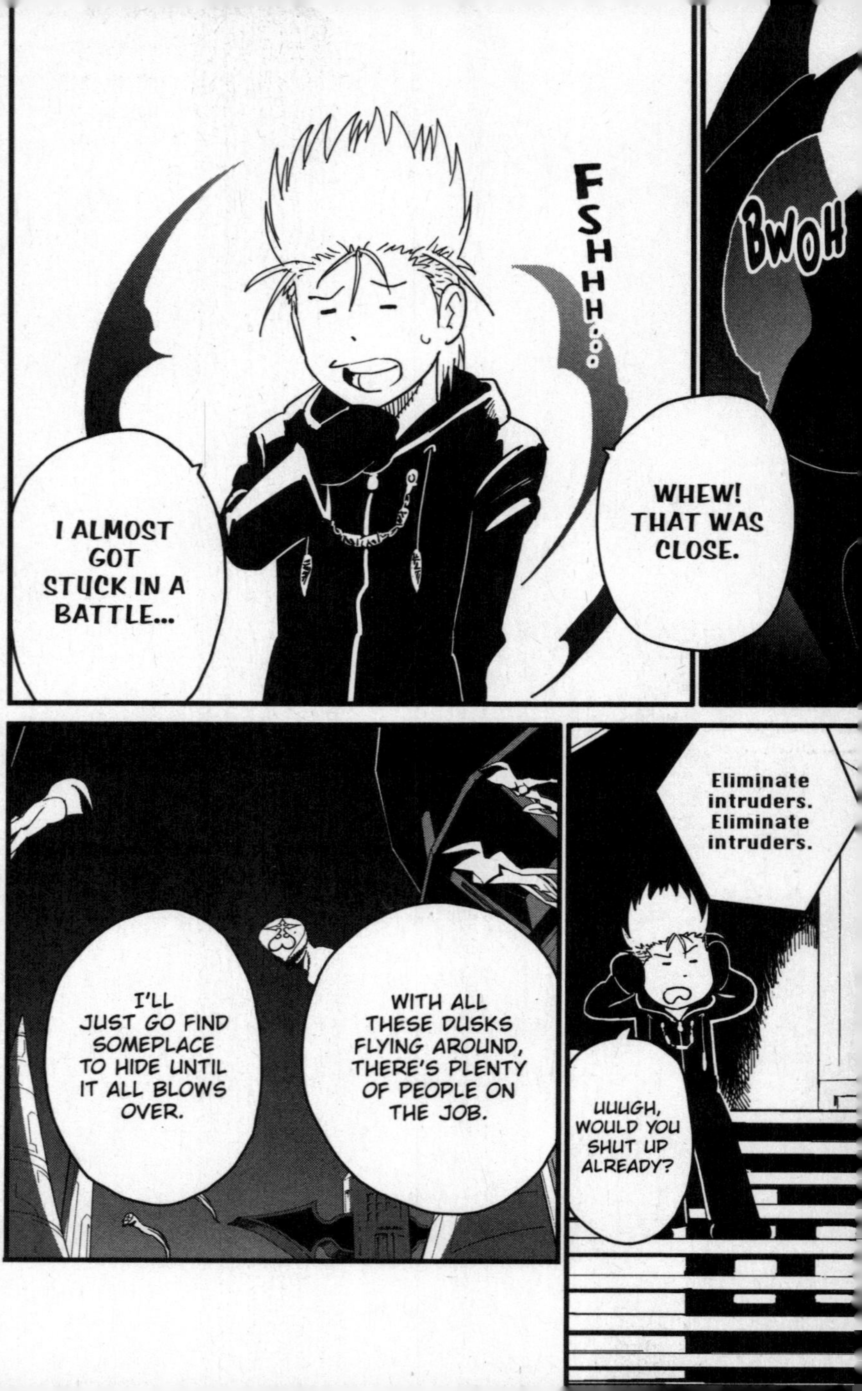
BWOH
FSHHH...
WHEW! THAT WAS CLOSE.
I ALMOST GOT STUCK IN A BATTLE...
Eliminate intruders. Eliminate intruders.
UUUGH, WOULD YOU SHUT UP ALREADY?
WITH ALL THESE DUSKS FLYING AROUND, THERE'S PLENTY OF PEOPLE ON THE JOB.
I'LL JUST GO FIND SOMEPLACE TO HIDE UNTIL IT ALL BLOWS OVER.

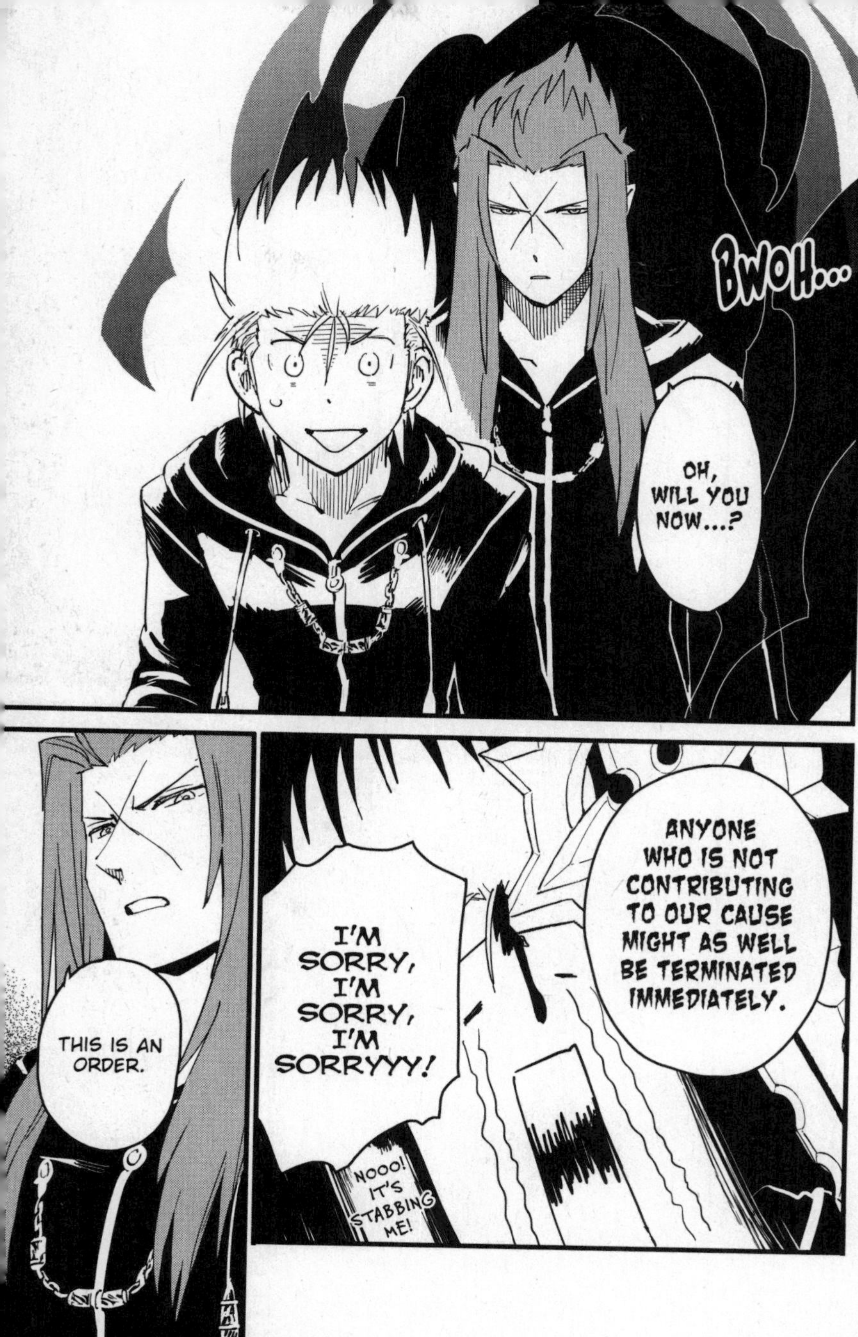
BWOH...
OH, WILL YOU NOW...?
ANYONE WHO IS NOT CONTRIBUTING TO OUR CAUSE MIGHT AS WELL BE TERMINATED IMMEDIATELY.
I'M SORRY, I'M SORRY, I'M SORRYYY!
NOOO! IT'S STABBING ME!
THIS IS AN ORDER.

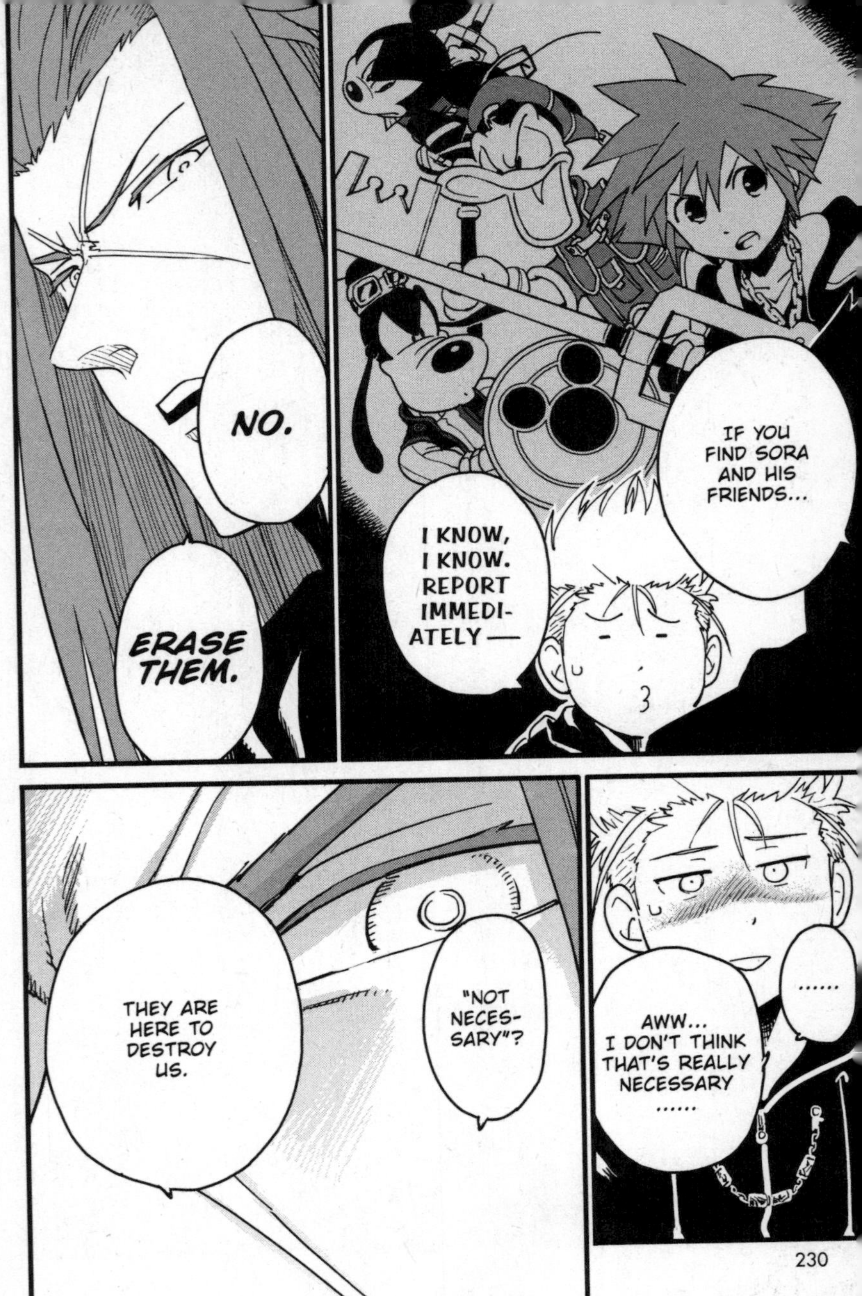
IF YOU FIND SORA AND HIS FRIENDS...
I KNOW, I KNOW. REPORT IMMEDI-ATELY—
NO.
ERASE THEM.
......
AWW... I DON'T THINK THAT'S REALLY NECESSARY ......
"NOT NECES-SARY"?
THEY ARE HERE TO DESTROY US.

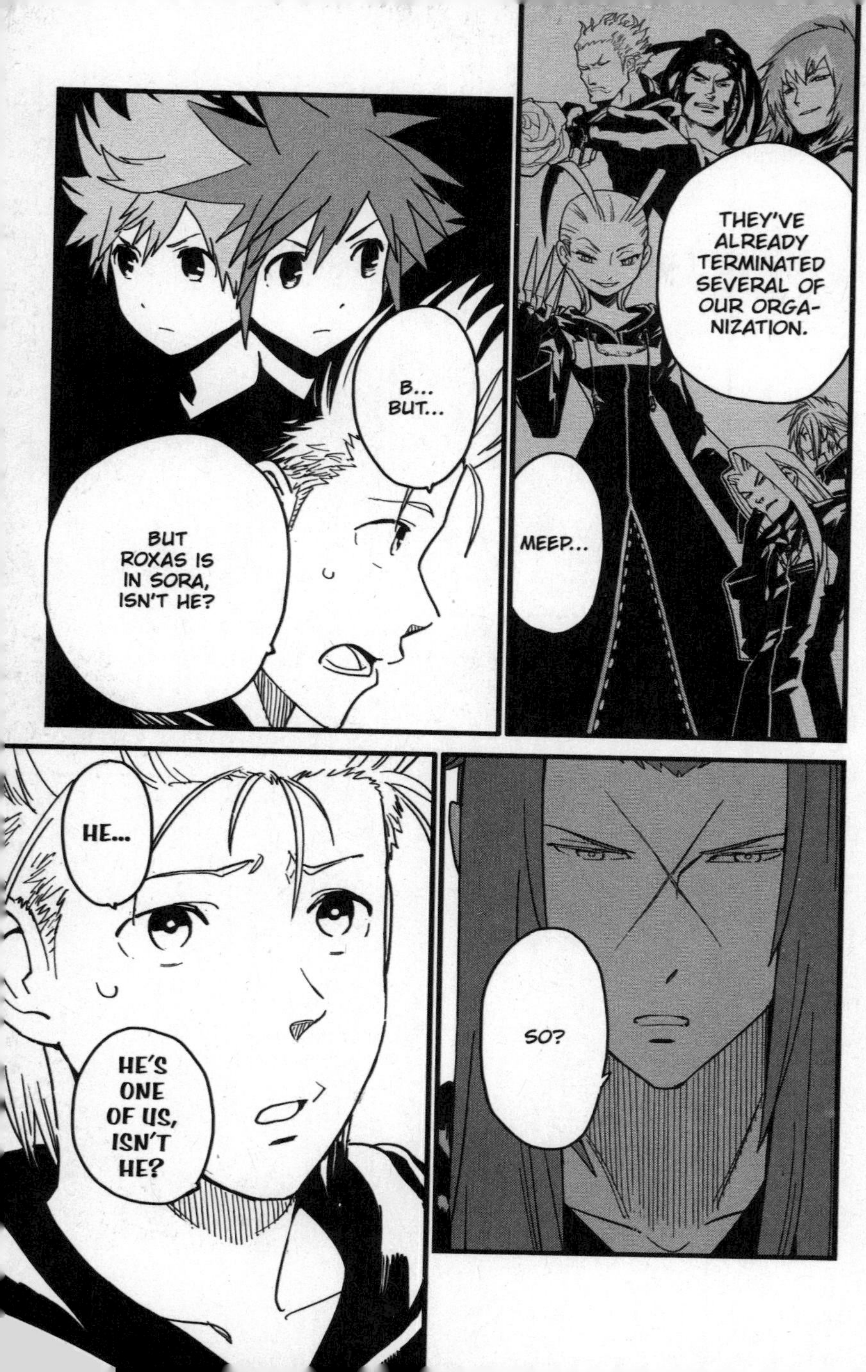
THEY'VE ALREADY TERMINATED SEVERAL OF OUR ORGA-NIZATION.
MEEP...
B... BUT...
BUT ROXAS IS IN SORA, ISN'T HE?
SO?
HE...
HE'S ONE OF US, ISN'T HE?

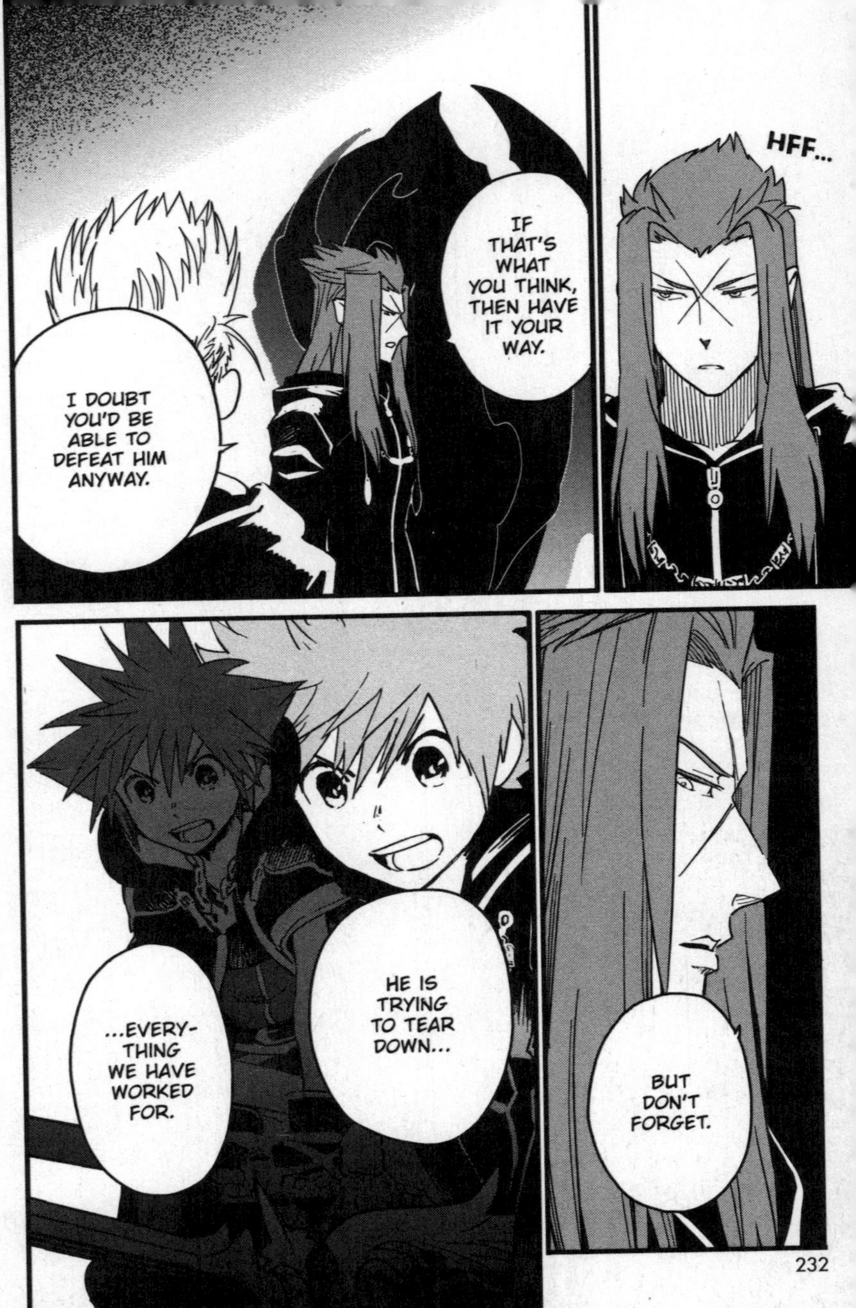
HFF...
IF THAT'S WHAT YOU THINK, THEN HAVE IT YOUR WAY.
I DOUBT YOU'D BE ABLE TO DEFEAT HIM ANYWAY.
BUT DON'T FORGET.
HE IS TRYING TO TEAR DOWN...
...EVERY-THING WE HAVE WORKED FOR.

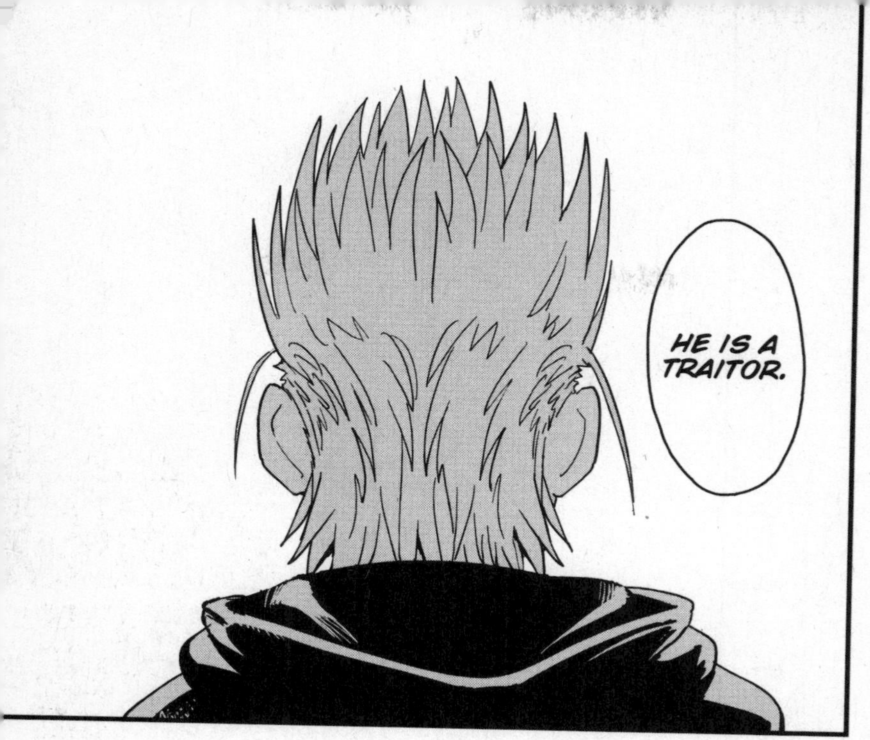
HE IS A TRAITOR.
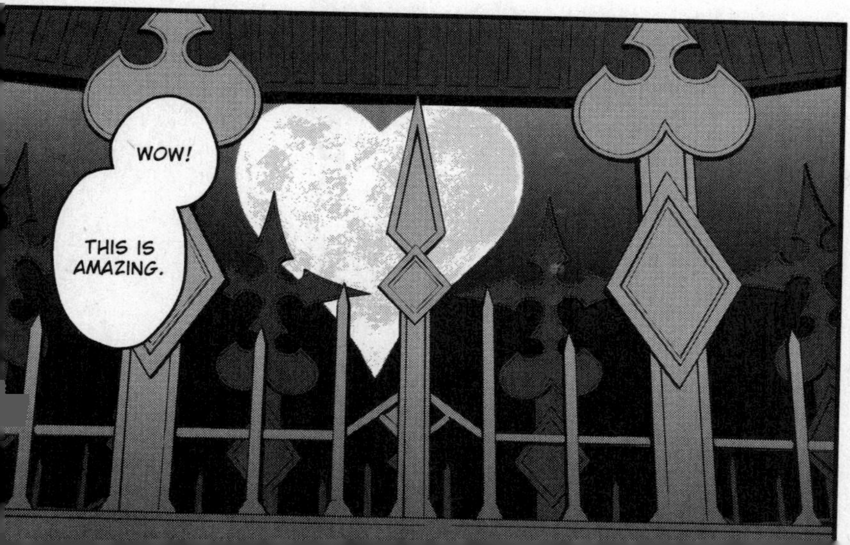
WOW!
THIS IS AMAZING.

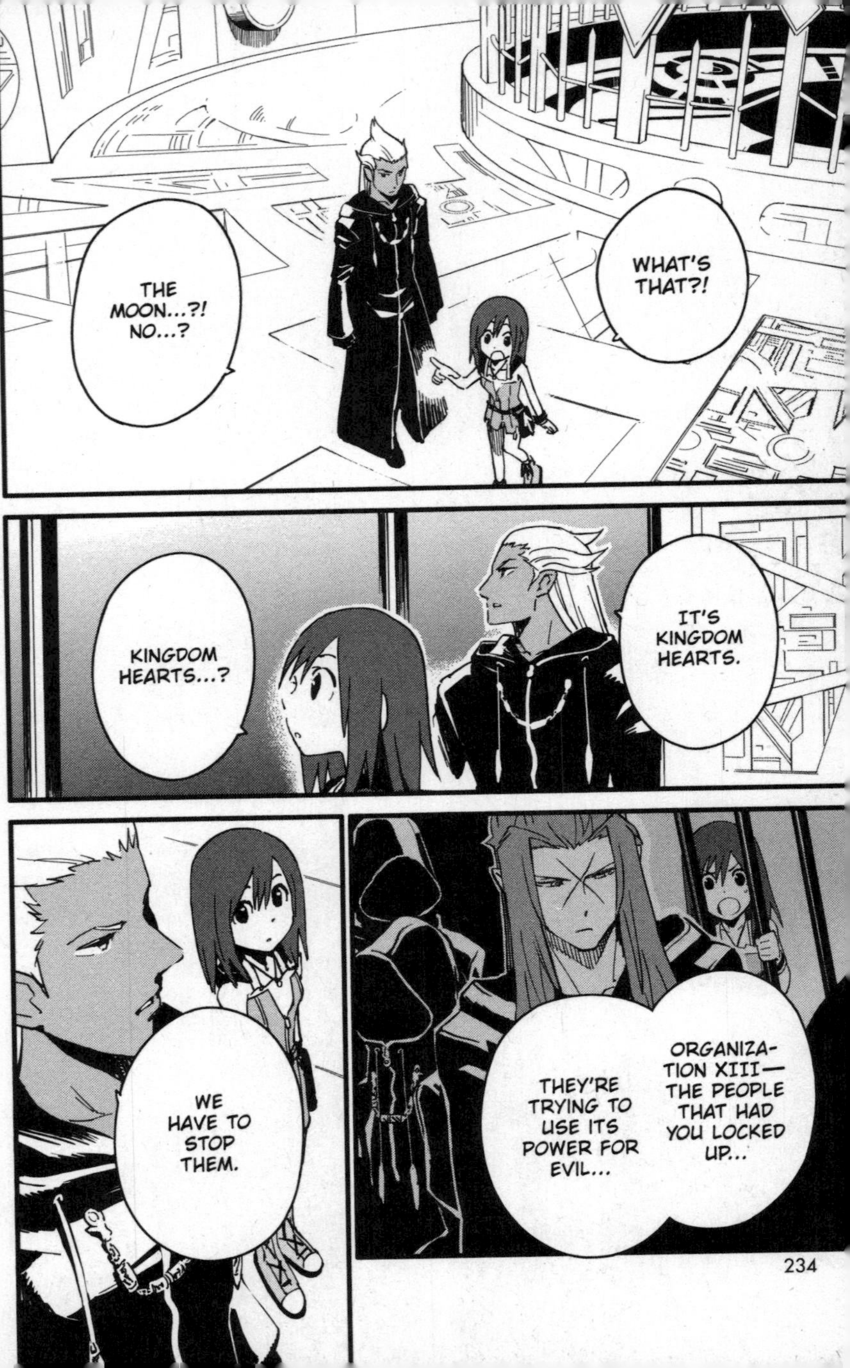
WHAT'S THAT?!
THE MOON...?! NO...?
IT'S KINGDOM HEARTS.
KINGDOM HEARTS...?
ORGANIZATION XIII—THE PEOPLE THAT HAD YOU LOCKED UP...
THEY'RE TRYING TO USE ITS POWER FOR EVIL...
WE HAVE TO STOP THEM.

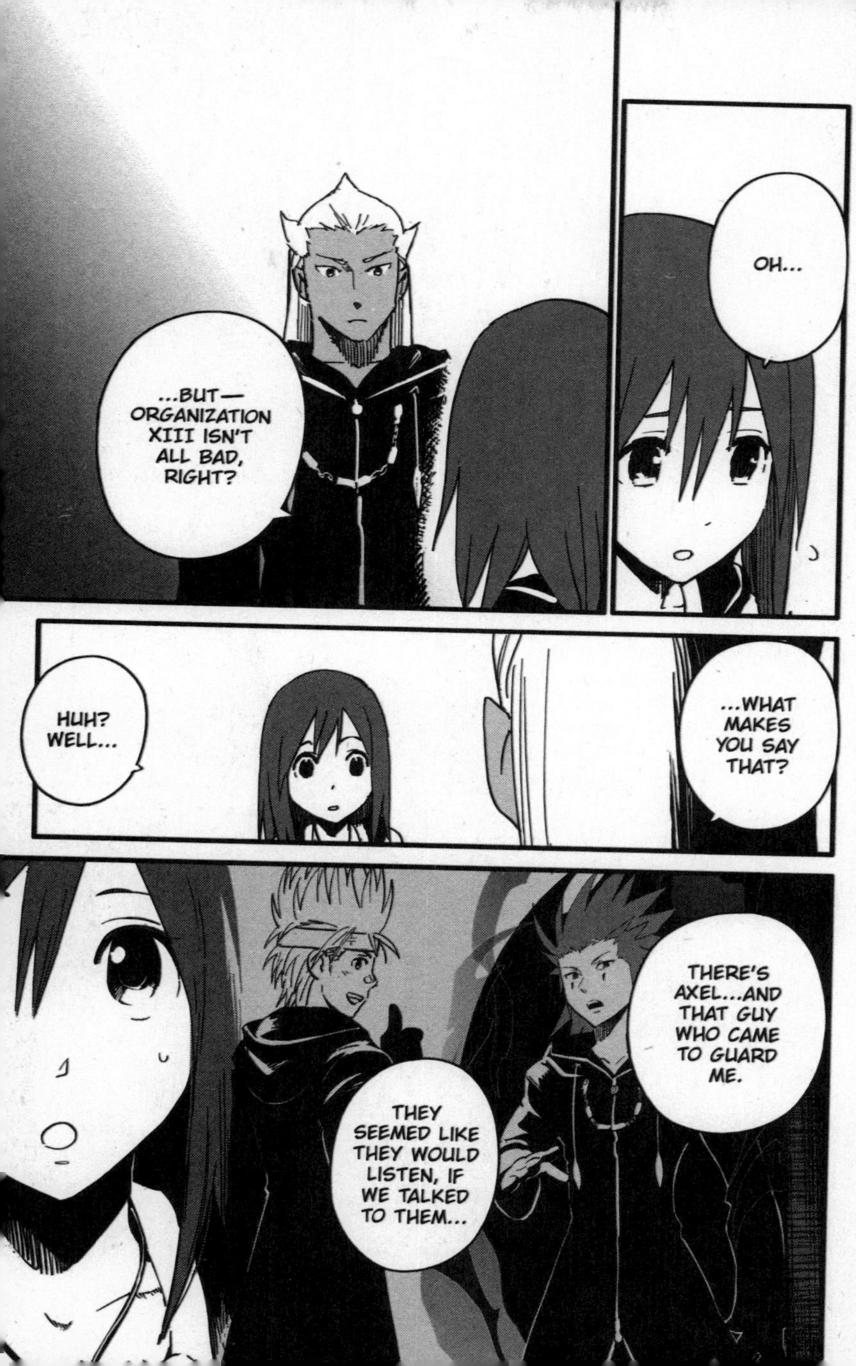
OH...
...BUT—ORGANIZATION XIII ISN'T ALL BAD, RIGHT?
...WHAT MAKES YOU SAY THAT?
HUH? WELL...
THERE'S AXEL...AND THAT GUY WHO CAME TO GUARD ME.
THEY SEEMED LIKE THEY WOULD LISTEN, IF WE TALKED TO THEM...

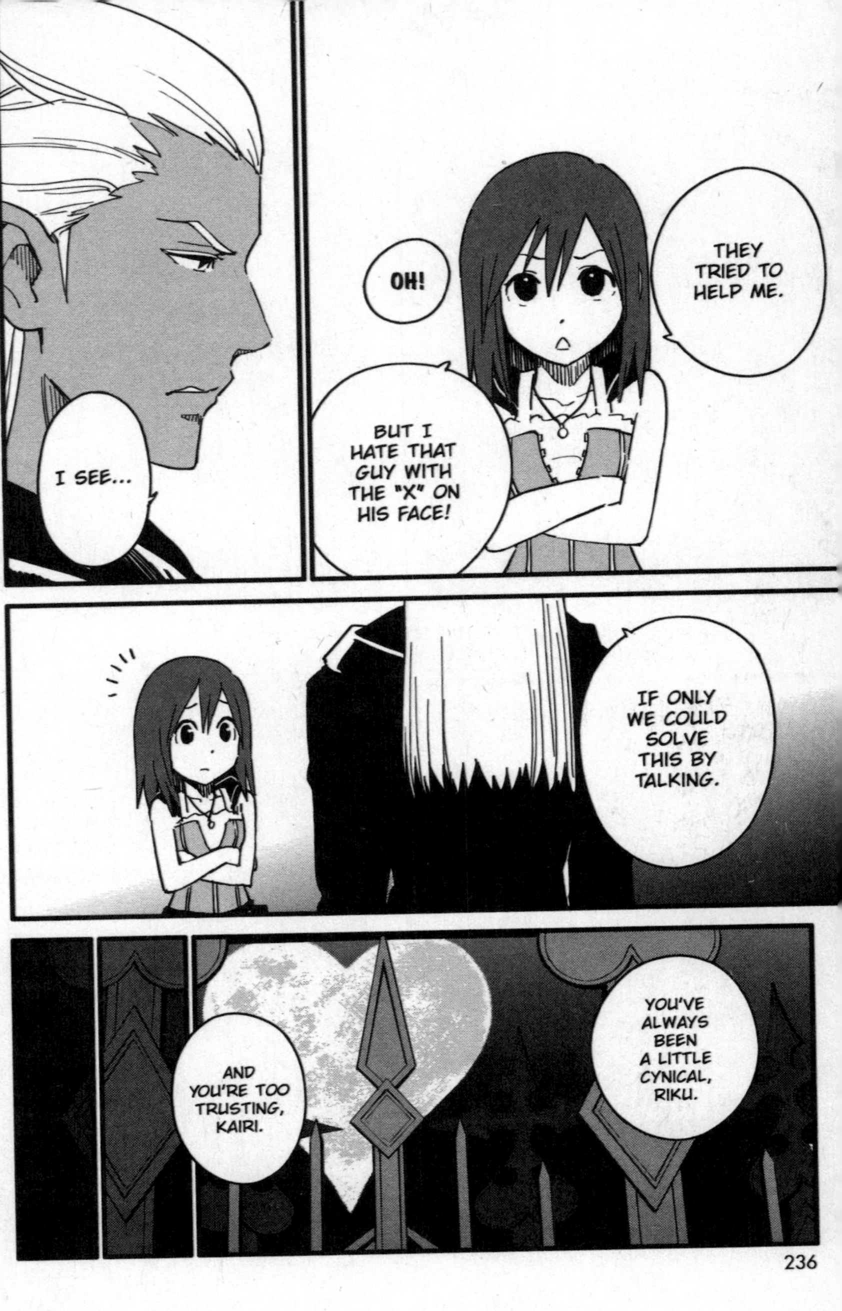
THEY TRIED TO HELP ME.
OH!
BUT I HATE THAT GUY WITH THE "X" ON HIS FACE!
I SEE...
IF ONLY WE COULD SOLVE THIS BY TALKING.
YOU'VE ALWAYS BEEN A LITTLE CYNICAL, RIKU.
AND YOU'RE TOO TRUSTING, KAIRI.

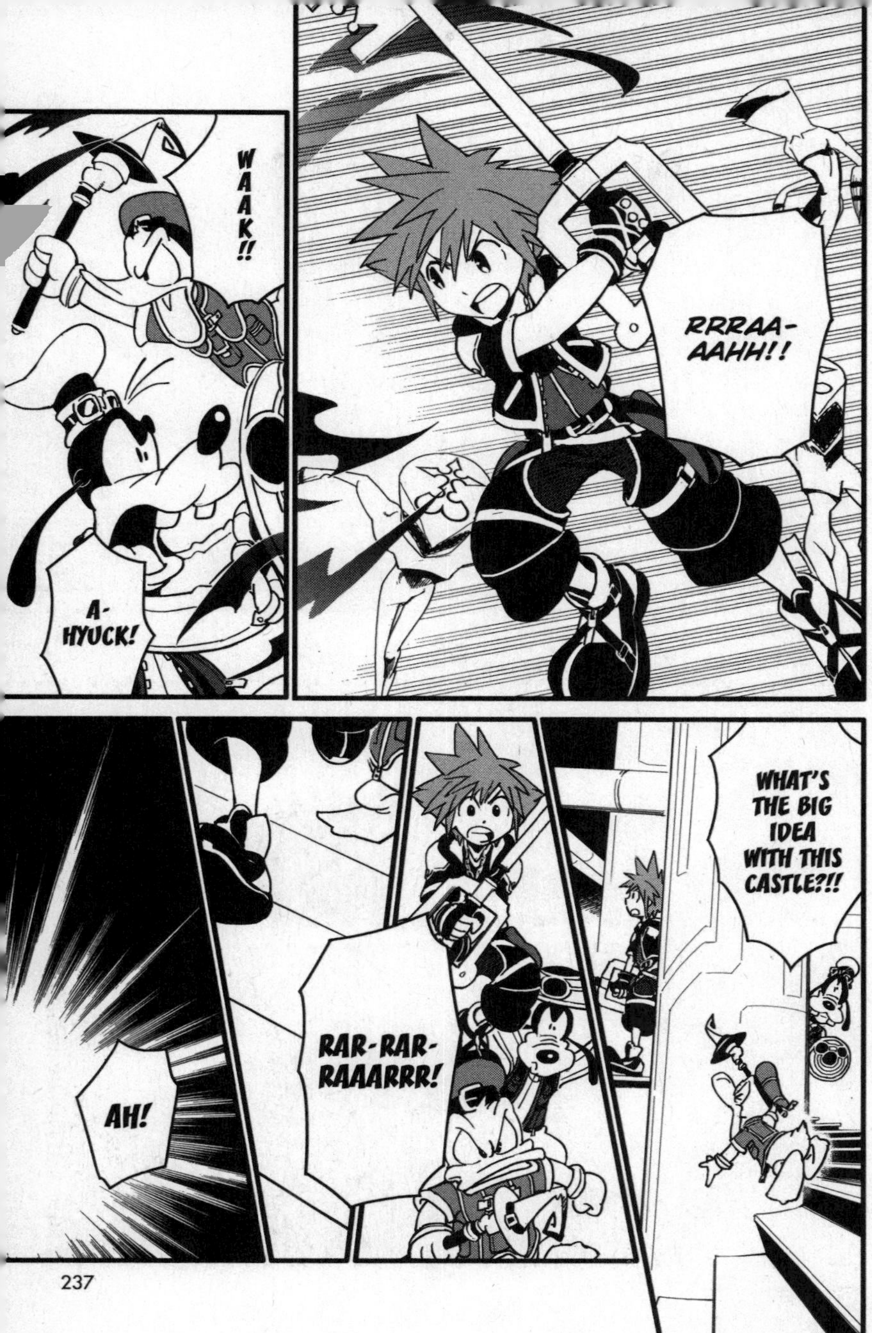
RRRAA-AAHH!!
WAAK!!
A-HYUCK!
WHAT'S THE BIG IDEA WITH THIS CASTLE?!!
RAR-RAR-RAAARRR!
AH!

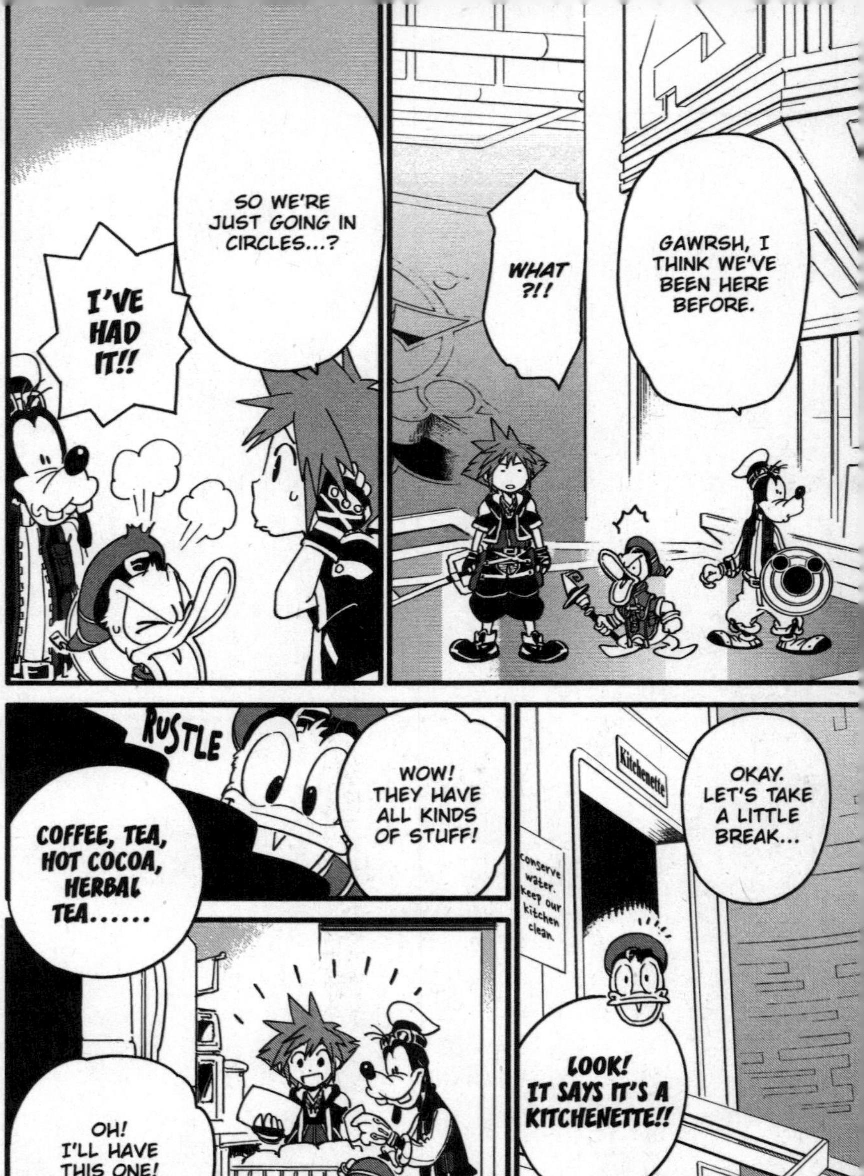
GAWRSH, I THINK WE'VE BEEN HERE BEFORE.
WHAT ?!!
SO WE'RE JUST GOING IN CIRCLES...?
I'VE HAD IT!!
OKAY. LET'S TAKE A LITTLE BREAK...
Kitchenette
Conserve water. Keep our kitchen clean.
LOOK! IT SAYS IT'S A KITCHENETTE!!
RUSTLE
WOW! THEY HAVE ALL KINDS OF STUFF!
COFFEE, TEA, HOT COCOA, HERBAL TEA......
OH! I'LL HAVE THIS ONE! INSTANT PILAF!!

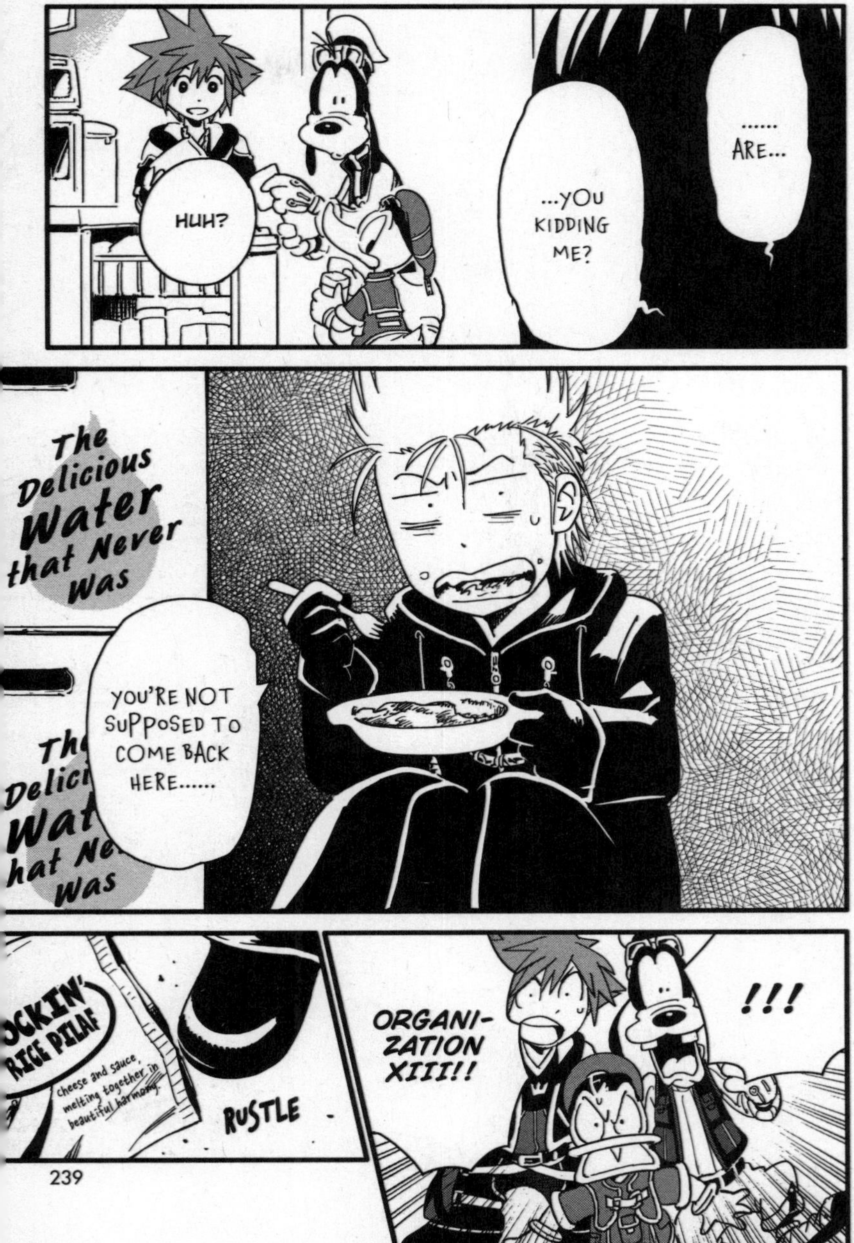
......ARE...
...YOU KIDDING ME?
HUH?
The Delicious Water that Never Was
YOU'RE NOT SUPPOSED TO COME BACK HERE......
!!!
ORGANI-ZATION XIII!!
OCKIN' RICE PILAF
cheese and sauce, melting together in beautiful harmony.
RUSTLE

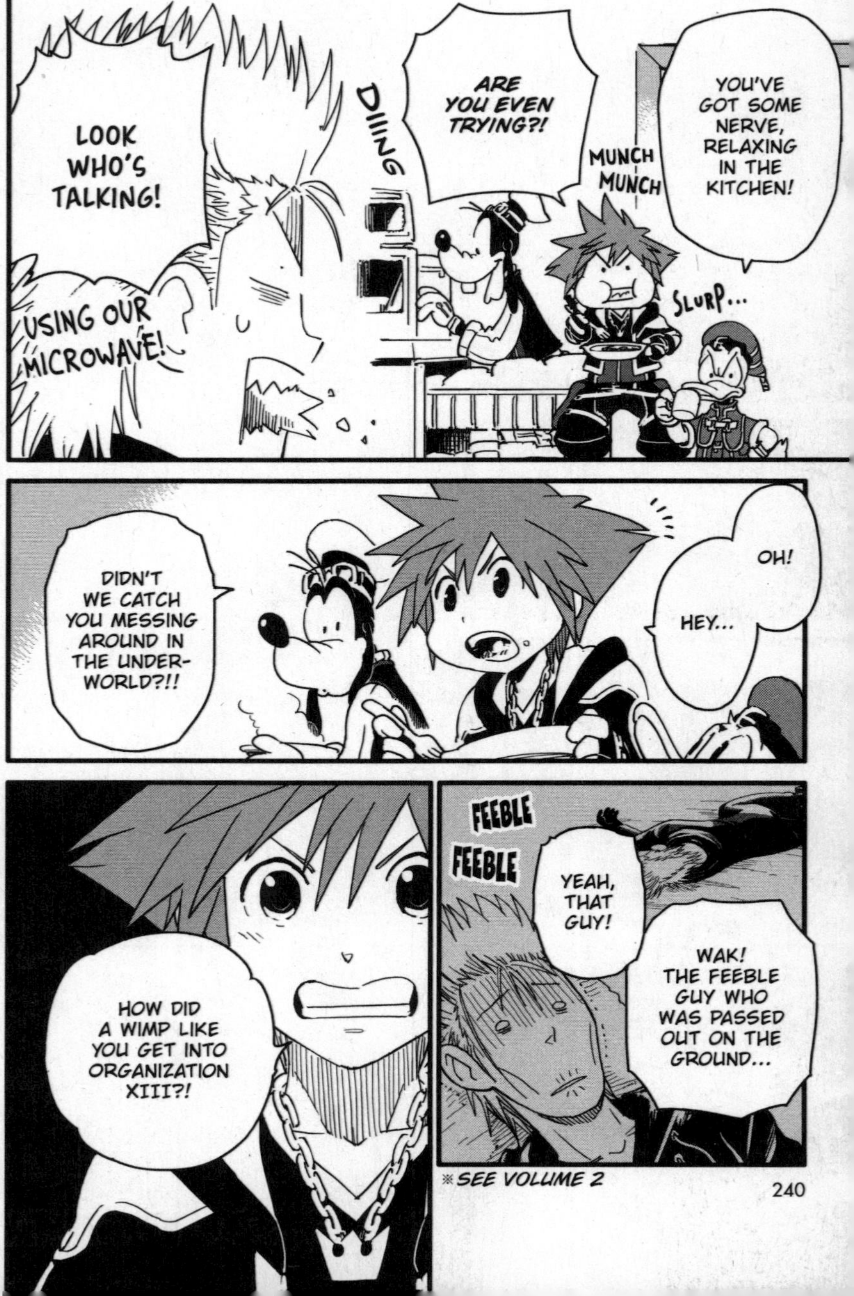
YOU'VE GOT SOME NERVE, RELAXING IN THE KITCHEN!
MUNCH MUNCH
SLURP...
ARE YOU EVEN TRYING?!
DIIING
LOOK WHO'S TALKING!
USING OUR MICROWAVE!
OH!
HEY...
DIDN'T WE CATCH YOU MESSING AROUND IN THE UNDER-WORLD?!!
FEEBLE
FEEBLE
WAK! THE FEEBLE GUY WHO WAS PASSED OUT ON THE GROUND...
YEAH, THAT GUY!
HOW DID A WIMP LIKE YOU GET INTO ORGANIZATION XIII?!

※SEE VOLUME 2

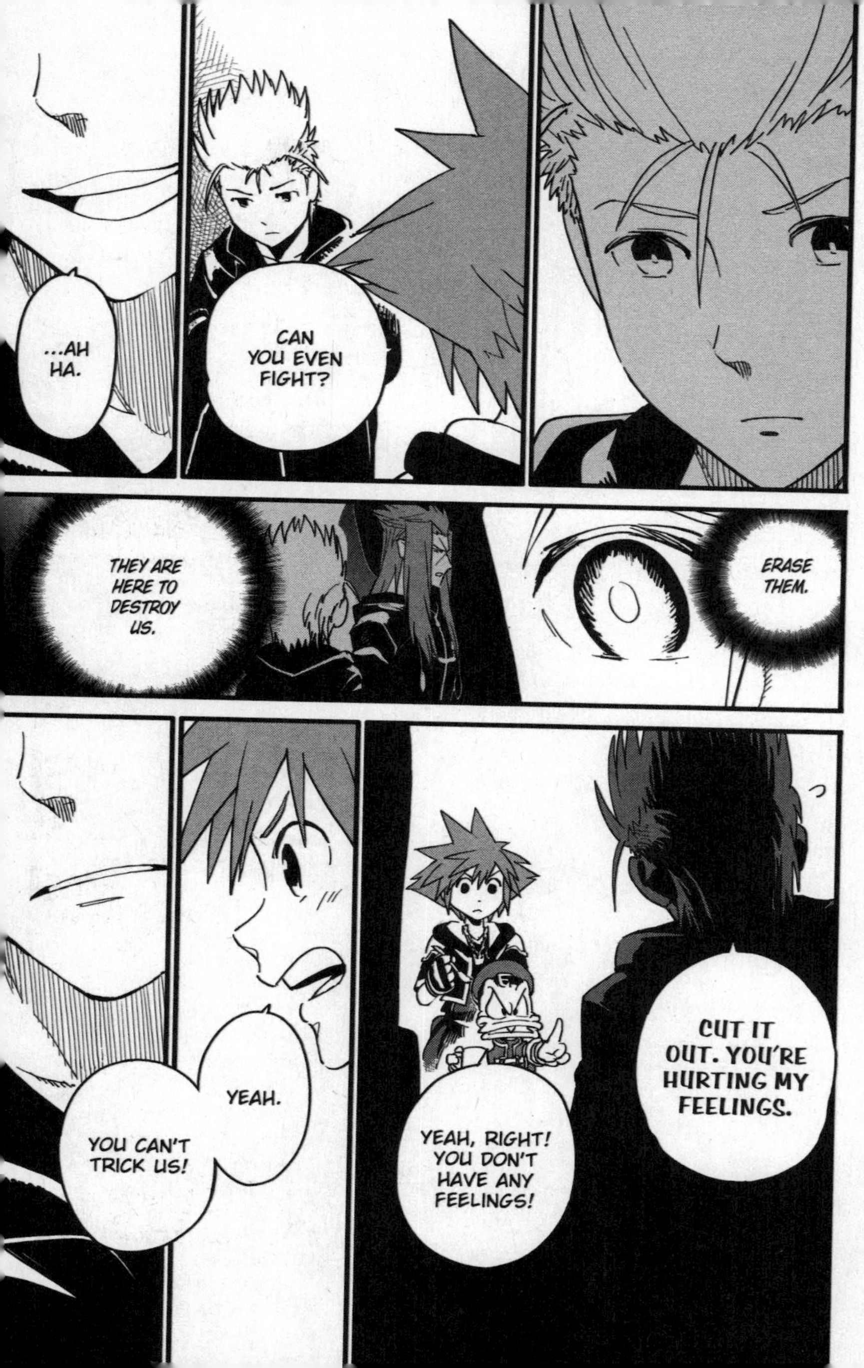
CAN YOU EVEN FIGHT?
...AH HA.
ERASE THEM.
THEY ARE HERE TO DESTROY US.
CUT IT OUT. YOU'RE HURTING MY FEELINGS.
YEAH, RIGHT! YOU DON'T HAVE ANY FEELINGS!
YEAH.
YOU CAN'T TRICK US!

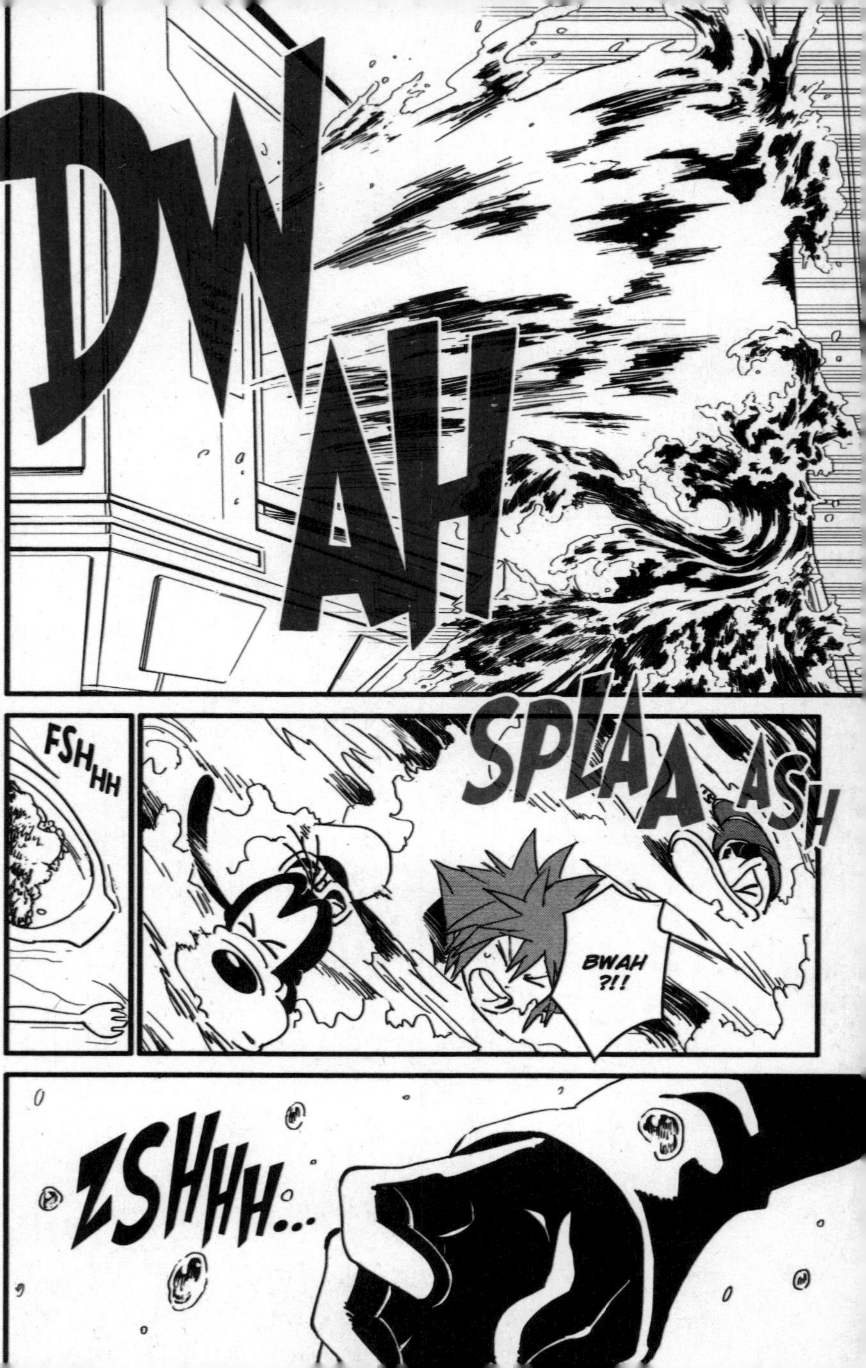
DWAH
SPLAAASH
BWAH ?!!
FSHHH
ZSHHH...

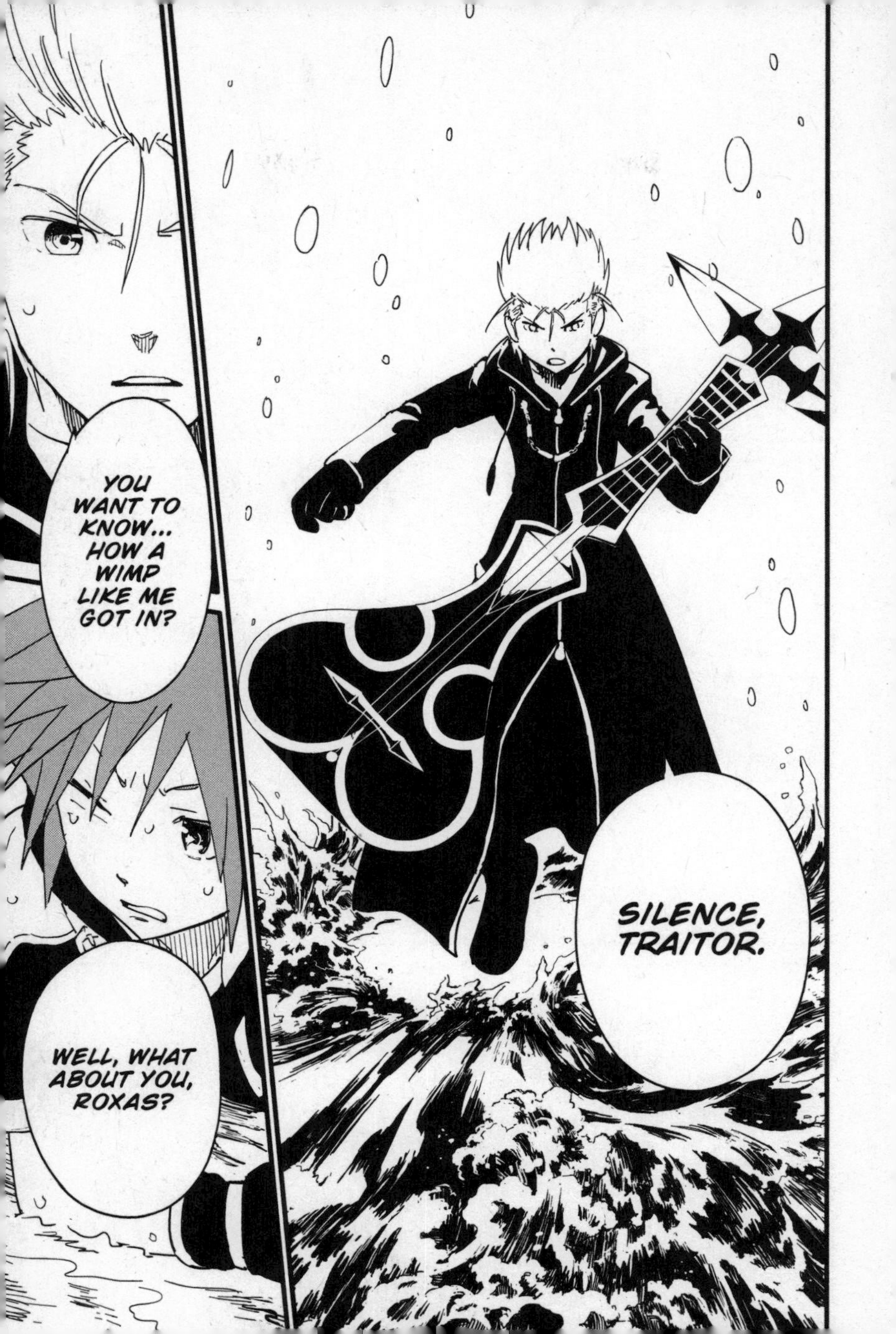

SILENCE, TRAITOR.
YOU WANT TO KNOW... HOW A WIMP LIKE ME GOT IN?
WELL, WHAT ABOUT YOU, ROXAS?

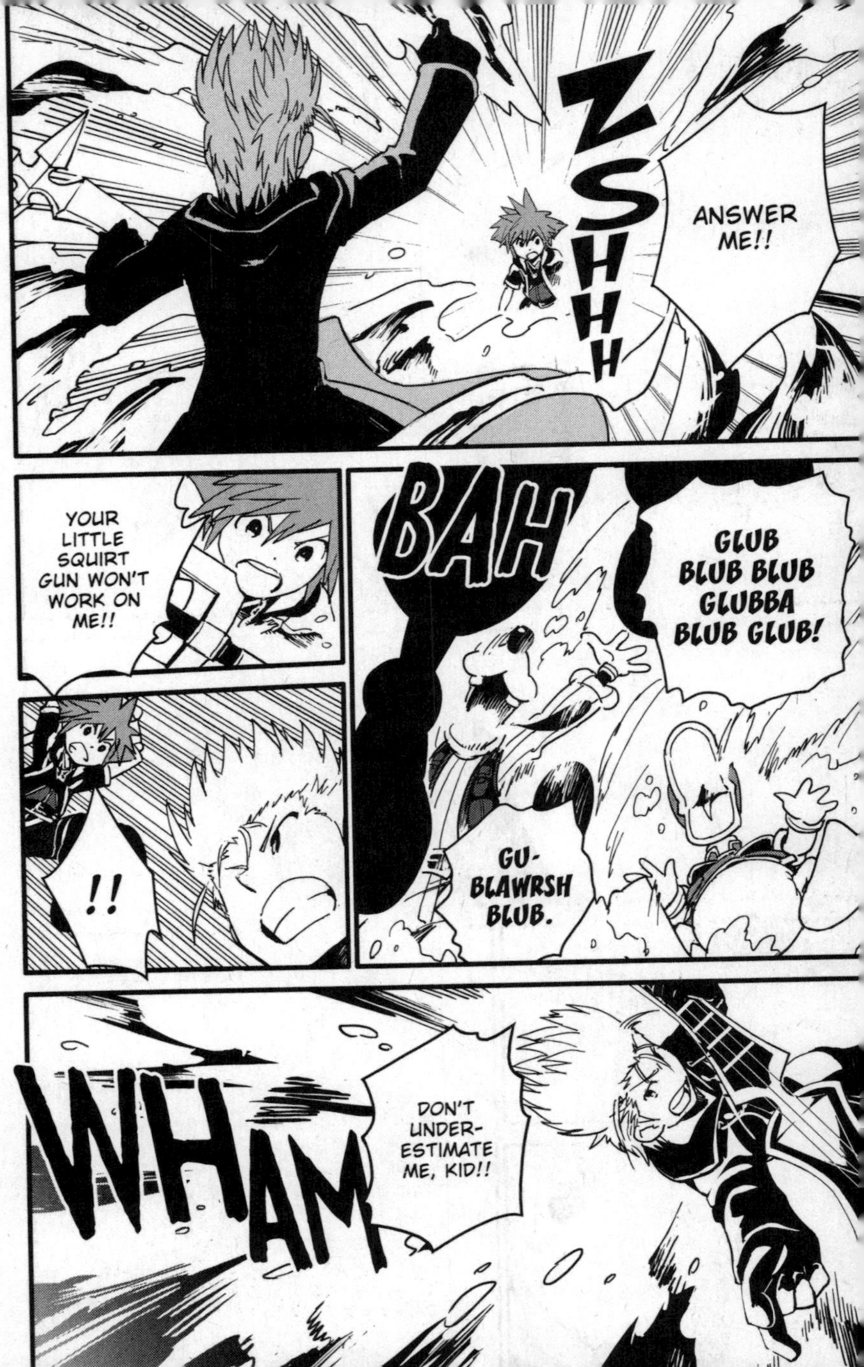
ZSHHH
ANSWER ME!!
GLUB BLUB BLUB GLUBBA BLUB GLUB!
BAH
GU-BLAWRSH BLUB.
YOUR LITTLE SQUIRT GUN WON'T WORK ON ME!!
!!
DON'T UNDER-ESTIMATE ME, KID!!
WHAM

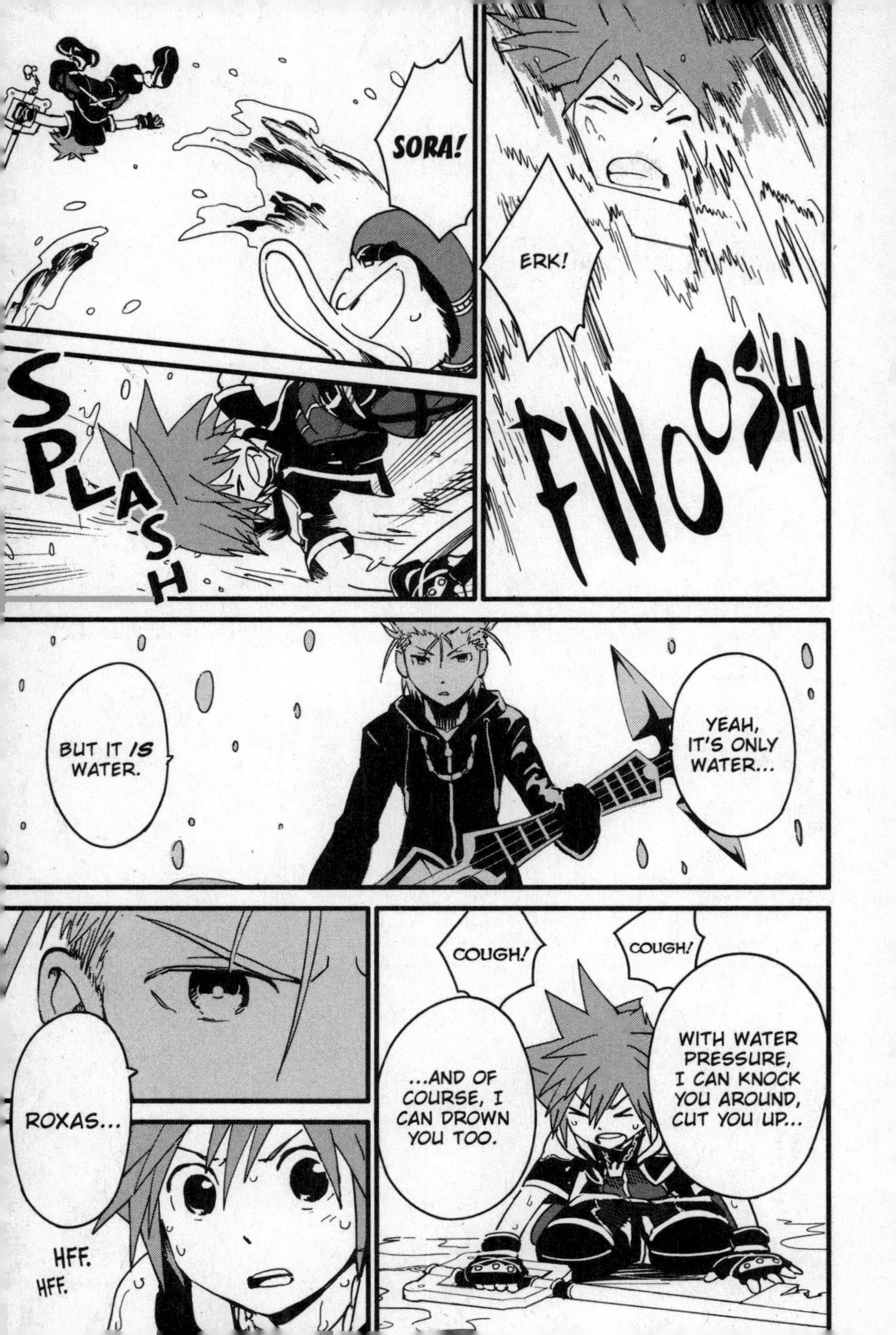
ERK!
FWOOSH
SORA!
SPLASH
YEAH, IT'S ONLY WATER...
BUT IT *IS* WATER.
COUGH!
COUGH!
WITH WATER PRESSURE, I CAN KNOCK YOU AROUND, CUT YOU UP...
...AND OF COURSE, I CAN DROWN YOU TOO.
ROXAS...
HFF. HFF.

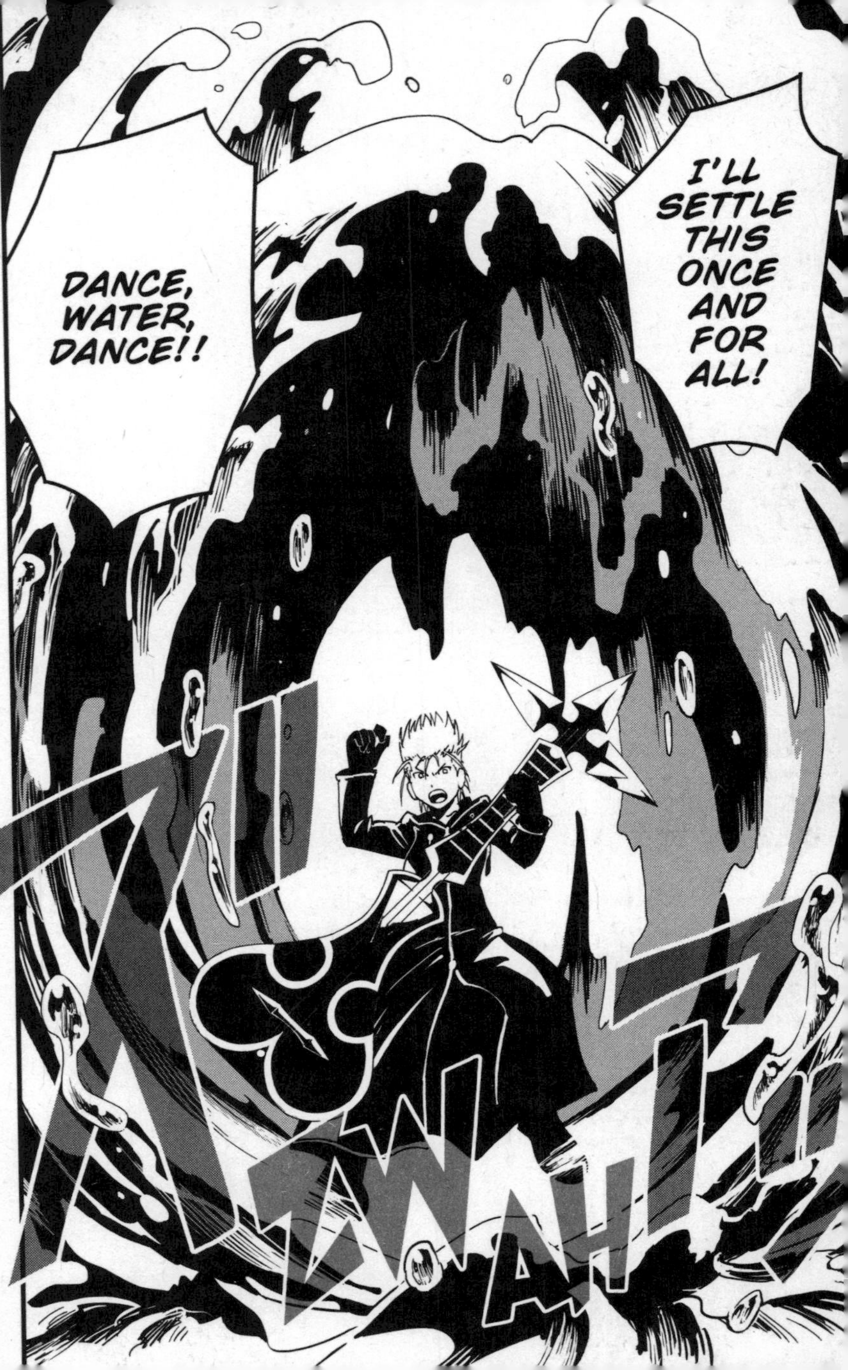
I'LL SETTLE THIS ONCE AND FOR ALL!
DANCE, WATER, DANCE!!

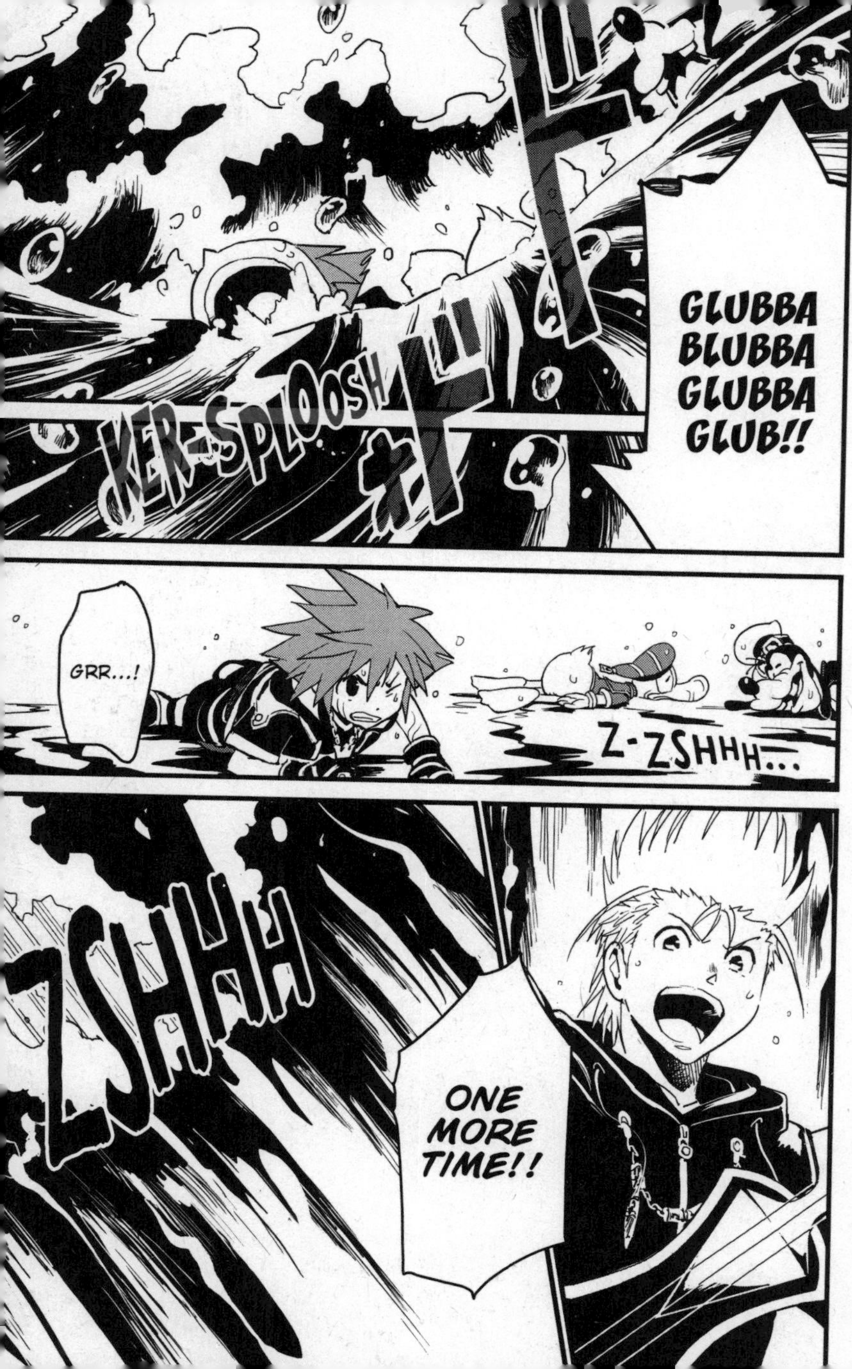
GLUBBA BLUBBA GLUBBA GLUB!!
KER-SPLOOSH
Z-ZSHHH...
GRR...!
ONE MORE TIME!!
ZSHHH

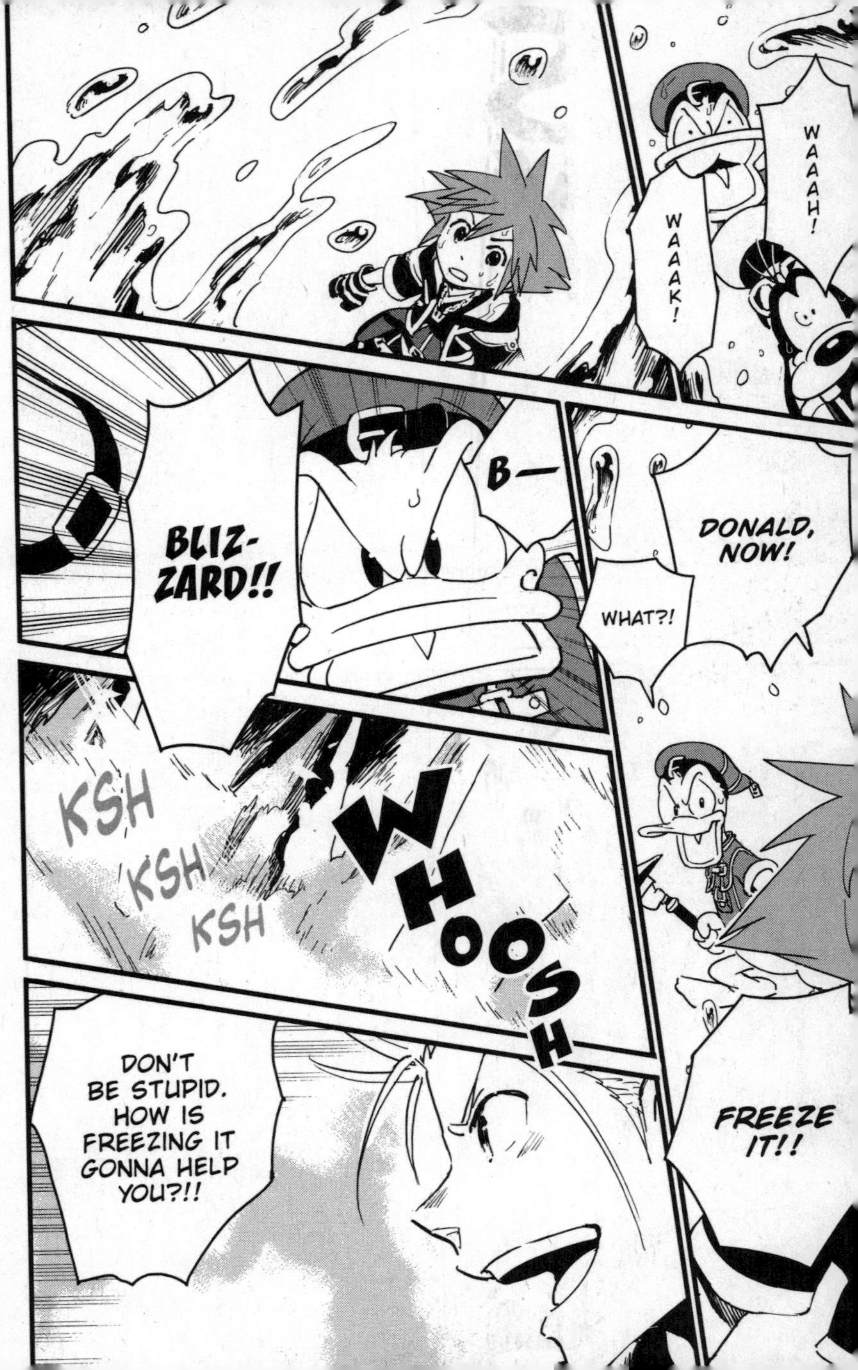
WAAAAH!
WAAAK!
DONALD, NOW!
WHAT?!
B—
BLIZ-ZARD!!
KSH
KSH
KSH
WHOOSH
FREEZE IT!!
DON'T BE STUPID. HOW IS FREEZING IT GONNA HELP YOU?!!

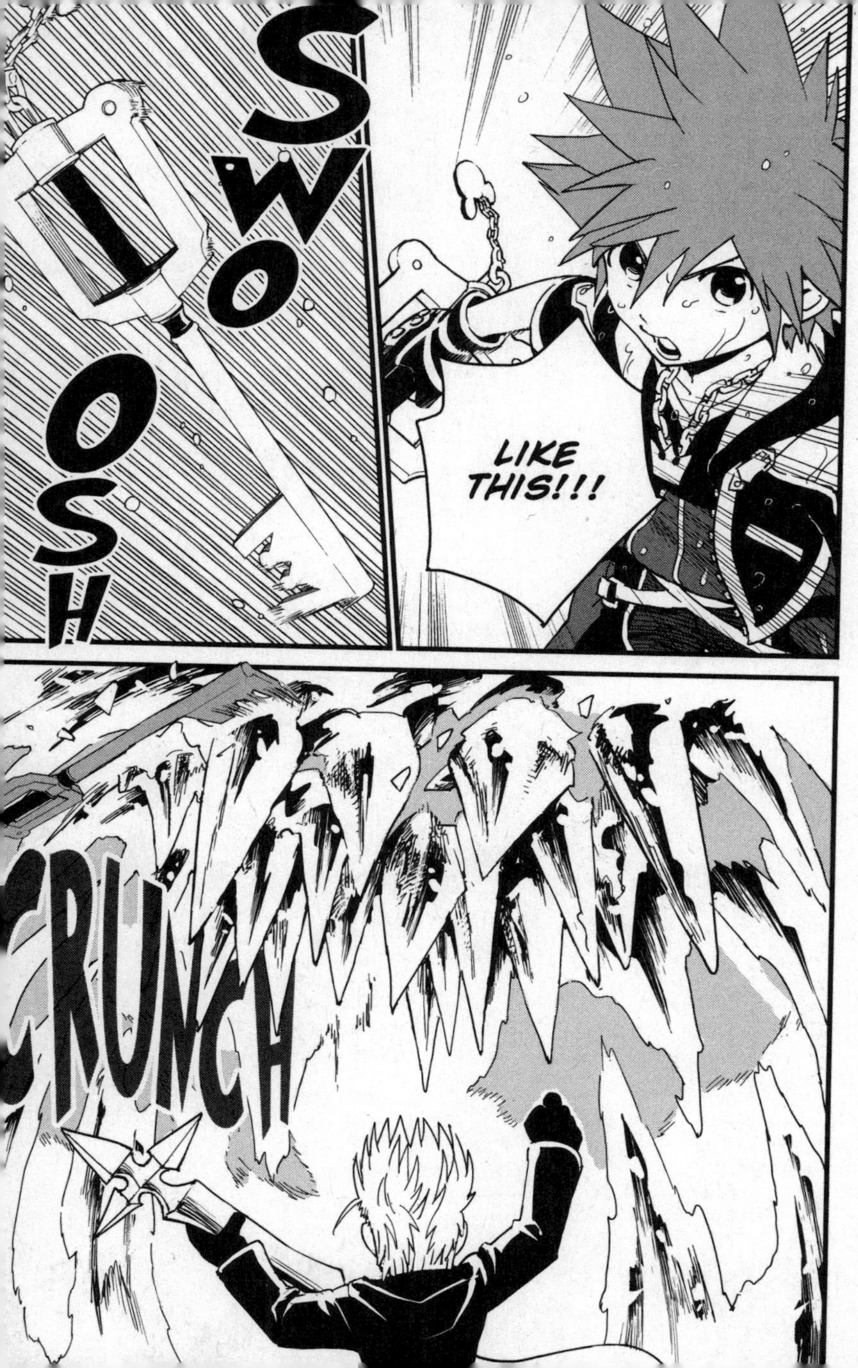
LIKE THIS!!!
SWOOSH
CRUNCH

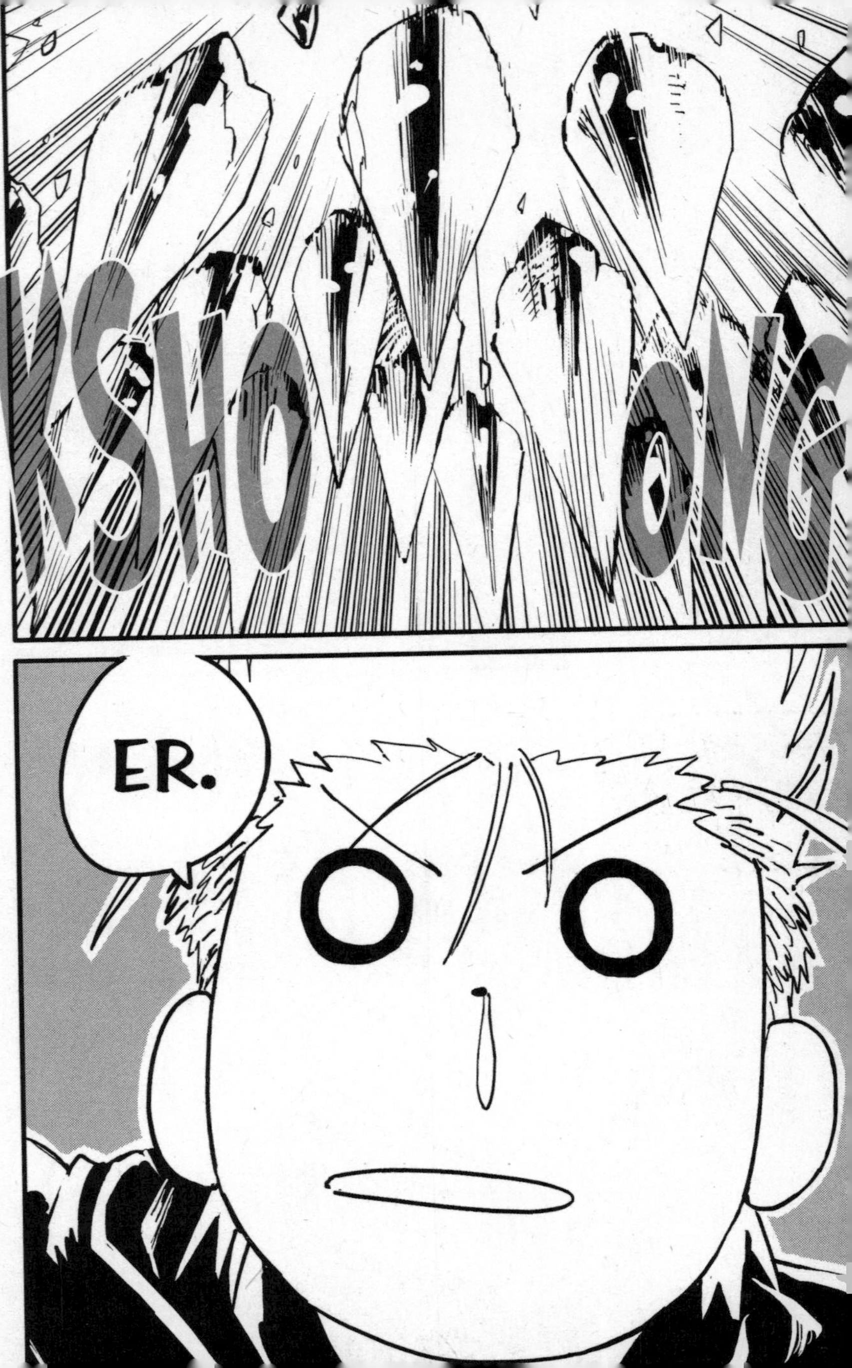
KSHOWWWONG
ER.

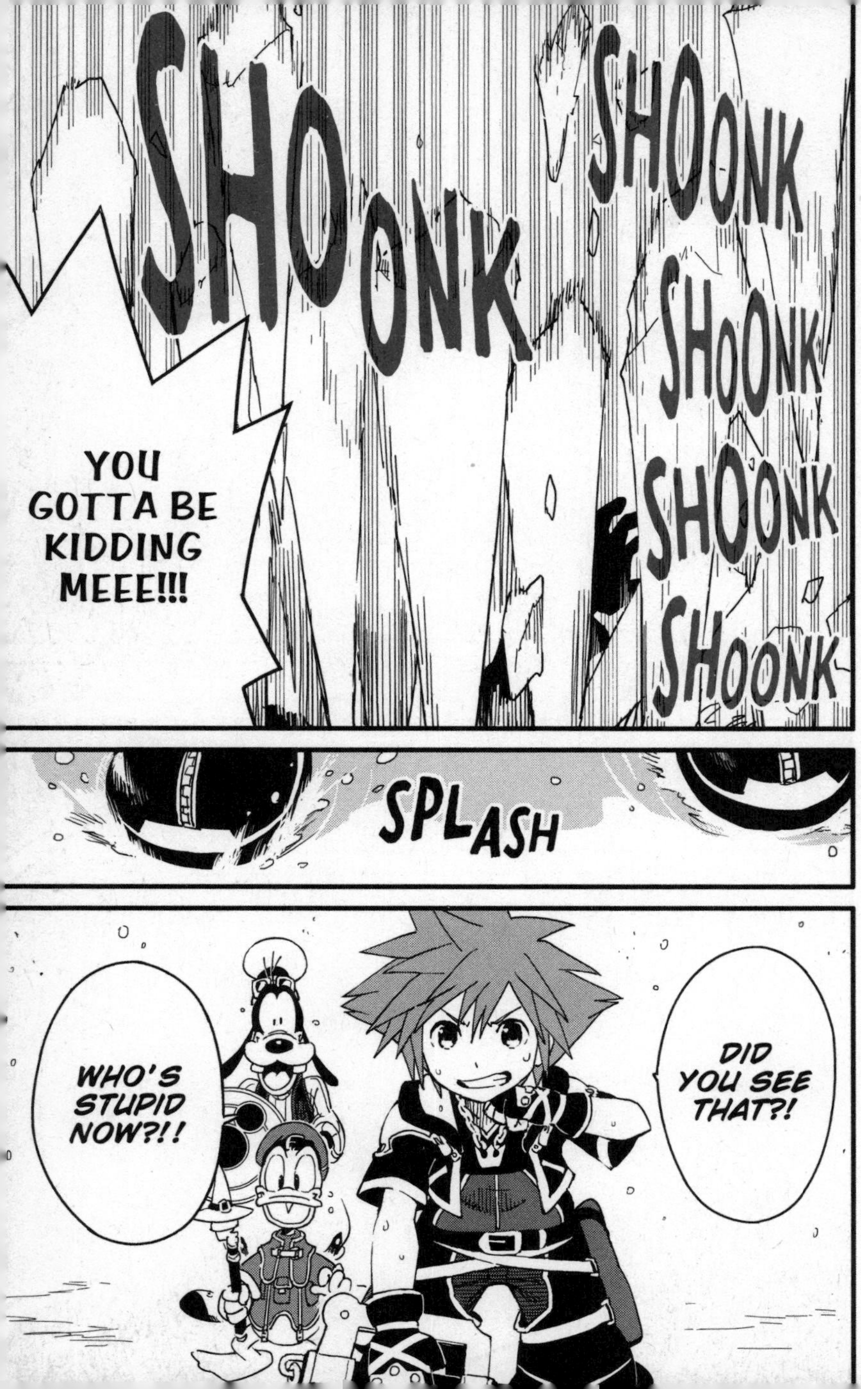
SHOONK
SHOONK
SHOONK
SHOONK
SHOONK
YOU GOTTA BE KIDDING MEEE!!!
SPLASH
DID YOU SEE THAT?!
WHO'S STUPID NOW?!!

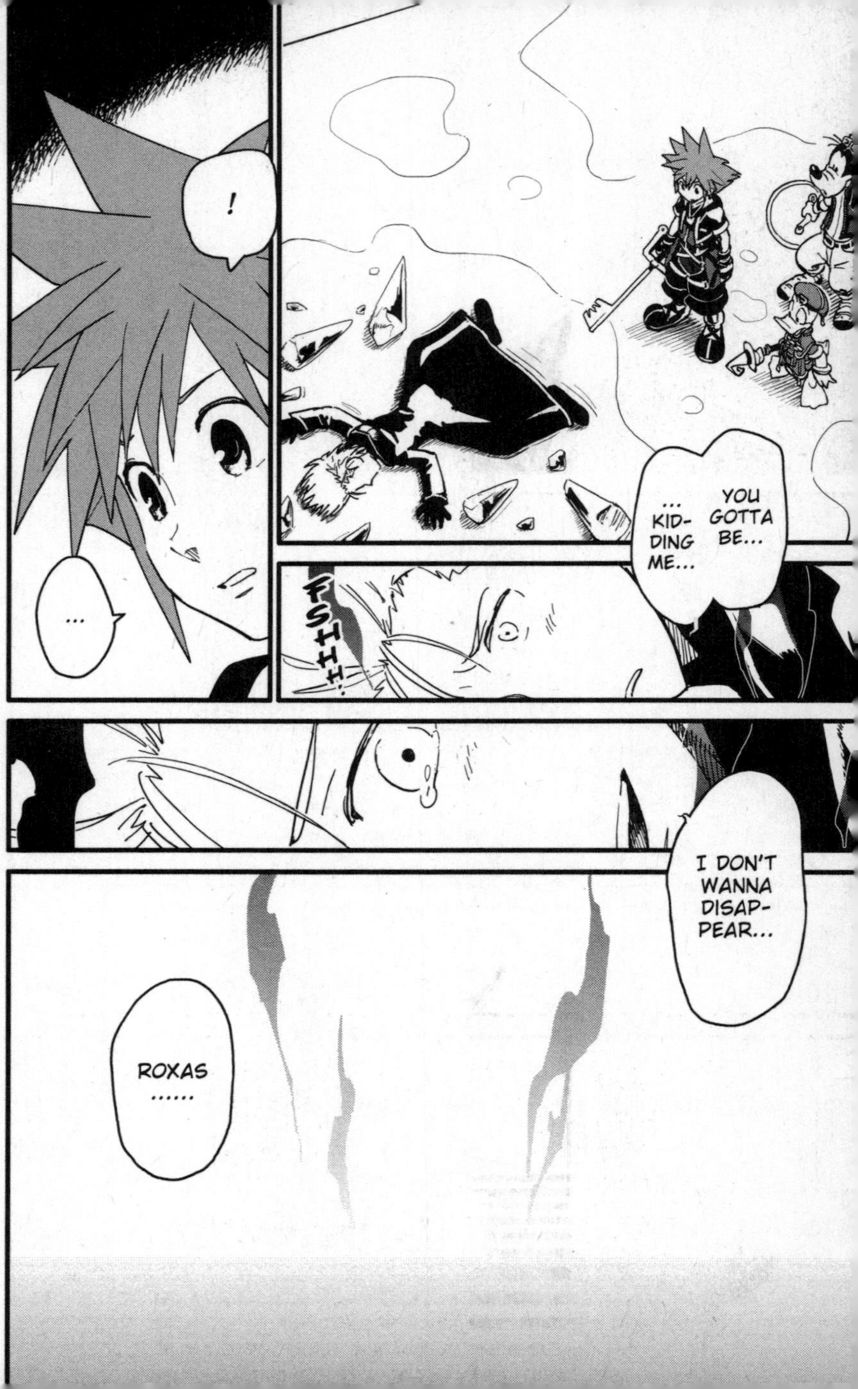
YOU GOTTA BE...
...KID-DING ME...
FSHHH!
!
...
I DON'T WANNA DISAP-PEAR...
ROXAS ......

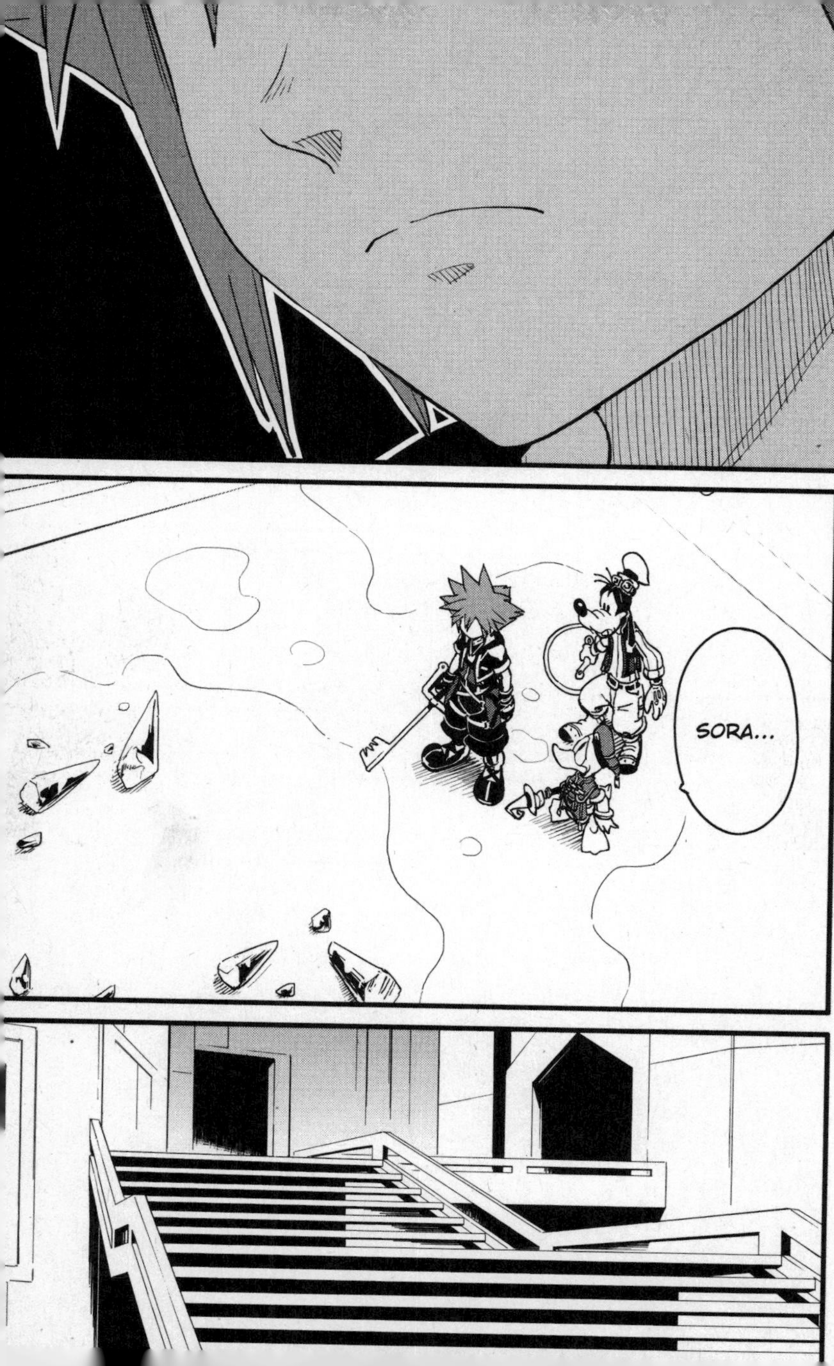
SORA...

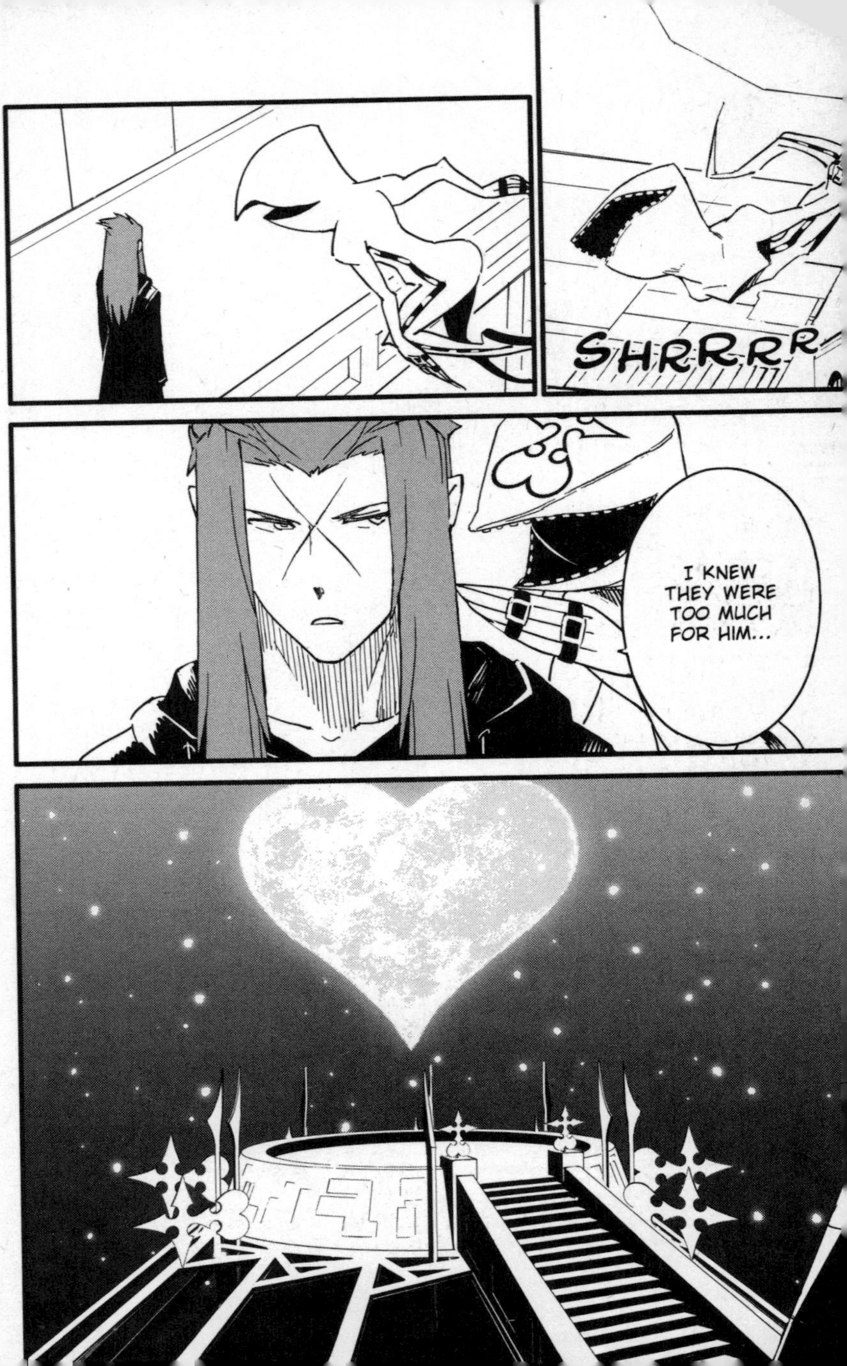
SHRRRR
I KNEW THEY WERE TOO MUCH FOR HIM...

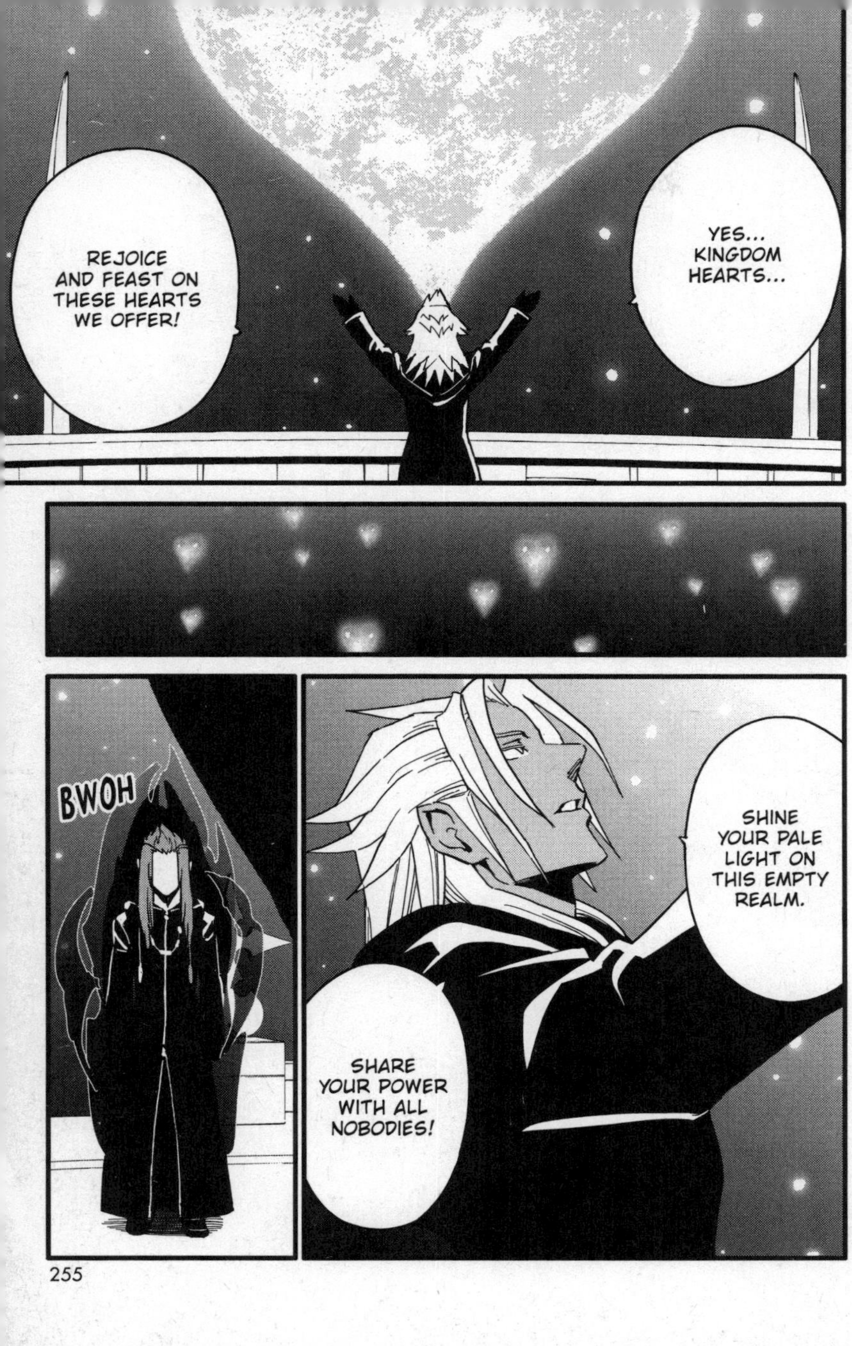
YES... KINGDOM HEARTS...
REJOICE AND FEAST ON THESE HEARTS WE OFFER!
SHINE YOUR PALE LIGHT ON THIS EMPTY REALM.
SHARE YOUR POWER WITH ALL NOBODIES!
BWOH

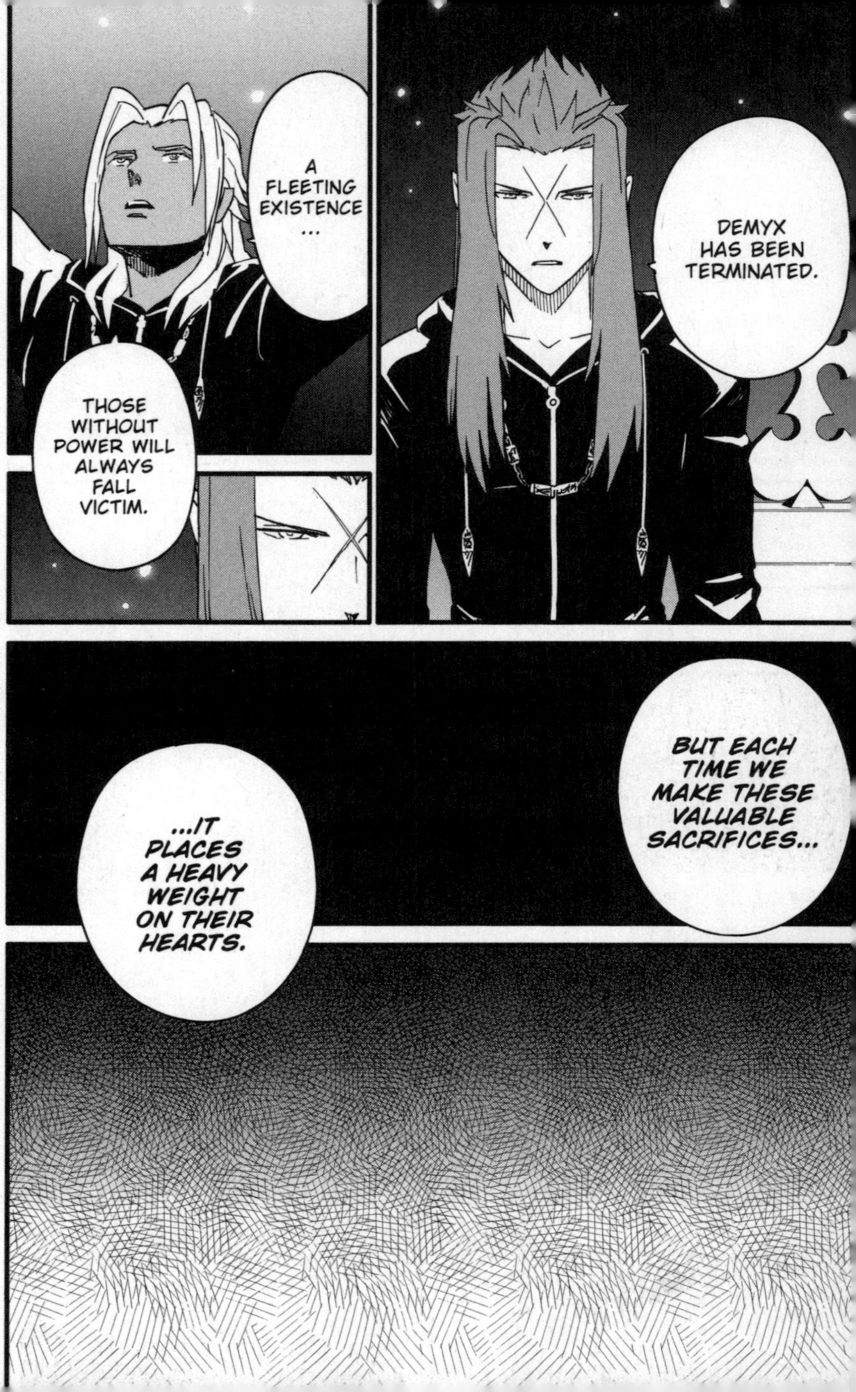
DEMYX HAS BEEN TERMINATED.
A FLEETING EXISTENCE ...
THOSE WITHOUT POWER WILL ALWAYS FALL VICTIM.
BUT EACH TIME WE MAKE THESE VALUABLE SACRIFICES...
...IT PLACES A HEAVY WEIGHT ON THEIR HEARTS.

Disney SQUARE ENIX

KINGDOM HEARTS

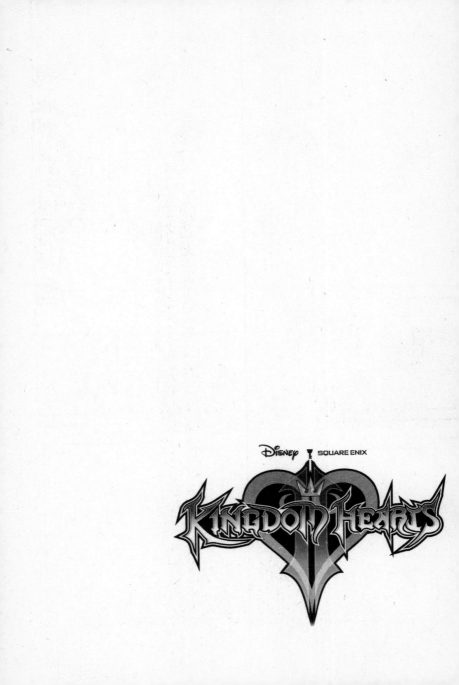

Chapter 61: Role-Reversing Princess

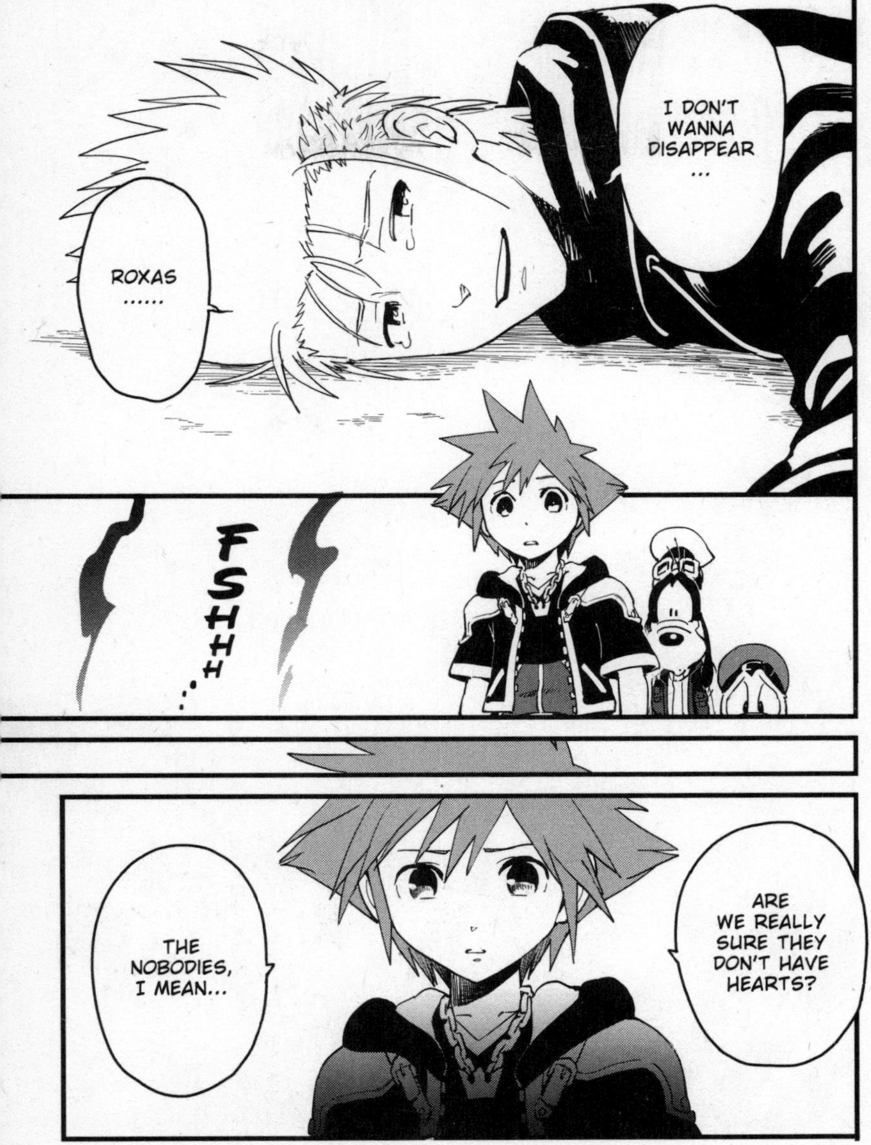
I DON'T WANNA DISAPPEAR ...
ROXAS ......
FSHHH...
ARE WE REALLY SURE THEY DON'T HAVE HEARTS?
THE NOBODIES, I MEAN...

Chapter 61: Role-Reversing Princess

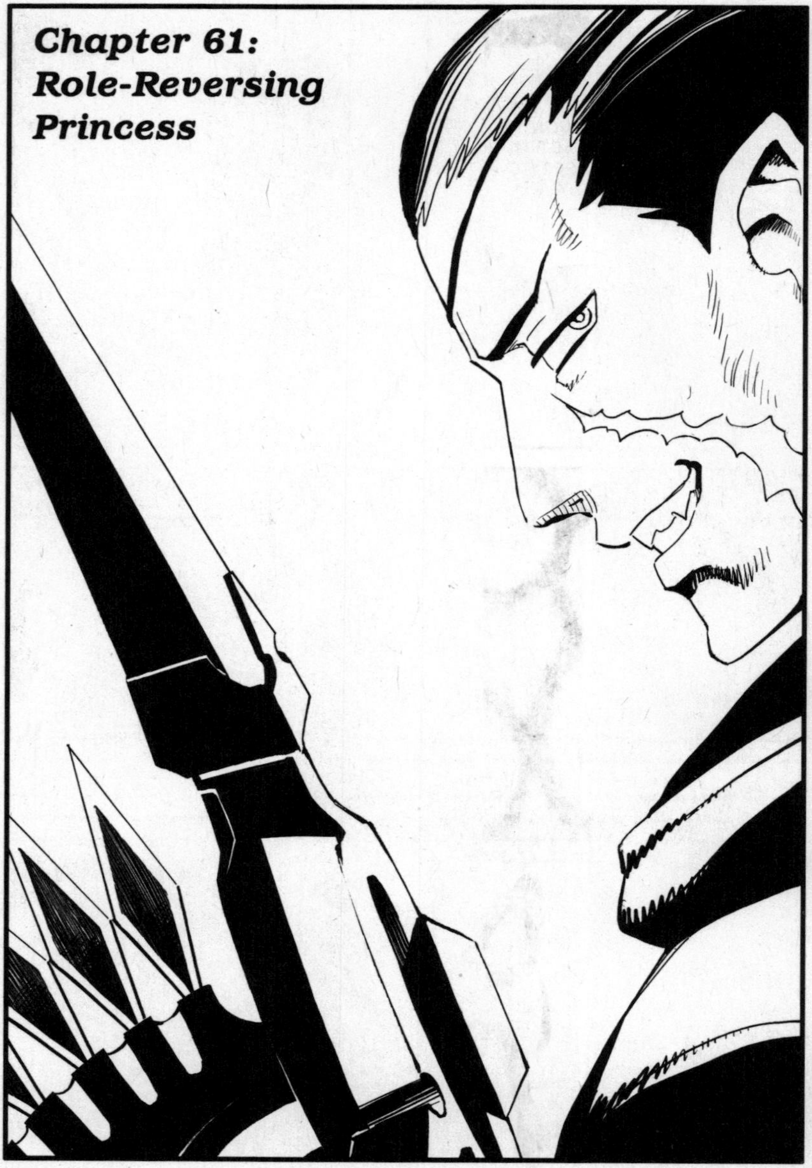

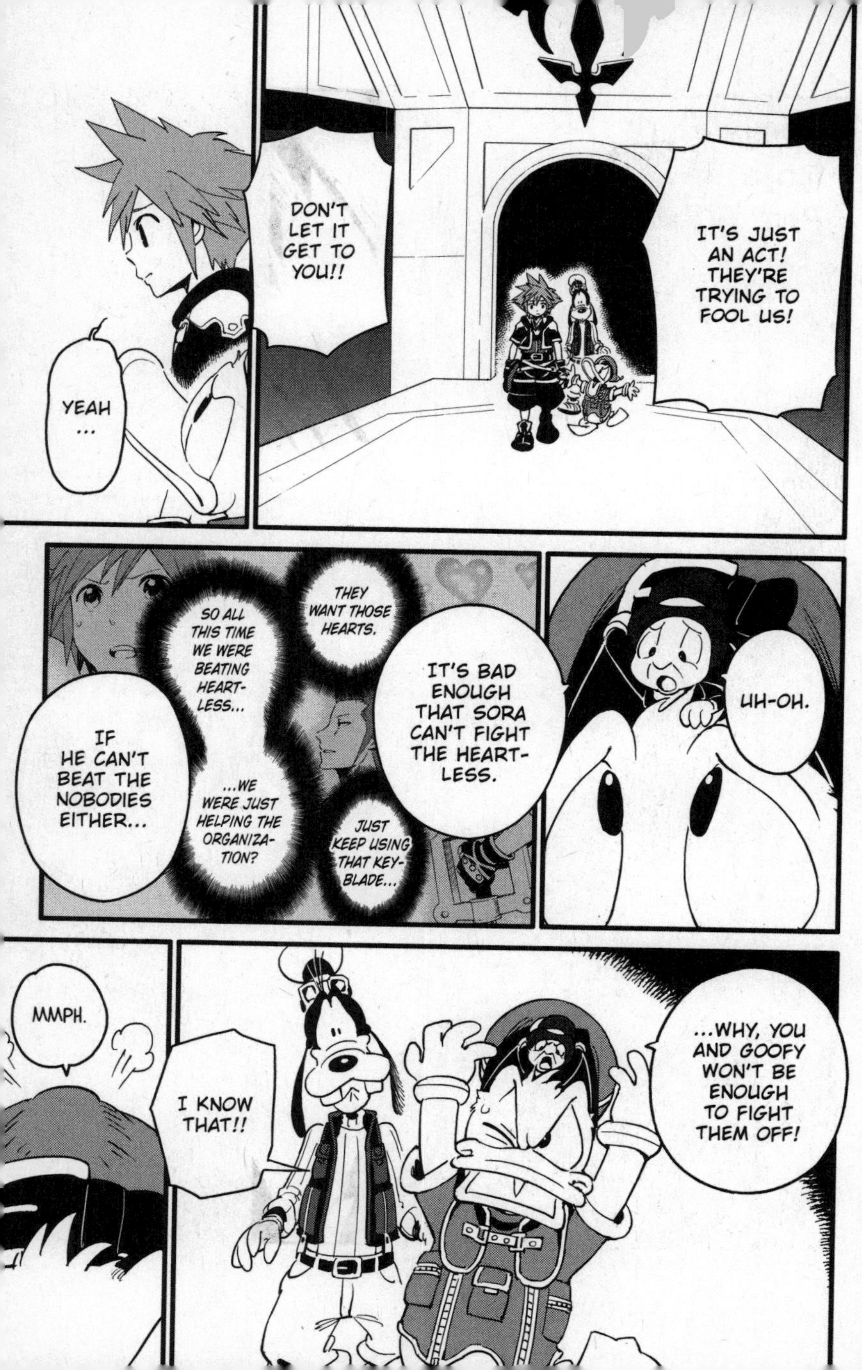
IT'S JUST AN ACT! THEY'RE TRYING TO FOOL US!
DON'T LET IT GET TO YOU!!
YEAH ...
UH-OH.
IT'S BAD ENOUGH THAT SORA CAN'T FIGHT THE HEART-LESS.
THEY WANT THOSE HEARTS.
SO ALL THIS TIME WE WERE BEATING HEART-LESS...
JUST KEEP USING THAT KEY-BLADE...
...WE WERE JUST HELPING THE ORGANIZA-TION?
IF HE CAN'T BEAT THE NOBODIES EITHER...
...WHY, YOU AND GOOFY WON'T BE ENOUGH TO FIGHT THEM OFF!
I KNOW THAT!!
MMPH.

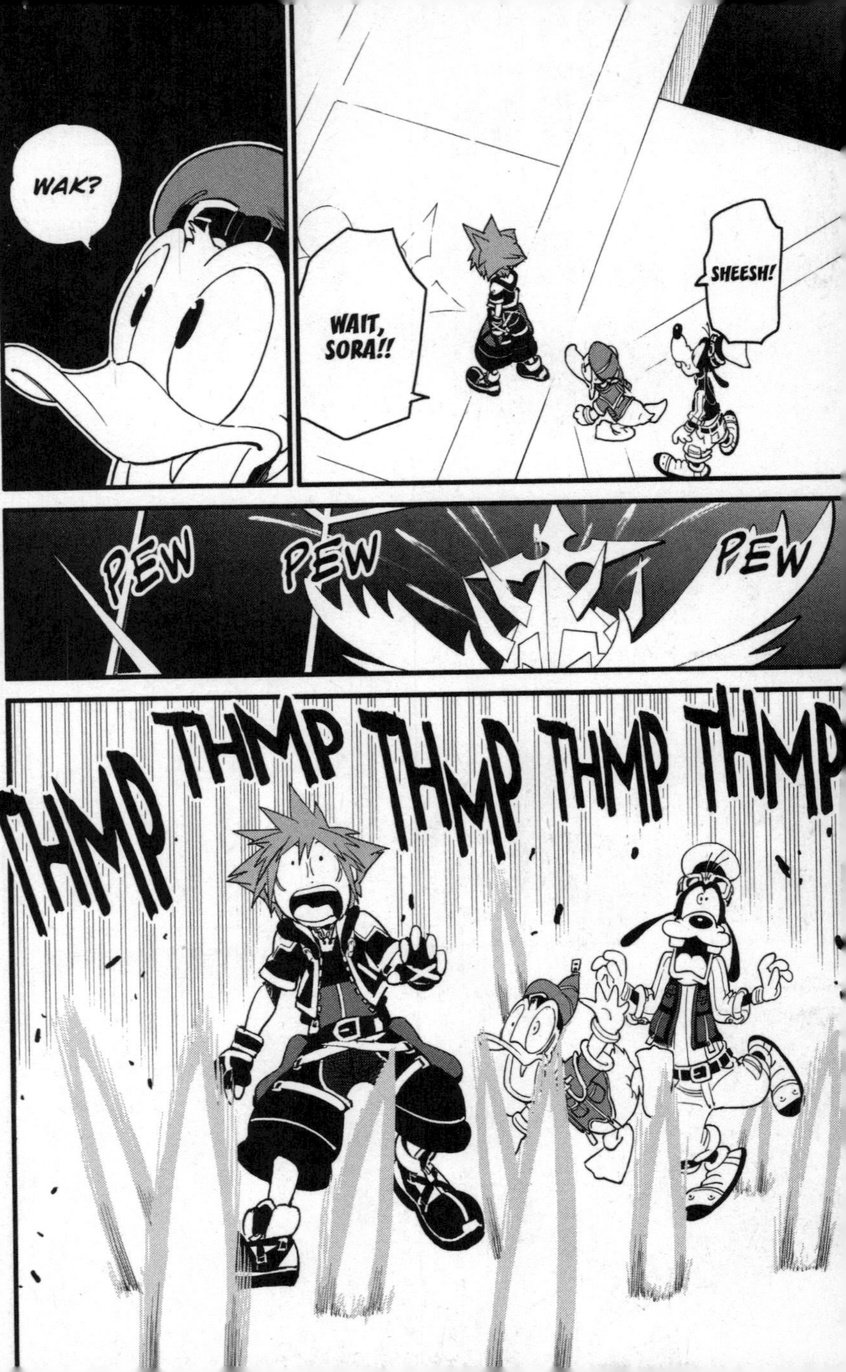
SHEESH!
WAIT, SORA!!
WAK?
PEW
PEW
PEW
THMP THMP THMP THMP THMP

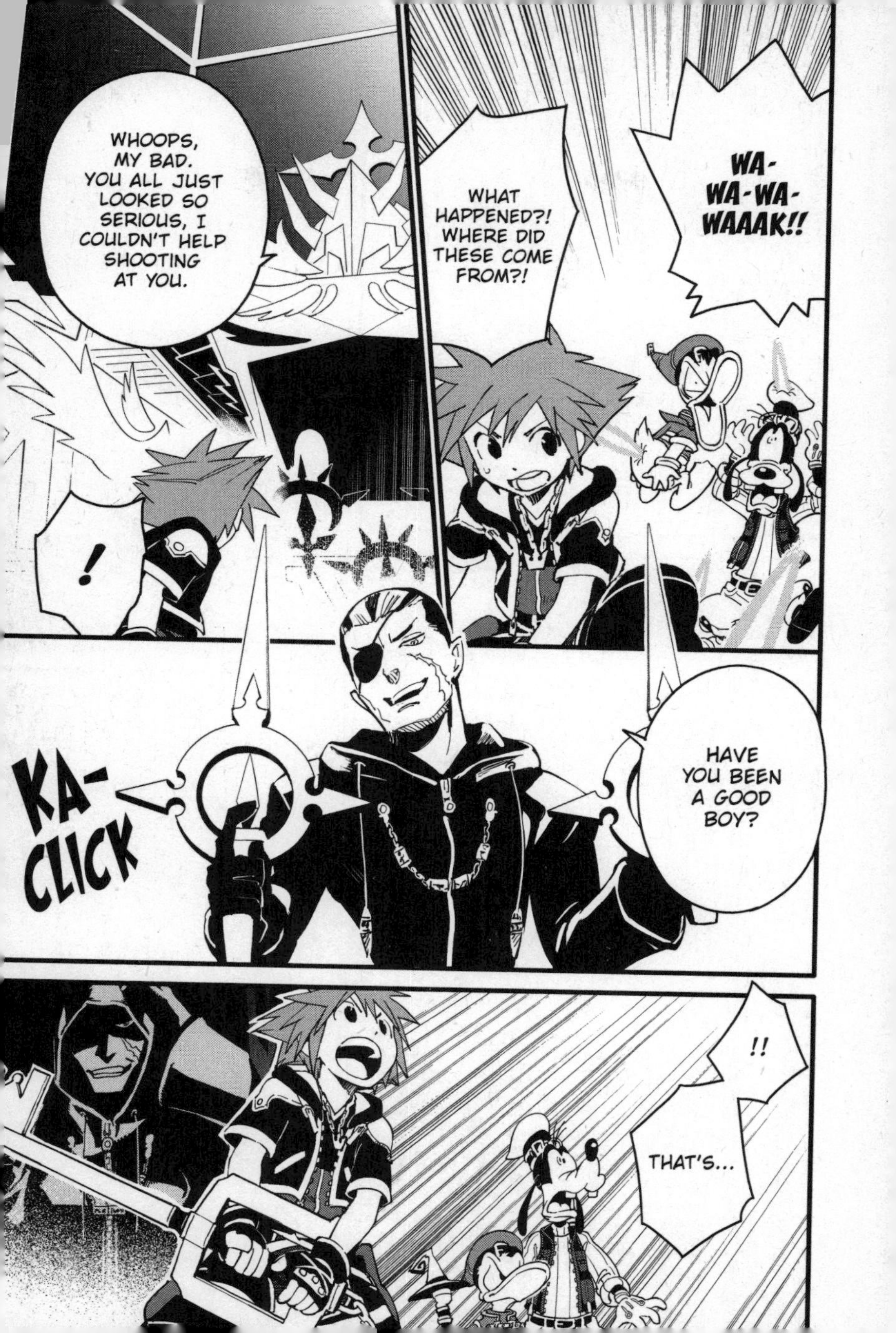
WA-WA-WA-WAAAK!!
WHAT HAPPENED?! WHERE DID THESE COME FROM?!
WHOOPS, MY BAD. YOU ALL JUST LOOKED SO SERIOUS, I COULDN'T HELP SHOOTING AT YOU.
!
HAVE YOU BEEN A GOOD BOY?
KA-CLICK
!!
THAT'S...

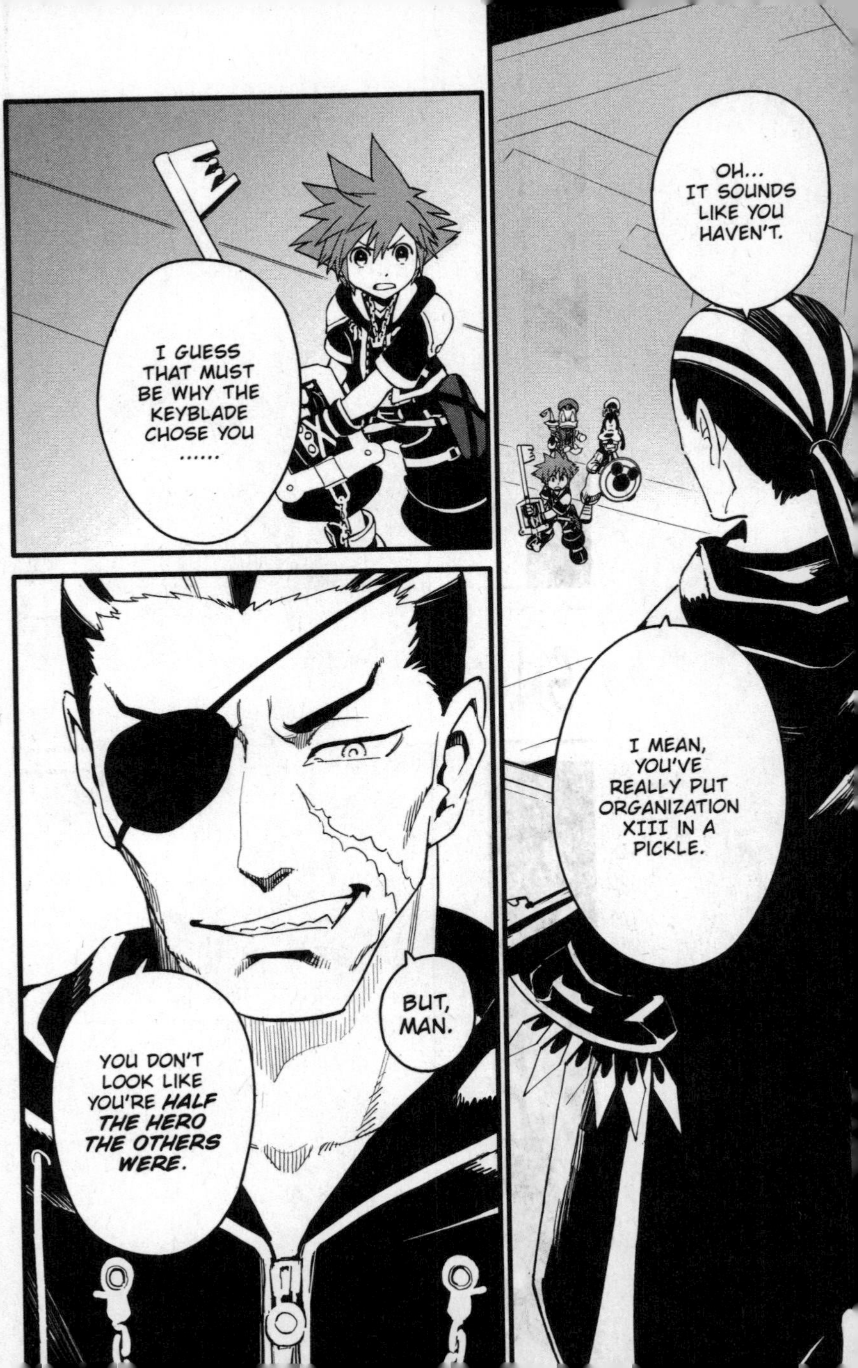
OH... IT SOUNDS LIKE YOU HAVEN'T.
I MEAN, YOU'VE REALLY PUT ORGANIZATION XIII IN A PICKLE.
I GUESS THAT MUST BE WHY THE KEYBLADE CHOSE YOU ......
BUT, MAN.
YOU DON'T LOOK LIKE YOU'RE *HALF THE HERO THE OTHERS WERE*.

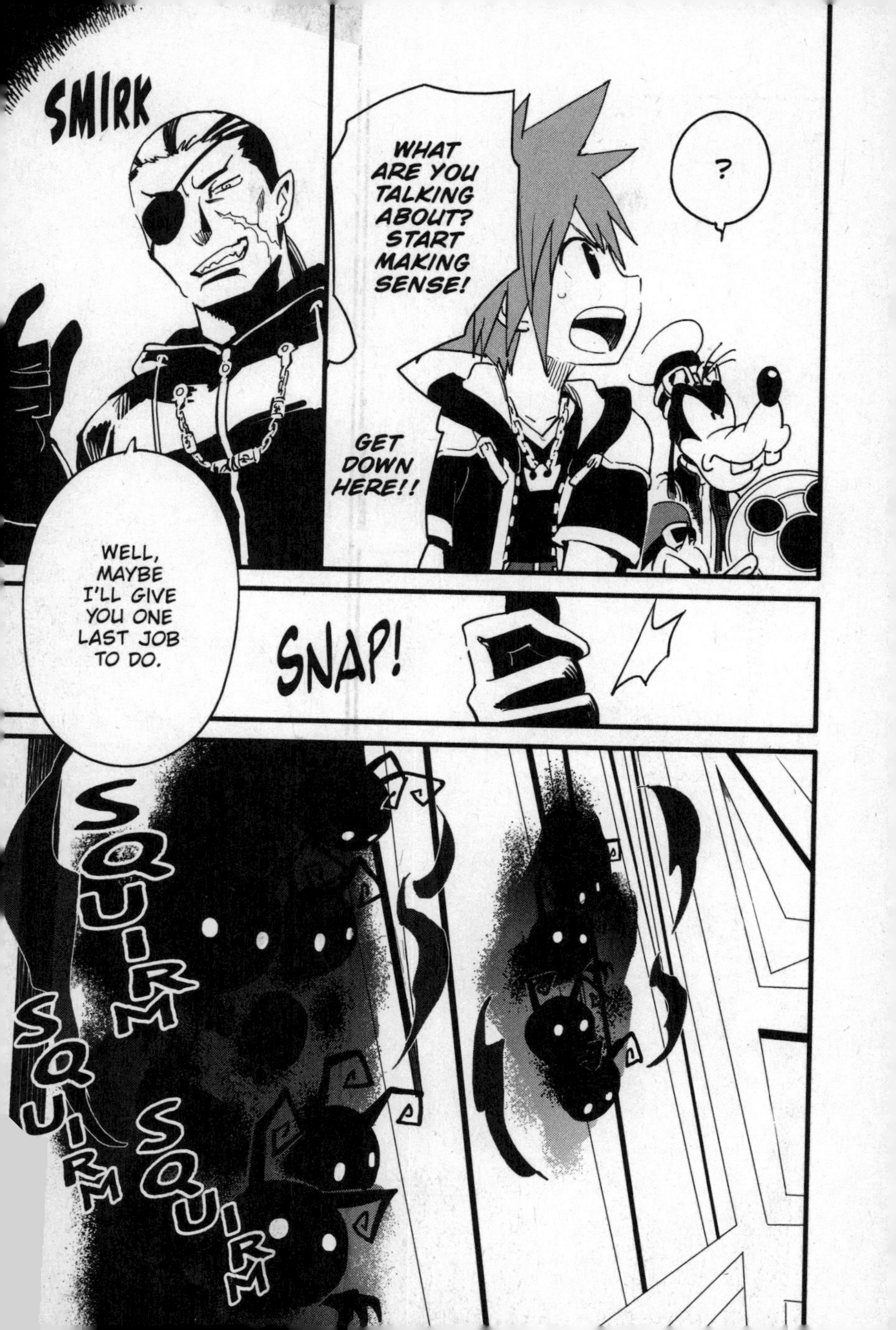
?
WHAT ARE YOU TALKING ABOUT? START MAKING SENSE!
GET DOWN HERE!!
SMIRK
WELL, MAYBE I'LL GIVE YOU ONE LAST JOB TO DO.
SNAP!
SQUIRM
SQUIRM
SQUIRM
SQUIRM

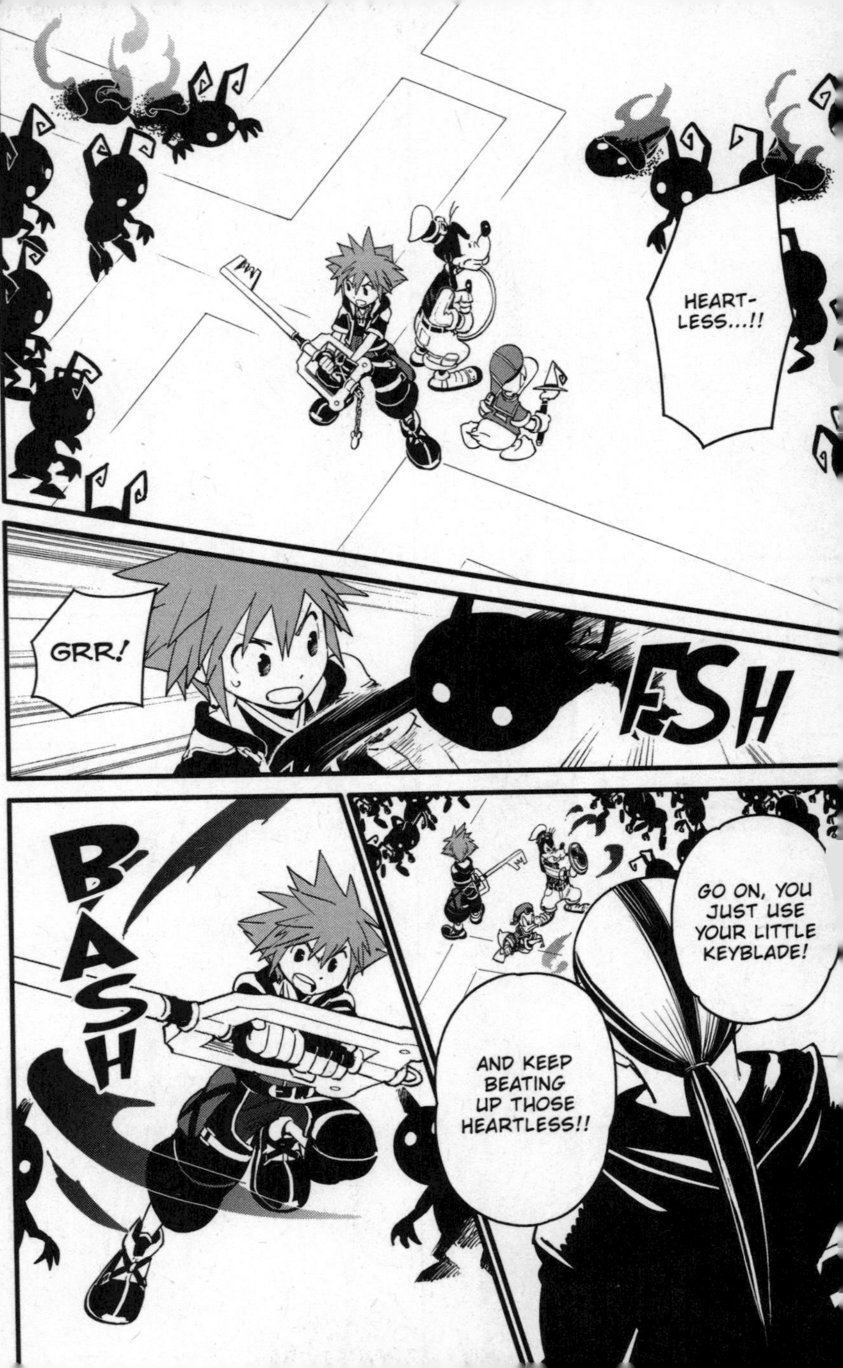
HEART-LESS...!!
GRR!
FSH
GO ON, YOU JUST USE YOUR LITTLE KEYBLADE!
AND KEEP BEATING UP THOSE HEARTLESS!!
BASH

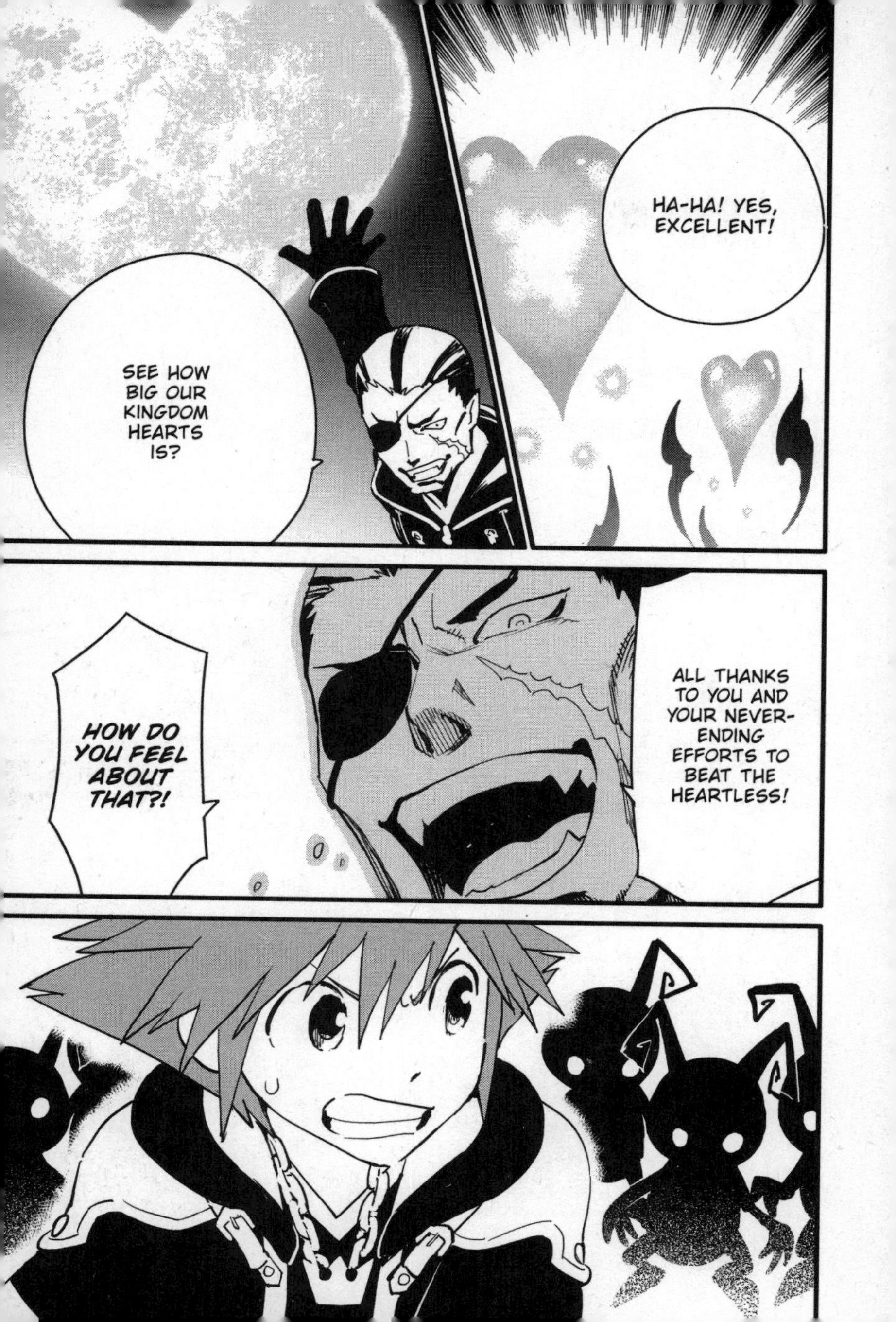
HA-HA! YES, EXCELLENT!
SEE HOW BIG OUR KINGDOM HEARTS IS?
ALL THANKS TO YOU AND YOUR NEVER-ENDING EFFORTS TO BEAT THE HEARTLESS!
HOW DO YOU FEEL ABOUT THAT?!

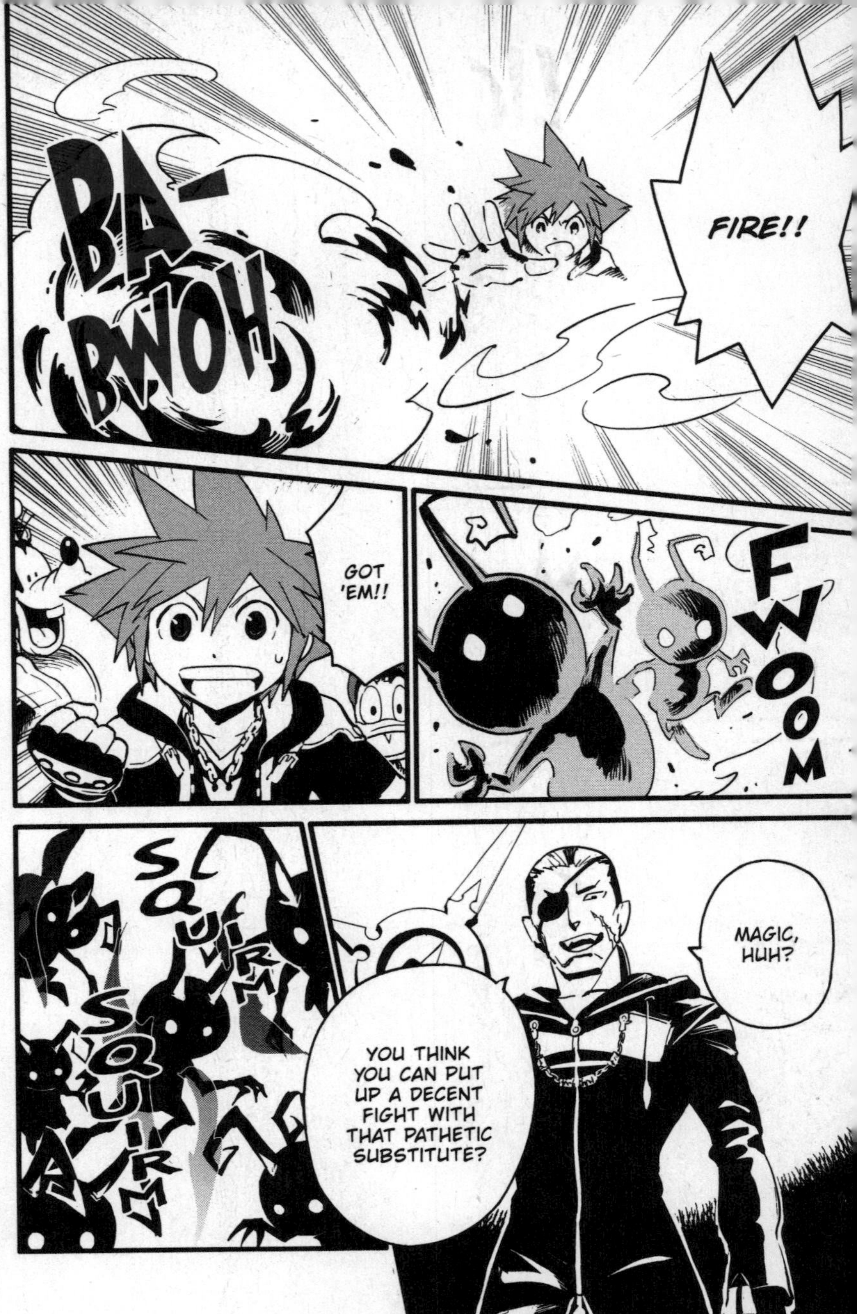
FIRE!!
BA-BWOH
FWOOM
GOT 'EM!!
MAGIC, HUH?
YOU THINK YOU CAN PUT UP A DECENT FIGHT WITH THAT PATHETIC SUBSTITUTE?
SQUIRM
SQUIRM

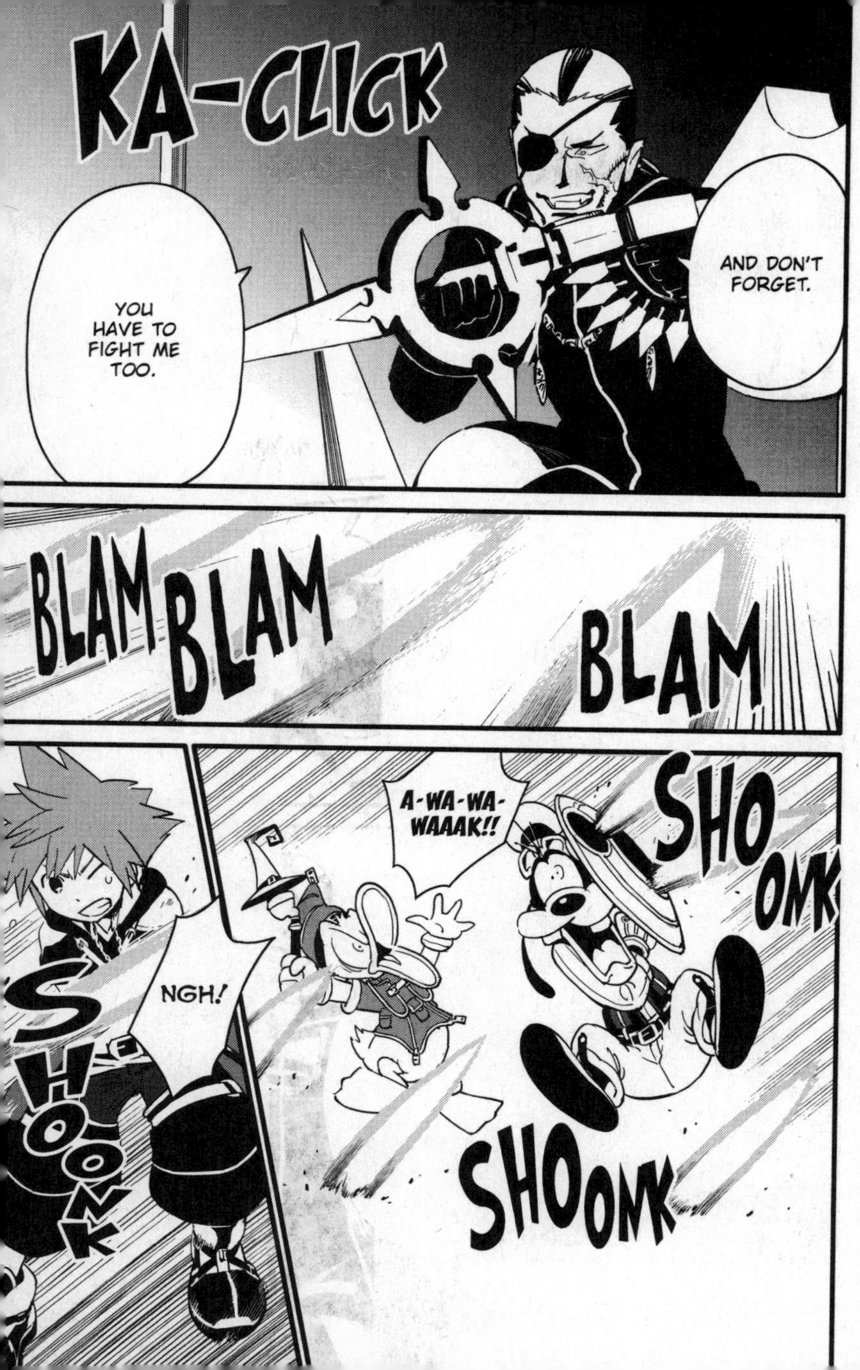
KA-CLICK
AND DON'T FORGET.
YOU HAVE TO FIGHT ME TOO.
BLAM
BLAM BLAM
SHOONK
A-WA-WA-WAAAK!!
SHOONK
NGH!
SHOONK

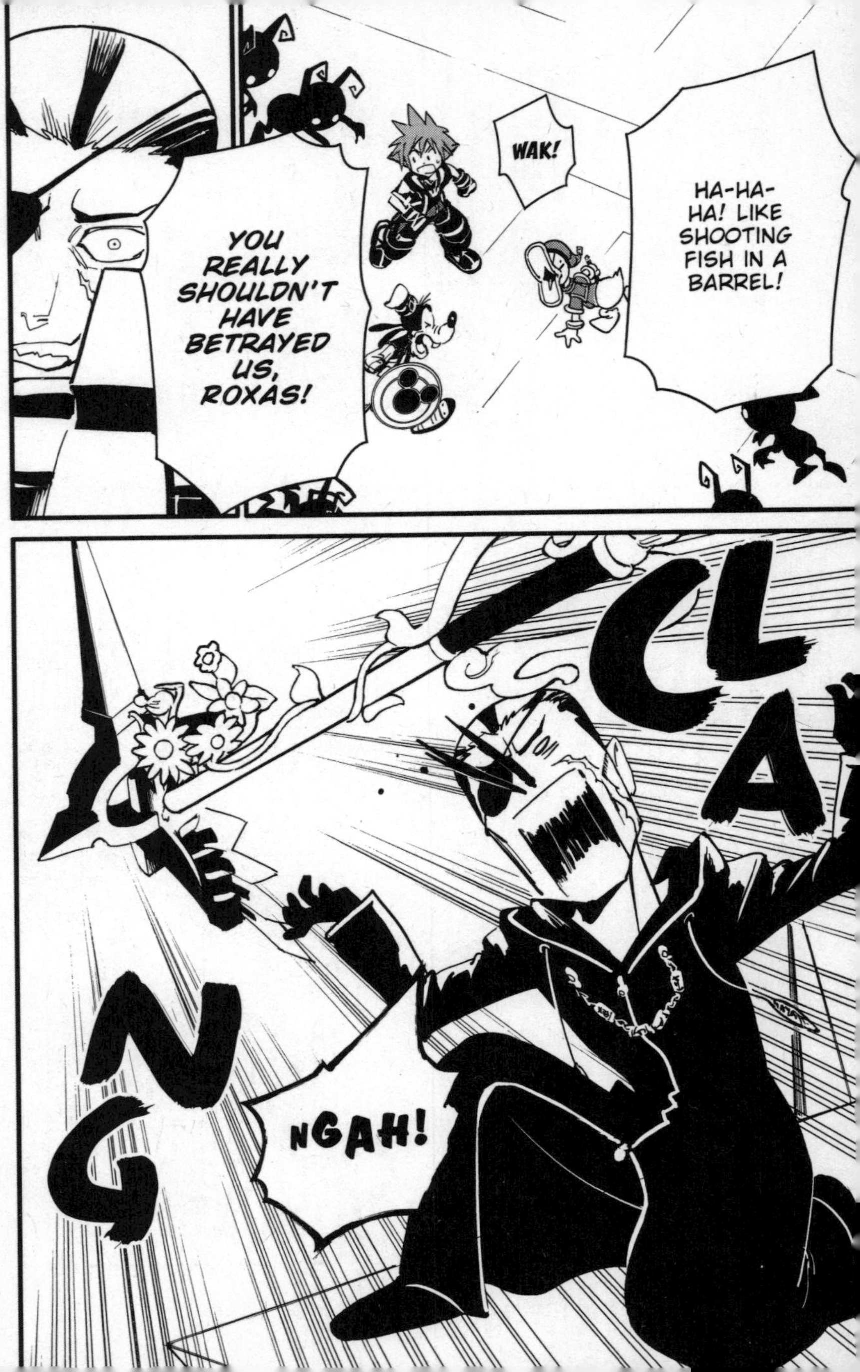
HA-HA-HA! LIKE SHOOTING FISH IN A BARREL!
WAK!
YOU REALLY SHOULDN'T HAVE BETRAYED US, ROXAS!
CLANG
NGAH!

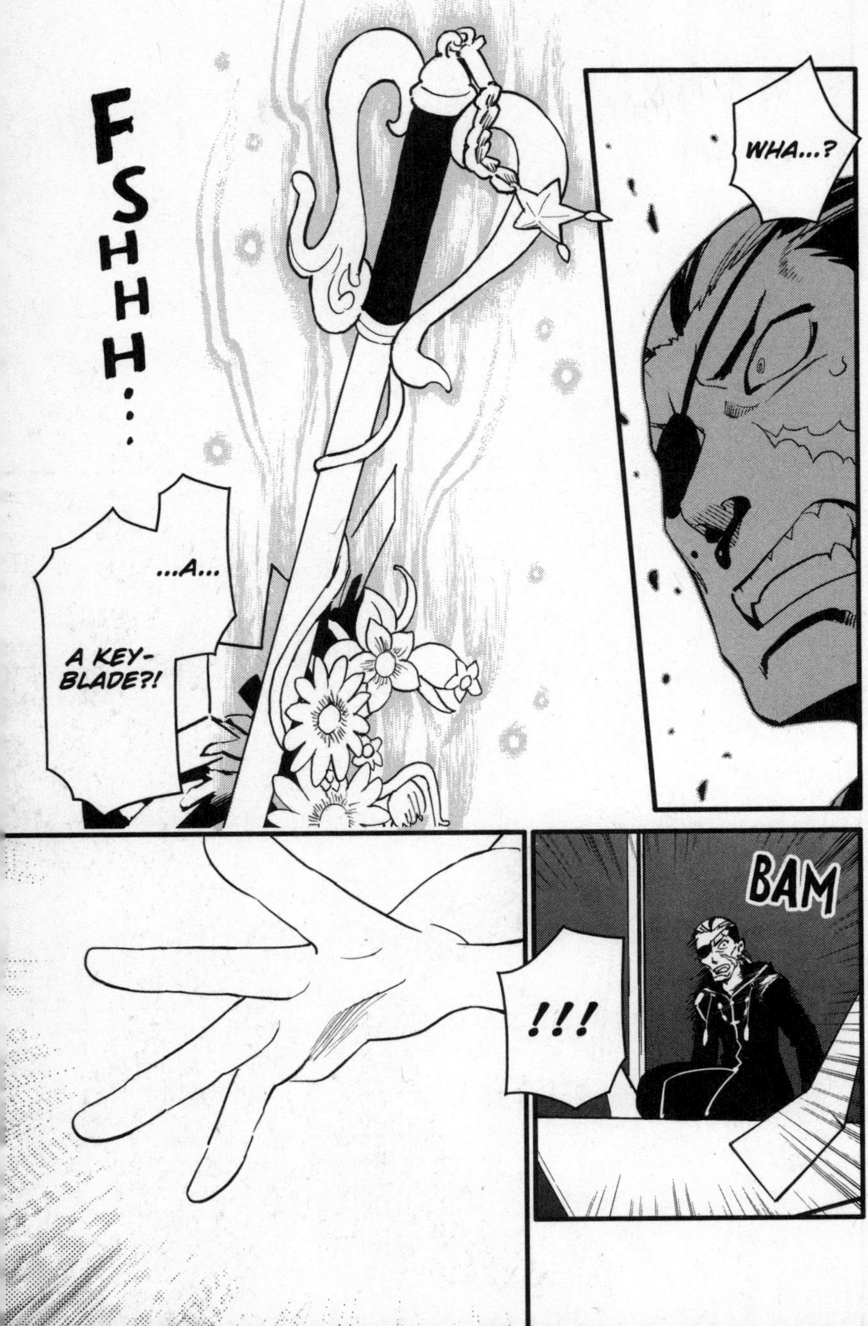
WHA...?
FSHHH...
...A...
A KEY-BLADE?!
BAM
!!!

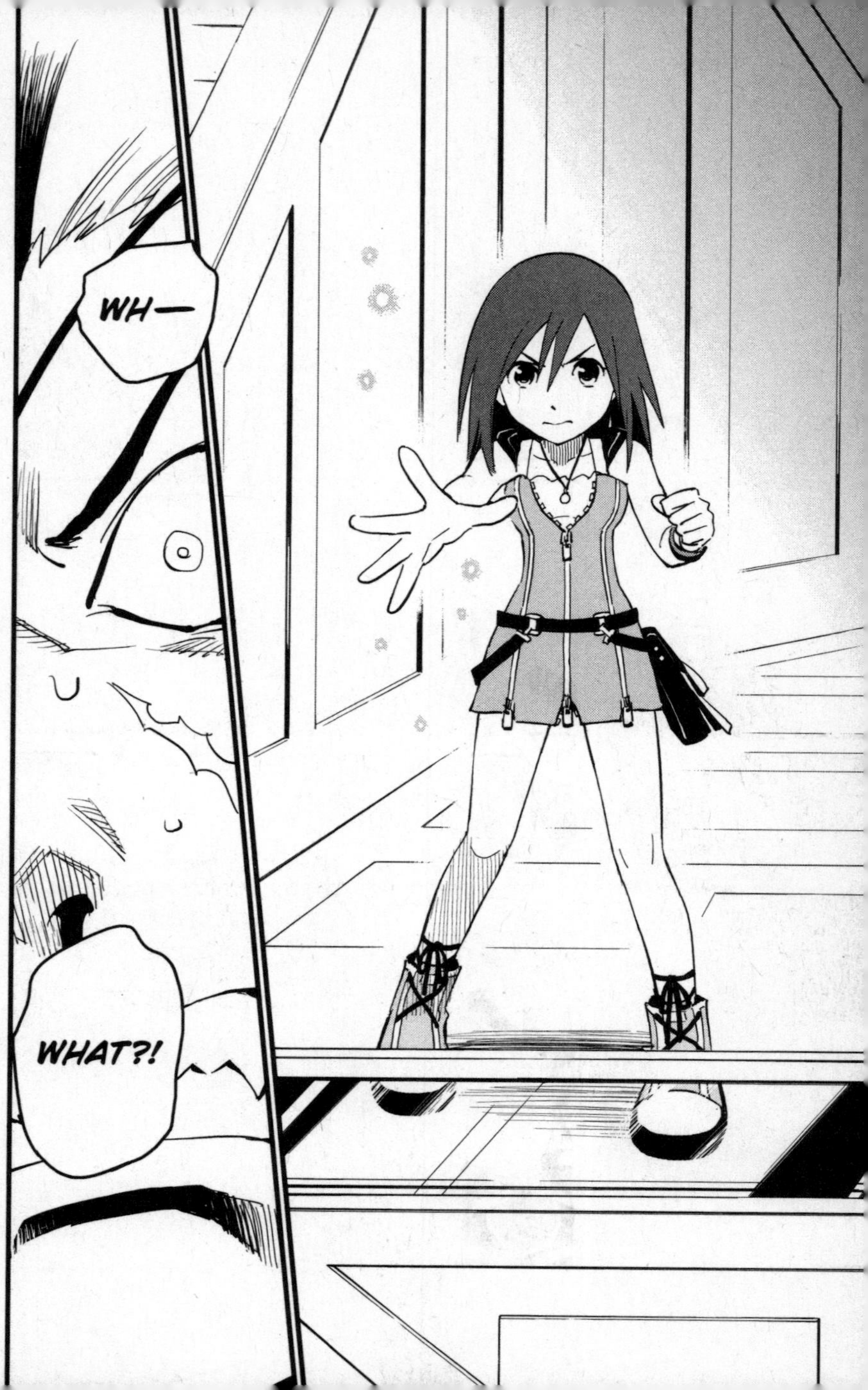
WH—
WHAT?!

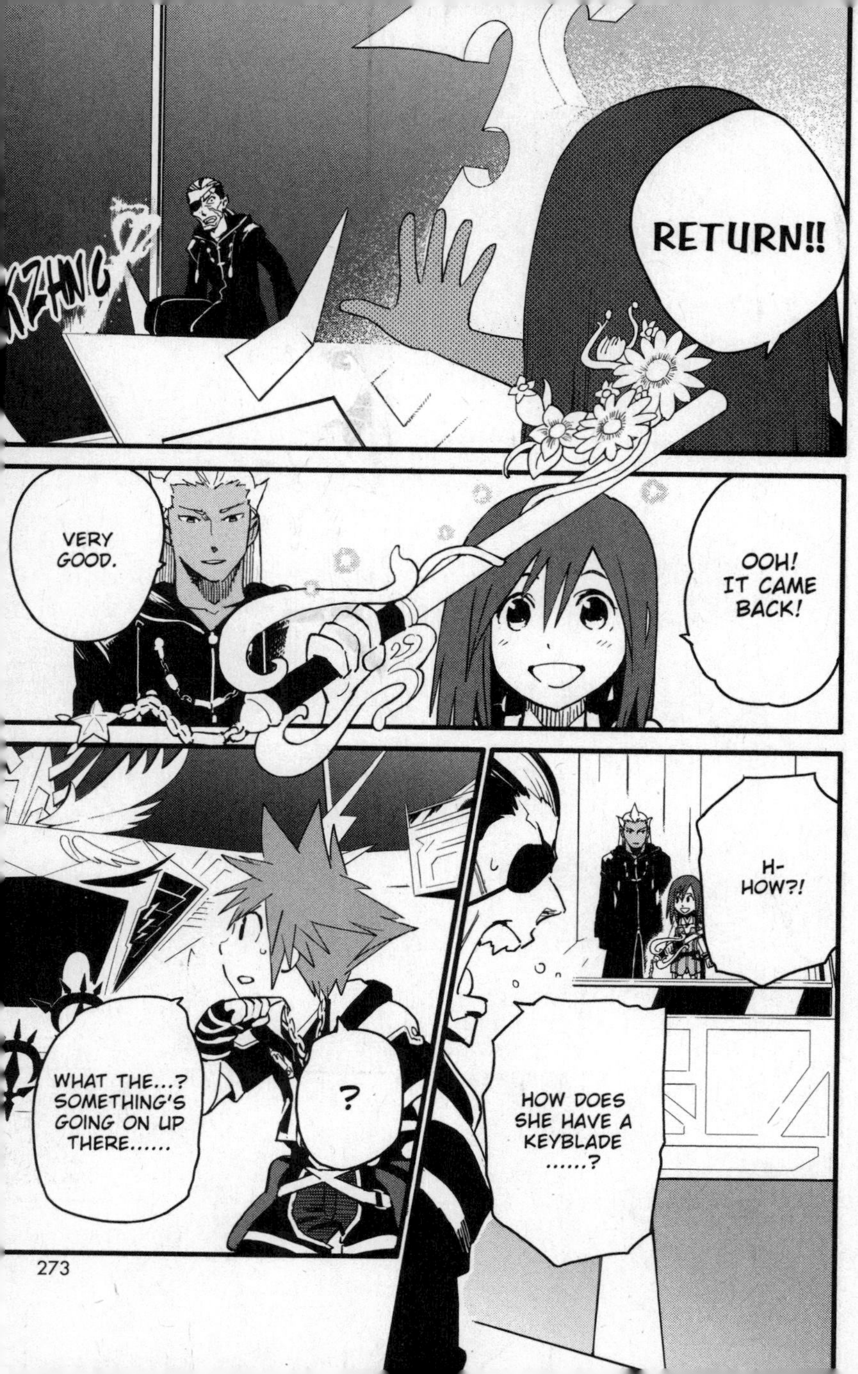
RETURN!!
KZHNG
OOH! IT CAME BACK!
VERY GOOD.
H- HOW?!
HOW DOES SHE HAVE A KEYBLADE ......?
?
WHAT THE...? SOMETHING'S GOING ON UP THERE......

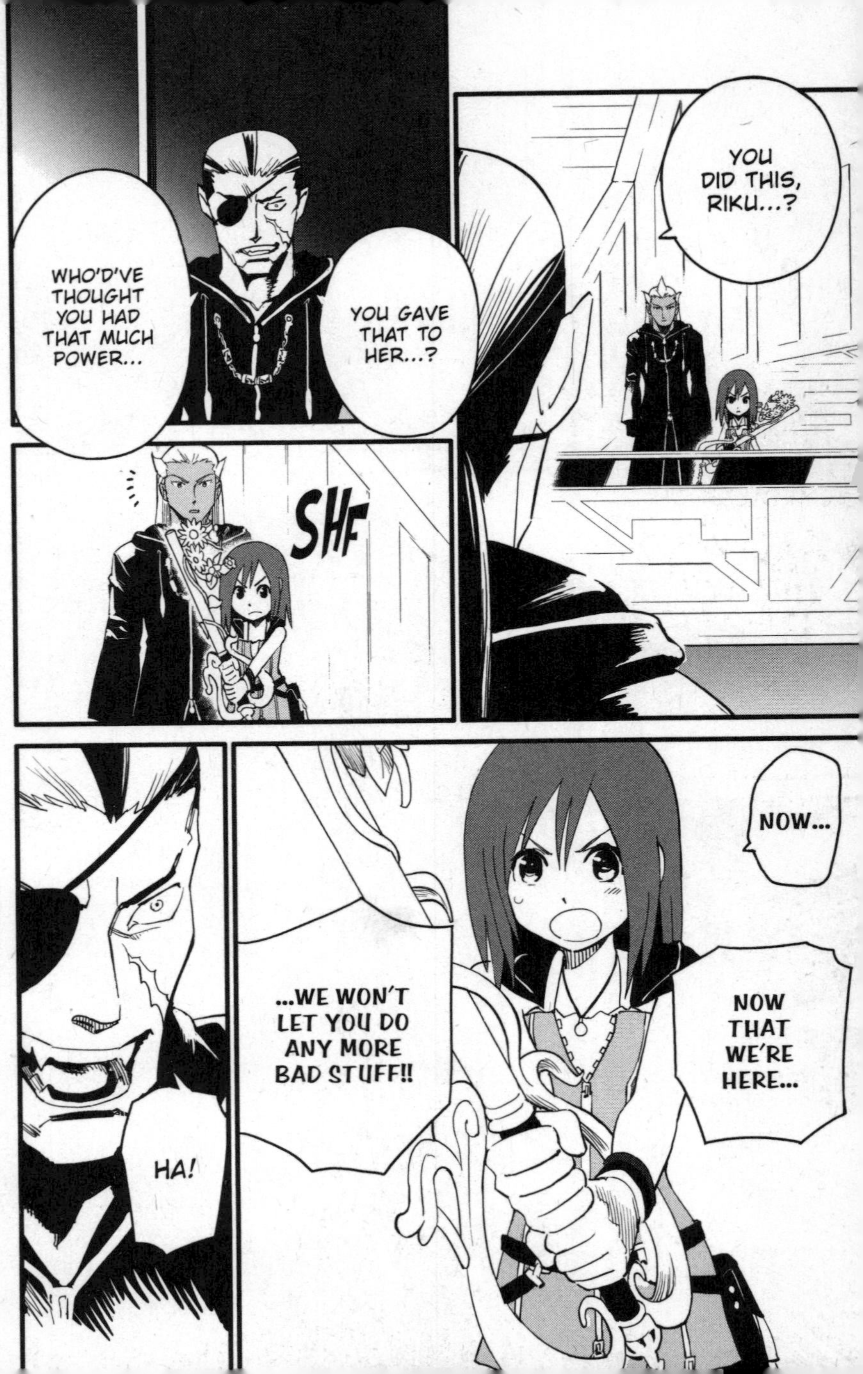
YOU DID THIS, RIKU...?
WHO'D'VE THOUGHT YOU HAD THAT MUCH POWER...
YOU GAVE THAT TO HER...?
SHF
NOW...
NOW THAT WE'RE HERE...
...WE WON'T LET YOU DO ANY MORE BAD STUFF!!
HA!

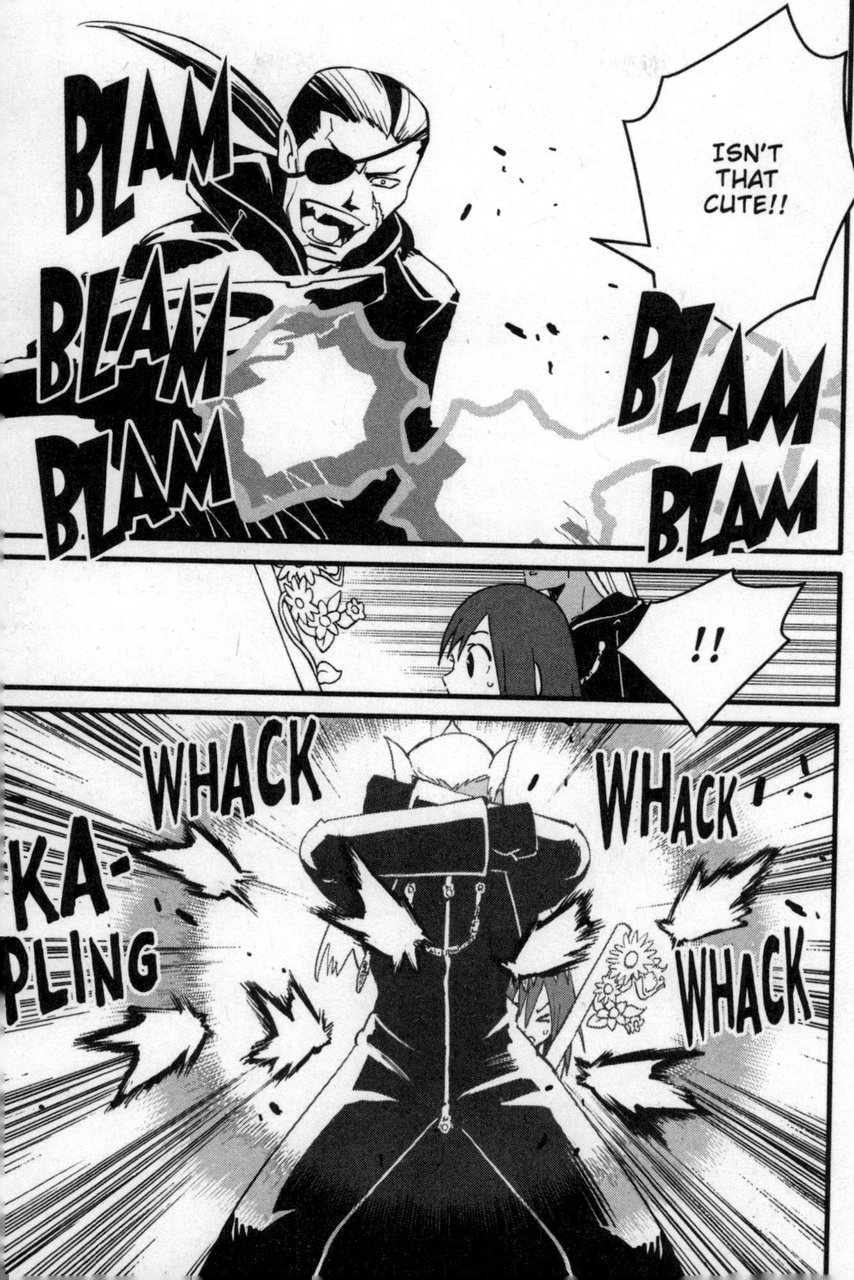
ISN'T THAT CUTE!!
BLAM BLAM
BLAM
BLAM BLAM BLAM
!!
WHACK
WHACK
WHACK
KA-PLING

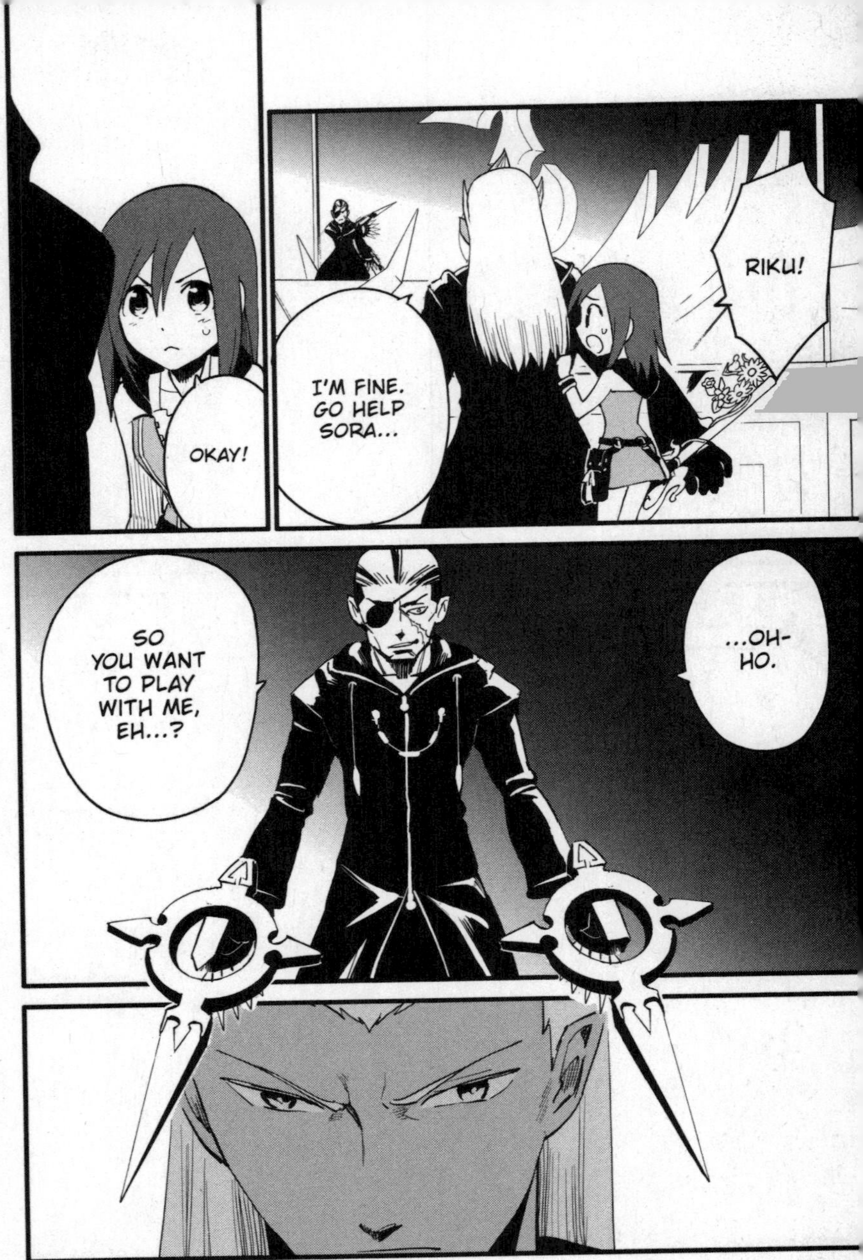
RIKU!
I'M FINE. GO HELP SORA...
OKAY!
...OH-HO.
SO YOU WANT TO PLAY WITH ME, EH...?

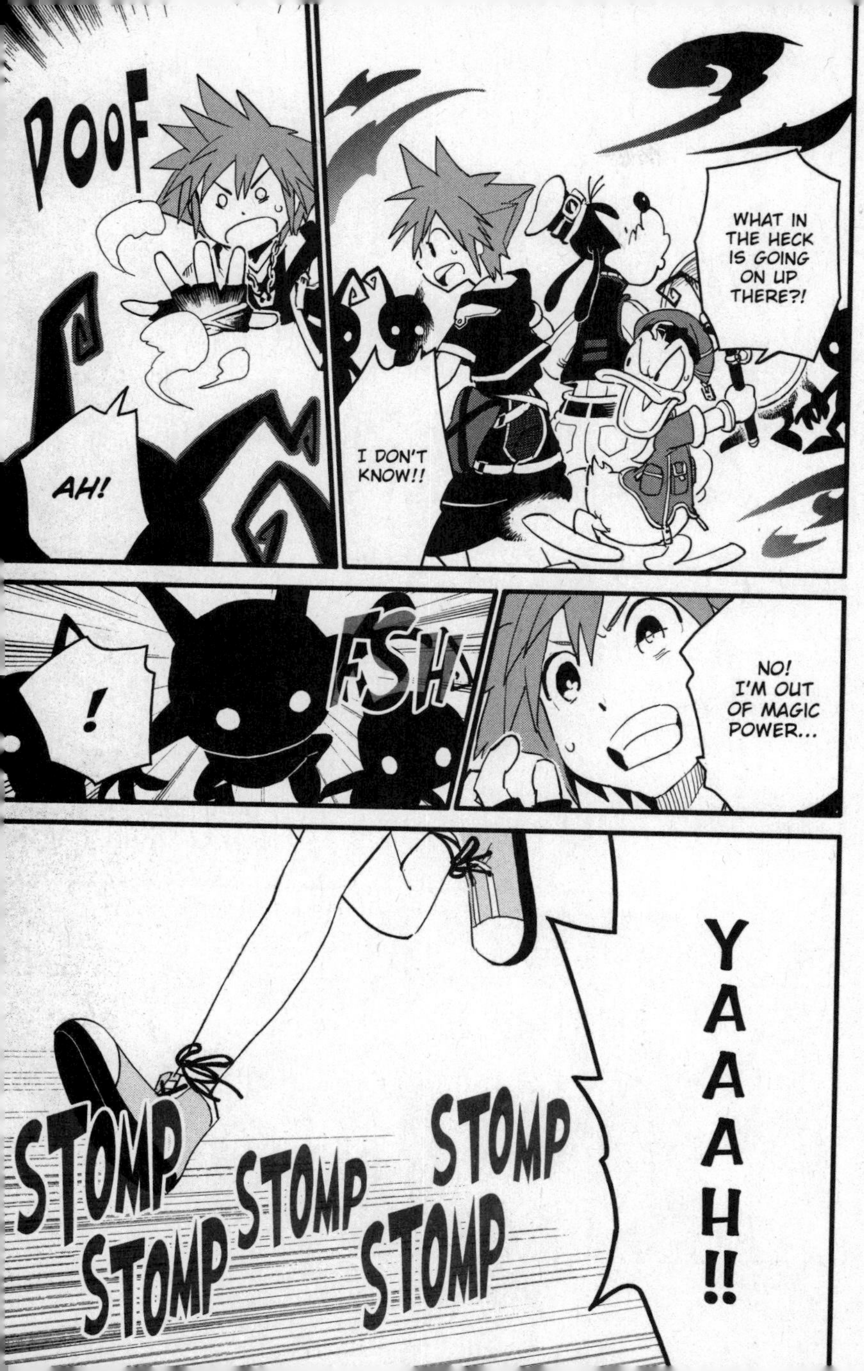
WHAT IN THE HECK IS GOING ON UP THERE?!
I DON'T KNOW!!
POOF
AH!
NO! I'M OUT OF MAGIC POWER...
FSH
!
YAAAAH!!
STOMP STOMP STOMP STOMP STOMP

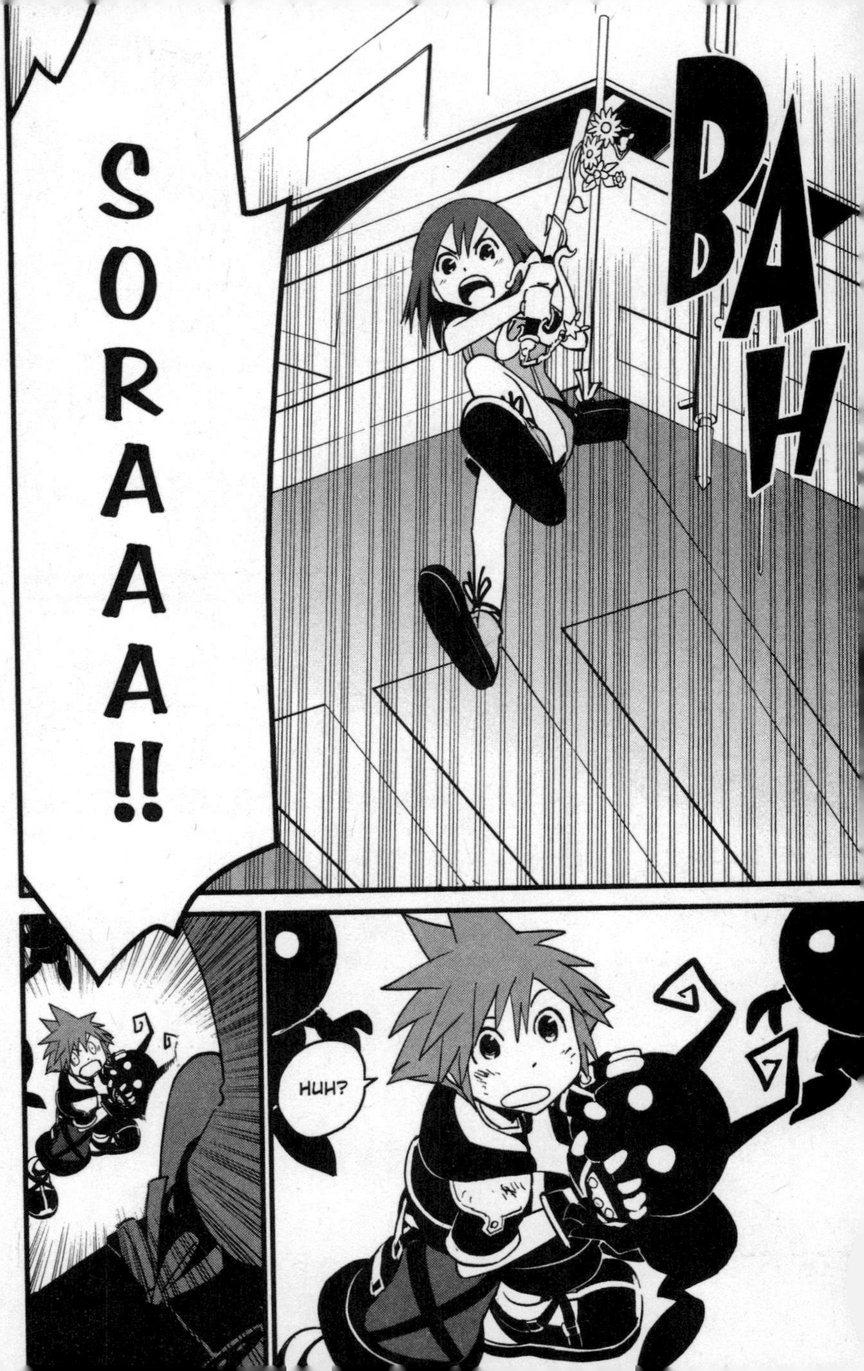
BAH
SORAAA!!
HUH?

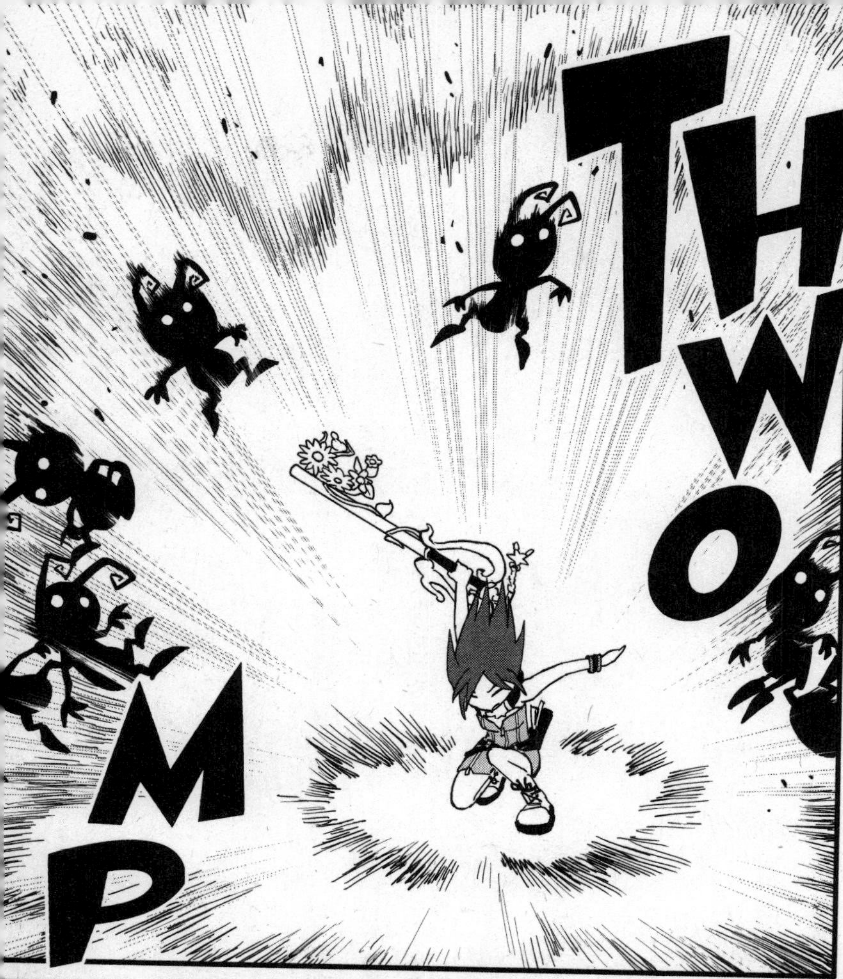
THWOMP

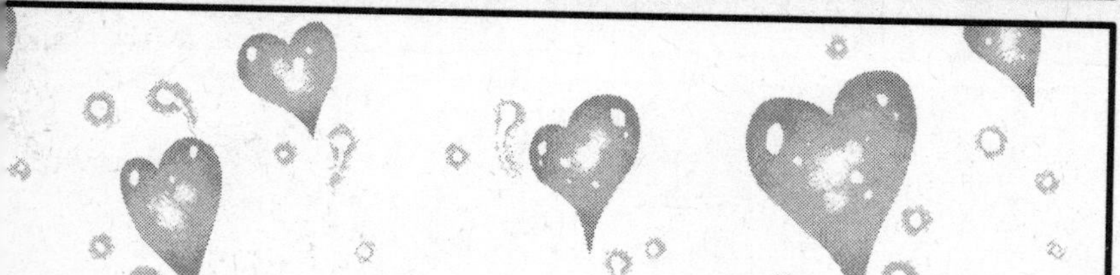

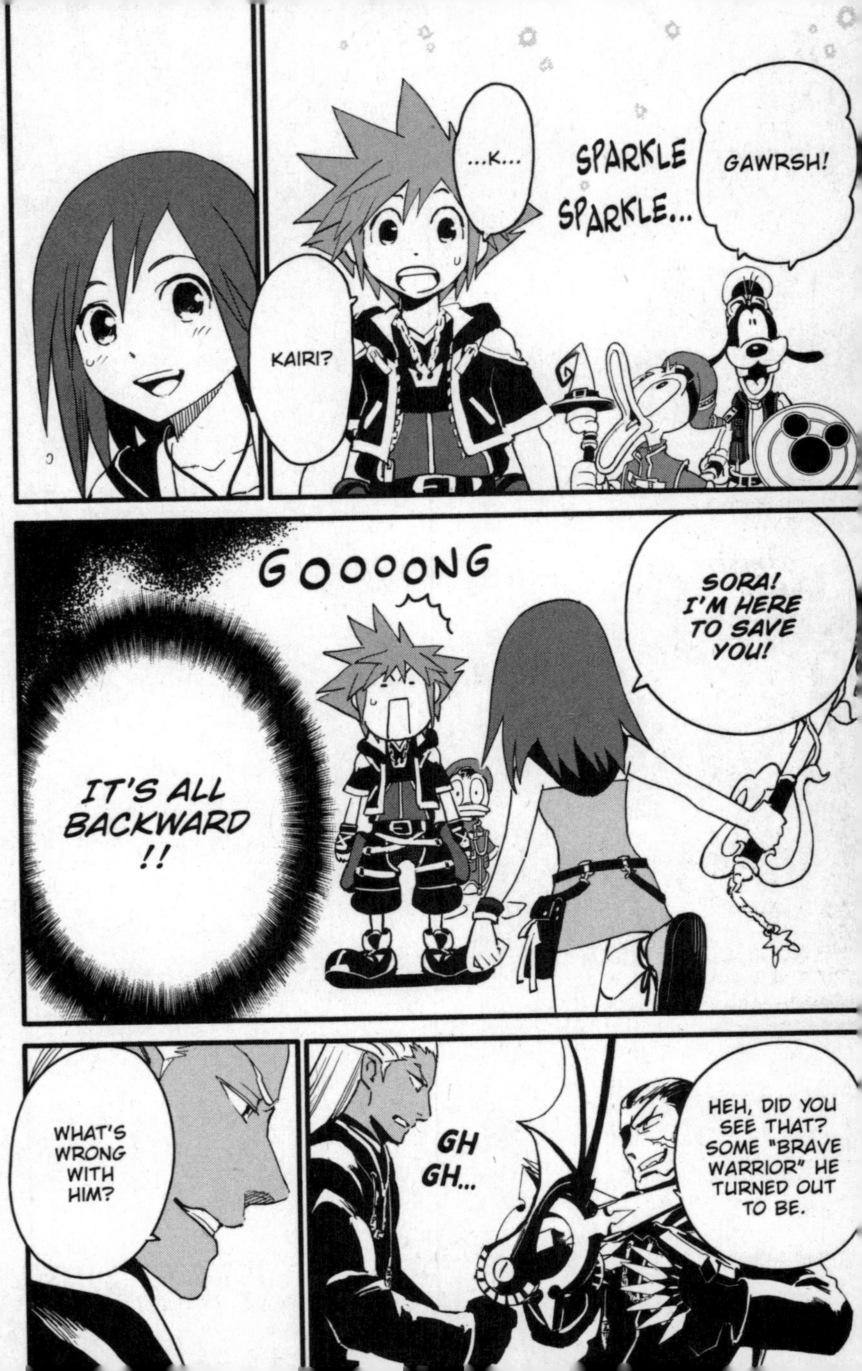
GAWRSH!
SPARKLE SPARKLE...
...K...
KAIRI?
SORA! I'M HERE TO SAVE YOU!
GOOOONG
IT'S ALL BACKWARD!!
HEH, DID YOU SEE THAT? SOME "BRAVE WARRIOR" HE TURNED OUT TO BE.
GH GH...
WHAT'S WRONG WITH HIM?

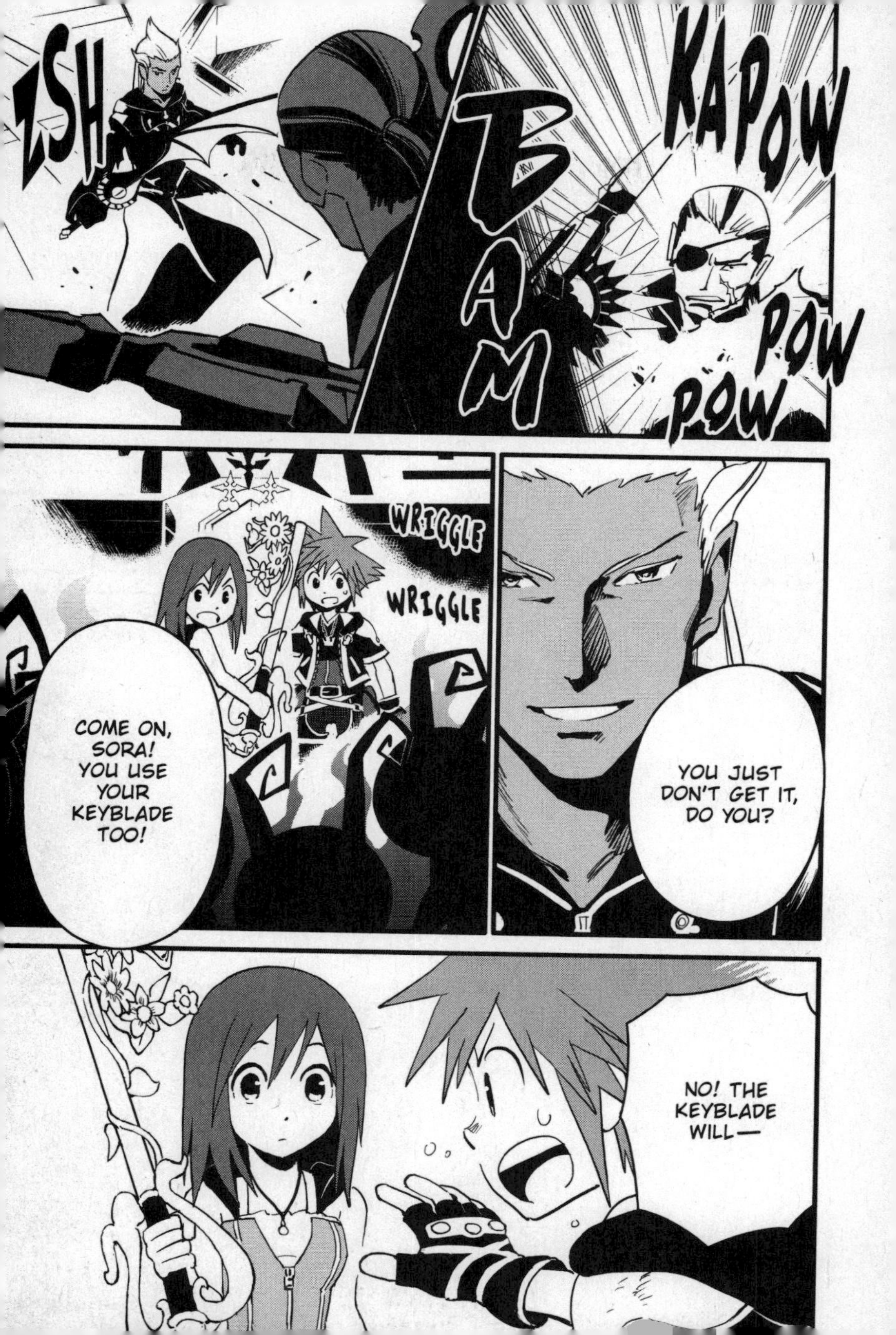
KAPOW
POW
POW
BAM
ZSH
YOU JUST DON'T GET IT, DO YOU?
WRIGGLE
WRIGGLE
COME ON, SORA! YOU USE YOUR KEYBLADE TOO!
NO! THE KEYBLADE WILL—

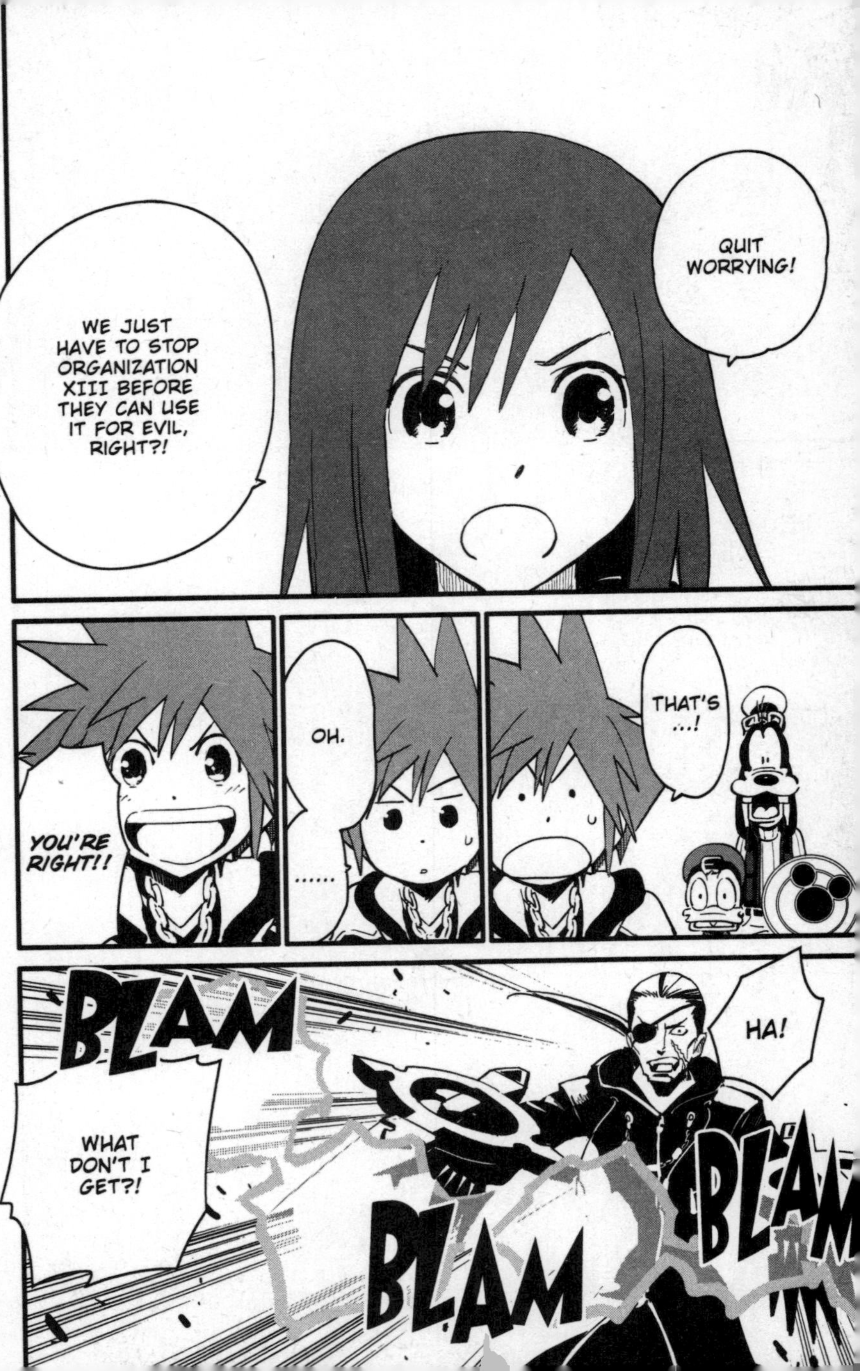
QUIT WORRYING!
WE JUST HAVE TO STOP ORGANIZATION XIII BEFORE THEY CAN USE IT FOR EVIL, RIGHT?!
THAT'S ...!
OH.
......
YOU'RE RIGHT!!
HA!
BLAM
BLAM
WHAT DON'T I GET?!
BLAM

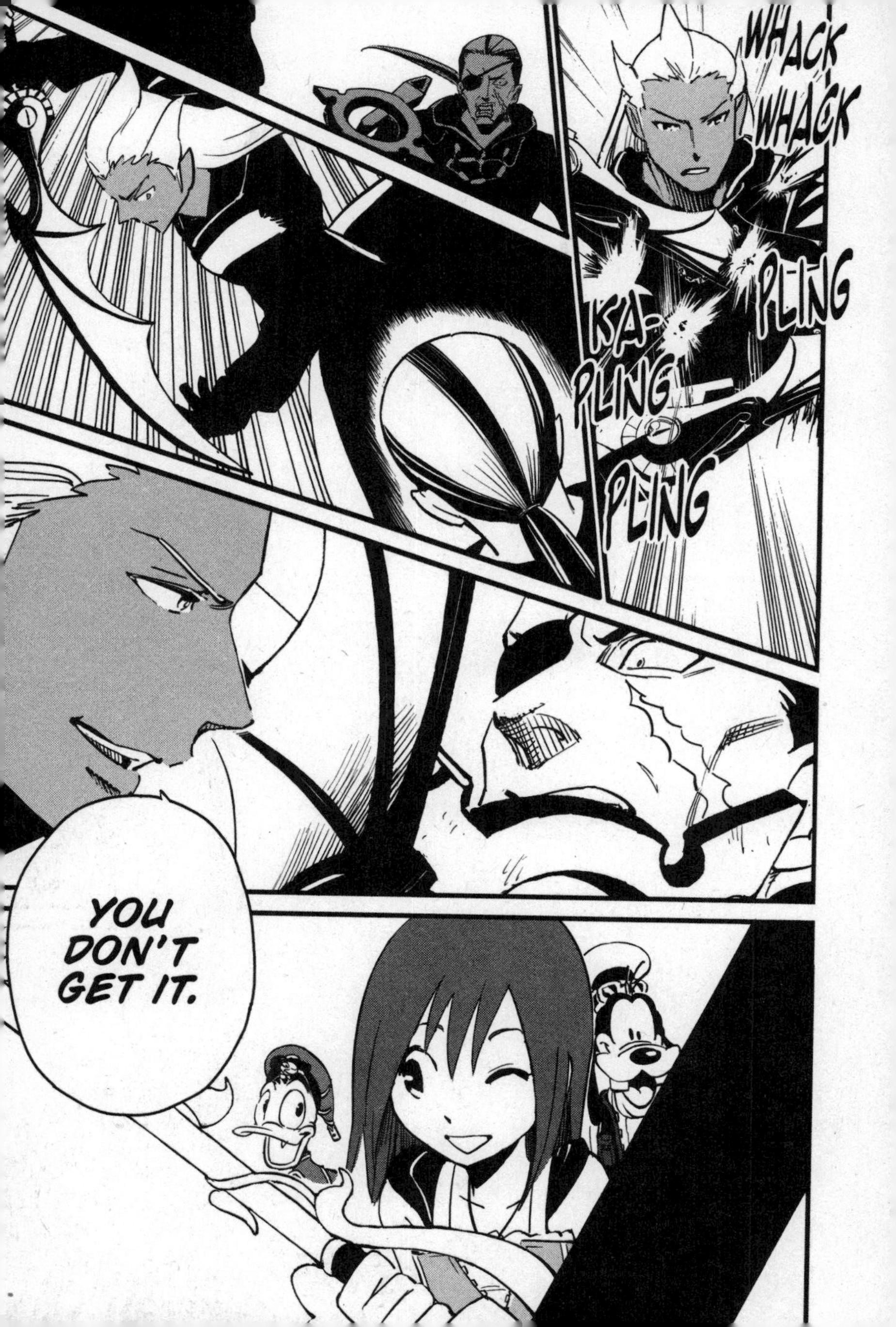
WHACK
WHACK
PLING
KA-PLING
PLING
YOU DON'T GET IT.

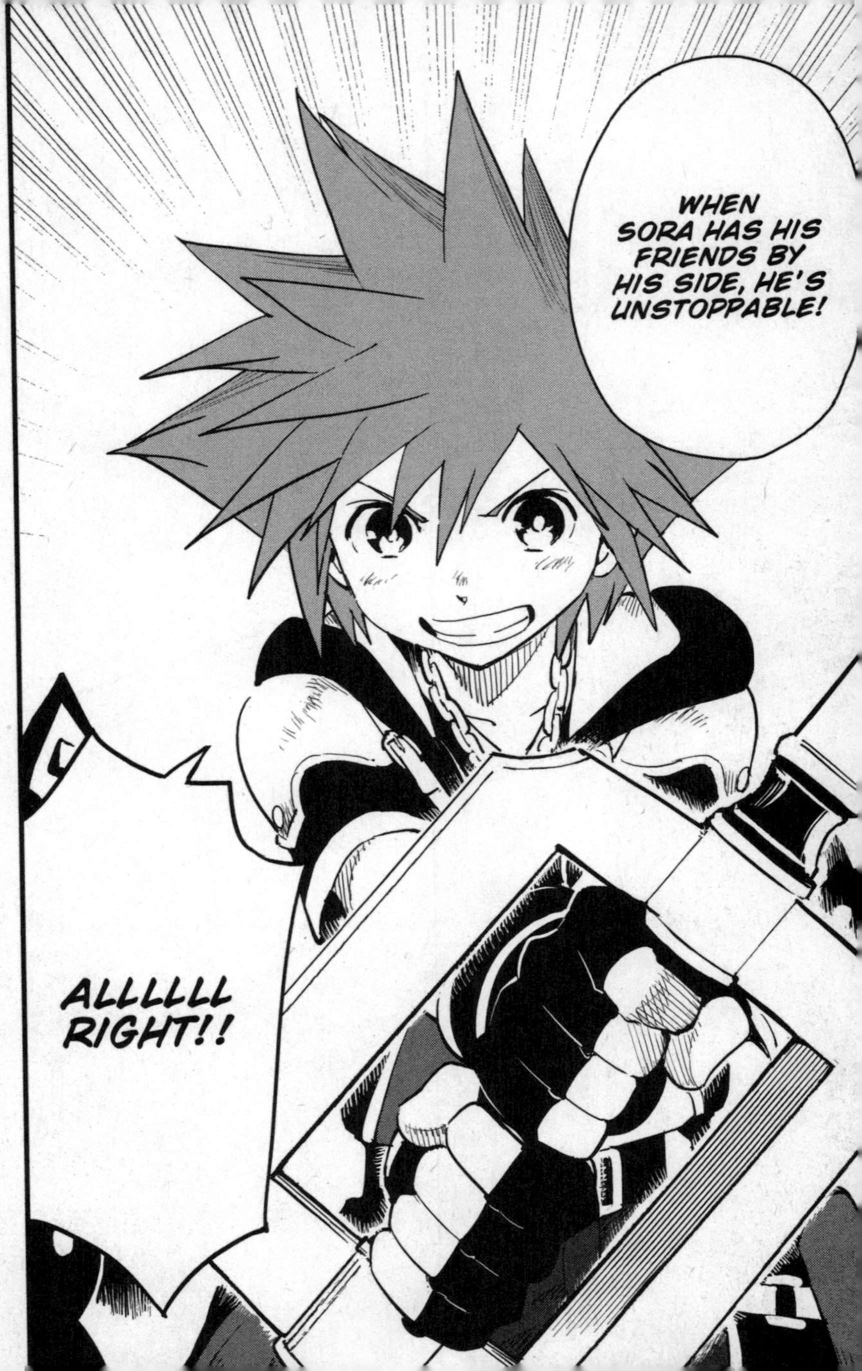
WHEN SORA HAS HIS FRIENDS BY HIS SIDE, HE'S UNSTOPPABLE!
ALLLLLL RIGHT!!

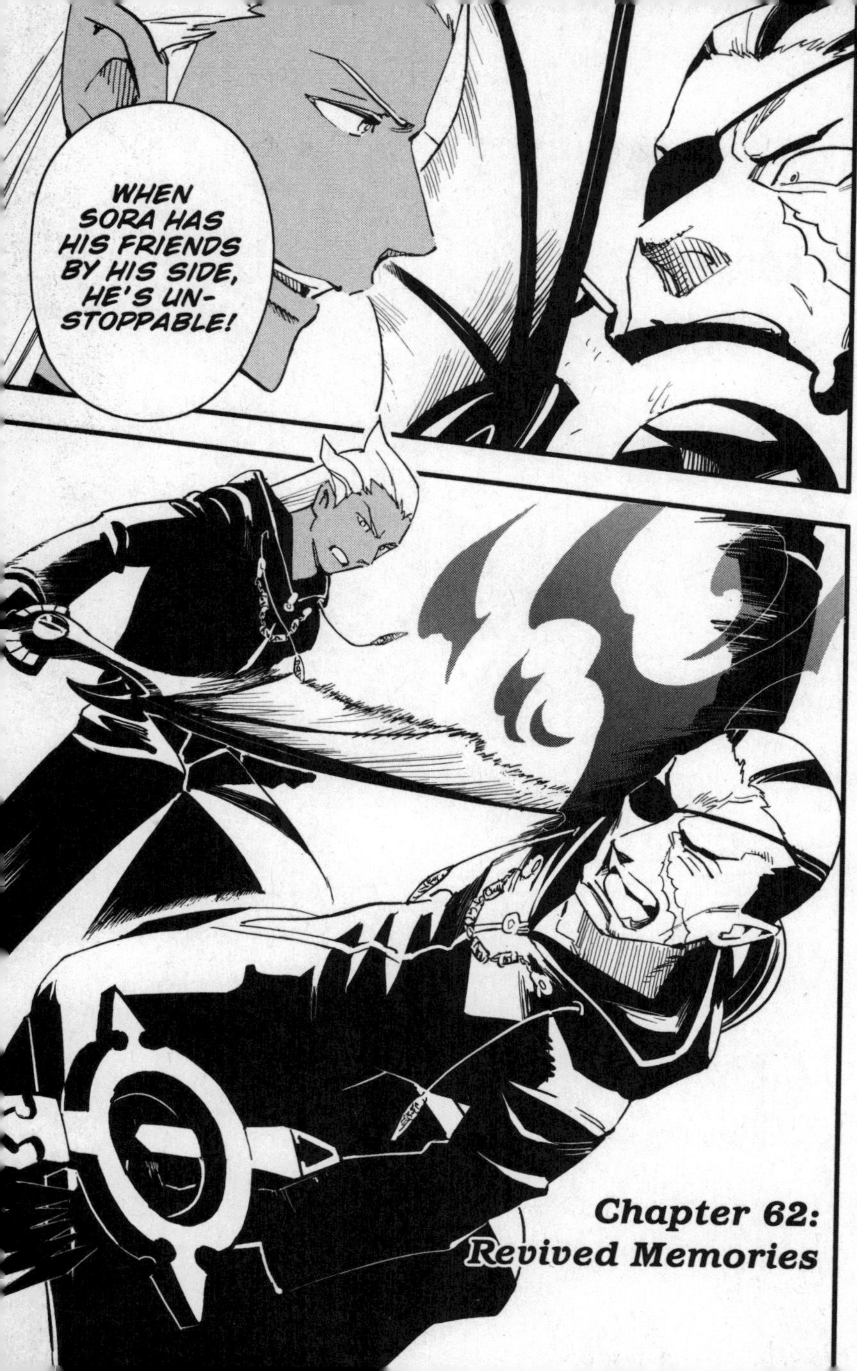
WHEN SORA HAS HIS FRIENDS BY HIS SIDE, HE'S UN-STOPPABLE!
Chapter 62: Revived Memories

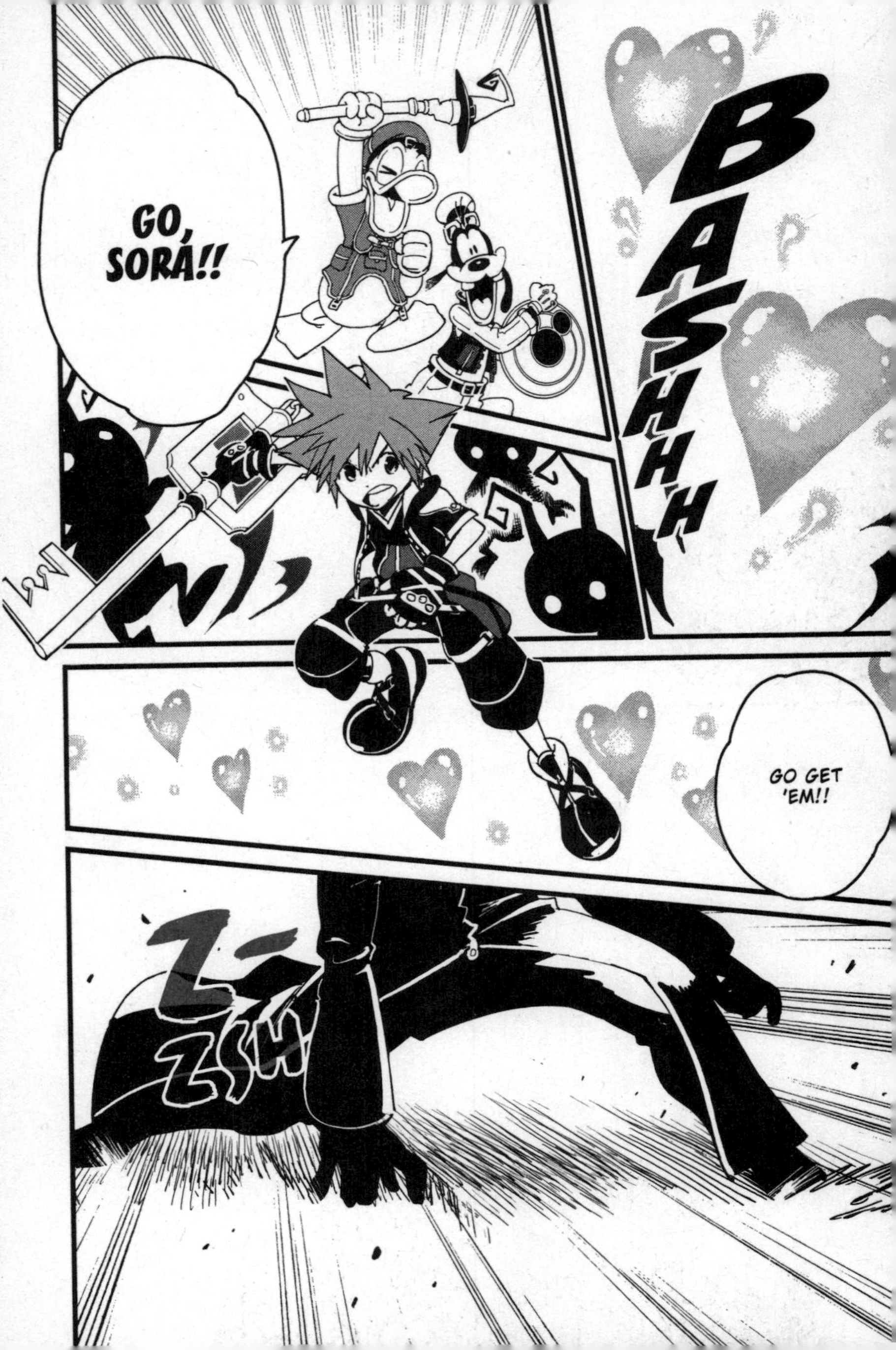
BASHHHH
GO, SORA!!
GO GET 'EM!!
ZSH

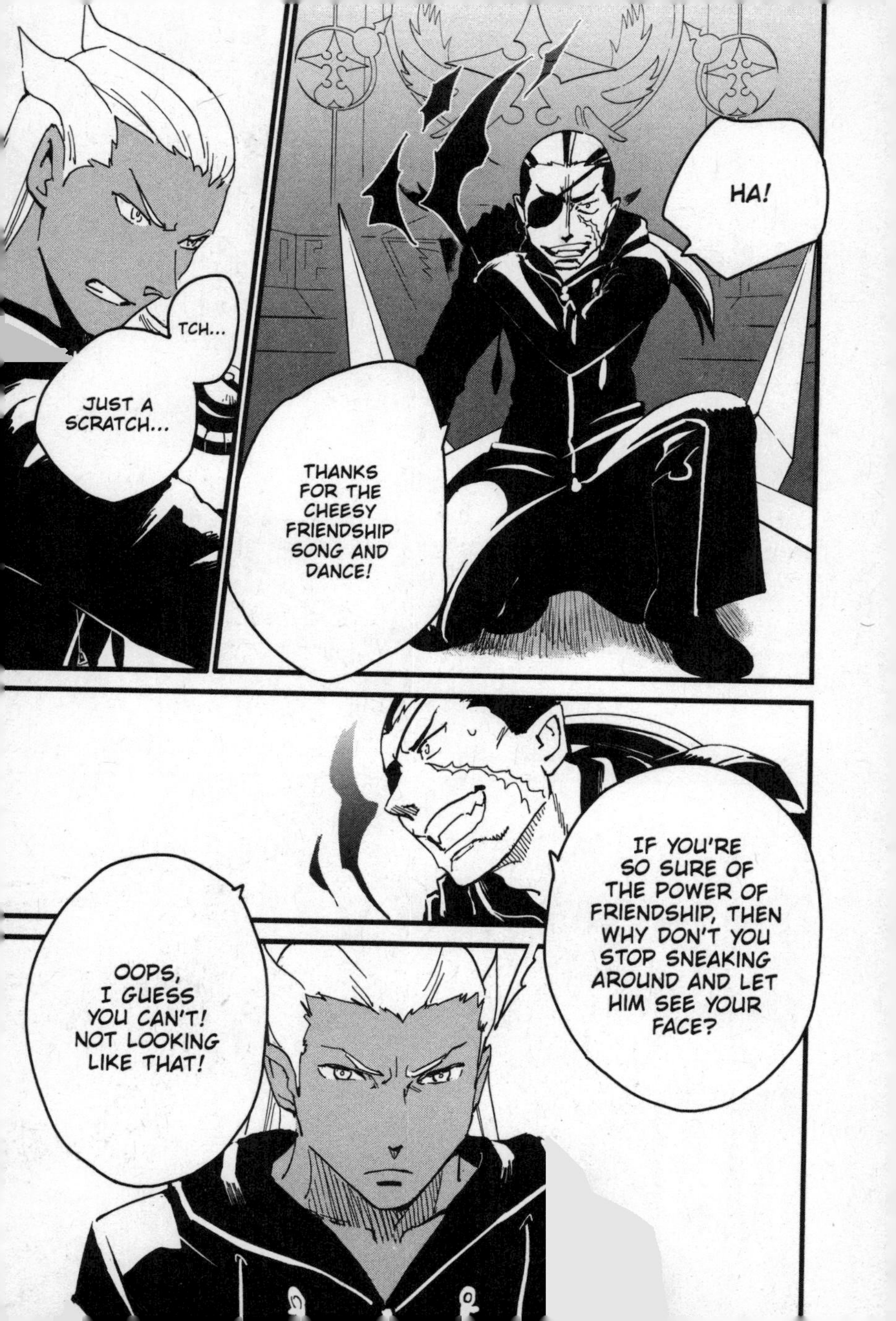
HA!
THANKS FOR THE CHEESY FRIENDSHIP SONG AND DANCE!
TCH...
JUST A SCRATCH...
IF YOU'RE SO SURE OF THE POWER OF FRIENDSHIP, THEN WHY DON'T YOU STOP SNEAKING AROUND AND LET HIM SEE YOUR FACE?
OOPS, I GUESS YOU CAN'T! NOT LOOKING LIKE THAT!

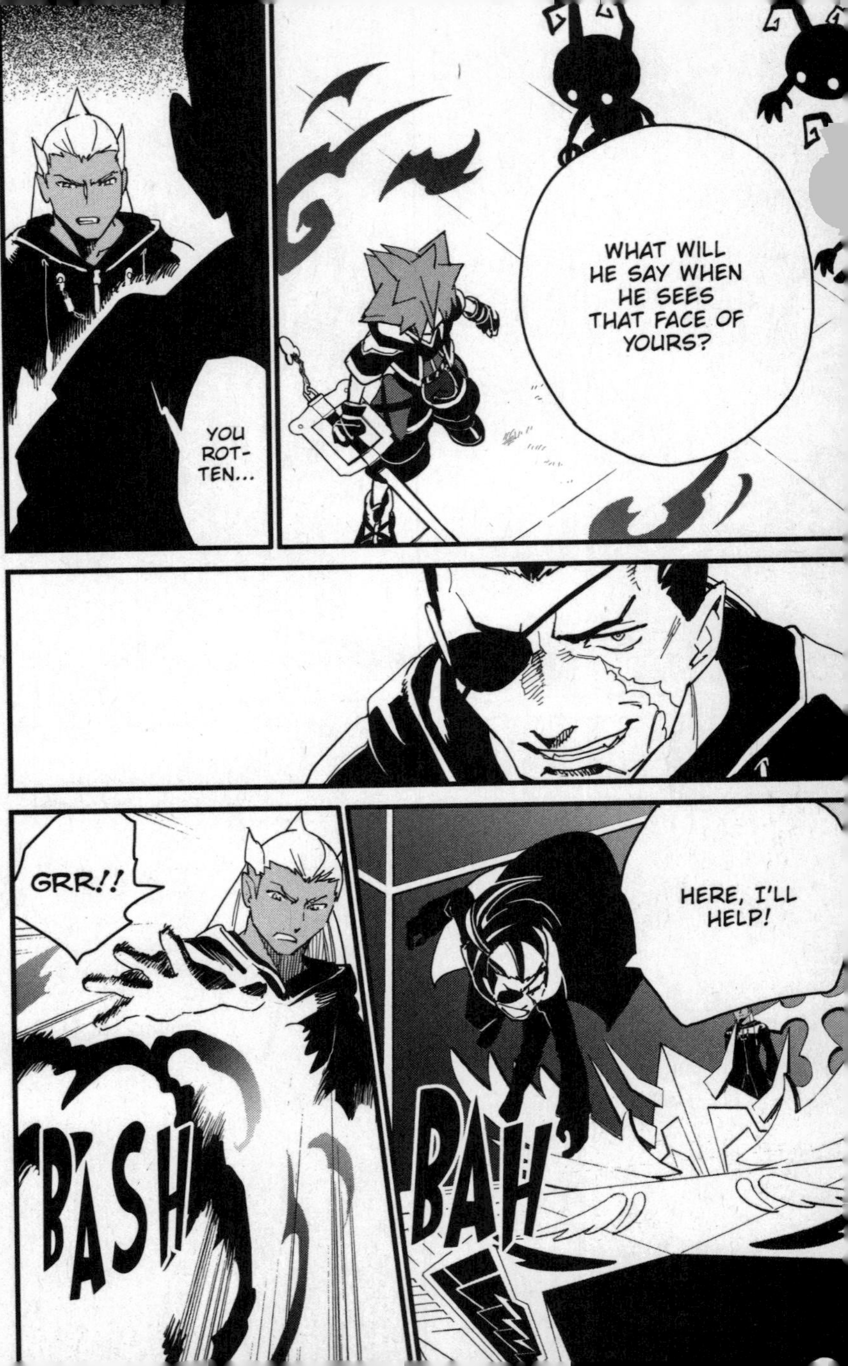
WHAT WILL HE SAY WHEN HE SEES THAT FACE OF YOURS?
YOU ROT-TEN...
HERE, I'LL HELP!
BAH
GRR!!
BASH

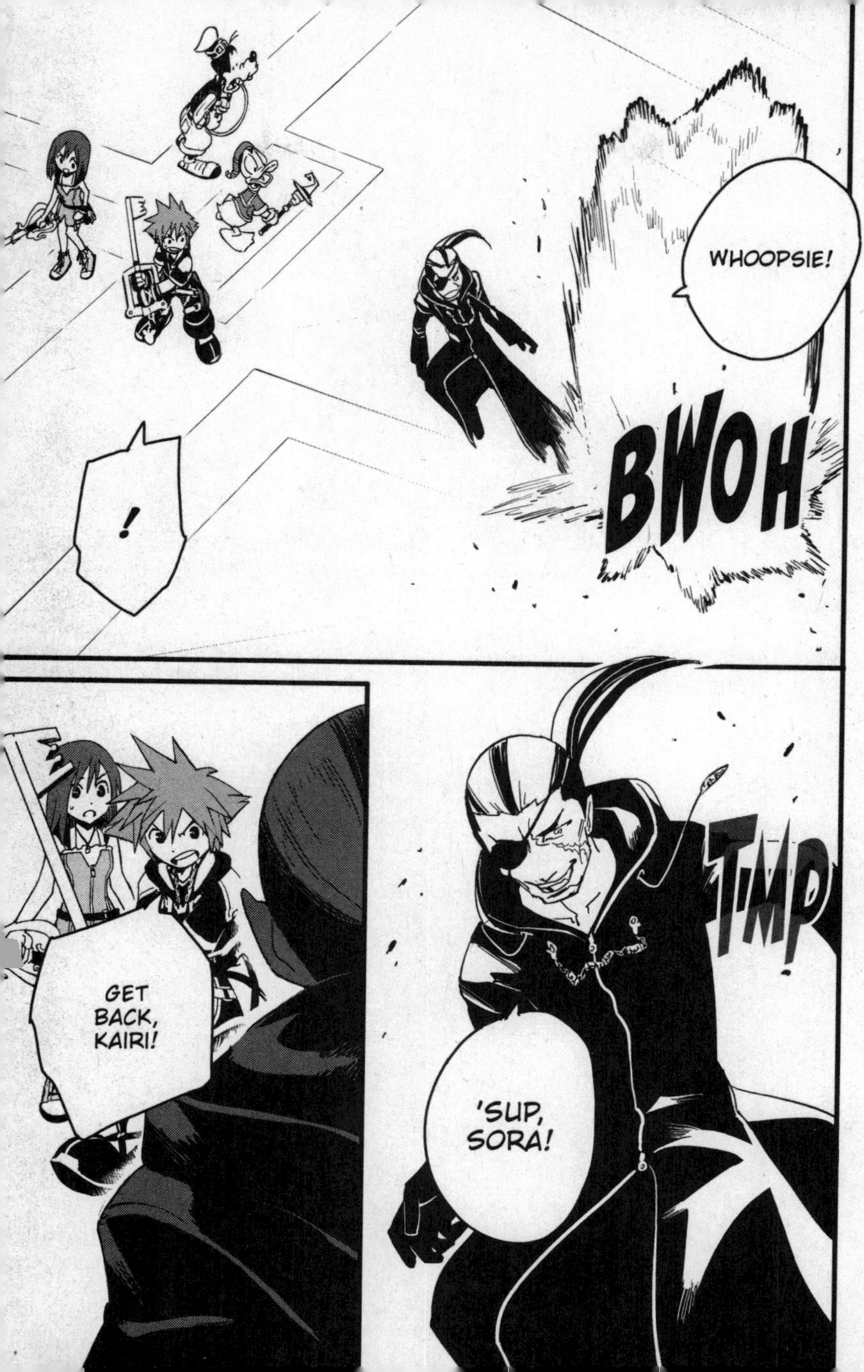
WHOOPSIE!
BWOH
!
TMP
'SUP, SORA!
GET BACK, KAIRI!

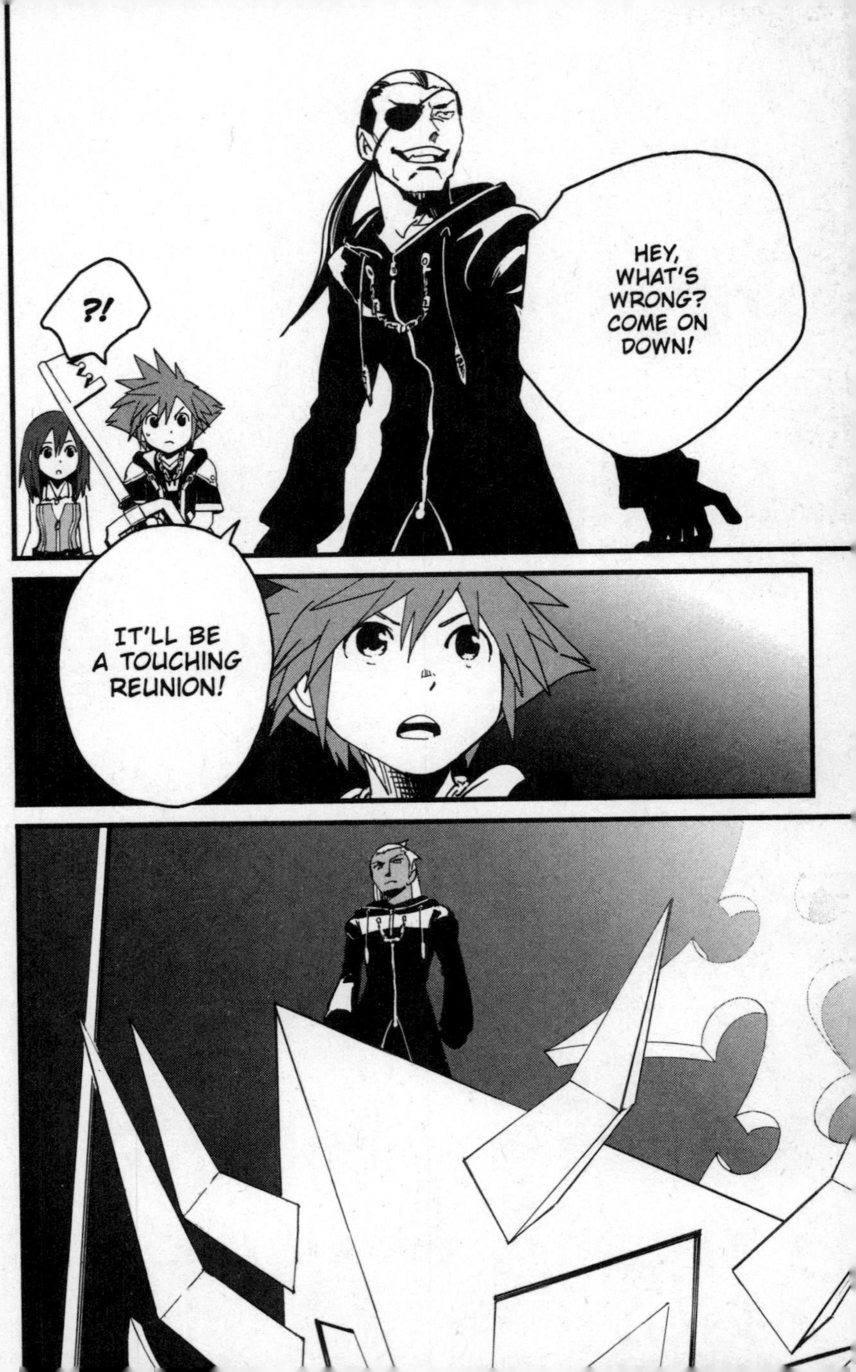
HEY, WHAT'S WRONG? COME ON DOWN!
?!
IT'LL BE A TOUCHING REUNION!

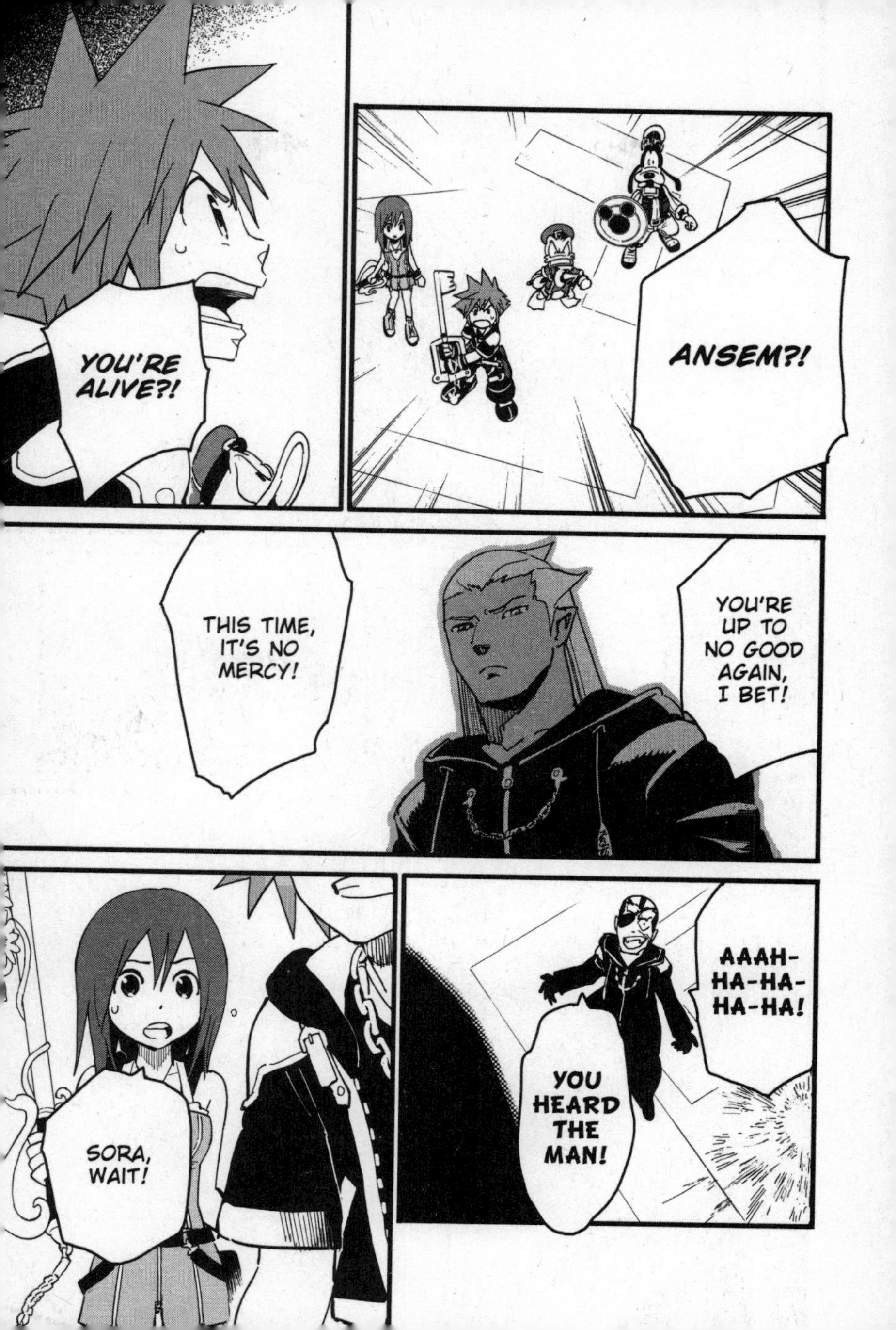
ANSEM?!
YOU'RE ALIVE?!
YOU'RE UP TO NO GOOD AGAIN, I BET!
THIS TIME, IT'S NO MERCY!
AAAH-HA-HA-HA-HA!
YOU HEARD THE MAN!
SORA, WAIT!

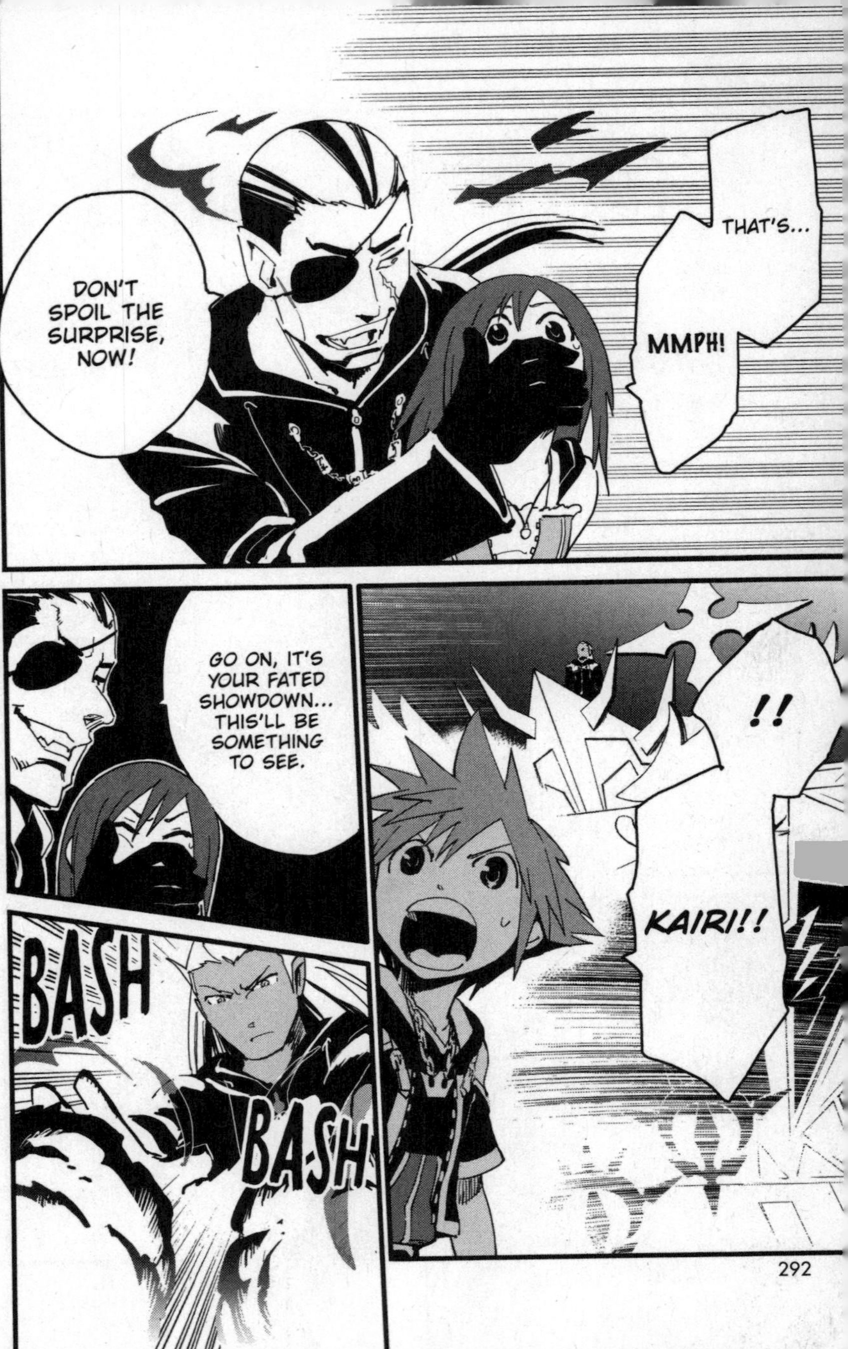
THAT'S...
MMPH!
DON'T SPOIL THE SURPRISE, NOW!
!!
KAIRI!!
GO ON, IT'S YOUR FATED SHOWDOWN... THIS'LL BE SOMETHING TO SEE.
BASH
BASH

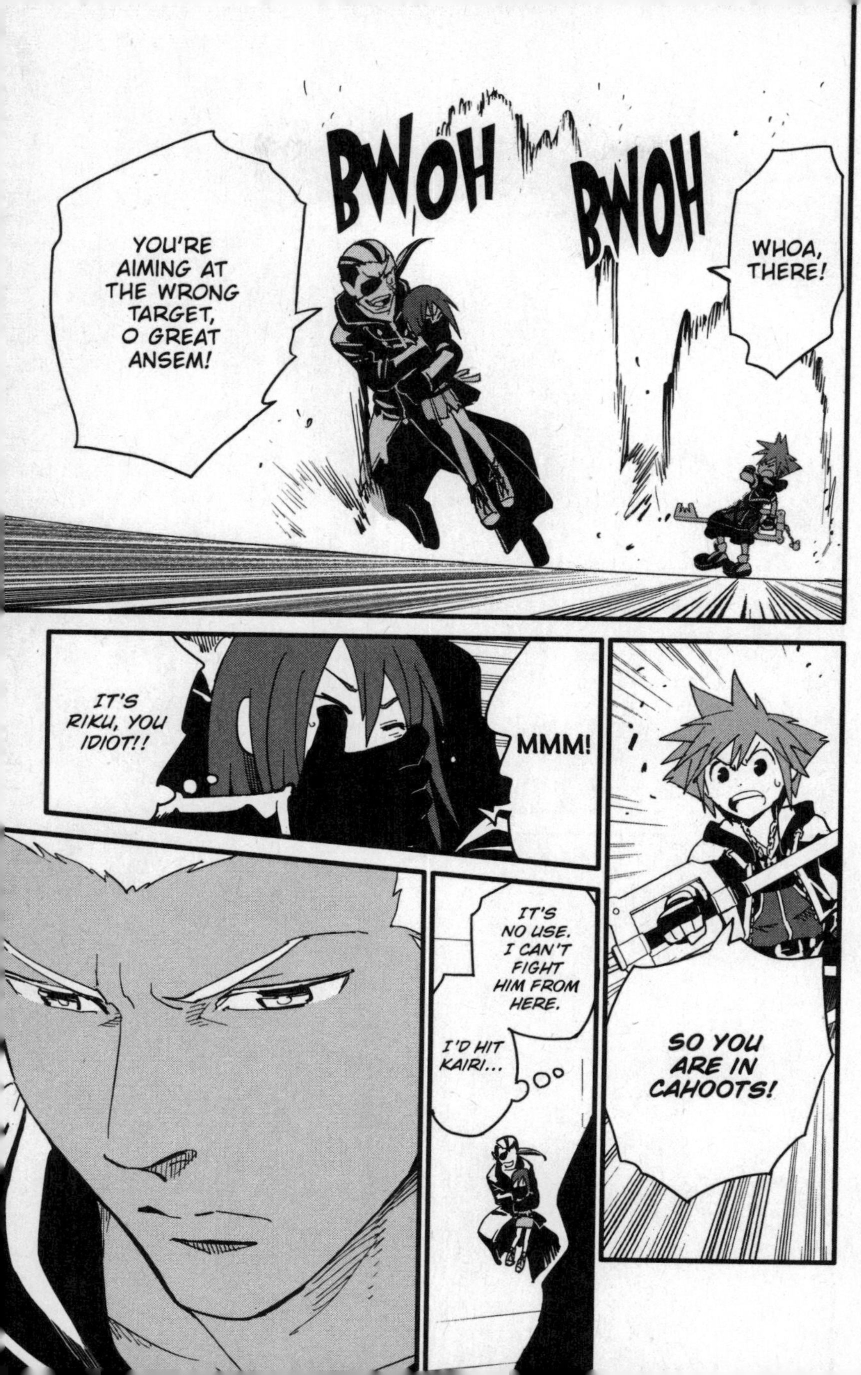
WHOA, THERE!
BWOH
BWOH
YOU'RE AIMING AT THE WRONG TARGET, O GREAT ANSEM!
SO YOU ARE IN CAHOOTS!
MMM!
IT'S RIKU, YOU IDIOT!!
IT'S NO USE. I CAN'T FIGHT HIM FROM HERE.
I'D HIT KAIRI...

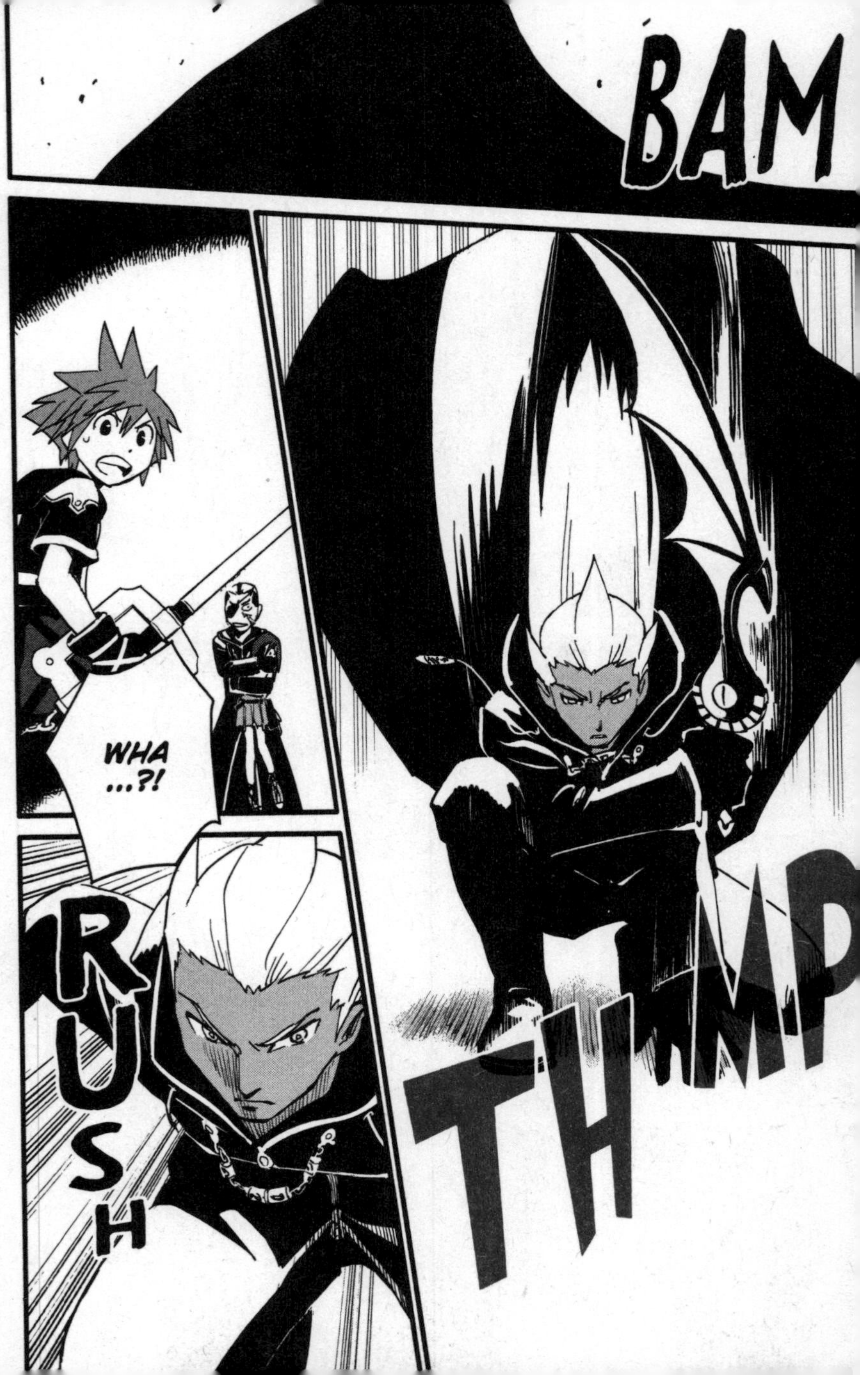
BAM
TH MP
WHA ...?!
RUSH

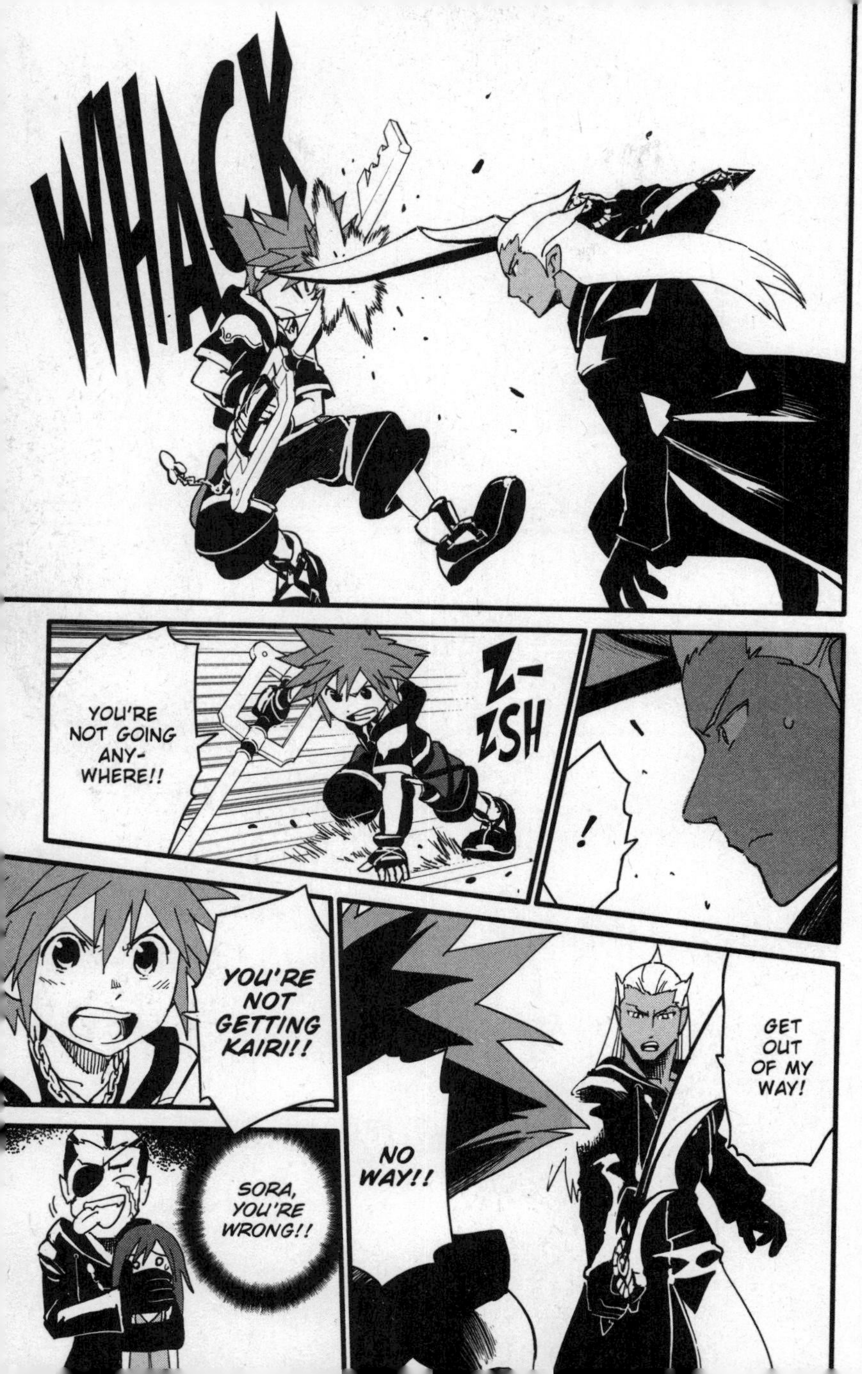
WHACK
!
Z-ZSH
YOU'RE NOT GOING ANY-WHERE!!
GET OUT OF MY WAY!
NO WAY!!
YOU'RE NOT GETTING KAIRI!!
SORA, YOU'RE WRONG!!

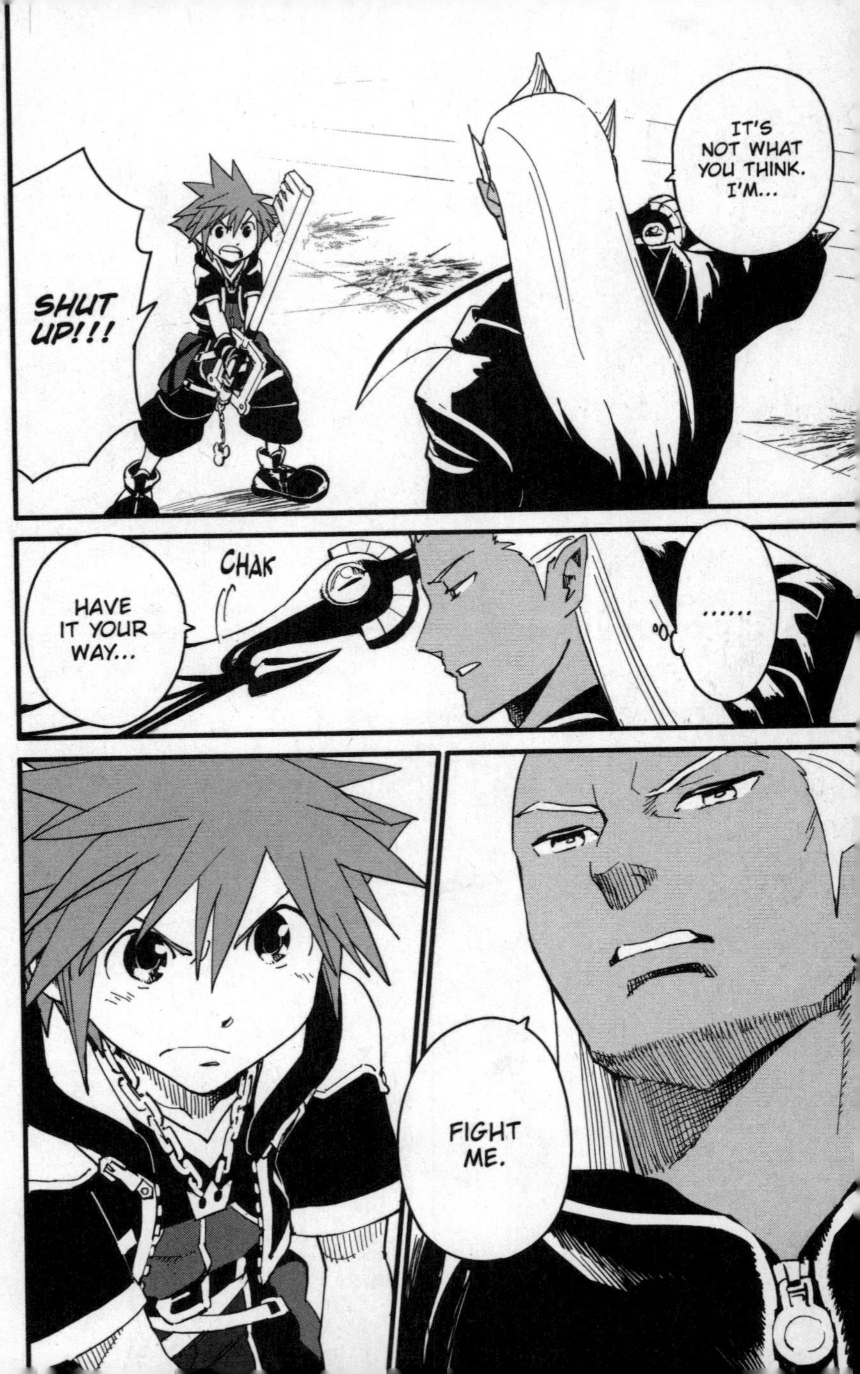
IT'S NOT WHAT YOU THINK. I'M...
SHUT UP!!!
......
CHAK
HAVE IT YOUR WAY...
FIGHT ME.

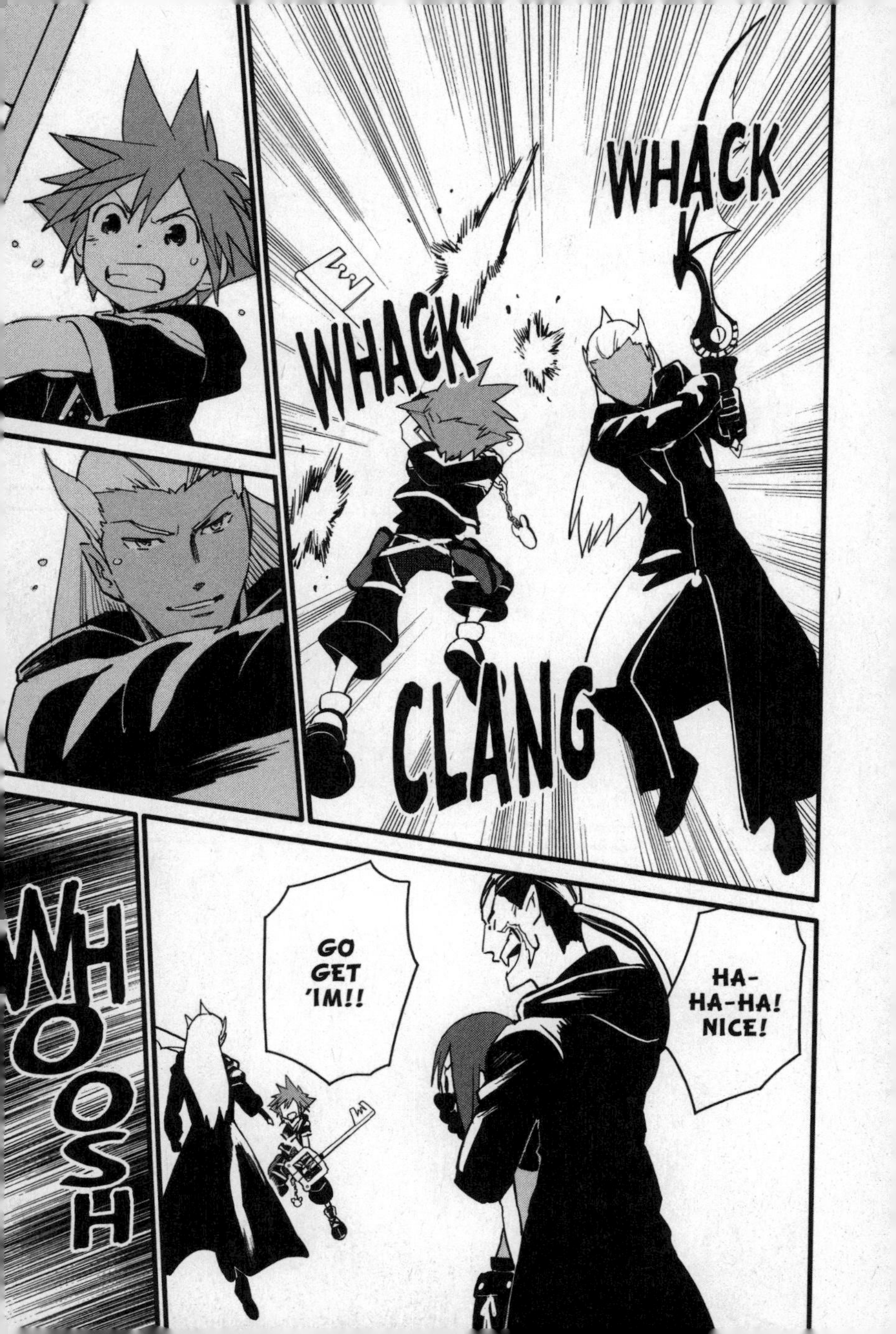
WHACK
WHACK
CLANG
HA-HA-HA! NICE!
GO GET 'IM!!
WHOOSH

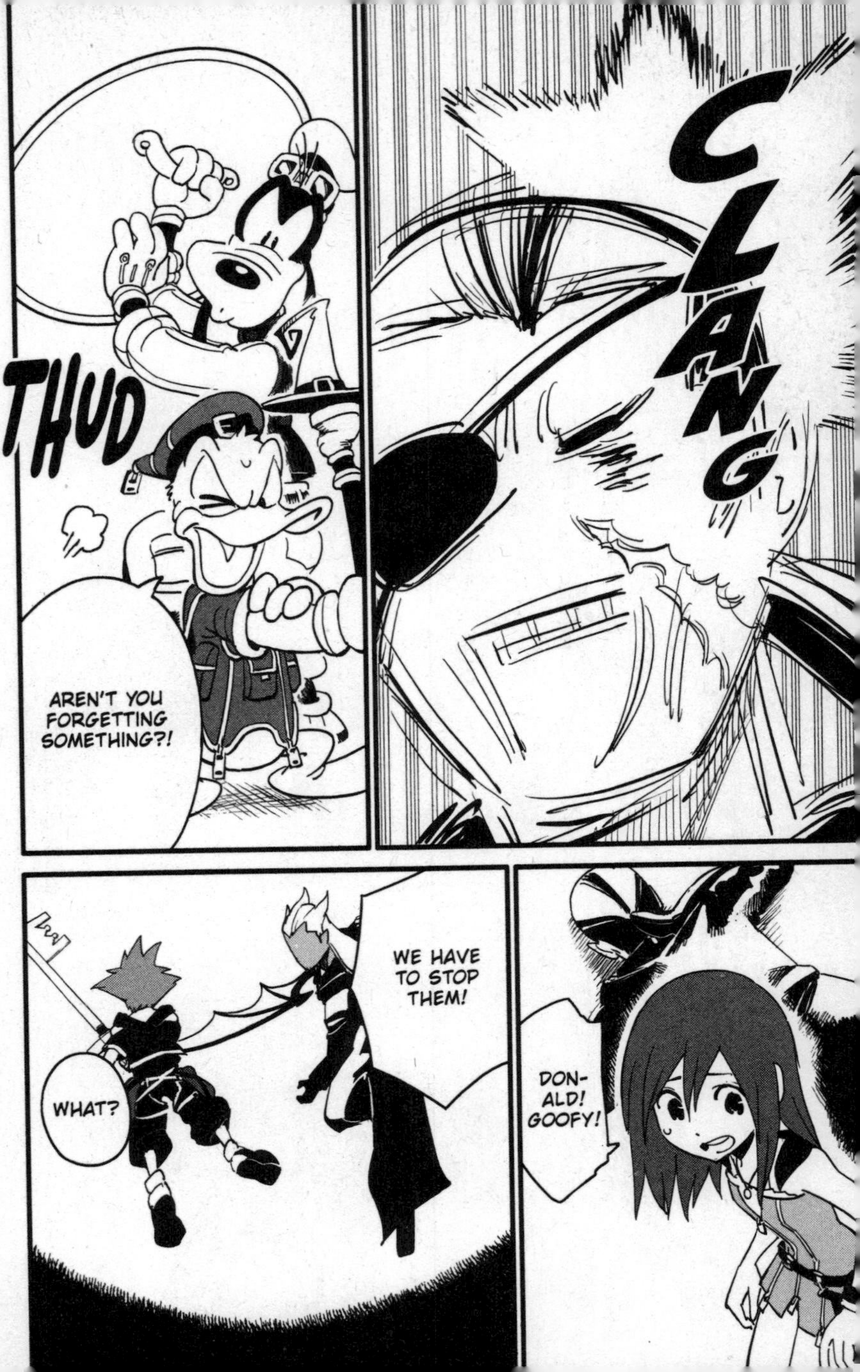
CLANG
THUD
AREN'T YOU FORGETTING SOMETHING?!
DON-ALD! GOOFY!
WE HAVE TO STOP THEM!
WHAT?

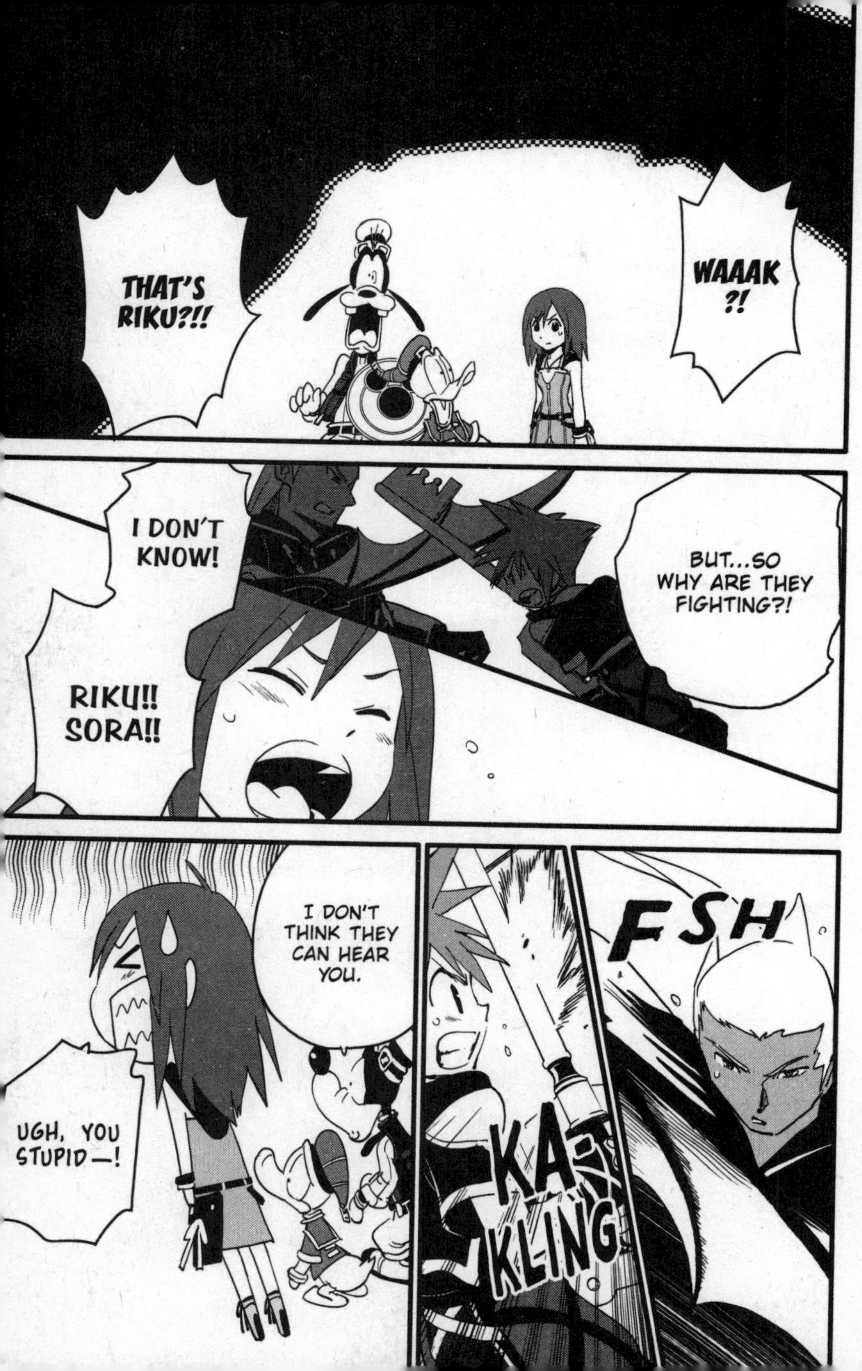
WAAAK ?!
THAT'S RIKU?!!
BUT...SO WHY ARE THEY FIGHTING?!
I DON'T KNOW!
RIKU!! SORA!!
FSH
KA-KLING!
I DON'T THINK THEY CAN HEAR YOU.
UGH, YOU STUPID—!

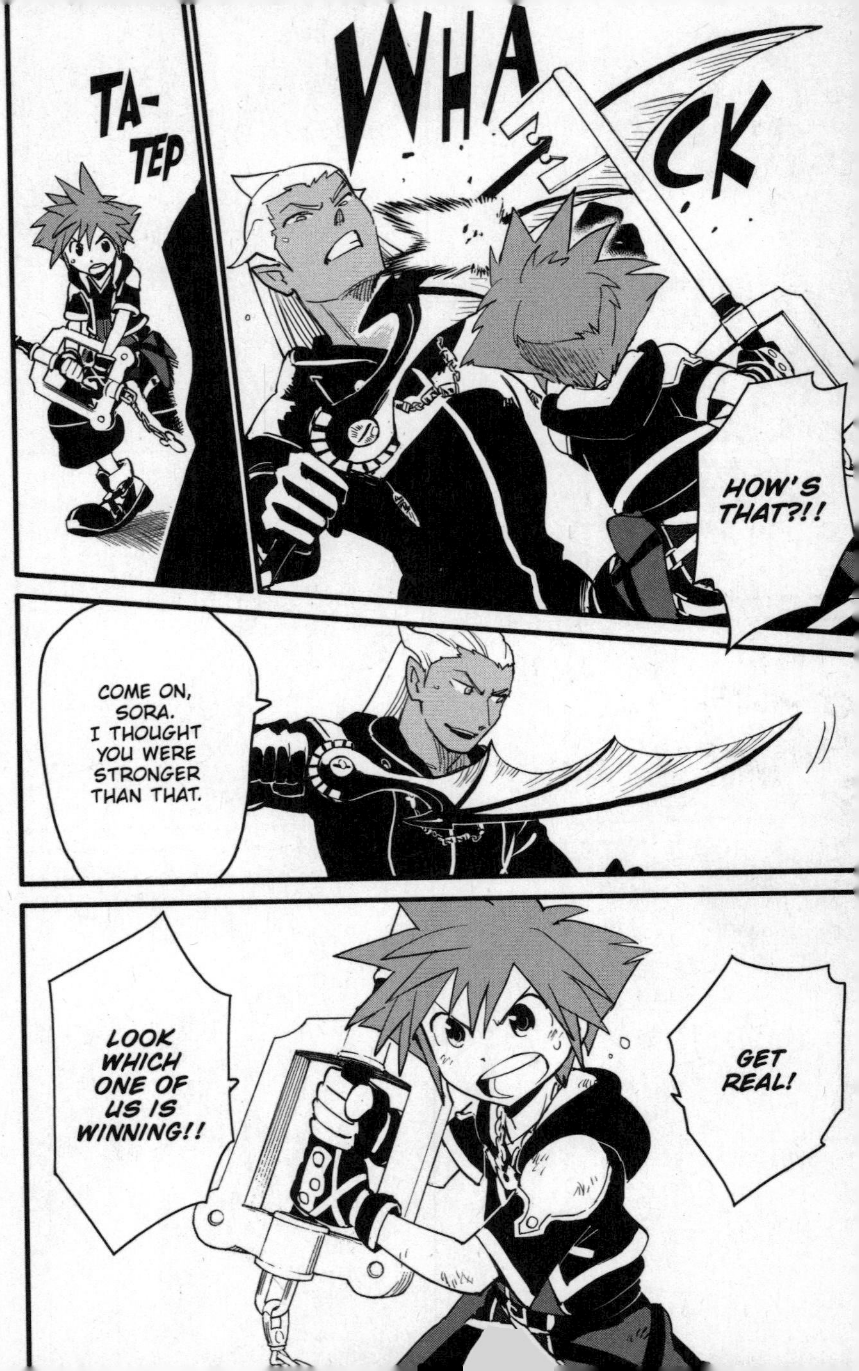
WHACK
HOW'S THAT?!!
TA-TEP
COME ON, SORA. I THOUGHT YOU WERE STRONGER THAN THAT.
GET REAL!
LOOK WHICH ONE OF US IS WINNING!!

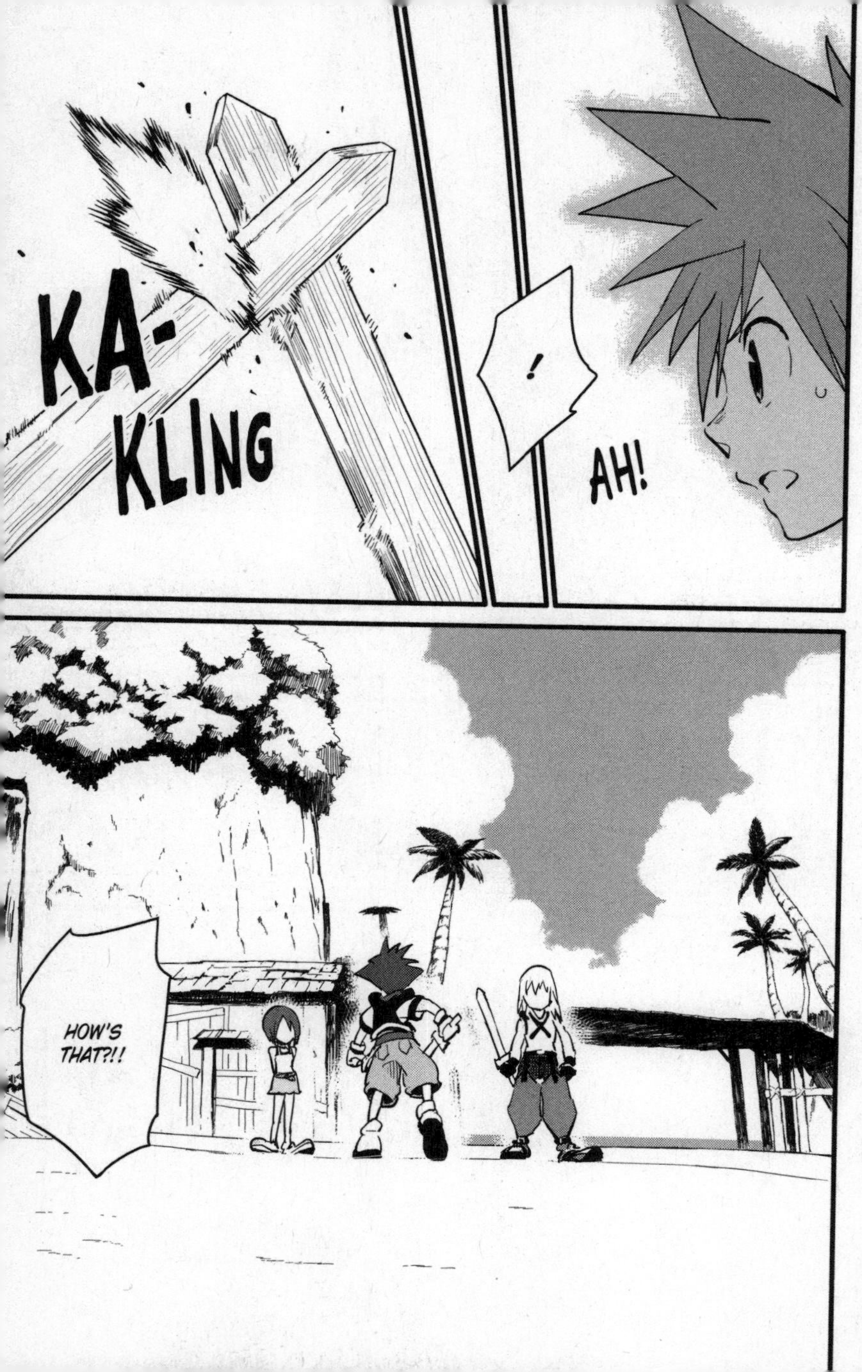
!
AH!
KA-KLING
HOW'S THAT?!!

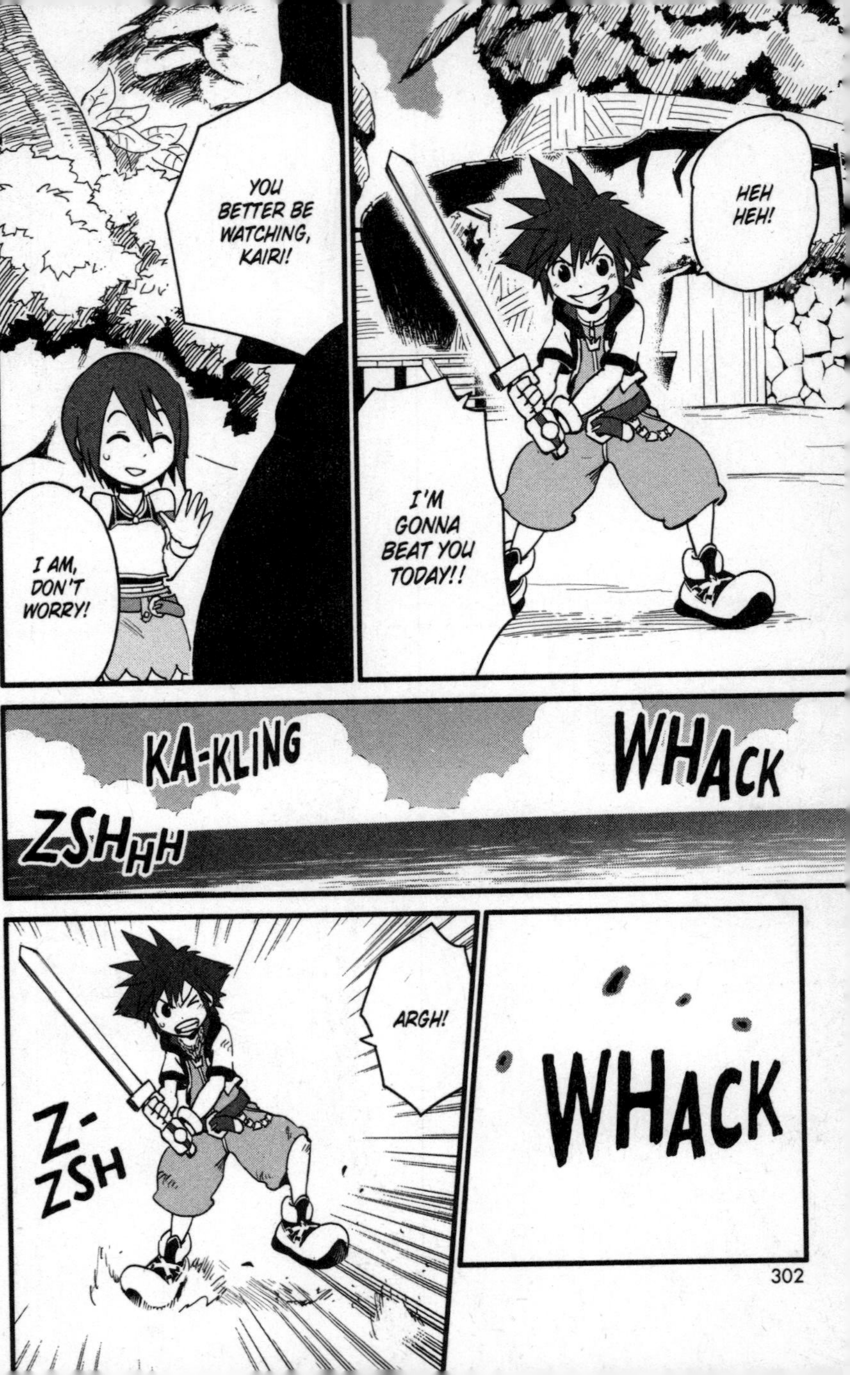
HEH HEH!
I'M GONNA BEAT YOU TODAY!!
YOU BETTER BE WATCHING, KAIRI!
I AM, DON'T WORRY!
WHACK
KA-KLING
ZSHHH
WHACK
ARGH!
Z-ZSH

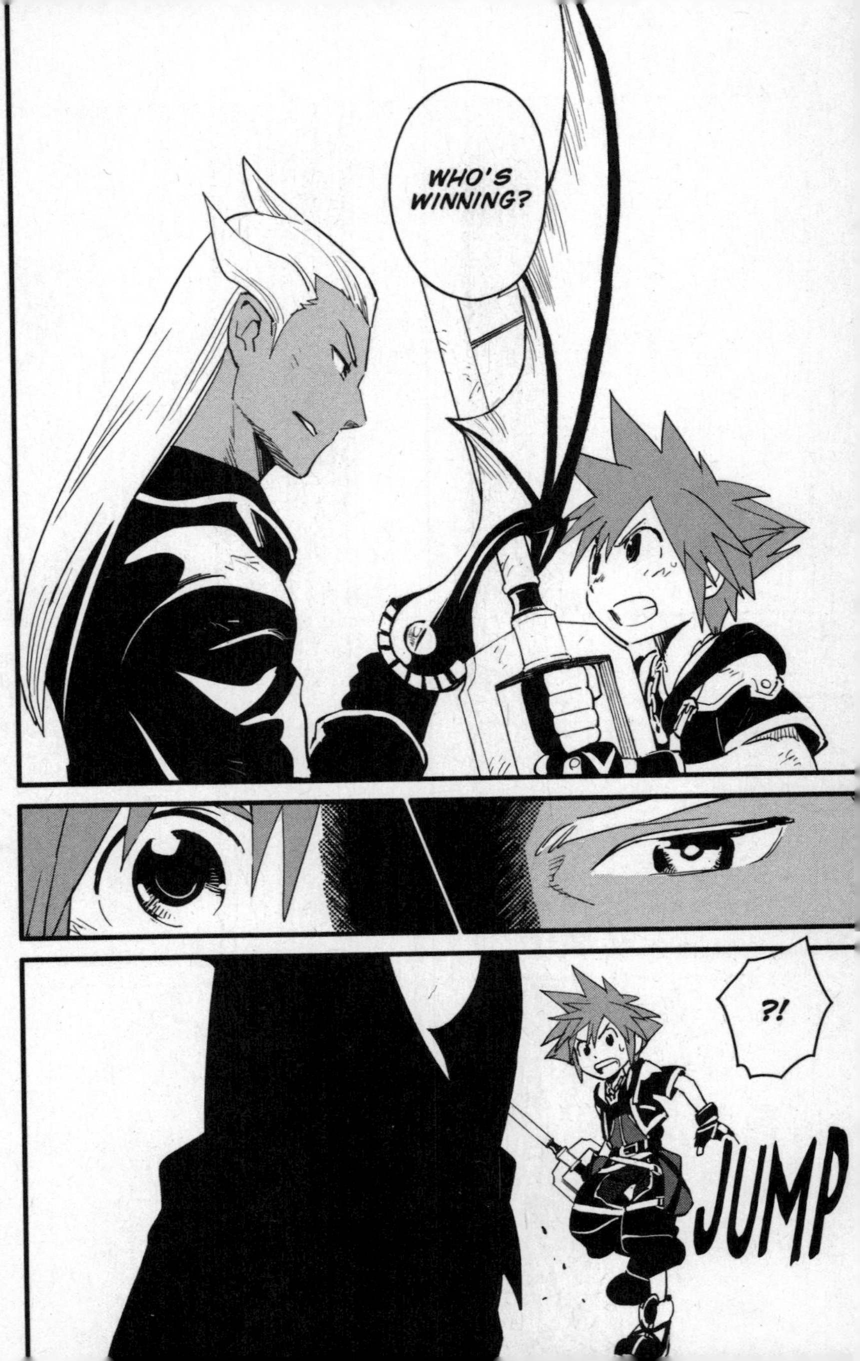
WHO'S WINNING?
?!
JUMP

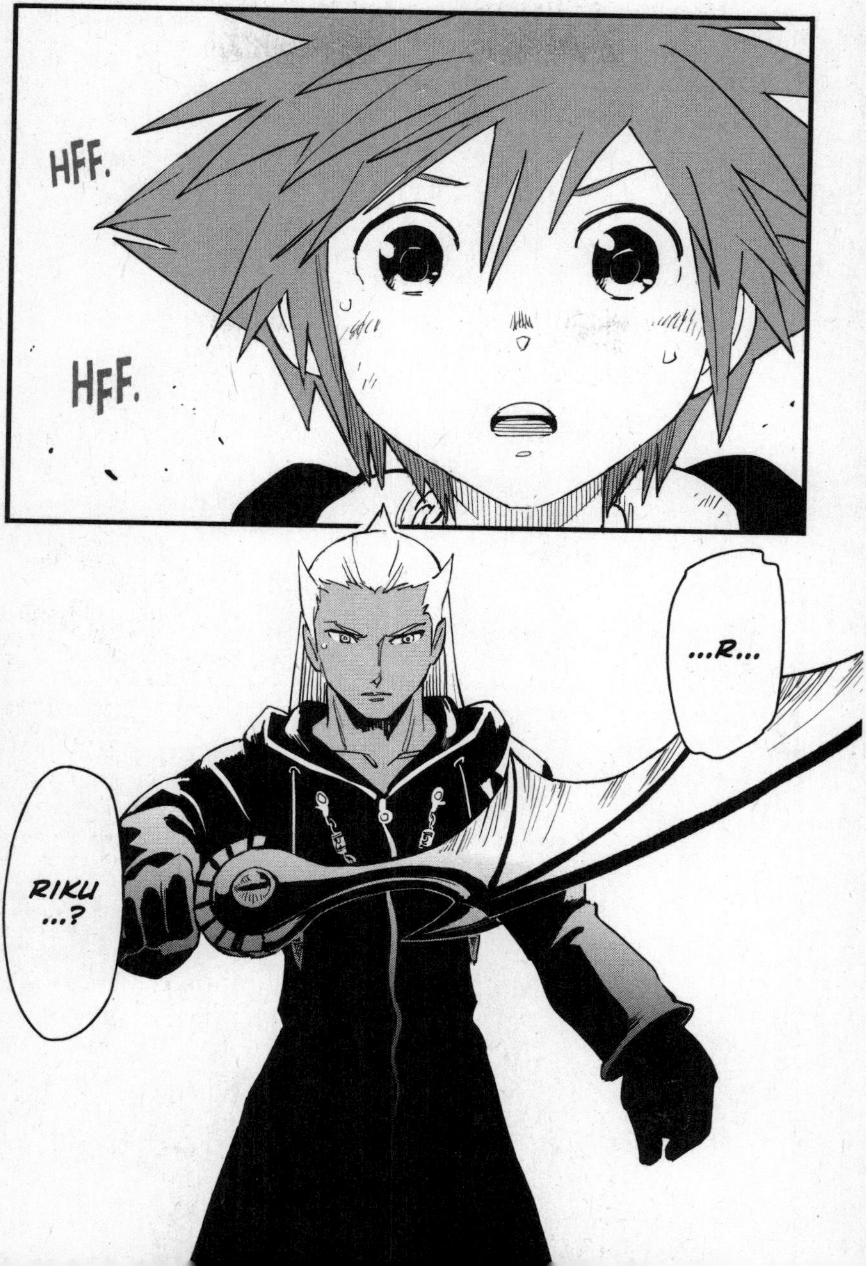
HFF.
HFF.
...R...
RIKU ...?

Disney SQUARE ENIX

KINGDOM HEARTS

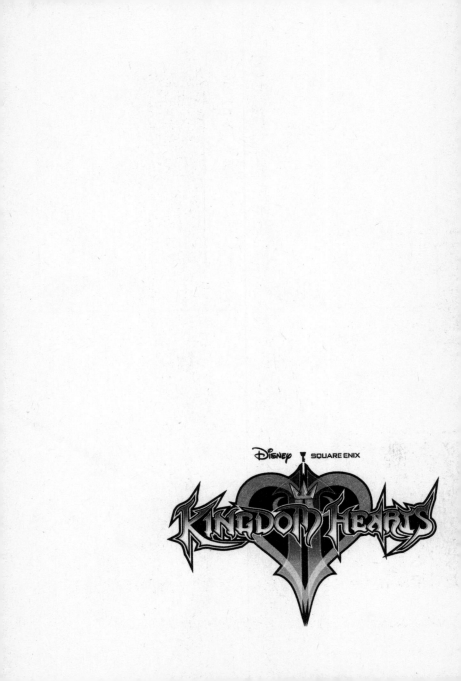

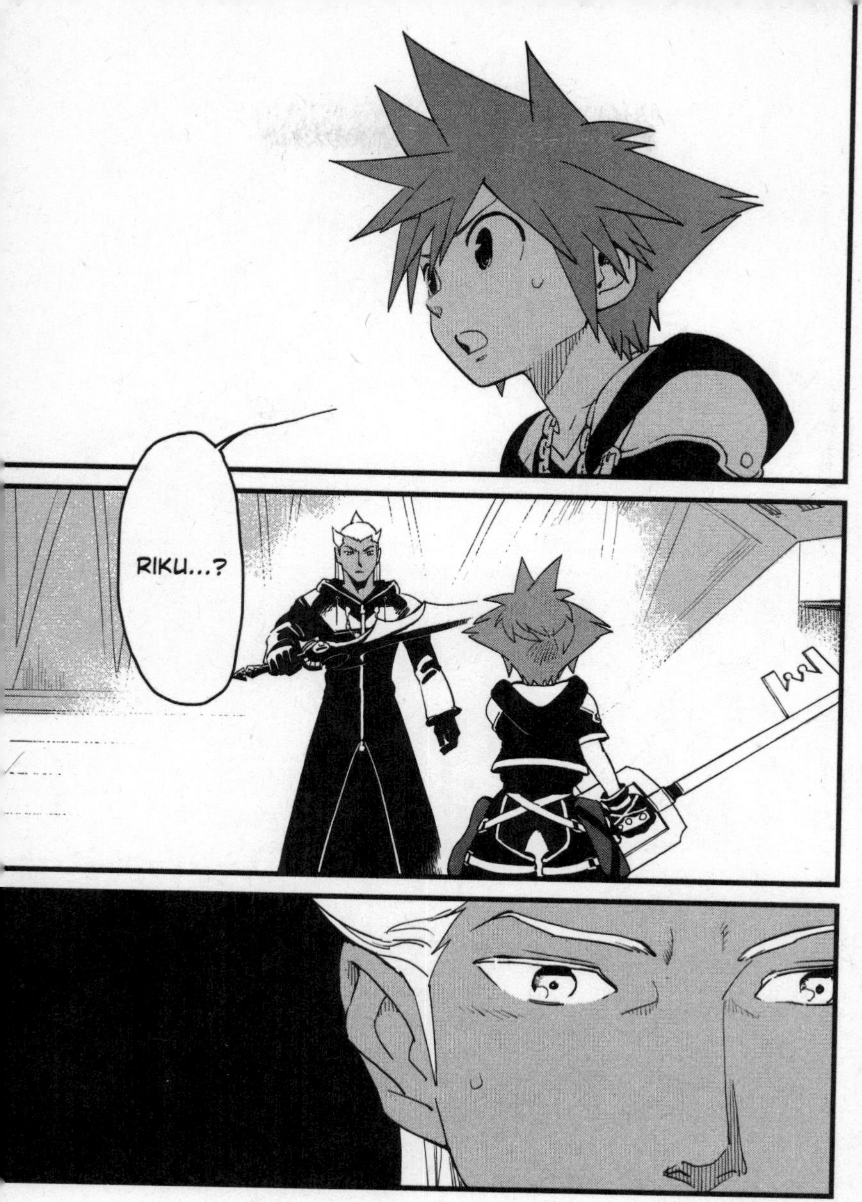
RIKU...?

Chapter 63: What the Heart Sees

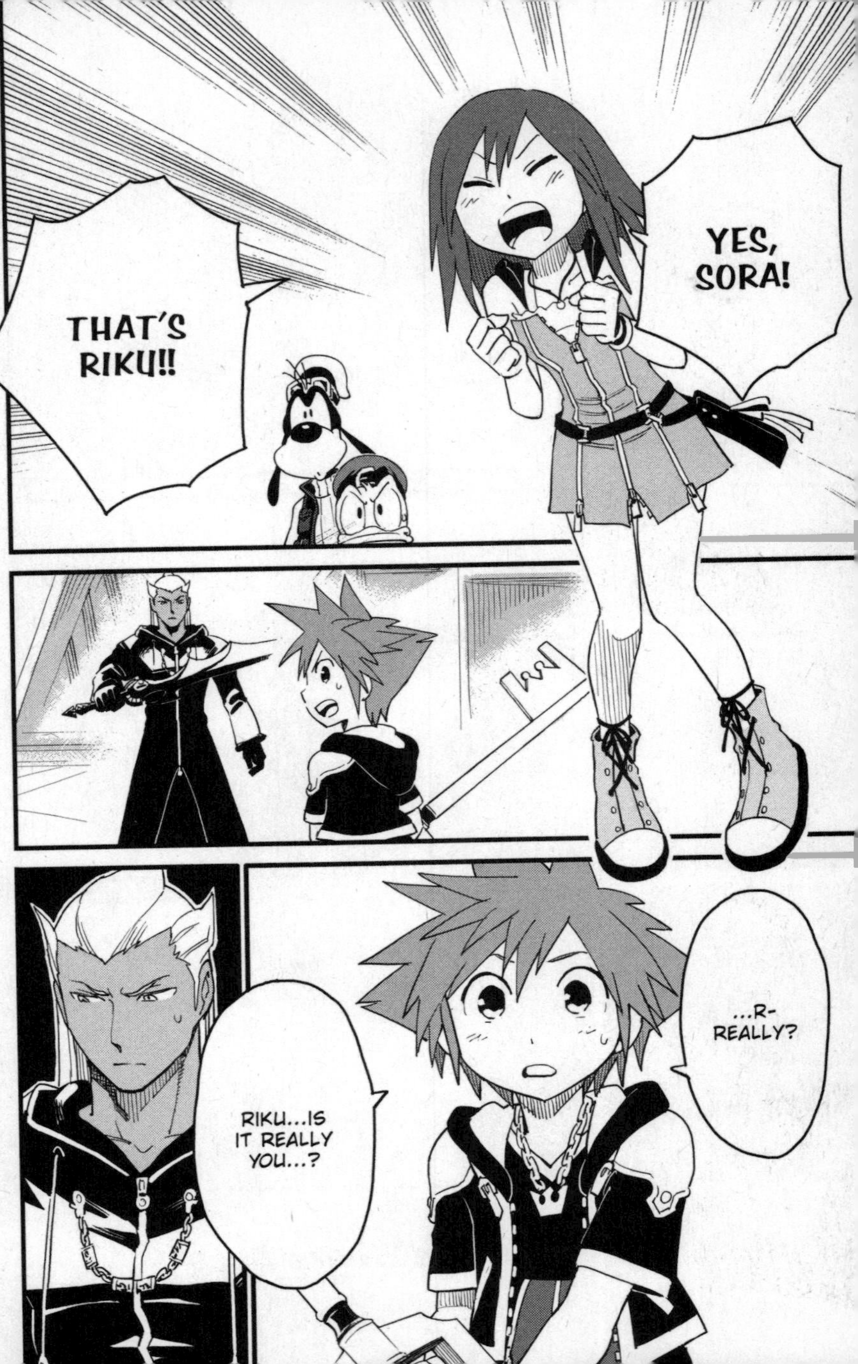
YES, SORA!
THAT'S RIKU!!
...R-REALLY?
RIKU...IS IT REALLY YOU...?

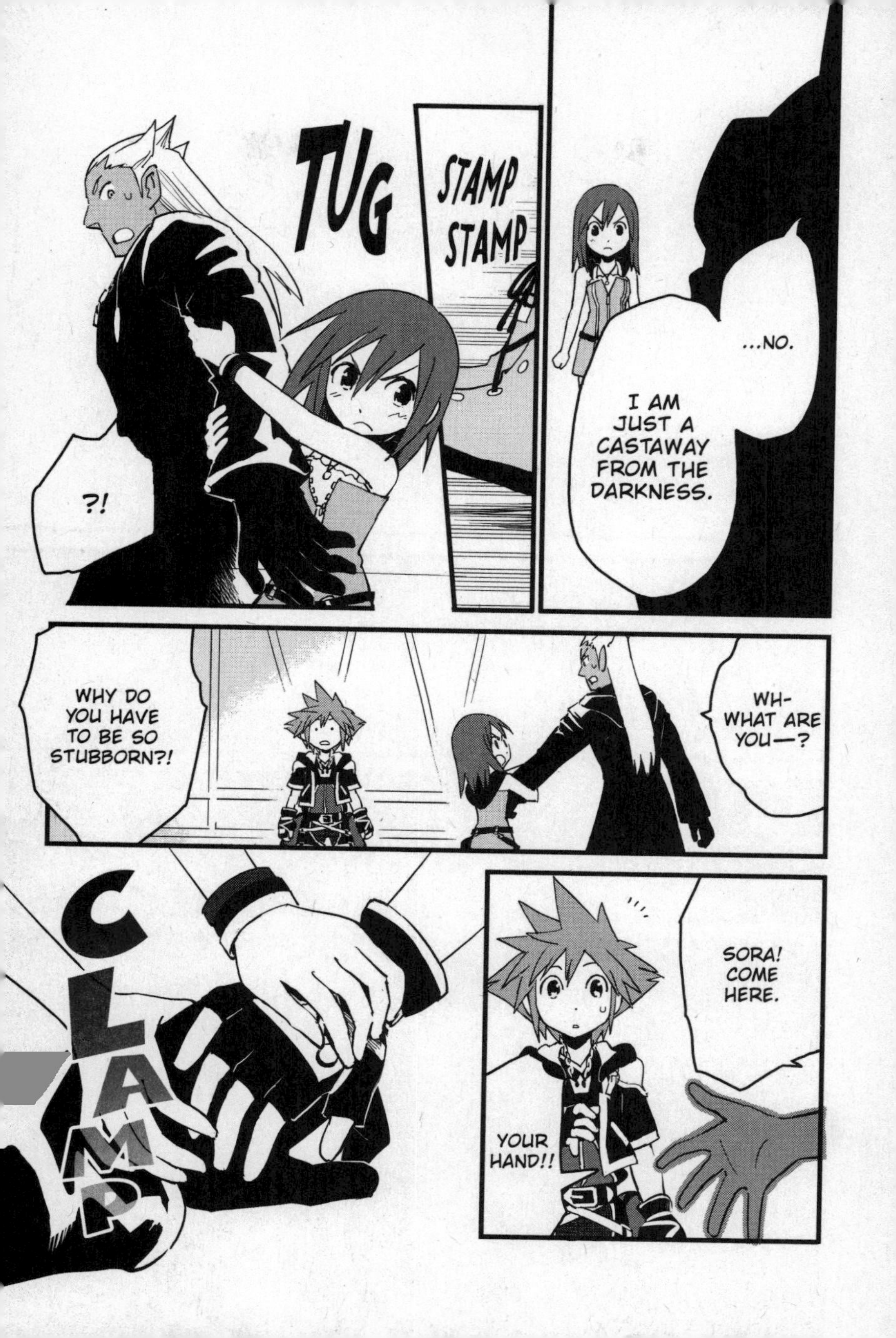
...NO.
I AM JUST A CASTAWAY FROM THE DARKNESS.
STAMP STAMP
TUG
?!
WH- WHAT ARE YOU—?
WHY DO YOU HAVE TO BE SO STUBBORN?!
SORA! COME HERE.
YOUR HAND!!
CLAMP

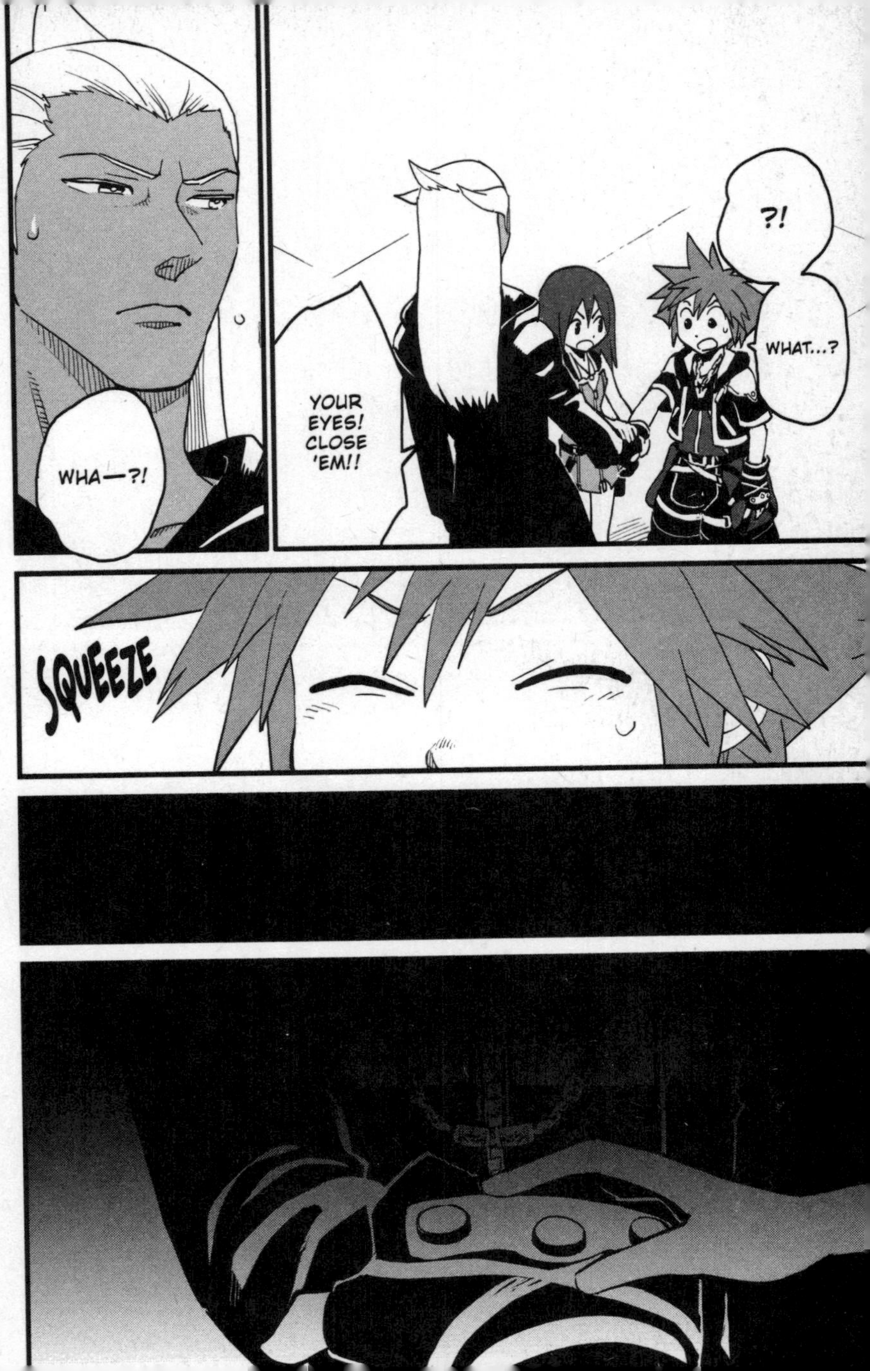
?!
WHAT...?
YOUR EYES! CLOSE 'EM!!
WHA—?!
SQUEEZE

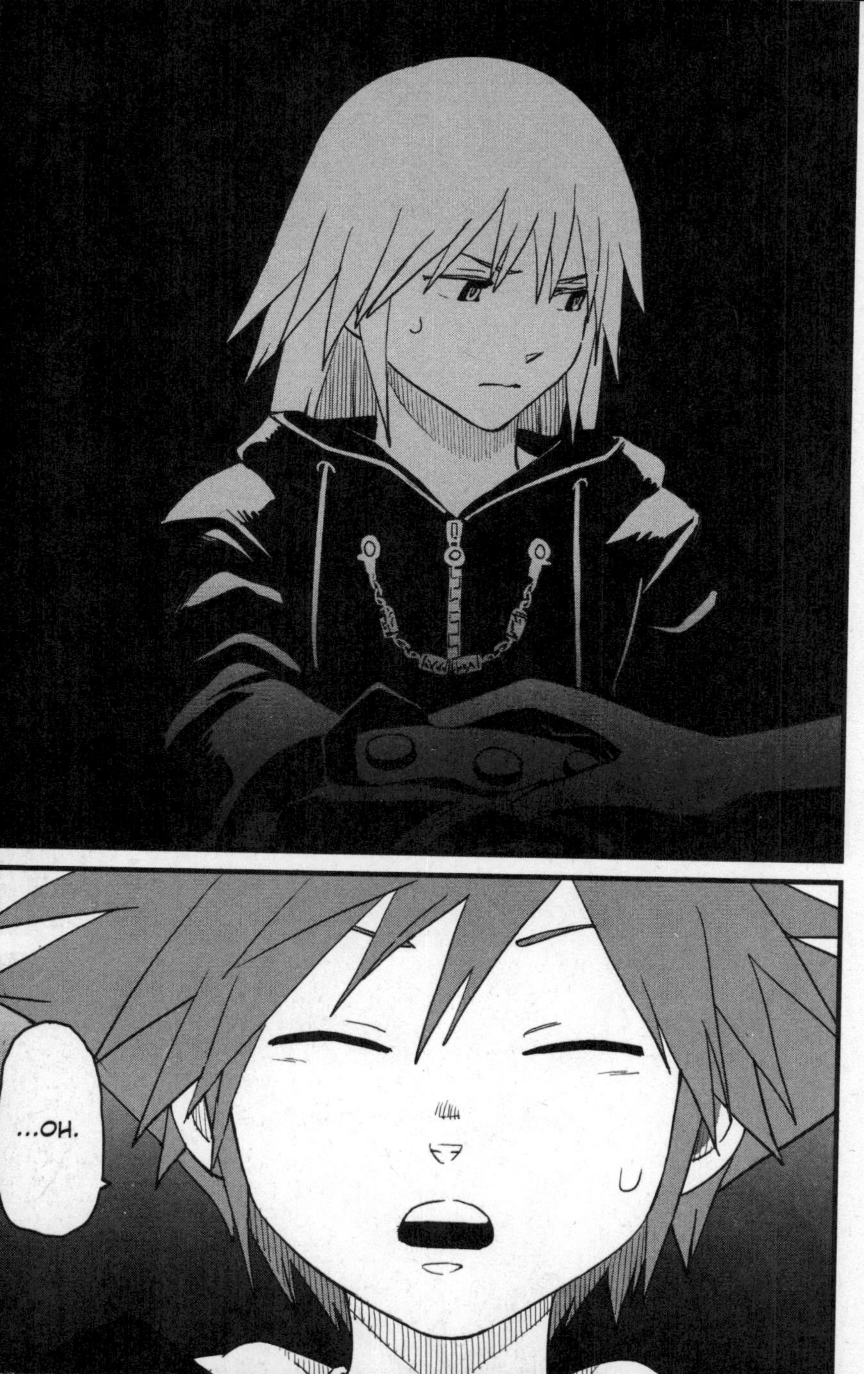
...OH.

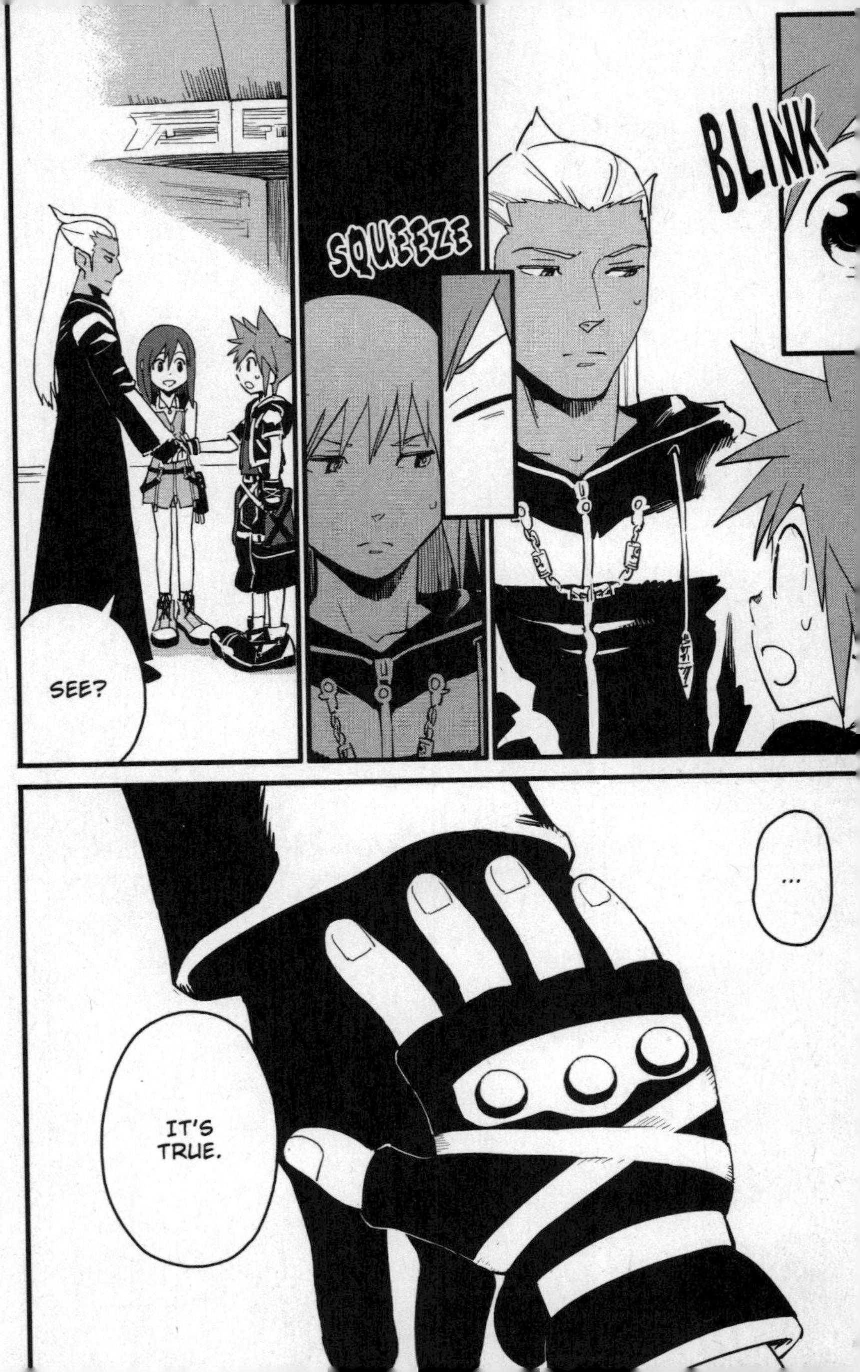
BLINK
SQUEEEZE
SEE?
...
IT'S TRUE.

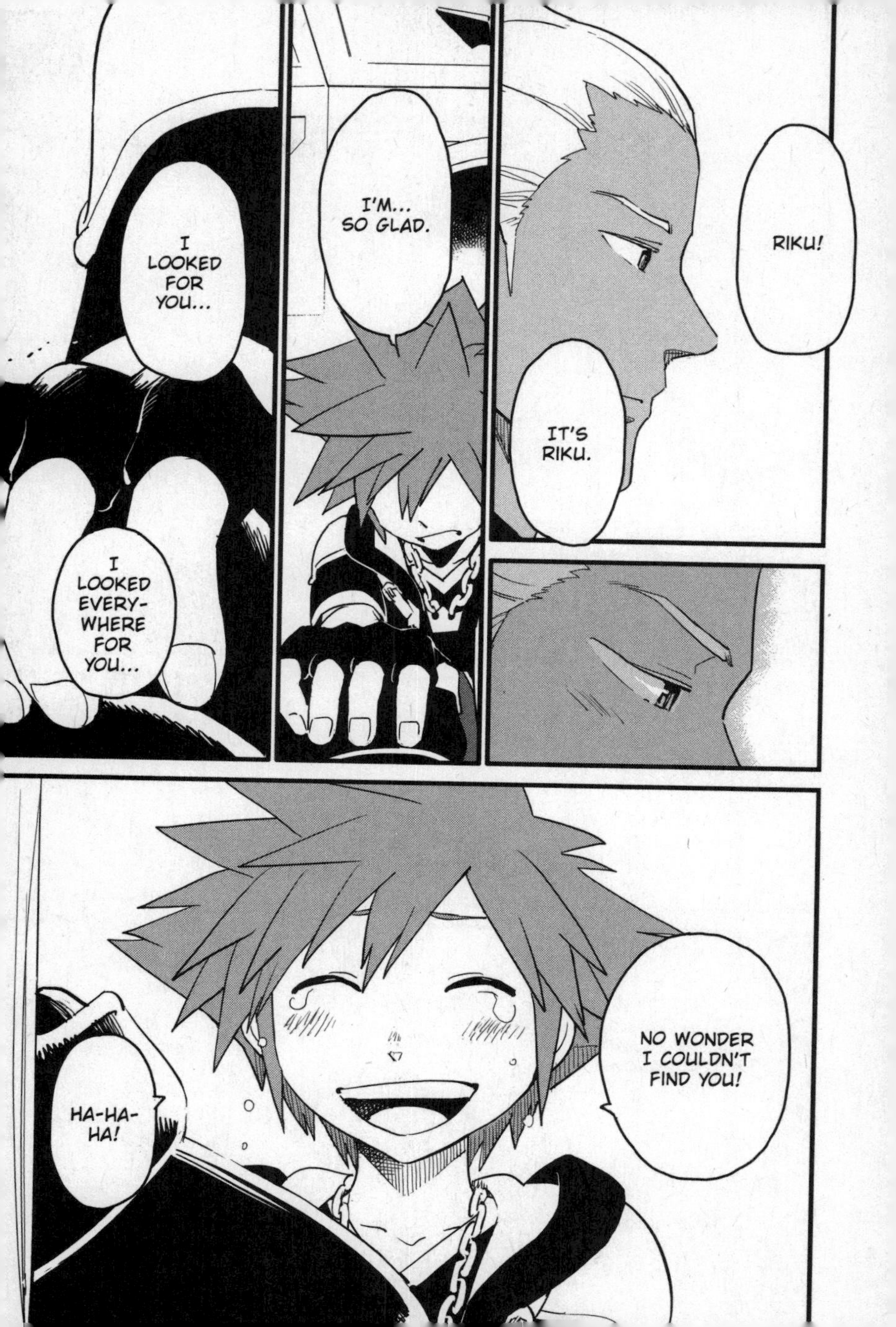
RIKU!
IT'S RIKU.
I'M... SO GLAD.
I LOOKED FOR YOU...
I LOOKED EVERY-WHERE FOR YOU...
NO WONDER I COULDN'T FIND YOU!
HA-HA-HA!

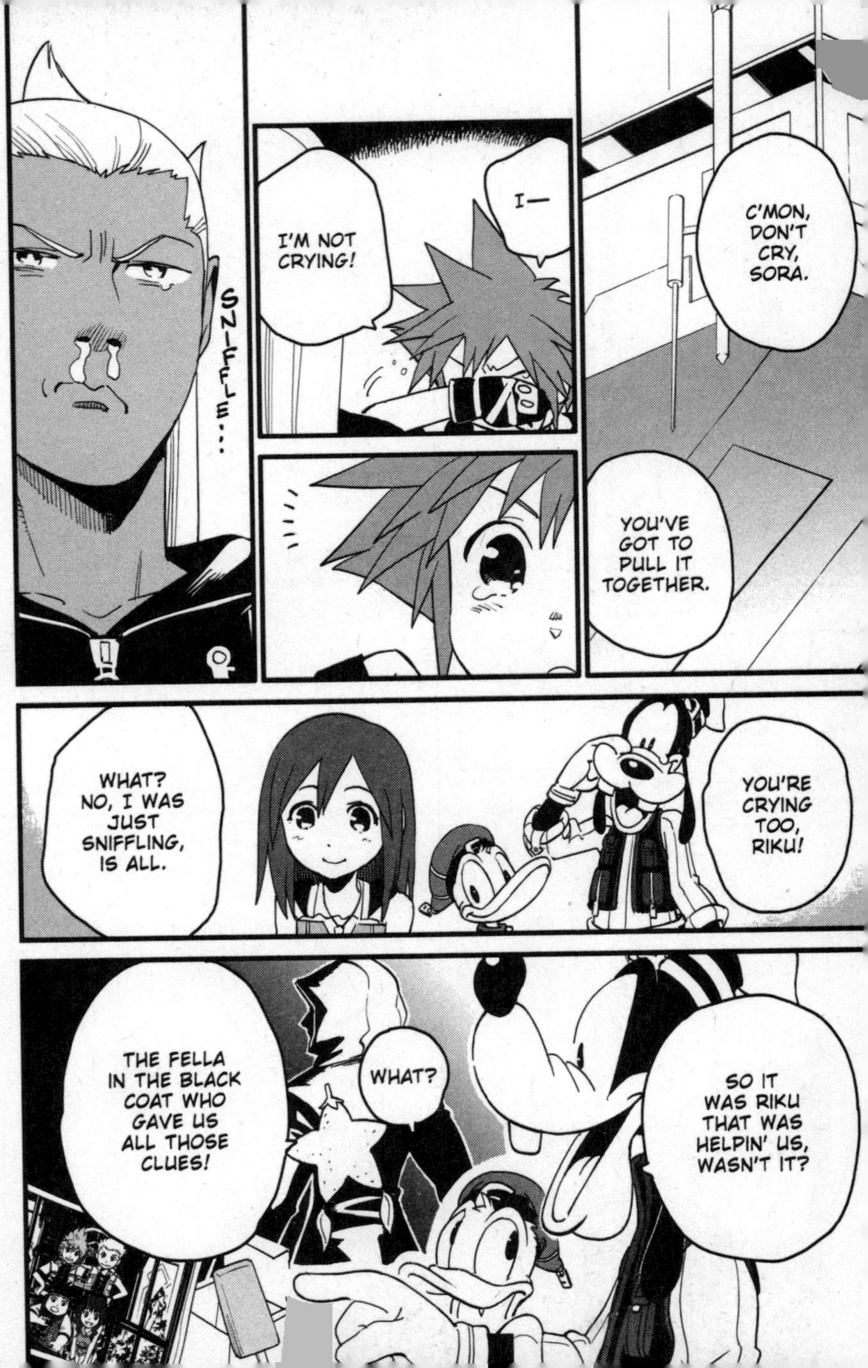
C'MON, DON'T CRY, SORA.
YOU'VE GOT TO PULL IT TOGETHER.
I—
I'M NOT CRYING!
SNIFFLE...
YOU'RE CRYING TOO, RIKU!
WHAT? NO, I WAS JUST SNIFFLING, IS ALL.
SO IT WAS RIKU THAT WAS HELPIN' US, WASN'T IT?
WHAT?
THE FELLA IN THE BLACK COAT WHO GAVE US ALL THOSE CLUES!

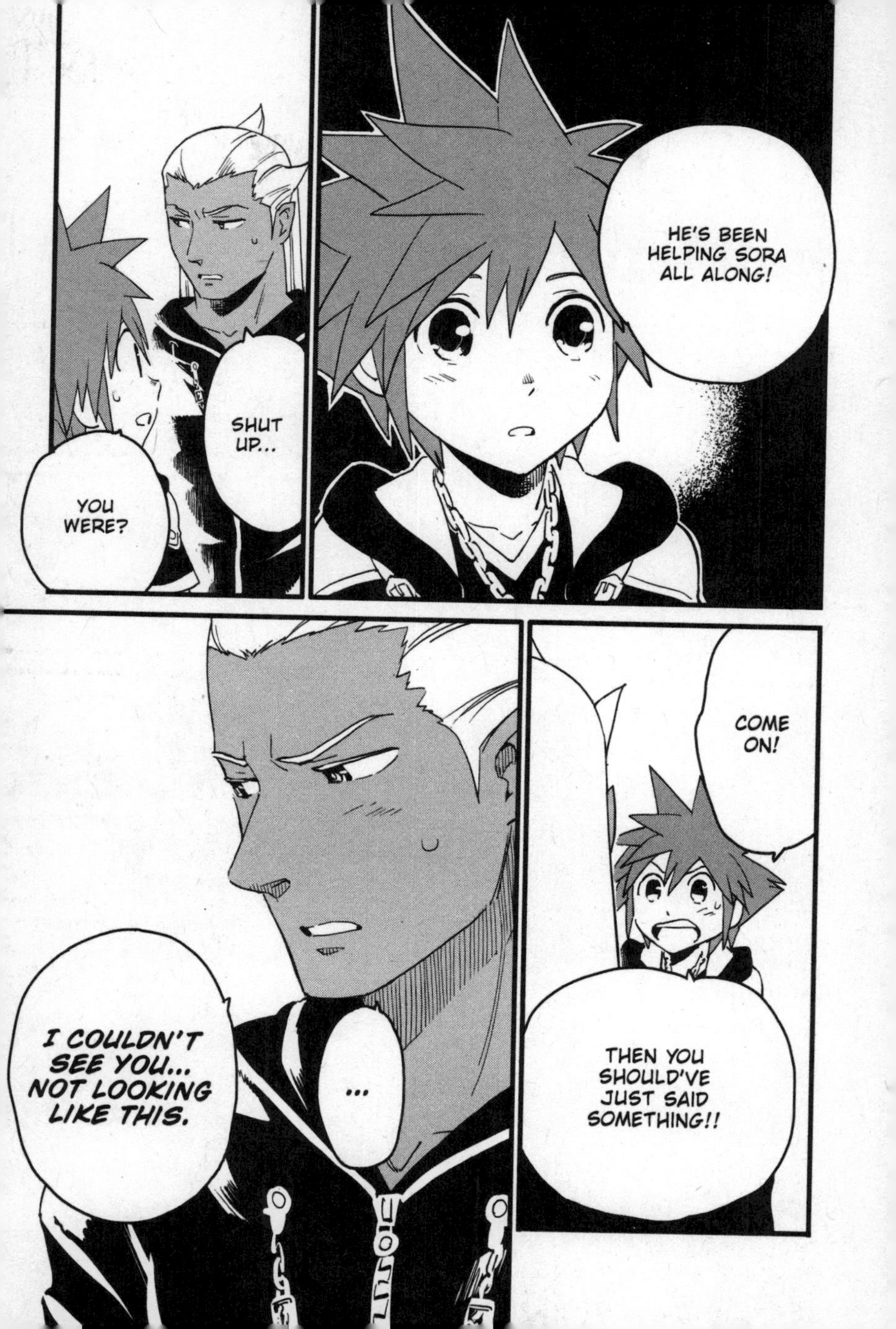
HE'S BEEN HELPING SORA ALL ALONG!
SHUT UP...
YOU WERE?
COME ON!
THEN YOU SHOULD'VE JUST SAID SOMETHING!!
...
I COULDN'T SEE YOU... NOT LOOKING LIKE THIS.

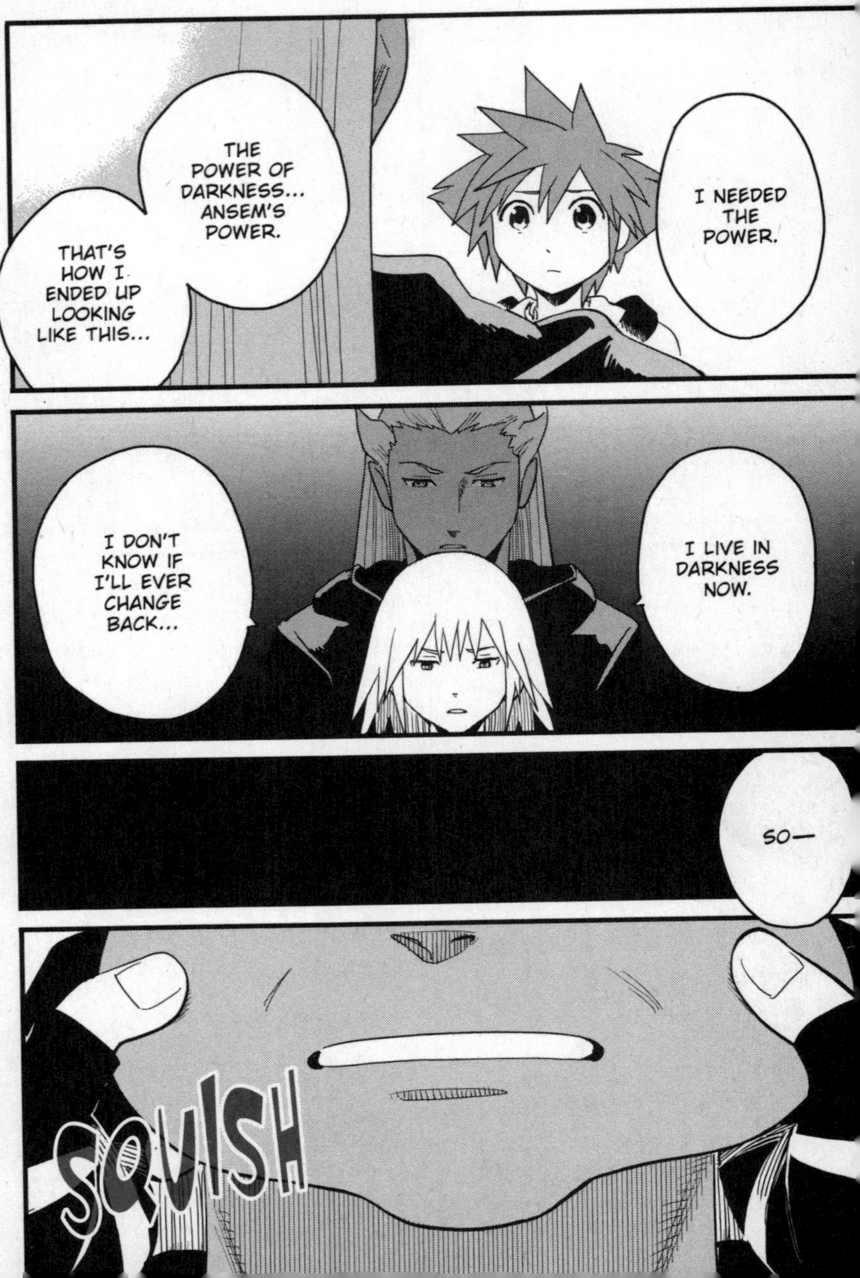
I NEEDED THE POWER.
THE POWER OF DARKNESS... ANSEM'S POWER.
THAT'S HOW I ENDED UP LOOKING LIKE THIS...
I LIVE IN DARKNESS NOW.
I DON'T KNOW IF I'LL EVER CHANGE BACK...
SO—
SQUISH

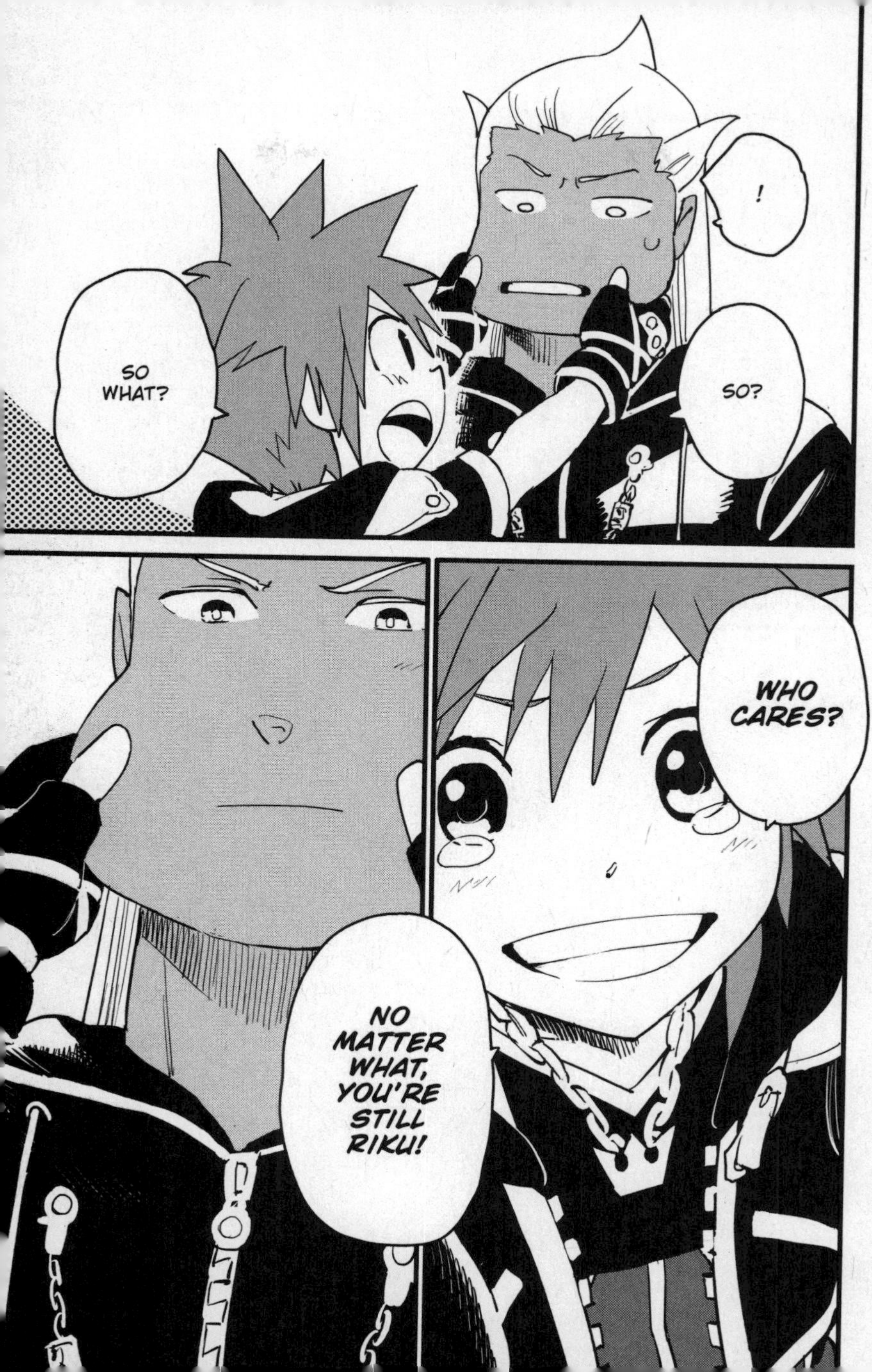
!
SO?
SO WHAT?
WHO CARES?
NO MATTER WHAT, YOU'RE STILL RIKU!

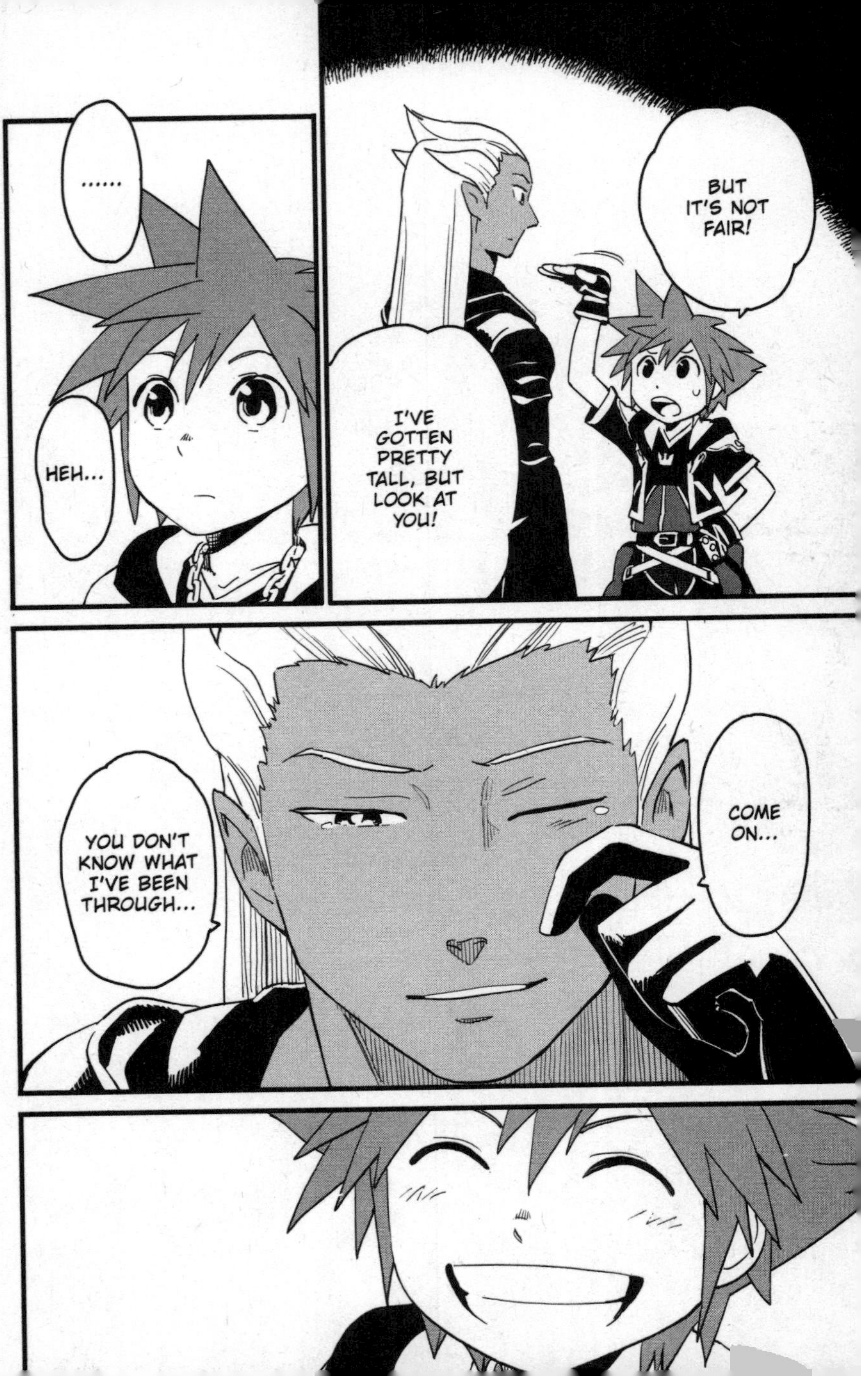
BUT IT'S NOT FAIR!
I'VE GOTTEN PRETTY TALL, BUT LOOK AT YOU!
......
HEH...
COME ON...
YOU DON'T KNOW WHAT I'VE BEEN THROUGH...

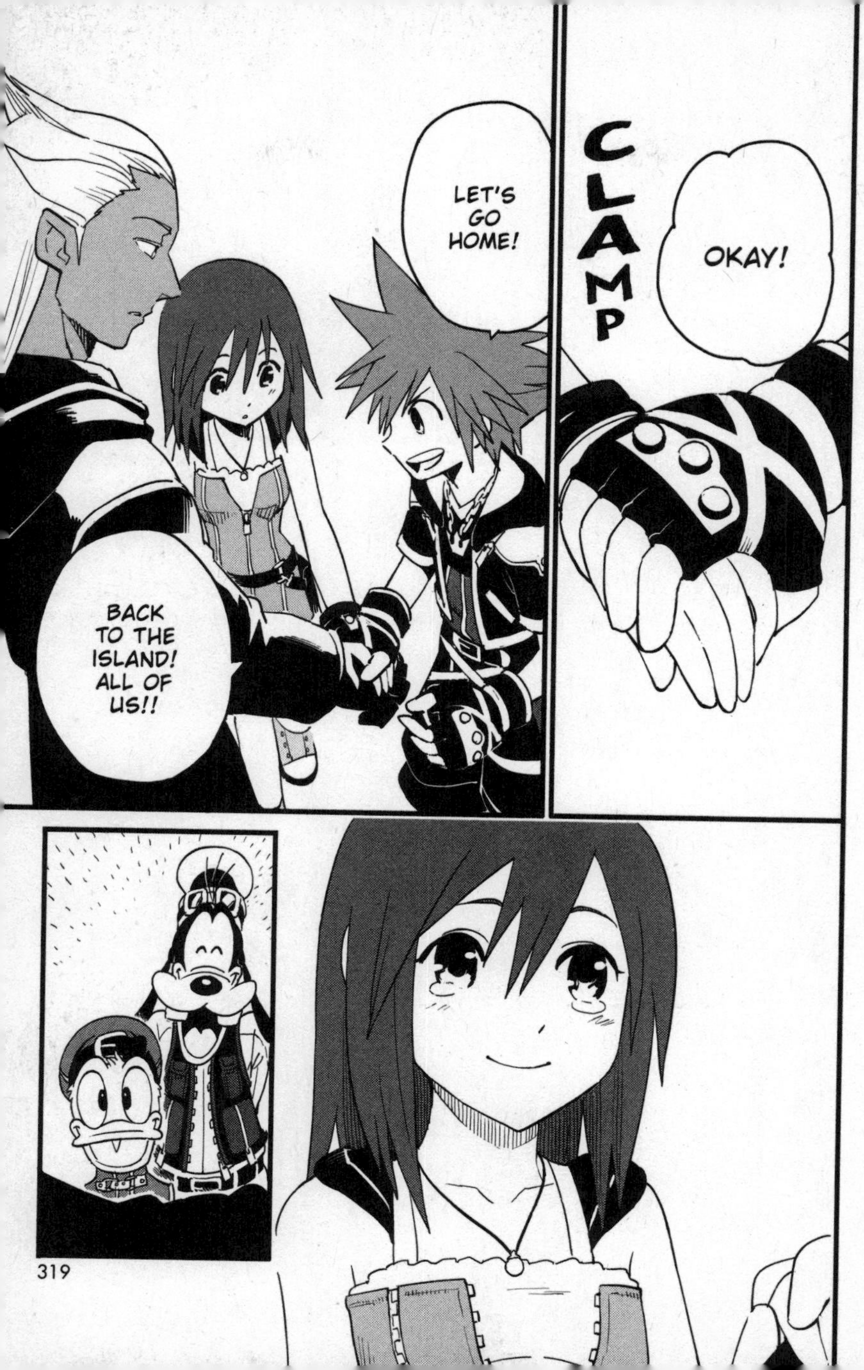
OKAY!
CLAMP
LET'S GO HOME!
BACK TO THE ISLAND! ALL OF US!!

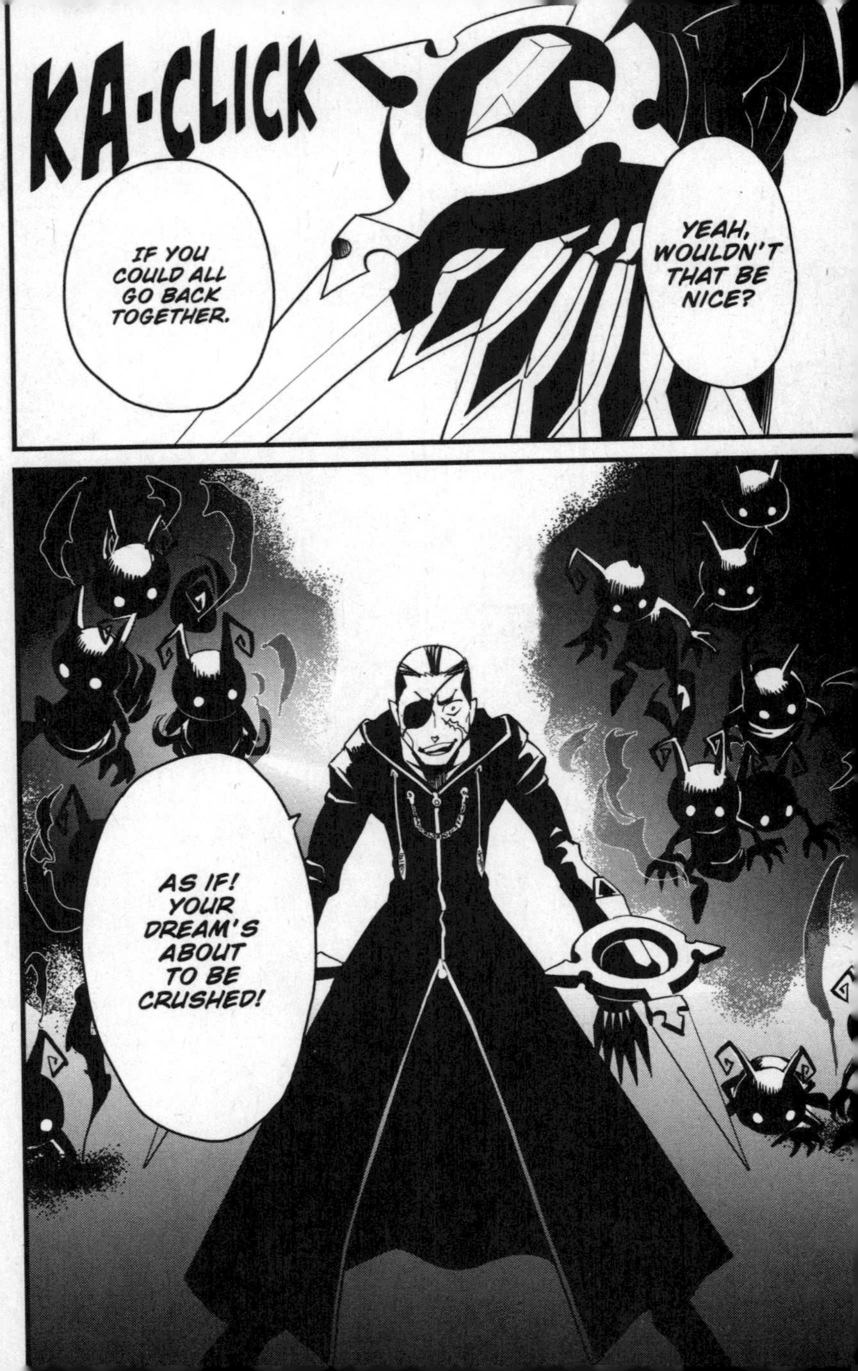
KA-CLICK
YEAH, WOULDN'T THAT BE NICE?
IF YOU COULD ALL GO BACK TOGETHER.
AS IF! YOUR DREAM'S ABOUT TO BE CRUSHED!

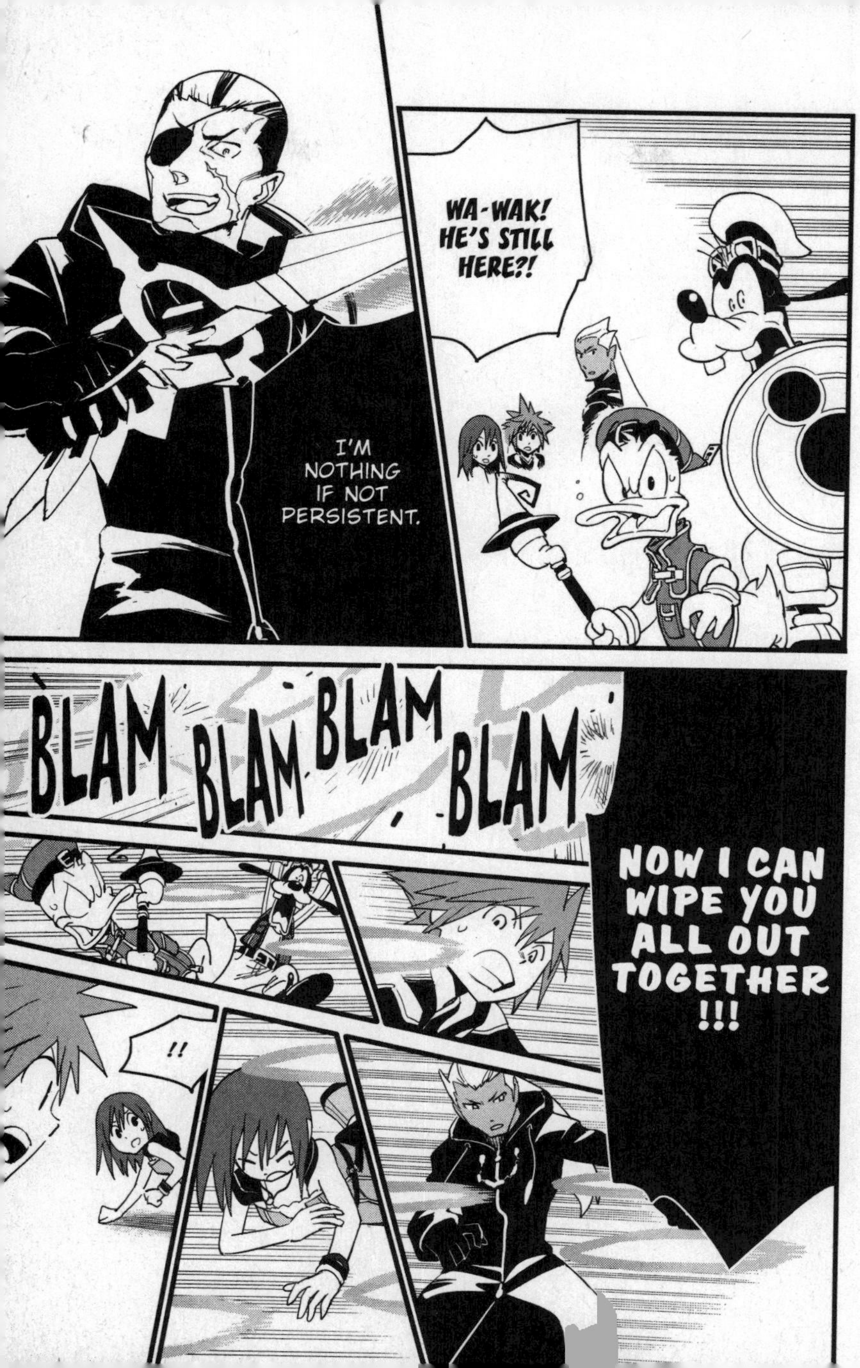
WA-WAK! HE'S STILL HERE?!
I'M NOTHING IF NOT PERSISTENT.
BLAM
BLAM
BLAM
BLAM
NOW I CAN WIPE YOU ALL OUT TOGETHER !!!
!!

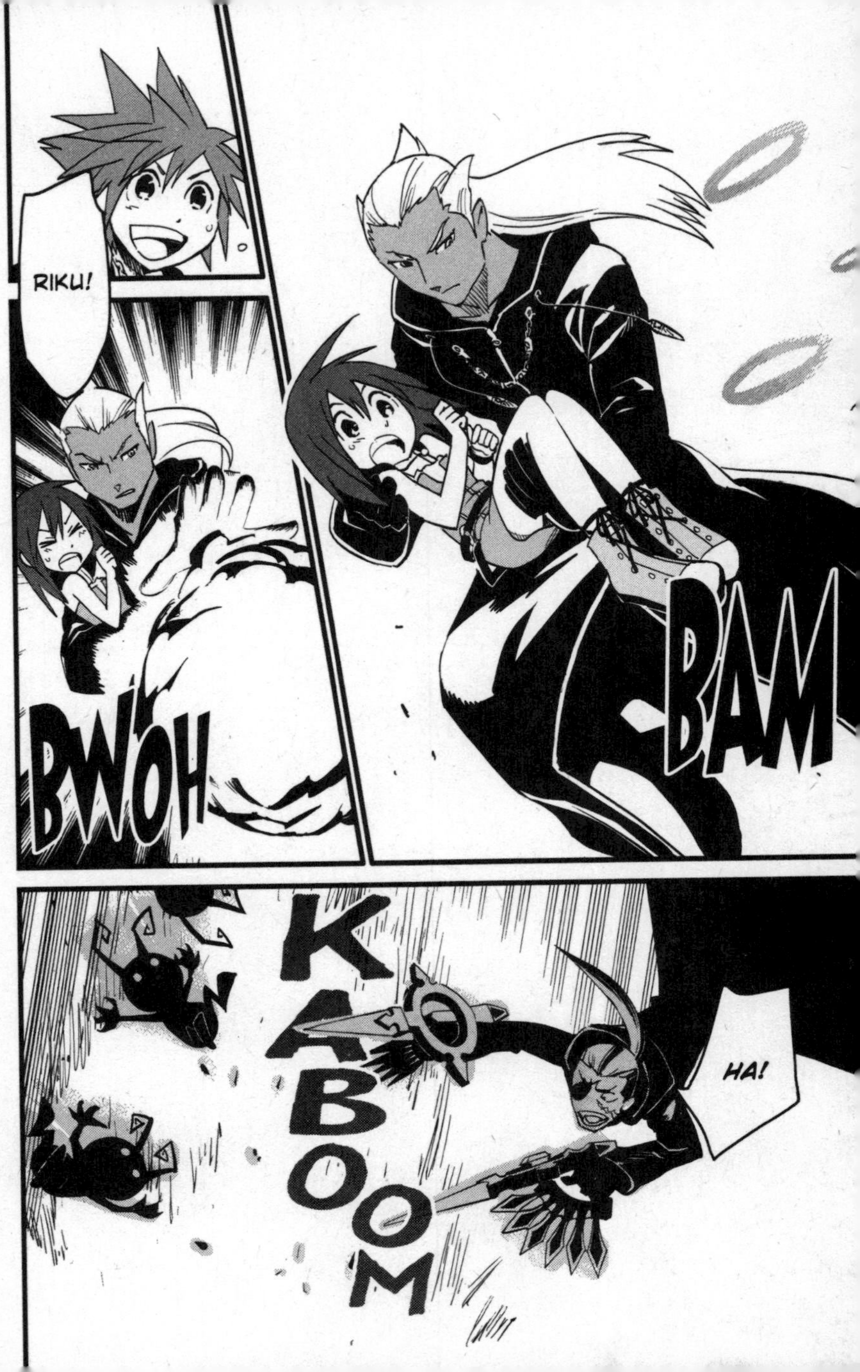
BAM
RIKU!
BWOH
KABOOM
HA!

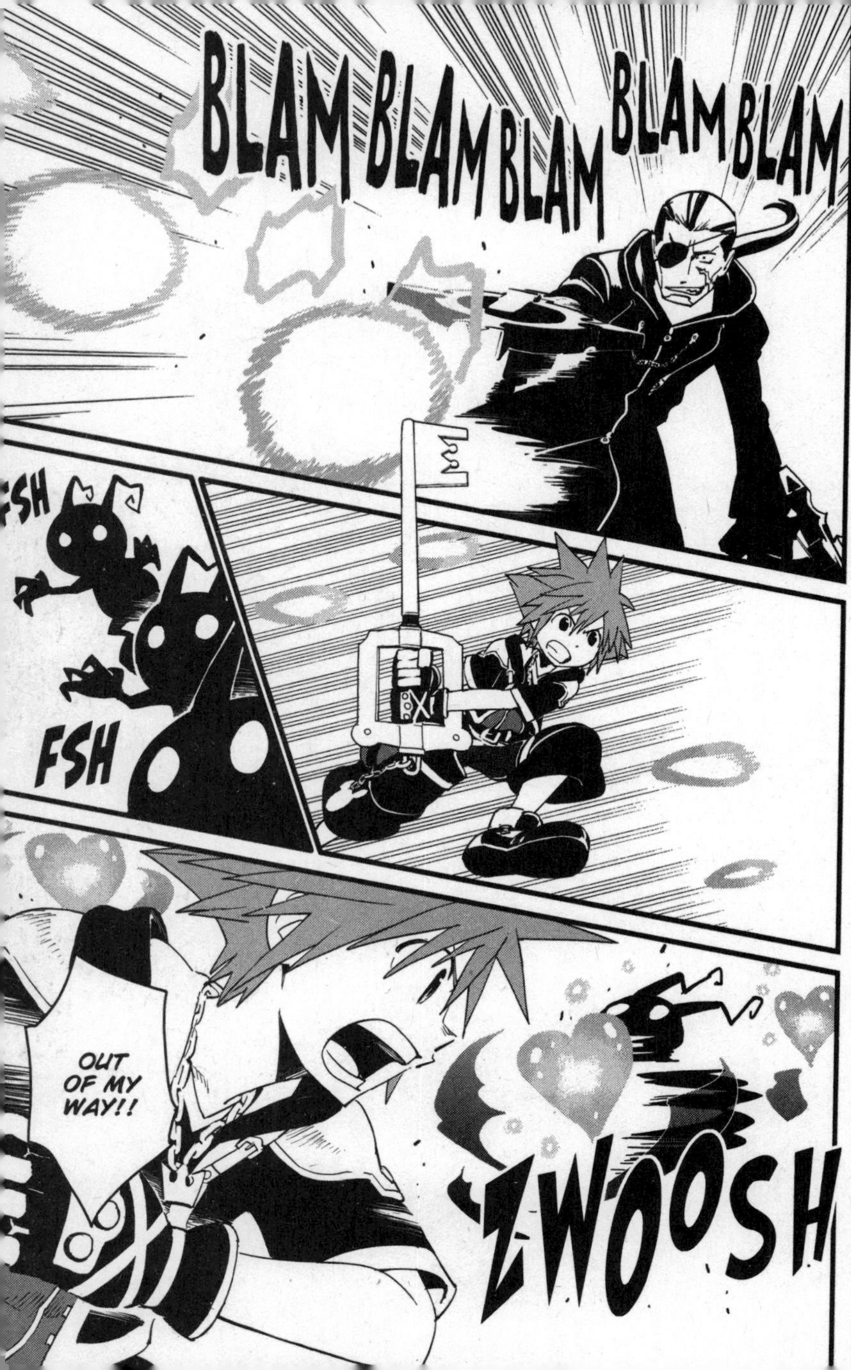
BLAM BLAM BLAM BLAM BLAM
FSH
FSH
OUT OF MY WAY!!
ZWOOSH

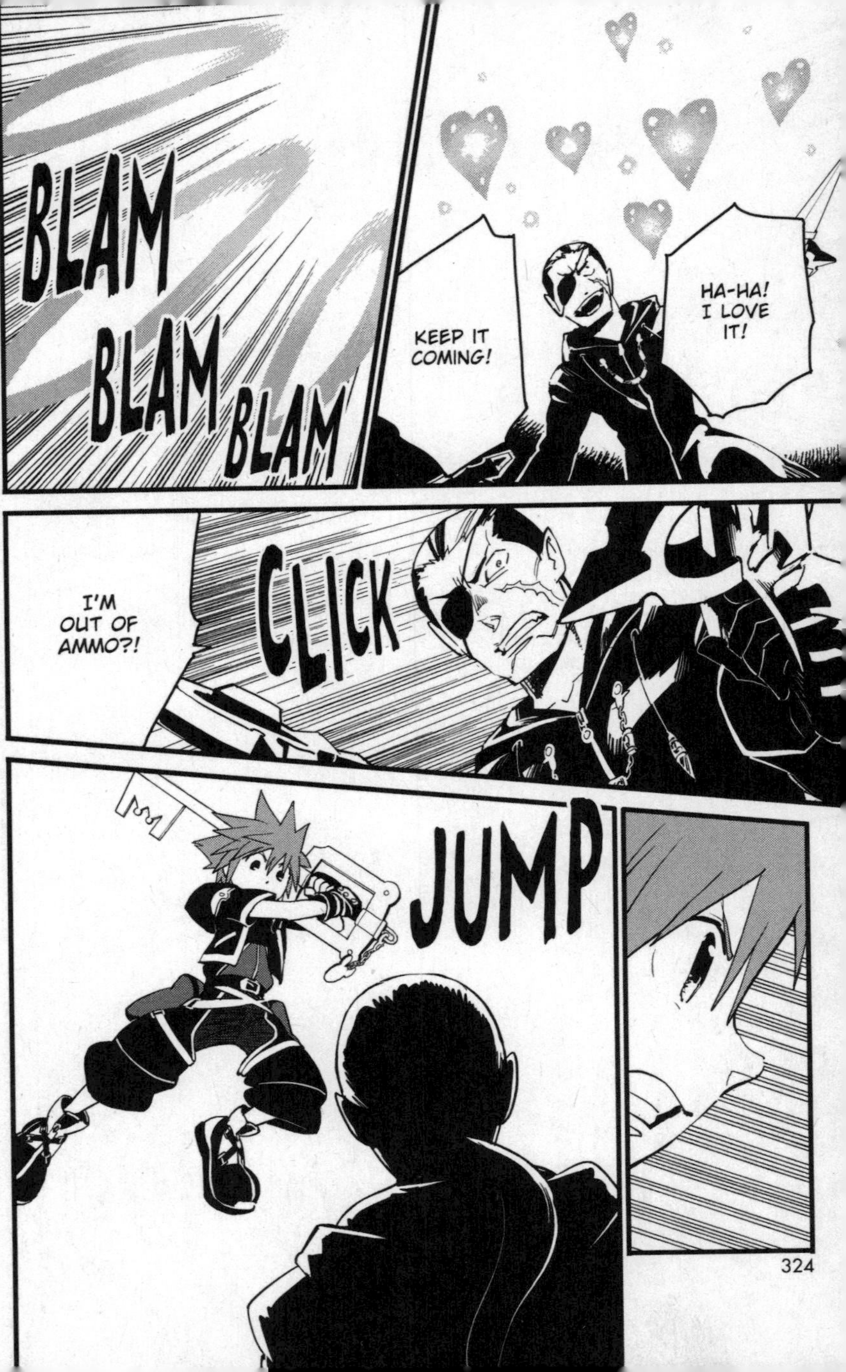
HA-HA! I LOVE IT!
KEEP IT COMING!
BLAM
BLAM
BLAM
CLICK
I'M OUT OF AMMO?!
JUMP

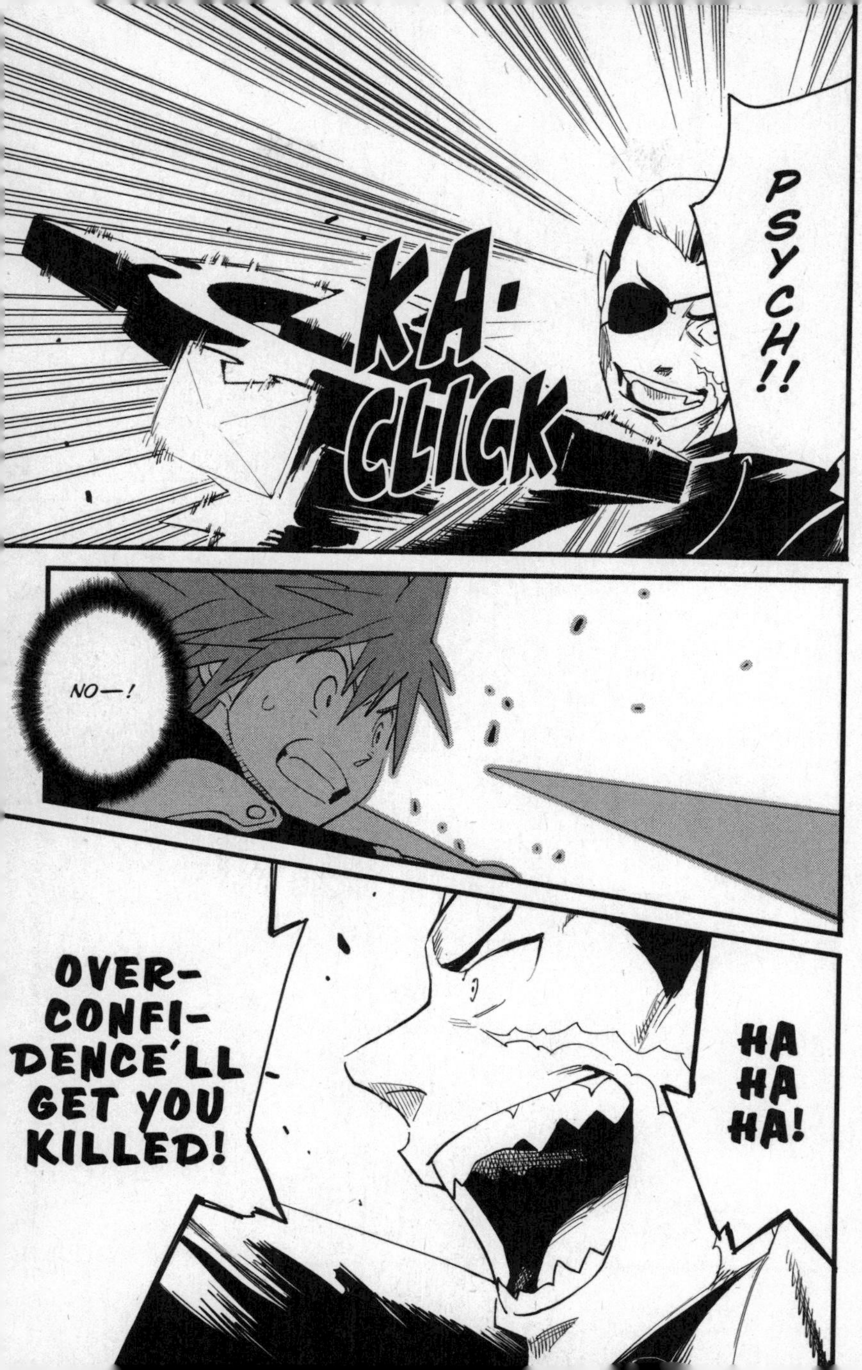
PSYCH!!
KA-CLICK
NO—!
HA HA HA!
OVER-CONFI-DENCE'LL GET YOU KILLED!

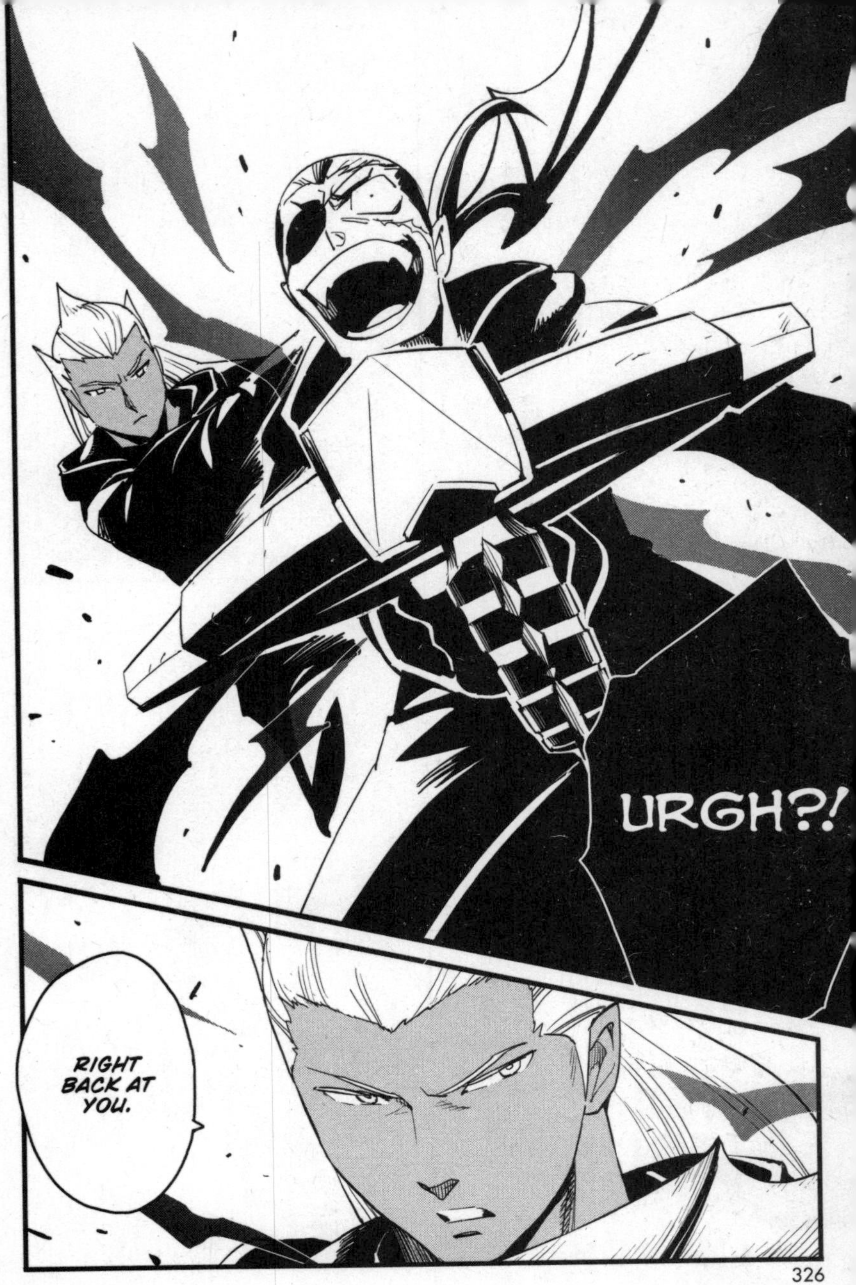
URGH?!
RIGHT BACK AT YOU.

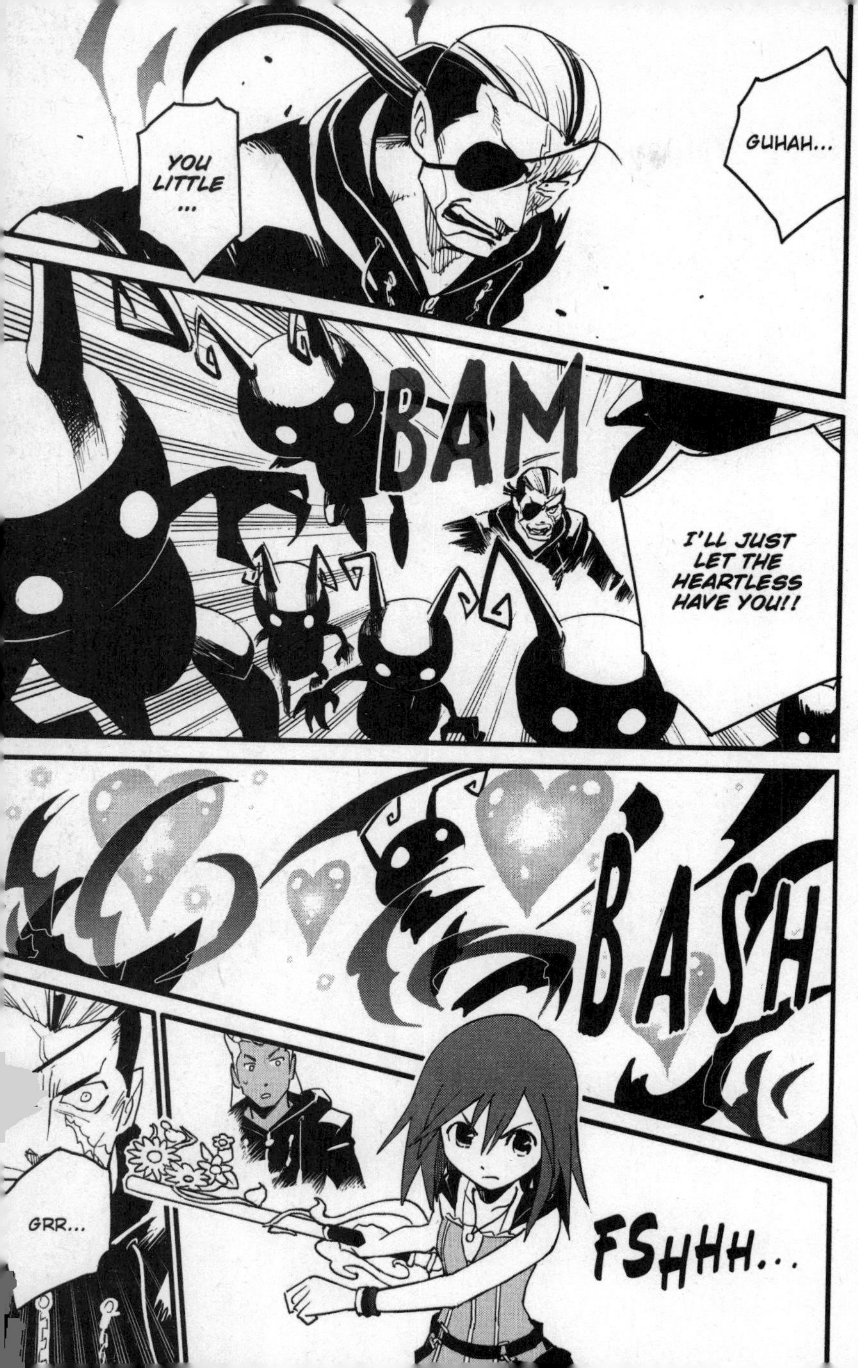
GUHAH...
YOU LITTLE ...
I'LL JUST LET THE HEARTLESS HAVE YOU!!
BAM
BASH
FSHHH...
GRR...

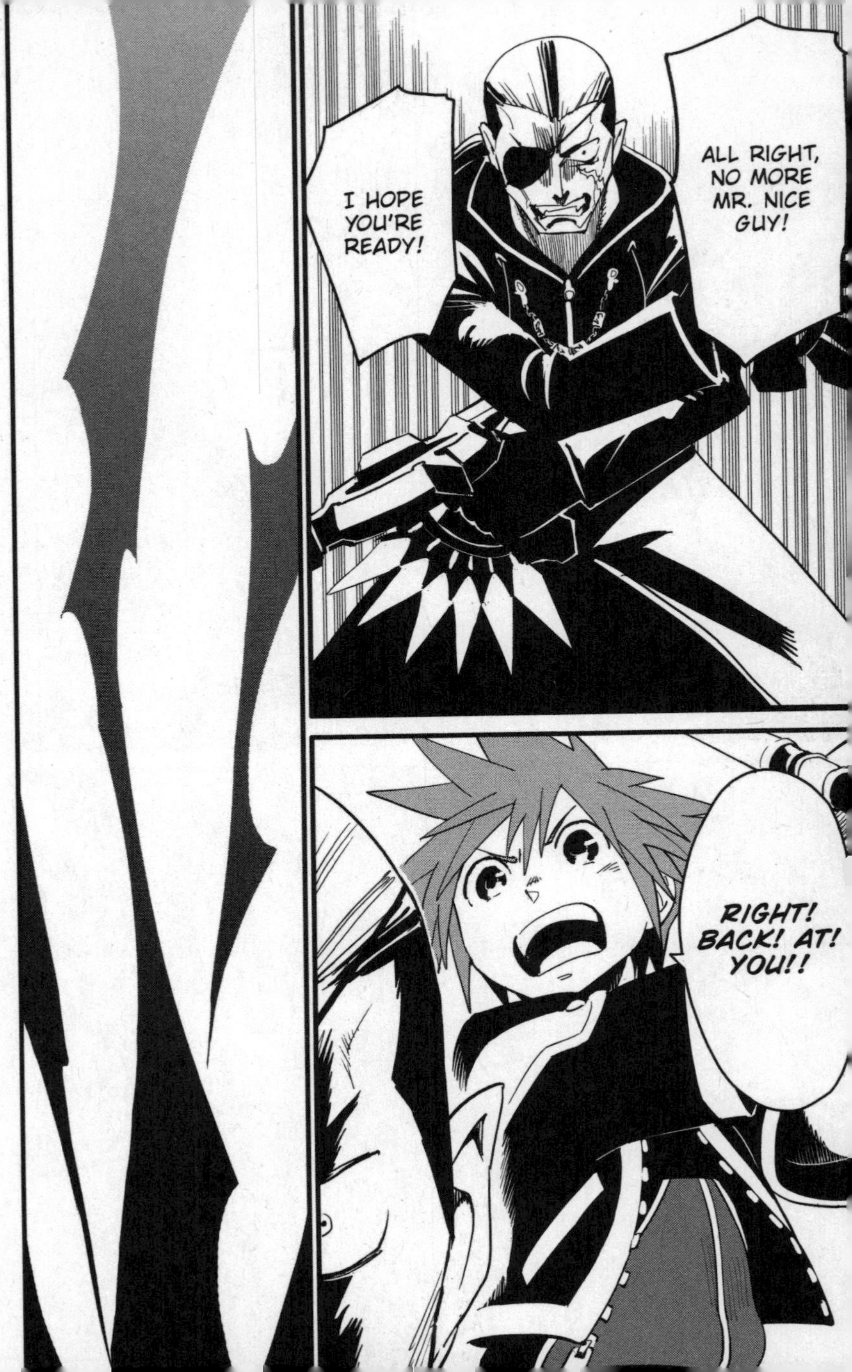
ALL RIGHT, NO MORE MR. NICE GUY!
I HOPE YOU'RE READY!
RIGHT! BACK! AT! YOU!!

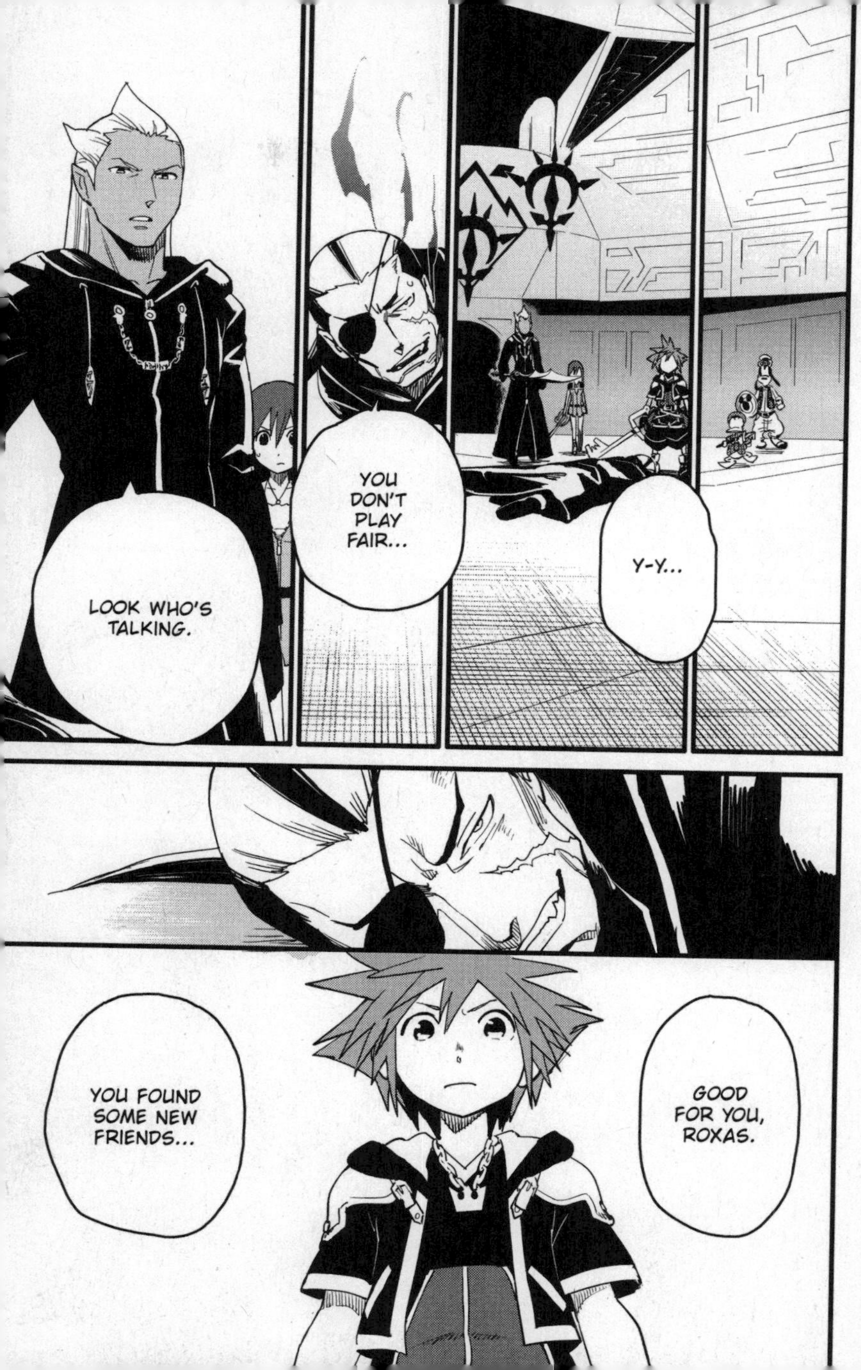
Y-Y...
YOU DON'T PLAY FAIR...
LOOK WHO'S TALKING.
GOOD FOR YOU, ROXAS.
YOU FOUND SOME NEW FRIENDS...

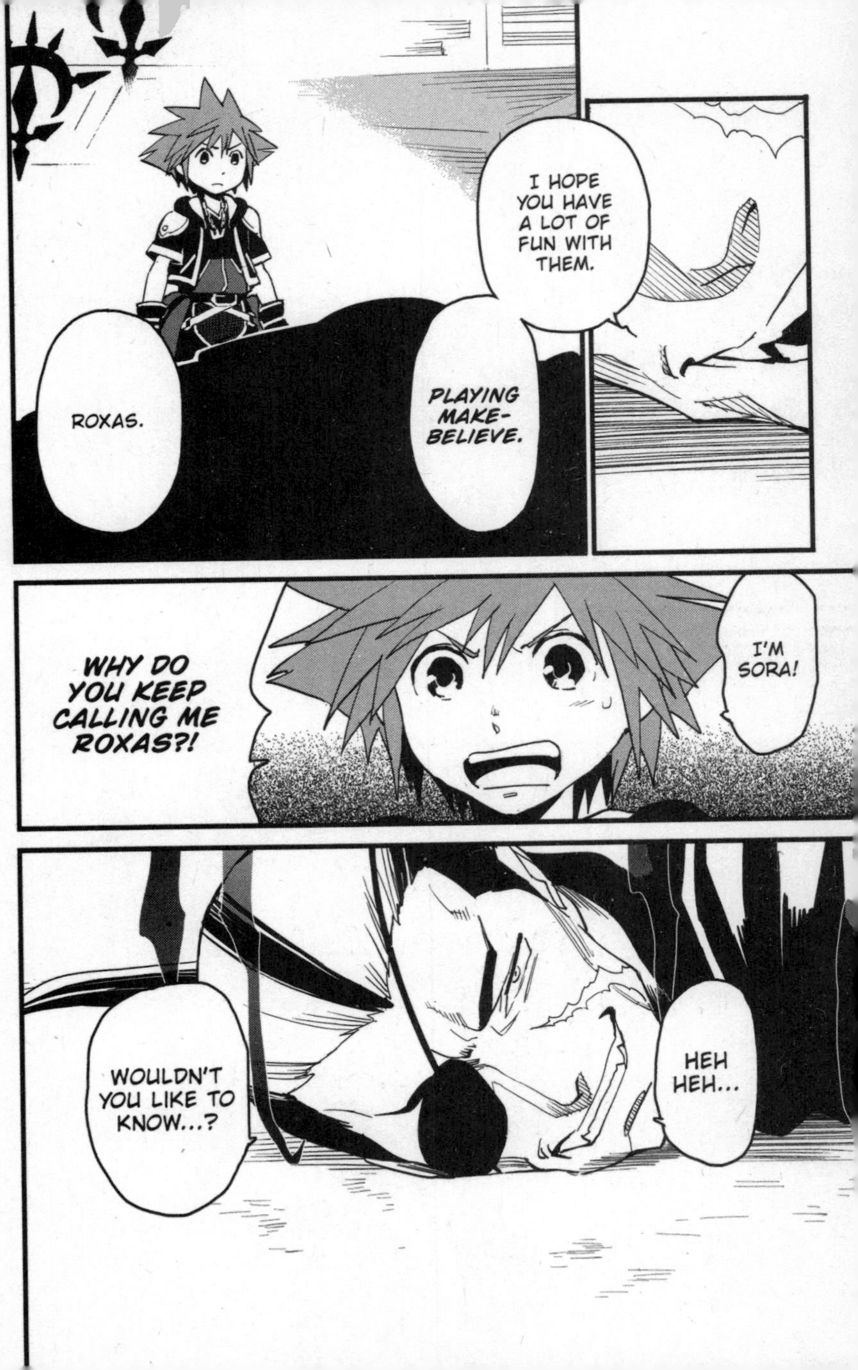
I HOPE YOU HAVE A LOT OF FUN WITH THEM.
PLAYING MAKE-BELIEVE.
ROXAS.
I'M SORA!
WHY DO YOU KEEP CALLING ME ROXAS?!
HEH HEH...
WOULDN'T YOU LIKE TO KNOW...?

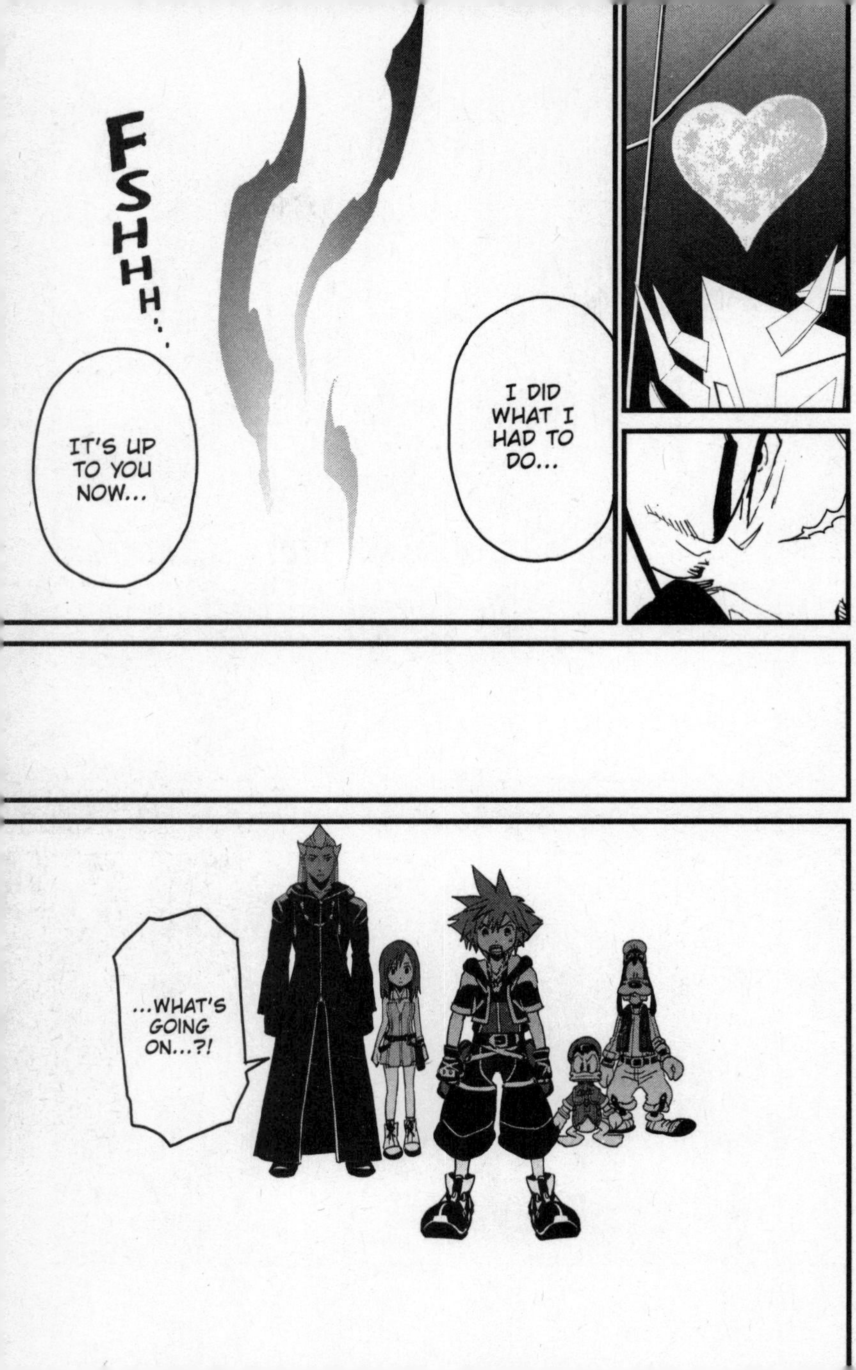
I DID WHAT I HAD TO DO...
FSHHH...
IT'S UP TO YOU NOW...
...WHAT'S GOING ON...?!

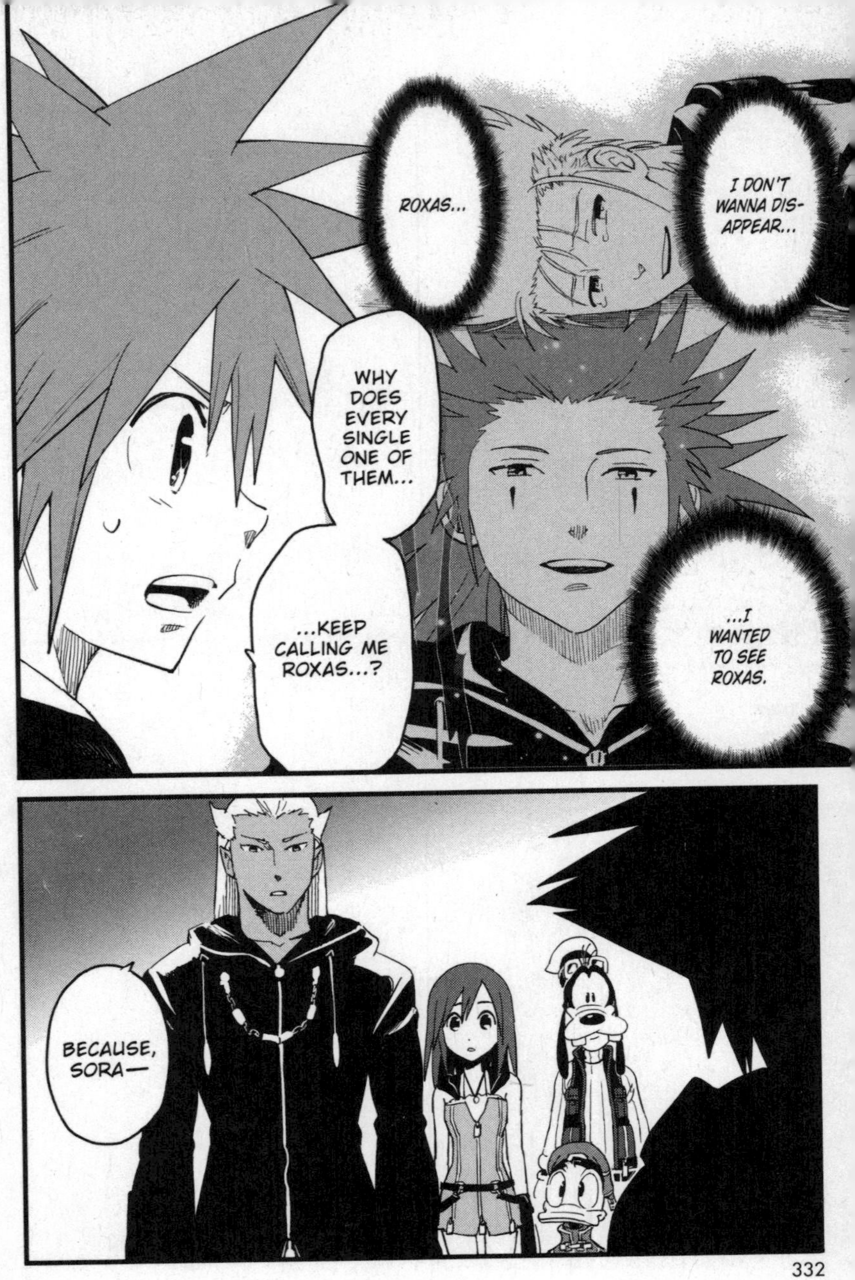
I DON'T WANNA DIS-APPEAR...
ROXAS...
WHY DOES EVERY SINGLE ONE OF THEM...
...I WANTED TO SEE ROXAS.
...KEEP CALLING ME ROXAS...?
BECAUSE, SORA—

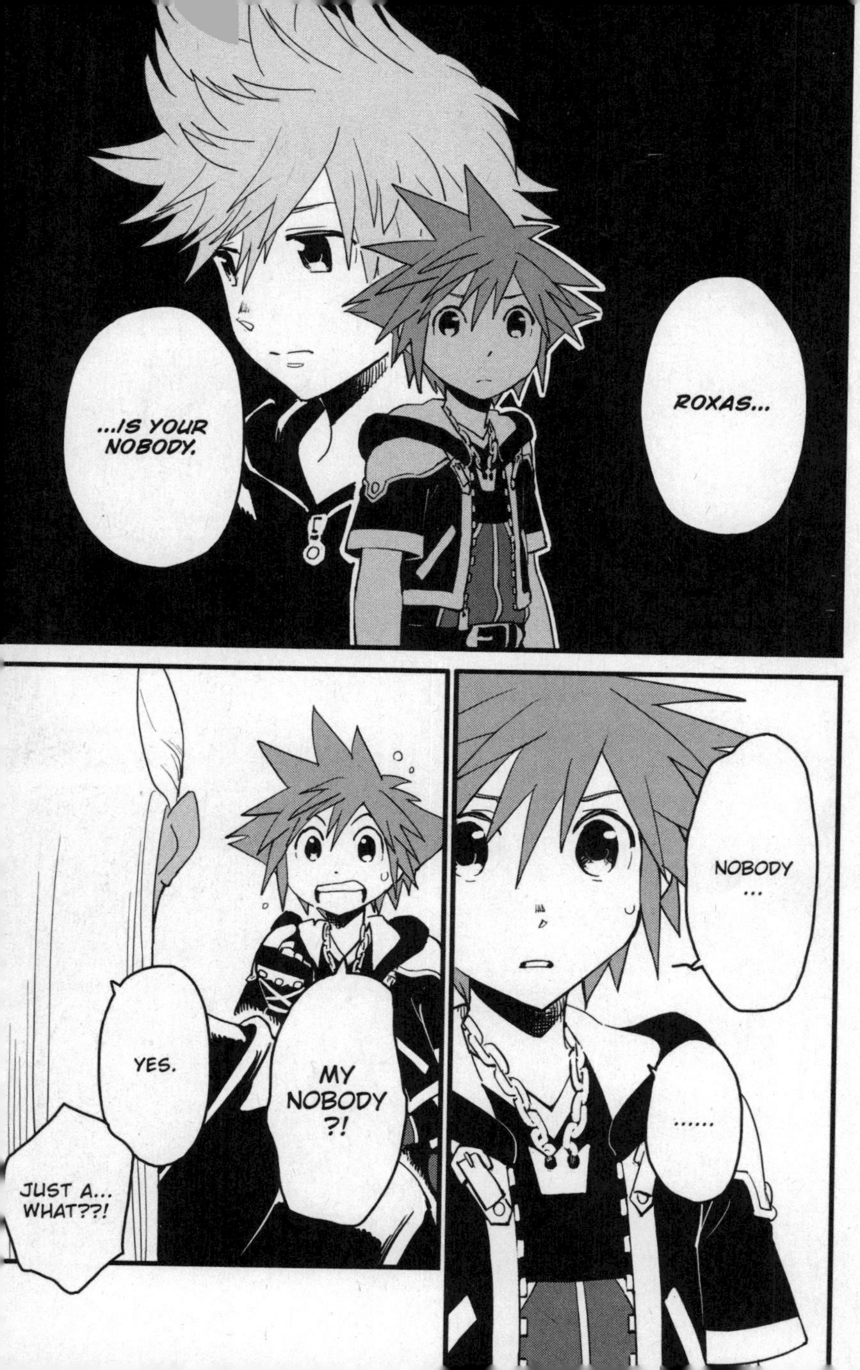
ROXAS...
...IS YOUR NOBODY.
NOBODY ...
......
MY NOBODY ?!
YES.
JUST A... WHAT??!

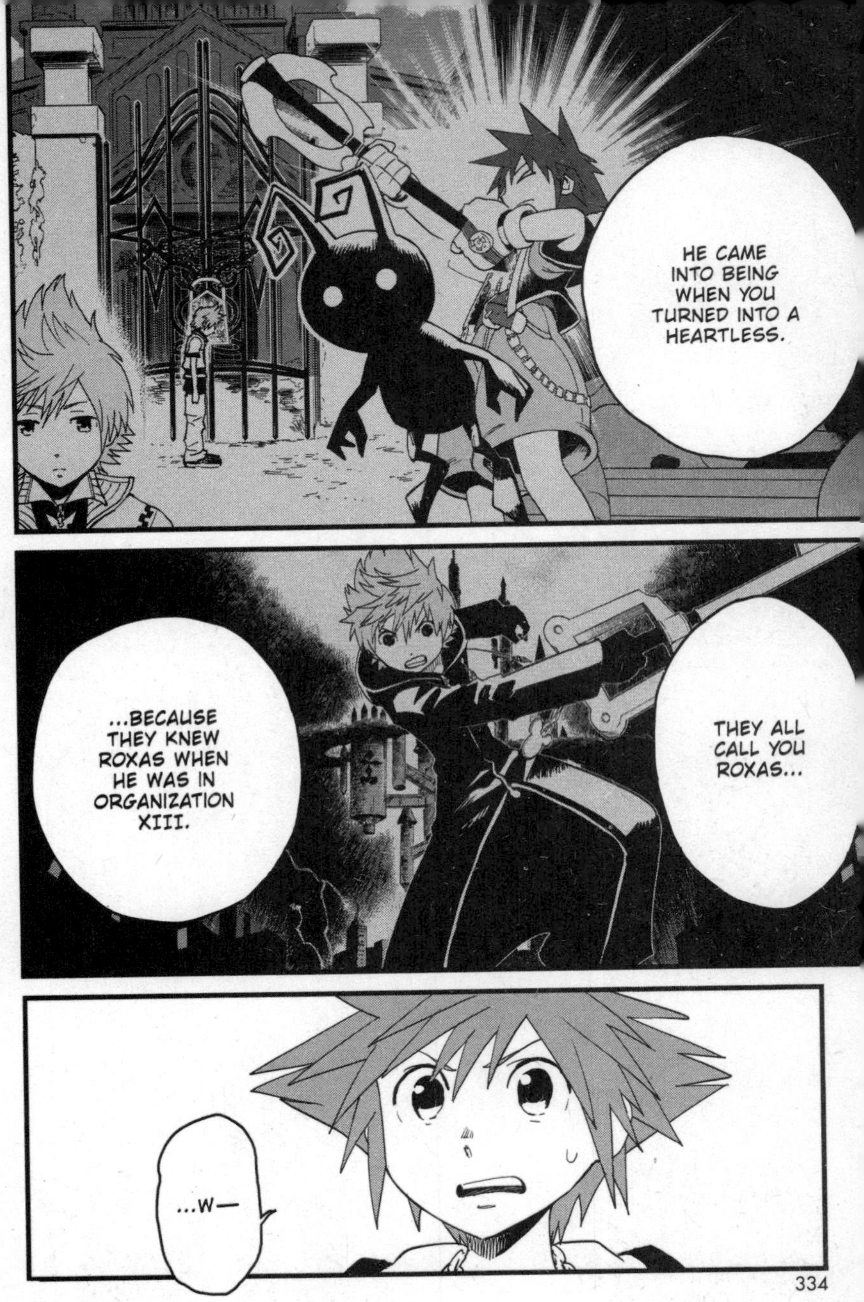
HE CAME INTO BEING WHEN YOU TURNED INTO A HEARTLESS.
THEY ALL CALL YOU ROXAS...
...BECAUSE THEY KNEW ROXAS WHEN HE WAS IN ORGANIZATION XIII.
...W—

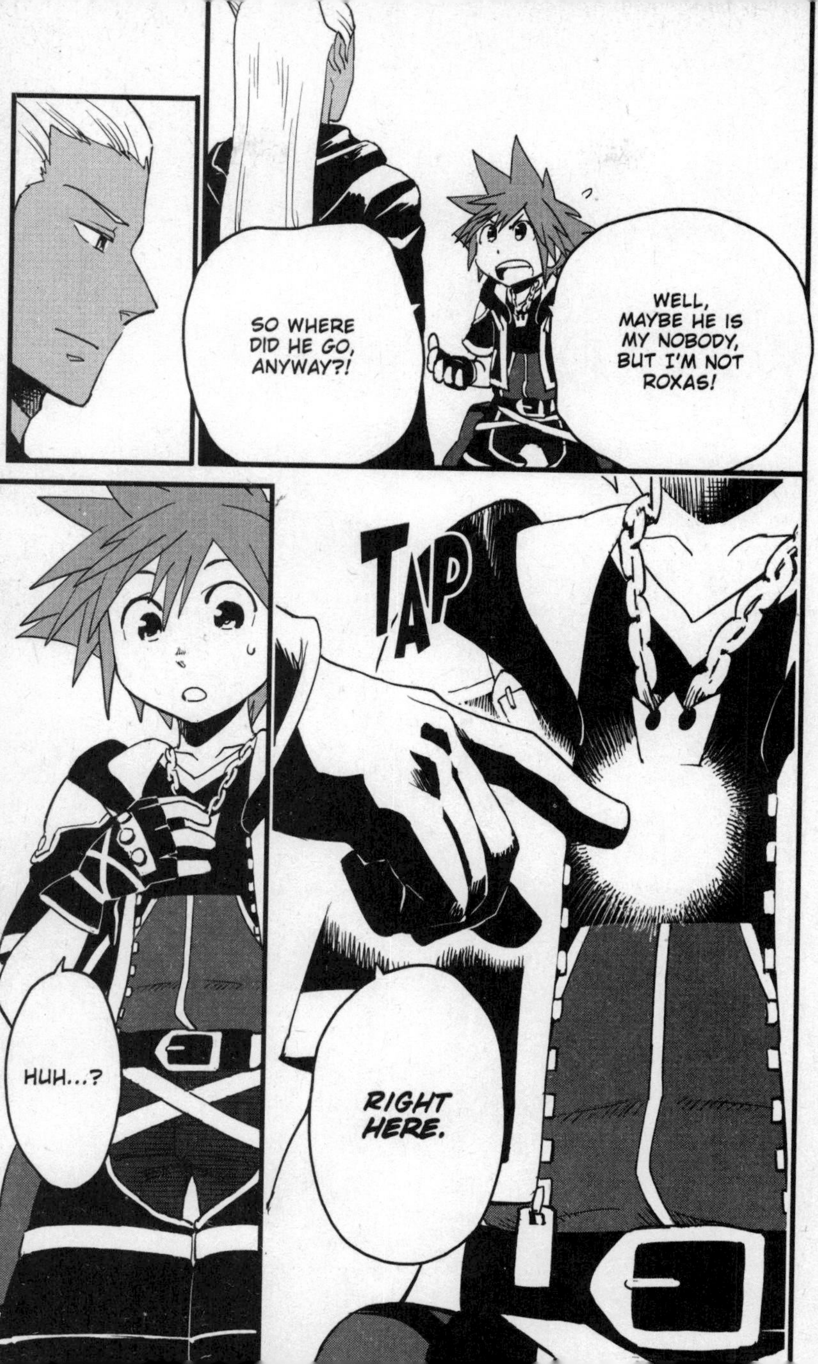
WELL, MAYBE HE IS MY NOBODY, BUT I'M NOT ROXAS!
SO WHERE DID HE GO, ANYWAY?!
TAP
RIGHT HERE.
HUH...?

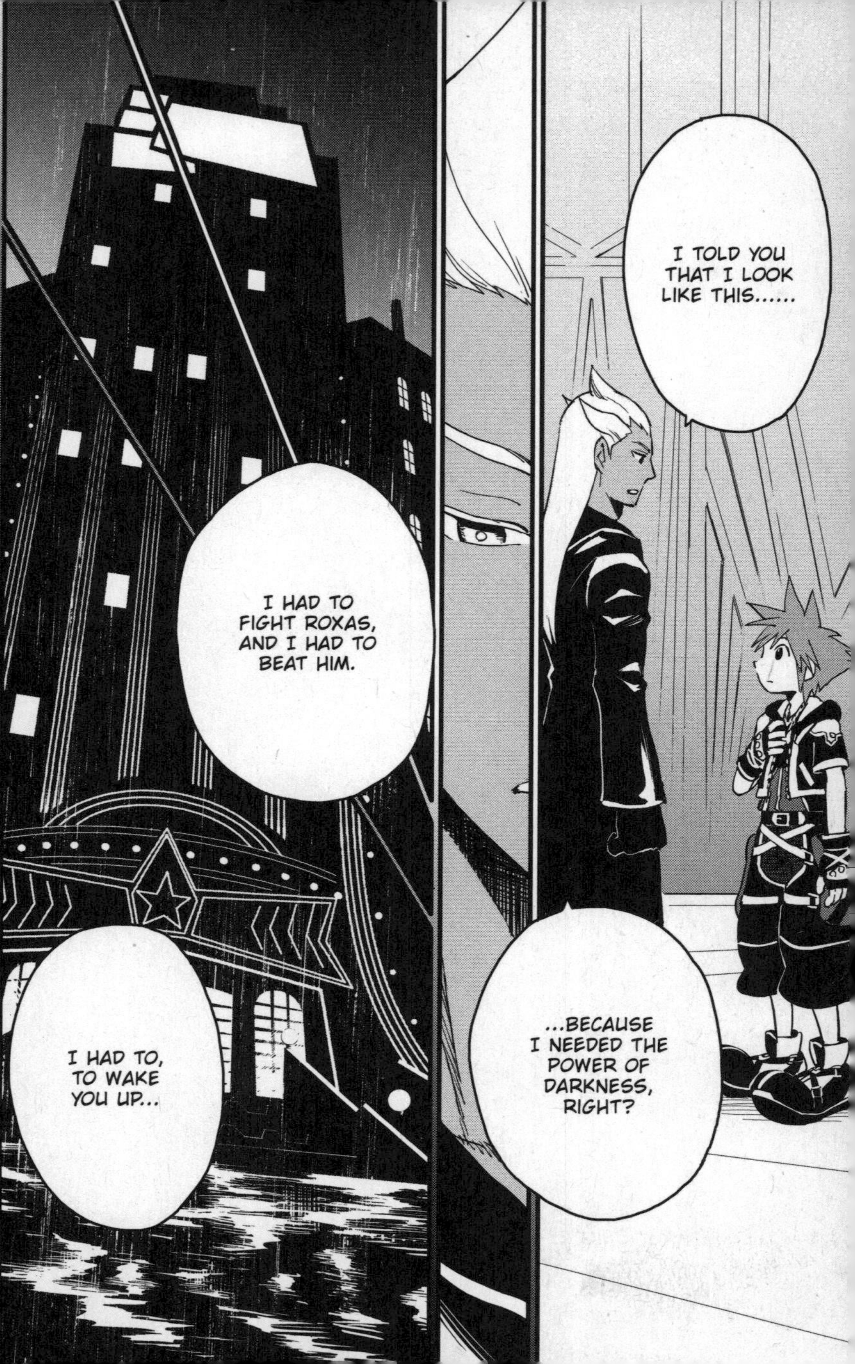
I TOLD YOU THAT I LOOK LIKE THIS......
...BECAUSE I NEEDED THE POWER OF DARKNESS, RIGHT?
I HAD TO FIGHT ROXAS, AND I HAD TO BEAT HIM.
I HAD TO, TO WAKE YOU UP...

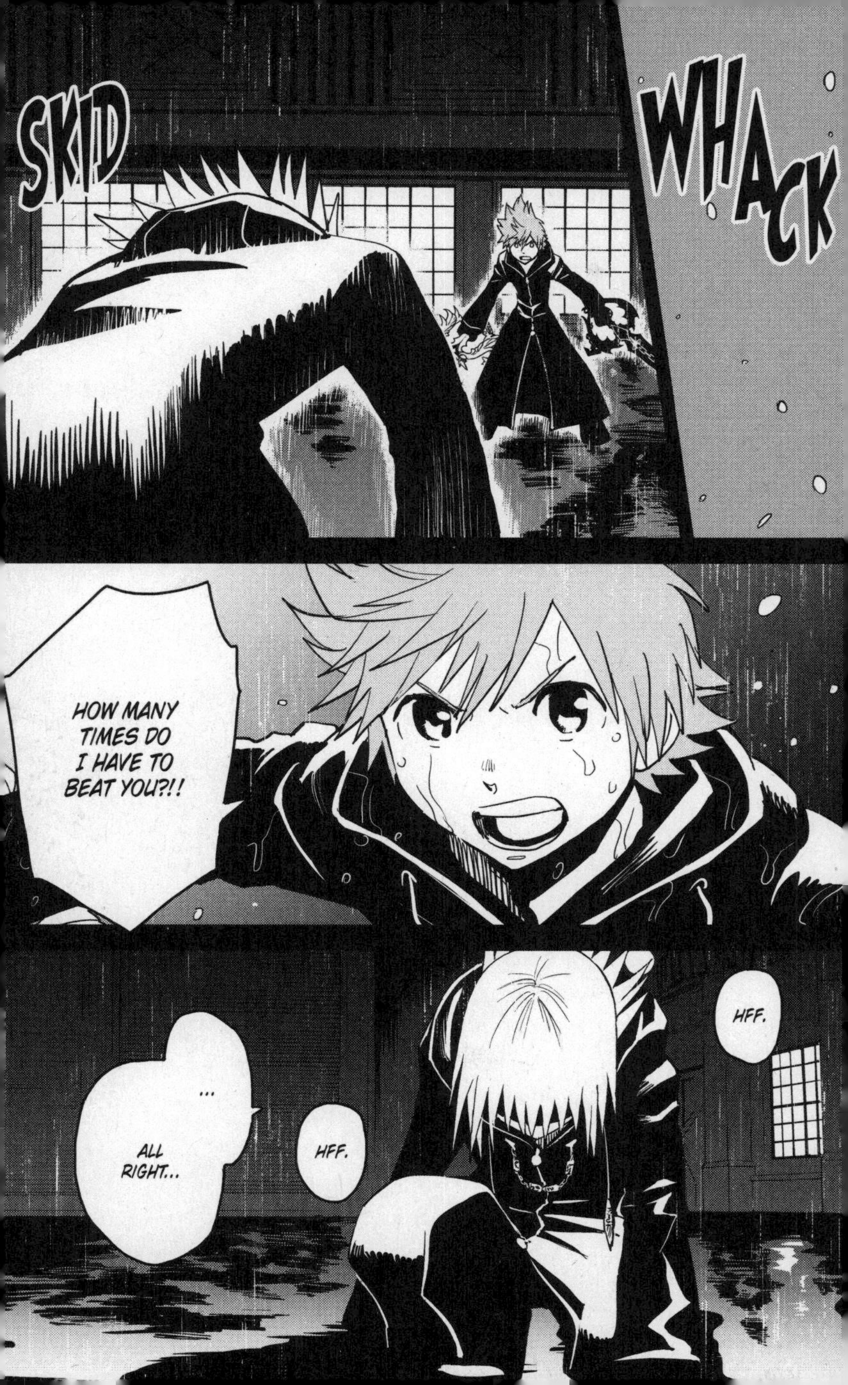
WHACK
SKID
HOW MANY TIMES DO I HAVE TO BEAT YOU?!!
HFF.
HFF.
...
ALL RIGHT...

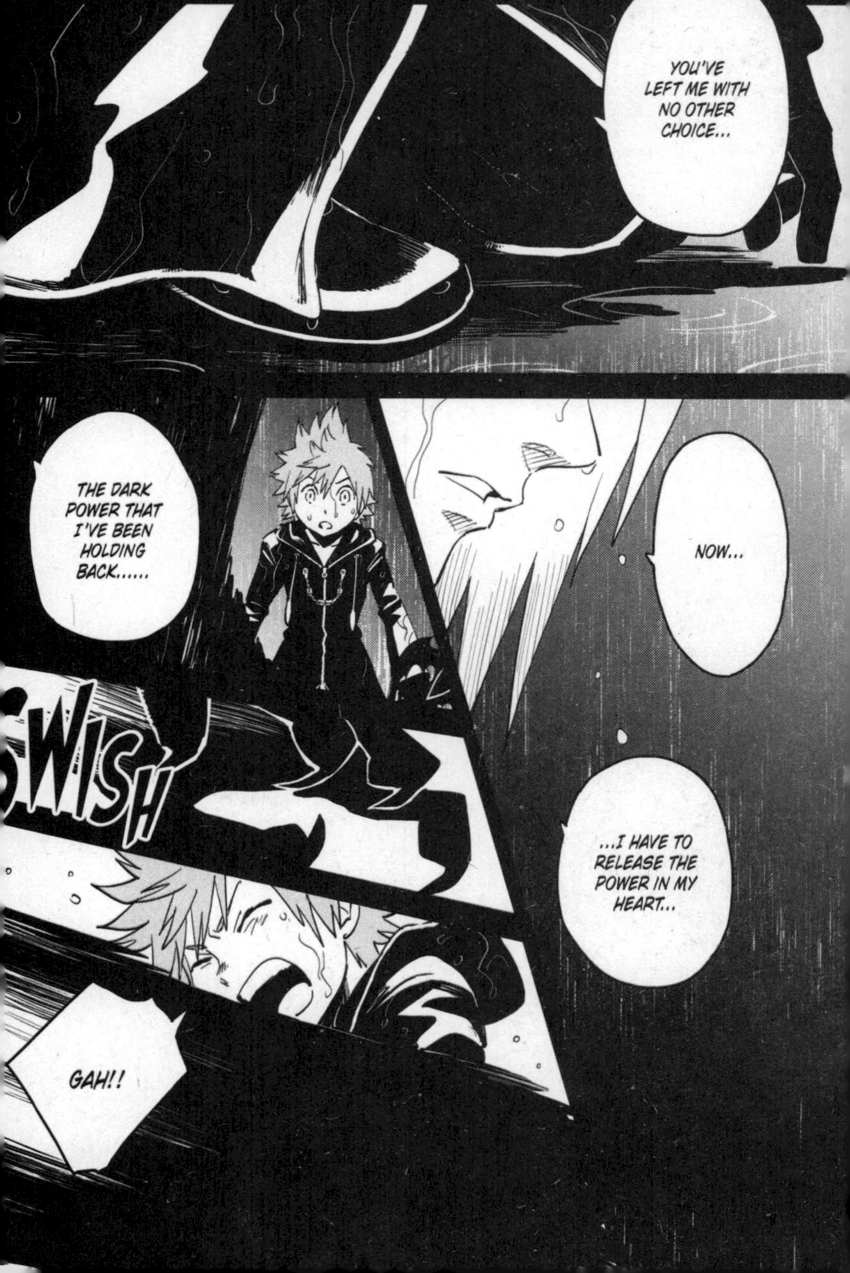
YOU'VE LEFT ME WITH NO OTHER CHOICE...
NOW...
...I HAVE TO RELEASE THE POWER IN MY HEART...
THE DARK POWER THAT I'VE BEEN HOLDING BACK......
SWISH
GAH!!

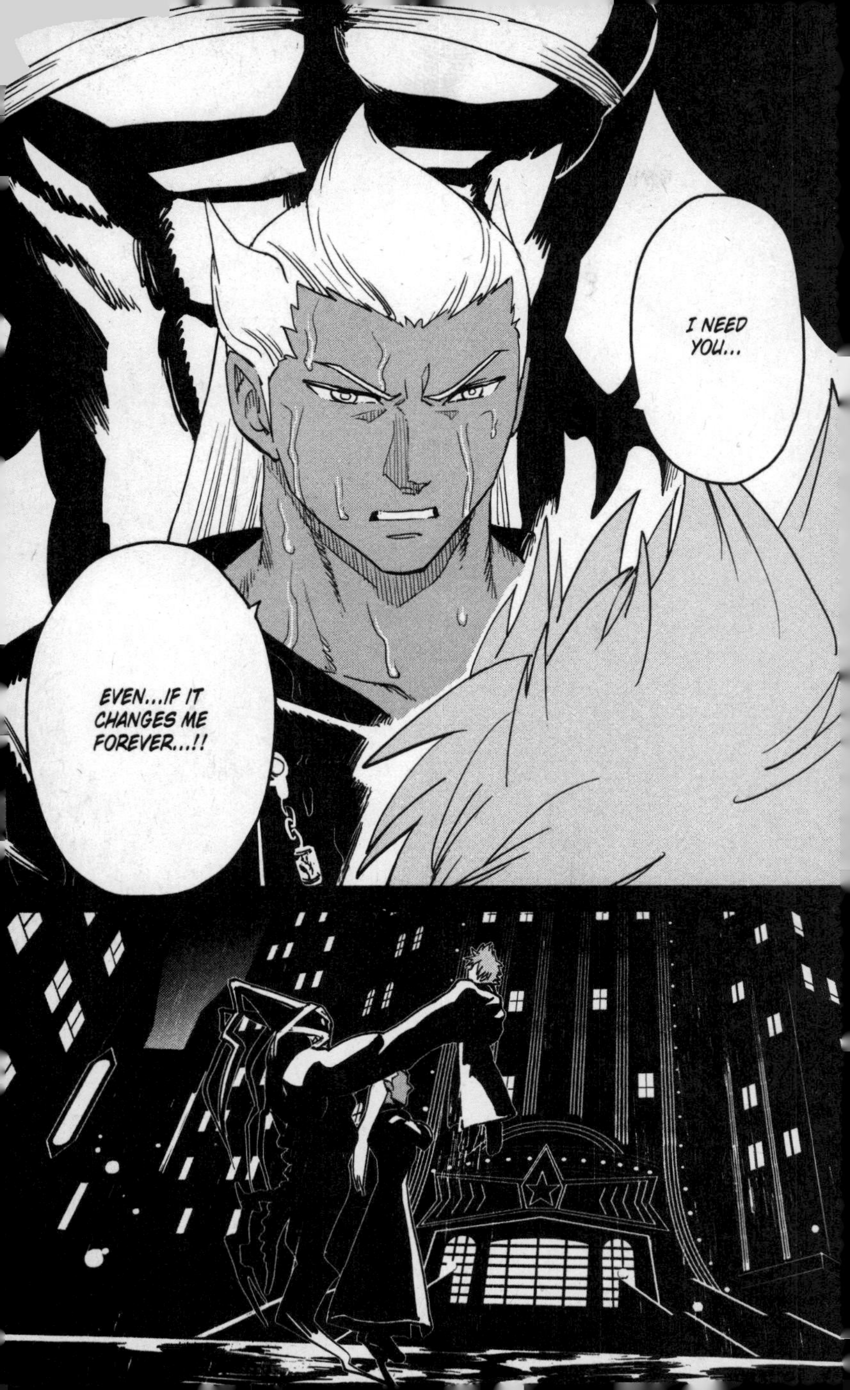
I NEED YOU...
EVEN...IF IT CHANGES ME FOREVER...!!

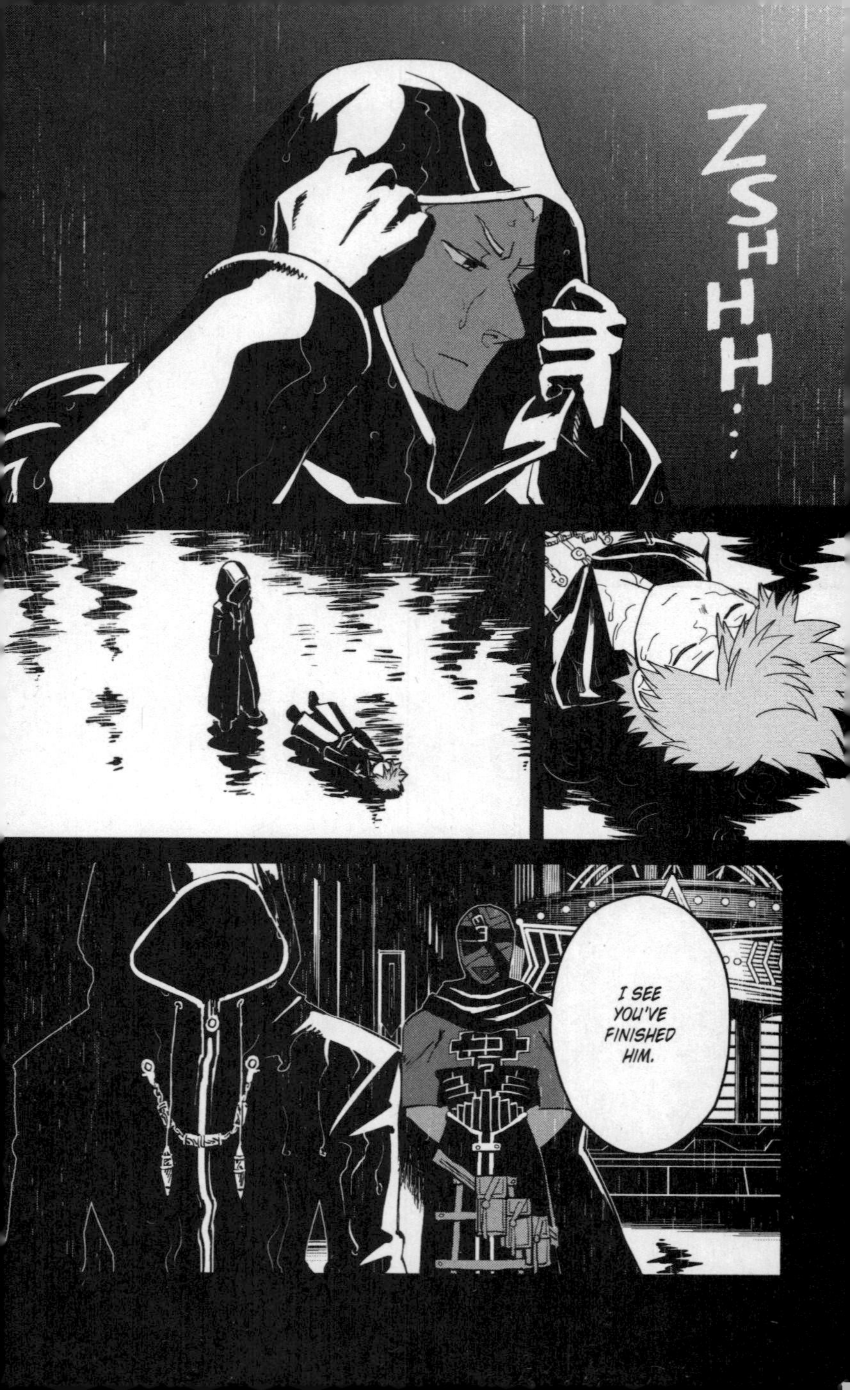
ZSHHH...
I SEE YOU'VE FINISHED HIM.

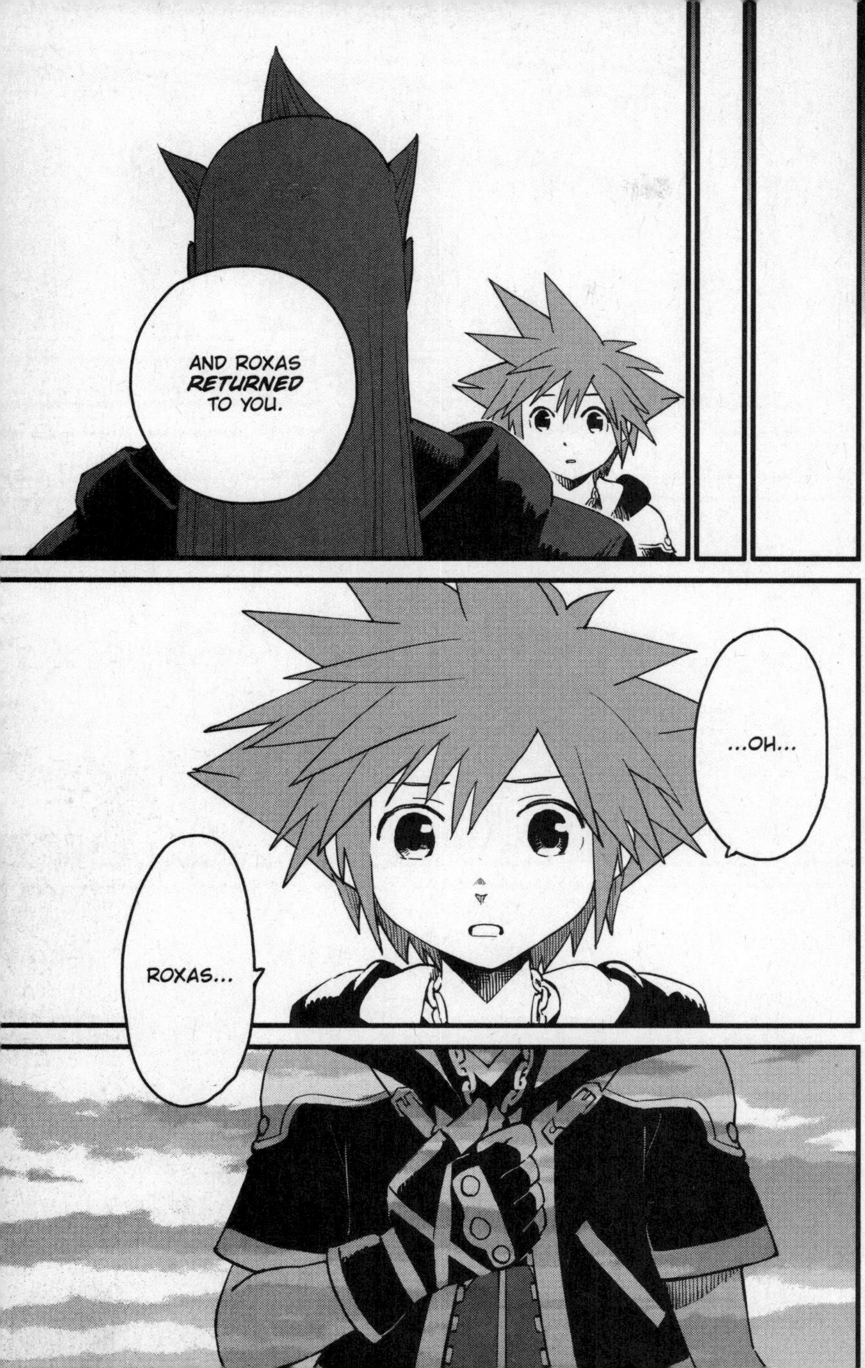
AND ROXAS RETURNED TO YOU.
...OH...
ROXAS...

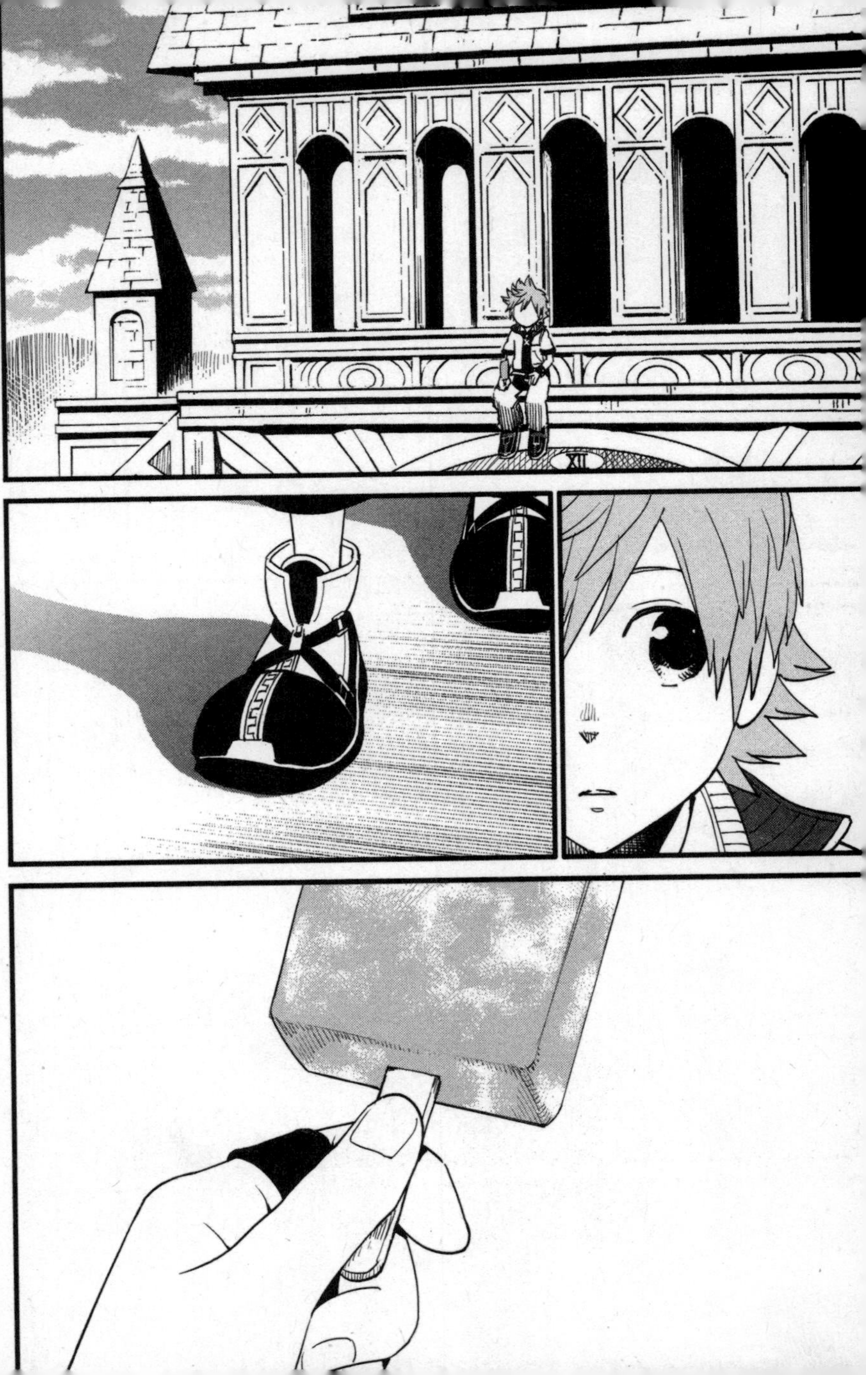

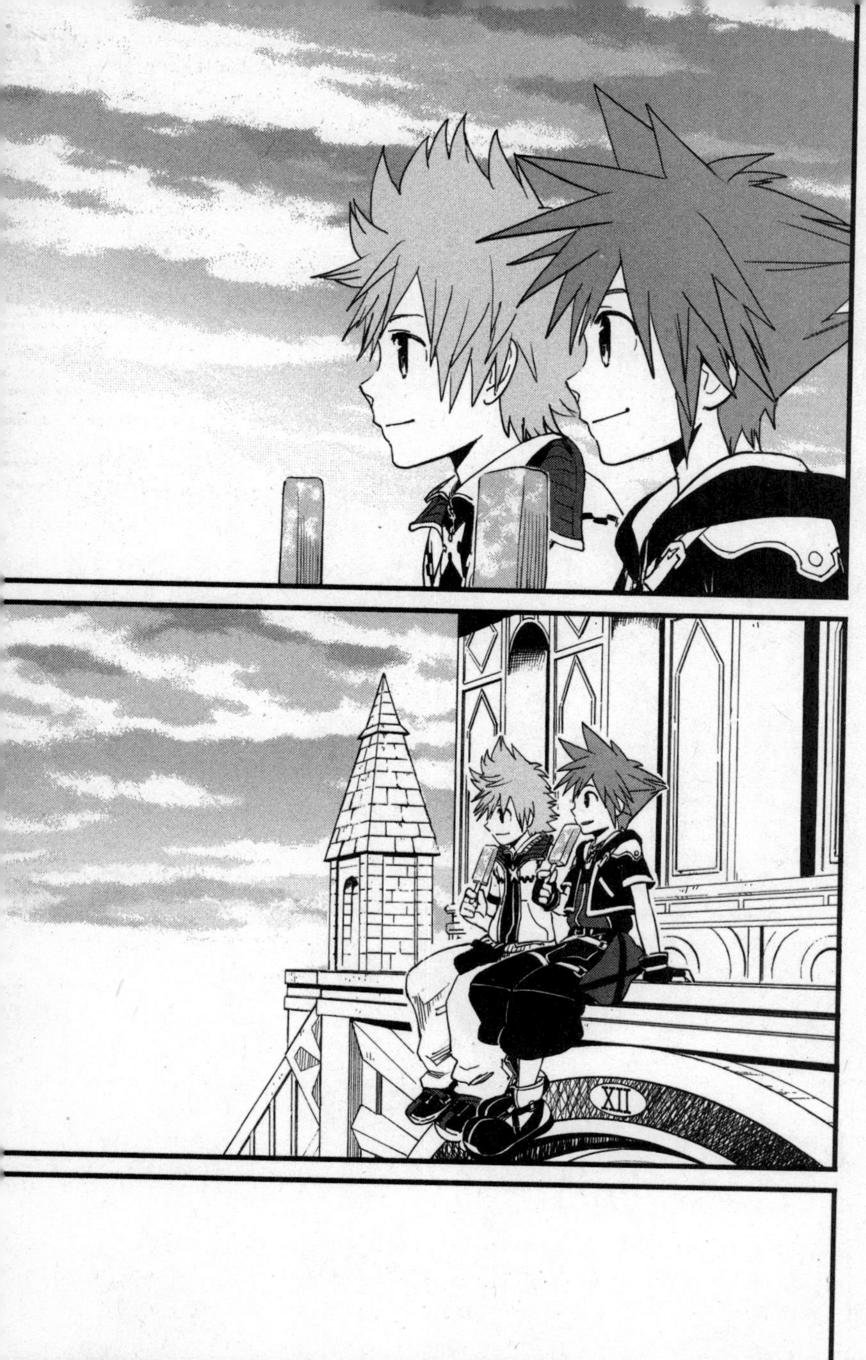
XII

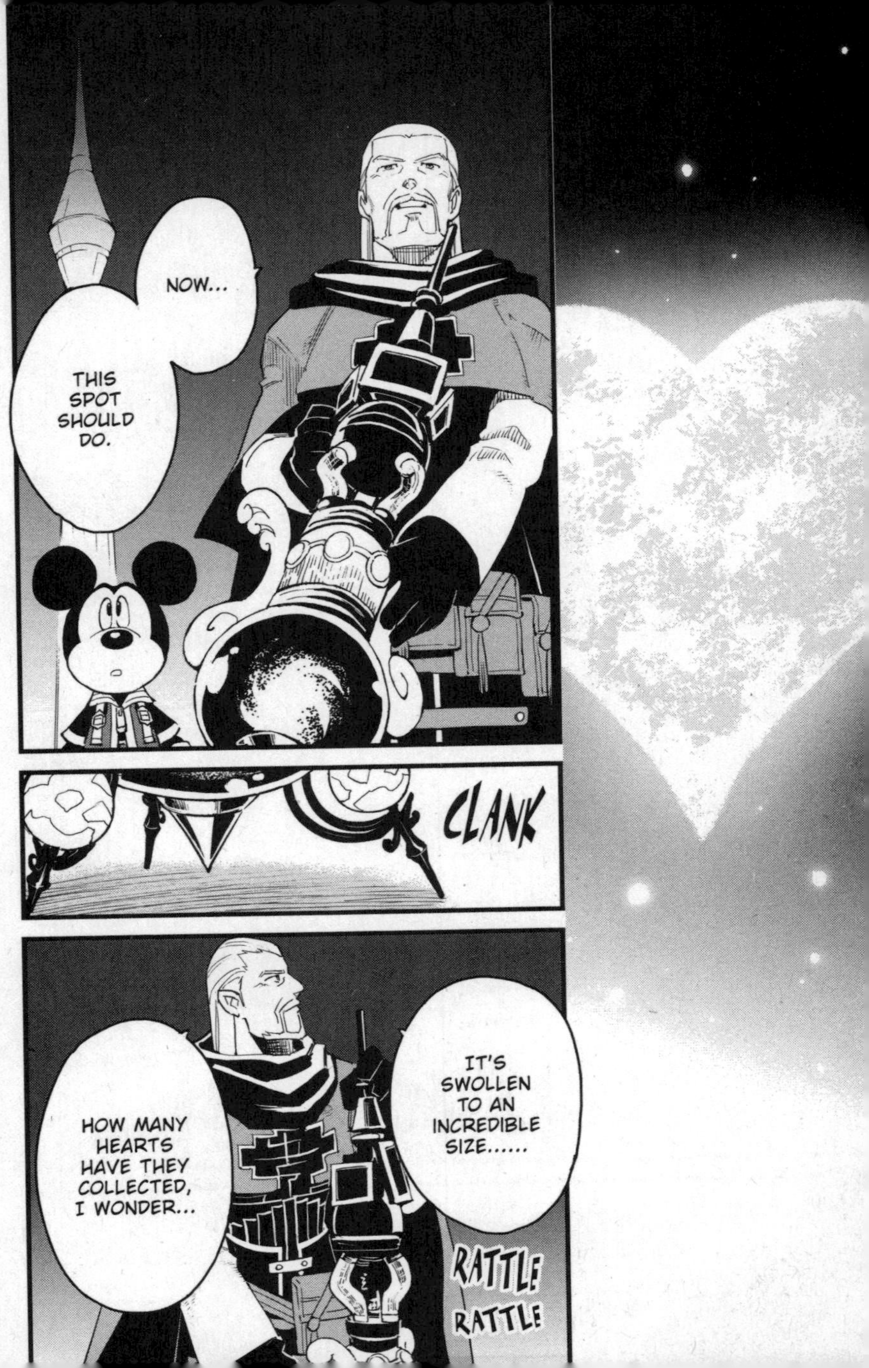
NOW...
THIS SPOT SHOULD DO.
CLANK
IT'S SWOLLEN TO AN INCREDIBLE SIZE......
HOW MANY HEARTS HAVE THEY COLLECTED, I WONDER...
RATTLE RATTLE

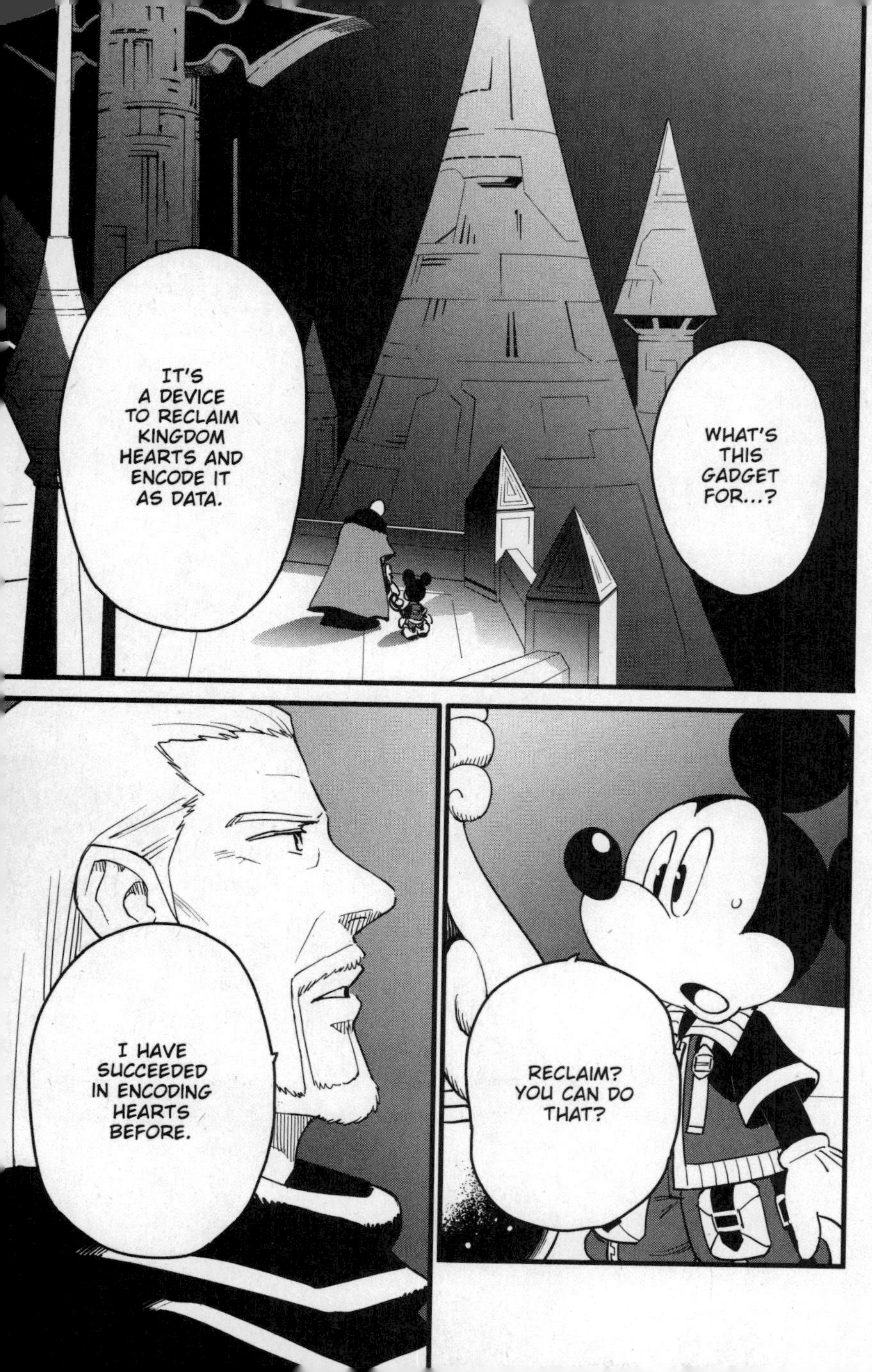
WHAT'S THIS GADGET FOR...?
IT'S A DEVICE TO RECLAIM KINGDOM HEARTS AND ENCODE IT AS DATA.
RECLAIM? YOU CAN DO THAT?
I HAVE SUCCEEDED IN ENCODING HEARTS BEFORE.

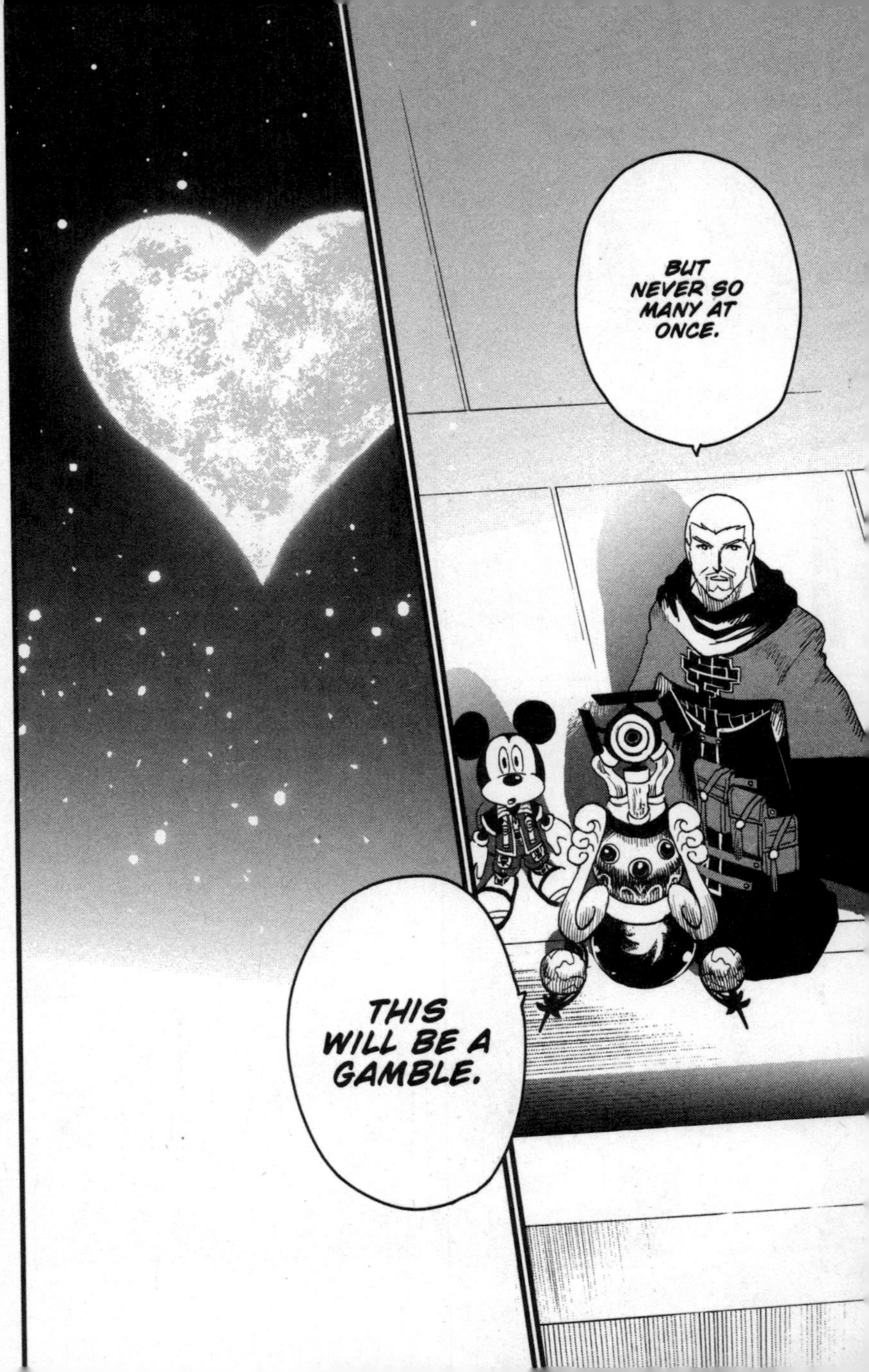
BUT NEVER SO MANY AT ONCE.
THIS WILL BE A GAMBLE.

Chapter 64: Odds of Winning

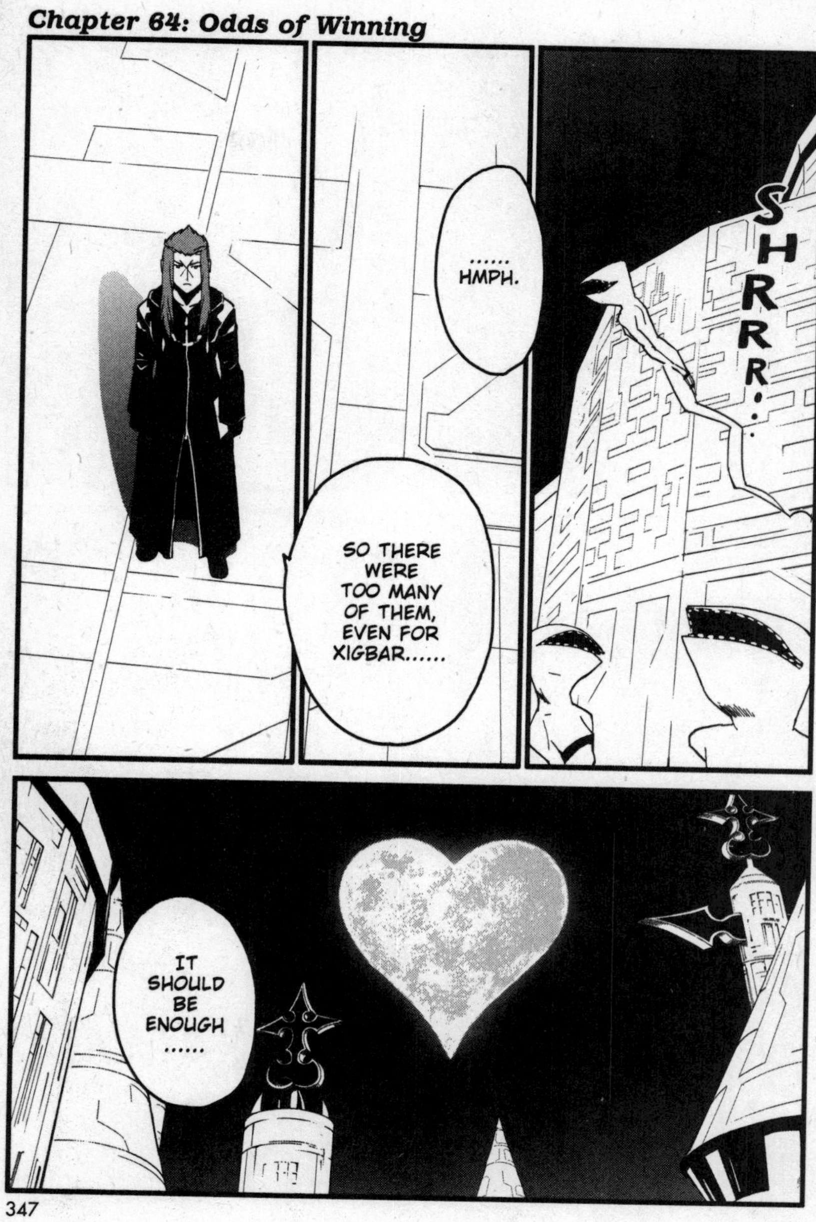
SHRRR..
...... HMPH.
SO THERE WERE TOO MANY OF THEM, EVEN FOR XIGBAR......
IT SHOULD BE ENOUGH ......

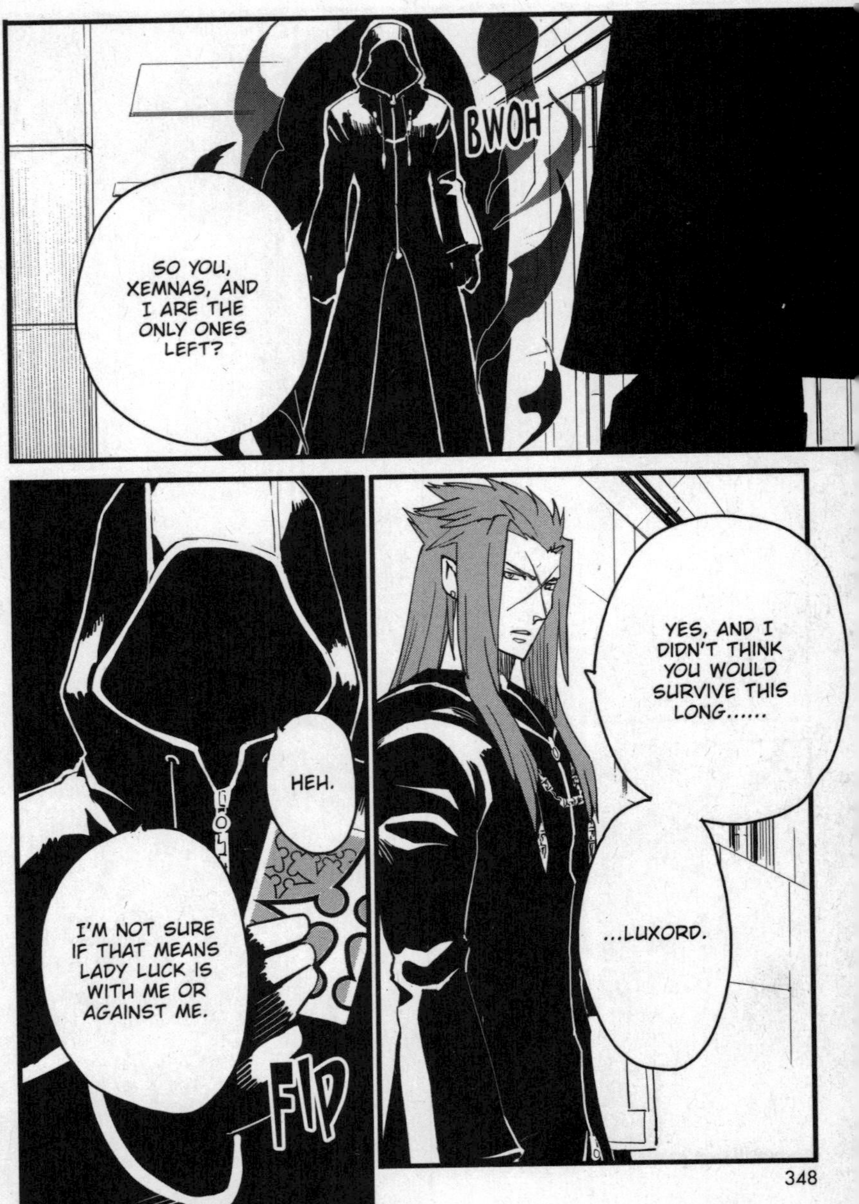
BWOH
SO YOU, XEMNAS, AND I ARE THE ONLY ONES LEFT?
YES, AND I DIDN'T THINK YOU WOULD SURVIVE THIS LONG......
...LUXORD.
HEH.
I'M NOT SURE IF THAT MEANS LADY LUCK IS WITH ME OR AGAINST ME.
FID

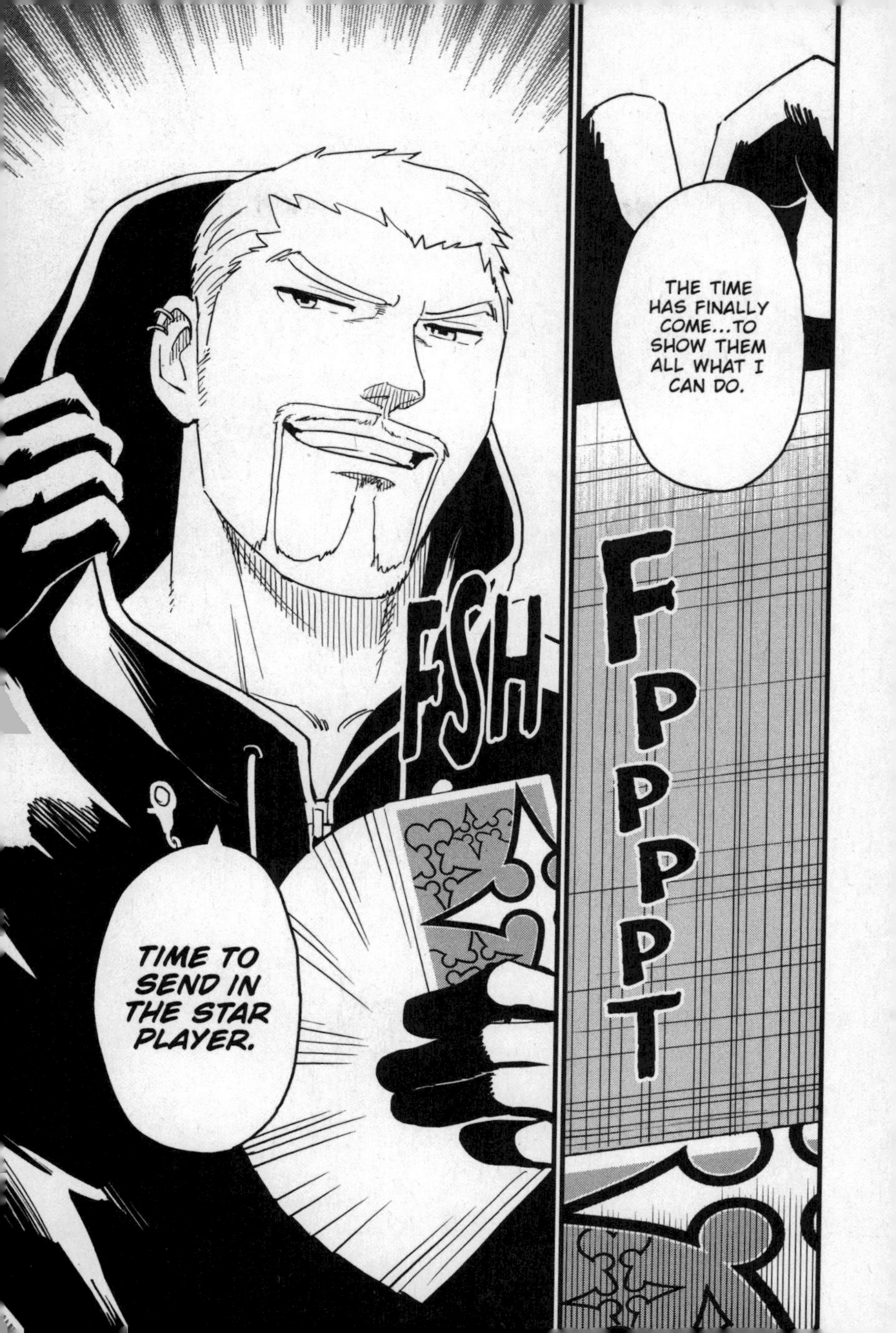
THE TIME HAS FINALLY COME...TO SHOW THEM ALL WHAT I CAN DO.
FPPPT
FSH
TIME TO SEND IN THE STAR PLAYER.

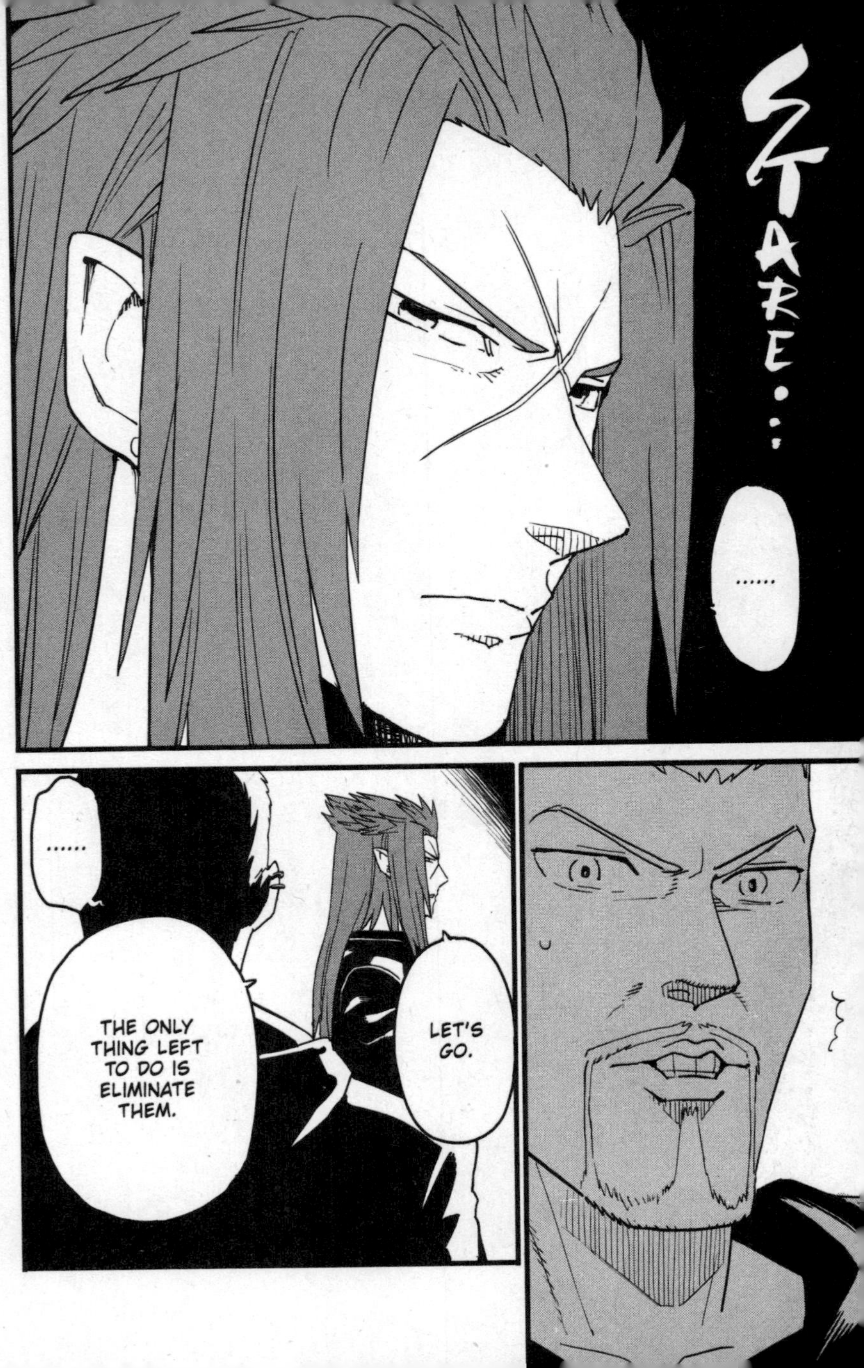
STARE...
......
......
THE ONLY THING LEFT TO DO IS ELIMINATE THEM.
LET'S GO.

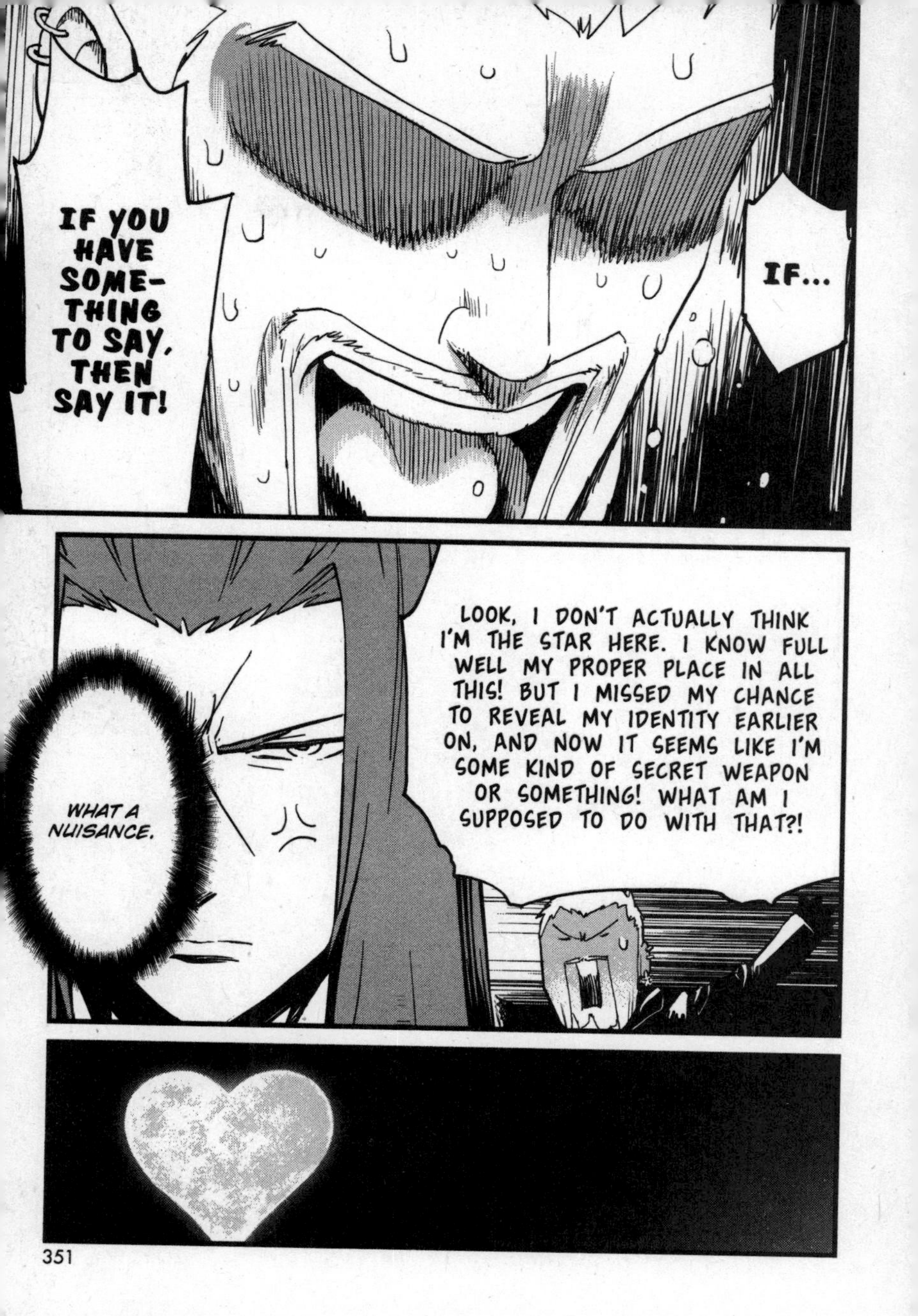
IF...
IF YOU HAVE SOME-THING TO SAY, THEN SAY IT!
LOOK, I DON'T ACTUALLY THINK I'M THE STAR HERE. I KNOW FULL WELL MY PROPER PLACE IN ALL THIS! BUT I MISSED MY CHANCE TO REVEAL MY IDENTITY EARLIER ON, AND NOW IT SEEMS LIKE I'M SOME KIND OF SECRET WEAPON OR SOMETHING! WHAT AM I SUPPOSED TO DO WITH THAT?!
WHAT A NUISANCE.

Chapter 64: Odds of Winning

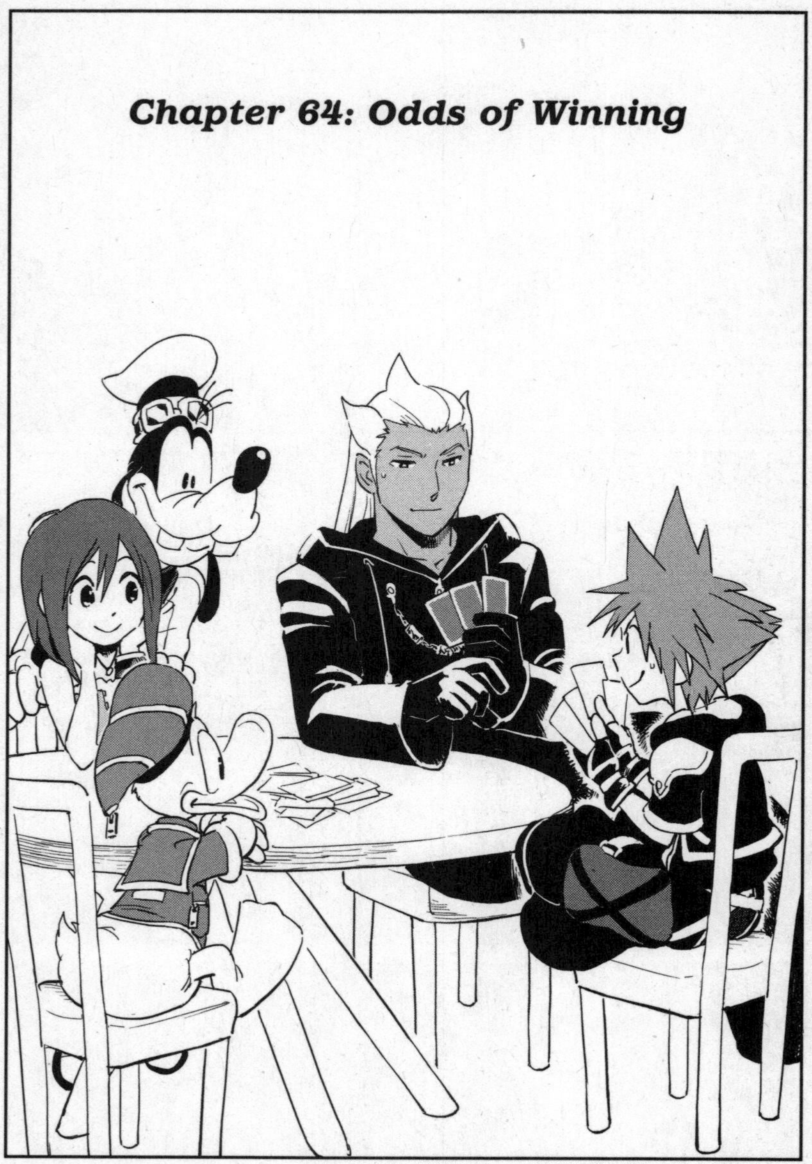

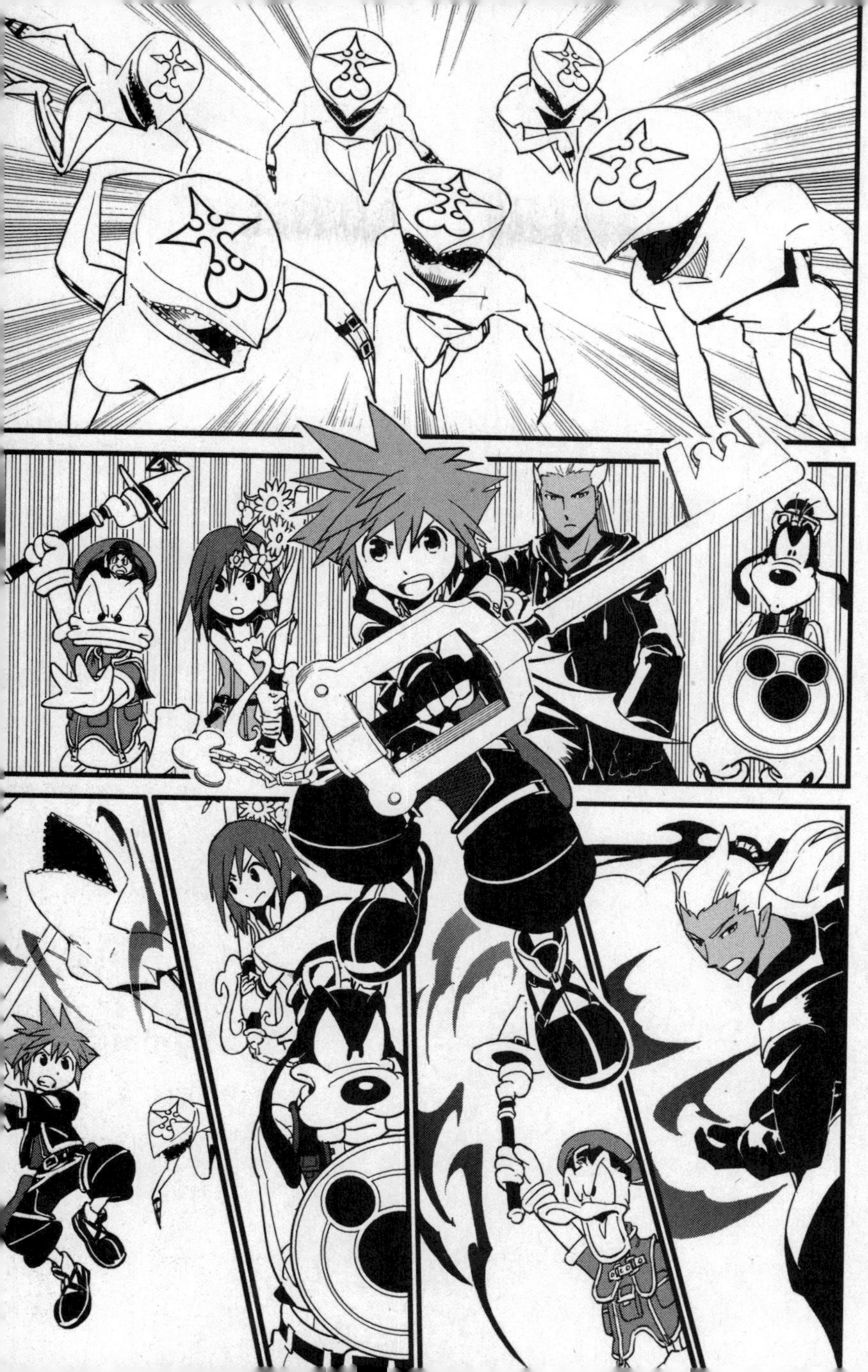

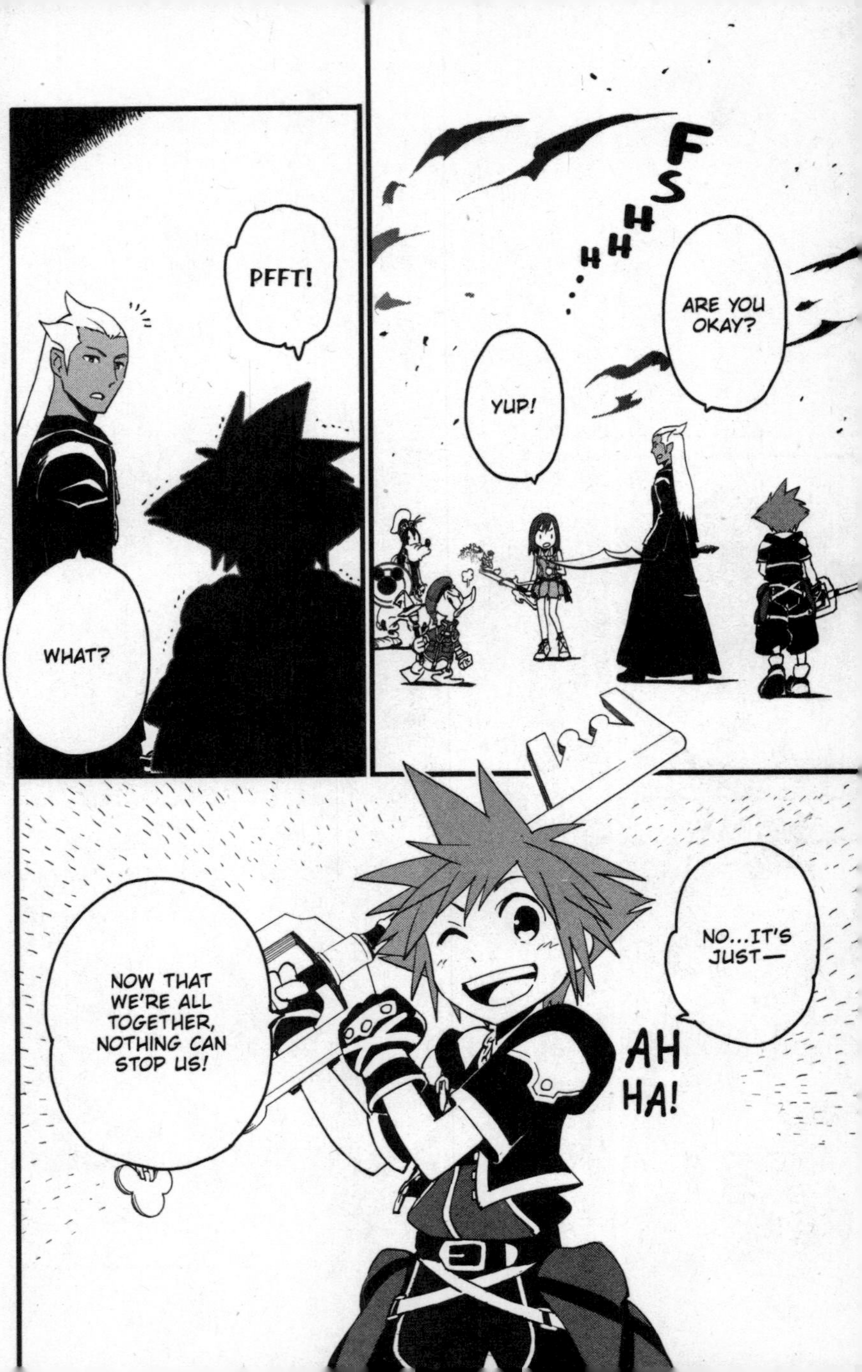
FSHHH...
ARE YOU OKAY?
YUP!
PFFT!
WHAT?
NO...IT'S JUST—
AH HA!
NOW THAT WE'RE ALL TOGETHER, NOTHING CAN STOP US!

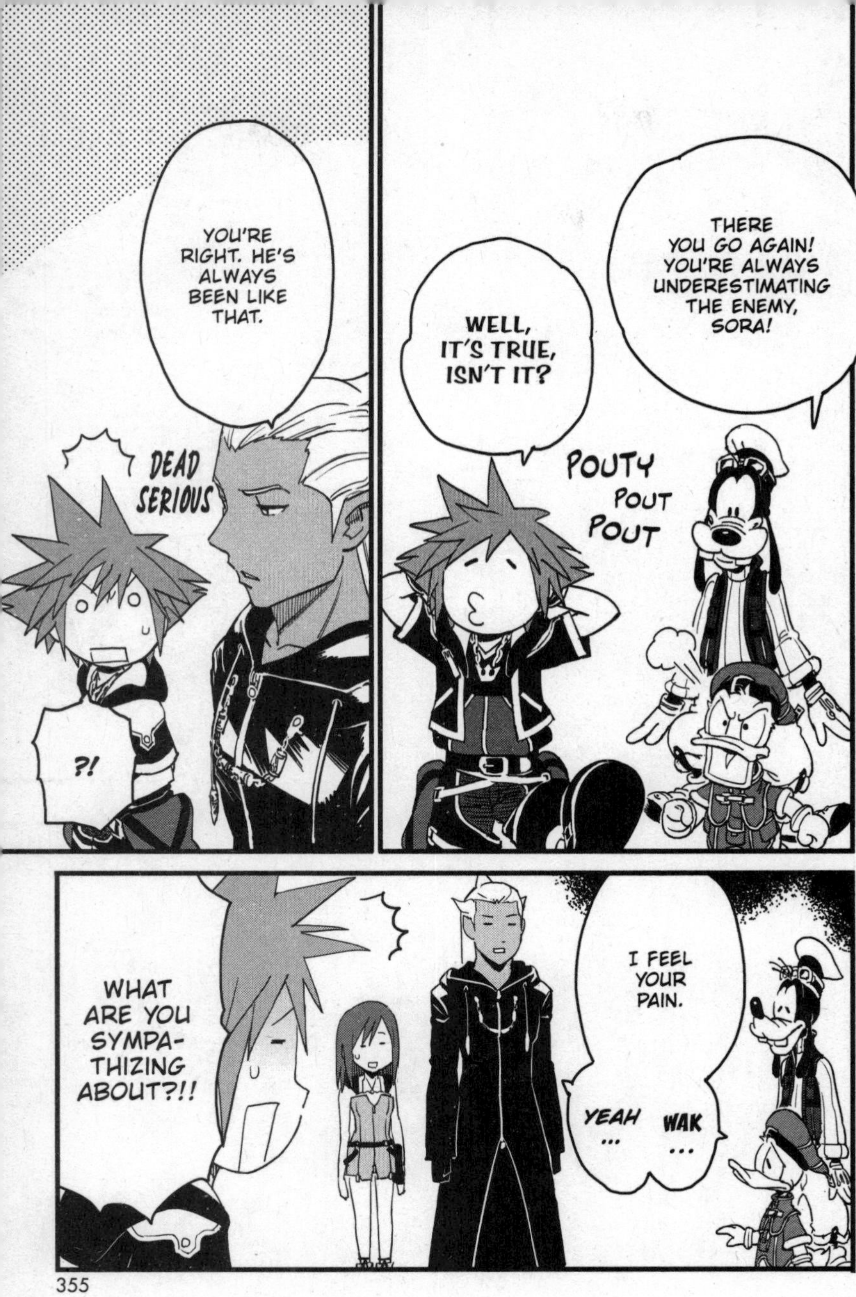
THERE YOU GO AGAIN! YOU'RE ALWAYS UNDERESTIMATING THE ENEMY, SORA!
WELL, IT'S TRUE, ISN'T IT?
POUTY POUT POUT
YOU'RE RIGHT. HE'S ALWAYS BEEN LIKE THAT.
DEAD SERIOUS
?!
I FEEL YOUR PAIN.
YEAH ...
WAK ...
WHAT ARE YOU SYMPA-THIZING ABOUT?!!

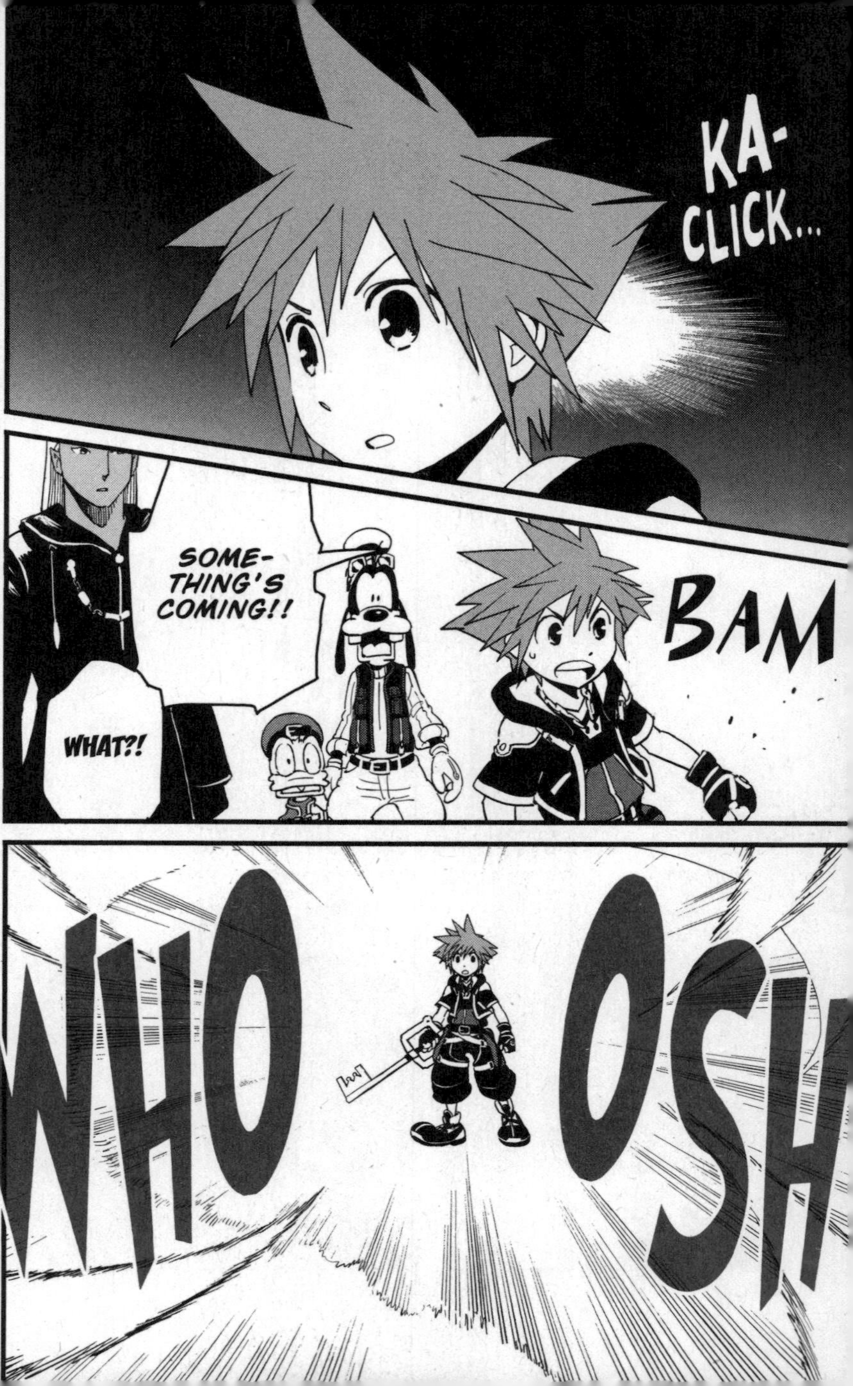
KA-CLICK...
BAM
SOME-THING'S COMING!!
WHAT?!
WHOOSH

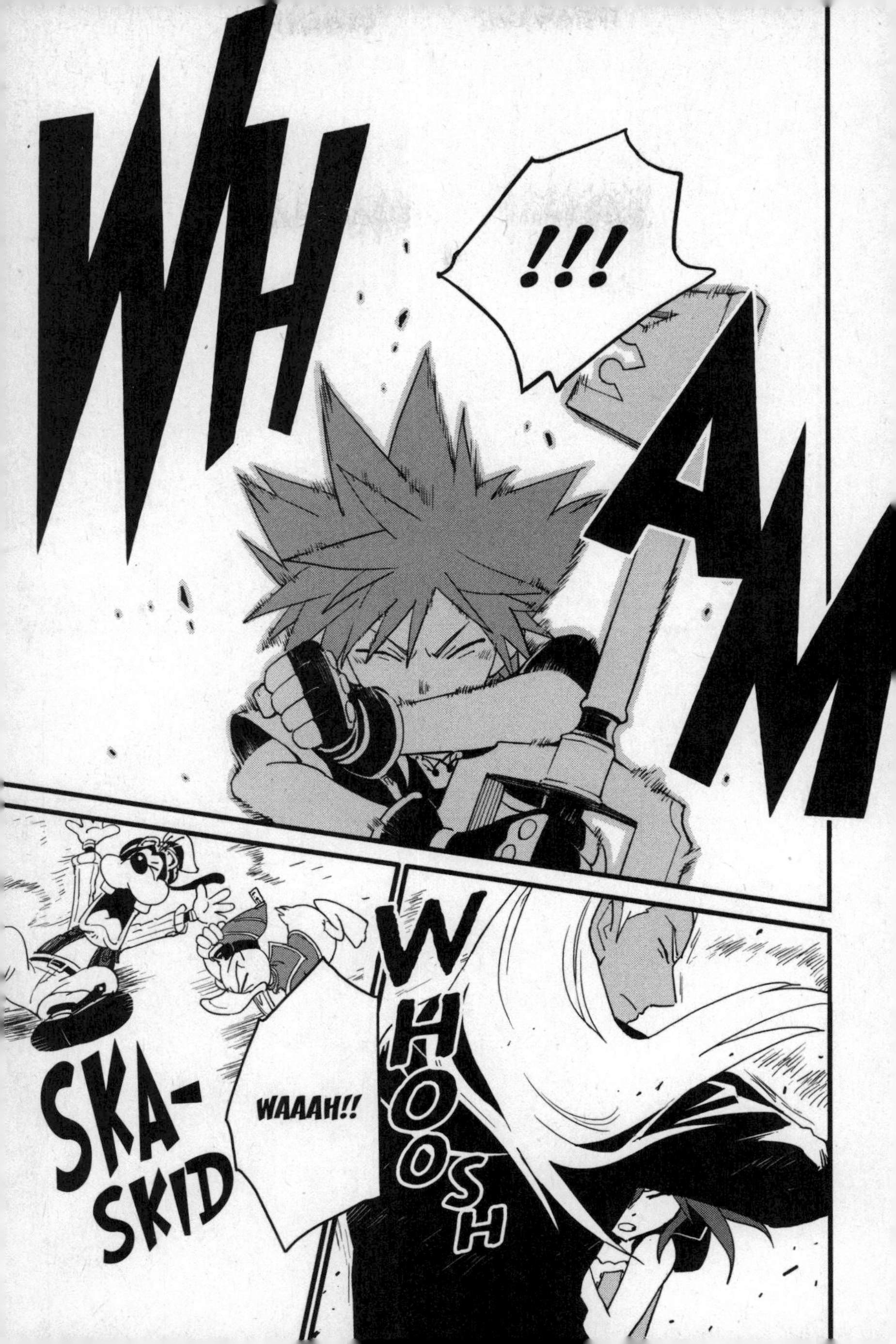
WHAM
!!!
WHOOSH
WAAAH!!
SKA-SKID

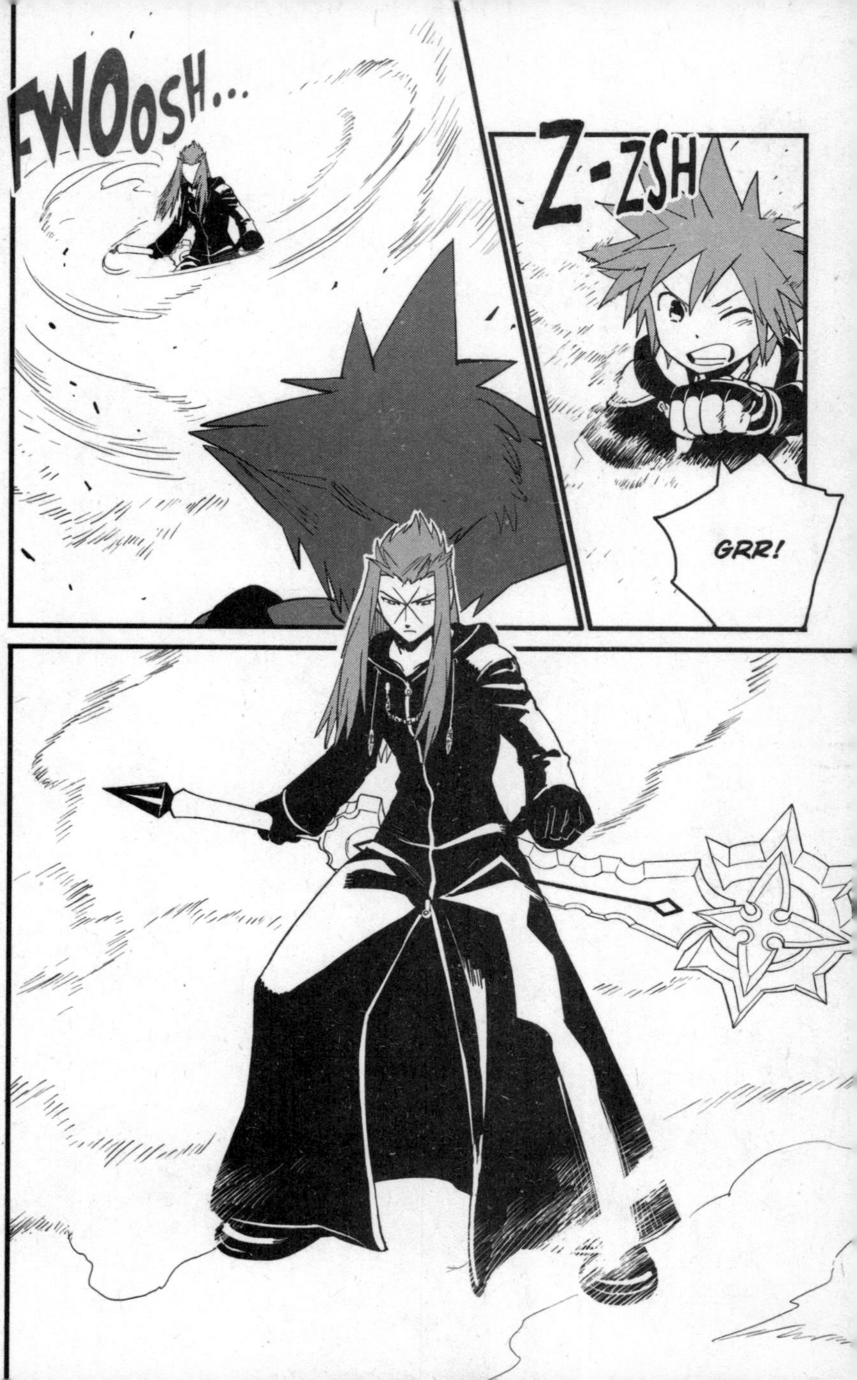
Z-ZSH
GRR!
FWOOSH...

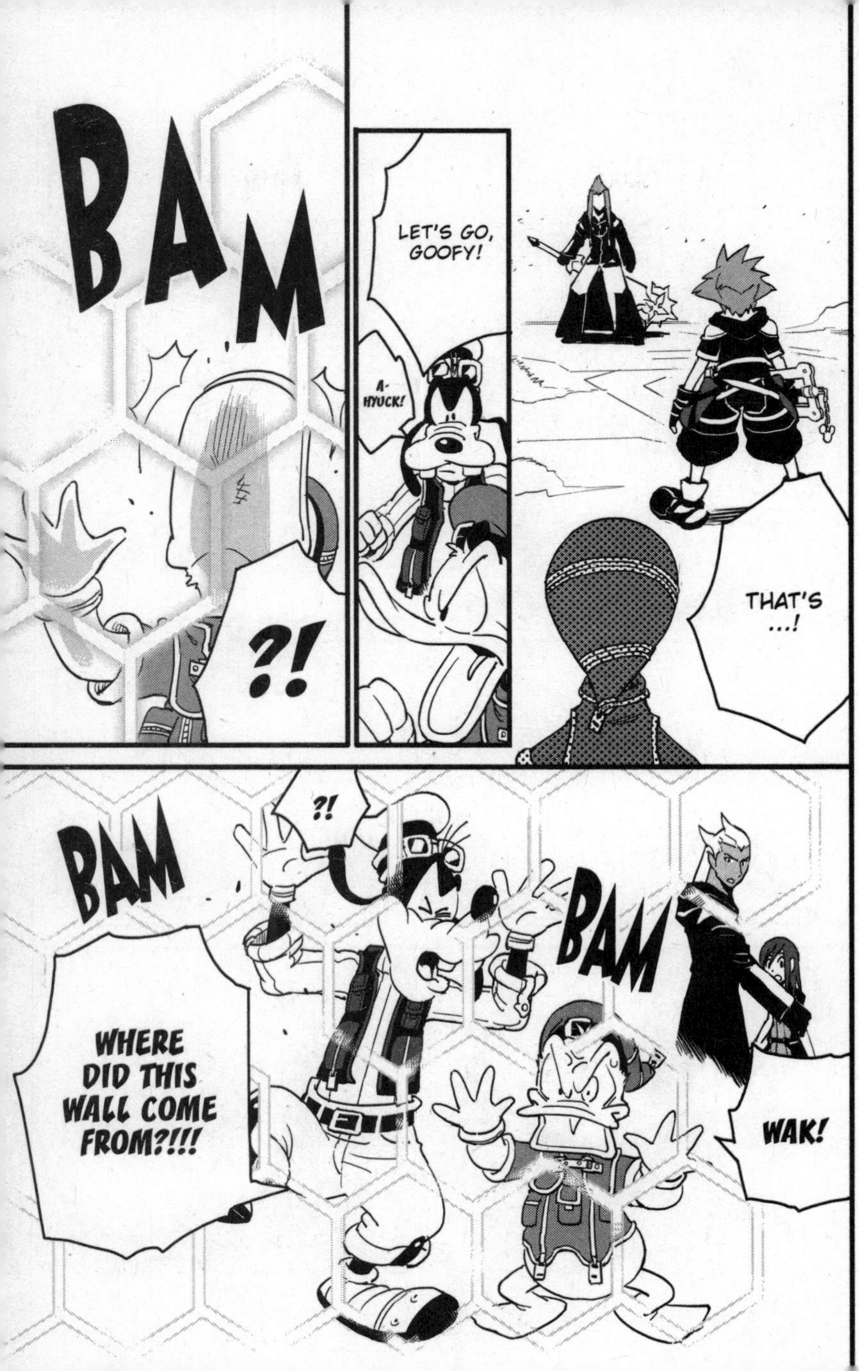
THAT'S ...!
LET'S GO, GOOFY!
A-HYUCK!
BAM
?!
WAK!
BAM
?!
BAM
WHERE DID THIS WALL COME FROM?!!!

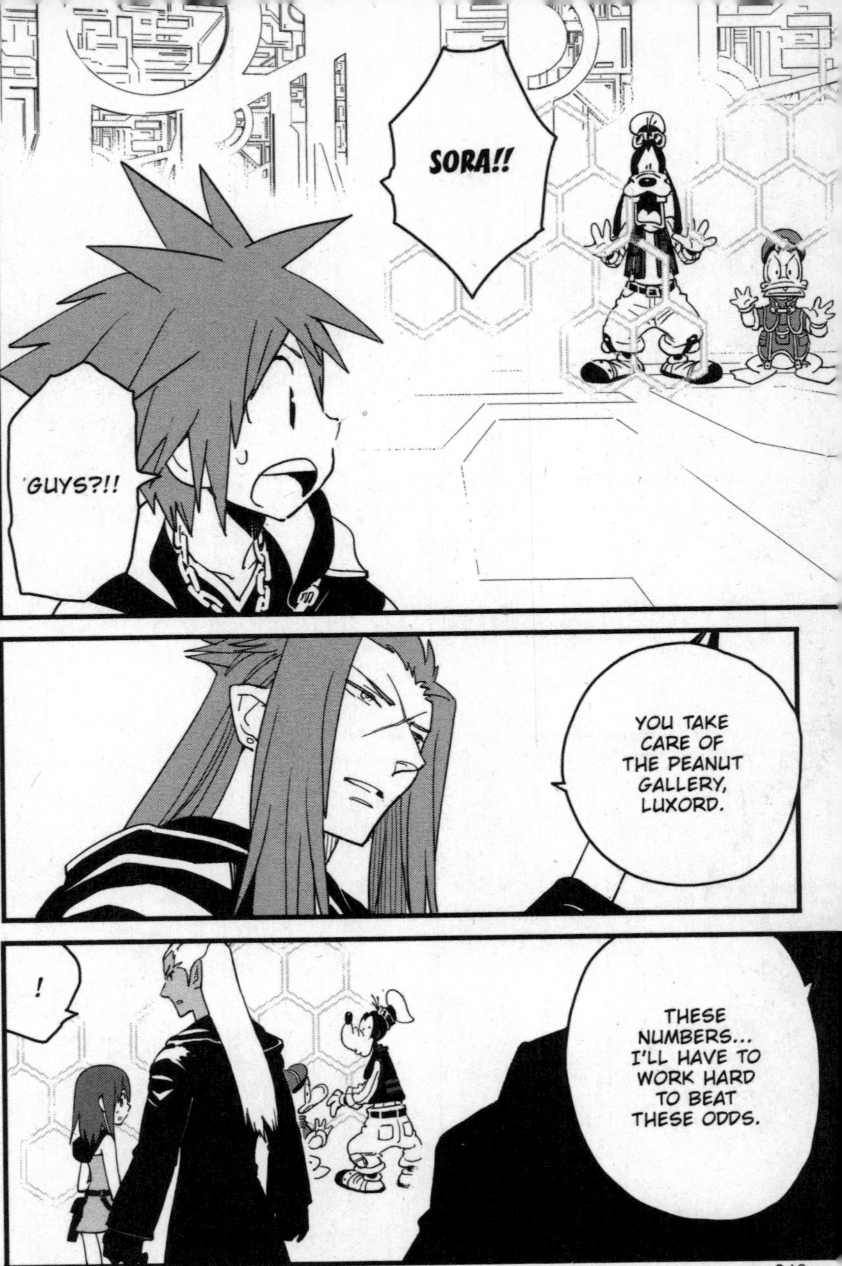
SORA!!
GUYS?!!
YOU TAKE CARE OF THE PEANUT GALLERY, LUXORD.
THESE NUMBERS... I'LL HAVE TO WORK HARD TO BEAT THESE ODDS.
!

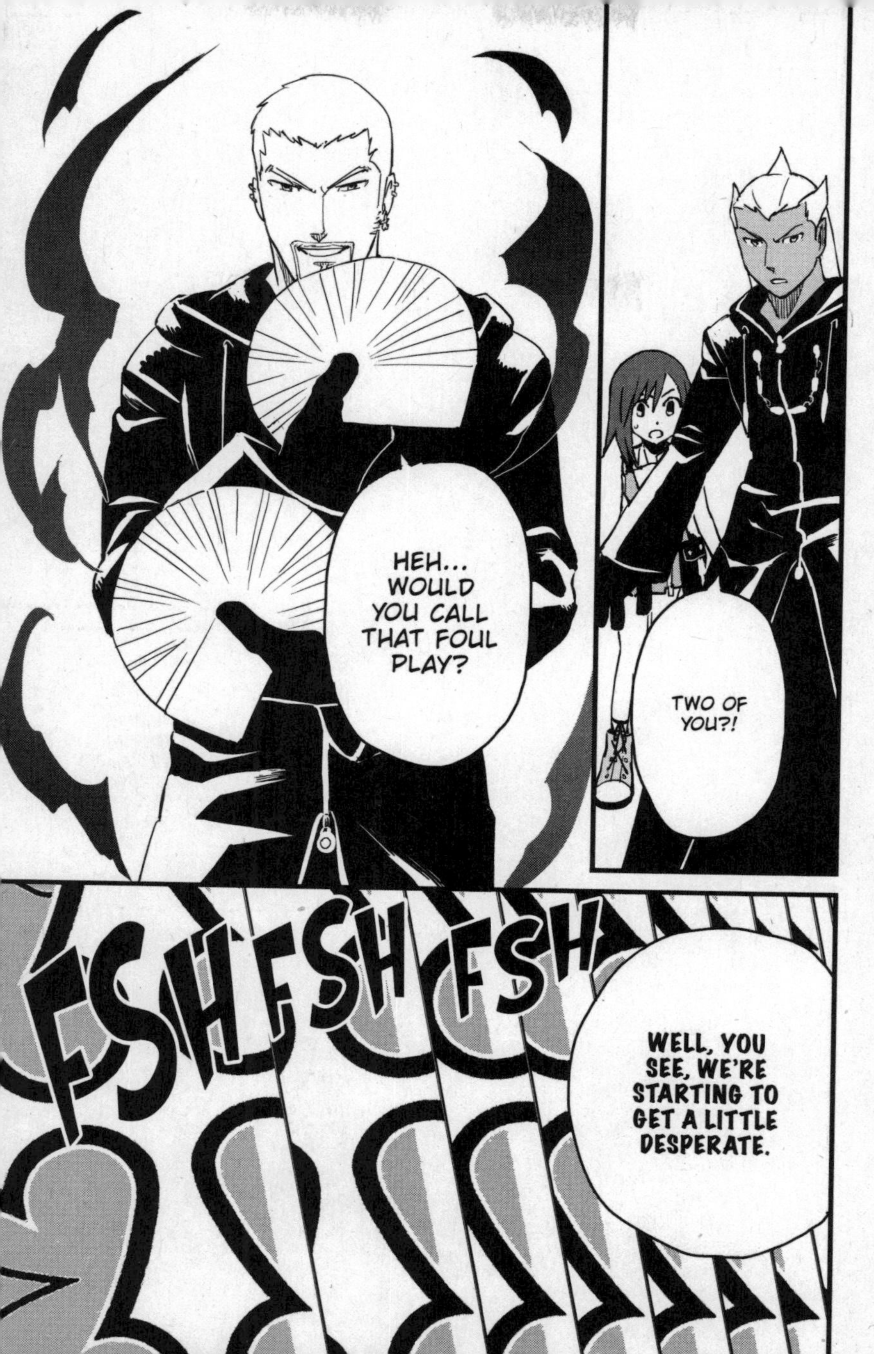
TWO OF YOU?!
HEH... WOULD YOU CALL THAT FOUL PLAY?
FSH FSH FSH
WELL, YOU SEE, WE'RE STARTING TO GET A LITTLE DESPERATE.

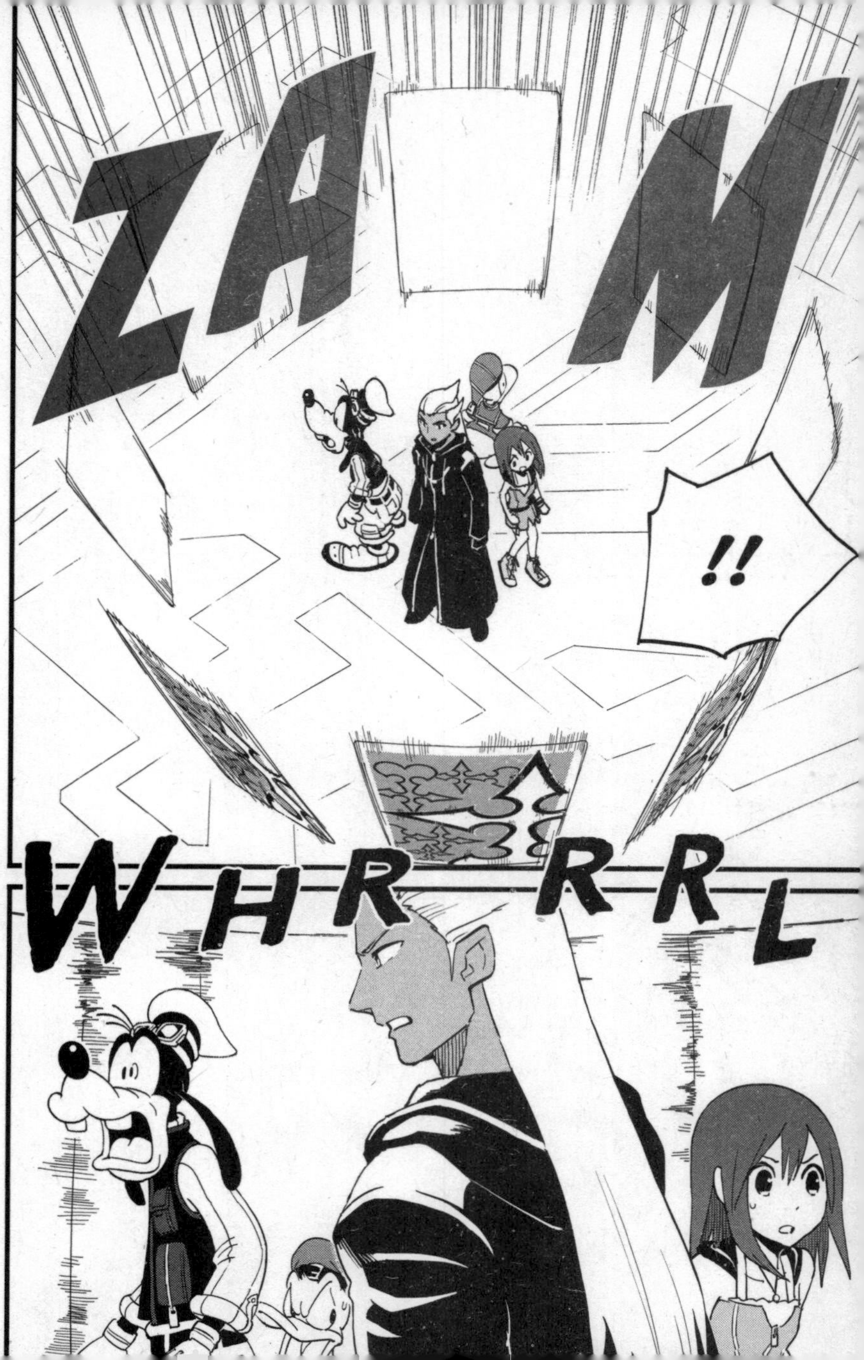
ZAM
!!
WHRRRL

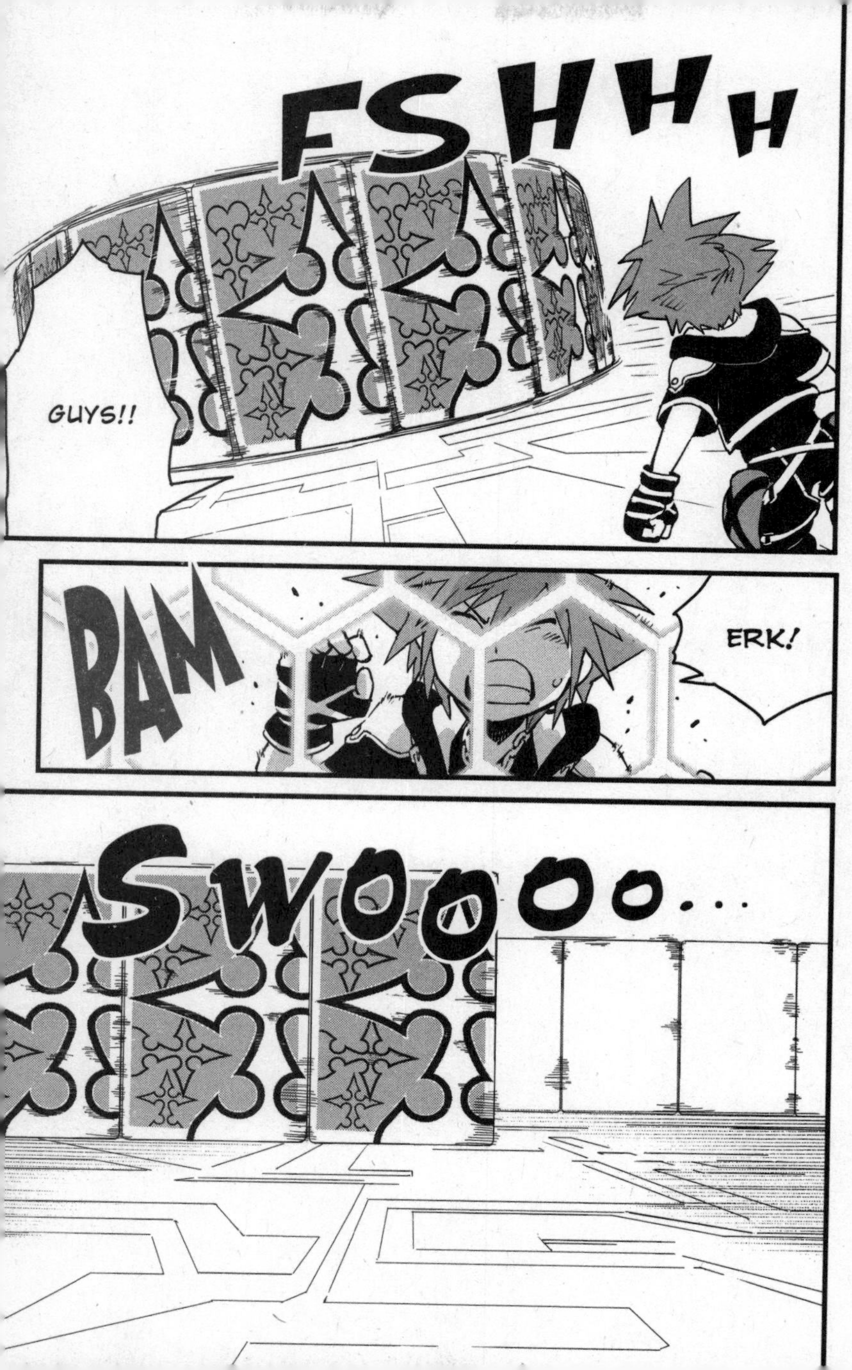
FSHHHH
GUYS!!
ERK!
BAM
SWOOOOO...

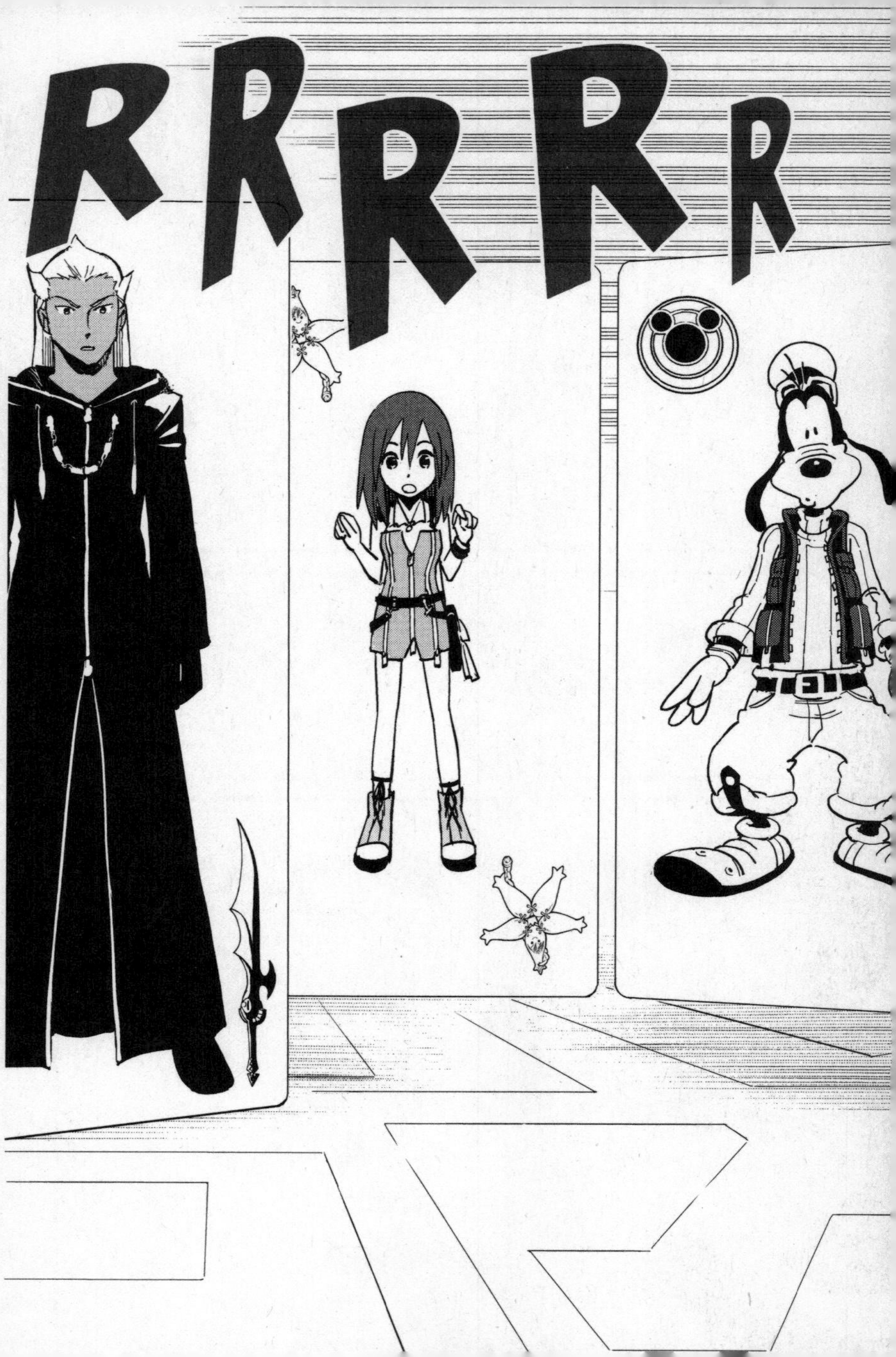
RRRRR

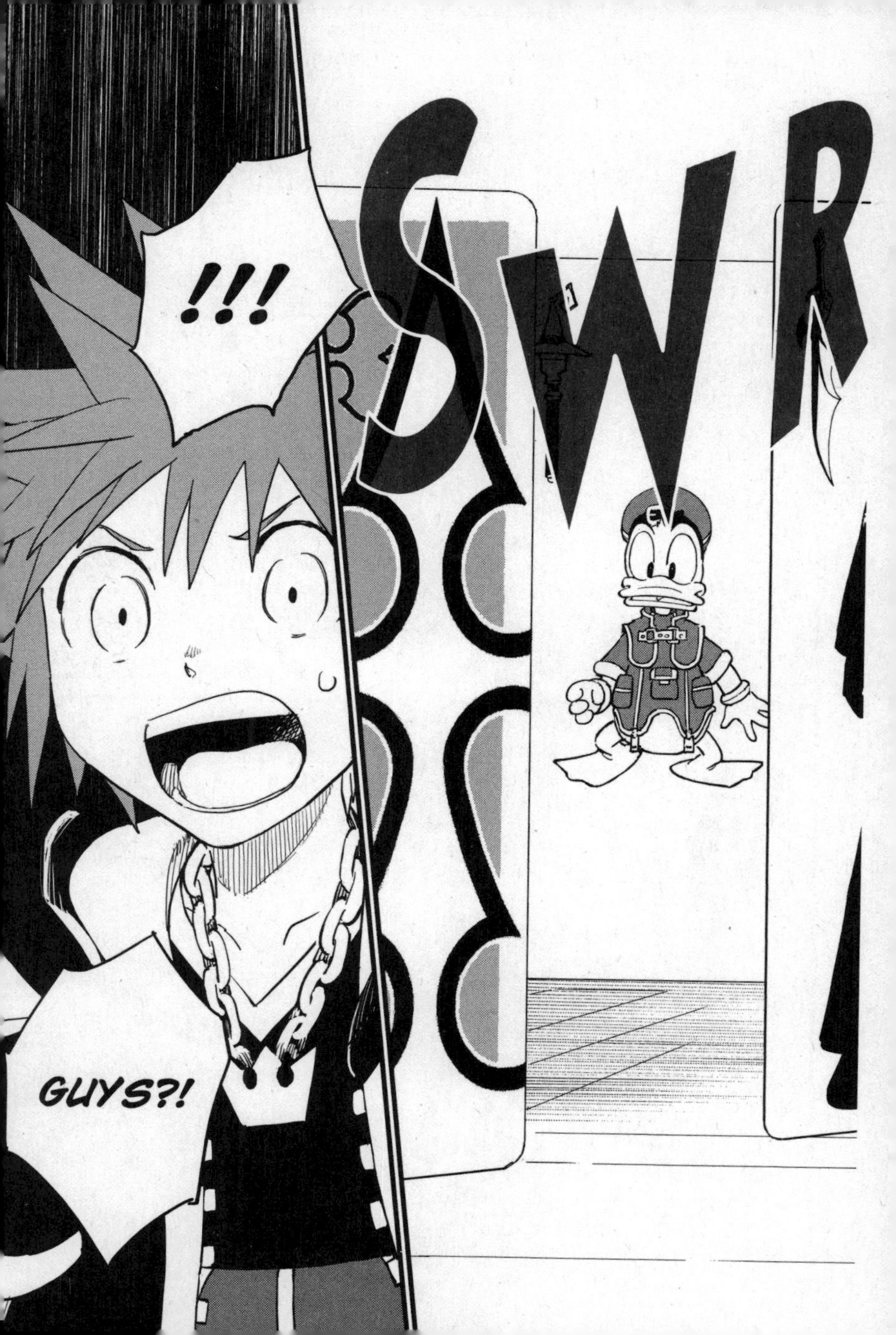
SWR
!!!
GUYS?!

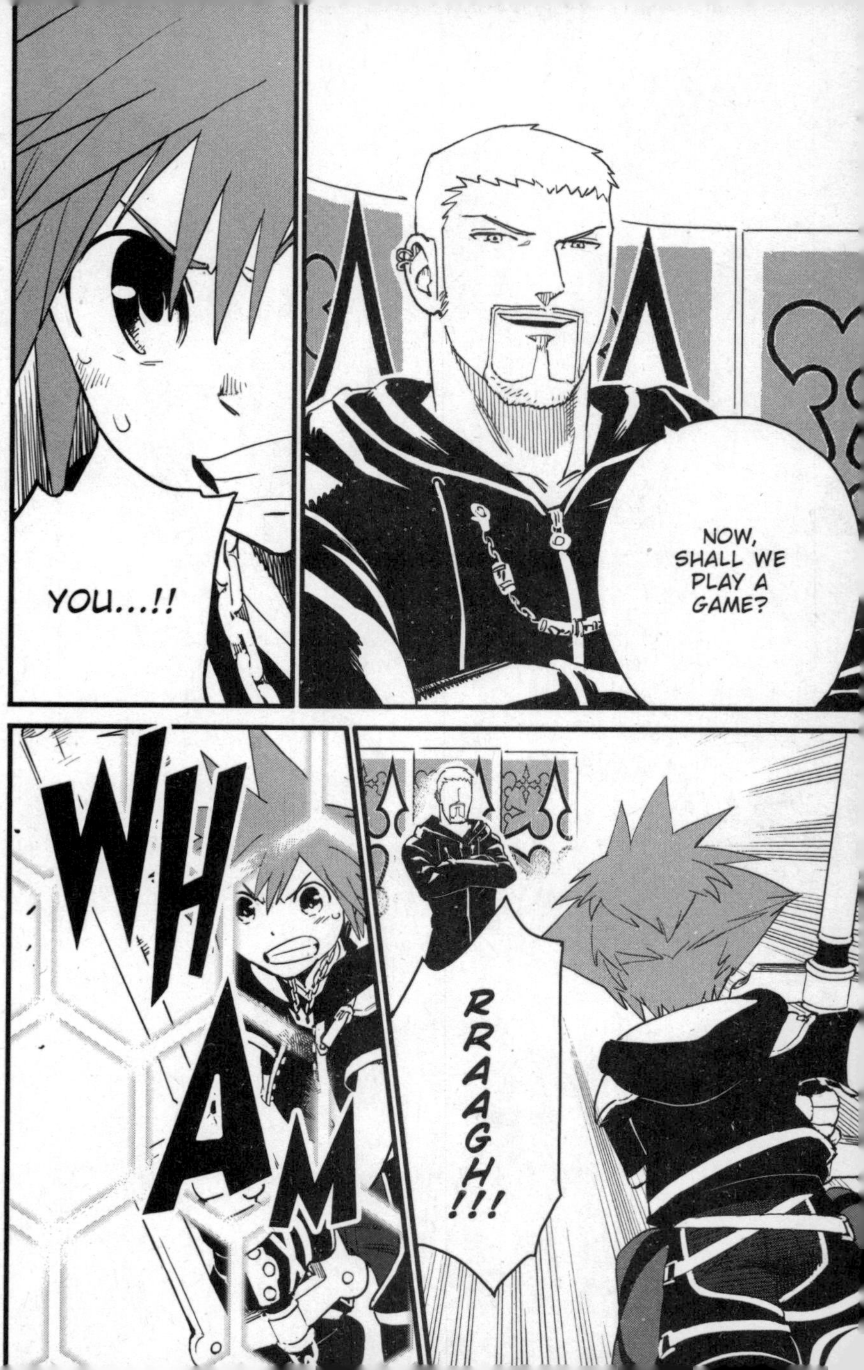
NOW, SHALL WE PLAY A GAME?
YOU...!!
RRAAGH!!!
WHAM

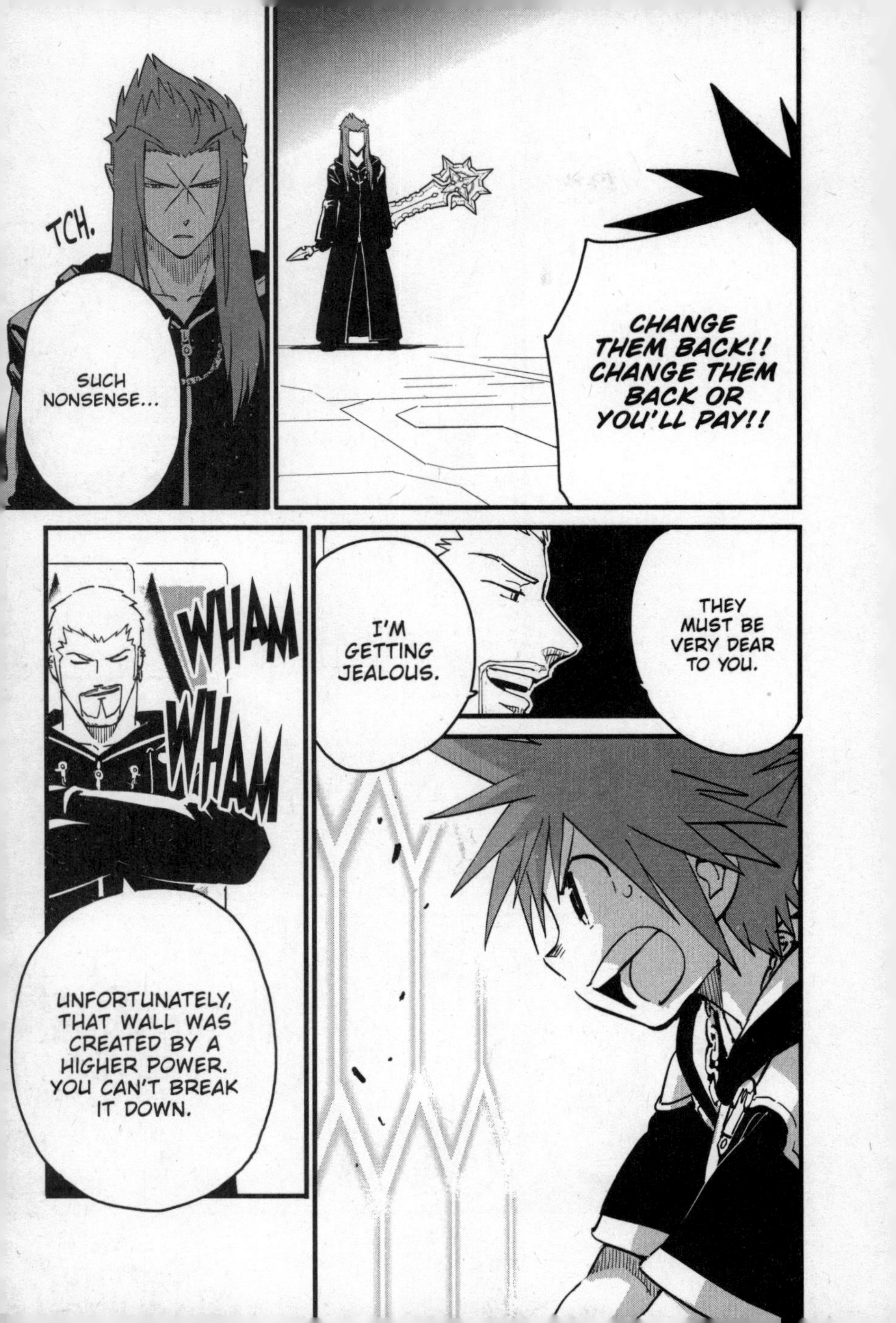
CHANGE THEM BACK!! CHANGE THEM BACK OR YOU'LL PAY!!
TCH.
SUCH NONSENSE...
THEY MUST BE VERY DEAR TO YOU.
I'M GETTING JEALOUS.
WHAM
WHAM
UNFORTUNATELY, THAT WALL WAS CREATED BY A HIGHER POWER. YOU CAN'T BREAK IT DOWN.

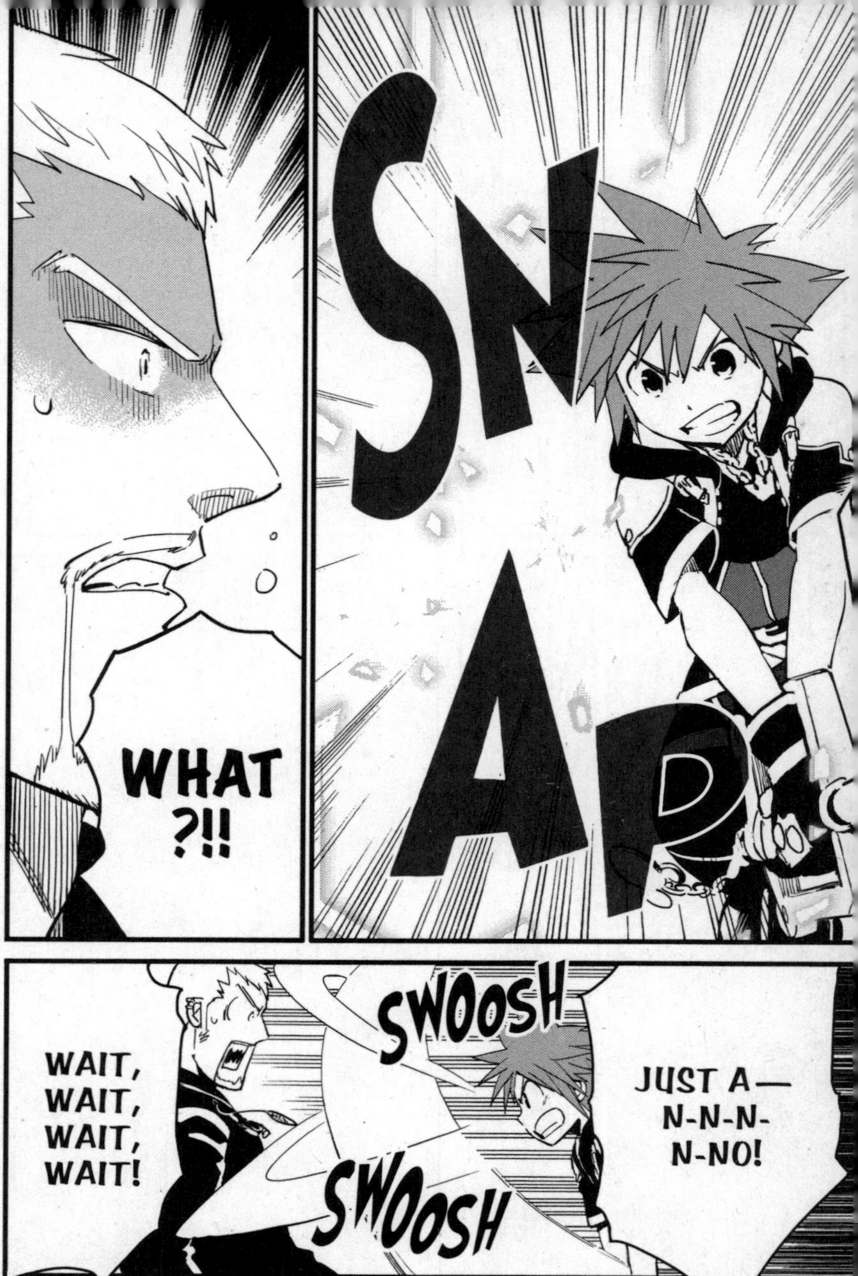
SNAP
WHAT ?!!
JUST A— N-N-N-N-NO!
SWOOSH
WAIT, WAIT, WAIT, WAIT!
SWOOSH

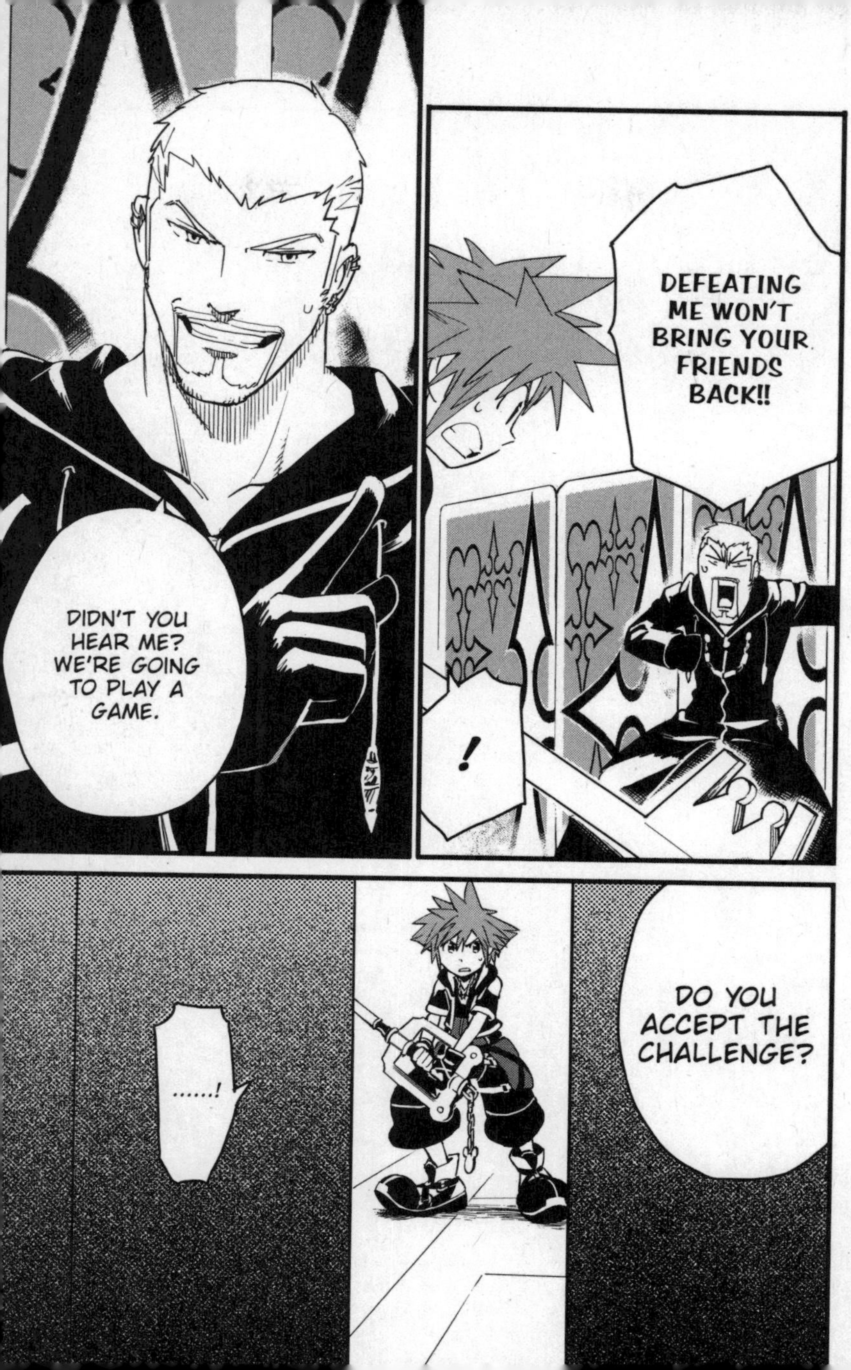
DEFEATING ME WON'T BRING YOUR FRIENDS BACK!!
!
DIDN'T YOU HEAR ME? WE'RE GOING TO PLAY A GAME.
DO YOU ACCEPT THE CHALLENGE?
......!

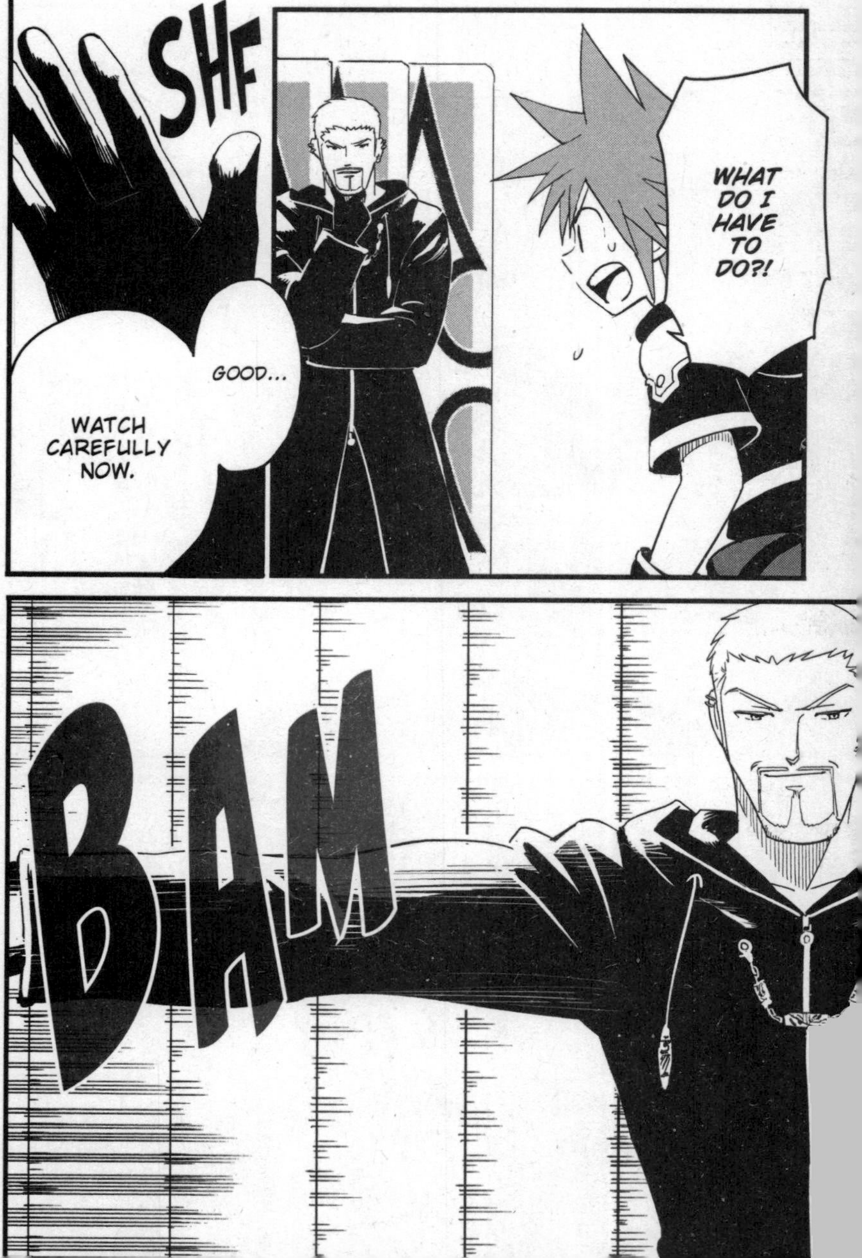
WHAT DO I HAVE TO DO?!
GOOD...
WATCH CAREFULLY NOW.
SHF
BAM

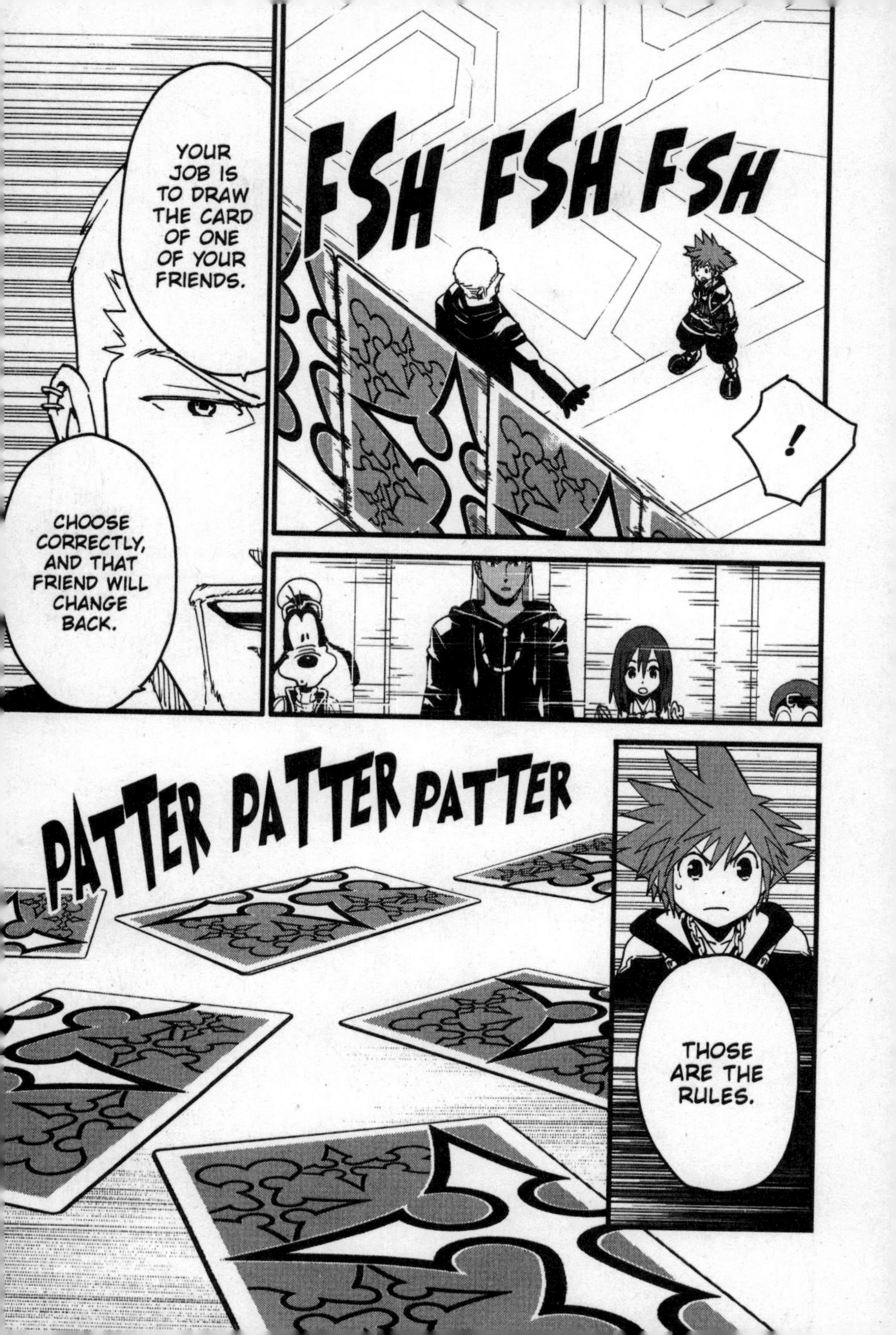
FSH FSH FSH
!
YOUR JOB IS TO DRAW THE CARD OF ONE OF YOUR FRIENDS.
CHOOSE CORRECTLY, AND THAT FRIEND WILL CHANGE BACK.
THOSE ARE THE RULES.
PATTER PATTER PATTER

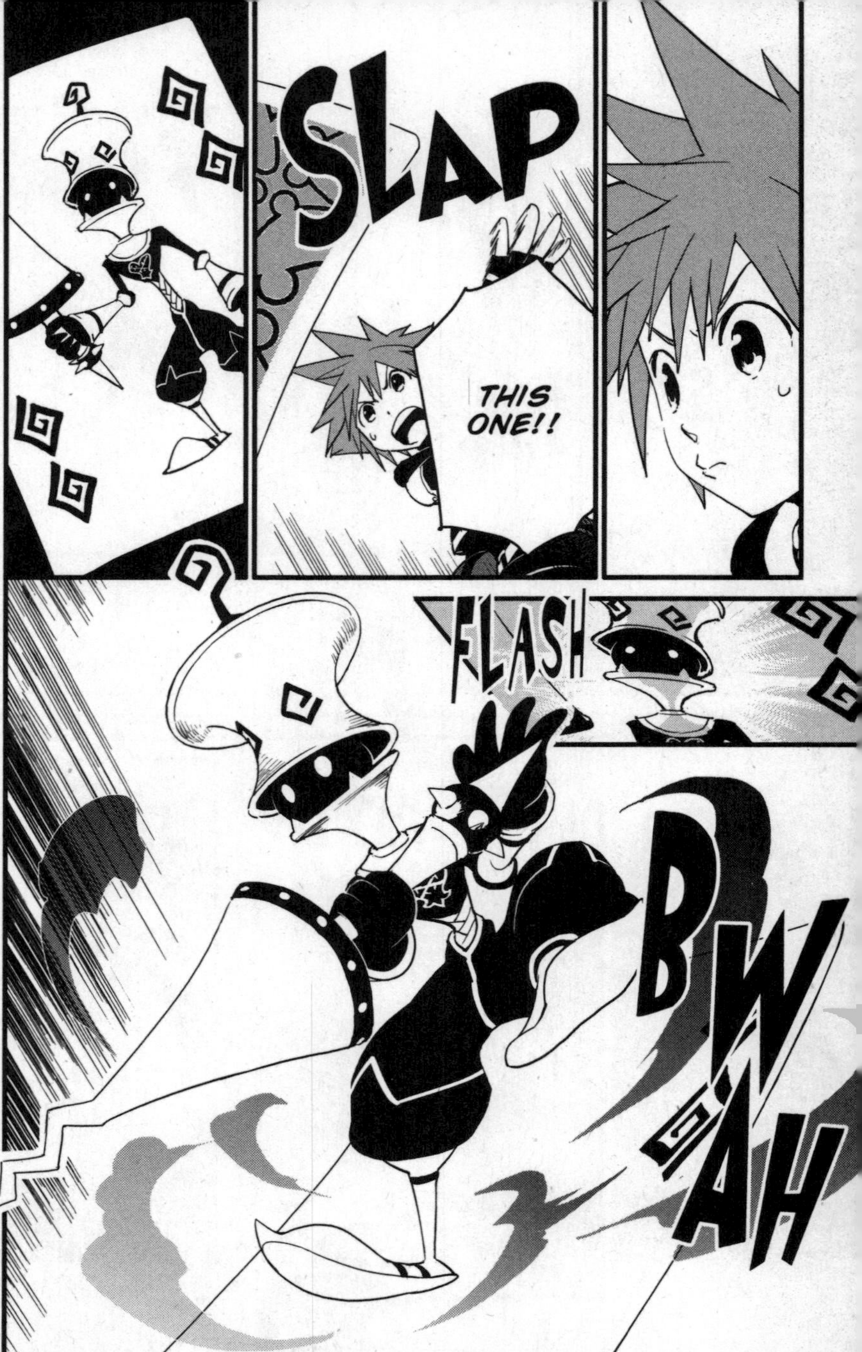
SLAP
THIS ONE!!
FLASH
BWAAH

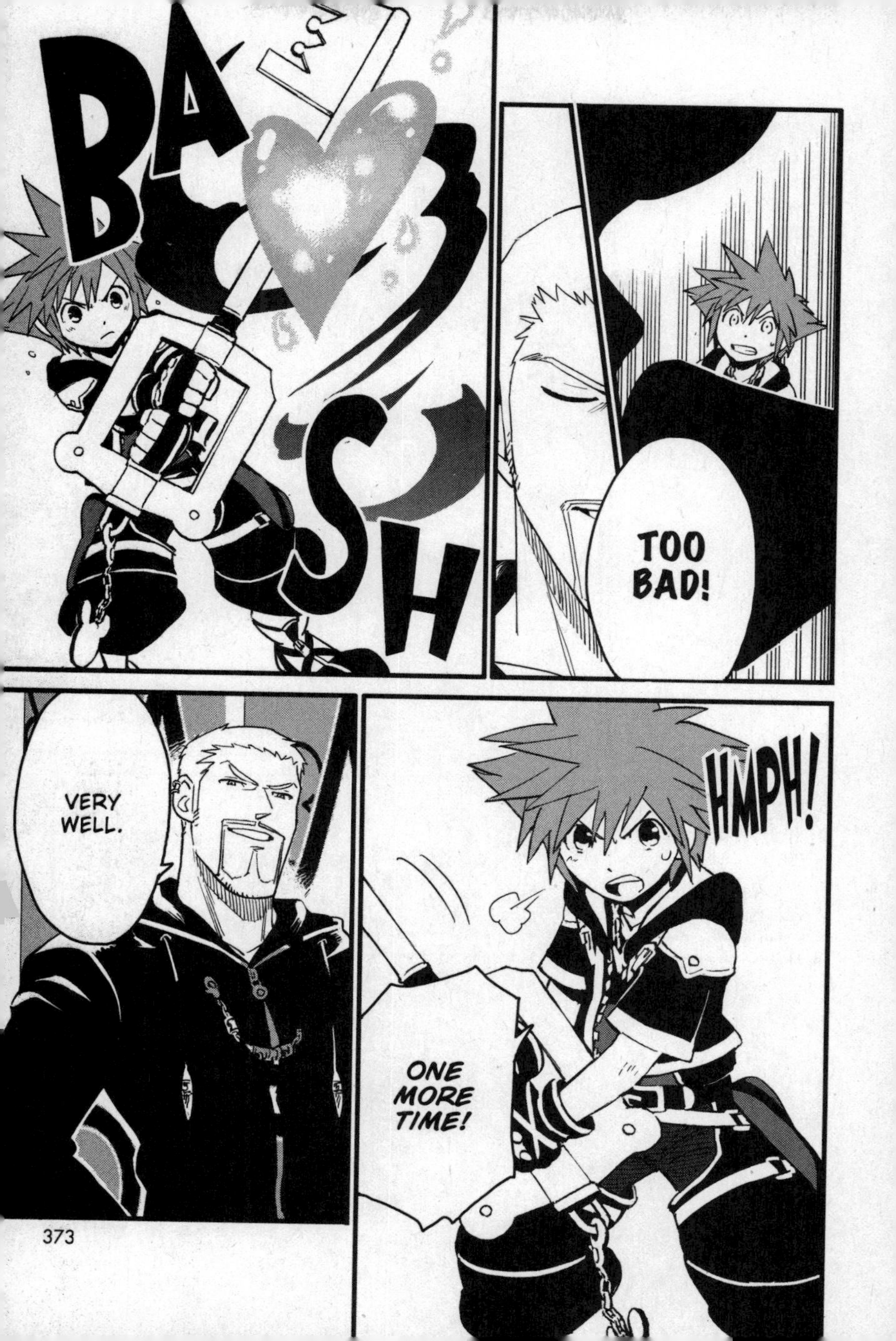
TOO BAD!
BASH
HMPH!
ONE MORE TIME!
VERY WELL.

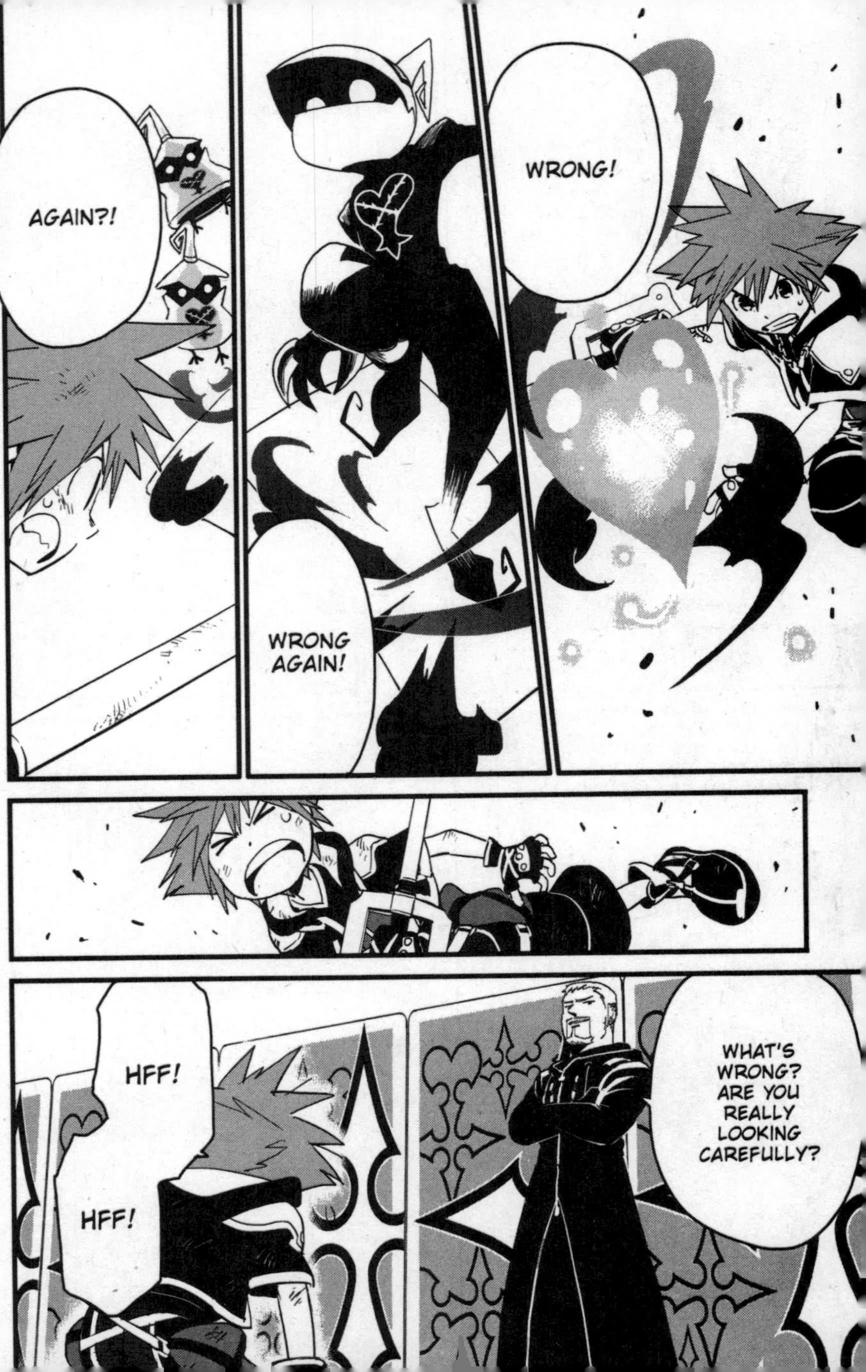
WRONG!
WRONG AGAIN!
AGAIN?!
WHAT'S WRONG? ARE YOU REALLY LOOKING CAREFULLY?
HFF!
HFF!

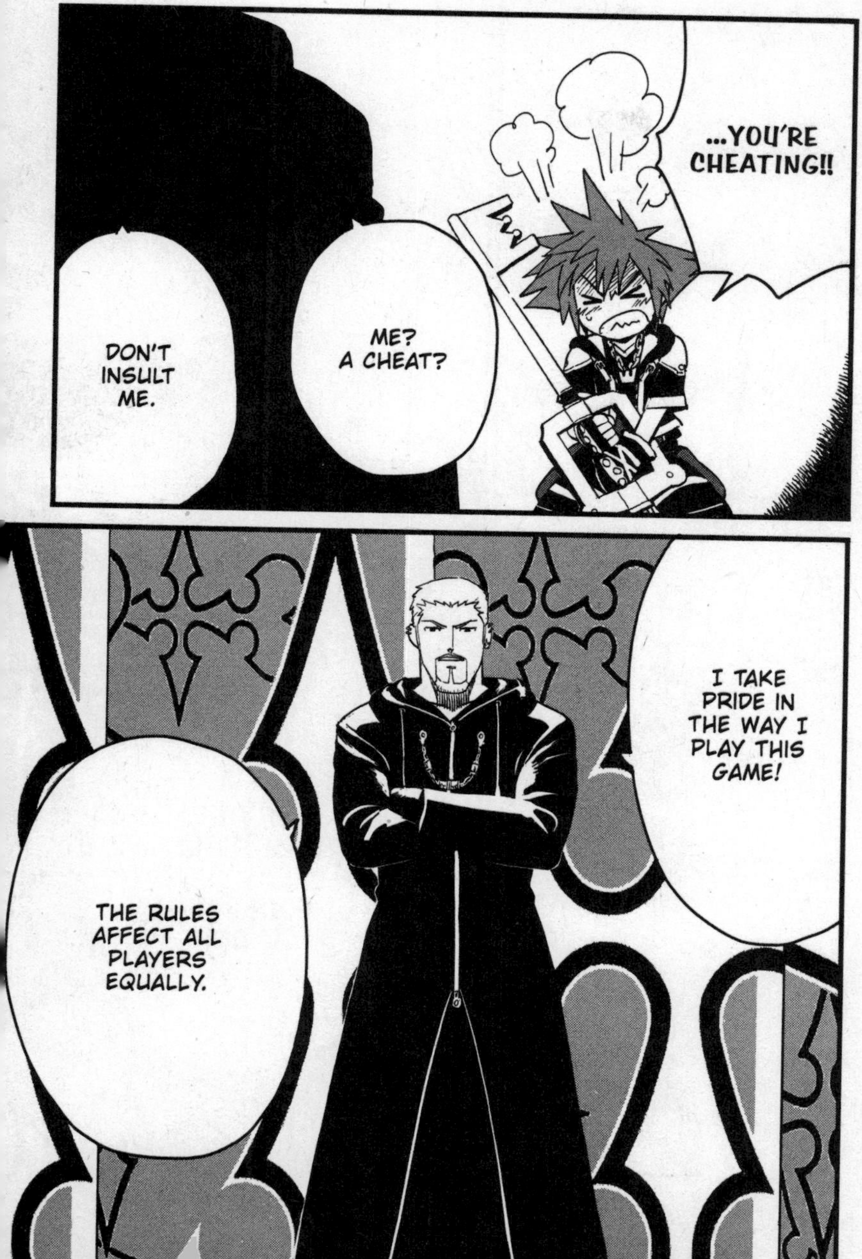
...YOU'RE CHEATING!!
ME? A CHEAT?
DON'T INSULT ME.
I TAKE PRIDE IN THE WAY I PLAY THIS GAME!
THE RULES AFFECT ALL PLAYERS EQUALLY.

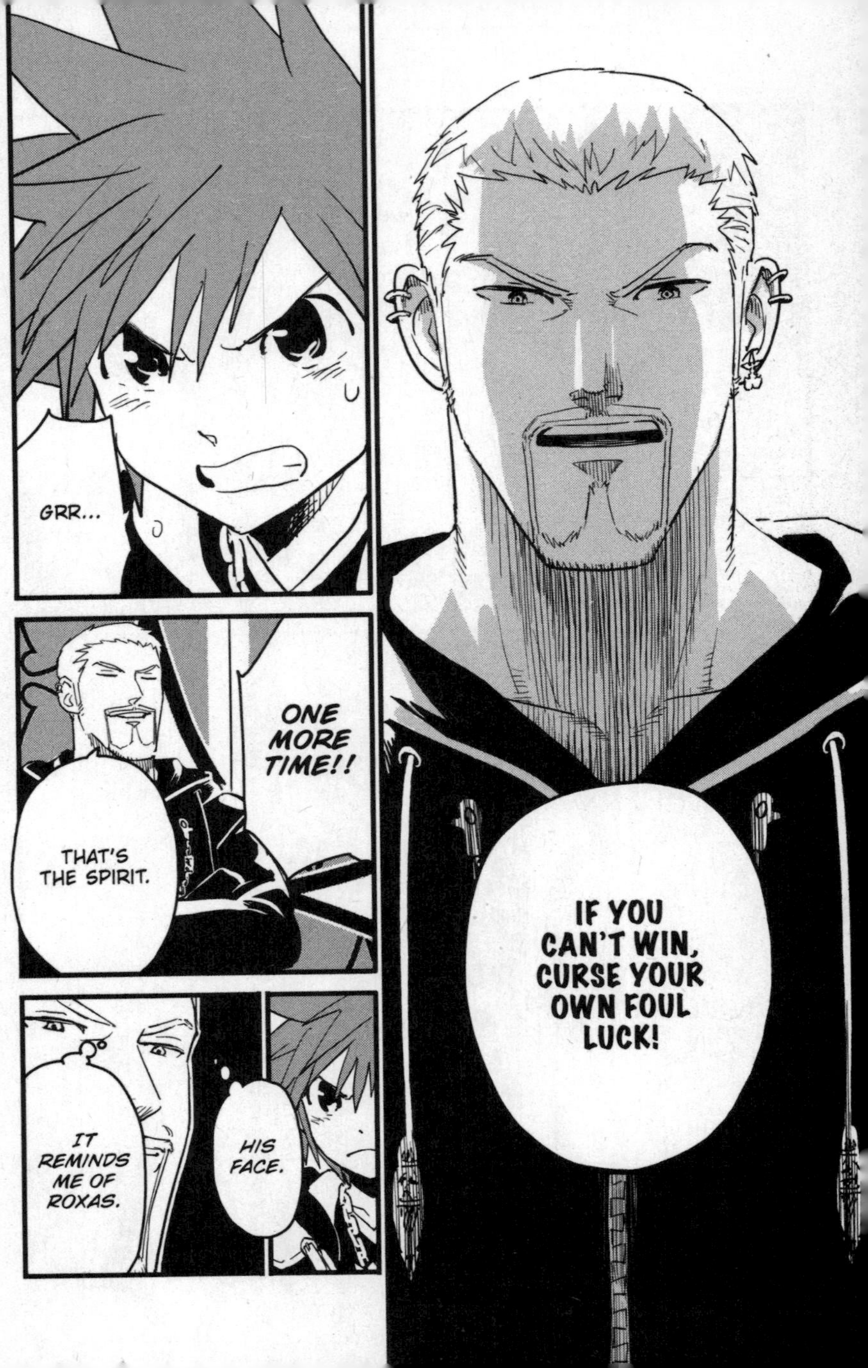
IF YOU CAN'T WIN, CURSE YOUR OWN FOUL LUCK!
GRR...
ONE MORE TIME!!
THAT'S THE SPIRIT.
HIS FACE.
IT REMINDS ME OF ROXAS.

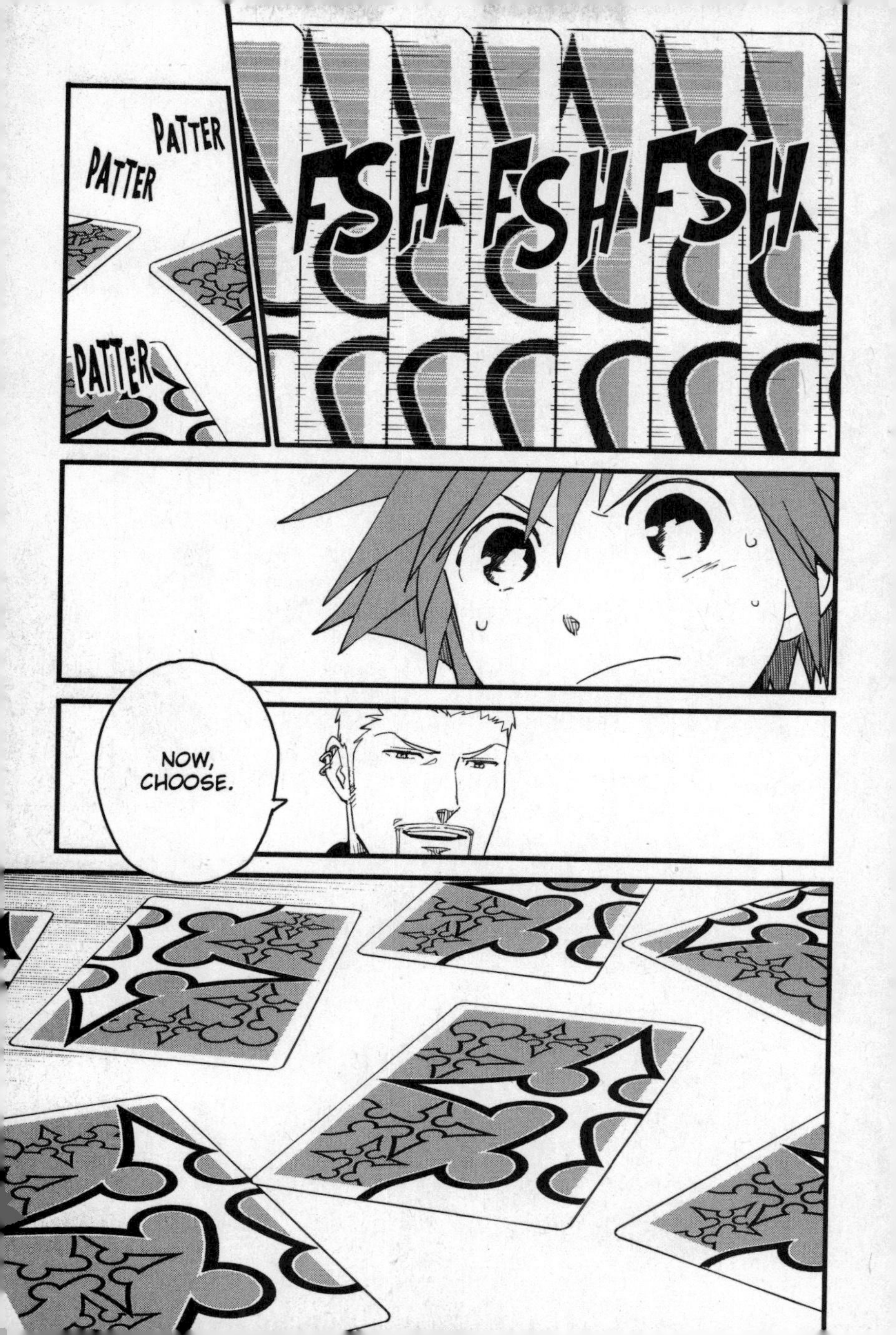
FSH FSH FSH
PATTER
PATTER
PATTER
NOW, CHOOSE.

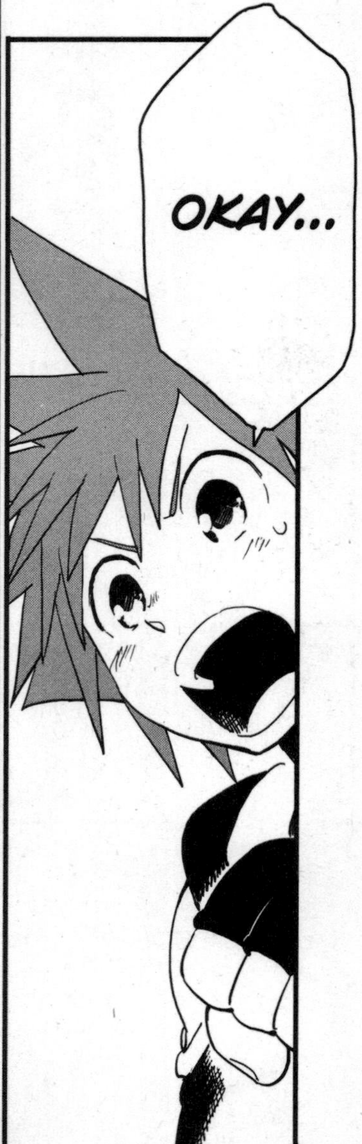
OKAY...
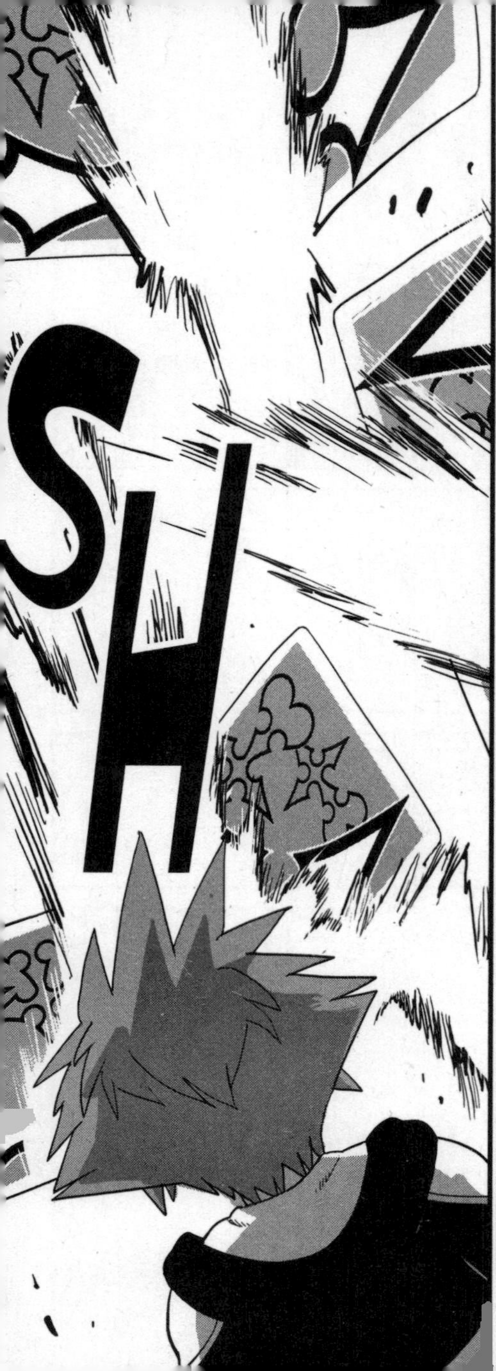
SH

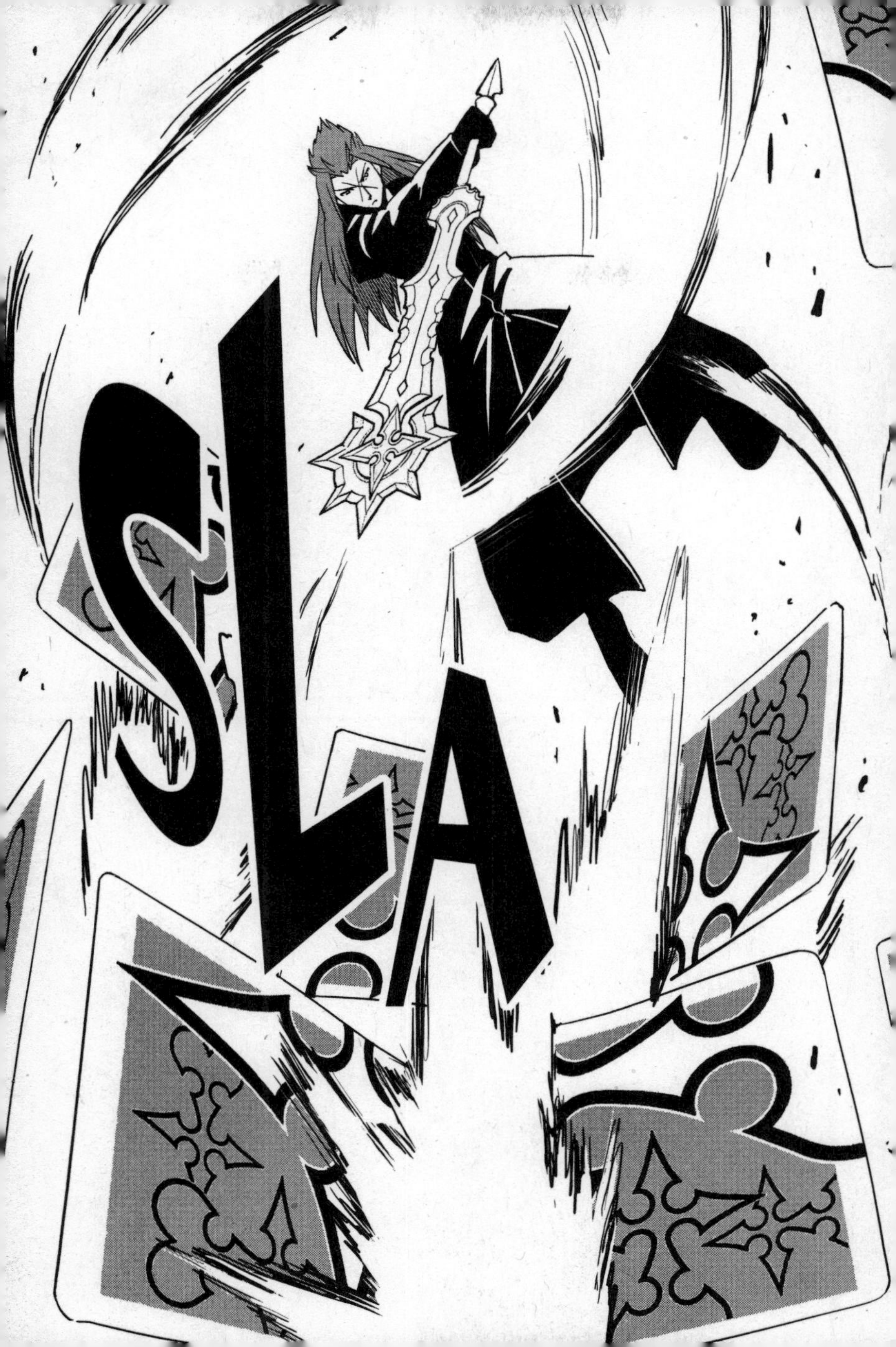
SLA

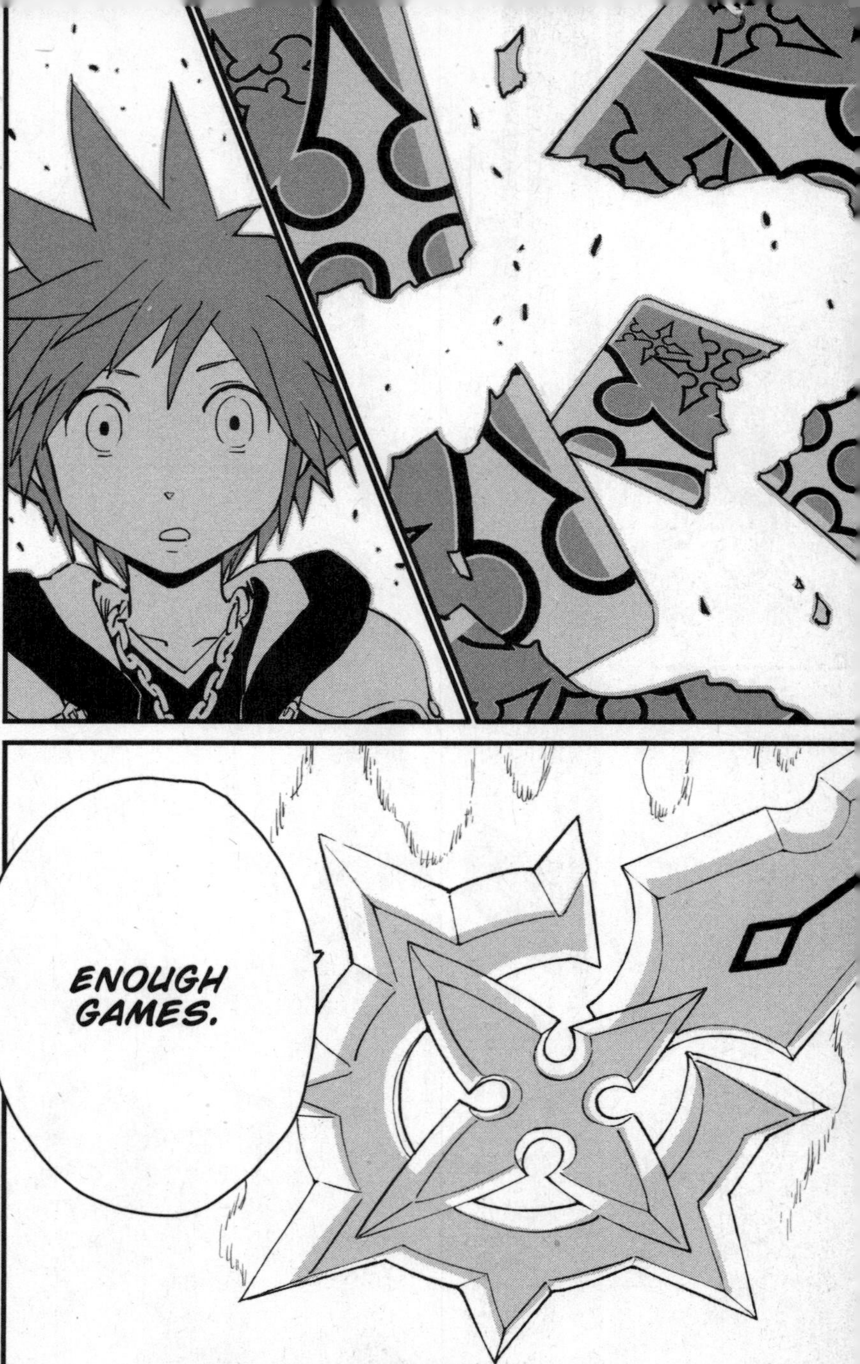
ENOUGH GAMES.

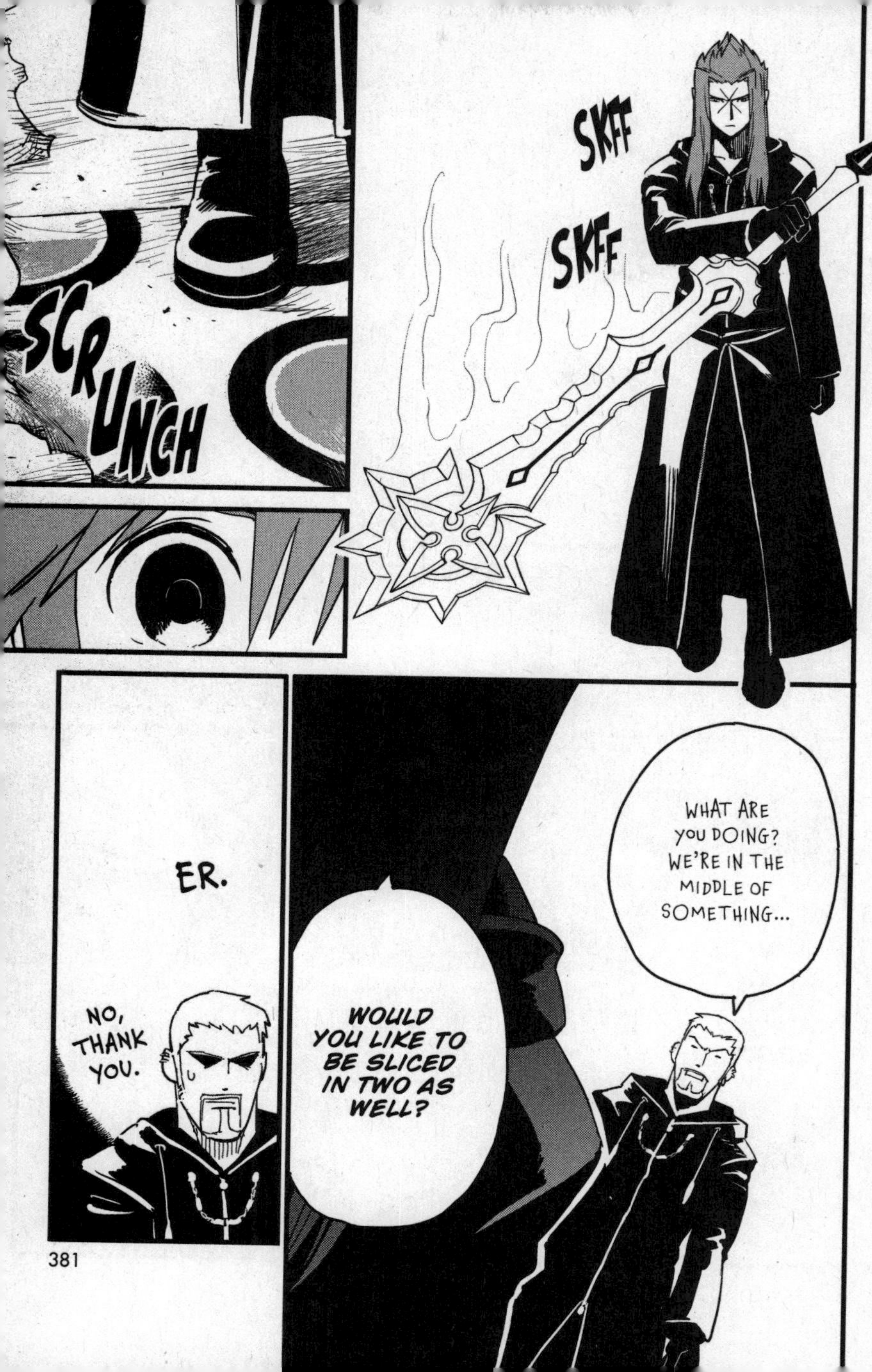
SKFF
SKFF
SCRUNCH
WHAT ARE YOU DOING? WE'RE IN THE MIDDLE OF SOMETHING...
WOULD YOU LIKE TO BE SLICED IN TWO AS WELL?
ER.
NO, THANK YOU.

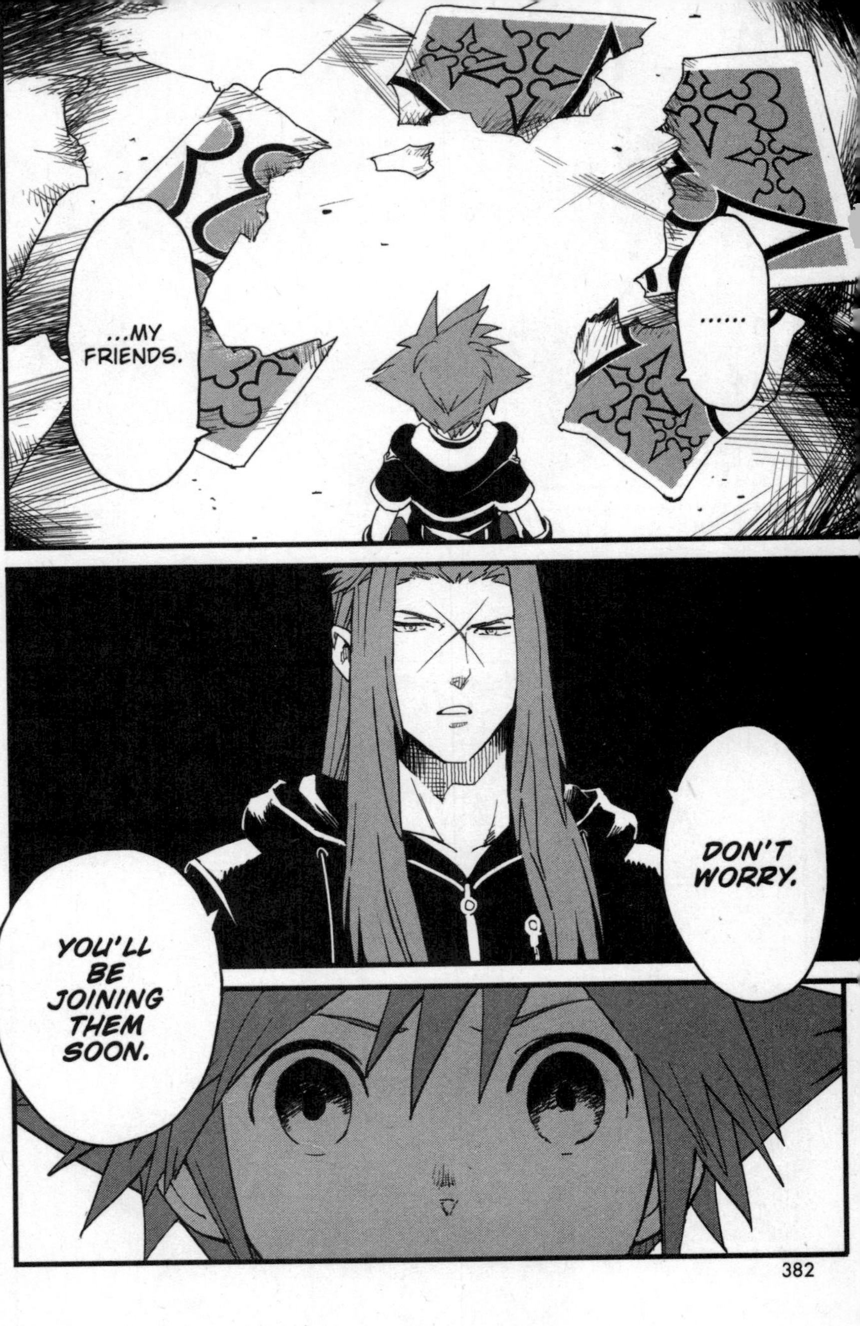
......
...MY FRIENDS.
DON'T WORRY.
YOU'LL BE JOINING THEM SOON.

Disney SQUARE ENIX

KINGDOM HEARTS

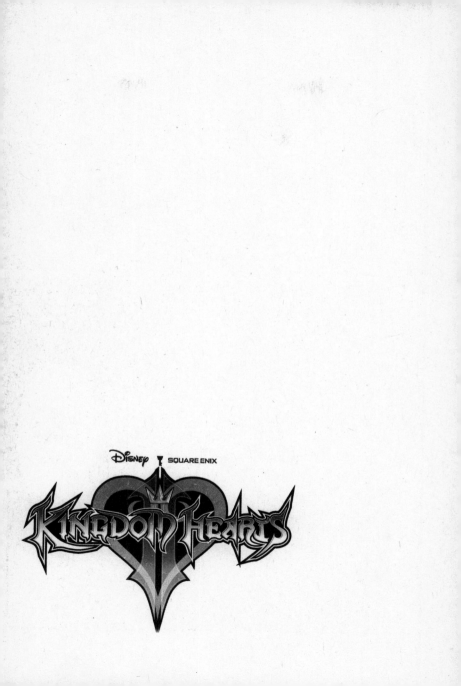

Disney SQUARE ENIX

KINGDOM HEARTS

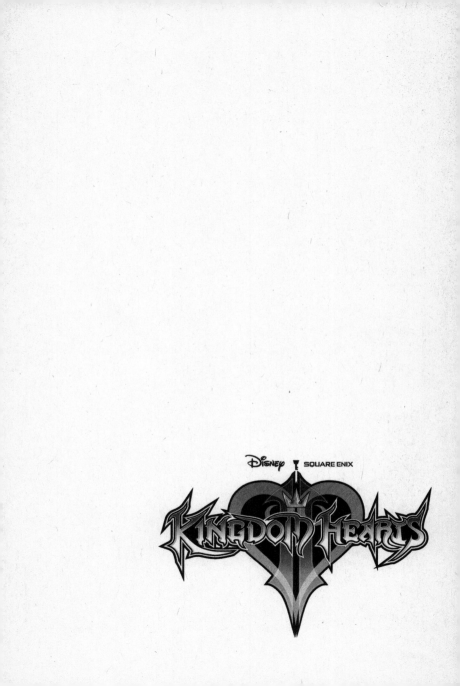

Chapter 65: The Reason I Fight

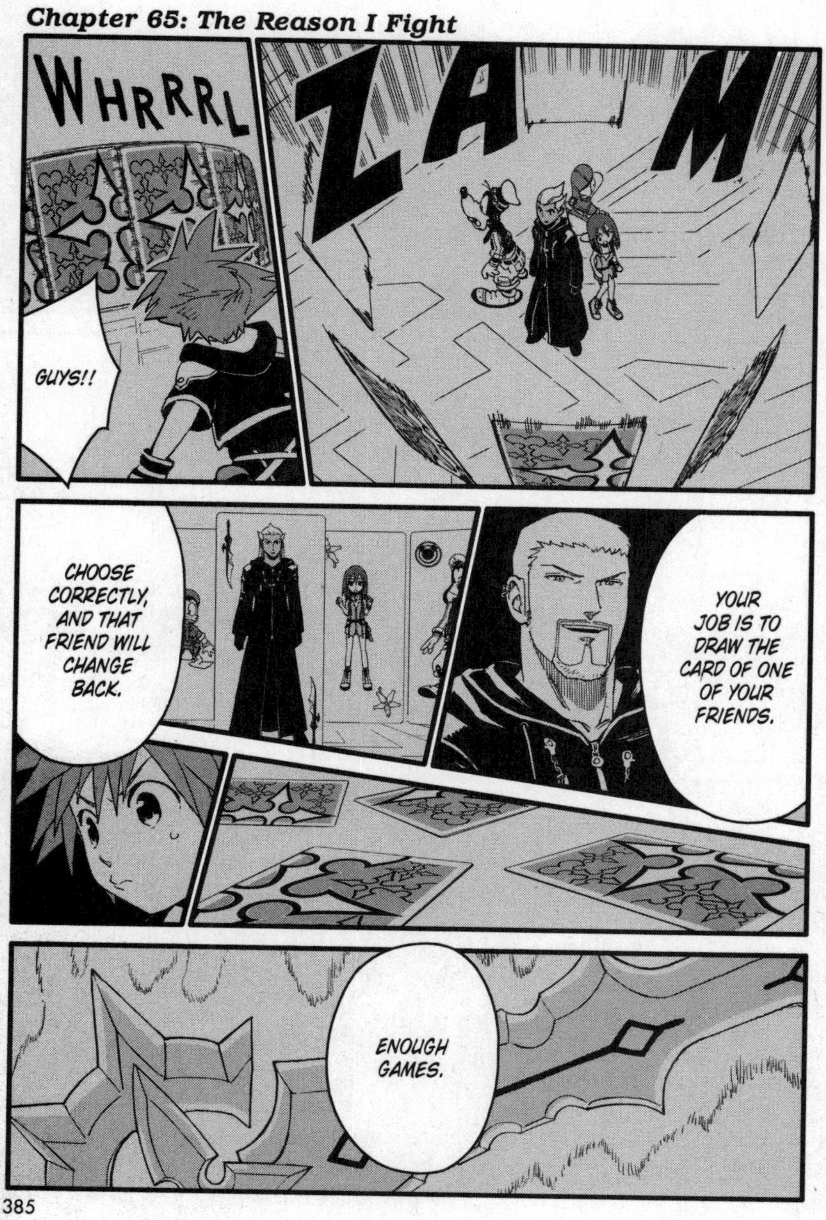
ZAM
WHRRRL
GUYS!!
YOUR JOB IS TO DRAW THE CARD OF ONE OF YOUR FRIENDS.
CHOOSE CORRECTLY, AND THAT FRIEND WILL CHANGE BACK.
ENOUGH GAMES.

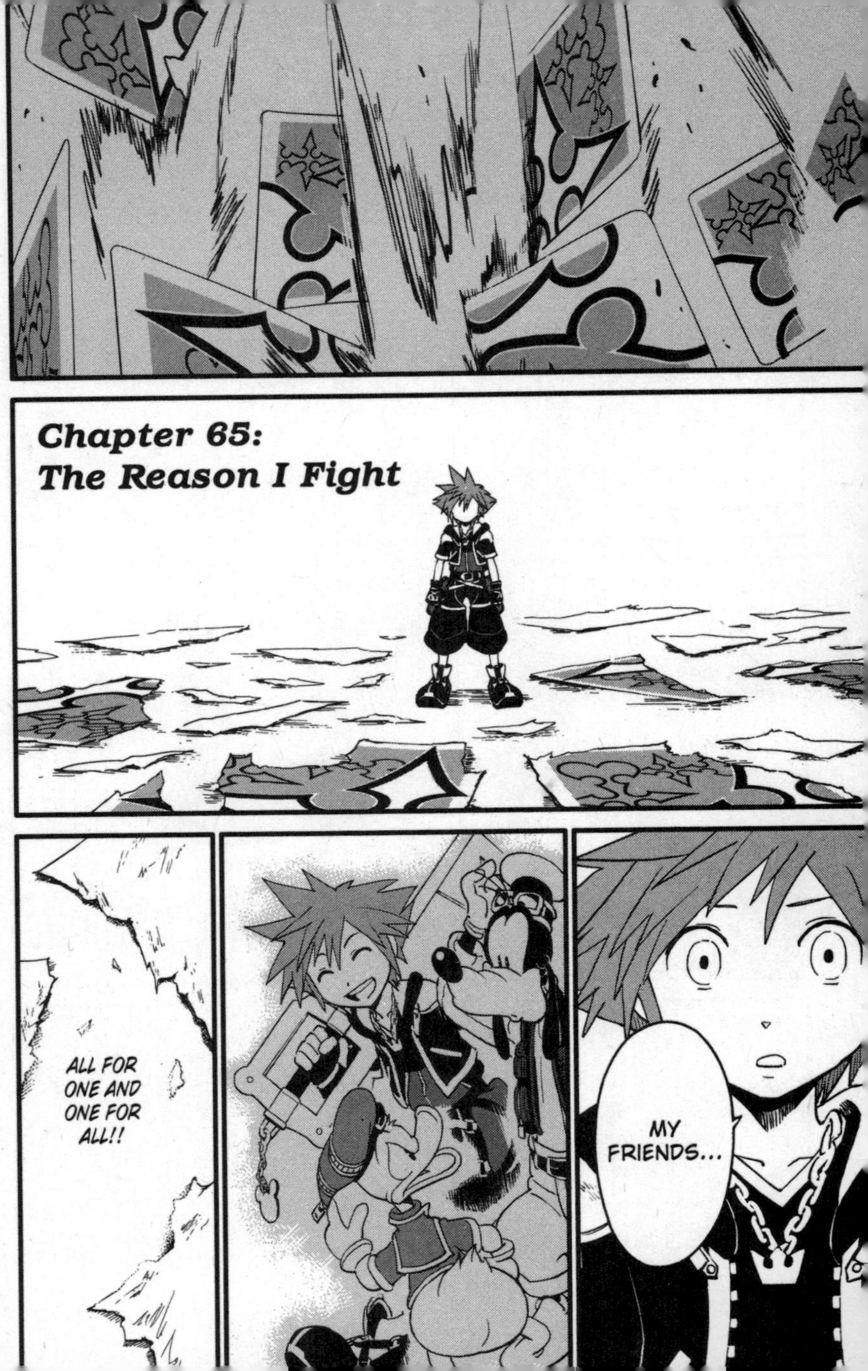
Chapter 65:
The Reason I Fight
MY FRIENDS...
ALL FOR ONE AND ONE FOR ALL!!

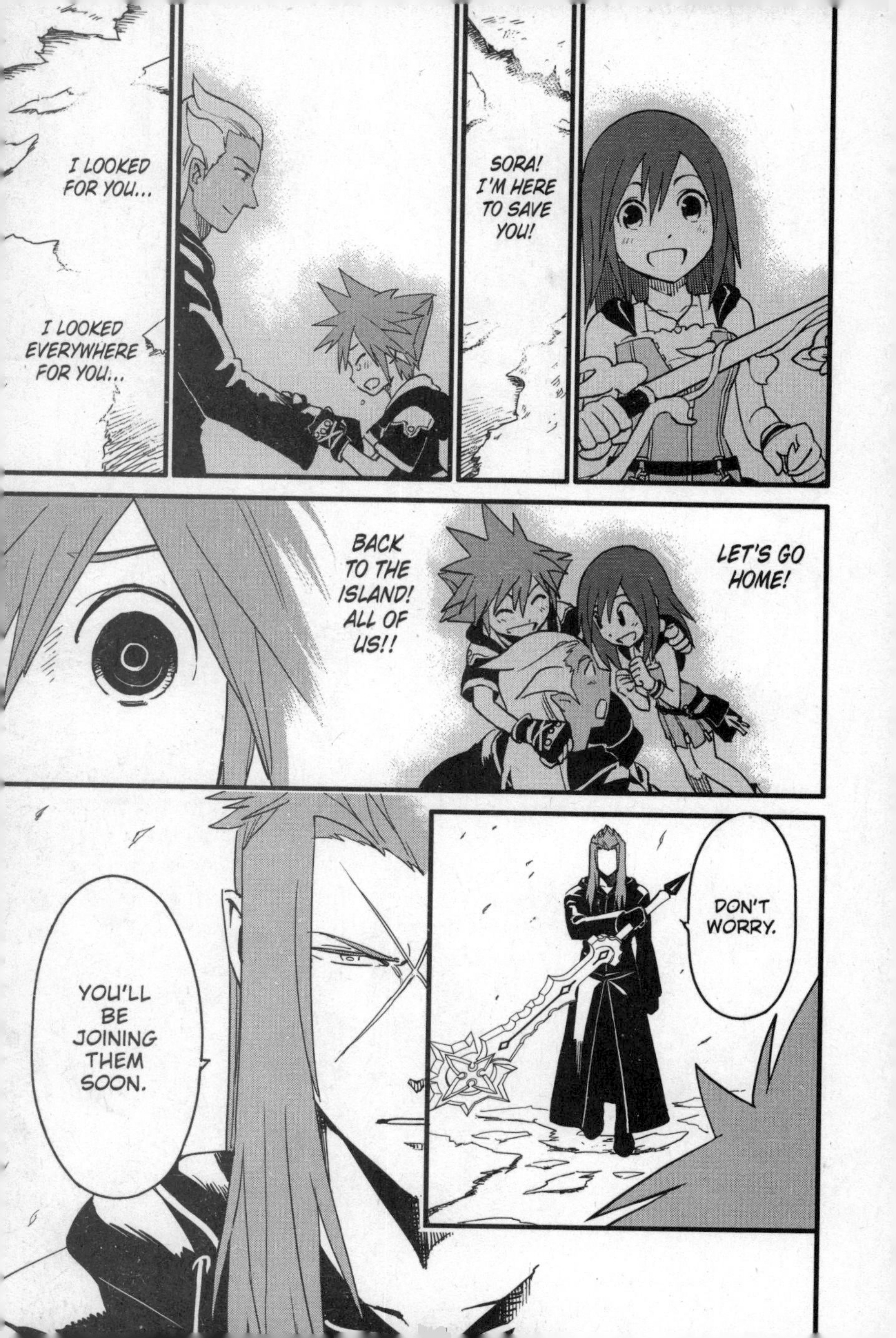
SORA! I'M HERE TO SAVE YOU!
I LOOKED FOR YOU...
I LOOKED EVERYWHERE FOR YOU...
LET'S GO HOME!
BACK TO THE ISLAND! ALL OF US!!
DON'T WORRY.
YOU'LL BE JOINING THEM SOON.

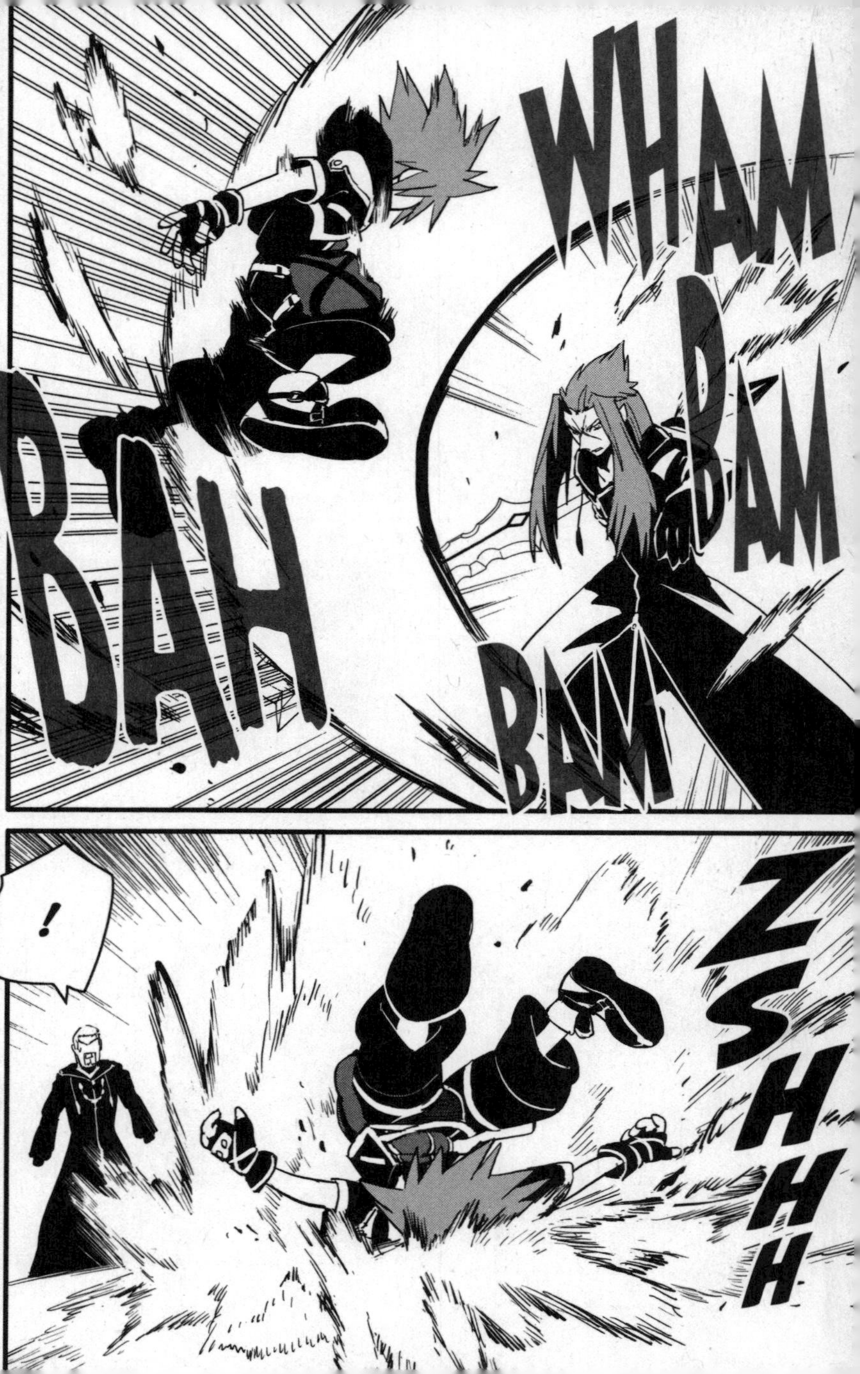
WHAM
BAM
BAM
BAH
ZSHHHH
!

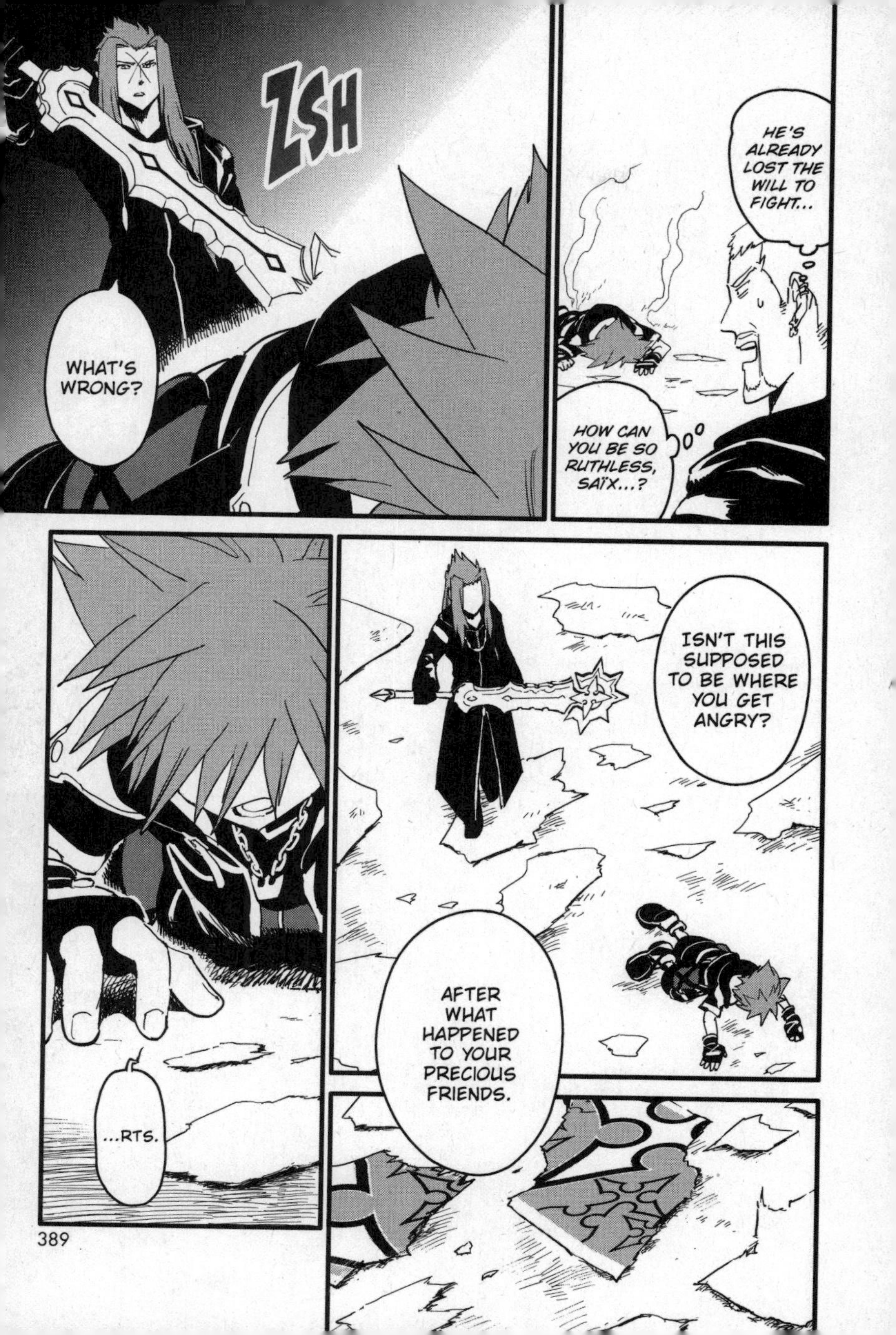
HE'S ALREADY LOST THE WILL TO FIGHT...
HOW CAN YOU BE SO RUTHLESS, SAÏX...?
ZSH
WHAT'S WRONG?
ISN'T THIS SUPPOSED TO BE WHERE YOU GET ANGRY?
AFTER WHAT HAPPENED TO YOUR PRECIOUS FRIENDS.
...RTS.

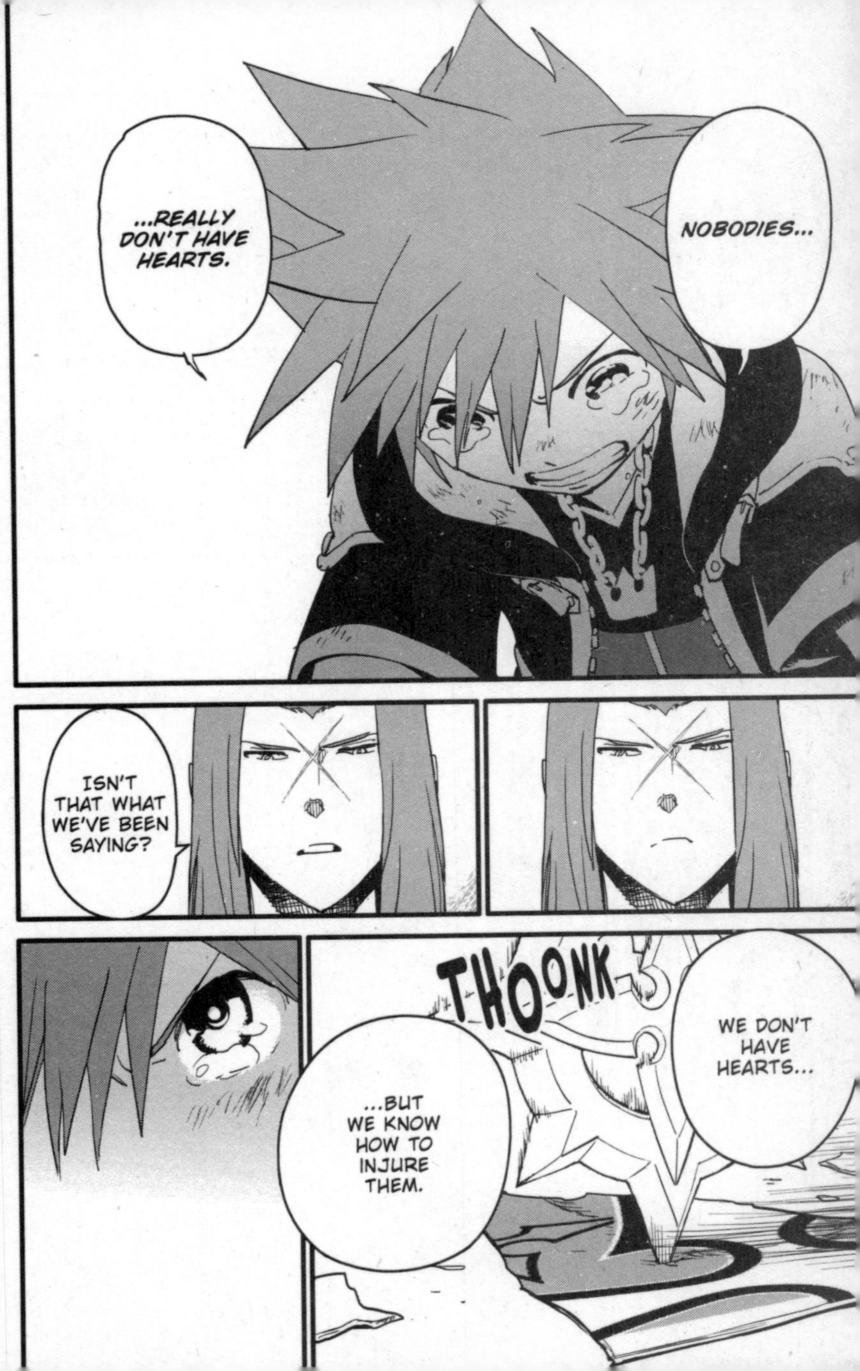
NOBODIES...
...REALLY DON'T HAVE HEARTS.
ISN'T THAT WHAT WE'VE BEEN SAYING?
THOONK
WE DON'T HAVE HEARTS...
...BUT WE KNOW HOW TO INJURE THEM.

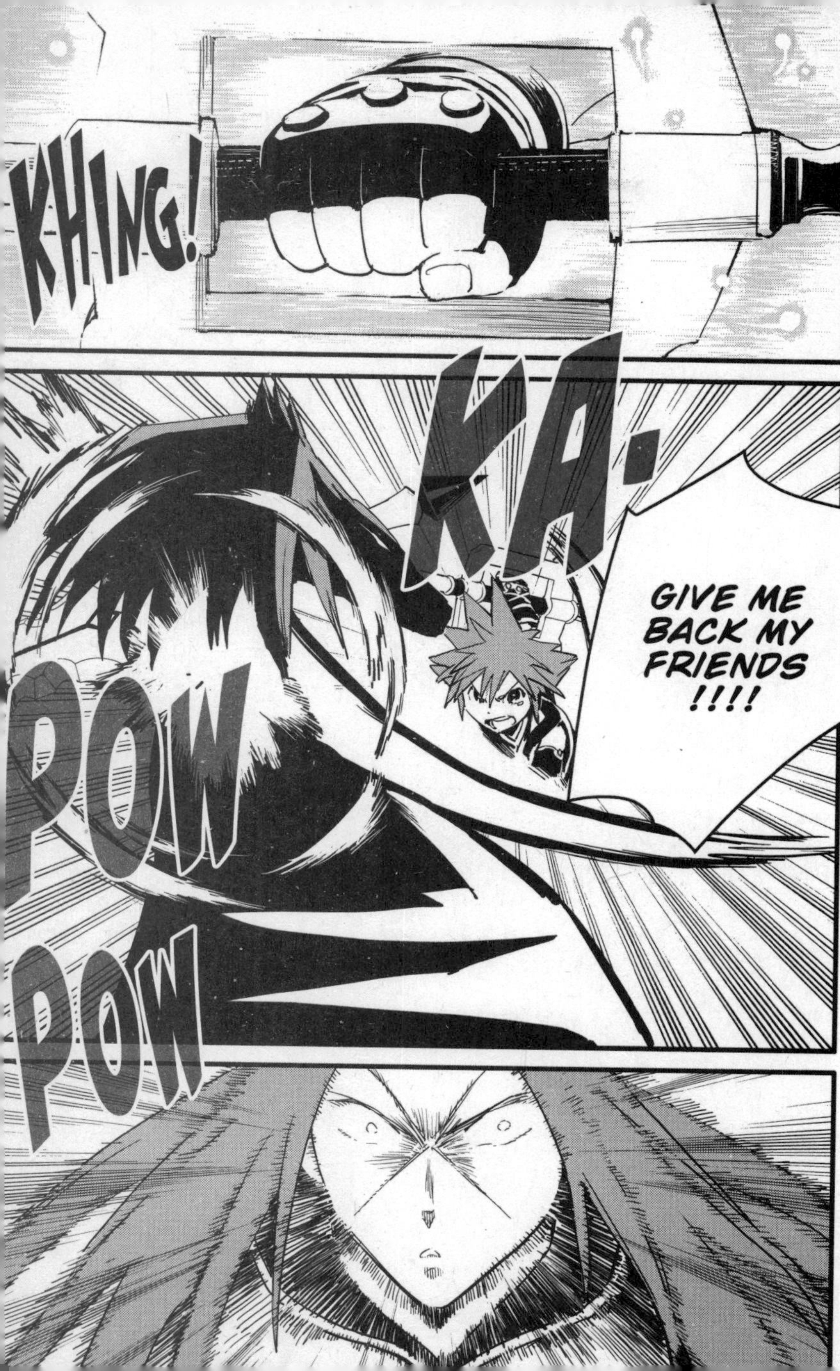
KHING!
KA-
GIVE ME BACK MY FRIENDS !!!!
POW
POW

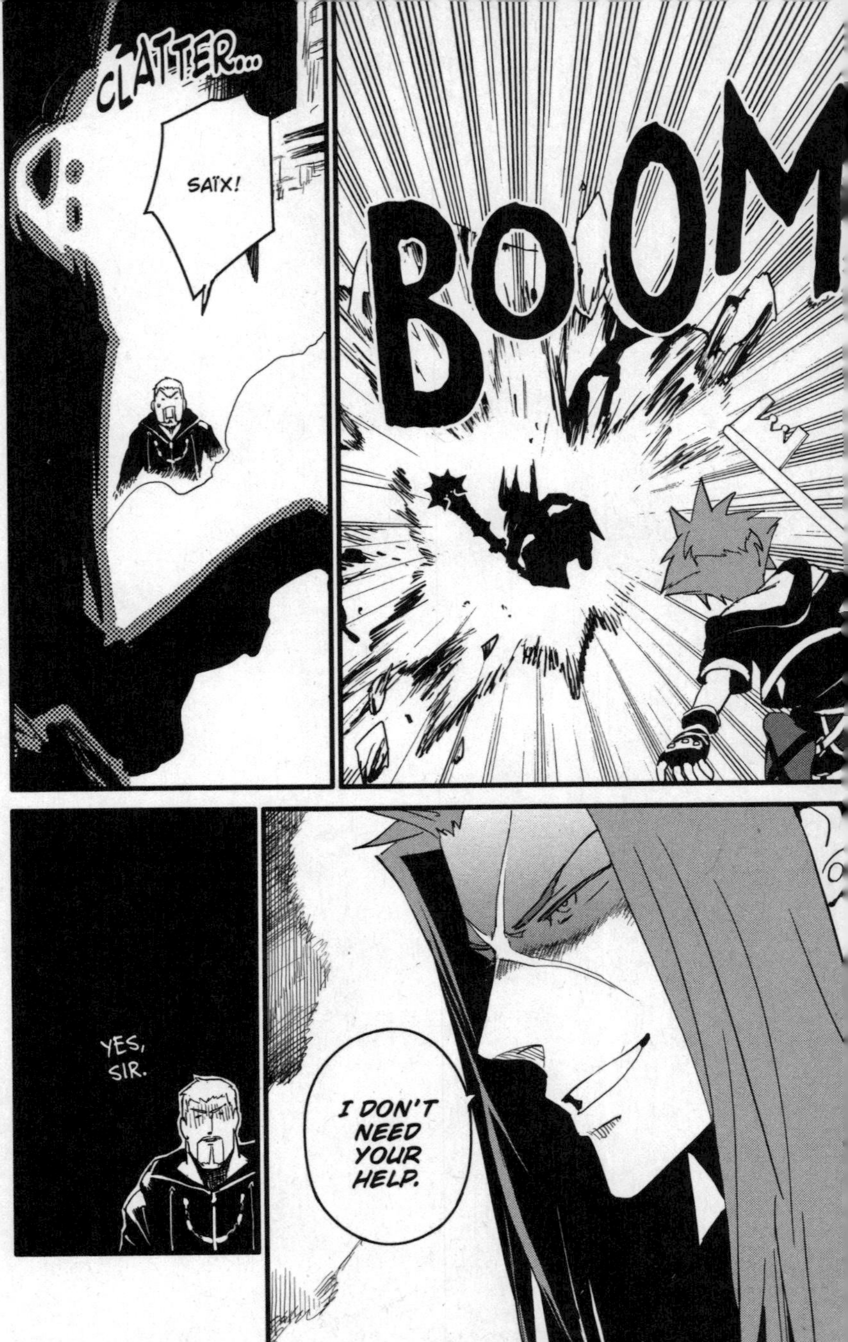
BOOM
CLATTER...
SAÏX!
I DON'T NEED YOUR HELP.
YES, SIR.

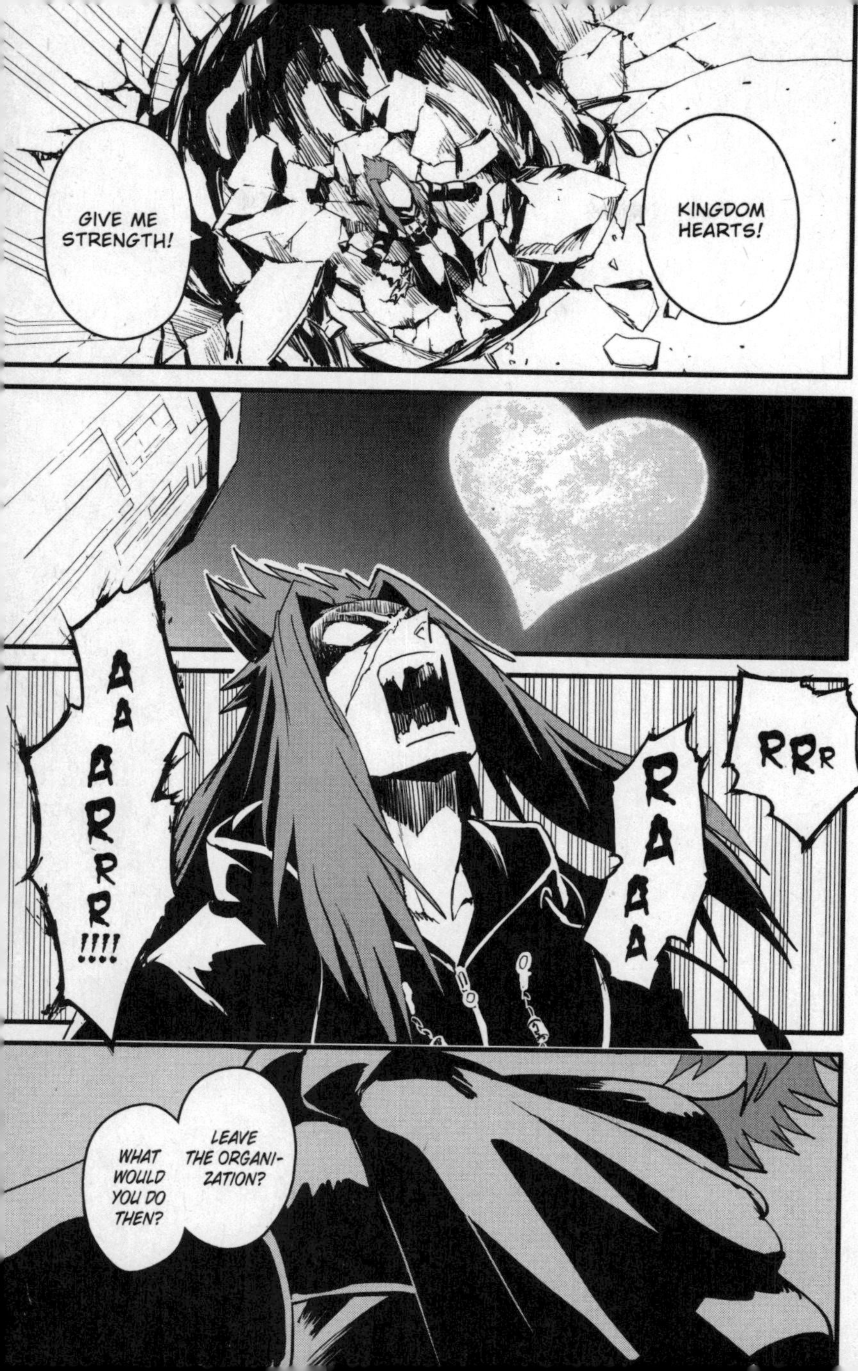
KINGDOM HEARTS!
GIVE ME STRENGTH!
RRr
RAAA
AAARRRR!!!!
LEAVE THE ORGANI-ZATION?
WHAT WOULD YOU DO THEN?

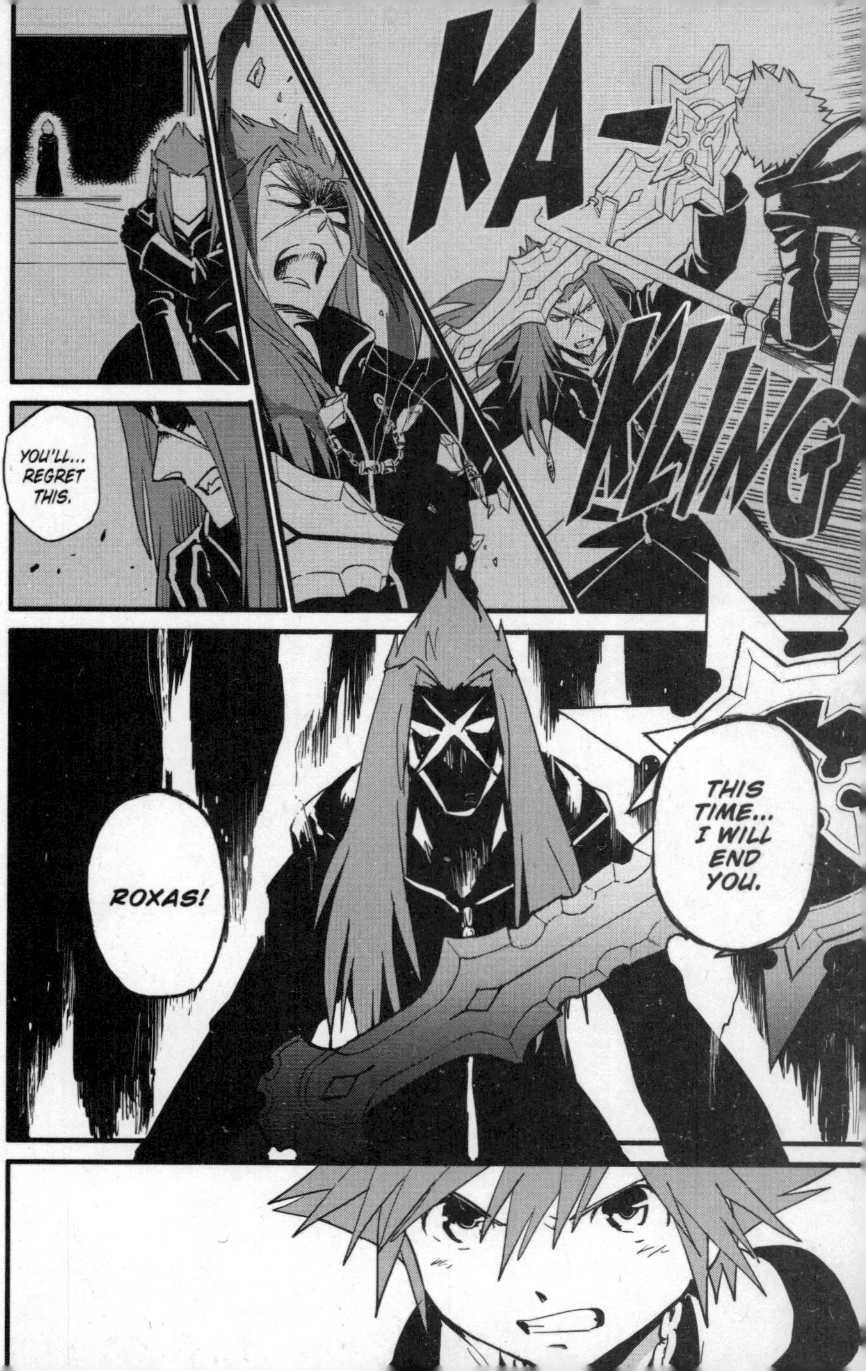
KA-KLING
YOU'LL... REGRET THIS.
THIS TIME... I WILL END YOU.
ROXAS!

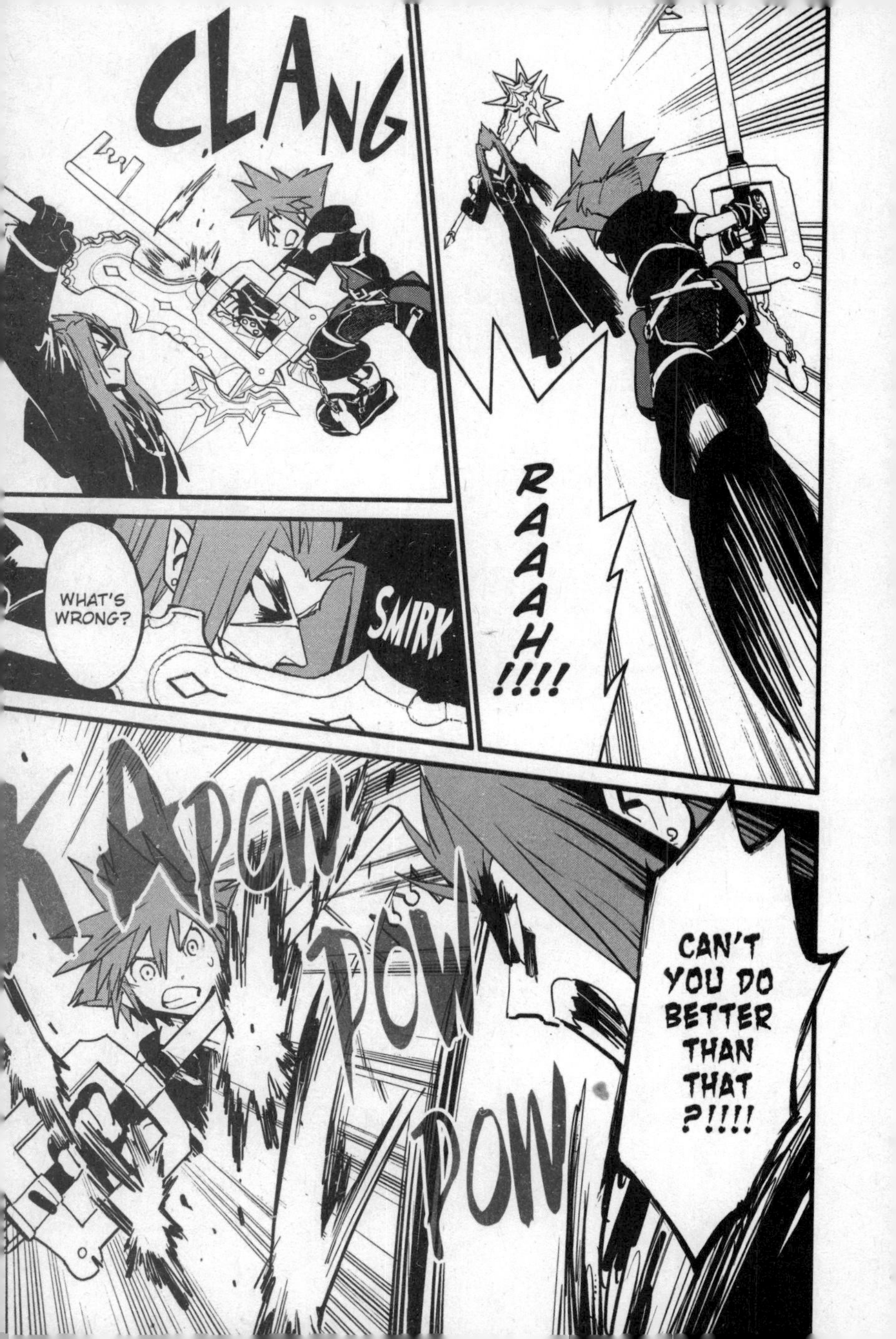
RAAAAH!!!!
CLANG
WHAT'S WRONG?
SMIRK
KAPOW
POW
POW
CAN'T YOU DO BETTER THAN THAT?!!!!

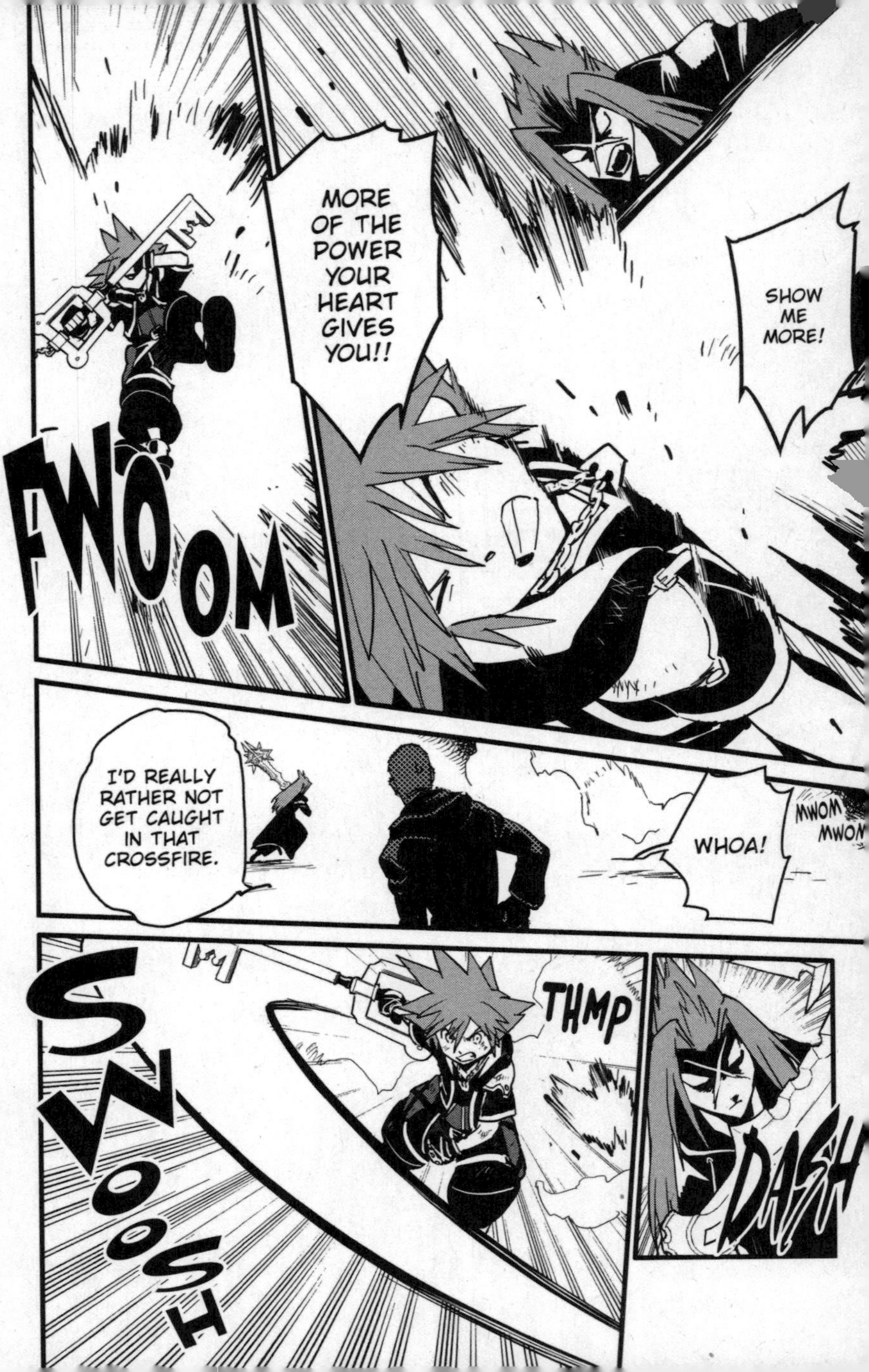
SHOW ME MORE!
MORE OF THE POWER YOUR HEART GIVES YOU!!
FWOOM
MWOM MWOM
WHOA!
I'D REALLY RATHER NOT GET CAUGHT IN THAT CROSSFIRE.
DASH
THMP
SWOOSH

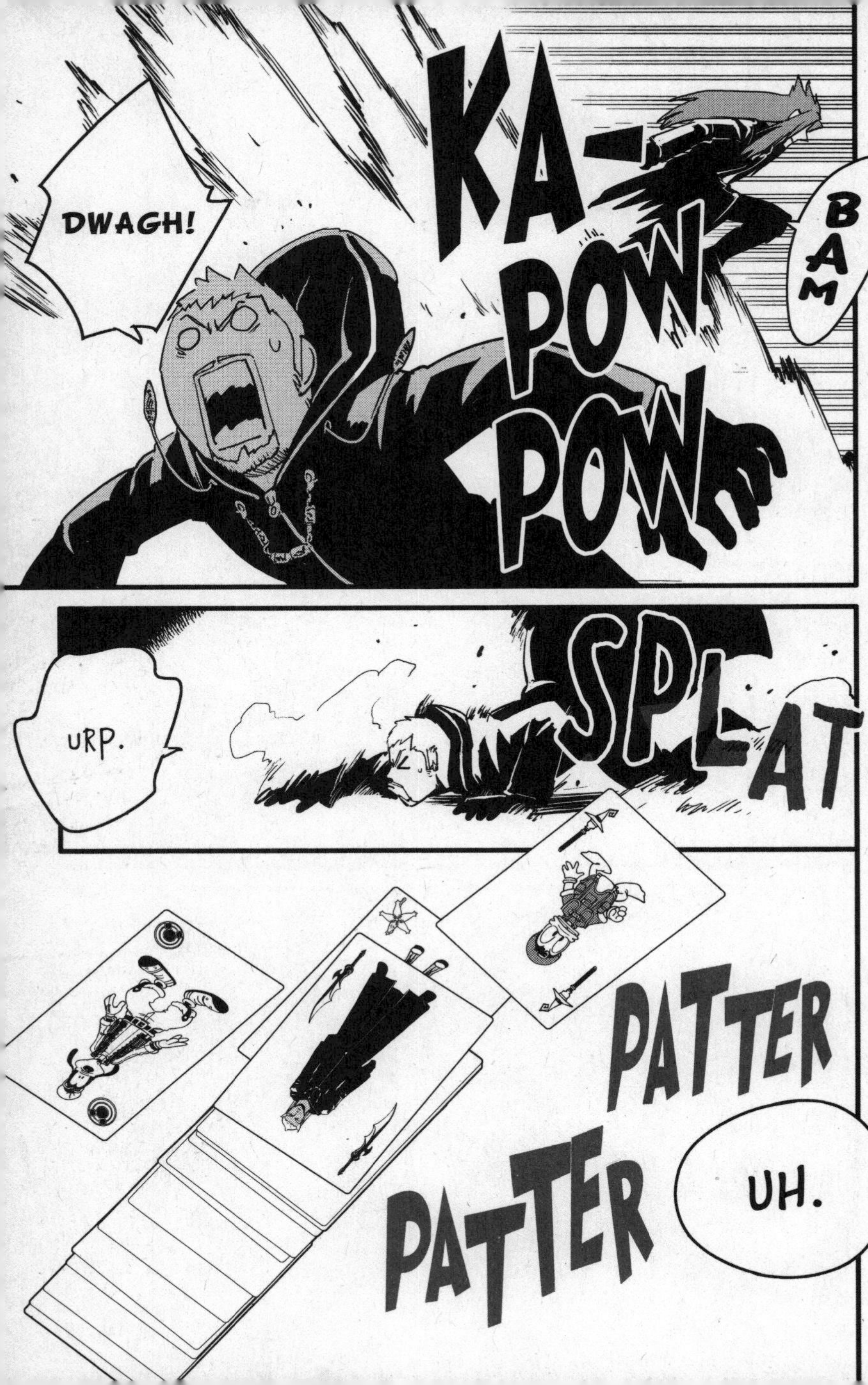
BAM
KA-POW POW
DWAGH!
SPLAT
URP.
PATTER PATTER
UH.

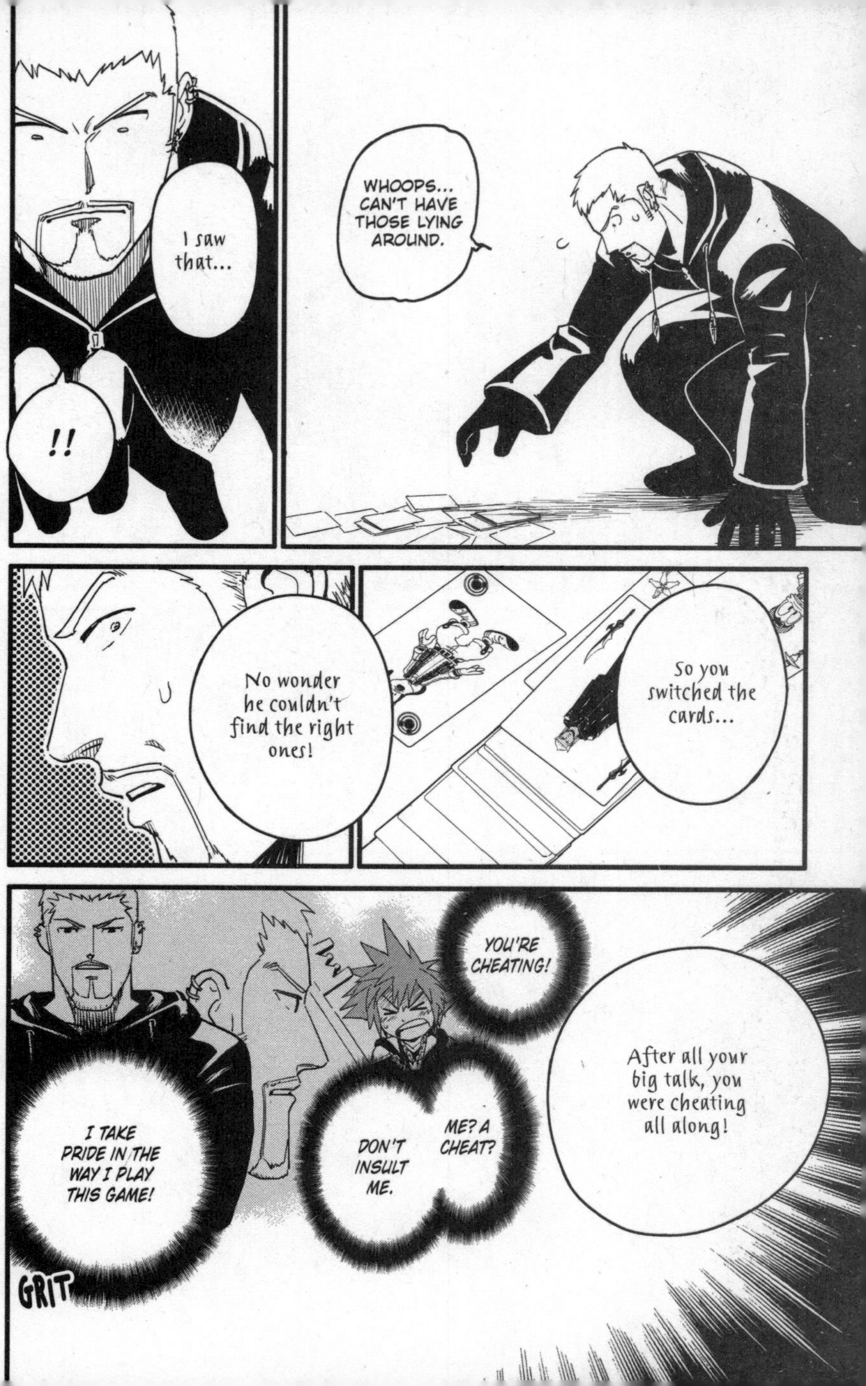
WHOOPS... CAN'T HAVE THOSE LYING AROUND.
I saw that...
!!
So you switched the cards...
No wonder he couldn't find the right ones!
YOU'RE CHEATING!
After all your big talk, you were cheating all along!
ME? A CHEAT?
DON'T INSULT ME.
I TAKE PRIDE IN THE WAY I PLAY THIS GAME!
GRIT

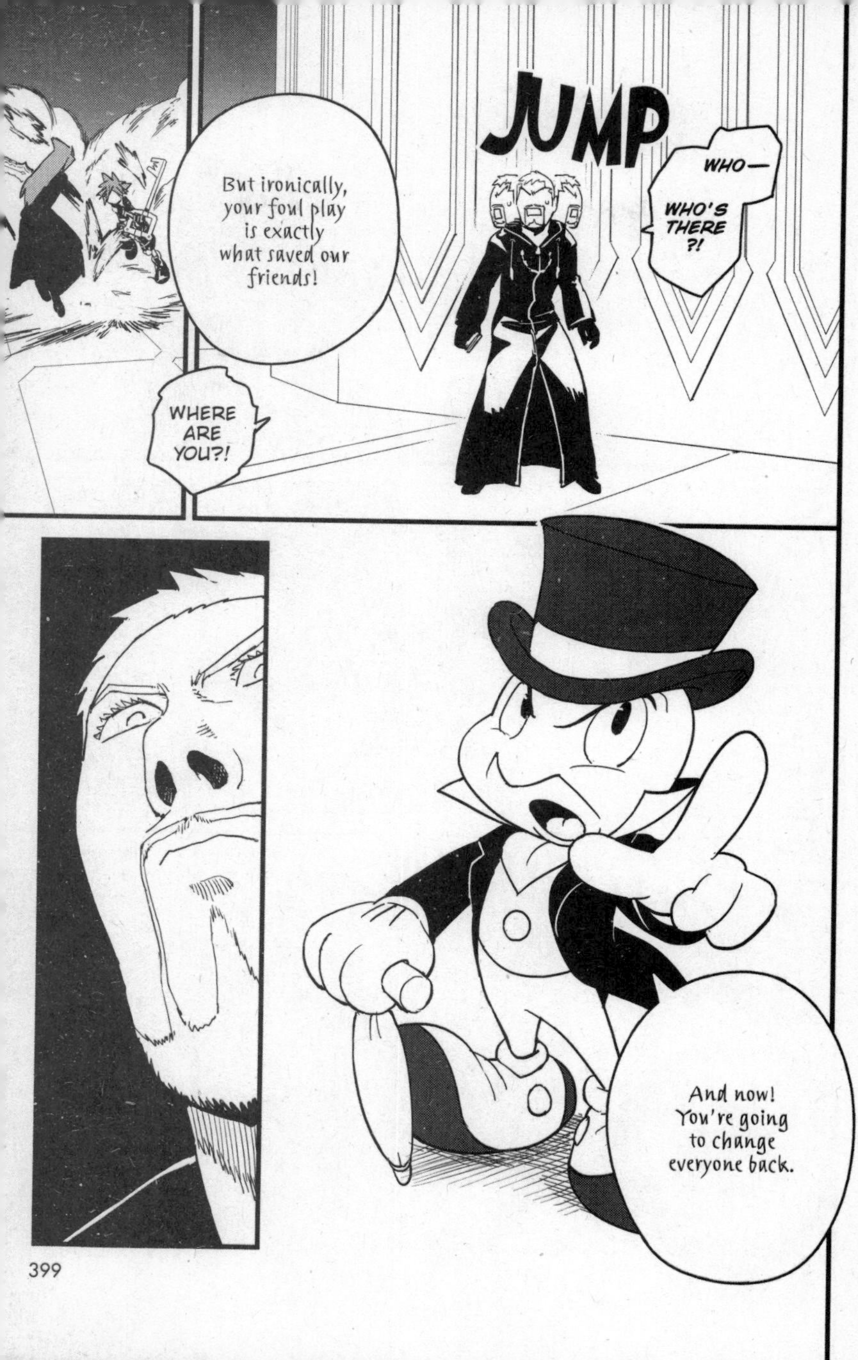
JUMP
WHO—
WHO'S THERE ?!
But ironically, your foul play is exactly what saved our friends!
WHERE ARE YOU?!
And now! You're going to change everyone back.

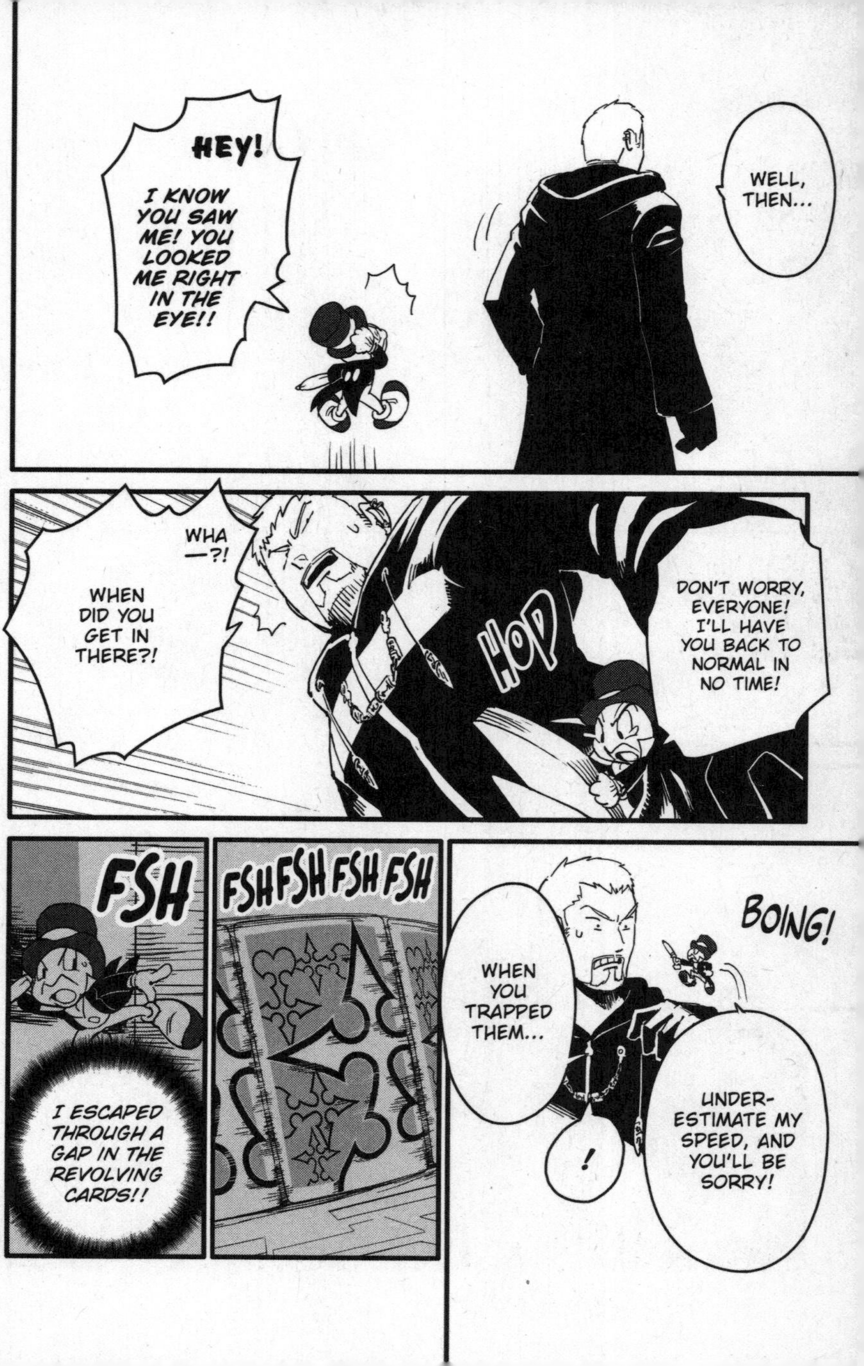
WELL, THEN...
HEY!
I KNOW YOU SAW ME! YOU LOOKED ME RIGHT IN THE EYE!!
DON'T WORRY, EVERYONE! I'LL HAVE YOU BACK TO NORMAL IN NO TIME!
HOP
WHA—?!
WHEN DID YOU GET IN THERE?!
BOING!
WHEN YOU TRAPPED THEM...
UNDER-ESTIMATE MY SPEED, AND YOU'LL BE SORRY!
!
FSHFSH FSH FSH
FSH
I ESCAPED THROUGH A GAP IN THE REVOLVING CARDS!!

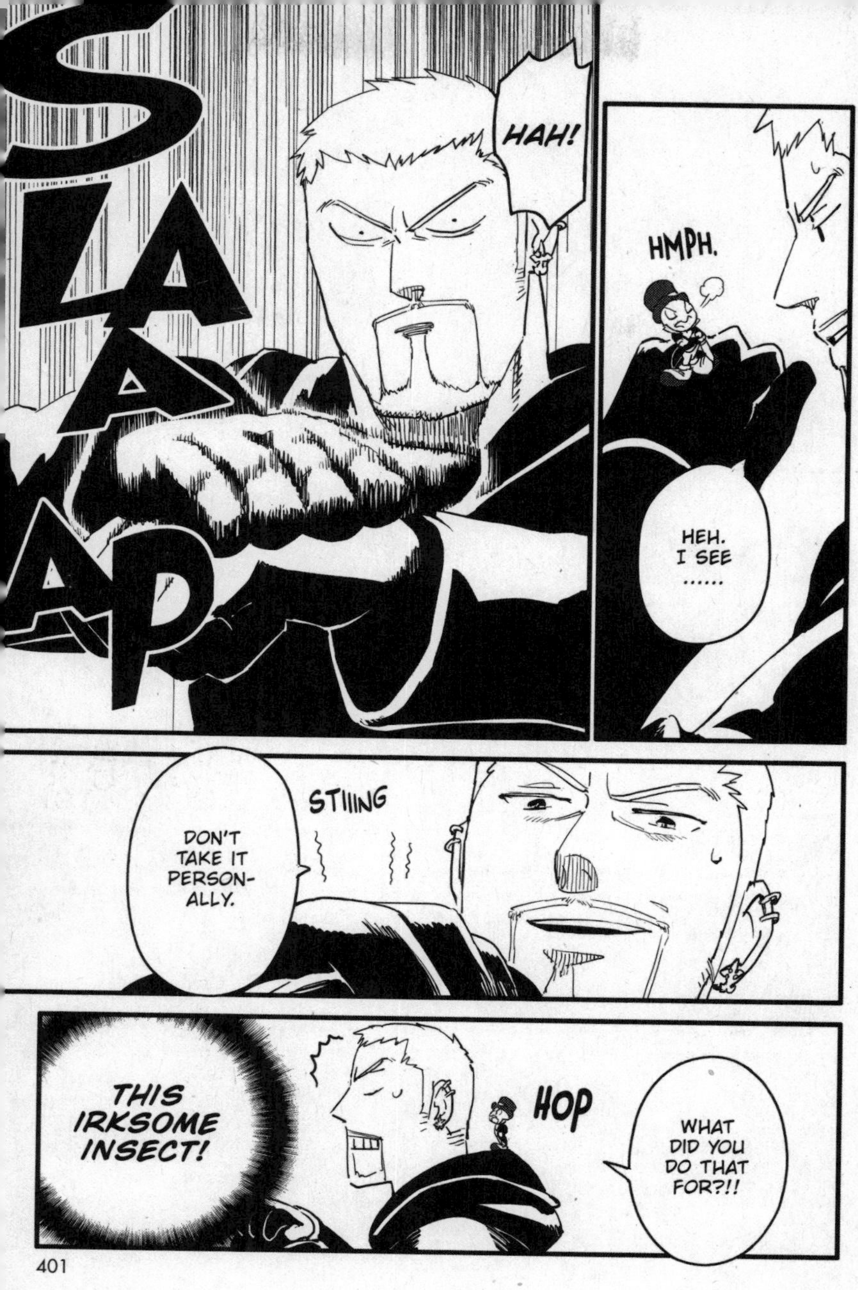
HMPH.
HEH. I SEE ......
SLAAAP
HAH!
STIIING
DON'T TAKE IT PERSON-ALLY.
WHAT DID YOU DO THAT FOR?!!
HOP
THIS IRKSOME INSECT!

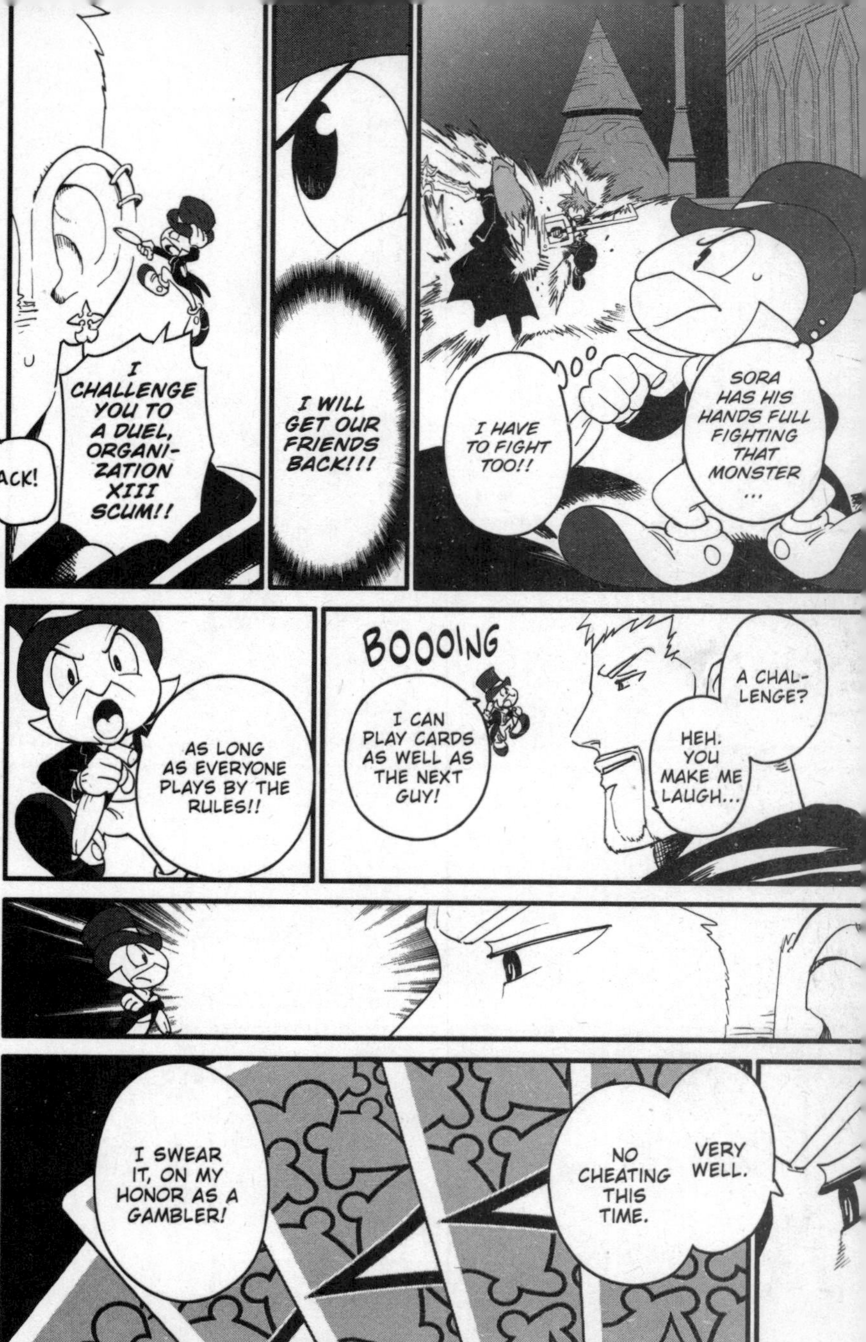
SORA HAS HIS HANDS FULL FIGHTING THAT MONSTER ...
I HAVE TO FIGHT TOO!!
I WILL GET OUR FRIENDS BACK!!!
I CHALLENGE YOU TO A DUEL, ORGANIZATION XIII SCUM!!
ACK!
A CHALLENGE?
HEH. YOU MAKE ME LAUGH...
BOOOING
I CAN PLAY CARDS AS WELL AS THE NEXT GUY!
AS LONG AS EVERYONE PLAYS BY THE RULES!!
VERY WELL.
NO CHEATING THIS TIME.
I SWEAR IT, ON MY HONOR AS A GAMBLER!

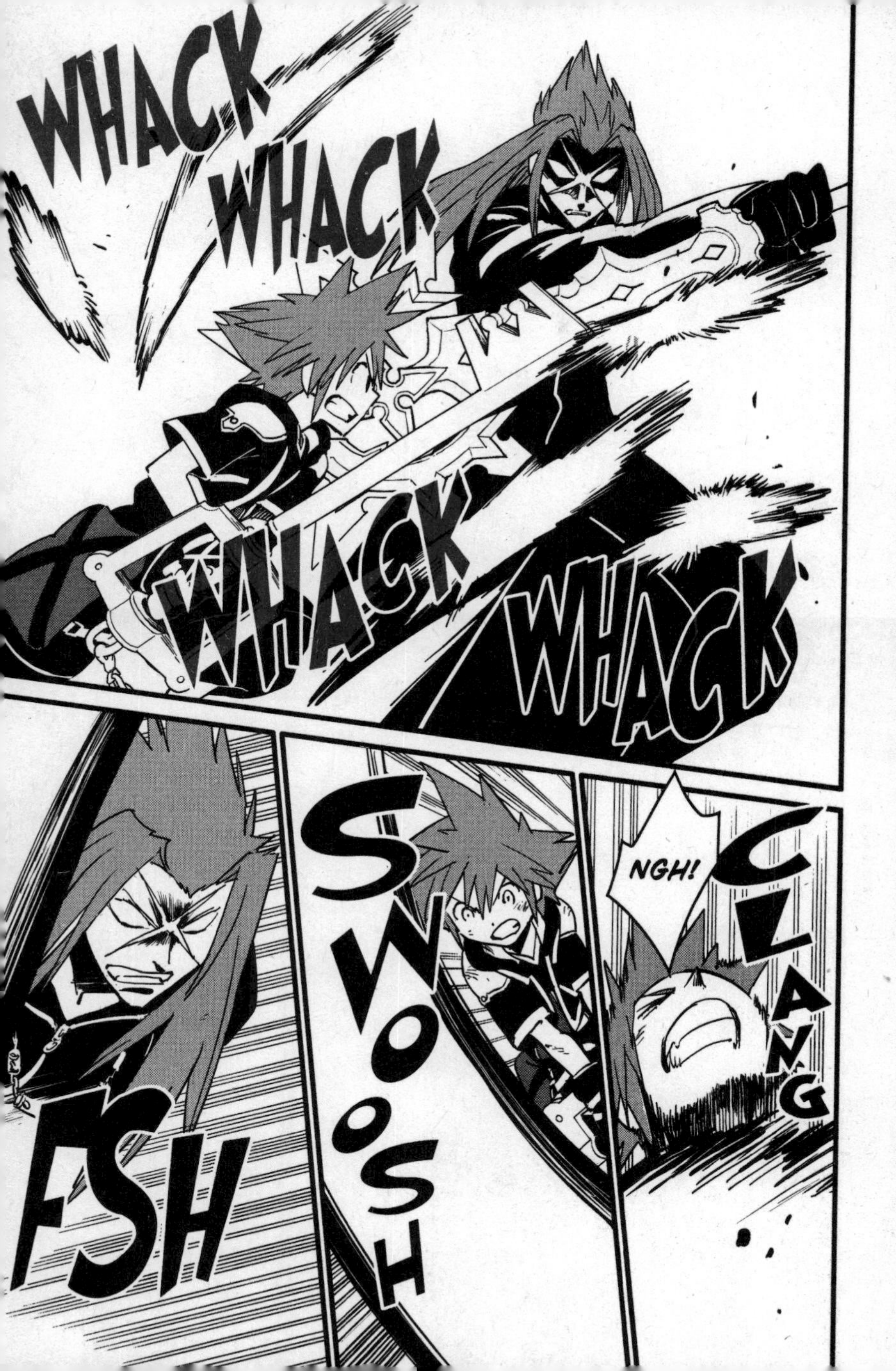
WHACK
WHACK
WHACK
WHACK
NGH!
CLANG
SWOOSH
FSH

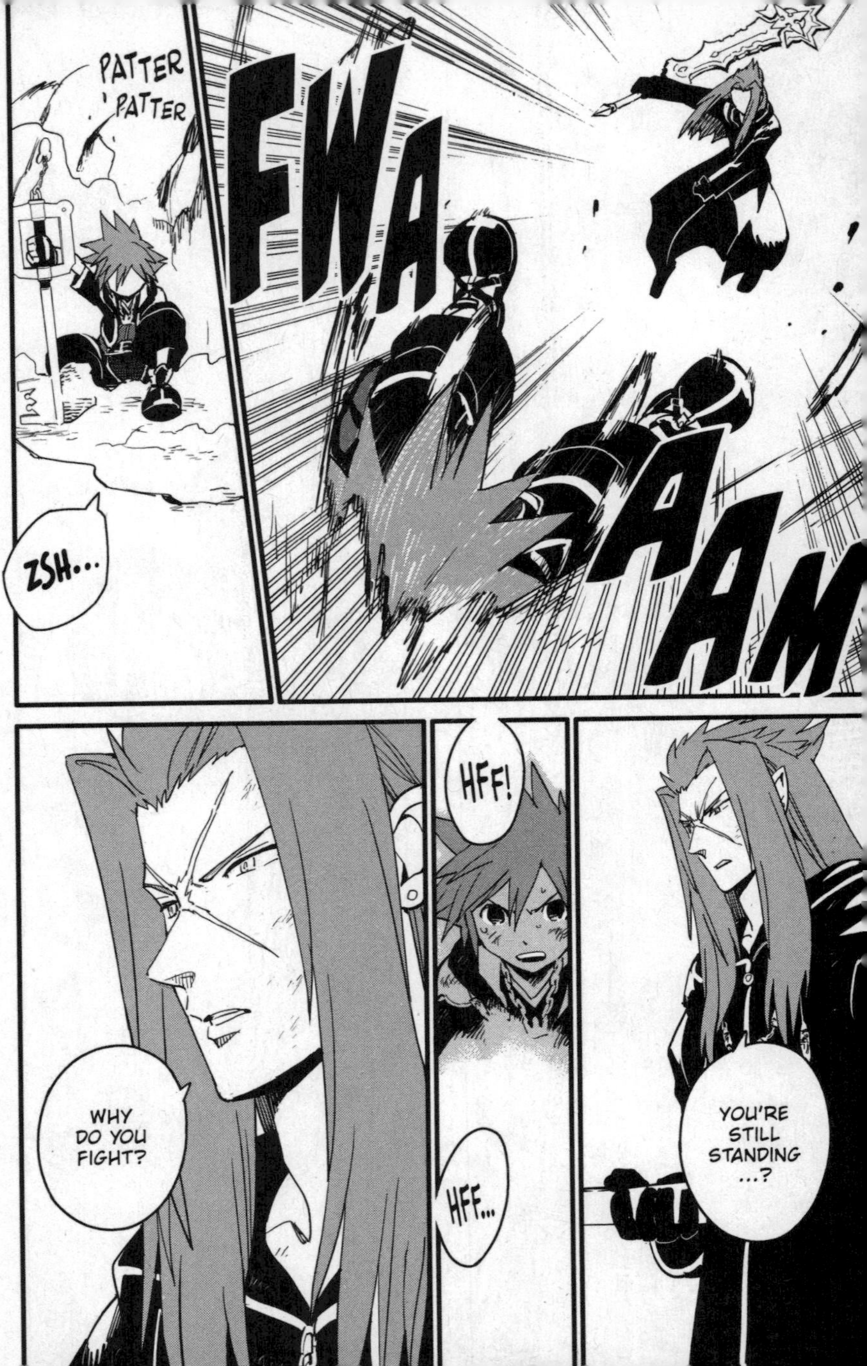
FWA
AAM
PATTER PATTER
ZSH...
YOU'RE STILL STANDING ...?
HFF!
HFF...
WHY DO YOU FIGHT?

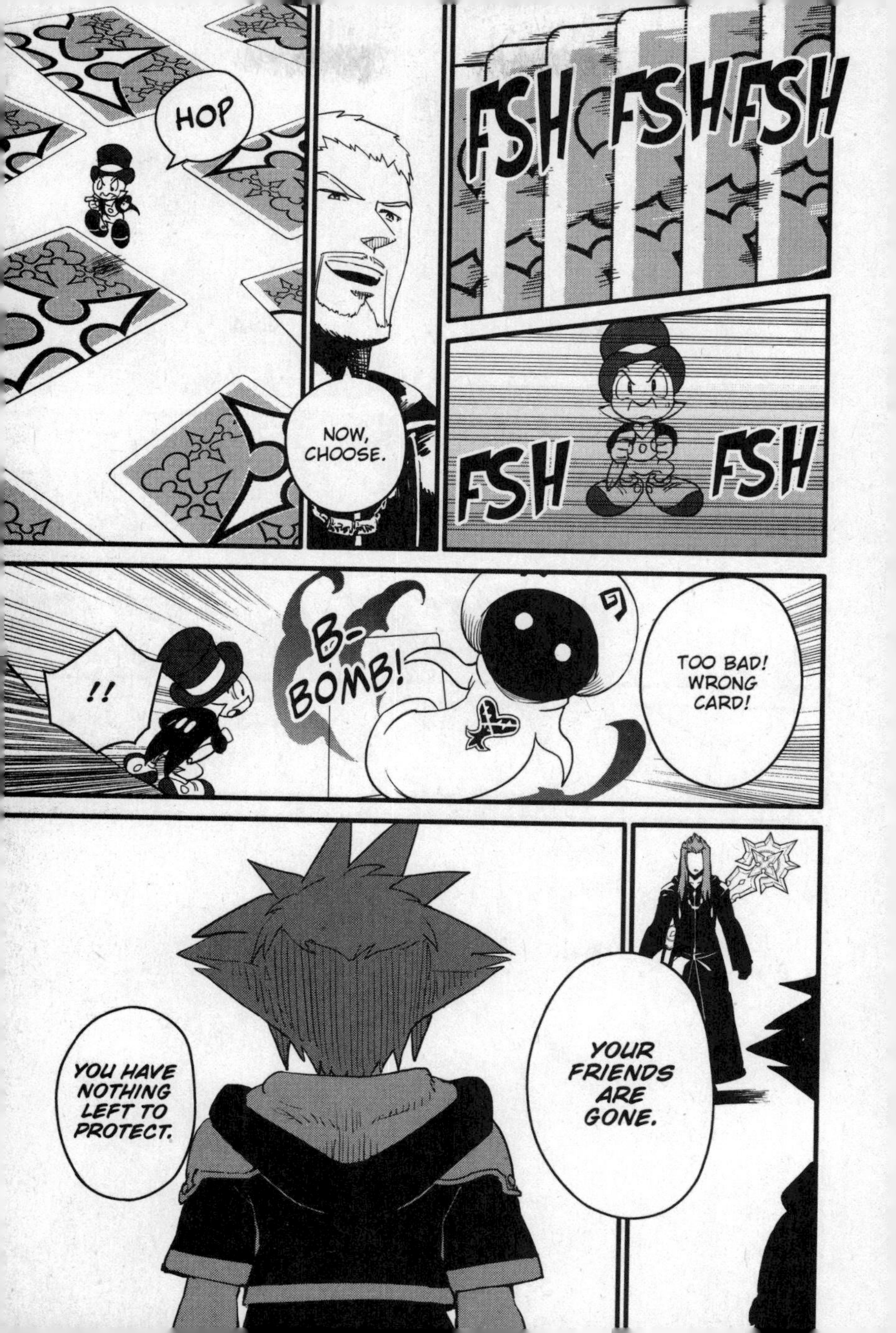
FSH FSH FSH
FSH
FSH
NOW, CHOOSE.
HOP
TOO BAD! WRONG CARD!
B-BOMB!
!!
YOUR FRIENDS ARE GONE.
YOU HAVE NOTHING LEFT TO PROTECT.

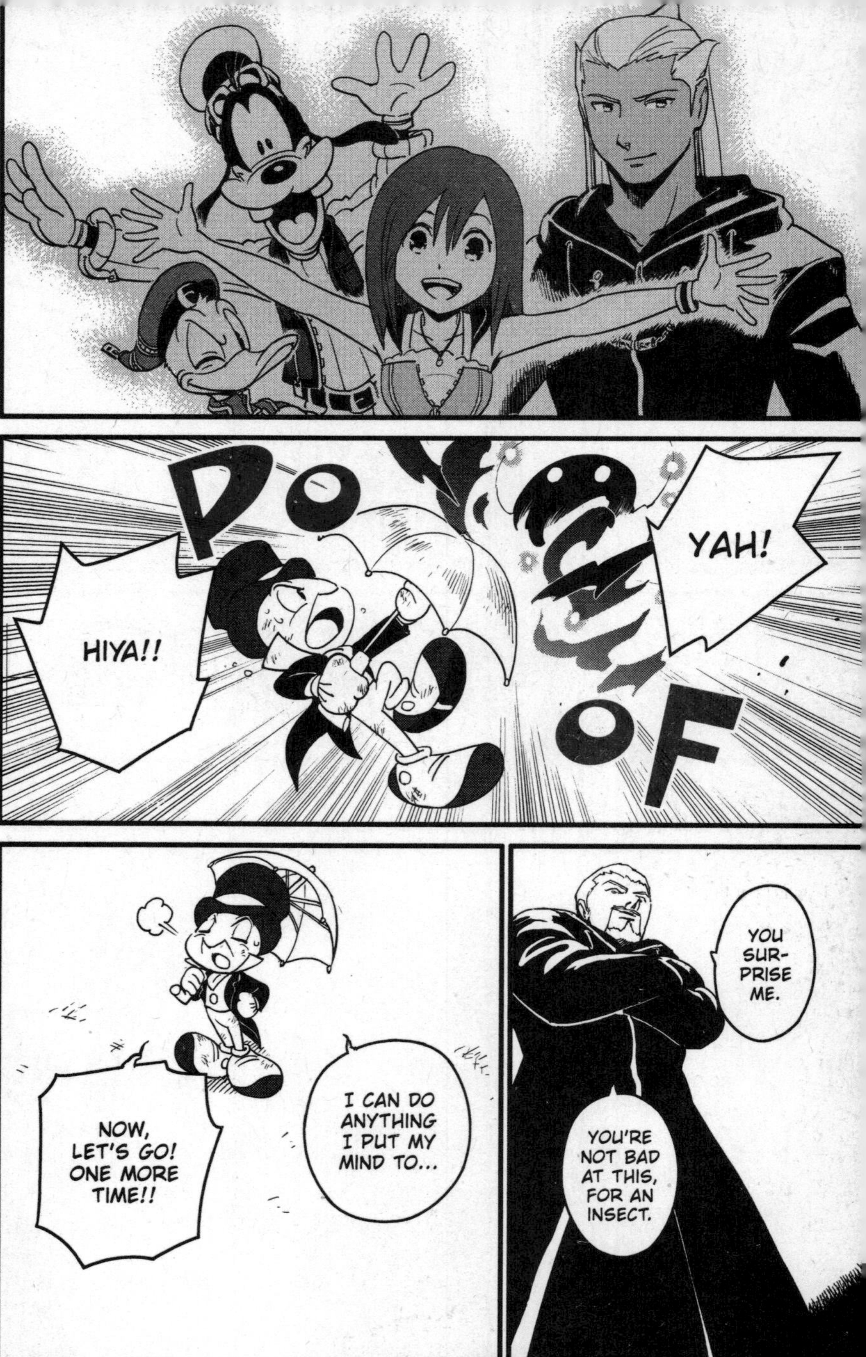
YAH!
POOF
HIYA!!
YOU SURPRISE ME.
YOU'RE NOT BAD AT THIS, FOR AN INSECT.
I CAN DO ANYTHING I PUT MY MIND TO...
NOW, LET'S GO! ONE MORE TIME!!

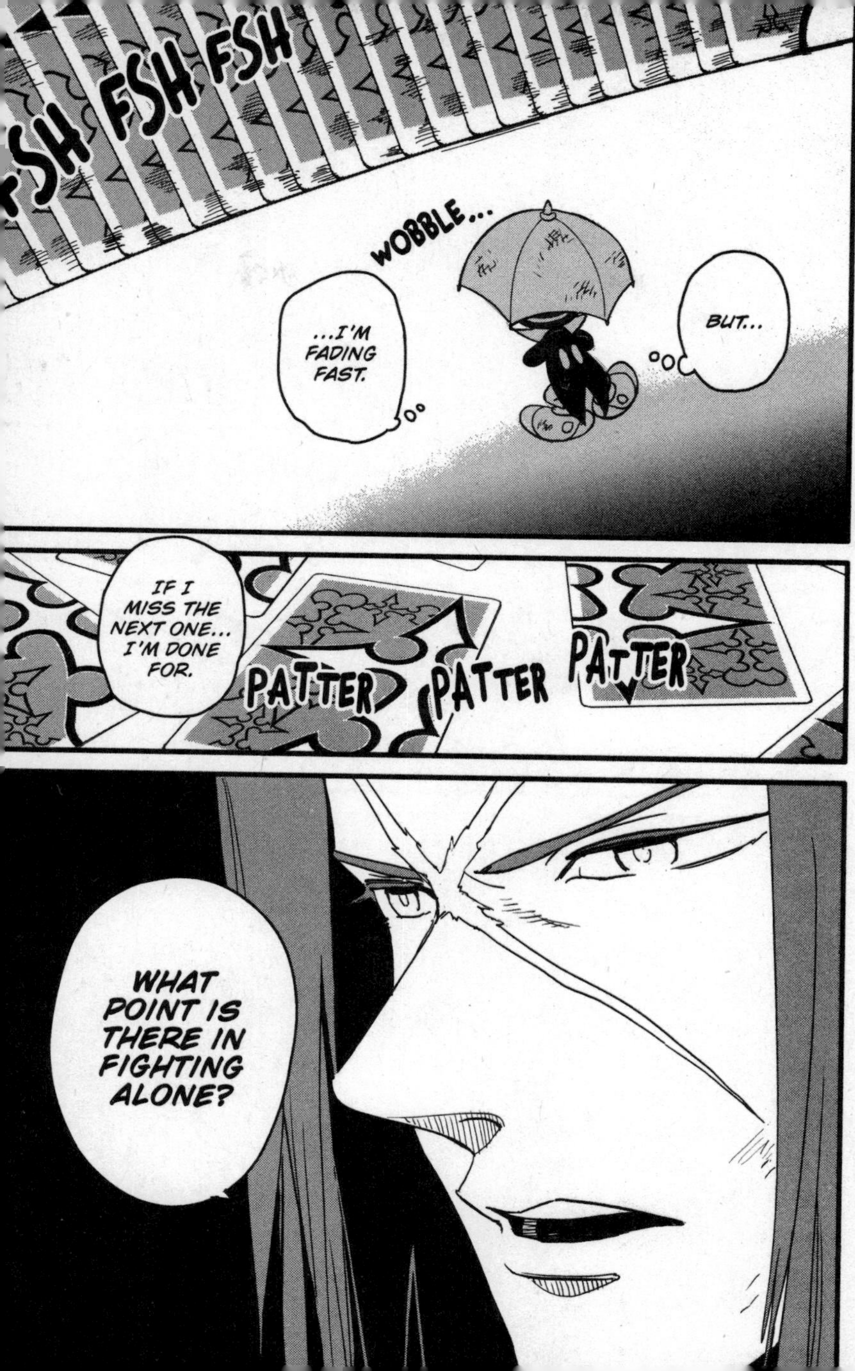
FSH FSH FSH
WOBBLE...
BUT...
...I'M FADING FAST.
IF I MISS THE NEXT ONE... I'M DONE FOR.
PATTER PATTER PATTER
WHAT POINT IS THERE IN FIGHTING ALONE?

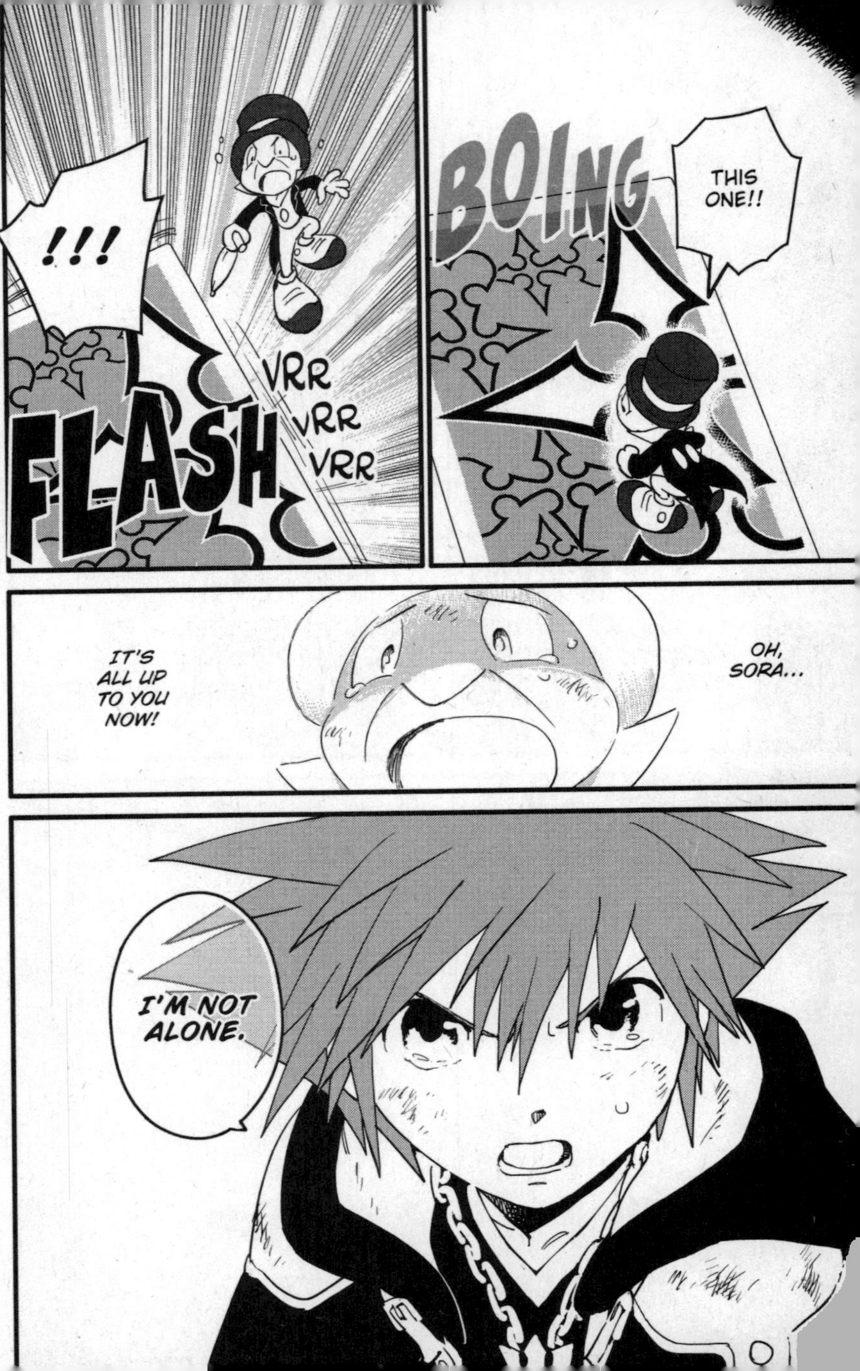
BOING
THIS ONE!!
!!!
FLASH
VRR VRR VRR
OH, SORA...
IT'S ALL UP TO YOU NOW!
I'M NOT ALONE.

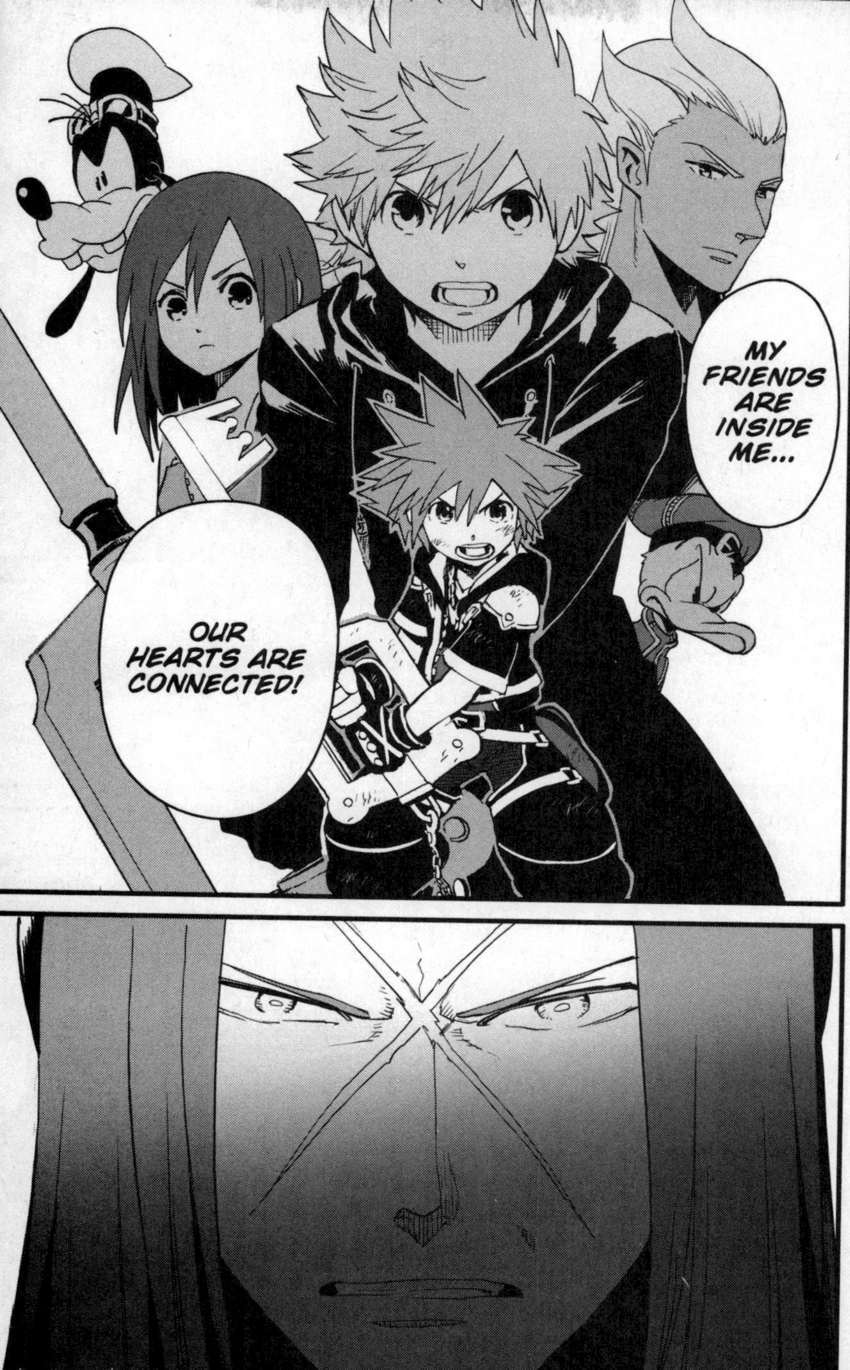
MY FRIENDS ARE INSIDE ME...
OUR HEARTS ARE CONNECTED!

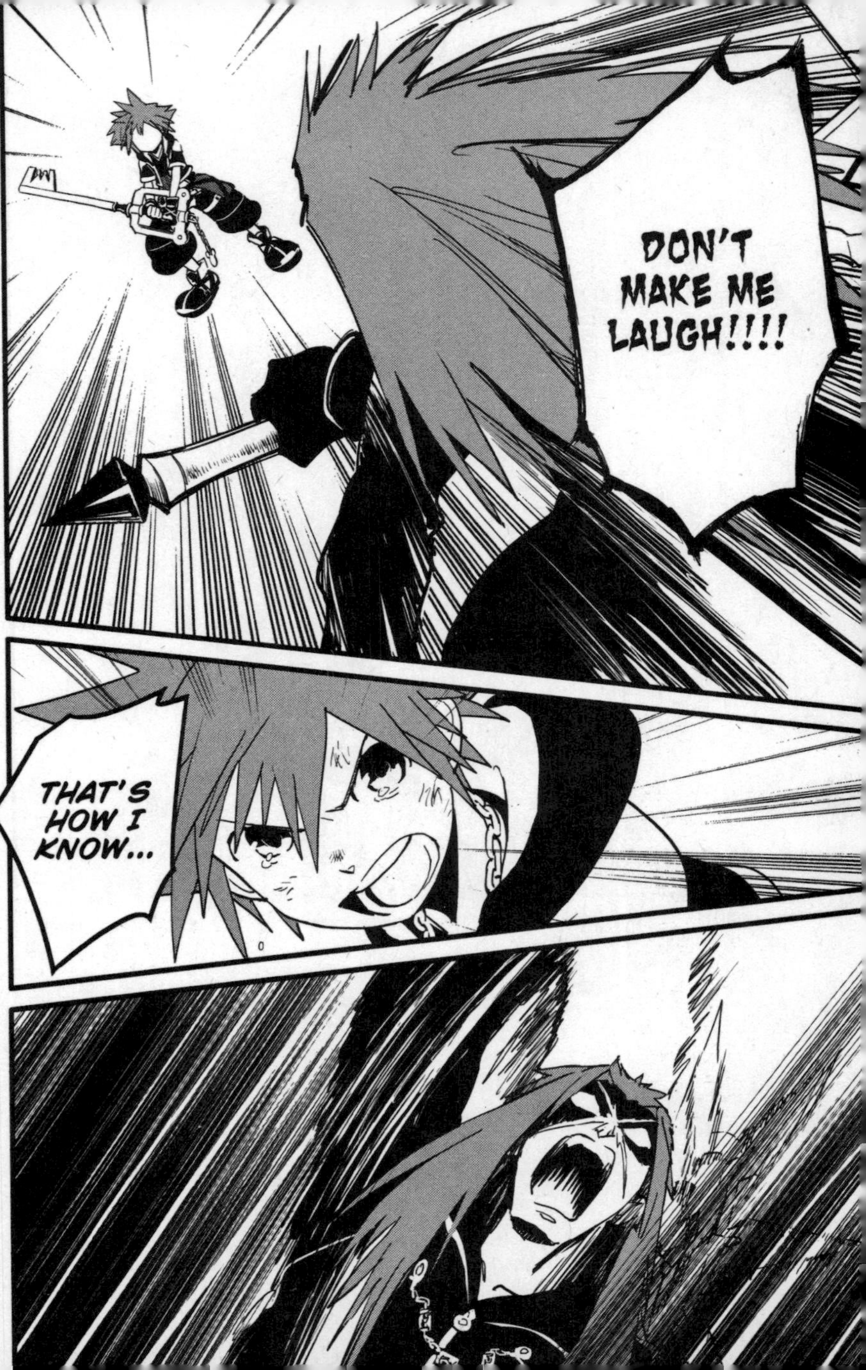
DON'T MAKE ME LAUGH!!!!
THAT'S HOW I KNOW...

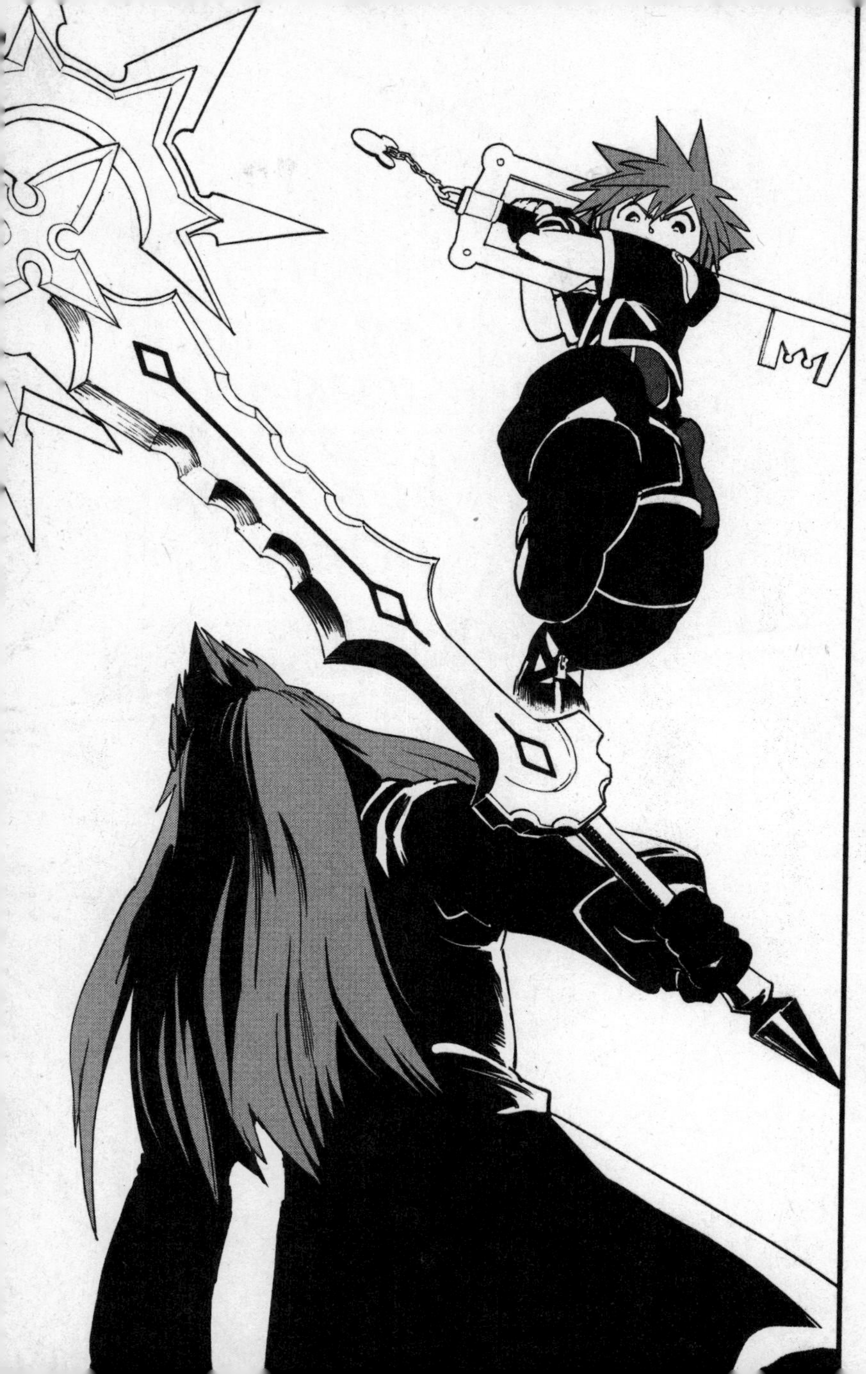

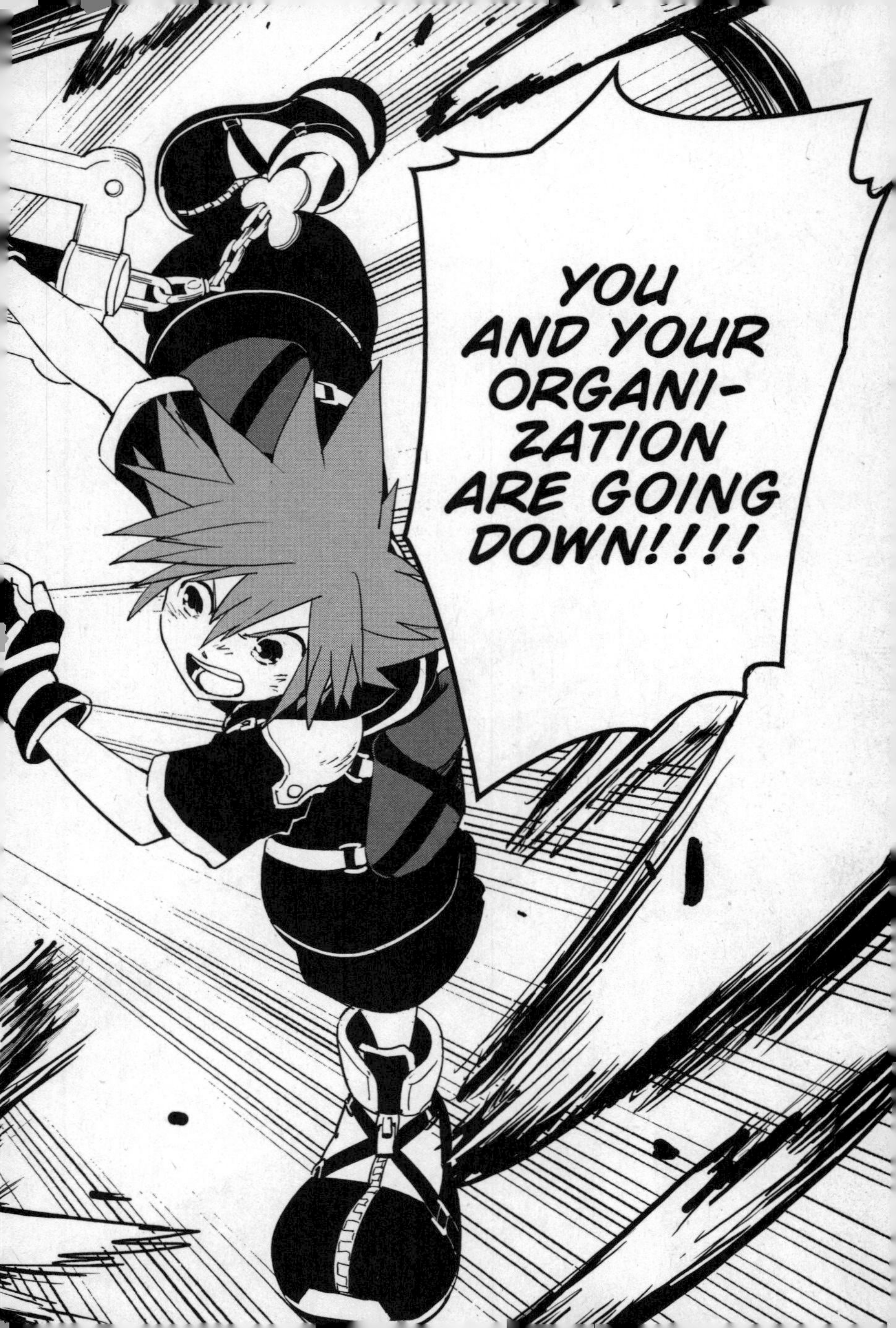
YOU AND YOUR ORGANI-ZATION ARE GOING DOWN!!!!

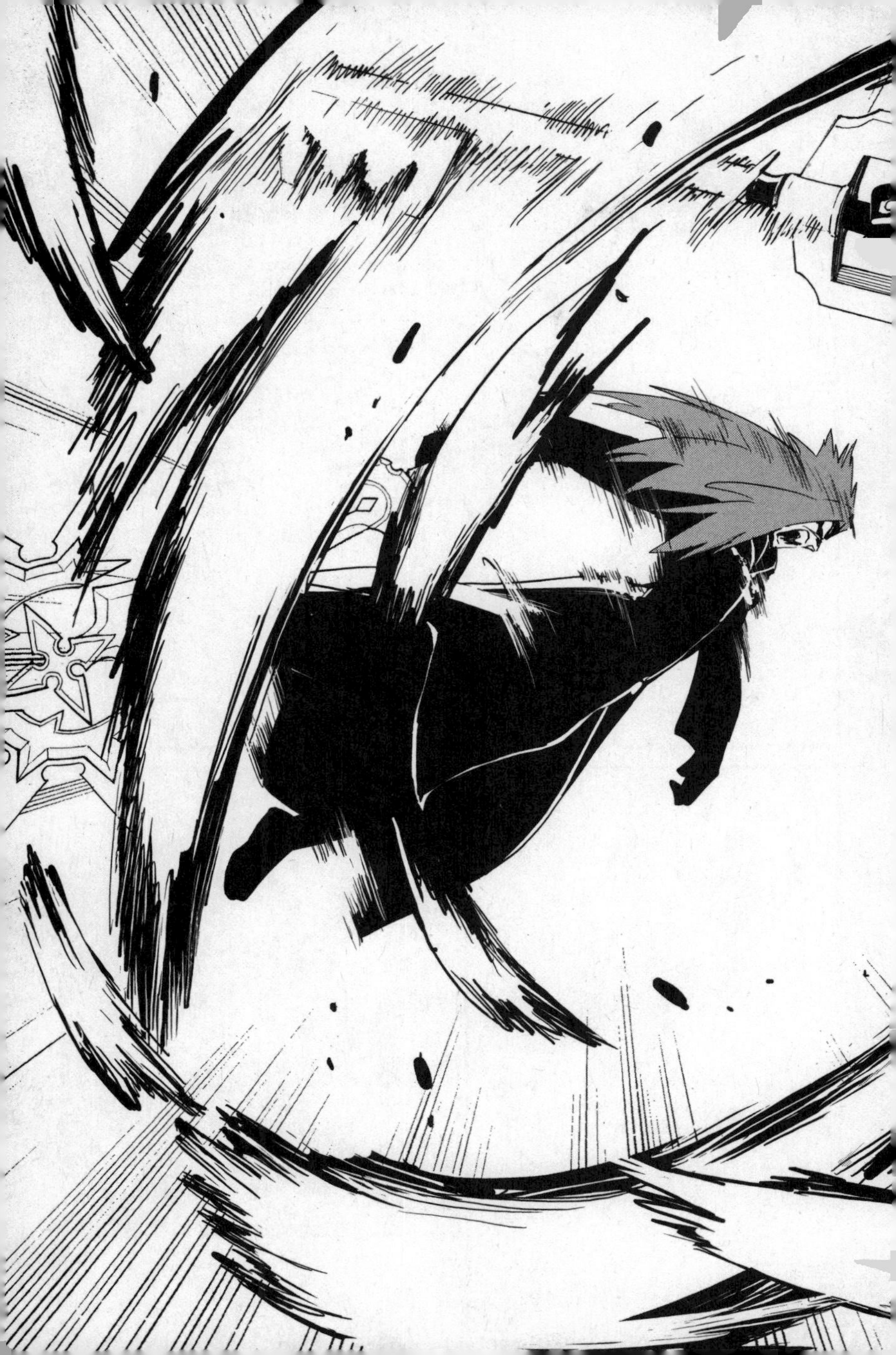

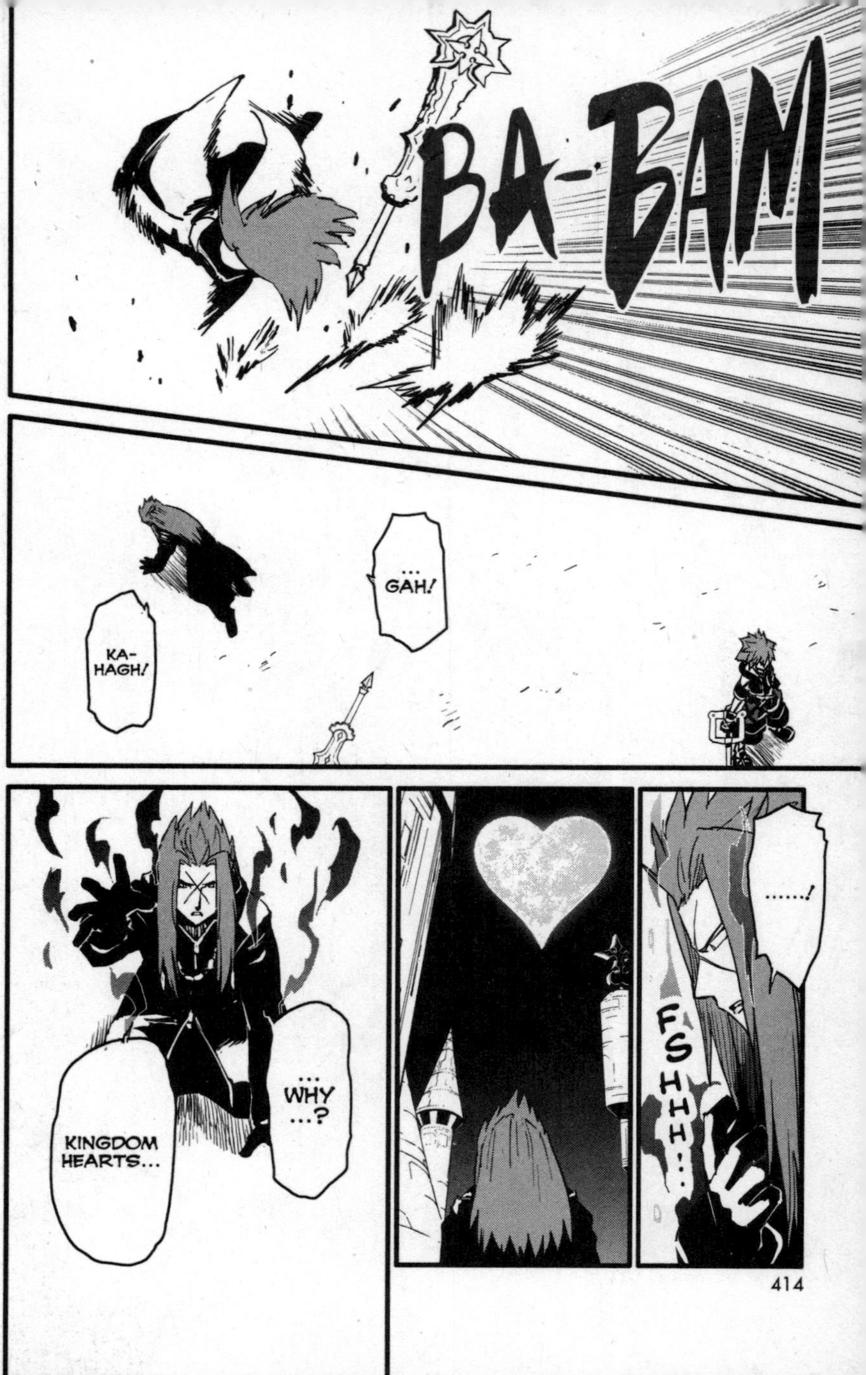
BA-BAM
... GAH!
KA-HAGH!
......!
FSHHH!...
... WHY ...?
KINGDOM HEARTS...

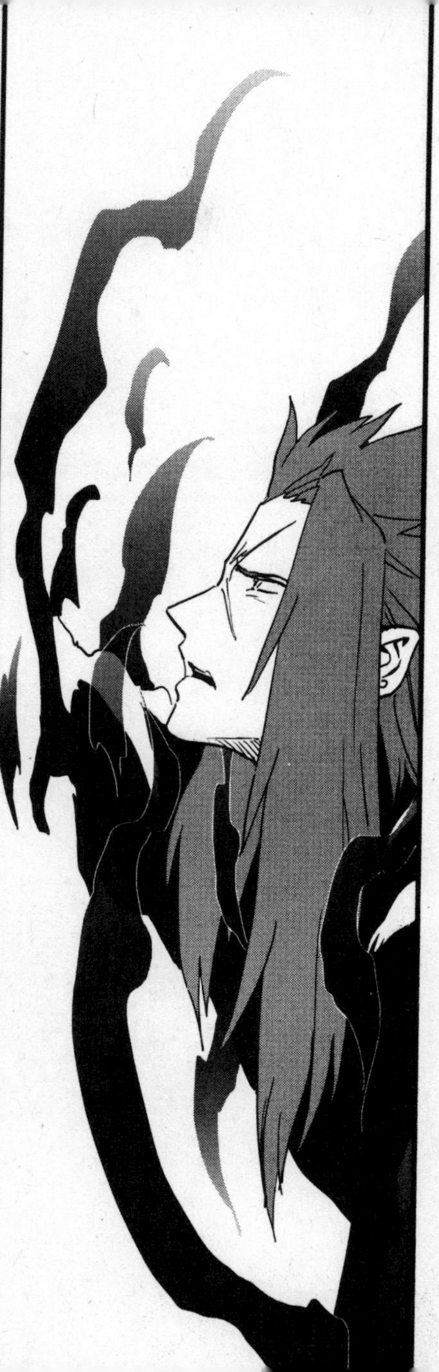
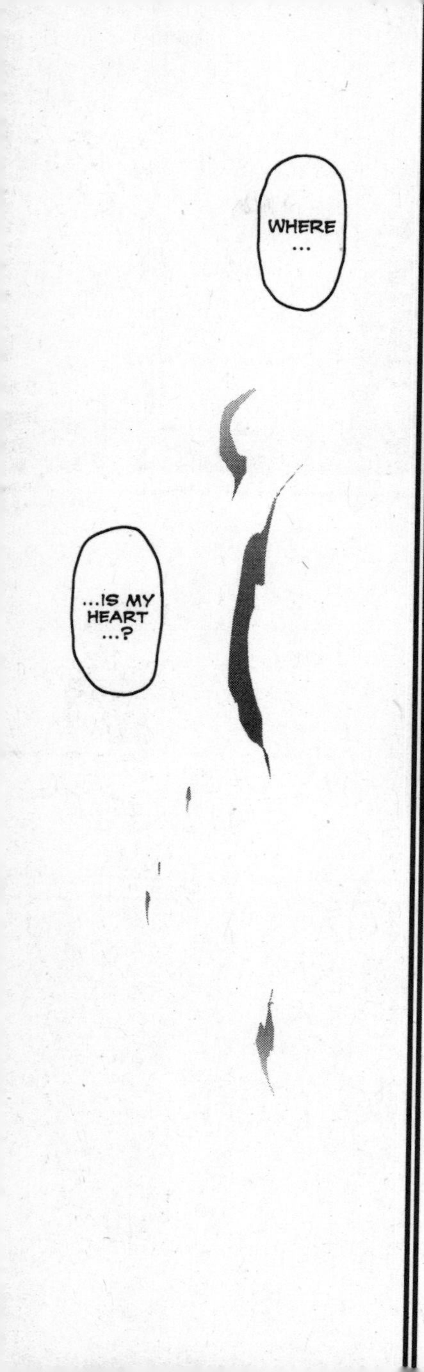
WHERE ...
...IS MY HEART ...?

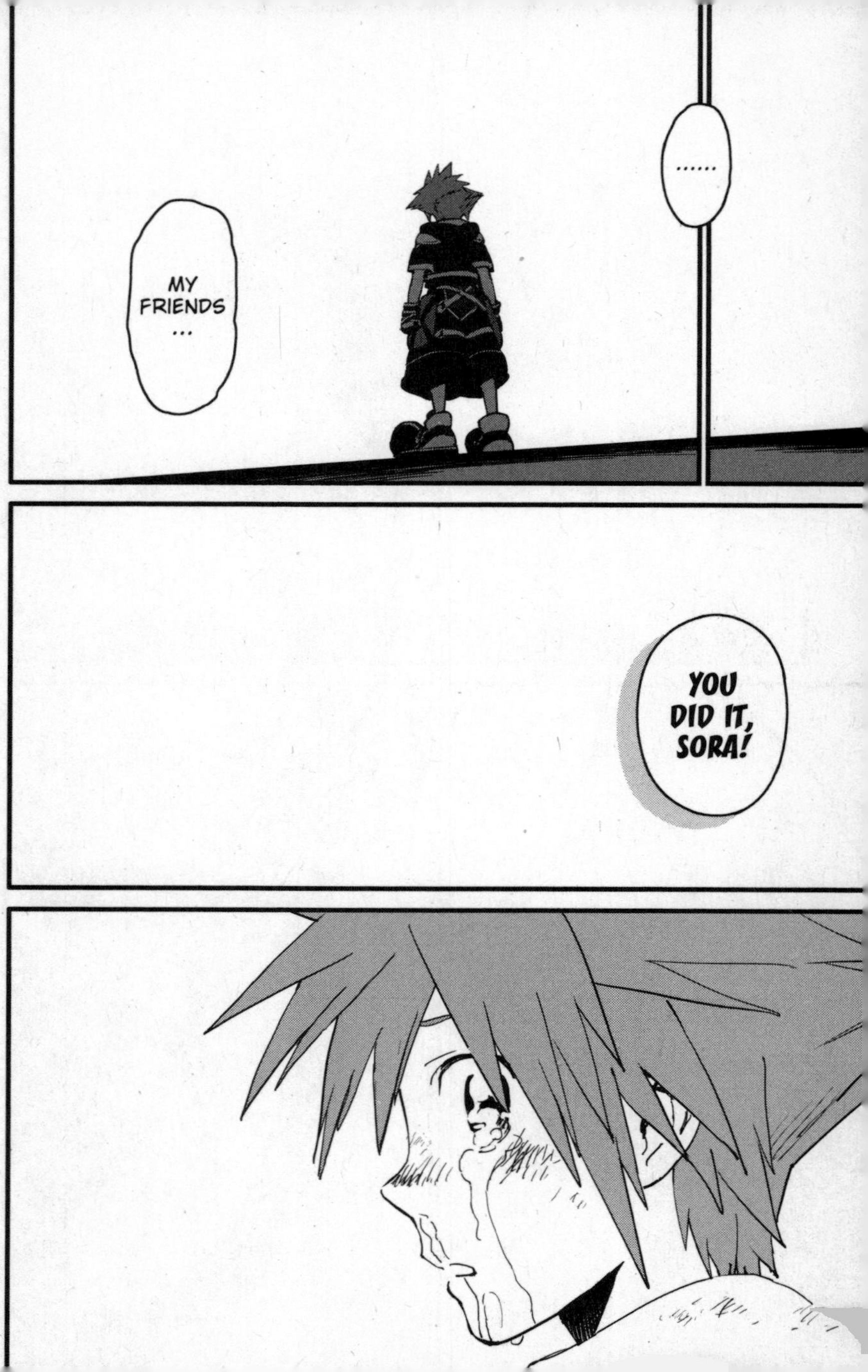
......
MY FRIENDS ...
YOU DID IT, SORA!

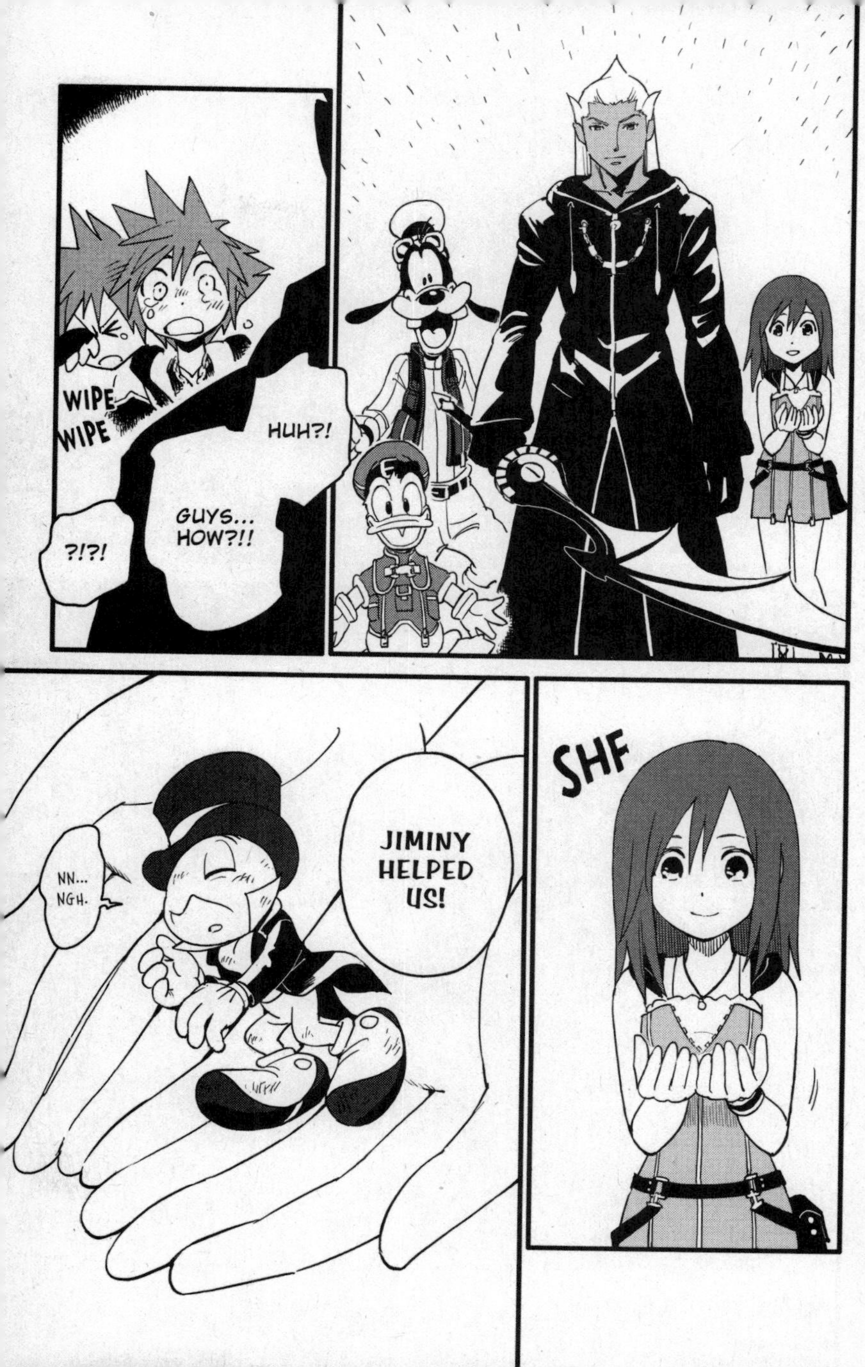
HUH?!
WIPE WIPE
GUYS... HOW?!!
?!?!
SHF
JIMINY HELPED US!
NN... NGH.

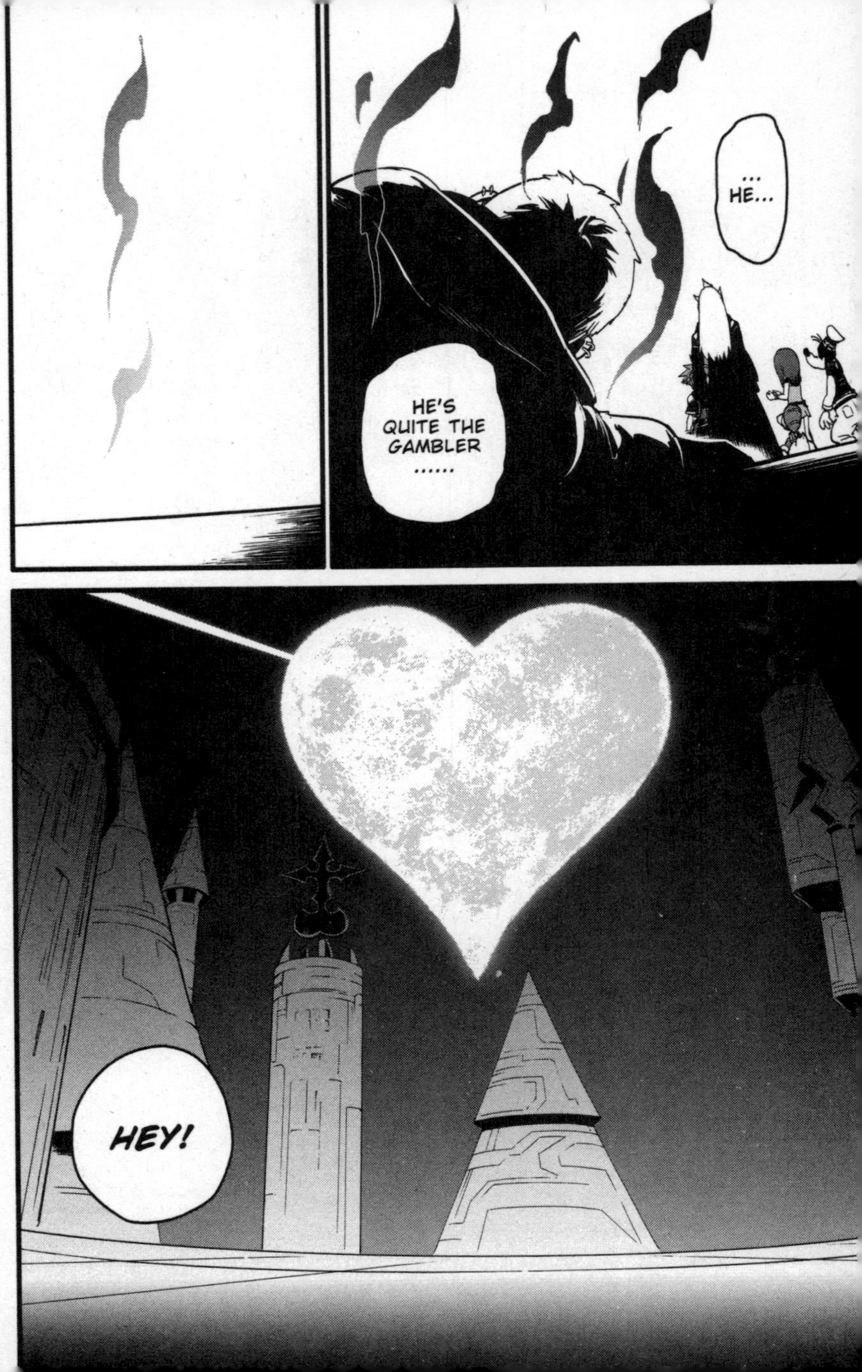
... HE...
HE'S QUITE THE GAMBLER ......
HEY!

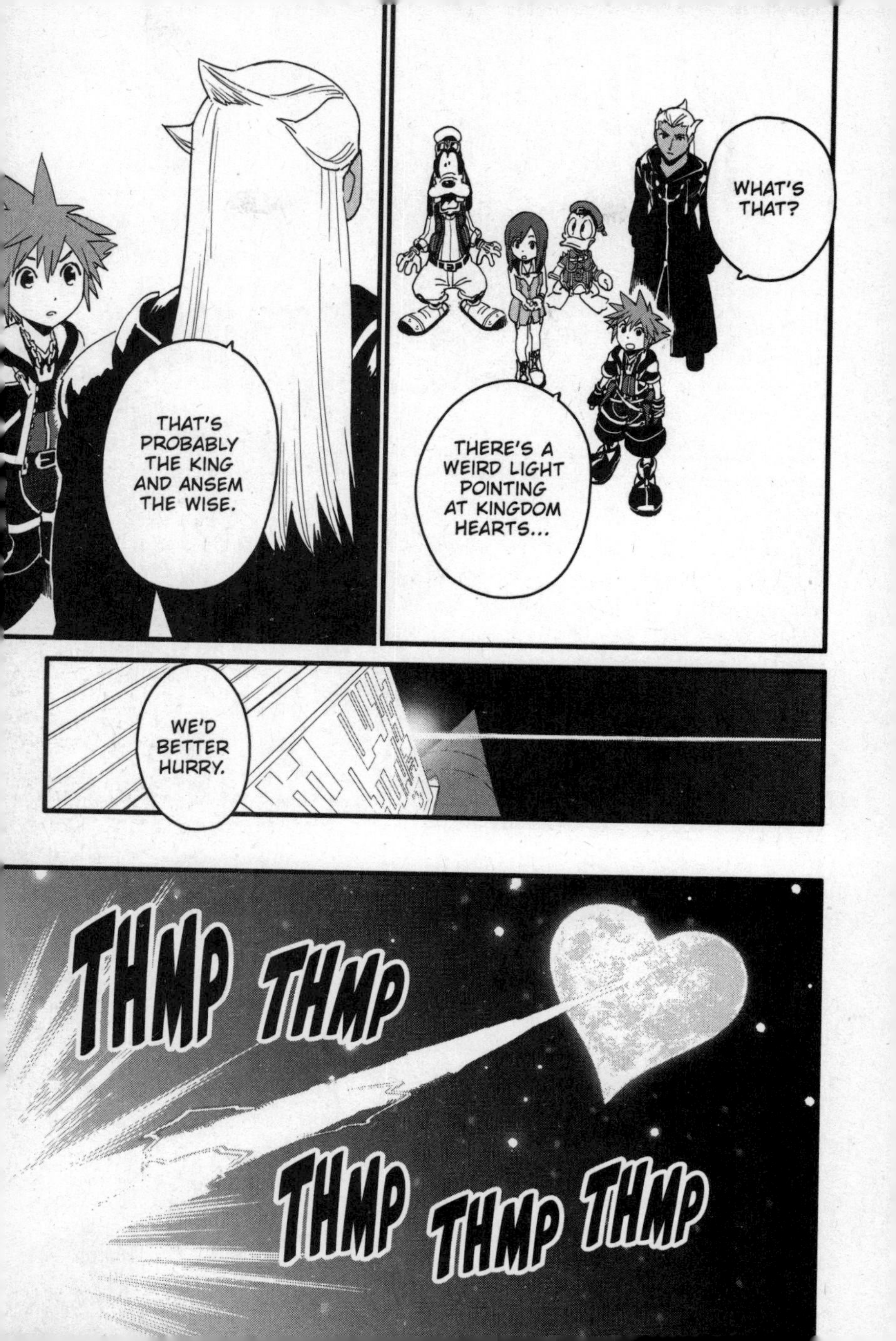
WHAT'S THAT?
THERE'S A WEIRD LIGHT POINTING AT KINGDOM HEARTS...
THAT'S PROBABLY THE KING AND ANSEM THE WISE.
WE'D BETTER HURRY.
THMP THMP
THMP THMP THMP

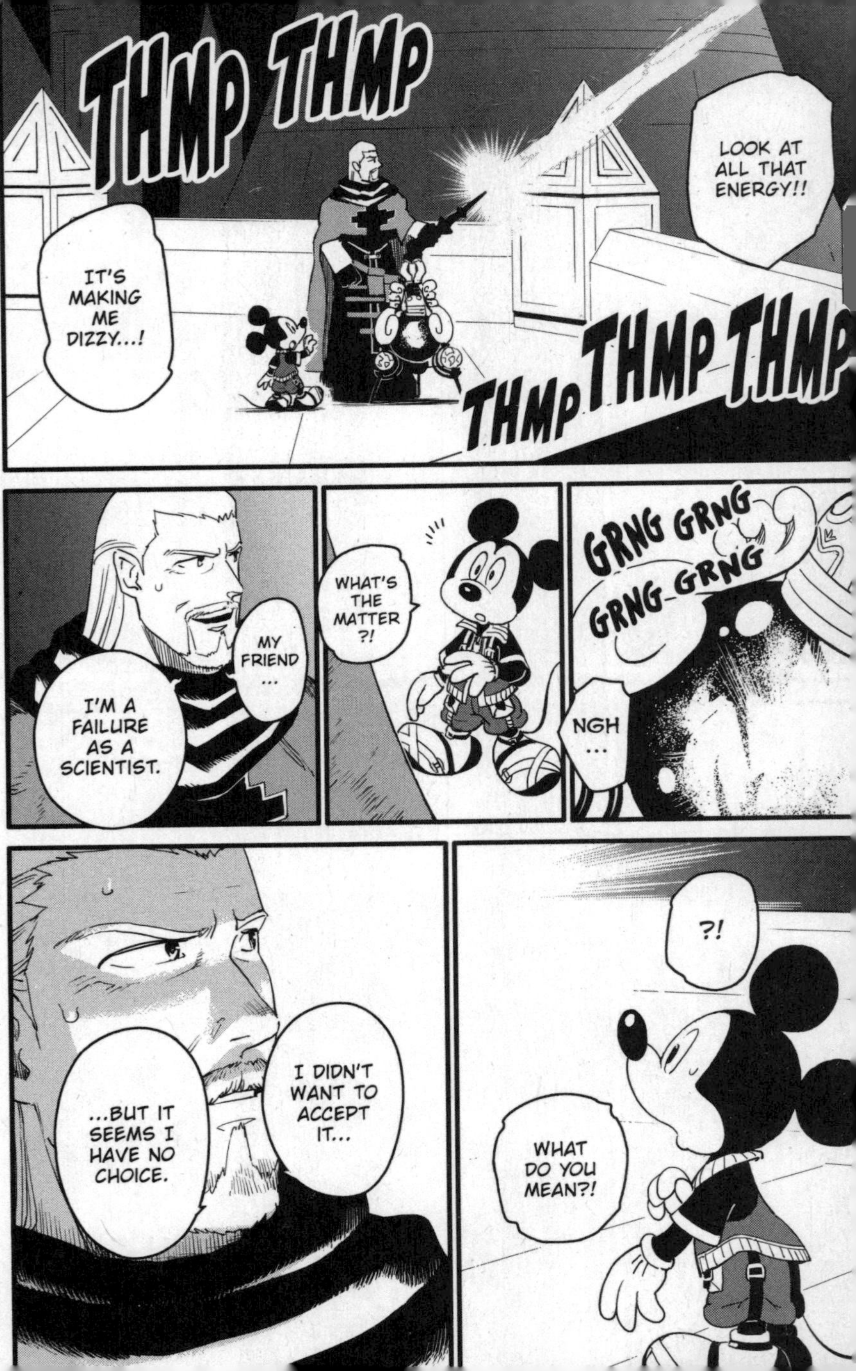
LOOK AT ALL THAT ENERGY!!
THMP THMP
IT'S MAKING ME DIZZY...!
THMP THMP THMP
GRNG GRNG GRNG GRNG
NGH...
WHAT'S THE MATTER?!
MY FRIEND...
I'M A FAILURE AS A SCIENTIST.
?!
WHAT DO YOU MEAN?!
I DIDN'T WANT TO ACCEPT IT...
...BUT IT SEEMS I HAVE NO CHOICE.

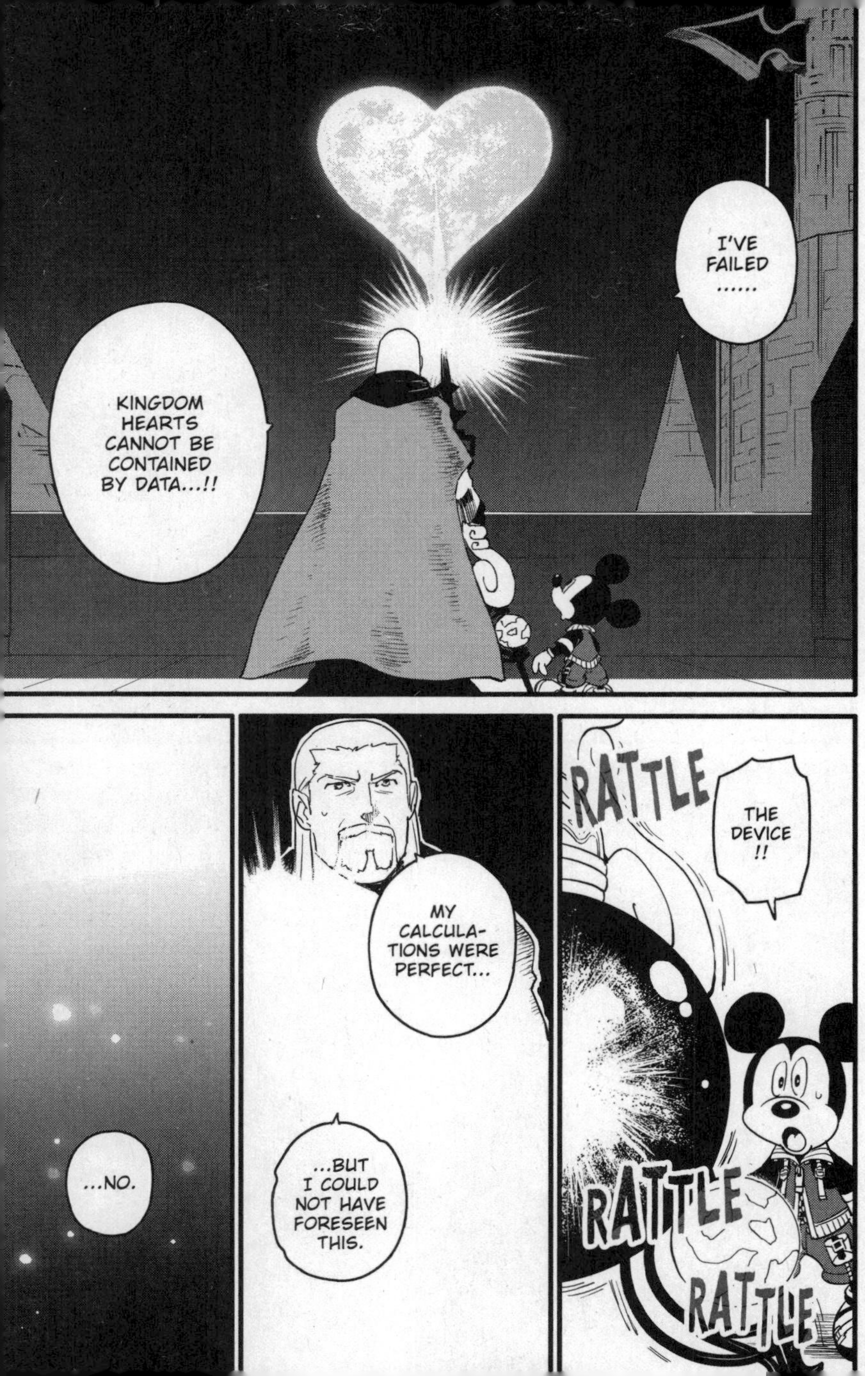
I'VE FAILED ......
KINGDOM HEARTS CANNOT BE CONTAINED BY DATA...!!
THE DEVICE !!
RATTLE
RATTLE
RATTLE
MY CALCULA-TIONS WERE PERFECT...
...BUT I COULD NOT HAVE FORESEEN THIS.
...NO.

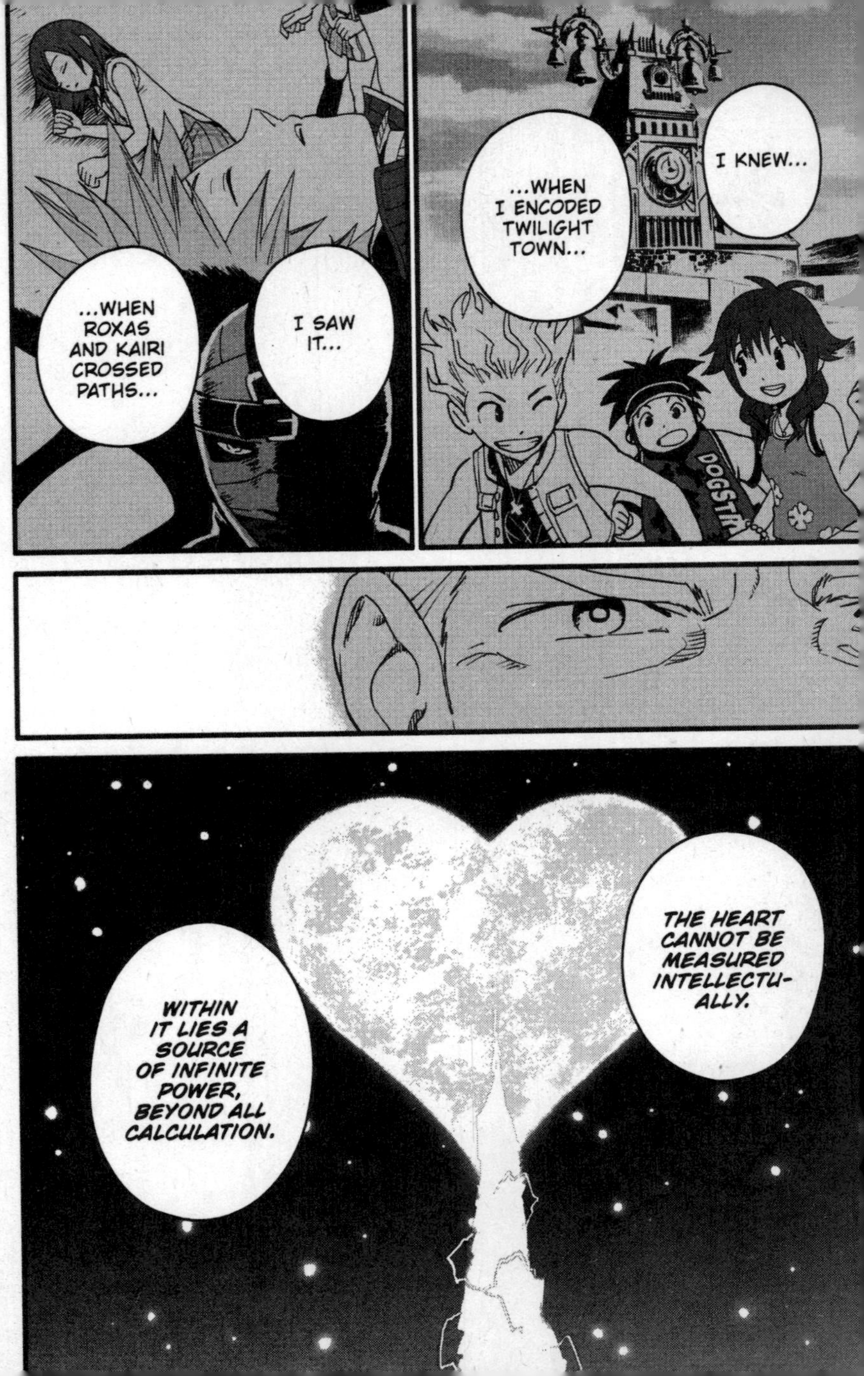
I KNEW...
...WHEN I ENCODED TWILIGHT TOWN...
I SAW IT...
...WHEN ROXAS AND KAIRI CROSSED PATHS...
THE HEART CANNOT BE MEASURED INTELLECTU-ALLY.
WITHIN IT LIES A SOURCE OF INFINITE POWER, BEYOND ALL CALCULATION.

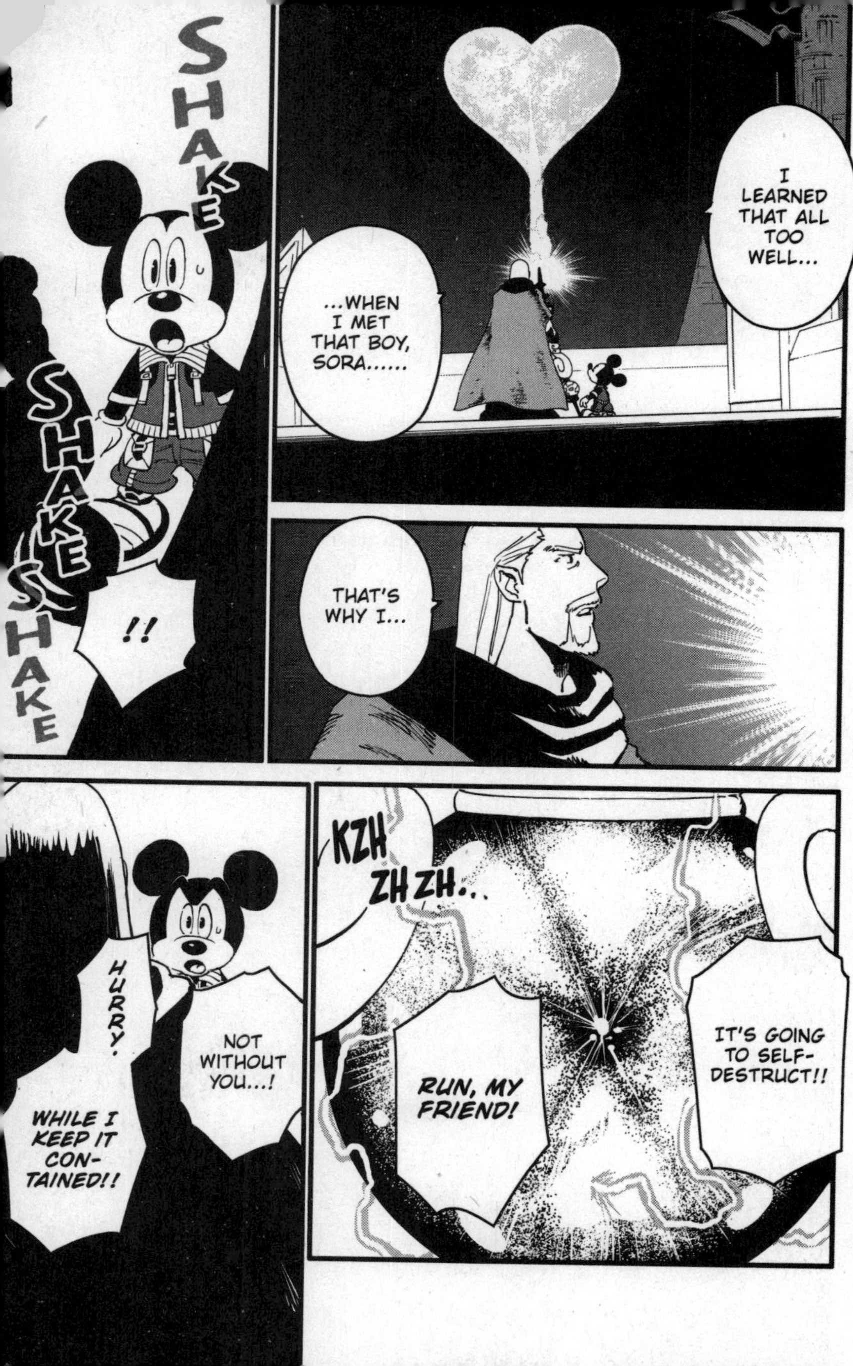
I LEARNED THAT ALL TOO WELL...
...WHEN I MET THAT BOY, SORA......
THAT'S WHY I...
SHAKE
SHAKE
SHAKE
SHAKE
!!
KZH ZH ZH...
IT'S GOING TO SELF-DESTRUCT!!
RUN, MY FRIEND!
NOT WITHOUT YOU...!
HURRY.
WHILE I KEEP IT CON-TAINED!!

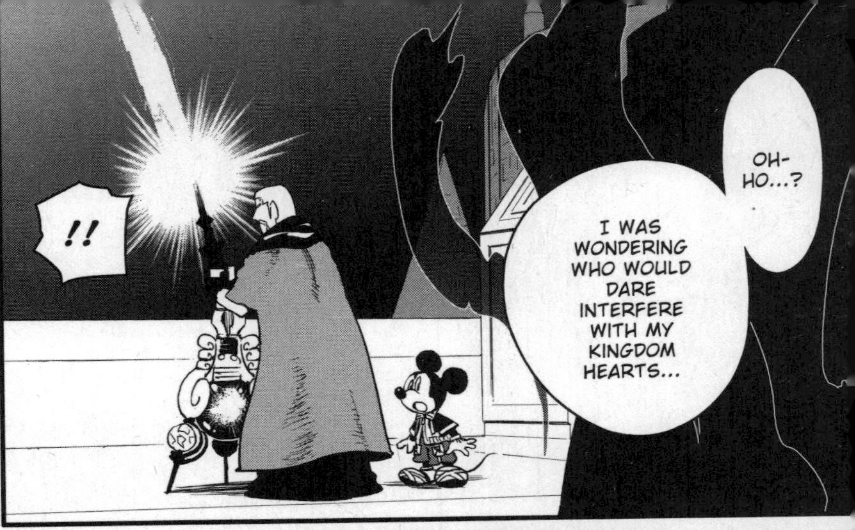
OH-HO...?
I WAS WONDERING WHO WOULD DARE INTERFERE WITH MY KINGDOM HEARTS...
!!
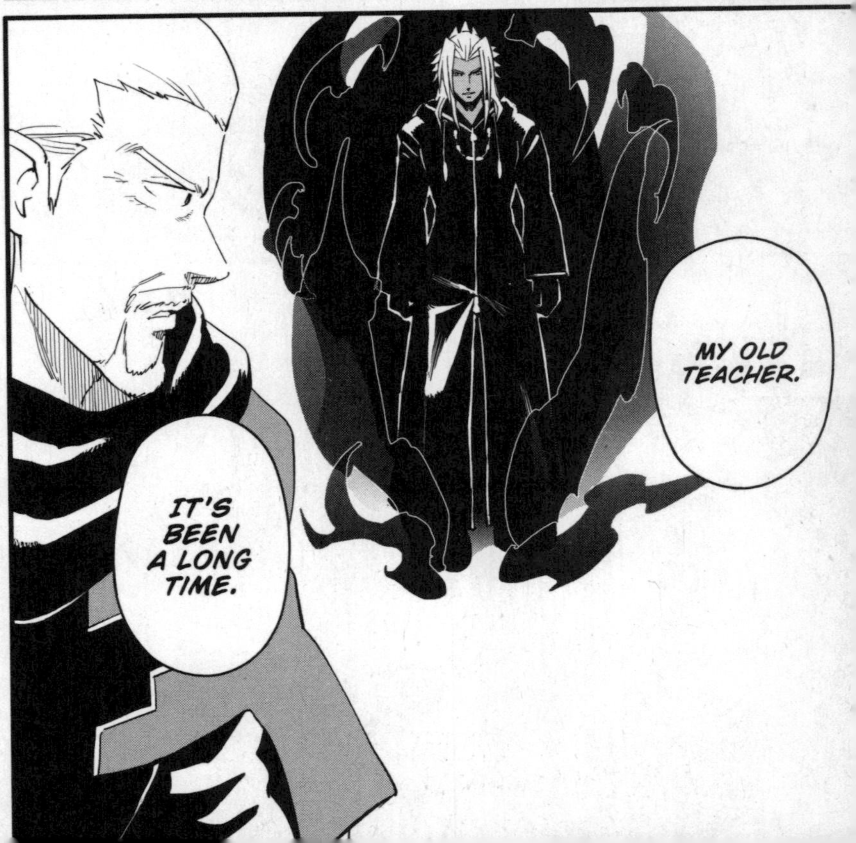
MY OLD TEACHER.
IT'S BEEN A LONG TIME.

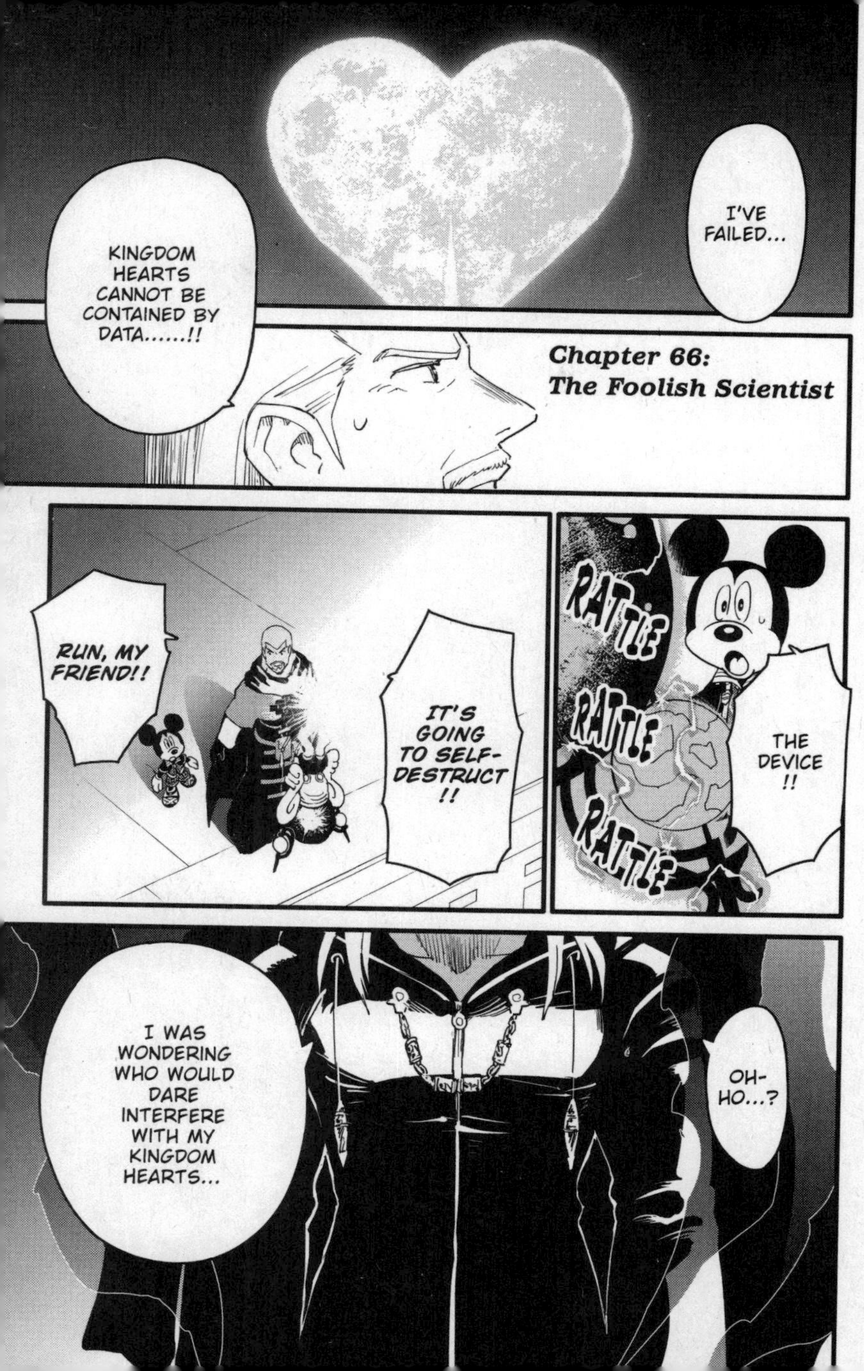
I'VE FAILED...
KINGDOM HEARTS CANNOT BE CONTAINED BY DATA......!!
Chapter 66: The Foolish Scientist
RATTLE
RATTLE
RATTLE
THE DEVICE !!
IT'S GOING TO SELF-DESTRUCT !!
RUN, MY FRIEND!!
OH-HO...?
I WAS WONDERING WHO WOULD DARE INTERFERE WITH MY KINGDOM HEARTS...

Chapter 66: The Foolish Scientist

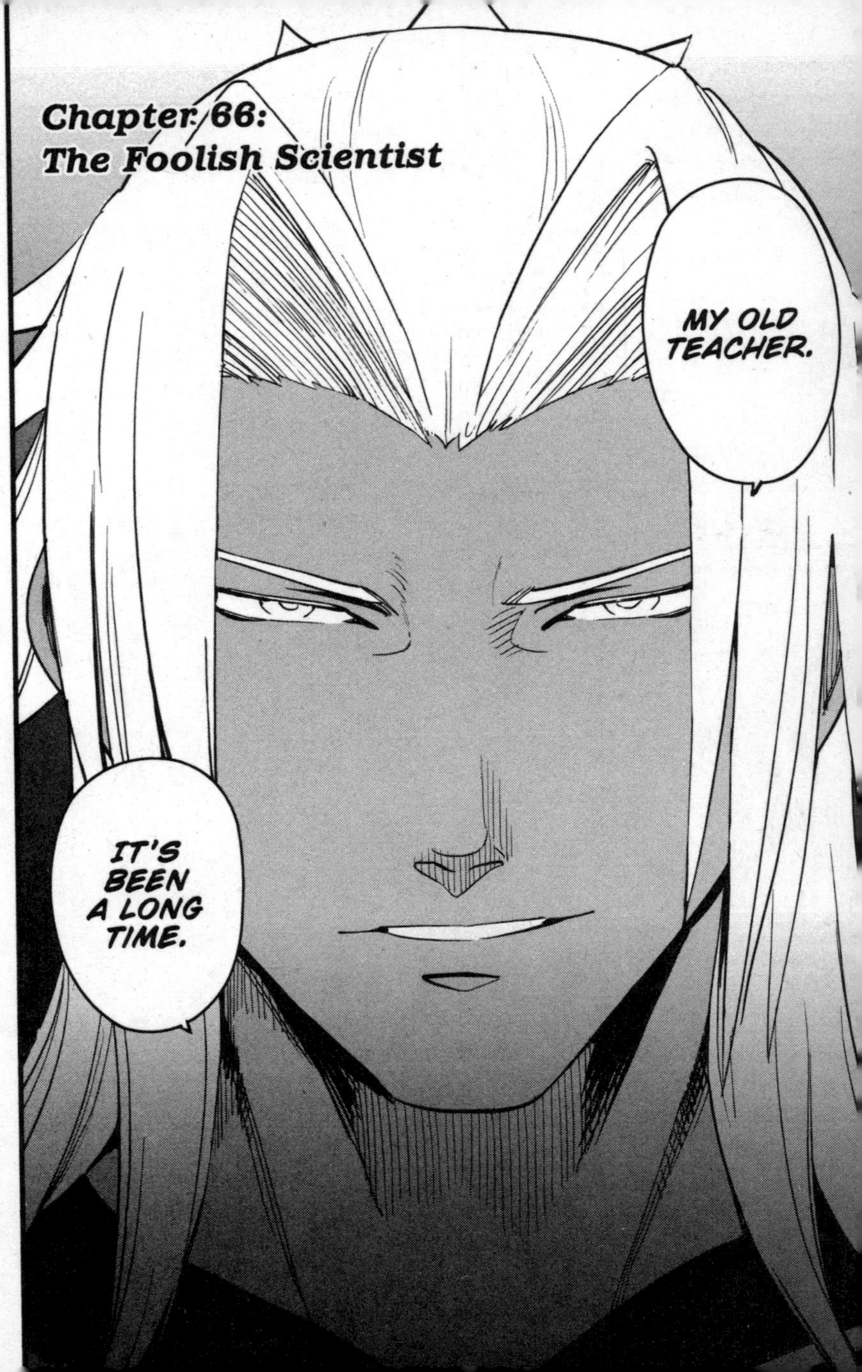
MY OLD TEACHER.
IT'S BEEN A LONG TIME.

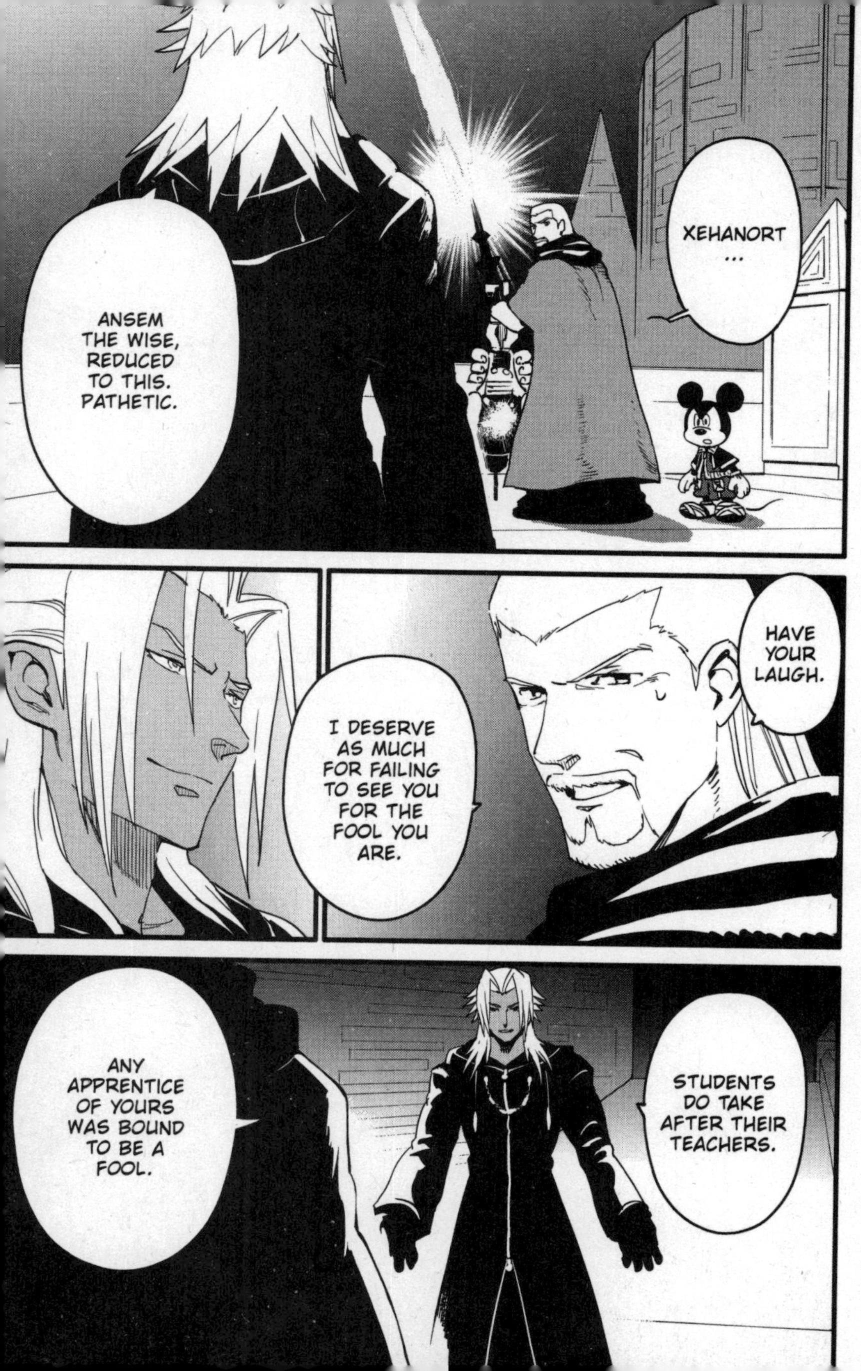
XEHANORT ...
ANSEM THE WISE, REDUCED TO THIS. PATHETIC.
HAVE YOUR LAUGH.
I DESERVE AS MUCH FOR FAILING TO SEE YOU FOR THE FOOL YOU ARE.
STUDENTS DO TAKE AFTER THEIR TEACHERS.
ANY APPRENTICE OF YOURS WAS BOUND TO BE A FOOL.

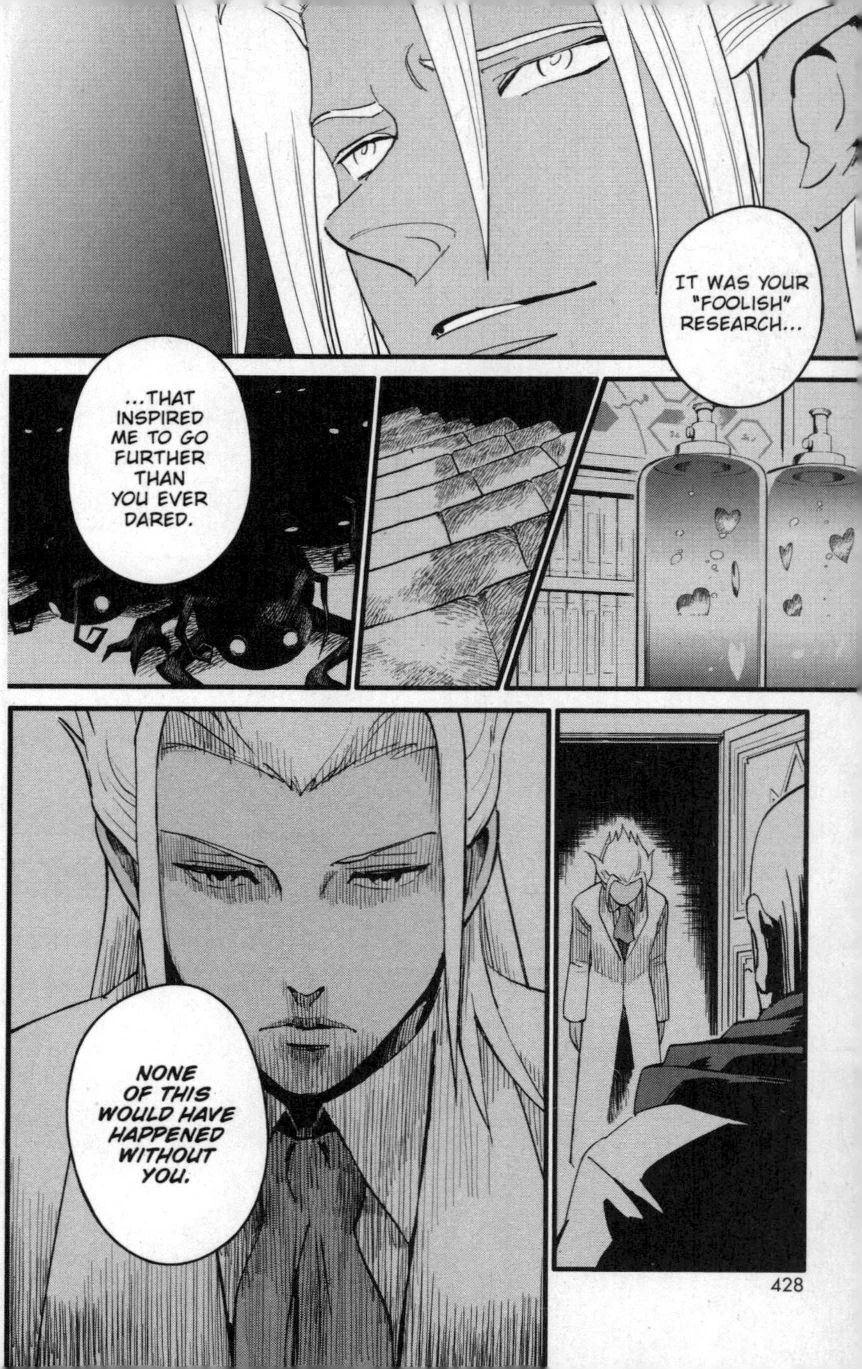
IT WAS YOUR "FOOLISH" RESEARCH...
...THAT INSPIRED ME TO GO FURTHER THAN YOU EVER DARED.
NONE OF THIS WOULD HAVE HAPPENED WITHOUT YOU.

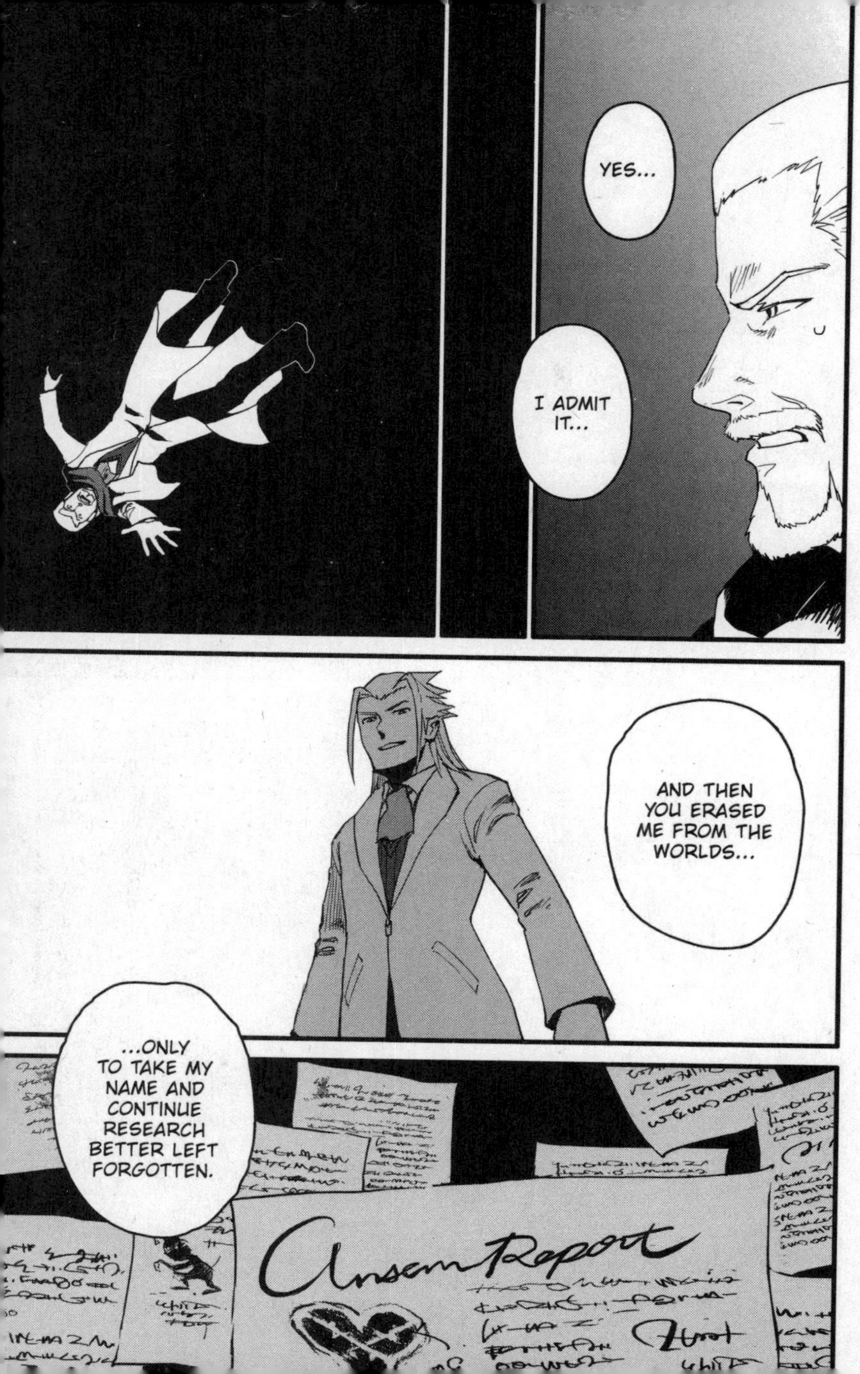
YES...
I ADMIT IT...
AND THEN YOU ERASED ME FROM THE WORLDS...
...ONLY TO TAKE MY NAME AND CONTINUE RESEARCH BETTER LEFT FORGOTTEN.
Ansem Report

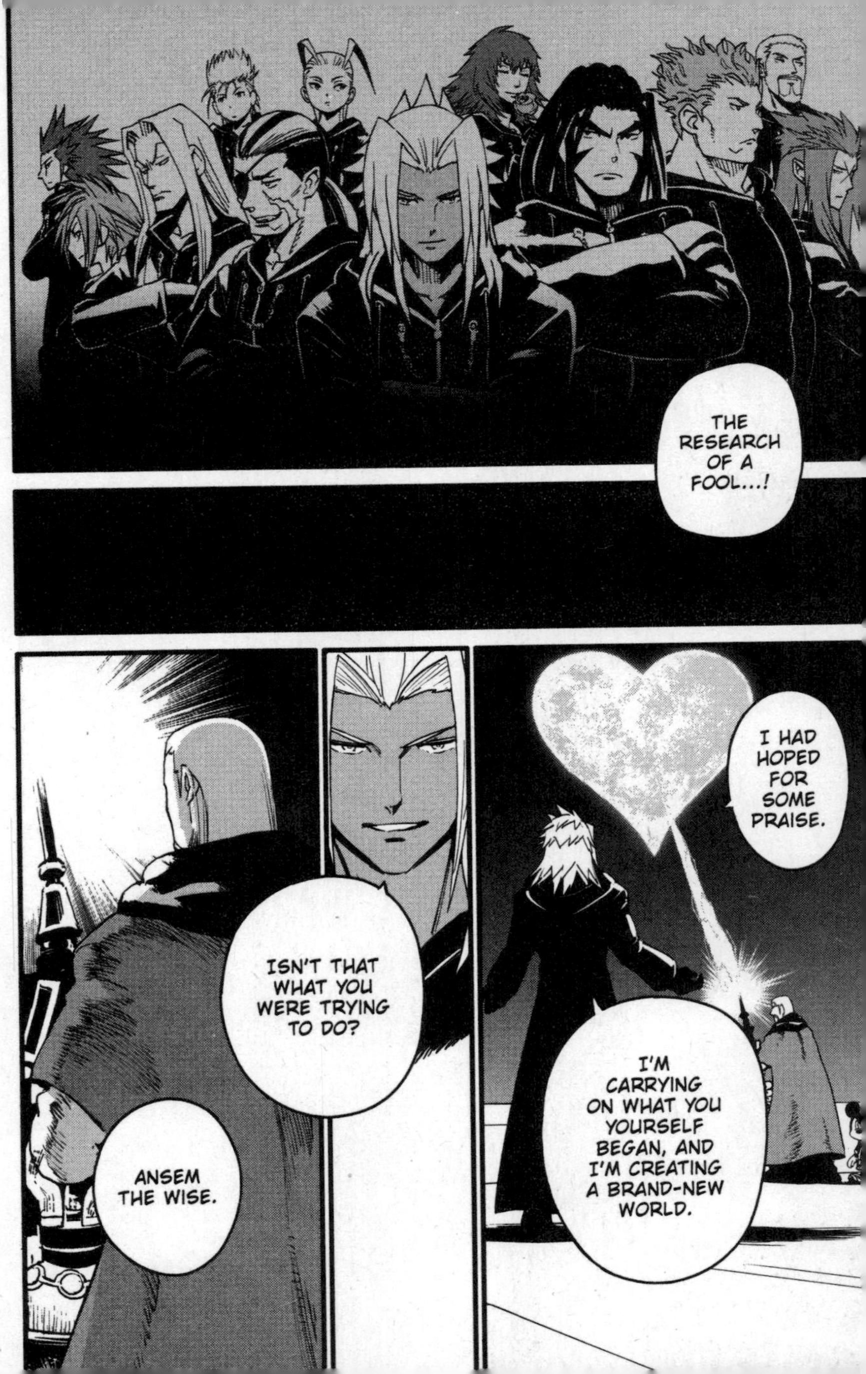
THE RESEARCH OF A FOOL...!
I HAD HOPED FOR SOME PRAISE.
I'M CARRYING ON WHAT YOU YOURSELF BEGAN, AND I'M CREATING A BRAND-NEW WORLD.
ISN'T THAT WHAT YOU WERE TRYING TO DO?
ANSEM THE WISE.

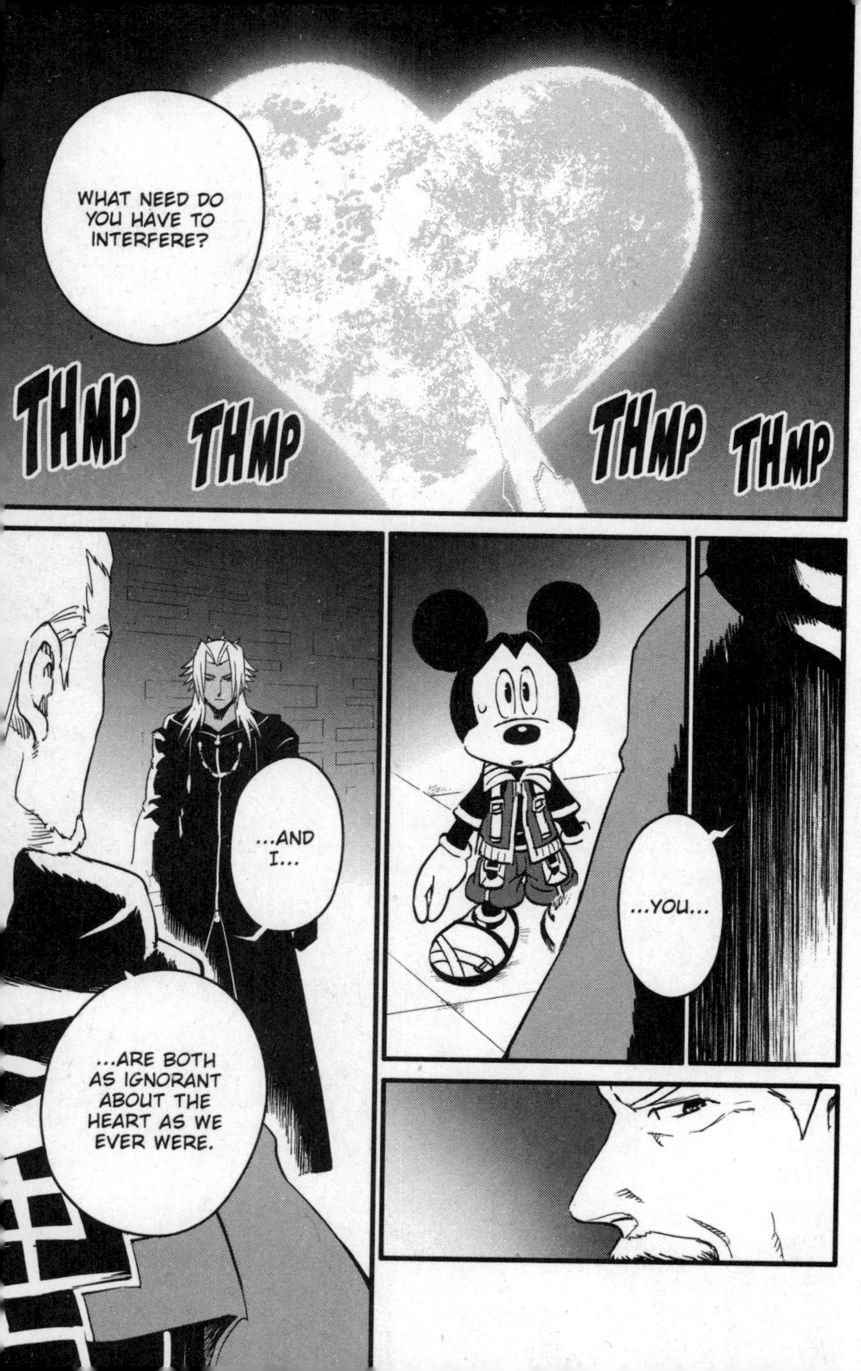
WHAT NEED DO YOU HAVE TO INTERFERE?
THMP
THMP
THMP
THMP
...YOU...
...AND I...
...ARE BOTH AS IGNORANT ABOUT THE HEART AS WE EVER WERE.

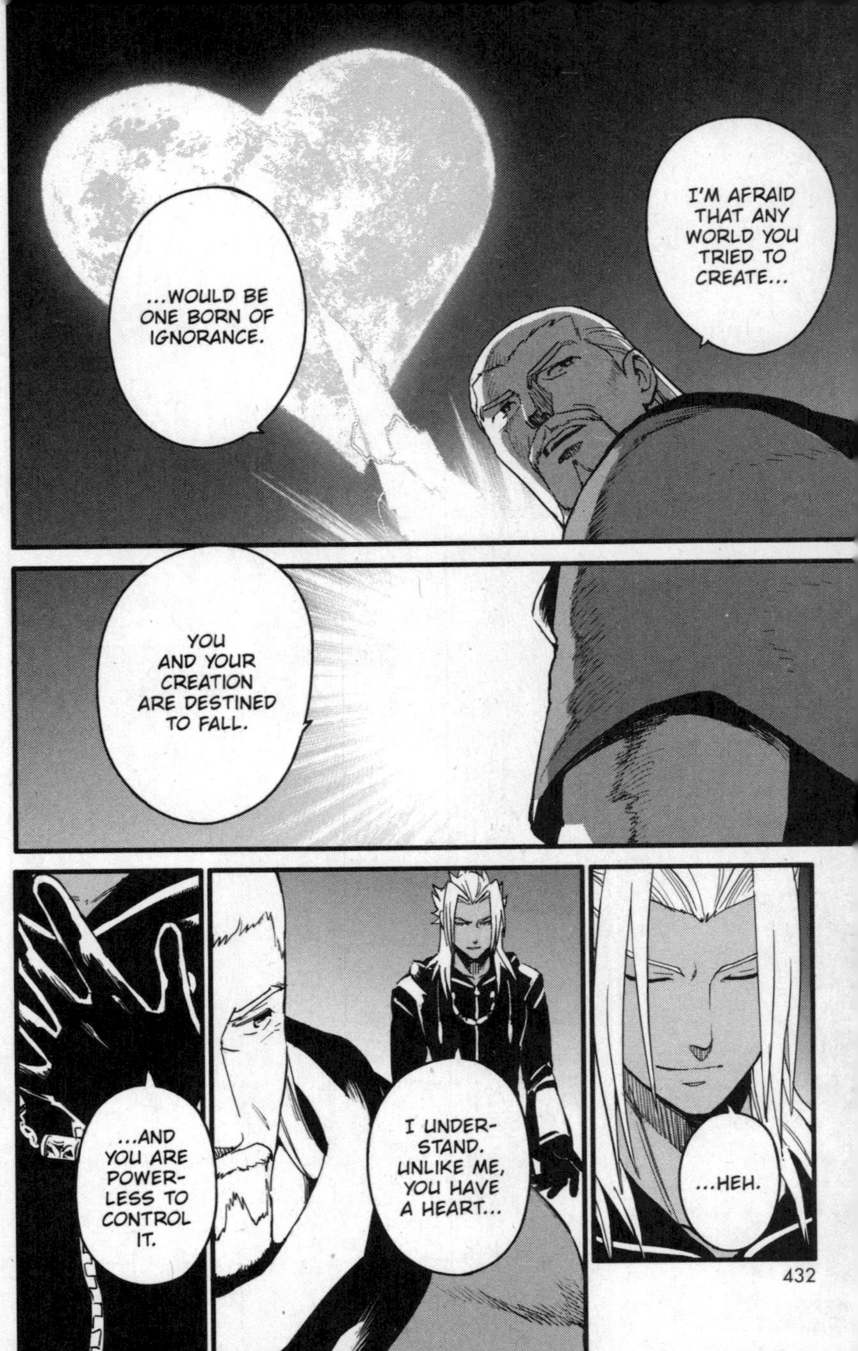
I'M AFRAID THAT ANY WORLD YOU TRIED TO CREATE...
...WOULD BE ONE BORN OF IGNORANCE.
YOU AND YOUR CREATION ARE DESTINED TO FALL.
...HEH.
I UNDER-STAND. UNLIKE ME, YOU HAVE A HEART...
...AND YOU ARE POWER-LESS TO CONTROL IT.

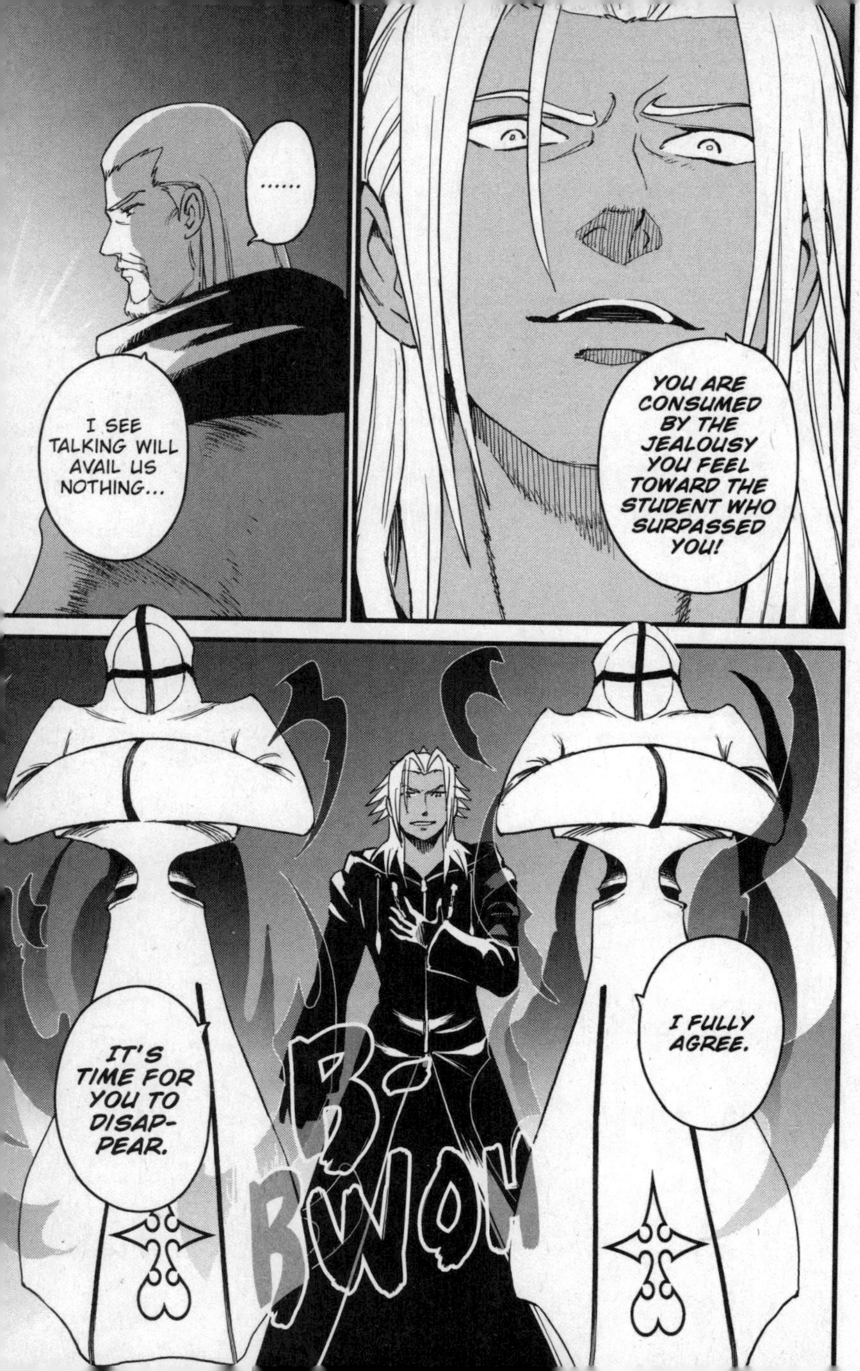
YOU ARE CONSUMED BY THE JEALOUSY YOU FEEL TOWARD THE STUDENT WHO SURPASSED YOU!
......
I SEE TALKING WILL AVAIL US NOTHING...
I FULLY AGREE.
IT'S TIME FOR YOU TO DISAP-PEAR.
BWOH

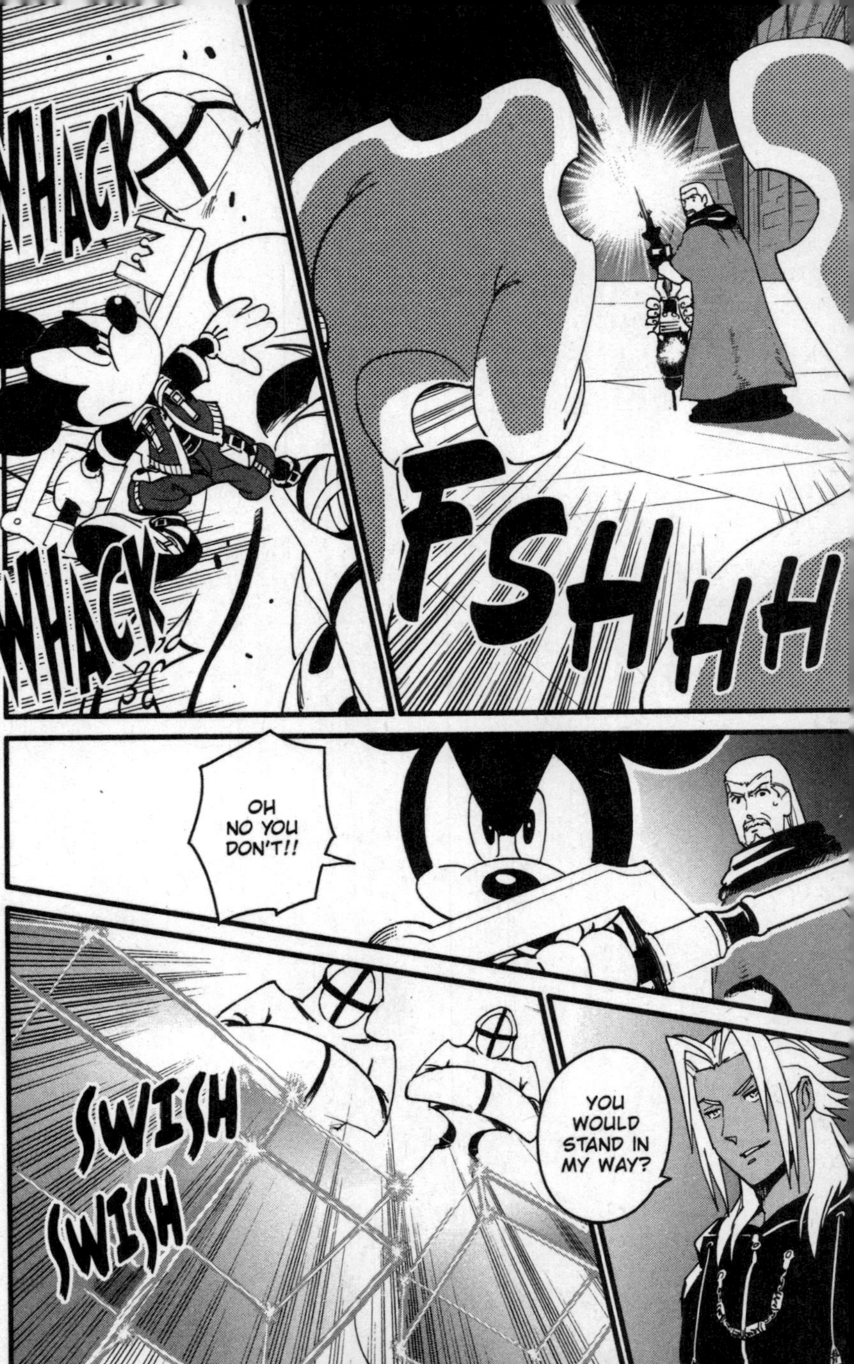
FSHHHH
WHACK
WHACK
OH NO YOU DON'T!!
YOU WOULD STAND IN MY WAY?
SWISH
SWISH

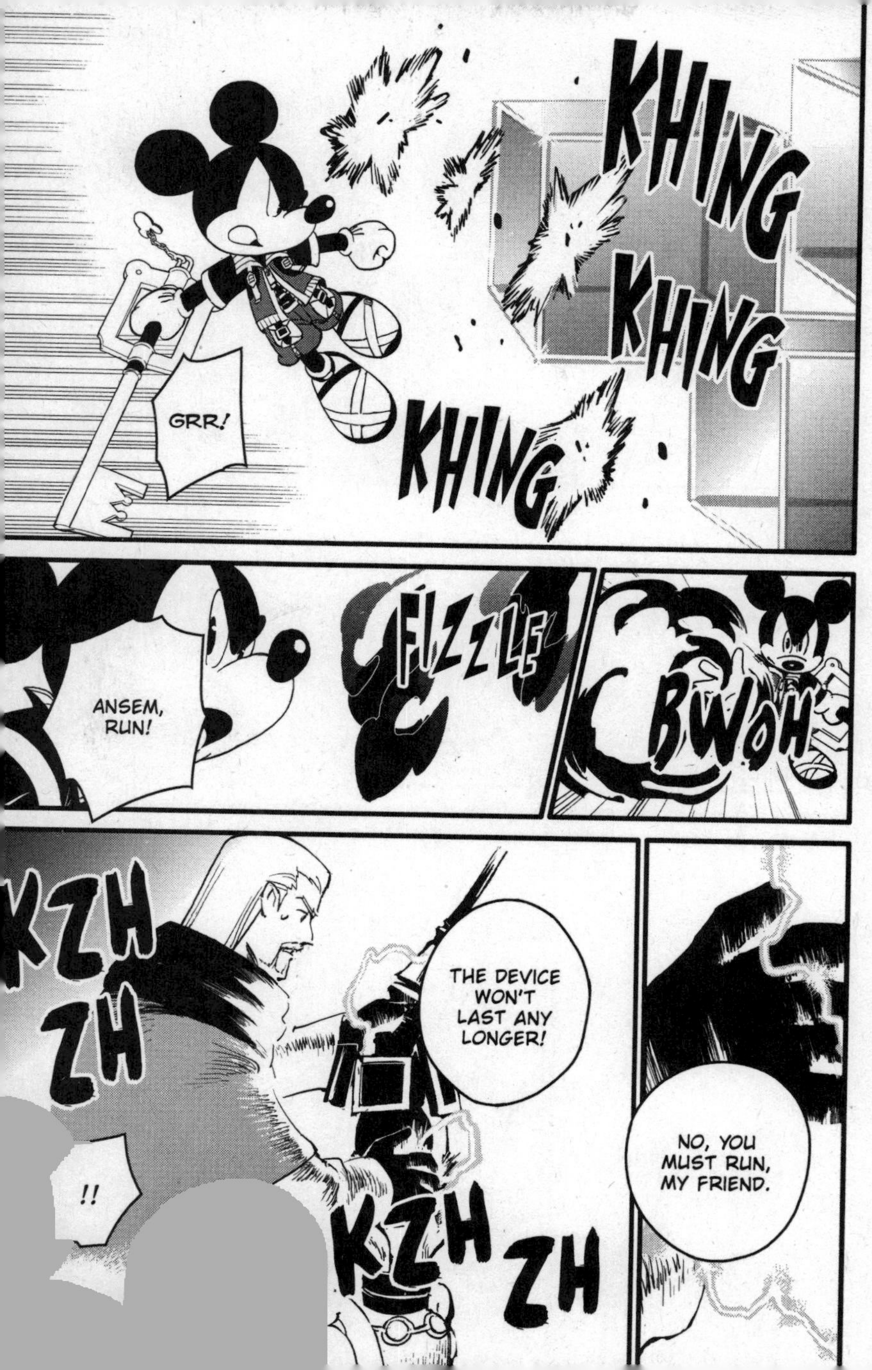
KHING
KHING
KHING
GRR!
BWOH
FIZZLE
ANSEM, RUN!
NO, YOU MUST RUN, MY FRIEND.
THE DEVICE WON'T LAST ANY LONGER!
KZH ZH
!!
KZH ZH

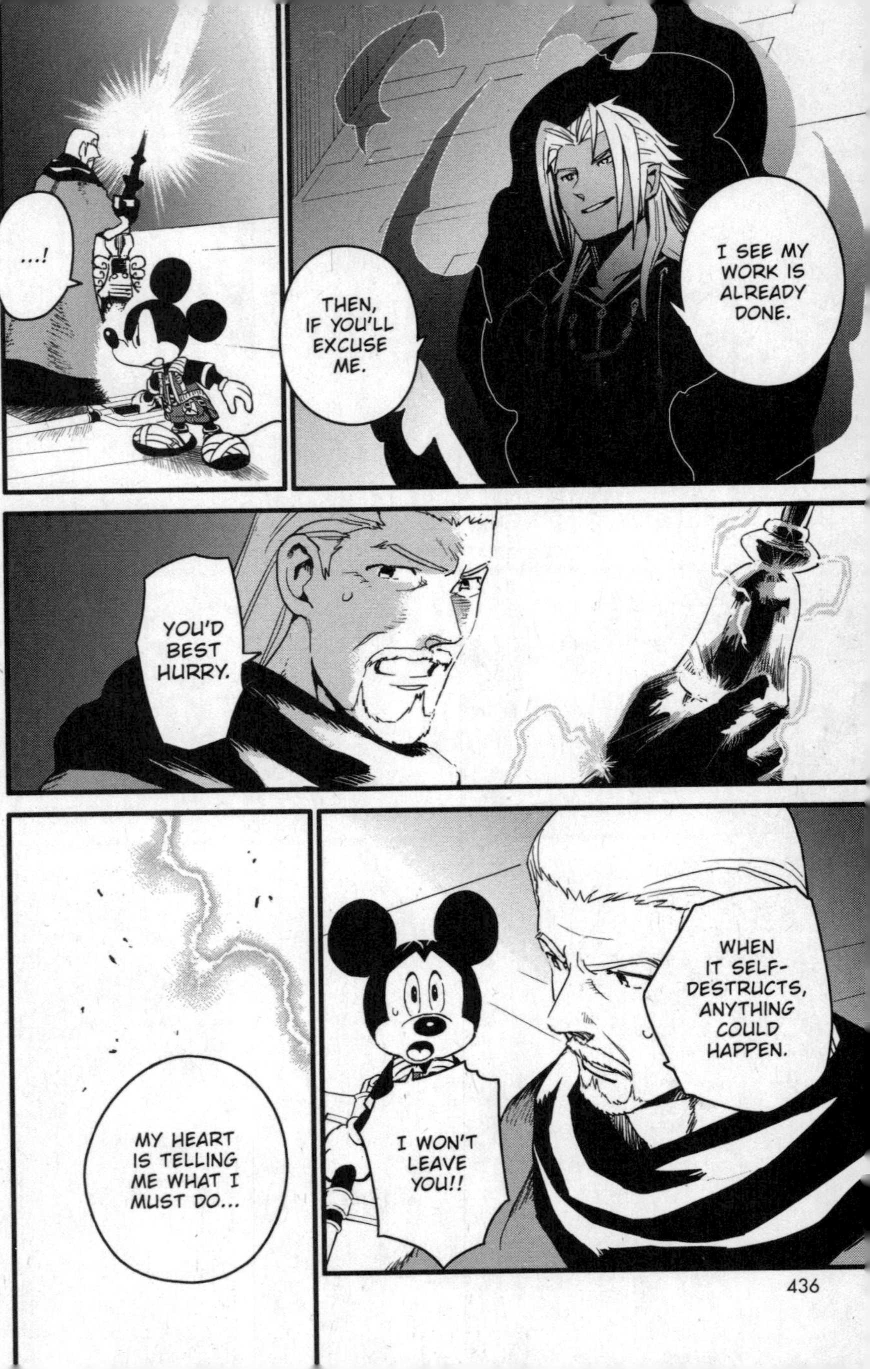
I SEE MY WORK IS ALREADY DONE.
THEN, IF YOU'LL EXCUSE ME.
...!
YOU'D BEST HURRY.
WHEN IT SELF-DESTRUCTS, ANYTHING COULD HAPPEN.
I WON'T LEAVE YOU!!
MY HEART IS TELLING ME WHAT I MUST DO...

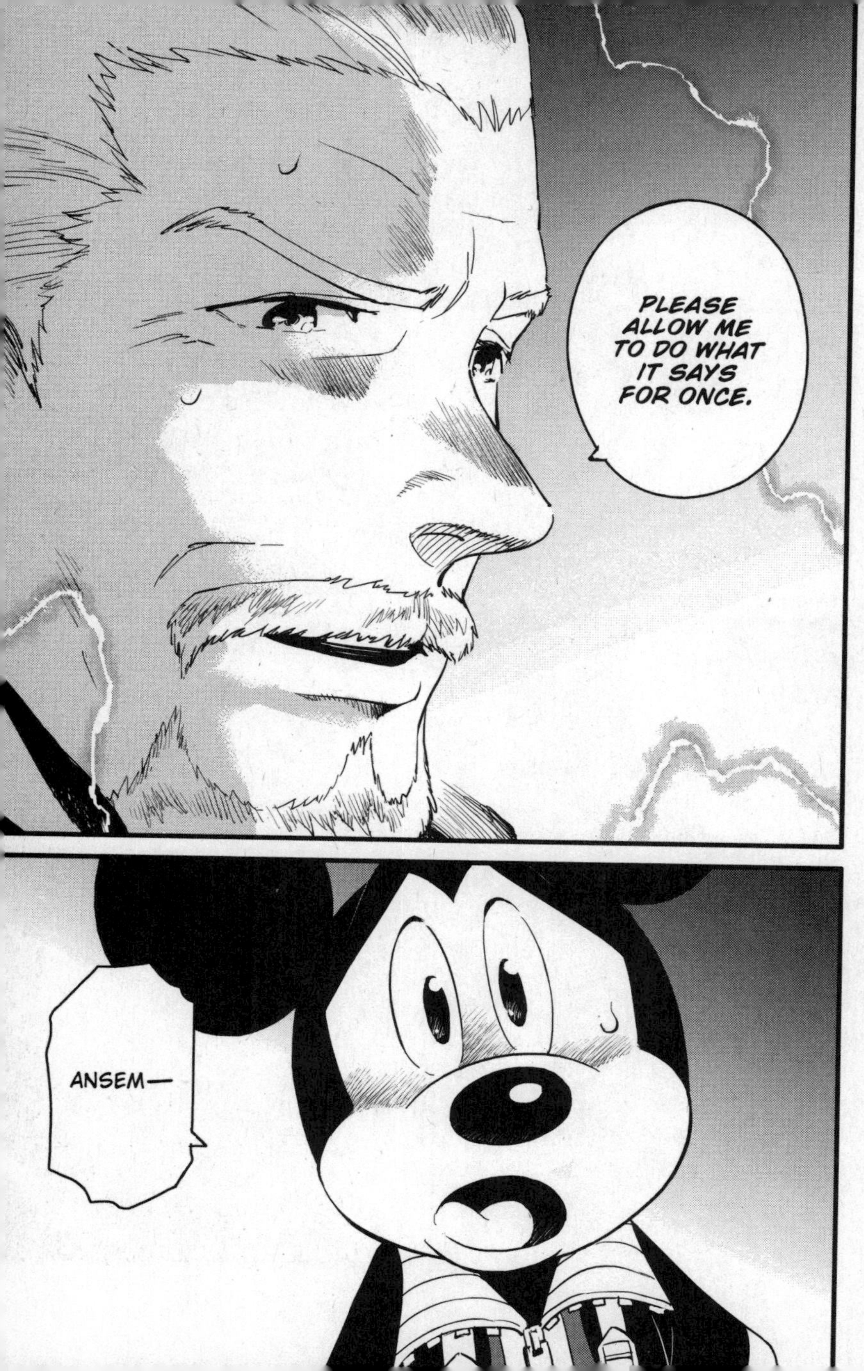
PLEASE ALLOW ME TO DO WHAT IT SAYS FOR ONCE.
ANSEM—

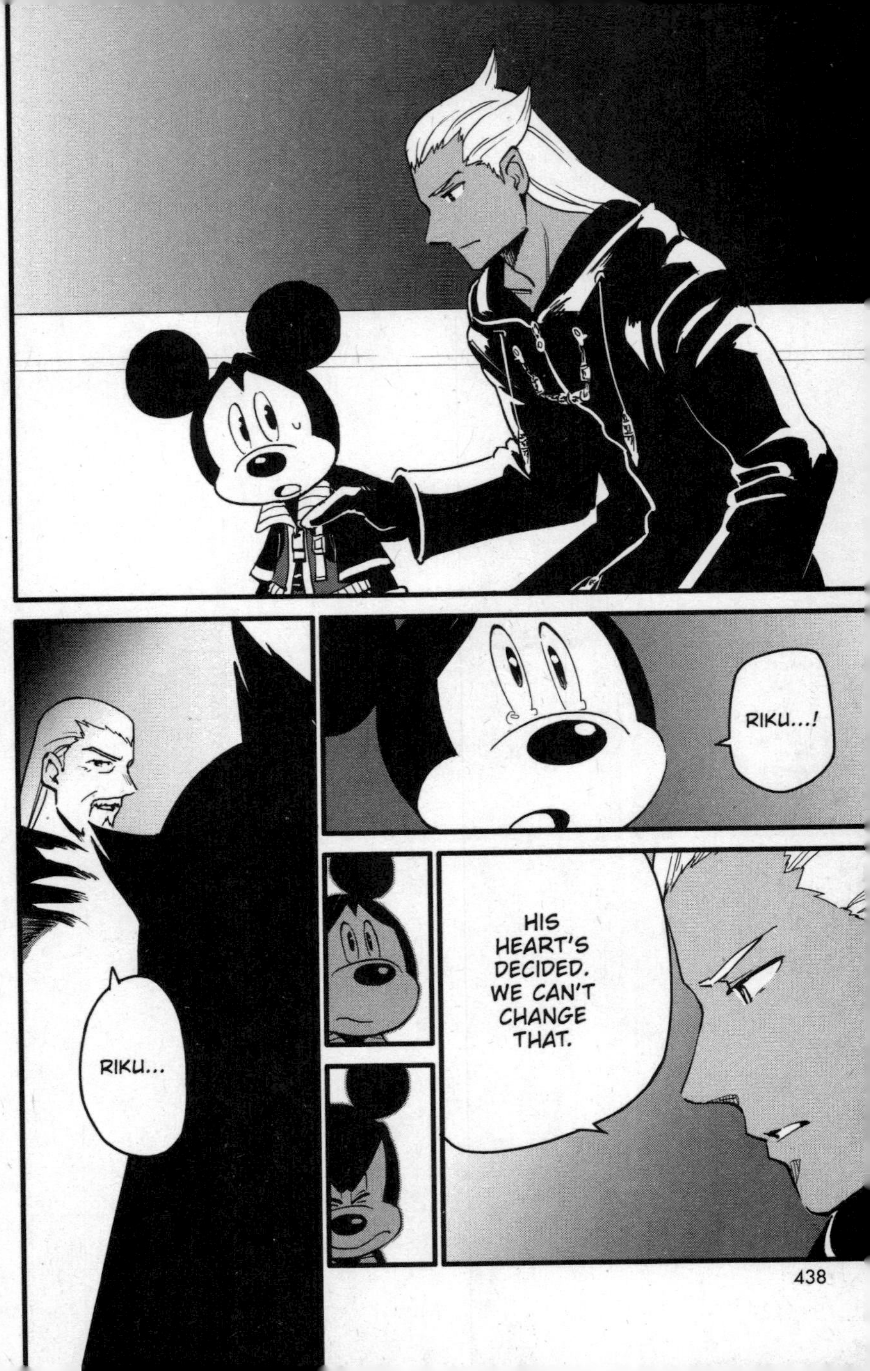
RIKU...!
HIS HEART'S DECIDED. WE CAN'T CHANGE THAT.
RIKU...

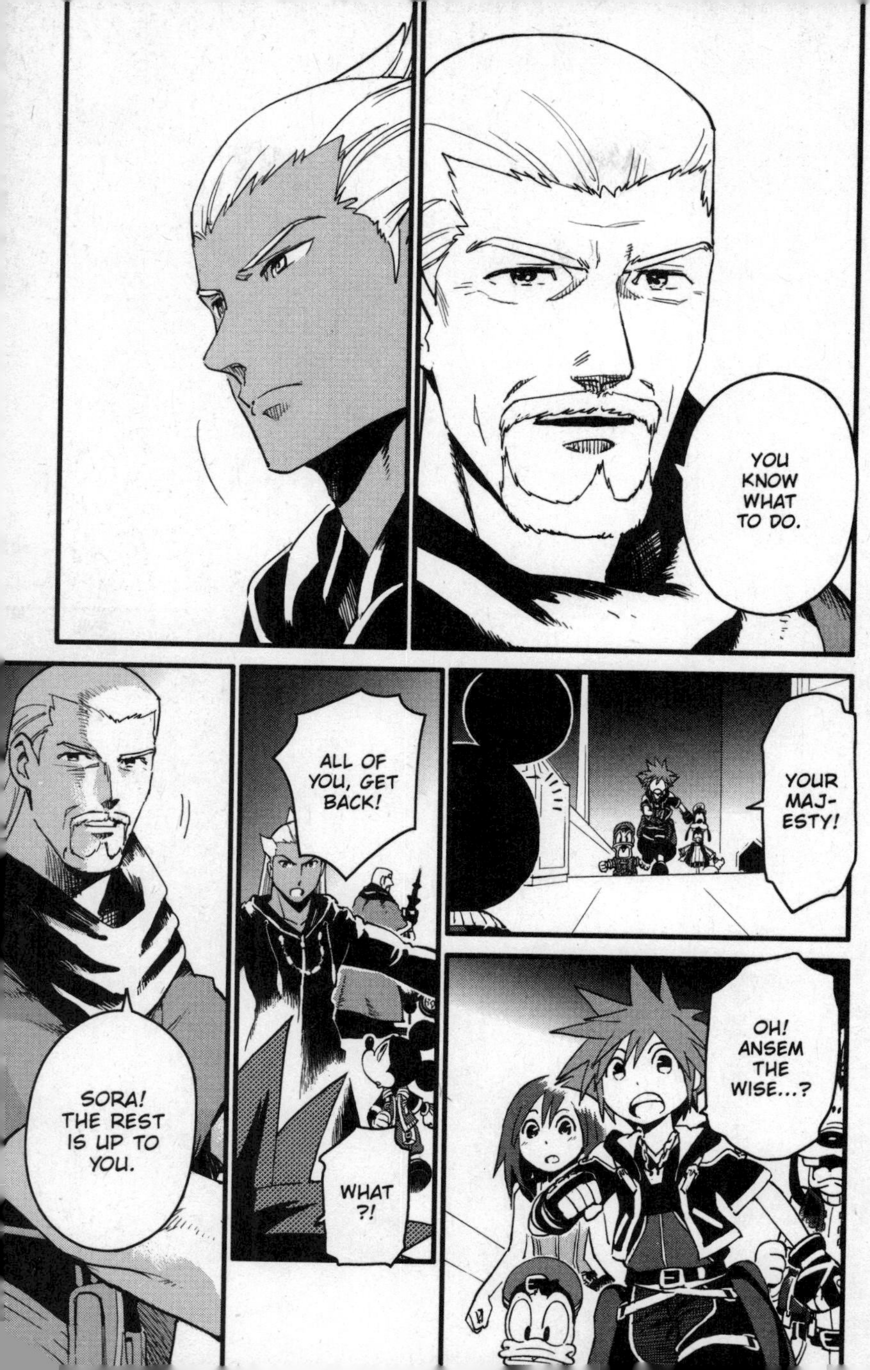
YOU KNOW WHAT TO DO.
YOUR MAJ-ESTY!
OH! ANSEM THE WISE...?
ALL OF YOU, GET BACK!
WHAT?!
SORA! THE REST IS UP TO YOU.

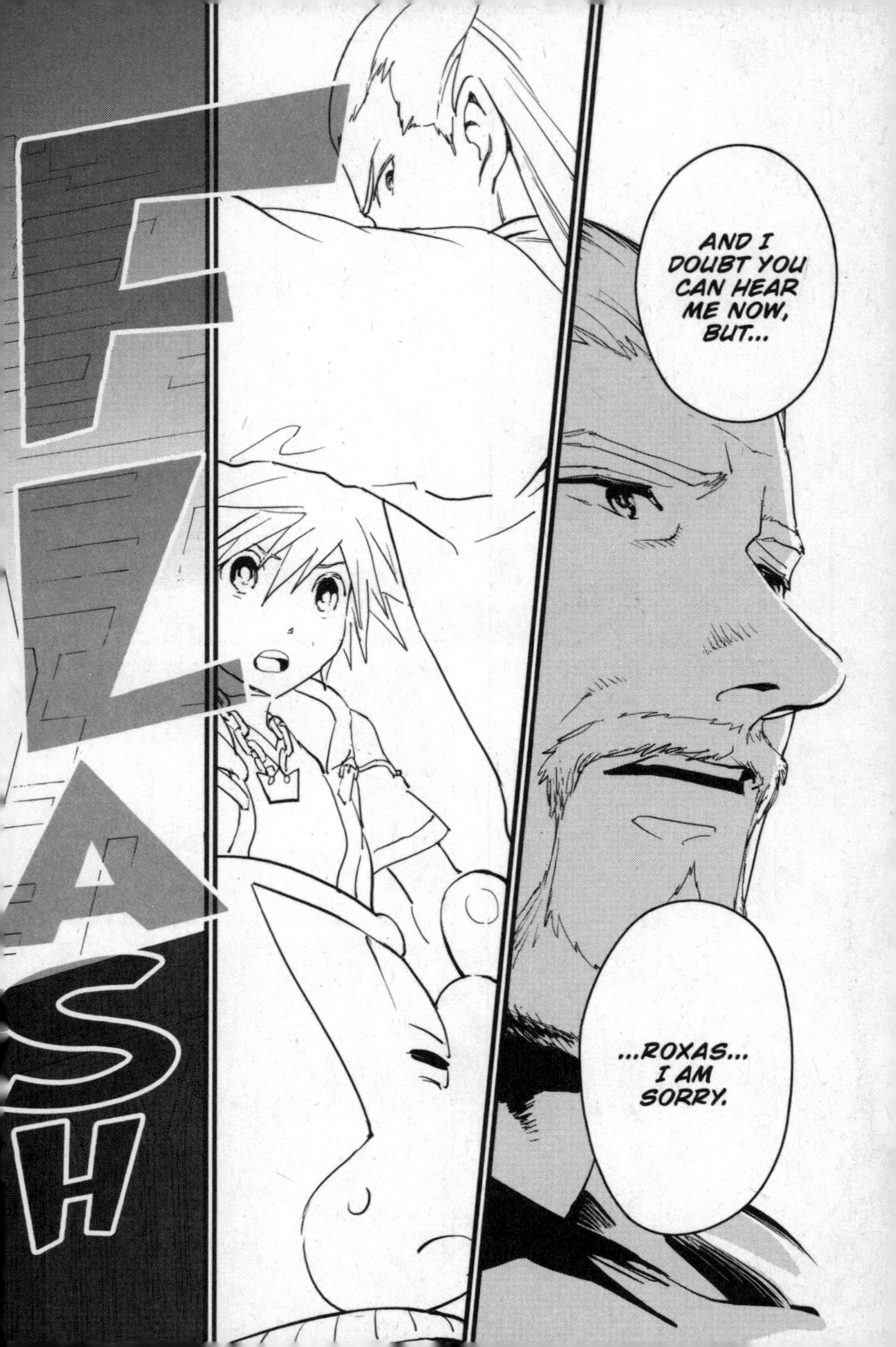
AND I DOUBT YOU CAN HEAR ME NOW, BUT...
...ROXAS... I AM SORRY.
FLASH

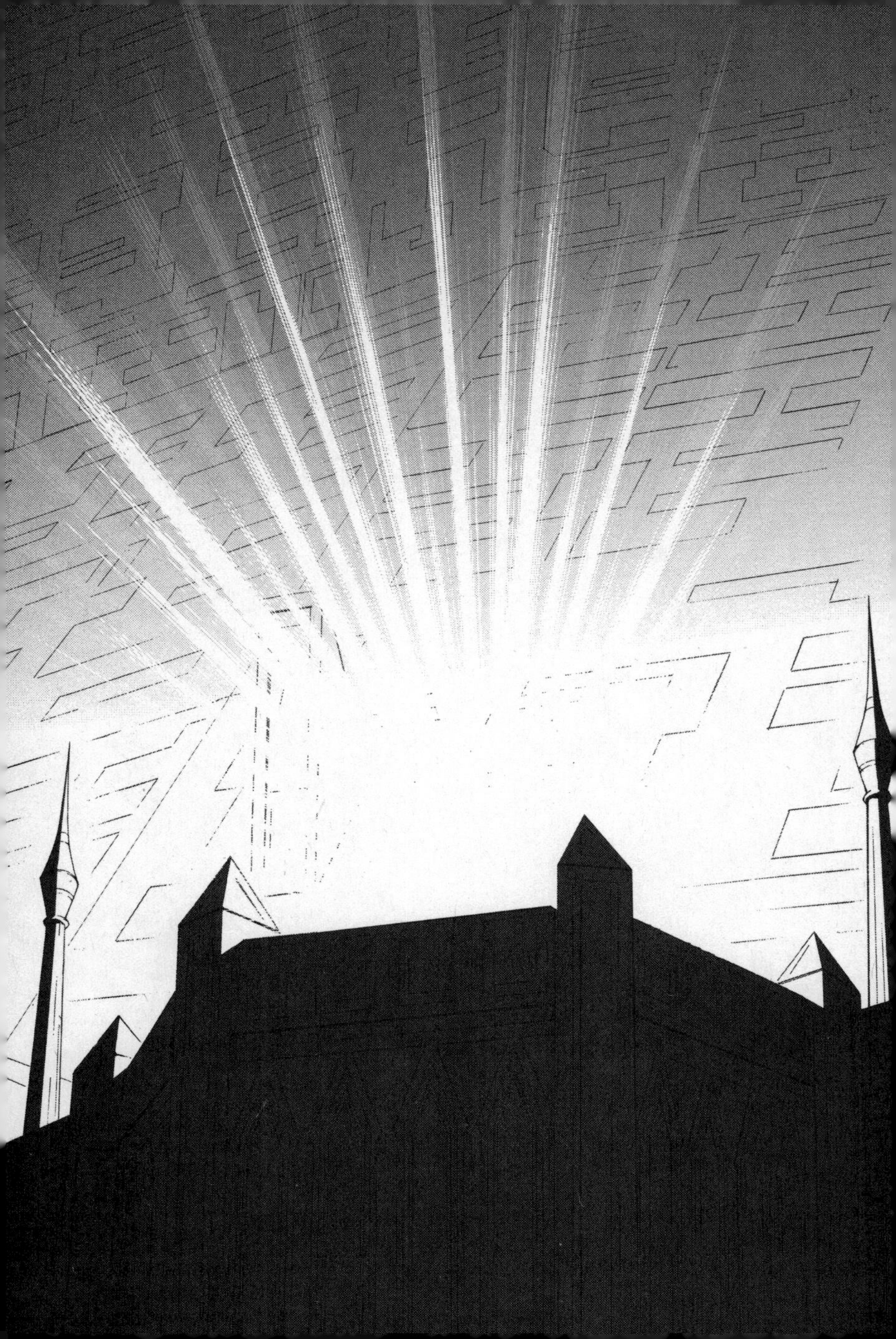

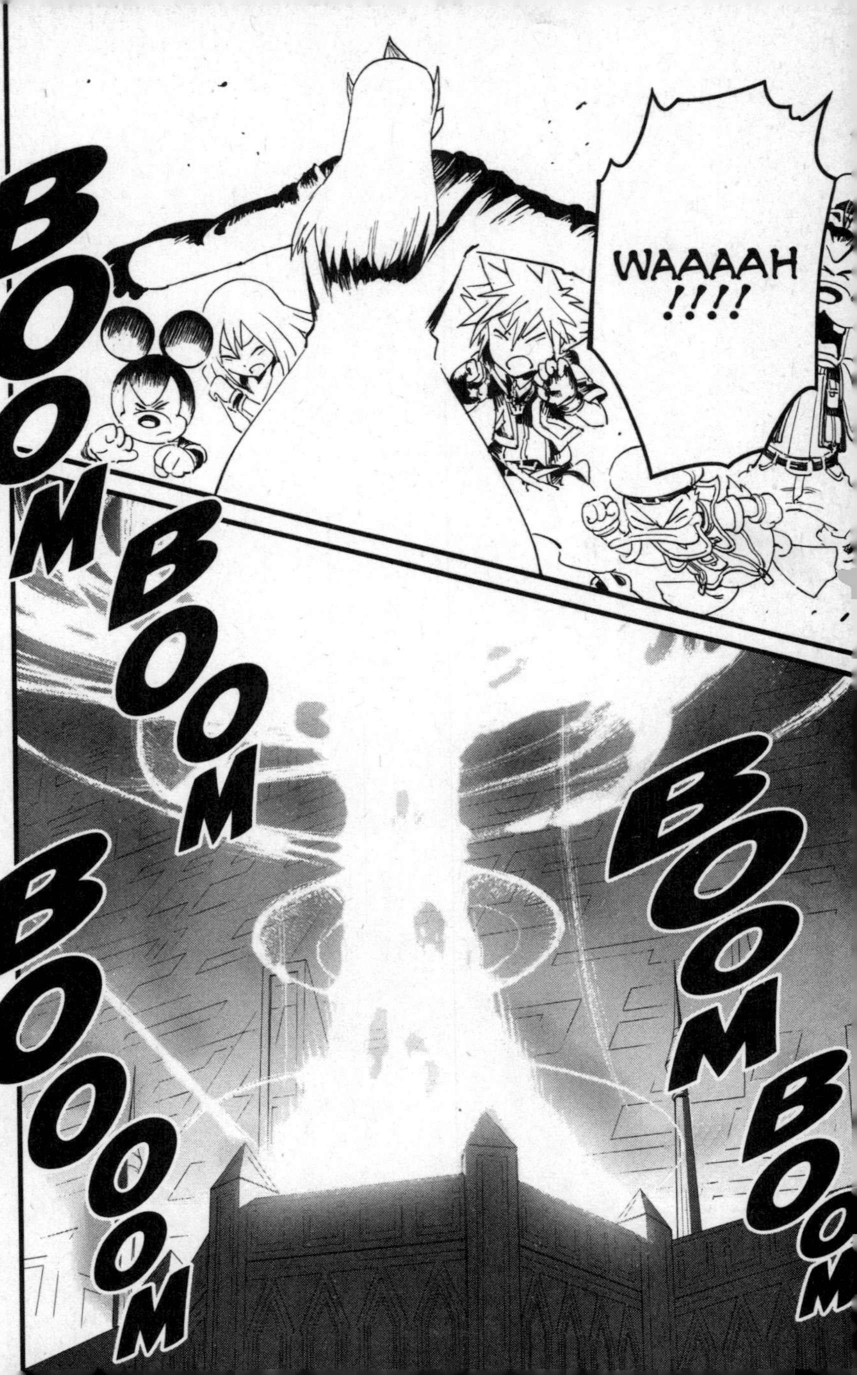
WAAAAH !!!!
BOOM
BOOM
BOOMBOOM
BOOOOOM

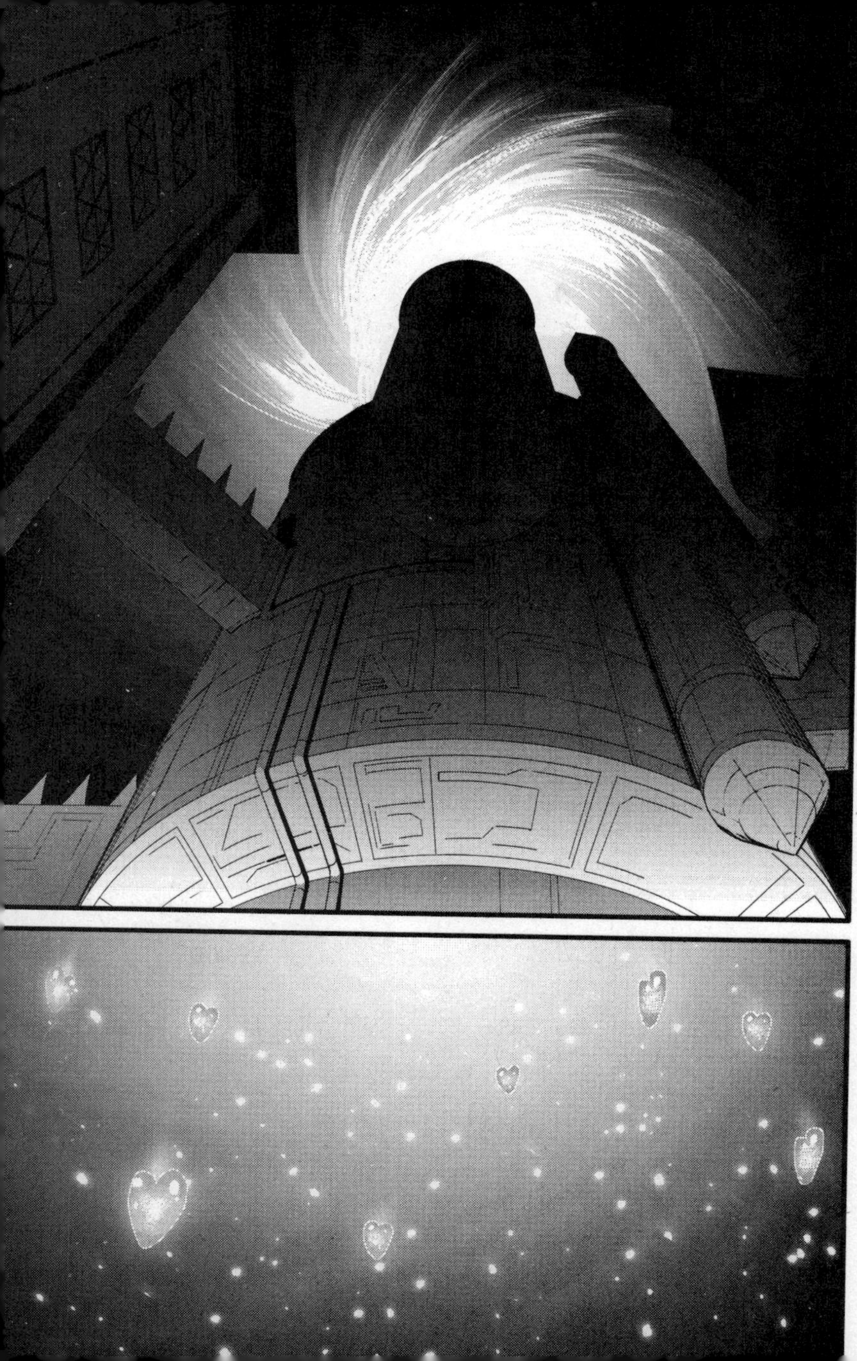

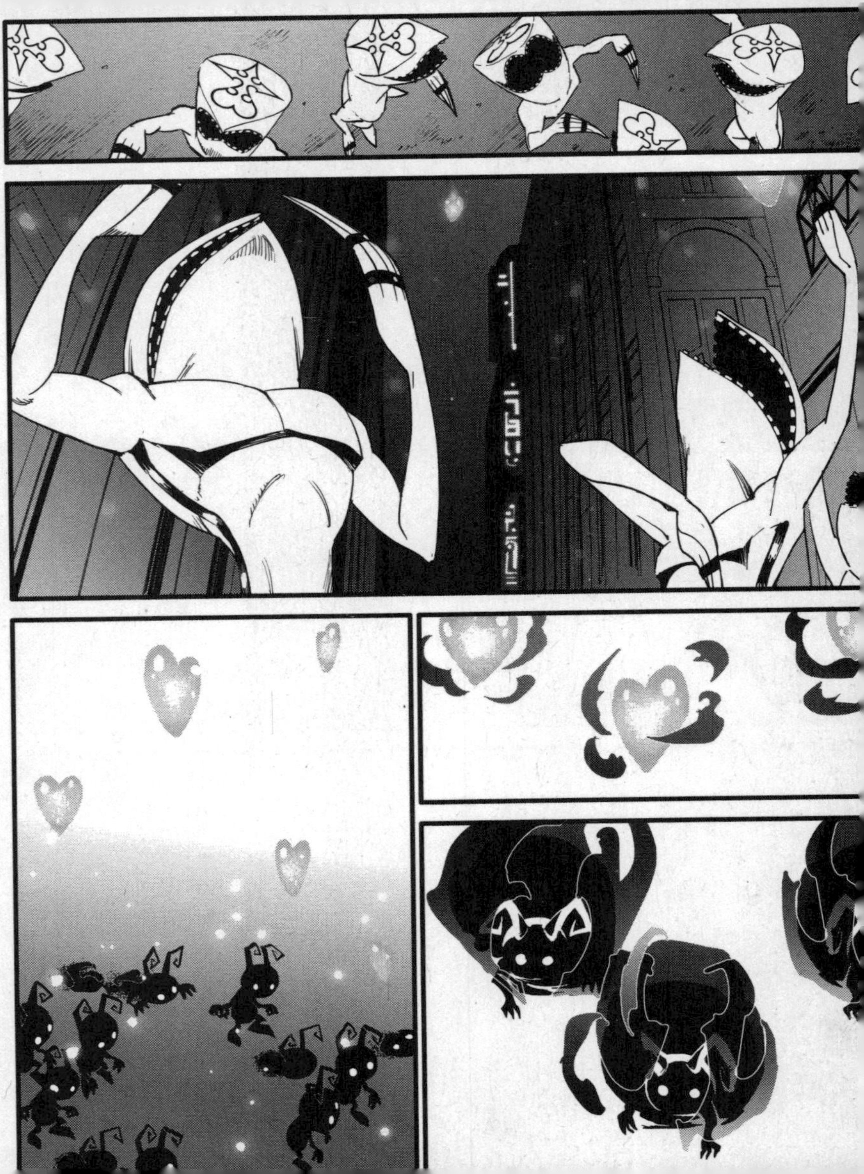

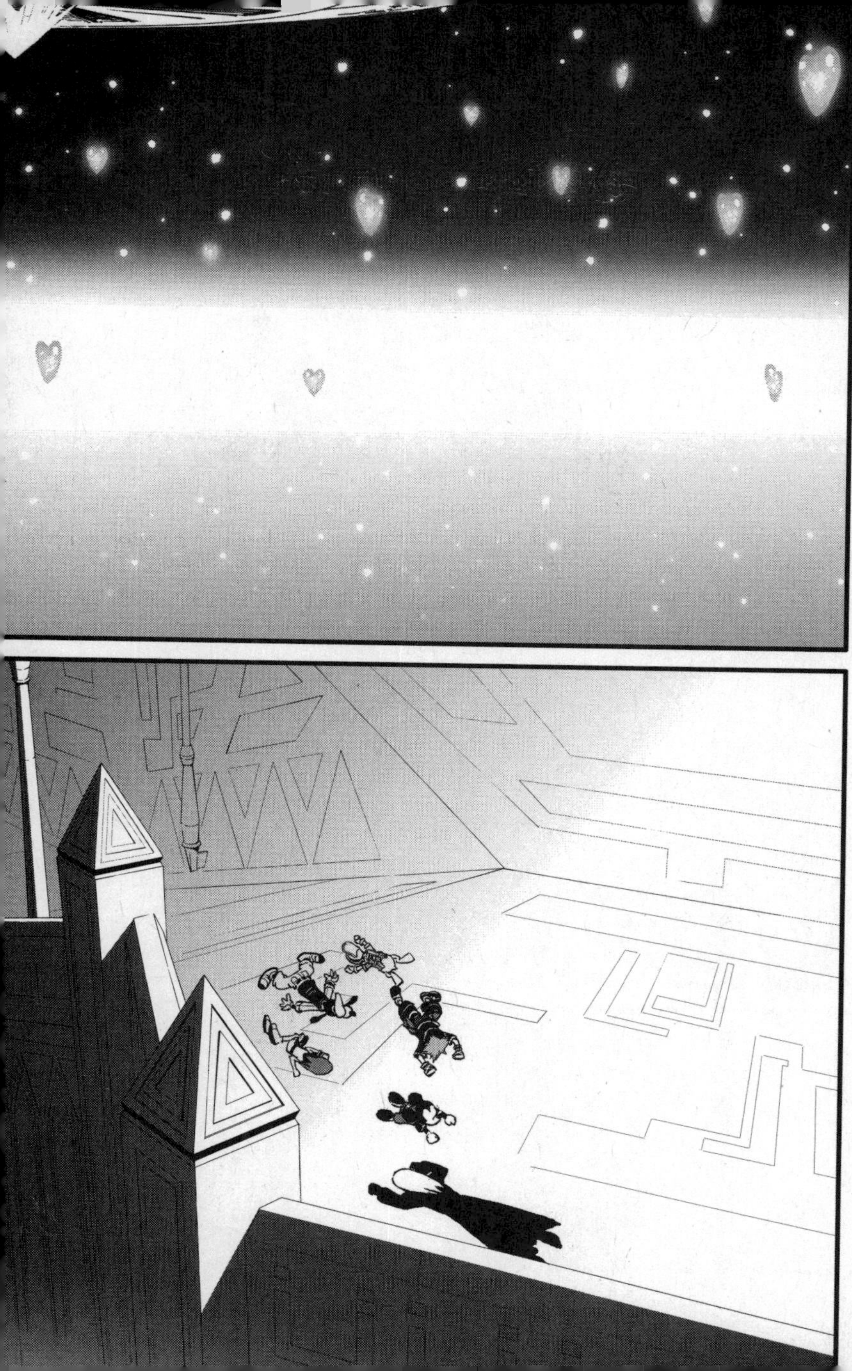

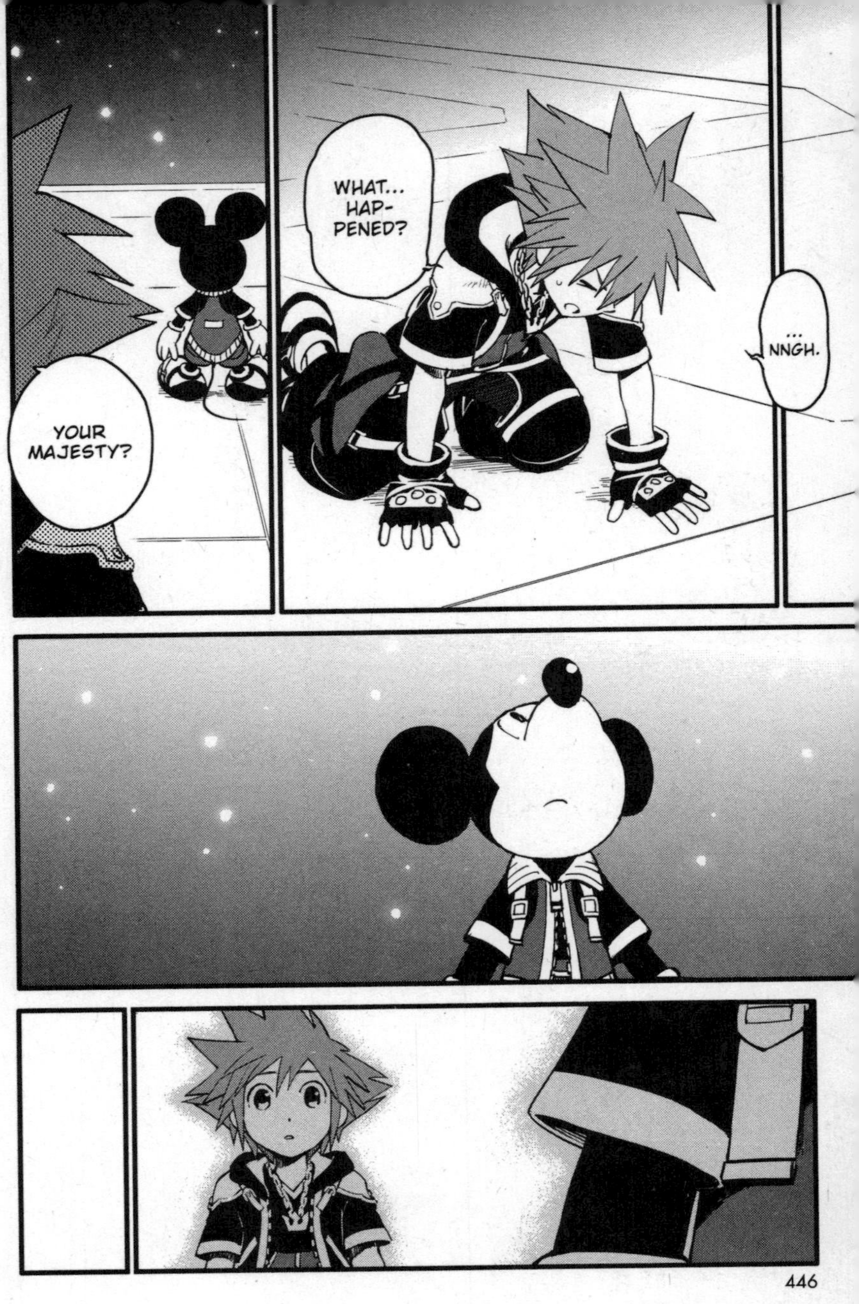
...NNGH.
WHAT... HAP-PENED?
YOUR MAJESTY?

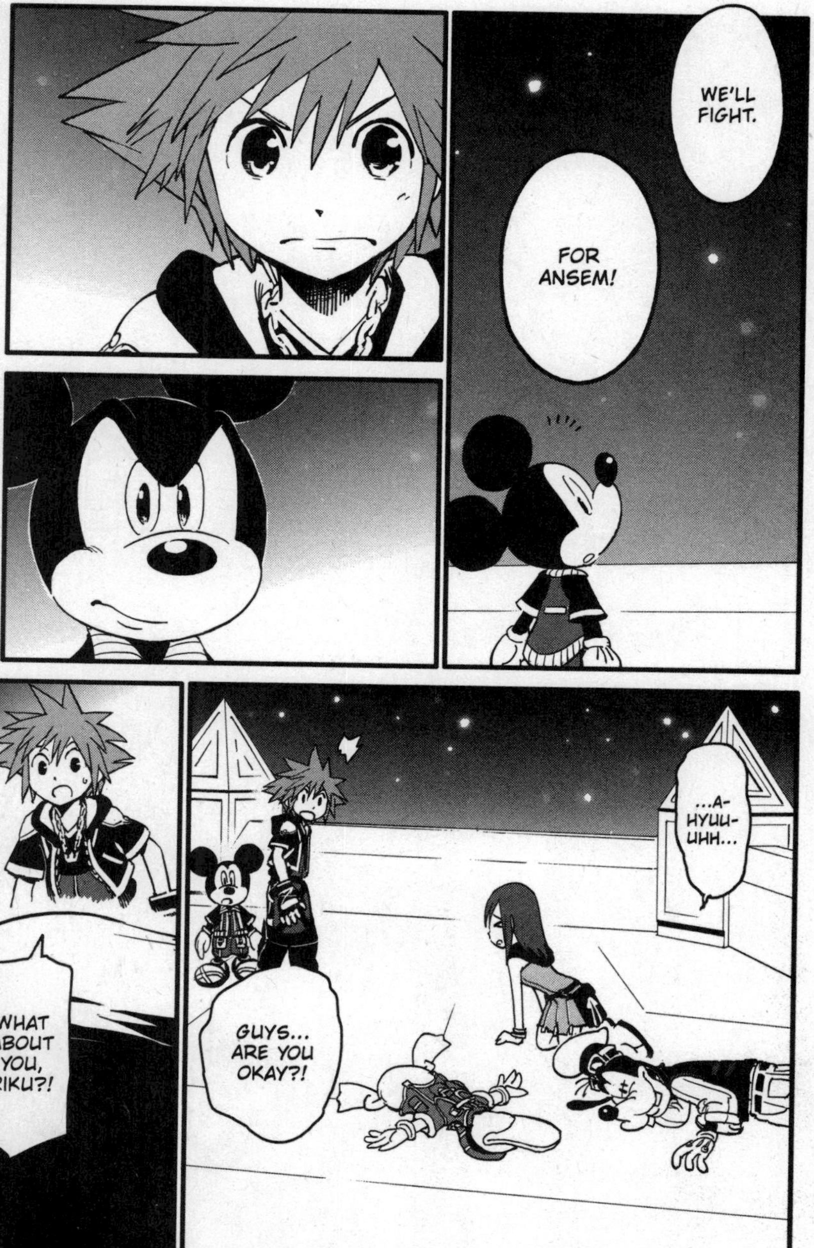
WE'LL FIGHT.
FOR ANSEM!
...A-HYUUU-UHH...
GUYS... ARE YOU OKAY?!
WHAT ABOUT YOU, RIKU?!

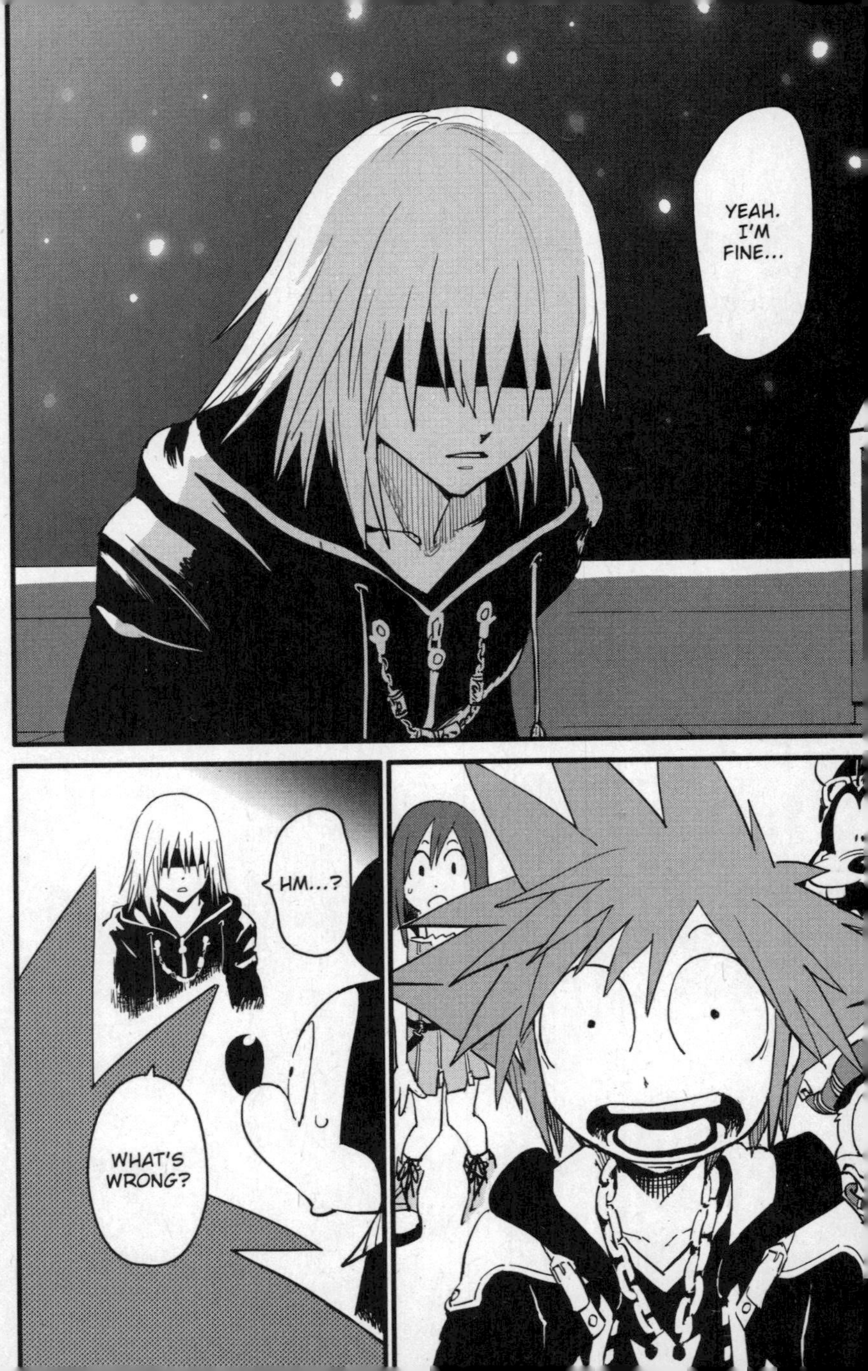
YEAH. I'M FINE...
HM...?
WHAT'S WRONG?

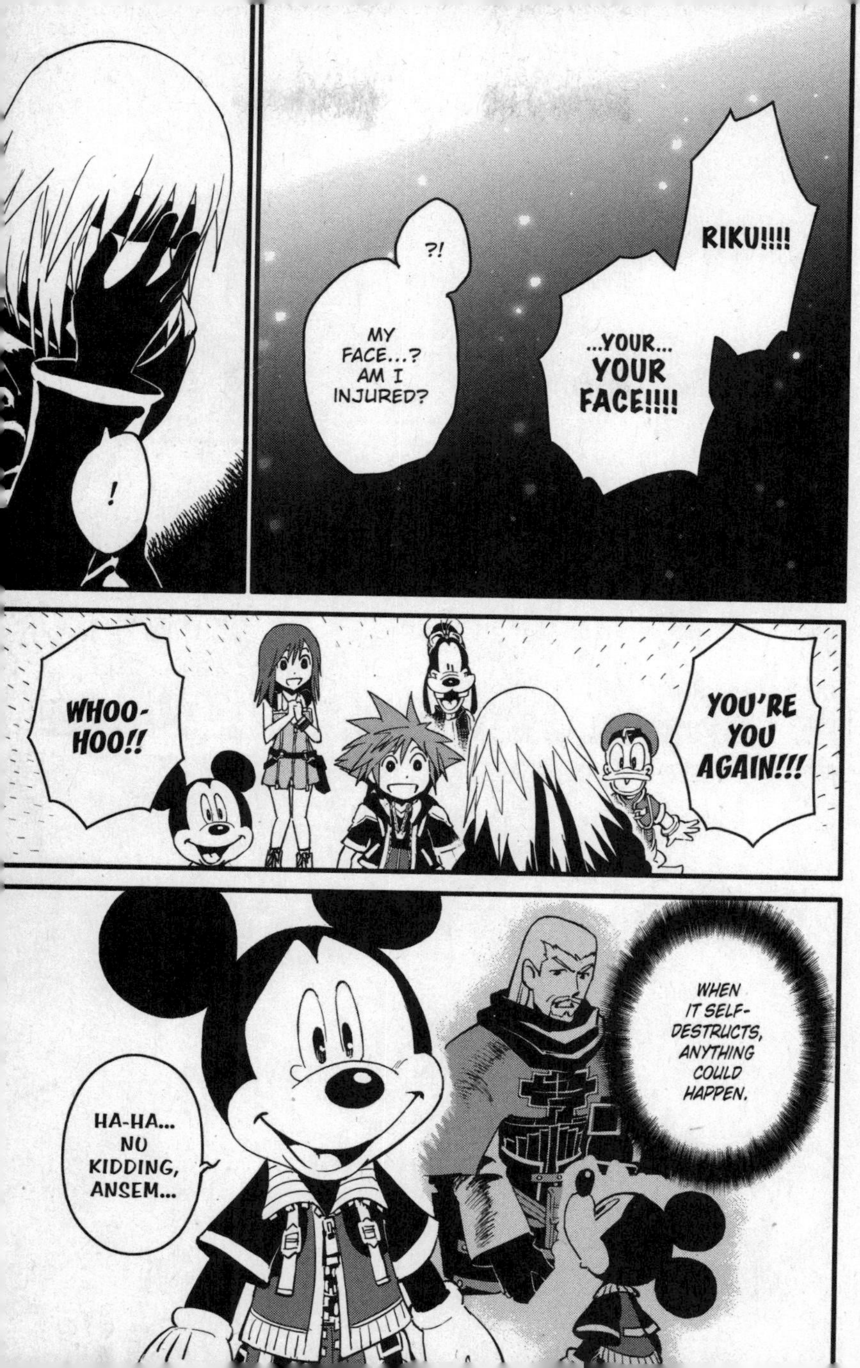
RIKU!!!!
?!
...YOUR... YOUR FACE!!!!
MY FACE...? AM I INJURED?
!
YOU'RE YOU AGAIN!!!
WHOO-HOO!!
WHEN IT SELF-DESTRUCTS, ANYTHING COULD HAPPEN.
HA-HA... NO KIDDING, ANSEM...

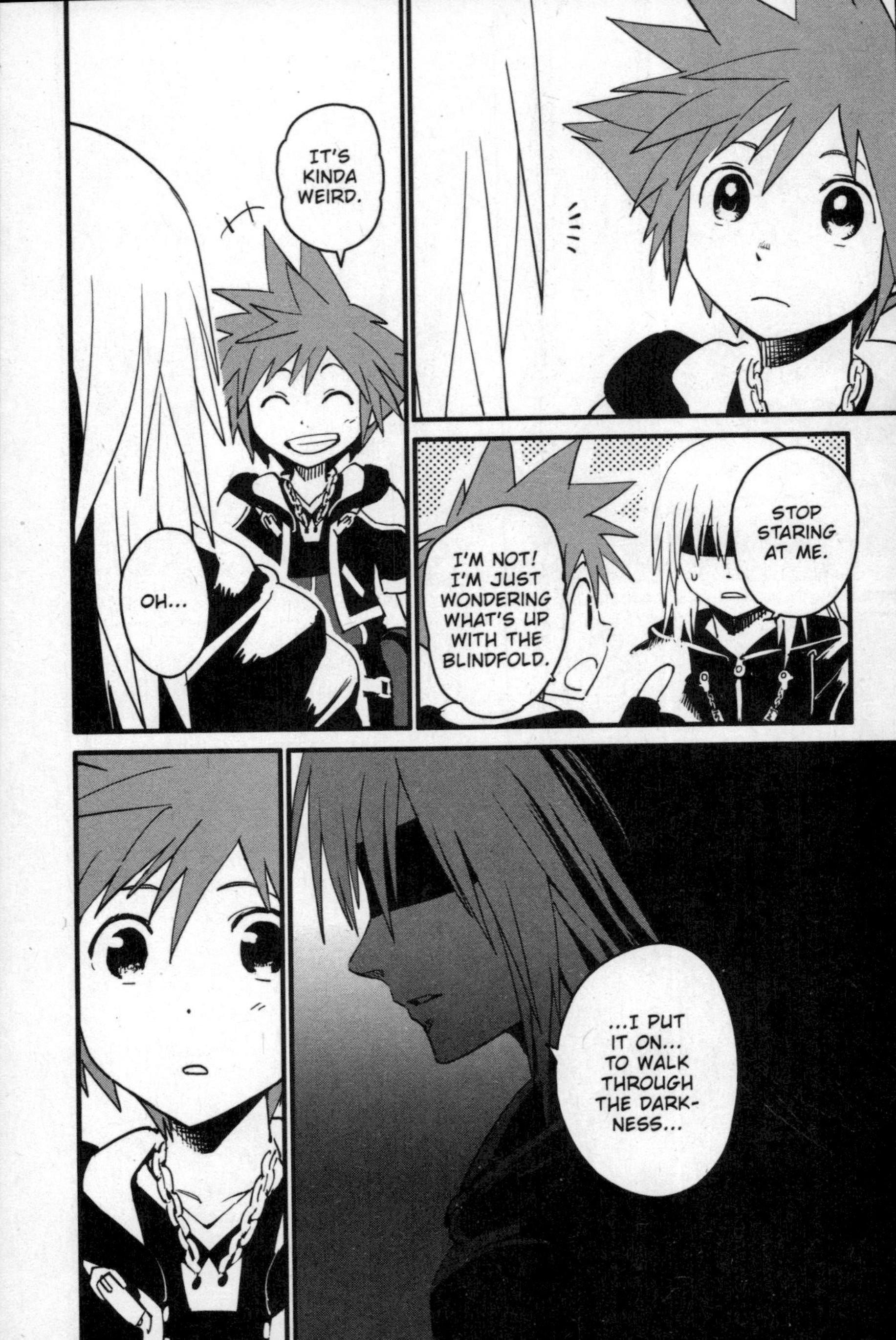
STOP STARING AT ME.
I'M NOT! I'M JUST WONDERING WHAT'S UP WITH THE BLINDFOLD.
IT'S KINDA WEIRD.
OH...
...I PUT IT ON... TO WALK THROUGH THE DARK-NESS...

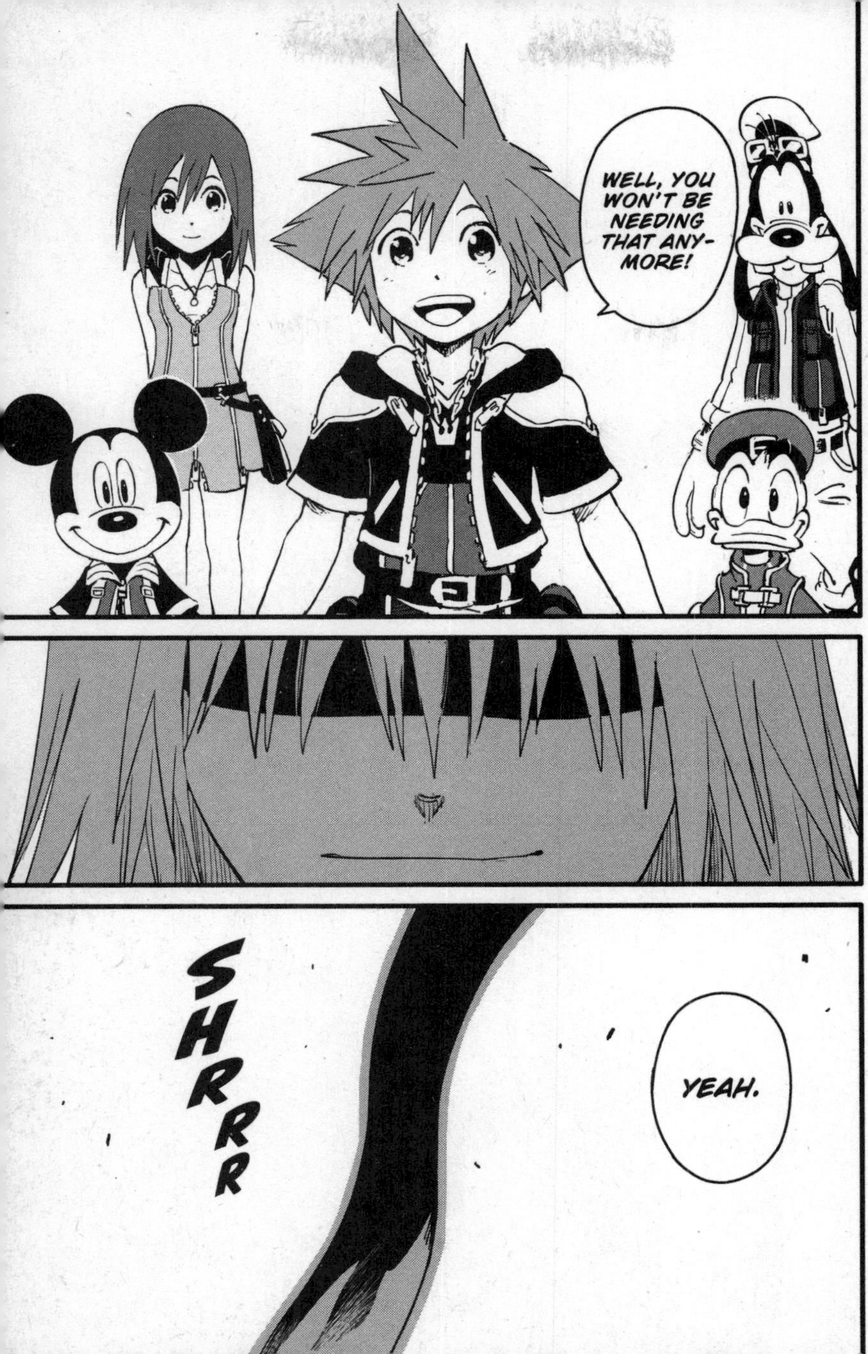
WELL, YOU WON'T BE NEEDING THAT ANY-MORE!
YEAH.
SHRRR

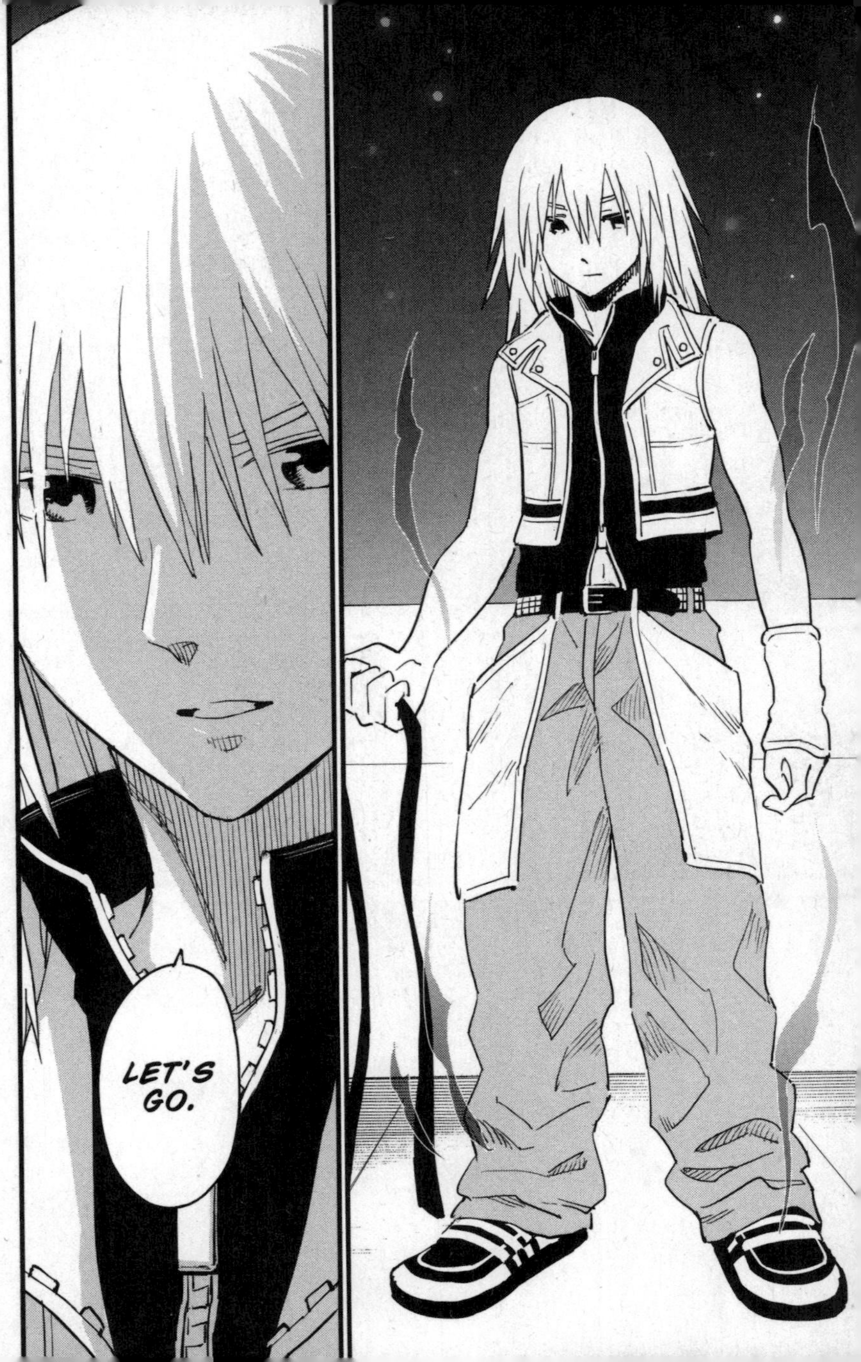
LET'S GO.

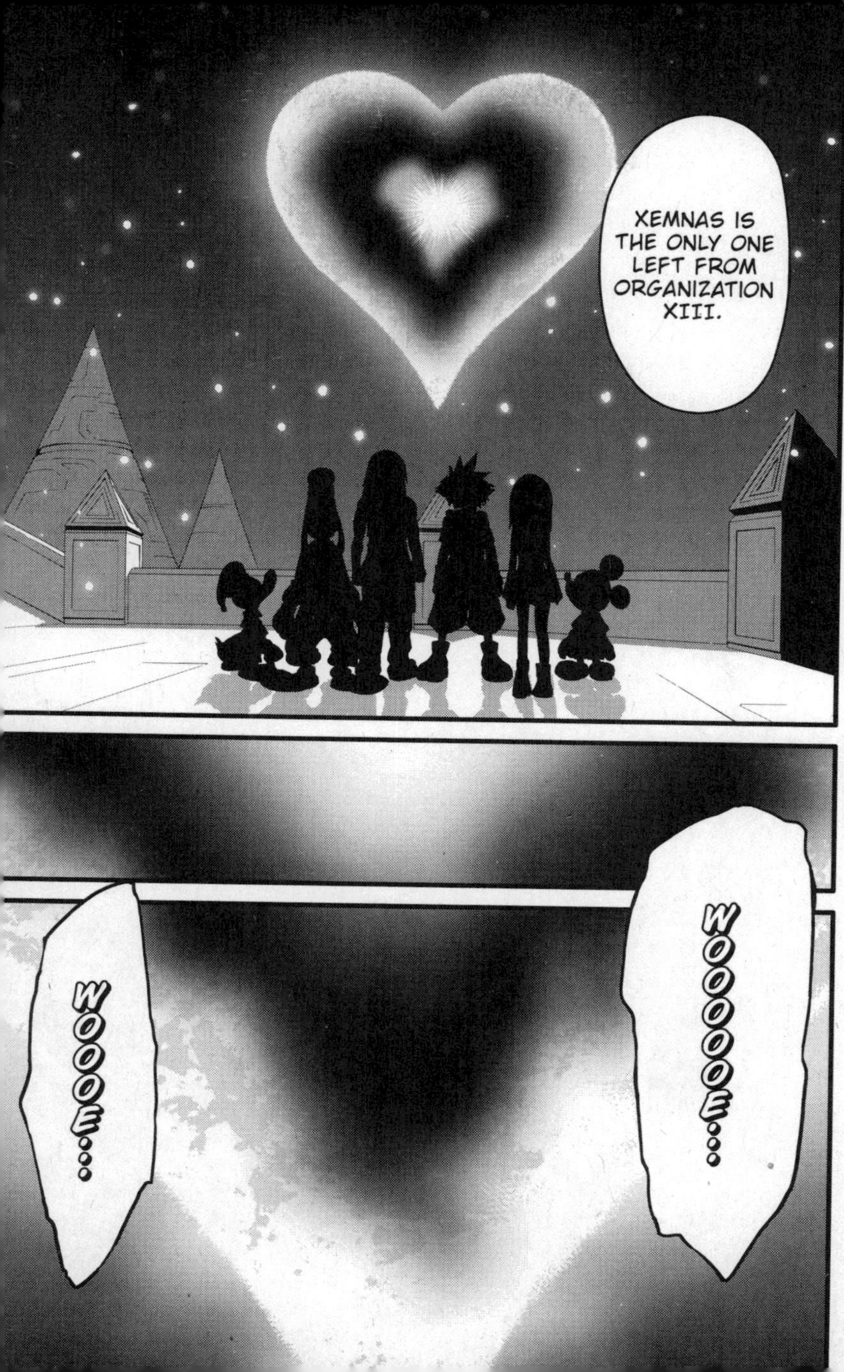
XEMNAS IS THE ONLY ONE LEFT FROM ORGANIZATION XIII.
WOOOOOE...
WOOOE...

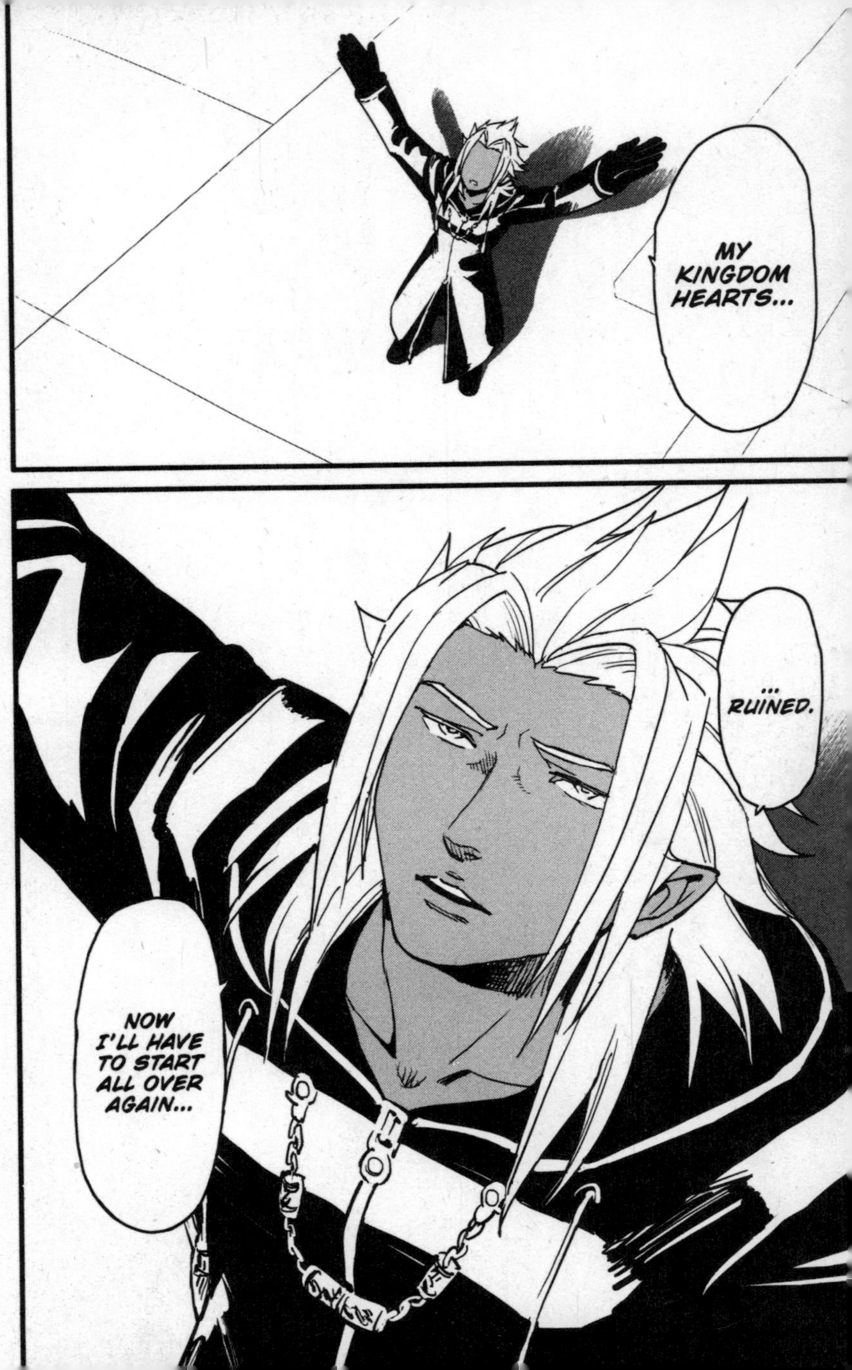
MY KINGDOM HEARTS...
... RUINED.
NOW I'LL HAVE TO START ALL OVER AGAIN...

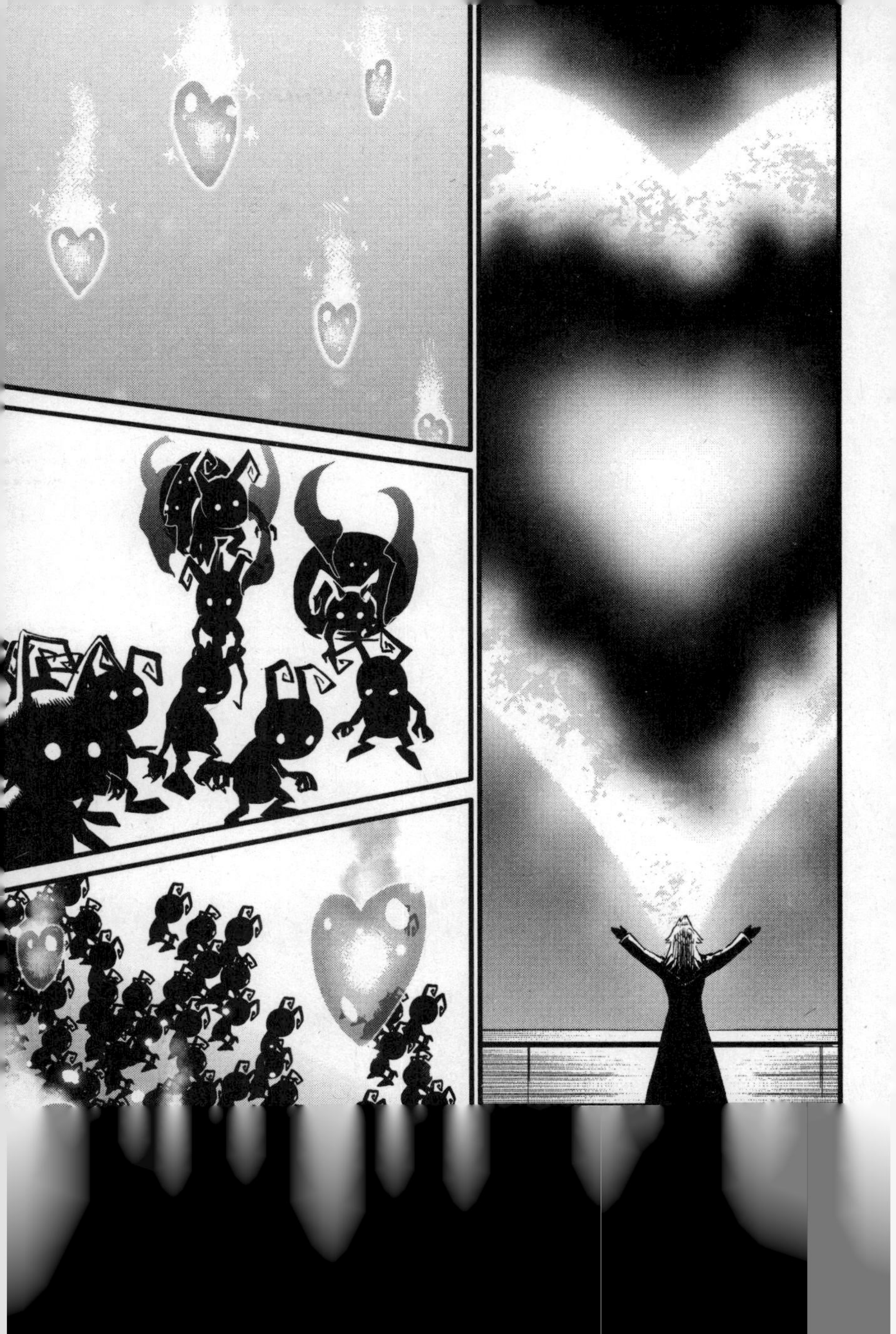

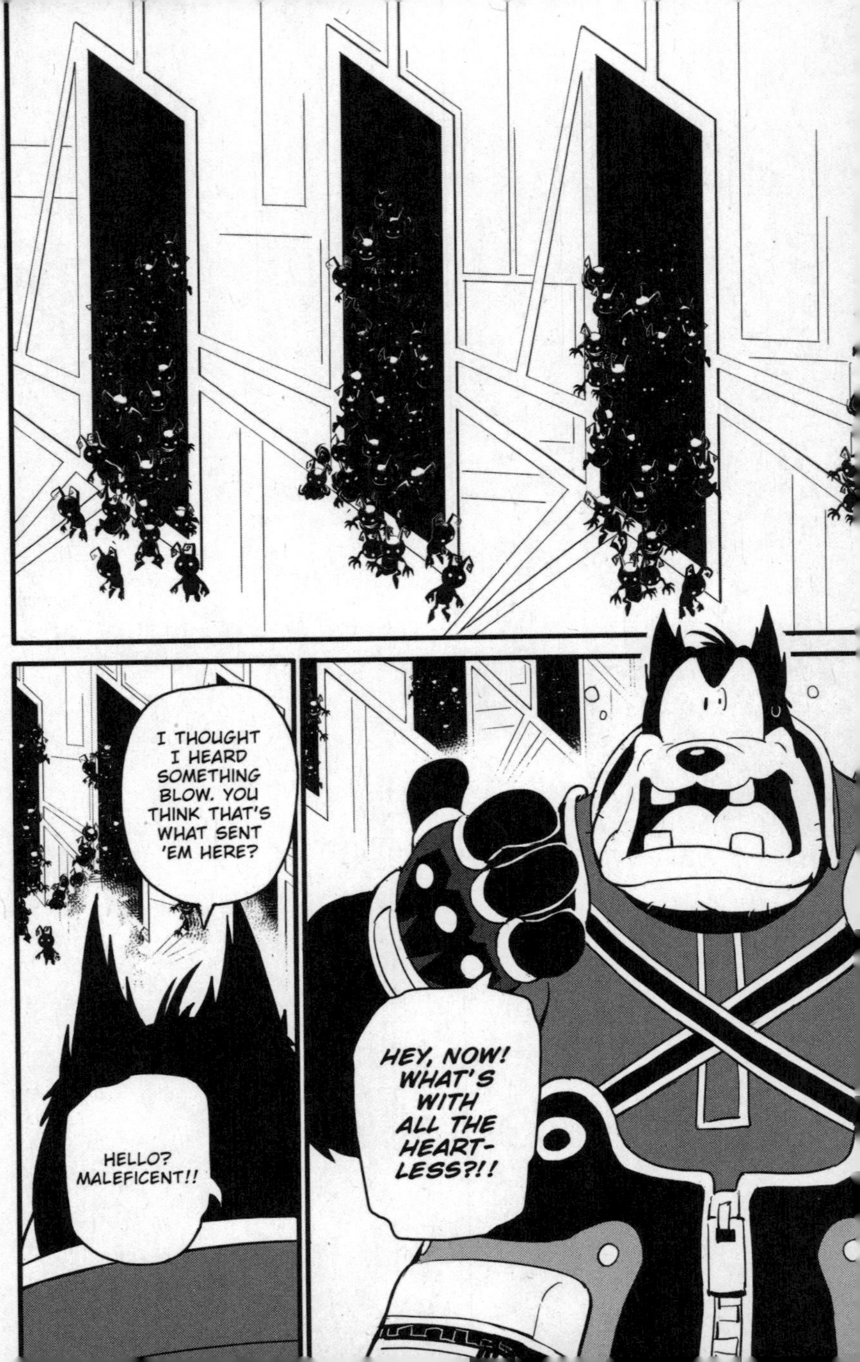
HEY, NOW! WHAT'S WITH ALL THE HEART-LESS?!!
I THOUGHT I HEARD SOMETHING BLOW. YOU THINK THAT'S WHAT SENT 'EM HERE?
HELLO? MALEFICENT!!

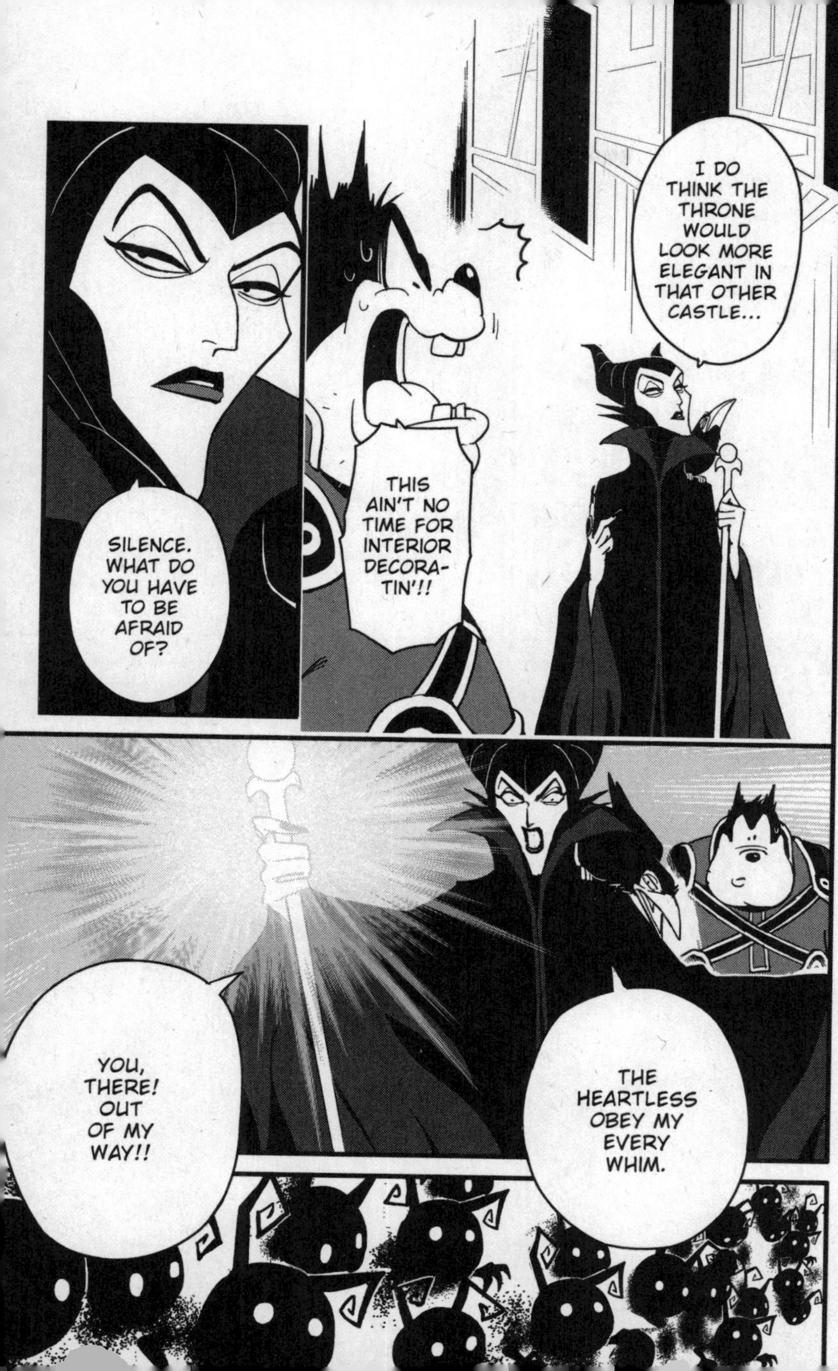
I DO THINK THE THRONE WOULD LOOK MORE ELEGANT IN THAT OTHER CASTLE...
THIS AIN'T NO TIME FOR INTERIOR DECORA-TIN'!!
SILENCE. WHAT DO YOU HAVE TO BE AFRAID OF?
THE HEARTLESS OBEY MY EVERY WHIM.
YOU, THERE! OUT OF MY WAY!!

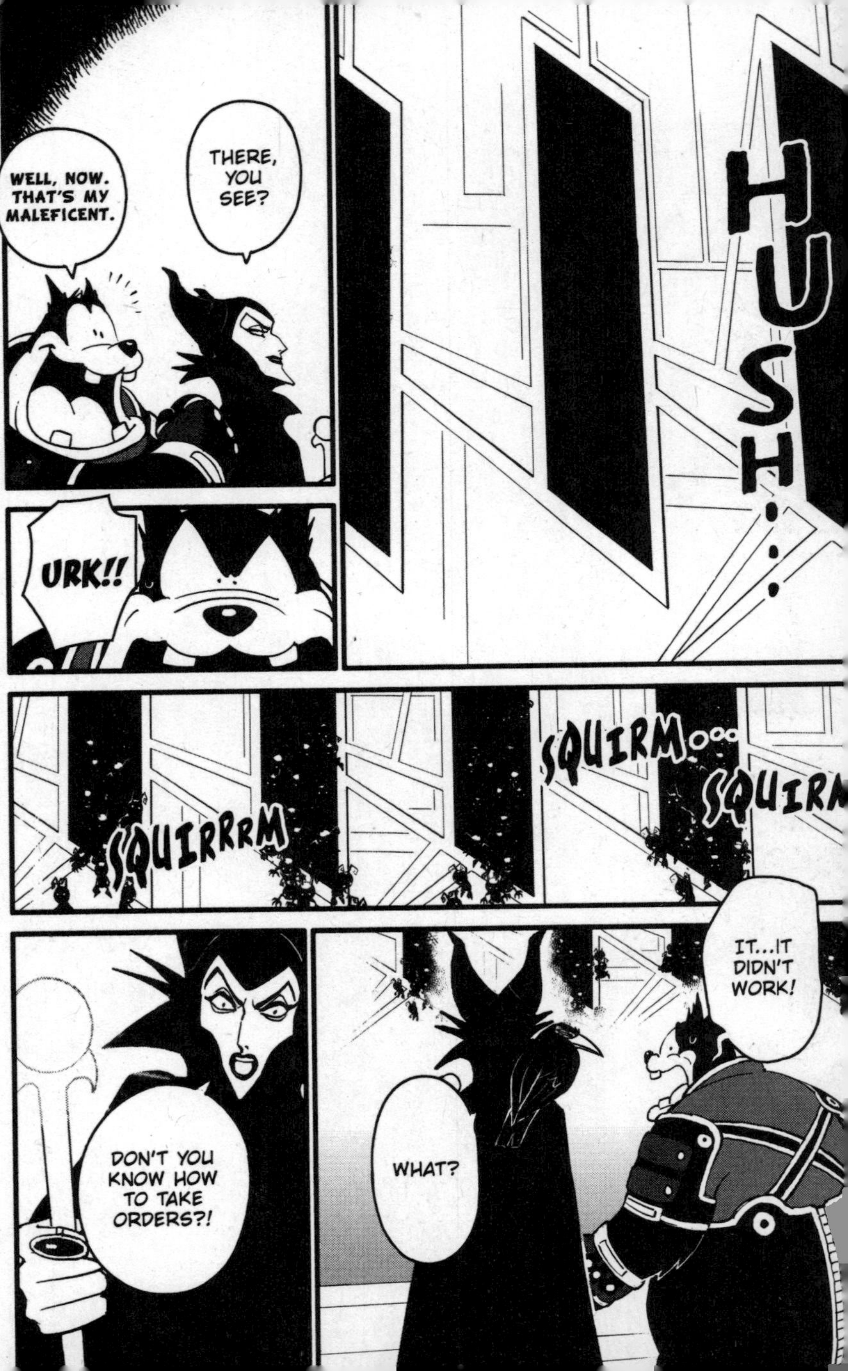
HUSH...
THERE, YOU SEE?
WELL, NOW. THAT'S MY MALEFICENT.
URK!!
SQUIRM...
SQUIRRRM
IT...IT DIDN'T WORK!
WHAT?
DON'T YOU KNOW HOW TO TAKE ORDERS?!

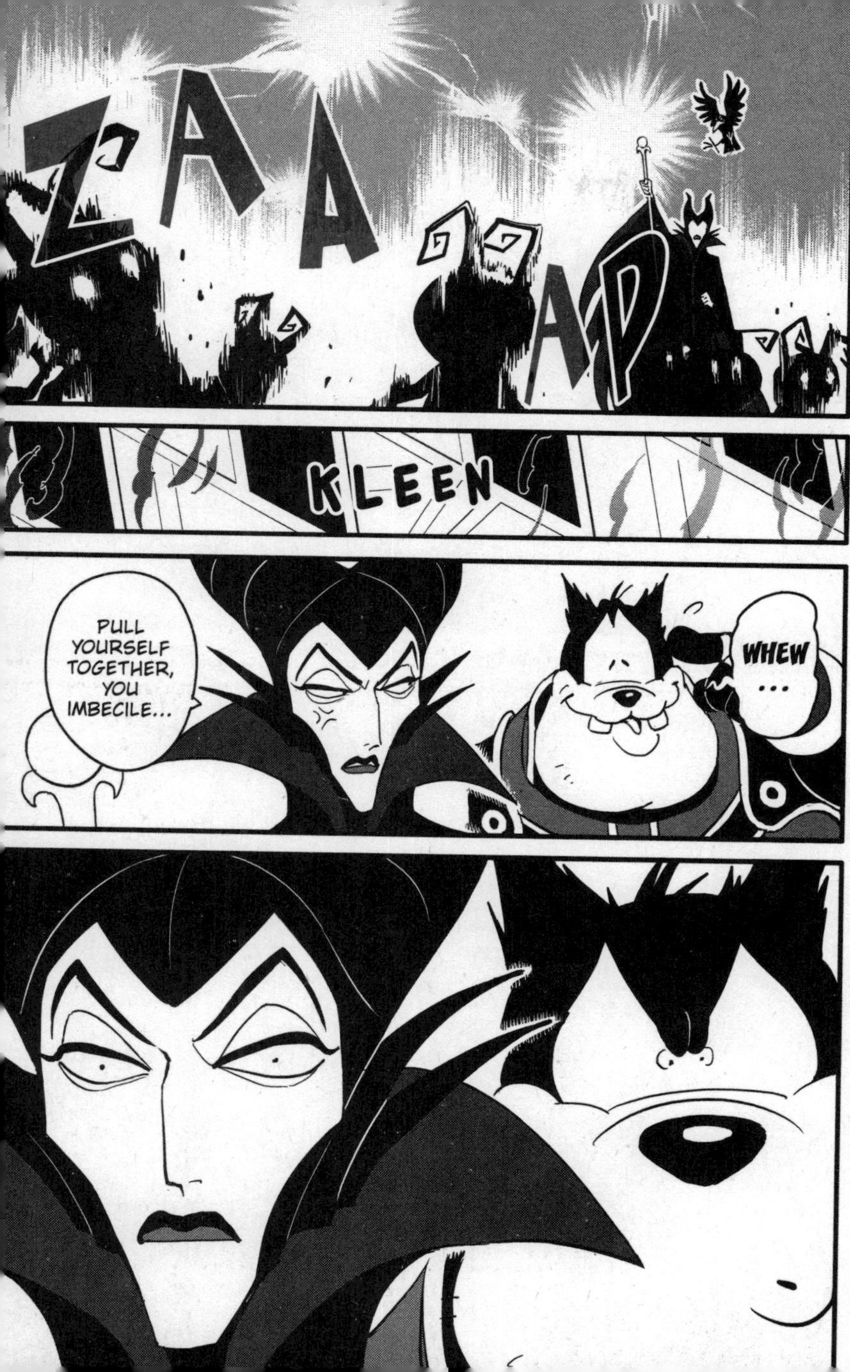
ZAAAP
KLEEN
WHEW ...
PULL YOURSELF TOGETHER, YOU IMBECILE...

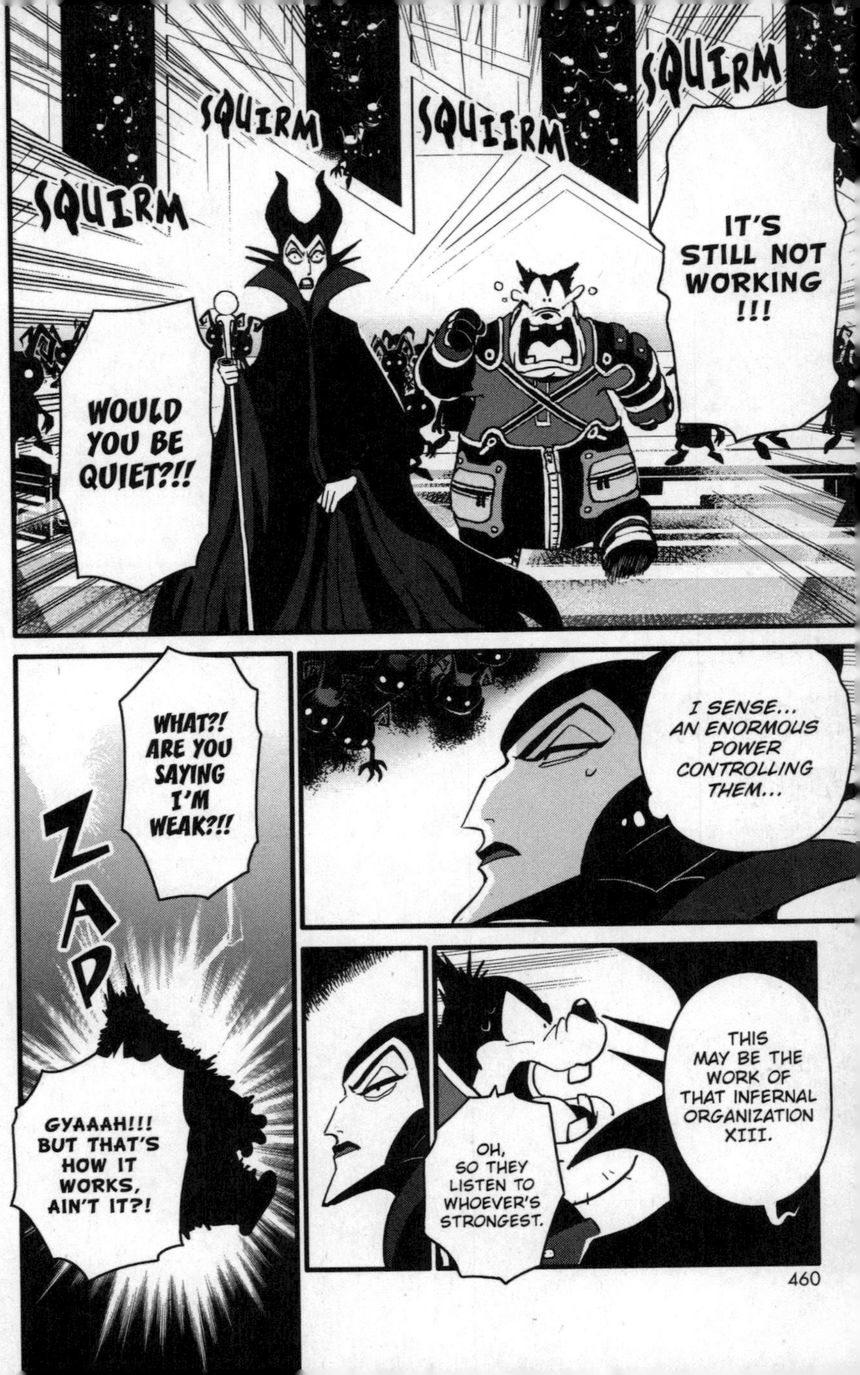

SQUIRM
SQUIIRM
SQUIRM
SQUIRM
IT'S STILL NOT WORKING !!!
WOULD YOU BE QUIET?!!
I SENSE... AN ENORMOUS POWER CONTROLLING THEM...
THIS MAY BE THE WORK OF THAT INFERNAL ORGANIZATION XIII.
OH, SO THEY LISTEN TO WHOEVER'S STRONGEST.
WHAT?! ARE YOU SAYING I'M WEAK?!!
ZAP
GYAAAH!!! BUT THAT'S HOW IT WORKS, AIN'T IT?!

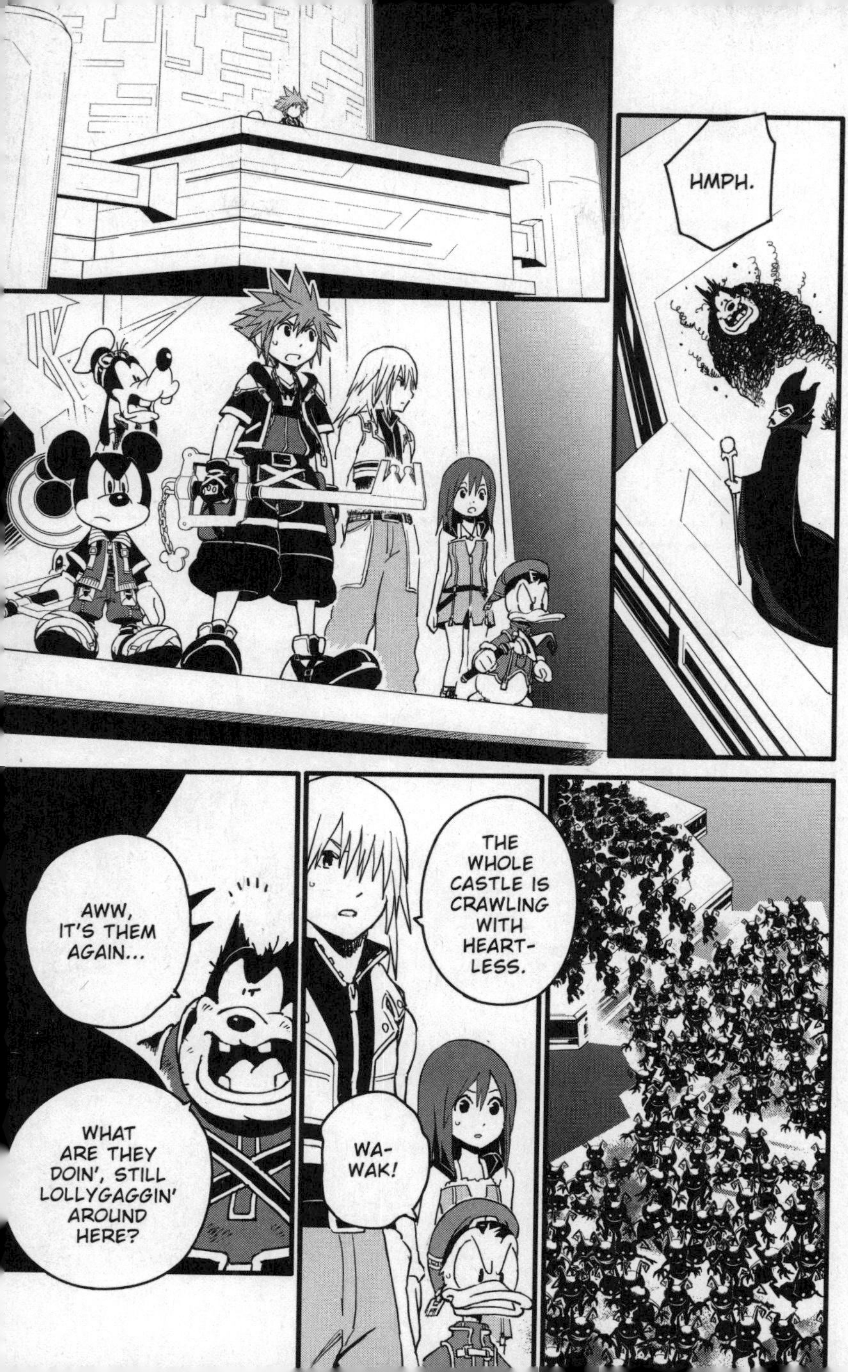
HMPH.
THE WHOLE CASTLE IS CRAWLING WITH HEART-LESS.
WA-WAK!
AWW, IT'S THEM AGAIN...
WHAT ARE THEY DOIN', STILL LOLLYGAGGIN' AROUND HERE?

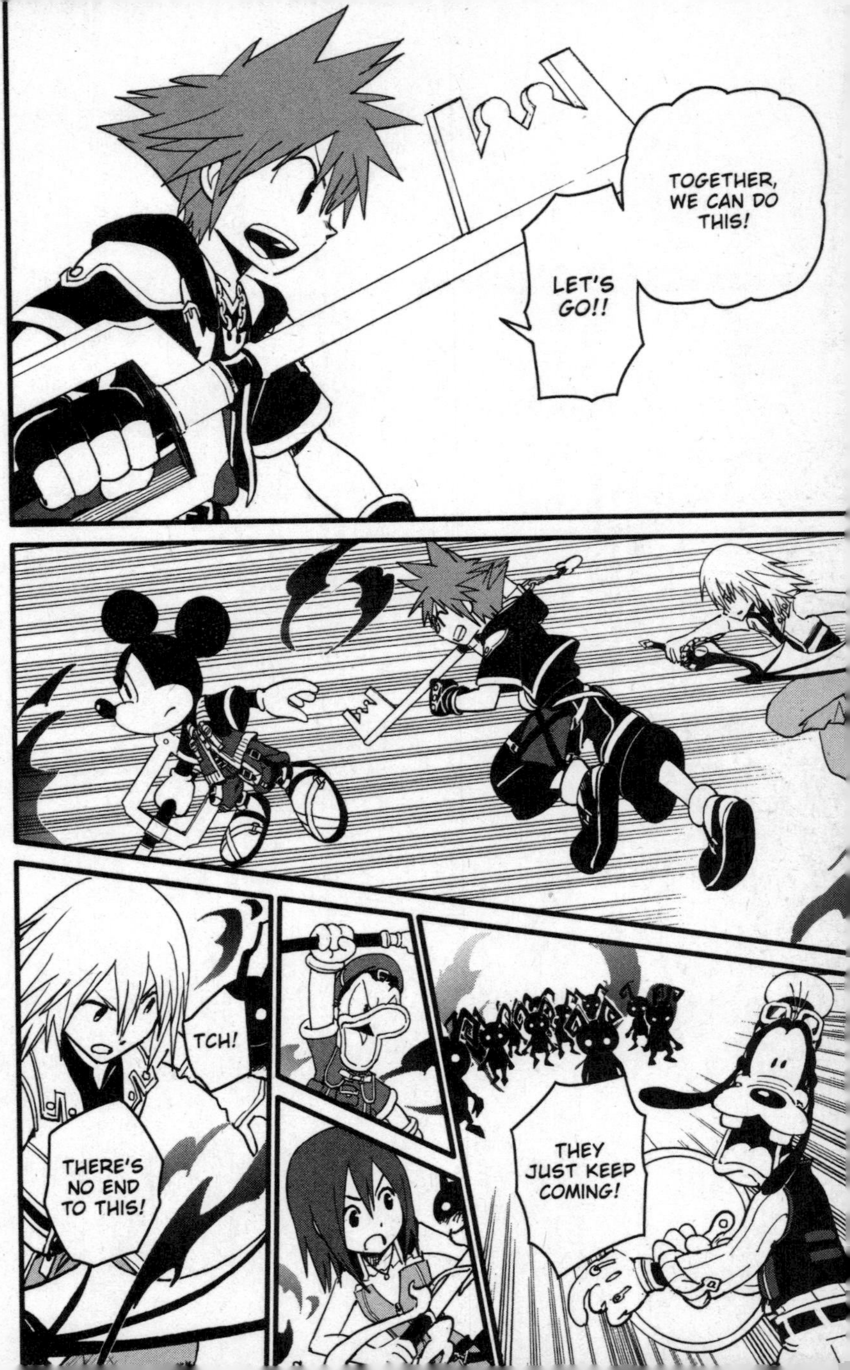
TOGETHER, WE CAN DO THIS!
LET'S GO!!
THEY JUST KEEP COMING!
TCH!
THERE'S NO END TO THIS!

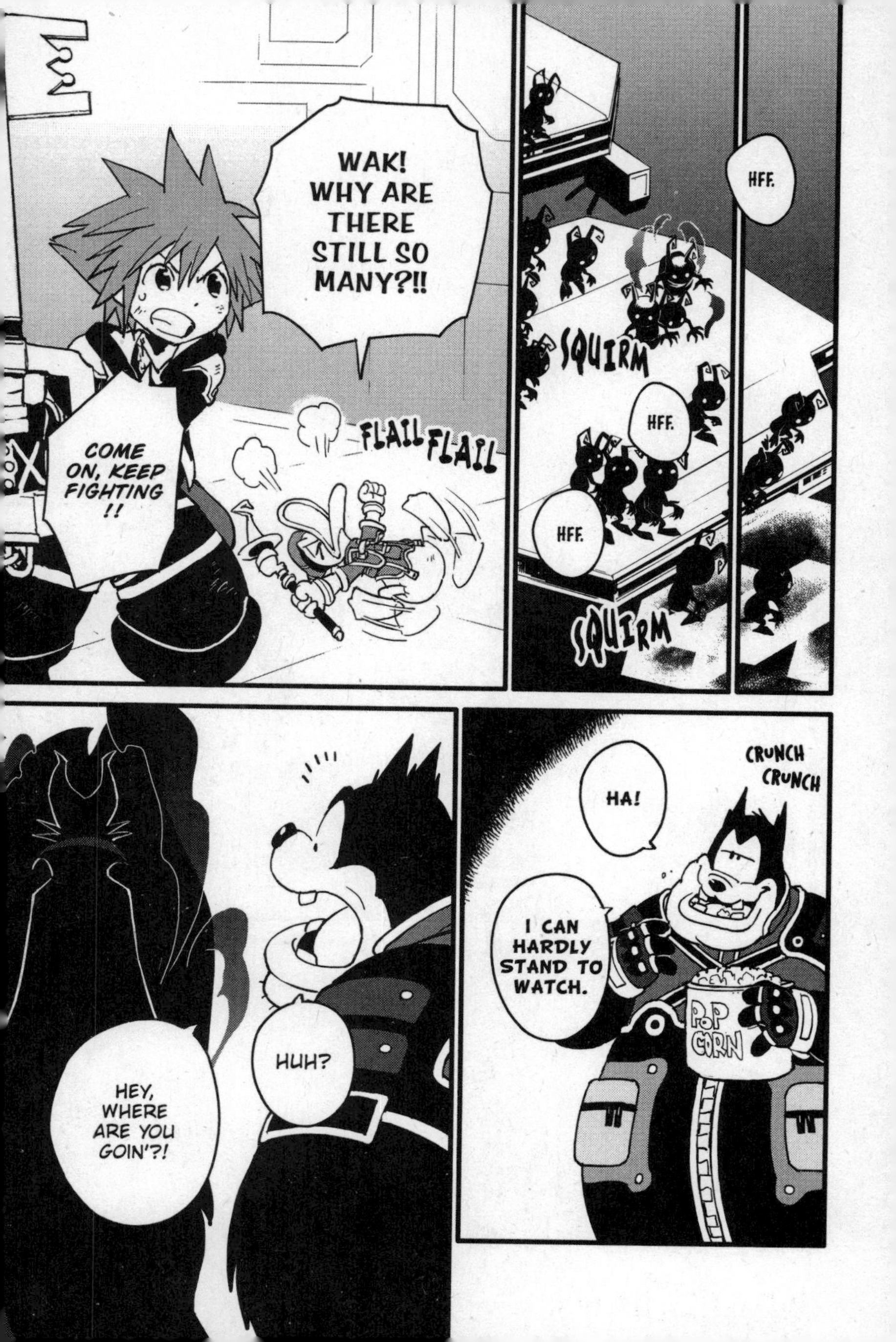
HFF.
SQUIRM
HFF.
HFF.
SQUIRM
WAK! WHY ARE THERE STILL SO MANY?!!
FLAIL FLAIL
COME ON, KEEP FIGHTING !!
CRUNCH CRUNCH
HA!
I CAN HARDLY STAND TO WATCH.
POP CORN
HUH?
HEY, WHERE ARE YOU GOIN'?!

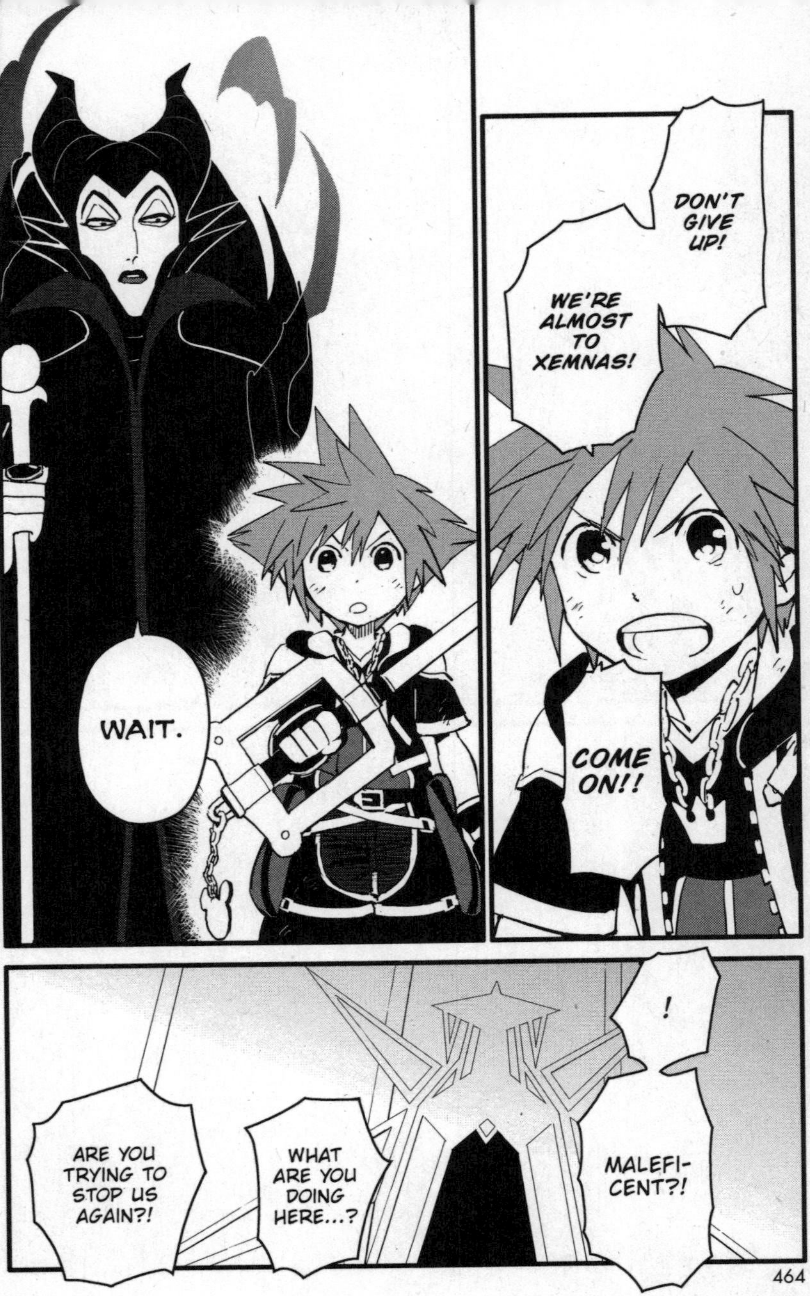
DON'T GIVE UP!
WE'RE ALMOST TO XEMNAS!
COME ON!!
WAIT.
!
MALEFI-CENT?!
WHAT ARE YOU DOING HERE...?
ARE YOU TRYING TO STOP US AGAIN?!

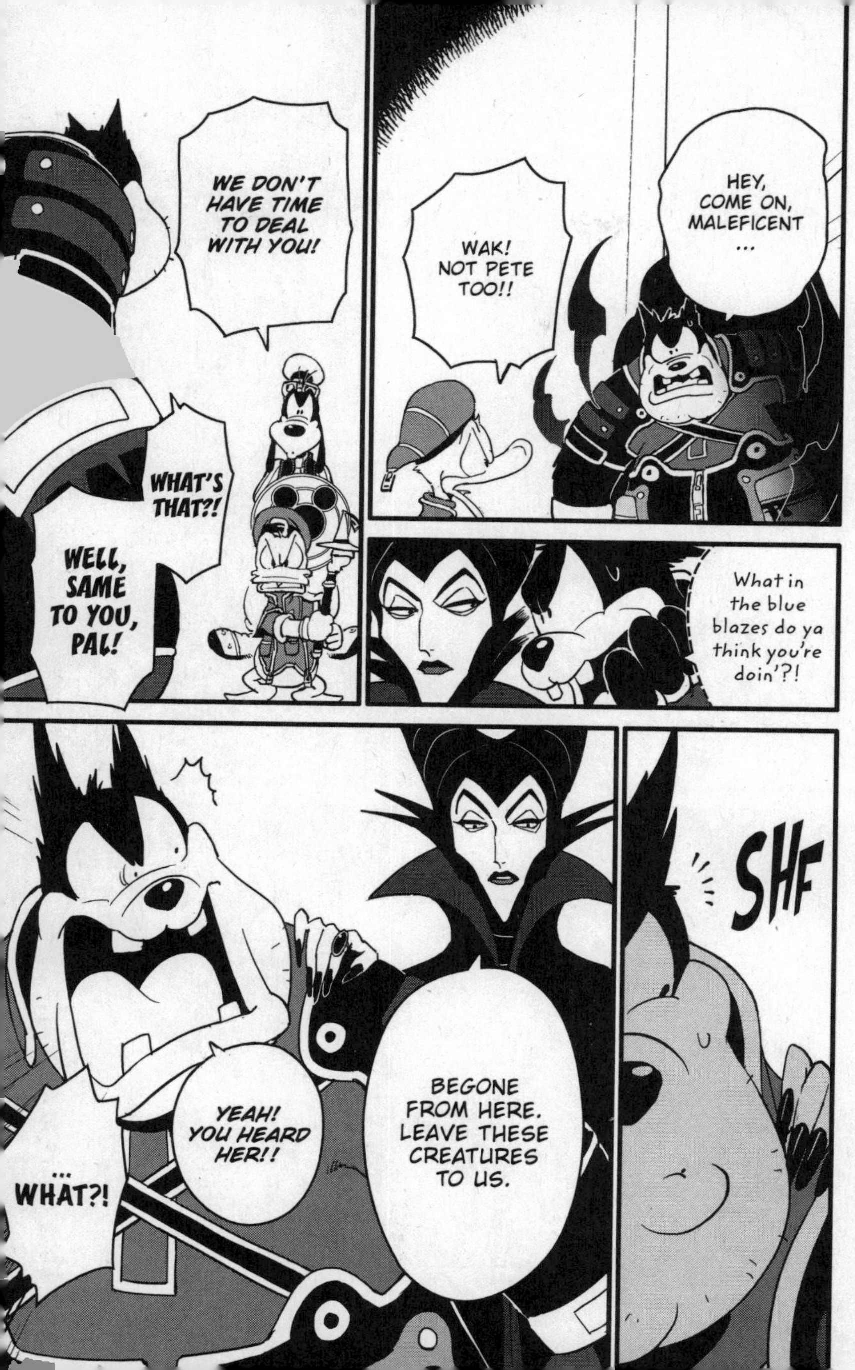
HEY, COME ON, MALEFICENT ...
WAK! NOT PETE TOO!!
What in the blue blazes do ya think you're doin'?!
WE DON'T HAVE TIME TO DEAL WITH YOU!
WHAT'S THAT?!
WELL, SAME TO YOU, PAL!
SHF
BEGONE FROM HERE. LEAVE THESE CREATURES TO US.
YEAH! YOU HEARD HER!!
... WHAT?!

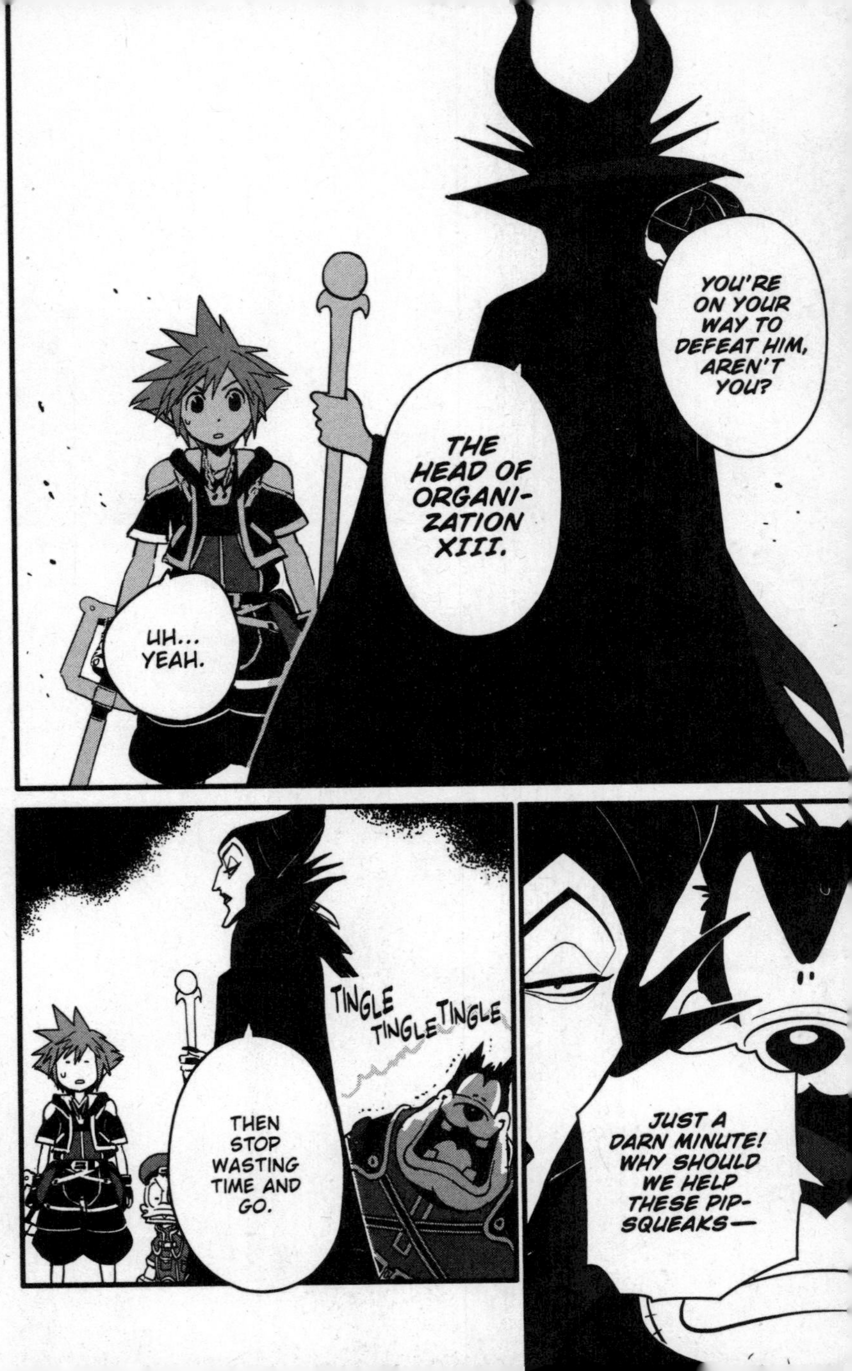
YOU'RE ON YOUR WAY TO DEFEAT HIM, AREN'T YOU?
THE HEAD OF ORGANI-ZATION XIII.
UH... YEAH.
JUST A DARN MINUTE! WHY SHOULD WE HELP THESE PIP-SQUEAKS—
TINGLE TINGLE TINGLE
THEN STOP WASTING TIME AND GO.

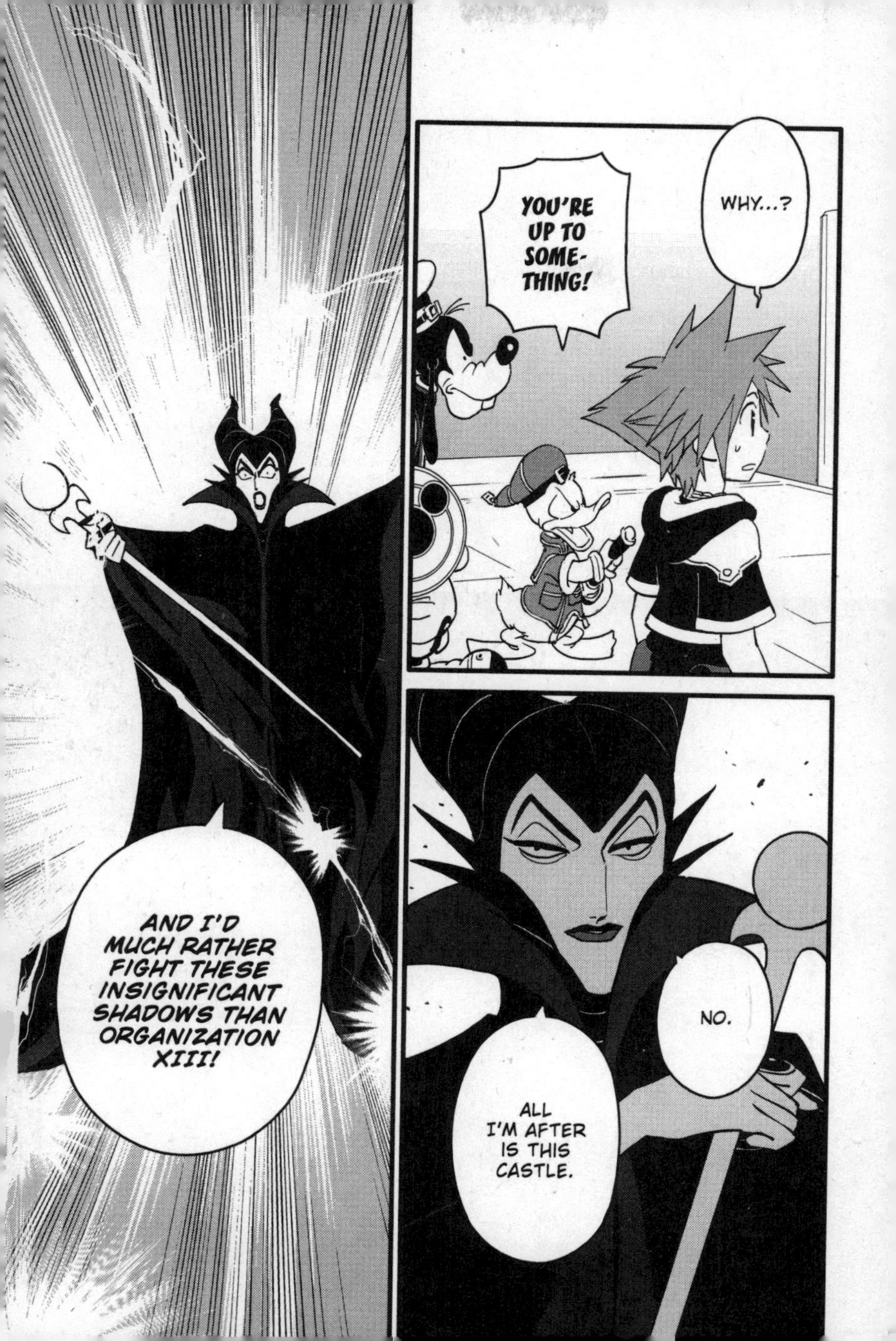
WHY...?
YOU'RE UP TO SOME-THING!
NO.
ALL I'M AFTER IS THIS CASTLE.
AND I'D MUCH RATHER FIGHT THESE INSIGNIFICANT SHADOWS THAN ORGANIZATION XIII!

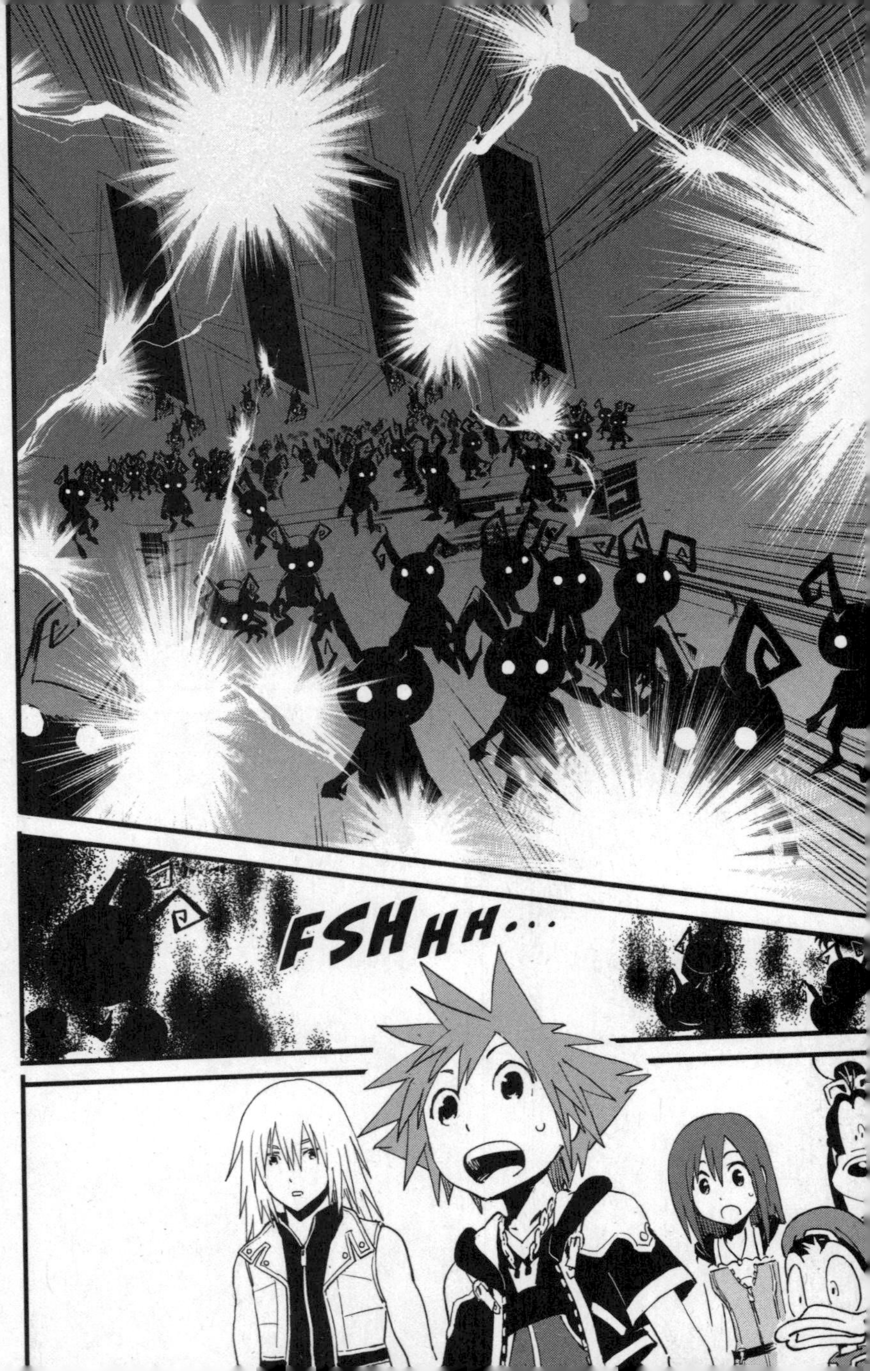
FSHHH...

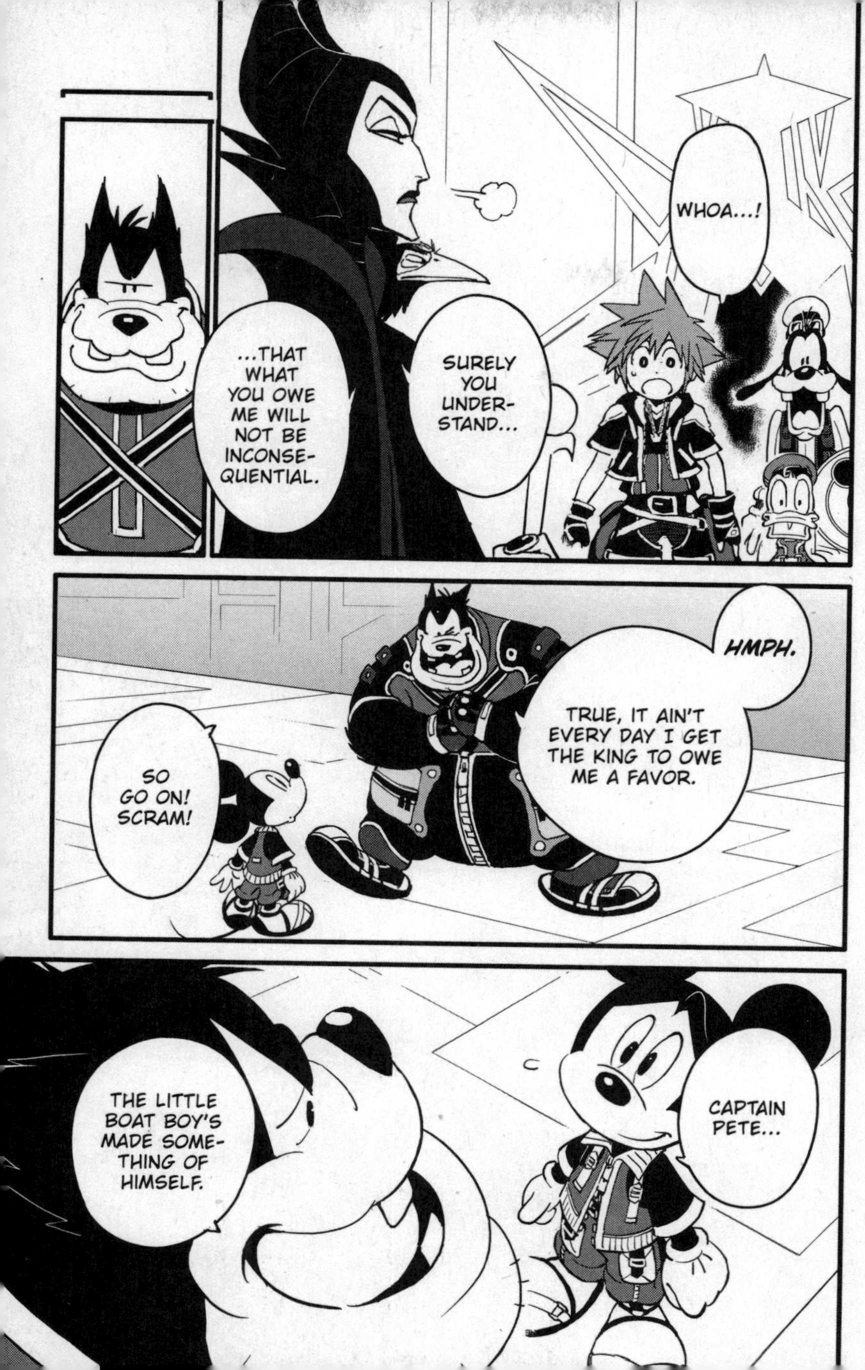
WHOA...!
SURELY YOU UNDERSTAND...
...THAT WHAT YOU OWE ME WILL NOT BE INCONSEQUENTIAL.
HMPH.
TRUE, IT AIN'T EVERY DAY I GET THE KING TO OWE ME A FAVOR.
SO GO ON! SCRAM!
CAPTAIN PETE...
THE LITTLE BOAT BOY'S MADE SOMETHING OF HIMSELF.

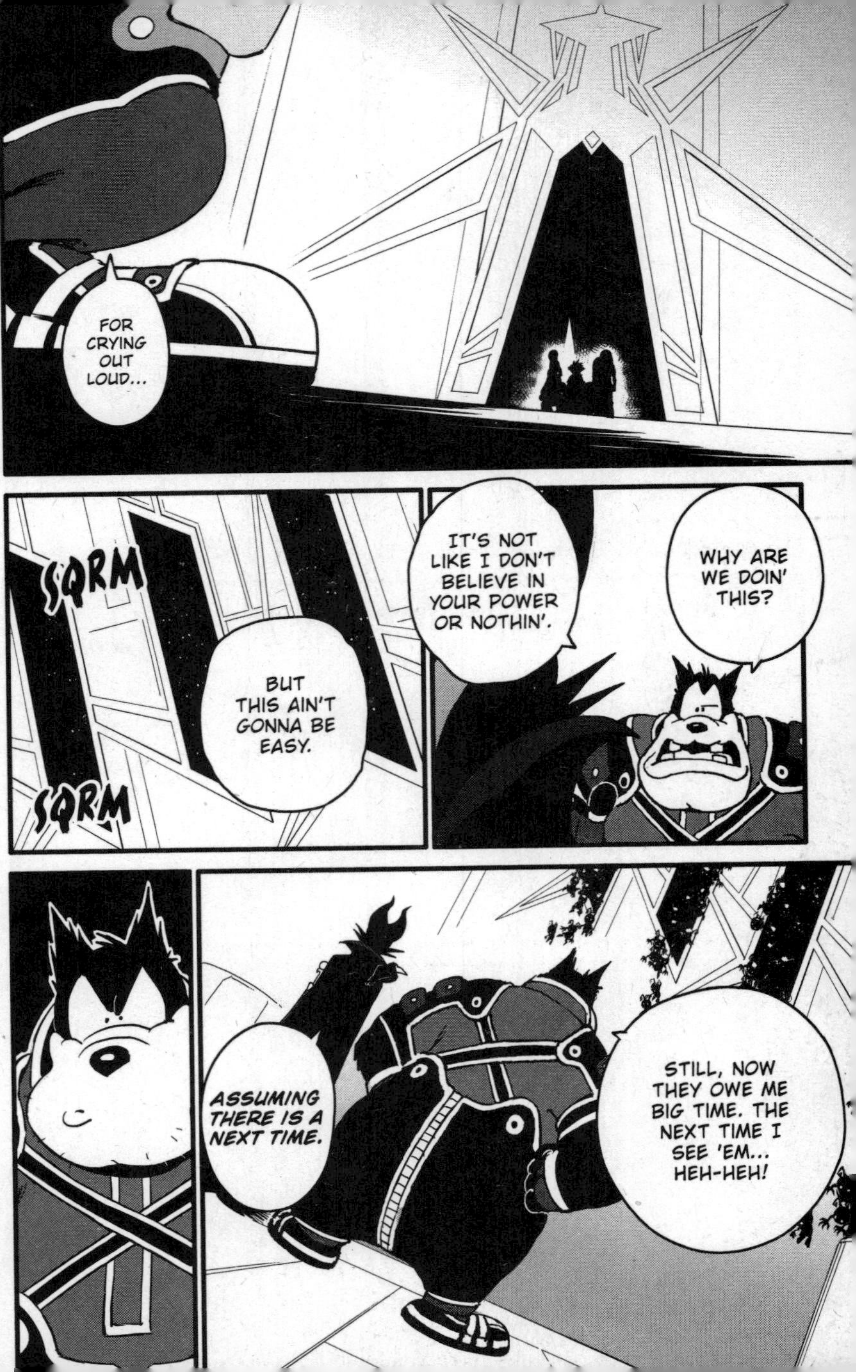
FOR CRYING OUT LOUD...
WHY ARE WE DOIN' THIS?
IT'S NOT LIKE I DON'T BELIEVE IN YOUR POWER OR NOTHIN'.
BUT THIS AIN'T GONNA BE EASY.
SQRM
SQRM
STILL, NOW THEY OWE ME BIG TIME. THE NEXT TIME I SEE 'EM... HEH-HEH!
ASSUMING THERE IS A NEXT TIME.

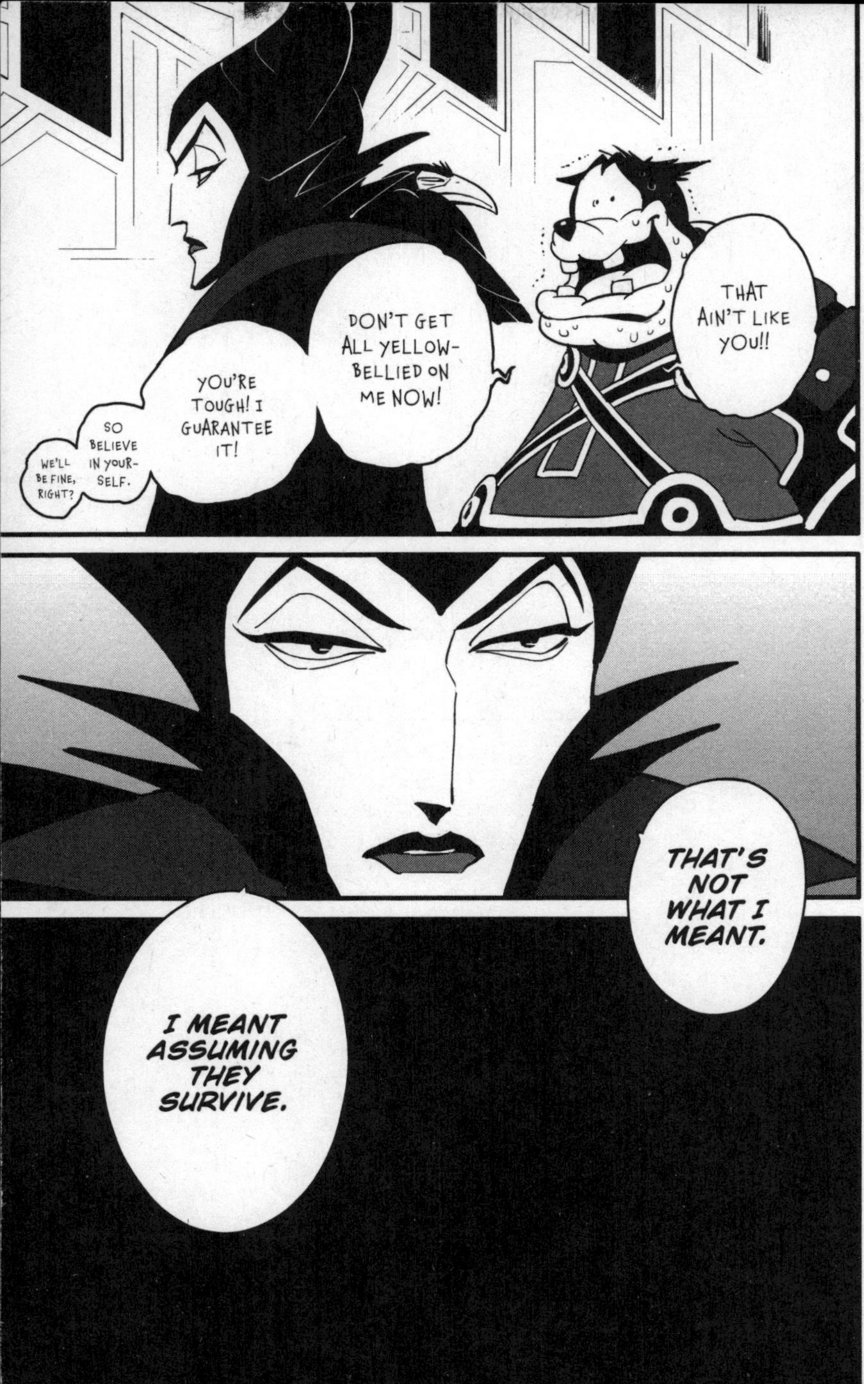
THAT AIN'T LIKE YOU!!
DON'T GET ALL YELLOW-BELLIED ON ME NOW!
YOU'RE TOUGH! I GUARANTEE IT!
SO BELIEVE IN YOUR-SELF.
WE'LL BE FINE, RIGHT?
THAT'S NOT WHAT I MEANT.
I MEANT ASSUMING THEY SURVIVE.

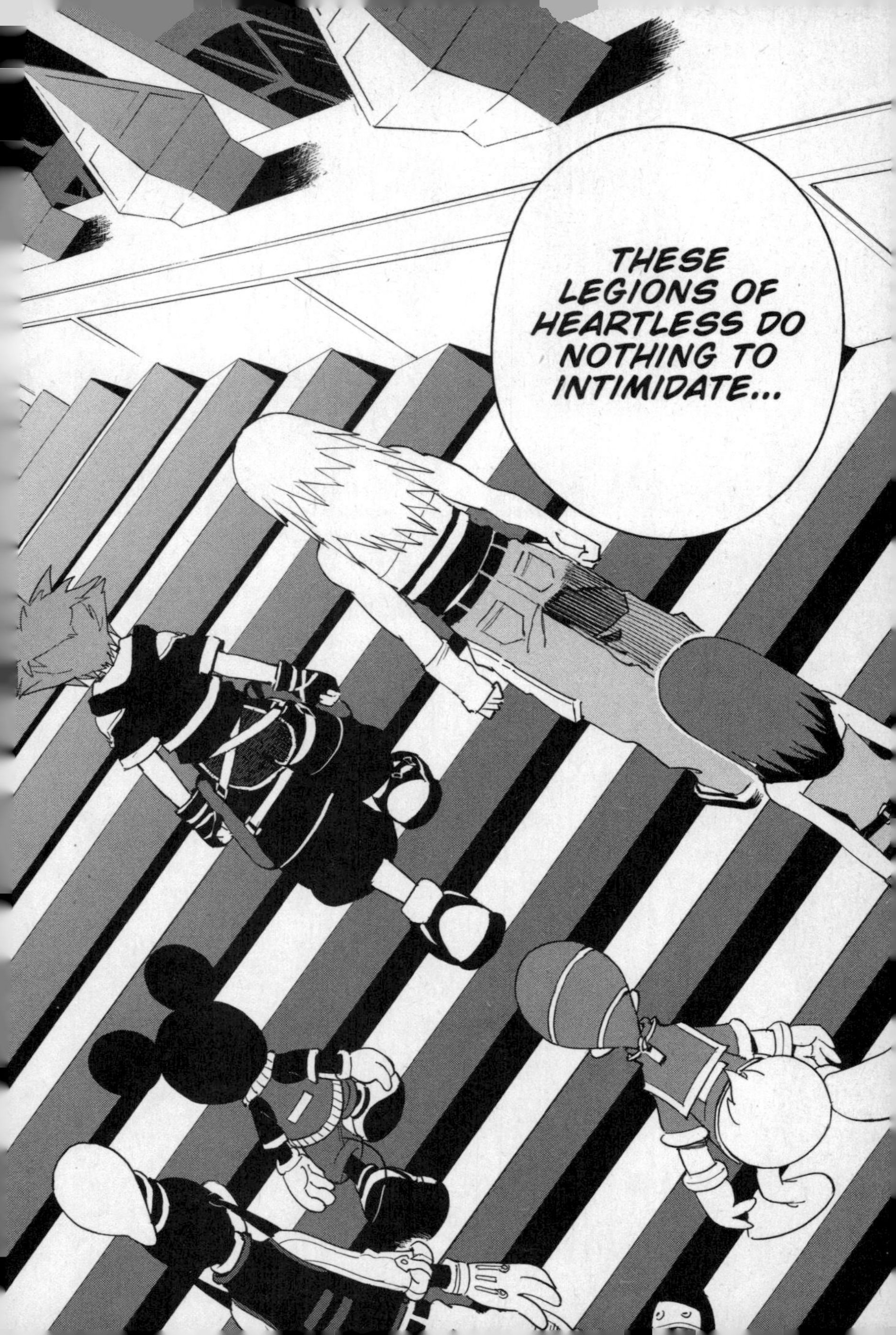
THESE LEGIONS OF HEARTLESS DO NOTHING TO INTIMIDATE...

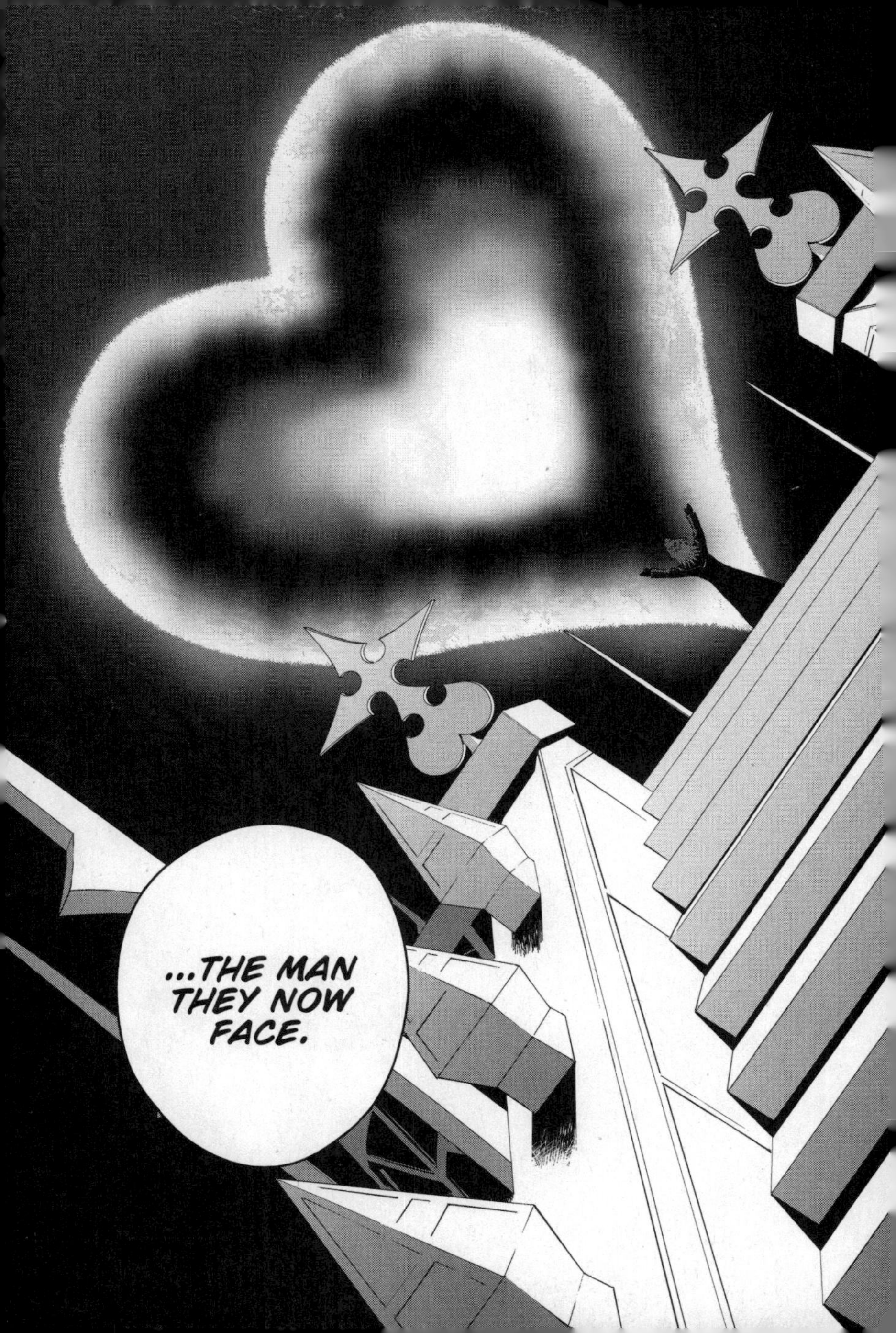
...THE MAN THEY NOW FACE.

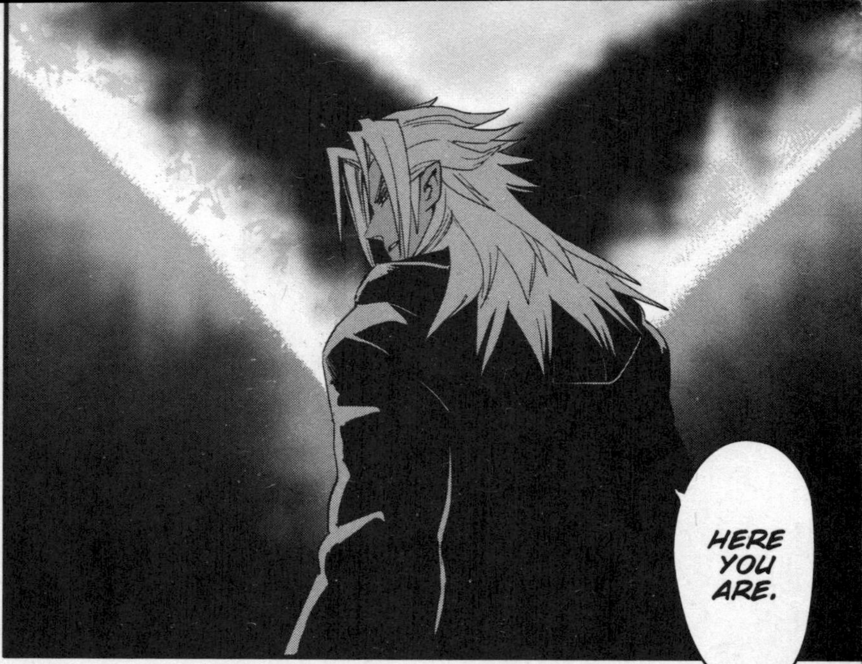
HERE YOU ARE.
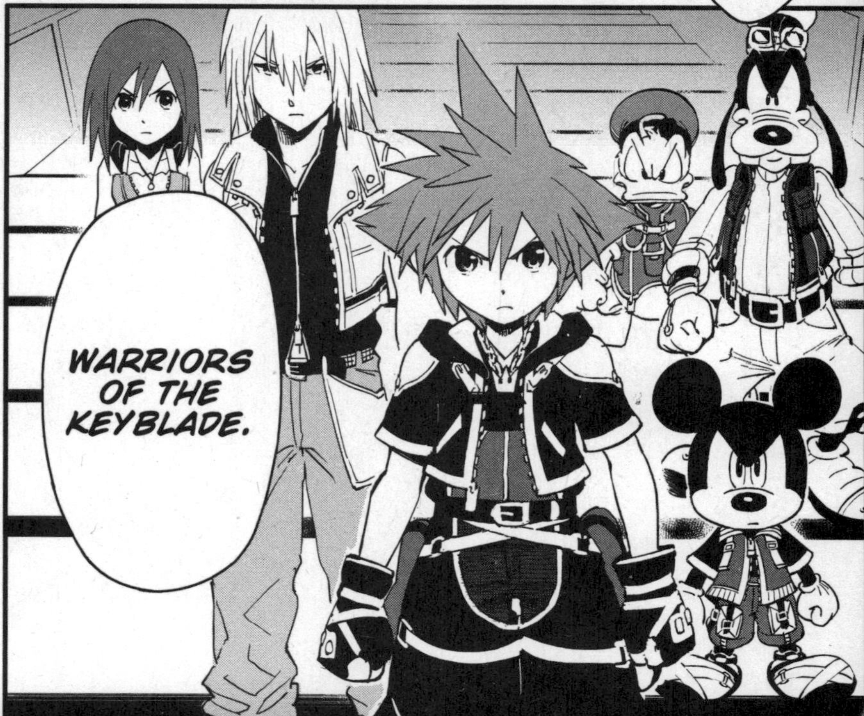
WARRIORS OF THE KEYBLADE.

Chapter 67: The Power of the Heart

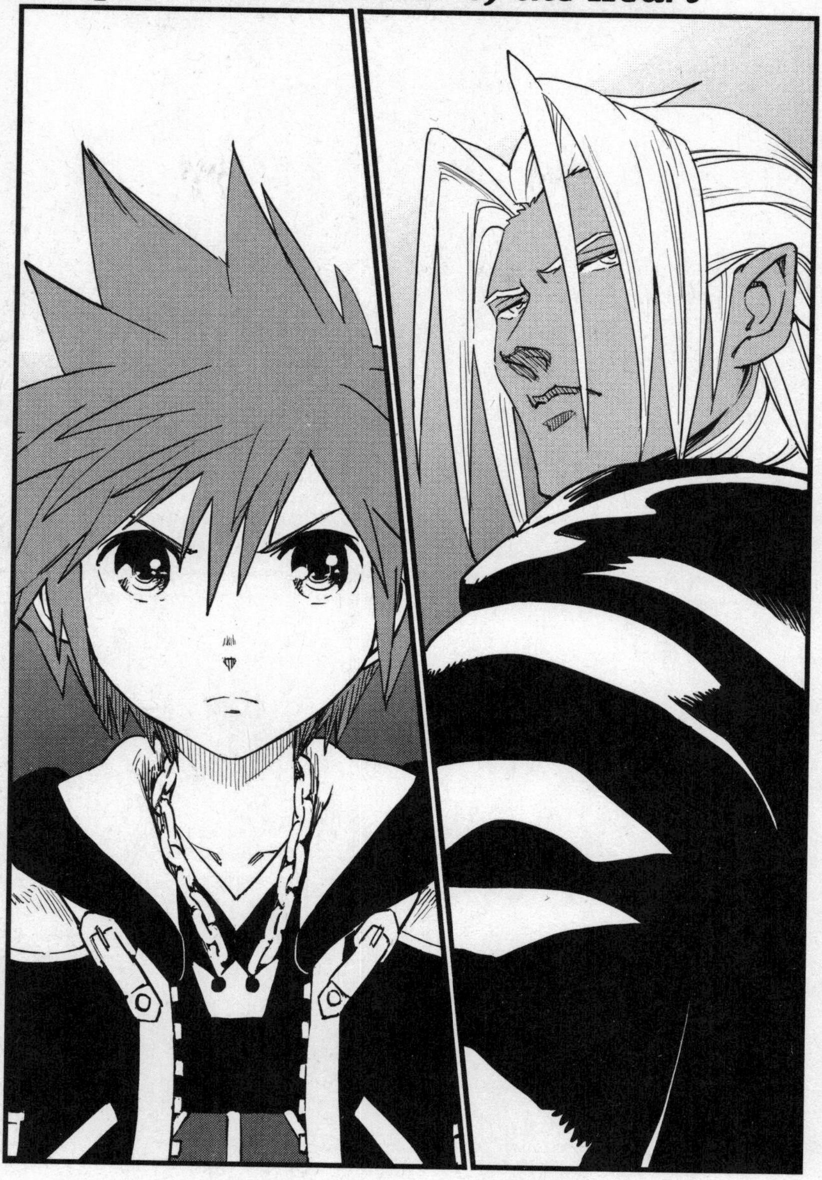

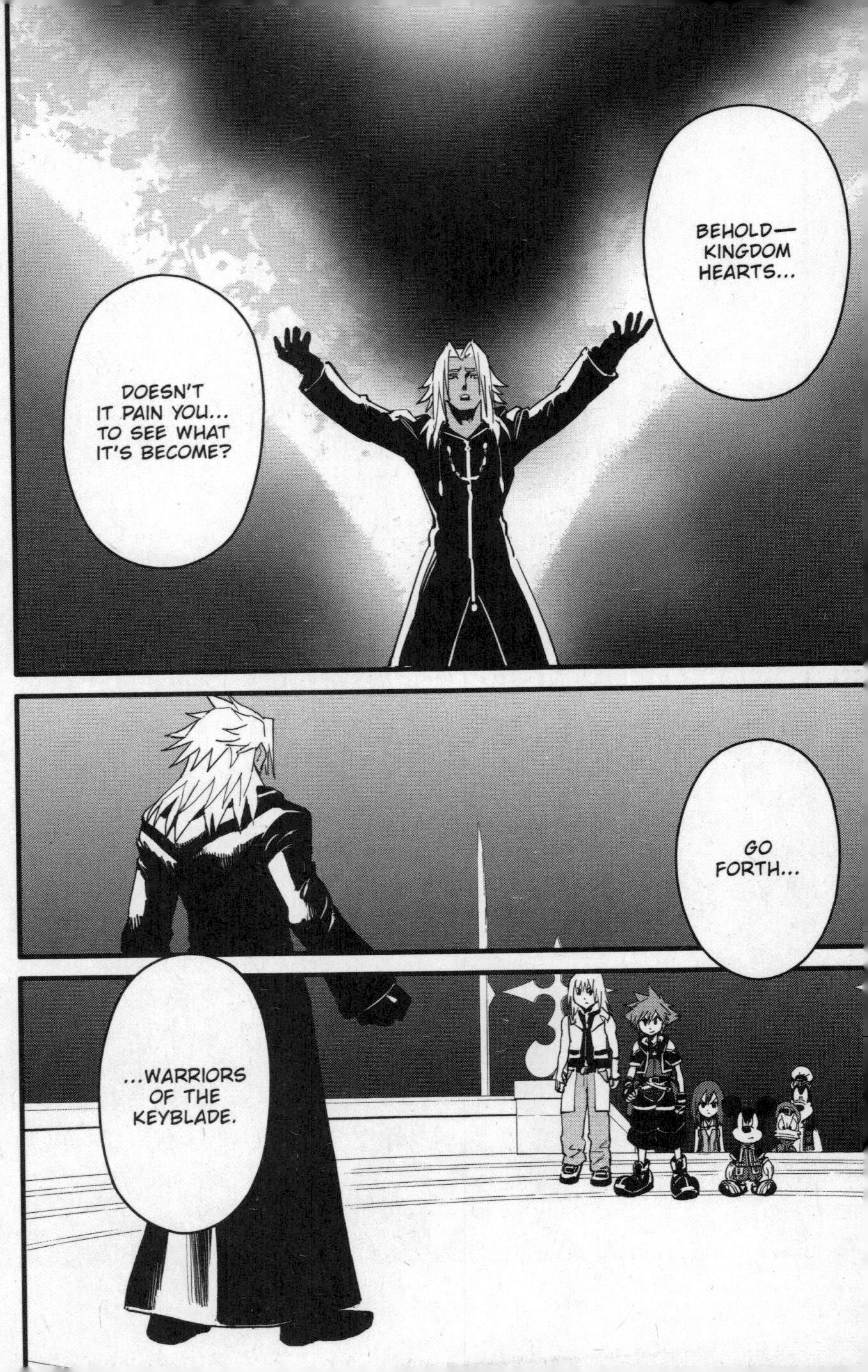
BEHOLD—KINGDOM HEARTS...
DOESN'T IT PAIN YOU... TO SEE WHAT IT'S BECOME?
GO FORTH...
...WARRIORS OF THE KEYBLADE.

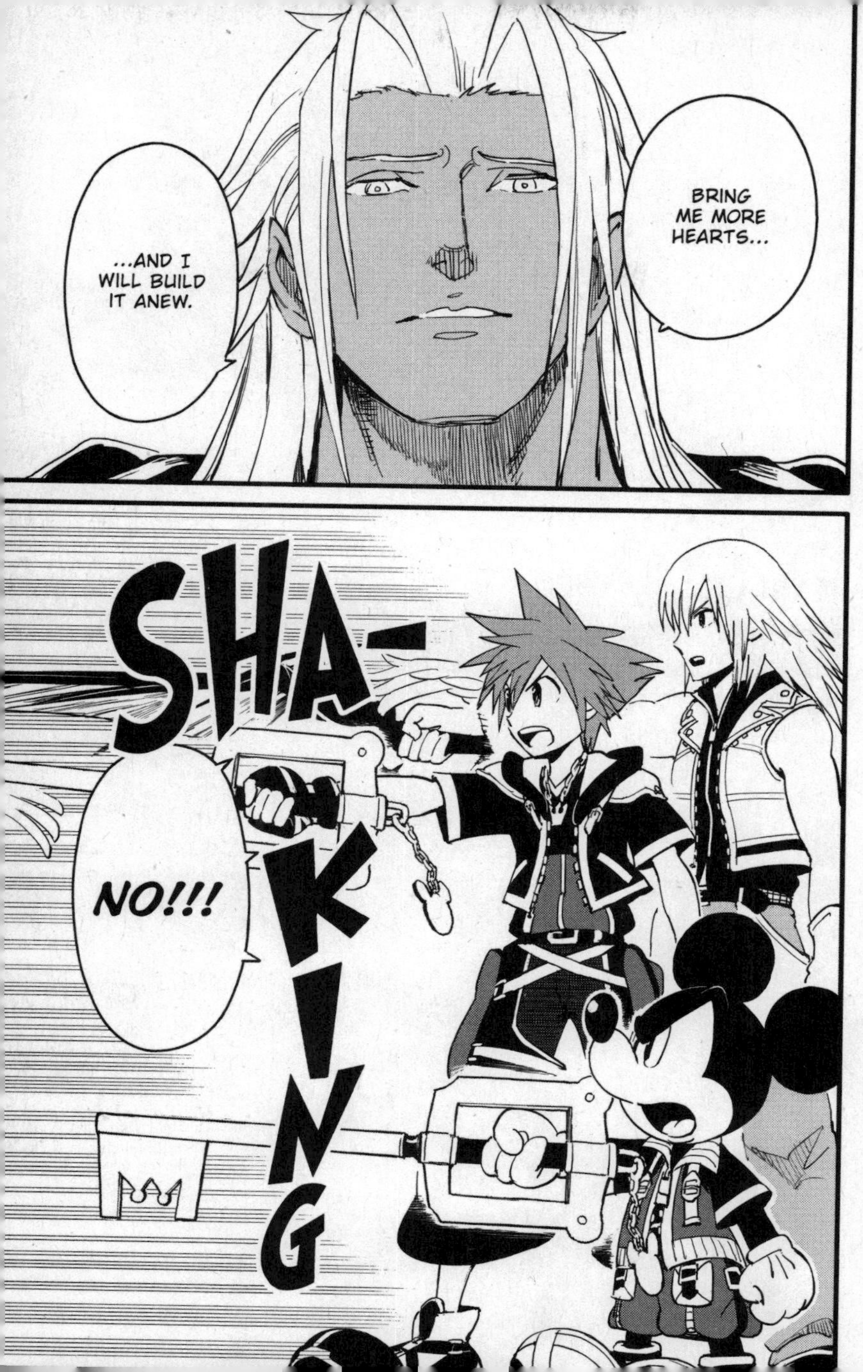
BRING ME MORE HEARTS...
...AND I WILL BUILD IT ANEW.
SHA-KING
NO!!!

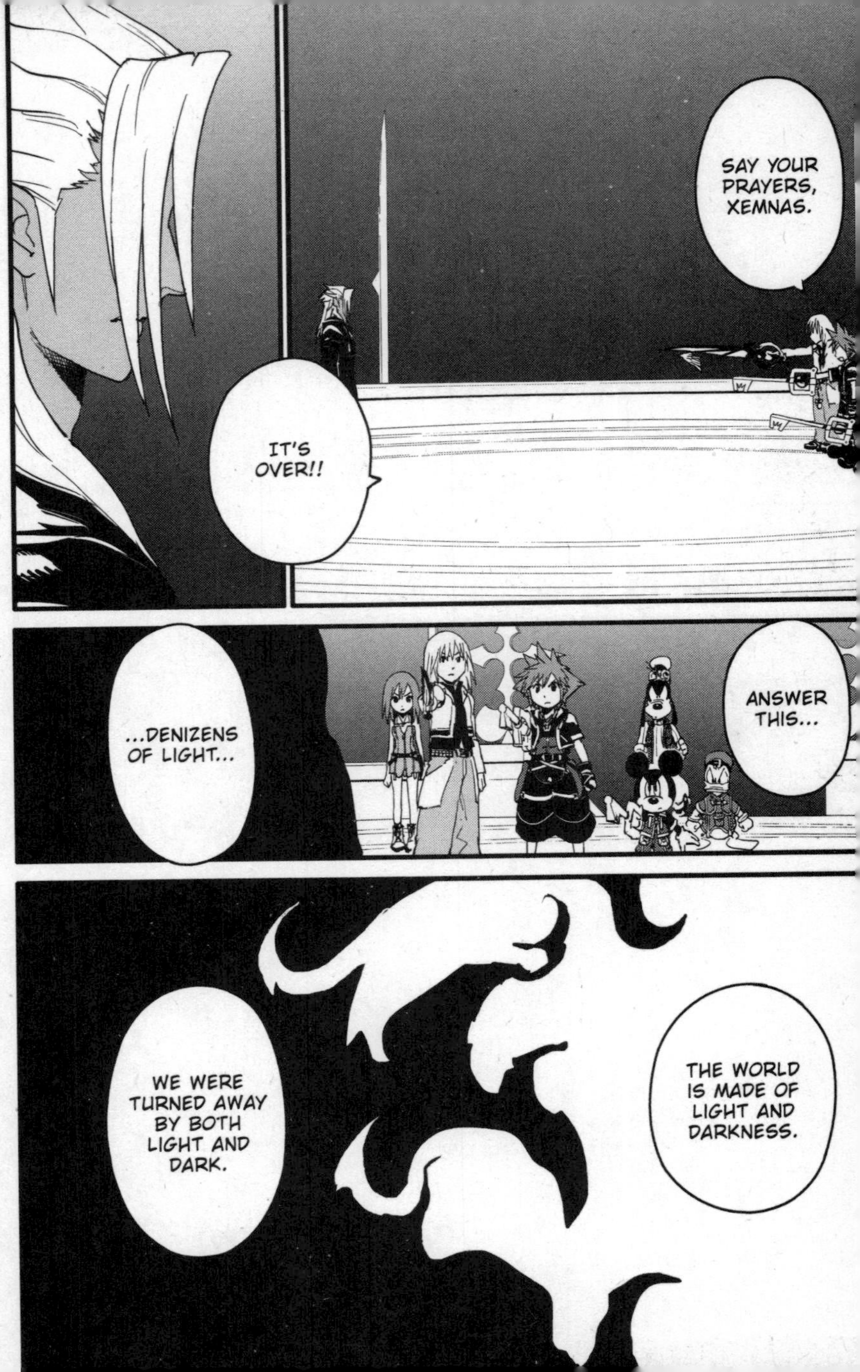
SAY YOUR PRAYERS, XEMNAS.
IT'S OVER!!
ANSWER THIS...
...DENIZENS OF LIGHT...
THE WORLD IS MADE OF LIGHT AND DARKNESS.
WE WERE TURNED AWAY BY BOTH LIGHT AND DARK.

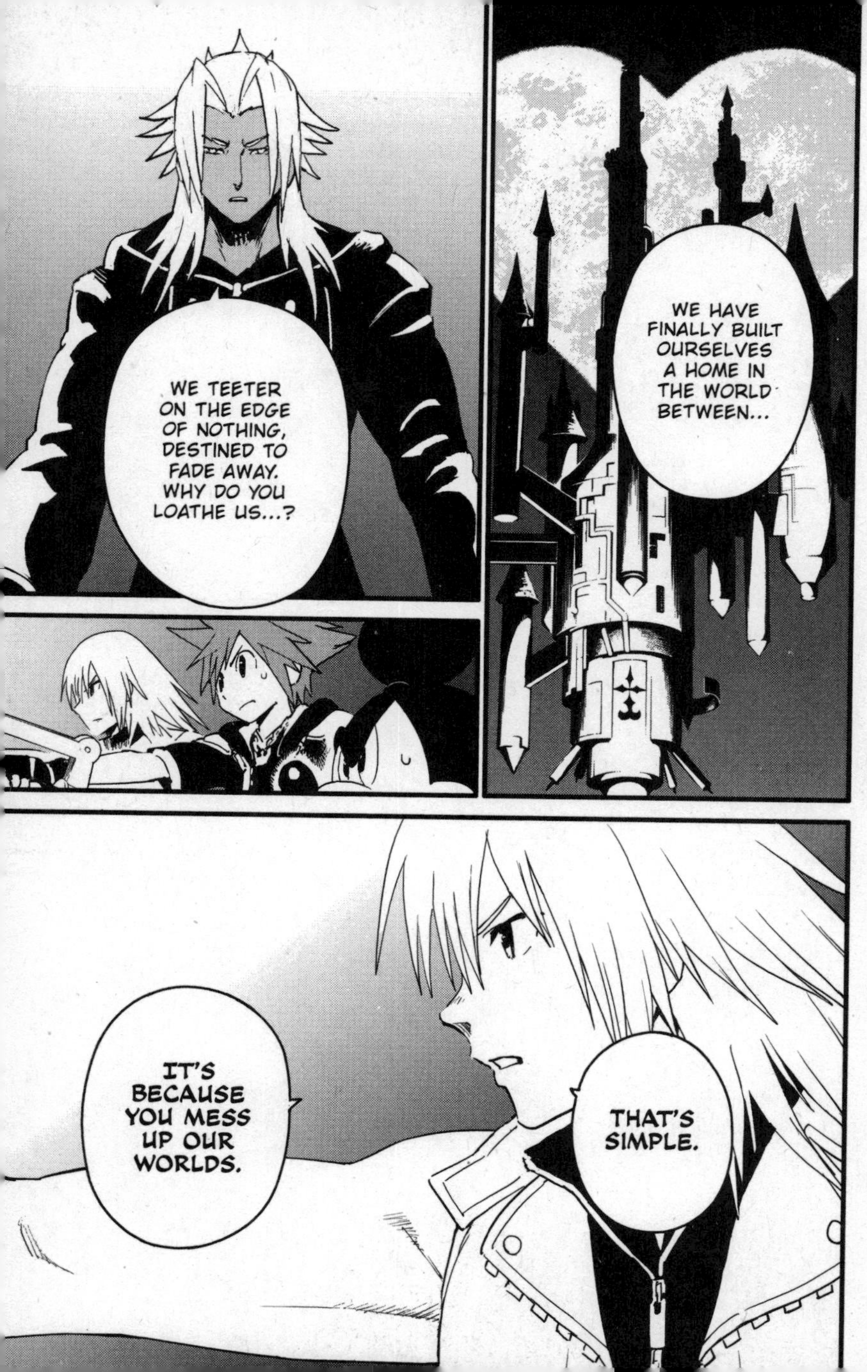
WE HAVE FINALLY BUILT OURSELVES A HOME IN THE WORLD BETWEEN...
WE TEETER ON THE EDGE OF NOTHING, DESTINED TO FADE AWAY. WHY DO YOU LOATHE US...?
THAT'S SIMPLE.
IT'S BECAUSE YOU MESS UP OUR WORLDS.

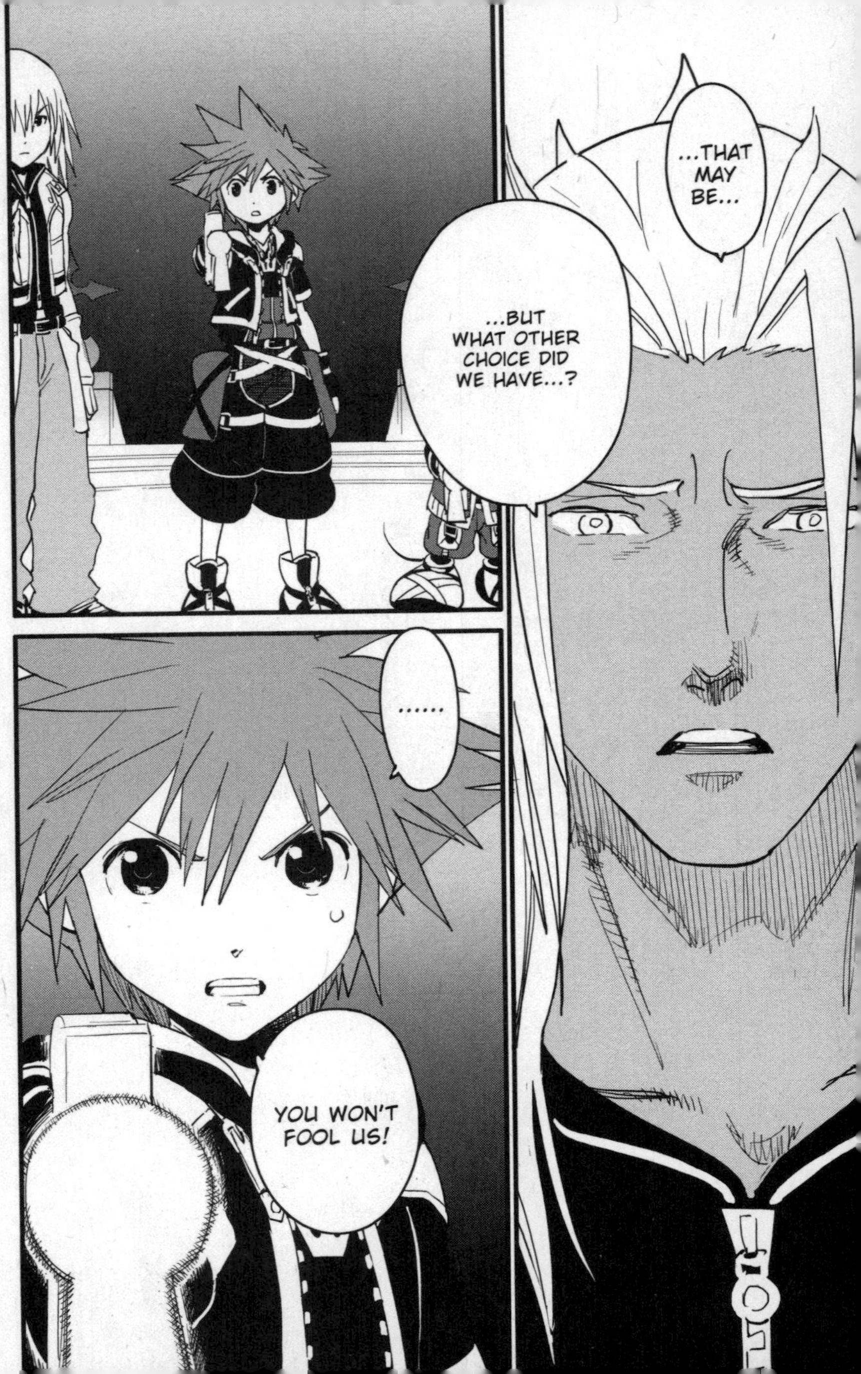
...THAT MAY BE...
...BUT WHAT OTHER CHOICE DID WE HAVE...?
......
YOU WON'T FOOL US!

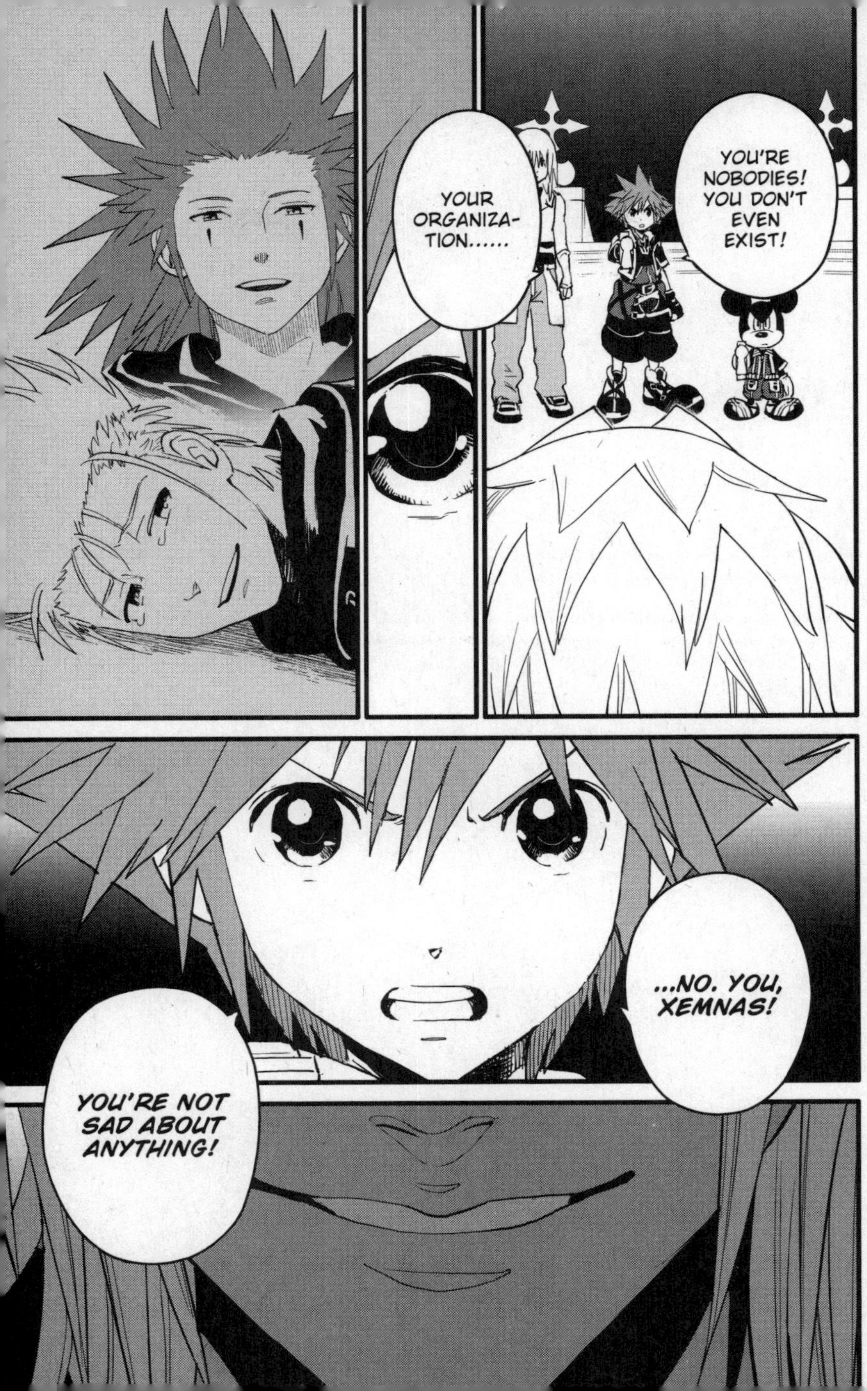
YOU'RE NOBODIES! YOU DON'T EVEN EXIST!
YOUR ORGANIZA-TION......
...NO. YOU, XEMNAS!
YOU'RE NOT SAD ABOUT ANYTHING!

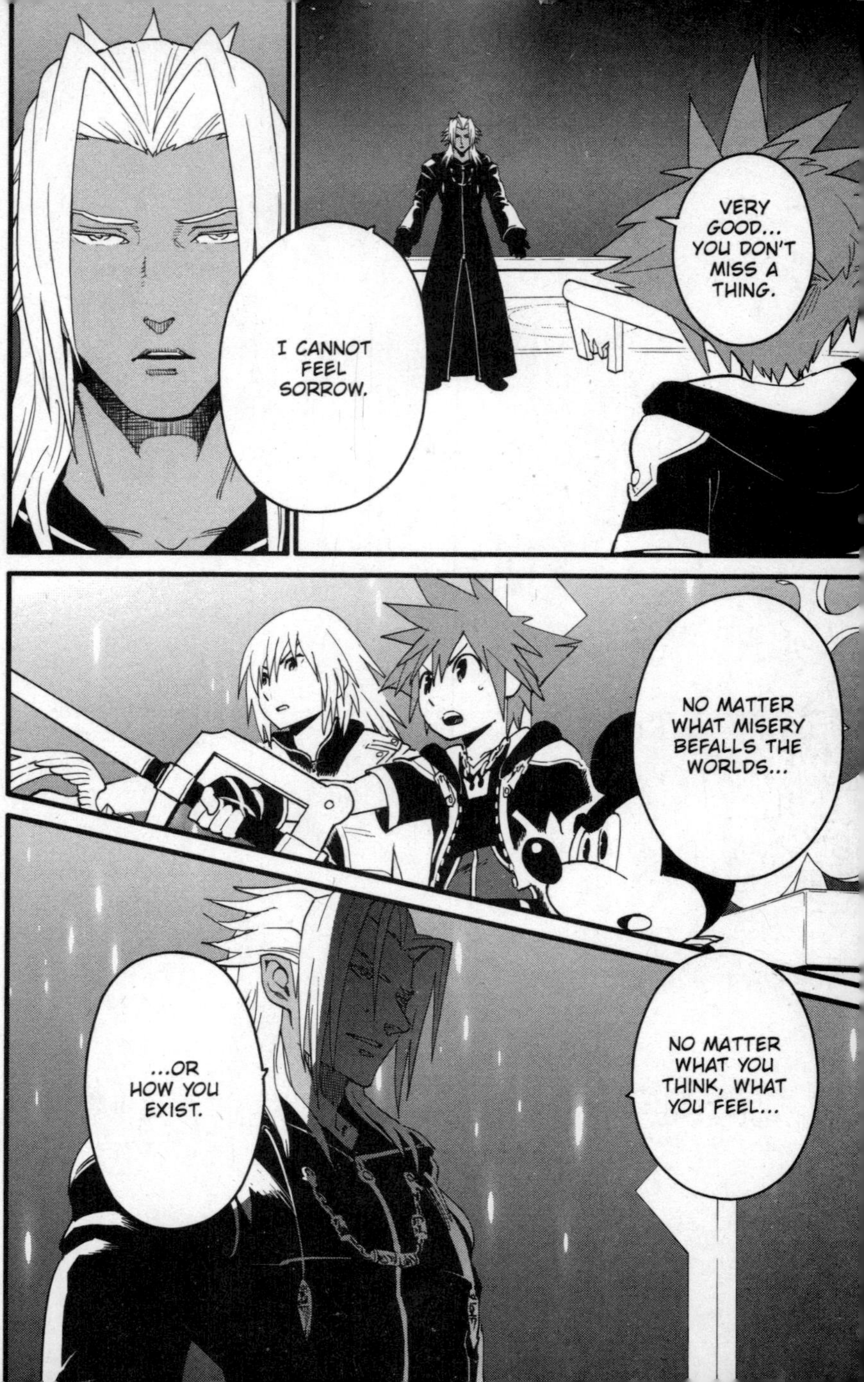
VERY GOOD... YOU DON'T MISS A THING.
I CANNOT FEEL SORROW.
NO MATTER WHAT MISERY BEFALLS THE WORLDS...
NO MATTER WHAT YOU THINK, WHAT YOU FEEL...
...OR HOW YOU EXIST.

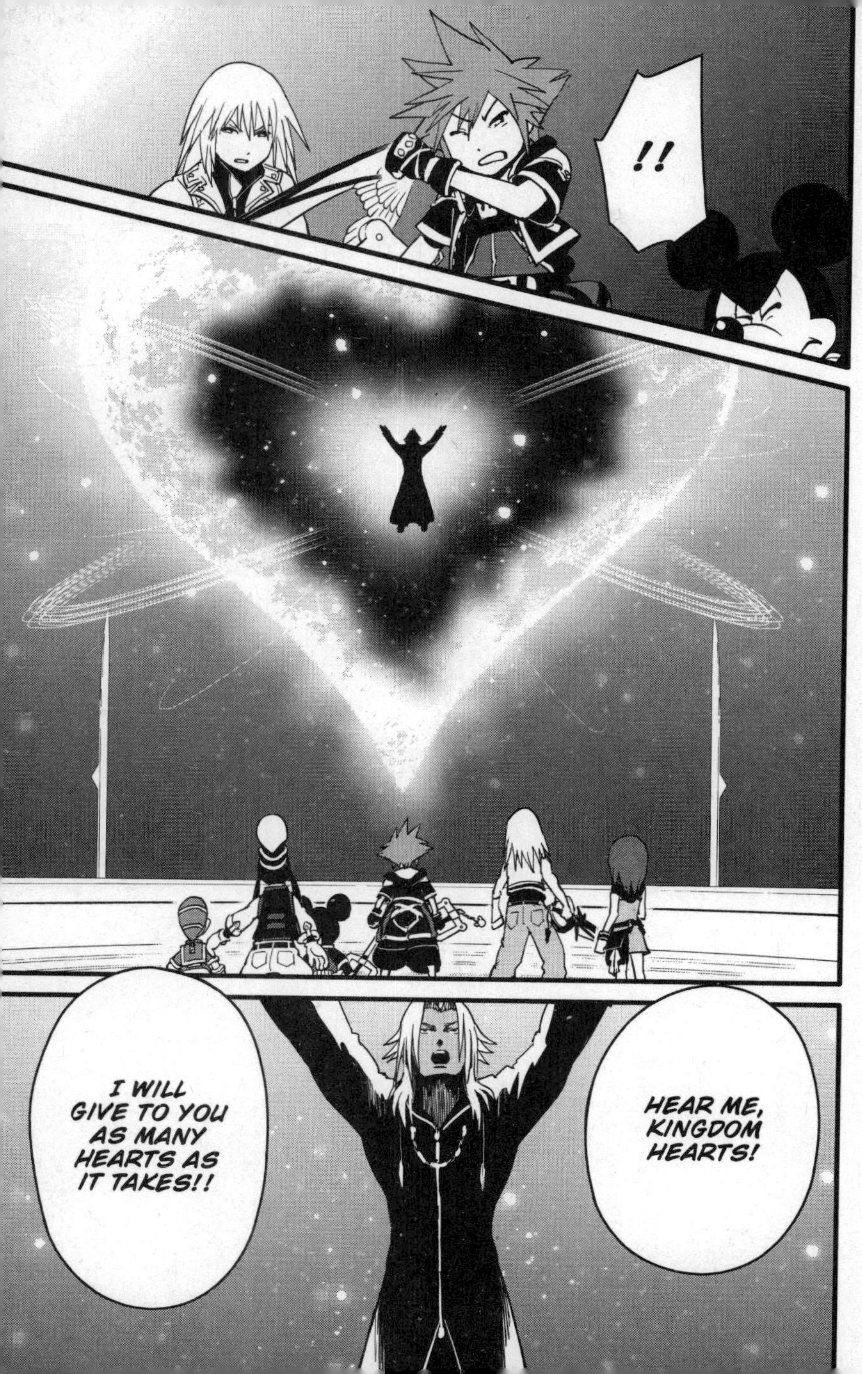
!!
HEAR ME, KINGDOM HEARTS!
I WILL GIVE TO YOU AS MANY HEARTS AS IT TAKES!!

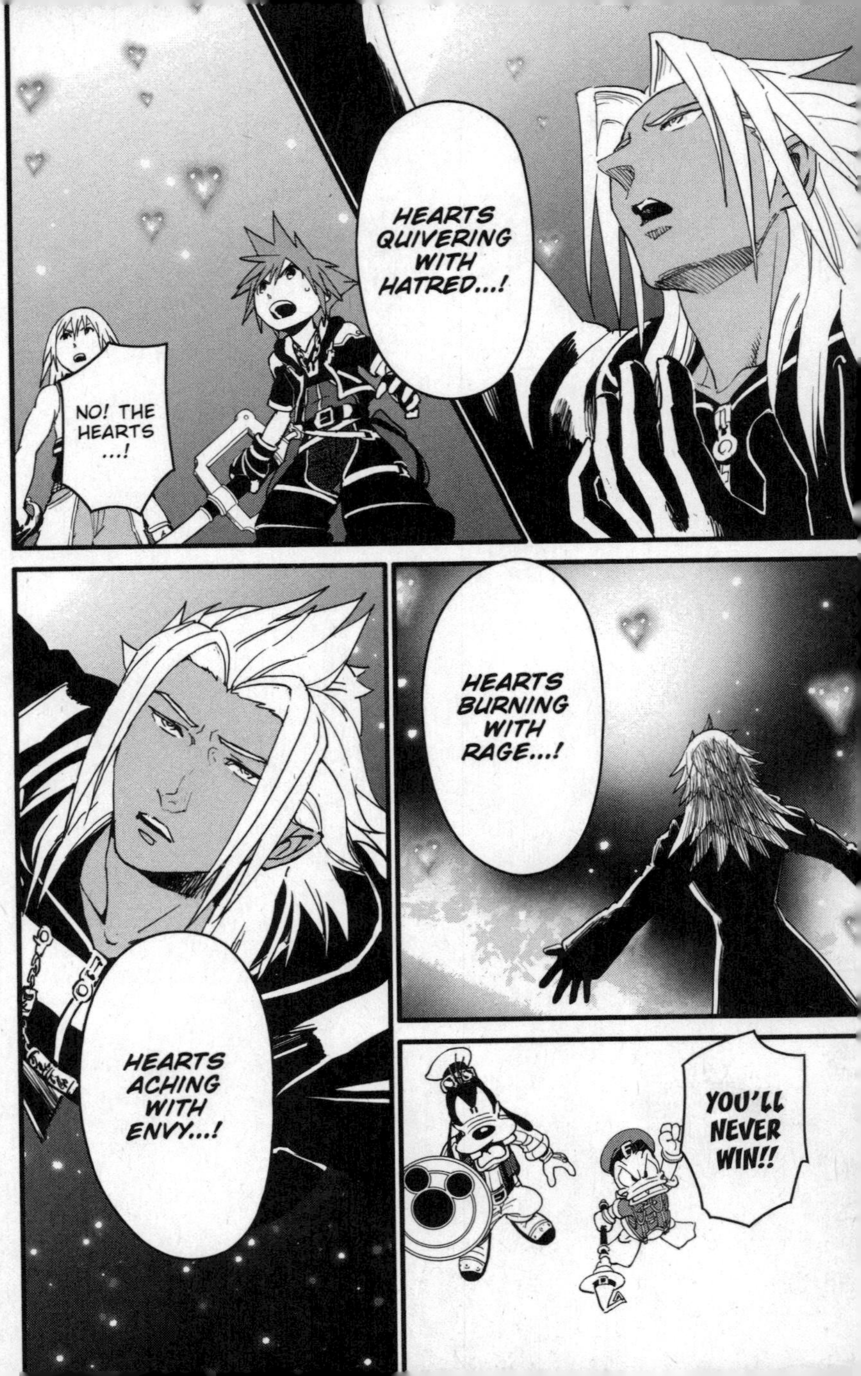
HEARTS QUIVERING WITH HATRED...!
NO! THE HEARTS ...!
HEARTS BURNING WITH RAGE...!
YOU'LL NEVER WIN!!
HEARTS ACHING WITH ENVY...!

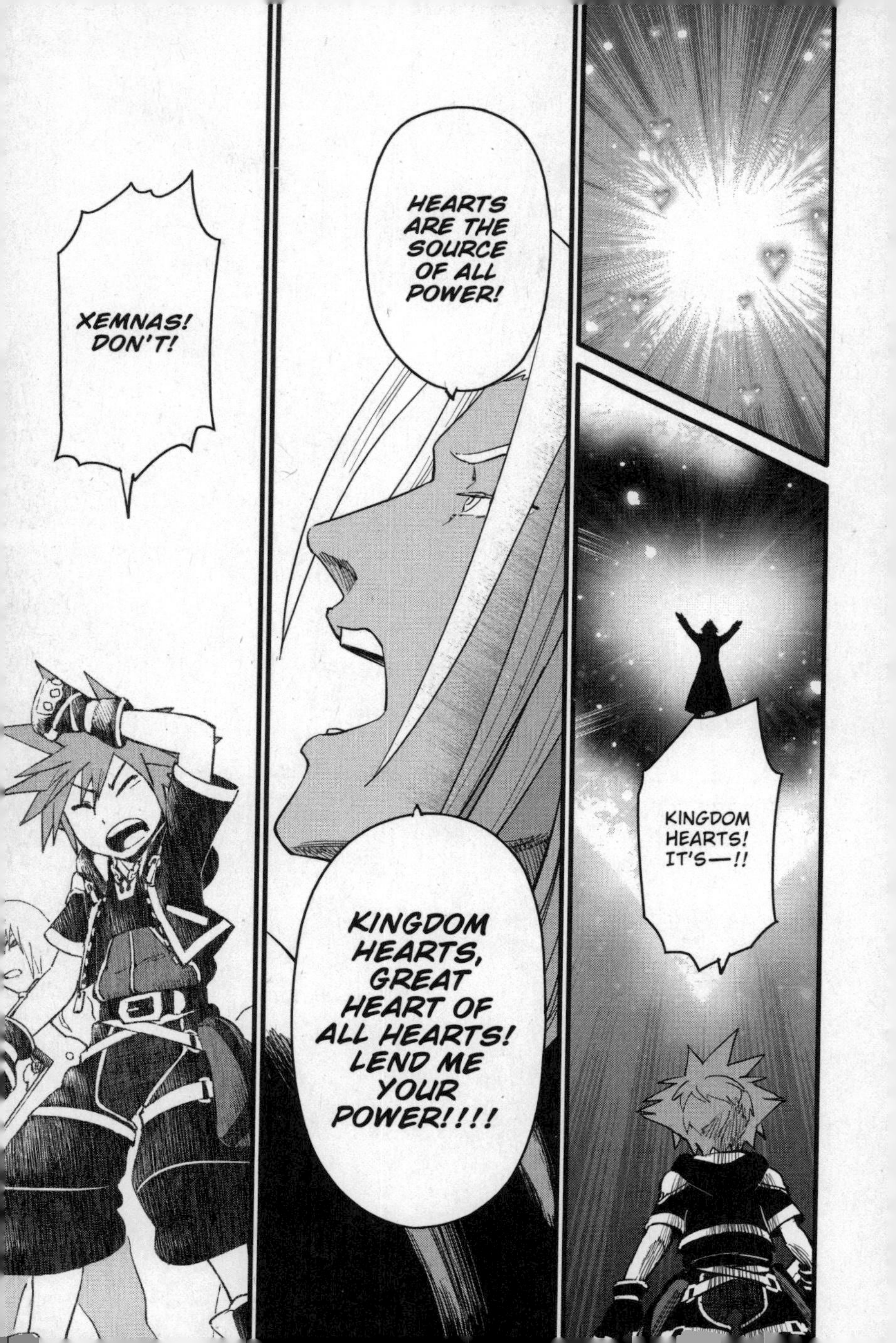
KINGDOM HEARTS! IT'S—!!
HEARTS ARE THE SOURCE OF ALL POWER!
KINGDOM HEARTS, GREAT HEART OF ALL HEARTS! LEND ME YOUR POWER!!!!
XEMNAS! DON'T!

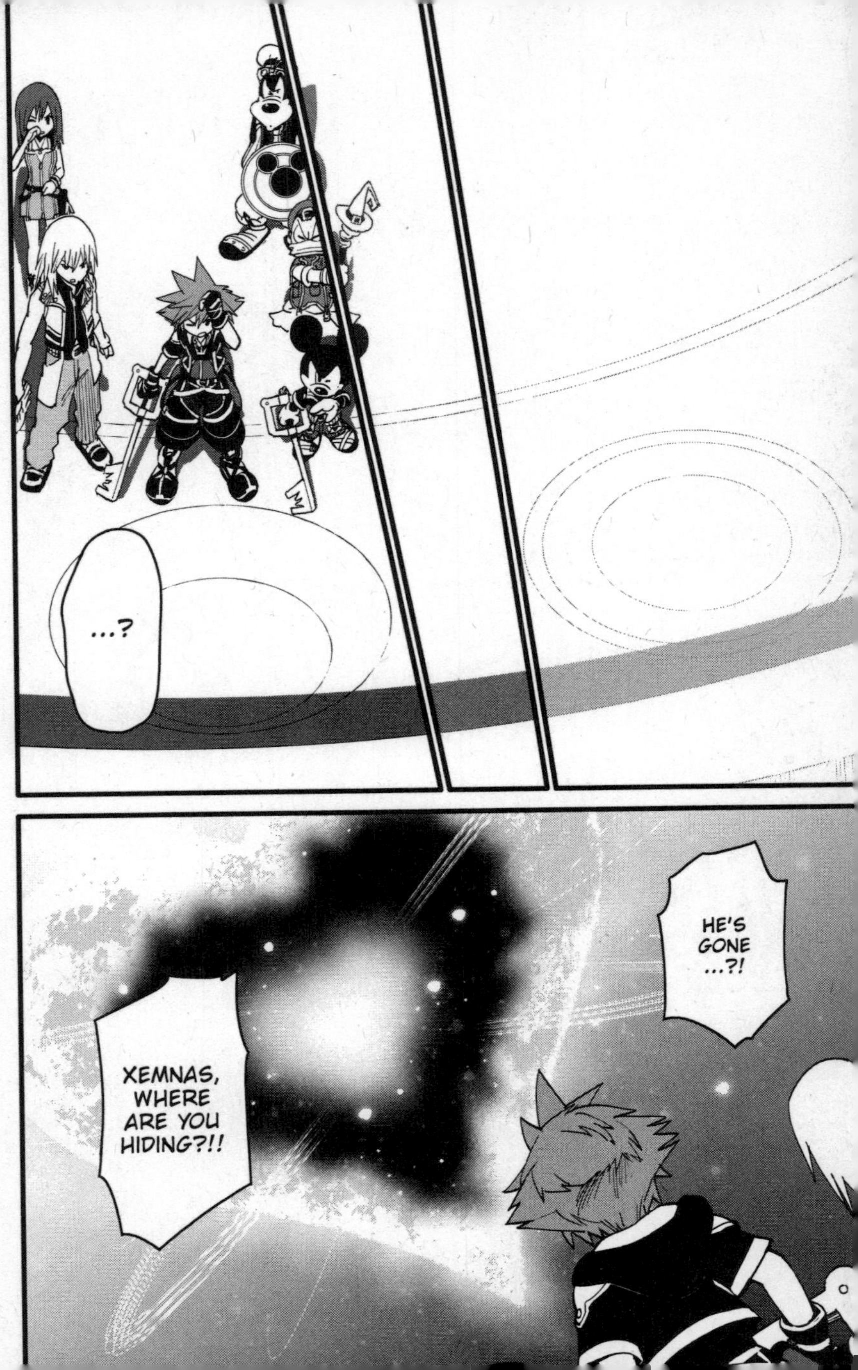
...?
HE'S GONE ...?!
XEMNAS, WHERE ARE YOU HIDING?!!

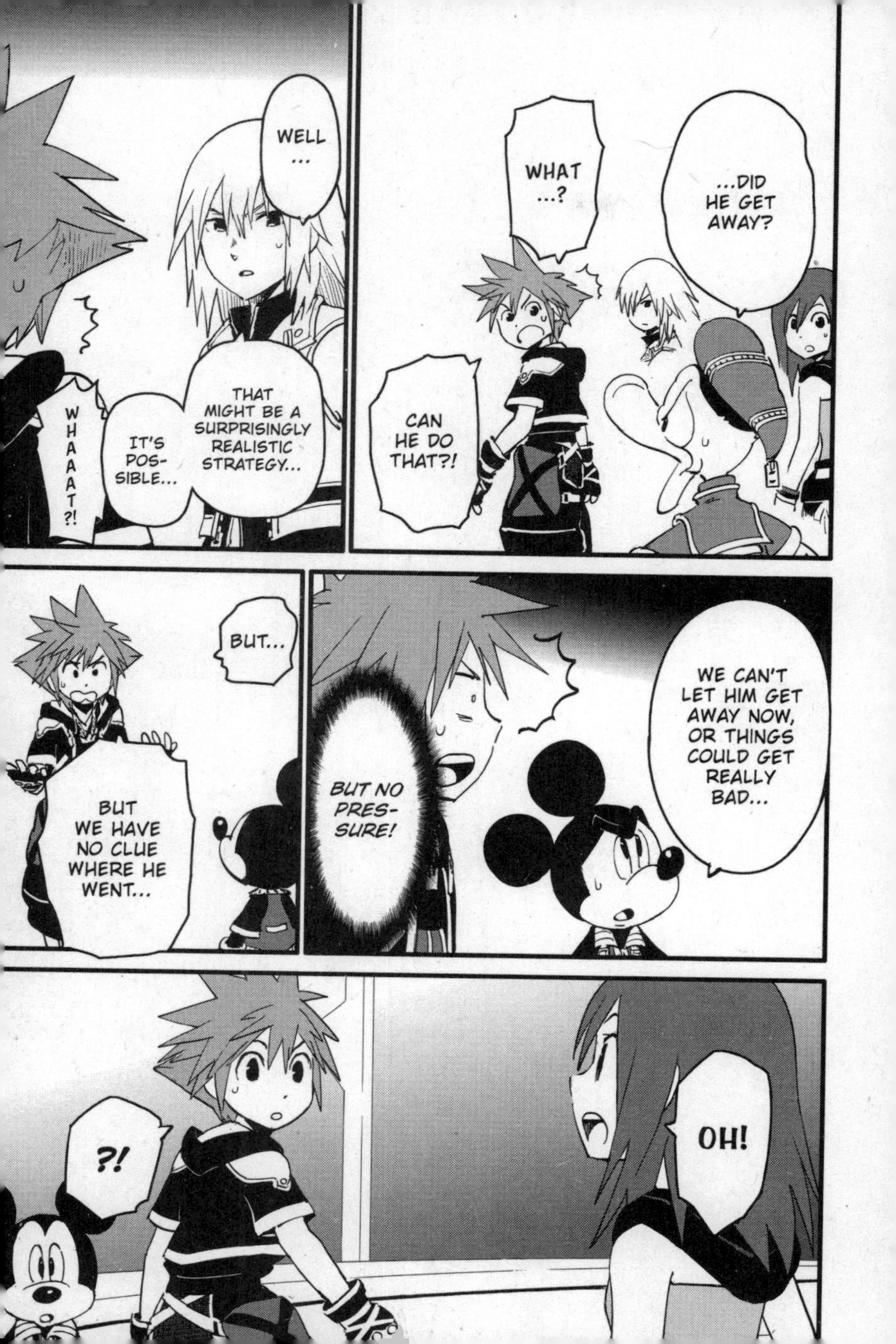
...DID HE GET AWAY?
WHAT ...?
CAN HE DO THAT?!
WELL ...
THAT MIGHT BE A SURPRISINGLY REALISTIC STRATEGY...
IT'S POS-SIBLE...
WHAAAAT?!
WE CAN'T LET HIM GET AWAY NOW, OR THINGS COULD GET REALLY BAD...
BUT NO PRES-SURE!
BUT...
BUT WE HAVE NO CLUE WHERE HE WENT...
OH!
?!

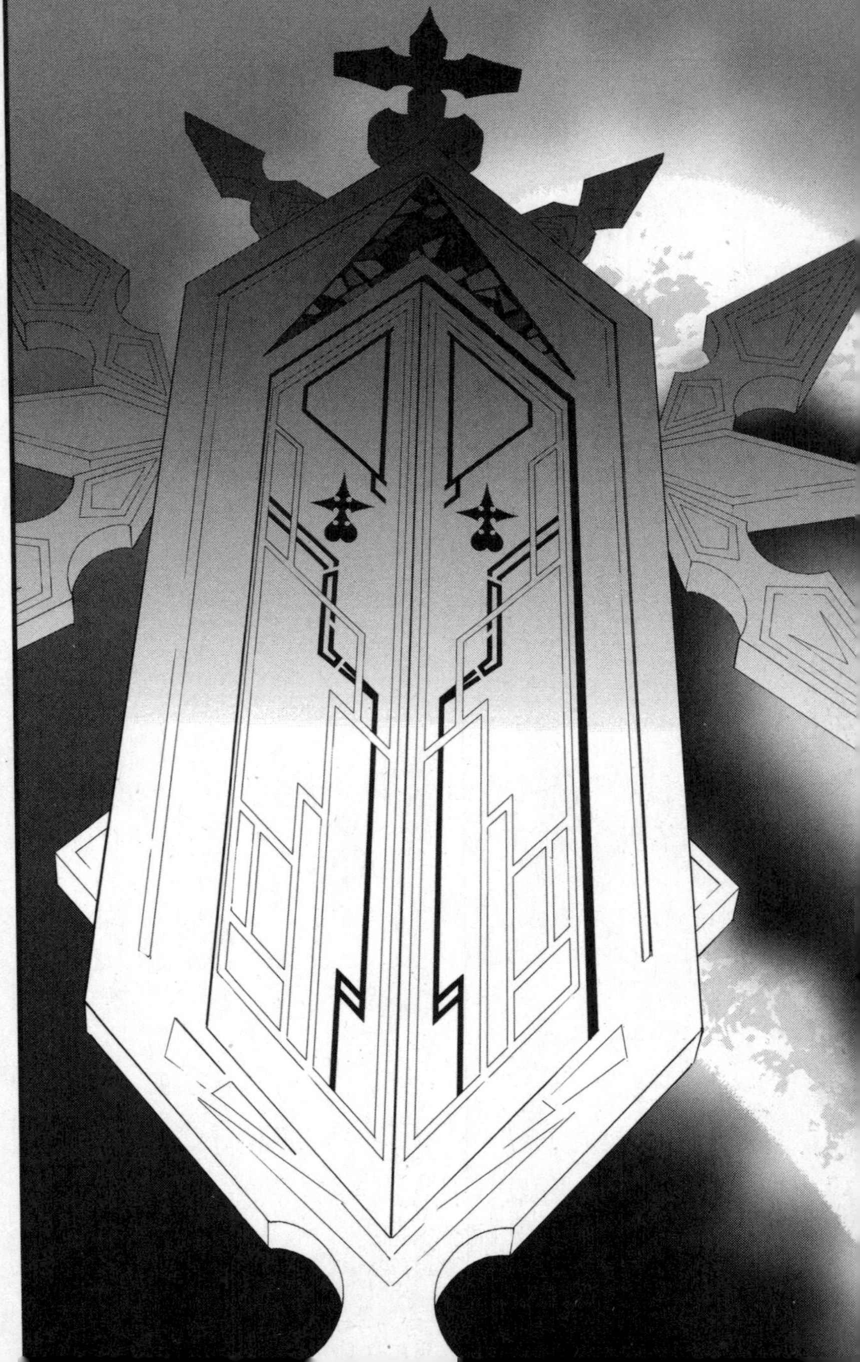

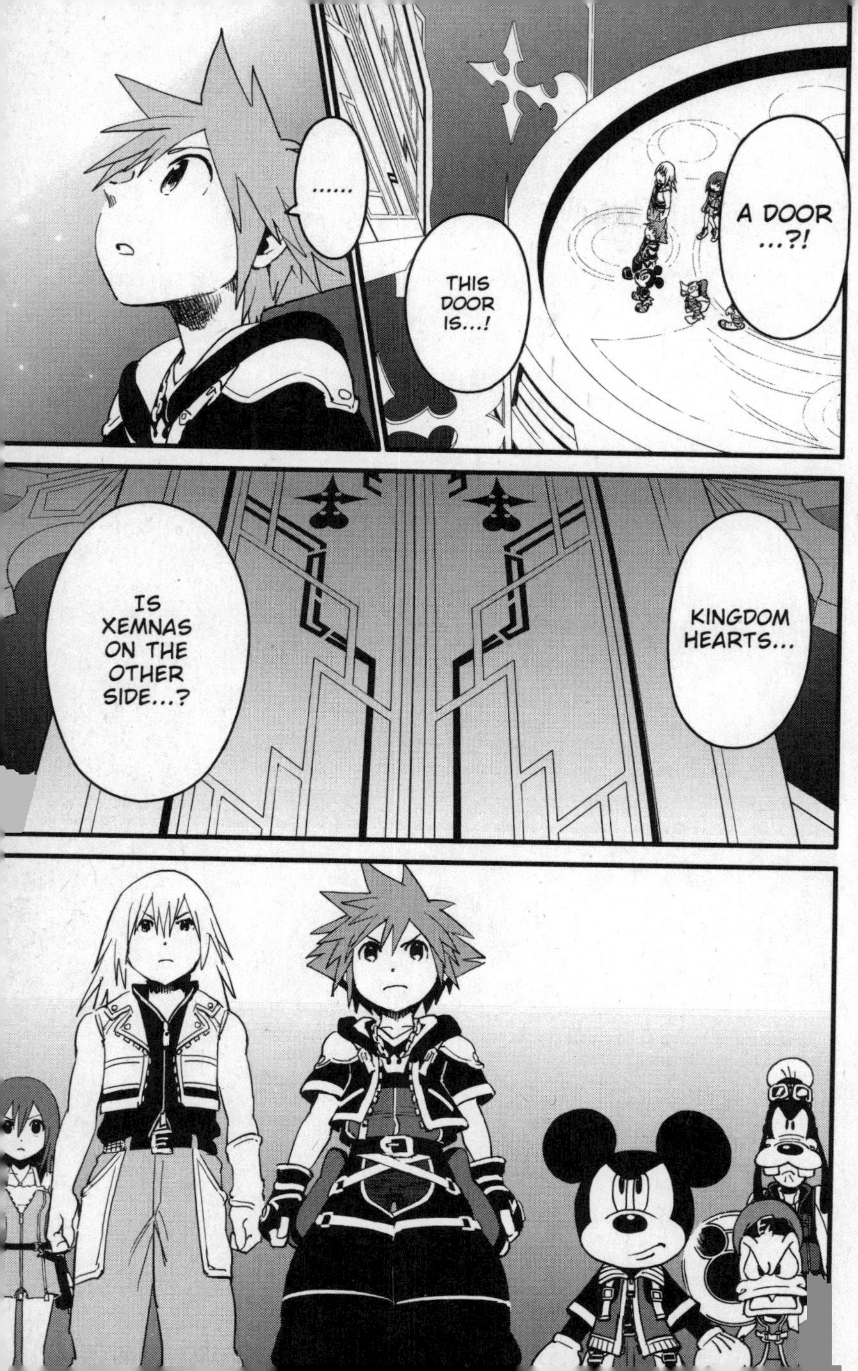
A DOOR ...?!
THIS DOOR IS...!
......
KINGDOM HEARTS...
IS XEMNAS ON THE OTHER SIDE...?

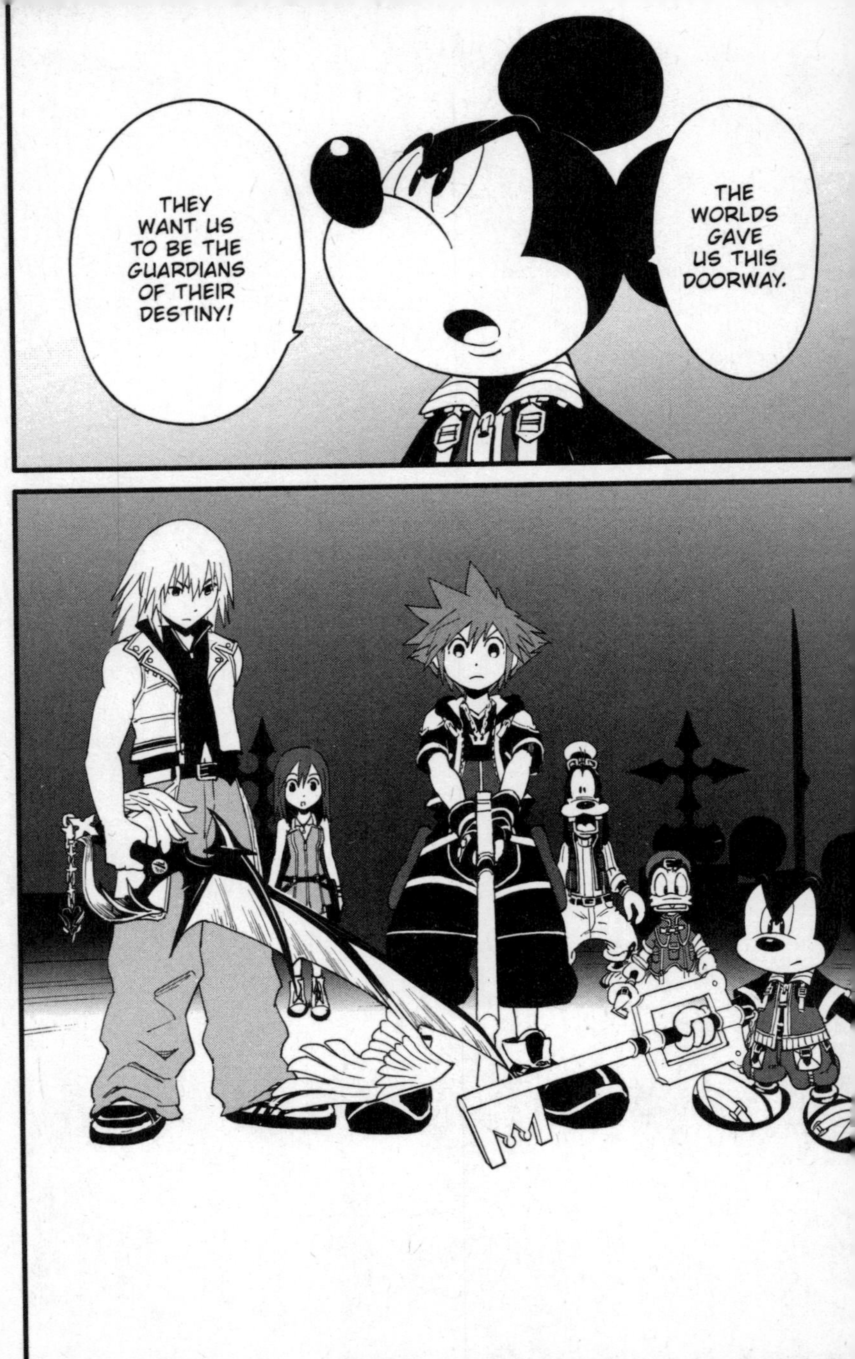
THE WORLDS GAVE US THIS DOORWAY.
THEY WANT US TO BE THE GUARDIANS OF THEIR DESTINY!

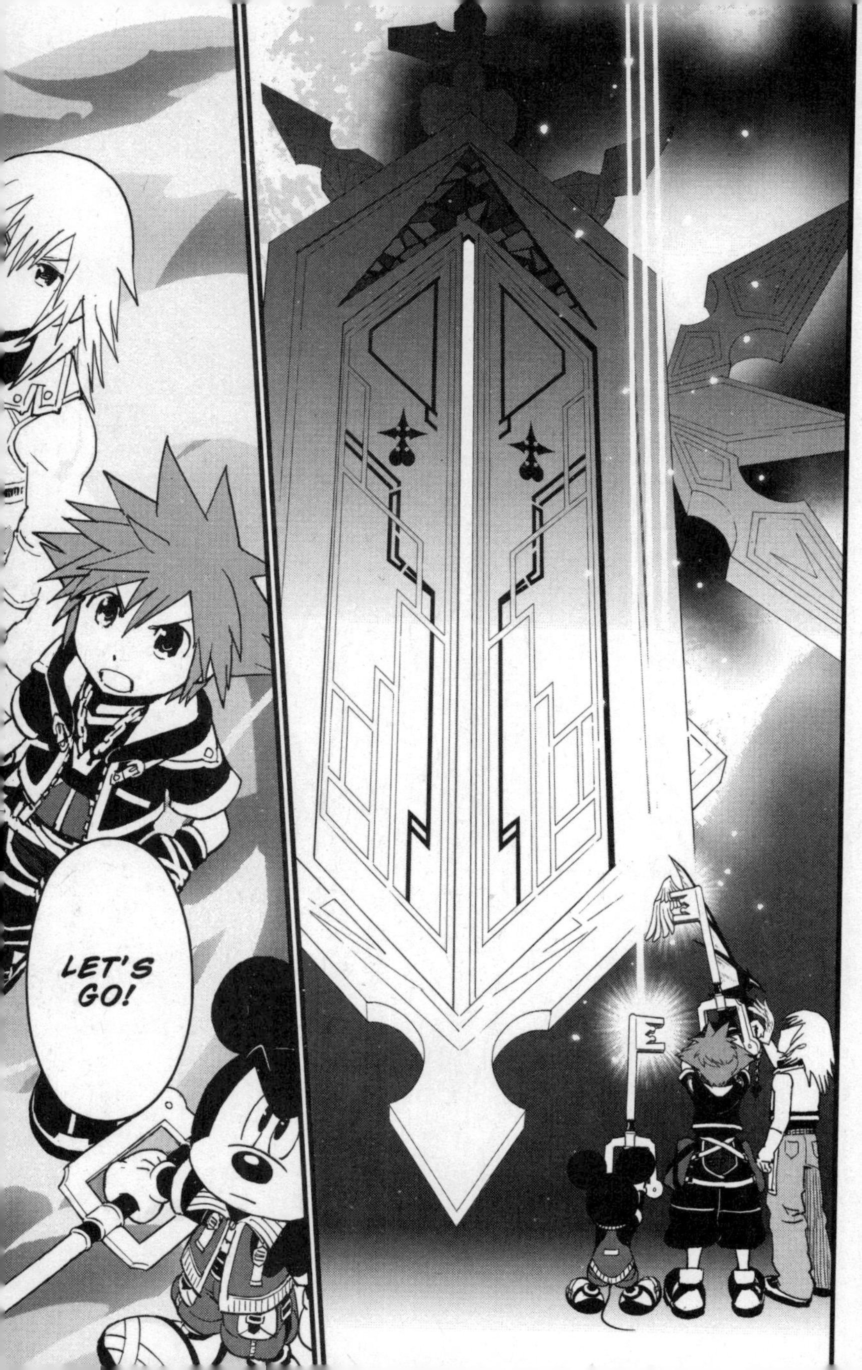
LET'S GO!

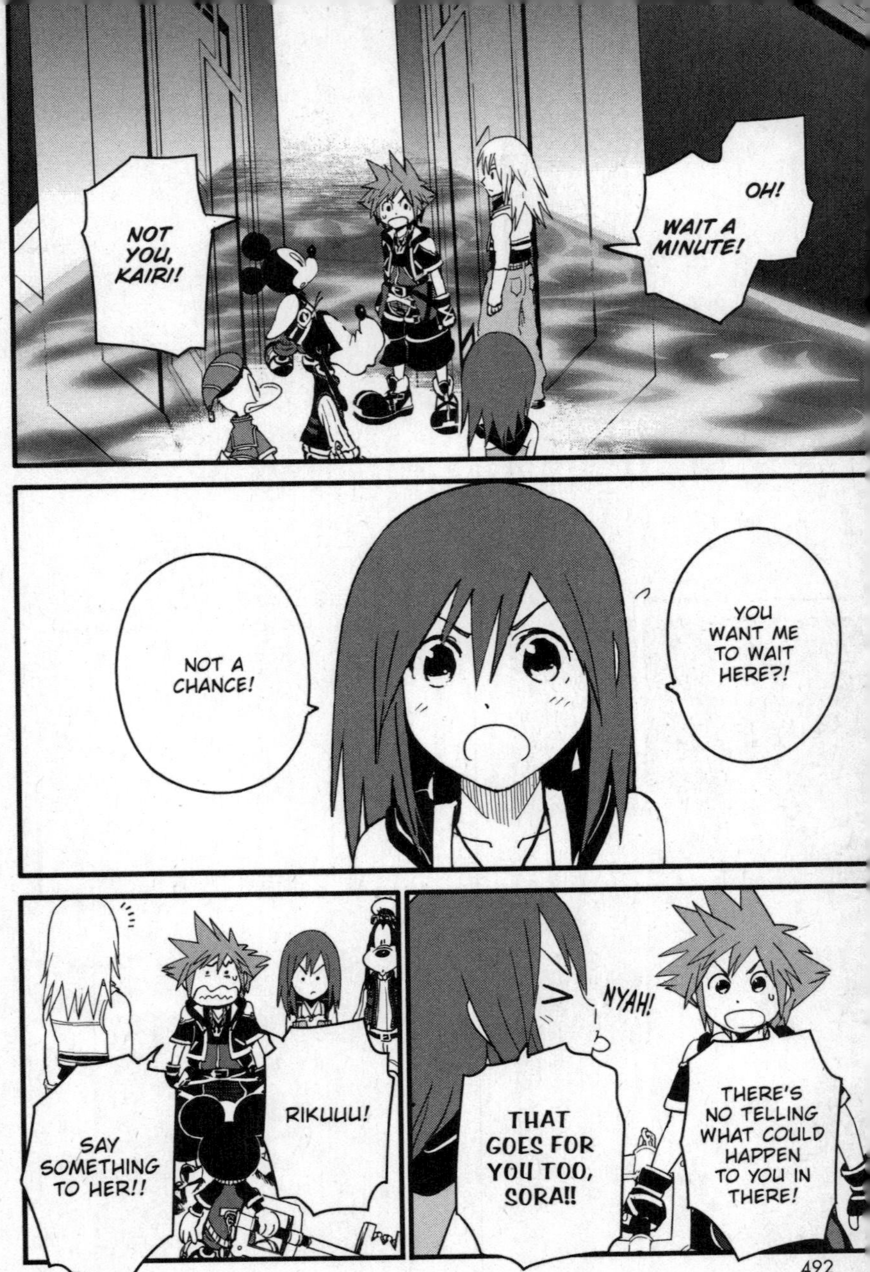
OH!
WAIT A MINUTE!
NOT YOU, KAIRI!
YOU WANT ME TO WAIT HERE?!
NOT A CHANCE!
THERE'S NO TELLING WHAT COULD HAPPEN TO YOU IN THERE!
NYAH!
THAT GOES FOR YOU TOO, SORA!!
RIKUUU!
SAY SOMETHING TO HER!!

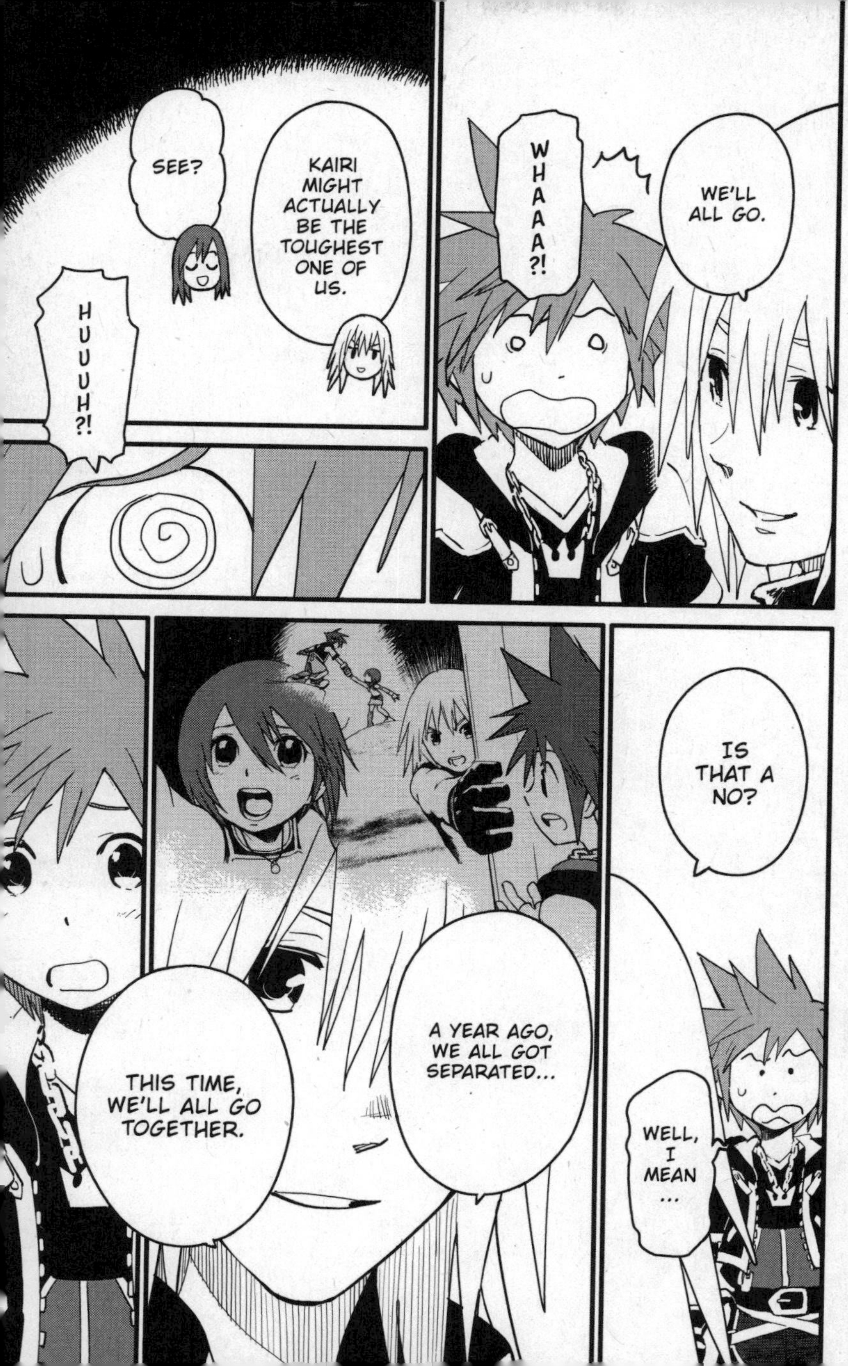
WE'LL ALL GO.
WHAAAA?!
KAIRI MIGHT ACTUALLY BE THE TOUGHEST ONE OF US.
SEE?
HUUUUH?!
IS THAT A NO?
WELL, I MEAN...
A YEAR AGO, WE ALL GOT SEPARATED...
THIS TIME, WE'LL ALL GO TOGETHER.

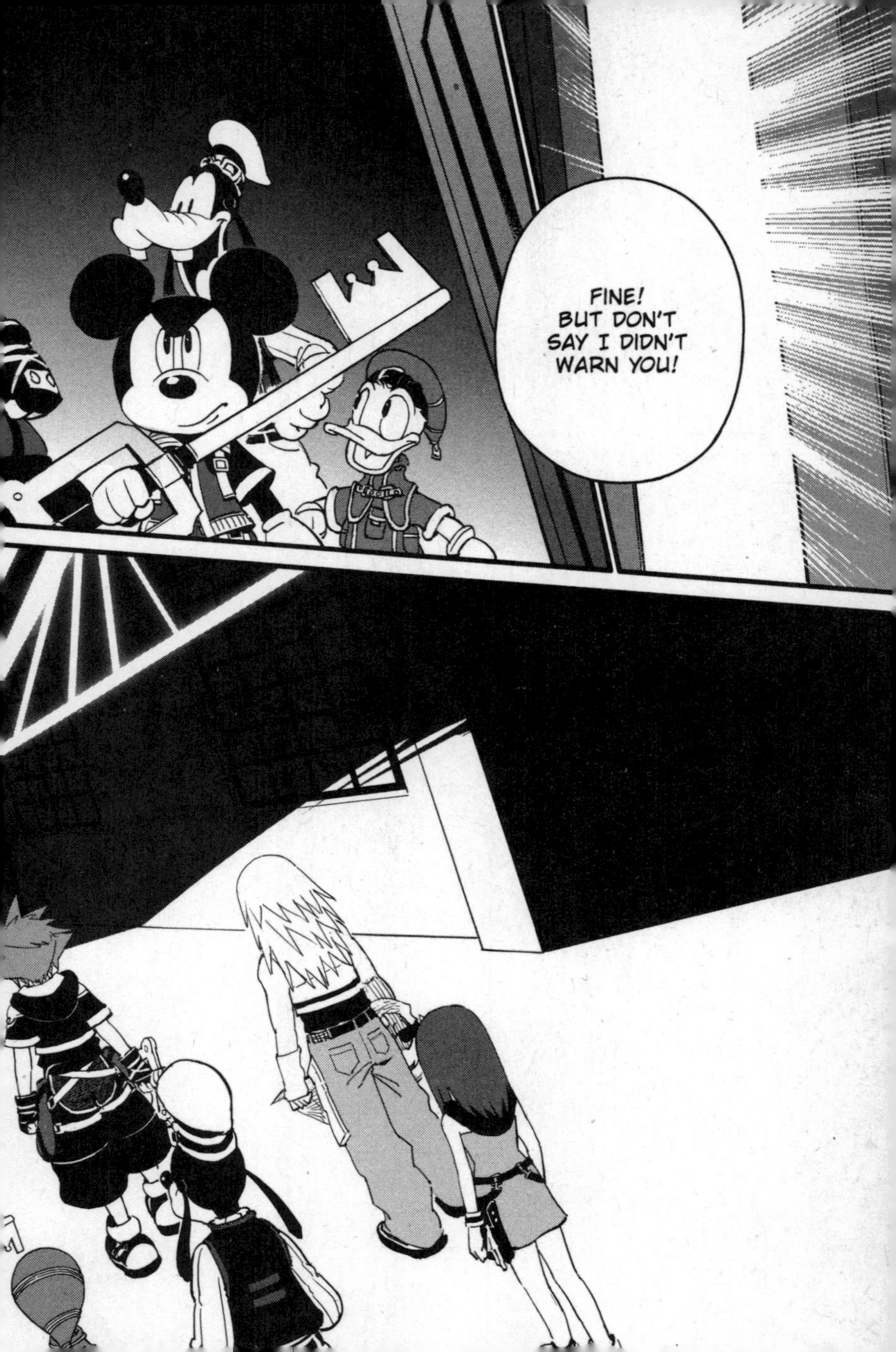
FINE! BUT DON'T SAY I DIDN'T WARN YOU!

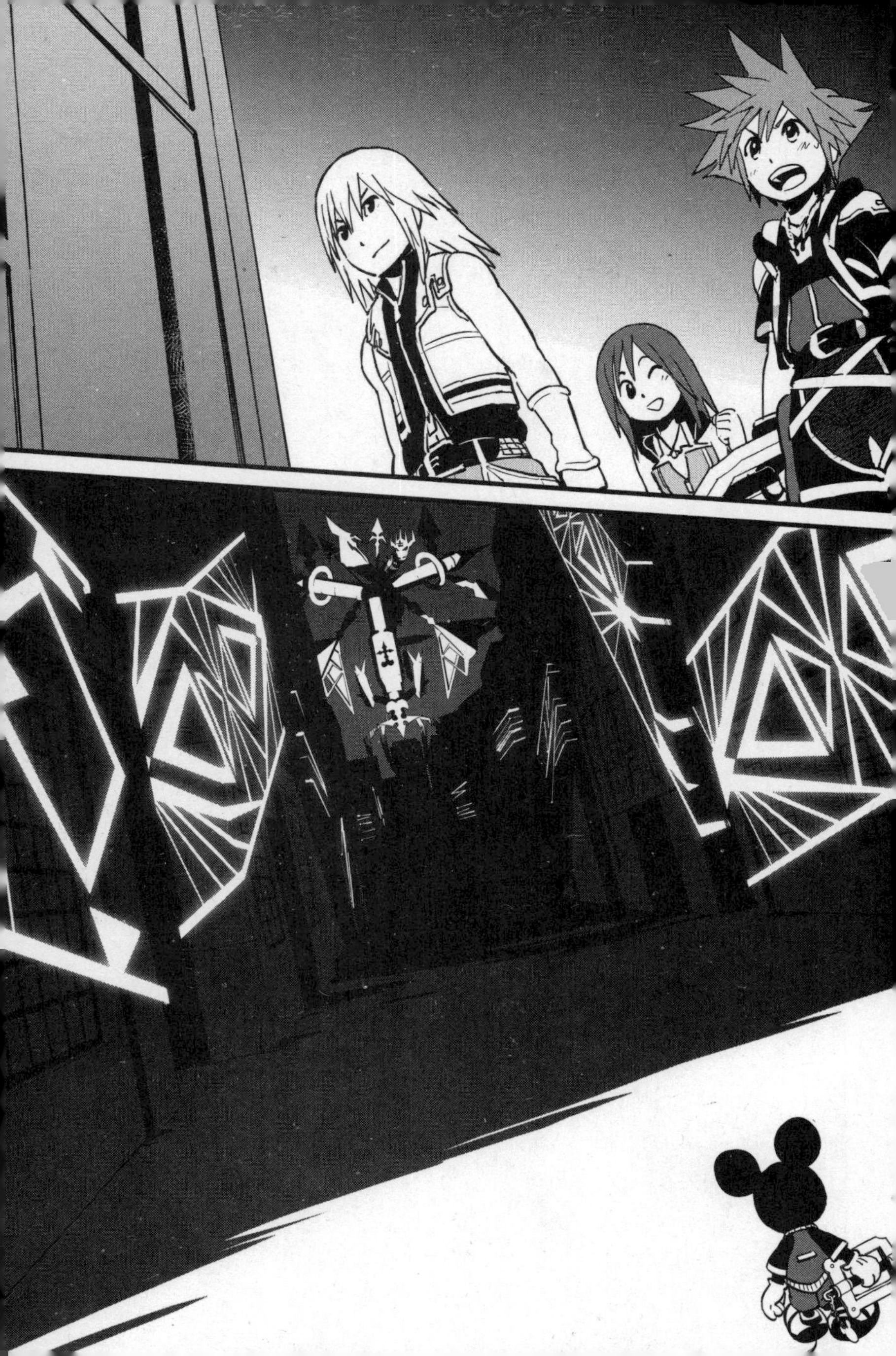

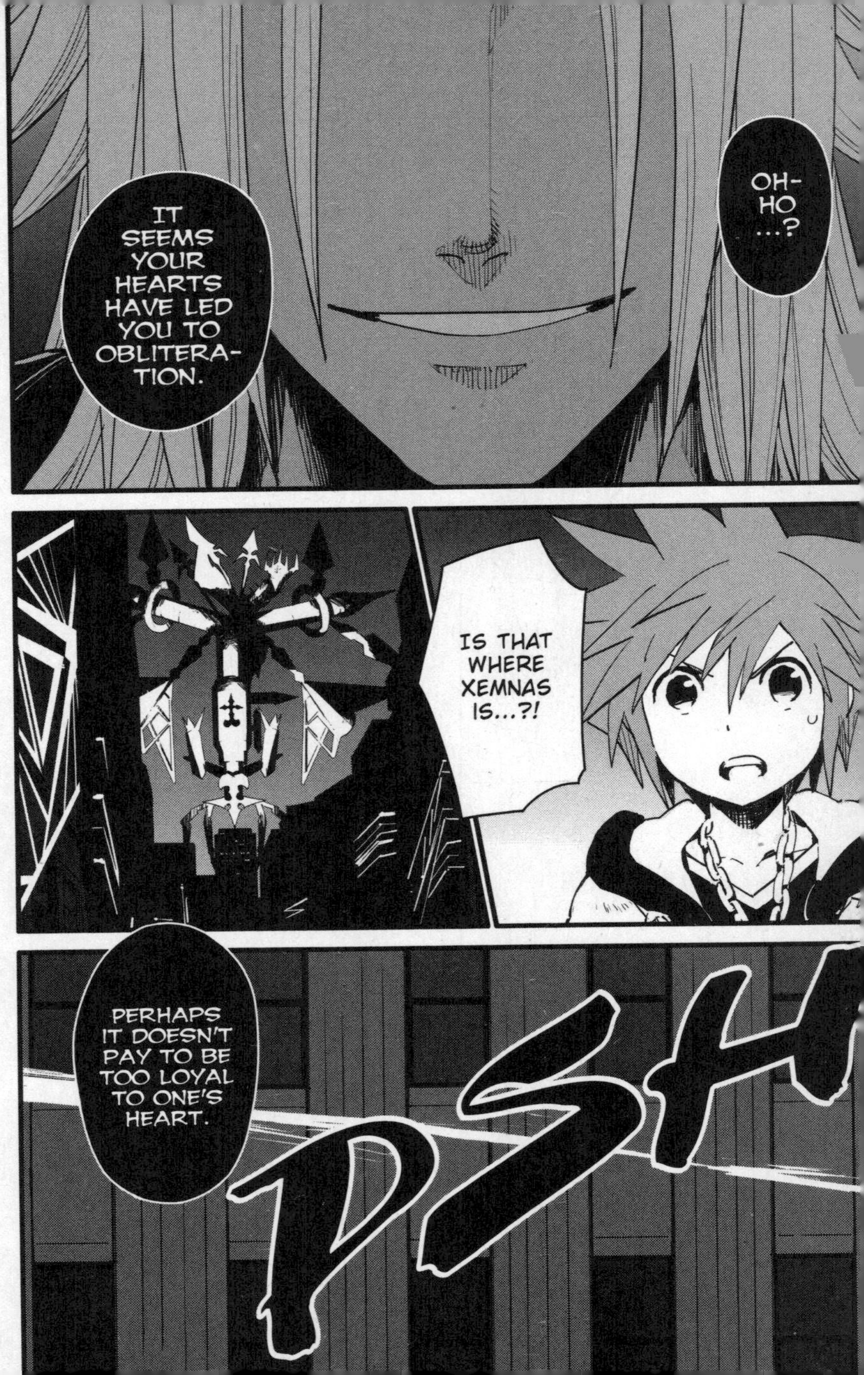
OH-HO...?
IT SEEMS YOUR HEARTS HAVE LED YOU TO OBLITERATION.
IS THAT WHERE XEMNAS IS...?!
PERHAPS IT DOESN'T PAY TO BE TOO LOYAL TO ONE'S HEART.
DSH

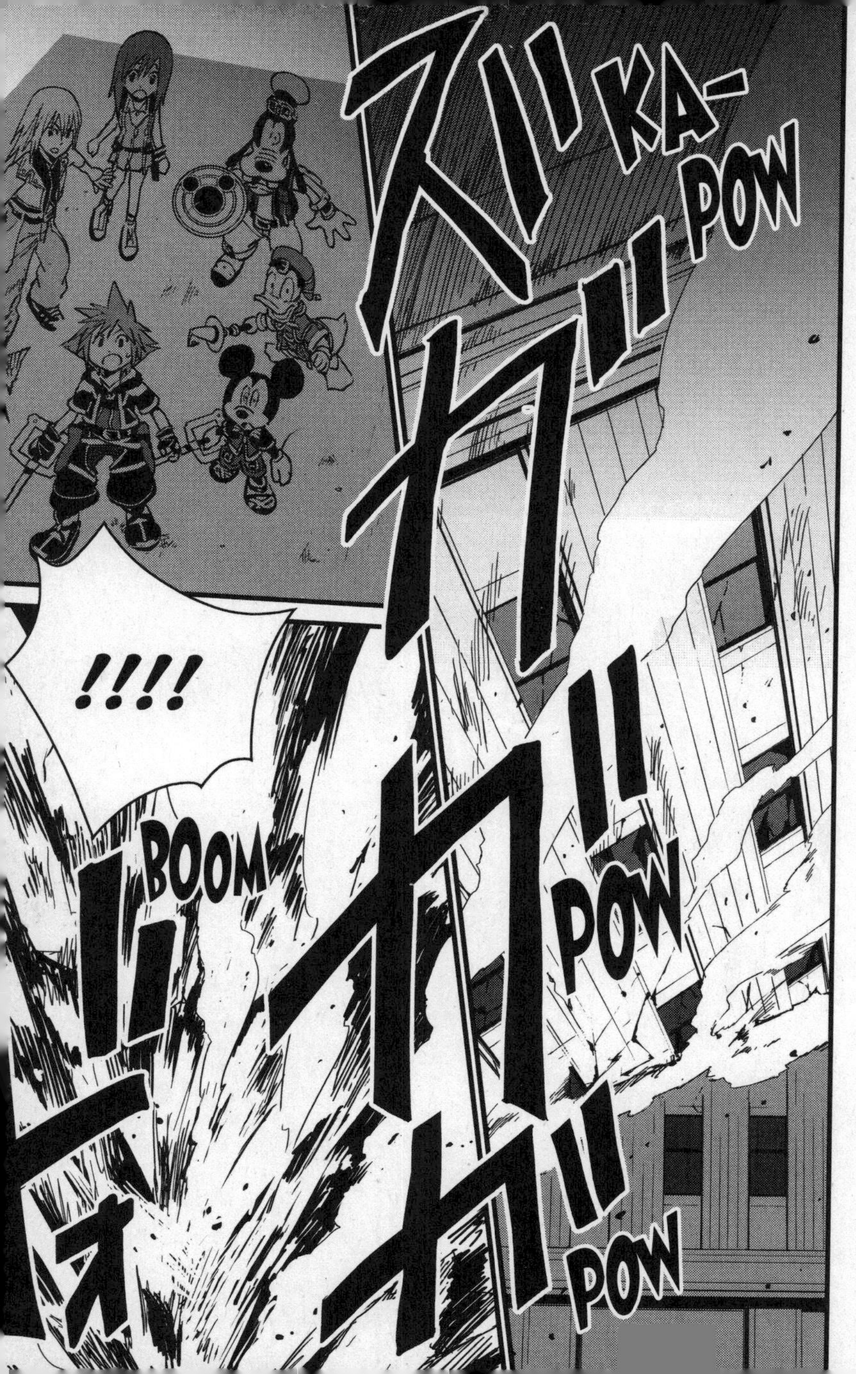
KA-POW
POW
POW
!!!!
BOOM

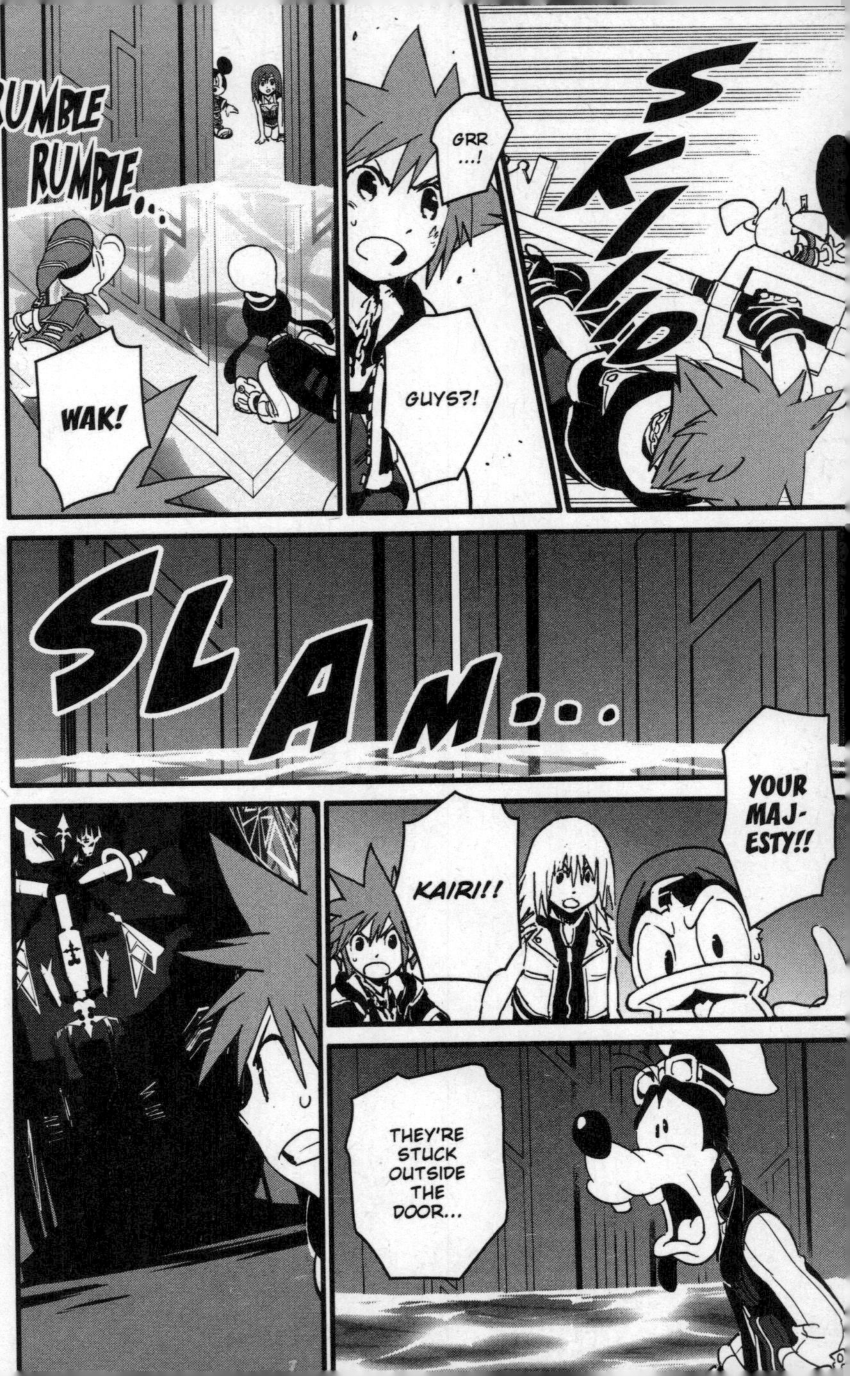

SKIID
GRR ...!
GUYS?!
RUMBLE RUMBLE...
WAK!
SLAM...
YOUR MAJ-ESTY!!
KAIRI!!
THEY'RE STUCK OUTSIDE THE DOOR...

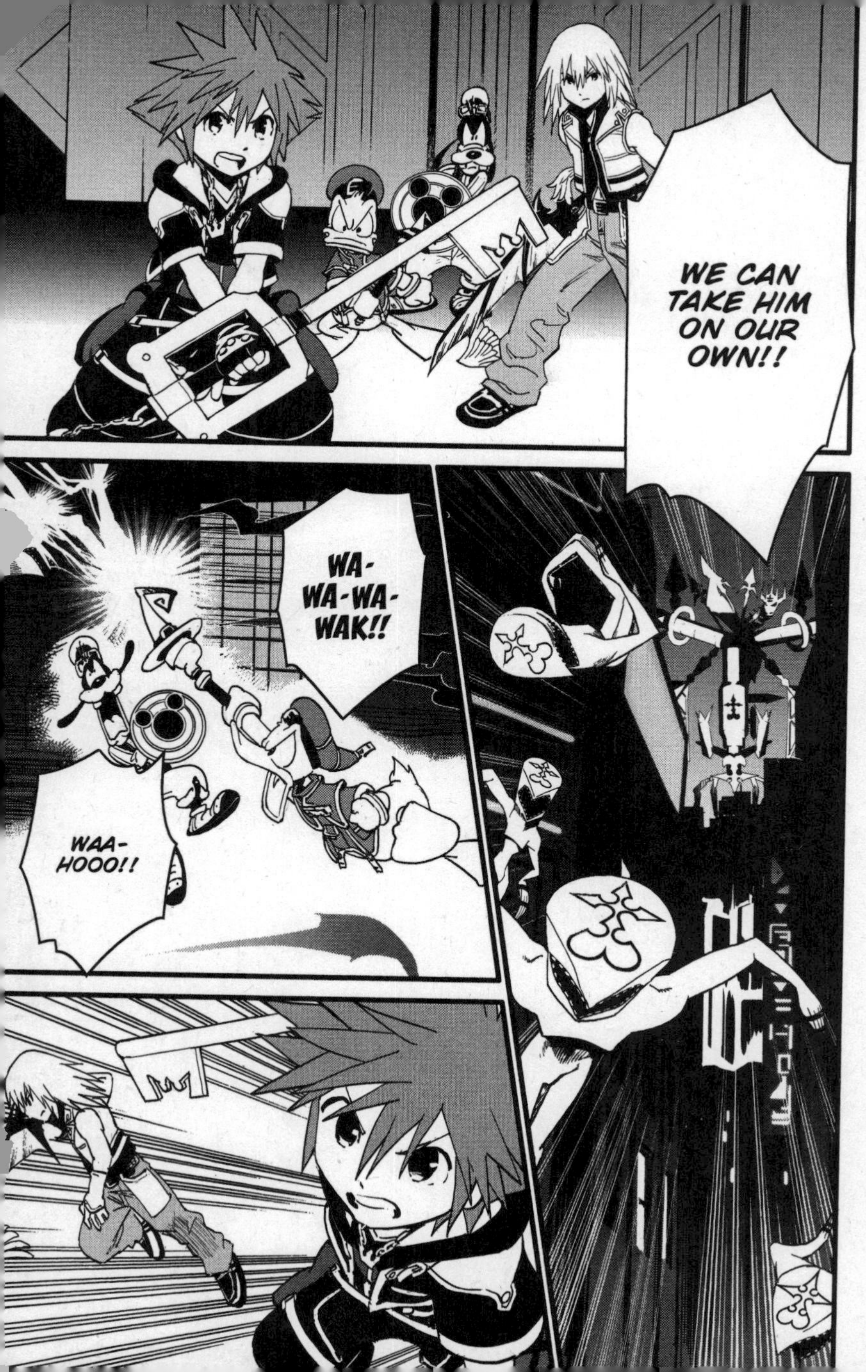
WE CAN TAKE HIM ON OUR OWN!!
WA-WA-WA-WAK!!
WAA-HOOO!!

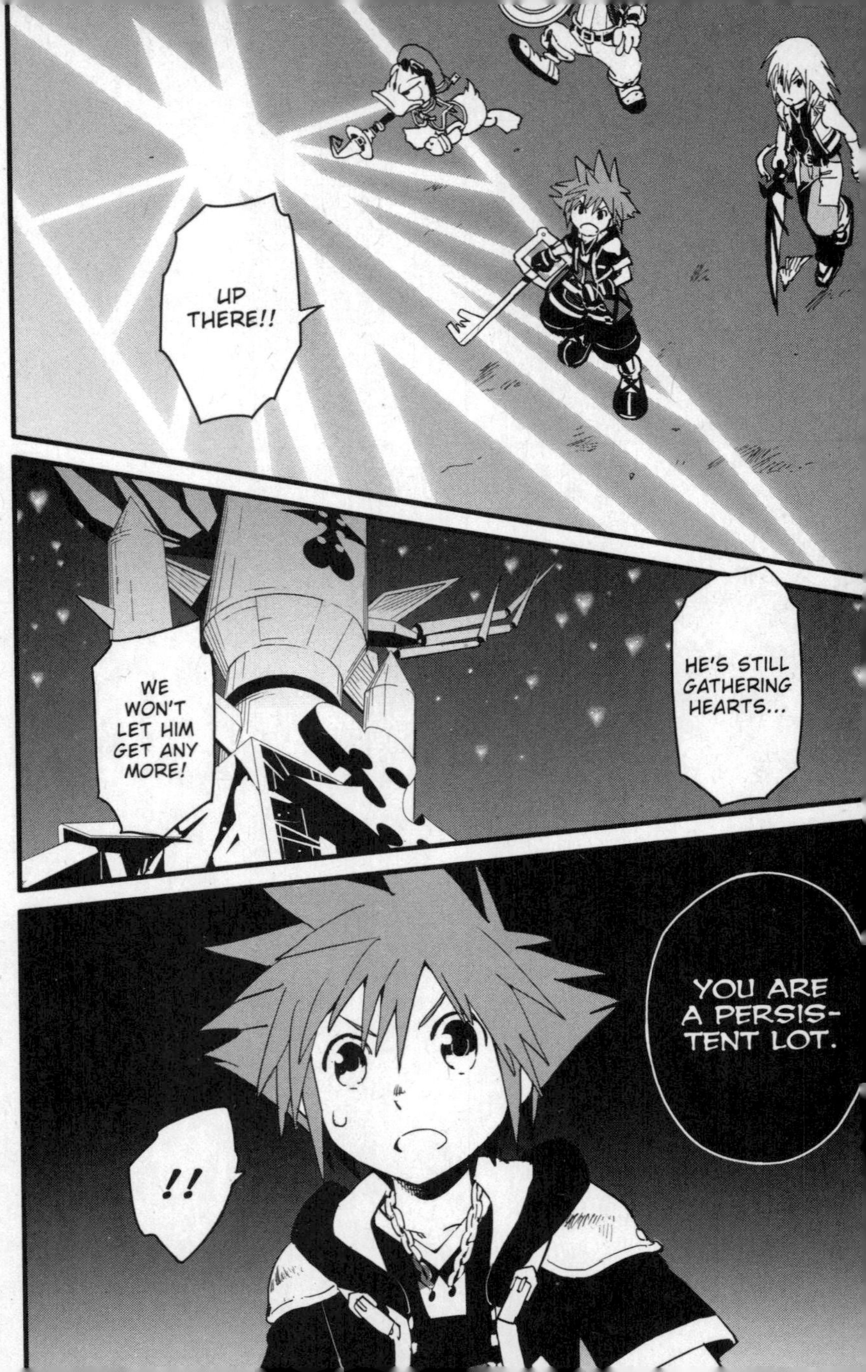
UP THERE!!
HE'S STILL GATHERING HEARTS...
WE WON'T LET HIM GET ANY MORE!
YOU ARE A PERSIS-TENT LOT.
!!

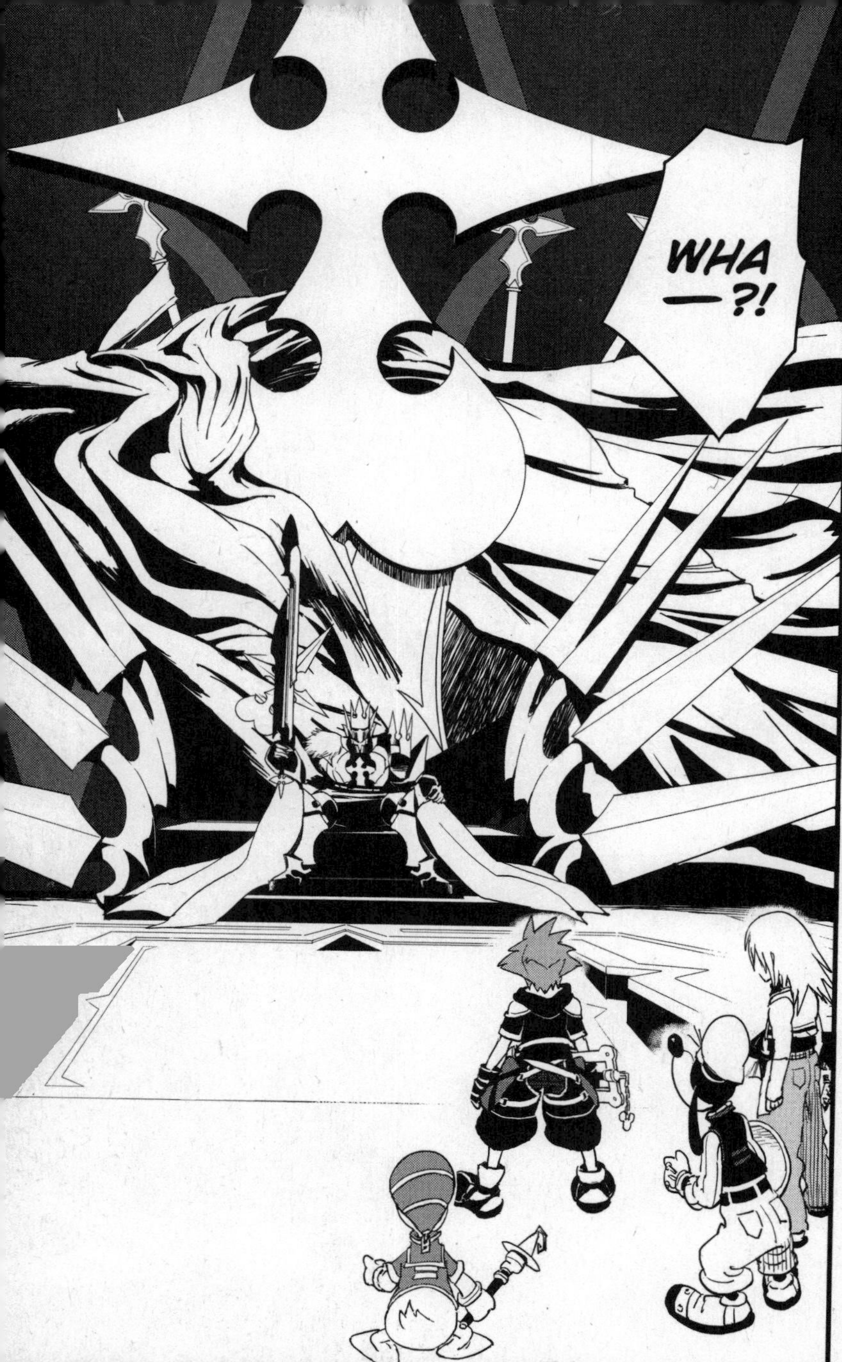
WHA—?!

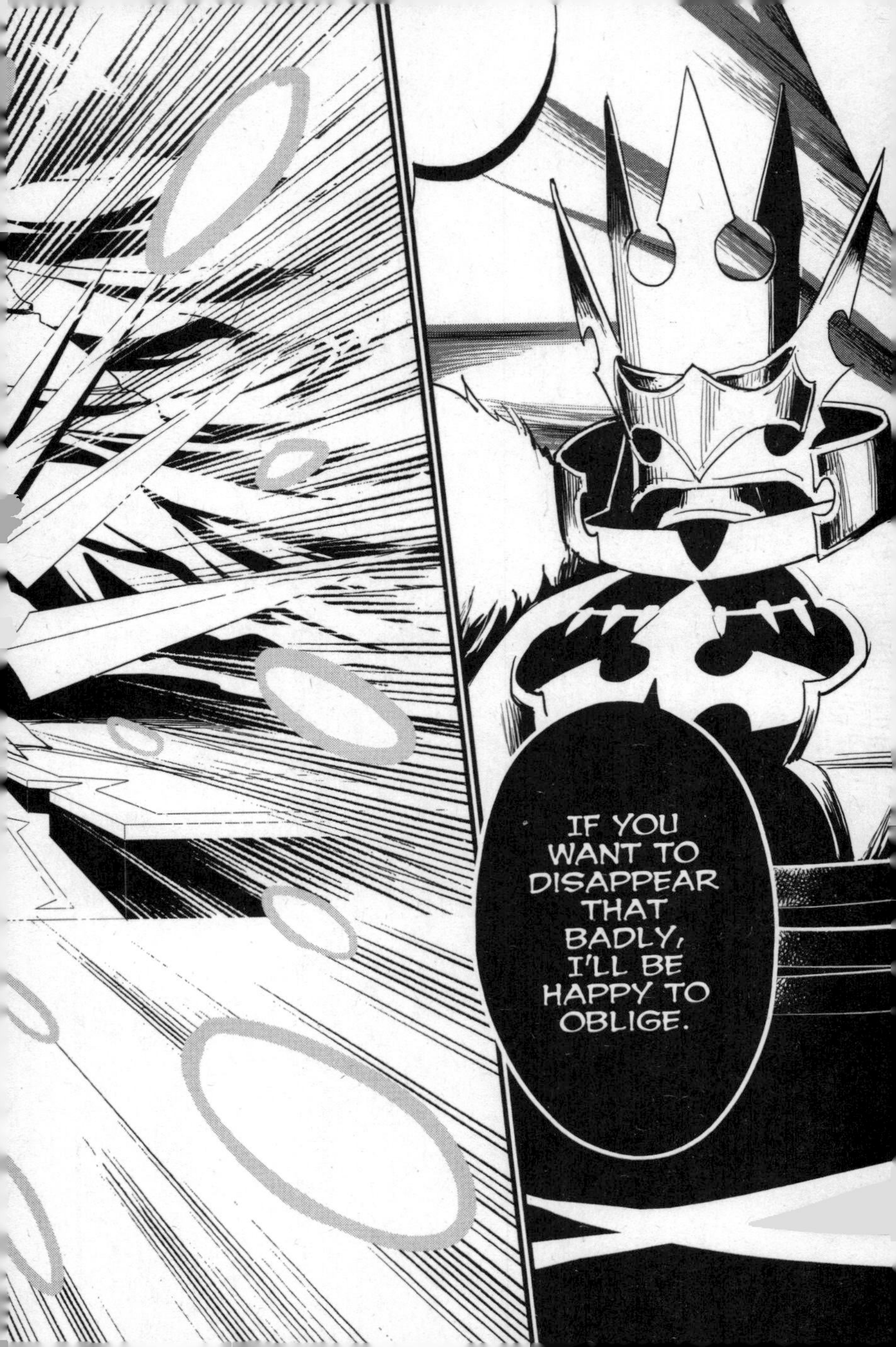
IF YOU WANT TO DISAPPEAR THAT BADLY, I'LL BE HAPPY TO OBLIGE.

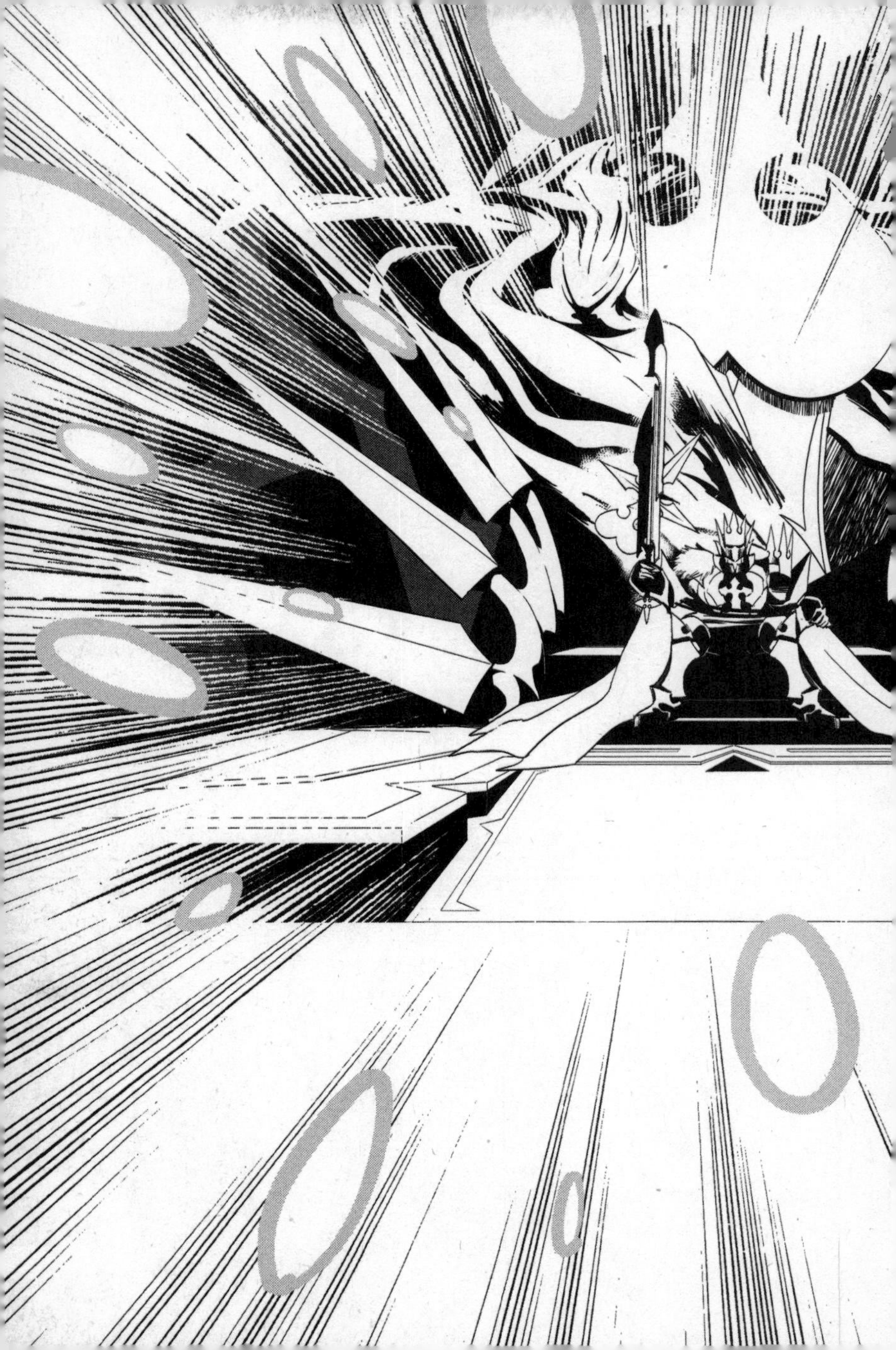

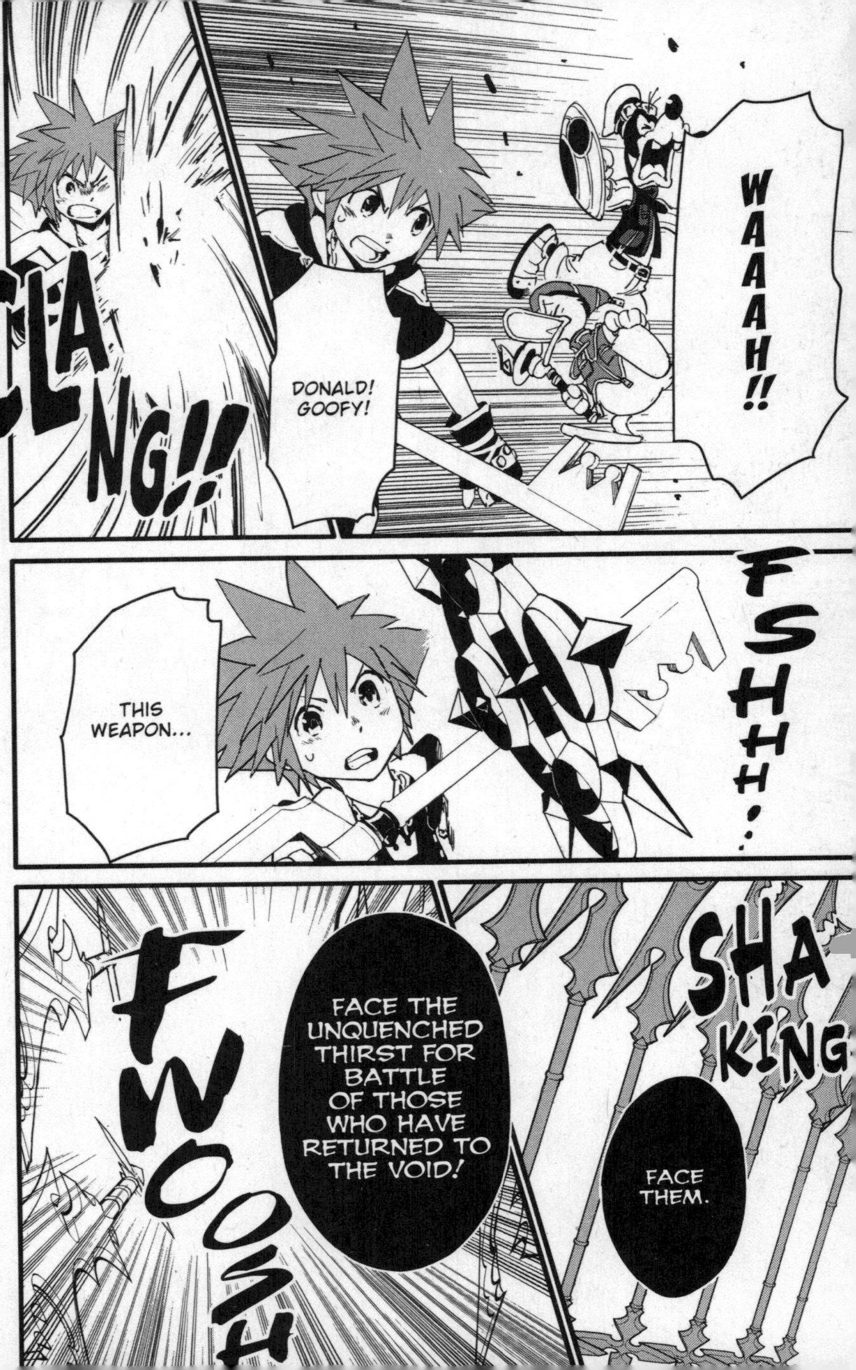
WAAAAH!!
DONALD! GOOFY!
CLANG!!
FSHHH...
THIS WEAPON...
SHAKING
FACE THE UNQUENCHED THIRST FOR BATTLE OF THOSE WHO HAVE RETURNED TO THE VOID!
FACE THEM.
FWOOSH

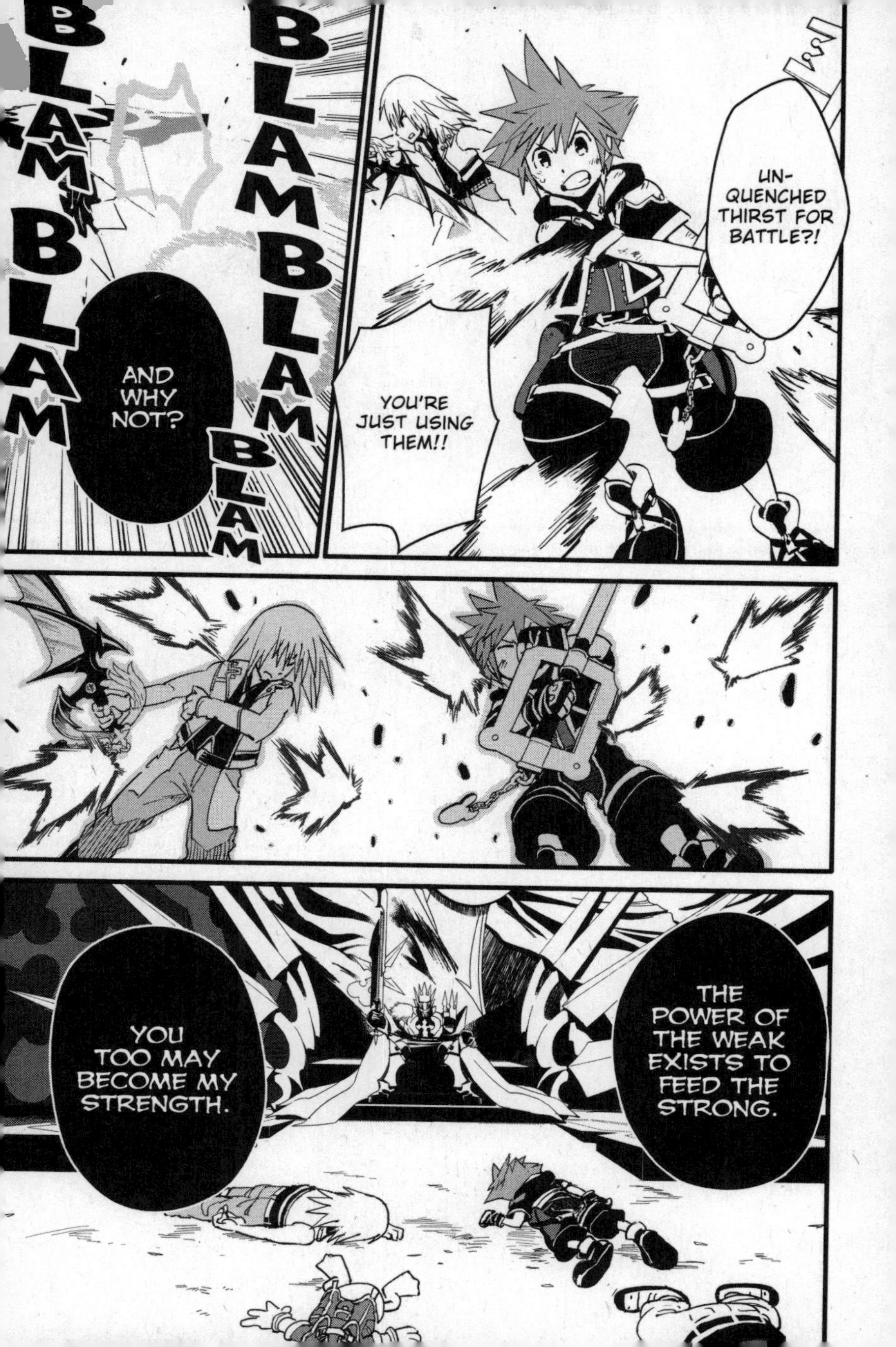
UN-QUENCHED THIRST FOR BATTLE?!
YOU'RE JUST USING THEM!!
BLAM BLAM
AND WHY NOT?
BLAM
BLAM BLAM
THE POWER OF THE WEAK EXISTS TO FEED THE STRONG.
YOU TOO MAY BECOME MY STRENGTH.

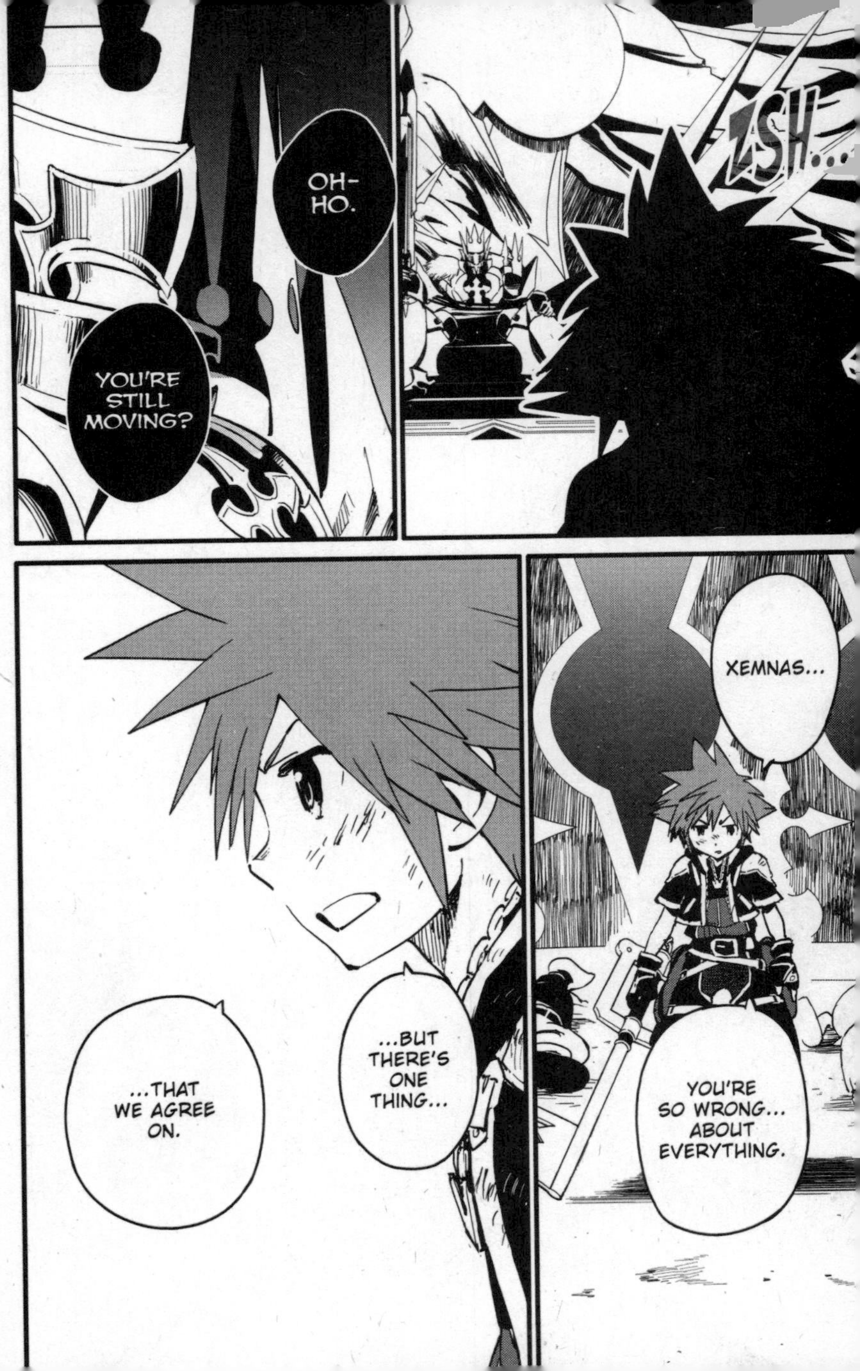
ASH...
OH-HO.
YOU'RE STILL MOVING?
XEMNAS...
YOU'RE SO WRONG... ABOUT EVERYTHING.
...BUT THERE'S ONE THING...
...THAT WE AGREE ON.

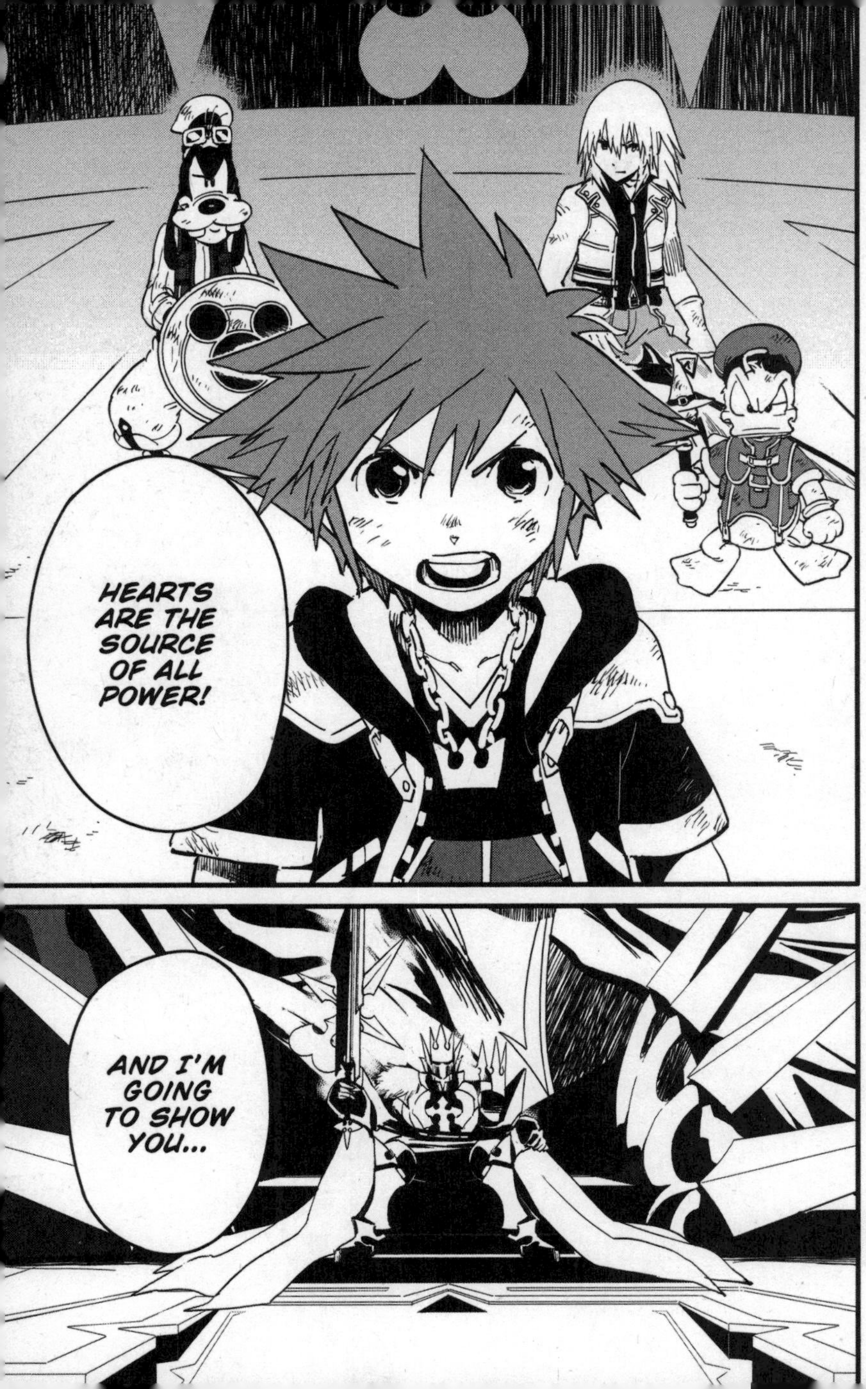
HEARTS ARE THE SOURCE OF ALL POWER!
AND I'M GOING TO SHOW YOU...

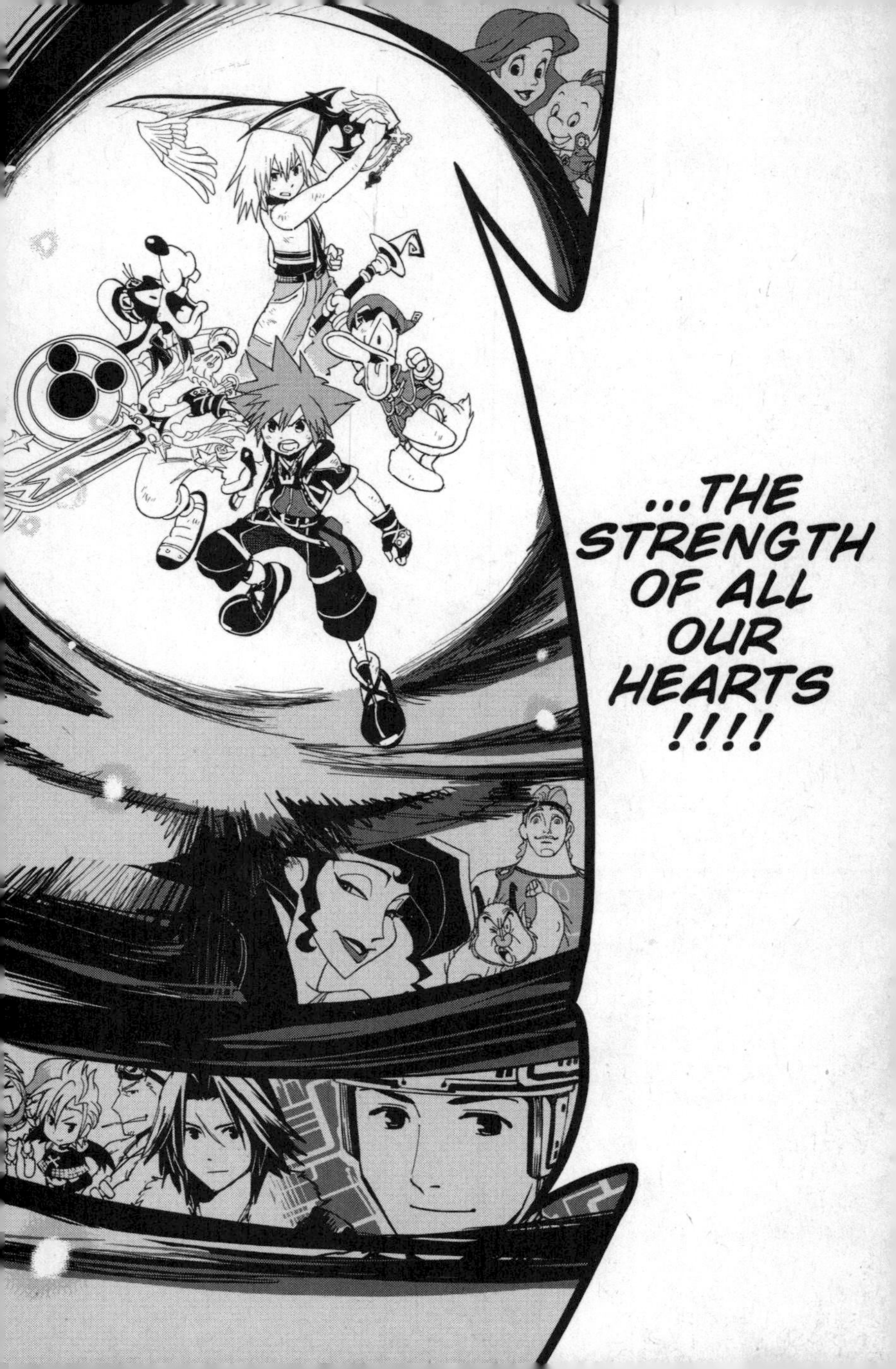
...THE STRENGTH OF ALL OUR HEARTS !!!!

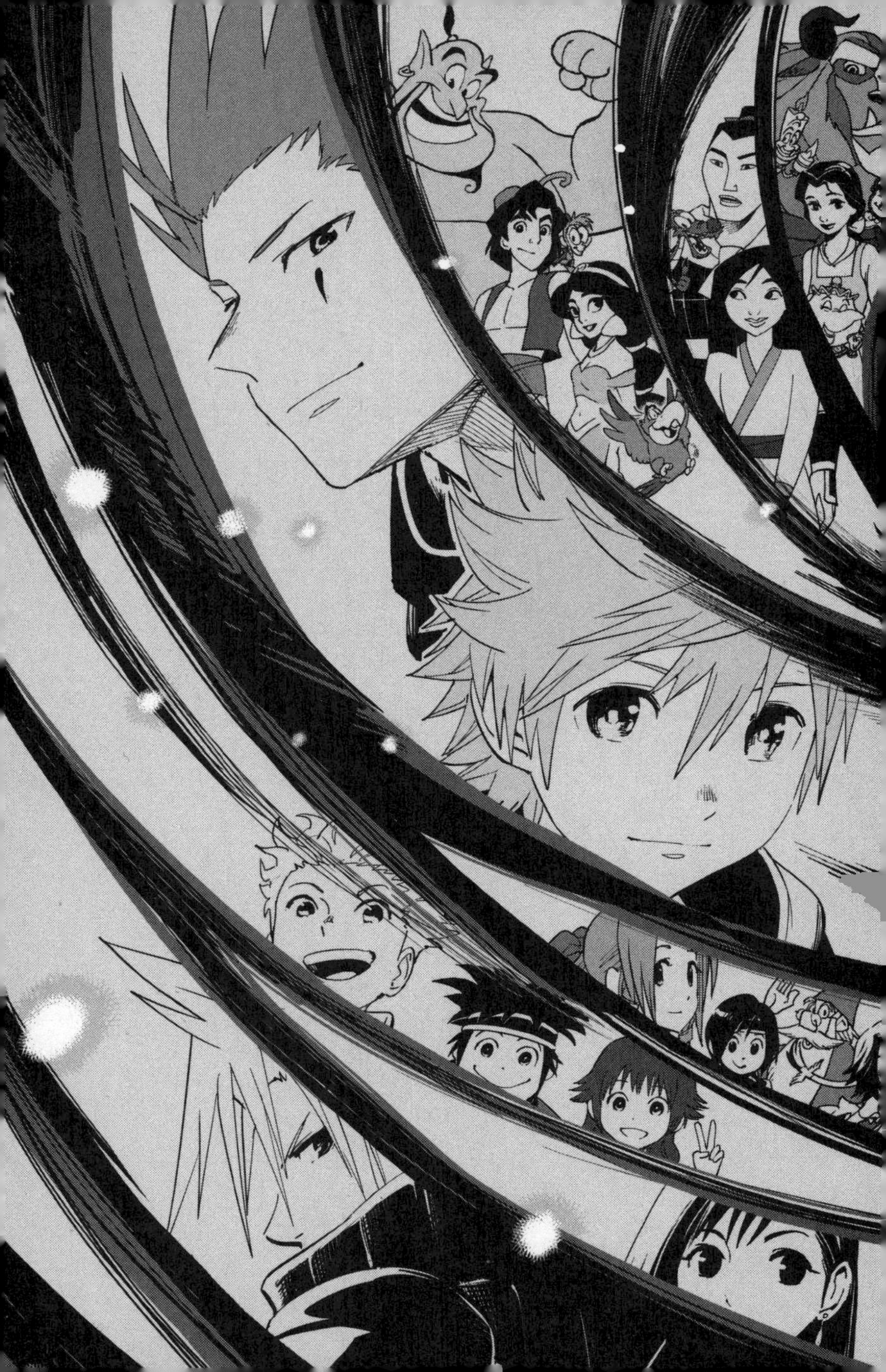

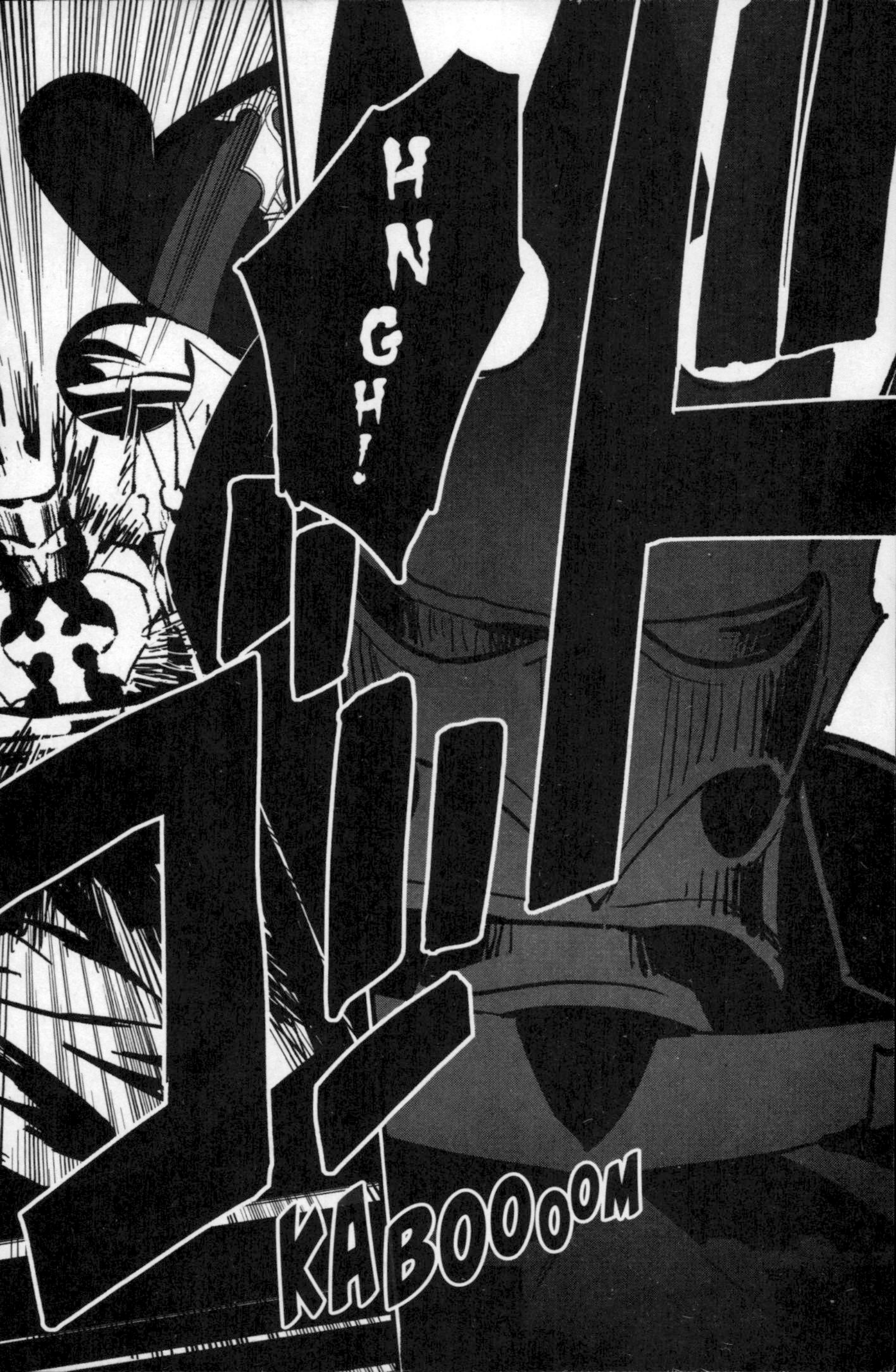
HNGH!
KABOOOOM

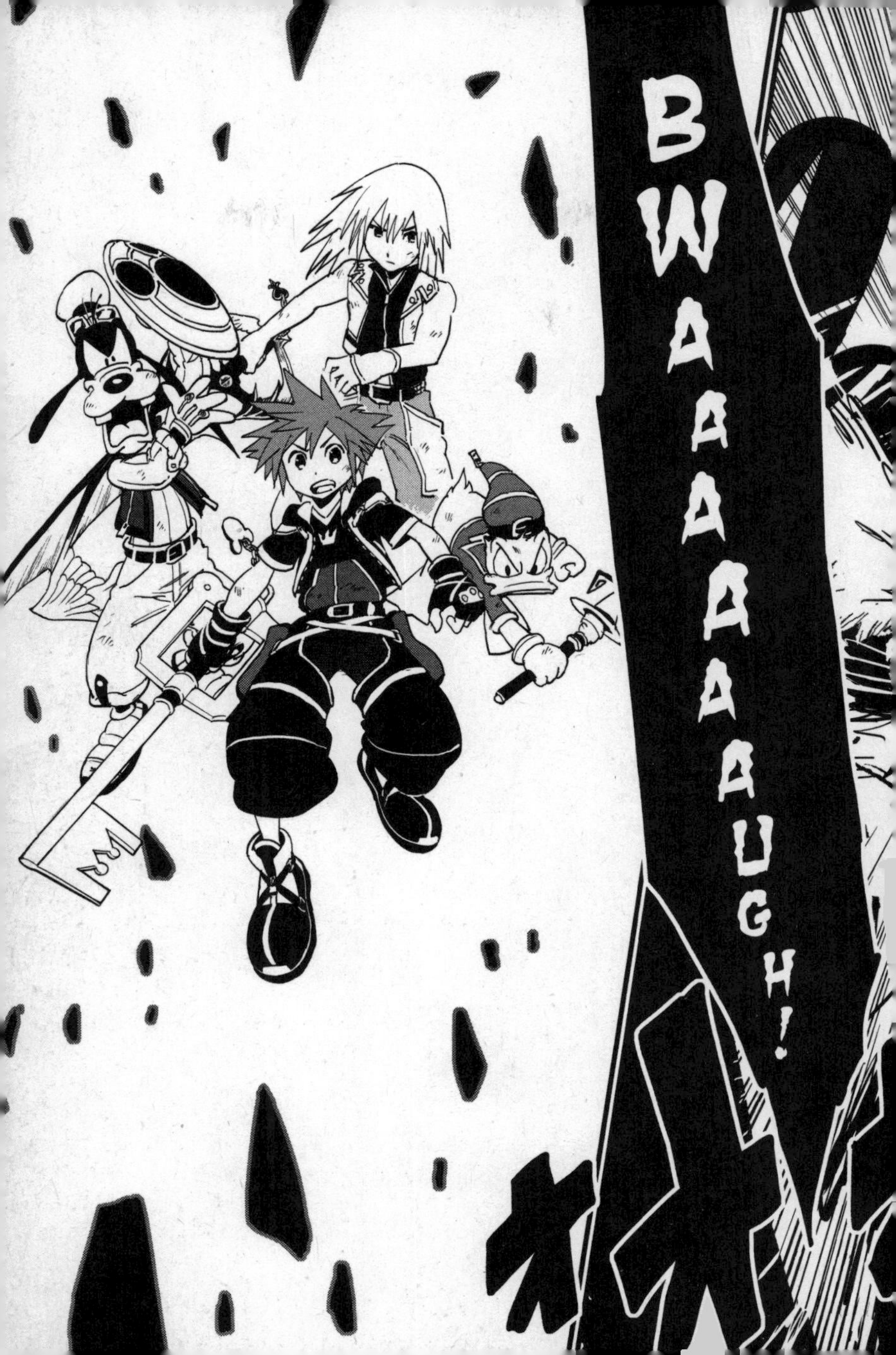
BWAAAAAUGH!

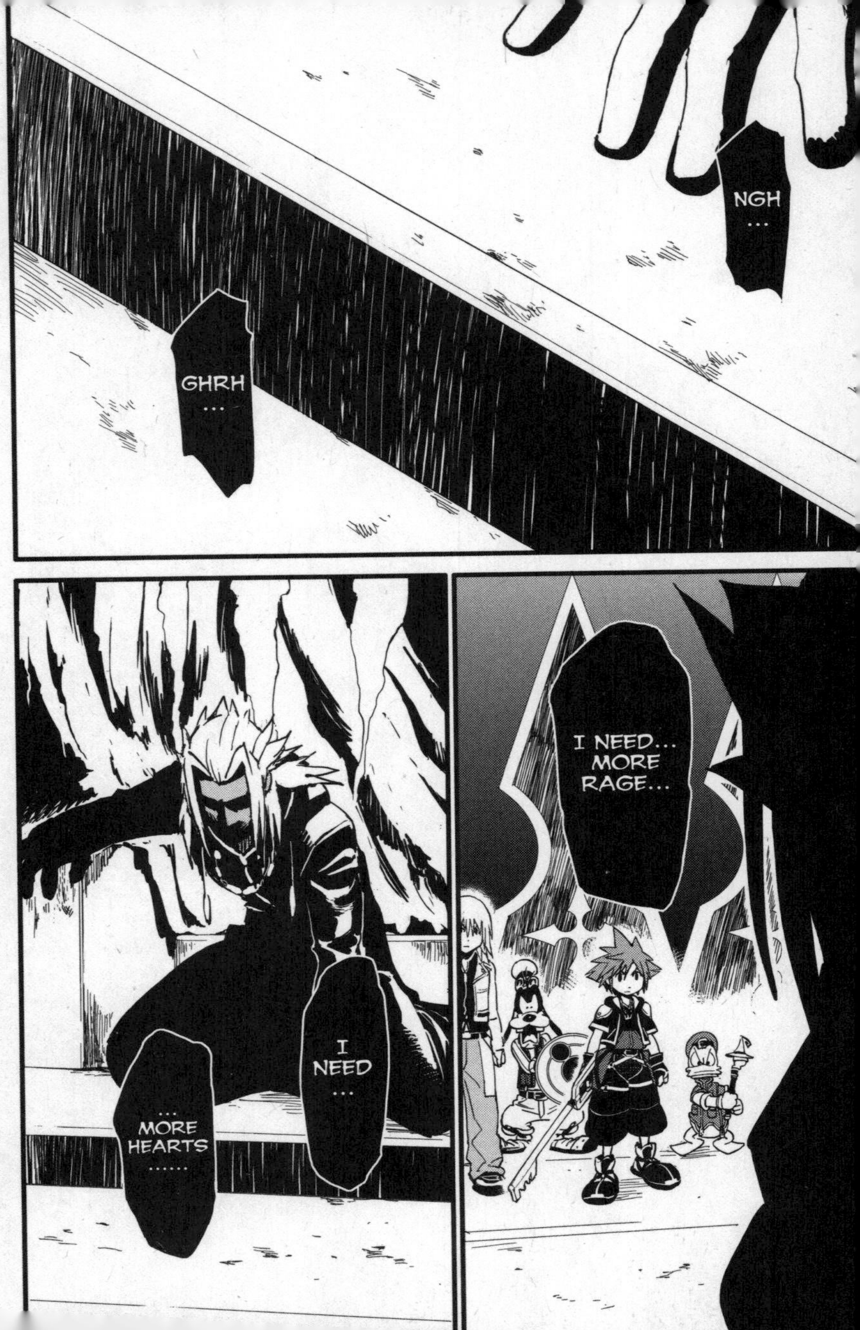
NGH...
GHRH...
I NEED... MORE RAGE...
I NEED...
...MORE HEARTS......

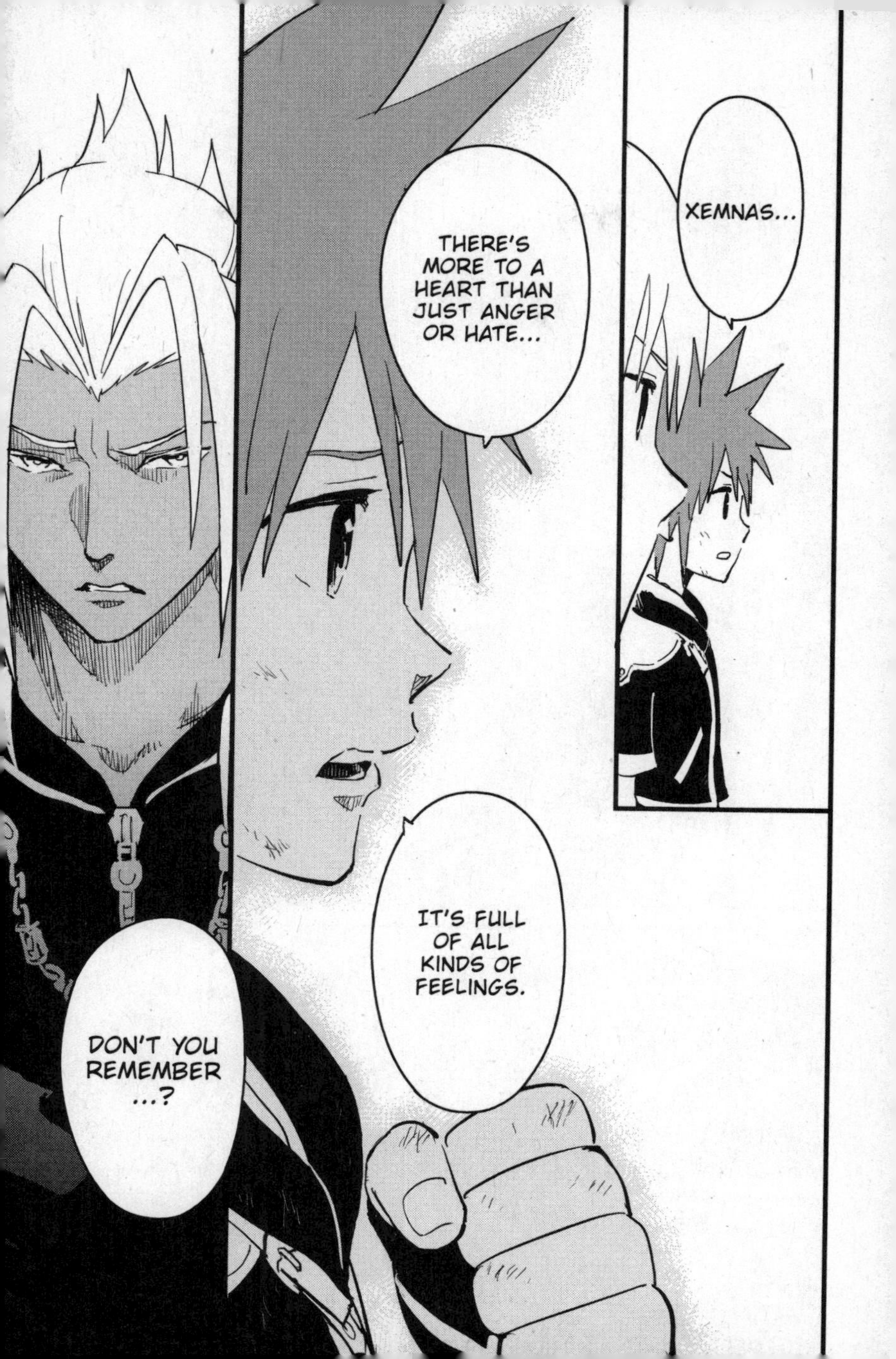
XEMNAS...
THERE'S MORE TO A HEART THAN JUST ANGER OR HATE...
IT'S FULL OF ALL KINDS OF FEELINGS.
DON'T YOU REMEMBER ...?

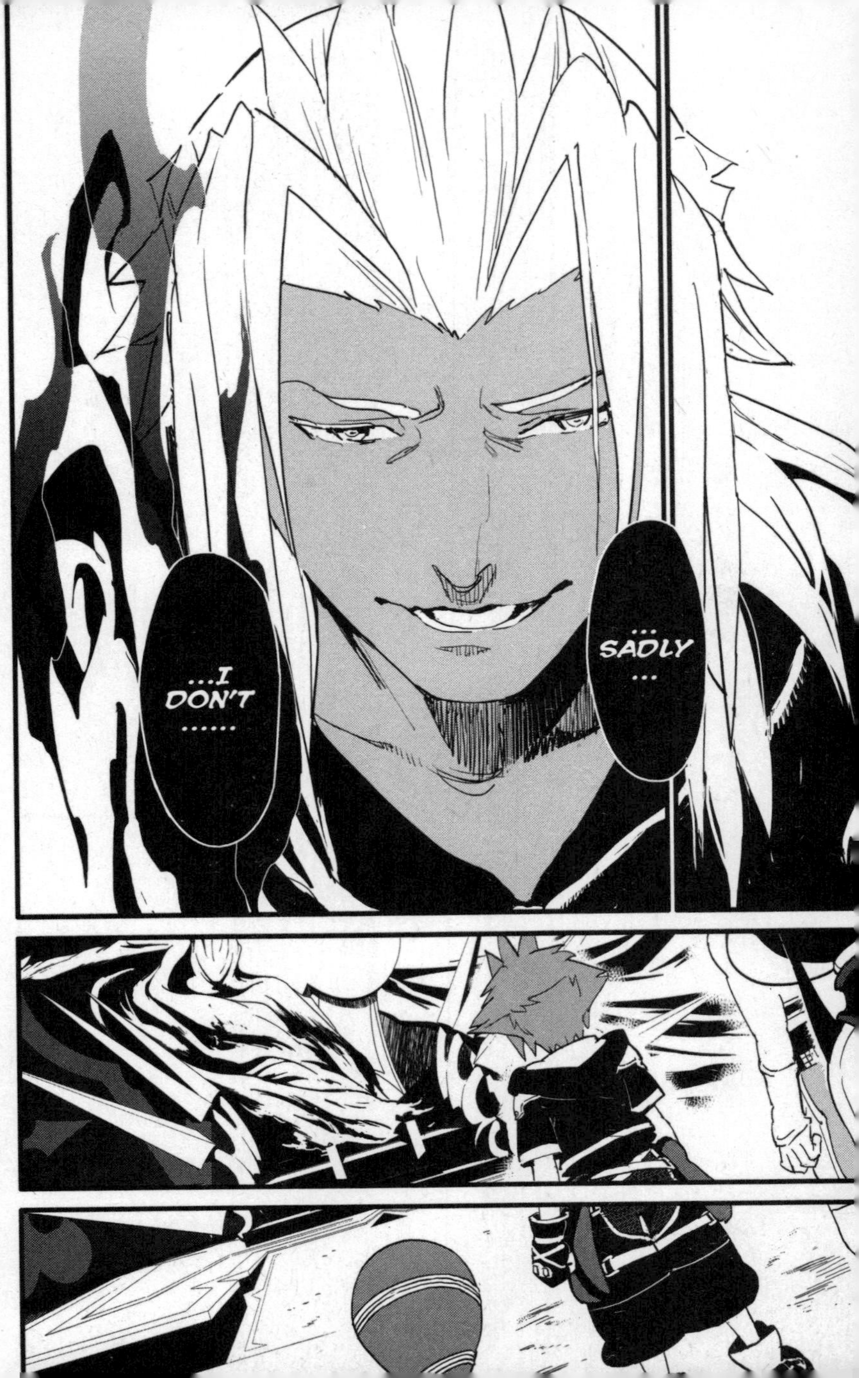
...SADLY...
...I DON'T ......

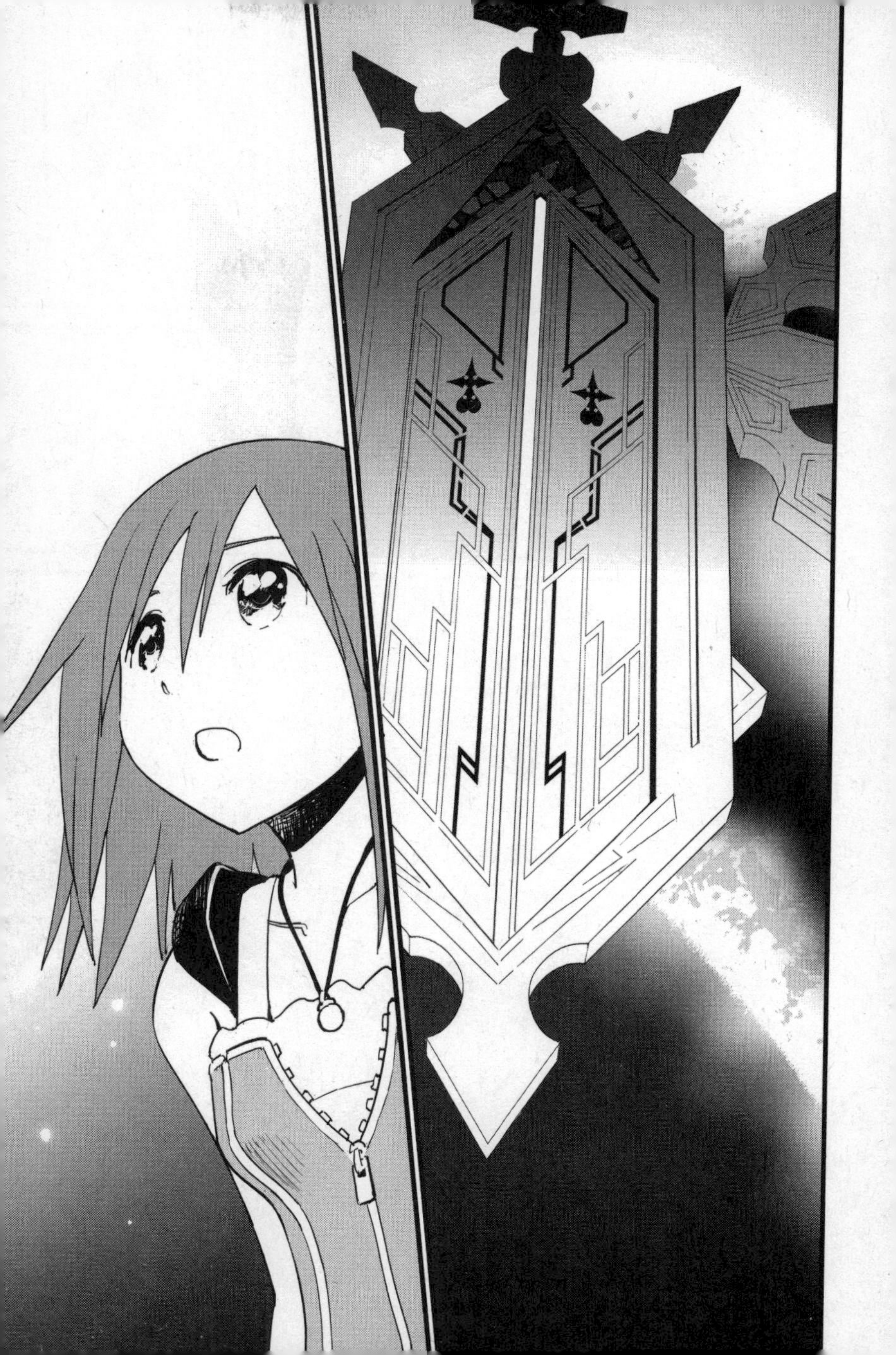

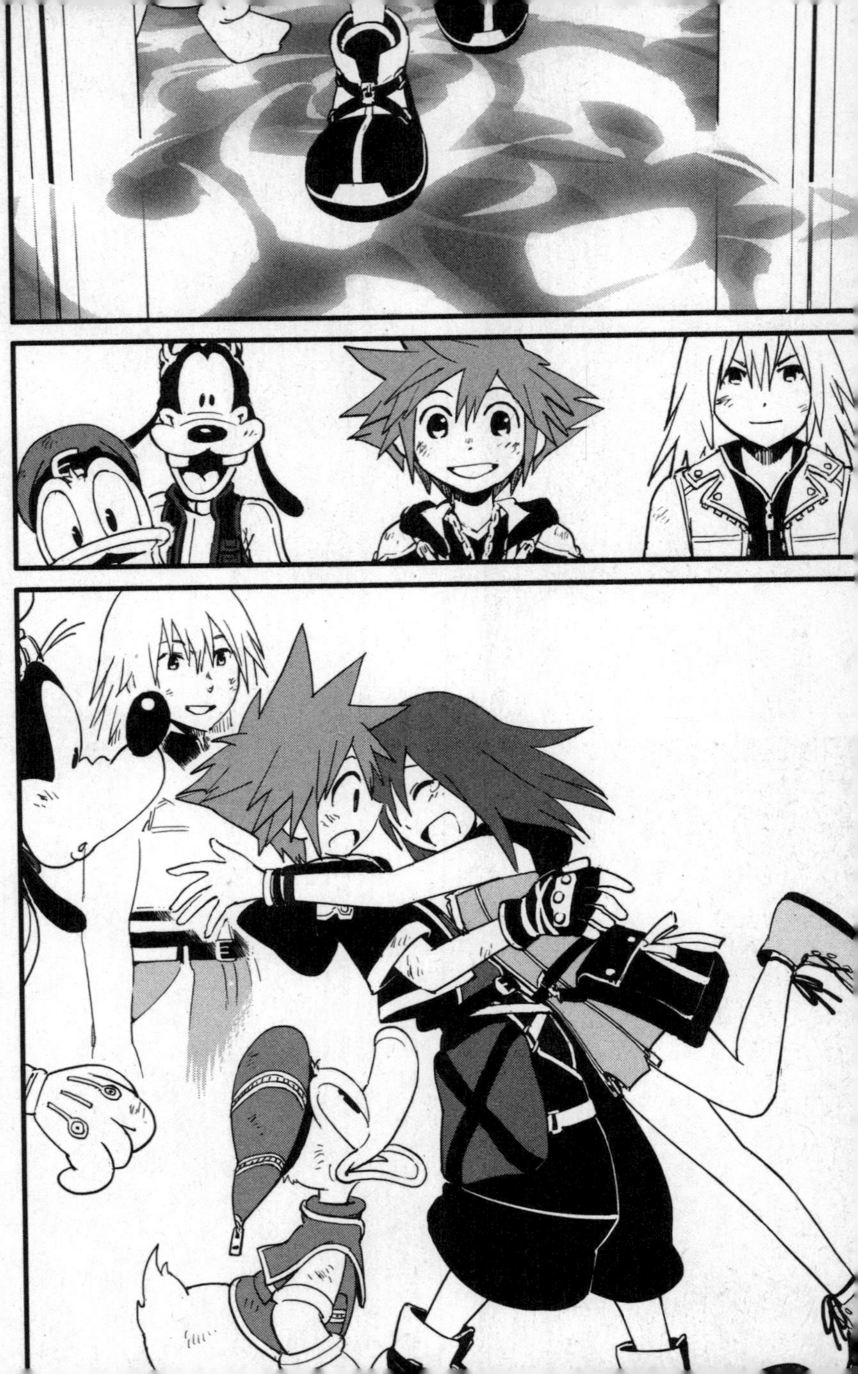

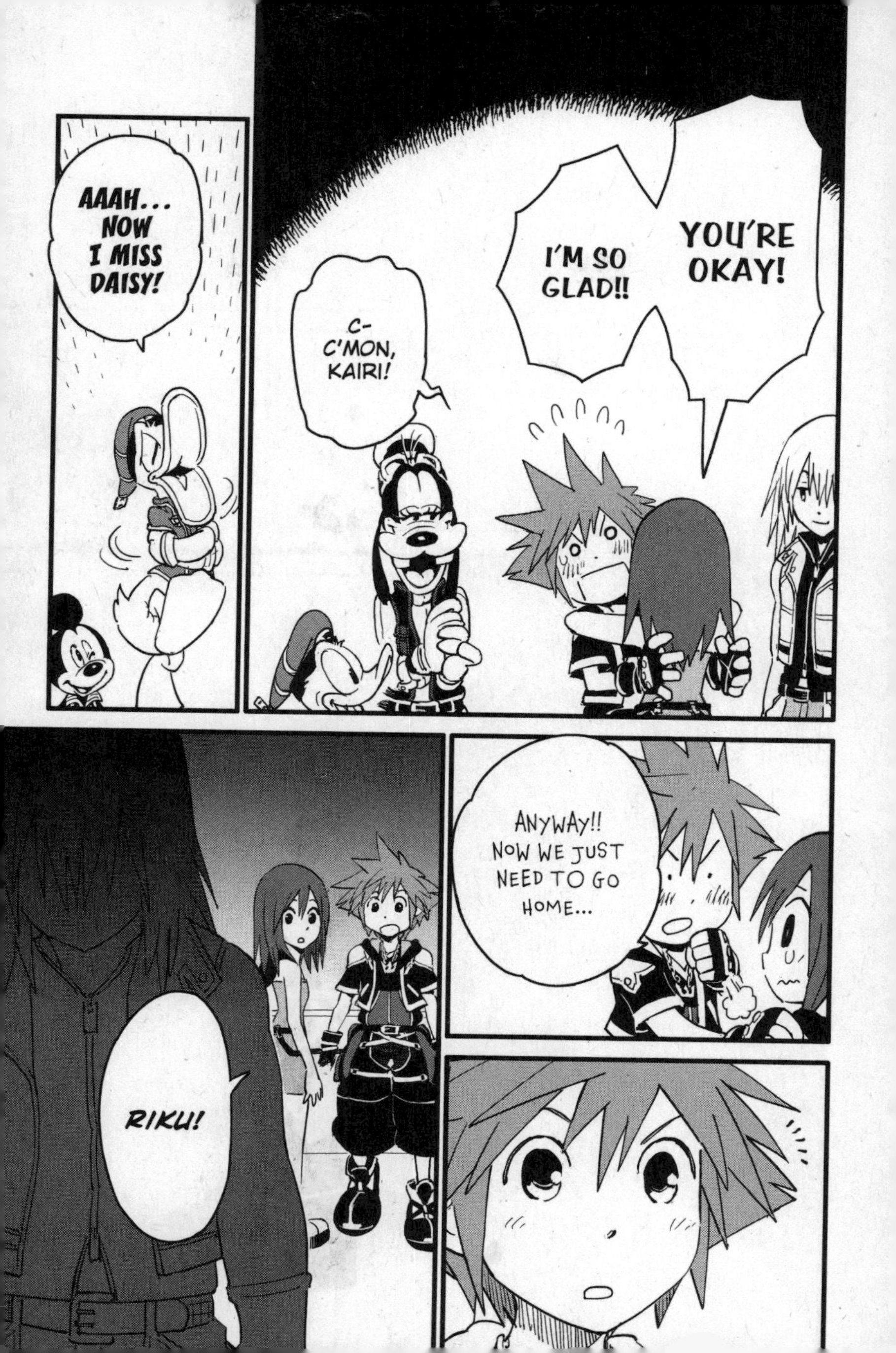
YOU'RE OKAY!
I'M SO GLAD!!
C-C'MON, KAIRI!
AAAH... NOW I MISS DAISY!
ANYWAY!! NOW WE JUST NEED TO GO HOME...
RIKU!

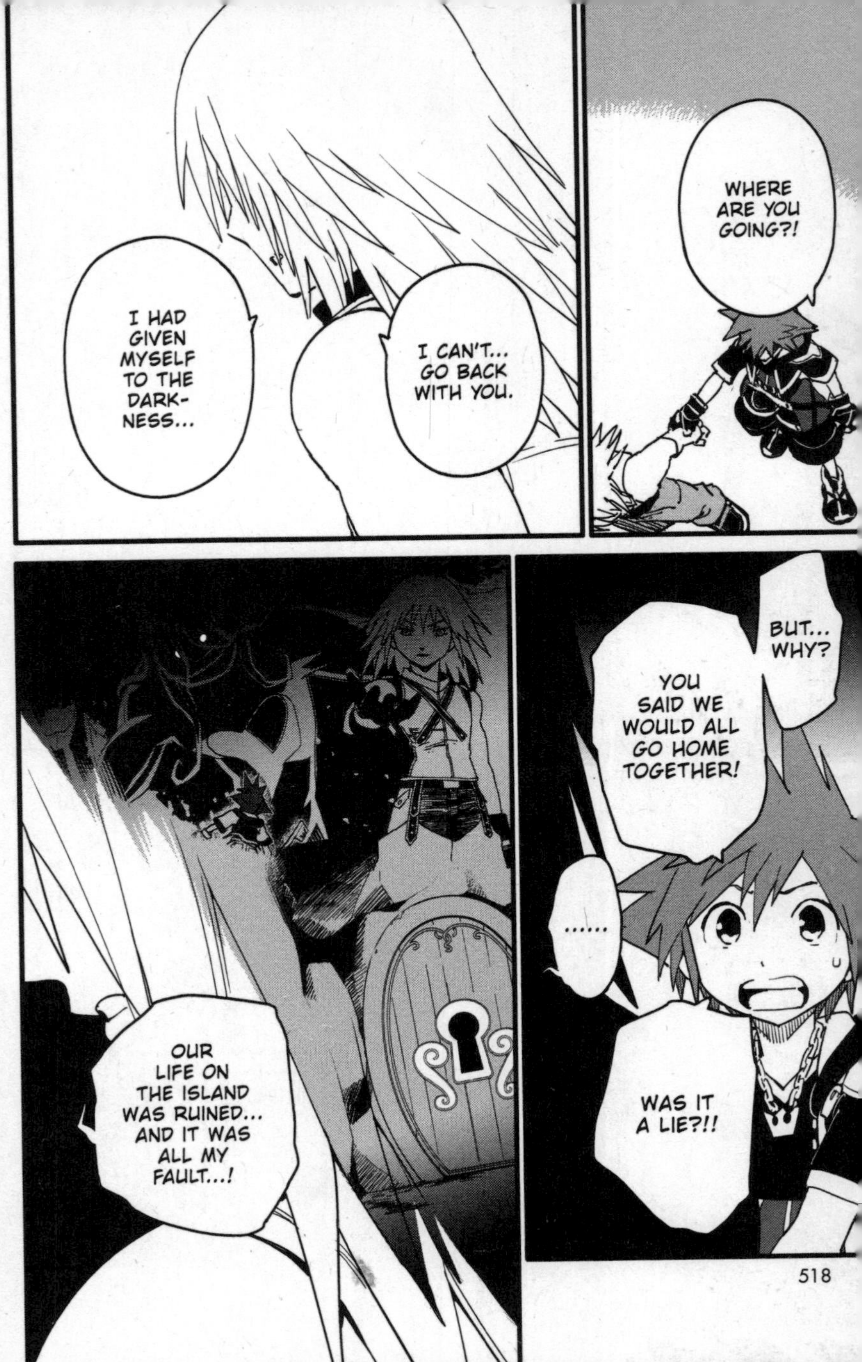
WHERE ARE YOU GOING?!
I CAN'T... GO BACK WITH YOU.
I HAD GIVEN MYSELF TO THE DARK-NESS...
BUT... WHY?
YOU SAID WE WOULD ALL GO HOME TOGETHER!
......
WAS IT A LIE?!!
OUR LIFE ON THE ISLAND WAS RUINED... AND IT WAS ALL MY FAULT...!

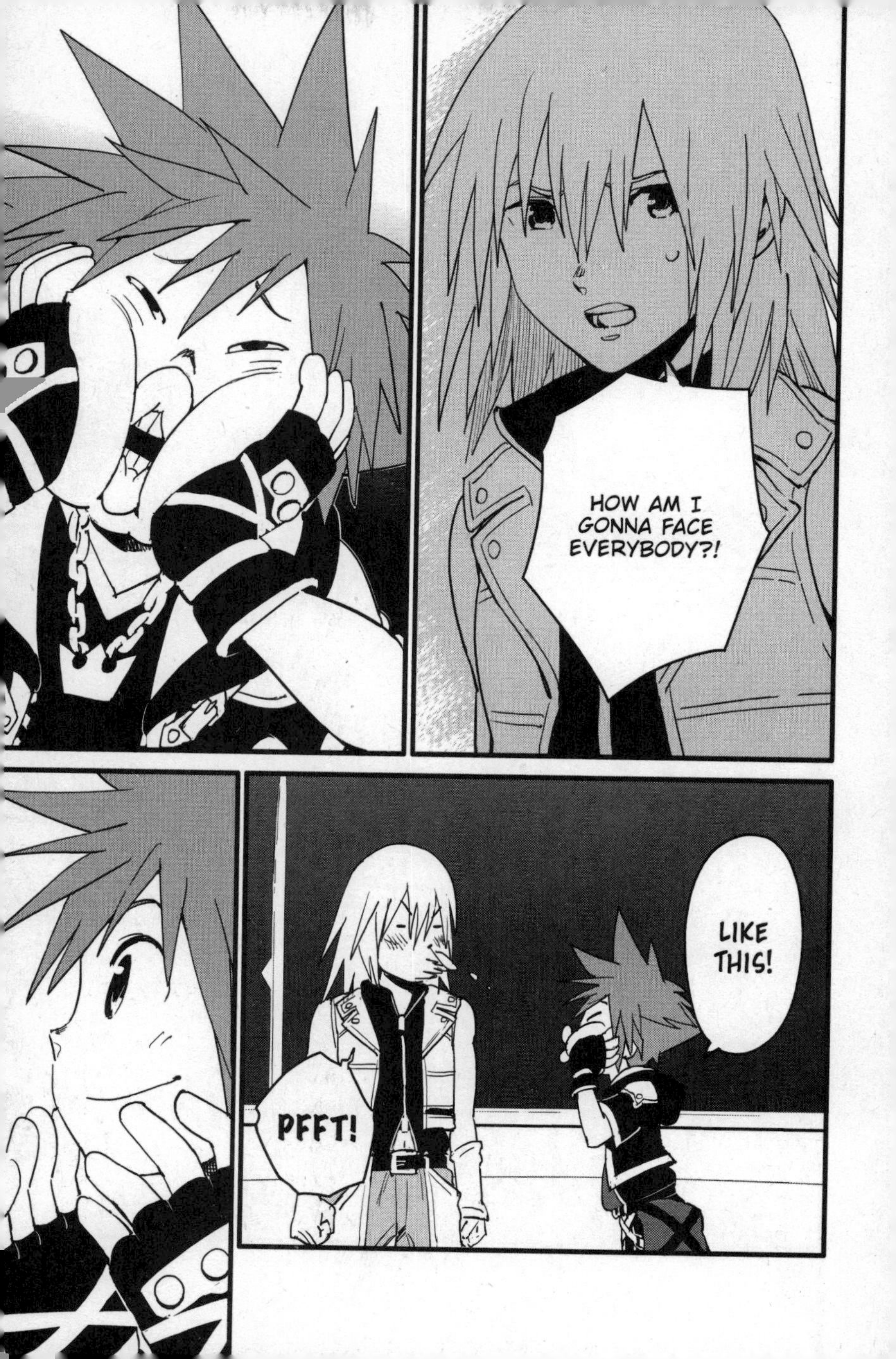
HOW AM I GONNA FACE EVERYBODY?!
LIKE THIS!
PFFT!

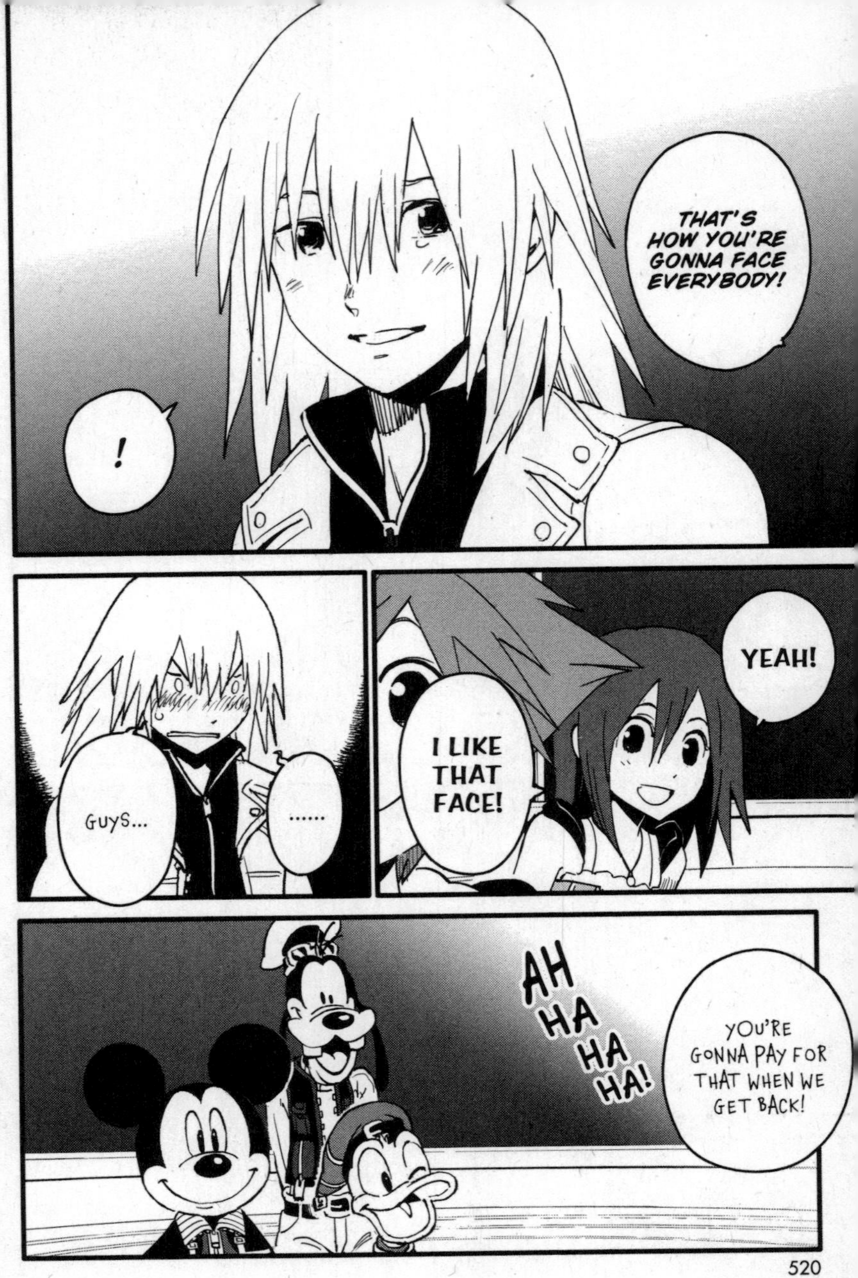
THAT'S HOW YOU'RE GONNA FACE EVERYBODY!
!
YEAH!
I LIKE THAT FACE!
......
GUYS...
YOU'RE GONNA PAY FOR THAT WHEN WE GET BACK!
AH HA HA HA!

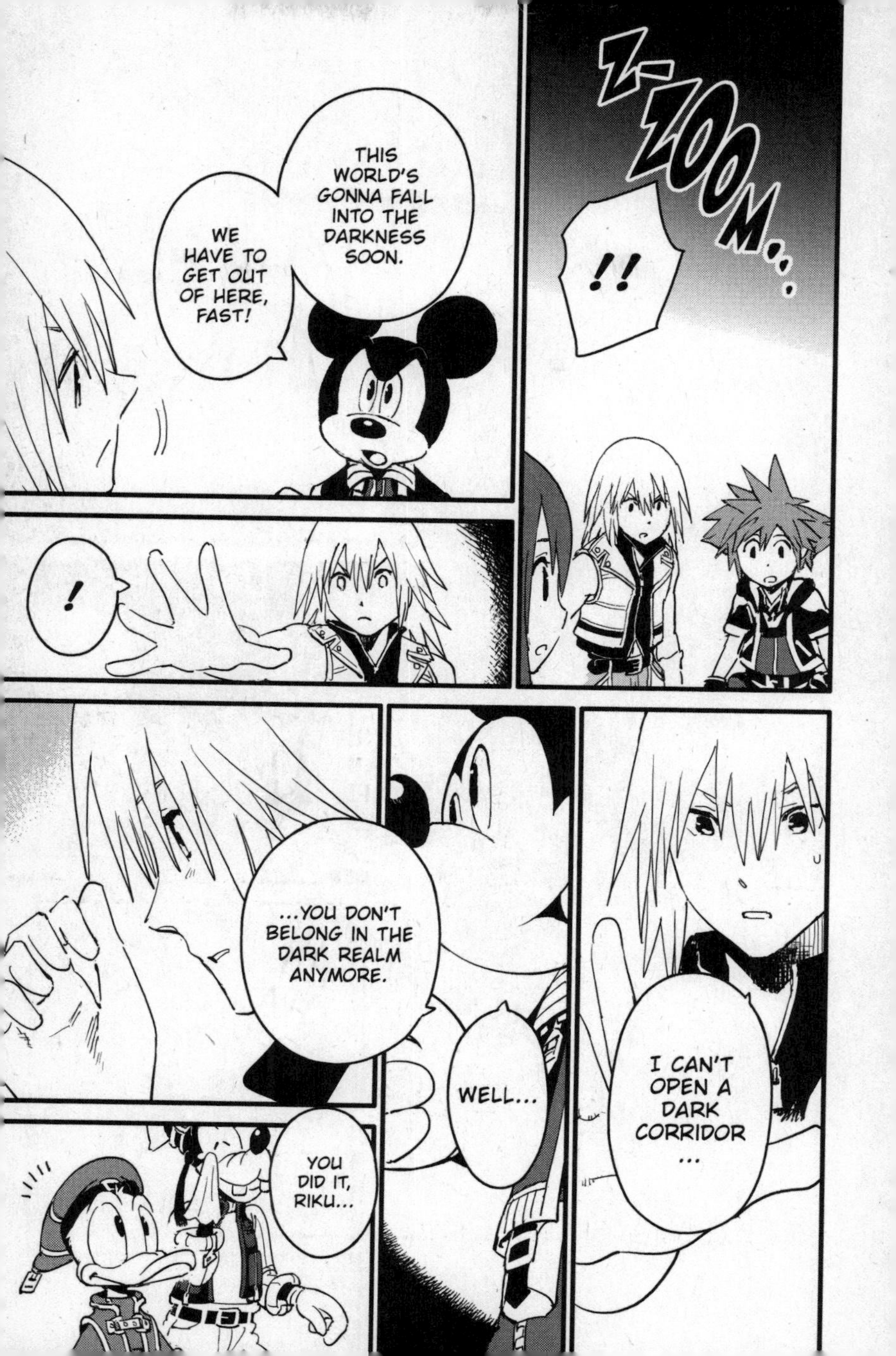

Z-ZOOM...
!!
THIS WORLD'S GONNA FALL INTO THE DARKNESS SOON.
WE HAVE TO GET OUT OF HERE, FAST!
!
I CAN'T OPEN A DARK CORRIDOR...
WELL...
...YOU DON'T BELONG IN THE DARK REALM ANYMORE.
YOU DID IT, RIKU...

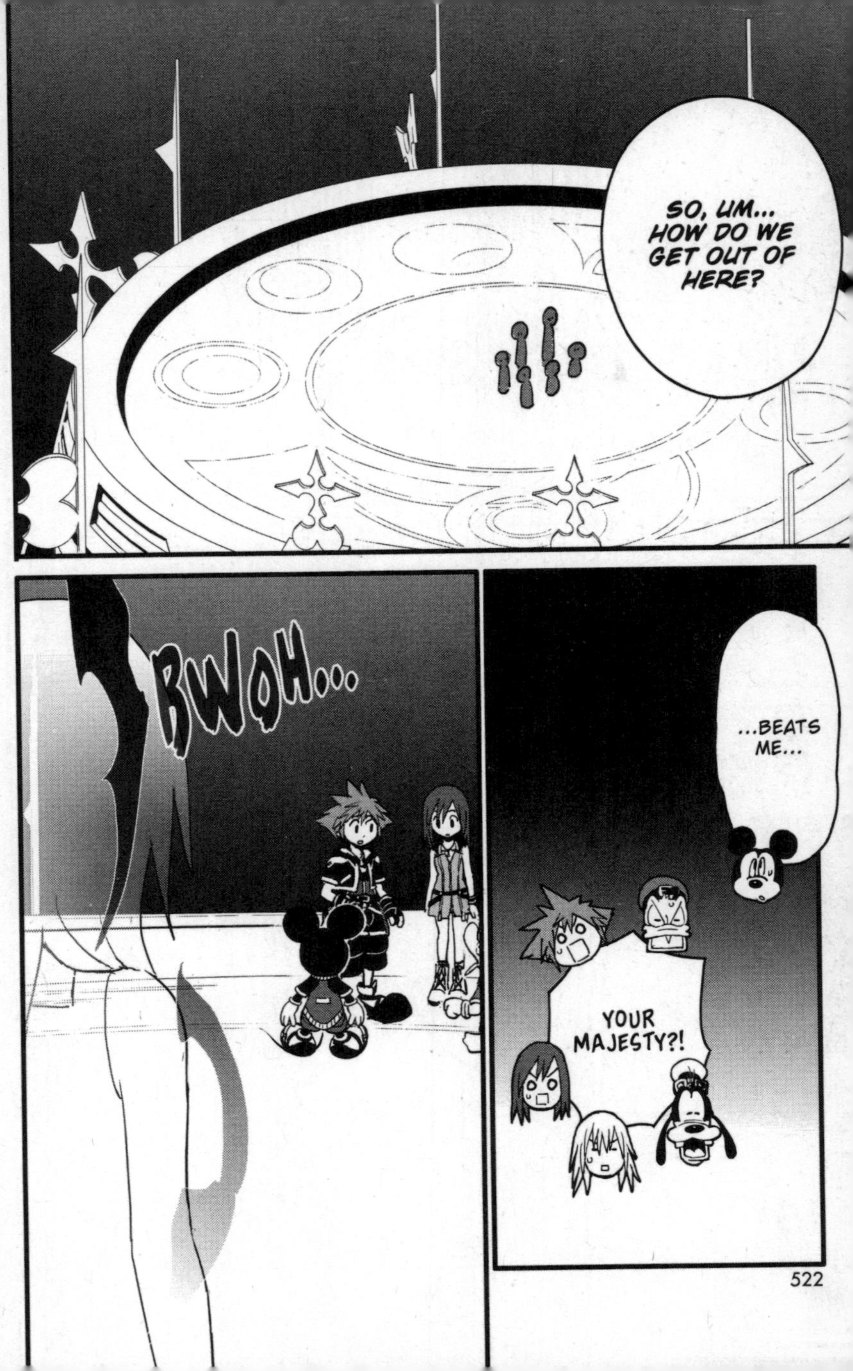
SO, UM... HOW DO WE GET OUT OF HERE?
...BEATS ME...
YOUR MAJESTY?!
BWOH...

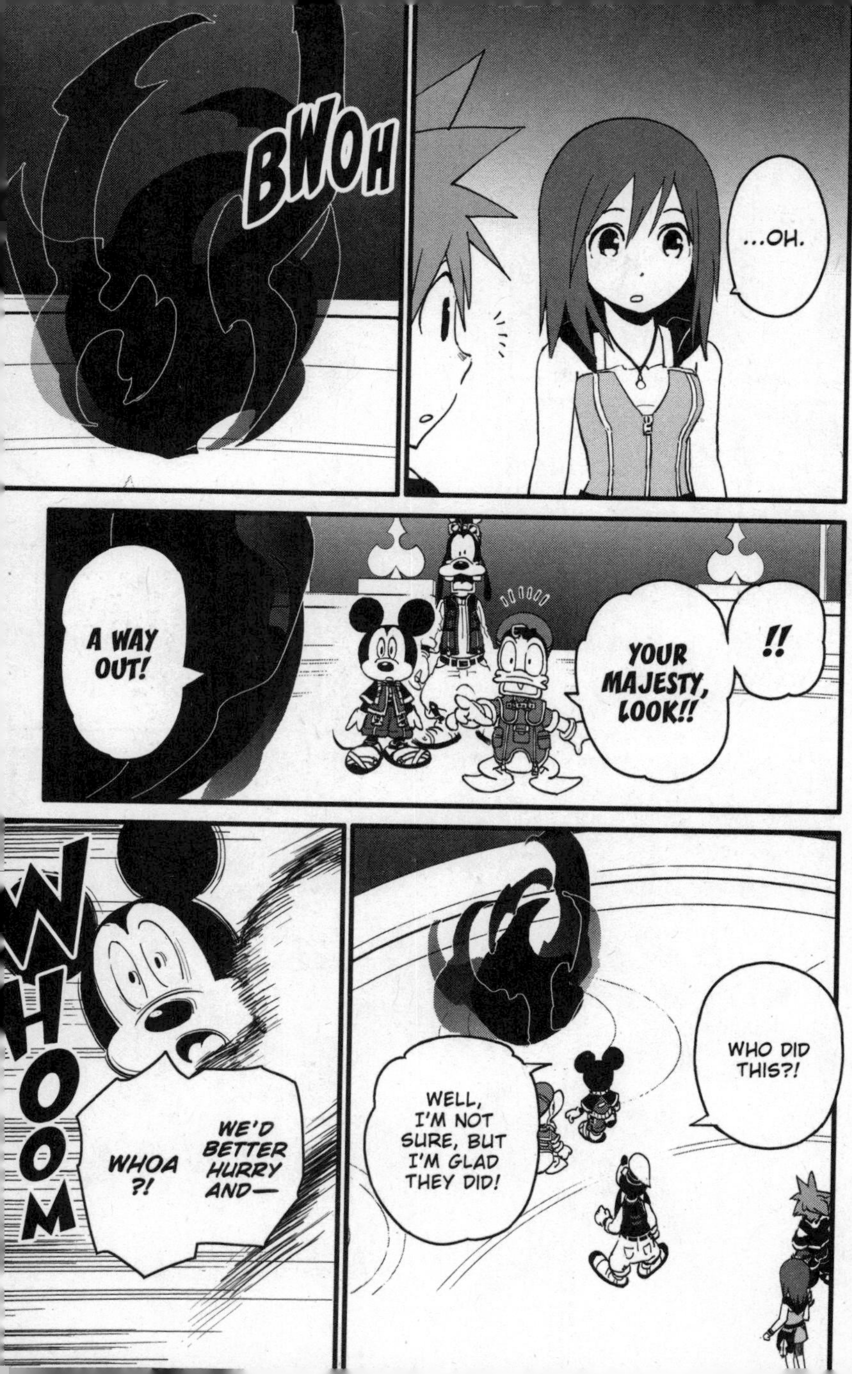
...OH.
BWOH
!!
YOUR MAJESTY, LOOK!!
A WAY OUT!
WHO DID THIS?!
WELL, I'M NOT SURE, BUT I'M GLAD THEY DID!
WHOOM
WE'D BETTER HURRY AND—
WHOA ?!

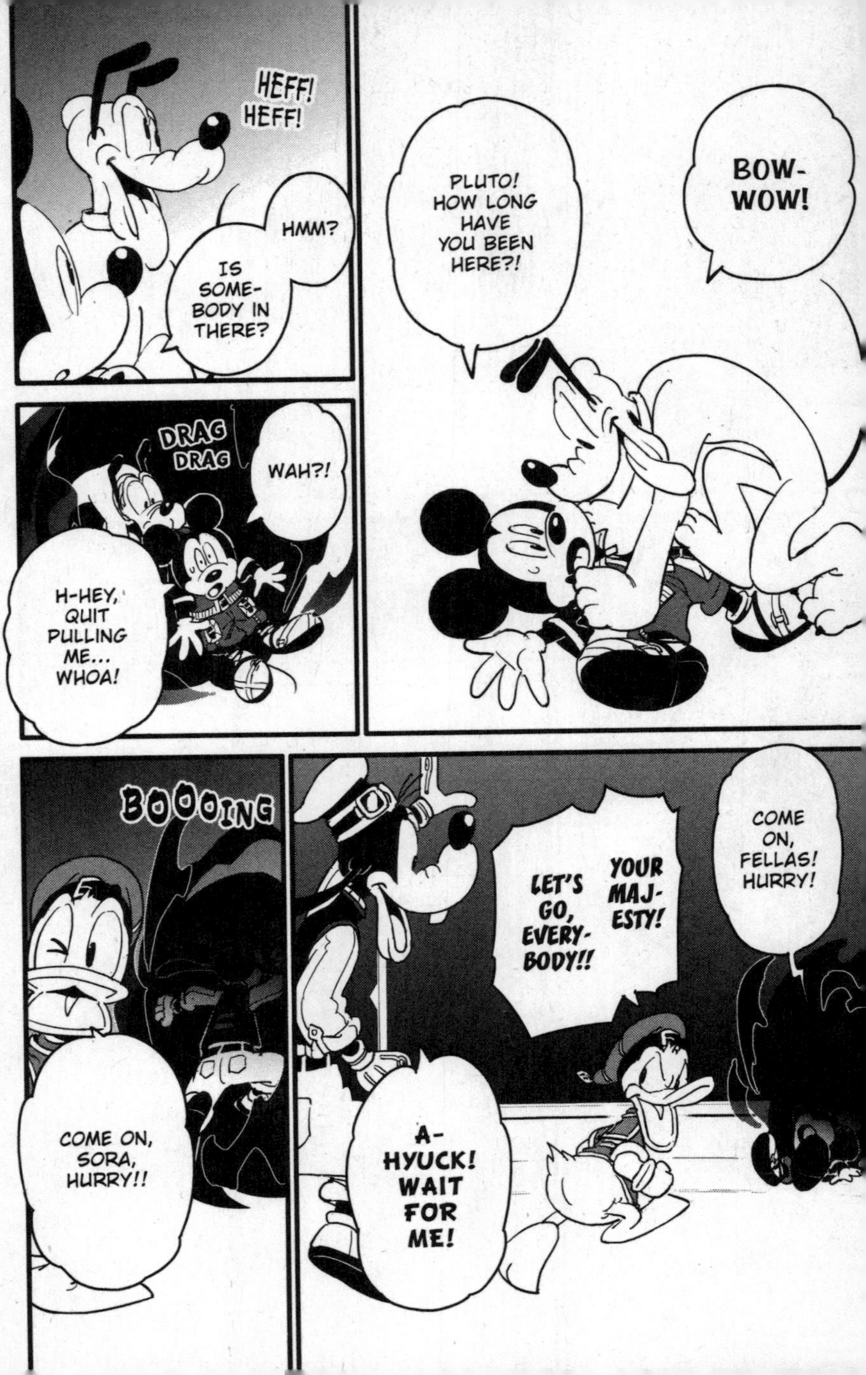
BOW-WOW!
PLUTO! HOW LONG HAVE YOU BEEN HERE?!
HEFF! HEFF!
HMM?
IS SOMEBODY IN THERE?
WAH?!
DRAG DRAG
H-HEY, QUIT PULLING ME... WHOA!
COME ON, FELLAS! HURRY!
YOUR MAJESTY!
LET'S GO, EVERYBODY!!
A-HYUCK! WAIT FOR ME!
BOOOING
COME ON, SORA, HURRY!!

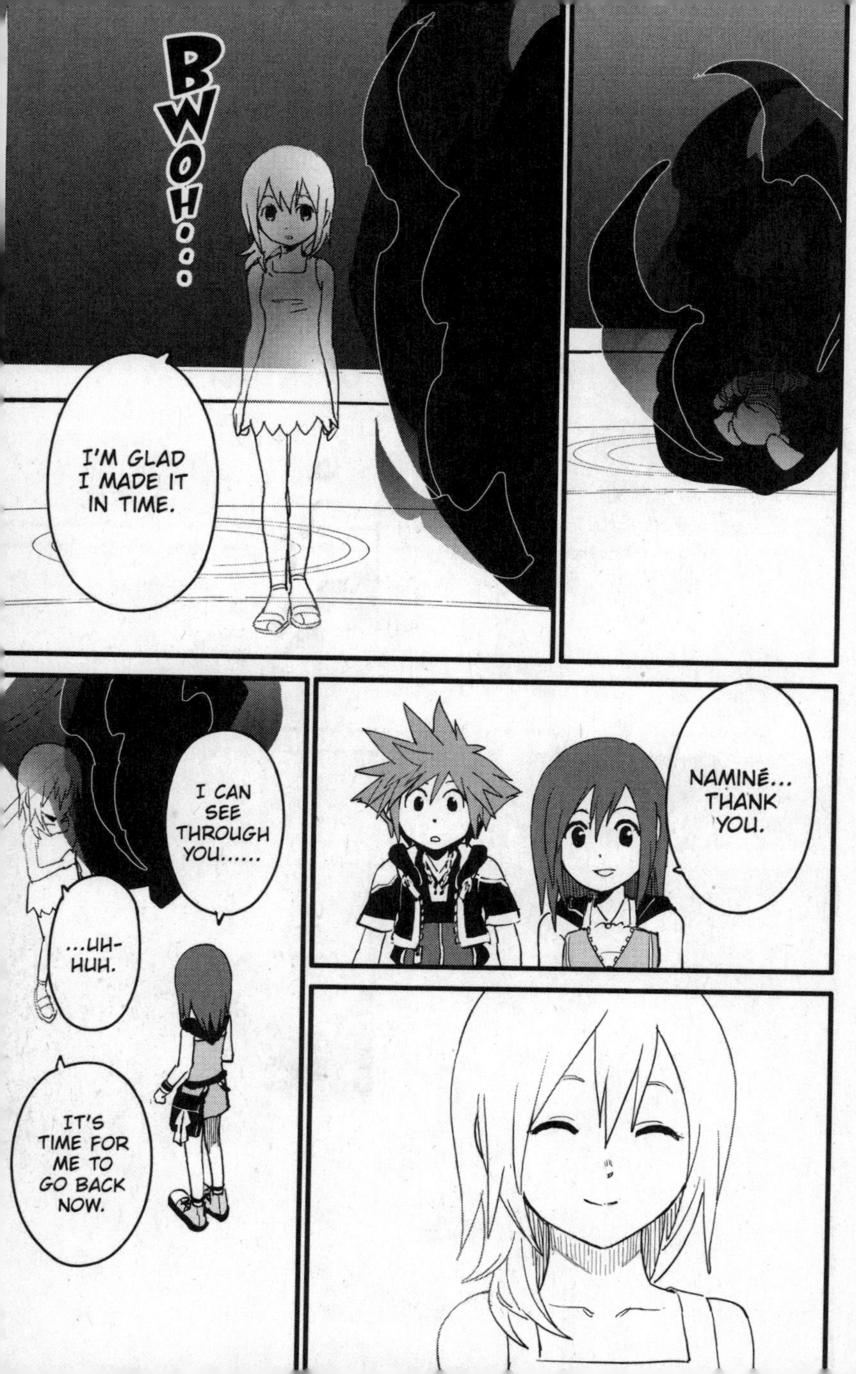
BWOHOOO
I'M GLAD I MADE IT IN TIME.
NAMINÉ... THANK YOU.
I CAN SEE THROUGH YOU......
...UH-HUH.
IT'S TIME FOR ME TO GO BACK NOW.

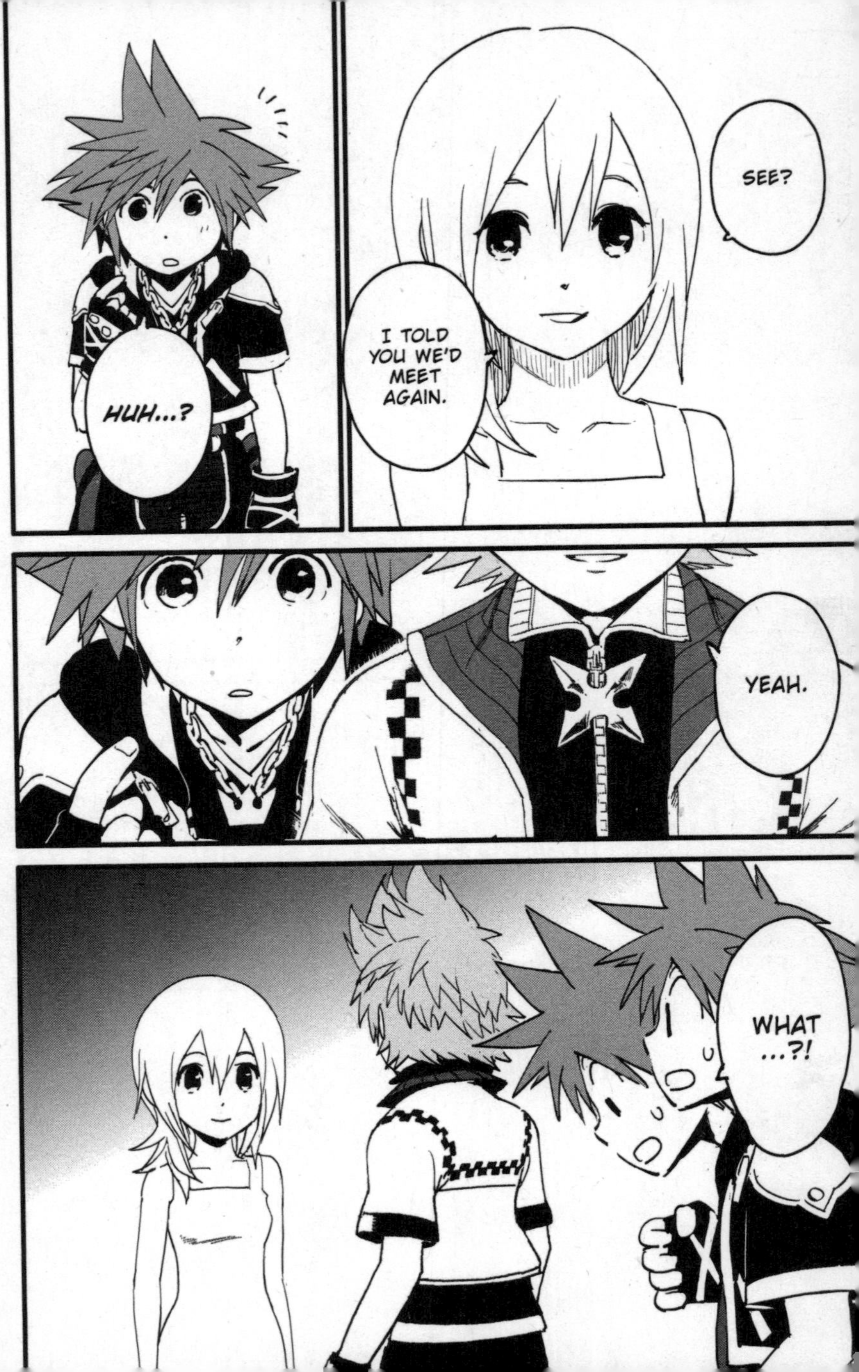
SEE?
I TOLD YOU WE'D MEET AGAIN.
HUH...?
YEAH.
WHAT ...?!

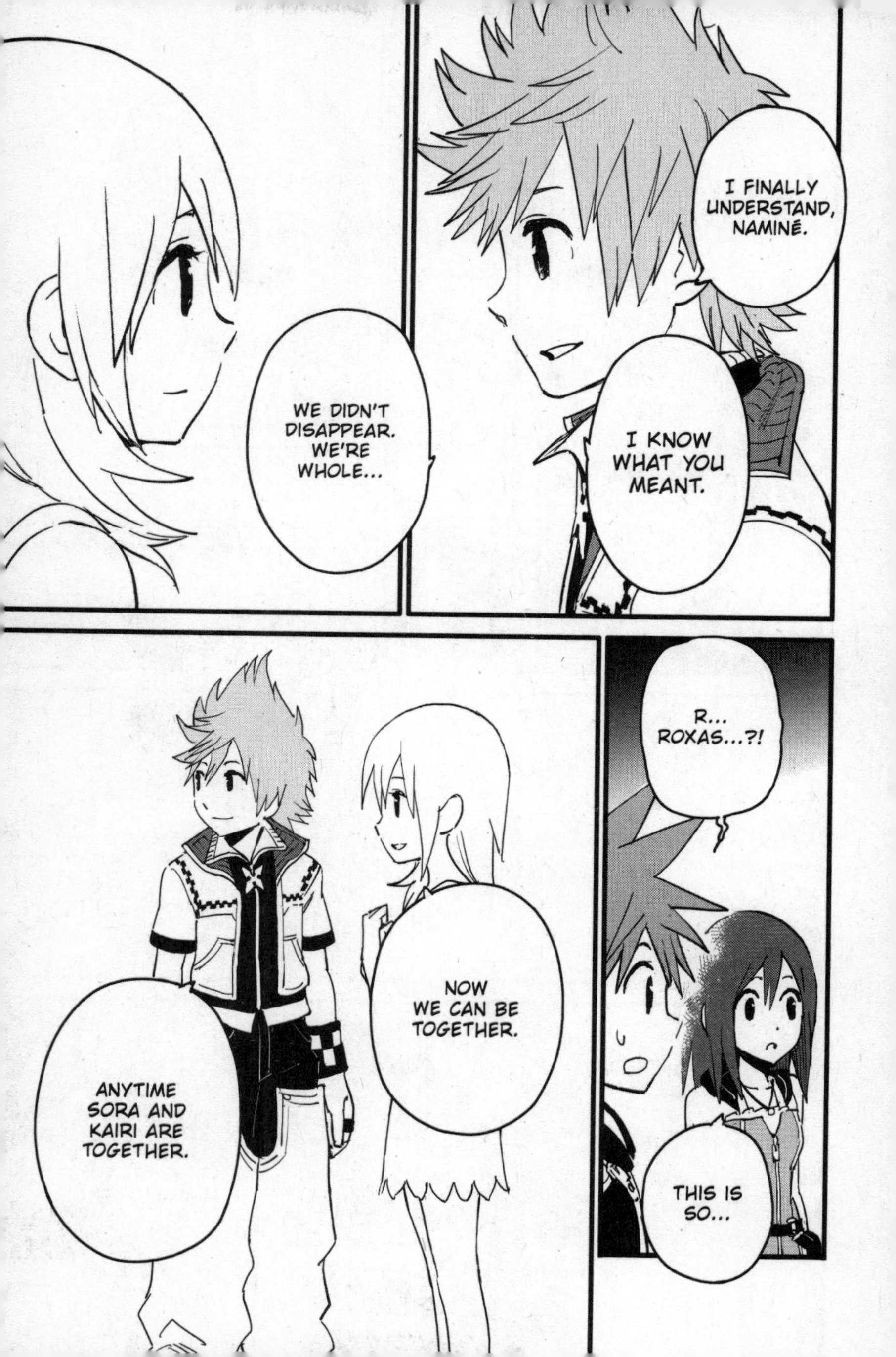
I FINALLY UNDERSTAND, NAMINÉ.
I KNOW WHAT YOU MEANT.
WE DIDN'T DISAPPEAR. WE'RE WHOLE...
R... ROXAS...?!
THIS IS SO...
NOW WE CAN BE TOGETHER.
ANYTIME SORA AND KAIRI ARE TOGETHER.

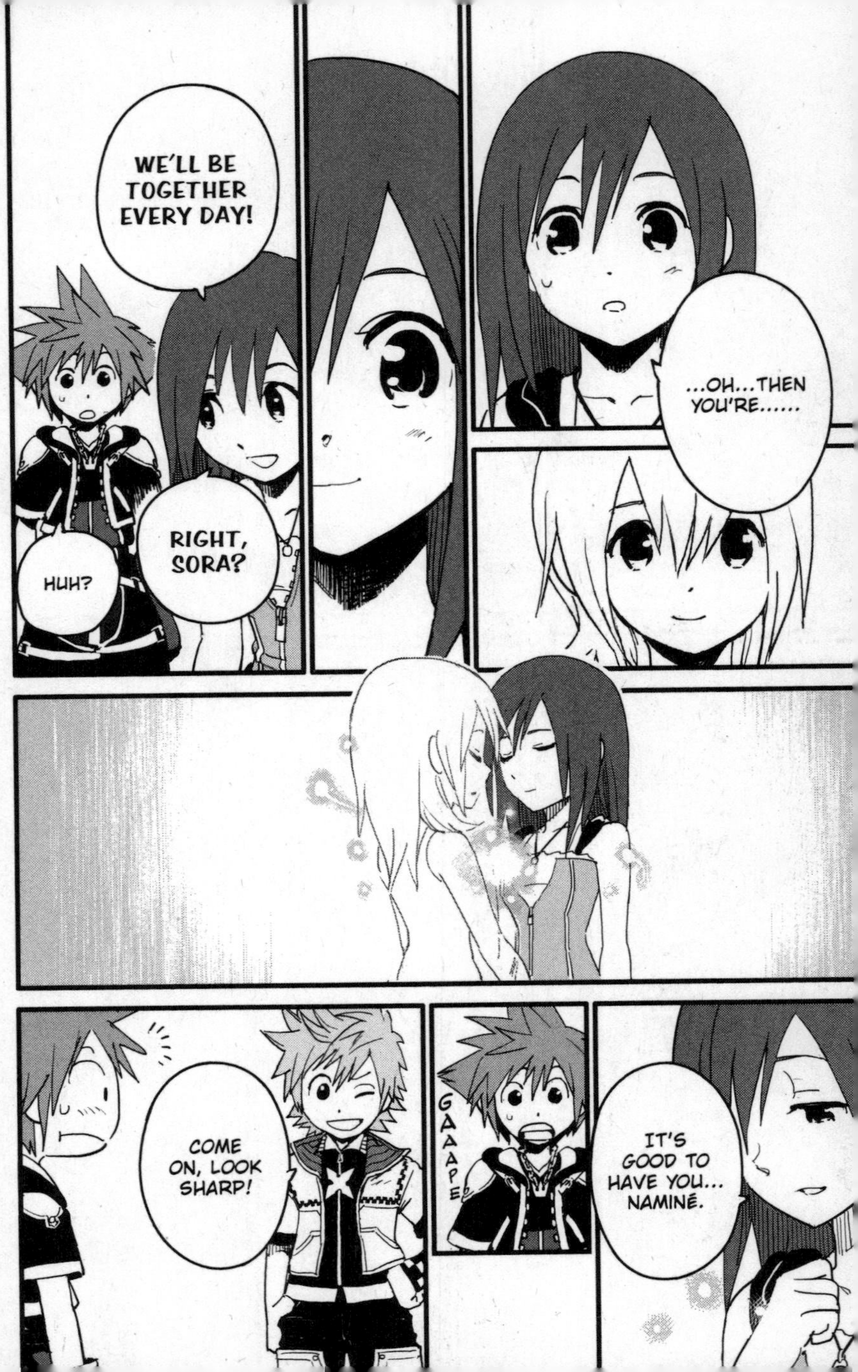
...OH...THEN YOU'RE......
WE'LL BE TOGETHER EVERY DAY!
RIGHT, SORA?
HUH?
IT'S GOOD TO HAVE YOU... NAMINÉ.
GAAAPE
COME ON, LOOK SHARP!

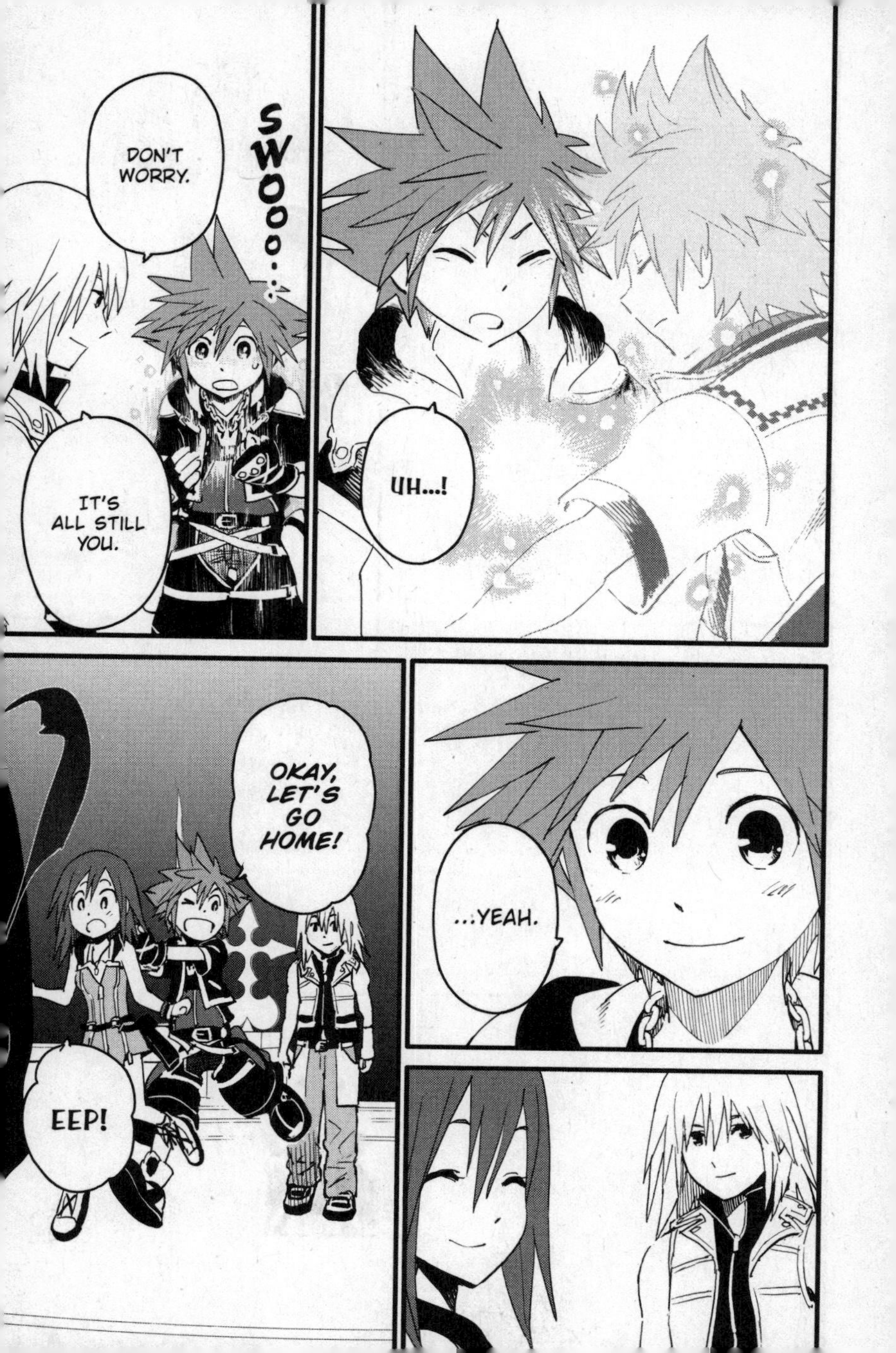
UH...!
SWOOO...
DON'T WORRY.
IT'S ALL STILL YOU.
...YEAH.
OKAY, LET'S GO HOME!
EEP!

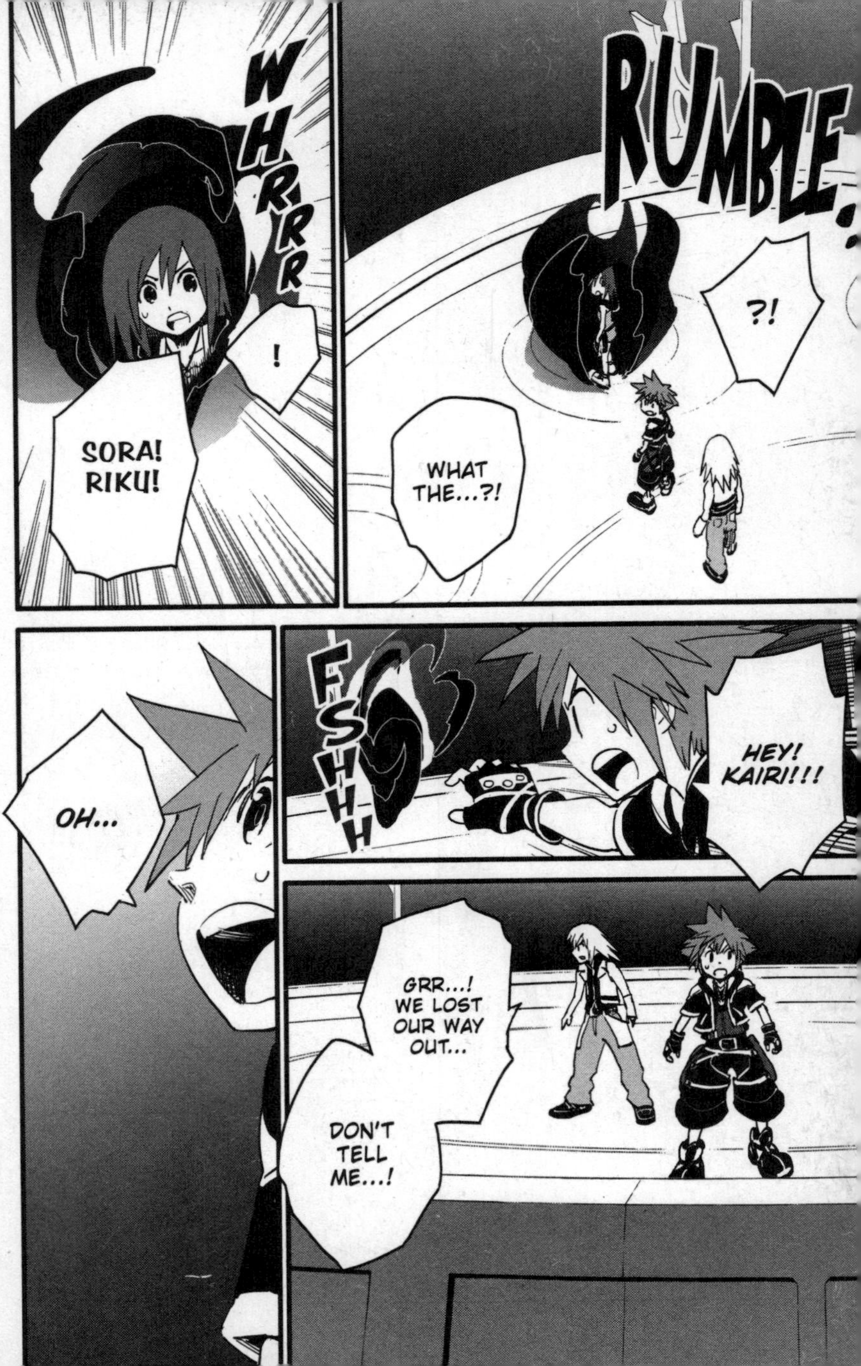
RUMBLE...
?!
WHAT THE...?!
WHRRR
!
SORA! RIKU!
FSHHHH
HEY! KAIRI!!!
GRR...! WE LOST OUR WAY OUT...
DON'T TELL ME...!
OH...

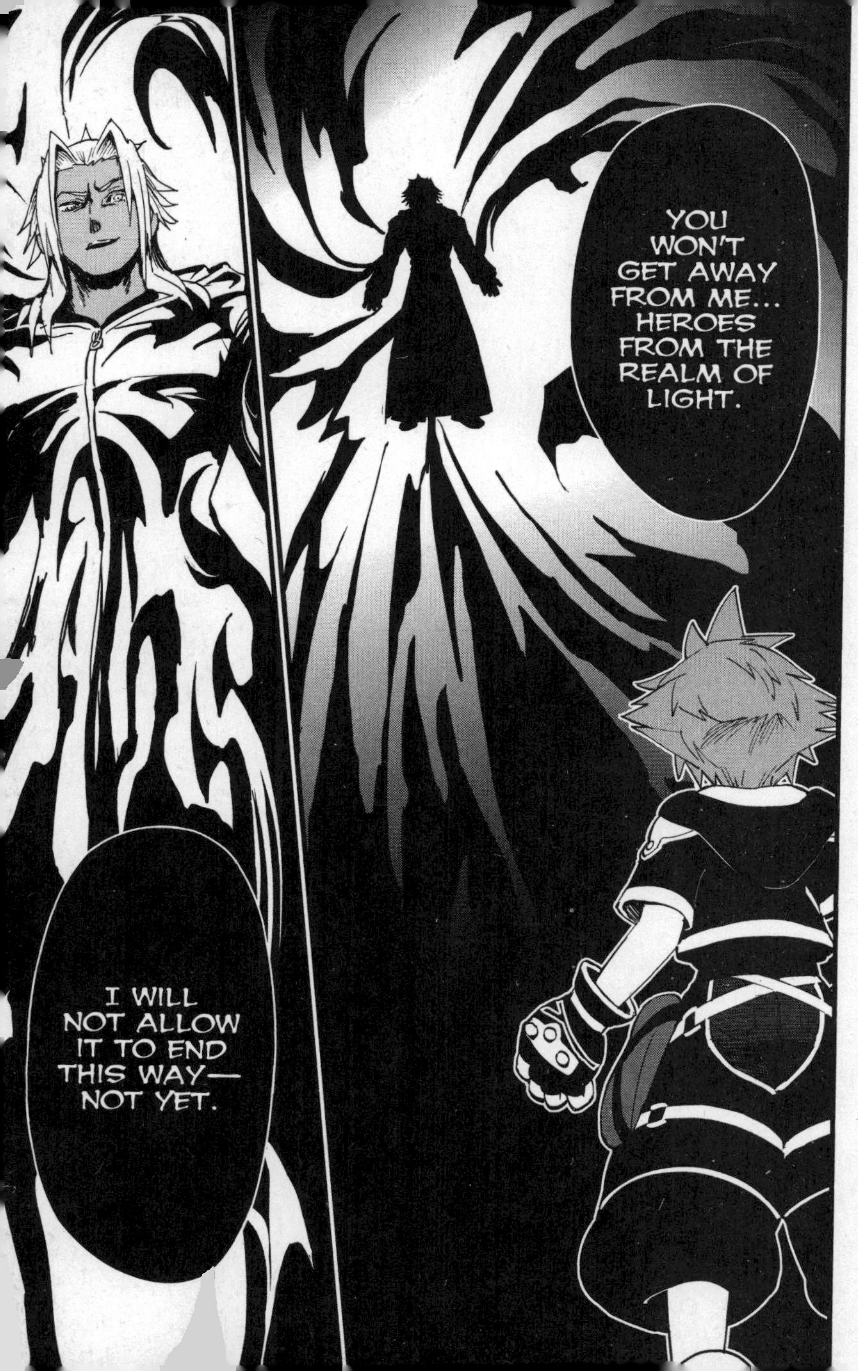
YOU WON'T GET AWAY FROM ME... HEROES FROM THE REALM OF LIGHT.
I WILL NOT ALLOW IT TO END THIS WAY—NOT YET.

Disney SQUARE ENIX

KINGDOM HEARTS

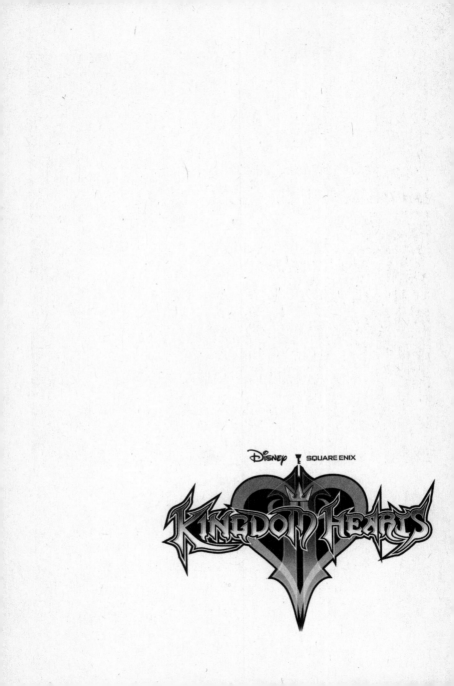

Final Chapter: The Door to Light

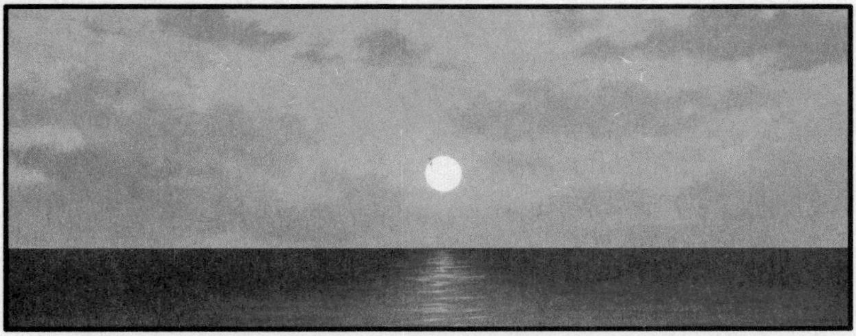

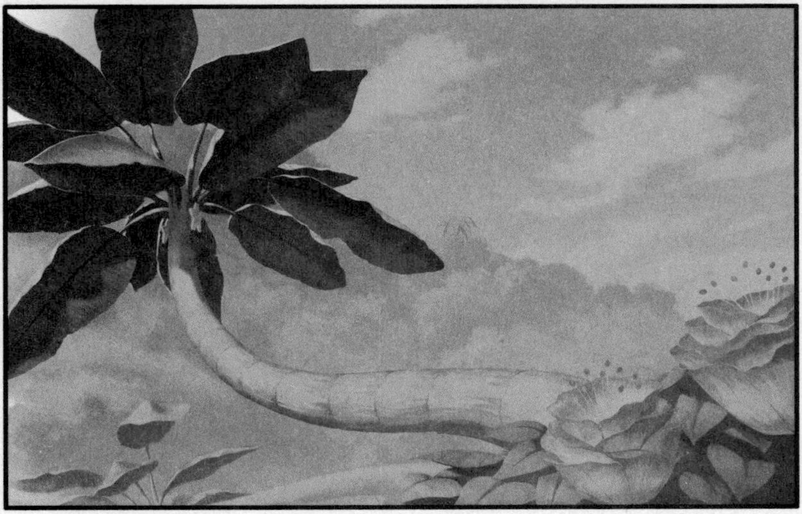

THINKING OF YOU, WHEREVER YOU ARE.

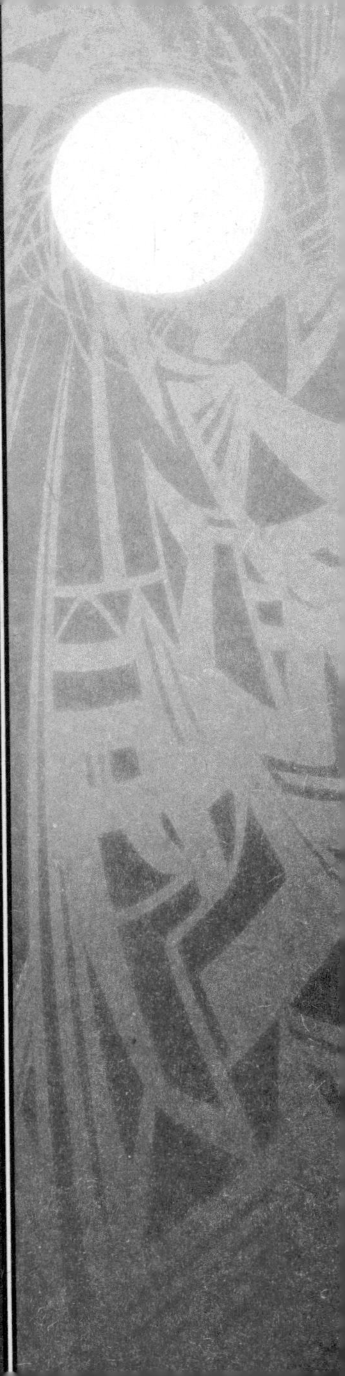

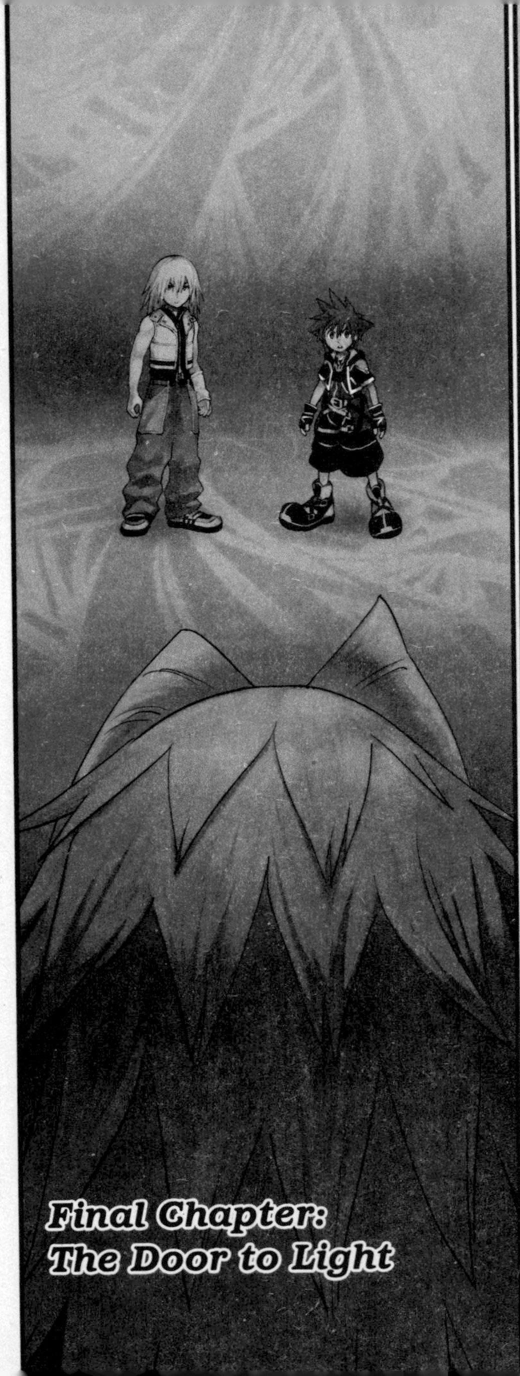

Final Chapter: The Door to Light

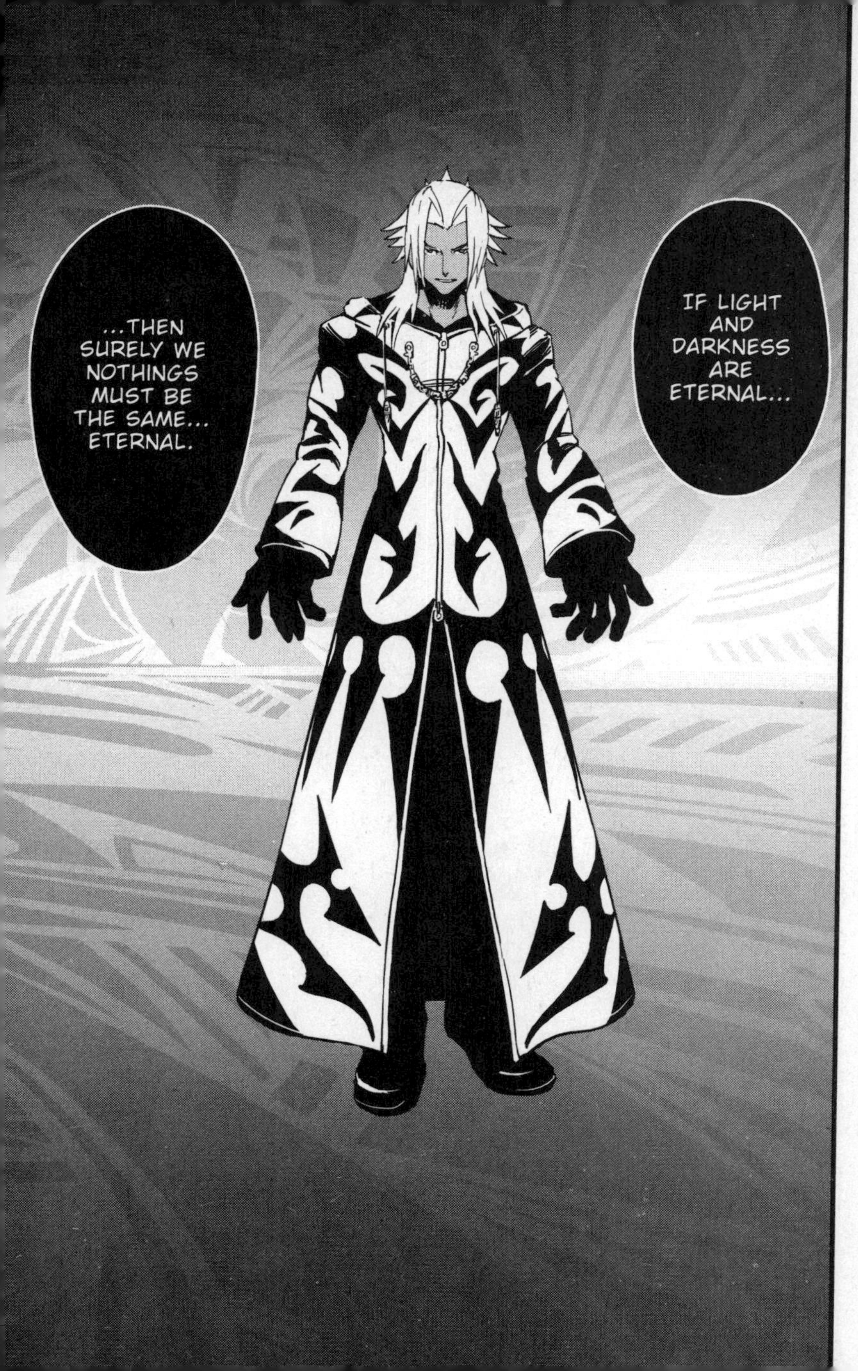
IF LIGHT AND DARKNESS ARE ETERNAL...
...THEN SURELY WE NOTHINGS MUST BE THE SAME... ETERNAL.

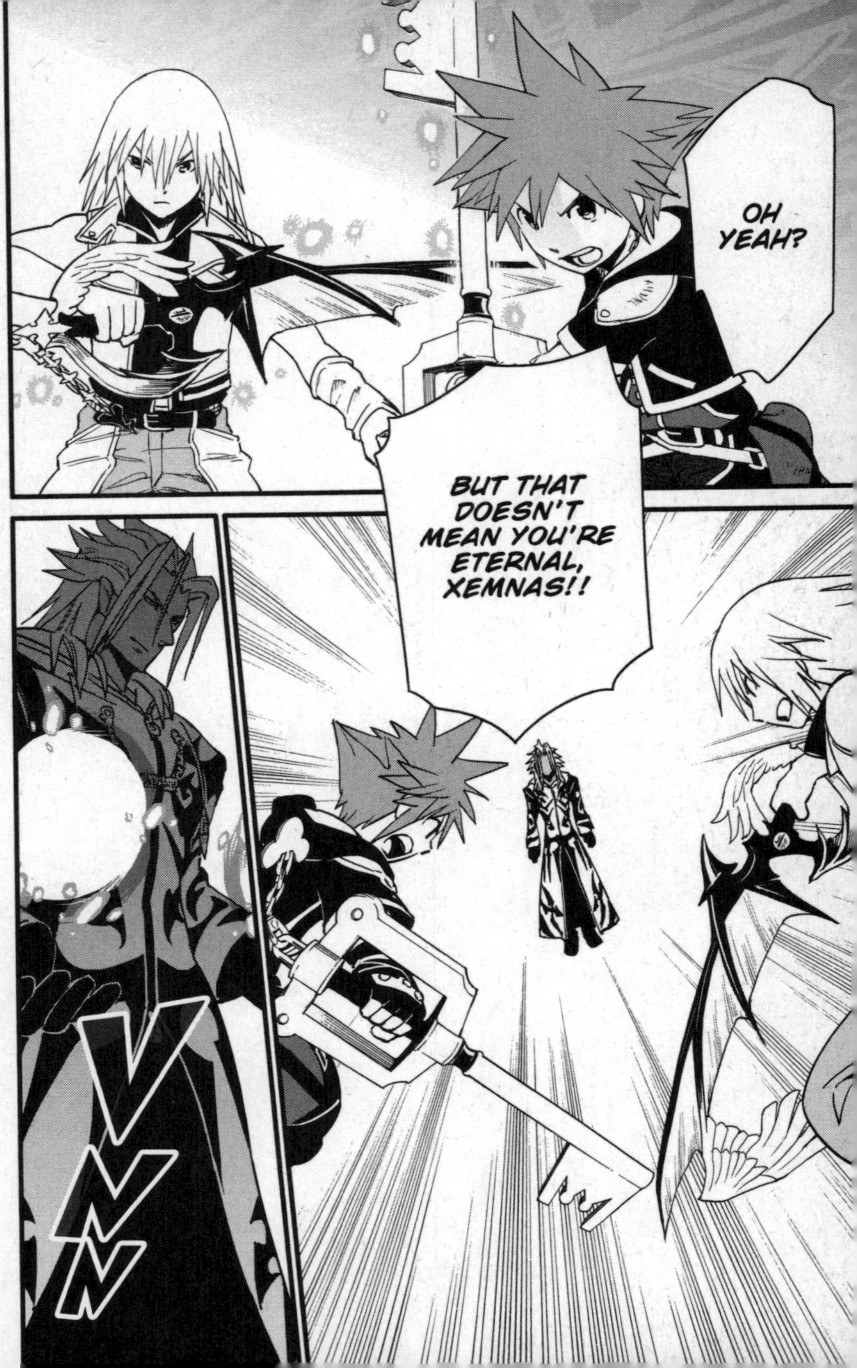
OH YEAH?
BUT THAT DOESN'T MEAN YOU'RE ETERNAL, XEMNAS!!

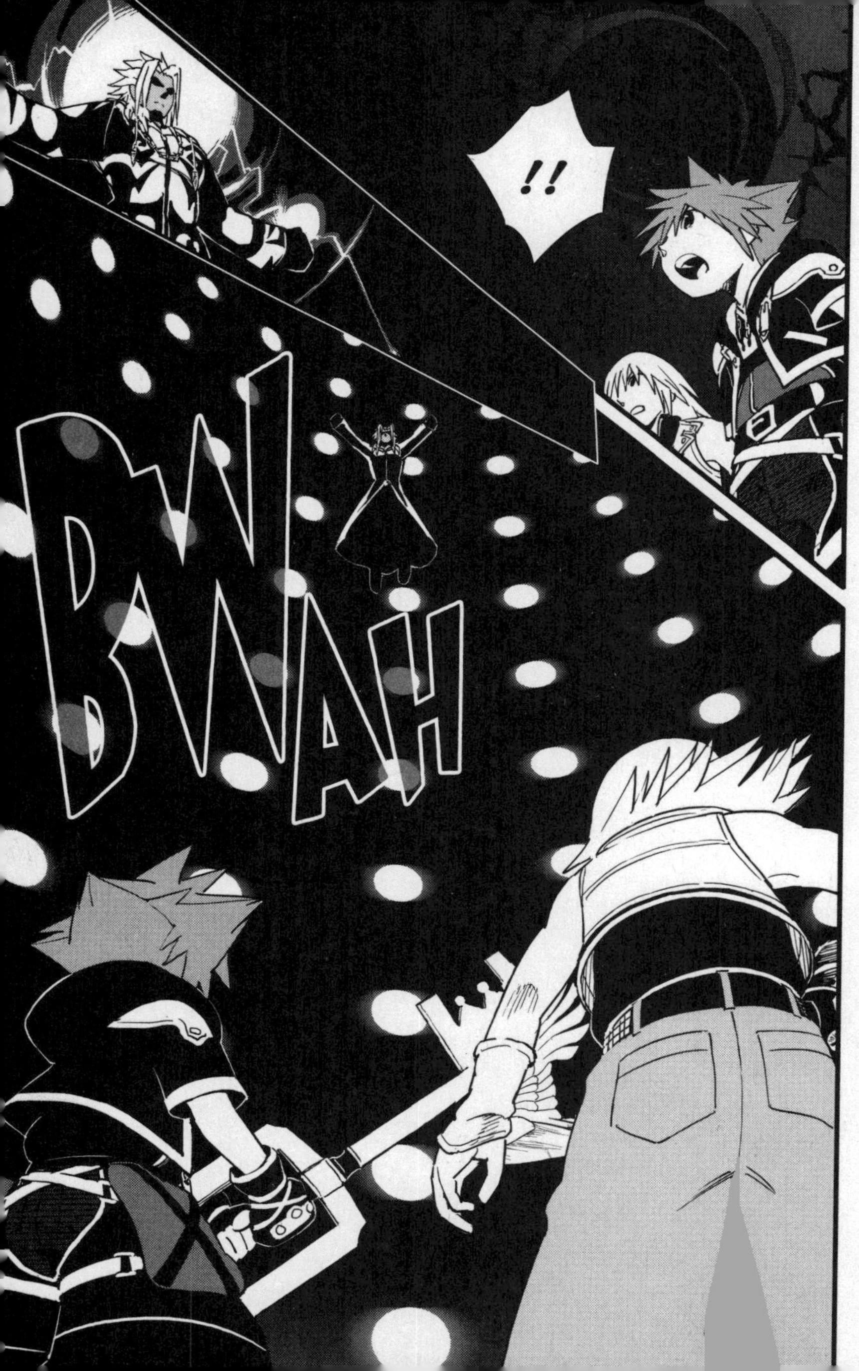
!!
BWAH

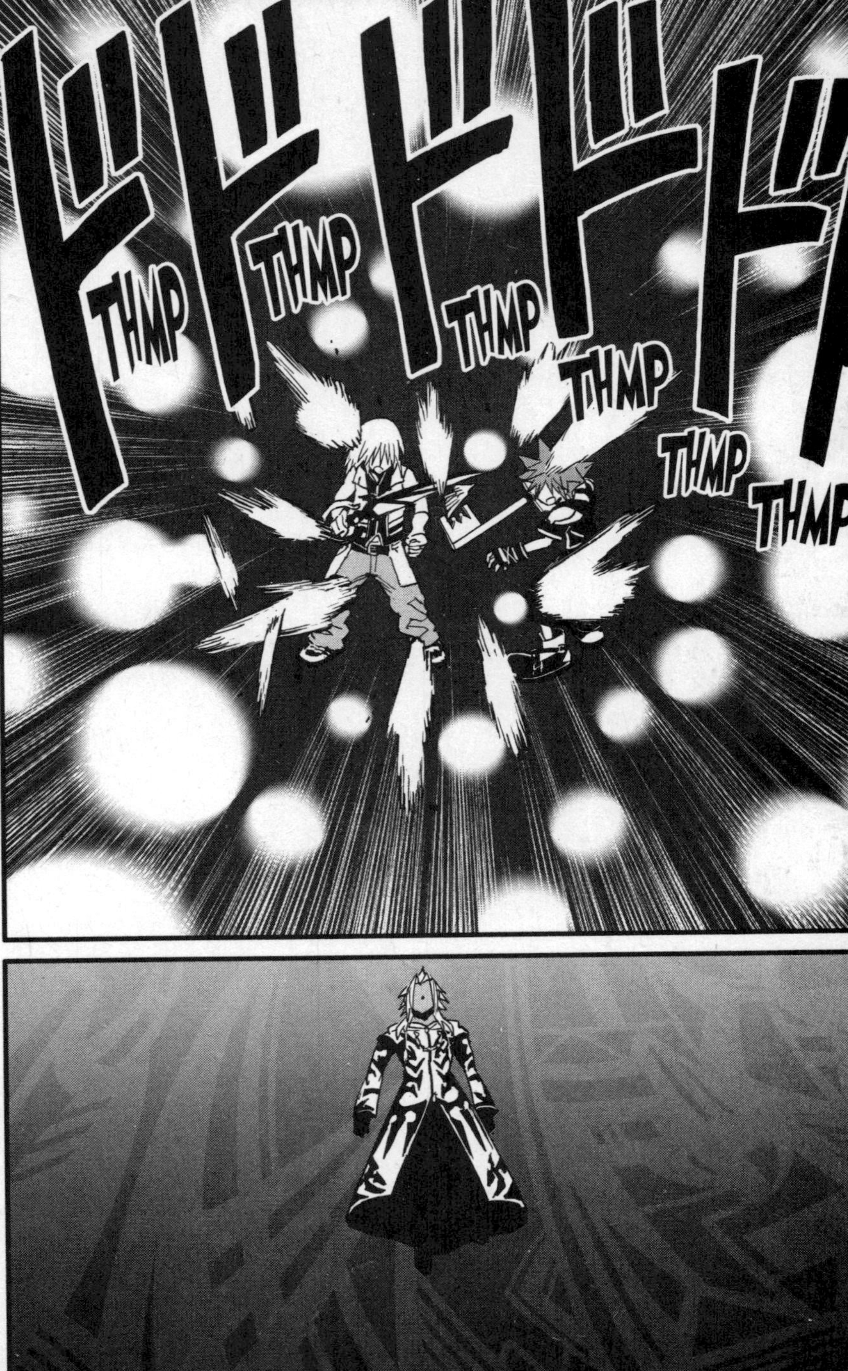
THMP
THMP
THMP
THMP
THMP
THMP

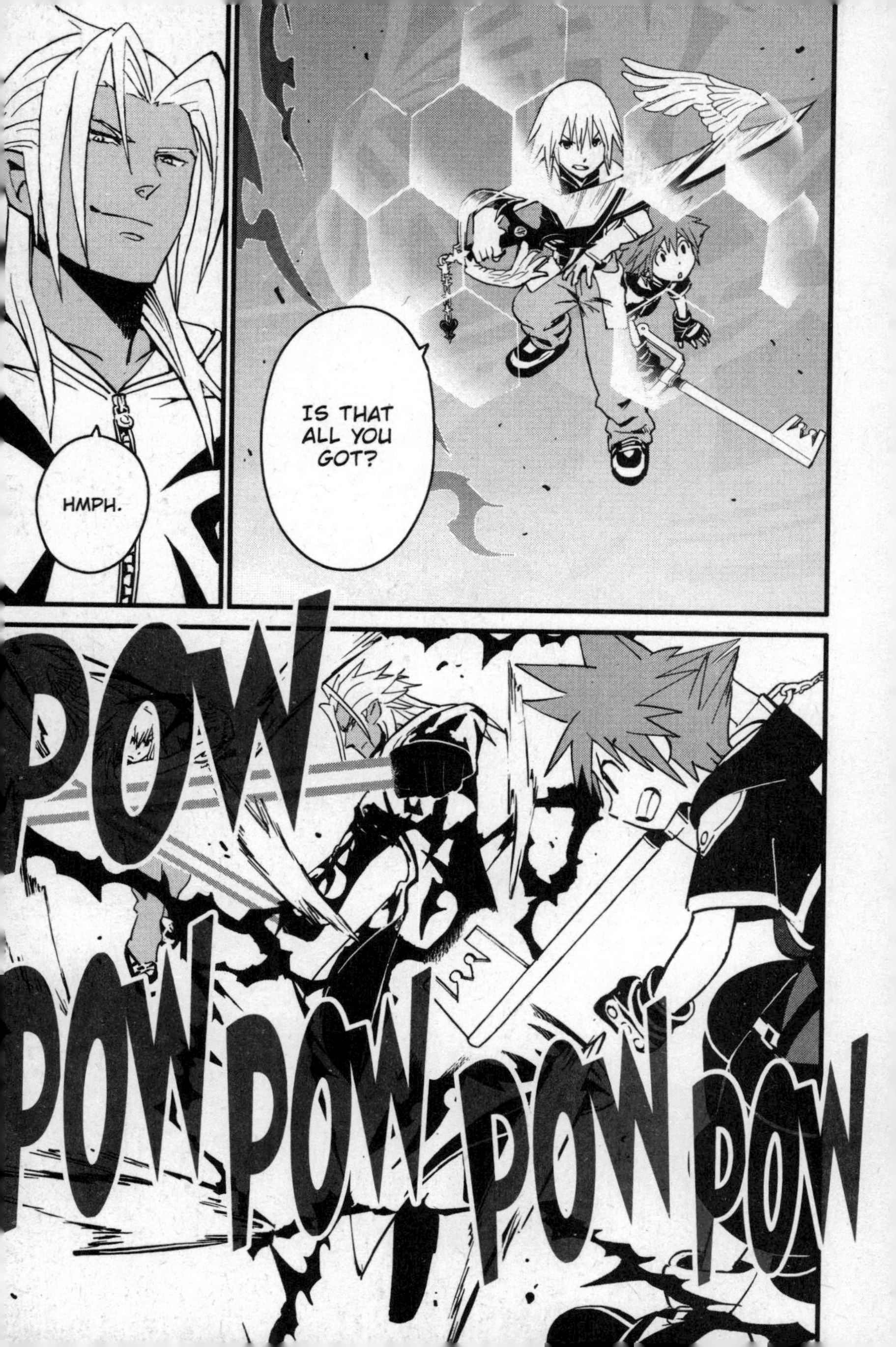
IS THAT ALL YOU GOT?
HMPH.
POW
POW POW POW POW

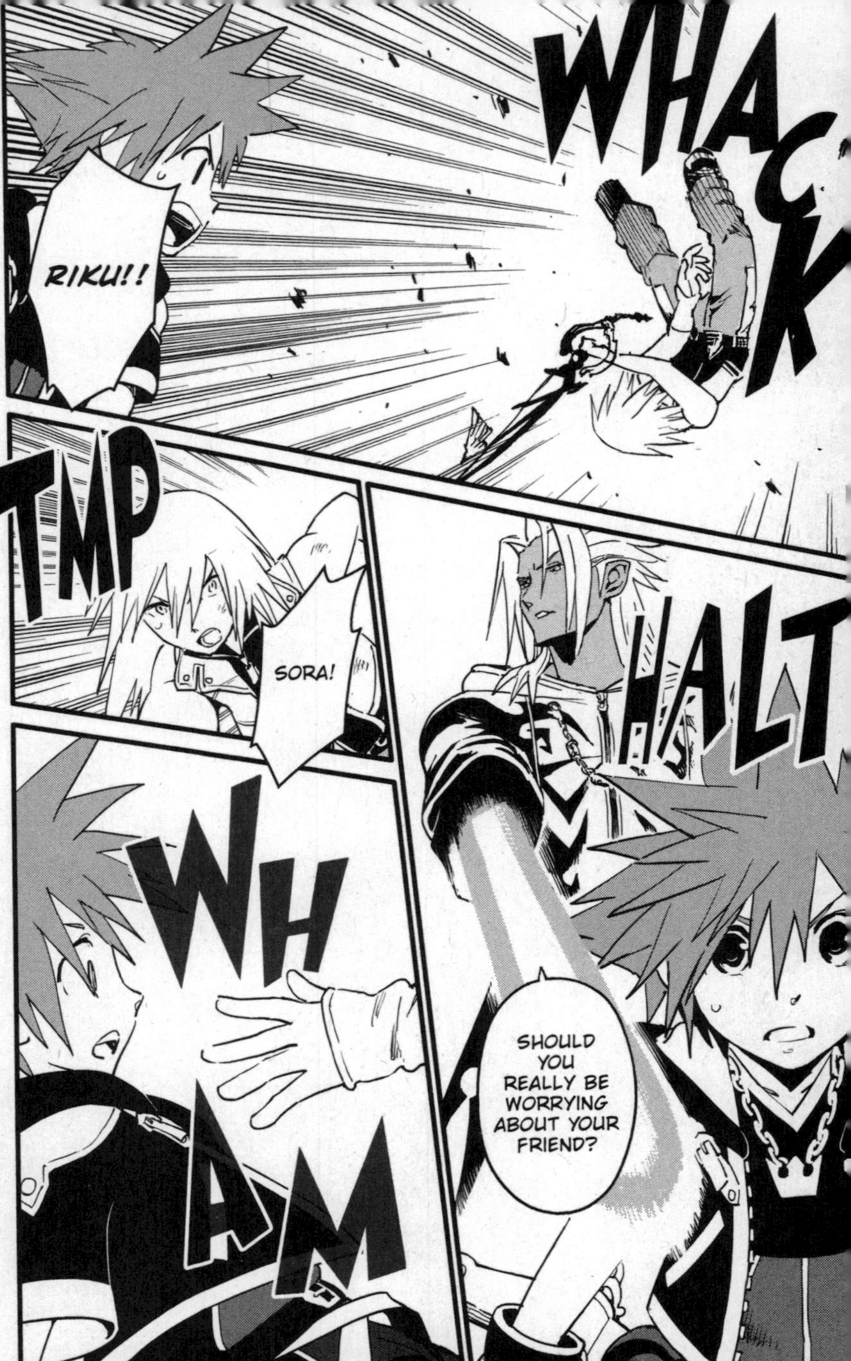
WHACK
RIKU!!
HALT
SHOULD YOU REALLY BE WORRYING ABOUT YOUR FRIEND?
TMP
SORA!
WHAM

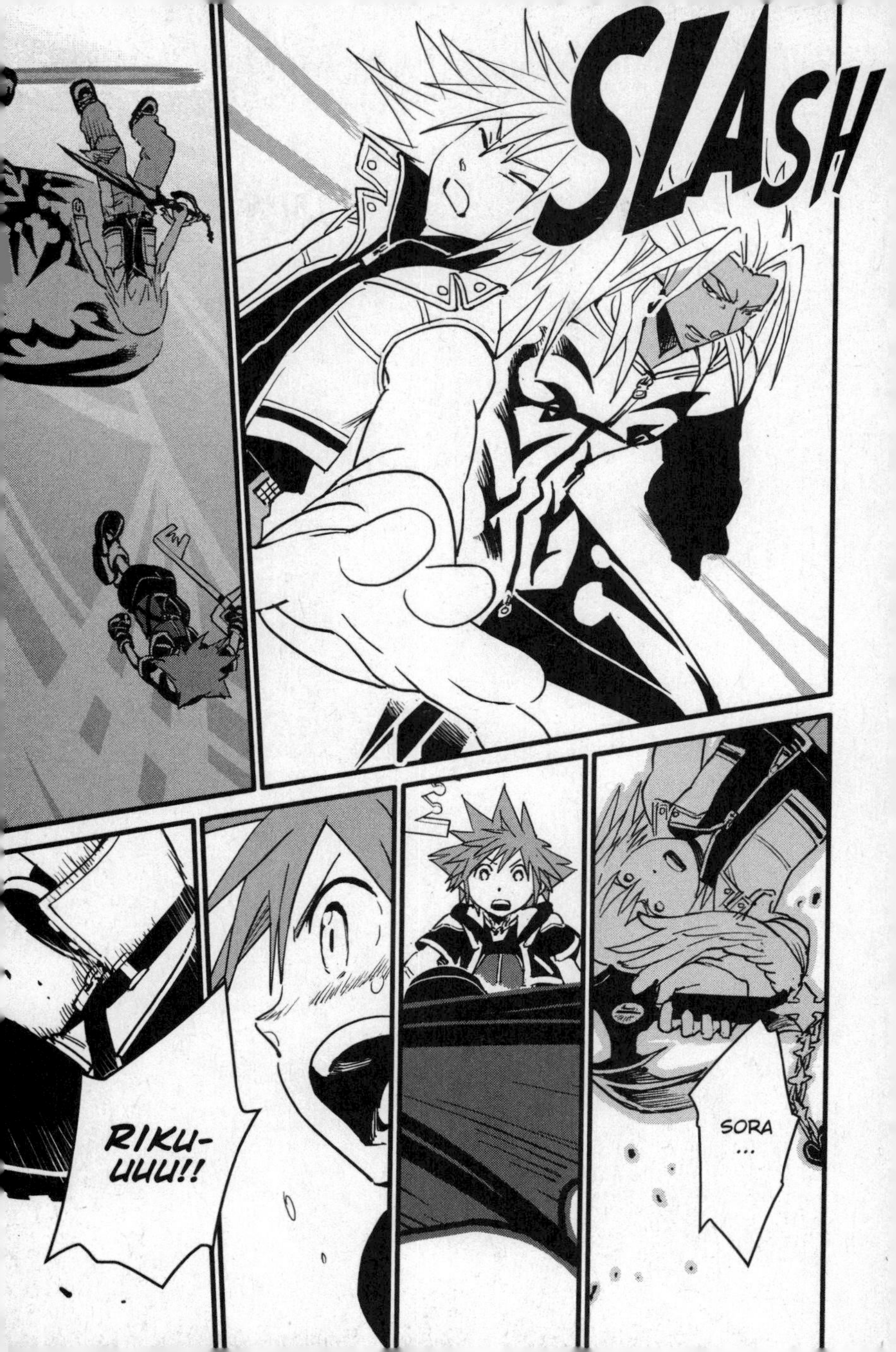
SLASH
SORA ...
RIKU-UUU!!

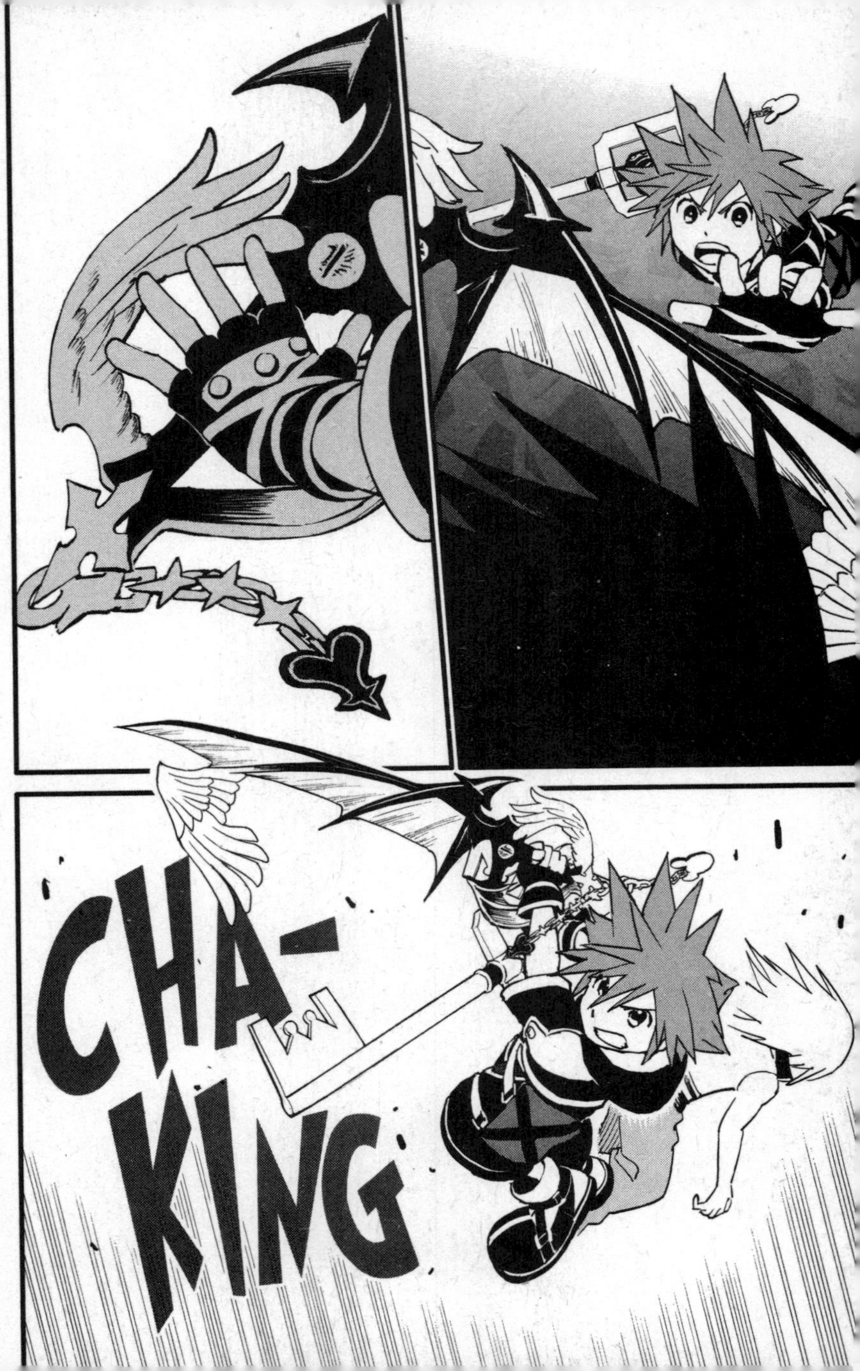
CHA-
KING

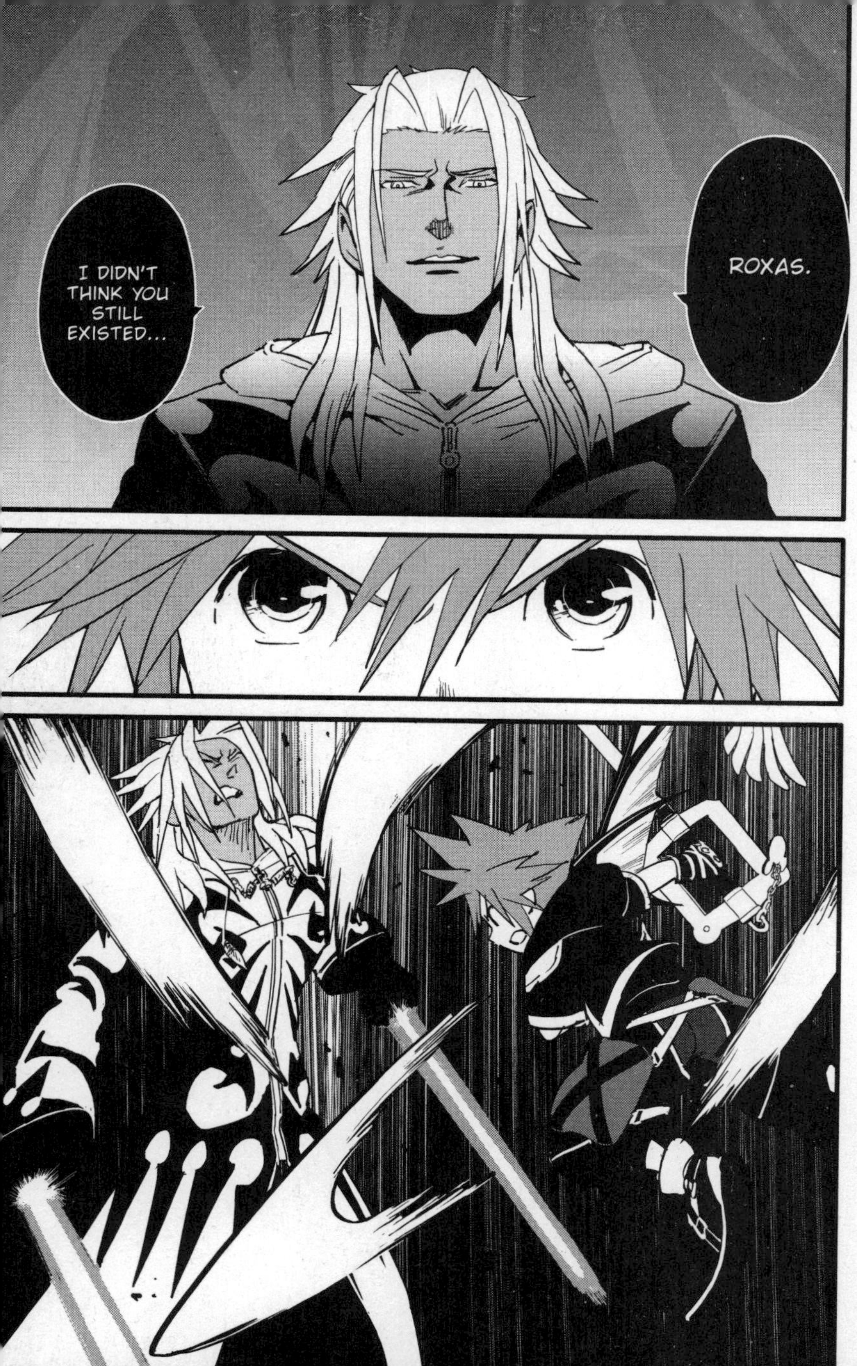
ROXAS.
I DIDN'T THINK YOU STILL EXISTED...

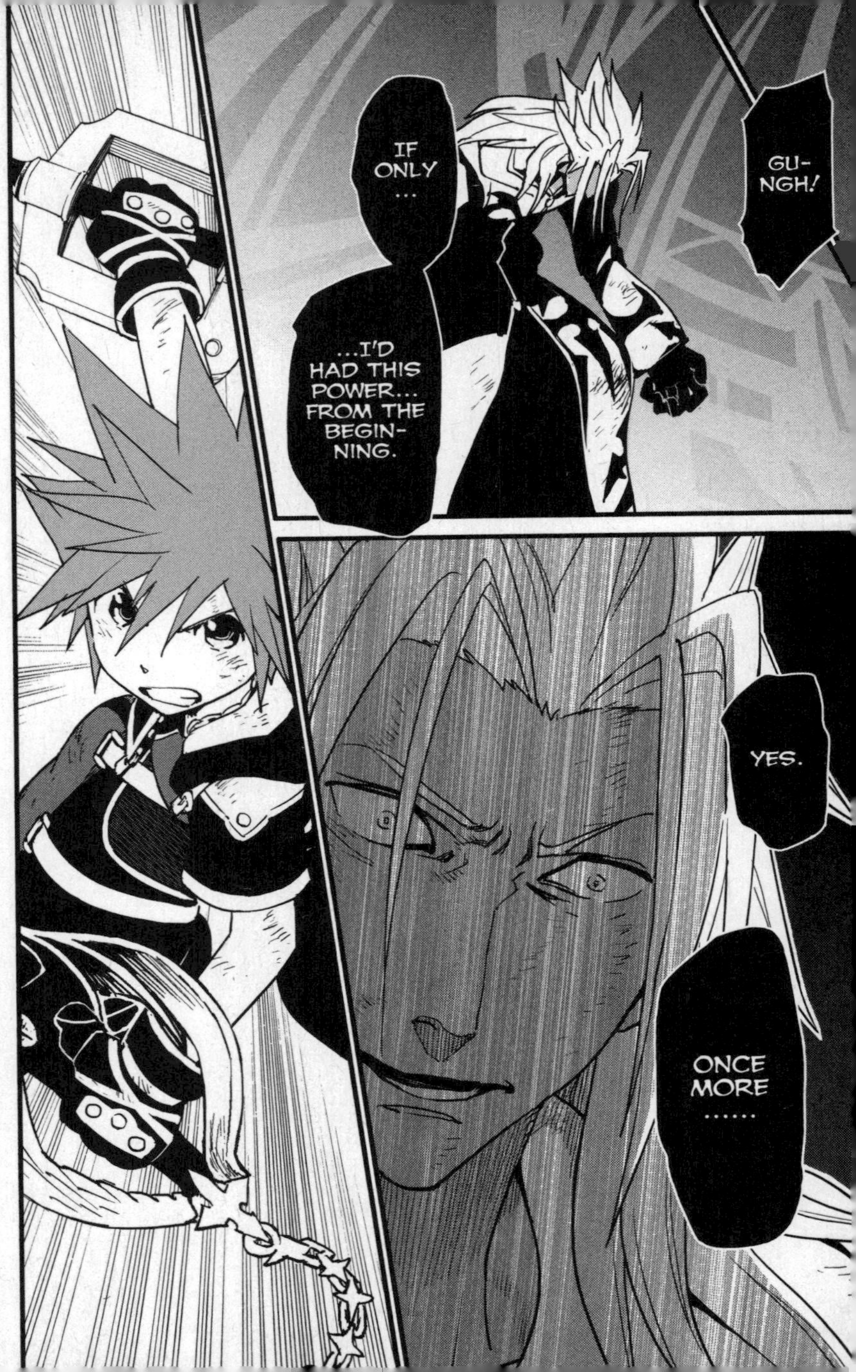
GU-NGH!
IF ONLY...
...I'D HAD THIS POWER... FROM THE BEGIN-NING.
YES.
ONCE MORE......

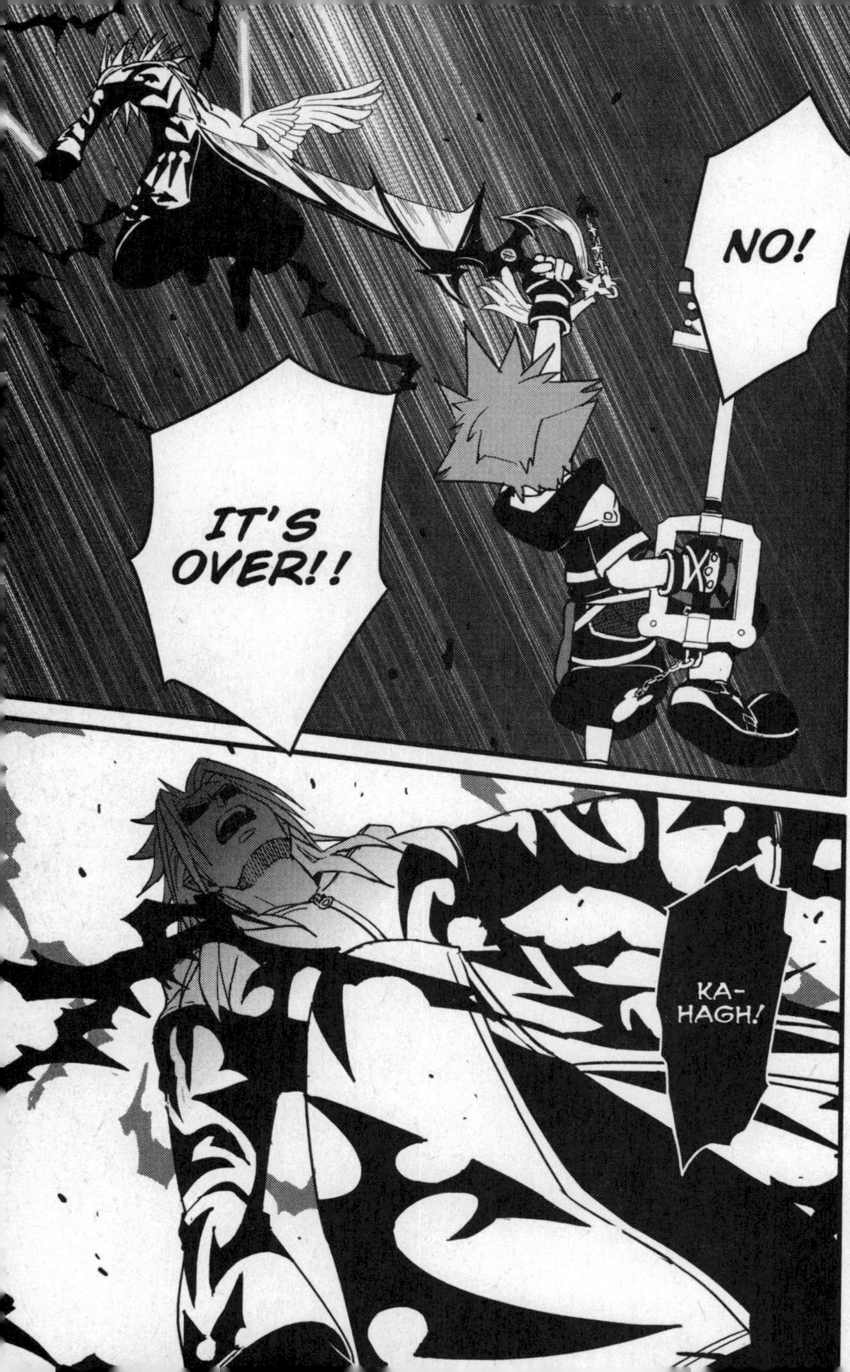
NO!
IT'S OVER!!
KA-HAGH!

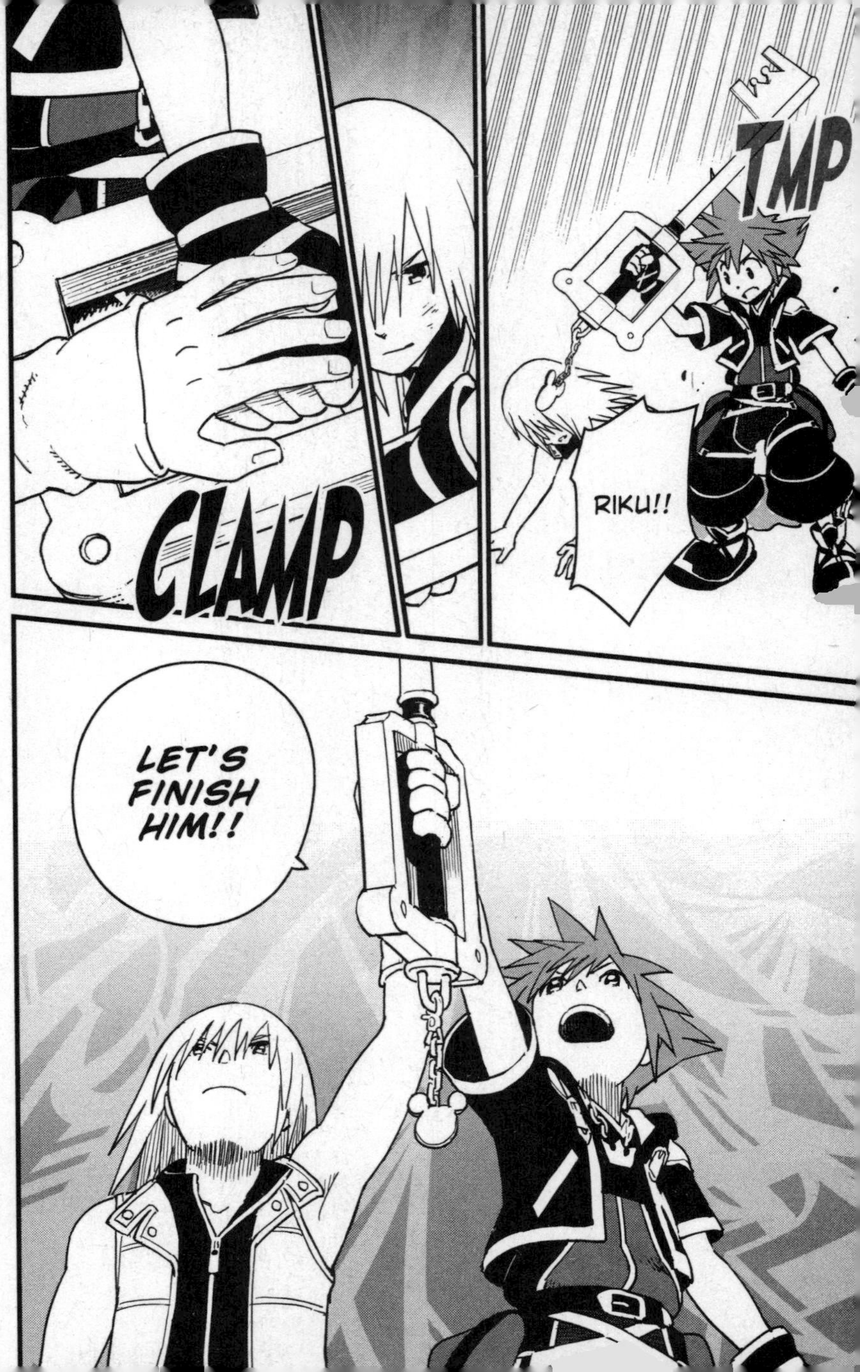
TMP
RIKU!!
CLAMP
LET'S FINISH HIM!!

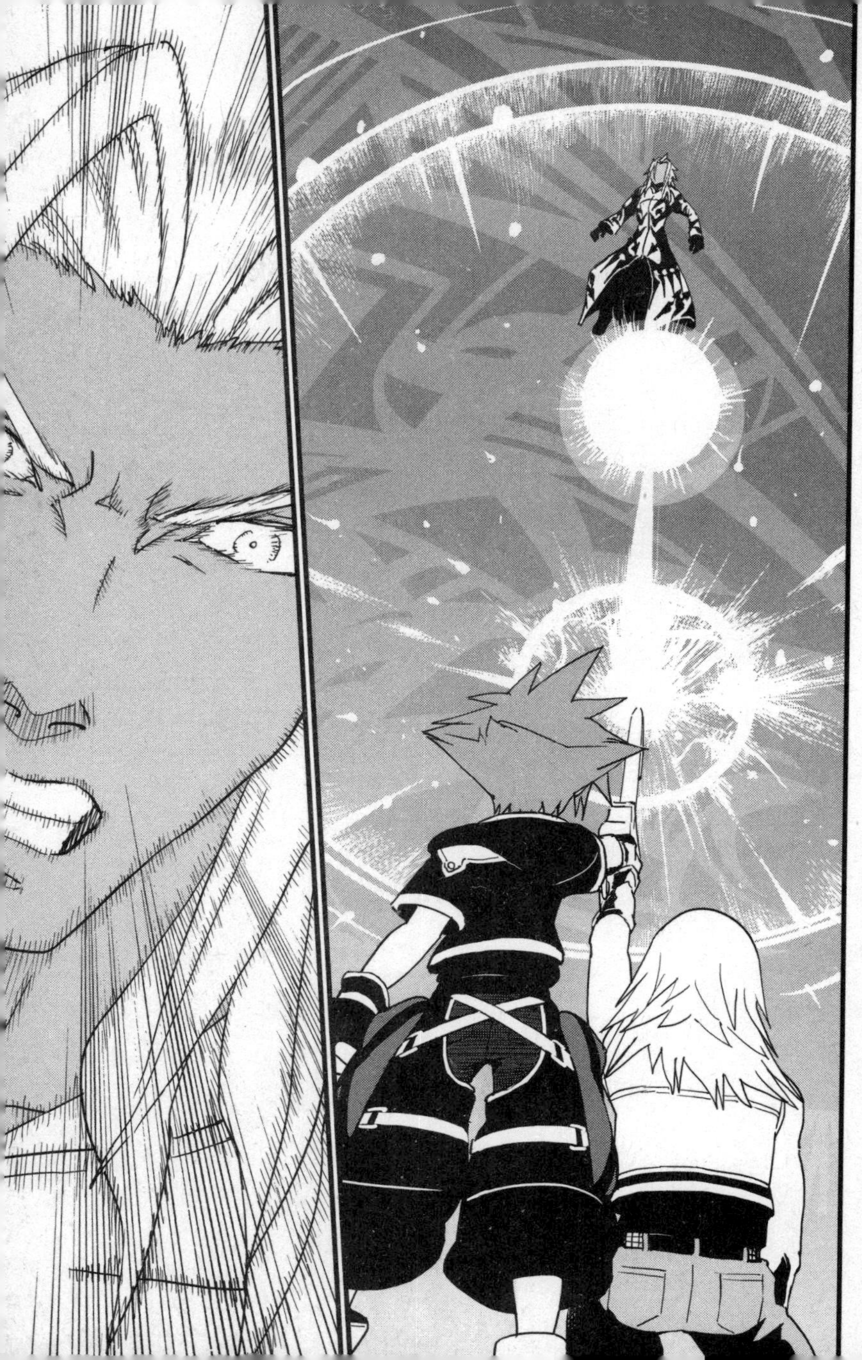

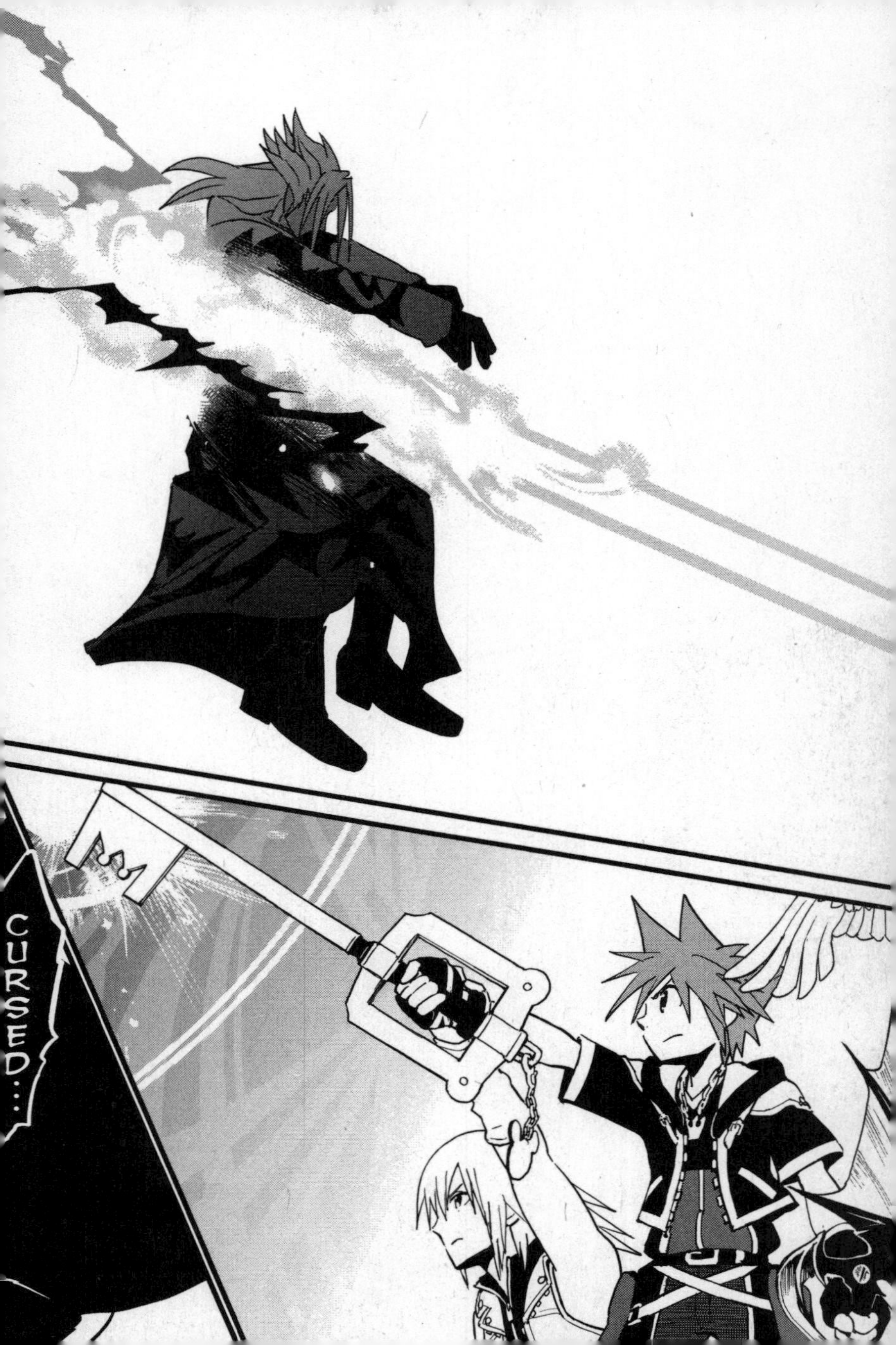
CURSED...

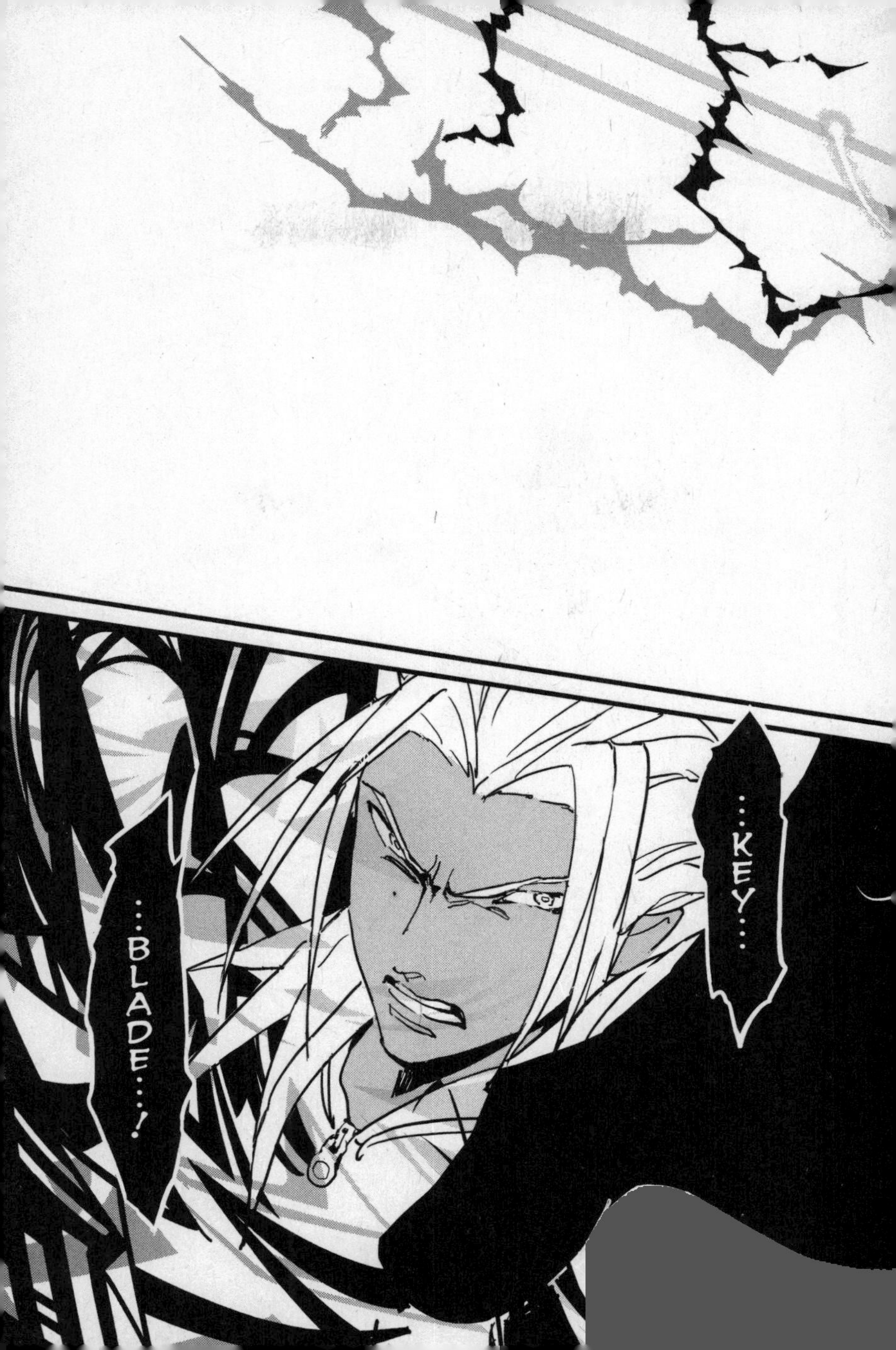
...KEY...
...BLADE...!

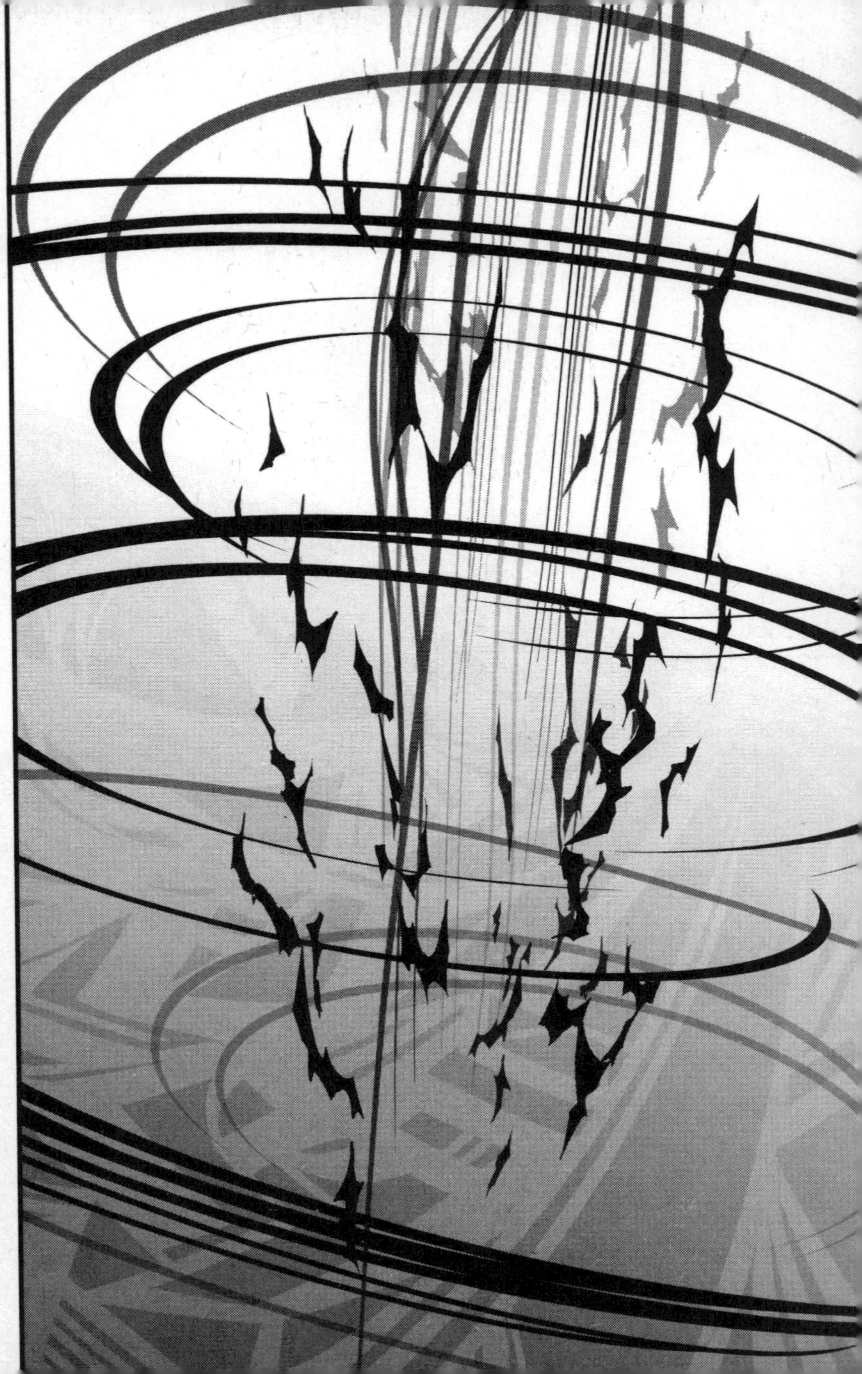

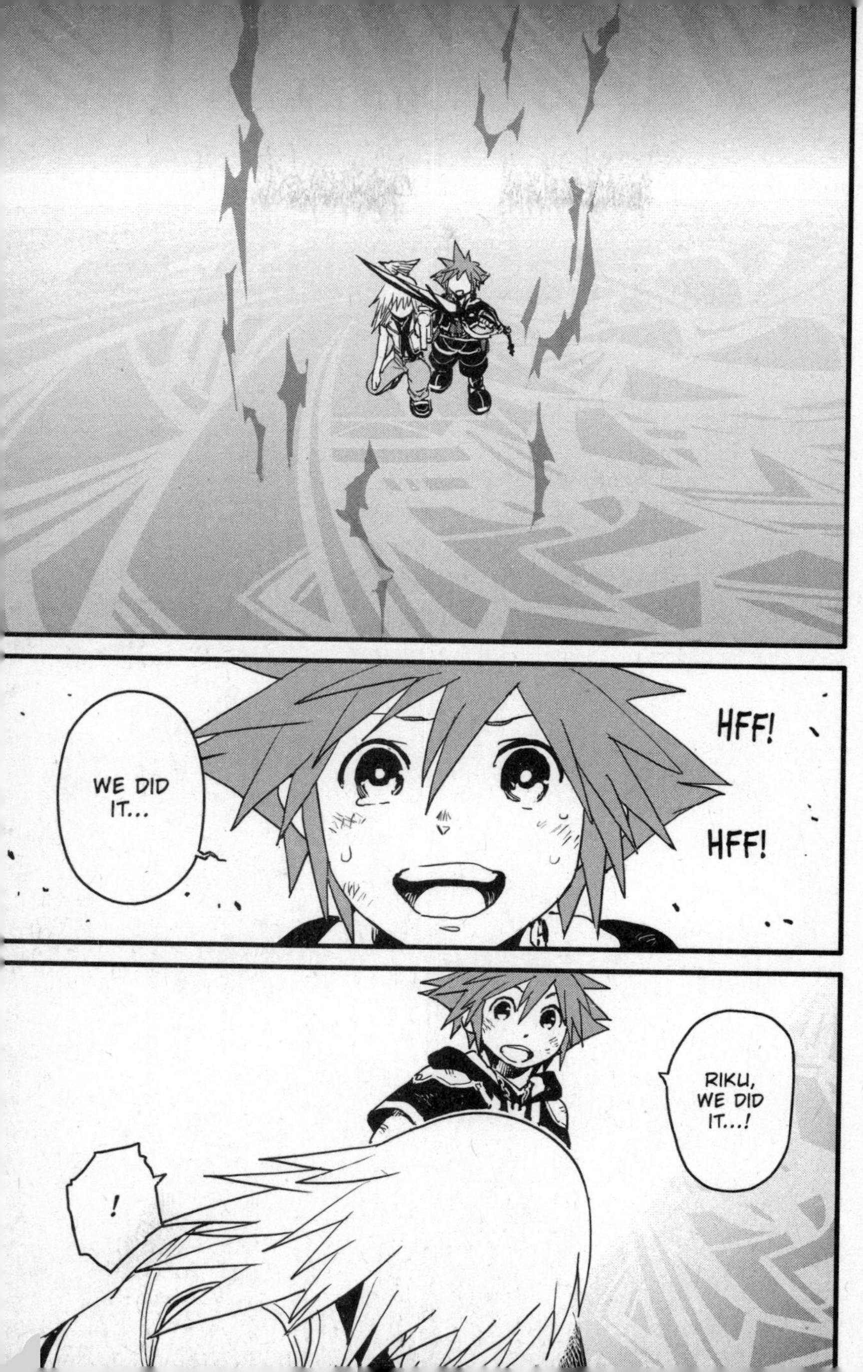
HFF!
HFF!
WE DID IT...
RIKU, WE DID IT...!
!

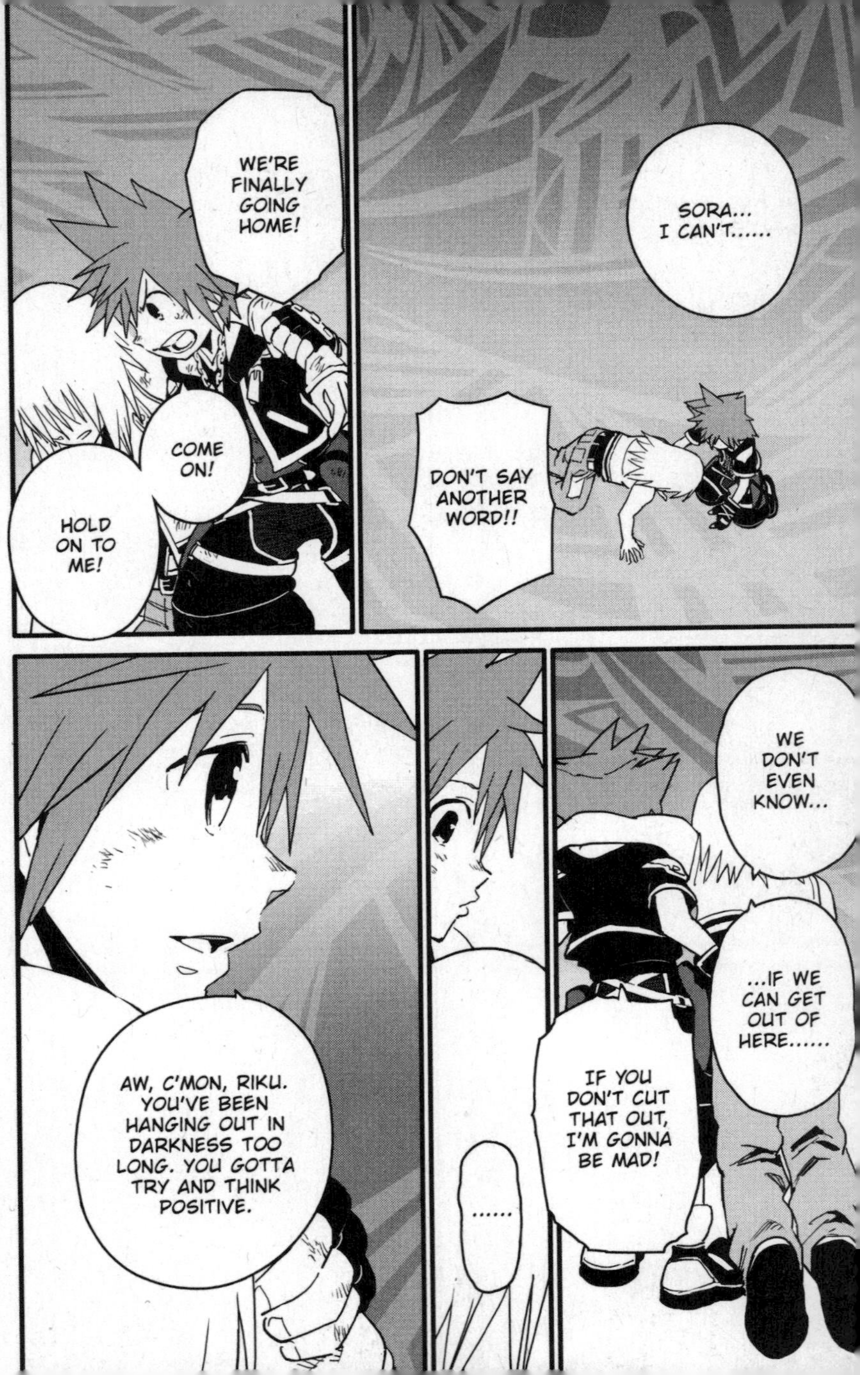
SORA... I CAN'T......
DON'T SAY ANOTHER WORD!!
WE'RE FINALLY GOING HOME!
COME ON!
HOLD ON TO ME!
WE DON'T EVEN KNOW...
...IF WE CAN GET OUT OF HERE......
IF YOU DON'T CUT THAT OUT, I'M GONNA BE MAD!
......
AW, C'MON, RIKU. YOU'VE BEEN HANGING OUT IN DARKNESS TOO LONG. YOU GOTTA TRY AND THINK POSITIVE.

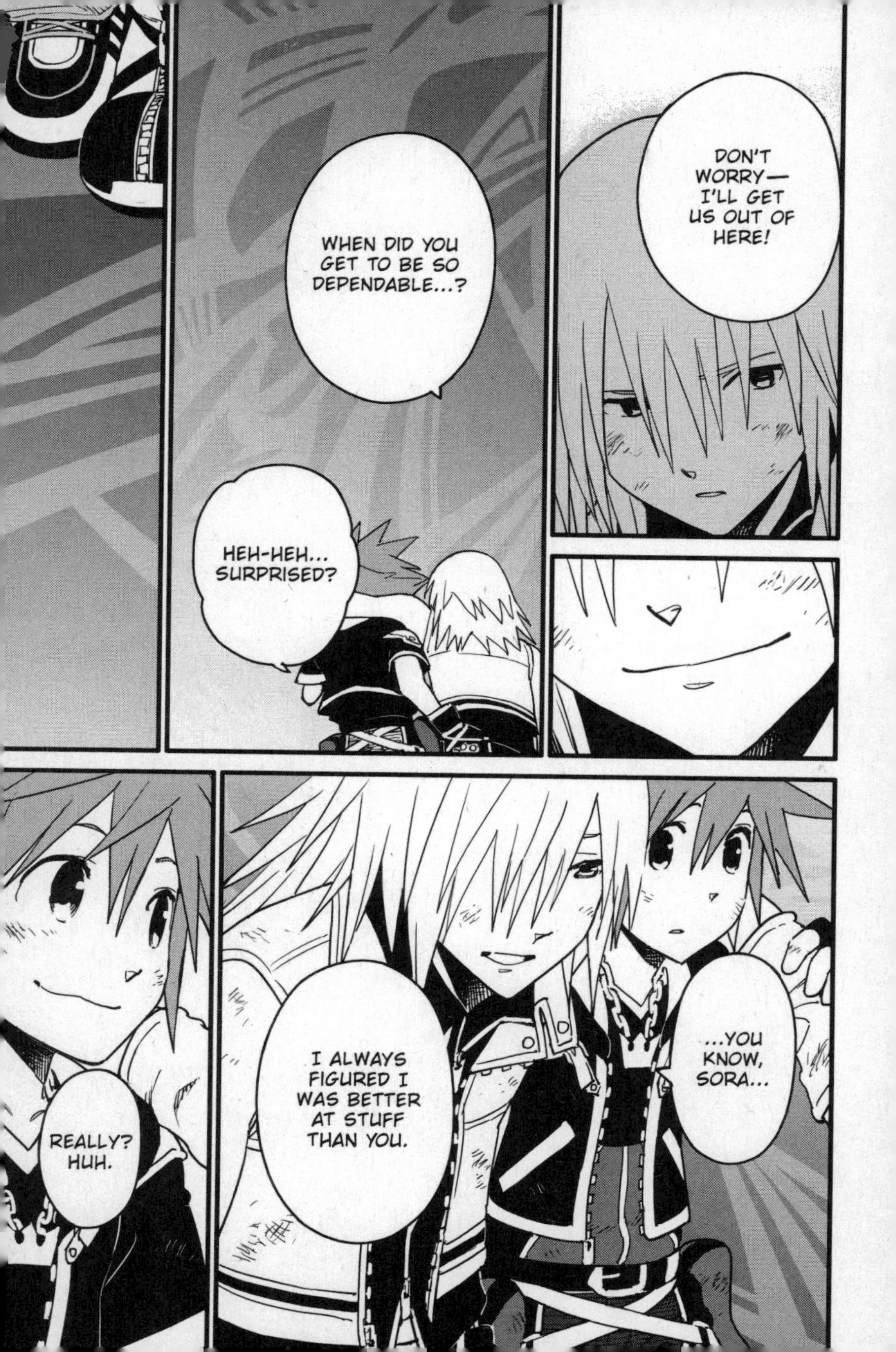
DON'T WORRY— I'LL GET US OUT OF HERE!
WHEN DID YOU GET TO BE SO DEPENDABLE...?
HEH-HEH... SURPRISED?
...YOU KNOW, SORA...
I ALWAYS FIGURED I WAS BETTER AT STUFF THAN YOU.
REALLY? HUH.

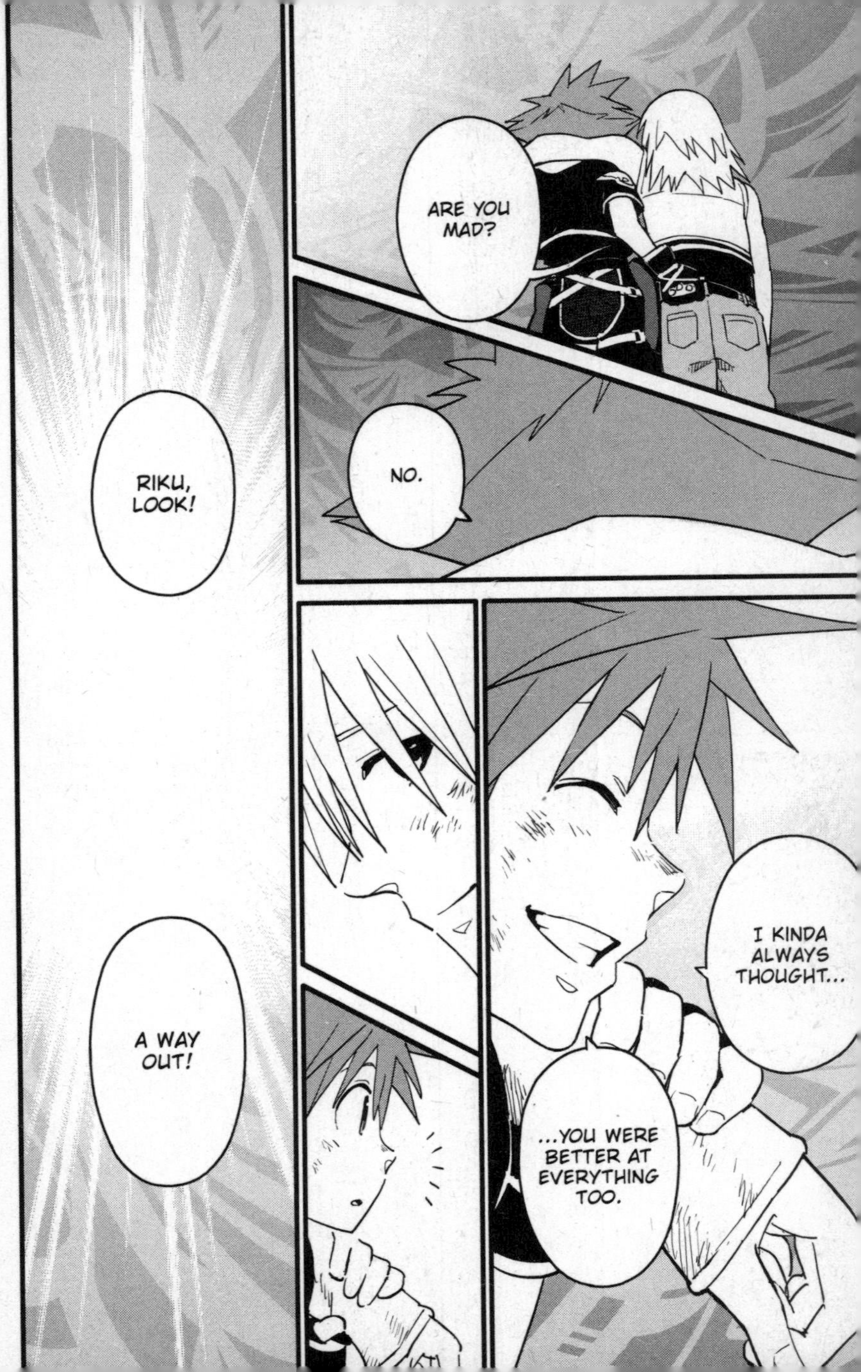
ARE YOU MAD?
NO.
I KINDA ALWAYS THOUGHT...
...YOU WERE BETTER AT EVERYTHING TOO.
RIKU, LOOK!
A WAY OUT!

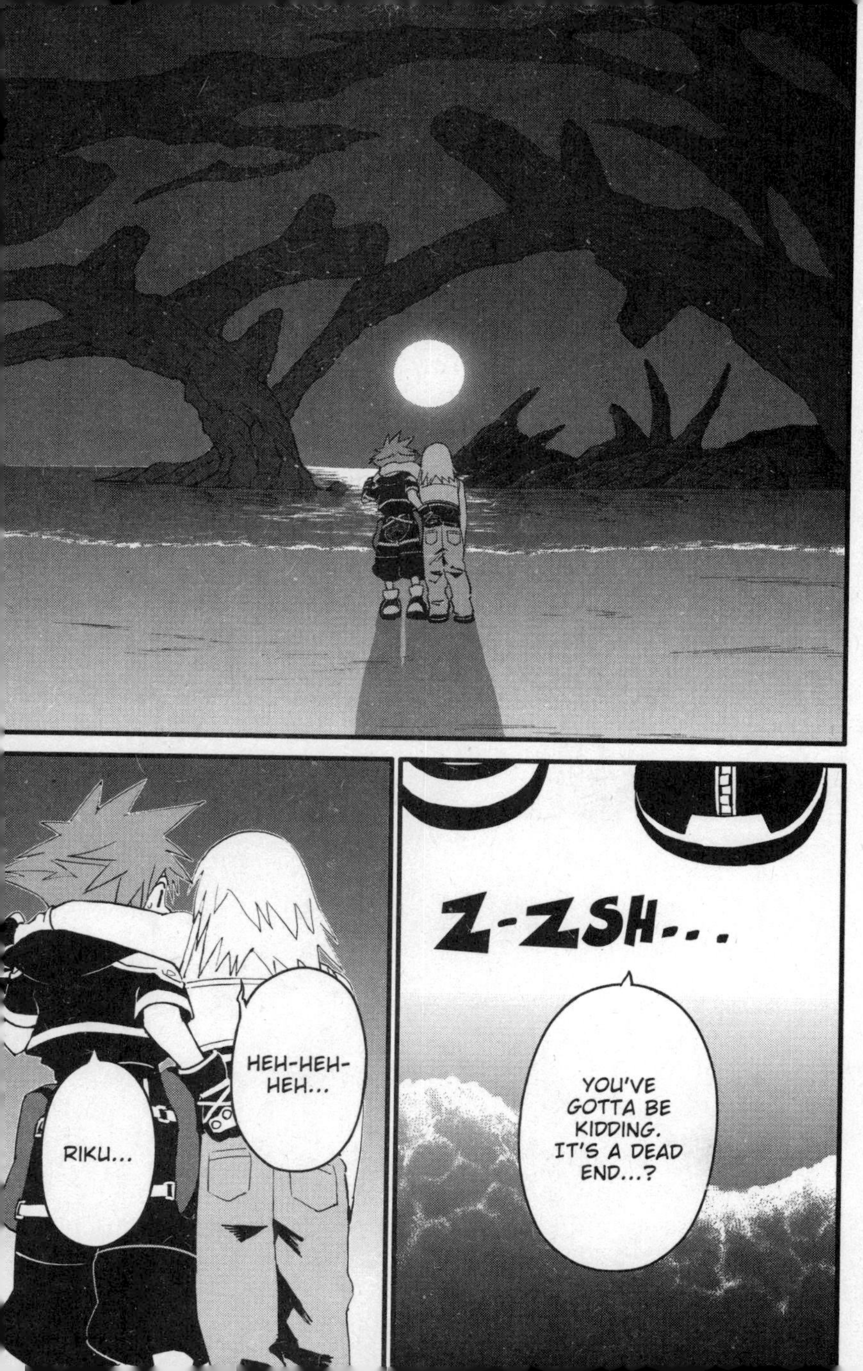
Z-ZSH...
YOU'VE GOTTA BE KIDDING. IT'S A DEAD END...?
HEH-HEH-HEH...
RIKU...

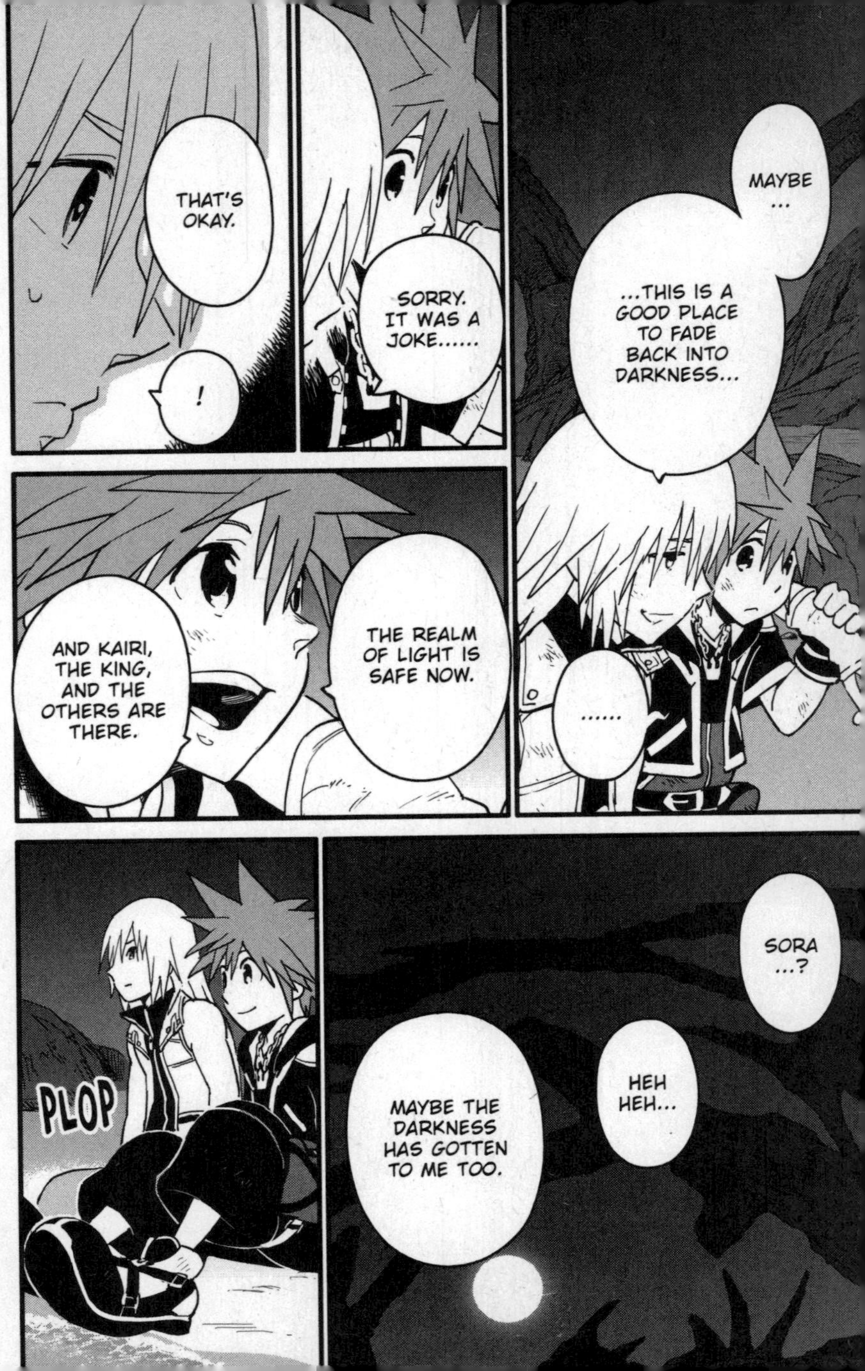
MAYBE ...
...THIS IS A GOOD PLACE TO FADE BACK INTO DARKNESS...
......
SORRY. IT WAS A JOKE......
THAT'S OKAY.
!
THE REALM OF LIGHT IS SAFE NOW.
AND KAIRI, THE KING, AND THE OTHERS ARE THERE.
SORA ...?
HEH HEH...
MAYBE THE DARKNESS HAS GOTTEN TO ME TOO.
PLOP

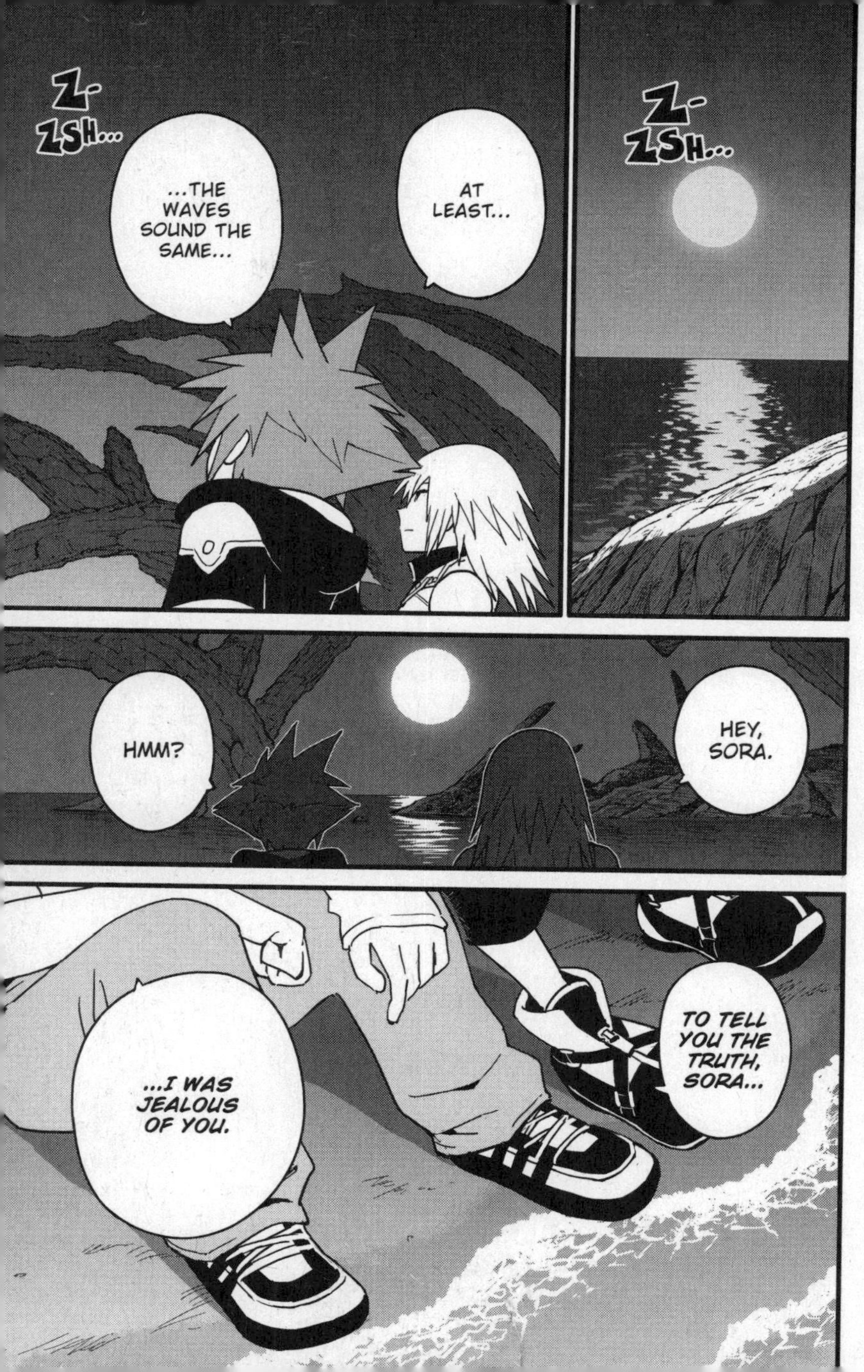

Z-ZSH...
Z-ZSH...
AT LEAST...
...THE WAVES SOUND THE SAME...
HEY, SORA.
HMM?
TO TELL YOU THE TRUTH, SORA...
...I WAS JEALOUS OF YOU.

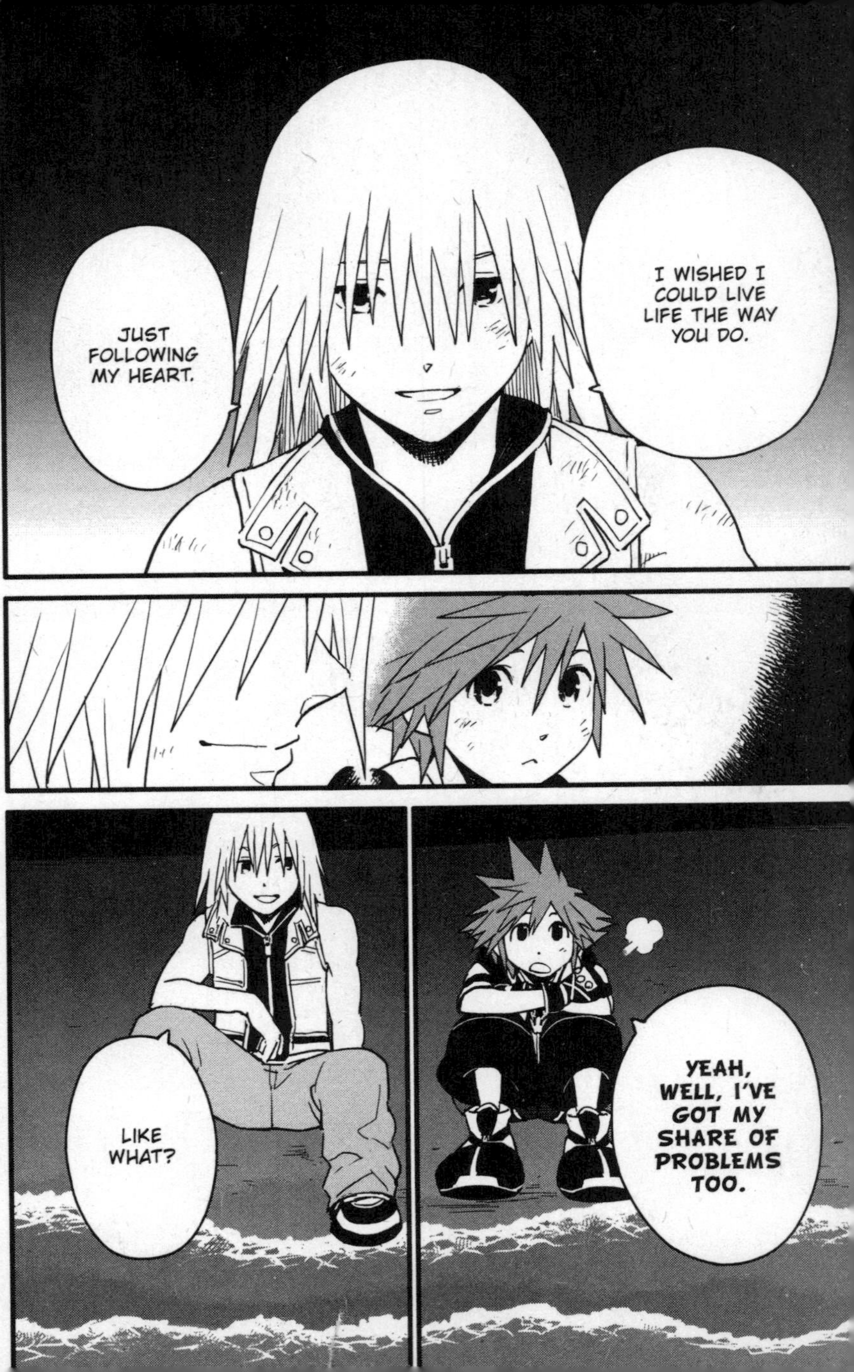
I WISHED I COULD LIVE LIFE THE WAY YOU DO.
JUST FOLLOWING MY HEART.
YEAH, WELL, I'VE GOT MY SHARE OF PROBLEMS TOO.
LIKE WHAT?

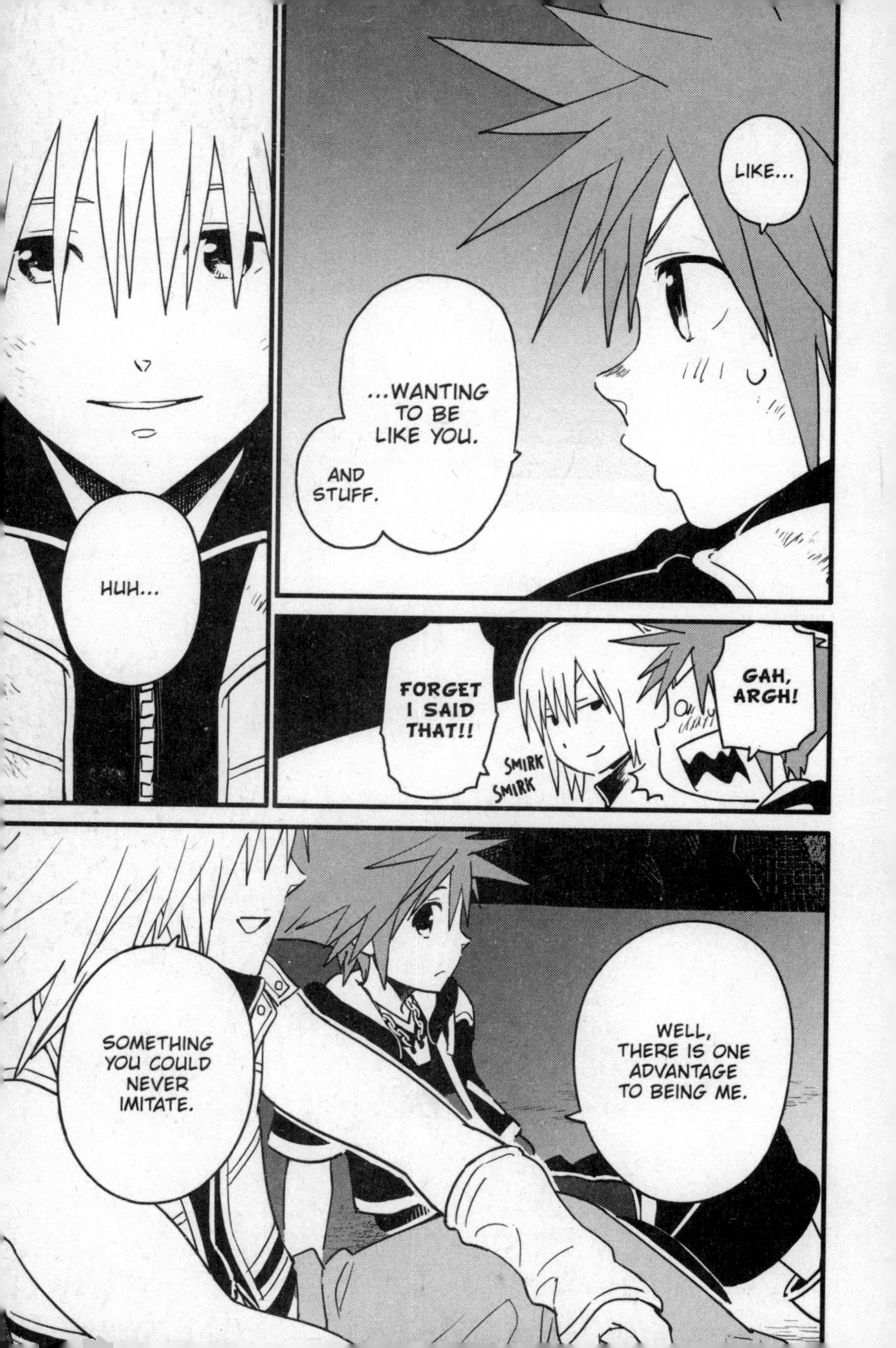
LIKE...
...WANTING TO BE LIKE YOU.
AND STUFF.
GAH, ARGH!
FORGET I SAID THAT!!
SMIRK SMIRK
HUH...
WELL, THERE IS ONE ADVANTAGE TO BEING ME.
SOMETHING YOU COULD NEVER IMITATE.

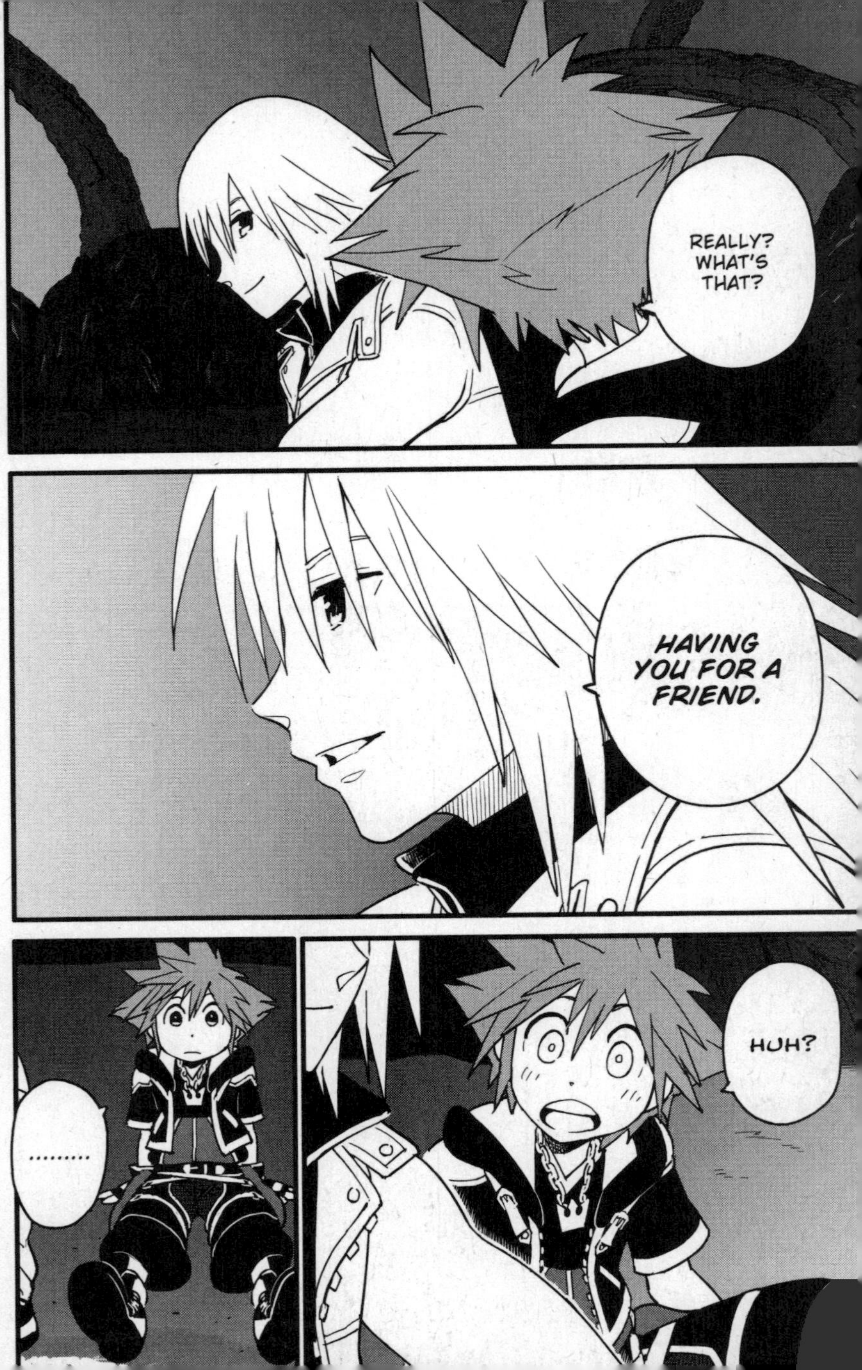
REALLY? WHAT'S THAT?
HAVING YOU FOR A FRIEND.
HUH?
....

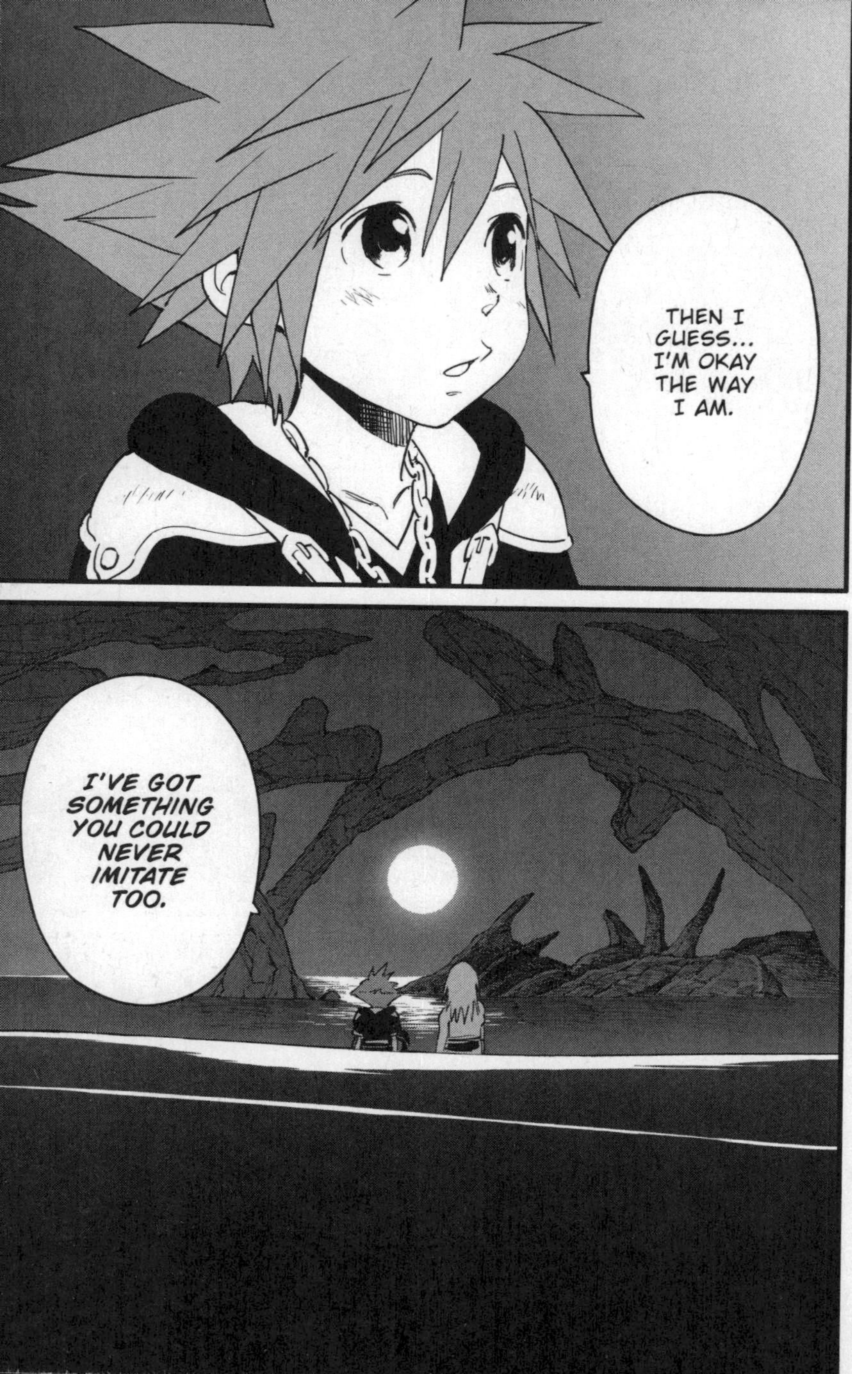
THEN I GUESS... I'M OKAY THE WAY I AM.
I'VE GOT SOMETHING YOU COULD NEVER IMITATE TOO.

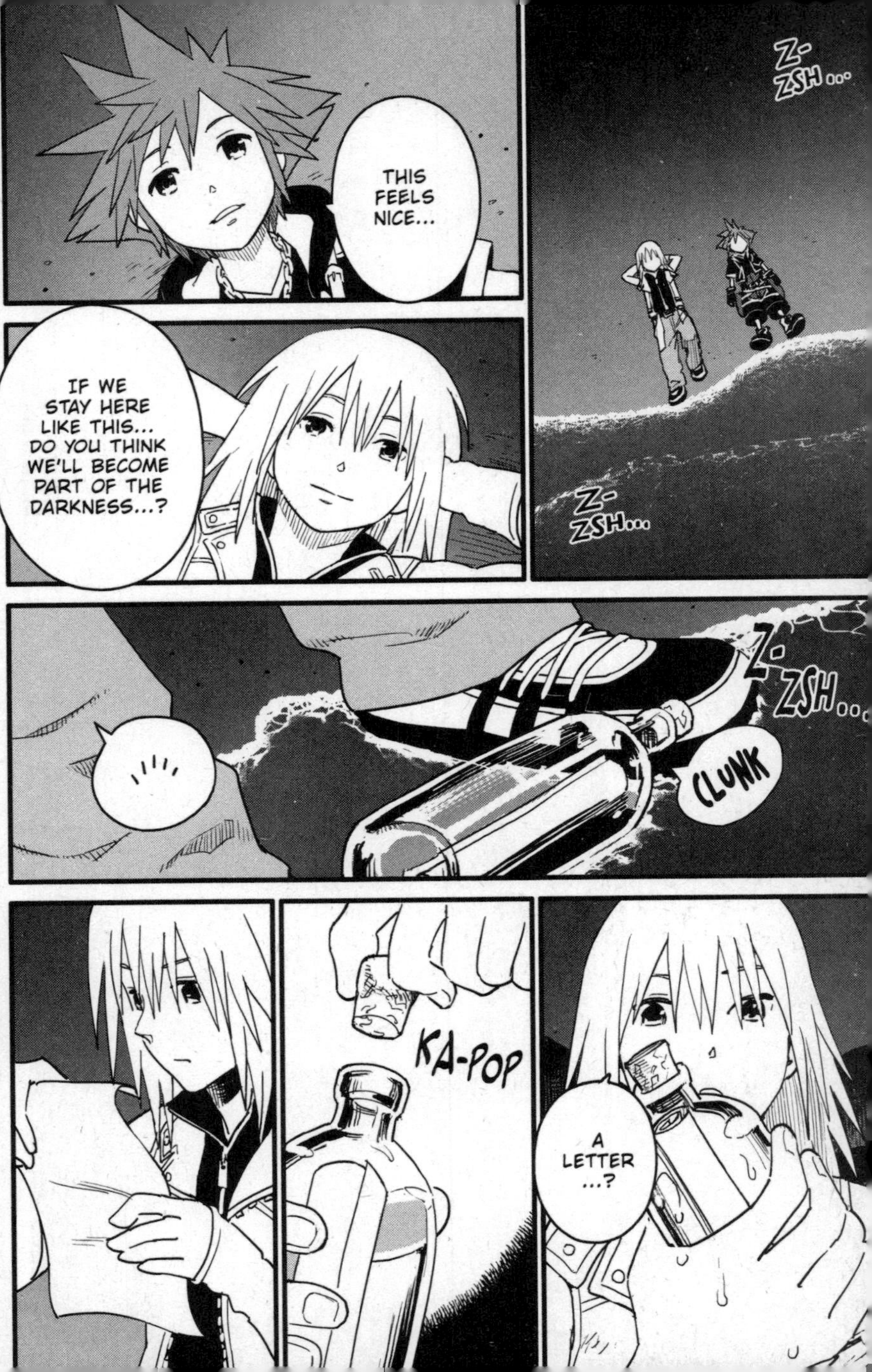
Z-ZSH...
Z-ZSH...
THIS FEELS NICE...
IF WE STAY HERE LIKE THIS... DO YOU THINK WE'LL BECOME PART OF THE DARKNESS...?
Z-ZSH...
CLUNK
A LETTER ...?
KA-POP

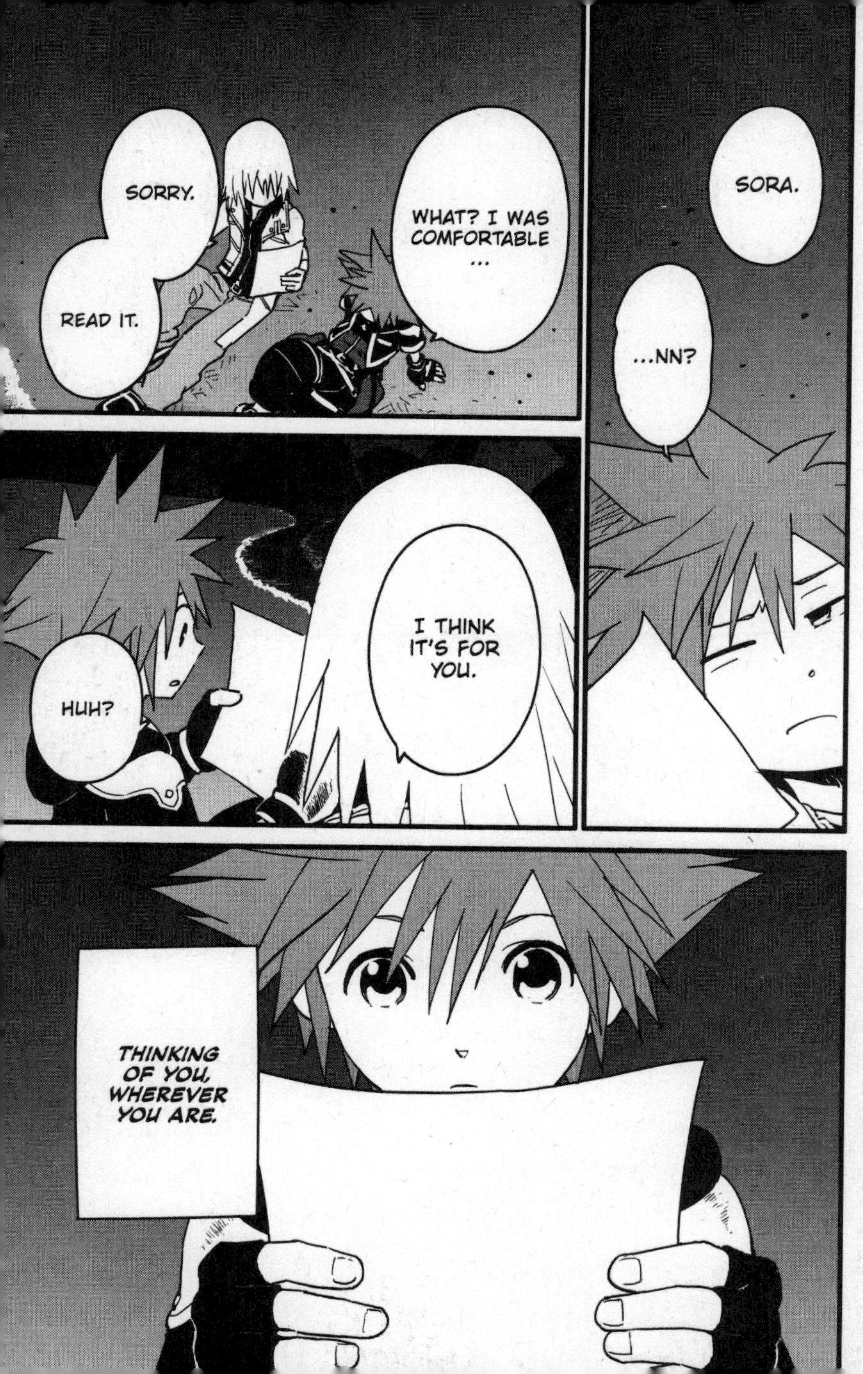
SORA.
...NN?
WHAT? I WAS COMFORTABLE ...
SORRY.
READ IT.
I THINK IT'S FOR YOU.
HUH?
THINKING OF YOU, WHEREVER YOU ARE.

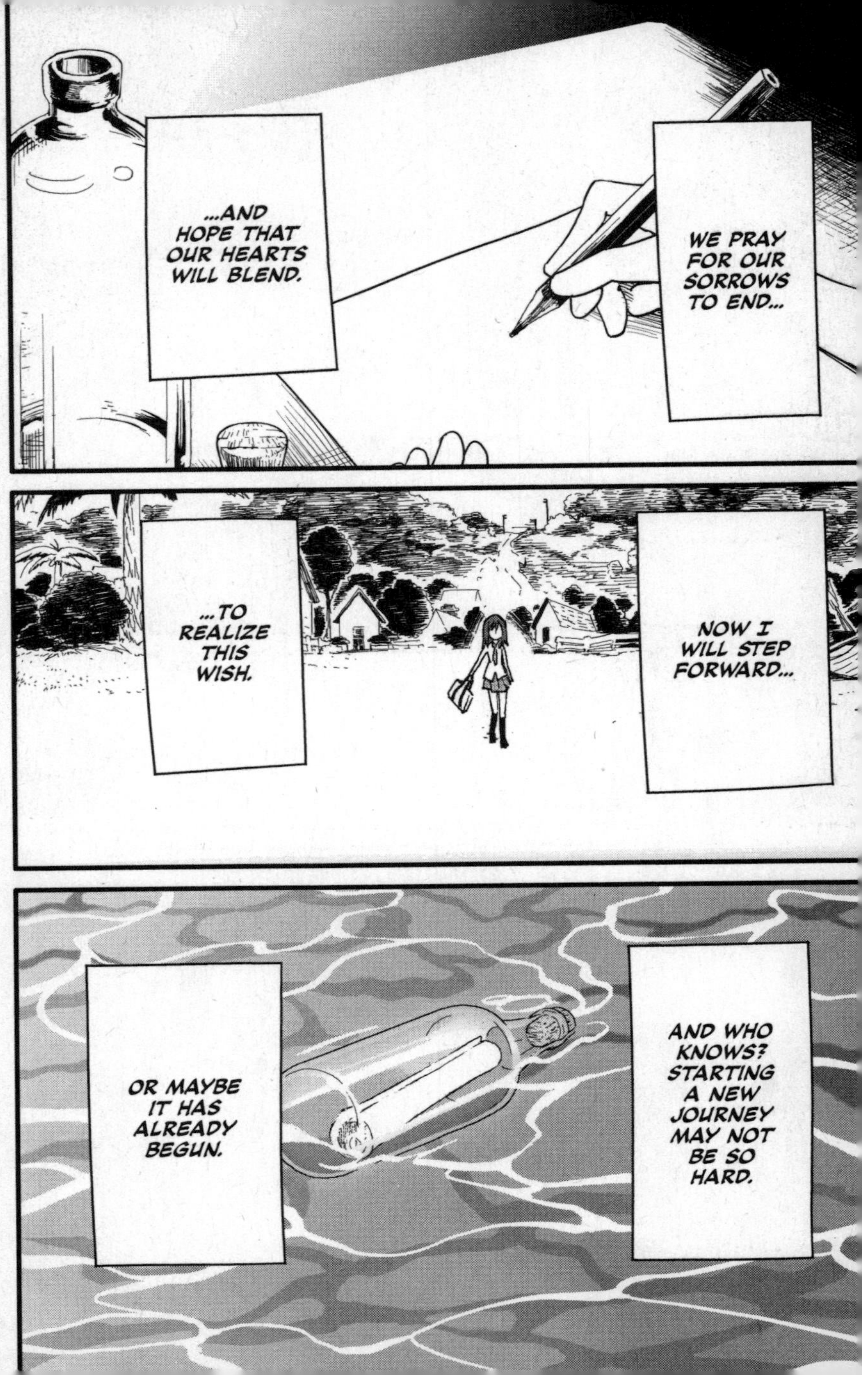
WE PRAY FOR OUR SORROWS TO END...
...AND HOPE THAT OUR HEARTS WILL BLEND.
NOW I WILL STEP FORWARD...
...TO REALIZE THIS WISH.
AND WHO KNOWS? STARTING A NEW JOURNEY MAY NOT BE SO HARD.
OR MAYBE IT HAS ALREADY BEGUN.

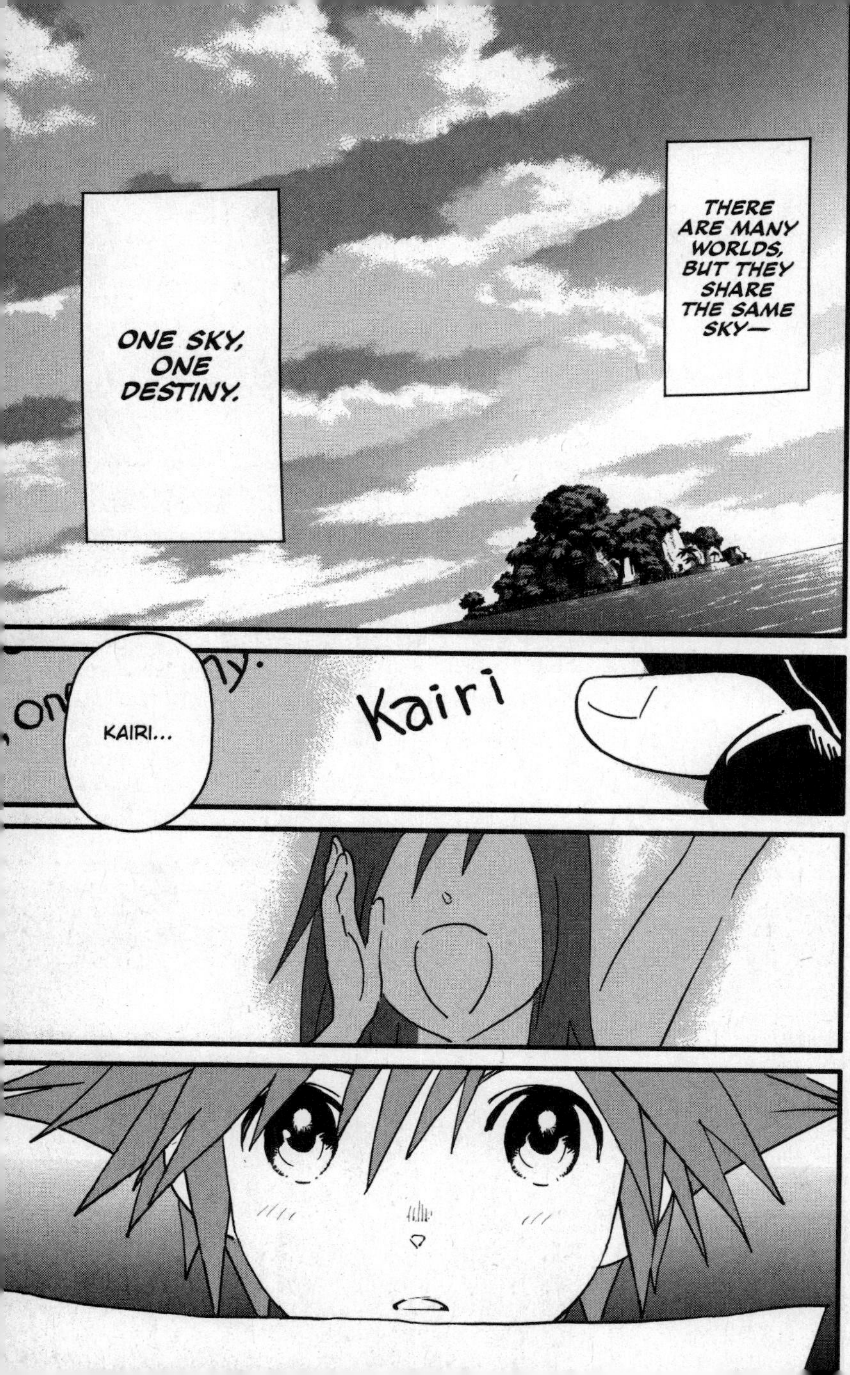
THERE ARE MANY WORLDS, BUT THEY SHARE THE SAME SKY—
ONE SKY, ONE DESTINY.
Kairi
KAIRI...

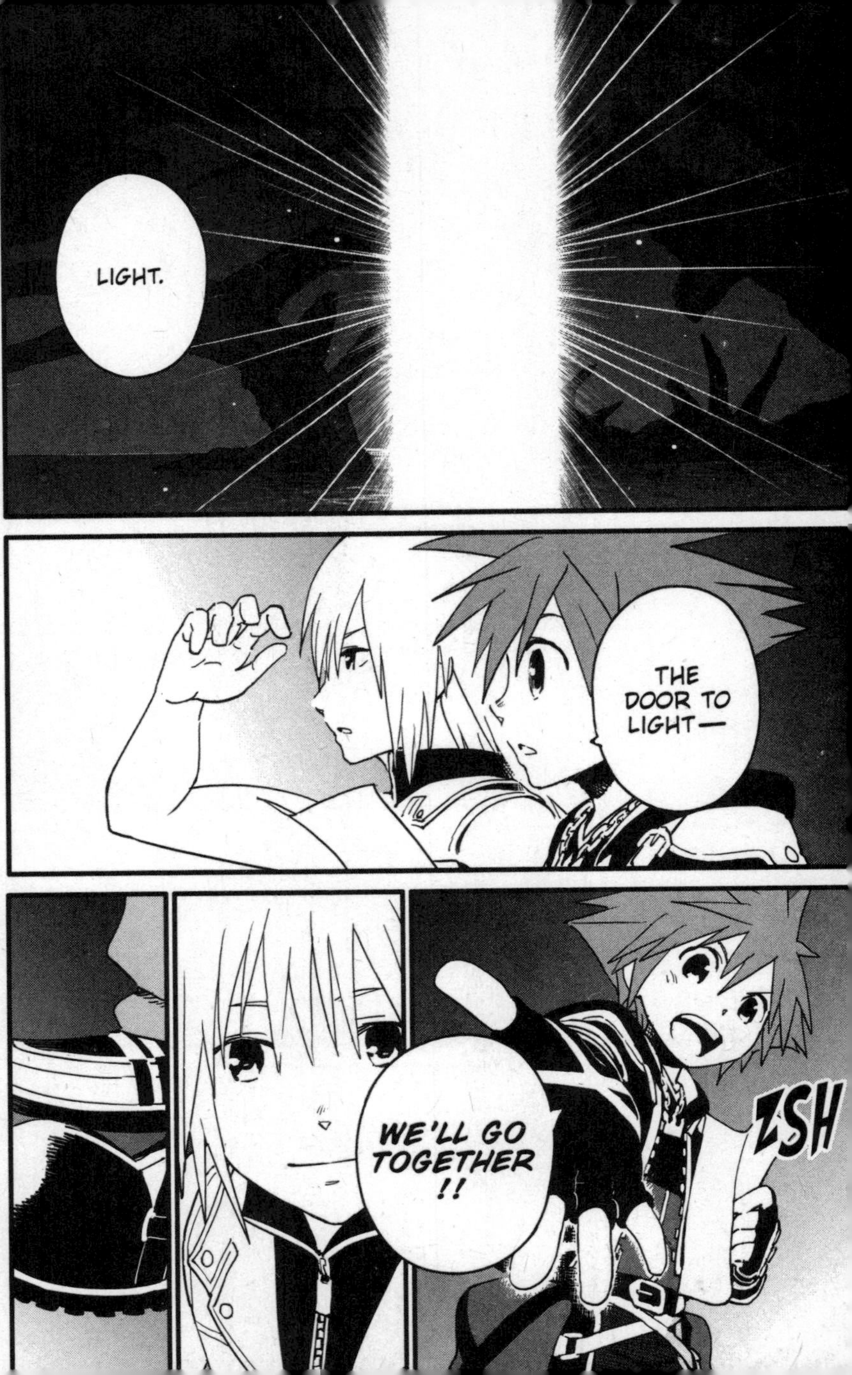
LIGHT.
THE DOOR TO LIGHT—
WE'LL GO TOGETHER !!
ZSH

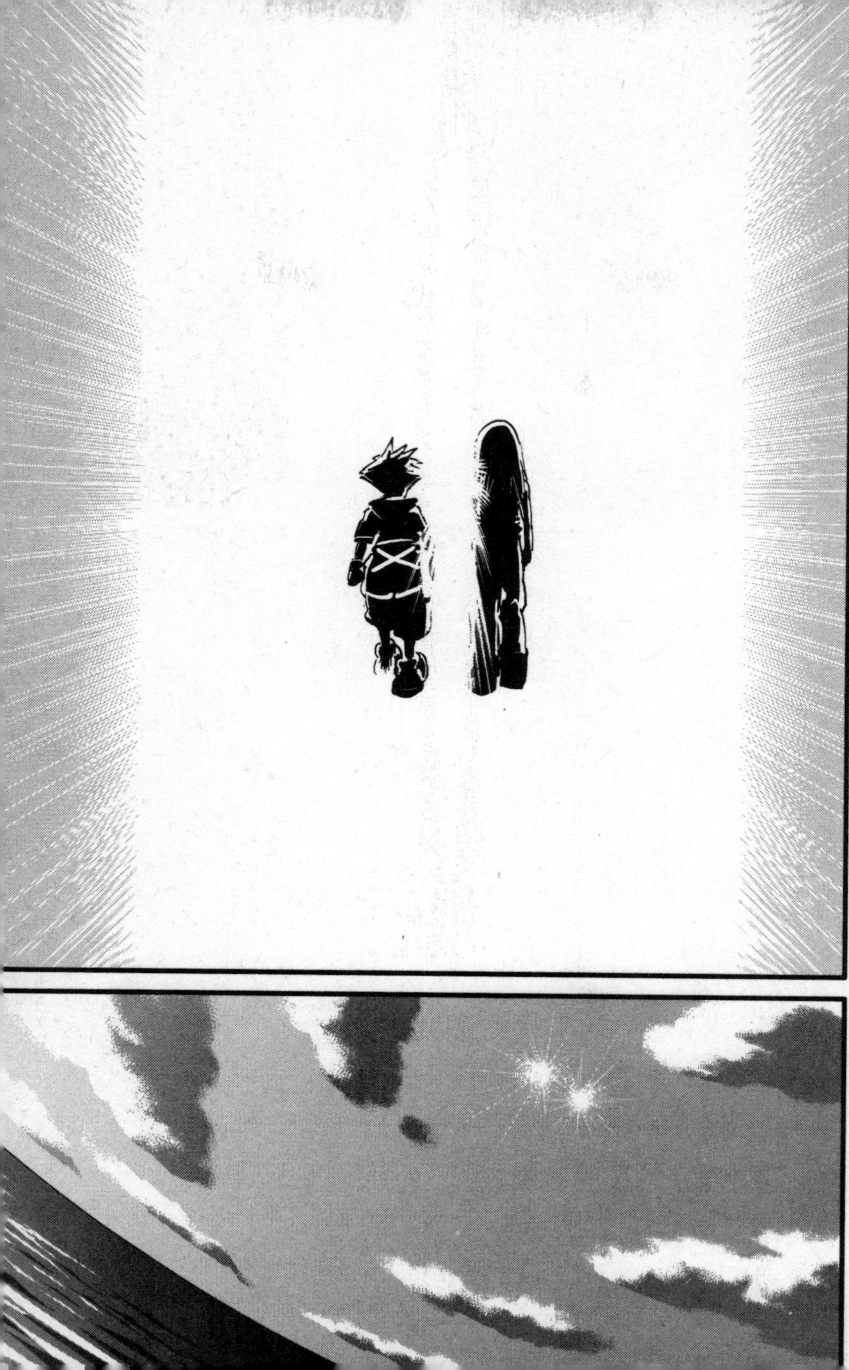

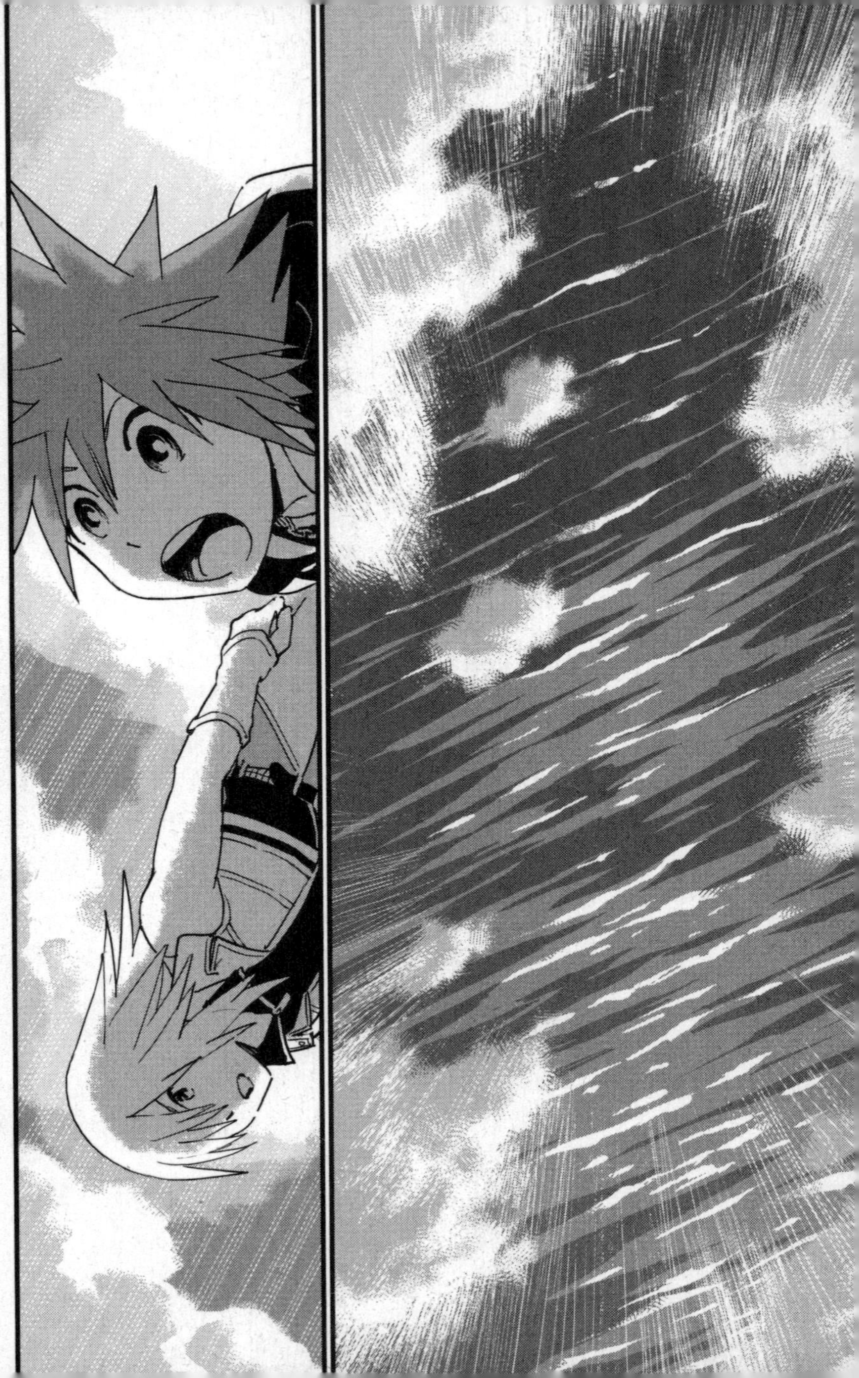

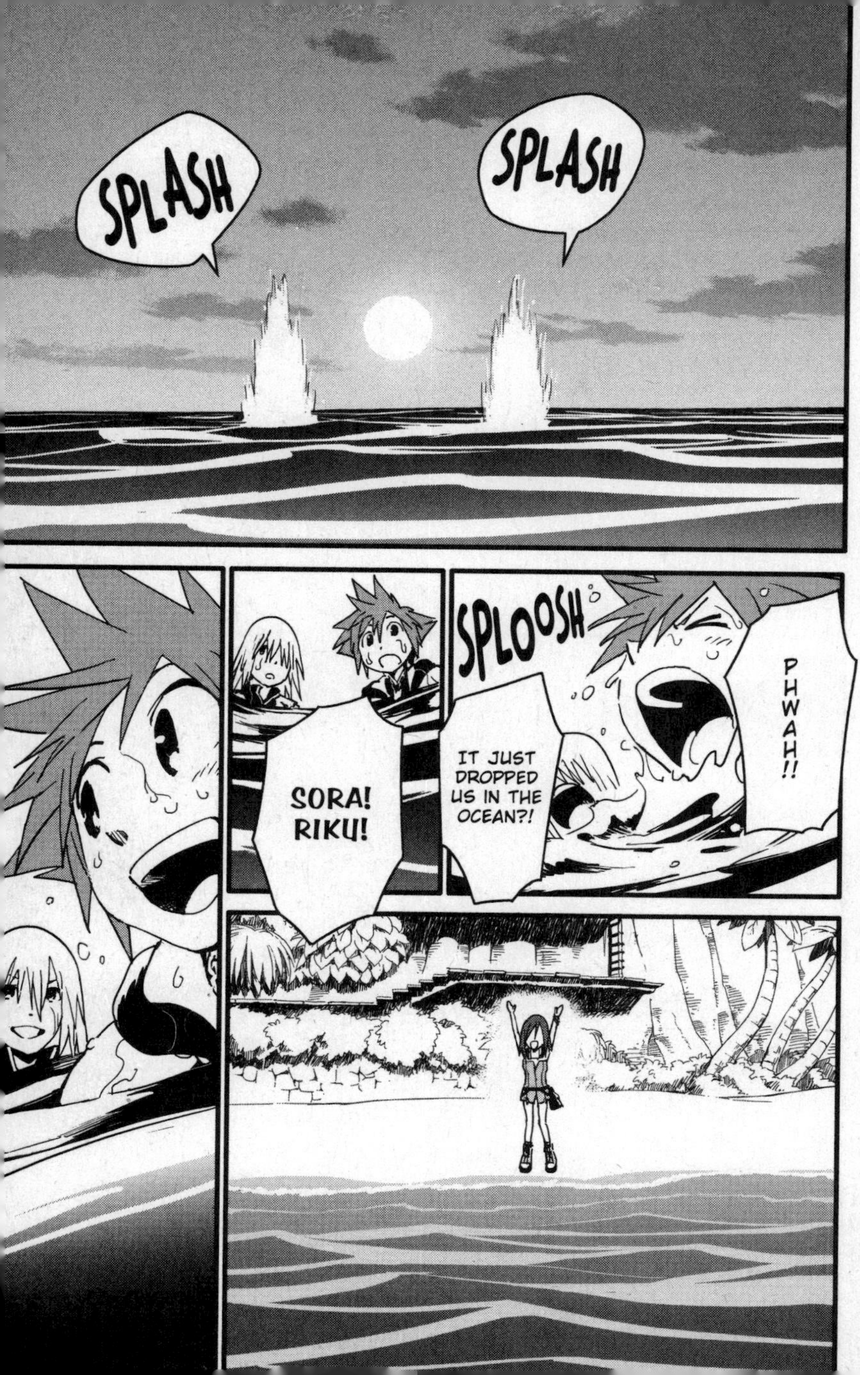
SPLASH
SPLASH
SPLOOSH
PHWAH!!
IT JUST DROPPED US IN THE OCEAN?!
SORA! RIKU!

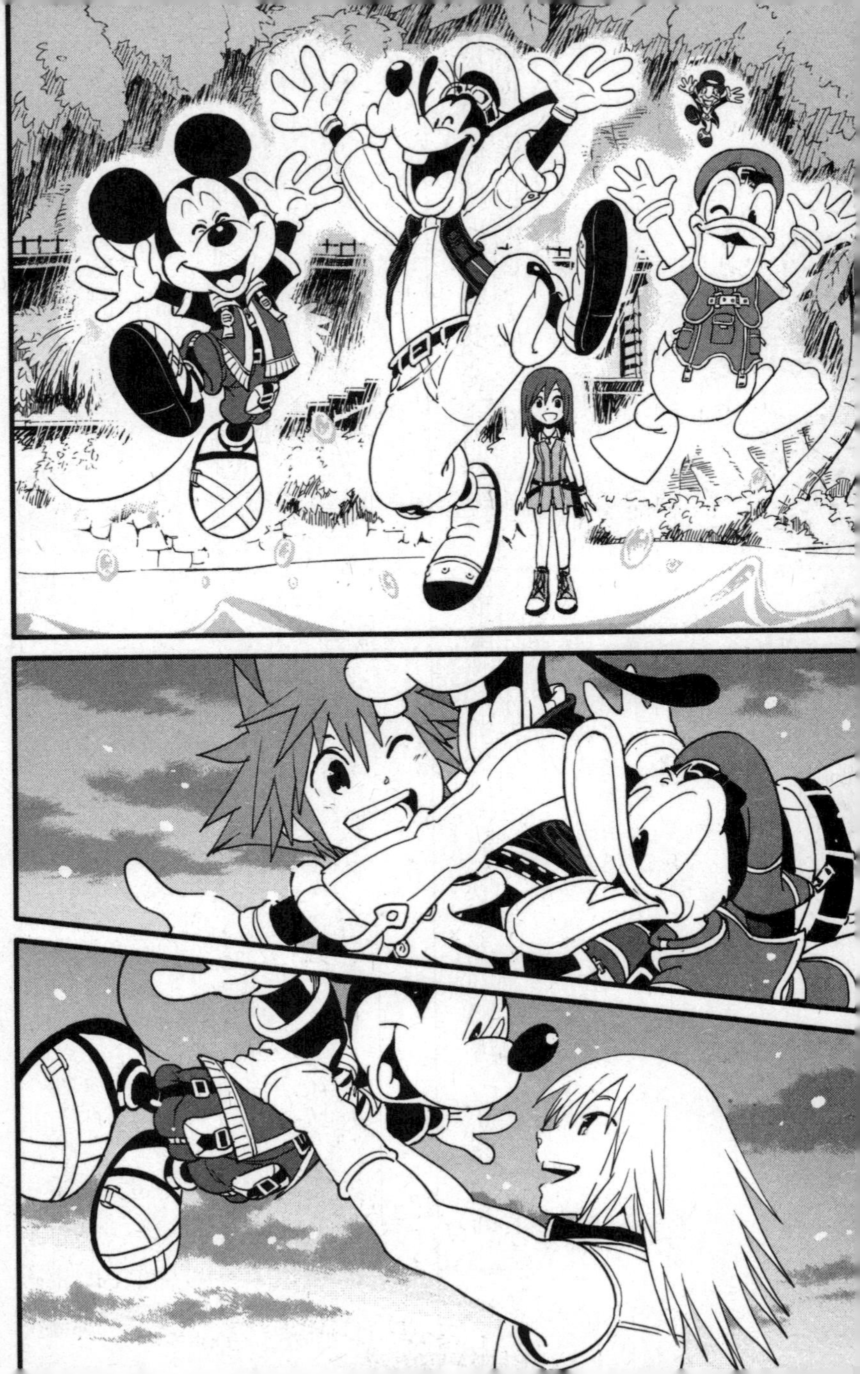

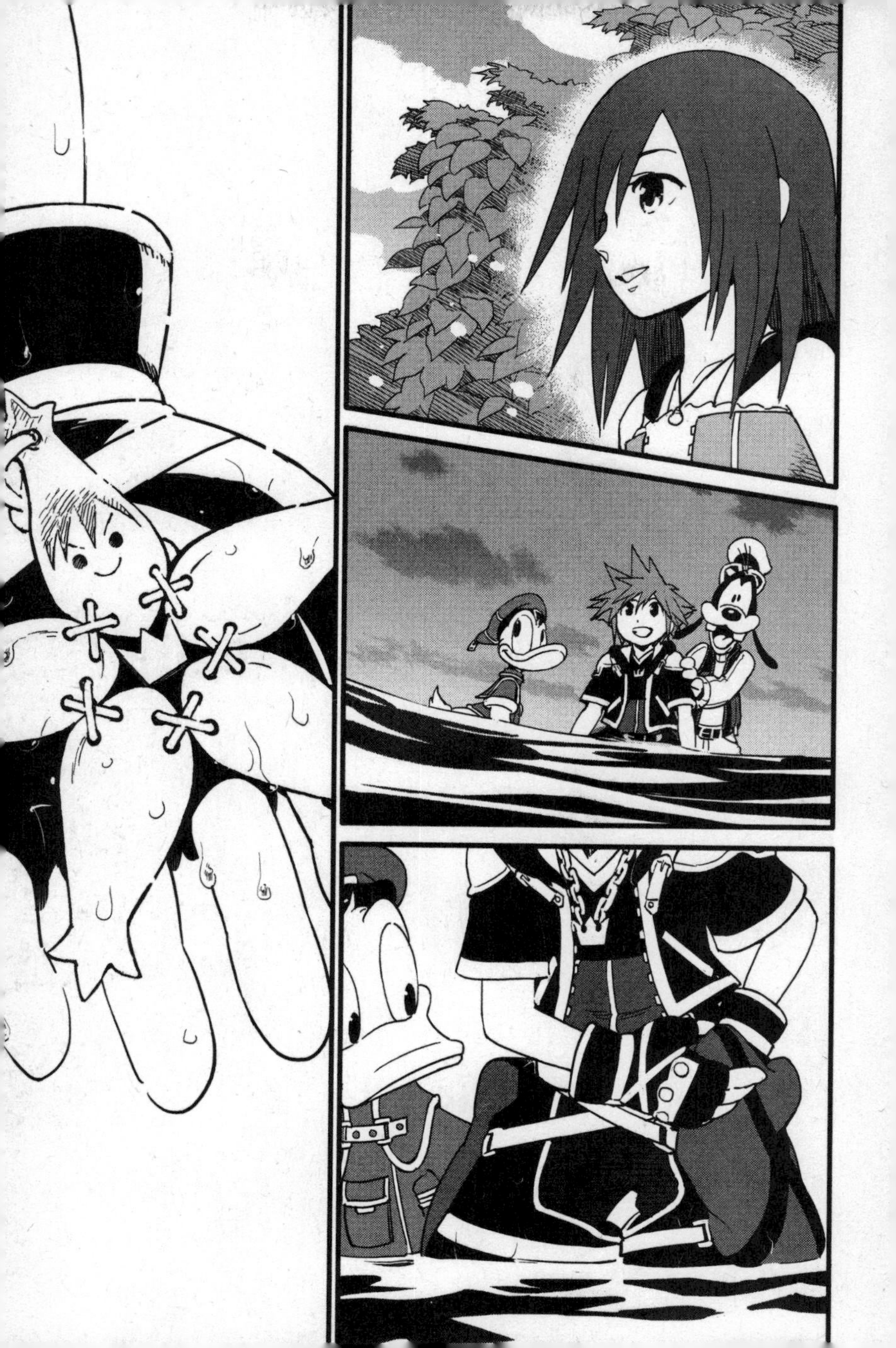

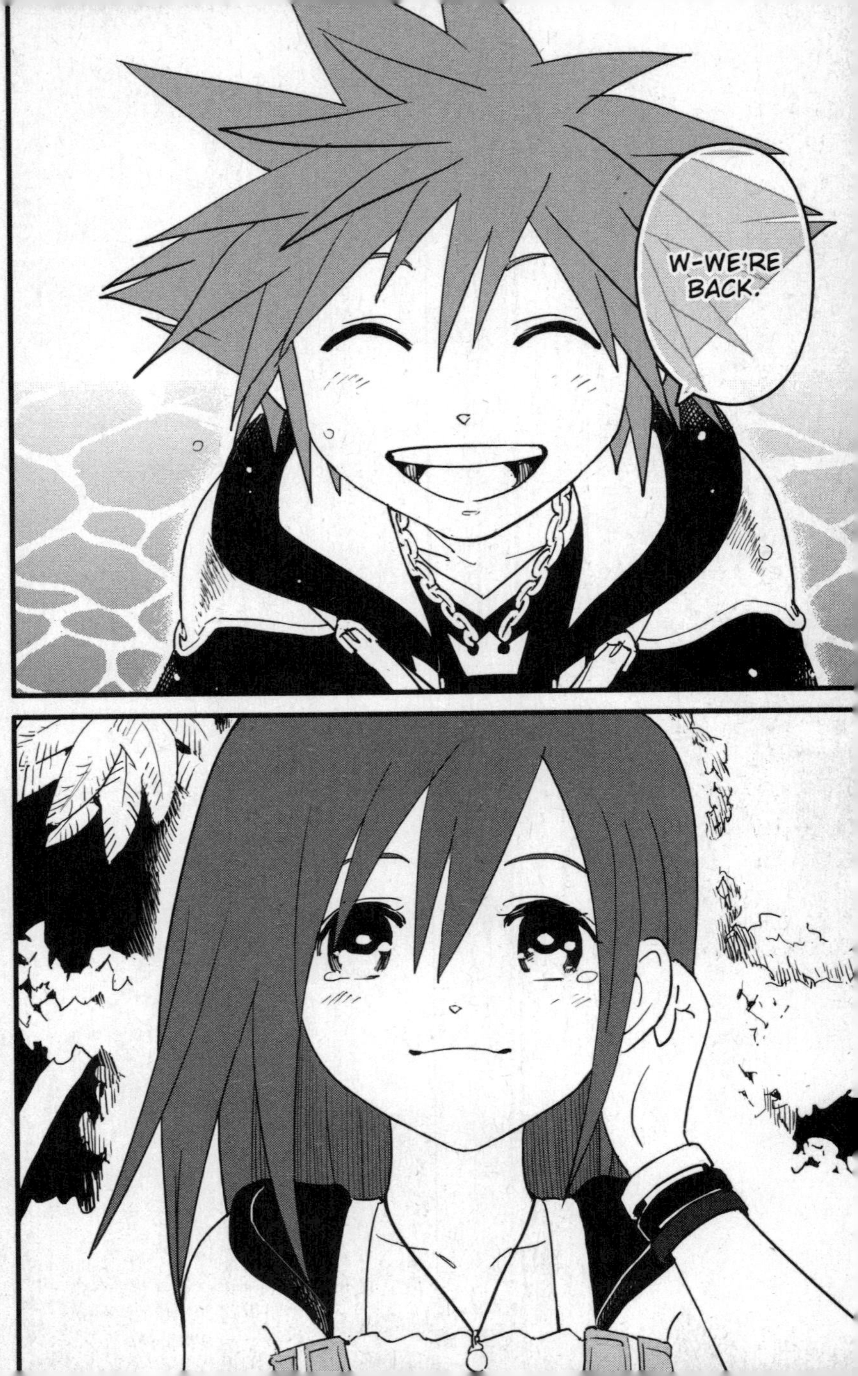
W-WE'RE BACK.

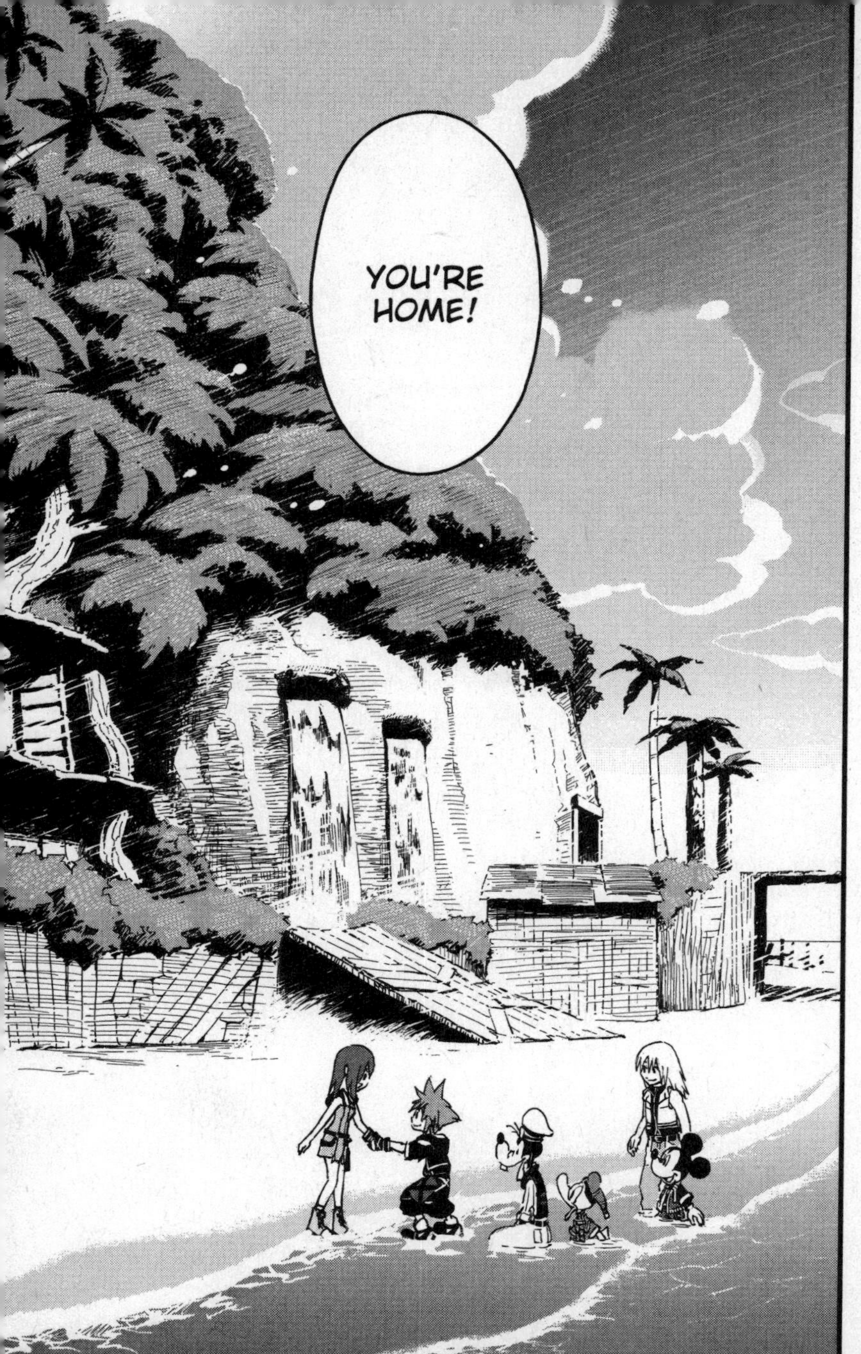
YOU'RE HOME!

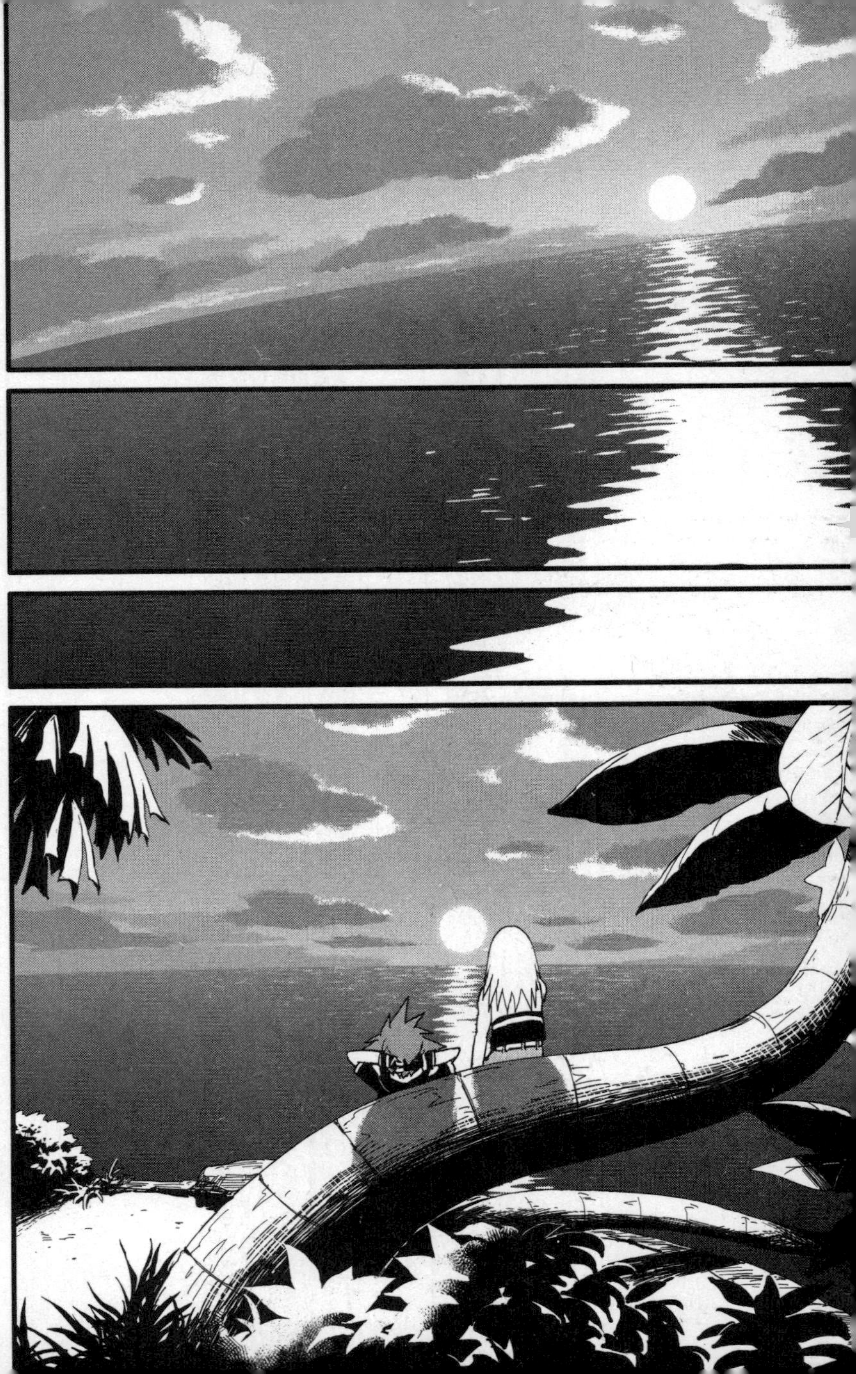

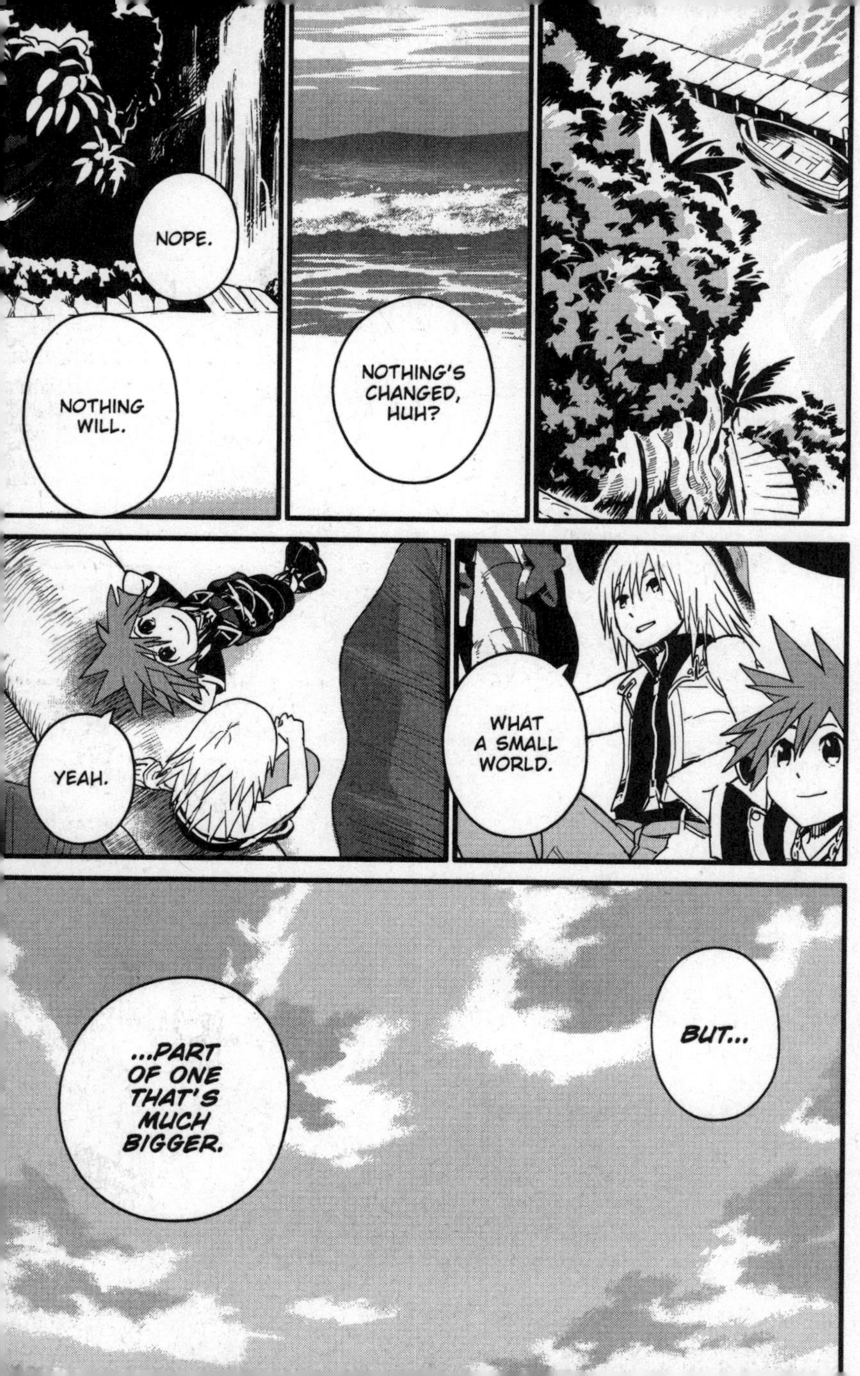
NOTHING'S CHANGED, HUH?
NOPE.
NOTHING WILL.
WHAT A SMALL WORLD.
YEAH.
BUT...
...PART OF ONE THAT'S MUCH BIGGER.

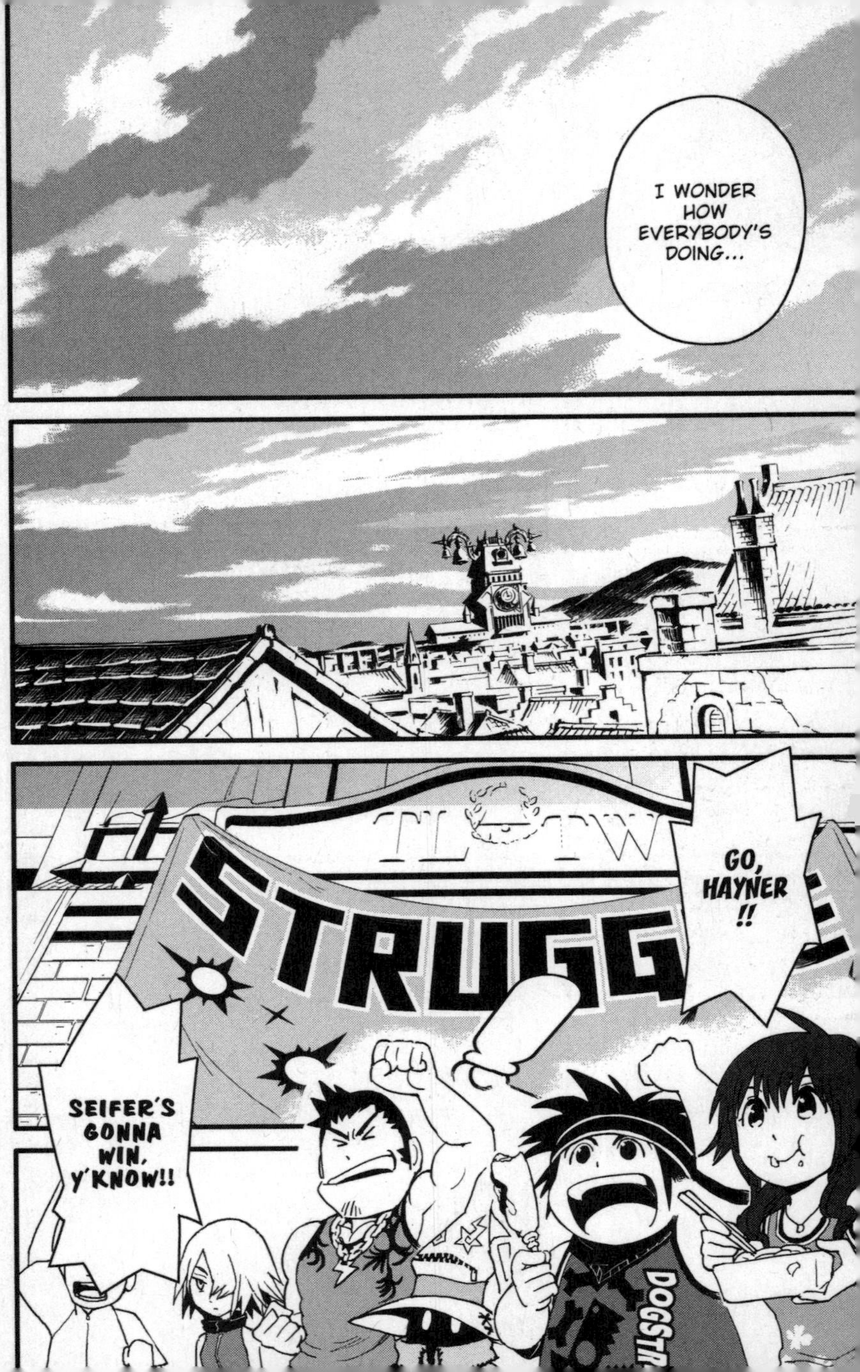
I WONDER HOW EVERYBODY'S DOING...
GO, HAYNER!!
SEIFER'S GONNA WIN, Y'KNOW!!

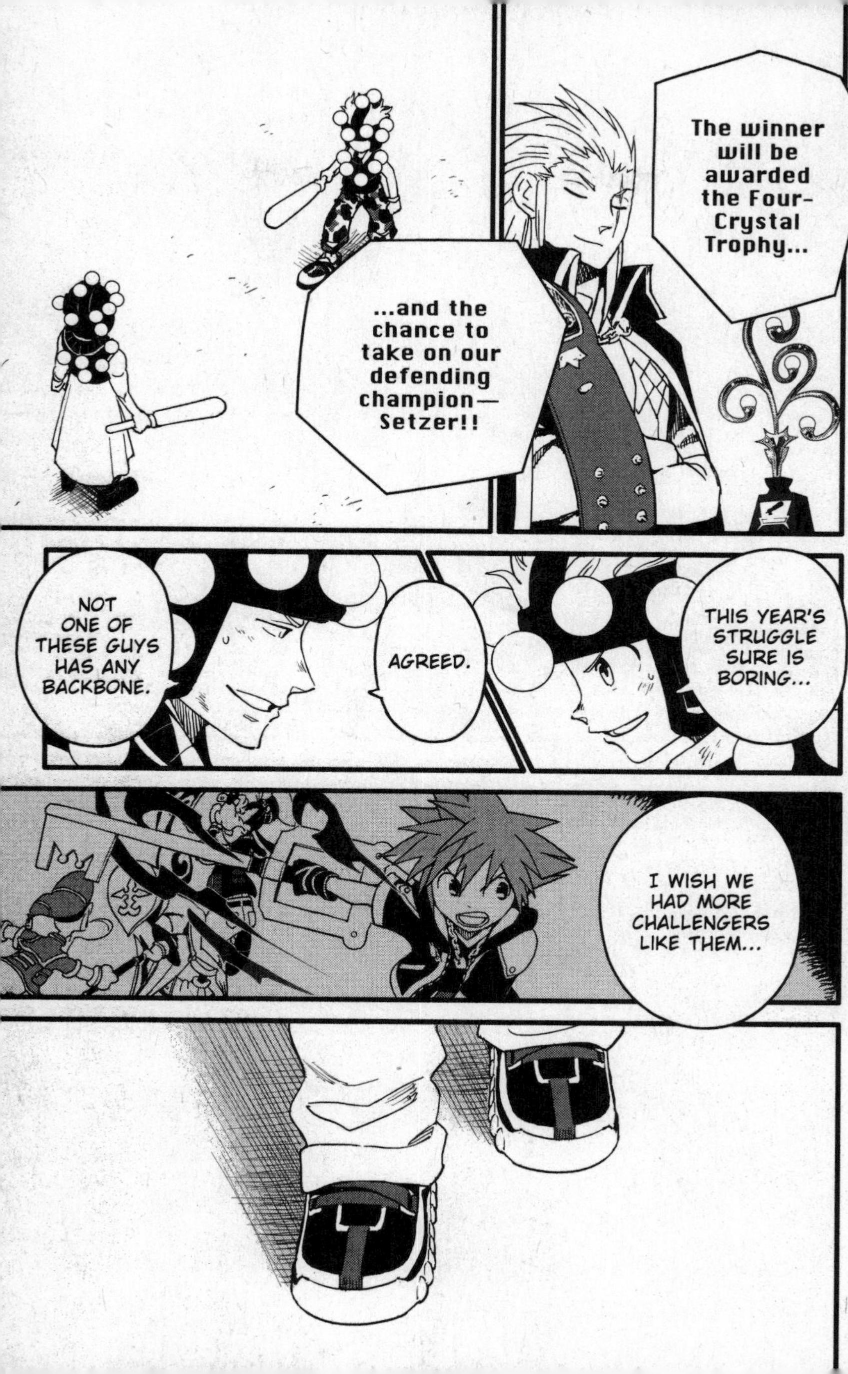
The winner will be awarded the Four-Crystal Trophy...
...and the chance to take on our defending champion—Setzer!!
THIS YEAR'S STRUGGLE SURE IS BORING...
AGREED.
NOT ONE OF THESE GUYS HAS ANY BACKBONE.
I WISH WE HAD MORE CHALLENGERS LIKE THEM...

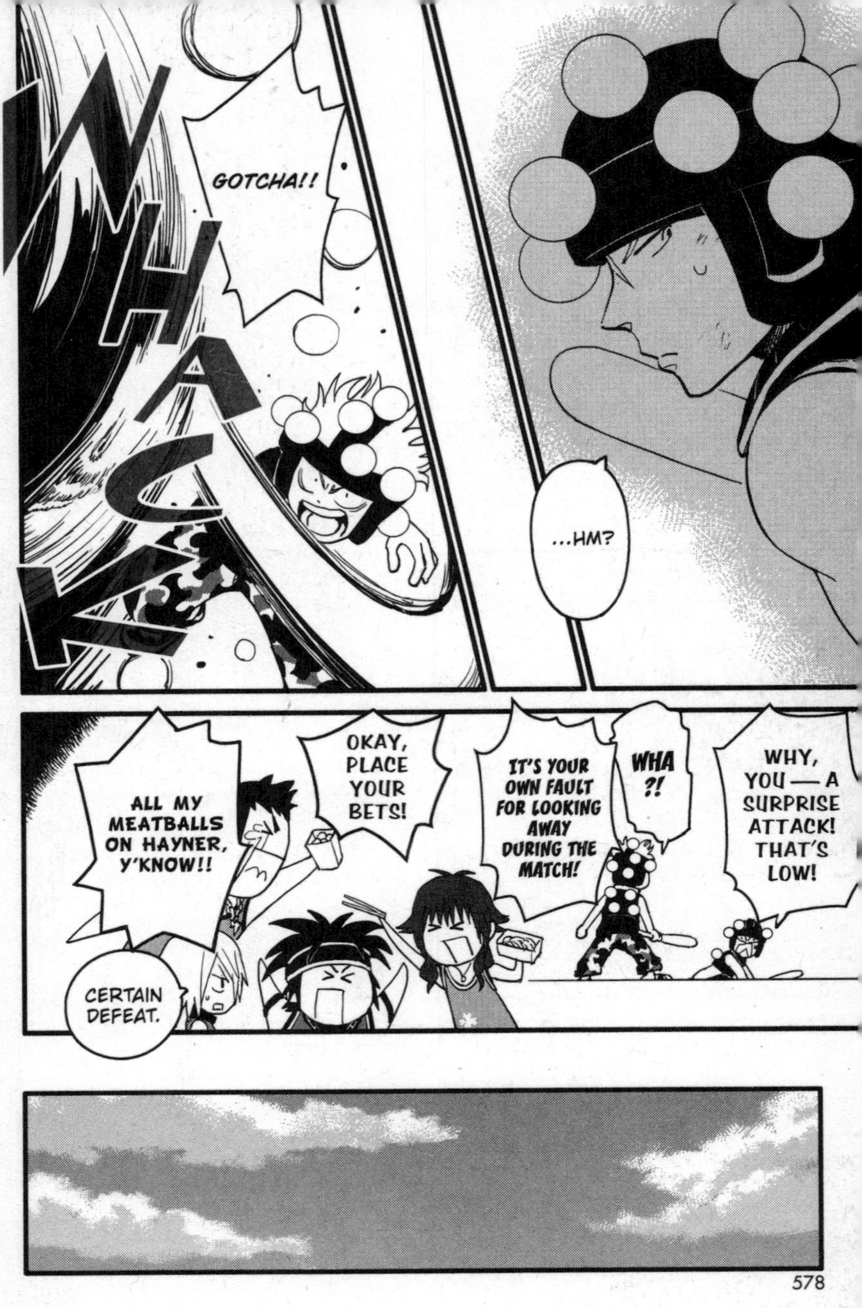
...HM?
GOTCHA!!
WHACK
WHY, YOU — A SURPRISE ATTACK! THAT'S LOW!
WHA?!
IT'S YOUR OWN FAULT FOR LOOKING AWAY DURING THE MATCH!
OKAY, PLACE YOUR BETS!
ALL MY MEATBALLS ON HAYNER, Y'KNOW!!
CERTAIN DEFEAT.

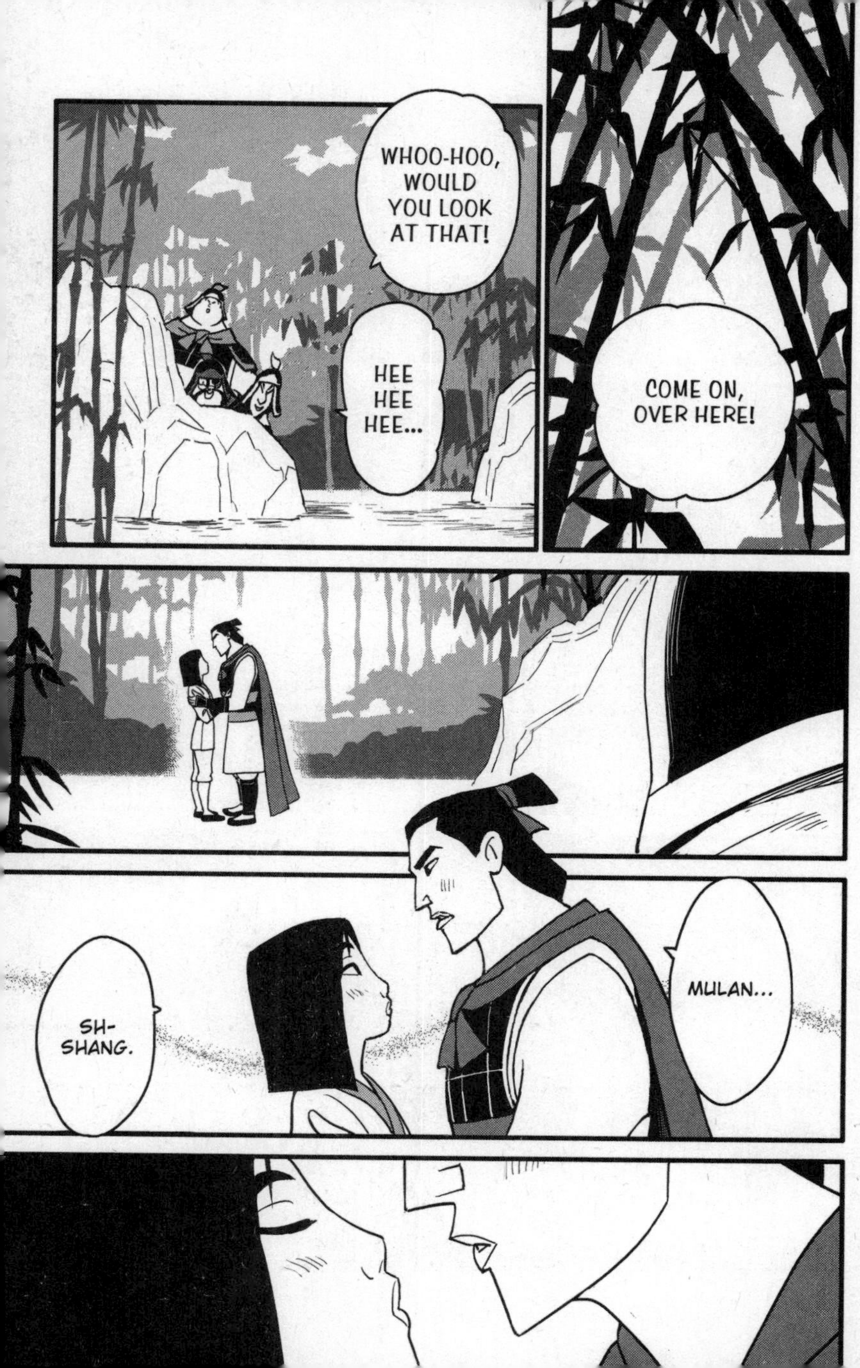
COME ON, OVER HERE!
WHOO-HOO, WOULD YOU LOOK AT THAT!
HEE HEE HEE...
MULAN...
SH-SHANG.

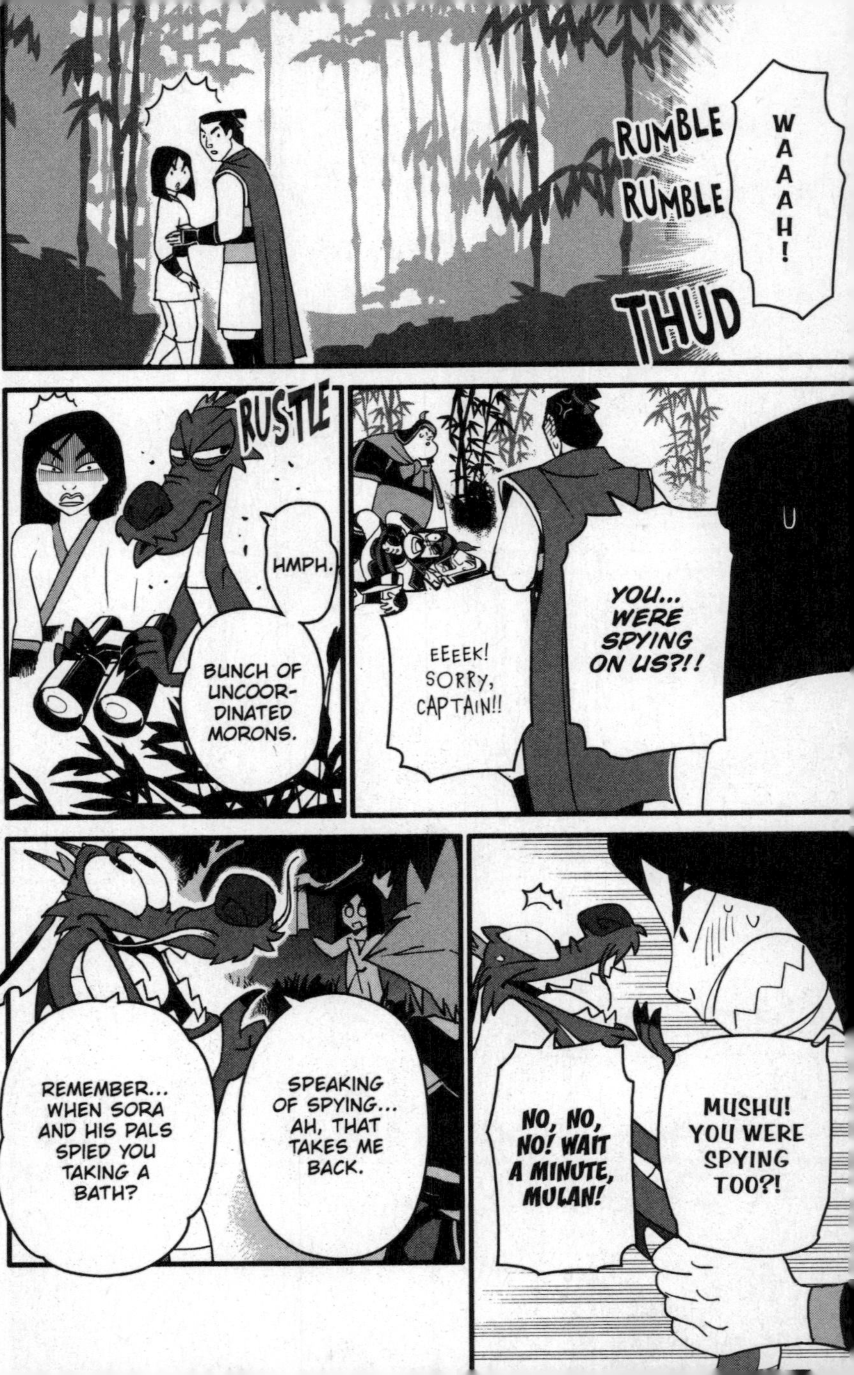
WAAAAH!
RUMBLE RUMBLE
THUD
YOU... WERE SPYING ON US?!!
EEEEK! SORRY, CAPTAIN!!
RUSTLE
HMPH.
BUNCH OF UNCOORDINATED MORONS.
MUSHU! YOU WERE SPYING TOO?!
NO, NO, NO! WAIT A MINUTE, MULAN!
SPEAKING OF SPYING... AH, THAT TAKES ME BACK.
REMEMBER... WHEN SORA AND HIS PALS SPIED YOU TAKING A BATH?

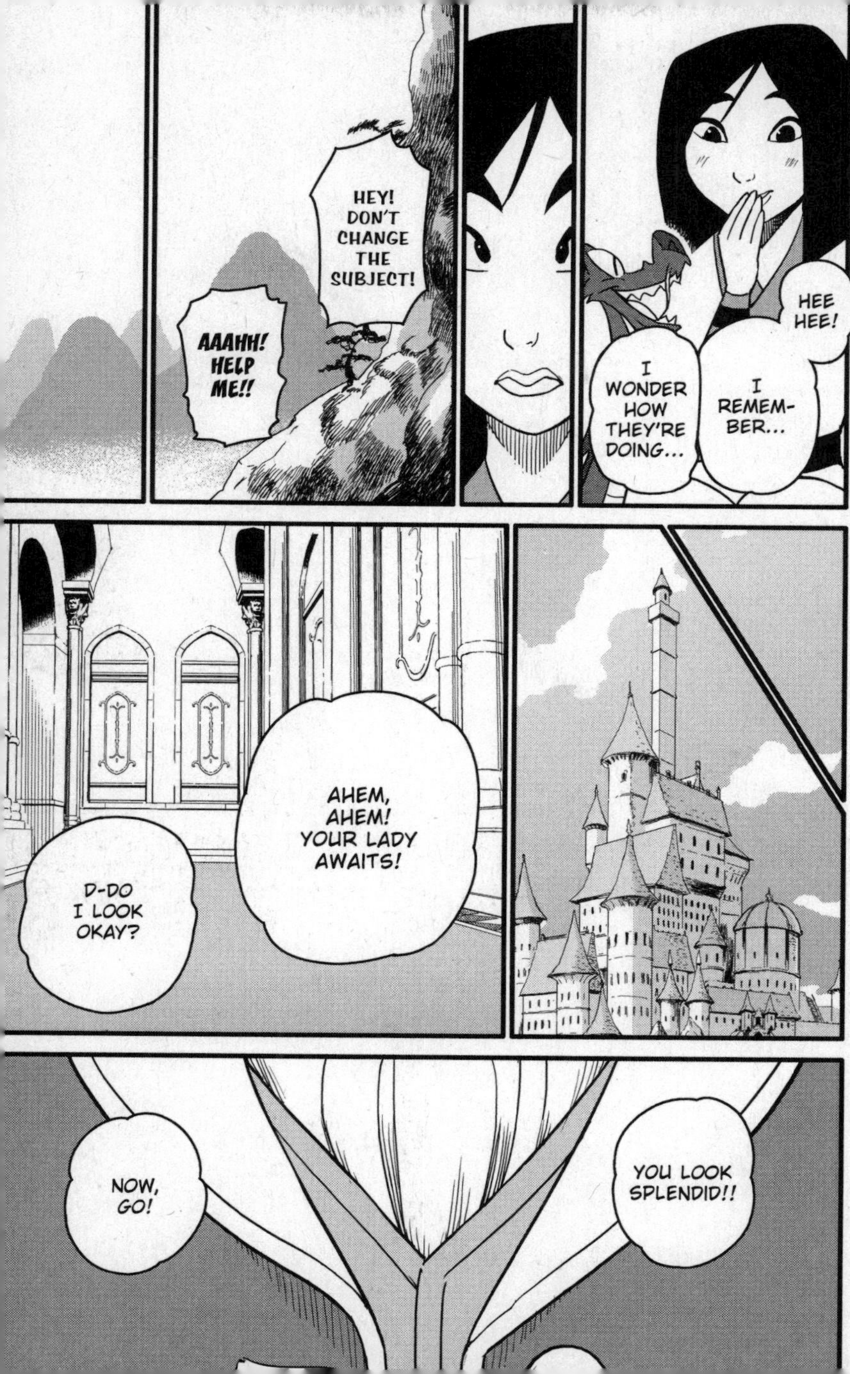
HEE HEE!
I REMEMBER...
I WONDER HOW THEY'RE DOING...
HEY! DON'T CHANGE THE SUBJECT!
AAAHH! HELP ME!!
AHEM, AHEM! YOUR LADY AWAITS!
D-DO I LOOK OKAY?
YOU LOOK SPLENDID!!
NOW, GO!

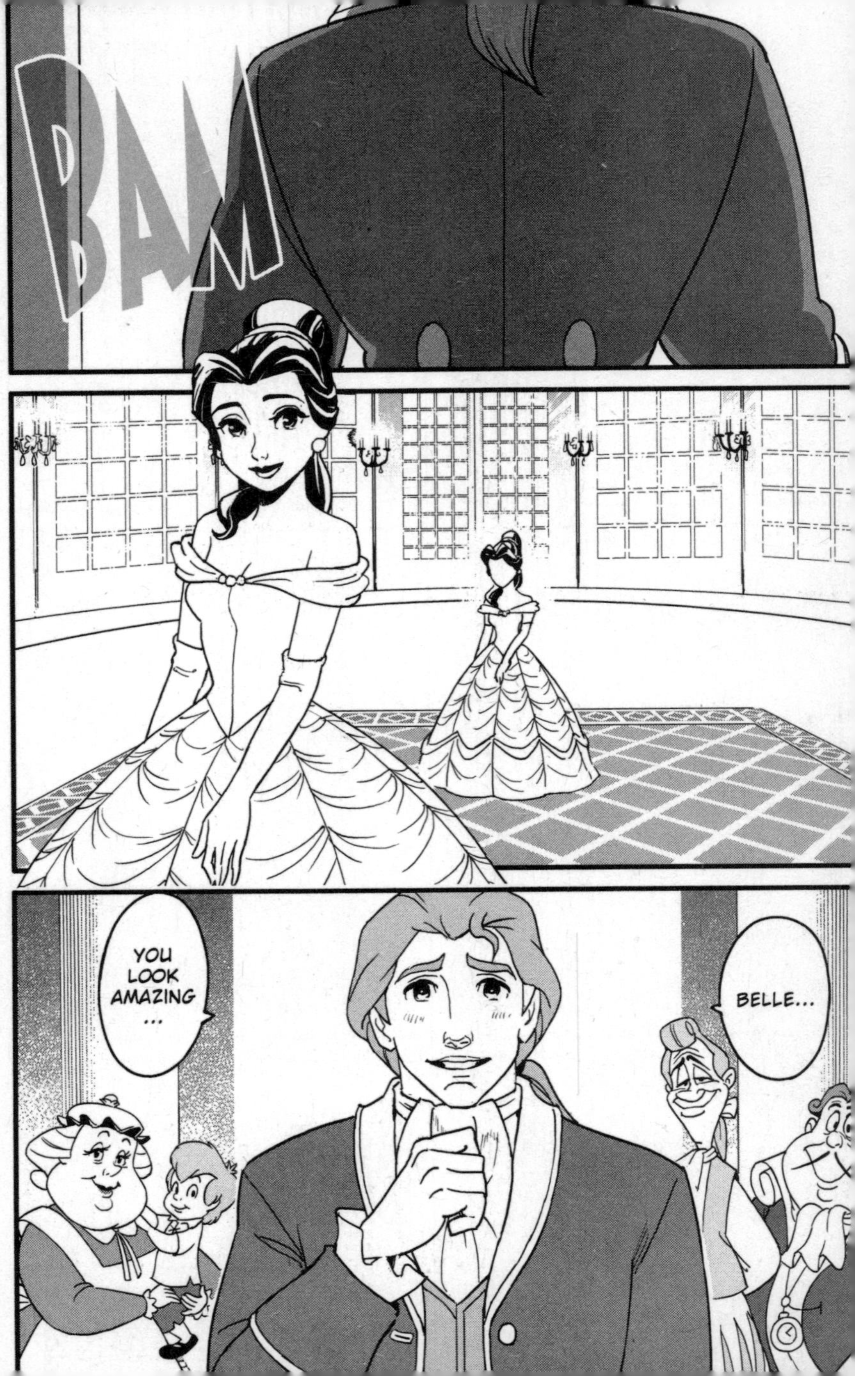
BAM
BELLE...
YOU LOOK AMAZING...

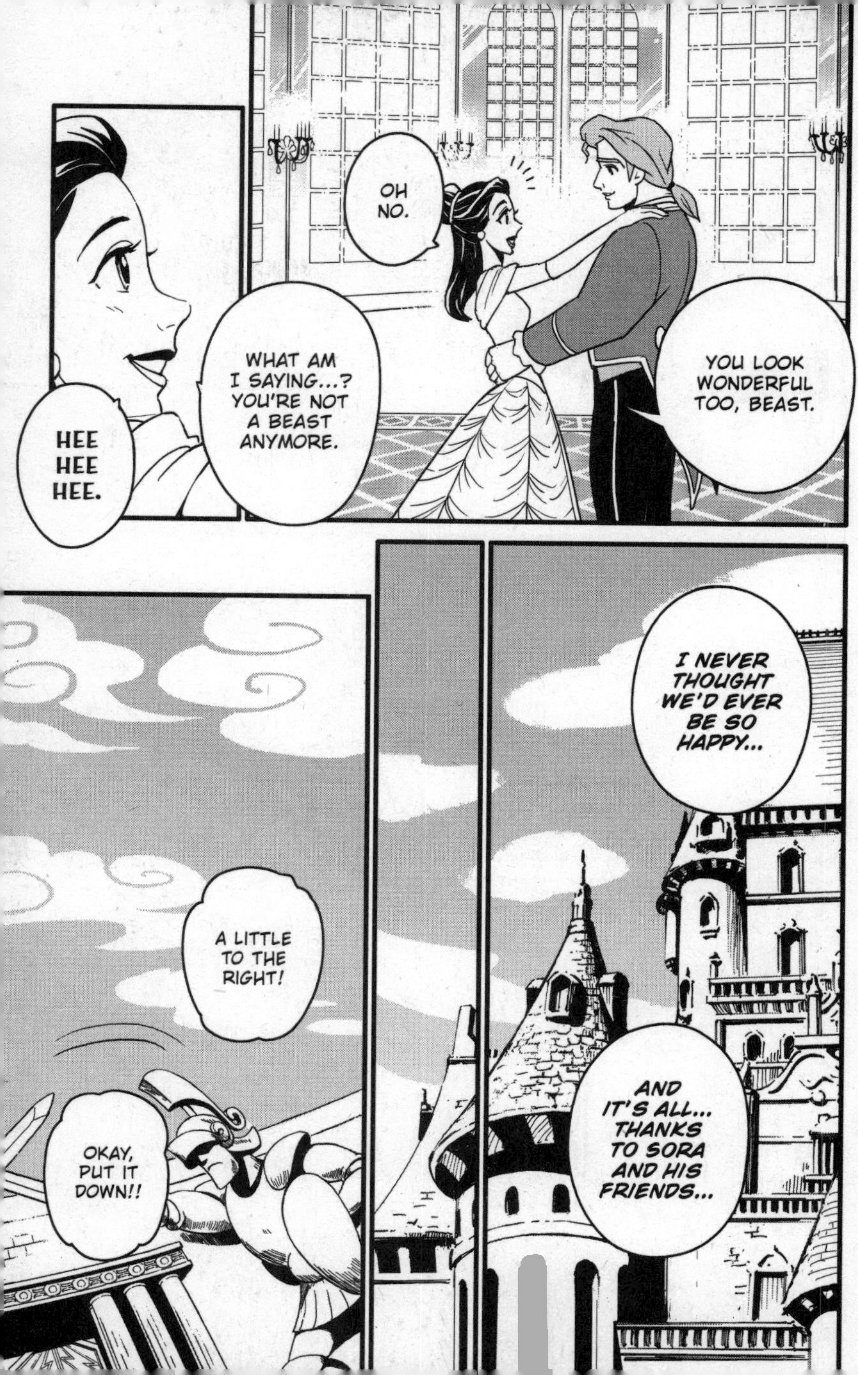

YOU LOOK WONDERFUL TOO, BEAST.
OH NO.
WHAT AM I SAYING...? YOU'RE NOT A BEAST ANYMORE.
HEE HEE HEE.
I NEVER THOUGHT WE'D EVER BE SO HAPPY...
AND IT'S ALL... THANKS TO SORA AND HIS FRIENDS...
A LITTLE TO THE RIGHT!
OKAY, PUT IT DOWN!!

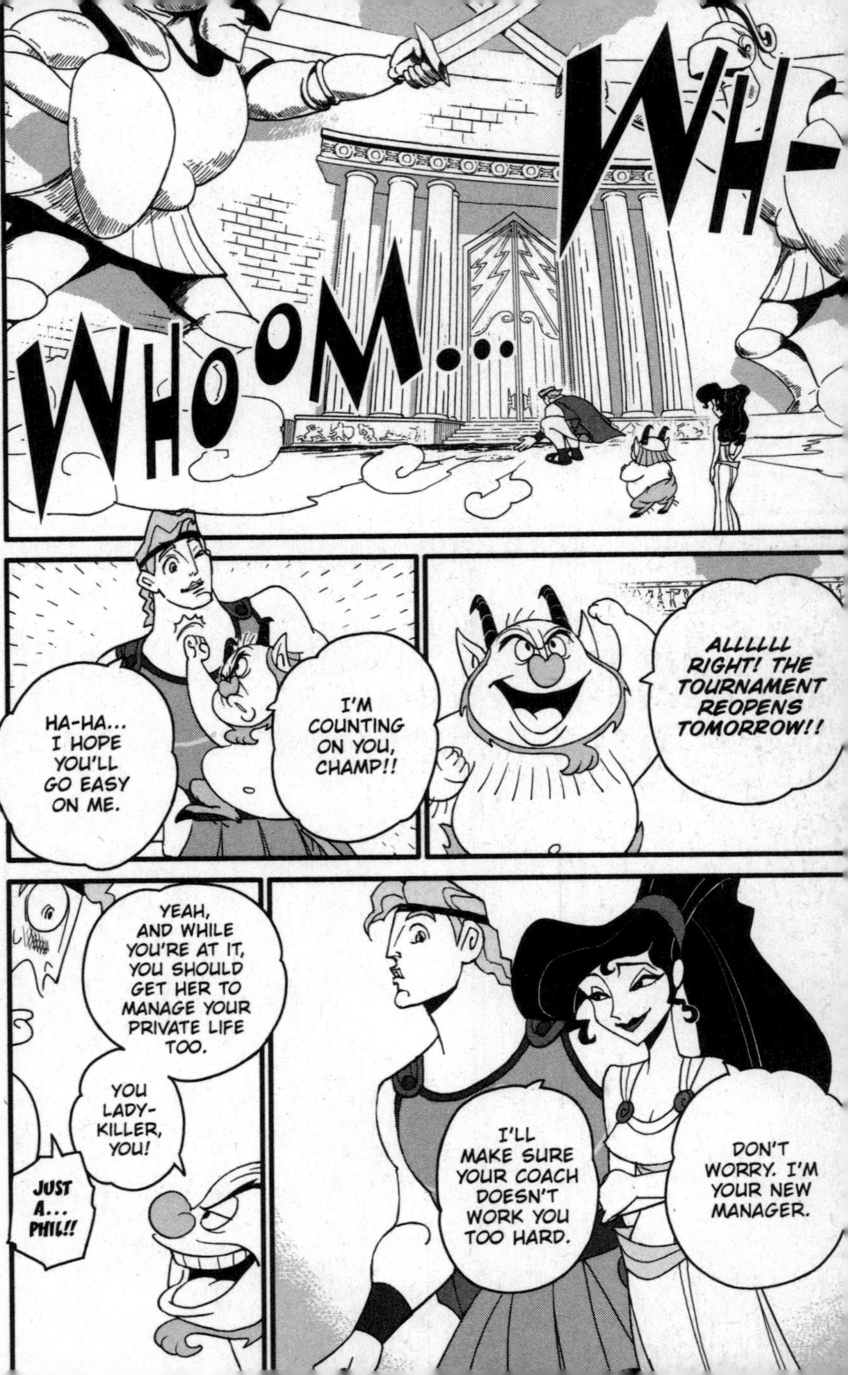
WH-
WHOOM...
ALLLLLL RIGHT! THE TOURNAMENT REOPENS TOMORROW!!
I'M COUNTING ON YOU, CHAMP!!
HA-HA... I HOPE YOU'LL GO EASY ON ME.
DON'T WORRY. I'M YOUR NEW MANAGER.
I'LL MAKE SURE YOUR COACH DOESN'T WORK YOU TOO HARD.
YEAH, AND WHILE YOU'RE AT IT, YOU SHOULD GET HER TO MANAGE YOUR PRIVATE LIFE TOO.
YOU LADY-KILLER, YOU!
JUST A... PHIL!!

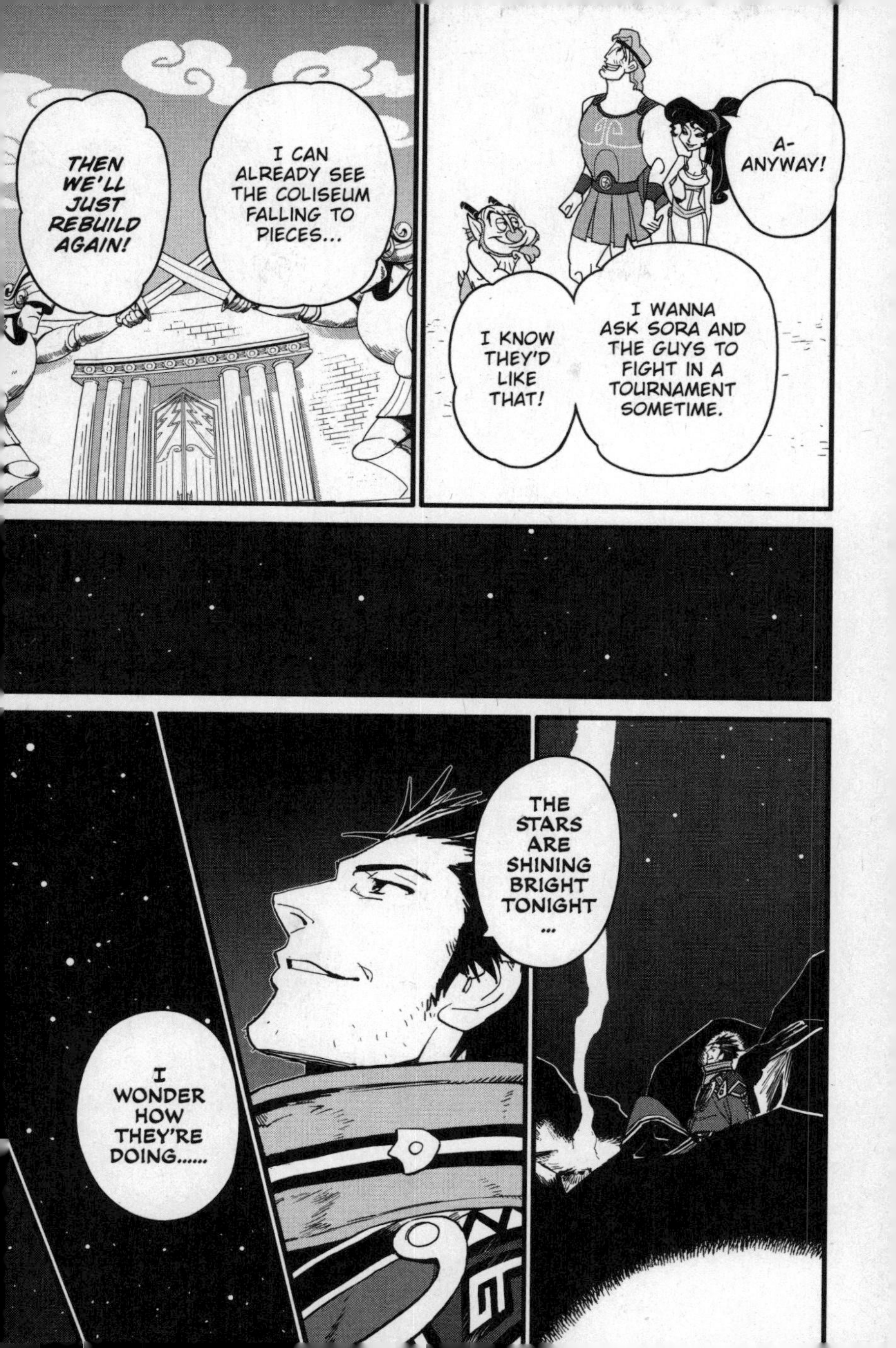
A-ANYWAY!
I WANNA ASK SORA AND THE GUYS TO FIGHT IN A TOURNAMENT SOMETIME.
I KNOW THEY'D LIKE THAT!
I CAN ALREADY SEE THE COLISEUM FALLING TO PIECES...
THEN WE'LL JUST REBUILD AGAIN!
THE STARS ARE SHINING BRIGHT TONIGHT...
I WONDER HOW THEY'RE DOING......

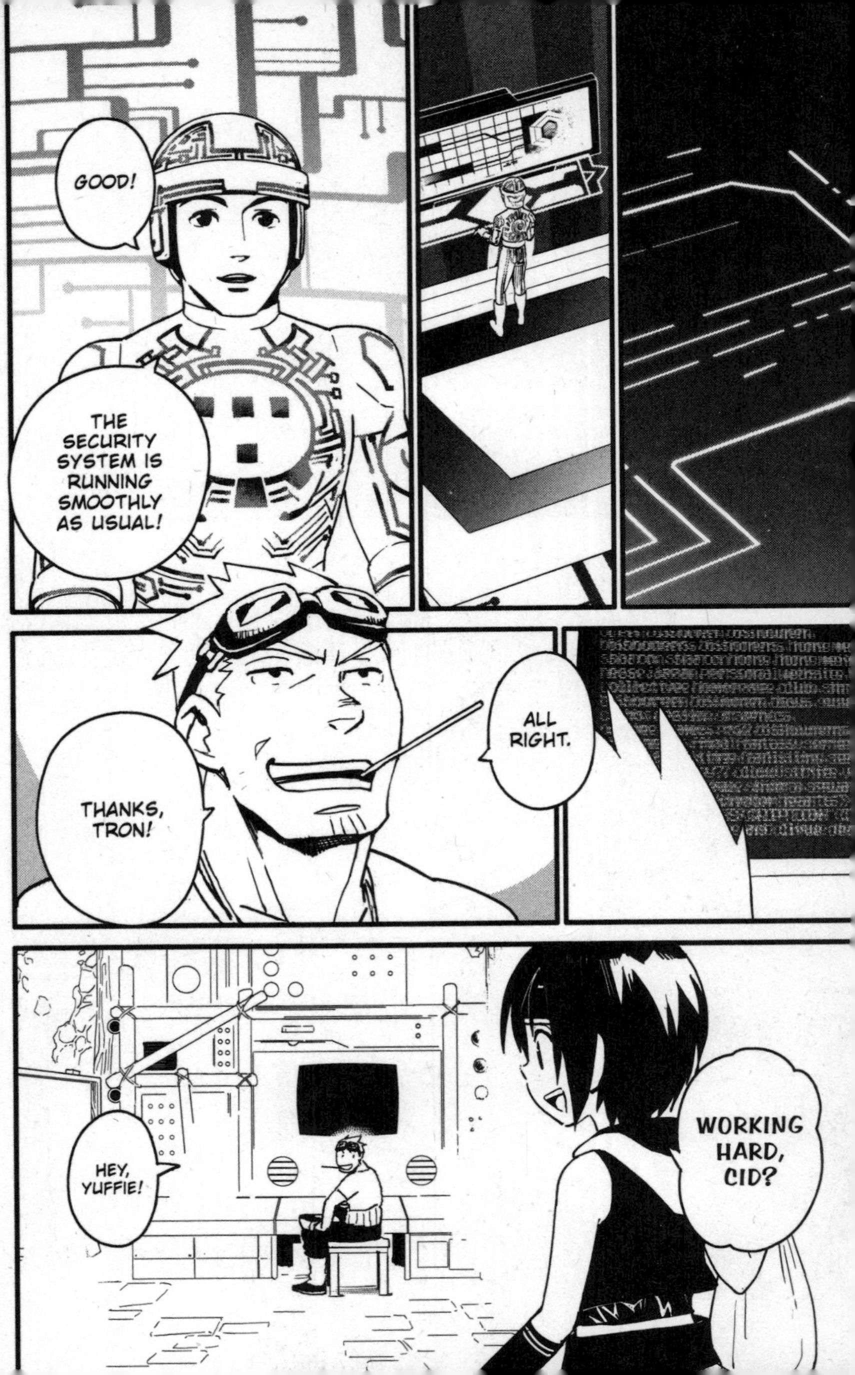
GOOD!
THE SECURITY SYSTEM IS RUNNING SMOOTHLY AS USUAL!
ALL RIGHT.
THANKS, TRON!
WORKING HARD, CID?
HEY, YUFFIE!

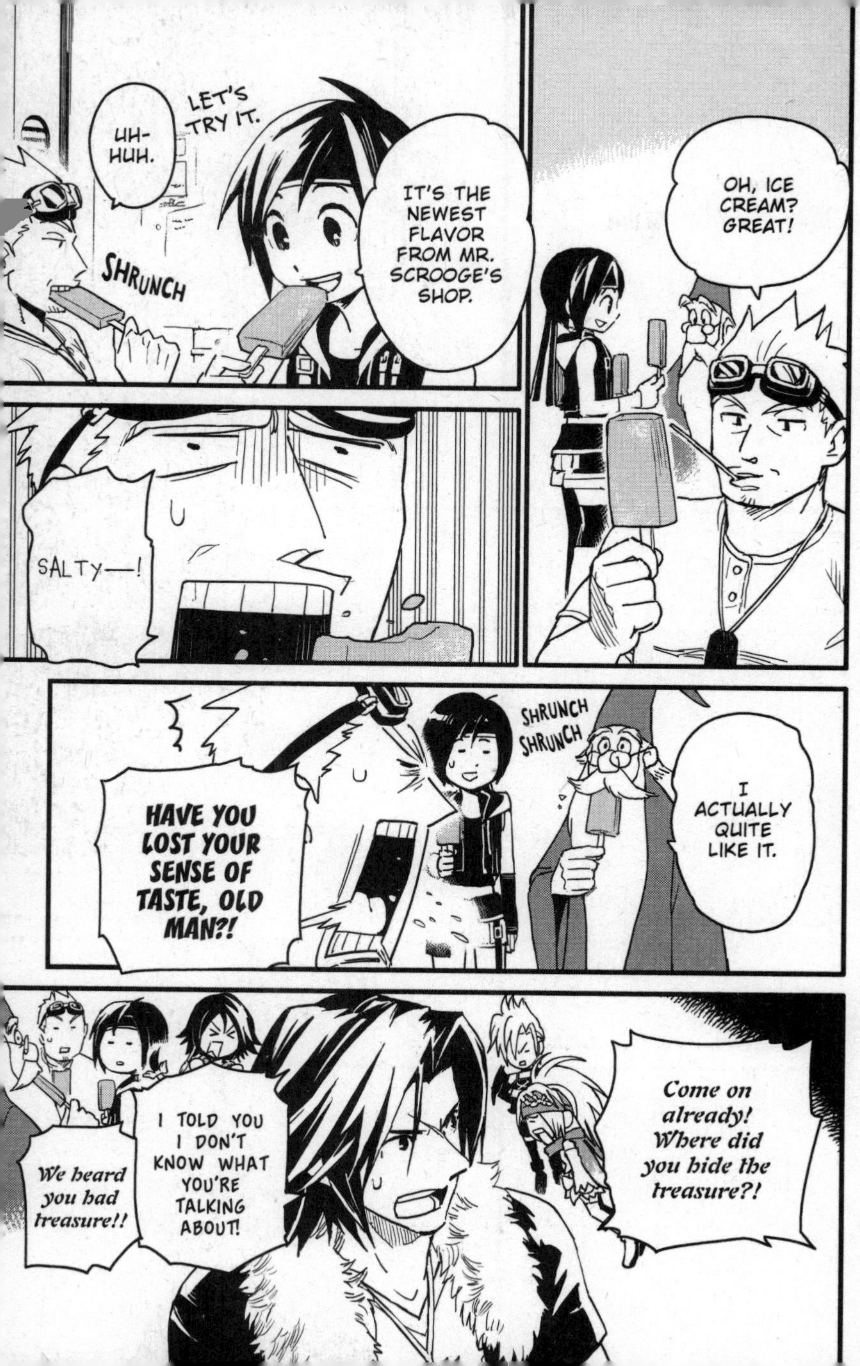
OH, ICE CREAM? GREAT!
IT'S THE NEWEST FLAVOR FROM MR. SCROOGE'S SHOP.
LET'S TRY IT.
UH-HUH.
SHRUNCH
SALTY—!
I ACTUALLY QUITE LIKE IT.
SHRUNCH SHRUNCH
HAVE YOU LOST YOUR SENSE OF TASTE, OLD MAN?!
Come on already! Where did you hide the treasure?!
I TOLD YOU I DON'T KNOW WHAT YOU'RE TALKING ABOUT!
We heard you had treasure!!

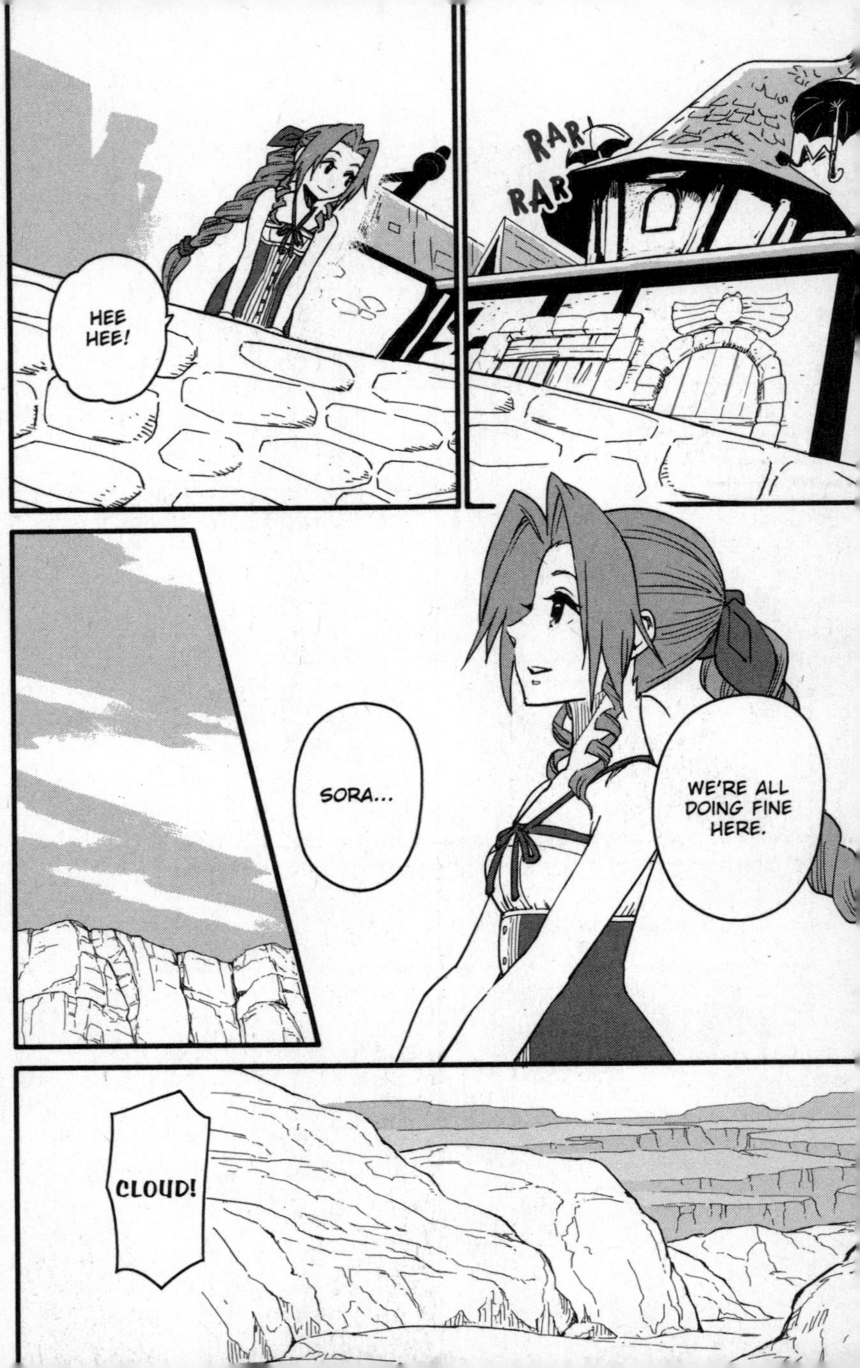
RAR RAR
HEE HEE!
WE'RE ALL DOING FINE HERE.
SORA...
CLOUD!

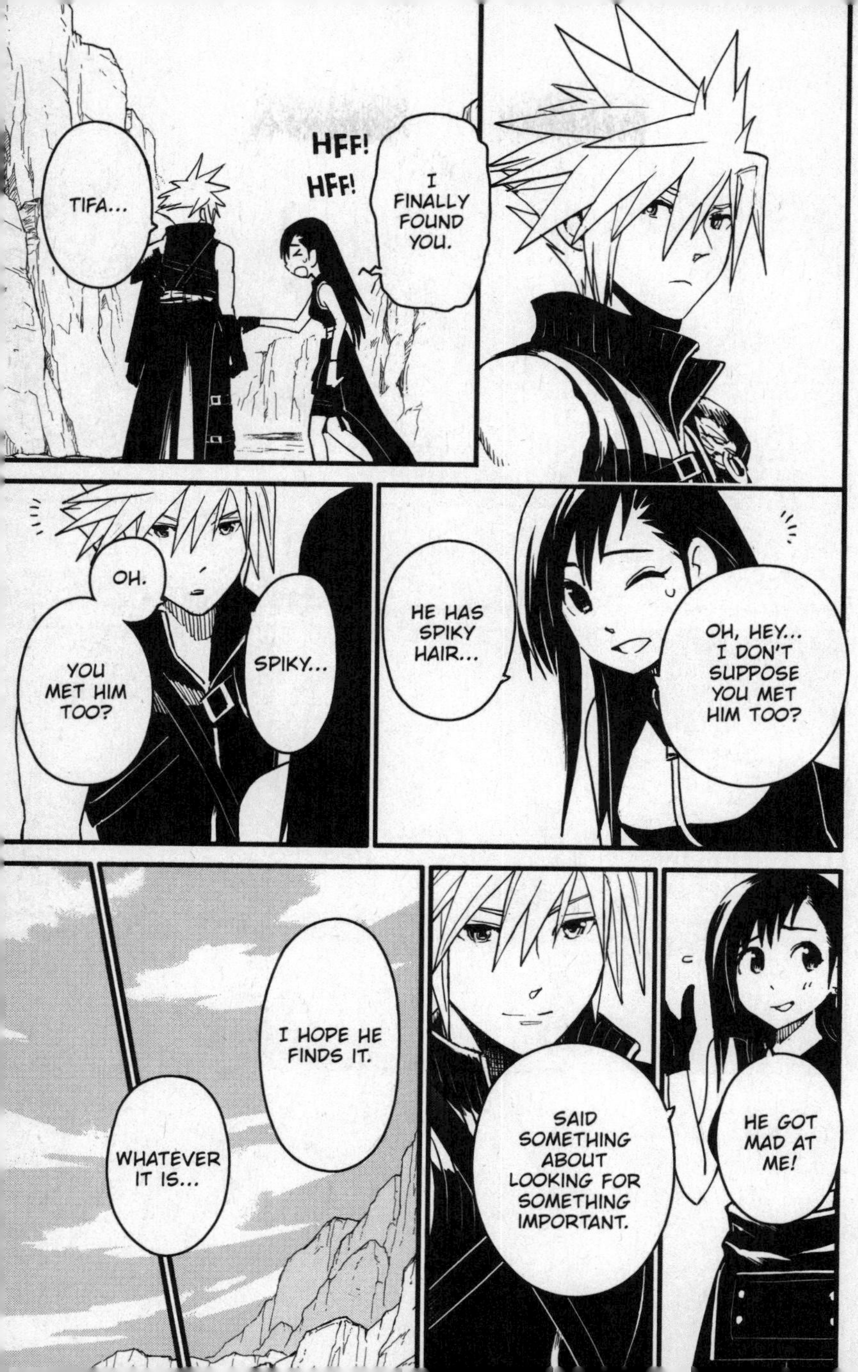
I FINALLY FOUND YOU.
HFF!
HFF!
TIFA...
OH, HEY... I DON'T SUPPOSE YOU MET HIM TOO?
HE HAS SPIKY HAIR...
SPIKY...
OH.
YOU MET HIM TOO?
HE GOT MAD AT ME!
SAID SOMETHING ABOUT LOOKING FOR SOMETHING IMPORTANT.
I HOPE HE FINDS IT.
WHATEVER IT IS...

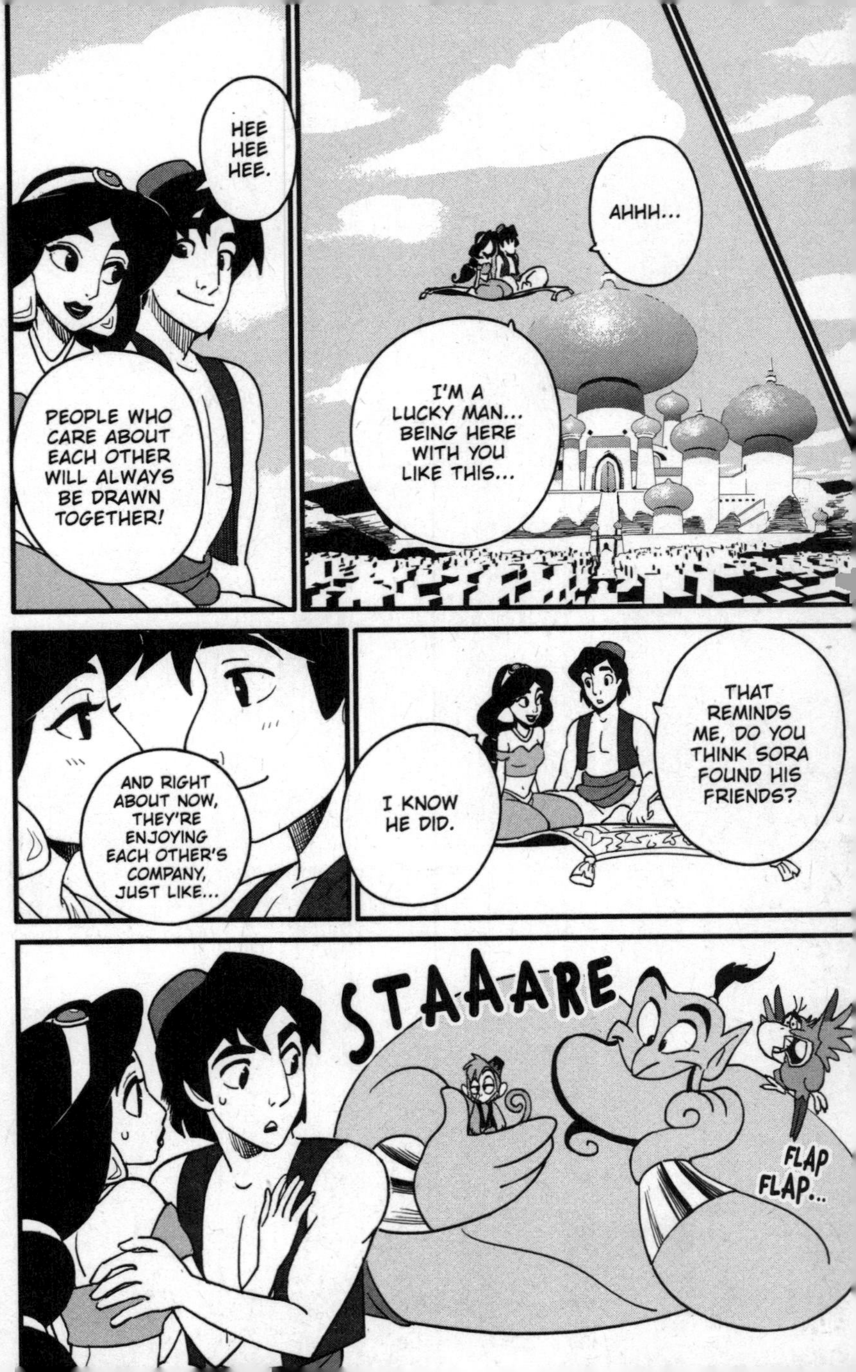
AHHH...
I'M A LUCKY MAN... BEING HERE WITH YOU LIKE THIS...
HEE HEE HEE.
PEOPLE WHO CARE ABOUT EACH OTHER WILL ALWAYS BE DRAWN TOGETHER!
THAT REMINDS ME, DO YOU THINK SORA FOUND HIS FRIENDS?
I KNOW HE DID.
AND RIGHT ABOUT NOW, THEY'RE ENJOYING EACH OTHER'S COMPANY, JUST LIKE...
STAAARE
FLAP FLAP...

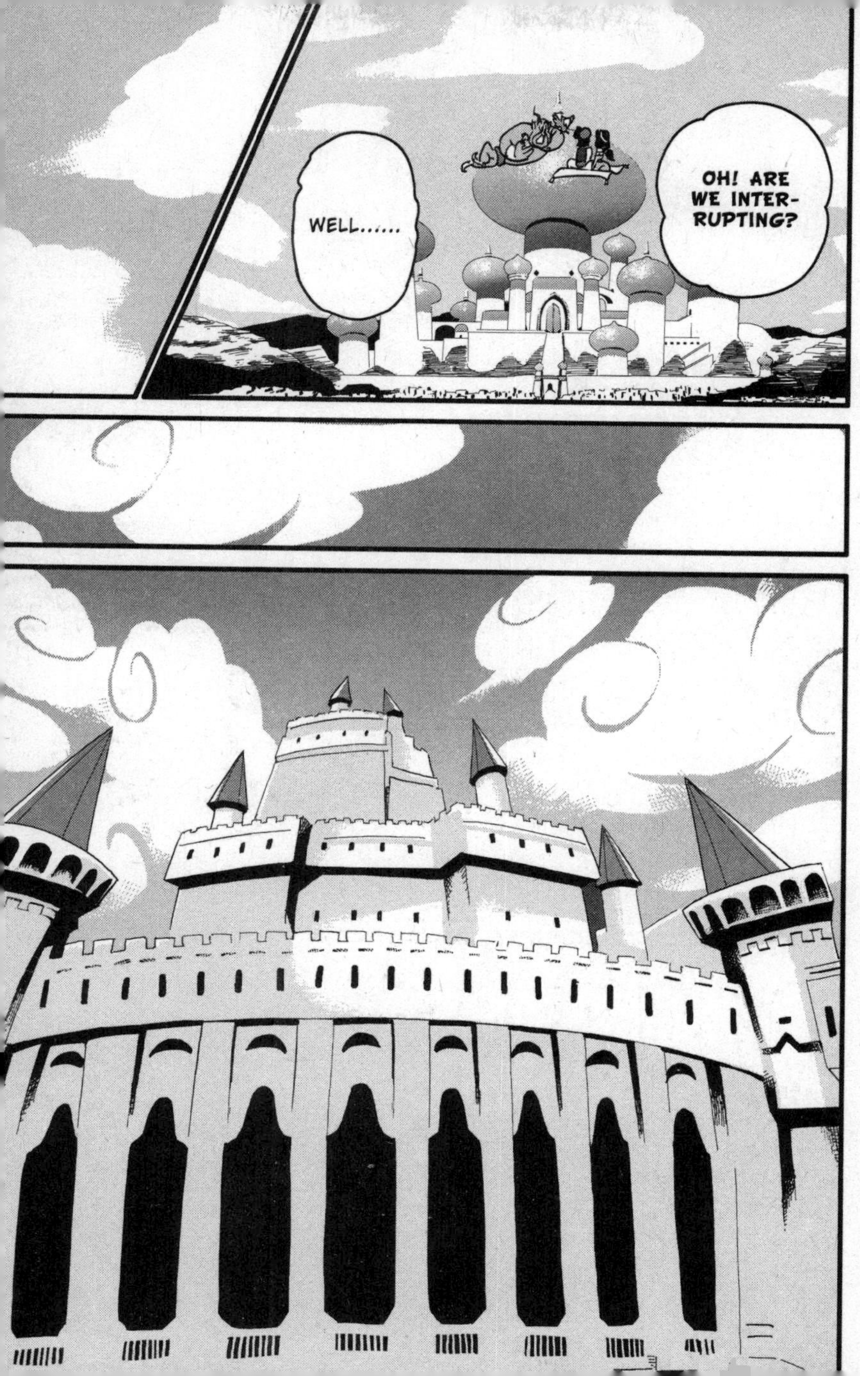
OH! ARE WE INTER-RUPTING?
WELL......

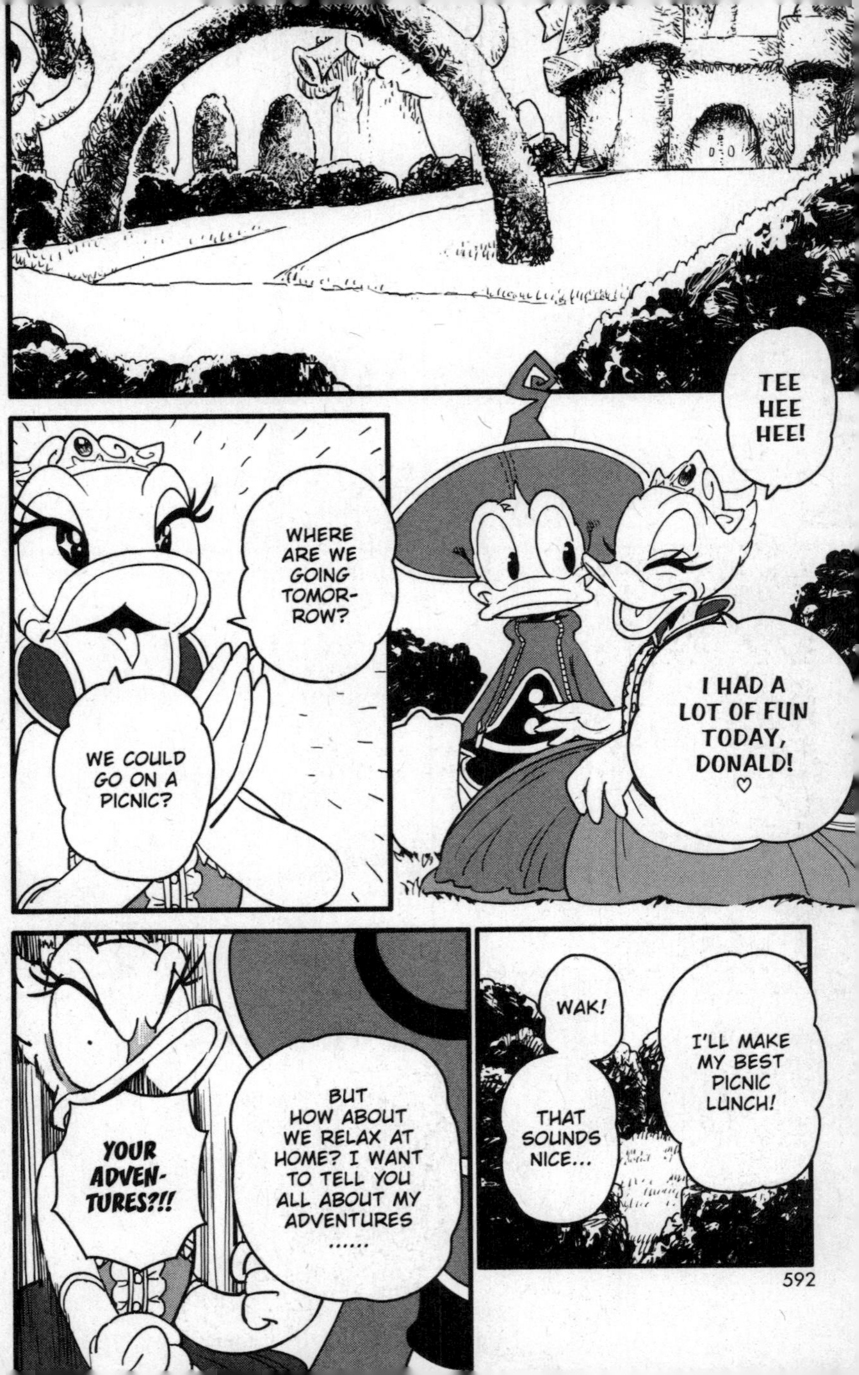
TEE HEE HEE!
I HAD A LOT OF FUN TODAY, DONALD! ♡
WHERE ARE WE GOING TOMOR-ROW?
WE COULD GO ON A PICNIC?
I'LL MAKE MY BEST PICNIC LUNCH!
WAK!
THAT SOUNDS NICE...
BUT HOW ABOUT WE RELAX AT HOME? I WANT TO TELL YOU ALL ABOUT MY ADVENTURES ......
YOUR ADVEN-TURES?!!

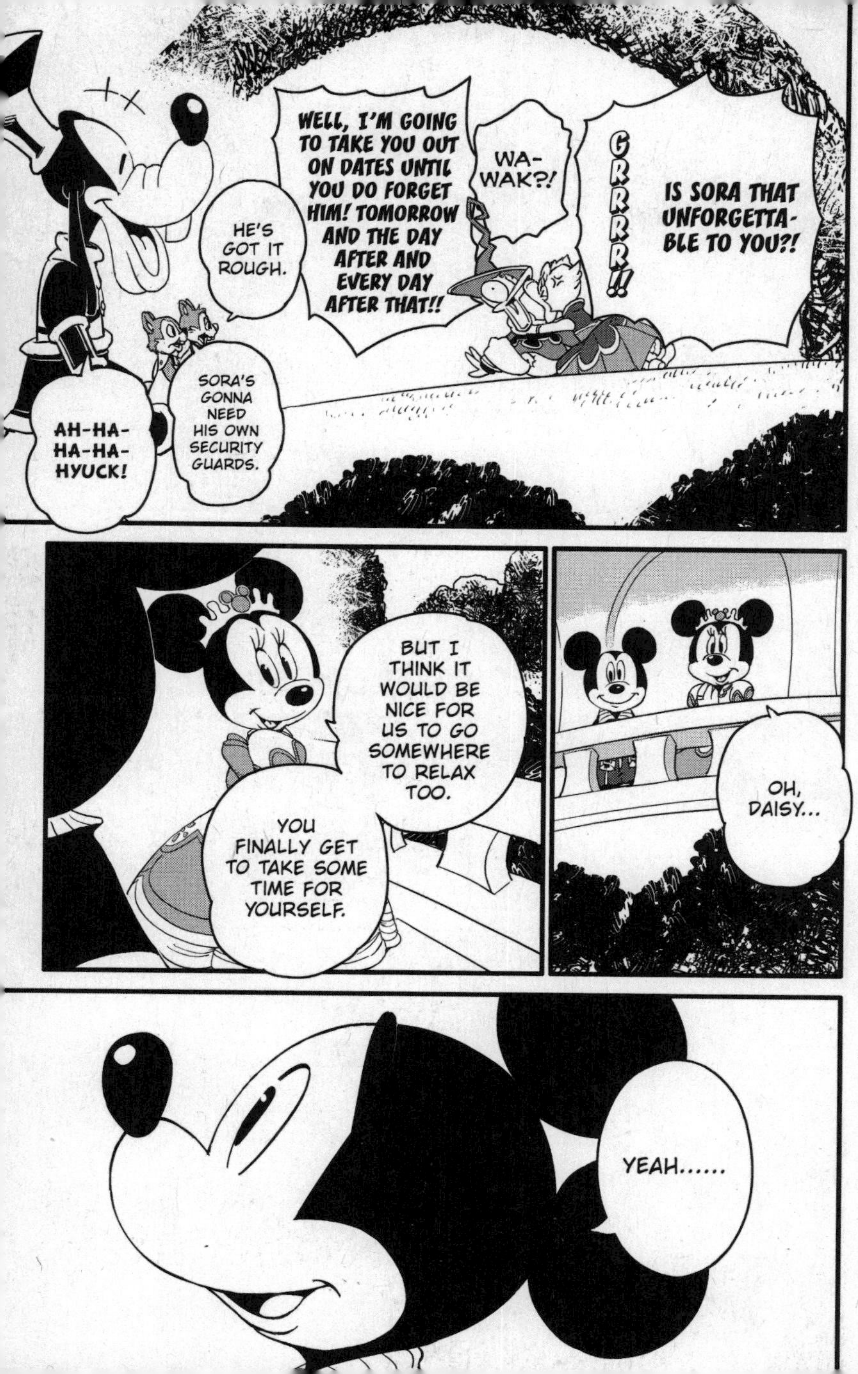
IS SORA THAT UNFORGETTABLE TO YOU?!
GRRRRR!!
WA-WAK?!
WELL, I'M GOING TO TAKE YOU OUT ON DATES UNTIL YOU DO FORGET HIM! TOMORROW AND THE DAY AFTER AND EVERY DAY AFTER THAT!!
HE'S GOT IT ROUGH.
SORA'S GONNA NEED HIS OWN SECURITY GUARDS.
AH-HA-HA-HA-HYUCK!
OH, DAISY...
YOU FINALLY GET TO TAKE SOME TIME FOR YOURSELF.
BUT I THINK IT WOULD BE NICE FOR US TO GO SOMEWHERE TO RELAX TOO.
YEAH......

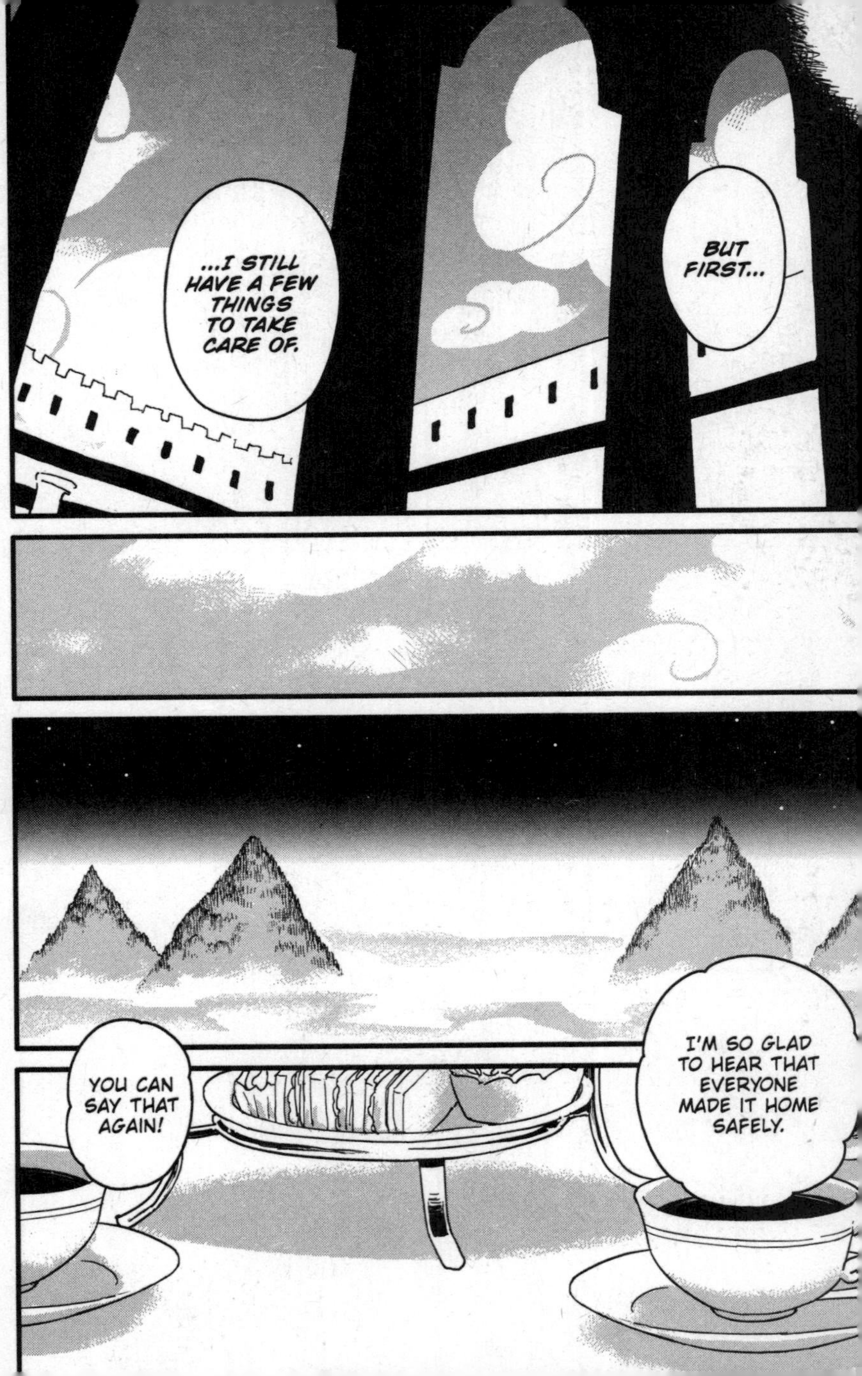
BUT FIRST...
...I STILL HAVE A FEW THINGS TO TAKE CARE OF.
I'M SO GLAD TO HEAR THAT EVERYONE MADE IT HOME SAFELY.
YOU CAN SAY THAT AGAIN!

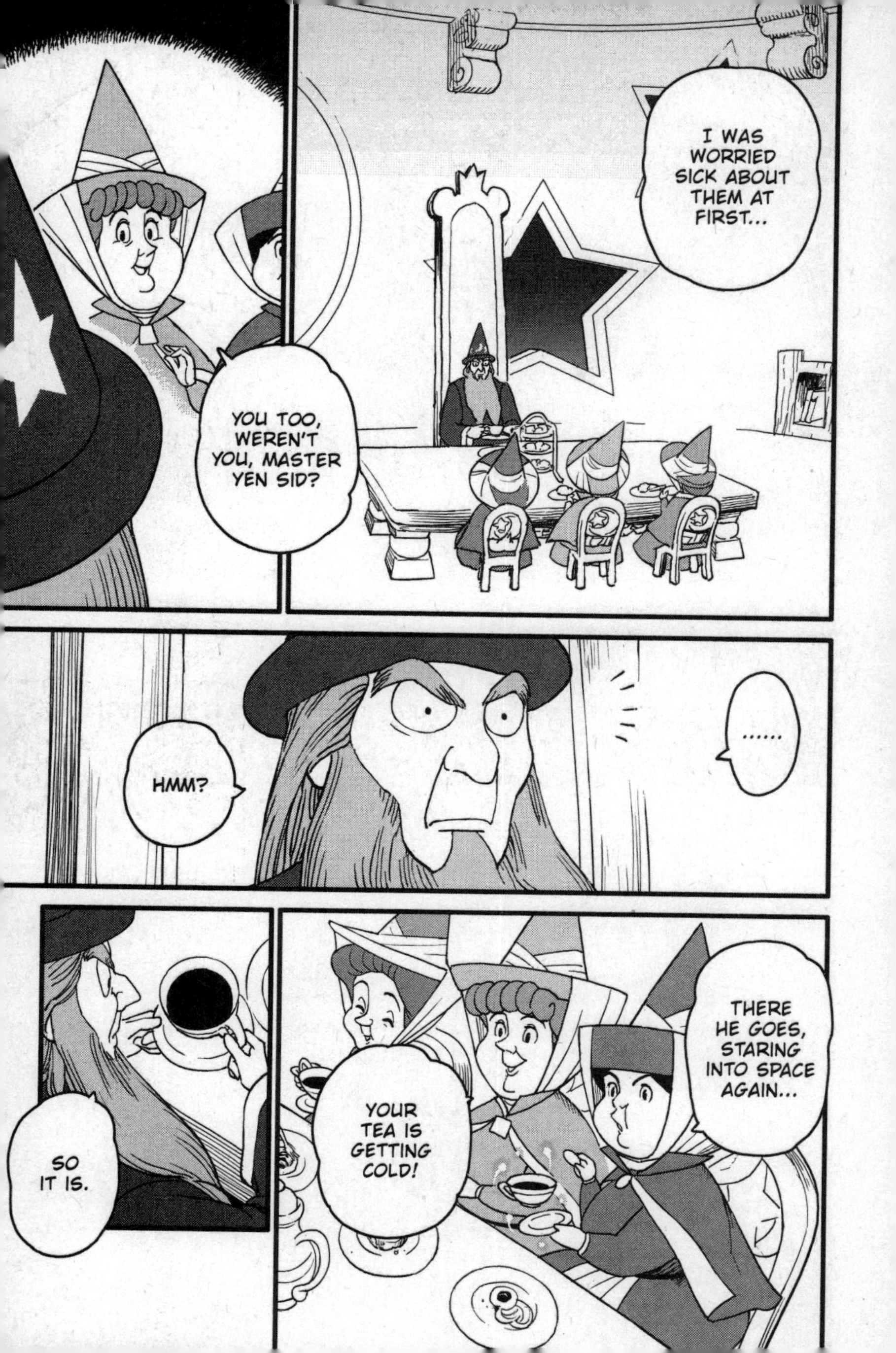
I WAS WORRIED SICK ABOUT THEM AT FIRST...
YOU TOO, WEREN'T YOU, MASTER YEN SID?
......
HMM?
THERE HE GOES, STARING INTO SPACE AGAIN...
YOUR TEA IS GETTING COLD!
SO IT IS.

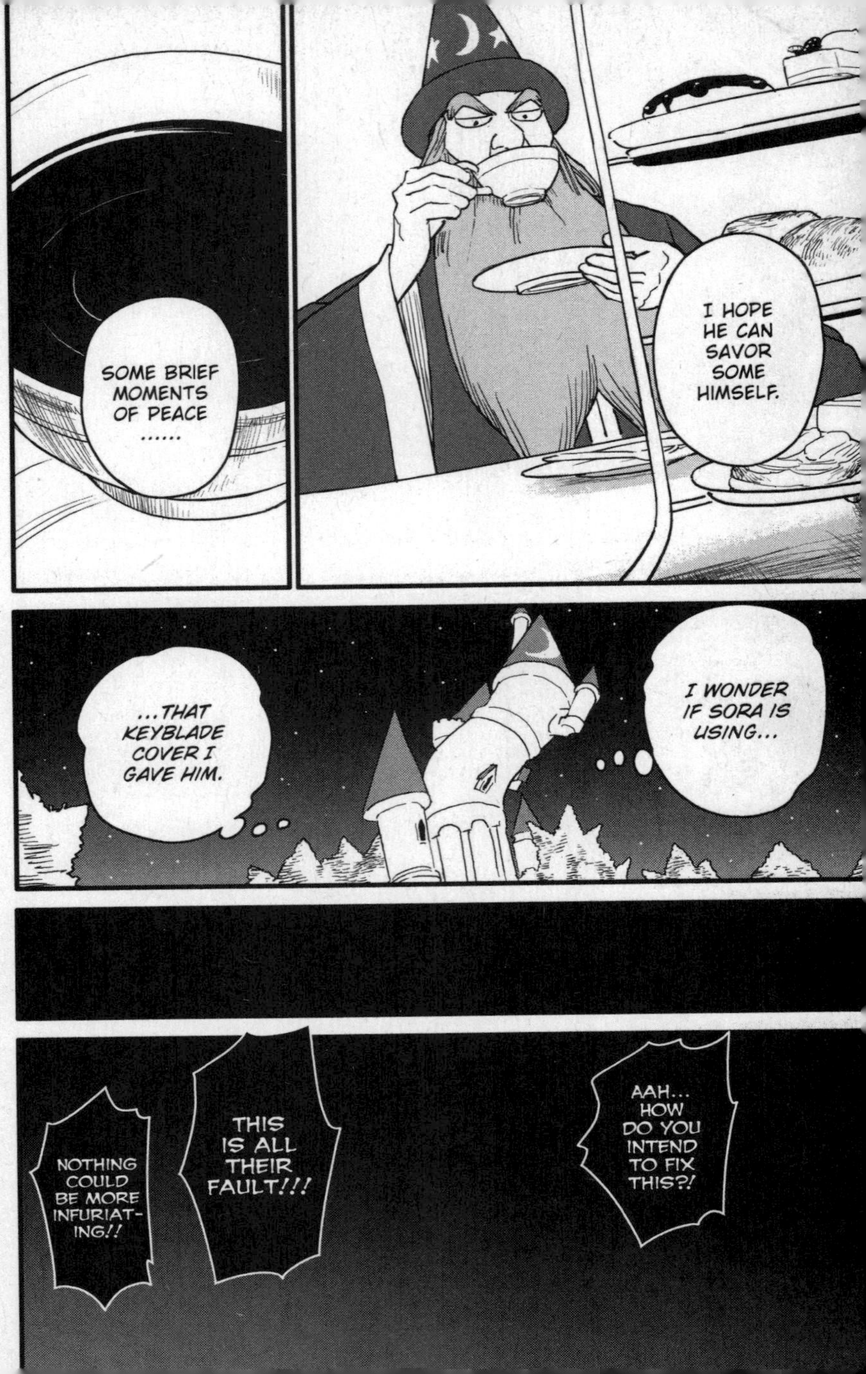
I HOPE HE CAN SAVOR SOME HIMSELF.
SOME BRIEF MOMENTS OF PEACE ......
I WONDER IF SORA IS USING...
...THAT KEYBLADE COVER I GAVE HIM.
AAH... HOW DO YOU INTEND TO FIX THIS?!
THIS IS ALL THEIR FAULT!!!
NOTHING COULD BE MORE INFURIATING!!

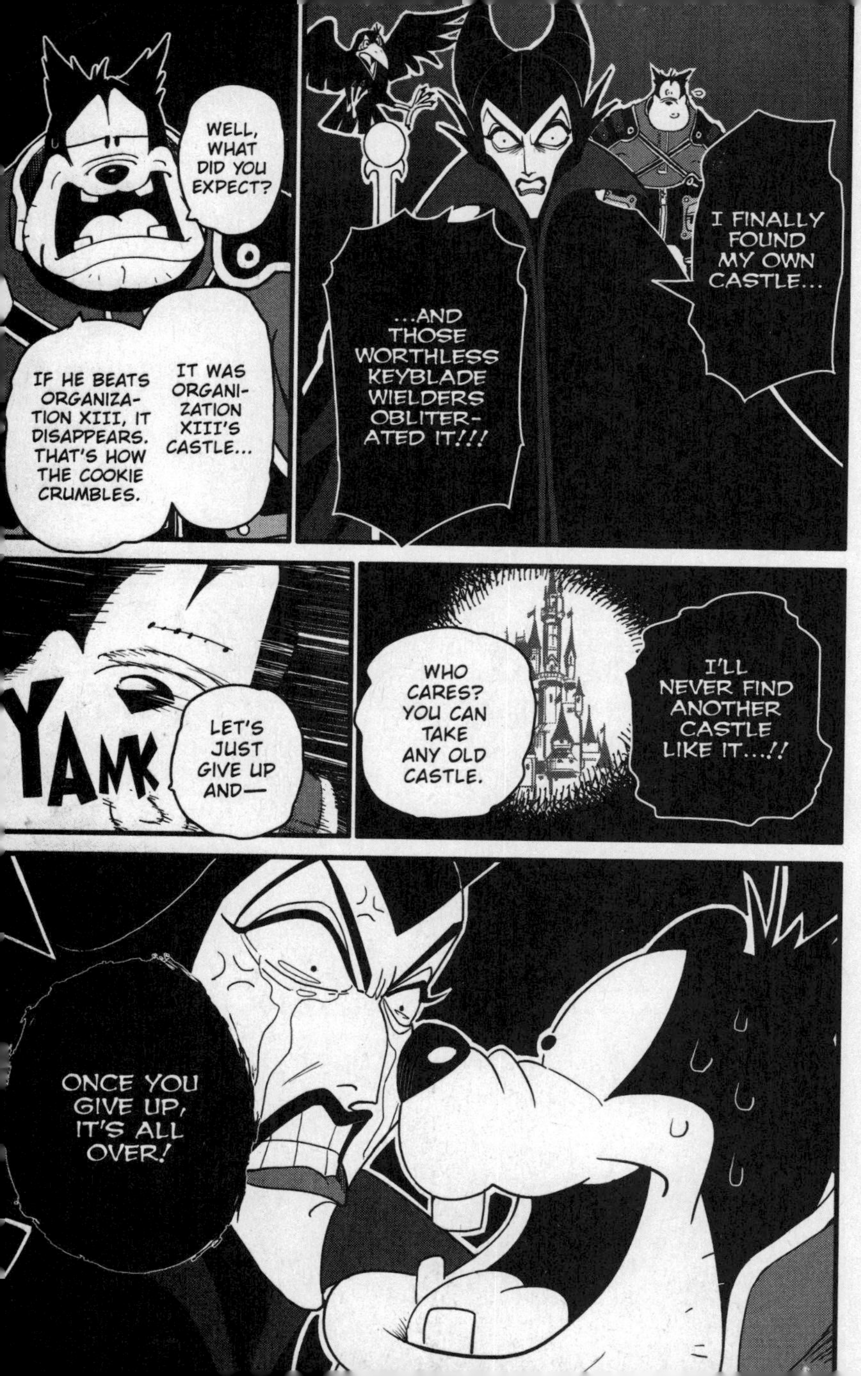
I FINALLY FOUND MY OWN CASTLE...
...AND THOSE WORTHLESS KEYBLADE WIELDERS OBLITERATED IT!!!
WELL, WHAT DID YOU EXPECT?
IT WAS ORGANIZATION XIII'S CASTLE...
IF HE BEATS ORGANIZATION XIII, IT DISAPPEARS. THAT'S HOW THE COOKIE CRUMBLES.
I'LL NEVER FIND ANOTHER CASTLE LIKE IT...!!
WHO CARES? YOU CAN TAKE ANY OLD CASTLE.
LET'S JUST GIVE UP AND—
YANK
ONCE YOU GIVE UP, IT'S ALL OVER!

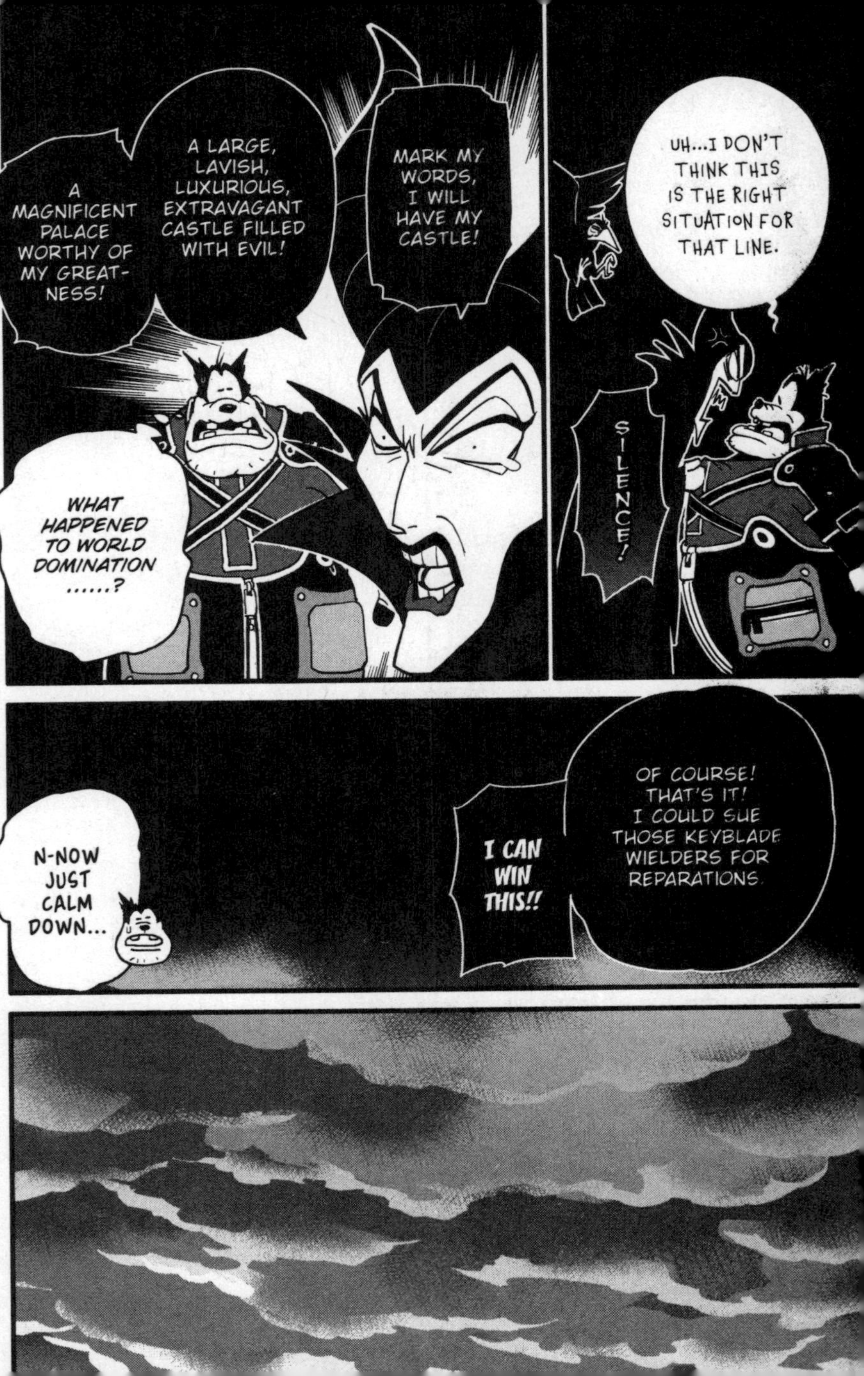

A MAGNIFICENT PALACE WORTHY OF MY GREAT-NESS!
A LARGE, LAVISH, LUXURIOUS, EXTRAVAGANT CASTLE FILLED WITH EVIL!
WHAT HAPPENED TO WORLD DOMINATION ......?
MARK MY WORDS, I WILL HAVE MY CASTLE!
UH...I DON'T THINK THIS IS THE RIGHT SITUATION FOR THAT LINE.
SILENCE!
N-NOW JUST CALM DOWN...
OF COURSE! THAT'S IT! I COULD SUE THOSE KEYBLADE WIELDERS FOR REPARATIONS.
I CAN WIN THIS!!

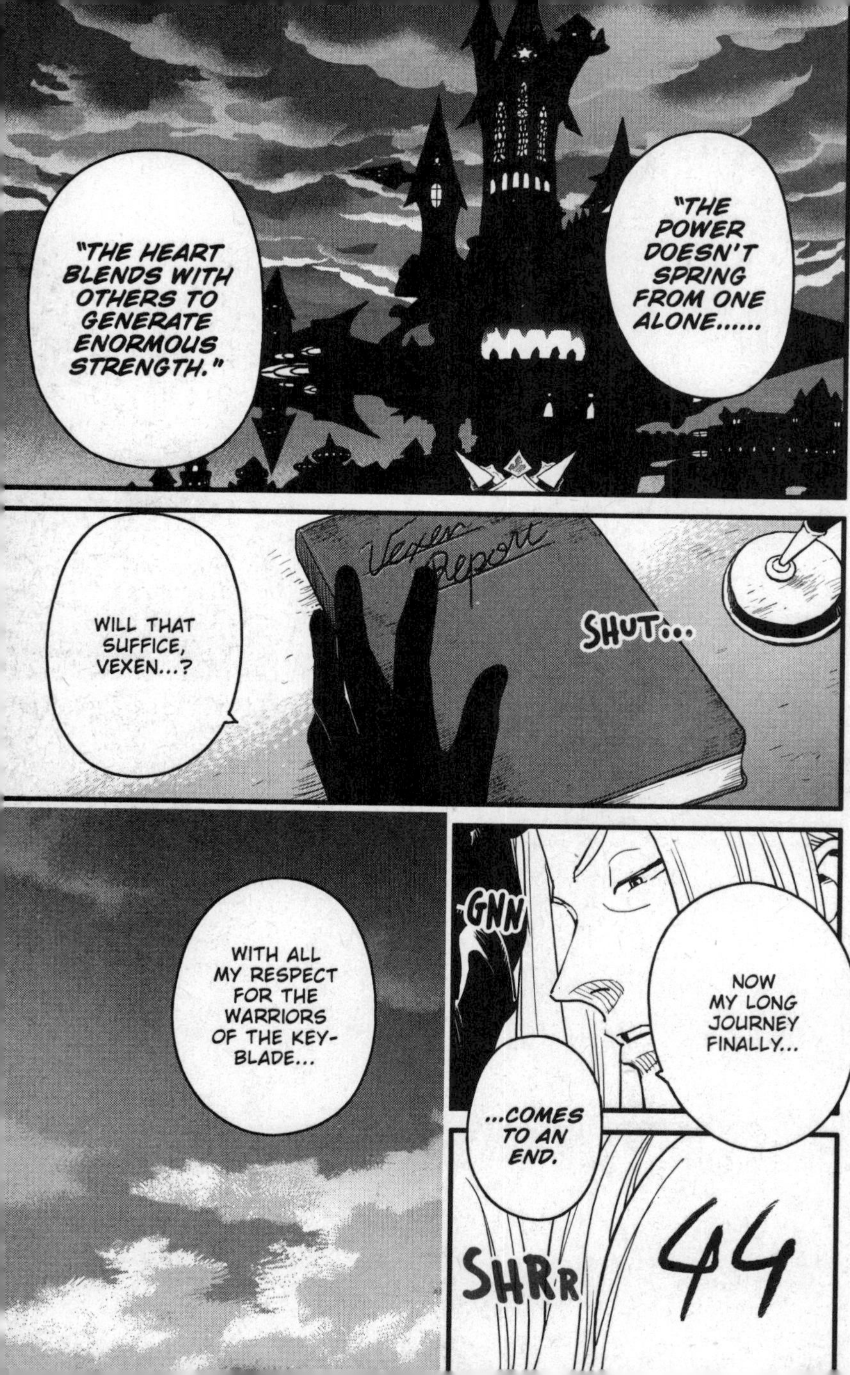
"THE POWER DOESN'T SPRING FROM ONE ALONE......
"THE HEART BLENDS WITH OTHERS TO GENERATE ENORMOUS STRENGTH."
Vexen Report
SHUT...
WILL THAT SUFFICE, VEXEN...?
GNN
NOW MY LONG JOURNEY FINALLY...
...COMES TO AN END.
SHRR
44
WITH ALL MY RESPECT FOR THE WARRIORS OF THE KEY-BLADE...

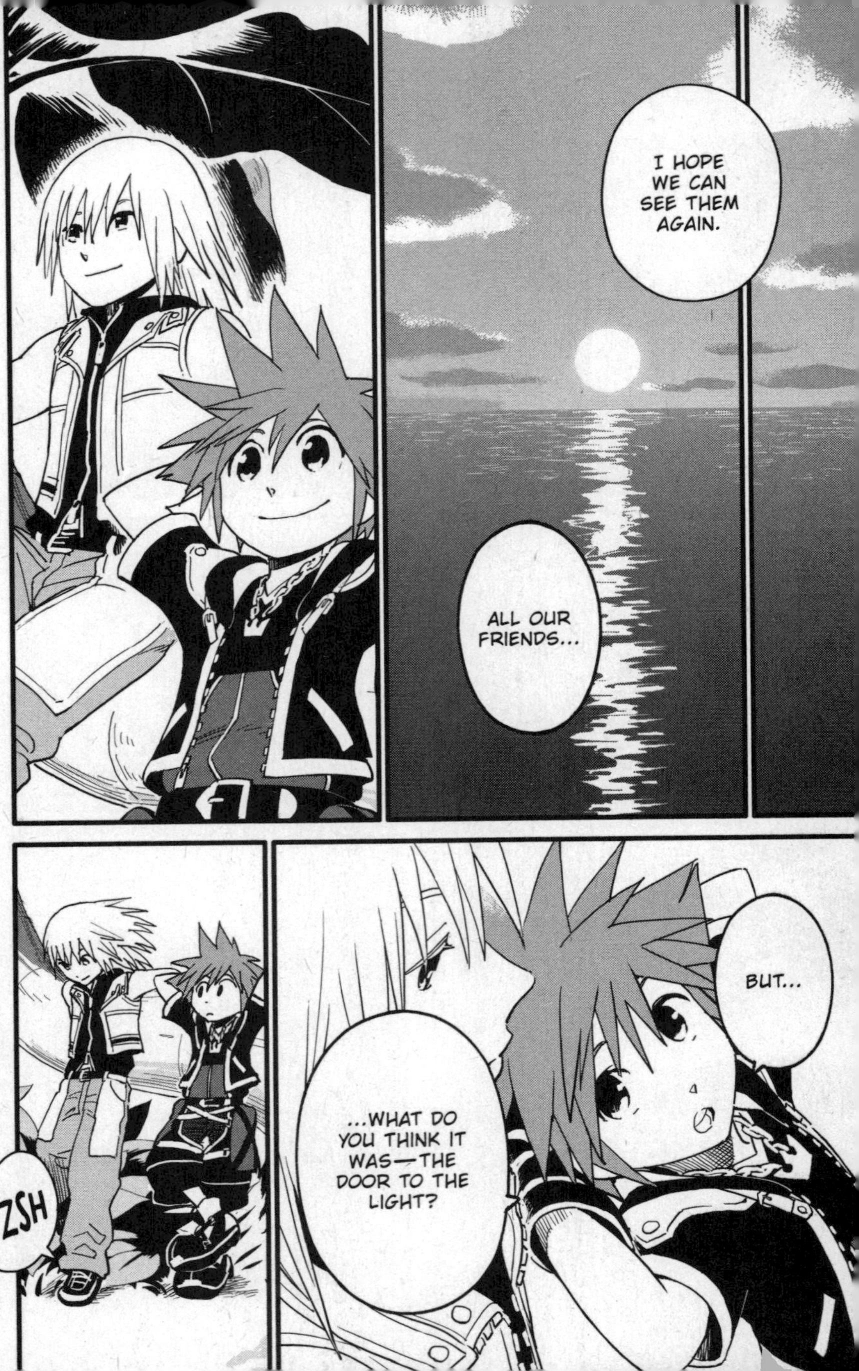
I HOPE WE CAN SEE THEM AGAIN.
ALL OUR FRIENDS...
BUT...
...WHAT DO YOU THINK IT WAS—THE DOOR TO THE LIGHT?
ZSH

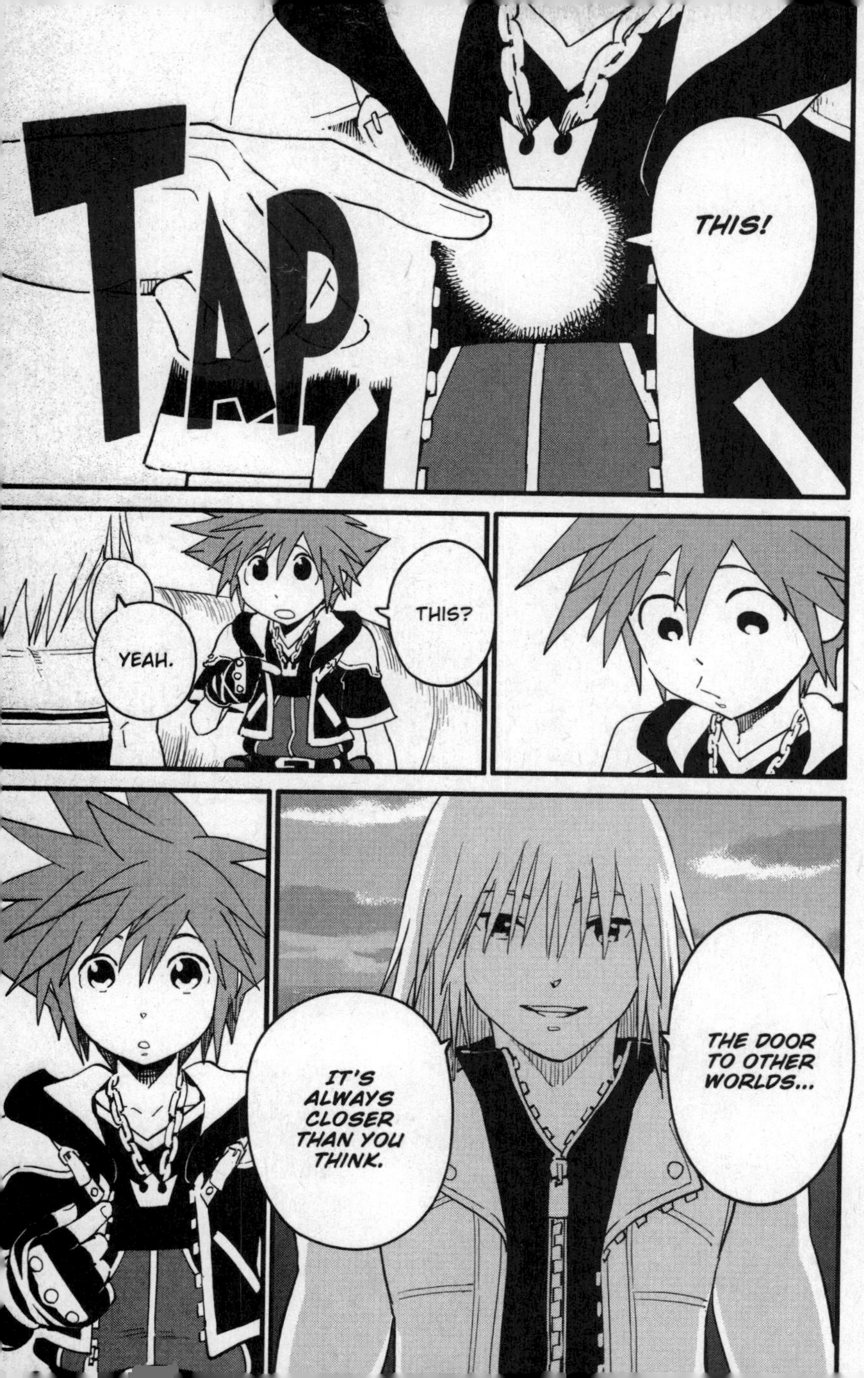
THIS!
TAP
THIS?
YEAH.
THE DOOR TO OTHER WORLDS...
IT'S ALWAYS CLOSER THAN YOU THINK.

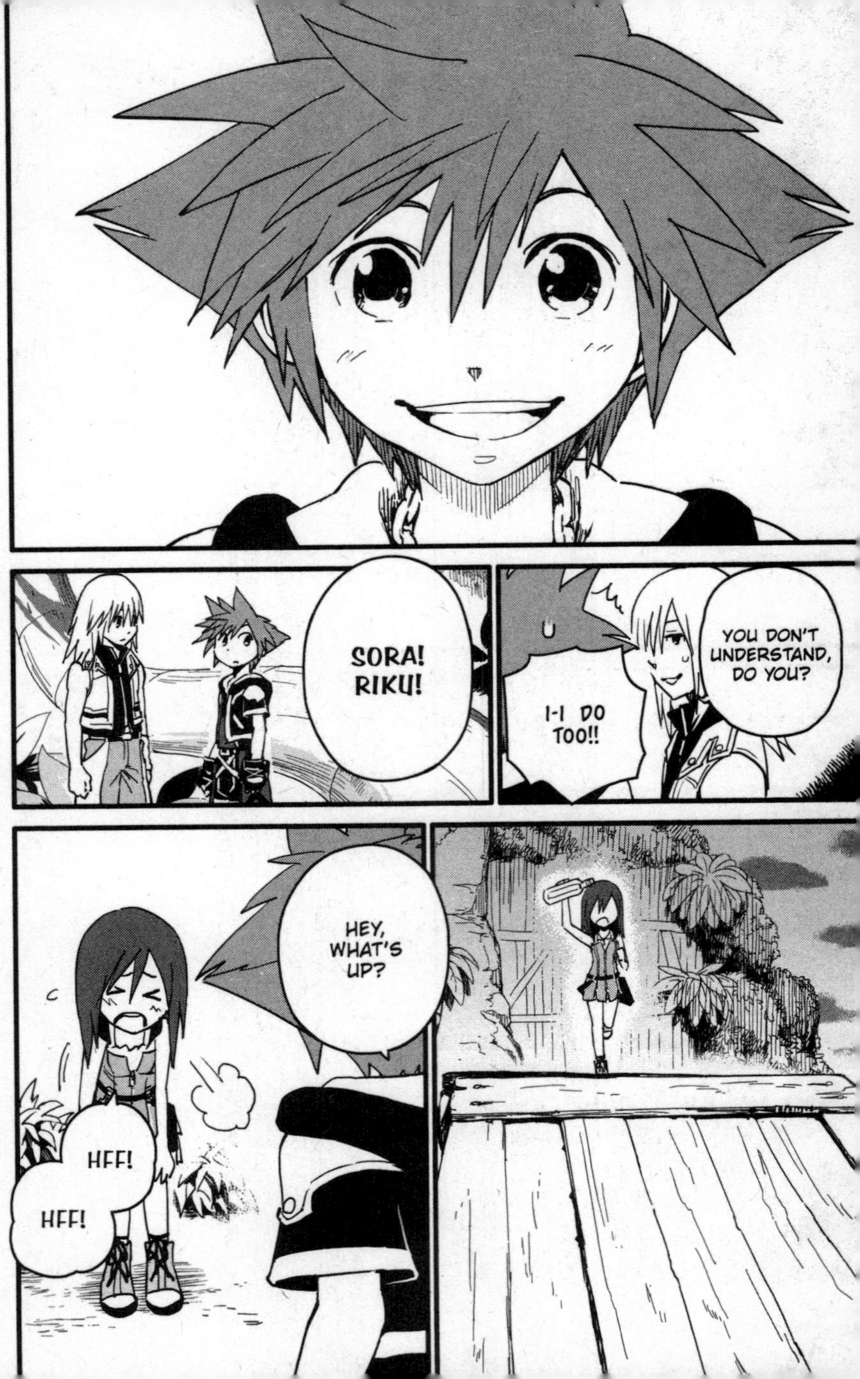
YOU DON'T UNDERSTAND, DO YOU?
I-I DO TOO!!
SORA! RIKU!
HEY, WHAT'S UP?
HFF!
HFF!

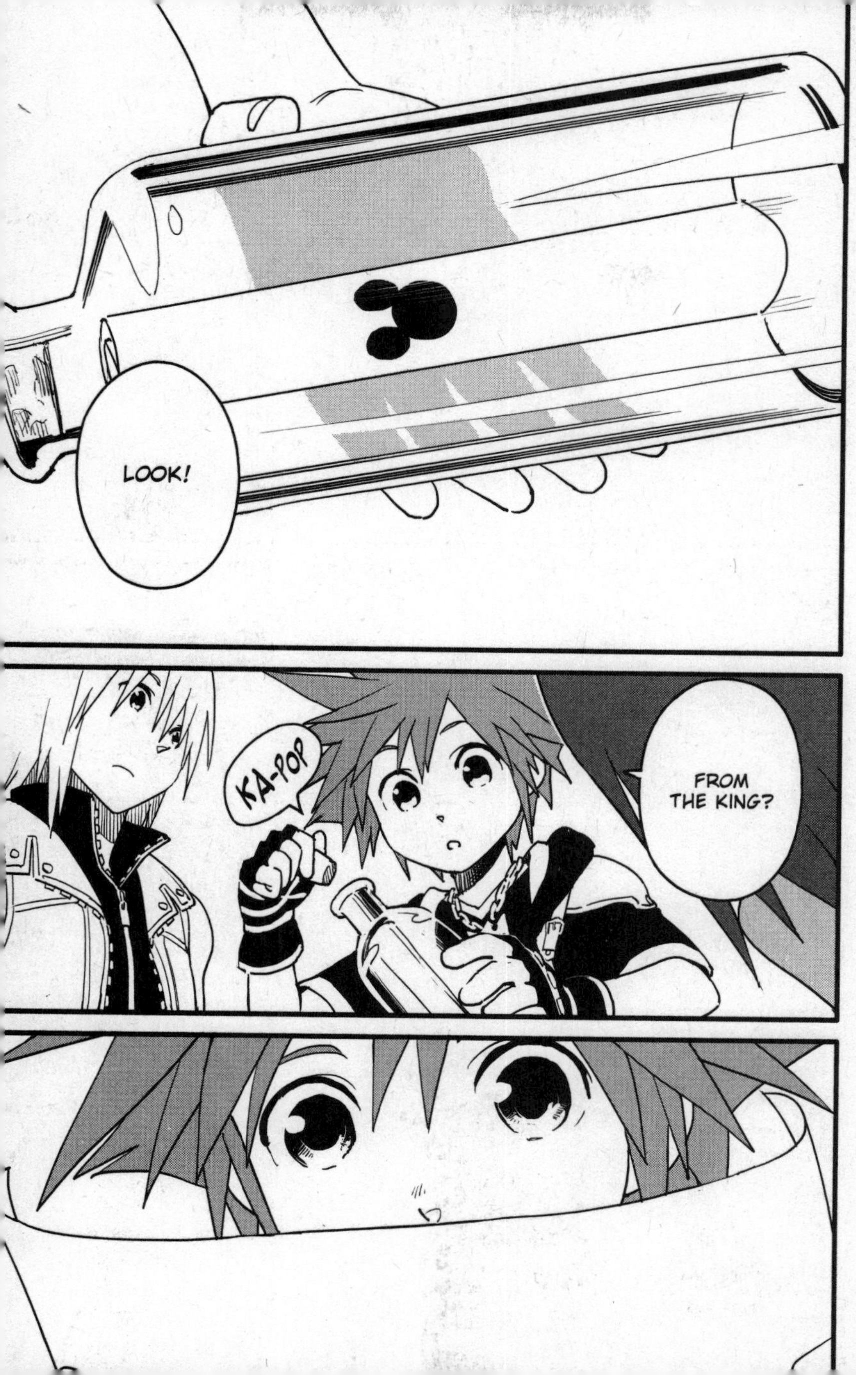
LOOK!
FROM THE KING?
KA-POP

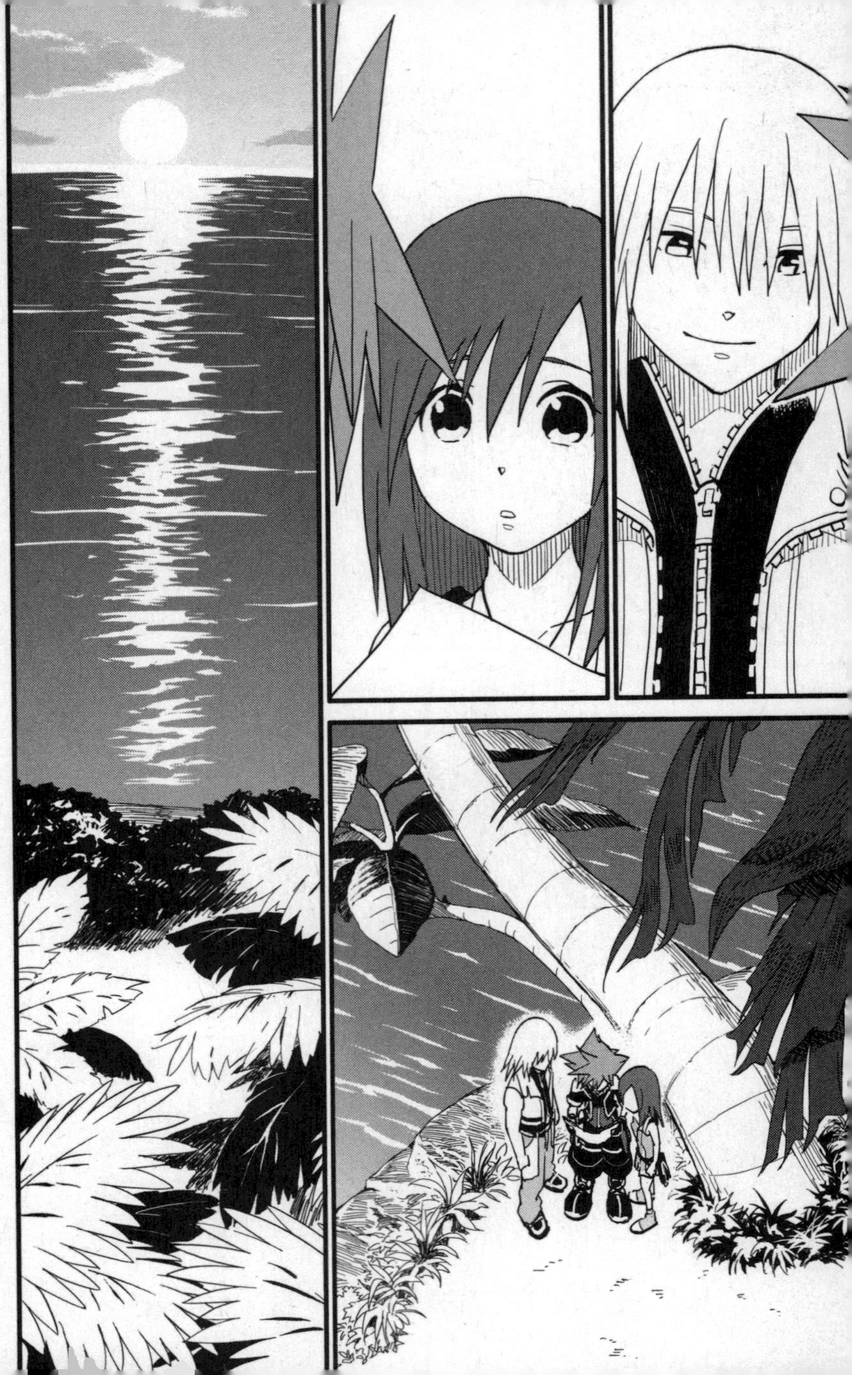

*THERE ARE MANY WORLDS,
BUT THEY SHARE THE SAME SKY—
ONE SKY, ONE DESTINY.*

KINGDOM HEARTS II④ *End*

Disney SQUARE ENIX

KINGDOM HEARTS

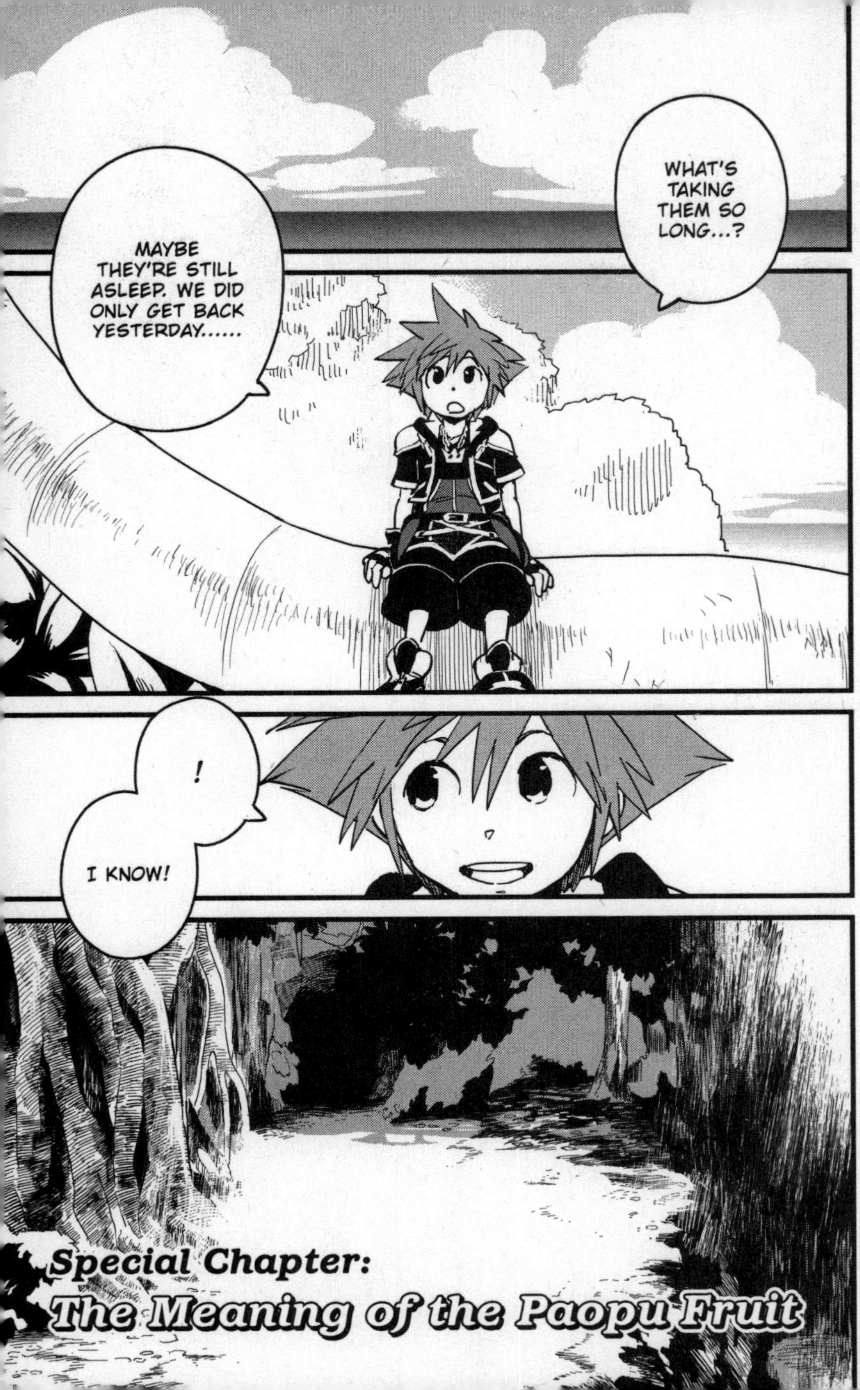
WHAT'S TAKING THEM SO LONG...?
MAYBE THEY'RE STILL ASLEEP. WE DID ONLY GET BACK YESTERDAY......
!
I KNOW!
Special Chapter:
The Meaning of the Paopu Fruit

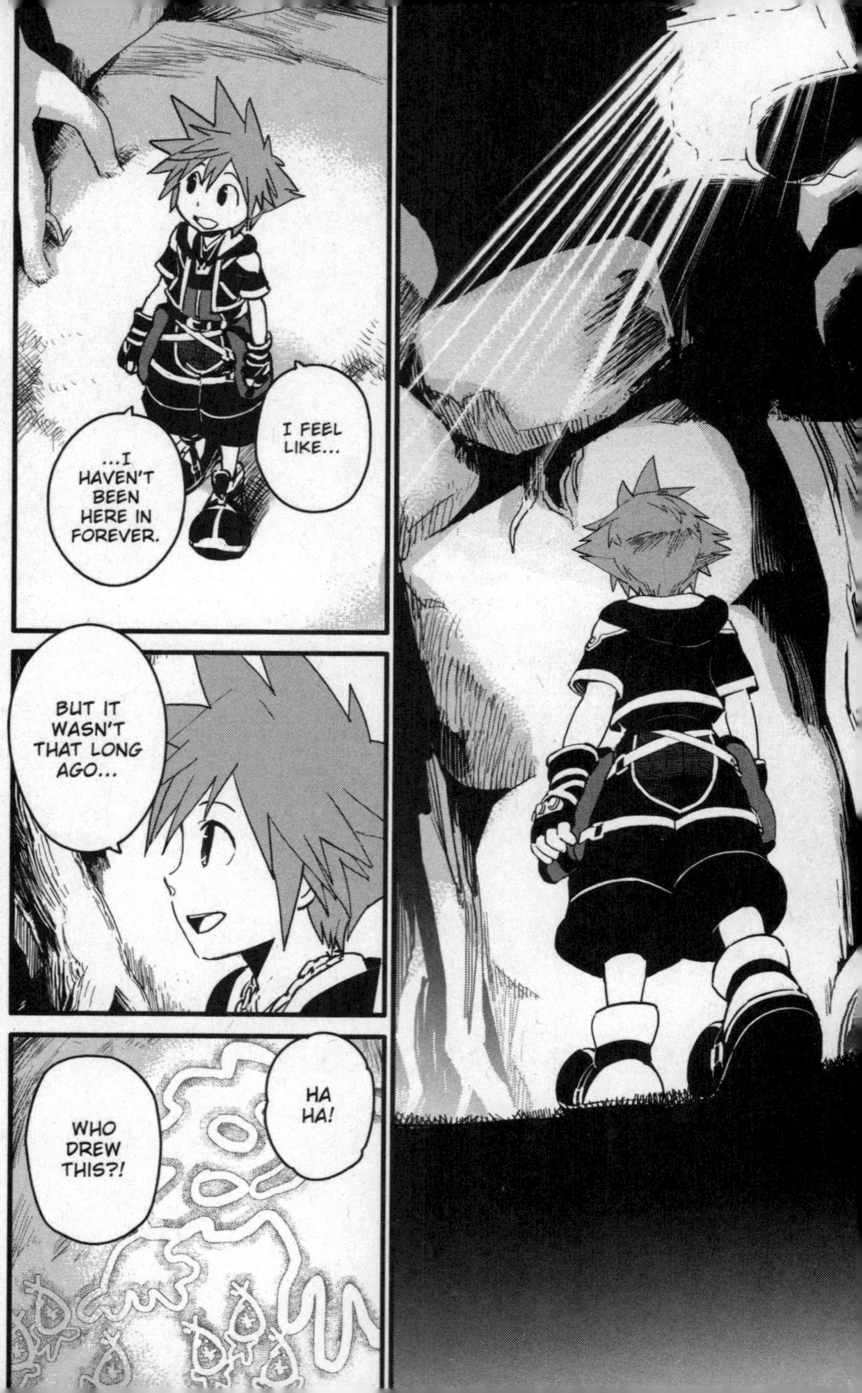
I FEEL LIKE...
...I HAVEN'T BEEN HERE IN FOREVER.
BUT IT WASN'T THAT LONG AGO...
HA HA!
WHO DREW THIS?!

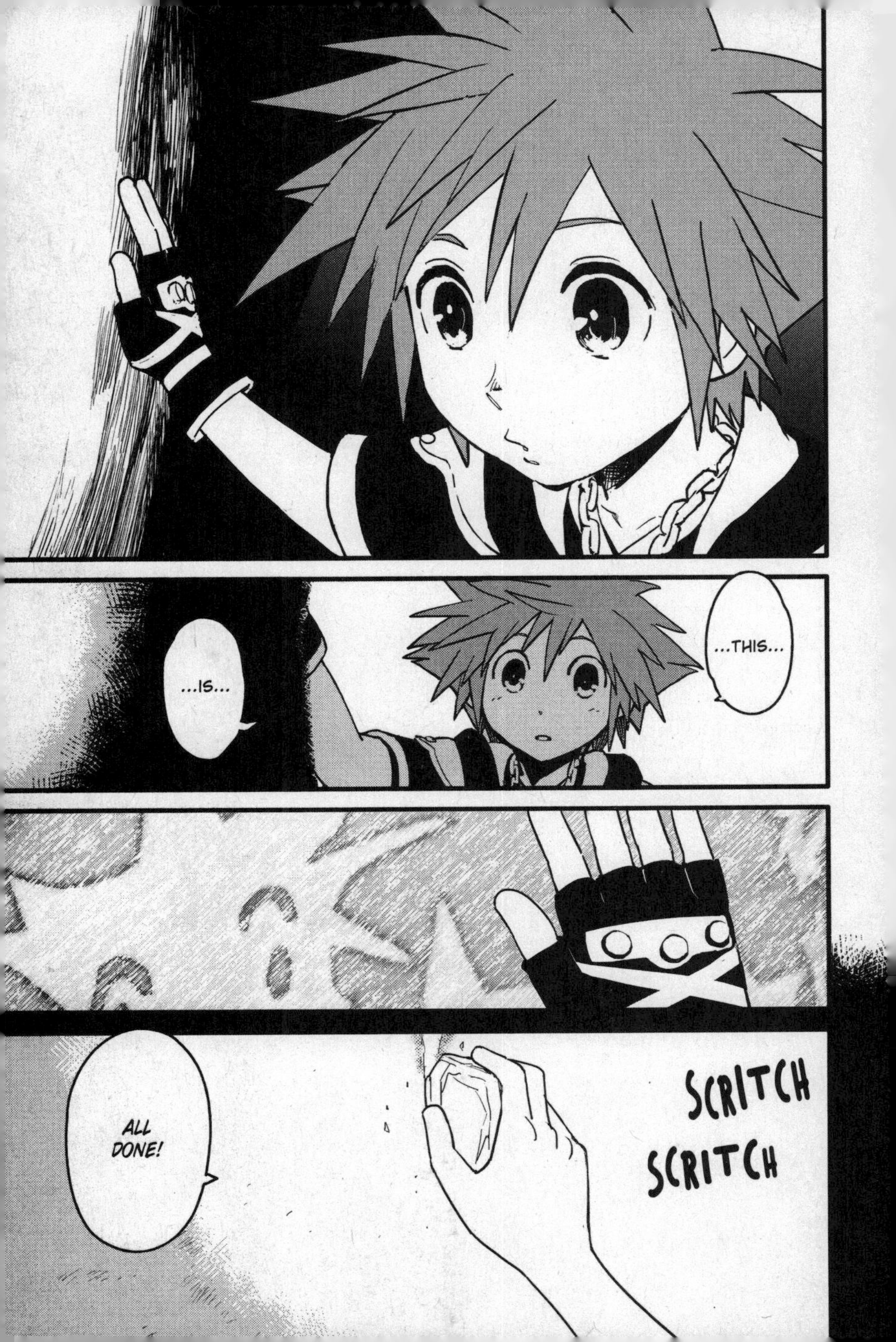
...THIS...
...IS...
SCRITCH
SCRITCH
ALL DONE!

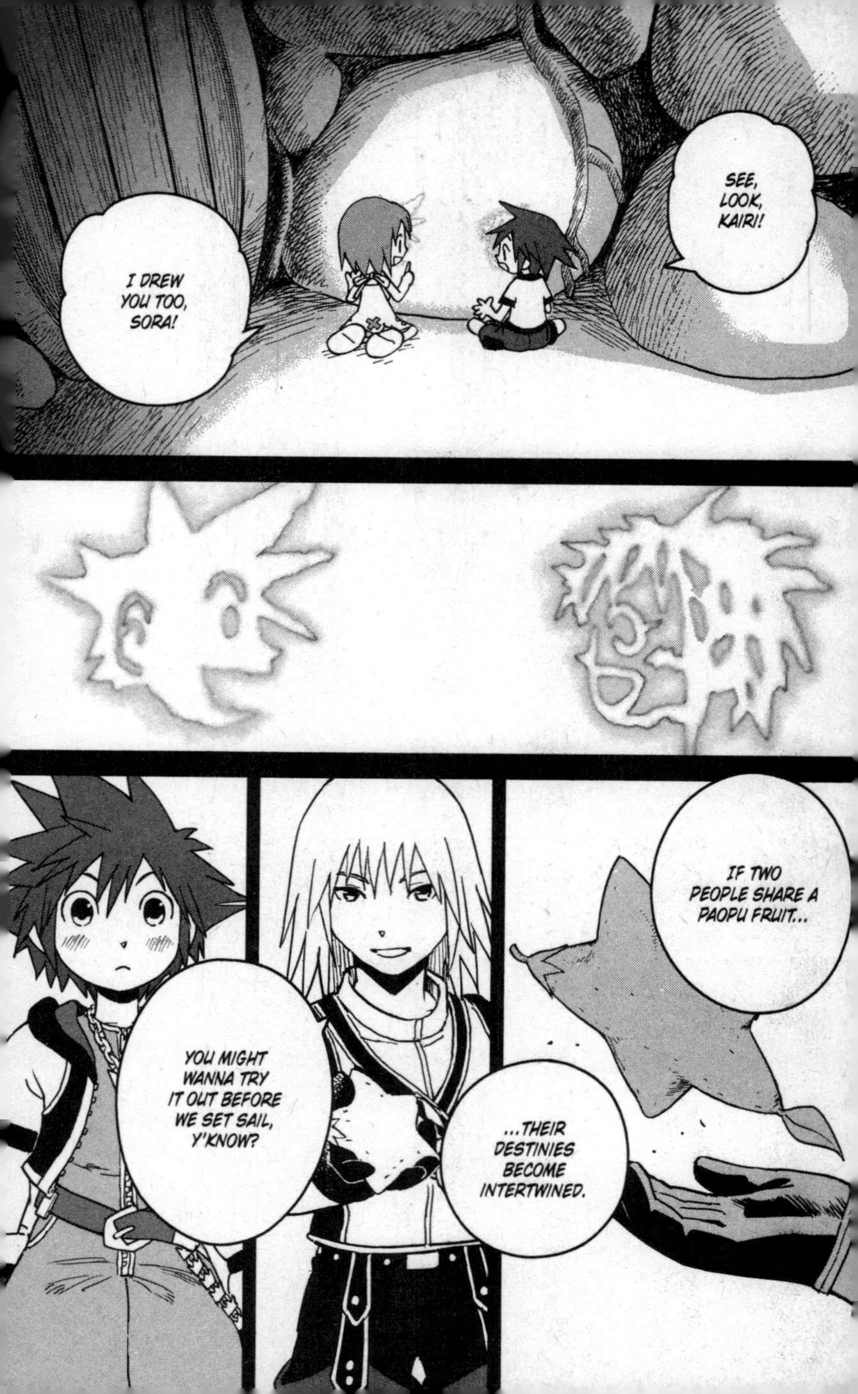
SEE, LOOK, KAIRI!
I DREW YOU TOO, SORA!
IF TWO PEOPLE SHARE A PAOPU FRUIT...
...THEIR DESTINIES BECOME INTERTWINED.
YOU MIGHT WANNA TRY IT OUT BEFORE WE SET SAIL, Y'KNOW?

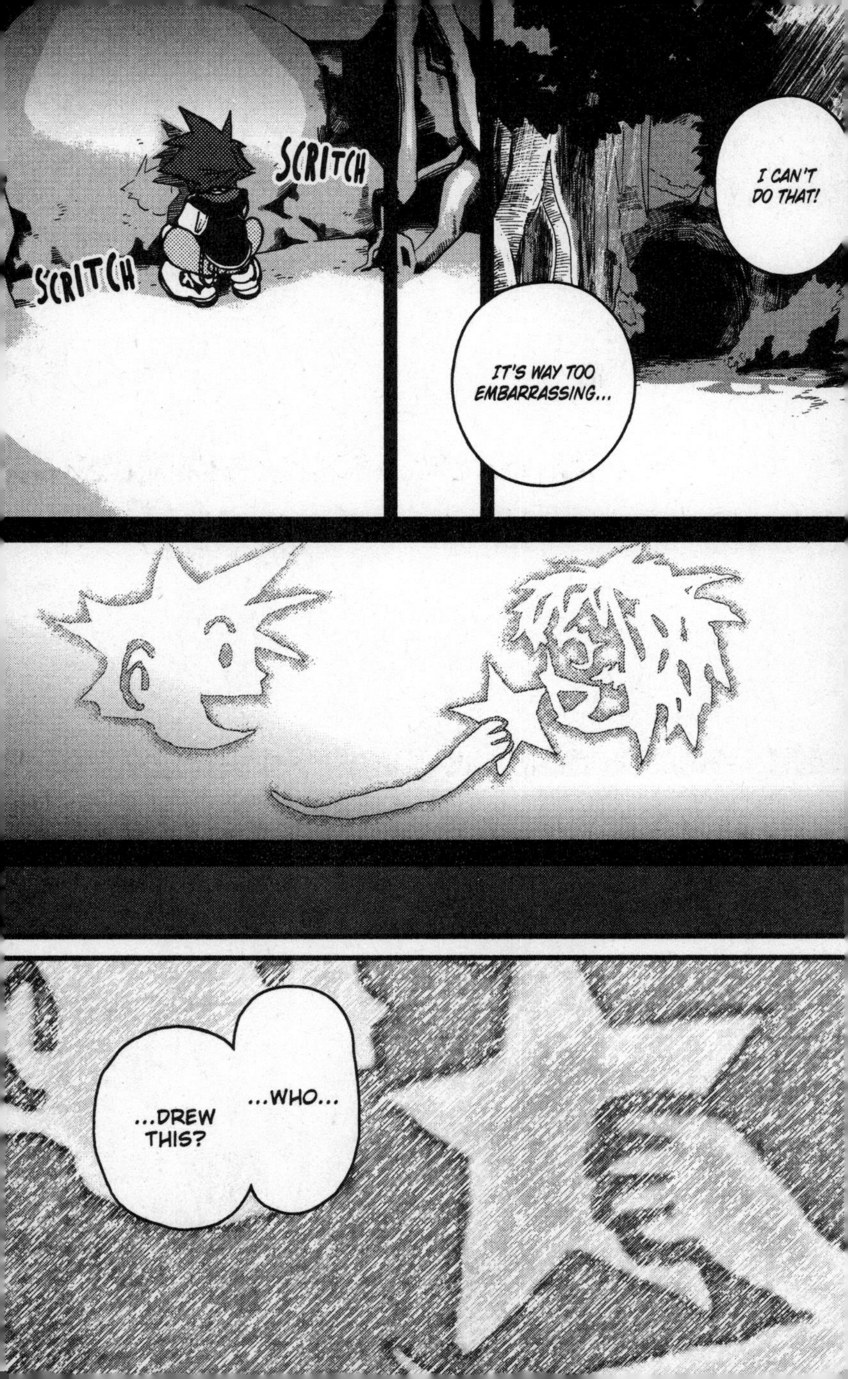
I CAN'T DO THAT!
IT'S WAY TOO EMBARRASSING...
SCRITCH
SCRITCH
...WHO...
...DREW THIS?

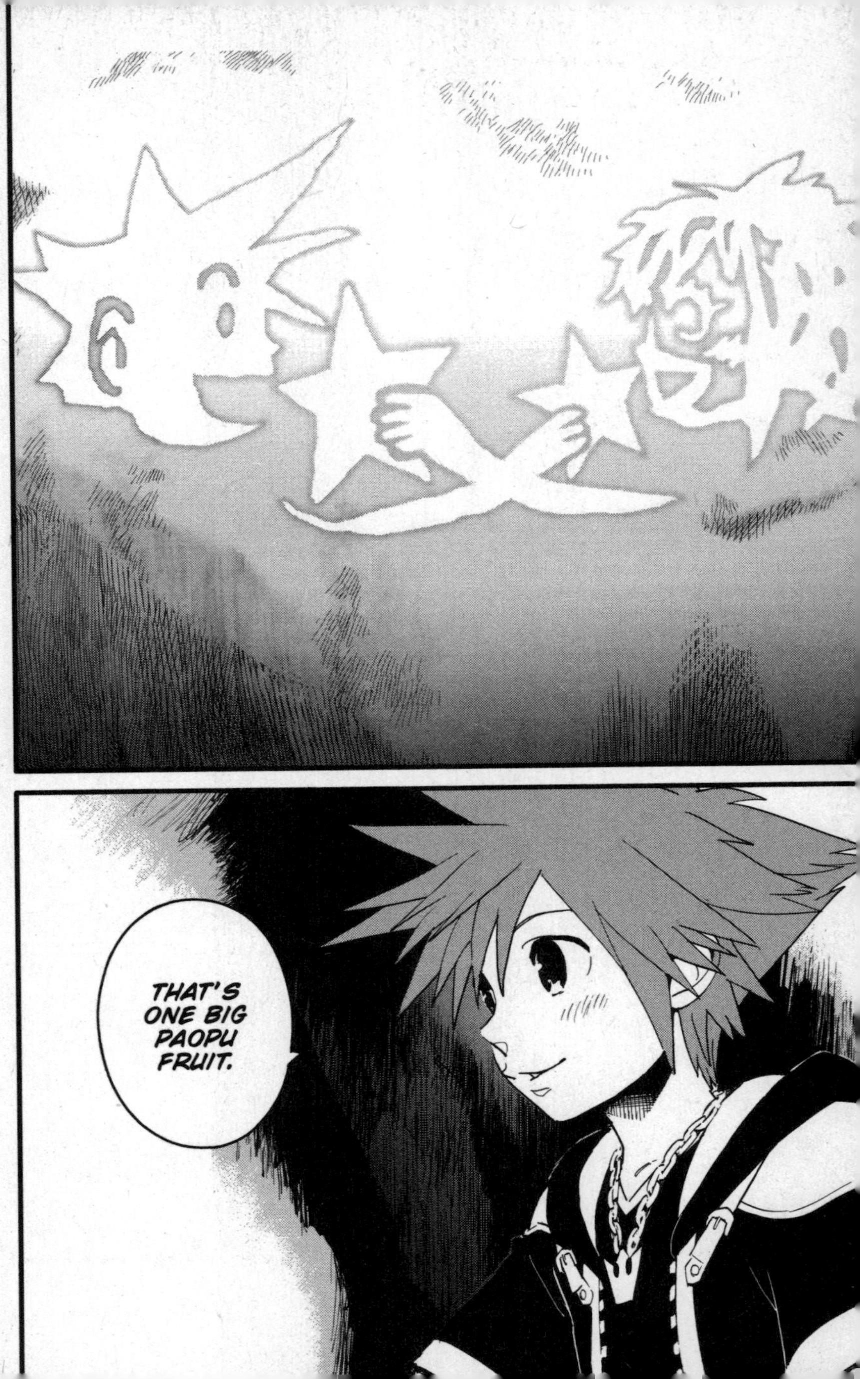
THAT'S ONE BIG PAOPU FRUIT.

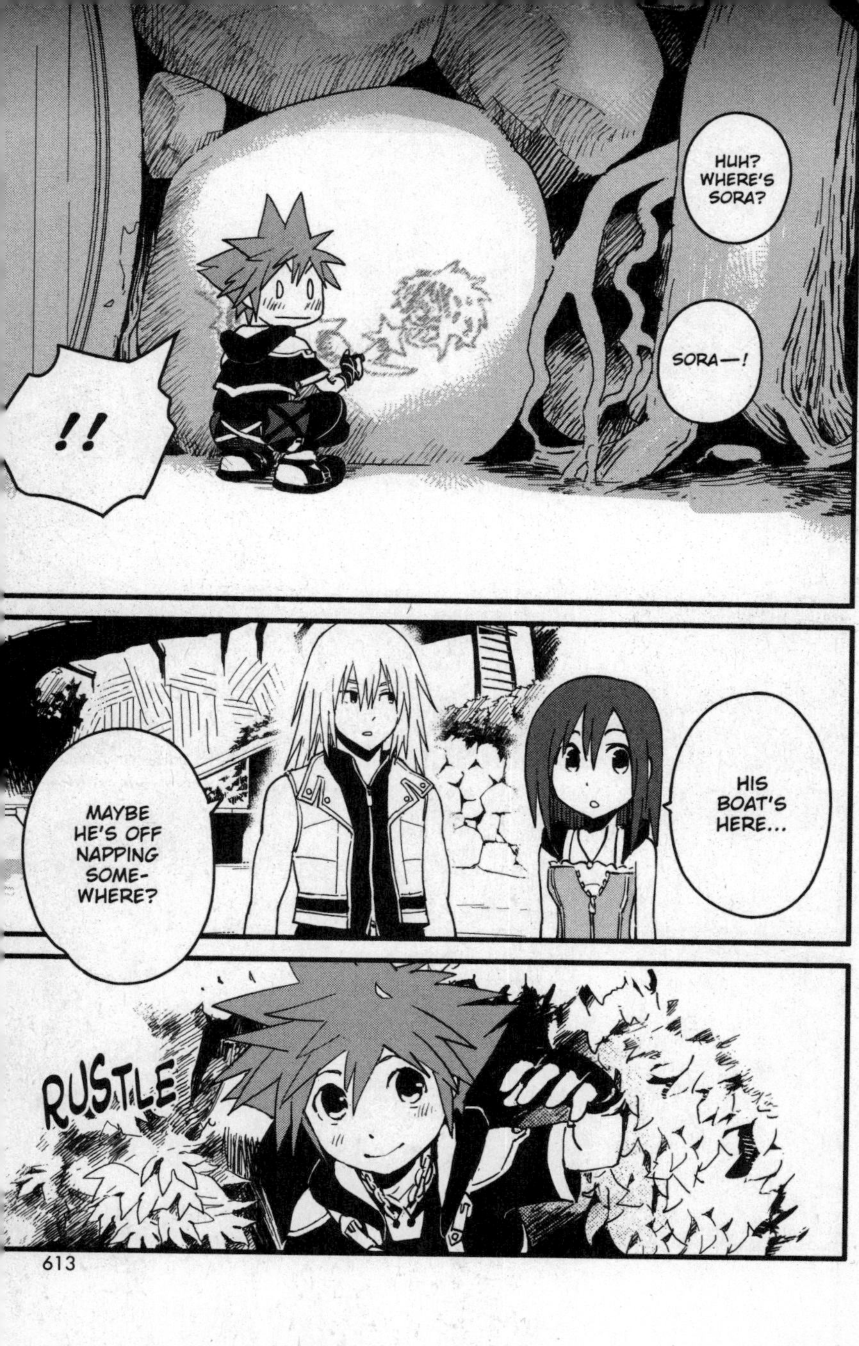
HUH? WHERE'S SORA?
SORA—!
!!
HIS BOAT'S HERE...
MAYBE HE'S OFF NAPPING SOME-WHERE?
RUSTLE

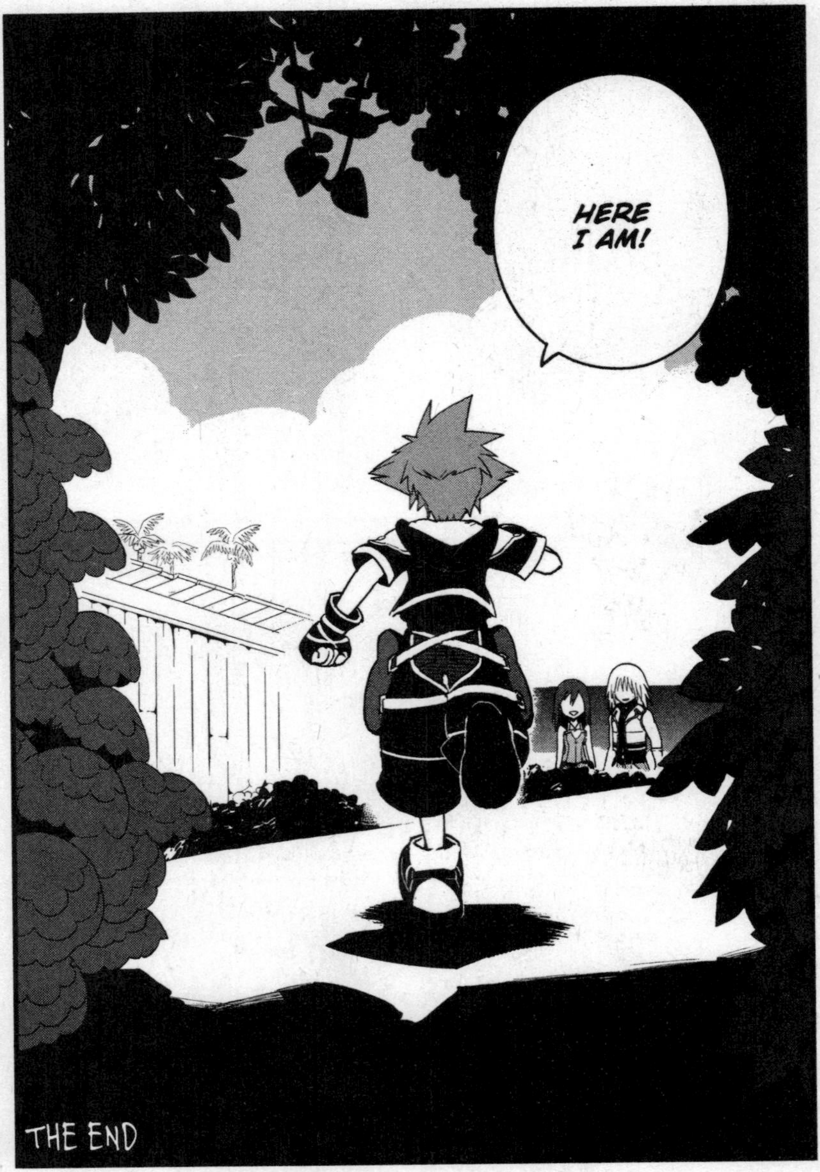
HERE I AM!
THE END

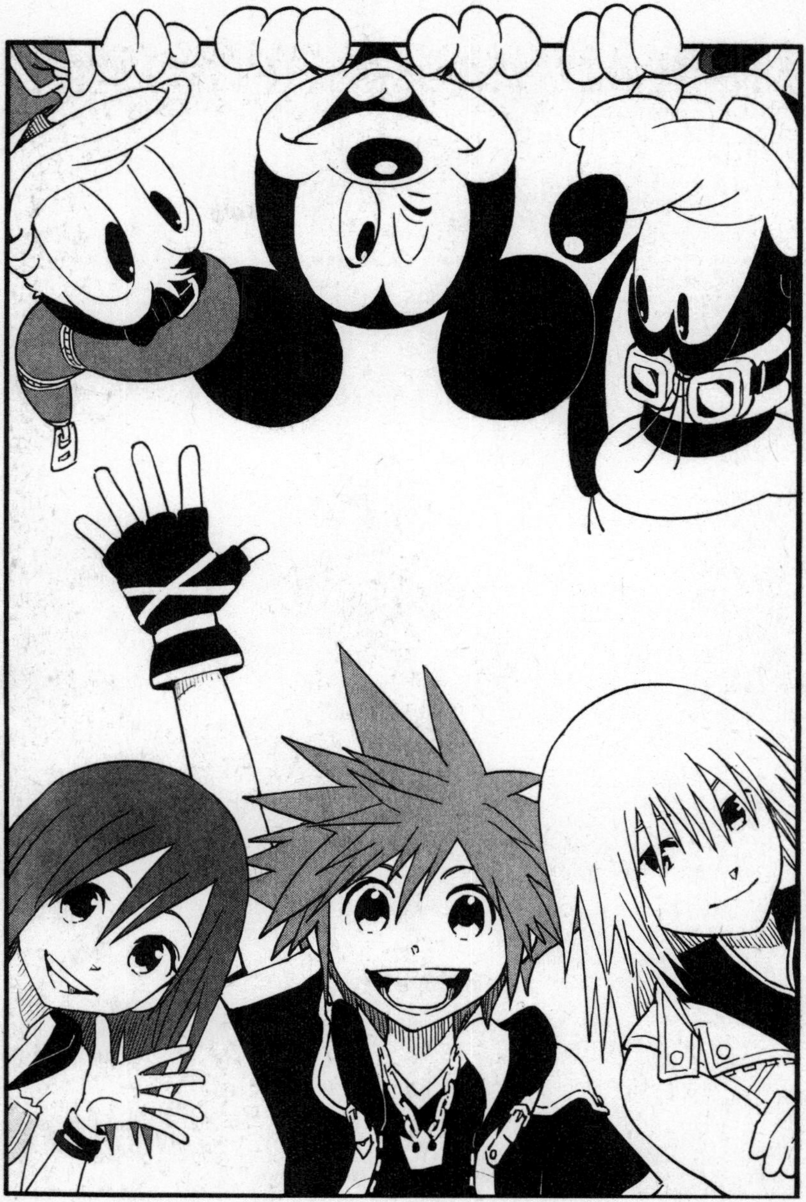

KINGDOM HEARTS II ④

SHIRO AMANO

ORIGINAL CONCEPT:
TETSUYA NOMURA

Translation: Alethea and Athena Nibley • Lettering: Lys Blakeslee

Yen Press
1290 Avenue of the Americas
New York, NY 10104

Visit us at yenpress.com
facebook.com/yenpress
twitter.com/yenpress
yenpress.tumblr.com
instagram.com/yenpress

First Yen Press Edition: May 2017

Yen Press is an imprint of Yen Press, LLC.
The Yen Press name and logo are trademarks of Yen Press, LLC.

The publisher is not responsible for websites (or their content) that are not owned by the publisher.

Library of Congress Control Number: 2014378925

ISBN: 978-0-316-38272-4

10 9 8 7 6 5 4

WOR

Printed in the United States of America

Turn to the back
for a sneak peek of
*Kingdom Hearts II:
The Novel*, Volume 1,
coming June 2017!

Roxas, Hayner, and Olette all ran to look in the box.

"What? How? All our —————— are gone?" Olette said, and then touched her throat, looking nervously at Roxas.

Not only were their things gone—the word itself was gone…?

"Stolen…," Roxas said. "Even the word —————— got stolen?"

Hayner nodded and caught his eye. "There's no way Seifer could've done this."

Roxas nodded in reply.

"Okay. Time for some recon!" Hayner dashed out of their hangout. Pence and Olette followed him.

"All right!" Roxas moved to catch up—and the world began spinning. "…Huh?"

The strength drained from his legs, but by the time he realized he was crumpling to the floor, darkness was swallowing his mind.

A deep voice spoke from somewhere.

"His heart is returning. Doubtless he'll awaken very soon."

But…Roxas didn't know who it was.

It's already been one year since I promised him, Naminé thought.

Sora was asleep in the flower-bud capsule. It had been a year since he went in.

She looked away, down at the floor. *Maybe we're just being used.*

"…Naminé."

Slowly she turned to face the person addressing her.

The man wore a black cloak, the same as those in the organization. There was kindness in the eyes that she glimpsed beneath the hood—eyes that could never lie.

She'd spent this past year doing nothing but drawing pictures… but for *him*, it had been a very hard year.

"It won't be much longer." His gaze was fixed on the sleeping Sora.

Everything he *does is for Sora…and for all the worlds. So what about me? What am I doing here?* Naminé asked herself.

"He seems lonely, somehow," he said.

"I wouldn't worry."

A small smile curled the edges of Naminé's mouth.

off?" he said to the others.

"Yeah, that's just wrong," Pence agreed, angrily shaking his head, though his bristly black hair didn't ruffle in the slightest. It looked coarse enough to hurt if it were to fall in his eyes—maybe that was why he wore it bound up in a headband. He wore an oversize basketball shirt by Dog Street, featuring the brand's logo and stylized dog character chasing bones. It suited his sturdy build perfectly.

"Seifer's gone too far this time," Olette added. Her orange tank top with the four-leaf-clover design at the hip was her favorite shirt. She always regarded everyone with kindness, no matter what. Even Seifer.

"I mean, it's true that stuff's been getting stolen around town. And we've never gotten along with Seifer. So if he wants to think we did it, I can't really blame him. What's really driving me nuts is that he's going around tellin' everybody that we're the thieves! Now the whole town is treating us like a bunch of criminals! Have you ever been this mad in your *life*?" Hayner ranted all in one breath, and jumped down from the wooden crate that made his usual perch, shaking a fist. "'Cause I haven't. Nuh-uh, never. So, what to do...?"

Hayner turned and stared at Roxas, who hadn't quite been listening.

Roxas paused, surprise crossing his face, and then he jumped to his feet. "Um, well... We could find the real thieves. That would set the record straight."

"Hey, that sounds kinda fun," Pence said, getting out of his chair.

Not quite satisfied, Hayner stuck out his lips in a pout. "What about Seifer?"

Beside him, Pence rushed to the box that they called the treasure chest and rummaged through it.

"First, we gotta clear our names," Roxas said. "Once we find the real culprit, everyone will get off our back."

"Oh no!" Pence looked up from the box, holding a compact camera.

"Now what?" Hayner shot Pence a look, offended by the interruption.

"They're gone! Our —— are gone!"

CHAPTER 1
The First Day

UNDER THE SOFT LIGHT SPILLING IN THROUGH THE
window, Roxas slowly opened his eyes.

"Another dream about him…," he mumbled, then stood up on
his bed to fling the window wide open. The warm, faintly humid
summer air rushed in. His chestnut hair shone honey-gold in the
light. From his room on the second floor, Roxas could see a broad
swath of the town.

A dream… Ever since the beginning of summer vacation,
Roxas had been having the same dreams every night. Dreams of
a vivid blue sky over a brilliant sea of the same color, and a boy,
named for that sky. The boy's name was…

"……Sora."

Roxas murmured it to himself and blinked his blue eyes.

The boy in the dream, Sora, had a smile as bright as the sky. *He
seems nice enough*, Roxas thought. But he couldn't quite say how
he felt about the boy.

From a distance, he heard the bells ringing. That was the town's
distinctive landmark—the clock tower above the station. The
two bells that stuck out from it on each side told time for all the
citizens of Twilight Town.

Roxas stretched and hopped off his bed. He took off his
pajamas—a plain white shirt and shorts—and dressed in a white
jacket and black pants before leaving his room.

Roxas headed to the usual spot—an old storage space under
the train tracks. His friends, Hayner and Pence and Olette, were
already there, chatting about something.

"Hey, Roxas," Olette said, noticing him.

"Oh—hi." Roxas looked back at his friends, each seated in a
corner.

"Roxas, you gotta hear this, too!" Hayner blurted, a bit loud,
as usual. He wore pants and shoes with a camouflage pattern and
a black T-shirt emblazoned with a skull, and as always, his wavy,
light-brown hair was impeccably styled. "Man, doesn't it tick you

"Who are you?" he asked the other man.

"I'm what's left. An empty shell. Or maybe I'm all there ever was."

He frowned slightly at the man's evasive reply. "I meant your name."

Yes—he wanted to know the *name* of the person standing before him.

"My name is of no importance. What about you? Do you remember your true name?"

It sounded almost like the man was taunting him. He opened his mouth to respond...

To say *his* name. The name of the one in the very depths of his memory.

"My true name...is..."

And here...the story begins.

"It is beyond your comprehension for now. Until we meet again," the man replied softly. The blades disappeared from his hands.

"Wait—who *are* you?!"

"I am...but a mere shell." With that, the man vanished like smoke into the air.

Still clutching the Keyblade, Sora stared in confusion. And then a voice he knew spoke.

"Good work, Sora."

He turned to find Leon standing there. "Are we back...?"

"Something wrong, Sora?" Leon asked, seeing him looking so bewildered.

"No... It's nothing." Sora grinned and ran ahead to the final battle—the fight against Ansem.

When he came to, he was standing somewhere else. It was the edge of the world—or so he felt. Jagged, crumbling rocks jutted up from a dark seashore.

But come to think of it, hadn't he sat in a place sort of like this, talking about the future?

A blue sea...a blue sky...

The scene simply floated up in his mind, and he shook his head. *That couldn't have happened.*

Then he glanced down at himself. He was wearing unfamiliar black clothes—a cloak, to be precise. He knew he was seeing himself for the first time, but strangely, nothing about his appearance seemed wrong.

"So, you've arrived," said a voice behind him.

He turned and saw a figure much like himself—someone wearing a black cloak, face completely hidden under a hood. His own expression was most likely concealed from the other man, too.

"I've been to see him."

Him?

He nearly asked who the other man meant, but he had a vague sense that he already knew. He bit back the question.

"He looks a lot like you."

Right—and I probably look a lot like him. He and I are two sides of the same coin...

PROLOGUE
Episode One

AFTER THEY CLOSED THE KEYHOLE, SORA AND HIS friends thought they would find the princesses standing at the door in Hollow Bastion, awaiting their return. But instead they stepped through the door into a strange place shrouded in mist.

"Huh…?" Donald cocked his head.

"Now where are we…?" Sora mumbled, looking around. Then a strange sensation came over him.

"Ah. It seems you are special, too."

At the sudden voice behind him, Sora turned. "Who are you?!"

He saw a man standing there alone, wearing a black cloak, looking down at Sora from beneath a hood.

"Ansem…?" Goofy said uncertainly, and readied his shield behind Sora.

The man seemed like Ansem. But the hood covering his face made it hard to tell who it was. Tensed for a fight, Sora and his friends glared at the mysterious figure.

"That name rings familiar…," the man murmured, as if to himself, and then spoke to Sora again. "You remind me of him."

"What's that supposed to mean?!" Sora shot back, taking a stance with the Keyblade. He had no idea who the man was talking about.

"It means you are not whole. You are incomplete. Allow me… to test your strength."

The man approached, gliding over the floor, and flung orbs of light from his hands. The attack struck Sora and sent him sprawling.

"Sora!" Goofy cried, running to his defense, but the man drew twin swords from his cloak and knocked Goofy back.

"*Firaga! Thundaga! Blizzaga!*" Donald hurled spells at the man, but they all dissipated harmlessly without even singeing the black cloak.

"…Impressive," said the man. "This will be enjoyable."

"What are you talking about…?!" Sora shouted, springing to his feet.

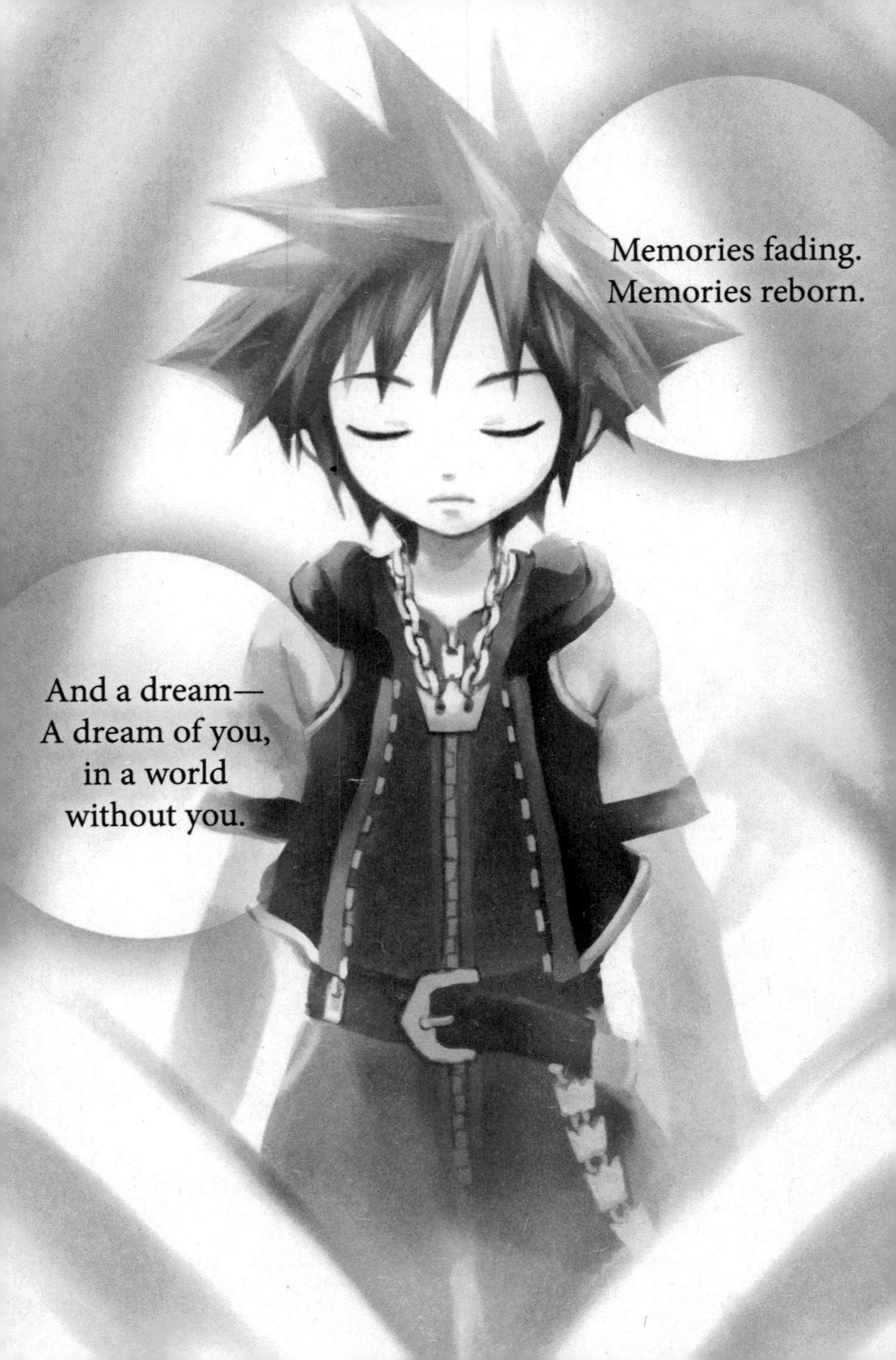
Memories fading.
Memories reborn.
And a dream—
A dream of you,
in a world
without you.

What's happening to me...?
Falling...falling into darkness.........?

DISNEY · SQUARE ENIX

KINGDOM HEARTS

THE NOVEL

VOL.1
PREVIEW

Tomoco Kanemaki

Original Concept
Tetsuya Nomura
Kazushige Nojima

Illustrations
Shiro Amano

YEN ON